Raymond CHANDLER

The Big Sleep

The High Window

The Lady in the Lake

The Long Goodbye

Playback

Farewell My Lovely

CHANCELLOR
PRESS

Raymond CHANDLER

The Big Sleep first published in Great Britain in 1939
by Hamish Hamilton

The High Window first published in Great Britain in 1943
by Hamish Hamilton

The Lady in the Lake first published in Great Britain in 1944
by Hamish Hamilton

The Long Goodbye first published in Great Britain in 1953
by Hamish Hamilton

Playback first published in Great Britain in 1958
by Hamish Hamilton

Farewell My Lovely first published in Great Britain in 1940
by Hamish Hamilton

This omnibus volume first published in 1977

This edition published jointly in Great Britain in 1985 by

William Heinemann Limited
10 Upper Grosvenor Street
London W1

Martin Secker & Warburg Limited
54 Poland Street
London W1

and
Chancellor Press
an imprint of the Octopus Publishing Group p.l.c.
59 Grosvenor Street
London W1

ISBN 0 907486 84 3

The Big Sleep   11

The High Window   133

The Lady in the Lake   265

The Long Goodbye   403

Playback   619

Farewell My Lovely   715

Raymond CHANDLER

The Big Sleep

Raymond CHANDLER

THE BIG SLEEP

I

It was about eleven o'clock in the morning, mid October, with the sun not shining and a look of hard wet rain in the clearness of the foothills. I was wearing my powder-blue suit, with dark blue shirt, tie and display handkerchief, black brogues, black wool socks with dark blue clocks on them. I was neat, clean, shaved and sober, and I didn't care who knew it. I was everything the well-dressed private detective ought to be. I was calling on four million dollars.

The main hallway of the Sternwood place was two stories high. Over the entrance doors, which would have let in a troop of Indian elephants, there was a broad stained-glass panel showing a knight in dark armour rescuing a lady who was tied to a tree and didn't have any clothes on but some very long and convenient hair. The knight had pushed the vizor of his helmet back to be sociable, and he was fiddling with the knots on the ropes that tied the lady to the tree and not getting anywhere. I stood there and thought that if I lived in the house, I would sooner or later have to climb up there and help him. He didn't seem to be really trying.

There were French doors at the back of the hall, beyond them a wide sweep of emerald grass to a white garage, in front of which a slim dark young chauffeur in shiny black leggings was dusting a maroon Packard convertible. Beyond the garage were some decorative trees trimmed as carefully as poodle dogs. Beyond them a large greenhouse with a domed roof. Then more trees and beyond everything the solid, uneven, comfortable line of the foothills.

On the east side of the hall a free staircase, tile-paved, rose to a gallery with a wrought-iron railing and another piece of stained-glass romance. Large hard chairs with rounded red plush seats were backed into the vacant spaces of the wall round about. They didn't look as if anybody had ever sat in them. In the middle of the west wall there was a big empty fireplace with a brass screen in four hinged panels, and over the fireplace a marble mantel with cupids at the corners. Above the mantel there was a large oil portrait, and above the portrait two bullet-torn or moth-eaten cavalry pennants crossed in a glass frame. The portrait was a stiffly posed job of an officer in full regimentals of about the time of the Mexican War. The officer had a neat black imperial, black mustachios, hot hard coal-black eyes, and the general look of a man it would pay to get along with. I thought this might be General Sternwood's grandfather. It could hardly be the General himself, even though I had heard he was pretty far gone in years to have a couple of daughters still in the dangerous twenties.

I was still staring at the hot black eyes when a door opened far back under the stairs. It wasn't the butler coming back. It was a girl.

She was twenty or so, small and delicately put together, but she looked durable. She wore pale blue slacks and they looked well on her. She walked as if she were floating. Her hair was a fine tawny wave cut much shorter than the current fashion of pageboy tresses curled in at the bottom. Her eyes were slate-grey, and had almost no expression when they looked at me. She came over near me and smiled with her mouth and she had little sharp predatory teeth, as white as fresh orange pith and as shiny as porcelain. They glistened between her thin too taut lips. Her face lacked colour and didn't look too healthy.

'Tall, aren't you?' she said.

'I didn't mean to be.'

Her eyes rounded. She was puzzled. She was thinking. I could see, even on that short acquaintance, that thinking was always going to be a bother to her.

'Handsome too,' she said. 'And I bet you know it.'

I grunted.

'What's your name?'

'Reilly,' I said. 'Doghouse Reilly.'

'That's a funny name.' She bit her lip and turned her head a little and looked at me along her eyes. Then she lowered her lashes until they almost cuddled her cheeks and slowly raised them again, like a theatre curtain. I was to get to know that trick. That was supposed to make me roll over on my back with all four paws in the air.

'Are you a prizefighter?' she asked, when I didn't.

'Not exactly. I'm a sleuth.'

'A—a—' She tossed her head angrily, and the rich colour of it glistened in the rather dim light of the big hall. 'You're making fun of me.'

'Uh-uh.'

'What?'

'Get on with you,' I said. 'You heard me.'

'You didn't say anything. You're just a big tease.' She put a thumb up and bit it. It was a curiously shaped thumb, thin and narrow like an extra finger, with no curve in the first joint. She bit it and sucked it slowly, turning it around in her mouth like a baby with a comforter.

'You're awfully tall,' she said. Then she giggled with secret merriment. Then she turned her body slowly and lithely, without lifting her feet. Her hands dropped limp at her sides. She tilted herself towards me on her toes. She fell straight back into my arms. I had to catch her or let her crack her head on the tessellated floor. I caught her under her arms and she went rubber-legged on me instantly. I had to hold her close to hold her up. When her head was against my chest she screwed it around and giggled at me.

'You're cute,' she giggled. 'I'm cute too.'

I didn't say anything. So the butler chose that convenient moment to come back through the French doors and see me holding her.

It didn't seem to bother him. He was a tall thin silver man, sixty or close to it or a little past it. He had blue eyes as remote as eyes could be. His skin was smooth and bright and he moved like a man with very sound muscles. He walked slowly across the floor towards us and the girl jerked away from me. She flashed across the room to the foot of the stairs and went up them like a deer. She was gone before I could draw a long breath and let it out.

The butler said tonelessly: 'The General will see you now, Mr Marlowe.'

I pushed my lower jaw up off my chest and nodded at him. 'Who was that?'

'Miss Carmen Sternwood, sir.'

'You ought to wean her. She looks old enough.'

He looked at me with grave politeness and repeated what he had said.

2

We went out at the French doors and along a smooth red-flagged path that skirted the far side of the lawn from the garage. The boyish-looking chauffeur had a big black and chromium sedan out now and was dusting that. The path took us along to the side of the greenhouse and the butler opened a door for me and stood aside. It opened into a sort of vestibule that was about as warm as a slow oven. He came in after me, shut the outer door, opened an inner door and we went through that. Then it was really hot. The air was thick, wet, steamy and larded with the cloying smell of tropical orchids in bloom. The glass walls and roof were heavily misted and big drops of moisture splashed down on the plants. The light had an unreal greenish colour, like light filtered through an aquarium tank. The plants filled the place, a forest of them, with nasty meaty leaves and stalks like the newly washed fingers of dead men. They smelled as overpowering as boiling alcohol under a blanket.

The butler did his best to get me through without being smacked in the face by the sodden leaves, and after a while we came to a clearing in the middle of the jungle, under the domed roof. Here, in a space of hexagonal flags, an old red Turkish rug was laid down and on the rug was a wheel chair, and in the wheel chair an old and obviously dying man watched us come with black eyes from which all fire had died long ago, but which still had the coal-black directness of the eyes in the portrait that hung above the mantel in the hall. The rest of his face was a leaden mask, with the bloodless lips and the sharp nose and the sunken temples and the outward-turning ear-lobes of approaching dissolution. His long narrow body was wrapped—in that heat—in a travelling rug and a faded red bathrobe. His thin clawlike hands were folded loosely on the rug, purple-nailed. A few locks of dry white hair clung to his scalp, like wild flowers fighting for life on a bare rock.

The butler stood in front of him and said: 'This is Mr Marlowe, General.'

The old man didn't move or speak, or even nod. He just looked at me lifelessly. The butler pushed a damp wicker chair against the backs of my legs and I sat down. He took my hat with a deft scoop.

Then the old man dragged his voice up from the bottom of a well and said: 'Brandy, Norris. How do you like your brandy, sir?'

'Any way at all,' I said.

The butler went away among the abominable plants. The General spoke again, slowly, using his strength as carefully as an out-of-work showgirl uses her last good pair of stockings.

'I used to like mine with champagne. The champagne as cold as Valley Forge and about a third of a glass of brandy beneath it. You may take your coat off, sir. It's too hot in here for a man with blood in his veins.'

I stood up and peeled off my coat and got a handkerchief out and mopped my face and neck and the backs of my wrists. St Louis in August had nothing on that place. I sat down again and felt automatically for a cigarette and then stopped. The old man caught the gesture and smiled faintly.

'You may smoke, sir. I like the smell of tobacco.'

I lit the cigarette and blew a lungful at him and he sniffed at it like a terrier at a rat-hole. The faint smile pulled at the shadowed corners of his mouth.

'A nice state of affairs when a man has to indulge his vices by proxy,' he said dryly. 'You are looking at a very dull survival of a rather gaudy life, a cripple paralysed in both legs and with only half of his lower belly. There's very little that I can eat and my sleep is so close to waking that it is hardly worth the name. I seem to exist largely on heat, like a newborn spider, and the orchids are an excuse for the heat. Do you like orchids?'

'Not particularly,' I said.

The General half closed his eyes. 'They are nasty things. Their flesh is too much like the flesh of men. And their perfume has the rotten sweetness of a prostitute.'

I stared at him with my mouth open. The soft wet heat was like a pall around us. The old man nodded, as if his neck was afraid of the weight of his head. Then the butler came pushing back through the jungle with a tea-wagon, mixed me a brandy and soda, swathed the copper ice bucket with a damp napkin, and went softly away among the orchids. A door opened and shut behind the jungle.

I sipped the drink. The old man licked his lips watching me, over and over again, drawing one lip slowly across the other with a funeral absorption, like an undertaker dry-washing his hands.

'Tell me about yourself, Mr Marlowe. I suppose I have a right to ask?'

'Sure, but there's very little to tell. I'm thirty-three years old, went to college once and can still speak English if there's any demand for it. There isn't much in my trade. I worked for Mr Wilde, the District Attorney, as an investigator once. His chief investigator, a man named Bernie Ohls, called me and told me you wanted to see me. I'm unmarried because I don't like policemen's wives.'

'And a little bit of a cynic,' the old man smiled. 'You didn't like working for Wilde?'

'I was fired. For insubordination. I test very high on insubordination, General.'

'I always did myself, sir. I'm glad to hear it. What do you know about my family?'

'I'm told you are a widower and have two young daughters, both pretty and both wild. One of them has been married three times, the last time to an ex-bootlegger, who went in the trade by the name of Rusty Regan. That's all I heard, General.'

'Did any of it strike you as peculiar?'

'The Rusty Regan part, maybe. But I always got along with bootleggers myself.'

He smiled his faint economical smile. 'It seems I do too. I'm very fond of Rusty. A big curly-headed Irishman from Clonmel, with sad eyes and a smile as wide as Wilshire Boulevard. The first time I saw him I thought he might be what you are probably thinking he was, an adventurer who happened to get himself wrapped up in some velvet.'

'You must have liked him,' I said. 'You learned to talk the language.'

He put his thin bloodless hands under the edge of the rug. I put my cigarette stub out and finished my drink.

'He was the breath of life to me—while he lasted. He spent hours with me, sweating like a pig, drinking brandy by the quart, and telling me stories of the Irish revolution. He had been an officer in the I.R.A. He wasn't even legally in the United States. It was a ridiculous marriage of course, and it probably didn't last a month, as a marriage. I'm telling you the family secrets, Mr Marlowe.'

'They're still secrets,' I said. 'What happened to him?'

The old man looked at me woodenly. 'He went away, a month ago. Abruptly, without a word to anyone. Without saying good-bye to me. That hurt a little, but he had been raised in a rough school. I'll hear from him one of these days. Meantime I am being blackmailed again.'

I said: 'Again?'

He brought his hands from under the rug with a brown envelope in them. 'I should have been very sorry for anybody who tried to blackmail me while Rusty was around. A few months before he came—that is to say about nine or ten months ago—I paid a man named Joe Brody five thousand dollars to let my younger daughter Carmen alone.'

'Ah,' I said.

He moved his thin white eyebrows. 'That means what?'

'Nothing,' I said.

He went on staring at me, half frowning. Then he said: 'Take this envelope and examine it. And help yourself to the brandy.'

I took the envelope off his knees and sat down with it again. I wiped off the palms of my hands and turned it around. It was addressed to General Guy Sternwood, 3765 Alta Brea Crescent, West Hollywood, California. The address was in ink, in the slanting printing engineers use. The envelope was slit. I opened it up and took out a brown card and three slips of stiff paper. The card was of thin brown linen, printed in gold: 'Mr Arthur Gwynn Geiger.' No address. Very small in the lower lefthand corner: 'Rare Books and De Luxe Editions.' I turned the card over. More of the slanted printing on the back. 'Dear Sir: In spite of the legal uncollectibility of the enclosed, which frankly represent gambling debts, I assume you might wish them honoured. Respectfully, A. G. Geiger.'

I looked at the slips of stiffish white paper. They were promissory notes filled out in ink, dated on several dates early in the month before, September. 'On Demand I promise to pay to Arthur Gwynn Geiger or Order the sum of One Thousand Dollars ($1000.00) without interest. Value Received. Carmen Sternwood.'

The written part was in a sprawling moronic handwriting with a lot of fat curlicues and circles for dots. I mixed myself another drink and sipped it and put the exhibit aside.

'Your conclusions?' the General asked.

'I haven't any yet. Who is this Arthur Gwynn Geiger?'

'I haven't the faintest idea.'

'What does Carmen say?'

'I haven't asked her. I don't intend to. If I did, she would suck her thumb and look coy.'

I said: 'I met her in the hall. She did that to me. Then she tried to sit in my lap.'

Nothing changed in his expression. His clasped hands rested peacefully on the edge of the rug, and the heat, which made me feel like a New England boiled dinner, didn't seem to make him even warm.

'Do I have to be polite?' I asked. 'Or can I just be natural?'

'I haven't noticed that you suffer from many inhibitions, Mr Marlowe.'

'Do the two girls run around together?'

'I think not. I think they go their separate and slightly divergent roads to perdition. Vivian is spoiled, exacting, smart and quite ruthless. Carmen is a child who likes to pull wings off flies. Neither of them has any more moral sense than a cat. Neither have I. No Sternwood ever had. Proceed.'

'They're well educated, I suppose. They know what they're doing.'

'Vivian went to good schools of the snob type and to college. Carmen went to half a dozen schools of greater and greater liberality, and ended up where she started. I presume they both had, and still have, all the usual vices. If I sound a little sinister as a parent, Mr Marlowe, it is because my hold on life is too slight to include any Victorian hypocrisy.' He leaned his head back and closed his eyes, then opened them again suddenly. 'I need not add that a man who indulges in parenthood for the first time at the age of fifty-four deserves all he gets.'

I sipped my drink and nodded. The pulse in his lean grey throat throbbed visibly and yet so slowly that it was hardly a pulse at all. An old man two-thirds dead and still determined to believe he could take it.

'Your conclusions?' he asked suddenly.

'I'd pay him.'

'Why?'

'It's a question of a little money against a lot of annoyance. There has to be something behind it. But nobody's going to break your heart, if it hasn't been done already. And it would take an awful lot of chisellers an awful lot of time to rob you of enough so that you'd even notice it.'

'I have pride, sir,' he said coldly.

'Somebody's counting on that. It's the easiest way to fool them. That or the police. Geiger can collect on these notes, unless you can show fraud. Instead of that he makes you a present of them and admits they are gambling debts, which gives you a defence, even if he had kept the notes. If he's a crook, he knows his onions, and if he's an honest man doing a little loan business on the side, he ought to have his money. Who was this Joe Brody you paid the five thousand dollars to?'

'Some kind of gambler. I hardly recall. Norris would know. My butler.'

'Your daughters have money in their own right, General?'

'Vivian has, but not a great deal. Carmen is still a minor under her mother's will. I give them both generous allowances.'

I said: 'I can take this Geiger off your back, General, if that's what you want. Whoever he is and whatever he has. It may cost you a little money, besides what you pay me. And, of course, it won't get you anything. Sugaring them never does. You're already listed on their book of nice names.'

'I see.' He shrugged his wide sharp shoulders in the faded red bath-robe. 'A moment ago you said pay him. Now you say it won't get me anything.'

'I mean it might be cheaper and easier to stand for a certain amount of squeeze. That's all.'

'I'm afraid I'm rather an impatient man, Mr Marlowe. What are your charges?'

'I get twenty-five a day and expenses—when I'm lucky.'

'I see. It seems reasonable enough for removing morbid growths from people's backs. Quite a delicate operation. You realize that, I hope. You'll make your operation as little of a shock to the patient as possible? There might be several of them, Mr Marlowe.'

I finished my second drink and wiped my lips and my face. The heat didn't get any less hot with the brandy in me. The General blinked at me and plucked at the edge of his rug.

'Can I make a deal with this guy, if I think he's within hooting distance of being on the level?'

'Yes. The matter is now in your hands. I never do things by halves.'

'I'll take him out,' I said. 'He'll think a bridge fell on him.'

'I'm sure you will. And now I must excuse myself. I am tired.' He reached out and touched the bell on the arm of his chair. The cord was plugged into a black cable that wound along the side of the deep dark green boxes in which the orchids grew and festered. He closed his eyes, opened them again in a brief bright stare, and settled back among his cushions. The lids dropped again and he didn't pay any more attention to me.

I stood up and lifted my coat off the back of the damp wicker chair and went off with it among the orchids, opened the two doors and stood outside in the brisk October air getting myself some oxygen. The chauffeur over by the garage had gone away. The butler came along the red path with smooth light steps and his back as straight as an ironing board. I shrugged into my coat and watched him come.

He stopped about two feet from me and said gravely: 'Mrs Regan would like to see you before you leave, sir. And in the matter of money the General has instructed me to give you a cheque for whatever seems desirable.'

'Instructed you how?'

He looked puzzled, then he smiled. 'Ah, I see, sir. You are, of course, a detective. By the way he rang his bell.'

'You write his cheques?'

'I have that privilege.'

'That ought to save you from a pauper's grave. No money now, thanks. What does Mrs Regan want to see me about?'

His blue eyes gave me a smooth level look. 'She has a misconception of the purpose of your visit, sir.'

'Who told her anything about my visit?'

'Her windows command the greenhouse. She saw us go in. I was obliged to tell her who you were.'

'I don't like that,' I said.

His blue eyes frosted. 'Are you attempting to tell me my duties, sir?'

'No. But I'm having a lot of fun trying to guess what they are.'

We stared at each other for a moment. He gave me a blue glare and turned away.

3

This room was too big, the ceiling was too high, the doors were too tall, and the white carpet that went from wall to wall looked like a fresh fall of snow at Lake Arrowhead. There were full-length mirrors and crystal doodads all over the place. The ivory furniture had chromium on it, and the enormous ivory drapes lay tumbled on the white carpet a yard from the windows. The white made the ivory look dirty and the ivory made the white look bled out. The windows stared towards the darkening foothills. It was going to rain soon. There was pressure in the air already.

I sat down on the edge of a deep soft chair and looked at Mrs Regan. She was worth a stare. She was trouble. She was stretched out on a modernistic chaise-longue with her slippers off, so I stared at her legs in the sheerest silk stockings. They seemed to be arranged to stare at. They were visible to the knee and one of them well beyond. The knees were dimpled, not bony and sharp. The calves were beautiful, the ankles long and slim and with enough melodic line for a tone poem. She was tall and rangy and strong-looking. Her head was against an ivory satin cushion. Her hair was black and wiry and parted in the middle and she had the hot black eyes of the portrait in the hall. She had a good mouth and a good chin. There was a sulky droop to her lips and the lower lip was full.

She had a drink. She took a swallow from it and gave me a cool level stare over the rim of the glass.

'So you're a private detective,' she said. 'I didn't know they really existed, except in books. Or else they were greasy little men snooping around hotels.'

There was nothing in that for me, so I let it drift with the current. She put her glass down on the flat arm of the chaise-longue and flashed an emerald and touched her hair. She said slowly: 'How did you like Dad?'

'I liked him,' I said.

'He liked Rusty. I suppose you know who Rusty is?'

'Uh-huh.'

'Rusty was earthy and vulgar at times, but he was very real. And he was a lot of fun for Dad. Rusty shouldn't have gone off like that. Dad feels very badly about it, although he won't say so. Or did he?'

'He said something about it.'

'You're not much of a gusher, are you, Mr Marlowe? But he wants to find him, doesn't he?'

I stared at her politely through a pause. 'Yes and no,' I said.

'That's hardly an answer. Do you think you can find him?'

'I didn't say I was going to try. Why not try the Missing Persons Bureau? They have the organization. It's not a one-man job.'

'Oh, Dad wouldn't hear of the police being brought into it.' She looked at me smoothly across her glass again, emptied it, and rang a bell. A maid came into the room by a side door. She was a middle-aged woman with a long yellow gentle face, a long nose, no chin, large wet eyes. She looked like a nice old horse that had been turned out to pasture after long service. Mrs Regan waved the empty glass at her and she mixed another drink and handed it to her and left the room, without a word, without a glance in my direction.

When the door shut Mrs Regan said: 'Well, how will you go about it then?'

'How and when did he skip out?'

'Didn't Dad tell you?'

I grinned at her with my head on one side. She flushed. Her hot black eyes looked mad. 'I don't see what there is to be cagey about,' she snapped. 'And I don't like your manners.'

'I'm not crazy about yours,' I said. 'I didn't ask to see you. You sent for me. I don't mind your ritzing me or drinking your lunch out of a Scotch bottle. I don't mind your showing me your legs. They're very swell legs and it's a pleasure to make their acquaintance. I don't mind if you don't like my manners. They're pretty bad. I grieve over them during the long winter evenings. But don't waste your time trying to cross-examine me.'

She slammed her glass down so hard that it slopped over on an ivory cushion. She swung her legs to the floor and stood up with her eyes sparking fire and her nostrils wide. Her mouth was open and her bright teeth glared at me. Her knuckles were white.

'People don't talk like that to me,' she said thickly.

I sat there and grinned at her. Very slowly she closed her mouth and looked down at the spilled liquor. She sat down on the edge of the chaise-longue and cupped her chin in one hand.

'My God, you big dark handsome brute! I ought to throw a Buick at you.'

I snicked a match on my thumbnail and for once it lit. I puffed smoke into the air and waited.

'I loathe masterful men,' she said. 'I simply loathe them.'

'Just what is it you're afraid of, Mrs Regan?'

Her eyes whitened. Then they darkened until they seemed to be all pupil. Her nostrils looked pinched.

'That wasn't what he wanted with you at all,' she said in a strained voice that still had shreds of anger clinging to it. 'About Rusty. Was it?'

'Better ask him.'

She flared up again. 'Get out! Damn you, get out!'

I stood up. 'Sit down!' she snapped. I sat down. I flicked a finger at my palm and waited.

'Please,' she said. 'Please. You could find Rusty–if Dad wanted you to.'

That didn't work either. I nodded and asked: 'When did he go?'

'One afternoon a month back. He just drove away in his car without saying a word. They found the car in a private garage somewhere.'

'They?'

She got cunning. Her whole body seemed to go lax. Then she smiled at me winningly. 'He didn't tell you then.' Her voice was almost gleeful, as if she had outsmarted me. Maybe she had.

'He told me about Mr Regan, yes. That's not what he wanted to see me about. Is that what you've been trying to get me to say?'

'I'm sure I don't care what you say.'

I stood up again. 'Then I'll be running along.' She didn't speak. I went over to the tall white door I had come in at. When I looked back she had her lip between her teeth and was worrying it like a puppy at the fringe of a rug.

I went out, down the tile staircase to the hall, and the butler drifted out of somewhere with my hat in his hand. I put it on while he opened the door for me.

'You made a mistake,' I said. 'Mrs Regan didn't want to see me.'

He inclined his silver head and said politely: 'I'm sorry, sir. I make many mistakes.' He closed the door against my back.

I stood on the step breathing my cigarette smoke and looking down a succession of terraces with flowerbeds and trimmed trees to the high iron fence with gilt spears that hemmed in the estate. A winding driveway dropped down between retaining walls to the open iron gates. Beyond the fence the hill sloped for several miles. On this lower level faint and far off I could just barely see some of the old wooden derricks of the oilfield from which the Sternwoods had made their money. Most of the field was public park now, cleaned up and donated to the city by General Sternwood. But a little of it was still producing in groups of wells pumping five or six barrels a day. The Sternwoods, having moved up the hill, could no longer smell the stale sump water or the oil, but they could still look out of their front windows and see what had made them rich. If they wanted to. I don't suppose they would want to.

I walked down a brick path from terrace to terrace, followed along inside the fence and so out of the gates to where I had left my car under a pepper tree on the street. Thunder was crackling in the foothills now and the sky above them was purple-black. It was going to rain hard. The air had the damp foretaste of rain. I put the top up on my convertible before I started down-town.

She had lovely legs. I would say that for her. They were a couple of pretty smooth citizens, she and her father. He was probably just trying me out; the job he had given me was a lawyer's job. Even if Mr Arthur Gwynn Geiger, 'Rare Books and De Luxe Edition', turned out to be a blackmailer, it was still a lawyer's job. Unless there was a lot more to it than met the eye. At a casual glance I thought I might have a lot of fun finding out.

I drove down to the Hollywood public library and did a little superficial research in a stuffy volume called *Famous First Editions*. Half an hour of it made me need my lunch.

4

A. G. Geiger's place was a store frontage on the north side of the boulevard near Las Palmas. The entrance door was set far back in the middle and there was a copper trim on the windows, which were backed with Chinese screens, so I couldn't see into the store. There was a lot of Oriental junk in the windows. I didn't know whether it was any good, not being a collector of antiques, except unpaid bills. The entrance door was plate glass, but I couldn't see much through that either, because the store was very dim. A building entrance adjoined it on one side and on the other was a glittering credit jewellery establishment. The jeweller stood in his entrance, teetering on his heels and looking bored, a tall handsome white-haired Jew in lean dark clothes, with about nine carats of diamond on his right hand. A faint knowing smile curved his lips when I turned into Geiger's store. I let the door close softly behind me and walked on a thick blue rug that paved the floor from wall to wall. There were blue leather easy chairs with smoke stands beside them. A few sets of tooled leather bindings were set out on narrow polished tables, between book ends. There were more tooled bindings in glass cases on the walls. Nice-looking merchandise, the kind a rich promoter would buy by the yard and have somebody paste his book-plate in. At the back there was a grained wood partition with a door in the middle of it, shut. In the corner made by the partition and one wall a woman sat behind a small desk with a carved wooden lantern on it.

She got up slowly and swayed towards me in a tight black dress that didn't reflect any light. She had long thighs and she walked with a certain something I hadn't often seen in bookstores. She was an ash blonde with greenish eyes, beaded lashes, hair waved smoothly back from ears in which large jet buttons glittered. Her fingernails were silvered. In spite of her get-up she looked as if she would have a hall bedroom accent.

She approached me with enough sex appeal to stampede a businessmen's lunch and tilted her head to finger a stray, but not very stray, tendril of softly glowing hair. Her smile was tentative, but could be persuaded to be nice.

'Was it something?' she inquired.

I had my horn-rimmed sun-glasses on. I put my voice high and let a bird twitter in it. 'Would you happen to have a *Ben Hur* 1860?'

She didn't say: 'Huh?' but she wanted to. She smiled bleakly. 'A first edition?'

'Third,' I said. 'The one with the erratum on page 116.'

'I'm afraid not—at the moment.'

'How about a *Chevalier Audubon* 1840—the full set, of course?'

'Er—not at the moment,' she said harshly. Her smile was now hanging by its teeth and eyebrows and wondering what it would hit when it dropped.

'You *do* sell books?' I said in my polite falsetto.

She looked me over. No smile now. Eyes medium to hard. Pose very straight and stiff. She waved silver finger-nails at the glassed-in shelves. 'What do they look like—grapefruit?' she inquired tartly.

'Oh, that sort of thing hardly interests me, you know. Probably has duplicate sets of steel engravings, tuppence coloured and a penny plain. The usual vulgarity. No. I'm sorry. No.'

'I see.' She tried to jack the smile back upon her face. She was as sore as an alderman with the mumps. 'Perhaps Mr Geiger—but he's not in at the moment.' Her eyes studied me carefully. She knew as much about rare books as I knew about handling a flea circus.

'He might be in later?'

'I'm afraid not until late.'

'Too bad,' I said. 'Ah, too bad. I'll sit down and smoke a cigarette in one of these charming chairs. I have rather a blank afternoon. Nothing to think about but my trigonometry lesson.'

'Yes,' she said. 'Ye—es, of course.'

I stretched out in one and lit a cigarette with the round nickel lighter on the smoking stand. She still stood, holding her lower lip with her teeth, her eyes vaguely troubled. She nodded at last, turned slowly and walked back to her little desk in the corner. From behind the lamp she stared at me. I crossed my ankles and yawned. Her silver nails went out to the cradle phone on the desk, didn't touch it, dropped and began to tap on the desk.

Silence for about five minutes. The door opened and a tall hungry-looking bird with a cane and a big nose came in neatly, shut the door behind him against the pressure of the door-closer, marched over to the desk and placed a wrapped parcel on the desk. He took a pin-seal wallet with gold corners from his pocket and showed the blonde something. She pressed a button on the desk. The tall bird went to the door in the panelled partition and opened it barely enough to slip through.

I finished my cigarette and lit another. The minutes dragged by. Horns tooted and grunted on the boulevard. A big red interurban car grumbled past. A traffic light gonged. The blonde leaned on her elbow and cupped a hand over her eyes and stared at me behind it. The partition door opened and the tall bird with the cane slid out. He had another wrapped parcel, the shape of a large book. He went over to the desk and paid money. He left as he had come, walking on the balls of his feet, breathing with his mouth open, giving me a sharp side glance as he passed.

I got to my feet, tipped my hat to the blonde and went out after him. He walked west, swinging his cane in a small tight arc just above his right shoe. He was easy to follow. His coat was cut from a rather loud piece of horse robe with shoulders so wide that his neck stuck up out of it like a celery stalk and his head wobbled on it as he walked. We went a block and a half. At the Highland Avenue traffic signal I pulled up beside him and let him see me. He gave me a casual, then a suddenly sharpened side glance, and quickly turned away. We crossed Highland with the green light and made another block. He stretched his long legs and had twenty yards on me at the corner. He turned right. A hundred feet up the hill he stopped and hooked his cane over his arm and fumbled a leather cigarette-case out of an inner pocket. He put a cigarette in his mouth, dropped his match, looked back when he picked it up, saw me watching him from the corner, and straightened up as if somebody had booted him from behind. He almost raised dust going up the block, walking with long gawky strides and jabbing his cane into the pavement. He turned left again. He had at least half a block on me when I reached the place where he had turned. He had me wheezing. This was a narrow tree-lined street with a retaining wall on one side and three bungalow courts on the other.

He was gone. I loafed along the block peering this way and that. At the second bungalow court I saw something. It was called The La Baba, a quiet dim place with a double row of tree-shaded bungalows. The central walk was lined with Italian cypresses trimmed short and chunky, something the shape of the oil jars in *Ali Baba and the Forty Thieves*. Behind the third jar a loud-patterned sleeve edge moved.

I leaned against a pepper tree in the parkway and waited. The thunder in the foothills was rumbling again. The glare of lightning was reflected on piled-up black clouds off to the south. A few tentative raindrops splashed down on the pavement and made spots as large as nickels. The air was as still as the air in General Sternwood's orchid house.

The sleeve behind the tree showed again, then a big nose and one eye and some sandy hair without a hat on it. The eye stared at me. It disappeared. Its mate reappeared like a woodpecker on the other side of the tree. Five minutes went by. It got him. His type are half nerves. I heard a match strike and then whistling started. Then a dim shadow slipped along the grass to the next tree. Then he was out on the walk coming straight towards me, swinging the cane and whistling. A sour whistle with jitters in it. I stared vaguely up at the dark sky. He passed within ten feet of me and didn't give me a glance. He was safe now. He had ditched it.

I watched him out of sight and went up the central walk of The La Baba and parted the branches of the third cypress. I drew out a wrapped book and put it under my arm and went away from there. Nobody yelled at me.

5

Back on the boulevard I went into a drugstore phone booth and looked up Mr Arthur Gwynn Geiger's residence. He lived on Laverne Terrace, a hillside street off Laurel Canyon Boulevard. I dropped my nickel and dialled his number just for fun. Nobody answered. I turned to the classified section and noted a couple of bookstores within blocks of where I was.

The first I came to was on the north side, a large lower floor devoted to stationery and office supplies, a mass of books on the mezzanine. It didn't look the right place. I crossed the street and walked two blocks east to the other one. This was more like it, a narrowed cluttered little shop stacked with books from floor to ceiling and four or five browsers taking their time putting thumb marks on the new jackets. Nobody paid any attention to them. I shoved on back into the store, passed through a partition and found a small dark woman reading a law book at a desk.

I flipped my wallet open on her desk and let her look at the buzzer pinned to the flap. She looked at it, took her glasses off and leaned back in her chair. I put the wallet away. She had the fine-drawn face of an intelligent Jewess. She stared at me and said nothing.

I said: 'Would you do me a favour, a very small favour?'

'I don't know. What is it?' She had a smoothly husky voice.

'You know Geiger's store across the street, two blocks west?'

'I think I may have passed it.'

'It's a bookstore,' I said. 'Not your kind of bookstore. You know darn well.'

She curled her lips slightly and said nothing. 'You know Geiger by sight?' I asked.

'I'm sorry. I don't know Mr Geiger.'

'Then you couldn't tell me what he looks like?'

Her lip curled some more. 'Why should I?'

'No reason at all. If you don't want to, I can't make you.'

She looked out through the partition door and leaned back again. 'That was a sheriff's star, wasn't it?'

'Honorary deputy. Doesn't mean a thing. It's worth a dime cigar.'

'I see.' She reached for a pack of cigarettes and shook one loose and reached for it with her lips. I held a match for her. She thanked me, leaned back again and regarded me through smoke. She said carefully:

'You wish to know what he looks like and you don't want to interview him?'

'He's not there,' I said.

'I presume he will be. After all, it's his store.'

'I don't want to interview him just yet,' I said.

She looked out through the open doorway again. I said: 'Know anything about rare books?'

'You could try me.'

'Would you have a *Ben Hur*, 1860, third edition, the one with the duplicated line on page 116?'

She pushed her yellow law book to one side and reached a fat volume up on the desk, leafed it through, found her page, and studied it. 'Nobody would,' she said without looking up. 'There isn't one.'

'Right.'

'What in the world are you driving at?'

'The girl in Geiger's store didn't know that.'

She looked up. 'I see. You interest me. Rather vaguely.'

'I'm a private dick on a case. Perhaps I ask too much. It didn't seem much to me somehow.'

She blew a soft grey smoke ring and poked her finger through. It came to pieces in frail wisps. She spoke smoothly, indifferently. 'In his early forties, I should judge. Medium height, fattish. Would weigh about a hundred and sixty pounds. Fat face, Charlie Chan moustache, thick soft neck. Soft all over. Well dressed, goes without a hat, affects a knowledge of antiques and hasn't any. Oh yes. His left eye is glass.'

'You'd make a good cop,' I said.

She put the reference book back on an open shelf at the end of her desk, and opened the law book in front of her again. 'I hope not,' she said. She put her glasses on.

I thanked her and left. The rain had started. I ran for it, with the wrapped book under my arm. My car was on a side street pointing at the boulevard almost opposite Geiger's store. I was well sprinkled before I got there. I tumbled into the car and ran both windows up and wiped my parcel off with my handkerchief. Then I opened it up.

I knew about what it would be, of course. A heavy book, well bound, handsomely printed in handset type on fine paper. Larded with full-page arty photographs. Photos and letterpress were alike of an indescribable filth. The book was not new. Dates were stamped on the front endpaper, in and out dates. A rent book. A lending library of elaborate smut.

I re-wrapped the book and locked it up behind the seat. A racket like that, out in the open on the boulevard, seemed to mean plenty of protection. I sat there and poisoned myself with cigarette smoke and listened to the rain and thought about it.

6

Rain filled the gutters and splashed knee-high off the pavement. Big cops in slickers that shone like gun barrels had a lot of fun carrying giggling girls across the bad places. The rain drummed hard on the roof of the car and the burbank top began to leak. A pool of water formed on the floorboards for me to keep my feet in. It was too early in the fall for that kind of rain. I struggled into a trench coat and made a dash for the nearest drugstore and bought myself a pint of whisky. Back in the car I used enough of it to keep warm and interested. I was long overparked, but the cops were too busy carrying girls and blowing whistles to bother about that.

In spite of the rain, or perhaps even because of it, there was business done at Geiger's. Very nice cars stopped in front and very nice-looking people went in and out with wrapped parcels. They were not all men.

He showed about four o'clock. A cream-coloured coupé stopped in front of the store and I caught a glimpse of the fat face and the Charlie Chan moustache as he dodged out of it and into the store. He was hatless and wore a belted green leather raincoat. I couldn't see his glass eye at that distance. A tall and very good-looking kid in a jerkin came out of the store and rode the coupé off around the corner and came back walking, his glistening black hair plastered with rain.

Another hour went by. It got dark and the rain-clouded lights of the stores were soaked up by the black street. Street-car bells jangled crossly. At around five-fifteen the tall boy in the jerkin came out of Geiger's with an umbrella and went after the cream-coloured coupé. When he had it in front Geiger came out and the tall boy held the umbrella over Geiger's bare head. He folded it, shook it off and handed it into the car. He dashed back into the store. I started my motor.

The coupé went west on the boulevard, which forced me to make a left turn and a lot of enemies, including a motorman who stuck his head out into the rain to bawl me out. I was two blocks behind the coupé before I got in the groove. I hoped Geiger was on his way home. I caught sight of him two or three times and then made him turning north into Laurel Canyon Drive. Half-way up the grade he turned left and took a curving ribbon of wet concrete which was called Laverne Terrace. It was a narrow street with a high bank on one side and a scattering of cabin-like houses built down the slope on the other side, so that their roofs were not very much above road level. Their front windows were masked by hedges and shrubs. Sodden trees dripped all over the landscape.

Geiger had his lights on and I hadn't. I speeded up and passed him on a curve, picked a number off a house as I went by and turned at the end of the block. He had already stopped. His car lights were tilted in at the garage of a small house with a square box hedge so arranged that it masked the front door completely. I watched him come out of the garage with his umbrella up and go in through the hedge. He didn't act as if he expected anybody to be tailing him. Light went on in the house. I drifted down to the next house above it, which seemed empty but had no signs out. I parked, aired out the convertible, had a drink from my bottle, and sat. I didn't know what I was waiting for, but something told me to wait. Another army of sluggish minutes dragged by. .

Two cars came up the hill and went over the crest. It seemed to be a very quiet street. At a little after six more bright lights bobbed through the driving rain. It was pitch-black by then. A car dragged to a stop in front of Geiger's house. The filaments of its lights glowed dimly and died. The door opened and a woman got out. A small slim woman in a vagabond hat and a transparent raincoat. She went in through the box maze. A bell rang faintly, light through the rain, a closing door, silence.

I reached a flash out of my car pocket and went down-grade and looked at the car. It was a Packard convertible, maroon or dark brown. The left window was down. I felt for the licence-holder and poked light at it. The registration read: Carmen Sternwood, 3765 Alta Brea Crescent, West Hollywood. I went back to my car again and sat and sat. The top dripped on my knees and my stomach burned from the whisky. No more cars came up the hill. No lights went on in the house before which I was parked. It seemed like a nice neighbourhood to have bad habits in.

At seven-twenty a single flash of hard white light shot out of Geiger's house like a wave of summer lightning. As the darkness folded back on it and ate it up a thin tinkling scream echoed out and lost itself among the rain-drenched trees. I was out of the car and on my way before the echoes died.

There was no fear in the scream. It had a sound of half-pleasurable shock, an accent of drunkenness, an overtone of pure idiocy. It was a nasty sound. It made me think of men in white and barred windows and hard narrow cots with leather wrist and ankle straps fastened to them. The Geiger hideaway was perfectly silent again when I hit the gap in the hedge and dodged around the angle that masked the front door. There was an iron ring in a lion's mouth for a knocker. I reached for it, I had hold of it. At that exact instant, as if somebody had been waiting for the cue, three shots boomed in the house. There was a sound that might have been a long harsh sigh. Then a soft messy thump. And then rapid footsteps in the house—going away.

The door fronted on a narrow run, like a footbridge over a gully, that filled the gap between the house wall and the edge of the bank. There was no porch, no solid ground, no way to get around to the back. The back entrance was at the top of a flight of wooden steps that rose from the alley-like street below. I knew this because I heard a clatter of feet on the steps, going down. Then I heard the sudden roar of a starting car. It faded swiftly into the distance. I thought the sound was echoed by another car, but I wasn't sure. The house in front of me was as silent as a vault. There wasn't any hurry. What was in there was in there.

I straddled the fence at the side of the runway and leaned far out to the draped but unscreened French window and tried to look in at the crack where the drapes came together. I saw lamplight on a wall and one end of a bookcase. I got back on the runway and took all of it and some of the hedge and gave the front door the heavy shoulder. This was foolish. About the only part of a California house you can't put your foot through is the front door. All it did was hurt my shoulder and make me mad. I climbed over the railing again and kicked the French window in, used my hat for a glove and pulled out most of the lower small pane of glass. I could now reach in and draw a bolt that fastened the window to the sill. The rest was easy. There was no top bolt. The catch gave. I climbed in and pulled the drapes off my face.

Neither of the two people in the room paid any attention to the way I came in, although only one of them was dead.

7

It was a wide room, the whole width of the house. It had a low beamed ceiling and brown plaster walls decked out with strips of Chinese embroidery, and Chinese and Japanese prints in grained wood frames. There were low bookshelves, there was a thick pinkish Chinese rug in which a gopher could have spent a week without showing his nose above the nap. There were floor cushions, bits of odd silk tossed around, as if whoever lived there had to have a piece he could reach out and thumb. There was a broad low divan of old rose tapestry. It had a wad of clothes on it, including lilac-coloured silk underwear. There was a big carved lamp on a pedestal, two other standing lamps with jade-green shades and long tassels. There was a black desk with carved gargoyles at the corners and behind it a yellow satin cushion on a polished black chair with carved arms and back. The room contained an odd assortment of odours, of which the most emphatic at the moment seemed to be the pungent aftermath of cordite and the sickish aroma of ether.

On a sort of low dais at one end of the room there was a high-backed teakwood chair in which Miss Carmen Sternwood was sitting on a fringed orange shawl. She was sitting very straight, with her hands on the arms of the chair, her knees close together, her body stiffly erect in the pose of an Egyptian goddess, her chin level, her small bright teeth shining between her parted lips. Her eyes were wide open. The dark slate colour of the iris had devoured the pupil. They were mad eyes. She seemed to be unconscious, but she didn't have the pose of unconsciousness. She looked as if, in her mind, she was doing something very important and making a fine job of it. Out of her mouth came a tinny chuckling noise which didn't change her expression or even move her lips.

She was wearing a pair of long jade earrings. They were nice earrings and had probably cost a couple of hundred dollars. She wasn't wearing anything else.

She had a beautiful body, small, lithe, compact, firm, rounded. Her skin in the lamplight had the shimmering lustre of a pearl. Her legs didn't quite have the raffish grace of Mrs Regan's legs, but they were very nice. I looked her over without either embarrassment or ruttishness. As a naked girl she was not there in that room at all. She was just a dope. To me she was always just a dope.

I stopped looking at her, and looked at Geiger. He was on his back on the floor, beyond the fringe of the Chinese rug, in front of a thing that looked like a totem pole. It had a profile like an eagle and its wide round eye was a camera lens. The lens was aimed at the naked girl in the chair. There was a blackened flash bulb clipped to the side of the totem pole. Geiger was wearing Chinese slippers with thick felt soles, and his legs were in black satin pyjamas and the upper part of him wore a Chinese embroidered coat, the front of which was mostly blood. His glass eye shone brightly up at me and was by far the most lifelike thing about him. At a glance none of the three shots I heard had missed. He was very dead.

The flash bulb was the sheet lightning I had seen. The crazy scream was the doped and naked girl's reaction to it. The three shots had been somebody else's idea of how the proceedings might be given a new twist. The idea of the lad who had gone down the back steps and slammed into a car and raced away. I could see merit in his point of view.

A couple of fragile gold-veined glasses rested on a red lacquer tray on the end of the black desk, beside a pot-bellied flagon of brown liquid. I took the stopper out and sniffed at it. It smelled of ether and something else, possibly laudanum. I had never tried the mixture but it seemed to go pretty well with the Geiger *ménage*.

I listened to the rain hitting the roof and the north windows. Beyond was no other sound, no cars, no siren, just the rain beating. I went over to the divan and peeled off my trench coat and pawed through the girl's clothes. There was a pale green rough wool dress of the pull-on type, with half sleeves. I thought I might be able to handle it. I decided to pass up her underclothes, not from feelings of delicacy, but because I couldn't see myself putting her pants on and snapping her brassiére. I took the dress over to the teak chair on the dais. Miss Sternwood smelled of ether also, at a distance of several feet. The tinny chuckling noise was still coming from her and a little froth oozed down her chin. I slapped her face. She blinked and stopped chuckling. I slapped her again.

'Come on,' I said brightly. 'Let's be nice. Let's get dressed.'

She peered at me, her slaty eyes as empty as holes in a mask. 'Gugugoterell,' she said.

I slapped her around a little more. She didn't mind the slaps. They didn't bring her out of it. I set to work with the dress. She didn't mind that either. She let me hold her arms up and she spread her fingers out wide, as if that was cute. I got her hands through the sleeves, pulled the dress down over her back, and stood her up. She fell into my arms giggling. I set her back in the chair and got her stockings and shoes on her.

'Let's take a little walk,' I said. 'Let's take a nice little walk.'

We took a little walk. Part of the time her earrings banged against my chest and part of the time we did the splits in unison, like adagio dancers. We walked over to Geiger's body and back. I had her look at him. She thought he was cute. She giggled and tried to tell me so, but she just bubbled. I walked her over to the divan and spread her out on it. She hiccuped twice, giggled a little and went to sleep. I stuffed her belongings into my pockets and went over behind the totem pole thing. The camera was there all right, set inside it, but there was no plateholder in the camera. I looked around on the floor, thinking he might have got it out before he was shot. No plateholder. I took hold of his limp chilling hand and rolled him a little. No plateholder. I didn't like this development.

I went into a hall at the back of the room and investigated the house.

There was a bathroom on the right and a locked door, a kitchen at the back. The kitchen window had been jimmied. The screen was gone and the place where the hook had pulled out showed on the sill. The back door was unlocked. I left it unlocked and looked into a bedroom on the left side of the hall. It was neat, fussy, womanish. The bed had a flounced cover. There was perfume on the triple-mirrored dressing-table, beside a handkerchief, some loose money, a man's brushes, a keyholder. A man's clothes were in the closet and a man's slippers under the flounced edge of the bed cover. Mr Geiger's room. I took the keyholder back to the living-room and went through the desk. There was a locked steel box in the deep drawer. I used one of the keys on it. There was nothing in it but a blue leather book with an index and a lot of writing in code, in the same slanting printing that had written to General Sternwood. I put the notebook in my pocket, wiped the steel box where I had touched it, locked the desk up, pocketed the keys, turned the gas logs off in the fireplace, wrapped myself in my coat and tried to rouse Miss Sternwood. It couldn't be done. I crammed her vagabond hat on her head and swathed her in her coat and carried her out to her car. I went back and put all the lights out and shut the front door, dug her keys out of her bag and started the Packard. We went off down the hill without lights. It was less than ten minutes' drive to Alta Brea Crescent. Carmen spent them snoring and breathing ether in my face. I couldn't keep her head off my shoulder. It was all I could do to keep it out of my lap.

8

There was dim light behind narrow leaded panes in the side door of the Sternwood mansion. I stopped the Packard under the *porte-cochère* and emptied my pockets out on the seat. The girl snored in the corner, her hat tilted rakishly over her nose, her hands hanging limp in the folds of the raincoat. I got out and rang the bell. Steps came slowly, as if from a long dreary distance. The door opened and the straight, silvery butler looked out at me. The light from the hall made a halo of his hair.

He said: 'Good evening, sir' politely and looked past me at the Packard. His eyes came back to look at my eyes.

'Is Mrs Regan in?'

'No, sir.'

'The General is asleep, I hope?'

'Yes. The evening is his best time for sleeping.'

'How about Mrs Regan's maid?'

'Mathilda? She's here, sir.'

'Better get her down here. The job needs the woman's touch. Take a look in the car and you'll see why.'

He took a look in the car. He came back. 'I see,' he said. 'I'll get Mathilda.'

'Mathilda will do right by her,' I said.

'We all try to do right by her,' he said.

'I guess you'll have had practice,' I said.

He let that one go. 'Well, good night,' I said. 'I'm leaving it in your hands.'

'Very good, sir. May I call you a cab?'

'Positively not,' I said. 'As a matter of fact I'm not here. You're just seeing things.'

He smiled then. He gave me a duck of his head and I turned and walked down the driveway and out of the gates.

Ten blocks of that, winding down curved rainswept streets, under the steady drip of trees, past lighted windows in big houses in ghostly enormous grounds, vague clusters of eaves and gables and lighted windows high on the hillside, remote and inaccessible, like witch houses in a forest. I came out at a service station glaring with wasted light, where a bored attendant in a white cap and a dark blue windbreaker sat hunched on a stool, inside the steamed glass, reading a paper. I started in, then kept going. I was as wet as I could get already. And on a night like that you can grow a beard waiting for a taxi. And taxi drivers remember.

I made it back to Geiger's house in something over half an hour of nimble walking. There was nobody there, no car on the street except my own car in front of the next house. It looked as dismal as a lost dog. I dug my bottle of rye out of it and poured half of what was left down my throat and got inside to light a cigarette. I smoked half of it, threw it away, got out again and went down to Geiger's. I unlocked the door and stepped into the still warm darkness and stood there, dripping quietly on the floor and listening to the rain. I groped to a lamp and lit it.

The first thing I noticed was that a couple of strips of embroidered silk were gone from the wall. I hadn't counted them, but the spaces of brown plaster stood out naked and obvious. I went a little farther and put another lamp on. I looked at the totem pole. At its foot, beyond the margin of the Chinese rug, on the bare floor another rug had been spread. It hadn't been there before. Geiger's body had. Geiger's body was gone.

That froze me. I pulled my lips back against my teeth and leered at the glass eye in the totem pole. I went through the house again. Everything was exactly as it had been. Geiger wasn't in his flounced bed or under it or in his closet. He wasn't in the kitchen or the bathroom. That left the locked door on the right of the hall. One of Geiger's keys fitted the lock. The room inside was interesting, but Geiger wasn't in it. It was interesting because it was so different from Geiger's room. It was a hard bare masculine bedroom with a polished wood floor, a couple of small throw rugs in an Indian design, two straight chairs, a bureau in dark grained wood with a man's toilet set and two black candles in foot-high brass candlesticks. The bed was narrow and looked hard and had a maroon batik cover. The room felt cold. I locked it up again, wiped the knob off with my handkerchief, and went back to the totem pole. I knelt down and squinted along the nap of the rug to the front door. I thought I could see two parallel grooves pointing that way, as though heels had dragged. Whoever had done it had meant business. Dead men are heavier than broken hearts.

It wasn't the law. They would have been there still, just about getting warmed up with their pieces of string and chalk and their cameras and dusting powders and their nickel cigars. They would have been very much there. It wasn't the killer. He had left too fast. He must have seen the girl. He couldn't be sure she was too batty to see him. He would be on his way to distant places. I couldn't guess the answer, but it was all right with me if somebody wanted Geiger missing instead of just murdered. It gave me a chance to find out if I could tell it leaving Carmen Sternwood out. I locked up again, choked my car to life and rode off home to a shower, dry clothes and a late dinner. After that I sat around in the apartment and drank too much hot toddy trying to crack the code in Geiger's blue indexed notebook. All I could be sure of was that it was a list of names and addresses probably of the customers. There were over four hundred of them. That made it a nice racket, not to mention any blackmail angles, and there were probably plenty of those. Any name on the list might be a prospect as the killer. I didn't envy the police their job when it was handed to them.

I went to bed full of whisky and frustration and dreamed about a man in a bloody Chinese coat who chased a naked girl with long jade earrings while I ran after them and tried to take a photograph with an empty camera.

9

The next morning was bright, clear and sunny. I woke up with a motorman's glove in my mouth, drank two cups of coffee and went through the morning papers. I didn't find any reference to Mr Arthur Gwynn Geiger in either of them. I was shaking the wrinkles out of my damp suit when the phone rang. It was Bernie Ohls, the DA's chief investigator, who had given me the lead to General Sternwood.

'Well, how's the boy?' he began. He sounded like a man who had slept well and didn't owe too much money.

'I've got a hangover,' I said.

'Tsk, tsk.' He laughed absently and then his voice became a shade too casual, a cagey cop voice. 'Seen General Sternwood yet?'

'Uh-huh.'

'Done anything for him?'

'Too much rain,' I answered, if that was an answer.

'They seem to be a family things happen to. A big Buick belonging to one of them is washing about in the surf off Lido fish pier.'

I held the telephone tight enough to crack it. I also held my breath.

'Yeah,' Ohls said cheerfully. 'A nice new Buick sedan all messed up with sand and sea water. . . . Oh, I almost forgot. There's a guy inside it.'

I let my breath out so slowly that it hung on my lips. 'Regan?' I asked.

'Huh? Who? Oh, you mean the ex-legger the eldest girl picked up and went and married. I never saw him. What would he be doing down there?'

'Quit stalling. What would anybody be doing down there?'

'I don't know, pal. I'm dropping down to look-see. Want to go along?'

'Yes.'

'Snap it up,' he said. 'I'll be in my hutch.'

Shaved, dressed and lightly breakfasted I was at the Hall of Justice in less than an hour. I rode up to the seventh floor and went along to the group of small offices used by the DA's men. Ohls's was no larger than the others, but he had it to himself. There was nothing on his desk but a blotter, a cheap pen set, his hat and one of his feet. He was a medium-sized blondish man with stiff white eyebrows, calm eyes and well-kept teeth. He looked like anybody you would pass on the street. I happened to know he had killed nine men—three of them when he was covered, or somebody thought he was.

He stood up and pocketed a flat tin of toy cigars called Entractes, jiggled the one in his mouth up and down and looked at me carefully along his nose, with his head thrown back.

'It's not Regan,' he said. 'I checked. Regan's a big guy, as tall as you and a shade heavier. This is a young kid.'

I didn't say anything.

'What made Regan skip out?' Ohls asked. 'You interested in that?'

'I don't think so,' I said.

'When a guy out of the liquor traffic marries into a rich family and then waves good-bye to a pretty dame and a couple million legitimate bucks—that's enough to make even me think. I guess you thought that was a secret.'

'Uh-huh.'

'Okey, keep buttoned, kid. No hard feelings.' He came around the desk tapping his pockets and reaching for his hat.

'I'm not looking for Regan,' I said.

He fixed the lock on his door and we went down to the official parking lot and got into a small blue sedan. We drove out Sunset, using the siren once in a while to beat a signal. It was a crisp morning, with just enough snap in the air to make life seem simple and sweet, if you didn't have too much on your mind. I had.

It was thirty miles to Lido on the coast highway, the first ten of them through traffic. Ohls made the run in three-quarters of an hour. At the end of that time we skidded to a stop in front of a faded stucco arch and I took my feet out of the floorboards and we got out. A long pier railed with white two-by-fours stretched seaward from the arch. A knot of people leaned out at the far end and a motor-cycle officer stood under the arch keeping another group of people from going out on the pier. Cars were parked on both sides of the highway, the usual ghouls, of both sexes. Ohls showed the motor-cycle officer his badge and we went out on the pier, into a loud fish smell which one night's hard rain hadn't even dented.

'There she is—on the power barge,' Ohls said, pointing with one of his toy cigars.

A low black barge with a wheelhouse like a tug's was crouched against the pilings at the end of the pier. Something that glistened in the morning sunlight was on its deck, with hoist chains still around it, a large black and chromium car. The arm of the hoist had been swung back into position and lowered to deck level. Men stood around the car. We went down slippery steps to the deck.

Ohls said hello to a deputy in green khaki and a man in plain clothes. The barge crew of three men leaned against the front of the wheelhouse and chewed tobacco. One of them was rubbing at his wet hair with a dirty bath-towel. That would be the man who had gone down into the water to put the chains on.

We looked the car over. The front bumper was bent, one headlight smashed, the other bent up but the glass still unbroken. The radiator shell had a big dent in it, and the paint and nickel were scratched up all over the car. The upholstery was sodden and black. None of the tyres seemed to be damaged.

The driver was still draped around the steering post with his head at an unnatural angle to his shoulders. He was a slim dark-haired kid who had been good-looking not so long ago. Now his face was bluish white and his eyes were a faint dull gleam under the lowered lids and his open mouth had sand in it. On the left side of his forehead there was a dull bruise that stood out against the whiteness of the skin.

Ohls backed away, made a noise in his throat and put a match to his little cigar. 'What's the story?'

The uniformed man pointed up at the rubbernecks on the end of the pier. One of them was fingering a place where the white two-by-fours had been broken through in a wide space. The splintered wood showed yellow and clean, like fresh-cut pine.

'Went through there. Must have hit pretty hard. The rain stopped early down here, around 9 p.m. The broken wood's dry inside. That puts it after the rain stopped. She fell in plenty of water not to be banged up worse, not more than half tide or she'd have drifted farther, and not more than half tide going out or she'd have crowded the piles. That makes it around ten last night. Maybe nine-thirty, not earlier. She shows under the water when the boys come down to fish this morning, so we get the barge to hoist her out and we find the dead guy.'

The plain-clothes man scuffed at the deck with the toe of his shoe. Ohls looked sideways along his eyes at me, and twitched his little cigar like a cigarette.

'Drunk?' he asked, of nobody in particular.

The man who had been towelling his head went over to the rail and cleared his throat in a loud hawk that made everyone look at him. 'Got some sand,' he said, and spat. 'Not as much as the boy friend got—but some.'

The uniformed man said: 'Could have been drunk. Showing off all alone in the rain. Drunks will do anything.'

'Drunk, hell,' the plain-clothes man said. 'The hand throttle's set half-way down and the guy's been sapped on the side of the head. Ask me and I'll call it murder.'

Ohls looked at the man with the towel. 'What do you think, buddy?'

The man with the towel looked flattered. He grinned. 'I say suicide, Mac. None of my business, but you ask me, I say suicide. First off the guy ploughed an awful straight furrow down that pier. You can read his tread marks all the way nearly. That puts it after the rain like the Sheriff said. Then he hit the pier hard and clean or he don't go through and land right side up. More likely turned over a couple of times. So he had plenty of speed and hit the rail square. That's more than half-throttle. He could have done that with his hand falling and he could have hurt his head falling too.'

Ohls said: 'You got eyes, buddy. Frisked him?' he asked the deputy. The deputy looked at me then, at the crew against the wheelhouse. 'Okey, save that,' Ohls said.

A small man with glasses and a tired face and a black bag came down the steps from the pier. He picked out a fairly clean spot on the deck and put the bag down. Then he took his hat off and rubbed the back of his neck and stared out to sea, as if he didn't know where he was or what he had come for.

Ohls said: 'There's your customer, Doc. Dived off the pier last night.

Around nine to ten. That's all we know.'

The small man looked in at the dead man morosely. He fingered the head, peered at the bruise on the temple, moved the head around with both hands, felt the man's ribs. He lifted a lax dead hand and stared at the fingernails. He let it fall and watched it fall. He stepped back and opened his bag and took out a printed pad of DOA forms and began to write over a carbon.

'Broken neck's the apparent cause of death,' he said, writing. 'Which means there won't be much water in him. Which means he's due to start getting stiff pretty quick now he's out in the air. Better get him out of the car before he does. You won't like doing it after.'

Ohls nodded. 'How long dead, Doc?'

'I wouldn't know.'

Ohls looked at him sharply and took the little cigar out of his mouth and looked at that sharply. 'Pleased to know you, Doc. A coroner's man that can't guess within five minutes has me beat.'

The little man grinned sourly and put his pad in his bag and clipped his pencil back on his waistcoat. 'If he ate dinner last night, I'll tell you—if I know what time he ate it. But not within five minutes.'

'How would he get that bruise—falling?'

The little man looked at the bruise again. 'I don't think so. That blow came from something covered. And it had already bled subcutaneously while he was alive.'

'Blackjack, huh?'

'Very likely.'

The little ME's man nodded, picked his bag off the deck and went back up the steps to the pier. An ambulance was backing into position outside the stucco arch. Ohls looked at me and said: 'Let's go. Hardly worth the ride, was it?'

We went back along the pier and got into Ohls's sedan again. He wrestled it around on the highway and drove back towards town along a three-lane highway washed clean by the rain, past low rolling hills of yellow-white sand terraced with pink moss. Seaward a few gulls wheeled and swooped over something in the surf and far out a white yacht looked as if it was hanging in the sky.

Ohls cocked his chin at me and said: 'Know him?'

'Sure. The Sternwood chauffeur. I saw him dusting that very car out there yesterday.'

'I don't want to crowd you, Marlowe. Just tell me, did the job have anything to do with him?'

'No. I don't even know his name.'

'Owen Taylor. How do I know? Funny about that. About a year or so back we had him in the cooler on a Mann Act rap. It seems he run Sternwood's hotcha daughter, the young one, off to Yuma. The sister ran after them and brought them back and had Owen heaved into the icebox. Then next day she comes down to the DA and gets him to beg the kid off with the US 'cutor. She says the kid meant to marry her sister and wanted to, only the sister can't see it. All *she* wanted was to kick a few high ones off the bar and have herself a party. So we let the kid go and then darned if they don't have him come back to work. And a little later we get the routine report on his prints from Washington, and he's got a prior back in Indiana, attempted hold-up six years ago. He got off with a six months in the county jail, the very one Dillinger bust out of. We hand that to the Sternwoods and they keep him on just the same. What do you think of that?'

'They seem to be a screwy family,' I said. 'Do they know about last night?'

'No. I gotta go up against them now.'

'Leave the old man out of it, if you can.'

'Why?'·

'He has enough troubles and he's sick.'

'You mean Regan?'

I scowled. 'I don't know anything about Regan, I told you. I'm not looking for Regan. Regan hasn't bothered anybody that I know of.'

Ohls said: 'Oh,' and stared thoughtfully out to sea and the sedan nearly went off the road. For the rest of the drive back to town he hardly spoke. He dropped me off in Hollywood near the Chinese Theatre and turned back west to Alta Brea Crescent. I ate lunch at a counter and looked at an afternoon paper and couldn't find anything about Geiger in it.

After lunch I walked east on the boulevard to have another look at Geiger's store.

IO

The lean black-eyed credit jeweller was standing in his entrance in the same position as the afternoon before. He gave me the same knowing look as I turned in. The store looked just the same. The same lamp glowed on the small desk in the corner and the same ash blonde in the same black suéde-like dress got up from behind it and came towards me with the same tentative smile on her face.

'Was it—?' she said and stopped. Her silver nails twitched at her side. There was an overtone of strain in her smile. It wasn't a smile at all. It was a grimace. She just thought it was a smile.

'Back again,' I said airily, and waved a cigarette. 'Mr Geiger in to-day?'

'I'm–I'm afraid not. No–I'm afraid not. Let me see–you wanted—?'

I took my dark glasses off and tapped them delicately on the inside of my left wrist. If you can weigh a hundred and ninety pounds and look like a fairy, I was doing my best.

'That was just a stall about those first editions,' I whispered. 'I have to be careful. I've got something he'll want. Something he's wanted for a long time.'

The silver finger-nails touched the blonde hair over one small jet-buttoned ear. 'Oh, a salesman,' she said. 'Well–you might come in to-morrow. I think he'll be here to-morrow.'

'Drop the veil,' I said. 'I'm in the business too.'

Her eyes narrowed until they were a faint greenish glitter, like a forest pool far back in the shadow of trees. Her fingers clawed at her palm. She stared at me and chopped off a breath.

'Is he sick? I could go up to the house,' I said impatiently. 'I haven't got for ever.'

'You—a—you—a—' her throat jammed. I thought she was going to fall on her nose. Her whole body shivered and her face fell apart like a bride's pie crust. She put it together again slowly, as if lifting a great weight, by sheer will power. The smile came back, with a couple of corners badly bent.

'No,' she said. 'No. He's out of town. That—wouldn't be any use. Can't you—come in—to-morrow?'

I had my mouth open to say something when the partition door opened a foot. The tall dark handsome boy in the jerkin looked out, pale-faced and tight-lipped, saw me, shut the door quickly again, but not before I had seen on the floor behind him a lot of wooden boxes lined with newspapers and packed loosely with books. A man in very new overalls was fussing with them. Some of Geiger's stock was being moved out.

When the door shut I put my dark glasses on again and touched my hat. 'To-morrow, then. I'd like to give you a card but you know how it is.'

'Ye—es. I know how it is.' She shivered a little more and made a faint sucking noise between her bright lips. I went out of the store and west on the boulevard to the corner and north on the street to the alley which ran behind the stores. A small black truck with wire sides and no lettering on it was backed up to Geiger's place. The man in the very new overalls was just heaving a box up on the tailboard. I went back to the boulevard and along the block next to Geiger's and found a taxi standing at a fireplug. A fresh-faced kid was reading a horror magazine behind the wheel. I leaned in and showed him a dollar: 'Tail job?'

He looked me over. 'Cop?'

'Private.'

He grinned. 'My meat, Jack.' He tucked the magazine over his rear-view mirror and I got into the cab. We went around the block and pulled up across from Geiger's alley, beside another fireplug.

There were about a dozen boxes on the truck when the man in overalls closed the screened doors and hooked the tailboard up and got in behind the wheel.

'Take him,' I told my driver.

The man in overalls gunned his motor, shot a glance up and down the alley and ran away fast in the other direction. He turned left out of the alley. We did the same. I caught a glimpse of the truck turning east on Franklin and told my driver to close in a little. He didn't or couldn't do it. I saw the truck two blocks away when we got to Franklin. We had it in sight to Vine and across Vine and all the way to Western. We saw it twice after Western. There was a lot of traffic and the fresh-faced kid tailed from too far back. I was telling him about that without mincing words when the truck, now far ahead, turned north again. The street at which it turned was called Britanny Place. When we got to Britanny Place the truck had vanished.

The fresh-faced kid made comforting sounds at me through the panel and we went up the hill at four miles an hour looking for the truck behind bushes. Two blocks up, Britany Place swung to the east and met Randall Place in a tongue of land on which there was a white apartment house with its front on Randall Place and its basement garage opening on Britanny. We were going past that and the fresh-faced kid was telling me the truck couldn't be far away when I looked through the arched entranced of the garage and saw it back in the dimness with its rear doors open again.

We went around to the front of the apartment house and I got out. There was nobody in the lobby, no switchboard. A wooden desk was pushed back against the wall beside a panel of gilt mailboxes. I looked the names over. A man named Joseph Brody had Apartment 405. A man named Joe Brody had received five thousand dollars from General Sternwood to stop playing with Carmen and find some other little girl to play with. It could be the same Joe Brody. I felt like giving odds on it.

I went around an elbow of wall to the foot of tiled stairs and the shaft of the automatic elevator. The top of the elevator was level with the floor. There was a door beside the shaft lettered 'Garage'. I opened it and went down narrow steps to the basement. The automatic elevator was propped open and the man in new overalls was grunting hard as he stacked heavy boxes in it. I stood beside him and lit a cigarette and watched him. He didn't like my watching him.

After a while I said: 'Watch the weight, bud. She's only tested for half a ton. Where's the stuff going?'

'Brody, four-o-five,' he said. 'Manager?'

'Yeah. Looks like a nice lot of loot.'

He glared at me with pale white-rimmed eyes. 'Books,' he snarled. 'A hundred pounds a box, easy, and me with a seventy-five pound back.'

'Well, watch the weight,' I said.

He got into the elevator with six boxes and shut the doors. I went back up the steps to the lobby and out to the street and the cab took me down-town again to my office building. I gave the fresh-faced kid too much money and he gave me a dog-eared business card which for once I didn't drop into the majolica jar of sand beside the elevator bank.

I had a room and a half on the seventh floor at the back. The half-room was an office split in two to make reception-rooms. Mine had my name on it and nothing else, and that only on the reception-room. I always left this unlocked, in case I had a client, and the client cared to sit down and wait.

I had a client.

11

She wore brownish speckled tweeds, a mannish shirt and tie, hand-carved walking shoes. Her stockings were just as sheer as the day before, but she wasn't showing as much of her legs. Her black hair was glossy under a brown Robin Hood hat that might have cost fifty dollars and looked as if you could have made it with one hand out of a desk blotter.

'Well, you *do* get up,' she said, wrinkling her nose at the faded red settee, the two odd semi-easy chairs, the net curtains that needed laundering and the boy's size library table with the venerable magazines on it to give the place a professional touch. 'I was beginning to think perhaps you worked in bed, like Marcel Proust.'

'Who's he?' I put a cigarette in my mouth and stared at her. She looked a little pale and strained, but she looked like a girl who could function under a strain.

'A French writer, a connoisseur in degenerates. You wouldn't know him.'

'Tut, tut,' I said. 'Come into my boudoir.'

She stood up and said: 'We didn't get along very well yesterday. Perhaps I was rude.'

'We were both rude,' I said. I unlocked the communicating door and held it for her. We went into the rest of my suite, which contained a rust-red carpet, not very young, five green filing cases, three of them full of California climate, an advertising calendar showing the Quins rolling around on a sky-blue floor, in pink dresses, with seal-brown hair and sharp black eyes as large as mammoth prunes. There were three near-walnut chairs, the usual desk with the usual blotter, pen set, ashtray and telephone, and the usual squeaky swivel chair behind it.

'You don't put on much of a front,' she said, sitting down at the customer's side of the desk.

I went over to the mail slot and picked up six envelopes, two letters and four pieces of advertising matter. I hung my hat on the telephone and sat down.

'Neither do the Pinkertons,' I said. 'You can't make much money at this trade, if you're honest. If you have a front, you're making money—or expect to.'

'Oh—are you honest?' she asked and opened her bag. She picked a cigarette out of a French enamel case, lit it with a pocket lighter, dropped case and lighter back into the bag and left the bag open.

'Painfully.'

'How did you ever get into this slimy kind of business then?'

'How did you come to marry a bootlegger?'

'My God, let's not start quarrelling again. I've been trying to get you on the phone all morning. Here and at your apartment.'

'About Owen?'

Her face tightened sharply. Her voice was soft. 'Poor Owen,' she said. 'So you know about that.'

'A DA's man took me down to Lido. He thought I might know something about it. But he knew much more than I did. He knew Owen wanted to marry your sister—once.'

She puffed silently at her cigarette and considered me with steady black eyes. 'Perhaps it wouldn't have been a bad idea,' she said quietly. 'He was in love with her. We don't find much of that in our circle.'

'He had a police record.'

She shrugged. She said negligently: 'He didn't know the right people. That's all a police record means in this rotten crime-ridden country.'

'I wouldn't go that far.'

She peeled her right glove off and bit her index finger at the first joint, looking at me with steady eyes. 'I didn't come to see you about Owen. Do you feel yet that you can tell me what my father wanted to see you about?'

'Not without his permission.'

'Was it about Carmen?'

'I can't even say that.' I finished filling a pipe and put a match to it. She watched the smoke for a moment. Then her hand went into her open bag and came out with a thick white envelope. She tossed it across the desk.

'You'd better look at it anyway,' she said.

I picked it up. The address was typewritten to Mrs Vivian Regan, 3765 Alta Brea Crescent, West Hollywood. Delivery had been by messenger service and the office stamp showed 8.35 a.m. as the time out. I opened the envelope and drew out the shiny $4\frac{1}{4}$ by $3\frac{1}{4}$ photo that was all there was inside.

It was Carmen sitting in Geiger's high-backed teakwood chair on the dais, in her earrings and her birthday suit. Her eyes looked even a little crazier than as I remembered them. The back of the photo was blank. I put it back in the envelope.

'How much do they want?' I asked.

'Five thousand–for the negative and the rest of the prints. The deal has to be closed to-night, or they give the stuff to some scandal sheet.'

'The demand came how?'

'A woman telephoned me, about half an hour after this thing was delivered.'

'There's nothing in the scandal sheet angle. Juries convict without leaving the box on that stuff nowadays. What else is there?'

'Does there have to be something else?'

'Yes.'

She stared at me, a little puzzled. 'There is. The woman said there was a police jam connected with it and I'd better lay it on the line fast, or I'd be talking to my little sister through a wire screen.'

'Better,' I said. 'What kind of jam?'

'I don't know.'

'Where is Carmen now?'

'She's at home. She was sick last night. She's still in bed, I think.'

'Did she go out last night?'

'No. I was out, but the servants say she wasn't. I was down at Las Olindas, playing roulette at Eddie Mars's Cypress Club. I lost my shirt.'

'So you like roulette. You would.'

She crossed her legs and lit another cigarette. 'Yes. I like roulette. All the Sternwoods like losing games, like roulette and marrying men that walk out on them and riding steeplechases at fifty-eight years old and being rolled on by a jumper and crippled for life. The Sternwoods have money. All it has bought them is a rain cheque.'

'What was Owen doing last night with your car?'

'Nobody knows. He took it without permission. We always let him take a car on his night off, but last night wasn't his night off.' She made a wry mouth. 'Do you think—?'

'He knew about this nude photograph? How would I be able to say? I don't rule him out. Can you get five thousand in cash right away?'

'Not unless I tell Dad–or borrow it. I could probably borrow it from Eddie Mars. He ought to be generous with me, Heaven knows.'

'Better try that. You may need it in a hurry.'

She leaned back and hung an arm over the back of the chair. 'How about telling the police?'

'It's a good idea. But you won't do it.'

'Won't I?'

'No. You have to protect your father and your sister. You don't know what the police might turn up. It might be something they couldn't sit on. Though they usually try in blackmail cases.'

'Can you do anything?'

'I think I can. But I can't tell you why or how.'

'I like you,' she said suddenly. 'You believe in miracles. Would you have a drink in the office?'

I unlocked my deep drawer and got out my office bottle and two pony glasses. I filled them and we drank. She snapped her bag shut and pushed her chair back.

'I'll get the five grand,' she said. 'I've been a good customer of Eddie Mars. There's another reason why he should be nice to me, which you may not know.' She gave me one of those smiles the lips have forgotten before they reach the eyes. 'Eddie's blonde wife is the lady Rusty ran away with.'

I didn't say anything. She stared tightly at me and added: 'That doesn't interest you?'

'It ought to make it easier to find him—if I was looking for him. You don't think he's in this mess, do you?'

She pushed her empty glass at me. 'Give me another drink. You're the hardest guy to get anything out of. You don't even move your ears.'

I filled the little glass. 'You've got all you wanted out of me—a pretty good idea I'm not looking for your husband.'

She put the drink down very quickly. It made her gasp—or gave her an opportunity to gasp. She let a breath out slowly.

'Rusty was no crook. If he had been, it wouldn't have been for nickels. He carried fifteen thousand dollars, in bills. He called it his mad money. He had it when I married him and he had it when he left me. No—Rusty's not in on any cheap blackmail racket.'

She reached for the envelope and stood up. 'I'll keep in touch with you,' I said. 'If you want to leave me a message, the phone girl at my apartment house will take care of it.'

We walked over to the door. Tapping the white envelope against her knuckles, she said: 'You still feel you can't tell me what Dad—'

'I'd have to see him first.'

She took the photo out and stood looking at it, just inside the door. 'She has a beautiful little body, hasn't she?'

'Uh-huh.'

She leaned a little towards me. 'You ought to see mine,' she said gravely.

'Can it be arranged?'

She laughed suddenly and sharply and went half-way through the door, then turned her head to say coolly: 'You're as cold-blooded a beast as I ever met, Marlowe. Or can I call you Phil?'

'Sure.'

'You can call me Vivian.'

'Thanks, Mrs Regan.'

'Oh, go to hell, Marlowe.' She went on out and didn't look back.

I let the door shut and stood with my hand on it, staring at the hand. My face felt a little hot. I went back to the desk and put the whisky away and rinsed out the two pony glasses and put them away.

I took my hat off the phone and called the DA's office, and asked for Bernie Ohls.

He was back in his cubby-hole. 'Well, I let the old man alone,' he said. 'The butler said he or one of the girls would tell him. This Owen Taylor lived over the garage and I went through his stuff. Parents at Dubuque, Iowa. I wired the Chief of Police there to find out what they want done. The Sternwood family will pay for it.'

'Suicide?' I asked.

'No can tell. He didn't leave any notes. He had no leave to take the car. Everybody was home last night but Mrs Regan. She was down at Las Olindas with a playboy named Larry Cobb. I checked on that. I know a lad on one of the tables.'

'You ought to stop some of that flash gambling,' I said.

'With the syndicate we got in this county? Be your age, Marlowe. That sap mark on the boy's head bothers me. Sure you can't help me on this?'

I liked his putting it that way. It let me say no without actually lying. We said good-bye and I left the office, bought all three afternoon papers and rode a taxi down to the Hall of Justice to get my car out of the lot. There was nothing in any of the papers about Geiger. I took another look at his blue notebook, but the code was just as stubborn as it had been the night before.

12

The trees on the upper side of Laverne Terrace had fresh green leaves after the rain. In the cool afternoon sunlight I could see the steep drop of the hill and the flight of steps down which the killer had run after his three shots in the darkness. Two small houses fronted on the street below. They might or might not have heard the shots.

There was no activity in front of Geiger's house or anywhere along the block. The box hedge looked green and peaceful and the shingles on the roof were still damp. I drove past slowly, gnawing at an idea. I hadn't looked in the garage the night before. Once Geiger's body slipped away I hadn't really wanted to find it. It would force my hand. But dragging him to the garage, to his own car and driving that off into one of the hundred-odd lonely canyons around Los Angeles would be a good way to dispose of him for days or even for weeks. That supposed two things: a key to his car and two in the party. It would narrow the sector of search quite a lot, especially as I had had his personal keys in my pocket when it happened.

I didn't get a chance to look at the garage. The doors were shut and padlocked and something moved behind the hedge as I drew level. A woman in a green and white check coat and a small button of a hat on soft blonde hair stepped out of the maze and stood looking wild-eyed at my car, as if she hadn't heard it come up the hill. Then she turned swiftly and dodged back out of sight. It was Carmen Sternwood, of course.

I went on up the street and parked and walked back. In the daylight it seemed an exposed and dangerous thing to do. I went in through the hedge. She stood there straight and silent against the locked front door. One hand went slowly up to her teeth and her teeth bit at her funny thumb. There were purple smears under her eyes and her face was gnawed white by nerves.

She half smiled at me. She said: 'Hello,' in a thin, brittle voice. 'What—what—?' That tailed off and she went back to the thumb.

'Remember me?' I said. 'Doghouse Reilly, the man that grew too tall. Remember?'

She nodded and a quick jerky smile played across her face.

'Let's go in,' I said. 'I've got a key. Swell, huh?'

'Wha—wha—?'

I pushed her to one side and put the key in the door and opened it and pushed her in through it. I shut the door again and stood there sniffing. The place was horrible by daylight. The Chinese junk on the walls, the rug, the fussy lamps, the teakwood stuff, the sticky riot of colours, the totem pole, the flagon of ether and laudanum—all this in the daytime had a stealthy nastiness, like a fag party.

The girl and I stood looking at each other. She tried to keep a cute little smile on her face but her face was too tired to be bothered. It kept going blank on her. The smile would wash off like water off sand and her pale skin had a harsh granular texture under the stunned and stupid blankness of her eyes. A whitish tongue licked at the corners of her mouth. A pretty, spoiled and not very bright little girl who had gone very, very wrong, and nobody was doing anything about it. To hell with the rich. They made me sick. I rolled a cigarette in my fingers and pushed some books out of the way and sat on the end of the black desk. I lit my cigarette, puffed a plume of smoke and watched the thumb and tooth act for a while in silence. Carmen stood in front of me, like a bad girl in the principal's office.

'What are you doing here?' I asked her finally.

She picked at the cloth of her coat and didn't answer.

'How much do you remember of last night?'

She answered that—with a foxy glitter rising at the back of her eyes. 'Remember what? I was sick last night. I was home.' Her voice was a cautious throaty sound that just reached my ears.

'Like hell you were.'

Her eyes flicked up and down very swiftly.

'Before you went home,' I said. 'Before I took you home. Here. In that chair'—I pointed to it—'on that orange shawl. You remember all right.'

A slow flush crept up her throat. That was something. She could blush. A glint of white showed under the clogged grey irises. She chewed hard on her thumb.

'You—were the one?' she whispered.

'Me. How much of it stays with you?'

She said vaguely: 'Are you the police?'

'No. I'm a friend of your father's.'

'You're not the police?'

'No.'

She let out a thin sigh. 'Wha—what do you want?'

'Who killed him?'

Her shoulders jerked, but nothing more moved in her face. 'Who else—knows?'

'About Geiger? I don't know. Not the police, or they'd be camping here. Maybe Joe Brody.'

It was a stab in the dark but it got her. 'Joe Brody! Him!'

Then we were both silent. I dragged at my cigarette and she ate her thumb.

'Don't get clever, for God's sake,' I urged her. 'This is a spot for a little old-fashioned simplicity. Did Brody kill him?'

'Kill who?'

'Oh, Christ,' I said.

She looked hurt. Her chin came down an inch. 'Yes,' she said solemnly. 'Joe did it.'

'Why?'

'I don't know.' She shook her head, persuading herself that she didn't know.

'Seen much of him lately?'

Her hands went down and made small white knots. 'Just once or twice. I hate him.'

'Then you know where he lives.'

'Yes.'

'And you don't like him any more?'

'I hate him!'

'Then you'd like him for the spot.'

A little blank again. I was going too fast for her. It was hard not to. 'Are you willing to tell the police it was Joe Brody?' I probed.

Sudden panic flamed all over her face. 'If I can kill the nude photo angle, of course,' I added soothingly.

She giggled. That gave me a nasty feeling. If she had screeched or wept or even nose-dived to the floor in a dead faint, that would have been all right. She just giggled. It was suddenly a lot of fun. She had had her photo taken as Isis and somebody had swiped it and somebody had bumped Geiger off in front of her and she was drunker than a Legion convention, and it was suddenly a lot of nice clean fun. So she giggled. Very cute. The giggles got louder and ran around the corners of the room like rats behind the wainscoting. She started to go hysterical. I slid off the desk and stepped up close to her and gave her a smack on the side of the face.

'Just like last night,' I said. 'We're a scream together. Reilly and Sternwood, two stooges in search of a comedian.'

The giggles stopped dead, but she didn't mind the slap any more than last night. Probably all her boy friends got around to slapping her sooner or later. I could understand how they might. I sat down on the end of the black desk again.

'Your name isn't Reilly,' she said seriously. 'It's Philip Marlowe. You're a private detective. Viv told me. She showed me your card.' She smoothed the cheek I had slapped. She smiled at me, as if I was nice to be with.

'Well, you do remember,' I said. 'And you came back to look for that photo and you couldn't get into the house. Didn't you?'

Her chin ducked down and up. She worked the smile. I was having the eye put on me. I was being brought into camp. I was going to yell 'Yippee!' in a minute and ask her to go to Yuma.

'The photo's gone,' I said. 'I looked last night, before I took you home. Probably Brody took it with him. You're not kidding me about Brody?'

She shook her head earnestly.

'It's a pushover,' I said. 'You don't have to give it another thought. Don't tell a soul you were here, last night or to-day. Not even Vivian. Just forget you were here. Leave it to Reilly.'

'Your name isn't—' she began, and then stopped and shook her head vigorously in agreement with what I had said or with what she had just thought of. Her eyes became narrow and almost black and as shallow as enamel on a cafeteria tray. She had had an idea. 'I have to go home now,' she said, as if we had been having a cup of tea.

'Sure.'

I didn't move. She gave me another cute glance and went on towards the front door. She had her hand on the knob when we both heard a car coming. She looked at me with questions in her eyes. I shrugged. The car stopped, right in front of the house. Terror twisted her face. There were steps and the bell rang. Carmen stared back at me over her shoulder, her hand clutching the door knob, almost drooling with fear. The bell kept on ringing. Then the ringing stopped. A key tickled at the door and Carmen jumped away from it and stood frozen. The door swung open. A man stepped through it briskly and stopped dead, staring at us quietly, with complete composure.

13

He was a grey man, all grey, except for his polished black shoes and two scarlet diamonds in his grey satin tie that looked like the diamonds on roulette layouts. His shirt was grey and his double-breasted suit of soft, beautifully cut flannel. Seeing Carmen he took a grey hat off and his hair underneath it was grey and as fine as if it had been sifted through gauze. His thick grey eyebrows had that indefinably sporty look. He had a long chin, a nose with a hook to it, thoughtful grey eyes that had a slanted look because the fold of skin over his upper lid came down over the corner of the lid itself.

He stood there politely, one hand touching the door at his back, the other holding the grey hat and flapping it gently against his thigh. He looked hard, not the hardness of the tough guy. More like the hardness of a well-weathered horseman. But he was no horseman. He was Eddie Mars.

He pushed the door shut behind him and put that hand in the lap-seamed pocket of his coat and left the thumb outside to glisten in the rather dim light of the room. He smiled at Carmen. He had a nice easy smile. She licked her lips and stared at him. The fear went out of her face. She smiled back.

'Excuse the casual entrance,' he said. 'The bell didn't seem to rouse anybody. Is Mr Geiger around?'

I said: 'No. We don't know just where he is. We found the door a little open. We stepped inside.'

He nodded and touched his long chin with the brim of his hat. 'You're friends of his, of course?'

'Just business acquaintances. We dropped by for a book.'

'A book, eh?' He said that quickly and brightly and, I thought, a little slyly, as if he knew all about Geiger's books. Then he looked at Carmen again and shrugged.

I moved towards the door. 'We'll trot along now,' I said. I took hold of her arm. She was staring at Eddie Mars. She liked him.

'Any message—if Geiger comes back?' Eddie Mars asked gently.

'We won't bother you.'

'That's too bad,' he said, with too much meaning. His grey eyes twinkled and then hardened as I went past him to open the door. He added in a casual tone: 'The girl can dust. I'd like to talk to you a little, soldier.'

I let go of her arm. I gave him a blank stare. 'Kidder, eh?' he said nicely. 'Don't waste it. I've got two boys outside in a car that always do just what I want them to.'

Carmen made a sound at my side and bolted through the door. Her steps faded rapidly downhill. I hadn't seen her car, so she must have left it down below. I started to say: 'What the hell—!'

'Oh, skip it,' Eddie Mars sighed. 'There's something wrong around here. I'm going to find out what it is. If you want to pick lead out of your belly, get in my way.'

'Well, well,' I said, 'a tough guy.'

'Only when necessary, soldier.' He wasn't looking at me any more. He was walking around the room, frowning, not paying any attention to me. I looked out above the broken pane of the front window. The top of a car showed over the hedge. Its motor idled.

Eddie Mars found the purple flagon and the two gold-veined glasses on the desk. He sniffed at one of the glasses, then at the flagon. A disgusted smile wrinkled his lips. 'The lousy pimp,' he said tonelessly.

He looked at a couple of books, grunted, went on around the desk and stood in front of the little totem pole with the camera eye. He studied it, dropped his glance to the floor in front of it. He moved the small rug with his foot, then bent swiftly, his body tense. He went down on the floor with one grey knee. The desk hid him from me partly. There was a sharp exclamation and he came up again. His arm flashed under his coat and a black Luger appeared in his hand. He held it in long brown fingers, not pointing it at me, not pointing it at anything.

'Blood,' he said. 'Blood on the floor there, under the rug. Quite a lot of blood.'

'Is that so?' I said, looking interested.

He slid into the chair behind the desk and hooked the mulberry-coloured phone towards him and shifted the Luger to his left hand. He frowned sharply at the telephone, bringing his thick grey eyebrows close together and making a hard crease in the weathered skin at the top of his hooked nose. 'I think we'll have some law,' he said.

I went over and kicked at the rug that lay where Geiger had lain. 'It's old blood,' I said. 'Dried blood.'

'Just the same we'll have some law.'

'Why not?' I said.

His eyes went narrow. The veneer had flaked off him, leaving a well-dressed hard boy with a Luger. He didn't like my agreeing with him.

'Just who the hell are you, soldier?'

'Marlowe is the name. I'm a sleuth.'

'Never heard of you. Who's the girl?'

'Client. Geiger was trying to throw a loop on her with some blackmail. We came to talk it over. He wasn't here. The door being open we walked in to wait. Or did I tell you that?'

'Convenient,' he said. 'The door being open. When you didn't have a key.'

'Yes. How come *you* had a key?'

'Is that any of your business, soldier?'

'I could make it my business.'

He smiled tightly and pushed his hat back on his grey hair. 'And I could make your business my business.'

'You wouldn't like it. The pay's too small.'

'All right, bright eyes. I own this house. Geiger is my tenant. Now what do you think of that?'

'You know such lovely people.'

'I take them as they come. They come all kinds.' He glanced down at the Luger, shrugged and tucked it back under his arm. 'Got any good ideas, soldier?'

'Lots of them. Somebody gunned Geiger. Somebody got gunned by Geiger, who ran away. Or it was two other fellows. Or Geiger was running a cult and made blood sacrifices in front of that totem pole. Or he had chicken for dinner and liked to kill his chickens in the front parlour.'

The grey man scowled at me.

'I give up,' I said. 'Better call your friends down-town.'

'I don't get it,' he said. 'I don't get your game here.'

'Go ahead, call the buttons. You'll get a big reaction from it.'

He thought that over without moving. His lips went back against his teeth. 'I don't get that, either,' he said tightly.

'Maybe it just isn't your day. I know you, Mr Mars. The Cypress Club at Las Olindas. Flash gambling for flash people. The local law in your pocket and a well-greased line into LA. In other words, protection. Geiger was in a racket that needed that too. Perhaps you spared him a little now and then, seeing he's your tenant.'

His mouth became a hard white grimace. 'Geiger was in what racket?'

'The smut book racket.'

He stared at me for long level minute. 'Somebody got to him,' he said softly. 'You know something about it. He didn't show at the store to-day. They don't know where he is. He didn't answer the phone here. I came up to see about it. I find blood on the floor, under a rug. And you and a girl here.'

'A little weak,' I said. 'But maybe you can sell the story to a willing buyer. You missed a little something, though. Somebody moved his books out of the store to-day–the nice books he rented out.'

He snapped his fingers sharply and said: 'I should have thought of that, soldier. You seem to get around. How do you figure it?'

'I think Geiger was rubbed. I think that is his blood. And the books being moved out gives a motive for hiding the body for a while. Somebody is taking over the racket and wants a little time to organize.'

'They can't get away with it,' Eddie Mars said grimly.

'Who says so? You and a couple of gunmen in your car outside? This is a big town now, Eddie. Some very tough people have checked in here lately. The penalty of growth.'

'You talk too damned much,' Eddie Mars said. He bared his teeth and whistled twice, sharply. A car door slammed outside and running steps came through the hedge. Mars flicked the Luger out again and pointed it at my chest. 'Open the door.'

The knob rattled and a voice called out. I didn't move. The muzzle of the Luger looked like the mouth of the Second Street tunnel, but I didn't move. Not being bullet-proof is an idea I had had to get used to.

'Open it yourself, Eddie. Who the hell are you to give me orders? Be nice and I might help you out.'

He came to his feet rigidly and moved around the end of the desk and over to the door. He opened it without taking his eyes off me. Two men tumbled into the room, reaching busily under their arms. One was an obvious pug, a good-looking pale-faced boy with a bad nose and one ear like a club steak. The other man was slim, blond, deadpan, with close-set eyes and no colour in them.

Eddie Mars said: 'See if this bird is wearing any iron.'

The blond flicked a short-barrelled gun out and stood pointing it at me. The pug sidled over flatfooted and felt my pockets with care. I turned around for him like a bored beauty modelling an evening gown.

'No gun,' he said in a burry voice.

'Find out who he is.'

The pug slipped a hand into my breast pocket and drew out my wallet. He flipped it open and studied the contents. 'Name's Philip Marlowe, Eddie. Lives at the Hobart Arms on Franklin. Private licence, deputy's badge and all. A shamus.' He slipped the wallet back in my pocket, slapped my face lightly and turned away.

'Beat it,' Eddie Mars said.

The two gunmen went out again and closed the door. There was the sound of them getting back into the car. They started its motor and kept it idling once more.

'All right. Talk,' Eddie Mars said. The peaks of his eyebrows made sharp angles against his forehead.

'I'm not ready to give out. Killing Geiger to grab his racket would be a dumb trick and I'm not sure it happened that way, assuming he has been killed. But I'm sure that whoever got the books knows what's what, and I'm sure that the blonde lady down at his store is scared batty about something or other. And I have a guess who got the books.'

'Who?'

'That's the part I'm not ready to give out. I've got a client, you know.'

He wrinkled his nose. 'That—' he chopped it off quickly.

'I expected you would know the girl,' I said.

'Who got the books, soldier?'

'Not ready to talk, Eddie. Why should I?'

He put the Luger down on the desk and slapped it with his open palm. 'This,' he said. 'And I might make it worth your while.'

'That's the spirit. Leave the gun out of it. I can always hear the sound of money. How much are you clinking at me?'

'For doing what?'

'What did you want done?'

He slammed the desk hard. 'Listen, soldier. I ask you a question and you ask me another. We're not getting anywhere. I want to know where Geiger is, for my own personal reasons. I didn't like his racket and I didn't protect him. I happen to own this house. I'm not so crazy about that right now. I can believe that whatever you know about all this is under glass, or there would be a flock of johns squeaking sole leather around this dump. You haven't got anything to sell. My guess is you need a little protection yourself. So cough up.'

It was a good guess, but I wasn't going to let him know it. I lit a cigarette and blew the match out and flicked it at the glass eye of the totem pole. 'You're right,' I said. 'If anything has happened to Geiger, I'll have to give what I have to the law. Which puts it in the public domain and doesn't leave me anything to sell. So with your permission I'll just drift.'

His face whitened under the tan. He looked mean, fast and tough for a moment. He made a movement to lift the gun. I added casually: 'By the way, how is Mrs Mars these days?'

I thought for a moment I had kidded him a little too far. His hand jerked at the gun, shaking. His face was stretched out by hard muscles. 'Beat it,' he said quite softly. 'I don't give a damn where you go or what you do when you get there. Only take a word of advice, soldier. Leave me out of your plans or you'll wish your name was Murphy and you lived in Limerick.'

'Well, that's not so far from Clonmel,' I said. 'I hear you had a pal came from there.'

He leaned down on the desk, frozen-eyed, unmoving. I went over to the door and opened it and looked back at him. His eyes had followed me, but his lean grey body had not moved. There was hate in his eyes. I went out and through the hedge and up the hill to my car and got into it. I turned it around and drove up over the crest. Nobody shot at me. After a few blocks I turned off, cut the motor and sat for a few moments. Nobody followed me either. I drove back into Hollywood.

14

It was ten minutes to five when I parked near the lobby entrance of the apartment house on Randall Place. A few windows were lit and radios were bleating at the dusk. I rode the automatic elevator up to the fourth floor and went along a wide hall carpeted in green and panelled in ivory. A cool breeze blew down the hall from the open screened door to the fire escape.

There was a small ivory pushbutton beside the door marked '405'. I pushed it and waited what seemed a long time. Then the door opened noiselessly about a foot. There was a steady, furtive air in the way it opened. The man was long-legged, long-waisted, high-shouldered and he had dark brown eyes in a brown expressionless face that had learned to control its expressions long ago. Hair like steel wool grew far back on his head and gave him a great deal of domed brown forehead that might at a careless glance have seemed a dwelling-place for brains. His sombre eyes probed at me impersonally. His long thin brown fingers held the edge of the door. He said nothing.

I said: 'Geiger?'

Nothing in the man's face changed that I could see. He brought a cigarette from behind the door and tucked it between his lips and drew a little smoke from it. The smoke came towards me in a lazy, contemptuous puff and behind it words in a cool, unhurried voice that had no more inflection than the voice of a faro dealer.

'You said what?'

'Geiger. Arthur Gwynn Geiger. The guy that has the books.'

The man considered that without any haste. He glanced down at the tip of his cigarette. His other hand, the one that had been holding the door, dropped out of sight. His shoulder had a look as though his hidden hand might be making motions.

'Don't know anybody by that name,' he said. 'Does he live around here?' I smiled. He didn't like the smile. His eyes got nasty. I said: 'You're Joe Brody?'

The brown face hardened. 'So what? Got a grift, brother—or just amusing yourself?'

'So you're Joe Brody,' I said. 'And you don't know anybody named Geiger. That's very funny.'

'Yeah? You got a funny sense of humour maybe. Take it away and play on it somewhere else.'

I leaned against the door and gave him a dreamy smile. 'You got the books, Joe. I got the sucker list. We ought to talk things over.'

He didn't shift his eyes from my face. There was a faint sound in the room behind him, as though a metal curtain ring clicked lightly on a metal rod. He glanced sideways into the room. He opened the door wider.

'Why not—if you think you've got something?' he said coolly. He stood aside from the door. I went past him into the room.

It was a cheerful room with good furniture and not too much of it. French windows in the end wall opened on a stone porch and looked across the dusk at the foothills. Near the windows a closed door in the west wall and near the entrance door another door in the same wall. This last had a plush curtain drawn across it on a thin brass rod below the lintel.

That left the east wall, in which there were no doors. There was a davenport backed against the middle of it, so I sat down on the davenport. Brody shut the door and walked crab-fashion to a tall oak desk studded with square nails. A cedarwood box with gilt hinges lay on the lower leaf of the desk. He carried the box to an easy chair midway between the other two doors and sat down. I dropped my hat on the davenport and waited.

'Well, I'm listening,' Brody said. He opened the cigar box and dropped his cigarette stub into a dish at his side. He put a long thin cigar in his mouth. 'Cigar?' He tossed one at me through the air.

I reached for it. Brody took a gun out of the cigar box and pointed it at my nose. I looked at the gun. It was a black Police .38. I had no argument against it at the moment.

'Neat, huh?' Brody said. 'Just kind of stand up a minute. Come forward just about two yards. You might grab a little air while you're doing that.' His voice was the elaborately casual voice of the tough guy in pictures. Pictures have made them all like that.

'Tsk, tsk,' I said, not moving at all. 'Such a lot of guns around town and so few brains. You're the second guy I've met within hours who seems to think a gat in the hand means a world by the tail. Put it down and don't be silly, Joe.'

His eyebrows came together and he pushed his chin at me. His eyes were mean.

'The other guy's name is Eddie Mars,' I said. 'Ever heard of him?'

'No.' Brody kept the gun pointed at me.

'If he ever gets wise to where you were last night in the rain, he'll wipe you off the way a check raiser wipes a check.'

'What would I be to Eddie Mars?' Brody asked coldly. But he lowered the gun to his knee.

'Not even a memory,' I said.

We stared at each other. I didn't look at the pointed black slipper that showed under the plush curtain on the doorway to my left.

Brody said quietly: 'Don't get me wrong. I'm not a tough guy—just careful. I don't know hell's first whisper about you. You might be a lifetaker for all I know.'

'You're not careful enough,' I said. 'That play with Geiger's books was terrible.'

He drew a long slow breath and let it out silently. Then he leaned back and crossed his long legs and held the Colt on his knee.

'Don't kid yourself I won't use this heat, if I have to,' he said. 'What's your story?'

'Have your friend with the pointed slippers come on in. She gets tired of holding her breath.'

Brody called out without moving his eyes off my stomach. 'Come on in, Agnes.'

The curtain swung aside and the green-eyed, thigh-swinging ash blonde from Geiger's store joined us in the room. She looked at me with a kind of mangled hatred. Her nostrils were pinched and her eyes had darkened a couple of shades. She looked very unhappy.

'I knew damn well you were trouble,' she snapped at me. 'I told Joe to watch his step.'

'It's not his step, it's the back of his lap he ought to watch,' I said.

'I suppose that's funny,' the blonde said.

'It has been,' I said. 'But it probably isn't any more.'

'Save the gags,' Brody advised me. 'Joe's watchin' his step plenty. Put some light on so I can see to pop this guy, if it works out that way.'

The blonde snicked on a light in a big square standing lamp. She sank down into a chair beside the lamp and sat stiffly, as if her girdle was too tight. I put my cigar in my mouth and bit the end off. Brody's Colt took a close interest in me while I got matches out and lit the cigar. I tasted the smoke and said:

'The sucker list I spoke of is in code. I haven't cracked it yet, but there are about five hundred names. You got twelve boxes of books that I know of. You should have at least five hundred books. There'll be a bunch more out on loan, but say five hundred is the full crop, just to be cautious. If it's a good active list and you could run it even fifty per cent down the line, that would be one hundred and twenty-five thousand rentals. Your girl friend knows all about that. I'm only guessing. Put the average rental as low as you like, but it won't be less than a dollar. That merchandise costs money. At a dollar a rental you take one hundred and twenty-five grand and you still have your capital. I mean, you still have Geiger's capital. That's enough to stop a guy for.'

The blonde said: 'You're crazy, you goddam egg-headed—!'

Brody put his teeth sideways at her and snarled: 'Pipe down, for Chrissake. Pipe down!'

She subsided into an outraged mixture of slow anguish and bottled fury. Her silvery nails scraped on her knees.

'It's no racket for bums,' I told Brody almost affectionately. 'It takes a smooth worker like you, Joe. You've got to get confidence and keep it. People who spend their money for secondhand sex jags are as nervous as dowagers who can't find the rest-room. Personally I think the blackmail angles are a big mistake. I'm for shedding all that and sticking to legitimate sales and rentals.'

Brody's dark brown stare moved up and down my face. His Colt went on hungering for my vital organs. 'You're a funny guy,' he said tonelessly. 'Who has this lovely racket?'

'*You* have,' I said. 'Almost.'

The blonde choked and clawed her ear. Brody didn't say anything. He just looked at me.

'What?' the blonde called. 'You sit there and try to tell us Mr Geiger ran that kind of business right down on the main drag? You're nuts!'

I leered at her politely. 'Sure I do. Everybody knows the racket exists. Hollywood's made to order for it. If a thing like that has to exist, then right out on the street is where all practical coppers want it to exist. For the same reason they favour red light districts. They know where to flush the game when they want to.'

'My God,' the blonde said. 'You let this cheese-head sit there and insult me, Joe? You with a gun in your hand and him holding nothing but a cigar and his thumb?'

'I like it,' Brody said. 'The guy's got good ideas. Shut your trap and keep it shut, or I'll slap it shut for you with this.' He flicked the gun around in an increasingly negligent manner.

The blonde gasped and turned her face to the wall. Brody looked at me and said cunningly: '*How* have I got that lovely racket?'

'You shot Geiger to get it. Last night in the rain. It was dandy shooting weather. The trouble is he wasn't alone when you whiffed him. Either you didn't notice that, which seems unlikely, or you got the wind up and lammed. But you had nerve enough to take the plate out of his camera and you had nerve enough to come back later on and hide his corpse, so you could tidy up on the books before the law knew it had a murder to investigate.'

'Yah,' Brody said contemptuously. The Colt wobbled on his knee. His brown face was as hard as a piece of carved wood. 'You take chances, mister. It's kind of goddamned lucky for you I *didn't* bop Geiger.'

'You can step off for it just the same,' I told him cheerfully. 'You're made to order for the rap.'

Brody's voice went rough. 'Think you got me framed for it?'

'Positive.'

'How come?'

'There's somebody who'll tell it that way. I told you there was a witness. Don't go simple on me, Joe.'

He exploded then. 'That goddamned little hot pants!' he shouted. 'She would, goddamn her! She would—just that!'

I leaned back and grinned at him. 'Swell. I thought you had those nude photos of her.'

He didn't say anything. The blonde didn't say anything. I let them chew on it. Brody's face cleared slowly, with a sort of greyish relief. He put his Colt down on the end table beside his chair but kept his right hand close to it. He knocked ash from his cigar on the carpet and stared at me with eyes that were a tight shine between narrowed lids.

'I guess you think I'm dumb,' Brody said.

'Just average, for a grifter. Get the pictures.'

'What pictures?'

I shook my head. 'Wrong play, Joe. Innocence gets you nowhere. You were either there last night, or you got the nude photo from somebody that was there. You know *she* was there because you had your girl friend threaten Mrs Regan with a police rap. The only ways you could know enough to do that would be by seeing what happened or by holding the photo and knowing where and when it was taken. Cough up and be sensible.'

'I'd have to have a little dough,' Brody said. He turned his head a little to look at the green-eyed blonde. Not now green-eyed and only superficially a blonde. She was as limp as a fresh-killed rabbit.

'No dough,' I said.

He scowled bitterly. 'How d'you get to me?'

I flicked my wallet out and let him look at my buzzer. 'I was working on Geiger—for a client. I was outside last night, in the rain. I heard the shots. I crashed in. I didn't see the killer. I saw everything else.'

'And kept your lip buttoned,' Brody sneered.

I put my wallet away. 'Yes,' I admitted. 'Up till now. Do I get the photos or not?'

'About these books,' Brody said. 'I don't get that.'

'I tailed them here from Geiger's store. I have a witness.'

'That punk kid?'

'What punk kid?'

He scowled again. 'The kid that works at the store. He skipped out after the truck left. Agnes don't even know where he flops.'

'That helps,' I said, grinning at him. 'That angle worried me a little. Either of you ever been in Geiger's house—before last night?'

'Not even last night,' Brody said sharply. 'So she says I gunned him, eh?'

'With the photos in hand I might be able to convince her she was wrong. There was a little drinking being done.'

Brody sighed. 'She hates my guts. I bounced her out. I got paid, sure, but I'd have had to do it anyway. She's too screwy for a simple guy like me.' He cleared his throat. 'How about a little dough? I'm down to nickels. Agnes and me gotta move on.'

'Not from my client.'

'Listen—'

'Get the pictures, Brody.'

'Oh, hell,' he said. 'You win.' He stood up and slipped the Colt into his side pocket. His left hand went up inside his coat. He was holding it there, his face twisted with disgust, when the door buzzer rang and kept on ringing.

15

He didn't like that. His lower lip went in under his teeth, and his eyebrows drew down sharply at the corners. His whole face became sharp and foxy and mean.

The buzzer kept up its song. I didn't like it either. If the visitors should happen to be Eddie Mars and his boys, I might get chilled off just for being there. If it was the police, I was caught with nothing to give them but a smile and a promise. And if it was some of Brody's friends—supposing he had any—they might turn out to be tougher than he was.

The blonde didn't like it. She stood up in a surge and chipped at the air with one hand. Nerve tension made her face old and ugly.

Watching me, Brody jerked a small drawer in the desk and picked a bone-handled automatic out of it. He held it at the blonde. She slid over to him and took it, shaking.

'Sit down next to him,' Brody said. 'Hold it on him low down, away from the door. If he gets funny use your own judgment. We ain't licked yet, baby.'

'Oh, Joe,' the blonde wailed. She came over and sat next to me on the davenport and pointed the gun at my leg artery. I didn't like the jerky look in her eyes.

The door buzzer stopped humming and a quick impatient rapping on the wood followed it. Brody put his hand in his pocket, on his gun, and walked over to the door and opened it with his left hand. Carmen Sternwood pushed him back into the room by putting a little revolver against his lean brown lips.

Brody backed away from her with his mouth working and an expression of panic on his face. Carmen shut the door behind her and looked neither at me nor at Agnes. She stalked Brody carefully, her tongue sticking out a little between her teeth. Brody took both hands out of his pockets and gestured placatingly at her. His eyebrows designed themselves into an odd assortment of curves and angles. Agnes turned the gun away from me and swung it at Carmen. I shot my hand out and closed my fingers down hard over her hand and jammed my thumb on the safety catch. It was already on. I kept it on. There was a short silent tussle, to which neither Brody nor Carmen paid any attention whatever. I had the gun. Agnes breathed deeply and shivered the whole length of her body. Carmen's face had a bony scraped look and her breath hissed. Her voice said without tone:

'I want my pictures, Joe.'

Brody swallowed and tried to grin. 'Sure, kid, sure.' He said it in a small flat voice that was as much like the voice he had used to me as a scooter is like a ten-ton truck.

Carmen said: 'You shot Arthur Geiger. I saw you. I want my pictures.' Brody turned green.

'Hey, wait a minute, Carmen,' I called.

Blonde Agnes came to life with a rush. She ducked her head and sank her teeth in my right hand. I made more noises and shook her off.

'Listen, kid,' Brody said. 'Listen a minute—'

The blonde spat at me and threw herself on my leg and tried to bite that. I cracked her on the head with the gun, not very hard, and tried to stand up. She rolled down my legs and wrapped her arms around them. I fell back on the davenport. The blonde was strong with the madness of love or fear, or a mixture of both, or maybe she was just strong.

Brody grabbed for the little revolver that was so close to his face. He missed. The gun made a sharp rapping noise that was not very loud. The bullet broke glass in a folded-back French window. Brody groaned horribly and fell down on the floor and jerked Carmen's feet from under her. She landed in a heap and the little revolver went skidding off into a corner. Brody jumped up on his knees and reached for his pocket.

I hit Agnes on the head with less delicacy than before, kicked her off my feet, and stood up. Brody flicked his eyes at me. I showed him the automatic. He stopped trying to get his hand into his pocket.

'Christ!' he whined. 'Don't let her kill me!'

I began to laugh. I laughed like an idiot, without control. Blonde Agnes was sitting up on the floor with her hands flat on the carpet and her mouth wide open and a wick of metallic blonde hair down over her right eye. Carmen was crawling on her hands and knees, still hissing. The metal of her little revolver glistened against the baseboard over in the corner. She crawled towards it relentlessly.

I waved my share of the guns at Brody and said: 'Stay put. You're all right.'

I stepped past the crawling girl and picked the gun up. She looked at me and began to giggle. I put her gun in my pocket and patted her on the back. 'Get up, angel. You look like a Pekinese.'

I went over to Brody and put the automatic against his midriff and reached his Colt out of his side pocket. I now had all the guns that had been exposed to view. I stuffed them into my pockets and held my hand out to him.

'Give.'

He nodded, licking his lips, his eyes still scared. He took a fat envelope out of his breast pocket and gave it to me. There was a developed plate in the envelope and five glossy prints.

'Sure these are all?'

He nodded again. I put the envelope in my own breast pocket and turned away. Agnes was back on the davenport, straightening her hair. Her eyes ate Carmen with a green distillation of hate. Carmen was up on her feet too, coming towards me with her hand out, still giggling and hissing. There was a little froth at the corners of her mouth. Her small white teeth glinted close to her lips.

'Can I have them now?' she asked me with a coy smile.

'I'll take care of them for you. Go on home.'

'Home?'

I went to the door and looked out. The cool night breeze was blowing peacefully down the hall. No excited neighbours hung out of doorways. A small gun had gone off and broken a pane of glass, but noises like that don't mean much any more. I held the door open and jerked my head at Carmen. She came towards me, smiling uncertainly.

'Go on home and wait for me,' I said soothingly.

She put her thumb up. Then she nodded and slipped past me into the hall. She touched my cheek with her fingers as she went by. 'You'll take care of Carmen, won't you?' she said.

'Check.'

'You're cute.'

'What you see is nothing,' I said. 'I've got a Bali dancing girl tattooed on my right thigh.'

Her eyes rounded. She said: 'Naughty,' and wagged a finger at me. Then she whispered: 'Can I have my gun?'

'Not now. Later. I'll bring it to you.'

She grabbed me suddenly around the neck and kissed me on the mouth. 'I like you,' she said. 'Carmen likes you a lot.' She ran off down the hall as gay as a thrush, waved at me from the stairs and ran down the stairs out of my sight.

I went back into Brody's apartment.

16

I went over to the folded-back French window and looked at the small broken pane in the upper part of it. The bullet from Carmen's gun had smashed the glass like a blow. It had not made a hole. There was a small hole in the plaster which a keen eye would find quickly enough. I pulled the drapes over the broken pane and took Carmen's gun out of my pocket. It was a Banker's Special, .22 calibre, hollow point cartridges. It had a pearl grip, and a small round silver plate set into the butt was engraved: 'Carmen from Owen'. She made saps of all of them.

I put the gun back in my pocket and sat down close to Brody and stared into his bleak brown eyes. A minute passed. The blonde adjusted her face by the aid of a pocket mirror. Brody fumbled around with a cigarette and jerked: 'Satisfied?'

'So far. Why did you put the bite on Mrs Regan instead of the old man?'

'Tapped the old man once. About six, seven months ago. I figure maybe he gets sore enough to call in some law.'

'What made you think Mrs Regan wouldn't tell him about it?'

He considered that with some care, smoking his cigarette and keeping his eyes on my face. Finally he said: 'How well you know her?'

'I've met her twice. You must know her a lot better to take a chance on that squeeze with the photo.'

'She skates around plenty. I figure maybe she has a couple of soft spots she don't want the old man to know about. I figure she can raise five grand easy.'

'A little weak,' I said. 'But pass it. You're broke, eh?'

'I been shaking two nickels together for a month, trying to get them to mate.'

'What you do for a living?'

'Insurance. I got desk rooms in Puss Walgreen's office, Fulwider Building, Western and Santa Monica.'

'When you open up, you open up. The books here in your apartment?'

He snapped his teeth and waved a brown hand. Confidence was oozing back into his manner. 'Hell, no. In storage.'

'You had a man bring them here and then you had a storage outfit come and take them away again right afterwards?'

'Sure. I don't want them moved direct from Geiger's place, do I?'

'You're smart,' I said admiringly. 'Anything incriminating in the joint right now?'

He looked worried again. He shook his head sharply.

'That's fine,' I told him. I looked across at Agnes. She had finished fixing her face and was staring at the wall, blank-eyed hardly listening. Her face had the drowsiness which strain and shock induce, after their first incidence.

Brody flicked his eyes warily. 'Well?'

'How'd you come by the photo?'

He scowled. 'Listen, you got what you came after, got it plenty cheap. You done a nice neat job. Now go peddle it to your top man. I'm clean. I don't know nothing about any photo, do I, Agnes?'

The blonde opened her eyes and looked at him with vague but uncomplimentary speculation. 'A half-smart guy,' she said with a tired sniff. 'That's all I ever draw. Never once a guy that's smart all the way around the course. Never once.'

I grinned at her. 'Did I hurt your head much?'

'You and every other man I ever met.'

I looked back at Brody. He was pinching his cigarette between his fingers, with a sort of twitch. His hand seemed to be shaking a little. His brown poker face was still smooth.

'We've got to agree on a story,' I said. 'For instance, Carmen wasn't here. That's very important. She wasn't here. That was a vision you saw.'

'Huh!' Brody sneered. 'If you say so, pal, and if—' he put his hand out palm up and cupped the fingers and rolled the thumb gently against the index and middle fingers.

I nodded. 'We'll see. There might be a small contribution. You won't count it in grands, though. Now where did you get the picture?'

'A guy slipped it to me.'

'Uh-huh. A guy you just passed in the street. You wouldn't know him again. You never saw him before.'

Brody yawned. 'It dropped out of his pocket,' he said.

'Uh-huh. Got an alibi for last night, poker pan?'

'Sure. I was right here. Agnes was with me. Okey, Agnes?'

'I'm beginning to feel sorry for you again,' I said.

His eyes flicked wide and his mouth hung loose, the cigarette balanced on his lower lip.

'You think you're smart and you're so goddamned dumb,' I told him. 'Even if you don't dance off up in Quentin, you have such a bleak long lonely time ahead of you.'

His cigarette jerked and dropped ash on his waistcoat.

'Thinking about how smart you are,' I said.

'Take the air,' he growled suddenly. 'Dust. I got enough chinning with you. Beat it.'

'Okey.' I stood up and went over to the tall oak desk and took his two guns out of my pockets, laid them side by side on the blotter so that the barrels were exactly parallel. I reached my hat off the floor beside the davenport and started for the door.

Brody called: 'Hey!'

I turned and waited. His cigarette was jiggling like a doll on a coiled spring. 'Everything's smooth, ain't it?' he asked.

'Why, sure. This is a free country. You don't have to stay out of jail, if you don't want to. That is, if you're a citizen. Are you a citizen?'

He just stared at me, jiggling the cigarette. The blonde Agnes turned her head slowly and stared at me along the same level. Their glances contained almost the exact same blend of foxiness, doubt and frustrated anger. Agnes reached her silvery nails up abruptly and yanked a hair out of her head and broke it between her fingers with a bitter jerk.

Brody said tightly: 'You're not going to any cops, brother. Not if it's the Sternwoods you're working for. I've got too much stuff on that family. You got your pictures and you got your hush. Go and peddle your papers.'

'Make your mind up,' I said. 'You told me to dust, I was on my way out, you hollered at me and I stopped, and now I'm on my way out again. Is that what you want?'

'You ain't got anything on me,' Brody said.

'Just a couple of murders. Small change in your circle.'

He didn't jump more than an inch, but it looked like a foot. The white cornea showed all around the tobacco-coloured iris of his eyes. The brown skin of his face took on a greenish tinge in the lamplight.

Blonde Agnes let out a low animal wail and buried her head in a cushion on the end of the davenport. I stood there and admired the long line of her thighs.

Brody moistened his lips slowly and said: 'Sit down, pal. Maybe I have a little more for you. What's that crack about two murders mean?'

I leaned against the door. 'Where were you last night about seven-thirty, Joe?'

His mouth drooped sulkily and he stared down at the floor. 'I was watching a guy, a guy who had a nice racket I figured he needed a partner in. Geiger. I was watching him now and then to see had he any tough connections. I figure he has friends or he don't work the racket as open as he does. But they don't go to his house. Only dames.'

'You didn't watch hard enough,' I said. 'Go on.'

'I'm there last night on the street below Geiger's house. It's raining hard and I'm buttoned up in my coupé and I don't see anything. There's a car in front of Geiger's and another car a little way up the hill. That's why I stay down below. There's a big Buick parked down where I am and after a while I go over and take a gander into it. It's registered to Vivian Regan. Nothing happens, so I scram. That's all.' He waved his cigarette. His eyes crawled up and down my face.

'Could be,' I said. 'Know where that Buick is now?'

'Why would I?'

'In the Sheriff's garage. It was lifted out of twelve feet of water off Lido fish pier this morning. There was a dead man in it. He had been sapped and the car pointed out the pier and the hand throttle pulled down.'

Brody was breathing hard. One of his feet tapped restlessly. 'Jesus, guy, you can't pin that one on me,' he said thickly.

'Why not? This Buick was down back of Geiger's according to you. Well, Mrs Regan didn't have it out. Her chauffeur, a lad named Owen Taylor, had it out. He went over to Geiger's place to have words with him, because Owen Taylor was sweet on Carmen, and he didn't like the kind of games Geiger was playing with her. He let himself in the back way with a jimmy and a gun and he caught Geiger taking a photo of Carmen without any clothes on. So his gun went off, as guns will, and Geiger fell down dead and Owen ran away, but not without the photo negative Geiger had just taken. So you ran after him and took the photo from him. How else would you have got hold of it?'

Brody licked his lips. 'Yeah,' he said. 'But that don't make me knock him off. Sure, I heard the shots and saw this killer come slamming down the back steps into the Buick and off. I took out after him. He hit the bottom of the canyon and went west on Sunset. Beyond Beverly Hills he skidded off the road and had to stop and I came up and played copper. He had a gun but his nerve was bad and I sapped him down. So I went through his clothes and found out who he was and I lifted the plateholder, just out of curiosity. I was wondering what it was all about and getting my neck wet when he came out of it all of a sudden and knocked me off the car. He was out of sight when I picked myself up. That's the last I saw of him.'

'How did you know it was Geiger he shot?' I asked gruffly.

Brody shrugged. 'I figure it was, but I can be wrong. When I had the plate developed and saw what was on it, I was pretty damn sure. And when Geiger didn't come down to the store this morning and didn't answer his phone I was plenty sure. So I figure it's a good time to move his books out and make a quick touch on the Sternwoods for travel money and blow for a while.'

I nodded. 'That seems reasonable. Maybe you didn't murder anybody at that. Where did you hide Geiger's body?'

He lifted his eyebrows. Then he grinned. 'Nix, nix. Skip it. You think I'd go back there and handle him, not knowing when a couple carloads of law would come tearing around the corner? Nix.'

'Somebody hid the body,' I said.

Brody shrugged. The grin stayed on his face. He didn't believe me. While he was still not believing me the door buzzer started to ring again. Brody stood up sharply, hardeyed. He glanced over at his guns on the desk.

'So she's back again,' he growled.

'If she is, she doesn't have her gun,' I comforted him. 'Don't you have any other friends?'

'Just about one,' he growled. 'I got enough of this puss-in-the-corner game.' He marched to the desk and took the Colt. He held it down at his side and went to the door. He put his left hand to the knob and twisted it and opened the door a foot and leaned into the opening, holding the gun tight against his thigh.

A voice said: 'Brody?'

Brody said something I didn't hear. The two quick reports were muffled. The gun must have been pressed tight against Brody's body. He tilted forward against the door and the weight of his body pushed it shut with a bang. He slid down the wood. His feet pushed the carpet away behind him. His left hand dropped off the knob and the arm slapped the floor with a thud. His head was wedged against the door. He didn't move. The Colt clung to his right hand.

I jumped across the room and rolled him enough to get the door open and crowd through. A woman peered out of a door almost opposite. Her face was full of fright and she pointed along the hall with a clawlike hand.

I raced down the hall and heard thumping feet going down the tile steps and went down after the sound. At the lobby level the front door was closing itself quietly and running feet slapped the pavement outside. I made the door before it was shut, clawed it open again and charged out.

A tall hatless figure in a leather jerkin was running diagonally across the street between the parked cars. The figure turned and flame spurted from it. Two heavy hammers hit the stucco wall beside me. The figure ran on, dodged between two cars, vanished.

A man came up beside me and asked: 'What happened?'

'Shooting going on,' I said.

'Jesus!' He scuttled into the apartment house.

I walked quickly down the pavement to my car and got in and started it. I pulled out from the kerb and drove down the hill, not fast. No other car started up on the other side of the street. I thought I heard steps, but I wasn't sure about that. I rode down the hill a block and a half, turned at the intersection and started to back up. The sound of a muted whistling came to me faintly along the pavement. Then steps. I double parked and slid between two cars and went down low. I took Carmen's little revolver out of my pocket.

The sound of the steps grew louder, and the whistling went on cheerfully. In a moment the jerkin showed. I stepped out between the two cars and said: 'Got a match, buddy?'

The boy spun towards me and his right hand darted up to go inside the jerkin. His eyes were a wet shine in the glow of the round electroliers. Moist dark eyes shaped like almonds, and a pallid handsome face with wavy black hair growing low on the forehead in two points. A very handsome boy indeed, the boy from Geiger's store.

He stood there looking at me silently, his right hand on the edge of the jerkin, but not inside it yet. I held the little revolver down at my side.

'You must have thought a lot of that queen,' I said.

'Go — yourself,' the boy said softly, motionless between the parked cars and the five-foot retaining wall on the inside of the pavement.

A siren wailed distantly coming up the long hill. The boy's head jerked towards the sound. I stepped in close and put my gun into his jerkin.

'Me or the cops?' I asked him.

His head rolled a little sideways as if I had slapped his face. 'Who are you?' he said.

'Friend of Geiger's.'

'Get away from me, you son of a bitch.'

'This is a small gun, kid. I'll give it you through the navel and it will take three months to get you well enough to walk. But you'll get well. So you can walk to the nice new gas chamber up in Quentin.'

He said: 'Go — yourself.' His hand moved inside the jerkin. I pressed harder on his stomach. He let out a long soft sigh, took his hand away from the jerkin and let it fall limp at his side. His wide shoulders sagged. 'What you want?' he whispered.

I reached inside the jerkin and plucked out the automatic. 'Get into my car, kid.'

He stepped past me and I crowded him from behind. He got into the car. 'Under the wheel, kid. You drive.'

He slid under the wheel and I got into the car beside him. I said: 'Let the prowl car pass up the hill. They'll think we moved over when we heard the siren. Then turn her downhill and we'll go home.'

I put Carmen's gun away and leaned the automatic against the boy's ribs. I looked back through the window. The whine of the siren was very loud now. Two red lights swelled in the middle of the street. They grew larger and blended into one and the car rushed by in a wild flurry of sound.

'Let's go,' I said.

The boy swung the car and started off down the hill.

'Let's go home,' I said. 'To Laverne Terrace.'

His smooth lips twitched. He swung the car west on Franklin. 'You're a simple-minded lad. What's your name?'

'Carol Lundgren,' he said lifelessly.

'You shot the wrong guy, Carol. Joe Brody didn't kill your queen.'

He spoke three words to me and kept on driving.

17

A moon half gone from the full glowed through a ring of mist among the high branches of the eucalyptus trees on Laverne Terrace. A radio sounded loudly from a house low down the hill. The boy swung the car over to the box hedge in front of Geiger's house, killed the motor and sat looking straight before him with both hands on the wheel. No light showed through Geiger's hedge.

I said: 'Anybody home, son?'

'You ought to know.'

'How would I know?'

'Go — yourself.'

'That's how people get false teeth.'

He showed me his in a tight grin. Then kicked the door open and got out. I scuttled out after him. He stood with his fists on his hips, looking silently at the house above the top of the hedge.

'All right,' I said. 'You have a key. Let's go on in.'

'Who said I had a key?'

'Don't kid me, son. The fag gave you one. You've got a nice clean manly little room in there. He shooed you out and locked it up when he had lady visitors. He was like Caesar, a husband to women and a wife to men. Think I can't figure people like him and you out?'

I still held his automatic more or less pointed at him, but he swung on me just the same. It caught me flush on the chin. I backstepped fast enough to keep from falling, but I took plenty of the punch. It was meant to be a hard one, but a pansy has no iron in his bones, whatever he looks like.

I threw the gun down at the kid's feet and said: 'Maybe you need this.'

He stooped for it like a flash. There was nothing slow about his movements. I sank a fist in the side of his neck. He toppled over sideways, clawing for the gun and not reaching it. I picked it up again and threw it in the car. The boy came up on all fours, leering with his eyes too wide open. He coughed and shook his head.

'You don't want to fight,' I told him. 'You're giving away too much weight.'

He wanted to fight. He shot at me like a plane from a catapult, reaching for my knees in a diving tackle. I sidestepped and reached for his neck and took it into chancery. He scraped the dirt hard and got his feet under him enough to use his hands on me where it hurt. I twisted him around and heaved him a little higher. I took hold of my right wrist with my left hand and turned my right hipbone into him and for a moment it was a balance of weights. We seemed to hang there in the misty moonlight, two grotesque creatures whose feet scraped on the road and whose breath panted with effort.

I had my right forearm against his windpipe now and all the strength of both arms in it. His feet began a frenetic shuffle and he wasn't panting any more. He was ironbound. His left foot sprawled off to one side and the knee went slack. I held on half a minute longer. He sagged on my arm, an enormous weight I could hardly hold up. Then I let go. He sprawled at my feet, out cold. I went to the car and got a pair of handcuffs out of the glove compartment and twisted his wrists behind him and snapped them on. I lifted him by the armpits and managed to drag him in behind the hedge, out of sight from the street. I went back to the car and moved it a hundred feet up the hill and locked it.

He was still out when I got back. I unlocked the door, dragged him into the house, shut the door. He was beginning to gasp now. I switched a lamp on. His eyes fluttered open and focused on me slowly.

I bent down, keeping out of the way of his knees and said: 'Keep quiet or you'll get the same and more of it. Just lie quiet and hold your breath. Hold it until you can't hold it any longer and then tell yourself that you have to breathe, that you're black in the face, that your eyeballs are popping out, and that you're going to breathe right now, but that you're sitting strapped in the chair in the clean little gas chamber up in San Quentin and when you take that breath you're fighting with all your soul not to take it, it won't be air you'll get, it will be cyanide fumes. And that's what they call humane execution in our state now.'

'Go — yourself,' he said with a soft stricken sigh.

'You're going to cop a plea, brother, don't ever think you're not. And you're going to say just what we want you to say and nothing we don't want you to say.'

'Go — yourself.'

'Say that again and I'll put a pillow under your head.'

His mouth twitched. I left him lying on the floor with his wrists shackled behind him and his cheek pressed into the rug and an animal brightness in his visible eye. I put on another lamp and stepped into the hallway at the back of the living-room. Geiger's bedroom didn't seem to have been touched. I opened the door, not locked now, of the bedroom across the hall from it. There was a dim flickering light in the room and a smell of sandalwood. Two cones of incense ash stood side by side on a small brass tray on the bureau. The light came from the two tall black candles in the foot-high candlesticks. They were standing on straight-backed chairs, one on either side of the bed.

Geiger lay on the bed. The two missing strips of Chinese tapestry made a St Andrew's Cross over the middle of his body, hiding the blood-smeared front of his Chinese coat. Below the cross his black-pyjama'd legs lay stiff and straight. His feet were in the slippers with thick white felt soles. Above the cross his arms were crossed at the wrists and his hands lay flat against his shoulders, palms down, fingers close together and stretched out evenly. His mouth was closed and his Charlie Chan moustache was as unreal as a toupee. His broad nose was pinched and white. His eyes were almost closed, but not entirely. The faint glitter of his glass eye caught the light and winked at me.

I didn't touch him. I didn't go very near him. He would be as cold as ice and as stiff as a board.

The black candles guttered in the draught from the open door. Drops of black wax crawled down their sides. The air of the room was poisonous and unreal. I went out and shut the door again and went back to the living-room. The boy hadn't moved. I stood still, listening for sirens. It was all a question of how soon Agnes talked and what she said. If she talked about Geiger, the police would be there any minute. But she might not talk for hours. She might even have got away.

I looked down at the boy. 'Want to sit up, son?'

He closed his eyes and pretended to go to sleep. I went over to the desk and scooped up the mulberry-coloured phone and dialled Bernie Ohls's office. He had left to go home at six o'clock. I dialled the number of his home. He was there.

'This is Marlowe,' I said. 'Did your boys find a revolver on Owen Taylor this morning?'

I could hear him clearing his throat and then I could hear him trying to keep the surprise out of his voice. 'That would come under the heading of police business,' he said.

'If they did, it had three empty shells in it.'

'How the hell did you know that?' Ohls asked quietly.

'Come over to 7244 Laverne Terrace, off Laurel Canyon Boulevard. I'll show you where the slugs went.'

'Just like that, huh?'

'Just like that.'

Ohls said: 'Look out the window and you'll see me coming round the corner. I thought you acted a little cagey on that one.'

'Cagey is no word for it,' I said.

18

Ohls stood looking down at the boy. The boy sat on the couch leaning sideways against the wall. Ohls looked at him silently, his pale eyebrows bristling and stiff and round like the little vegetable brushes the Fuller Brush man gives away.

He asked the boy: 'Do you admit shooting Brody?'

The boy said his favourite three words in a muffled voice.

Ohls sighed and looked at me. I said: 'He doesn't have to admit that. I have his gun.'

Ohls said: 'I wish to Christ I had a dollar for every time I've had that said to me. What's funny about it?'

'It's not meant to be funny,' I said.

'Well, that's something,' Ohls said. He turned away. 'I've called Wilde. We'll go over and see him and take this punk. He can ride with me and you can follow on behind in case he tries to kick me in the face.'

'How do you like what's in the bedroom?'

'I like it fine,' Ohls said. 'I'm kind of glad that Taylor kid went off the pier. I'd hate to have to help send him to the death-house for rubbing that skunk.'

I went back into the small bedroom and blew out the black candles and let them smoke. When I got back to the living-room Ohls had the boy up on his feet. The boy stood glaring at him with sharp black eyes in a face as hard and white as cold mutton fat.

'Let's go,' Ohls said, and took him by the arms as if he didn't like touching him. I put the lamps out and followed them out of the house. We got into our cars and I followed Ohls's twin tail-lights down the long curving hill. I hoped this would be my last trip to Laverne Terrace.

Taggart Wilde, the District Attorney, lived at the corner of Fourth and Lafayette Park, in a white frame house the size of a carbarn, with red sand-stone *porte-cochère* built on to one side and a couple of acres of soft rolling lawn in front. It was one of those solid old-fashioned houses which it used to be the thing to move bodily to new locations as the city grew westward. Wilde came of an old Los Angeles family and had probably been born in the house when it was on West Adams or Figueroa or St James's Park.

There were two cars in the driveway already, a big private sedan and a police car with a uniformed chauffeur who leaned smoking against his rear fender and admiring the moon. Ohls went over and spoke to him and the chauffeur looked in at the boy in Ohls's car.

We went up to the house and rang the bell. A slick-haired blond man opened the door and led us down the hall and through a huge sunken living-room crowded with heavy dark furniture and along another hall on the far side of it. He knocked at a door and stepped inside, then held the door wide and we went into a panelled study with an open French door at the end and a view of dark garden and mysterious trees. A smell of wet earth and flowers came in at the window. There were large dim oils on the walls, easy chairs, books, a smell of good cigar smoke which blended with the smell of wet earth and flowers.

Taggart Wilde sat behind a desk, a middle-aged plump man with clear blue eyes that managed to have a friendly expression without really having any expression at all. He had a cup of black coffee in front of him and he held a dappled thin cigar between the neat careful fingers of his left hand. Another man sat at the corner of the desk in a blue leather chair, a cold-eyed hatchet-faced man, as lean as a rake and as hard as the manager of a loan office. His neat well-kept face looked as if it had been shaved within the hour. He wore a well-pressed brown suit and there was a black pearl in his tie. He had the long nervous fingers of a man with a quick brain. He looked ready for a fight.

Ohls pulled a chair up and sat down and said: 'Evening, Cronjager. Meet Phil Marlowe, a private eye who's in a jam.' Ohls grinned.

Cronjager looked at me without nodding. He looked me over as if he was looking at a photograph. Then he nodded his chin about an inch. Wilde said: 'Sit down, Marlowe. I'll try to handle Captain Cronjager, but you know how it is. This is a big city now.'

I sat down and lit a cigarette. Ohls looked at Cronjager and asked: 'What did you get on the Randall Place killing?'

The hatchet-faced man pulled one of his fingers until the knuckle cracked. He spoke without looking up. 'A stiff, two slugs in him. Two guns that hadn't been fired. Down on the street we got a blonde trying to start a car that didn't belong to her. Hers was right next to it, the same model. She acted rattled so the boys brought her in and she spilled. She was in there when this guy Brody got it. Claims she didn't see the killer.'

'That all?' Ohls asked.

Cronjager raised his eyebrows a little. 'Only happened about an hour ago. What did you expect—moving pictures of the killing?'

'Maybe a description of the killer,' Ohls said.

'A tall guy in a leather jerkin—if you call that a description.'

'He's outside in my heap,' Ohls said. 'Handcuffed. Marlowe put the arm on him for you. Here's his gun.' Ohls took the boy's automatic out of his pocket and laid it on a corner of Wilde's desk. Cronjager looked at the gun but didn't reach for it.

Wilde chuckled. He was leaning back and puffing his dappled cigar without letting go of it. He bent forward to sip from his coffee cup. He took a silk handkerchief from the breast pocket of the dinner-jacket he was wearing and touched his lips with it and tucked it away again.

'There's a couple more deaths involved,' Ohls said, pinching the soft flesh at the end of his chin.

Cronjager stiffened visibly. His surly eyes became points of steely light.

Ohls said: 'You heard about a car being lifted out of the Pacific Ocean off Lido pier this morning with a dead guy in it?'

Cronjager said: 'No,' and kept on looking nasty.

'The dead guy in the car was chauffeur to a rich family,' Ohls said. 'The family was being blackmailed on account of one of the daughters. Mr Wilde recommended Marlowe to the family, through me. Marlowe played it kind of close to the waistcoat.'

'I love private dicks that play murders close to the waistcoat,' Cronjager said. 'You don't have to be so goddamned coy about it.'

'Yeah,' Ohls said. 'I don't have to be so goddamned coy about it. It's not so goddamned often I get a chance to be coy with a city copper. I spend most of my time telling them where to put their feet so they won't break an ankle.'

Cronjager whitened around the corners of his sharp nose. His breath made a soft hissing sound in the quiet room. He said very quietly: 'You haven't had to tell any of *my* men where to put their feet, smart guy.'

'We'll see about that,' Ohls said. 'This chauffeur I spoke of that's drowned off Lido shot a guy last night in your territory. A guy named Geiger who ran a dirty book racket in a store on Hollywood Boulevard. Geiger was living with the punk I got outside in my car. I mean living with him, if you get the idea.'

Cronjager was staring at him levelly now. 'That sounds like it might grow up to be a dirty story,' he said.

'It's my experience most police stories are,' Ohls growled and turned to me, his eyebrows bristling. 'You're on the air, Marlowe. Give it to him.'

I gave it to him.

I left out two things, not knowing just why, at the moment, I left out one of them. I left out Carmen's visit to Brody's apartment and Eddie Mars's visit to Geiger's in the afternoon. I told the rest of it just as it happened.

Cronjager never took his eyes off my face and no expression of any kind crossed his as I talked. At the end of it he was perfectly silent for a long minute. Wilde was silent, sipping his coffee, puffing gently at his dappled cigar, Ohls stared at one of this thumbs.

Cronjager leaned slowly back in his chair and crossed one ankle over his knee and rubbed the ankle-bone with his thin nervous hand. His lean face wore a harsh frown. He said with deadly politeness:

'So all you did was not report a murder that happened last night and then spend to-day foxing around so that this kid of Geiger's could commit a second murder this evening.'

'That's all,' I said. 'I was in a pretty tough spot. I guess I did wrong, but I wanted to protect my client and I hadn't any reason to think the boy would go gunning for Brody.'

'That kind of thinking is police business, Marlowe. If Geiger's death had been reported last night, the books could never have been moved from the store to Brody's apartment. The kid wouldn't have been led to Brody and wouldn't have killed him. Say Brody was living on borrowed time. His kind usually are. But a life is a life.'

'Right,' I said. 'Tell that to your coppers next time they shoot down some scared petty larceny crook running away up an alley with a stolen spare.'

Wilde put both his hands down on his desk with a solid smack. 'That's enough of that,' he snapped. 'What makes you so sure, Marlowe, that this Taylor boy shot Geiger? Even if the gun that killed Geiger was found on Taylor's body or in the car, it doesn't absolutely follow that he was the killer. The gun might have been planted—say by Brody, the actual killer.'

'It's physically possible,' I said, 'but morally impossible. It assumes too much coincidence and too much that's out of character for Brody and his girl, and out of character for what he was trying to do. I talked to Brody for a long time. He was a crook, but not a killer type. He had two guns, but he wasn't wearing either of them. He was trying to find a way to cut in on

Geiger's racket, which naturally he knew all about from the girl. He says he was watching Geiger off and on to see if he had any tough backers. I believe him. To suppose he killed Geiger in order to get his books, then scrammed with the nude photo Geiger had just taken of Carmen Sternwood, then planted the gun on Owen Taylor and pushed Taylor into the ocean off Lido, is to suppose a hell of a lot too much. Taylor had the motive, jealous rage, and the opportunity to kill Geiger. He was out in one of the family cars without permission. He killed Geiger right in front of the girl, which Brody would never have done, even if he had been a killer. I can't see anybody with a purely commercial interest in Geiger doing that. But Taylor would have done it. The nude photo business was just what would have made him do it.'

Wilde chuckled and looked along his eyes at Cronjager. Cronjager cleared his throat with a snort. Wilde asked: 'What's this business about hiding the body? I don't see the point of that.'

I said: 'The kid hasn't told us, but he must have done it. Brody wouldn't have gone into the house after Geiger was shot. The boy must have got home when I was away taking Carmen to her house. He was afraid of the police, of course, being what he is, and he probably thought it a good idea to have the body hidden until he had removed his effects from the house. He dragged it out of the front door, judging by the marks on the rug, and very likely put it in the garage. Then he packed up whatever belongings he had there and took them away. And later on, sometime in the night and before the body stiffened, he had a revulsion of feeling and thought he hadn't treated his dead friend very nicely. So he went back and laid him out on the bed. That's all guessing of course.'

Wilde nodded. 'Then this morning he goes down to the store as if nothing had happened and keeps his eyes open. And when Brody moved the books out he found out where they were going and assumed that whoever got them had killed Geiger just for that purpose. He may even have known more about Brody and the girl than they suspected. What do you think, Ohls?'

Ohls said: 'We'll find out—but that doesn't help Cronjager's troubles. What's eating him is all this happened last night and he's only just been rung in on it.'

Cronjager said sourly: 'I think I can find some way to deal with that angle too.' He looked at me sharply and immediately looked away again.

Wilde waved his cigar and said: 'Let's see the exhibits, Marlowe.'

I emptied my pockets and put the catch on his desk: the three notes and Geiger's card to General Sternwood, Carmen's photos, and the blue notebook with the code list of names and addresses. I had already given Geiger's keys to Ohls.

Wilde looked at what I gave him, puffing gently at his cigar. Ohls lit one of his own toy cigars and blew smoke peacefully at the ceiling. Cronjager leaned on the desk and looked at what I had given Wilde.

Wilde tapped the three notes signed by Carmen and said: 'I guess these were just a come-on. If General Sternwood paid them, it would be through fear of something worse. Then Geiger would have tightened the screws. Do you know what he was afraid of?' He was looking at me.

I shook my head.

'Have you told your story complete in all relevant details?'

'I left out a couple of personal matters. I intend to keep on leaving them out, Mr Wilde.'

Cronjager said: 'Hah!' and snorted with deep feeling.

'Why?' Wilde asked quietly.

'Because my client is entitled to that protection, short of anything but a Grand Jury. I have a licence to operate as a private detective. I suppose that word "private" has some meaning. The Hollywood Division has two murders on its hands, both solved. They have both killers. They have the motive, the instrument in each case. The blackmail angle has got to be suppressed, as far as the names of the parties are concerned.'

'Why?' Wilde asked again.

'That's okey,' Cronjager said dryly. 'We're glad to stooge for a shamus of his standing.'

I said: 'I'll show you.' I got up and went back out of the house to my car and got the book from Geiger's store out of it. The uniformed police driver was standing beside Ohls's car. The boy was inside it, leaning back sideways in the corner.

'Has he said anything?' I asked.

'He made a suggestion,' the copper said and spat. 'I'm letting it ride.'

I went back into the house, put the book on Wilde's desk and opened up the wrappings. Cronjager was using a telephone on the end of the desk. He hung up and sat down as I came in.

Wilde looked through the book, wooden-faced, closed it and pushed it towards Cronjager. Cronjager opened it, looked at a page or two, shut it quickly. A couple of red spots the size of half-dollars showed on his cheekbones.

I said: 'Look at the stamped dates on the front end-paper.'

Cronjager opened the book again and looked at them. 'Well?'

'If necessary,' I said, 'I'll testify under oath that that book came from Geiger's store. The blonde, Agnes, will admit what kind of business the store did. It's obvious to anybody with eyes that that store is just a front for something. But the Hollywood police allowed it to operate, for their own reasons. I dare say the Grand Jury would like to know what those reasons are.'

Wilde grinned. He said: 'Grand Juries do ask those embarrassing questions sometimes—in a rather vain effort to find out just why cities are run as they are run.'

Cronjager stood up suddenly and put his hat on. 'I'm one against three here,' he snapped. 'I'm a homicide man. If this Geiger was running indecent literature, that's no skin off my nose. But I'm ready to admit it won't help my division any to have it washed over in the papers. What do you birds want?'

Wilde looked at Ohls. Ohls said calmly: 'I want to turn a prisoner over to you. Let's go.'

He stood up. Cronjager looked at him fiercely and stalked out of the room. Ohls went after him. The door closed again. Wilde tapped on his desk and stared at me with his clear blue eyes.

'You ought to understand how any copper would feel about a cover-up like this,' he said. 'You'll have to make statements of all of it—at least for the files. I think it may be possible to keep the two killings separate and to keep General Sternwood's name out of both of them. Do you know why I'm not tearing your ear off?'

'No. I expected to get both ears torn off.'

'What are you getting for it all?'

'Twenty-five dollars a day and expenses.'

'That would make fifty dollars and a little gasolene so far.'

'About that.'

He put his head on one side and rubbed the back of his left little finger along the lower edge of his chin.

'And for that amount of money you're willing to get yourself in Dutch with half the law enforcement of this county?'

'I don't like it,' I said. 'But what the hell am I to do? I'm on a case. I'm selling what I have to sell to make a living. What little guts and intelligence the Lord gave me and a willingness to get pushed around in order to protect a client. It's against my principles to tell as much as I've told to-night, without consulting the General. As for the cover-up, I've been in police business myself, as you know. They come a dime a dozen in any big city. Cops get very large and emphatic when an outsider tries to hide anything, but they do the same things themselves every other day, to oblige their friends or anybody with a little pull. And I'm not through. I'm still on the case. I'd do the same thing again, if I had to.'

'Providing Cronjager doesn't get your licence,' Wilde grinned. 'You said you held back a couple of personal matters. Of what import?'

'I'm still on the case,' I said, and stared straight into his eyes.

Wilde smiled at me. He had the frank daring smile of an Irishman. 'Let me tell you something, son. My father was a close friend of old Sternwood. I've done all my office permits—and maybe a good deal more—to save the old man from grief. But in the long run it can't be done. Those girls of his are bound certain to hook up with something that can't be hushed, especially that little blonde brat. They ought not to be running around loose. I blame the old man for that. I guess he doesn't realize what the world is to-day. And there's another thing I might mention while we're talking man to man and I don't have to growl at you. I'll bet a dollar to a Canadian dime that the General's afraid his son-in-law, the ex-bootlegger, is mixed up in this somewhere, and what he really hoped you would find out is that he isn't. What do you think of that?'

'Regan didn't sound like a blackmailer, what I heard of him. He had a soft spot where he was and he walked out on it.'

Wilde snorted. 'The softness of that spot neither you nor I could judge. If he was a certain sort of man, it would not have been so very soft. Did the General tell you he was looking for Regan?'

'He told me he wished he knew where he was and that he was all right. He liked Regan and was hurt the way he bounced off without telling the old man good-bye.'

Wilde leaned back and frowned. 'I see,' he said in a changed voice. His hand moved the stuff on his desk around, laid Geiger's blue notebook to one side and pushed the other exhibits towards me. 'You may as well take these,' he said. 'I've no further use for them.'

19

It was close to eleven when I put my car away and walked around to the front of the Hobart Arms. The plate-glass door was put on the lock at ten, so I had to get my keys out. Inside, in the square barren lobby, a man put a green evening paper down beside a potted palm and flicked a cigarette butt into the tub the palm grew in. He stood up and waved his hat at me and said: 'The boss wants to talk to you. You sure keep your friends waiting, pal.'

I stood still and looked at his flattened nose and club steak ear.

'What about?'

'What do you care? Just keep your nose clean and everything will be jake.' His hand hovered near the upper buttonhole of his open coat.

'I smell of policemen,' I said. 'I'm too tired to talk, too tired to eat, too tired to think. But if you think I'm not too tired to take orders from Eddie Mars—try getting your gat out before I shoot your good ear off.'

'Nuts. You ain't got no gun.' He stared at me levelly. His dark wiry brows closed in together and his mouth made a downward curve.

'That was then,' I told him. 'I'm not always naked.'

He waved his left hand. 'Okey. You win. I wasn't told to blast anybody. You'll hear from him.'

'Too late will be too soon,' I said, and turned slowly as he passed me on his way to the door. He opened it and went out without looking back. I grinned at my own foolishness, went along to the elevator and upstairs to the apartment. I took Carmen's little gun out of my pocket and laughed at it. Then I cleaned it thoroughly, oiled it, wrapped it in a piece of canton flannel and locked it up. I made myself a drink and was drinking it when the phone rang. I sat down beside the table on which it stood.

'So you're tough to-night,' Eddie Mars's voice said.

'Big, fast, tough and full of prickles. What can I do for you?'

'Cops over there—you know where. You keep me out of it?'

'Why should I?'

'I'm nice to be nice to, soldier. I'm not nice not to be nice to.'

'Listen hard and you'll hear my teeth chattering.'

He laughed dryly. 'Did you—or did you?'

'I did. I'm damned if I know why. I guess it was just complicated enough without you.'

'Thanks, soldier. Who gunned him?'

'Read it in the paper to-morrow—maybe.'

'I want to know now.'

'Do you get everything you want?'

'No. Is that an answer, soldier?'

'Somebody you never heard of gunned him. Let it go at that.'

'If that's on the level, some day I may be able to do you a favour.'

'Hang up and let me go to bed.'

He laughed again. 'You're looking for Rusty Regan, aren't you?'

'A lot of people seem to think I am, but I'm not.'

'If you were, I could give you an idea. Drop in and see me down at the beach. Any time. Glad to see you.'

'Maybe.'

'Be seeing you then.' The phone clicked and I sat holding it with a savage patience. Then I dialled the Sternwoods' number and heard it ring four or five times and then the butler's suave voice saying: 'General Sternwood's residence.'

'This is Marlowe. Remember me? I met you about a hundred years ago—or was it yesterday?'

'Yes, Mr Marlowe. I remember, of course.'

'Is Mrs Regan home?'

'Yes, I believe so. Would you—'

I cut in on him with a sudden change of mind. 'No. You give her the message. Tell her I have the pictures, all of them, and that everything is all right.'

'Yes . . . yes. . . .' The voice seemed to shake a little. 'You have the pictures—all of them—and everything is all right. . . . Yes, sir. I may say—thank you very much, sir.'

The phone rang back in five minutes. I had finished my drink and it made me feel as if I could eat the dinner I had forgotten all about; I went out leaving the telephone ringing. It was ringing when I came back. It rang at intervals until half past twelve. At that time I put my lights out and opened the windows up and muffled the phone bell with a piece of paper and went to bed. I had a bellyful of the Sternwood family.

I read all three of the morning papers over my eggs and bacon the next morning. Their accounts of the affair came as close to the truth as newspaper stories usually come—as close as Mars is to Saturn. None of the three connected Owen Taylor, driver of the Lido Pier Suicide Car, with the Laurel Canyon Exotic Bungalow Slaying. None of them mentioned the Sternwoods, Bernie Ohls or me. Owen Taylor was 'chauffeur to a wealthy family'. Captain Cronjager of the Hollywood Division got all the credit for solving the two slayings in his district, which were supposed to arise out of a dispute over the proceeds from a wire service maintained by one Geiger in the back of the bookstore on Hollywood Boulevard. Brody had shot Geiger and Carol Lundgren had shot Brody in revenge. Police were holding Carol Lundgren in custody. He had confessed. He had a bad record—probably in high school. Police were also holding one Agnes Lozelle, Geiger's secretary, as a material witness.

It was a nice write-up. It gave the impression that Geiger had been killed the night before, that Brody had been killed about an hour later, and that Captain Cronjager had solved both murders while lighting a cigarette. The suicide of Taylor made Page One of Section II. There was a photo of the sedan on the deck of the power lighter, with the licence plate blacked out, and something covered with a cloth lying on the deck beside the running board. Owen Taylor had been despondent and in poor health. His family lived in Dubuque, and his body would be shipped there. There would be no inquest.

20

Captain Gregory of the Missing Persons Bureau laid my card down on his wide flat desk and arranged it so that its edges exactly paralleled the edges of the desk. He studied it with his head on one side, grunted, swung around in his swivel chair and looked out of his window at the barred top floor of the Hall of Justice half a block away. He was a burly man with tired eyes and the slow deliberate movements of a night watchman. His voice was toneless, flat and uninterested.

'Private dick, eh?' he said, not looking at me at all, but looking out of his window. Smoke wisped from the blackened bowl of a briar that hung on his eye tooth. 'What can I do for you?'

'I'm working for General Guy Sternwood, 3765 Alta Brea Crescent, West Hollywood.'

Captain Gregory blew a little smoke from the corner of his mouth without removing the pipe. 'On what?'

'Not exactly on what you're working on, but I'm interested. I thought you could help me.'

'Help you on what?'

'General Sternwood's a rich man,' I said. 'He's an old friend of the DA's father. If he wants to hire a full-time boy to run errands for him, that's no reflection on the police. It's just a luxury he is able to afford himself.'

'What makes you think I'm doing anything for him?'

I didn't answer that. He swung round slowly and heavily in his swivel chair and put his large feet flat on the bare linoleum that covered his floor. His office had the musty smell of years of routine. He stared at me bleakly.

'I don't want to waste your time, Captain,' I said and pushed my chair back—about four inches.

He didn't move. He kept on staring at me out of his washed-out tired eyes. 'You know the DA?'

'I've met him. I worked for him once. I know Bernie Ohls, his chief investigator, pretty well.'

Captain Gregory reached for a phone and mumbled into it: 'Get me Ohls at the DA's office.'

He sat holding the phone down on its cradle. Moments passed. Smoke drifted from his pipe. His eyes were heavy and motionless like his hand. The bell tinkled and he reached for my card with his left hand. 'Ohls? . . . Al Gregory at headquarters. A guy named Philip Marlowe is in my office. His card says he's a private investigator. He wants information from me. . . . Yeah? What does he look like? . . . Okey, thanks.'

He dropped the phone and took his pipe out of his mouth and tamped the tobacco with the brass cap of a heavy pencil. He did it carefully and solemnly, as if that was as important as anything he would have to do that day. He leaned back and stared at me some more.

'What you want?'

'An idea of what progress you're making, if any.'

He thought that over. 'Regan?' he asked finally.

'Sure.'

'Know him?'

'I never saw him. I hear he's a good-looking Irishman in his late thirties, that he was once in the liquor racket, that he married General Sternwood's older daughter and that they didn't click. I'm told he disappeared about a month back.'

'Sternwood oughta think himself lucky instead of hiring private talent to beat around in the tall grass.'

'The General took a big fancy to him. Such things happen. The old man is crippled and lonely. Regan used to sit around with him and keep him company.'

'What you think you can do that we can't do?'

'Nothing at all, in so far as finding Regan goes. But there's a rather mysterious blackmail angle. I want to make sure Regan isn't involved. Knowing where he is or isn't might help.'

'Brother, I'd like to help you, but I don't know where he is. He pulled down the curtain and that's that.'

'Pretty hard to do against your organization, isn't it, Captain?'

'Yeah—but it can be done—for a while.' He touched a bell button on the side of his desk. A middle-aged woman put her head in at a side door. 'Get me the file on Terence Regan, Abba.'

The door closed. Captain Gregory and I looked at each other in some more heavy silence. The door opened again and the woman put a tabbed green file on his desk. Captain Gregory nodded her out, put a pair of heavy horn-rimmed glasses on his veined nose and turned the papers in the file over slowly. I rolled a cigarette around in my fingers.

'He blew on the 16th of September,' he said. 'The only thing important about that is it was the chauffeur's day off and nobody saw Regan take his car out. It was late afternoon, though. We found the car four days later in a garage belonging to a ritzy bungalow court place near the Sunset Towers. A garage man reported it to the stolen car detail, said it didn't belong there. The place is called the Casa de Oro. There's an angle to that I'll tell you about in a minute. We couldn't find out anything about who put the car in there. We print the car but don't find any prints that are on the file anywhere. The car in that garage don't jibe with foul play, although there's a reason to suspect foul play. It jibes with something else I'll tell you about in a minute.'

I said: 'That jibes with Eddie Mars's wife being on the missing list.'

He looked annoyed. 'Yeah. We investigate the tenants and find she's living there. Left about the time Regan did, within two days anyway. A guy who sounds a bit like Regan had been seen with her, but we don't get a positive identification. It's goddamned funny in this police racket how an old woman can look out of a window and see a guy running and pick him out of a line-up six months later, but we can show hotel help a clear photo and they just can't be sure.'

'That's one of the qualifications for good hotel help,' I said.

'Yeah. Eddie Mars and his wife didn't live together, but they were friendly, Eddie says. Here's some of the possibilities. First off Regan carried fifteen grand, packed it in his clothes all the time. Real money, they tell me. Not just a top card and a bunch of hay. That's a lot of jack but this Regan might be the boy to have it around so he could take it out and look at it when somebody was looking at him. Then again maybe he wouldn't give a damn. His wife says he never made a nickel off old man Sternwood except room and board and a Packard 120 his wife gave him. Tie that for an ex-legger in the rich gravy.'

'It beats me,' I said.

'Well, here we are with a guy who ducks out and has fifteen grand in his pants and folks know it. Well, that's money. I might duck out myself, if I had fifteen grand, and me with two kids in high school. So the first thought is somebody rolls him for it and rolls him too hard, so they have to take him out in the desert and plant him among the cactuses. But I don't like that too well. Regan carried a gat and had plenty of experience using it, and not just in a greasy-faced liquor mob. I understand he commanded a whole brigade in the Irish troubles back in 1922 or whenever it was. A guy like that wouldn't be white meat to a heister. Then, his car being in that garage makes whoever rolled him know he was sweet on Eddie Mars's wife, which he was, I guess, but it ain't something every poolroom bum would know.'

'Got a photo?' I asked.

'Him, not her. That's funny too. There's a lot of funny angles to this case. Here.' He pushed a shiny print across the desk and I looked at an Irish face that was more sad than merry and more reserved than brash. Not the face of a tough guy and not the face of a man who could be pushed around much by anybody. Straight dark brows with strong bone under them. A forehead wide rather than high, a mat of dark clustering hair, a thin short nose, a wide mouth. A chin that had strong lines but was small for the mouth. A face that looked a little taut, the face of a man who would move fast and play for keeps. I passed the print back. I would know that face, if I saw it.

Captain Gregory knocked his pipe out and refilled it and tamped the tobacco down with his thumb. He lit it, blew smoke and began to talk again.

'Well, there could be people who would know he was sweet on Eddie Mars's frau. Besides Eddie himself. For a wonder *he* knew it. But he don't seem to give a damn. We check him pretty thoroughly around that time. Of course Eddie wouldn't have knocked him off out of jealousy. The set-up would point to him too obvious.'

'It depends how smart he is,' I said. 'He might try the double bluff.'

Captain Gregory shook his head. 'If he's smart enough to get by in his racket, he's too smart for that. I get your idea. He pulls the dumb act because he thinks we wouldn't expect him to pull the dumb play. From a police angle that's wrong. Because he'd have us in his hair so much it would interfere with his business. *You* might think a dumb play would be smart. I might think so. The rank and file wouldn't. They'd make his life miserable. I've ruled it out. If I'm wrong, you can prove it on me and I'll eat my chair cushion. Till then I'm leaving Eddie in the clear. Jealousy is a bad motive for his type. Top-flight racketeers have business brains. They learn to do things that are good policy and let their personal feelings take care of themselves. I'm leaving that out.'

'What are you leaving in?'

'The dame and Regan himself. Nobody else. She was a blonde then, but she won't be now. We don't find her car, so they probably left in it. They had a long start on us—fourteen days. Except for that car of Regan's I don't figure we'd have got the case at all. Of course I'm used to them that way, especially in good-class families. And of course everything I've done has had to be under the hat.'

He leaned back and thumped the arms of his chair with the heels of his large heavy hands.

'I don't see nothing to do but wait,' he said. 'We've got readers out, but it's too soon to look for results. Regan had fifteen grand we know of. The girl had some, maybe a lot in rocks. But they'll run out of dough some day. Regan will cash a cheque, drop a marker, write a letter. They're in a strange town and they've got new names, but they've got the same old appetites. They got to get back in the fiscal system.'

'What did the girl do before she married Eddie Mars?'

'Torcher.'

'Can't you get any old professional photos?'

'No. Eddie must have had some, but he won't loosen up. He wants her let alone. I can't make him. He's got friends in town, or he wouldn't be what he is.' He grunted. 'Any of this do you any good?'

I said: 'You'll never find either of them. The Pacific Ocean is too close.'

'What I said about my chair cushion still goes. We'll find him. It may take time. It could take a year or two.'

'General Sternwood may not live that long,' I said.

'We've done all we could, brother. If he wants to put out a reward and spend some money, we might get results. The city don't give me the kind of money it takes.' His large eyes peered at me and his scratchy eyebrows moved. 'You serious about thinking Eddie put them both down?'

I laughed. 'No. I was just kidding. I think what you think, Captain. That Regan ran away with a woman who meant more to him than a rich wife he didn't get along with. Besides, she isn't rich yet.'

'You met her, I suppose?'

'Yes. She'd make a jazzy week-end, but she'd be wearing for a steady diet.'

He grunted and I thanked him for his time and information and left. A grey Plymouth sedan tailed me away from the City Hall. I gave it a chance to catch up with me on a quiet street. It refused the offer, so I shook it off and went about my business.

21

I didn't go near the Sternwood family. I went back to the office and sat in my swivel chair and tried to catch up on my foot-dangling. There was a gusty wind blowing in at the windows and the soot from the oil burners of the hotel next door was down-draughted into the room and rolling across the top of the desk like tumbleweed drifting across a vacant lot. I was thinking about going out to lunch and that life was pretty flat and that it would probably be just as flat if I took a drink and that taking a drink all alone at that time of day wouldn't be any fun anyway. I was thinking this when

Norris called up. In his carefully polite manner he said that General Sternwood was not feeling very well and that certain items in the newspaper had been read to him and he assumed that my investigation was now completed.

'Yes, as regards Geiger,' I said. 'I didn't shoot him, you know.'

'The General didn't suppose you did, Mr Marlowe.'

'Does the General know anything about those photographs Mrs Regan was worrying about?'

'No, sir. Decidedly not.'

'Did you know what the General gave me?'

'Yes, sir. Three notes and a card, I believe.'

'Right. I'll return them. As to the photos I think I'd better just destroy them.'

'Very good, sir. Mrs Regan tried to reach you a number of times last night—'

'I was out getting drunk,' I said.

'Yes. Very necessary, sir, I'm sure. The General has instructed me to send you a cheque for five hundred dollars. Will that be satisfactory?'

'More than generous,' I said.

'And I presume we may now consider the incident closed?'

'Oh, sure. Tight as a vault with a busted time lock.'

'Thank you, sir. I am sure we all appreciate it. When the General is feeling a little better—possibly to-morrow—he would like to thank you in person.'

'Fine,' I said. 'I'll come out and drink some more of his brandy, maybe with champagne.'

'I shall see that some is properly iced,' the old boy said, almost with a smirk in his voice.

That was that. We said good-bye and hung up. The coffee shop smell from next door came in at the windows with the soot but failed to make me hungry. So I got out my office bottle and took the drink and let my self-respect ride its own race.

I counted it up on my fingers. Rusty Regan had run away from a lot of money and a handsome wife to go wandering with a vague blonde who was more or less married to a racketeer named Eddie Mars. He had gone suddenly without good-byes and there might be any number of reasons for that. The General had been too proud, or, at the first interview he gave me, too careful, to tell me the Missing Persons Bureau had the matter in hand. The Missing Persons people were dead on their feet on it and evidently didn't think it worth bothering over. Regan had done what he had done and that was his business. I agreed with Captain Gregory that Eddie Mars would have been very unlikely to involve himself in a double murder just because another man had gone to town with the blonde he was not even living with. It might have annoyed him, but business is business, and you have to hold your teeth clamped around Hollywood to keep from chewing on stray blondes. If there had been a lot of money involved, that would be different. But fifteen grand wouldn't be a lot of money to Eddie Mars. He was no two-bit chiseller like Brody.

Geiger was dead and Carmen would have to find some other shady character to drink exotic blends of hooch with. I didn't suppose she would have any trouble. All she would have to do would be to stand on the corner for five minutes and look coy. I hoped that the next grifter who dropped the hook on her would play her a little more smoothly, a little more for the long haul rather than the quick touch.

Mrs Regan knew Eddie Mars well enough to borrow money from him. That was natural, if she played roulette and was a good loser. Any gambling house owner would lend a good client money in a pinch. Apart from this they had an added bond of interest in Regan. He was her husband and he had gone off with Eddie Mars's wife.

Carol Lundgren, the boy killer with the limited vocabulary, was out of circulation for a long, long time, even if they didn't strap him in a chair over a bucket of acid. They wouldn't, because he would take a plea and save the county money. They all do when they don't have the price of a big lawyer. Agnes Lozelle was in custody as a material witness. They wouldn't need her for that, if Carol took a plea, and if he pleaded guilty on arraignment, they would turn her loose. They wouldn't want to open up any angles on Geiger's business, apart from which they had nothing on her.

That left me. I had concealed a murder and suppressed evidence for twenty-four hours, but I was still at large and had a five-hundred-dollar cheque coming. The smart thing for me to do was to take another drink and forget the whole mess.

That being the obviously smart thing to do, I called Eddie Mars and told him I was coming down to Las Olindas that evening to talk to him. That was how smart I was.

I got down there about nine, under a hard high October moon that lost itself in the top layers of a beach fog. The Cypress Club was at the far end of the town, a rambling frame mansion that had once been the summer residence of a rich man named De Cazens, and later had been a hotel. It was now a big dark outwardly shabby place in a thick grove of wind-twisted Monterey cypresses, which gave it its name. It had enormous scrolled porches, turrets all over the place, stained-glass trims around the big windows, big empty stables at the back, a general air of nostalgic decay. Eddie Mars had left the outside much as he found it, instead of making it over to look like an MGM set. I left my car on a street with sputtering arc lights and walked into the grounds along a damp gravel path to the main entrance. A doorman in a double-breasted guards coat let me into a huge dim silent lobby from which a white oak staircase curved majestically up to the darkness of an upper floor. I checked my hat and coat and waited, listening to music and confused voices behind heavy double doors. They seemed a long way off, and not quite of the same world as the building itself. Then the slim pasty-faced blond man who had been with Eddie Mars and the pug at Geiger's place came through a door under the staircase, smiled at me bleakly and took me back with him along a carpeted hall to the boss's office.

This was a square room with a deep old bay window and a stone fireplace in which a fire of juniper logs burned lazily. It was wainscoted in walnut and had a frieze of faded damask above the panelling. The ceiling was high and remote. There was a smell of cold sea.

Eddie Mars's dark sheenless desk didn't belong in the room, but neither did anything made after 1900. His carpet had a Florida suntan. There was a bartop radio in the corner and a Sèvres china tea set on a copper tray beside a samovar. I wondered who that was for. There was a door in the corner that had a time lock on it.

Eddie Mars grinned at me sociably and shook hands and moved his chin at the vault. 'I'm a pushover for a heist mob here except for that thing,' he said cheerfully. 'The local johns drop in every morning and watch me open it. I have an arrangement with them.'

'You hinted you had something for me,' I said. 'What is it?'

'What's your hurry? Have a drink and sit down.'

'No hurry at all. You and I haven't anything to talk about but business.'

'You'll have the drink and like it,' he said. He mixed a couple and put mine down beside a red leather chair and stood crosslegged against the desk himself, one hand in the side pocket of his midnight-blue dinner jacket, the thumb outside and the nail glistening. In dinner clothes he looked a little harder than in grey flannel, but he still looked like a horseman. We drank and nodded at each other.

'Ever been here before?' he asked.

'During prohibition. I don't get any kick out of gambling.'

'Not with money,' he smiled. 'You ought to look in tonight. One of your friends is outside betting the wheels. I hear she's doing pretty well. Vivian Regan.'

I sipped my drink and took one of his monogrammed cigarettes.

'I kind of liked the way you handled that yesterday,' he said. 'You made me sore at the time but I could see afterwards how right you were. You and I ought to get along. How much do I owe you?'

'For doing what?'

'Still careful, eh? I have my pipe-line into headquarters, or I wouldn't be here. I get them the way they happen, not the way you read them in the papers.' He showed me his large white teeth.

'How much have you got?' I asked.

'You're not talking money?'

'Information was the way I understood it.'

'Information about what?'

'You have a short memory. Regan.'

'Oh, that.' He waved his glistening nails in the quiet light from one of those bronze lamps that shoot a beam at the ceiling. 'I hear you got the information already. I felt I owed you a fee. I'm used to paying for nice treatment.'

'I didn't drive down here to make a touch. I get paid for what I do. Not much by your standards, but I make out. One customer at a time is a good rule. You didn't bump Regan off, did you?'

'No. Did you think I did?'

'I wouldn't put it past you.'

He laughed. 'You're kidding.'

I laughed. 'Sure, I'm kidding. I never saw Regan, but I saw his photo. You haven't got men for the work. And while we're on that subject don't send me any more gun punks with orders. I might get hysterical and blow one down.'

He looked through his glass at the fire, set it down on the end of the desk and wiped his lips with a sheer lawn handkerchief.

'You talk a good game,' he said. 'But I dare say you can break a hundred and ten. You're not really interested in Regan are you?'

'No, not professionally. I haven't been asked to be. But I know somebody who would like to know where he is.'

'She doesn't give a damn,' he said.

'I mean her father.'

He wiped his lips again and looked at the handkerchief almost as if he expected to find blood on it. He drew his thick grey eyebrows close together and fingered the side of his weatherbeaten nose.

'Geiger was trying to blackmail the General,' I said. 'The General wouldn't say so, but I figure he was at least half scared Regan might be behind it.'

Eddie Mars laughed. 'Uh-uh. Geiger worked that one on everybody. It was strictly his own idea. He'd get notes from people that looked legal–were legal, I dare say, except that he wouldn't have dared sue on them. He'd present notes, with a nice flourish, leaving himself empty-handed. If he drew an ace, he had a prospect that scared and he went to work. If he didn't draw an ace, he just dropped the whole thing.'

'Clever guy,' I said. 'He dropped it all right. Dropped it and fell on it. How come *you* know all this?'

He shrugged impatiently. 'I wish to Christ I didn't know half the stuff that's brought to me. Knowing other people's business is the worst investment a man can make in my circle. Then if it was just Geiger you were after, you're washed up on that angle.'

'Washed up and paid off.'

'I'm sorry about that. I wish old Sternwood would hire himself a soldier like you on a straight salary, to keep those girls of his home at least a few nights a week.'

'Why?'

His mouth looked sulky. 'They're plain trouble. Take the dark one. She's a pain in the neck around here. If she loses, she plunges and I end up with a fistful of paper which nobody will discount at any price. She has no money of her own except an allowance and what's in the old man's will is a secret. If she wins, she takes my money home with her.'

'You get it back the next night,' I said.

'I get some of it back. But over a period of time I'm loser.'

He looked earnestly at me, as if that was important to me. I wondered why he thought it necessary to tell me at all. I yawned and finished my drink.

'I'm going out and look the joint over,' I said.

'Yes, do.' He pointed to a door near the vault door. 'That leads to a door behind the tables.'

'I'd rather go in the way the suckers enter.'

'Okey. As you please. We're friends, aren't we, soldier?'

'Sure.' I stood up and we shook hands.

'Maybe I can do you a real favour some day,' he said. 'You got it all from Gregory this time.'

'So you own a piece of him too.'

'Oh not that bad. We're just friends.'

I stared at him for a moment, then went over to the door I had come in at. I looked back at him when I had it open.

'You don't have anybody tailing me around in a grey Plymouth sedan, do you?'

His eyes widened sharply. He looked jarred. 'Hell, no. Why should I?'

'I couldn't imagine,' I said, and went on out. I thought his surprise looked genuine enough to be believed. I thought he even looked a little worried. I couldn't think of any reason for that.

22

It was about ten-thirty when the little yellow-sashed Mexican orchestra got tired of playing a low-voiced prettied-up rhumba that nobody was dancing to. The gourd player rubbed his finger tips together as if they were sore and got a cigarette into his mouth almost with the same movement. The other four, with a timed simultaneous stoop, reached under their chairs for glasses from which they sipped, smacking their lips and flashing their eyes. Tequila, their manner said. It was probably mineral water. The pretence was as wasted as the music. Nobody was looking at them.

The room had been a ballroom once and Eddie Mars had changed it only as much as his business compelled him. No chromium glitter, no indirect lighting from behind angular cornices, no fused glass pictures, or chairs in violent leather and polished metal tubing, none of the pseudo-modernistic circus of the typical Hollywood night trap. The light was from heavy crystal chandeliers and the rose-damask panels of the wall were still the same rose damask, a little faded by time and darkened by dust, that had been matched long ago against the parquetry floor, of which only a small glass-smooth space in front of the little Mexican orchestra showed bare. The rest was covered by a heavy old-rose carpeting that must have cost plenty. The parquetry was made of a dozen kinds of hardwood, from Burma teak through half a dozen shades of oak and ruddy wood that looked like mahogany, and fading out to the hard pale wild lilac of the California hills, all laid in elaborate patterns, with the accuracy of a transit.

It was still a beautiful room and now there was roulette in it instead of measured, old-fashioned dancing. There were three tables close to the far wall. A low bronze railing joined them and made a fence around the croupiers. All three tables were working, but the crowd was at the middle one. I could see Vivian Regan's black head close to it, from across the room where I was leaning against the bar and turning a small glass of bacardi around on the mahogany.

The bartender leaned beside me watching the cluster of well-dressed people at the middle table. 'She's pickin' 'em tonight, right on the nose,' he said. 'That tall black-headed frail.'

'Who is she?'

'I wouldn't know her name. She comes here a lot though.'

'The hell you wouldn't know her name.'

'I just work here, mister,' he said without any animosity. 'She's all alone too. The guy was with her passed out. They took him out to his car.'

'I'll take her home,' I said.

'The hell you will. Well, I wish you luck anyways. Should I gentle up that bacardi or do you like it the way it is?'

'I like it the way it is as well as I like it at all,' I said.

'Me, I'd just as leave drink croup medicine,' he said.

The crowd parted and two men in evening clothes pushed their way out and I saw the back of her neck and her bare shoulders in the opening. She wore a low-cut dress of dull green velvet. It looked too dressy for the occasion. The crowd closed and hid all but her black head. The two men came across the room and leaned against the bar and asked for Scotch and soda. One of them was flushed and excited. He was mopping his face with a black-bordered handkerchief. The double satin stripes down the side of his trousers were wide enough for tyre tracks.

'Boy, I never saw such a run,' he said in a jittery voice. 'Eight wins and two stand-offs in a row on that red. That's roulette, boy, that's roulette.'

'It gives me the itch,' the other one said. 'She's betting a grand at a crack. She can't lose.' They put their beaks in their drinks, gurgled swiftly and went back.

'So wise the little men are,' the barkeeper said. 'A grand a crack, huh. I saw an old horseface in Havana once—'

The noise swelled over at the middle table and a chiselled foreign voice rose above it saying: 'If you will just be patient a moment, madam. The table cannot cover your bet. Mr Mars will be here in a moment.'

I left my bacardi and padded across the carpet. The little orchestra started to play a tango, rather loud. No one was dancing or intending to dance. I moved through a scattering of people in dinner clothes and full evening dress and sports clothes and business suits to the end table at the left. It had gone dead. Two croupiers stood behind it with their heads together and their eyes sideways. One moved a rake back and forth aimlessly over the empty layout. They were both staring at Vivian Regan.

Her long lashes twitched and her face looked unnaturally white. She was at the middle table, exactly opposite the wheel. There was a disordered pile of money and chips in front of her. It looked like a lot of money. She spoke to the croupier with a cool, insolent, ill-tempered drawl.

'What kind of a cheap outfit is this, I'd like to know. Get busy and spin that wheel, highpockets. I want one more play and I'm playing table stakes. You take it away fast enough I've noticed, but when it comes to dishing it out you start to whine.'

The croupier smiled a cold polite smile that had looked at thousands of boors and millions of fools. His tall dark disinterested manner was flawless. He said gravely: 'The table cannot cover your bet, madam. You have over sixteen thousand dollars there.'

'It's your money,' the girl jeered. 'Don't you want it back?'

A man beside her tried to tell her something. She turned swiftly and spat something at him and he faded back into the crowd red-faced. A door opened in the panelling at the far end of the enclosed place made by the bronze railing. Eddie Mars came through the door with a set indifferent smile on his face, his hands thrust into the pockets of his dinner jacket, both thumb-nails glistening outside. He seemed to like that pose. He strolled behind the croupiers and stopped at the corner of the middle table. He spoke with lazy calm, less politely than the croupier.

'Something the matter, Mrs Regan?'

She turned her face to him with a sort of lunge. I saw the curve of her cheek stiffen, as if with an almost unbearable inner tautness. She didn't answer him.

Eddie Mars said gravely: 'If you're not playing any more, you must let me send someone home with you.'

The girl flushed. Her cheekbones stood out white in her face. Then she laughed off-key. She said bitterly:

'One more play, Eddie. Everything I have on the red. I like red. It's the colour of blood.'

Eddie Mars smiled faintly, then nodded and reached into his inner breast pocket. He drew out a large pinseal wallet with gold corners and tossed it carelessly along the table to the croupier. 'Cover her bet in even thousands,' he said, 'if no one objects to this turn of the wheel being just for the lady.'

No one objected. Vivian Regan leaned down and pushed all her winnings savagely with both hands on to the large red diamond on the layout.

The croupier leaned over the table without haste. He counted and stacked her money and chips, placed all but a few chips and bills in a neat pile and pushed the rest back off the layout with his rake. He opened Eddie Mars's wallet and drew out two flat packets of thousand-dollar bills. He broke one, counted six bills out, added them to the unbroken packet, put the four loose bills in the wallet and laid it aside as carelessly as if it had been a packet of matches. Eddie Mars didn't touch the wallet. Nobody moved except the croupier. He spun the wheel lefthanded and sent the ivory ball skittering along the upper edge with a casual flirt of his wrist. Then he drew his hands back and folded his arms.

Vivian's lips parted slowly until her teeth caught the light and glittered like knives. The ball drifted lazily down the slope of the wheel and bounced on the chromium ridges above the numbers. After a long time and then very suddenly motion left it with a dry click. The wheel slowed, carrying the ball around with it. The croupier didn't unfold his arms until the wheel had entirely ceased to revolve.

'The red wins,' he said formally, without interest. The little ivory ball lay in Red 25, the third number from the Double Zero. Vivian Regan put her head back and laughed triumphantly.

The croupier lifted his rake and slowly pushed the stack of thousand-dollar bills across the layout, added them to the stake, pushed everything slowly out of the field of play.

Eddie Mars smiled, put his wallet back in his pocket, turned on his heel and left the room through the door in the panelling.

A dozen people let their breath out at the same time and broke for the bar. I broke with them and got to the far end of the room before Vivian had gathered up her winnings and turned away from the table. I went out into the large quiet lobby, got my hat and coat from the check girl, dropped a quarter in her tray and went out on the porch. The doorman loomed up beside me and said: 'Can I get your car for you, sir?'

I said: 'I'm just going for a walk.'

The scrollwork along the edge of the porch roof was wet with the fog. The fog dripped from the Monterey cypresses that shadowed off into nothing towards the cliff above the ocean. You could see a scant dozen feet in any direction. I went down the porch steps and drifted off through the trees, following an indistinct path until I could hear the wash of the surf licking at the fog, low down at the bottom of the cliff. There wasn't a gleam of light anywhere. I could see a dozen trees clearly at one time, another dozen dimly, then nothing at all but the fog. I circled to the left and drifted back towards the gravel path that went around to the stables where they parked the cars. When I could make out the outlines of the house I stopped. A little in front of me I had heard a man cough.

My steps hadn't made any sound on the soft moist turf. The man coughed again, then stifled the cough with a handkerchief or a sleeve. While he was still doing that I moved forward closer to him. I made him out, a vague shadow close to the path. Something made me step behind a tree and crouch down. The man turned his head. His face should have been a white blur when he did that. It wasn't. It remained dark. There was a mask over it.

I waited, behind the tree.

23

Light steps, the steps of a woman, came along the invisible pathway and the man in front of me moved forward and seemed to lean against the fog. I couldn't see the woman, then I could see her indistinctly. The arrogant carriage of her head seemed familiar. The man stepped out very quickly. The two figures blended in the fog, seemed to be part of the fog. There was dead silence for a moment. The man said:

'This is a gun, lady. Gentle now. Sound carries in the fog. Just hand me the bag.'

The girl didn't make a sound. I moved forward a step. Quite suddenly I could see the foggy fuzz on the man's hat brim. The girl stood motionless. Then her breathing began to make a rasping sound, like a small file on soft wood.

'Yell,' the man said, 'and I'll cut you in half.'

She didn't yell. She didn't move. There was a movement from him, and a dry chuckle. 'It better be in here,' he said. A catch clicked and a fumbling sound came to me. The man turned and came towards my tree. When he had taken three or four steps he chuckled again. The chuckle was something out of my own memories. I reached a pipe out of my pocket and held it like a gun.

I called out softly: 'Hi, Lanny.'

The man stopped dead and started to bring his hand up. I said: 'No. I told you never to do that, Lanny. You're covered.'

Nothing moved. The girl back on the path didn't move. I didn't move. Lanny didn't move.

'Put the bag down between your feet, kid,' I told him. 'Slow and easy.'

He bent down. I jumped out and reached him still bent over. He straightened up against me breathing hard. His hands were empty.

'Tell me I can't get away with it,' I said. I leaned against him and took the gun out of his overcoat pocket. 'Somebody's always giving me guns,' I told him. 'I'm weighted down with them till I walk all crooked. Beat it.'

Our breaths met and mingled, our eyes were like the eyes of two tomcats on a wall. I stepped back.

'On your way, Lanny. No hard feelings. You keep it quiet and I keep it quiet. Okey?'

'Okey,' he said thickly.

The fog swallowed him. The faint sound of his steps and then nothing. I picked the bag up and felt in it and went towards the path. She still stood there motionless, a grey fur coat held tight around her throat with an ungloved hand on which a ring made a faint glitter. She wore no hat. Her dark parted hair was part of the darkness of the night. Her eyes too.

'Nice work, Marlowe. Are you my bodyguard now?' Her voice had a harsh note.

'Looks that way. Here's the bag.'

She took it. I said: 'Have you a car with you?'

She laughed. 'I came with a man. What are you doing here?'

'Eddie Mars wanted to see me.'

'I didn't know you knew him. Why?'

'I don't mind telling you. He thought I was looking for somebody he thought had run away with his wife.'

'Were you?'

'No.'

'Then what did you come for?'

'To find out why he thought I was looking for somebody he thought had run away with his wife.'

'Did you find out?'

'No.'

'You leak information like a radio announcer,' she said. 'I suppose it's none of my business—even if the man was my husband. I thought you weren't interested in that.'

'People keep throwing it at me.'

She clicked her teeth in annoyance. The incident of the masked man with the gun seemed to have made no impression on her at all. 'Well, take me to the garage,' she said. 'I have to look in at my escort.'

We walked along the path and around a corner of the building and there was light ahead, then around another corner and came to a bright enclosed stable yard lit with two floodlights. It was still paved with brick and still sloped down to a grating in the middle. Cars glistened and a man in a brown smock got up off a stool and came forward.

'Is my boy friend still blotto?' Vivian asked him carelessly.

'I'm afraid he is, miss. I put a rug over him and run the windows up. He's okey, I guess. Just kind of resting.'

We went over to a big Cadillac and the man in the smock pulled the rear door open. On the wide back seat, loosely arranged, covered to the chin with a plaid robe, a man lay snoring with his mouth open. He seemed to be a big blond man who would hold a lot of liquor.

'Meet Mr Larry Cobb,' Vivian said. 'Mister Cobb—Mister Marlowe.'

I grunted.

'Mr Cobb was my escort,' she said. 'Such a nice escort, Mr Cobb. So attentive. You should see him sober. *I* should see him sober. Somebody should see him sober. I mean, just for the record. So it could become a part of history, that brief flashing moment, soon buried in time, but never forgotten—when Larry Cobb was sober.'

'Yeah,' I said.

'I've even thought of marrying him,' she went on in a high strained voice, as if the shock of the stick-up was just beginning to get to her. 'At odd times when nothing pleasant would come into my mind. We all have those spells. Lots of money, you know. A yacht, a place on Long Island, a place at Newport, a place at Bermuda, places dotted here and there all over the world probably—just a good Scotch bottle apart. And to Mr Cobb a bottle of Scotch is not very far.'

'Yeah,' I said. 'Does he have a driver to take him home?'

'Don't say "yeah". It's common.' She looked at me with arched eyebrows. The man in the smock was chewing his lower lip hard. 'Oh, undoubtedly a whole platoon of drivers. They probably do squads right in front of the garage every morning, buttons shining, harness gleaming, white gloves immaculate—a sort of West Point elegance about them.'

'Well, where the hell is this driver?' I asked.

'He drove hisself to-night,' the man in the smock said, almost apologetically. 'I could call his home and have somebody come down for him.'

Vivian turned around and smiled at him as if he had just presented her with a diamond tiara. 'That would be lovely,' she said. 'Would you do that? I really wouldn't want Mr Cobb to die like that—with his mouth open. Someone might think he had died of thirst.'

The man in the smock said: 'Not if they sniffed him, miss.'

She opened her bag and grabbed a handful of paper money and pushed it at him. 'You'll take care of him, I'm sure.'

'Jeeze,' the man said, pop-eyed. 'I sure will, miss.'

'Regan is the name, she said sweetly. 'Mrs Regan. You'll probably see me again. Haven't been here long, have you?'

'No'm.' His hands were doing frantic things with the fistful of money he was holding.

'You'll get to love it here,' she said. She took hold of my arm. 'Let's ride in your car, Marlowe.'

'It's outside on the street.'

'Quite all right with me, Marlowe. I love a nice walk in the fog. You meet such interesting people.'

'Oh, nuts,' I said.

She held on to my arm and began to shake. She held me hard all the way to the car. She had stopped shaking by the time we reached it. I drove down a curving lane of trees on the blind side of the house. The lane opened on De Cazens Boulevard, the main drag of Las Olindas. We passed under the ancient sputtering arc lights and after a while there was a town, buildings, dead-looking stores, a service station with a light over a night bell, and at last a drugstore that was still open.

'You better have a drink,' I said.

She moved her chin, a point of paleness in the corner of the seat. I turned diagonally into the kerb and parked. 'A little black coffee and a smattering of rye would go well,' I said.

'I could get as drunk as two sailors and love it.'

I held the door for her and she got out close to me, brushing my cheek with her hair. We went into the drugstore. I bought a pint of rye at the liquor counter and carried it over to the stools and set it down on the cracked marble counter.

'Two coffees,' I said. 'Black, strong and made this year.'

'You can't drink liquor in here,' the clerk said. He had a washed-out blue smock, was thin on top as to hair, had fairly honest eyes and his chin would never hit a wall before he saw it.

Vivian Regan reached into her bag for a packet of cigarettes and shook a couple loose just like a man. She held them towards me.

'It's against the law to drink liquor in here,' the clerk said.

I lit the cigarettes and didn't pay any attention to him. He drew two cups of coffee from a tarnished nickel urn and set them in front of us. He looked at the bottle of rye, muttered under his breath and said wearily: 'Okey, I'll watch the street while you pour it.'

He went and stood at the display window with his back to us and his ears hanging out.

'My heart's in my mouth doing this,' I said, and unscrewed the top of the whisky bottle and loaded the coffee. 'The law enforcement in this town is terrific. All through prohibition Eddie Mars's place was a night club and they had two uniformed men in the lobby every night–to see that the guests didn't bring their own liquor instead of buying it from the house.'

The clerk turned suddenly and walked back behind the counter and went in behind the little glass window of the prescription room.

We sipped our loaded coffee. I looked at Vivian's face in the mirror back of the coffee urn. It was taut, pale, beautiful and wild. Her lips were red and harsh.

'You have wicked eyes,' I said. 'What's Eddie Mars got on you?'

She looked at me in the mirror. 'I took plenty away from him to-night at roulette–starting with five grand I borrowed from him yesterday and didn't have to use.'.

'That might make him sore. You think he sent that loogan after you?'

'What's a loogan?'

'A guy with a gun.'

'Are you a loogan?'

'Sure,' I laughed. 'But strictly speaking a loogan is on the wrong side of the fence.'

'I often wonder if there is a wrong side.'

'We're losing the subject. What has Eddie Mars got on you?'

'You mean a hold on me of some sort?'

'Yes.'

Her lip curled. 'Wittier, please, Marlowe. Much wittier.'

'How's the General? I don't pretend to be witty.'

'Not too well. He didn't get up to-day. You could at least stop questioning me.'

'I remember a time when I thought the same about you. How much does the General know?'

'He probably knows everything.'

'Norris would tell him?'

'No. Wilde, the District Attorney, was out to see him. Did you burn those pictures?'

'Sure. You worry about your little sister, don't you–from time to time.'

'I think she's all I do worry about. I worry about Dad in a way, to keep things from him.'

'He hasn't many illusions,' I said, 'but I suppose he still has pride.'

'We're his blood. That's the hell of it.' She stared at me in the mirror with deep, distant eyes. 'I don't want him to die despising his own blood. It was always wild blood, but it wasn't always rotten blood.'

'Is it now?'

'I guess you think so.'

'Not yours. You're just playing the part.'

She looked down. I sipped some more coffee and lit another cigarette for us. 'So you shoot people,' she said quietly. 'You're a killer.'

'Me? How?'

'The papers and the police fixed it up nicely. But I don't believe everything I read.'

'Oh, you think I accounted for Geiger—or Brody—or both of them.'

She didn't say anything. 'I didn't have to,' I said. 'I might have, I suppose, and got away with it. Neither of them would have hesitated to throw lead at me.'

'That makes you just a killer at heart, like all cops.'

'Oh, nuts.'

'One of those dark deadly quiet men who have no more feelings than a butcher has for slaughtered meat. I knew it the first time I saw you.'

'You've got enough shady friends to know different.'

'They're all soft compared to you.'

'Thanks, lady. You're no English muffin yourself.'

'Let's get out of this rotten little town.'

I paid the check, put the bottle of rye in my pocket, and we left. The clerk still didn't like me.

We drove away from Las Olindas through a series of little dank beach towns with shack-like houses built down on the sand close to the rumble of the surf and larger houses built back on the slopes behind. A yellow window shone here and there, but most of the houses were dark. A smell of kelp came in off the water and lay on the fog. The tyres sang on the moist concrete of the boulevard. The world was a wet emptiness.

We were close to Del Rey before she spoke to me for the first time since we left the drugstore. Her voice had a muffled sound, as if something was throbbing deep under it.

'Drive down by the Del Ray beach club. I want to look at the water. It's the next street on the left.'

There was a winking yellow light at the intersection. I turned the car and slid down a slope with a high bluff on one side, interurban tracks to the right, a low straggle of lights far off beyond the tracks, and then very far off a glitter of pier lights and a haze in the sky over a city. That way the fog was almost gone. The road crossed the tracks where they turned to run under the bluff, then reached a paved strip of waterfront highway that bordered an open and uncluttered beach. Cars were parked along the pavement, facing out to sea, dark. The lights of the beach club were a few hundred yards away.

I braked the car against the kerb and switched the headlights off and sat with my hands on the wheel. Under the thinning fog the surf curled and creamed, almost without sound, like a thought trying to form itself on the edge of consciousness.

'Move closer,' she said almost thickly.

I moved out from under the wheel into the middle of the seat. She turned her body a little away from me as if to peer out of the window. Then she let herself fall backwards, without a sound, into my arms. Her head almost struck the wheel. Her eyes were closed, her face was dim. Then I saw that her eyes opened and flickered, the shine of them visible even in the darkness.

'Hold me close, you beast,' she said.

I put my arms around her loosely at first. Her hair had a harsh feeling against my face. I tightened my arms and lifted her up. I brought her face slowly up to my face. Her eyelids were flickering rapidly, like moth wings.

I kissed her tightly and quickly. Then a long slow clinging kiss. Her lips opened under mine. Her body began to shake in my arms.

'Killer,' she said softly, her breath going into my mouth.

I strained her against me until the shivering of her body was almost shaking mine. I kept on kissing her. After a long time she pulled her head away enough to say: 'Where do you live?'

'Hobart Arms. Franklin near Kenmore.'

'I've never seen it.'

'Want to?'

'Yes.'

'What has Eddie Mars got on you?'

Her body stiffened in my arms and her breath made a harsh sound. Her head pulled back until her eyes, wide open, ringed with white, were staring at me.

'So that's the way it is,' she said in a soft dull voice.

'That's the way it is. Kissing is nice, but your father didn't hire me to sleep with you.'

'You son of a bitch,' she said calmly, without moving.

I laughed in her face. 'Don't think I'm an icicle,' I said. 'I'm not blind or without senses. I have warm blood like the next guy. You're easy to take—too damned easy. What has Eddie Mars got on you?'

'If you say that again, I'll scream.'

'Go ahead and scream.'

She jerked away and pulled herself upright, far back in the corner of the car.

'Men have been shot for little things like that, Marlowe.'

'Men have been shot for practically nothing. The first time we met I told you I was a detective. Get it through your lovely head. I work at it, lady. I don't play at it.'

She fumbled in her bag and got a handkerchief out and bit on it, her head turned away from me. The tearing sound of the handkerchief came to me. She tore it with her teeth, slowly, time after time.

'What makes you think he has anything on me?' she whispered, her voice muffled by the handkerchief.

'He lets you win a lot of money and sends a gunpoke around to take it back for him. You're not more than mildly surprised. You didn't even thank me for saving it for you. I think the whole thing was just some kind of an act. If I wanted to flatter myself, I'd say it was at least partly for my benefit.'

'You think he can win or lose as he pleases.'

'Sure. On even money bets, four times out of five.'

'Do I have to tell you I loathe your guts, Mister Detective?'

'You don't owe me anything. I'm paid off.'

She tossed the shredded handkerchief out of the car window. 'You have a lovely way with women.'

'I like kissing you.'

'You kept your head beautifully. That's so flattering. Should I congratulate you, or my father?'

'I liked kissing you.'

Her voice became an icy drawl. 'Take me away from here, if you will be so kind. I'm quite sure I'd like to go home.'

'You won't be a sister to me?'

'If I had a razor, I'd cut your throat—just to see what ran out of it.'

'Caterpillar blood,' I said.

I started the car and turned it and drove back across the interurban tracks to the highway and so on into town and up to West Hollywood. She didn't speak to me. She hardly moved all the way back. I drove through the gates and up the sunken driveway to the *porte-cochère* of the big house. She jerked the car door open and was out of it before it had quite stopped. She didn't speak even then. I watched her back as she stood against the door after ringing the bell. The door opened and Norris looked out. She pushed past him quickly and was gone. The door banged shut and I was sitting there looking at it.

I turned back down the driveway and home.

24

The apartment house lobby was empty this time. No gunman waiting under the potted palm to give me orders. I took the automatic elevator up to my floor and walked along the hallway to the tune of a muted radio behind a door. I needed a drink and was in a hurry to get one. I didn't switch the light on inside the door. I made straight for the kitchenette and brought up short in three or four feet. Something was wrong. Something on the air, a scent. The shades were down at the windows and the street light leaking in at the sides made a dim light in the room. I stood still and listened. The scent on the air was a perfume, a heavy, cloying perfume.

There was no sound, no sound at all. Then my eyes adjusted themselves more to the darkness and I saw there was something across the floor in front of me that shouldn't have been there. I backed, reached the wall switch with my thumb and flicked the light on.

The bed was down. Something in it giggled. A blonde head was pressed into my pillow. Two bare arms curved up and the hands belonging to them were clasped on top of the blonde head. Carmen Sternwood lay on her back, in my bed, giggling at me. The tawny wave of her hair was spread out on the pillow as if by a careful and artificial hand. Her slaty eyes peered at me and had the effect, as usual, of peering from behind a barrel. She smiled. Her small sharp teeth glinted.

'Cute, aren't I?' she said.

I said harshly: 'Cute as a Filipino on Saturday night.'

I went over to a floor lamp and pulled the switch, went back to put off the ceiling light, and went across the room again to the chessboard on a card table under the lamp. There was a problem laid out on the board, a six-mover. I couldn't solve it, like a lot of my problems. I reached down and moved a knight, then pulled my hat and coat off and threw them somewhere. All this time the soft giggling went on from the bed, that sound that made me think of rats behind a wainscoting in an old house.

'I bet you can't even guess how I got in.'

I dug a cigarette out and looked at her with bleak eyes. 'I bet I can. You came through the keyhole, just like Peter Pan.'

'Who's he?'

'Oh, a fellow I used to know around the poolroom.'

She giggled. 'You're cute, aren't you?' she said.

I began to say: 'About that thumb—' but she was ahead of me. I didn't have to remind her. She took her right hand from behind her head and started sucking the thumb and eyeing me with very round and naughty eyes.

'I'm all undressed,' she said, after I smoked and stared at her for a minute.

'By God,' I said, 'it was right at the back of my mind. I was groping for it. I almost had it, when you spoke. In another minute I'd have said "I bet you're all undressed." I always wear my rubbers in bed myself, in case I wake up with a bad conscience and have to sneak away from it.'

'You're cute.' She rolled her head a little, kittenishly. Then she took her left hand from under her head, and took hold of the covers, paused dramatically, and swept them aside. She was undressed all right. She lay there on the bed in the lamplight, as naked and glistening as a pearl. The Sternwood girls were giving me both barrels that night.

I pulled a shred of tobacco off the edge of my lower lip.

'That's nice,' I said. 'But I've already seen it all. Remember? I'm the guy that keeps finding you without any clothes on.'

She giggled some more and covered herself up again. 'Well, how *did* you get in?' I asked her.

'The manager let me in. I showed him your card. I'd stolen if from Vivian. I told him you told me to come here and wait for you. I was—I was mysterious.' She glowed with delight.

'Neat,' I said. 'Managers are like that. Now I know how you got in tell me how you're going to go out.'

She giggled. 'Not going—not for a long time . . . I like it here. You're cute.'

'Listen,' I pointed my cigarette at her. 'Don't make me dress you again. I'm tired. I appreciate all you're offering me. It's just more than I could possibly take. Doghouse Reilly never let a pal down that way. I'm your friend. I won't let you down—in spite of yourself. You and I have to keep on being friends, and this isn't the way to do it. Now will you dress like a nice little girl?'

She shook her head from side to side.

'Listen,' I ploughed on, 'you don't really care anything about me. You're just showing how naughty you can be. But you don't have to show me. I knew it already. I'm the guy that found—'

'Put the light out,' she giggled.

I threw my cigarette on the floor and stamped on it. I took a handkerchief out and wiped the palms of my hands. I tried it once more.

'It isn't on account of the neighbours,' I told her. 'They don't really care a lot. There's a lot of stray broads in any apartment house and one more won't make the building rock. It's a question of professional pride. You know—professional pride. I'm working for your father. He's a sick man, very frail, very helpless. He sort of trusts me not to pull any stunts. Won't you please get dressed, Carmen?'

'Your name isn't Doghouse Reilly,' she said. 'It's Philip Marlowe. You can't fool me.'

'I looked down at the chessboard. The move with the knight was wrong. I put it back where I had moved it from. Knights had no meaning in this game. It wasn't a game for knights.

I looked at her again. She lay still now, her face pale against the pillow, her eyes large and dark and empty as rain barrels in a drought. One of her small five-fingered thumbless hands picked at the cover restlessly. There was a vague glimmer of doubt starting to get born in her somewhere. She didn't know about it yet. It's so hard for women—even nice women—to realize that their bodies are not irresistible.

I said: 'I'm going out in the kitchen and mix a drink. Want one?'

'Uh-huh.' Dark silent mystified eyes stared at me solemnly, the doubt growing larger in them, creeping into them noiselessly, like a cat in long grass stalking a young blackbird.

'If you're dressed when I get back, you'll get the drink. Okey?'

Her teeth parted and a faint hissing noise came out of her mouth. She didn't answer me. I went out of the kitchenette and got out some Scotch and fizzwater and mixed a couple of highballs. I didn't have anything really exciting to drink, like nitro-glycerine or distilled tiger's breath. She hadn't moved when I got back with the glasses. The hissing had stopped. Her eyes were dead again. Her lips started to smile at me. Then she sat up suddenly and threw all the covers off her body and reached.

'Gimme.'

'When you're dressed. Not *until* you're dressed.'

I put the two glasses down on the card table and sat down myself and lit another cigarette. 'Go ahead. I won't watch you.'

I looked away. Then I was aware of the hissing noise very sudden and sharp. It startled me into looking at her again. She sat there naked, propped on her hands, her mouth open a little, her face like scraped bone. The hissing noise came tearing out of her mouth as if she had nothing to do with it. There was something behind her eyes, blank as they were, that I had never seen in a woman's eyes.

Then her lips moved very slowly and carefully, as if they were artificial lips and had to be manipulated with springs.

She called me a filthy name.

I didn't mind that. I didn't mind what she called me, what anybody called me. But this was the room I had to live in. It was all I had in the way of a home. In it was everything that was mine, that had any association for me, any past, anything that took the place of a family. Not much; a few books, pictures, radio, chessmen, old letters, stuff like that. Nothing. Such as they were they had all my memories.

I couldn't stand her in that room any longer. What she called me only reminded me of that.

I said carefully: 'I'll give you three minutes to get dressed and out of here. If you're not out by then, I'll throw you out—by force. Just the way you are, naked. And I'll throw your clothes after you into the hall. Now—get started.'

Her teeth chattered and the hissing noise was sharp and animal. She swung her feet to the floor and reached for her clothes on a chair beside the bed. She dressed. I watched her. She dressed with stiff awkward fingers—for a woman—but quickly at that. She was dressed in a little over two minutes. I timed it.

She stood there beside the bed, holding a green bag tight against a fur-trimmed coat. She wore a rakish green hat crooked on her head. She stood there for a moment and hissed at me, her face still like scraped bone, her eyes still empty and yet full of some jungle emotion. Then she walked quickly to the door and opened it and went out, without speaking, without looking back. I heard the elevator lurch into motion and move in the shaft.

I walked to the windows and pulled the shades up and opened the windows wide. The night air came drifting in with a kind of stale sweetness that still remembered automobile exhausts and the streets of the city. I reached for my drink and drank it slowly. The apartment house door closed itself down below me. Steps tinkled on the quiet pavement. A car started up not far away. It rushed off into the night with a rough clashing of gears. I went back to the bed and looked down at it. The imprint of her head was still in the pillow, of her small corrupt body still on the sheets.

I put my empty glass down and tore the bed to pieces savagely.

25

It was raining again the next morning, a slanting grey rain like a swung curtain of crystal beads. I got up feeling sluggish and tired and stood looking out of the windows, with a dark harsh taste of Sternwoods still in my mouth. I was as empty of life as a scarecrow's pockets. I went out to the kitchenette and drank two cups of black coffee. You can have a hangover from other things than alcohol. I had one from women. Women made me sick.

I shaved and showered and dressed and got my raincoat out and went downstairs and looked out of the front door. Across the street, a hundred feet up, a grey Plymouth sedan was parked. It was the same one that had tried to trail me around the day before, the same one that I had asked Eddie Mars about. There might be a cop in it, if a cop had that much time on his hands and wanted to waste it following me around. Or it might be a smoothie in the detective business trying to get a noseful of somebody else's case in order to chisel a way into it. Or it might be the Bishop of Bermuda disapproving of my night life.

I went out back and got my convertible from the garage and drove it around front past the grey Plymouth. There was a small man in it, alone. He started up after me. He worked better in the rain. He stayed close enough so that I couldn't make a short block and leave that before he entered it, and he stayed back far enough so that other cars were between us most of the time. I drove down to the boulevard and parked in the lot next to my building and came out of there with my raincoat collar up and my hat brim low and the raindrops tapping icily at my face in between. The Plymouth was across the way at a fireplug. I walked down to the intersection and crossed with the green light and walked back, close to the edge of the pavement and the parked cars. The Plymouth hadn't moved. Nobody got out of it. I reached it and jerked open the door on the kerb side.

A small bright-eyed man was pressed back into the corner behind the wheel. I stood and looked in at him, the rain thumping my back. His eyes blinked behind the swirling smoke of a cigarette. His hands tapped restlessly on the thin wheel.

I said: 'Can't you make your mind up?'

He swallowed and the cigarette bobbed between his lips. 'I don't think I know you,' he said, in a tight little voice.

'Marlowe's the name. The guy you've been trying to follow around for a couple of days.'

'I ain't following anybody, doc.'

'This jaloppy is. Maybe you can't control it. Have it your own way. I'm now going to eat breakfast in the coffee shop across the street, orange juice, bacon and eggs, toast, honey, three or four cups of coffee, and a toothpick. I am then going up to my office, which is on the seventh floor of the building right opposite you. If you have anything that's worrying you beyond endurance, drop up and chew it over. I'll only be oiling my machine-gun.'

I left him blinking and walked away. Twenty minutes later I was airing the scrubwoman's Soirée d'Amour out of my office and opening up a thick rough envelope addressed in a fine old-fashioned pointed handwriting. The envelope contained a brief formal note and a large mauve cheque for five hundred dollars, payable to Philip Marlowe and signed, Guy de Brisay Sternwood, by Vincent Norris. That made it a nice morning. I was making out a bank slip when the buzzer told me somebody had entered my two by four reception-room. It was the little man from the Plymouth.

'Fine,' I said. 'Come in and shed your coat.'

He slid past me carefully as I held the door, as carefully as though he feared I might plant a kick in his minute buttocks. We sat down and faced each other across the desk. He was a very small man, not more than five feet three and would hardly weigh as much as a butcher's thumb. He had tight brilliant eyes that wanted to look hard, and looked as hard as oysters on the half-shell. He wore a double-breasted dark grey suit that was too wide in the shoulders and had too much lapel. Over this, open, an Irish tweed coat with some badly worn spots. A lot of foulard tie bulged out and was rain-spotted above his crossed lapels.

'Maybe you know me,' he said. 'I'm Harry Jones.'

I said I didn't know him. I pushed a flat tin of cigarettes at him. His small neat fingers speared one like a trout taking the fly. He lit it with the desk lighter and waved his hand.

'I been around,' he said. 'Know the boys and such. Used to do a little liquor-running down from Hueneme Point. A tough racket, brother. Riding the scout car with a gun in your lap and a wad on your hip that would choke a coal chute. Plenty of times we paid off four sets of law before we hit Beverly Hills. A tough racket.'

'Terrible,' I said.

He leaned back and blew smoke at the ceiling from the small tight corner of his small tight mouth.

'Maybe you don't believe me,' he said.

'Maybe I don't,' I said. 'And maybe I do. And then again maybe I haven't bothered to make my mind up. Just what is the build-up supposed to do to me?'

'Nothing,' he said tartly.

'You've been following me around for a couple of days,' I said. 'Like a fellow trying to pick up a girl and lacking the last inch of nerve. Maybe you're selling insurance. Maybe you knew a fellow called Joe Brody. That's a lot of maybes, but I have a lot on hand in my business.'

His eyes bulged and his lower lip almost fell in his lap. 'Christ, how'd you know that?' he said.

'I'm psychic. Shake your business up and pour it. I haven't got all day.'

The brightness of his eyes almost disappeared between the suddenly narrowed lids. There was silence. The rain pounded down on the flat tarred roof over the Mansion House lobby below my windows. His eyes opened a little, shined again, and his voice was full of thought.

'I was trying to get a line of you, sure,' he said. 'I've got something to sell—cheap, for a couple of C notes. How'd you tie me to Joe?'

I opened a letter and read it. It offered me a six months' correspondence course in fingerprinting at a special professional discount. I dropped it into the waste basket and looked at the little man again. 'Don't mind me. I was just guessing. You're not a cop. You don't belong to Eddie Mars's outfit. I asked him last night. I couldn't think of anybody else but Joe Brody's friends who would be that much interested in me.'

'Jesus,' he said and licked his lower lip. His face had turned white as paper when I mentioned Eddie Mars. His mouth drooped open and his cigarette hung to the corner of it by some magic, as if it had grown there. 'Aw, you're kidding me,' he said at last, with the sort of smile the operating-room sees.

'All right. I'm kidding you.' I opened another letter. This one wanted to send me a daily news-letter from Washington, all inside stuff, straight from the cook-house. 'I suppose Agnes is loose,' I added.

'Yeah. She sent me. You interested?'

'Well—she's a blonde.'

'Nuts. You made a crack when you were up there that night—the night Joe got squibbed off. Something about Brody must have known something good about the Sternwoods or he wouldn't have taken the chance on that picture he sent them.'

'Uh-huh. So he had? What was it?'

'That's what the two hundred bucks pays for.'

I dropped some more fan mail into the basket and lit myself a fresh cigarette.

'We gotta get out of town,' he said. 'Agnes is a nice girl. You can't hold that stuff on her. It's not so easy for a dame to get by these days.'

'She's too big for you,' I said. 'She'll roll on you and smother you.'

'That's kind of a dirty crack, brother,' he said with something that was near enough to dignity to make me stare at him.

I said: 'You're right. I've been meeting the wrong kind of people lately. Let's cut out the gabble and get down to cases. What have you got for the money?'

'Would you pay it?'

'If it does what?'

'If it helps you find Rusty Regan.'

'I'm not looking for Rusty Regan.'

'Says you. Want to hear it or not?'

'Go ahead and chirp. I'll pay for anything I use. Two C notes buys a lot of information in my circle.'

'Eddie Mars had Regan bumped off,' he said calmly, and leaned back as if he had just been made a vice-president.

I waved a hand in the direction of the door. 'I wouldn't even argue with you,' I said. 'I wouldn't waste the oxygen. On your way, small size.'

He leaned across the desk, white lines at the corners of his mouth. He snubbed his cigarette out carefully, over and over again, without looking at it. From behind a communicating door came the sound of a typewriter clacking monotonously to the bell, to the shift, line after line.

'I'm not kidding,' he said.

'Beat it. Don't bother me. I have work to do.'

'No you don't,' he said sharply. 'I ain't that easy. I came here to speak my piece and I'm speaking it. I knew Rusty myself. Not well, well enough to say "How's a boy?" and he'd answer me or he wouldn't, according to how he felt. A nice guy though. I always liked him. He was sweet on a singer named Mona Grant. Then she changed her name to Mars. Rusty got sore and married a rich dame that hung around the joints like she couldn't sleep well at home. You know all about her, tall, dark, enough looks for a Derby winner, but the type would put a lot of pressure on a guy. High-strung. Rusty wouldn't get along with her. But Jesus, he'd get along with her old man's dough, wouldn't he? That's what you think. This Regan was a cockeyed sort of buzzard. He had long-range eyes. He was looking over into the next valley all the time. He wasn't scarcely around where he was. I don't think he gave a damn about dough. And coming from me, brother, that's a compliment.'

The little man wasn't so dumb after all. A three for a quarter grifter wouldn't even think such thoughts, much less know how to express them.

I said: 'So he ran away.'

'He started to run away, maybe. With this girl Mona. She wasn't living with Eddie Mars, didn't like his rackets. Especially the side lines, like blackmail, bent cars, hideouts for hot boys from the east, and so on. The talk was Regan told Eddie one night, right out in the open, that if he ever messed Mona up in any criminal rap, he'd be around to see him.'

'Most of this is on the record, Harry,' I said. 'You can't expect money for that.'

'I'm coming to what isn't. So Regan blew. I used to see him every afternoon in Vardi's drinking Irish whisky and staring at the wall. He don't talk much any more. He'd give me a bet now and then, which was what I was there for, to pick up bets for Puss Walgreen.'

'I thought he was in the insurance business.'

'That's what it says on the door. I guess he'd sell you insurance at that, if you tramped on him. Well, about the middle of September I don't see Regan any more. I don't notice it right away. You know how it is. A guy's there and you see him and then he ain't there and you don't see him until something makes you think of it. What makes me think about it is I hear a guy say laughing that Eddie Mars's woman lammed out with Rusty Regan and Mars is acting like he was best man, instead of being sore. So I tell Joe Brody and Joe was smart.'

'Like hell he was,' I said.

'Not copper smart, but still smart. He's out for the dough. He gets to figuring could he get a line somehow on the two lovebirds he could maybe collect twice—once from Eddie Mars and once from Regan's wife. Joe knew the family a little.'

'Five grand worth,' I said. 'He nicked them for that a while back.'

'Yeah?' Harry Jones looked mildly surprised. 'Agnes ought to have told me that. There's a frail for you. Always holding out. Well, Joe and me watch the papers and we don't see anything, so we know old Sternwood has a blanket on it. Then one day I see Lash Canino in Vardi's. Know him?'

I shook my head.

'There's a boy that is tough like some guys think they are tough. He does a job for Eddie Mars when Mars needs him—trouble-shooting. He'd bump a guy off between drinks. When Mars don't need him he don't go near him. And he don't stay in LA. Well it might be something and it might not. Maybe they got a line on Regan and Mars has just been sitting back with a smile on his puss, waiting for the chance. Then again it might be something else entirely. Anyway I tell Joe and Joe gets on Canino's tail. He can tail. Me, I'm no good at it. I'm giving that one away. No charge. And Joe tails Canino out to the Sternwood place and Canino parks outside the estate and a car comes up beside him with a girl in it. They talk for a while and Joe thinks the girl passes something over, like maybe dough. The girl beats it. It's Regan's wife. Okey, she knows Canino and Canino knows Mars. So Joe figures Canino knows something about Regan and is trying to squeeze a little on the side for himself. Canino blows and Joe loses him. End of Act One.'

'What does this Canino look like?'

'Short, heavy set, brown hair, brown eyes, and always wears brown clothes and a brown hat. Even wears a brown suéde raincoat. Drives a brown coupé. Everything brown for Mr Canino.'

'Lets have Act Two,' I said.

'Without some dough that's all.'

'I don't see two hundred bucks in it. Mrs Regan married an ex-bootlegger out of the joints. She'd know other people of his sort. She knows Eddie Mars well. If she thought anything had happened to Regan, Eddie would be the very man she'd go to, and Canino might be the man Eddie would pick to handle the assignment. Is that all you have?'

'Would you give the two hundred to know where Eddie's wife is?' the little man asked calmly.

He had all my attention now. I almost cracked the arms of my chair leaning on them.

'Even if she was alone?' Harry Jones added in a soft, rather sinister tone. 'Even if she never run away with Regan at all, and was being kept now about forty miles from LA in a hideout—so the law would keep on thinking she had dusted with him? Would you pay two hundred bucks for that, shamus?'

I licked my lips. They tasted dry and salty. 'I think I would,' I said. 'Where?'

'Agnes found her,' he said grimly. 'Just by a lucky break. Saw her out riding and managed to tail her home. Agnes will tell you where that is—when she's holding the money in her hand.'

I made a hard face at him. 'You could tell the coppers for nothing, Harry. They have some good wreckers, down at Central these days. If they killed you trying, they still have Agnes.'

'Let 'em try,' he said. 'I ain't so brittle.'

'Agnes must have something I didn't notice.'

'She's a grifter, shamus. I'm a grifter. We're all grifters. So we sell each other out for a nickel. Okey. See can you make me.' He reached for another of my cigarettes, placed it neatly between his lips and lit it with a match the way I do myself, missing twice on his thumb-nail and then using his foot. He puffed evenly and stared at me level-eyed, a funny little hard guy I could have thrown from home plate to second base. A small man in a big man's world. There was something I liked about him.

'I haven't pulled anything in here,' he said steadily. 'I came in talking two C's. That's still the price. I come because I thought I'd get a take it or leave it, one right gee to another. Now you're waving cops at me. You oughta be ashamed of yourself.'

I said: 'You'll get the two hundred—for that information. I have to get the money myself first.'

He stood up and nodded and pulled his worn little Irish tweed coat tight around his chest. 'That's okey. After dark is better anyway. It's a leery job—buckin' guys like Eddie Mars. But a guy has to eat. The book's been pretty dull lately. I think the big boys have told Puss Walgreen to move on. Suppose you come over there to the office, Fulwider Building, Western and Santa Monica, four-twenty-eight at the back. You bring the money, I'll take you to Agnes.'

'Can't you tell me yourself? I've seen Agnes.'

'I promised her,' he said simply. He buttoned his overcoat, cocked his hat jauntily, nodded again and strolled to the door. He went out. His steps died along the hall.

I went down to the bank and deposited my five-hundred-dollar cheque and drew out two hundred in currency. I went upstairs again and sat in my chair thinking about Harry Jones and his story. It seemed a little too pat. It had the austere simplicity of fiction rather than the tangled woof of fact. Captain Gregory ought to have been able to find Mona Mars, if she was that close to his beat. Supposing, that is, he had tried.

I thought about it most of the day. Nobody came into the office. Nobody called me on the phone. It kept on raining.

26

At seven the rain had stopped for a breathing spell, but the gutters were still flooded. On Santa Monica the water was level with the pavement and a thin film of it washed over the top of the kerbing. A traffic cop in shining black rubber from boots to cap sloshed through the flood on his way from the shelter of a sodden awning. My rubber heels slithered on the pavement as I turned into the narrow lobby of the Fulwider Building. A single drop light burned far back, beyond an open, once-gilt elevator. There was a tarnished and well-missed spittoon on a gnawed rubber mat. A case of false teeth hung on the mustard-coloured wall like a fuse box in a screen porch. I shook the rain off my hat and looked at the building directory beside the case of teeth. Numbers with names and numbers without names. Plenty of vacancies or plenty of tenants who wished to remain anonymous. Painless dentists, shyster detective agencies, small sick businesses that had crawled there to die, mail order schools that would teach you how to become a railway clerk or a radio technician or a screen writer—if the postal inspectors didn't catch up with them first. A nasty building. A building in which the smell of stale cigar butts would be the cleanest odour.

An old man dozed in the elevator, on a ramshackle stool, with a burst-out cushion under him. His mouth was open, his veined temples glistened in the weak light. He wore a blue uniform coat that fitted him the way a stall fits a horse. Under that grey trousers with frayed cuffs, white cotton socks and black kid shoes, one of which was slit across a bunion. On the stool he slept miserably, waiting for a customer. I went past him softly, the clandestine air of the building prompting me, found the fire door and pulled it open. The fire stairs hadn't been swept in a month. Bums had slept on them, eaten on them, left crusts and fragments of greasy newspaper, matches, a gutted imitation-leather pocket-book. In a shadowy angle against the scribbled wall a pouched ring of pale rubber had fallen and had not been disturbed. A very nice building.

I came out at the fourth floor sniffing for air. The hallway had the same dirty spittoon and frayed mat, the same mustard walls, the same memories of low tide. I went down the line and turned a corner. The name: 'L.D. Walgreen—Insurance', showed on a dark pebbled glass door, on a second dark door, on a third behind which there was a light. One of the dark doors said: 'Entrance.'

A glass transom was open above the lighted door. Through it the sharp birdlike voice of Harry Jones spoke, saying:

'Canino? . . . Yeah, I've seen you around somewhere. Sure.'

I froze. The other voice spoke. It had a heavy purr, like a small dynamo behind a brick wall. It said: 'I thought you would.' There was a vaguely sinister note in that voice.

A chair scraped on linoleum, steps sounded, the transom above me squeaked shut. A shadow melted from behind the pebbled glass.

I went back to the first of the three doors marked with the name Walgreen. I tried it cautiously. It was locked. It moved in a loose frame, an old door fitted many years past, made of half-seasoned wood and shrunken now. I reached my wallet out and slipped the thick hard window of celluloid from over my driver's licence. A burglar's tool the law had forgotten to proscribe. I put my gloves on, leaned softly and lovingly against the door and pushed the knob hard away from the frame. I pushed the celluloid plate into the wide crack and felt for the slope of the spring lock. There was a dry click, like a small icicle breaking. I hung there motionless, like a lazy fish in the water. Nothing happened inside. I turned the knob and pushed the door back into darkness. I shut it behind me as carefully as I had opened it.

The lighted oblong of an uncurtained window faced me, cut by the angle of a desk. On the desk a hooded typewriter took form, then the metal knob of a communicating door. This was unlocked. I passed into the second of the three offices. Rain rattled suddenly against the closed window. Under its noise I crossed the room. A tight fan of light spread from an inch opening of the door into the lighted office. Everything very convenient. I walked like a cat on a mantel and reached the hinged side of the door, put an eye to the crack and saw nothing but light against the angle of the wood.

The purring voice was now saying quite pleasantly: 'Sure, a guy could sit on his fanny and crab what another guy done if he knows what it's all about. So you go to see this peeper. Well, that was your mistake. Eddie don't like it. The peeper told Eddie some guy in a grey Plymouth was tailing him. Eddie naturally wants to know who and why, see.'

Harry Jones laughed lightly. 'What makes it his business?'

'That don't get you no place.'

'You know why I went to the peeper. I already told you. Account of Joe Brody's girl. She has to blow and she's shatting on her uppers. She figures the peeper can get her some dough. I don't have any.'

The purring voice said gently: 'Dough for what? Peepers don't give that stuff out to punks.'

'He could raise it. He knows rich people.' Harry Jones laughed, a brave little laugh.

'Don't fuss with me, little man.' The purring voice had an edge, like sand in the bearings.

'Okey, okey. You know the dope on Brody's bump-off. That screwy kid done it all right, but the night it happened this Marlowe was right there in the room.'

'That's known, little man. He told it to the law.'

'Yeah—here's what isn't. Brody was trying to peddle a nudist photo of the young Sternwood girl. Marlowe got wise to him. While they were arguing about it the young Sternwood girl dropped around herself—with a gat. She took a shot at Brody. She lets one fly and breaks a window. Only the peeper didn't tell the coppers about that. And Agnes didn't neither. She figures it's railway fare for her not to.'

'This ain't got anything to do with Eddie?'

'Show me how.'

'Where's this Agnes at?'

'Nothing doing.'

'You'll tell me, little man. Here, or in the back room where the boys pitch dimes against the wall.'

'She's my girl now, Canino. I don't put my girl in the middle for anybody.'

A silence followed. I listened to the rain lashing the windows. The smell of cigarette smoke came through the crack of the door. I wanted to cough. I bit hard on a handkerchief.

The purring voice said, still gentle: 'From what I hear this blonde broad was just a shill for Geiger. I'll talk it over with Eddie. How much you tap the peeper for?'

'Two centuries.'

'Get it?'

Harry Jones laughed again. 'I'm seeing him to-morrow. I have hopes.'

'Where's Agnes?'

'Listen—'

'Where's Agnes?'

Silence.

'Look at it, little man.'

I didn't move. I wasn't wearing a gun. I didn't have to see through the crack of the door to know that a gun was what the purring voice was inviting Harry Jones to look at. But I didn't think Mr Canino would do anything with his gun beyond showing it. I waited.

'I'm looking at it,' Harry Jones said, his voice squeezed tight as if it could hardly get past his teeth. 'And I don't see anything I didn't see before. Go ahead and blast and see what it gets you.'

'A Chicago overcoat is what it would get *you*, little man.'

Silence.

'Where's Agnes?'

Harry Jones sighed. 'Okey,' he said wearily. 'She's in an apartment house at 28 Court Street, up on Bunker Hill. Apartment 301. I guess I'm yellow all right. Why should I front for that twist?'

'No reason. You got good sense. You and me'll go out and talk to her. All I want is to find out is she dummying up on you, kid. If it's the way you say it is, everything is jakeloo. You can put the bite on the peeper and be on your way. No hard feelings?'

'No,' Harry Jones said. 'No hard feelings, Canino.'

'Fine. Let's dip the bill. Got a glass?' The purring voice was now as false as an usherette's eyelashes and as slippery as a watermelon seed. A drawer was pulled open. Something jarred on wood. A chair squeaked. A scuffing sound on the floor. 'This is bond stuff,' the purring voice said.

There was a gurgling sound. 'Moths in your ermine, as the ladies say.'

Harry Jones said softly: 'Success.'

I heard a short sharp cough. Then a violent retching. There was a small thud on the floor, as if a thick glass had fallen. My fingers curled against my raincoat.

The purring voice said gently: 'You ain't sick from just one drink, are you, pal?'

Harry Jones didn't answer. There was laboured breathing for a short moment. Then thick silence folded down. Then a chair scraped.

'So long, little man,' said Mr Canino.

Steps, a click, the wedge of light died at my feet, a door opened and closed quietly. The steps faded, leisurely and assured.

I stirred around the edge of the door and pulled it wide and looked into blackness relieved by the dim shine of a window. The corner of a desk glittered faintly. A hunched shape took form in a chair behind it. In the close air there was a heavy clogged smell, almost a perfume. I went across to the corridor and listened. I heard the distant clang of the elevator.

I found the light switch and light glowed in a dusty glass bowl hanging from the ceiling by three brass chains. Harry Jones looked at me across the desk, his eyes wide open, his face frozen in a tight spasm, the skin bluish. His small dark head was tilted to one side. He sat upright against the back of the chair.

A tramcar bell clanged at an almost infinite distance and the sound came buffeted by innumerable walls. A brown half-pint of whisky stood on the desk with the cap off. Harry Jones's glass glinted against a castor of the desk. The second glass was gone.

I breathed shallowly, from the top of my lungs, and bent above the bottle.

Behind the charred smell of the bourbon another odour lurked, faintly, the odour of bitter almonds. Harry Jones dying had vomited on his coat. That made it cyanide.

I walked around him carefully and lifted a phone book from a hook on the wooden frame of the window. I let it fall again, reached the telephone as far as it would go from the little dead man. I dialled information. The voice answered.

'Can you give me the phone number of Apartment 301, 28 Court Street?'

'One moment, please.' The voice came to me borne on the smell of bitter almonds. A silence. 'The number is Wentworth 2528. It is listed under Glendower Apartments.'

I thanked the voice and dialled the number. The bell rang three times, then the line opened. A radio blared along the wire and was muted. A burly male voice said: 'Hello.'

'Is Agnes there?'

'No Agnes here, buddy. What number you want?'

'Wentworth two-five-two-eight.'

'Right number, wrong gal. Ain't that a shame?' The voice cackled.

I hung up and reached for the phone book again and looked up the Wentworth Apartments. I dialled the manager's number. I had a blurred vision of Mr Canino driving fast through rain to another appointment with death.

'Glendower Apartments. Mr Schiff speaking.'

'This is Wallis, Police Identification Bureau. Is there a girl named Agnes Lozelle registered in your place?'

'Who did you say you were?'

I told him again.

'If you'll give me your number I'll—'

'Cut the comedy,' I said sharply, 'I'm in a hurry. Is there or isn't there?'

'No. There isn't.' The voice was as stiff as a breadstick.

'Is there a tall blonde with green eyes registered in the flop?'

'Say, this isn't any flop—'

'Oh, can it, *can it!*' I rapped at him in a police voice. 'You want me to send the vice squad over there and shake the joint down? I know all about Bunker Hill apartment houses, mister. Especially the ones that have phone numbers listed for each apartment.'

'Hey, take it easy, officer. I'll co-operate. There's a couple of blondes here, sure. Where isn't there? I hadn't noticed their eyes much. Would yours be alone?'

'Alone, or with a little chap about five feet three, a hundred and ten, sharp black eyes, wears double-breasted dark grey suit and Irish tweed overcoat, grey hat. My information is Apartment 301, but all I get there is the big razzoo.'

'Oh, she ain't there. There's a couple of car salesmen living in three-o-one.'

'Thanks, I'll drop around.'

'Make it quiet, won't you? Come to my place, direct?'

'Much obliged, Mr Schiff.' I hung up.

I wiped sweat off my face. I walked to the far corner of the office and stood with my face to the wall, patted it with a hand. I turned around slowly and looked across at little Harry Jones grimacing in his chair.

'Well, you fooled him, Harry,' I said out loud, in a voice that sounded queer to me. 'You lied to him and you drank your cyanide like a little gentleman. You died like a poisoned rat, Harry, but you're no rat to me.'

I had to search him. It was a nasty job. His pockets yielded nothing about Agnes, nothing that I wanted at all. I didn't think they would, but I had to be sure. Mr Canino might be back. Mr Canino would be the kind of self-confident gentleman who would not mind returning to the scene of his crime.

I put the light out and started to open the door. The phone bell rang jarringly down on the baseboard. I listened to it, my jaw muscles drawn into a knot, aching. Then I shut the door and put the light on again and went across to it.

'Yeah?'

A woman's voice. Her voice. 'Is Harry around?'

'Not for a minute, Agnes.'

She waited a while on that. Then she said slowly: 'Who's talking?'

'Marlowe, the guy that's trouble to you.'

'Where is he?' sharply.

'I came over to give him two hundred bucks in return for certain information. The offer holds. I have the money. Where are you?'

'Didn't he tell you?'

'No.'

'Perhaps you'd better ask him. Where is he?'

'I can't ask him. Do you know a man named Canino?'

Her gasp came as clearly as though she had been beside me.

'Do you want the two C's or not?' I asked.

'I-I want it pretty bad, mister.'

'All right then. Tell me where to bring it.'

'I-I—' Her voice trailed off and came back with a panic rush. 'Where's Harry?'

'Got scared and blew. Meet me somewhere—anywhere at all—I have the money.'

'I don't believe you—about Harry. It's a trap.'

'Oh stuff. I could have had Harry hauled in long ago. There isn't anything to make a trap for. Canino got a line on Harry somehow and he blew. I want quiet, you want quiet, Harry wants quiet.' Harry already had it. Nobody could take it away from him. 'You don't think I'd stooge for Eddie Mars, do you, angel?'

'No-o, I guess not. Not that. I'll meet you in half an hour. Beside Bullocks Wilshire, the east entrance to the parking lot.'

'Right,' I said.

I dropped the phone in its cradle. The wave of almond odour flooded me again, and the sour smell of vomit. The little dead man sat silent in his chair, beyond fear, beyond change.

I left the office. Nothing moved in the dingy corridor. No pebbled glass door had light behind it. I went down the fire stairs to the second floor and from there looked down at the lighted roof of the elevator cage. I pressed the button. Slowly the car lurched into motion. I ran down the stairs again. The car was above me when I walked out of the building.

It was raining hard again. I walked into it with the heavy drops slapping my face. When one of them touched my tongue I knew that my mouth was

open and the ache at the side of my jaws told me it was open wide and
strained back, mimicking the rictus of death carved upon the face of Harry
Jones.

27

'Give me the money.'

The motor of the grey Plymouth throbbed under her voice and the rain
pounded above it. The violet light at the top of Bullocks green-tinged tower
was far above us, serene and withdrawn from the dark, dripping city. Her
black-gloved hand reached out and I put the bills in it. She bent over to
count them under the dim light of the dash. A bag clicked open, clicked
shut. She let a spent breath die on her lips. She leaned towards me.

'I'm leaving, copper. I'm on my way. This is a get-away stake and God
how I need it. What happened to Harry?'

'I told you he ran away. Canino got wise to him somehow. Forget Harry.
I've paid and I want my information.'

'You'll get it. Joe and I were out riding Foothill Boulevard Sunday before
last. It was late and the lights coming up and the usual mess of cars. We
passed a brown coupé and I saw the girl who was driving it. There was a
man beside her, a dark short man. The girl was a blonde. I'd seen her
before. She was Eddie Mars's wife. The guy was Canino. You wouldn't
forget either of them, if you ever saw them. Joe tailed the coupé from in
front. He was good at that. Canino, the watch-dog, was taking her out for
air. A mile or so east of Realito a road turns towards the foothills. That's
orange country to the south but to the north it's as bare as hell's back yard
and smack up against the hills there's a cyanide plant where they make the
stuff for fumigation. Just off the highway there's a small garage and paint-
shop run by a gee named Art Huck. Hot car drop, likely. There's a frame
house beyond this, and beyond the house nothing but the foothills and the
bare stone outcrop and the cyanide plant a couple of miles on. That's the
place where she's holed up. They turned off on this road and Joe swung
around and went back and we saw the car turn off the road where the frame
house was. We sat there half an hour looking through the cars going by.
Nobody came back out. When it was quite dark Joe sneaked up there and
took a look. He said there were lights in the house and a radio was going and
just the one car out in front, the coupé. So we beat it.'

She stopped talking and I listened to the swish of tyres on Wilshire. I
said: 'They might have shifted quarters since then but if that's what you
have to sell—that's what you have to sell. Sure you knew her?'

'If you ever see her, you won't make a mistake the second time. Good-
bye, copper, and wish me luck. I got a raw deal.'

'Like hell you did,' I said, and walked away across the street to my own
car.

The grey Plymouth moved forward, gathered speed, and darted around
the corner on to Sunset Place. The sound of its motor died, and with it
blonde Agnes wiped herself off the slate for good, so far as I was concerned.

Three men dead, Geiger, Brody, and Harry Jones, and the woman went riding off in the rain with my two hundred in her bag and not a mark on her. I kicked my starter and drove on down-town to eat. I ate a good dinner. Forty miles in the rain is a hike, and I hoped to make it a round trip.

I drove north across the river, on into Pasadena, through Pasadena and almost at once I was in orange groves. The tumbling rain was solid white spray in the headlights. The windshield wiper could hardly keep the glass clear enough to see through. But not even the drenched darkness could hide the flawless lines of the orange trees wheeling away like endless spokes into the night.

Cars passed with a tearing hiss and a wave of dirty spray. The highway jerked through a little town that was all packing houses and sheds, and railway sidings nuzzling them. The groves thinned out and dropped away to the south and the road climbed and it was cold and to the north the black foothills crouched closer and sent a bitter wind whipping down their flanks. Then faintly out of the dark two yellow vapour lights glowed high up in the air and a neon sign between them said: 'Welcome to Realito.'

Frame houses were spaced far back from a wide main street, then a sudden knot of stores, the lights of a drugstore behind fogged glass, the fly-cluster of cars in front of a movie theatre, a dark bank on a corner with a clock sticking out over the pavement and a group of people standing in the rain looking at its windows, as if they were some kind of a show. I went on. Empty fields closed in again.

Fate stage-managed the whole thing. Beyond Realito, just about a mile beyond, the highway took a curve and the rain fooled me and I went too close to the shoulder. My right front tyre let go with an angry hiss. Before I could stop the right rear went with it. I jammed the car to a stop, half on the pavement, half on the shoulder, got out and flashed a spotlight around. I had two flats and one spare. The flat butt of a heavy galvanized tack stared at me from the front tyre. The edge of the pavement was littered with them. They had been swept off, but not far enough off.

I snapped the flash off and stood there breathing rain and looking up a side road at a yellow light. It seemed to come from a skylight. The skylight could belong to a garage, the garage could be run by a man named Art Huck, and there could be a frame house next door to it. I tucked my chin down in my collar and started towards it, then went back to unstrap the licence-holder from the steering post and put it in my pocket. I leaned lower under the wheel. Behind a weighted flap, directly under my right leg as I sat in the car, there was a hidden compartment. There were two guns in it. One belonged to Eddie Mars's boy Lanny and one belonged to me. I took Lanny's. It would have had more practice than mine. I stuck it nose down in an inside pocket and started up the side road.

The garage was a hundred yards from the highway. It showed the highway a blank side wall. I played the flash on it quickly. 'Art Huck–Motor Repairs and Painting.' I chuckled, then Harry Jones's face rose up in front of me, and I stopped chuckling. The garage doors were shut, but there was an edge of light under them and a thread of light where the halves met. I went on past. The frame house was there, light in two front windows, shades down. It was set well back from the road, behind a thin clump of trees. A car stood on the gravel drive in front. It was dark, indistinct, but it would be a brown coupé and it would belong to Mr

Canino. It squatted there peacefully in front of the narrow wooden porch.

He would let her take it out for a spin once in a while, and sit beside her, probably with a gun handy. The girl Rusty Regan ought to have married, that Eddie Mars couldn't keep, the girl that hadn't run away with Regan. Nice Mr Canino.

I trudged back to the garage and banged on the wooden door with the butt of my flash. There was a hung instant of silence, as heavy as thunder. The light inside went out. I stood there grinning and licking the rain off my lip. I clicked the spot on the middle of the doors. I grinned at the circle of white. I was where I wanted to be.

A voice spoke through the door, a surly voice: 'What you want?'

'Open up. I've got two flats back on the highway and only one spare. I need help.'

'Sorry, mister. We're closed up. Realito's a mile west. Better try there.'

I didn't like that. I kicked the door hard. I kept on kicking it. Another voice made itself heard, a purring voice, like a small dynamo behind a wall. I liked this voice. It said: 'A wise guy, huh? Open up, Art.'

A bolt squealed and half of the door bent inward. My flash burned briefly on a gaunt face. Then something that glittered swept down and knocked the flash out of my hand. A gun had peaked at me. I dropped low where the flash burned on the wet ground and picked it up.

The surly voice said: 'Kill that spot, bo. Folks get hurt that way.'

I snapped the flash off and straightened. Light went on inside the garage, outlined a tall man in overalls. He backed away from the open door and kept a gun levelled at me.

'Step inside and shut the door, stranger. We'll see what we can do.'

I stepped inside, and shut the door behind my back. I looked at the gaunt man, but not at the other man who was shadowy over by a workbench, silent. The breath of the garage was sweet and sinister with the smell of hot pyroxylin paint.

'Ain't you got no sense?' the gaunt man chided me. 'A bank job was pulled at Realito this noon.'

'Pardon,' I said, remembering the people staring at the bank in the rain. 'I didn't pull it. I'm a stranger here.'

'Well, there was,' he said morosely. 'Some say it was a couple of punk kids and they got 'em cornered back here in the hills.'

'It's a nice night for hiding,' I said. 'I suppose they threw tacks out. I got some of them. I thought you just needed the business.'

'You didn't ever get socked in the kisser, did you?' the gaunt man asked me briefly.

'Not by anybody your weight.'

The purring voice from over in the shadows said: 'Cut out the heavy menace, Art. This guy's in a jam. You run a garage, don't you?'

'Thanks,' I said, and didn't look at him even then.

'Okey, okey,' the man in the overalls grumbled. He tucked his gun through a flap in his clothes and bit a knuckle, staring at me moodily over it. The smell of the pyroxylin paint was as sickening as ether. Over in the corner, under a drop light, there was a big new-looking sedan with a paint gun lying on its fender.

I looked at the man by the workbench now. He was short and thick-bodied with strong shoulders. He had a cool face and cool dark eyes. He wore a belted brown suéde raincoat that was heavily spotted with rain. His brown hat was tilted rakishly. He leaned his back against the workbench and looked me over without haste, without interest, as if he was looking at a slab of cold meat. Perhaps he thought of people that way.

He moved his dark eyes up and down slowly and then glanced at his finger-nails one by one, holding them up against the light and studying them with care, as Hollywood has taught it should be done. He spoke around a cigarette.

'Got two flats, huh? That's tough. They swept them tacks, I thought.'

'I skidded a little on the curve.'

'Stranger in town you said?'

'Travelling through. On the way to LA. How far is it?'

'Forty miles. Seems longer this weather. Where from, stranger?'

'Santa Rosa.'

'Come the long way, eh? Tahoe and Lone Pine?'

'Not Tahoe. Reno and Carson City.'

'Still the long way.' A fleeting smile curved his lips.

'Any law against it?' I asked him.

'Huh? No, sure not. Guess you think we're nosy. Just on account of that heist back there. Take a jack and get his flats, Art.'

'I'm busy,' the gaunt man growled. 'I've got work to do. I got this spray job. And it's raining, you might have noticed.'

The man in brown said pleasantly: 'Too damp for a good spray job, Art. Get moving.'

I said: 'They're front and rear, on the right side. You could use the spare for one spot, if you're busy.'

'Take two jacks, Art,' the brown man said.

'Now, listen—' Art began to bluster.

The brown man moved his eyes, looked at Art with a soft quiet-eyed stare, lowered them again almost shyly. He didn't speak. Art rocked as if a gust of wind had hit him. He stamped over to the corner and put a rubber coat over his overalls, a sou'wester on his head. He grabbed a socket wrench and a hand jack and wheeled a dolly jack over to the doors.

He went out silently, leaving the door yawning. The rain blustered in. The man in brown strolled over and shut it and strolled back to the workbench and put his hips exactly where they had been before. I could have taken him then. We were alone. He didn't know who I was. He looked at me lightly and threw his cigarette on the cement floor and stamped on it without looking down.

'I bet you could use a drink,' he said. 'Wet the inside and even up.' He reached a bottle from the workbench behind him and set it on the edge and set two glasses beside it. He poured a stiff jolt into each and held one out.

Walking like a dummy I went over and took it. The memory of the rain was still cold on my face. The smell of hot paint drugged the close air of the garage.

'That Art,' the brown man said. 'He's like all mechanics. Always got his face in a job he ought to have done last week. Business trip?'

I sniffed my drink delicately. It had the right smell. I watched him drink some of his before I swallowed mine. I rolled it around on my tongue. There was no cyanide in it. I emptied the little glass and put it down beside him and moved away.

'Partly,' I said. I walked over to the half-painted sedan with the big metal paint gun lying along its fender. The rain hit the flat roof hard. Art was out in it, cursing.

The brown man looked at the big car. 'Just a panel job, to start with,' he said casually, his purring voice still softer from the drink. 'But the guy had dough and his driver needed a few bucks. You know the racket.'

I said: 'There's only one that's older.' My lips felt dry. I didn't want to talk. I lit a cigarette. I wanted my tyres fixed. The minutes passed on tiptoe. The brown man and I were two strangers chance-met, looking at each other across a little dead man named Harry Jones. Only the brown man didn't know that yet.

Feet crunched outside and the door was pushed open. The light hit pencils of rain and made silver wires of them. Art trundled two muddy flats in sullenly, kicked the door shut, let one of the flats fall over on its side. He looked at me savagely.

'You sure pick spots for a jack to stand on,' he snarled.

The brown man laughed and took a rolled cylinder of nickels out of his pocket and tossed it up and down on the palm of his hand.

'Don't crab so much,' he said dryly. 'Fix those flats.'

'I'm fixin' them, ain't I?'

'Well, don't make a song about it.'

'Yah!' Art peeled his rubber coat and sou-wester off and threw them away from him. He heaved one tyre up on a spreader and tore the rim loose viciously. He had the tube out and cold-patched in nothing flat. Still scowling, he strode over to the wall beside me and grabbed an air hose, put enough air into the tube to give it body and let the nozzle of the air hose smack against the whitewashed wall.

I stood watching the roll of wrapped coins dance in Canino's hand. The moment of crouched intensity had left me. I turned my head and watched the gaunt mechanic beside me toss the air-stiffened tube up and catch it with his hands wide, one on each side of the tube. He looked it over sourly, glanced at a big galvanized tub of dirty water in the corner and grunted.

The teamwork must have been very nice. I saw no signal, no glance of meaning, no gesture that might have a special import. The gaunt man had the stiffened tube high in the air, staring at it. He half turned his body, took one long quick step, and slammed it down over my head and shoulders, a perfect ringer.

He jumped behind me and leaned hard on the rubber. His weight dragged on my chest, pinned my upper arms tight to my sides. I could move my hands, but I couldn't reach the gun in my pocket.

The brown man came almost dancing towards me across the floor. His hand tightened over the roll of nickels. He came up to me without sound, without expression. I bent forward and tried to heave Art off his feet.

The fist with the weighted tube inside it went through my spread hands like a stone through a cloud of dust. I had the stunned moment of shock when the lights danced and the visible world went out of focus but was still there. He hit me again. There was no sensation in my head. The bright glare got brighter. There was nothing but hard aching white light. Then there was darkness in which something red wriggled like a germ under a microscope. Then there was nothing bright or wriggling, just darkness and emptiness and a rushing wind and a falling as of great trees.

28

It seemed there was a woman and she was sitting near a lamp, which was where she belonged, in a good light. Another light shone hard on my face, so I closed my eyes again and tried to look at her through the lashes. She was so platinumed that her hair shone like a silver fruit bowl. She wore a green knitted dress with a broad white collar turned over it. There was a sharp-angled glossy bag at her feet. She was smoking and a glass of amber fluid was tall and pale at her elbow.

I moved my head a little, carefully. It hurt, but not more than I expected. I was trussed like a turkey ready for the oven. Handcuffs held my wrists behind me and a rope went from them to my ankles and then over the end of the brown davenport on which I was sprawled. The rope dropped out of sight over the davenport. I moved enough to make sure it was tied down.

I stopped these furtive movements and opened my eyes again and said: 'Hello.'

The woman withdrew her gaze from some distant mountain peak. Her small firm chin turned slowly. Her eyes were the blue of mountain lakes. Overhead the rain still pounded, with a remote sound, as if it was somebody else's rain.

'How do you feel?' It was a smooth silvery voice that matched her hair. It had a tiny tinkle in it, like bells in a doll's house. I thought that was silly as soon as I thought of it.

'Great,' I said. 'Somebody built a filling station on my jaw.'

'What did you expect, Mr Marlowe—orchids?'

'Just a plain pine box,' I said. 'Don't bother with bronze or silver handles. And don't scatter my ashes over the blue Pacific. I like the worms better. Did you know that worms are of both sexes and that any worm can love any other worm?'

'You're a little light-headed,' she said, with a grave stare.

'Would you mind moving this light?'

She got up and went behind the davenport. The light went off. The dimness was a benison.

'I don't think you're so dangerous,' she said. She was tall rather than short, but no bean-pole. She was slim, but not a dried crust. She went back to her chair.

'So you know my name.'

'You slept well. They had plenty of time to go through your pockets. They did everything but embalm you. So you're a detective.'

'Is that all they have on me?'

She was silent. Smoke floated dimly from the cigarette. She moved it in the air. Her hand was small and had shape, not the usual bony garden tool you see on women nowadays.

'What time is it?' I asked.

She looked sideways at her wrist, beyond the spiral of smoke, at the edge of the grave lustre of the lamplight. 'Ten-seventeen. You have a date?'

'I wouldn't be surprised. Is this the house next to Art Huck's garage?'

'Yes.'

'What are the boys doing–digging a grave?'

'They had to go somewhere.'

'You mean they left you here alone?'

Her head turned slowly again. She smiled. 'You don't look dangerous.'

'I thought they were keeping you a prisoner.'

It didn't seem to startle her. It even slightly amused her. 'What made you think that?'

'I know who you are.'

Her very blue eyes flashed so sharply that I could almost see the sweep of their glance, like the sweep of a sword. Her mouth tightened. But her voice didn't change.

'Then I'm afraid you're in a bad spot. And I hate killing.'

'And you Eddie Mars's wife? Shame on you.'

She didn't like that. She glared at me. I grinned. 'Unless you can unlock these bracelets, which I'd advise you not to do, you might spare me a little of that drink you're neglecting.'

She brought the glass over. Bubbles rose in it like false hopes. She bent over me. Her breath was as delicate as the eyes of a fawn. I gulped from the glass. She took it away from my mouth and watched some of the liquid run down my neck.

She bent over me again. Blood began to move around in me, like a prospective tenant looking over a house.

'Your face looks like a collision mat,' she said.

'Make the most of it. It won't last long even this good.'

She swung her head sharply and listened. For an instant her face was pale. The sounds were only the rain drifting against the walls. She went back across the room and stood with her side to me, bent forward a little, looking down at the floor.

'Why did you come here and stick your neck out?' she asked quietly. 'Eddie wasn't doing you any harm. You know perfectly well that if I hadn't hid out here, the police would have been certain Eddie murdered Rusty Regan.'

'He did,' I said.

She didn't move, didn't change position an inch. Her breath made a harsh quick sound. I looked around the room. Two doors, both in the same wall, one half open. A carpet of red and tan squares, blue curtains at the windows, a wallpaper with bright green pine trees on it. The furniture looked as if it had come from one of those places that advertise on bus benches. Gay, but full of resistance.

She said softly: 'Eddie didn't do anything to him. I haven't seen Rusty in months. Eddie's not that sort of man.'

'You left his bed and board. You were living alone. People at the place where you lived identified Regan's photo.'

'That's a lie,' she said coldly.

I tried to remember whether Captain Gregory had said that or not. My head was too fuzzy. I couldn't be sure.

'And it's none of your business,' she added.

'The whole thing is my business. I'm hired to find out.'

'Eddie's not that sort of man.'

'Oh, you like racketeers.'

'As long as people will gamble there will be places for them to gamble.'

'That's just protective thinking. Once outside the law you're all the way outside. You think he's just a gambler. I think he's a pornographer, a blackmailer, a hot car broker, a killer by remote control, and a suborner of crooked cops. He's whatever looks good to him, whatever has the cabbage pinned to it. Don't try to sell me on any high-souled racketeers. They don't come in that pattern.'

'He's not a killer.' She frowned.

'Not personally. He has Canino. Canino killed a man tonight, a harmless little guy who was trying to help somebody out. I almost saw him killed.'

She laughed wearily.

'All right,' I growled. 'Don't believe it. If Eddie is such a nice guy, I'd like to get to talk to him without Canino around. You know what Canino will do—beat my teeth out and then kick me in the stomach for mumbling.'

She put her head back and stood there thoughtful and withdrawn, thinking something out.

'I thought platinum hair was out of style,' I went on, just to keep sound alive in the room, just to keep from listening.

'It's a wig, silly. While mine grows out.' She reached up and yanked if off. Her own hair clipped short all over, like a boy's. She put the wig back on.

'Who did that to you?'

She looked surprised. 'I had it done. Why?'

'Yes. Why?'

'Why, to show Eddie I was willing to do what he wanted me to do—hide out. That he didn't need to have me guarded. I wouldn't let him down. I love him.'

'Good grief,' I groaned. 'And you have me right here in the room with you.'

She turned a hand over and stared at it. Then abruptly she walked out of the room. She came back with a kitchen knife. She bent and sawed at my rope.

'Canino has the key to the handcuffs,' she said. 'I can't do anything about those.'

She stepped back, breathing rapidly. She had cut the rope at every knot.

'You're a kick,' she said. 'Kidding with every breath—the spot you're in.'

'I thought Eddie wasn't a killer.'

She turned away quickly and went back to her chair by the lamp and sat down and put her face in her hands. I swung my feet to the floor and stood up. I tottered around, stiff-legged. The nerve on the left side of my face was jumping in all its branches. I took a step. I could still walk. I could run, if I had to.

'I guess you mean me to go,' I said.

She nodded without lifting her head.

'You'd better go with me—if you want to keep on living.'

'Don't waste time. He'll be back any minute.'

'Light a cigarette for me.'

I stood beside her, touching her knees. She came to her feet with a sudden lurch. Our eyes were only inches apart.

'Hello, Silver-Wig,' I said softly.

She stepped back, around the chair, and swept a package of cigarettes up off the table. She jabbed one loose and pushed it roughly into my mouth. Her hand was shaking. She snapped a small green leather lighter and held it to the cigarette. I drew in the smoke, staring into her lake-blue eyes. While she was still close to me I said:

'A little bird named Harry Jones led me to you. A little bird that used to hop in and out of cocktail bars picking up horse bets for crumbs. Picking up information too. This little bird picked up an idea about Canino. One way and another he and his friends found out where you were. He came to me to sell the information because he knew—how he knew is a long story—that I was working for General Sternwood. I got his information, but Canino got the little bird. He's a dead little bird now, with his feathers ruffled and his neck limp and a pearl of blood on his beak. Canino killed him. But Eddie Mars wouldn't do that, would he, Silver-Wig? He never killed anybody. He just hires it done.'

'Get out,' she said harshly. 'Get out of here quick.'

Her hand clutched in midair on the green lighter. The fingers strained. The knuckles were as white as snow.

'But Canino doesn't know I know that,' I said. 'About the little bird. All he knows is I'm nosing around.'

Then she laughed. It was almost a racking laugh. It shook her as the wind shakes a tree. I thought there was puzzlement in it, not exactly surprise, but as if a new idea had been added to something already known and it didn't fit. Then I thought that was too much to get out of a laugh.

'It's very funny,' she said breathlessly. 'Very funny, because, you see—I still love him. Women—' She began to laugh again.

I listened hard, my head throbbing. 'Let's go,' I said. 'Fast.'

She took two steps back and her face set hard. 'Get out, you! Get out! You can walk to Realito. You can make it—and you can keep your mouth shut—for an hour or two at least. You owe me that much.'

'Let's go,' I said. 'Got a gun, Silver-Wig?'

'You know I'm not going. You know that. Please, please get out of here quickly.'

I stepped up close to her, almost pressing against her. 'You're going to stay here after turning me loose? Wait for that killer to come back so you can say so sorry? A man who kills like swatting a fly. Not much. You're going with me, Silver-Wig.'

'No.'

'Suppose,' I said, 'your handsome husband *did* kill Regan? Or suppose Canino did, without Eddie's knowing it. Just suppose. How long will *you* last, after turning me loose?'

'I'm not afraid of Canino. I'm still his boss's wife.'

'Eddie's a handful of mush,' I snarled. 'Canino would take him with a teaspoon. He'll take him the way the cat took the canary. A handful of mush. The only time a girl like you goes for a wrong gee is when he's a handful of mush.'

'Get out!' she almost spat at me.

'Okey.' I turned away from her and moved out through the half-open door into a dark hallway. Then she rushed after me and pushed past to the front door and opened it. She peered out the wet blackness and listened. She motioned me forward.

'Good-bye,' she said under her breath. 'Good luck in everything but one thing. Eddie didn't kill Rusty Regan. You'll find him alive and well somewhere, when he wants to be found.'

I leaned against her and pressed her against the wall with my body. I pushed my mouth against her face. I talked to her that way.

'There's no hurry. All this was arranged in advance, rehearsed to the last detail, timed to the split second. Just like a radio programme. No hurry at all. Kiss me, Silver-Wig.'

Her face under my mouth was like ice. She put her hands up and took hold of my head and kissed me hard on the lips. Her lips were like ice, too.

I went out through the door and it closed behind me, without sound, and the rain blew in under the porch, not as cold as her lips.

29

The garage next door was dark. I crossed the gravel drive and a patch of sodden lawn. The road ran with small rivulets of water. It gurgled down a ditch on the far side. I had no hat. That must have fallen in the garage. Canino hadn't bothered to give it back to me. He hadn't thought I would need it any more. I imagined him driving back jauntily through the rain, alone, having left the gaunt and sulky Art and the probably stolen sedan in a safe place. She loved Eddie Mars and she was hiding to protect him. So he would find her there when he came back, calm beside the light and the untasted drink, and me tied up on the davenport. He would carry her stuff out to the car and go through the house carefully to make sure nothing incriminating was left. He would tell her to go out and wait. She wouldn't hear a shot. A blackjack is just as effective at short range. He would tell her he had left me tied up and I would get loose after a while. He would think she was that dumb. Nice Mr Canino.

The raincoat was open in front and I couldn't button it, being handcuffed. The skirts flapped against my legs like the wings of a large and tired bird. I came to the highway. Cars went by in a wide swirl of water illuminated by headlights. The tearing noise of their tyres died swiftly. I found my convertible where I had left it, both tyres fixed and mounted, so it could be driven away, if necessary. They thought of everything. I got into it and leaned down sideways under the wheel and fumbled aside the flap of leather that covered the pocket. I got the other gun, stuffed it up under my coat and started back. The world was small, shut in, black. A private world for Canino and me.

Half-way there the headlights nearly caught me. They turned swiftly off the highway and I slid down the bank into the wet ditch and flopped there breathing water. The car hummed by without slowing. I lifted my head, heard the rasp of its tyres as it left the road and took the gravel of the driveway. The motor died, the lights died, a door slammed. I didn't hear the house door shut, but a fringe of light trickled through the clump of trees, as though a shade had been moved aside from a window, or the light had been put on in the hall.

I came back to the soggy grass plot and sloshed across it. The car was between me and the house, the gun was down at my side, pulled as far around as I could get it, without pulling my left arm out by the roots. The car was dark, empty, warm. Water gurgled pleasantly in the radiator. I peered in at the door. The keys hung on the dash. Canino was very sure of himself. I went around the car and walked carefully across the gravel to the window and listened. I couldn't hear any voices, any sound but the swift bong-bong of the raindrops hitting the metal elbows at the bottom of the rain gutters.

I kept on listening. No loud voices, everything quiet and refined. He would be purring at her and she would be telling him she had let me go and I had promised to let them get away. He wouldn't believe me, as I wouldn't believe him. So he wouldn't be in there long. He would be on his way and take her with him. All I had to do was wait for him to come out.

I couldn't do it. I shifted the gun to my left hand and leaned down to scoop up a handful of gravel. I tossed it against the screen of the window. It was a feeble effort. Very little of it reached the glass above the screen, but the loose rattle of that little was like a dam bursting.

I ran back to the car and got on the running board behind it. The house had already gone dark. That was all. I dropped quietly on the running board and waited. No soap. Canino was too cagey.

I straightened up and got into the car backwards, fumbled around for the ignition key and turned it. I reached with my foot, but the starter button had to be on the dash. I found it at last, pulled it and the starter ground. The warm motor caught at once. It purred softly, contentedly. I got out of the car again and crouched down by the rear wheels.

I was shivering now but I knew Canino wouldn't like that last effect. He needed that car badly. A darkened window slid down inch by inch, only some shifting of light on the glass showing it moved. Flame spouted from it abruptly, the blended roar of three swift shots. Glass starred in the coupé. I yelled with agony. The yell went off into a wailing groan. The groan became a wet gurgle, choked with blood. I let the gurgle die sickeningly, on a choked gasp. It was nice work. I liked it. Canino liked it very much. I heard him laugh. It was a large booming laugh, not at all like the purr of his speaking voice.

Then silence for a little while, except for the rain and the quietly throbbing motor of the car. Then the house door crawled open, a deeper blackness in the black night. A figure showed in it cautiously, something white around the neck. It was her collar. She came out on the porch stiffly, a wooden woman. I caught the pale shine of her silver wig. Canino came crouched methodically behind her. It was so deadly it was almost funny.

She came down the steps. Now I could see the white stiffness of her face. She started towards the car. A bulwark of defence for Canino, in case I could still spit in his eye. Her voice spoke through the lisp of the rain, saying slowly, without any tone: 'I can't see a thing, Lash. The windows are misted.'

He grunted something and the girl's body jerked hard, as though he had jammed a gun into her back. She came on again and drew near the lightless car. I could see him behind her now, his hat, a side of his face, the bulk of his shoulder. The girl stopped rigid and screamed. A beautiful thin tearing scream that rocked me like a left hook.

'I can see him!' she screamed. 'Through the window. Behind the wheel, Lash!'

He fell for it like a bucket of lead. He knocked her roughly to one side and jumped forward, throwing his hand up. Three more spurts of flame cut the darkness. More glass scarred. One bullet went on through and smacked into a tree on my side. A ricochet whined off into the distance. But the motor went quietly on.

He was low down, crouched against the gloom, his face a greyness without form that seemed to come back slowly after the glare of the shots. If it was a revolver he had, it might be empty. It might not. He had fired six times, but he might have reloaded inside the house. I hoped he had. I didn't want him with an empty gun. But it might be an automatic.

I said: 'Finished?'

He whirled at me. Perhaps it would have been nice to allow him another shot or two, just like a gentleman of the old school. But his gun was still up and I couldn't wait any longer. Not long enough to be a gentleman of the old school. I shot him four times, the Colt straining against my ribs. The gun jumped out of his hand as if it had been kicked. He reached both his hands for his stomach. I could hear them smack hard against his body. He fell like that, straight forward, holding himself together with his broad hands. He fell face down in the wet gravel. And after that there wasn't a sound from him.

Silver-Wig didn't make a sound either. She stood rigid, with the rain swirling at her. I walked around Canino and kicked his gun, without any purpose. Then I walked after it and bent over sideways and picked it up. That put me close beside her. She spoke moodily, as if she was talking to herself.

'I—I was afraid you'd come back.'

I said: 'We had a date. I told you it was all arranged.' I began to laugh like a loon.

Then she was bending down over him, touching him. And after a little while she stood up with a small key on a thin chain.

She said bitterly: 'Did you have to kill him?'

I stopped laughing as suddenly as I had started. She went behind me and unlocked the handcuffs.

'Yes,' she said softly. 'I suppose you did.'

30

This was another day and the sun was shining again.

Captain Gregory of the Missing Persons Bureau looked heavily out of his office window at the barred upper floor of the Hall of Justice, white and clean after the rain. Then he turned ponderously in his swivel chair and tamped his pipe with a heat-scarred thumb and stared at me bleakly.

'So you got yourself in another jam.'

'Oh, you heard about it.'

'Brother, I sit here all day on my fanny and I don't look as if I had a brain in my head. But you'd be surprised what I hear. Shooting this Canino was all right I guess, but I don't figure the homicide boys pinned any medals on you.'

'There's been a lot of killings going on around me,' I said. 'I haven't been getting my share of it.'

He smiled patiently. 'Who told you this girl out there was Eddie Mars's wife?'

I told him. He listened carefully and yawned. He tapped his gold studded mouth with a palm like a tray. 'I guess you figure I ought to have found her.'

'That's a fair deduction.'

'Maybe I knew,' he said. 'Maybe I thought if Eddie and his woman wanted to play a little game like that, it would be smart—or as smart as I ever get—to let them think they were getting away with it. And then again maybe you think I was letting Eddie get away with it for more personal reasons.' He held his big hand out and revolved the thumb against the index and second fingers.

'No,' I said. 'I didn't really think that. Not even when Eddie seemed to know all about our talk here the other day.'

He raised his eyebrows as if raising them was an effort, a trick he was out of practice on. It furrowed his whole forehead and when it smoothed out it was full of white lines that turned reddish as I watched them.

'I'm a copper,' he said. 'Just a plain ordinary copper. Reasonably honest. As honest as you could expect a man to be in a world where it's out of style. That's mainly why I asked you to come in this morning. I'd like you to believe that. Being a copper I like to see the law win. I'd like to see the flashy well-dressed mugs like Eddie Mars spoiling their manicures in the rock quarry at Folsom, alongside of the poor little slum-bred hard guys that got knocked over on their first caper and never had a break since. That's what I'd like. You and me both lived too long to think I'm likely to see it happen. Not in this town, not in any town half this size, in any part of this wide, green and beautiful USA. We just don't run our country that way.'

I didn't say anything. He blew smoke with a backward jerk of his head, looked at the mouthpiece of his pipe and went on:

'But that don't mean I think Eddie Mars bumped off Regan or had any reason to or would have done it if he had. I just figured maybe he knows something about it, and maybe sooner or later something will sneak out into the open. Hiding his wife out at Realito was childish, but it's the kind of childishness a smart monkey thinks is smart. I had him in here last night, after the DA got through with him. He admitted the whole thing. He said he knew Canino as a reliable protection guy and that's what he had him for. He didn't know anything about his hobbies or want to. He didn't know Harry Jones. He didn't know Joe Brody. He did know Geiger, of course, but claims he didn't know about his racket. I guess you heard all that.'

'Yes.'

'You played it smart down there at Realito, brother. Not trying to cover up. We keep a file on unidentified bullets nowadays. Some day you might use that gun again. Then you'd be over a barrel.'

'I played it smart,' I said, and leered at him.

He knocked his pipe out and stared down at it broodingly. 'What happened to the girl?' he asked, not looking up.

'I don't know. They didn't hold her. We made statements, three sets of them, for Wilde, for the Sheriff's office, for the Homicide Bureau. They turned her loose. I haven't seen her since. I don't expect to.'

'Kind of a nice girl, they say. Wouldn't be one to play dirty games.'

'Kind of a nice girl,' I said.

Captain Gregory sighed and rumpled his mousy hair. 'There's just one more thing,' he said almost gently. 'You look like a nice guy, but you play too rough. If you really want to help the Sternwood family—leave 'em alone.'

'I think you're right, Captain.'

'How you feel?'

'Swell.' I said. 'I was standing on various pieces of carpet most of the night, being bawled out. Before that I got soaked to the skin and beaten up. I'm in perfect condition.'

'What the hell did you expect, brother?'

'Nothing else.' I stood up and grinned at him and started for the door. When I had almost reached it he cleared his throat suddenly and said in a harsh voice: 'I'm wasting my breath, huh? You still think you can find Regan.'

I turned round and looked him straight in the eyes. 'No, I don't think I can find Regan. I'm not even going to try. Does that suit you?'

He nodded slowly. Then he shrugged. 'I don't know what the hell I even said that for. Good luck, Marlowe. Drop around any time.'

'Thanks, Captain.'

I went down out of the City Hall and got my car from the parking lot and drove home to the Hobart Arms. I lay down on the bed with my coat off and stared at the ceiling and listened to the traffic sounds on the street outside and watched the sun move slowly across a corner of the ceiling. I tried to go to sleep, but sleep didn't come. I got up and took a drink, although it was the wrong time of day, and lay down again. I still couldn't go to sleep. My brain ticked like a clock. I sat up on the side of the bed and stuffed a pipe and said out loud:

'That old buzzard knows something.'

The pipe tasted as bitter as lye. I put it aside and lay down again. My mind drifted through waves of false memory, in which I seemed to do the same thing over and over again, go to the same places, meet the same people, say the same words to them, over and over again, and yet each time it seemed real, like something actually happening, and for the first time. I was driving hard along the highway through the rain, with Silver-Wig in the corner of the car, saying nothing, so that by the time we reached Los Angeles we seemed to be utter strangers again. I was getting out at an all-night drugstore and phoning Bernie Ohls that I had killed a man at Realito and was on my way over to Wilde's house with Eddie Mars's wife, who had seen me do it. I was pushing the car along the silent, rain-polished streets of Lafayette Park and up under the *porte-cochère* of Wilde's big frame house and the porch light was already on, Ohls having telephoned ahead that I was coming. I was in Wilde's study and he was behind his desk in a flowered dressing-gown and a tight hard face and a dappled cigar moved in his fingers and up to the bitter smile on his lips. Ohls was there and a slim grey scholarly man from the Sheriff's office who looked and talked more like a professor of economics than a cop. I was telling the story and they were listening quietly and Silver-Wig sat in a shadow with her hands folded in her lap, looking at nobody. There was a lot of telephoning. There were two men from the Homicide Bureau who looked at me as if I was some kind of strange beast escaped from a travelling circus. I was driving again, with one of them beside me, to the Fulwider Building. We were there in the room where Harry Jones was still in the chair behind the desk, the twisted stiffness of his dead face and the sour-sweet smell in the room. There was a medical examiner, very young and husky, with red bristles on his neck. There was a fingerprint man fussing around and I was telling him not to forget the latch of the transom. (He found Canino's thumbprint on it, the only print the brown man had left to back up my story.)

I was back again at Wilde's house, signing a typewritten statement his secretary had run off in another room. Then the door opened and Eddie Mars came in and an abrupt smile flashed to his face when he saw Silver-Wig, and he said: 'Hello, sugar', and she didn't look at him or answer him. Eddie Mars fresh and cheerful, in a dark business suit, with a fringed white scarf hanging outside his tweed overcoat. Then they were gone, everybody was gone out of the room but myself and Wilde, and Wilde was saying in a cold, angry voice: 'This is the last time, Marlowe. The next fast one you pull I'll throw you to the lions, no matter whose heart it breaks.'

It was like that, over and over again, lying on the bed and watching the patch of sunlight slide down the corner of the wall. Then the phone rang, and it was Norris, the Sternwood butler, with his usual untouchable voice.

'Mr Marlowe? I telephoned your office without success, so I took the liberty of trying to reach you at home.'

'I was out most of the night,' I said. 'I haven't been down.'

'Yes, sir. The General would like to see you this morning, Mr Marlowe, if it's convenient.'

'Half an hour or so,' I said. 'How is he?'

'He's in bed, sir, but not doing badly.'

'Wait till he sees me,' I said, and hung up.

I shaved, changed clothes and started for the door. Then I went back and got Carmen's little pearl-handled revolver and dropped it into my pocket. The sunlight was so bright that it danced. I got to the Sternwood place in twenty minutes and drove up under the arch at the side door. It was eleven-fifteen. The birds in the ornamental trees were crazy with song after the rain, the terraced lawns were as green as the Irish flag, and the whole estate looked as though it had been made about ten minutes before. I rang the bell. It was five days since I had rung it for the first time. It felt like a year.

A maid opened the door and led me along a side hall to the main hallway and left me there, saying Mr Norris would be down in a moment. The main hallway looked just the same. The portrait over the mantel had the same hot black eyes and the knight in the stained-glass window still wasn't getting anywhere untying the naked damsel from the tree.

In a few minutes Norris appeared, and he hadn't changed either. His acid-blue eyes were as remote as ever, his greyish-pink skin looked healthy and rested, and he moved as if he was twenty years younger than he really was. I was the one who felt the weight of the years.

We went up the tiled staircase and turned the opposite way from Vivian's room. With each step the house seemed to grow larger and more silent. We reached a massive old door that looked as if it had come out of a church. Norris opened it softly and looked in. Then he stood aside and I went in past him across what seemed to be about a quarter of a mile of carpet to a huge canopied bed like the one Henry the Eighth died in.

General Sternwood was propped up on pillows. His bloodless hands were clasped on top of the sheet. They looked grey against it. His black eyes were still full of fight and the rest of his face still looked like the face of a corpse.

'Sit down, Mr Marlowe.' His voice sounded weary and a little stiff.

I pulled a chair close to him and sat down. All the windows were shut tight. The room was sunless at that hour. Awnings cut off what glare there might be from the sky. The air had the faint sweetish smell of old age.

He stared at me silently for a long minute. He moved a hand as if to prove to himself that he could still move it, then folded it back over the other. He said lifelessly:

'I didn't ask you to look for my son-in-law, Mr Marlowe.'

'You wanted me to, though.'

'I didn't ask you to. You assume a great deal. I usually ask for what I want.'

I didn't say anything.

'You have been paid,' he went on coldly. 'The money is of no consequence one way or the other. I merely feel that you have, no doubt unintentionally, betrayed a trust.'

He closed his eyes on that. I said: 'Is that all you wanted to see me about?'

He opened his eyes again, very slowly, as though the lids were made of lead. 'I suppose you are angry at that remark,' he said.

I shook my head. 'You have an advantage over me, General. It's an advantage I wouldn't want to take away from you, not a hair of it. It's not much, considering what you have to put up with. You can say anything you like to me and I wouldn't think of getting angry. I'd like to offer you your money back. It may mean nothing to you. It might mean something to me.'

'What does it mean to you?'

'It means I have refused payment for an unsatisfactory job. That's all.'

'Do you do many unsatisfactory jobs?'

'A few. Everyone does.'

'Why did you go to see Captain Gregory?'

I leaned back and hung an arm over the back of the chair. I studied his face. It told me nothing. I didn't know the answer to his question—no satisfactory answer.

I said: 'I was convinced you put those Geiger notes up to me chiefly as a test, and that you were a little afraid Regan might somehow be involved in an attempt to blackmail you. I didn't know anything about Regan then. It wasn't until I talked to Captain Gregory that I realized Regan wasn't that sort of guy in all probability.'

'That is scarcely answering my question.'

I nodded. 'No. That is scarcely answering your question. I guess I just don't like to admit that I played a hunch. The morning I was here, after I left you out in the orchid house, Mrs Regan sent for me. She seemed to assume I was hired to look for her husband and she didn't seem to like it. She let drop however that "they" had found his car in a certain garage. The "they" could only be the police. Consequently the police must know something about it. If they did, the Missing Persons Bureau would be the department that would have the case. I didn't know whether you had reported it, of course, or somebody else, or whether they had found the car through somebody reporting it abandoned in a garage. But I know cops, and I knew that if they got that much, they would get a little more—especially as your driver happened to have a police record. I didn't know how much more they would get. That started me thinking about the Missing Persons Bureau. What convinced me was something in Mr Wilde's manner the night we had the conference over at his house about Geiger and so on. We were alone for a minute and he asked me whether you had told me you were looking for Regan. I said you had told me you wished you knew where he was and that he was all right. Wilde pulled his lip in and looked funny. I knew just as plainly as though he had said it that by "looking for Regan" he meant using the machinery of the law to look for him. Even then I tried to go up against Captain Gregory in such a way that I wouldn't tell him anything he didn't know already.'

'And you allowed Captain Gregory to think I had employed you to find Rusty?'

'Yeah. I guess I did—when I was sure he had the case.'

He closed his eyes. They twitched a little. He spoke with them closed: 'And do you consider that ethical?'

'Yes,' I said. 'I do.'

The eyes opened again. The piercing blackness of them was startling coming suddenly out of that dead face. 'Perhaps I don't understand,' he said.

'Maybe you don't. The head of a Missing Persons Bureau isn't a talker. He wouldn't be in that office if he was. This one is a very smart cagey guy who tries, with a lot of success at first, to give the impression he's a middle-aged hack fed up with his job. The game I play is not spillikins. There's always a large element of bluff connected with it. Whatever I might say to a cop, he would be apt to discount it. And to *that* cop it wouldn't make much difference what I said. When you hire a boy in my line of work it isn't like hiring a window-washer and showing him eight windows and saying: "Wash those and you're through." *You* don't know what I have to go through or over or under to do your job for you. I do it my way. I do my best to protect you and I may break a few rules, but I break them in your favour. The client comes first, unless he's crooked. Even then all I do is hand the job back to him and keep my mouth shut. After all you didn't tell me *not* to go to Captain Gregory.'

'That would have been rather difficult,' he said with a faint smile.

'Well, what have I done wrong? Your man Norris seemed to think when Geiger was eliminated the case was over. I don't see it that way. Geiger's method of approach puzzled me and still does. I'm not Sherlock Holmes or Philo Vance. I don't expect to go over ground the police have covered and pick up a broken pen point and build a case from it. If you think there is anybody in the detective business making a living doing that sort of thing, you don't know much about cops. It's not things like that they overlook if they overlook anything. I'm not saying they often overlook anything when they're really allowed to work. But if they do, it's apt to be something looser and vaguer, like a man of Geiger's type sending you his evidence of debt and asking you to pay like a gentleman—Geiger, a man in a shady racket, in a vulnerable position, protected by a racketeer and having at least some negative protection from some of the police. Why did he do that? Because he wanted to find out if there was anything putting pressure on you. If there was, you would pay him. If not, you would ignore him and wait for his next move. But there was something putting a pressure on you. Regan. You were afraid he was not what he had appeared to be, that he had stayed around and had been nice to you just long enough to find out how to play games with your bank account.'

He started to say something but I interrupted him. 'Even at that it wasn't your money you cared about. It wasn't even your daughters. You've more or less written them off. It's that you're still too proud to be played for a sucker—and you really liked Regan.'

There was a silence. Then the General said quietly: 'You talk too damn much, Marlowe. Am I to understand you are still trying to solve that puzzle?'

'No. I've quit. I've been warned off. The boys think I play too rough. That's why I thought I should give you back your money—because it isn't a completed job by my standards.'

He smiled. 'Quit nothing,' he said. 'I'll pay you another thousand dollars to find Rusty. He doesn't have to come back. I don't even have to know where he is. A man has a right to live his own life. I don't blame him for walking out on my daughter, nor even for going so abruptly. It was probably a sudden impulse. I want to know that he is all right wherever he is. I want to know it from him directly, and if he should happen to need money, I should want him to have that also. Am I clear?'

I said: 'Yes, General.'

He rested a little while, lax on the bed, his eyes closed and dark-lidded, his mouth tight and bloodless. He was used up. He was pretty nearly licked. He opened his eyes again and tried to grin at me.

'I guess I'm a sentimental old goat,' he said. 'And no soldier at all. I took a fancy to that boy. He seemed pretty clean to me. I must be a little too vain about my judgment of character. Find him for me, Marlowe. Just find him.'

'I'll try,' I said. 'You'd better rest now. I've talked your arm off.'

I got up quickly and walked across the wide floor and out. He had his eyes shut again before I opened the door. His hands lay limp on the sheet. He looked a lot more like a dead man than most dead men look. I shut the door quietly and went back along the upper hall and down the stairs.

31

The butler appeared with my hat. I put it on and said: 'What do you think of him?'

'He's not as weak as he looks, sir.'

'If he was, he'd be ready for burial. What did this Regan fellow have that bored into him so?'

The butler looked at me levelly and yet with a queer lack of expression. 'Youth, sir,' he said. 'And the soldier's eye.'

'Like yours,' I said.

'If I may say so, sir, not unlike yours.'

'Thanks. How are the ladies this morning?'

He shrugged politely.

'Just what I thought,' I said, and he opened the door for me.

I stood outside on the step and looked down the vistas of grassed terraces and trimmed trees and flowerbeds to the tall metal railing at the bottom of the gardens. I saw Carmen about half-way down, sitting on a stone bench, with her head between her hands, looking forlorn and alone.

I went down the red brick steps that led from terrace to terrace. I was quite close before she heard me. She jumped up and whirled like a cat. She wore the light blue slacks she had worn the first time I saw her. Her blonde hair was the same loose tawny wave. Her face was white. Red spots flared in her cheeks as she looked at me. Her eyes were slaty.

'Bored?' I said.

She smiled slowly, rather shyly, then nodded quickly. Then she whispered: 'You're not mad at me?'

'I thought you were mad at me.'

She put her thumb up and giggled. 'I'm not.' When she giggled I didn't like her any more. I looked around. A target hung on a tree about thirty feet away, with some darts sticking to it. There were three or four more on the stone bench where she had been sitting.

'For people with money you and your sister don't seem to have much fun,' I said.

She looked at me under her long lashes. This was the look that was supposed to make me roll over on my back. I said: 'You like throwing those darts?'

'Uh-huh.'

'That reminds me of something.' I looked back towards the house. By moving about three feet I made a tree hide me from it. I took her little pearl-handled gun out of my pocket. 'I brought you back your artillery. I cleaned it and loaded it up. Take my tip–don't shoot it at people, unless you get to be a better shot. Remember?'

Her face went paler and her thin thumb dropped. She looked at me, then at the gun I was holding. There was a fascination in her eyes. 'Yes,' she said, and nodded. Then suddenly: 'Teach me to shoot.'

'Huh?'

'Teach me how to shoot. I'd like that.'

'Here? It's against the law.'

She came close to me and took the gun out of my hand, cuddled her hand around the butt. Then she tucked it quickly inside her slacks, almost with a furtive movement, and looked around.

'I know where,' she said in a secret voice. 'Down by some of the old wells.' She pointed off down the hill. 'Teach me?'

I looked into her slaty blue eyes. I might as well have looked at a couple of bottle-tops. 'All right. Give me back the gun until I see if the place looks all right.'

She smiled and made a mouth, then handed it back with a secret naughty air, as if she was giving me a key to her room. We walked up the steps and around to my car. The gardens seemed deserted. The sunshine was as empty as a head waiter's smile. We got into the car and I drove down the sunken driveway and out through the gates.

'Where's Vivian?' I asked.

'Not up yet.' She giggled.

I drove on down the hill through the quiet, opulent streets with their faces washed by the rain, bore east to La Brea, then south. We reached the place she meant in about ten minutes.

'In there.' She leaned out of the window and pointed.

It was a narrow dirt road, not much more than a track, like the entrance to some foothill ranch. A wide five-barred gate was folded back against a stump and looked as if it hadn't been shut in years. The road was fringed with tall eucalyptus trees and deeply rutted. Trucks had used it. It was empty and sunny now, but not yet dusty. The rain had been too hard and too recent. I followed the ruts along and the noise of city traffic grew curiously and quickly faint, as if this were not in the city at all, but far away in a daydream land. Then the oil-stained, motionless walking-beam of a squat wooden derrick stuck up over a branch. I could see the rusty old steel cable that connected this walking-beam with half a dozen others. The beams didn't move, probably hadn't moved for a year. The wells were no longer pumping. There was a pile of rusted pipe, a loading platform that sagged at one end, half a dozen empty oil drums lying in a ragged pile. There was the stagnant, oil-scummed water of an old sump iridescent in the sunlight.

'Are they going to make a park of all this?' I asked.

She dipped her chin down and gleamed at me.

'It's about time. The smell of that sump would poison a herd of goats. This the place you had in mind?'

'Uh-huh. Like it?'

'It's beautiful.' I pulled up beside the loading platform. We got out. I listened. The hum of the traffic was a distant web of sound, like the buzzing of bees. The place was as lonely as a churchyard. Even after the rain the tall eucalyptus trees still looked dusty. They always look dusty. A branch broken off by the wind had fallen over the edge of the sump and the flat leathery leaves dangled in the water.

I walked around the sump and looked into the pumphouse. There was some junk in it, nothing that looked like recent activity. Outside a big wooden bull wheel was tilted against the wall. It looked like a good place all right.

I went back to the car. The girl stood beside it preening her hair and holding it out in the sun. 'Gimme,' she said, and held her hand out.

I took the gun out and put it in her palm. I bent down and picked up a rusty can.

'Take it easy now,' I said. 'It's loaded in all five. I'll go over and set this can in that square opening in the middle of that big wooden wheel. See?' I pointed. She ducked her head, delighted. 'That's about thirty feet. Don't start shooting until I get back beside you. Okey?'

'Okey,' she giggled.

I went back around the sump and set the can up in the middle of the bull wheel. It made a swell target. If she missed the can, which she was certain to do, she would probably hit the wheel. That would stop a small slug completely. However, she wasn't going to hit even that.

I went back towards her around the sump. When I was about ten feet from her, at the edge of the sump, she showed me all her sharp little teeth and brought the gun up and started to hiss.

I stopped dead, the sump water stagnant and stinking at my back.

'Stand there, you son of a bitch,' she said.

The gun pointed at my chest. Her hand seemed to be quite steady. The hissing sound grew louder and her face had the scraped bone look. Aged, deteriorated, become animal, and not a nice animal.

I laughed at her. I started to walk towards her. I saw her small finger tighten on the trigger and grow white at the tip. I was about six feet away from her when she started to shoot.

The sound of the gun made a sharp slap, without body, a brittle crack in the sunlight. I didn't see any smoke. I stopped again and grinned at her.

She fired twice more, very quickly. I don't think any of the shots would have missed. There were five in the little gun. She had fired four. I rushed her.

I didn't want the last one in my face, so I swerved to one side. She gave it to me quite carefully, not worried at all. I think I felt the hot breath of the powder blast a little.

I straightened up. 'My, but you're cute,' I said.

Her hand holding the empty gun began to shake violently. The gun fell out of it. Her mouth began to shake. Her whole face went to pieces. Then her head screwed up towards her left ear and froth showed on her lips. Her breath made a whining sound. She swayed.

I caught her as she fell. She was already unconscious. I prised her teeth open with both hands and stuffed a wadded handkerchief in between them. It took all my strength to do it. I lifted her up and got her into the car, then went back for the gun and dropped it into my pocket. I climbed in under the wheel, backed the car and drove back the way we had come along the rutted road, out of the gateway, back up the hill and so home.

Carmen lay crumpled in the corner of the car, without motion. I was half-way up the drive to the house before she stirred. Then her eyes suddenly opened wide and wild. She sat up.

'What happened?' she gasped.

'Nothing. Why?'

'Oh, yes it did,' she giggled. 'I wet myself.'

'They always do,' I said.

She looked at me with a sudden sick speculation and began to moan.

32

The gentle-eyed, horse-faced maid let me into the long grey and white upstairs sitting-room with the ivory drapes tumbled extravagantly on the floor and the white carpet from wall to wall. A screen star's boudoir, a place of charm and seduction, artificial as a wooden leg. It was empty at the moment. The door closed behind me with the unnatural softness of a hospital door. A breakfast table on wheels stood by the chaise-longue. Its silver glittered. There were cigarette ashes in the coffee cup. I sat down and waited.

It seemed a long time before the door opened again and Vivian came in. She was in oyster-white lounging pyjamas trimmed with white fur, cut as flowingly as a summer sea frothing on the beach of some small and exclusive island.

She went past me in long smooth strides and sat down on the edge of the chaise-longue. There was a cigarette in her lips, at the corner of her mouth. Her nails to-day were copper-red from quick to tip, without half-moons.

'So you're just a brute after all,' she said quietly, staring at me. 'An utter callous brute. You killed a man last night. Never mind how I heard it. I heard it. And now you have to come out here and frighten my kid sister into a fit.'

I didn't say a word. She began to fidget. She moved over to a slipper chair and put her head back against a white cushion that lay along the back of the chair against the wall. She blew pale grey smoke upwards and watched it float towards the ceiling and come apart in wisps that were for a little while distinguishable from the air and then melted and were nothing. Then very slowly she lowered her eyes and gave me a cool hard glance.

'I don't understand you,' she said. 'I'm thankful as hell one of us kept his head the night before last. It's bad enough to have a bootlegger in my past. Why don't you for Christ's sake say something?'

'How is she?'

'Oh, she's all right, I suppose. Fast asleep. She always goes to sleep. What did you do to her?'

'Not a thing. I came out of the house after seeing your father and she was out in front. She had been throwing darts at a target on a tree. I went down to speak to her because I had something that belonged to her. A little revolver Owen Taylor gave her once. She took it over to Brody's place the other evening, the evening he was killed. I had to take it away from her there. I didn't mention it, so perhaps you didn't know it.'

The black Sternwood eyes got large and empty. It was her turn not to say anything.

'She was pleased to get her little gun back and she wanted me to teach her how to shoot and she wanted to show me the old oil wells down the hill where your family made some of its money. So we went down there and the place was pretty creepy, all rusted metal and old wood and silent wells and greasy scummy sumps. Maybe that upset her. I guess you've been there yourself. It was kind of eerie.'

'Yes—it is.' It was a small breathless voice now.

'So we went in there and I stuck a can up in a bull wheel for her to pop at. She threw a wingding. Looked like a mild epileptic fit to me.'

'Yes.' The same minute voice. 'She has them once in a while. Is that all you wanted to see me about?'

'I guess you still wouldn't tell me what Eddie Mars has on you.'

'Nothing at all. And I'm getting a little tired of that question,' she said coldly.

'Do you know a man named Canino?'

She drew her fine black brows together in thought. 'Vaguely. I seem to remember the name.'

'Eddie Mars's trigger man. A tough hombre, they said. I guess he was. Without a little help from a lady I'd be where he is—in the morgue.'

'The ladies seem to—' She stopped dead and whitened. 'I can't joke about it,' she said simply.

'I'm not joking, and if I seem to talk in circles, it just seems that way. It all ties together—everything. Geiger and his cute little blackmail tricks, Brody and his pictures, Eddie Mars and his roulette tables, Canino and the girl Rusty Regan didn't run away with. It all ties together.'

'I'm afraid I don't even know what you're talking about.'

'Suppose you did—it would be something like this. Geiger got his hooks into your sister, which isn't very difficult, and got some notes from her and tried to blackmail your father with them, in a nice way. Eddie Mars was behind Geiger, protecting him and using him for a cat's-paw. Your father sent for me instead of paying up, which showed he wasn't scared about anything. Eddie Mars wanted to know that. He had something on you and he wanted to know if he had it on the General too. If he had, he could collect a lot of money in a hurry. If not, he would have to wait until you got your share of the family fortune, and in the meantime be satisfied with whatever spare cash he could take away from you across the roulette table. Geiger was killed by Owen Taylor, who was in love with your silly little sister and didn't like the kind of games Geiger played with her. That didn't mean anything to Eddie. He was playing a deeper game than Geiger knew anything about, or than Brody knew anything about, or anybody except you and Eddie and a tough guy named Canino. Your husband disappeared and Eddie, knowing everybody knew there had been bad blood between him and Regan, hid his wife out at Realito and put Canino to guard her, so that it would look as if she had run away with Regan. He even got Regan's car into the garage of the place where Mona Mars had been living. But that sounds a little silly taken merely as an attempt to divert suspicion that Eddie had killed your husband or had him killed. It isn't so silly, really. He had another motive. He was playing for a million or so. He knew where Regan had gone and why and he didn't want the police to have to find out. He wanted them to have an explanation of the disappearance that would keep them satisfied. Am I boring you?'

'You tire me,' she said in a dead, exhausted voice. 'God, how you tire me!'

'I'm sorry. I'm not just fooling around trying to be clever. Your father offered me a thousand dollars this morning to find Regan. That's a lot of money to me, but I can't do it.'

Her mouth jumped open. Her breath was suddenly strained and harsh. 'Give me a cigarette,' she said thickly. 'Why?' The pulse in her throat had begun to throb.

I gave her a cigarette and lit a match and held it for her. She drew in a lungful of smoke and let it out raggedly and then the cigarette seemed to be forgotten between her fingers. She never drew on it again.

'Well, the Missing Persons Bureau can't find him,' I said. 'It's not so easy. What they can't do it's not likely that I can do.'

'Oh.' There was a shade of relief in her voice.

'That's one reason. The Missing Persons people think he just disappeared on purpose, pulled down the curtain, as they call it. They don't think Eddie Mars did away with him.'

'Who said anybody did away with him?'

'We're coming to it,' I said.

For a brief instant her face seemed to come to pieces, to become merely a set of features without form or control. Her mouth looked like the prelude to a scream. But only for an instant. The Sternwood blood had to be good for something more than her black eyes and her recklessness.

I stood up and took the smoking cigarette from between her fingers and killed it in an ashtray. Then I took Carmen's little gun out of my pocket and laid it carefully, with exaggerated care, on her white satin knee. I balanced it there, and stepped back with my head on one side like a window-dresser getting the effect of a new twist of a scarf around a dummy's neck.

I sat down again. She didn't move. Her eyes came down millimetre by millimetre and looked at the gun.

'It's harmless,' I said. 'All five chambers empty. She fired them all. She fired them all at me.'

The pulse jumped wildly in her throat. Her voice tried to say something and couldn't. She swallowed.

'From a distance of five or six feet,' I said. 'Cute little thing, isn't she? Too bad I had loaded the gun with blanks.' I grinned nastily. 'I had a hunch about what she would do—if she got the chance.'

She brought her voice back from a long way off. 'You're a horrible man,' she said. 'Horrible.'

'Yeah. You're her big sister. What are you going to do about it?'

'You can't prove a word of it.'

'Can't prove what?'

'That she fired at you. You said you were down there around the wells with her, alone. You can't prove a word of what you say.'

'Oh that,' I said. 'I wasn't thinking of trying. I was thinking of another time—when the shells in the little gun had bullets in them.'

Her eyes were pools of darkness, much emptier than darkness.

'I was thinking of the day Regan disappeared,' I said. 'Late in the afternoon. When he took her down to those old wells to teach her to shoot and put up a can somewhere and told her to pop at it and stood near her while she shot. And she didn't shoot at the can. She turned the gun and shot him, just the way she tried to shoot me to-day, and for the same reason.'

She moved a little and the gun slid off her knee and fell to the floor. It was one of the loudest sounds I ever heard. Her eyes were riveted on my face. Her voice was a stretched whisper of agony. 'Carmen . . . Merciful God, Carmen! . . . Why?'

'Do I really have to tell you why she shot at me?'

'Yes.' Her eyes were still terrible. 'I'm—I'm afraid you do.'

'Night before last when I got home she was in my apartment. She'd kidded the manager into letting her in to wait for me. She was in my bed—naked. I threw her out on her ear. I guess maybe Regan did the same thing to her some time. But you can't do that to Carmen.'

She drew her lips back and made a half-hearted attempt to lick them. It made her, for a brief instant, look like a frightened child. The lines of her cheeks sharpened and her hand went up slowly like an artificial hand worked by wires and its fingers closed slowly and stiffly around the white fur at her collar. They drew the fur tight against her throat. After that she just sat staring.

'Money,' she croaked. 'I suppose you want money.'

'How much money?' I tried not to sneer.

'Fifteen thousand dollars?'

I nodded. 'That would be about right. That would be the established fee.

That was what he had in his pockets when she shot him. That would be what Mr Canino got for disposing of the body when you went to Eddie Mars for help. But that would be small change to what Eddie expects to collect one of these days, wouldn't it?'

'You son of a bitch!' she said.

'Uh-huh. I'm a very smart guy. I haven't a feeling or a scruple in the world. All I have the itch for is money. I am so money greedy that for twenty-five bucks a day and expenses, mostly gasolene and whisky, I do my thinking myself, what there is of it; I risk my whole future, the hatred of the cops and of Eddie Mars and his pals, I dodge bullets and eat saps, and say thank you very much, if you have any more trouble, I hope you'll think of me, I'll just leave one of my cards in case anything comes up. I do all this for twenty-five bucks a day–and maybe just a little to protect what little pride a broken and sick old man has left in his blood, in the thought that his blood is not poison, and that although his two little girls are a trifle wild, as many nice girls are these days, they are not perverts or killers. And that makes me a son of a bitch. All right. I don't care anything about that. I've been called that by people of all sizes and shapes, including your little sister. She called me worse than that for not getting into bed with her. I got five hundred dollars from your father, which I didn't ask for, but he can afford to give it to me. I can get another thousand for finding Mr Rusty Regan, if I could find him. Now you offer me fifteen grand. That makes me a big shot. With fifteen grand I could own a home and a new car and four suits of clothes. I might even take a vacation without worrying about losing a case. That's fine. What are you offering it to me for? Can I go on being a son of a bitch, or do I have to become a gentleman, like that lush that passed out in his car the other night?'

She was as silent as a stone woman.

'All right,' I went on heavily. 'Will you take her away? Somewhere far off from here where they can handle her type, where they will keep guns and knives and fancy drinks away from her? Hell, she might even get herself cured, you know. It's been done.'

She got up and walked slowly to the windows. The drapes lay in heavy ivory folds beside her feet. She stood among the folds and looked out, towards the quiet darkish foothills. She stood motionless, almost blending into the drapes. Her hands hung loose at her sides. Utterly motionless hands. She turned and came back along the room and walked past me blindly. When she was behind me she caught her breath sharply and spoke.

'He's in the sump,' she said. 'A horrible decayed thing. I did it. I did just what you said. I went to Eddie Mars. She came home and told me about it, just like a child. She's not normal. I knew the police would get it all out of her. In a little while she would even brag about it. And if dad knew, he would call them instantly and tell them the whole story. And some time in that night he would die. It's not his dying–it's what he would be thinking just before he died. Rusty wasn't a bad fellow. I didn't love him. He was all right, I guess. He just didn't mean anything to me, one way or another, alive or dead, compared with keeping it from dad.'

'So you let her run around loose,' I said, 'getting into other jams.'

'I was playing for time. Just for time. I played the wrong way, of course. I thought she might even forget it herself. I've heard they do forget what happens in those fits. Maybe she has forgotten it. I knew Eddie Mars would bleed me white, but I didn't care. I had to have help and I could only get it from somebody like him. . . . There have been times when I hardly believed it all myself. And other times when I had to get drunk quickly—whatever time of day it was. Awfully damn quickly.'

'You'll take her away,' I said. 'And do that awfully damn quickly.'

She still had her back to me. She said softly now: 'What about you?'

'Nothing about me. I'm leaving. I'll give you three days. If you're gone by then—okey. If you're not, out it comes. And don't think I don't mean that.'

She turned suddenly. 'I don't know what to say to you. I don't know how to begin.'

'Yeah. Get her out of here and see that she's watched every minute. Promise?'

'I promise. Eddie—'

'Forget Eddie. I'll go see him after I get some rest. I'll handle Eddie.'

'He'll try to kill you.'

'Yeah,' I said. 'His best boy couldn't. I'll take a chance on the others. Does Norris know?'

'He'll never tell.'

'I thought he knew.'

I went quickly away from her down the room and out and down the tiled staircase to the front hall. I didn't see anybody when I left. I found my hat alone this time. Outside the bright gardens had a haunted look, as though small wild eyes were watching me from behind the bushes, as though the sunshine itself had a mysterious something in its light. I got into my car and drove off down the hill.

What did it matter where you lay once you were dead? In a dirty sump or in a marble tower on top of a high hill? You were dead, you were sleeping the big sleep, you were not bothered by things like that. Oil and water were the same as wind and air to you. You just slept the big sleep, not caring about the nastiness of how you died or where you fell. Me, I was part of the nastiness now. Far more a part of it than Rusty Regan was. But the old man didn't have to be. He could lie quiet in his canopied bed, with his bloodless hands folded on the sheet, waiting. His heart was a brief, uncertain murmur. His thoughts were as grey as ashes. And in a little while he too, like Rusty Regan, would be sleeping the big sleep.

On the way downtown I stopped at a bar and had a couple of double Scotches. They didn't do me any good. All they did was make me think of Silver-Wig, and I never saw her again.

The High Window

Raymond CHANDLER

I

The house was on Dresden Avenue in the Oak Knoll section of Pasadena, a big solid cool-looking house with burgundy brick walls, a terra-cotta tile roof, and a white stone trim. The front windows were leaded downstairs. Upstairs windows were of the cottage type and had a lot of rococo imitation stonework trimming around them.

From the front wall and its attendant flowering bushes a half-acre or so of fine green lawn drifted in a gentle slope down to the street, passing on the way an enormous deodar around which it flowed like a cool green tide around a rock. The sidewalk and the parkway were both very wide and in the parkway were three white acacias that were worth seeing. There was a heavy scent of summer on the morning and everything that grew was perfectly still in the breathless air they get over there on what they call a nice cool day.

All I knew about the people was that they were a Mrs Elizabeth Bright Murdock and family and that she wanted to hire a nice clean private detective who wouldn't drop cigar ashes on the floor and never carried more than one gun. And I knew she was the widow of an old coot with whiskers named Jasper Murdock who had made a lot of money helping out the community, and got his photograph in the Pasadena paper every year on his anniversary, with the years of his birth and death underneath, and the legend: *His Life Was His Service.*

I left my car on the street and walked over a few dozen stumble stones set into the green lawn, and rang the bell in the brick portico under a peaked roof. A low red brick wall ran along the front of the house the short distance from the door to the edge of the driveway. At the end of the walk, on a concrete block, there was a little painted Negro in white riding-breeches and a green jacket and a red cap. He was holding a whip, and there was an iron hitching ring in the block at his feet. He looked a little sad, as if he had been waiting there a long time and was getting discouraged. I went over and patted his head while I was waiting for somebody to come to the door.

After a while a middle-aged sourpuss in a maid's costume opened the front door about eight inches and gave me the beady eye.

'Philip Marlowe,' I said. 'Calling on Mrs Murdock. By appointment.'

The middle-aged sourpuss ground her teeth, snapped her eyes shut, snapped them open and said in one of those angular hardrock pioneer-type voices: 'Which one?'

'Huh?'

'Which Mrs Murdock?' she almost screamed at me.

'Mrs Elizabeth Bright Murdock,' I said. 'I didn't know there was more than one.'

'Well, there is,' she snapped. 'Got a card?'

She still had the door a scant eight inches open. She poked the end of her nose and a thin muscular hand into the opening. I got my wallet out and got one of the cards with just my name on it and put it in the hand. The hand and nose went in and the door slammed in my face.

I thought that maybe I ought to have gone to the back door. I went over and patted the little Negro on the head again.

'Brother,' I said, 'you and me both.'

Time passed, quite a lot of time. I stuck a cigarette in my mouth, but didn't light it. The Good Humour man went by in his little blue and white wagon, playing 'Turkey in the Straw' on his music box. A large black and gold butterfly fishtailed in and landed on a hydrangea bush almost at my elbow, moved its wings slowly up and down a few times, then took off heavily and staggered away through the motionless hot scented air.

The front door came open again. The sourpuss said: 'This way.'

I went in. The room beyond was large and square and sunken and cool and had the restful atmosphere of a funeral chapel and something the same smell. Tapestry on the blank roughened stucco walls, iron grilles imitating balconies outside high side windows, heavy carved chairs with plush seats and tapestry backs and tarnished gilt tassels hanging down their sides. At the back a stained-glass window about the size of a tennis-court. Curtained French doors underneath it. An old musty, fusty, narrow-minded, clean and bitter room. It didn't look as if anybody ever sat in it or would ever want to. Marble-topped tables with crooked legs, gilt clocks, pieces of small statuary in two colours of marble. A lot of junk that would take a week to dust. A lot of money, and all wasted. Thirty years before, in the wealthy close-mouthed provincial town Pasadena then was, it must have seemed like quite a room. We left it and went along a hallway and after a while the sourpuss opened a door and motioned me in.

'Mr Marlowe,' she said through the door in a nasty voice, and went away grinding her teeth.

2

It was a small room looking out on the back garden. It had an ugly red and brown carpet and was furnished as an office. It contained what you would expect to find in a small office. A thin, fragile-looking, blondish girl in shell glasses sat behind a desk with a typewriter on a pulled-out leaf at her left. She had her hands poised on the keys, but she didn't have any paper in the machine. She watched me come into the room with the stiff, half-silly expression of a self-conscious person posing for a snapshot. She had a clear, soft voice, asking me to sit down.

'I am Miss Davis. Mrs Murdock's secretary. She wanted me to ask you for a few references.'

'References?'

'Certainly. References. Does that surprise you?'

I put my hat on her desk and the unlighted cigarette on the brim of the hat. 'You mean she sent for me without knowing anything about me?'

Her lip trembled and she bit it. I didn't know whether she was scared or annoyed or just having trouble being cool and business-like. But she didn't look happy.

'She got your name from the manager of a branch of the California-Security Bank. But he doesn't know you personally,' she said.

'Get your pencil ready,' I said.

She held it up and showed me that it was freshly sharpened and ready to go.

I said: 'First off, one of the vice-presidents of that same bank. George S. Leake. He's in the main office. Then State Senator Huston Oglethorpe. He may be in Sacramento, or he may be at his office in the State Building in Los Angeles. Then Sidney Dreyfuss, Jr, of Dreyfuss, Turner & Swayne, attorneys in the Title-Insurance Building. Got that?'

She wrote fast and easily. She nodded without looking up. The light danced on her blonde hair.

'Oliver Fry of the Fry-Kranz Corporation, Oil Well Tools. They're over on East Ninth, in the industrial district. Then, if you would like a couple of cops, Bernard Ohls of the D.A.'s staff, and Detective-Lieutenant Carl Randall of the Central Homicide Bureau. You think maybe that would be enough?'

'Don't laugh at me,' she said. 'I'm only doing what I'm told.'

'Better not call the last two, unless you know what the job is,' I said. 'I'm not laughing at you. Hot, isn't it?'

'It's not hot for Pasadena,' she said, and hoisted her phone book up on the desk and went to work.

While she was looking up the numbers and telephoning hither and yon I looked her over. She was pale with a sort of natural paleness and she looked healthy enough. Her coarse-grained coppery blonde hair was not ugly in itself, but it was drawn back so tightly over her narrow head that it almost lost the effect of being hair at all. Her eyebrows were thin and unusually straight and were darker than her hair, almost a chestnut colour. Her nostrils had the whitish look of an anaemic person. Her chin was too small, too sharp and looked unstable. She wore no make-up except orange-red on her mouth and not much of that. Her eyes behind the glasses were very large, cobalt blue with big irises and a vague expression. Both lids were tight so that the eyes had a slightly oriental look, or as if the skin of her face was naturally so tight that it stretched her eyes at the corners. The whole face had a sort of off-key neurotic charm that only needed some clever make-up to be striking.

She wore a one-piece linen dress with short sleeves and no ornament of any kind. Her bare arms had down on them, and a few freckles.

I didn't pay much attention to what she said over the telephone. Whatever was said to her she wrote down in shorthand, with deft easy strokes of the pencil. When she was through she hung the phone book back on a hook and stood up and smoothed the linen dress over her thighs and said:

'If you will just wait for a few moments—' and went towards the door.

Half-way there she turned back and pushed a top drawer of her desk shut at the side. She went out. The door closed. There was silence. Outside the window bees buzzed. Far off I heard the whine of a vacuum cleaner. I picked the unlighted cigarette off my hat, put it in my mouth and stood up. I went around the desk and pulled open the drawer she had come back to shut.

It wasn't any of my business. I was just curious. It wasn't any of my business that she had a small Colt automatic in the drawer. I shut it and sat down again.

She was gone about four minutes. She opened the door and stayed at it and said: 'Mrs Murdock will see you now.'

We went along some more hallway and she opened half of a double glass door and stood aside. I went in and the door was closed behind me.

It was so dark in there that at first I couldn't see anything but the outdoors light coming through thick bushes and screens. Then I saw that the room was a sort of sun porch that had been allowed to get completely overgrown outside. It was furnished with grass rugs and reed stuff. There was a reed chaise-longue over by the window. It had a curved back and enough cushions to stuff an elephant and there was a woman leaning back on it with a wine-glass in her hand. I could smell the thick scented alcoholic odour of the wine before I could see her properly. Then my eyes got used to the light and I could see her.

She had a lot of face and chin. She had pewter-coloured hair set in a ruthless permanent, a hard beak and large moist eyes with the sympathetic expression of wet stones. There was lace at her throat, but it was the kind of throat that would have looked better in a football sweater. She wore a greyish silk dress. Her thick arms were bare and mottled. There were jet buttons in her ears. There was a low glass-topped table beside her and a bottle of port on the table. She sipped from the glass she was holding and looked at me over it and said nothing.

I stood there. She let me stand while she finished the port in her glass and put the glass on the table and filled it again. Then she tapped her lips with a handkerchief. Then she spoke. Her voice had a hard baritone quality and sounded as if it didn't want any nonsense.

'Sit down, Mr Marlowe. Please do not light that cigarette. I'm asthmatic.'

I sat down in a reed rocker and tucked the still unlighted cigarette behind the handkerchief in my outside pocket.

'I've never had any dealing with private detectives, Mr Marlowe. I don't know anything about them. Your references seem satisfactory. What are your charges?'

'To do what, Mrs Murdock?'

'It's a very confidential matter, naturally. Nothing to do with the police. If it had to do with the police, I should have called the police.'

'I charge twenty-five dollars a day, Mrs Murdock. And, of course, expenses.'

'It seems high. You must make a great deal of money.' She drank some more of her port. I don't like port in hot weather, but it's nice when they let you refuse it.

'No,' I said. 'It isn't. Of course, you can get detective work done at any price—just like legal work. Or dental work. I'm not an organization. I'm just one man and I work at just one case at a time. I take risks, sometimes quite big risks, and I don't work all the time. No, I don't think twenty-five dollars a day is too much.'

'I see. And what is the nature of the expenses?'

'Little things that come up here and there. You never know.'

'I should prefer to know,' she said acidly.

'You'll know,' I said. 'You'll get it all down in black and white. You'll have a chance to object, if you don't like it.'

'And how much retainer would you expect?'

'A hundred dollars would hold me,' I said.

'I should hope it would,' she said, and finished her port and poured the glass full again without even waiting to wipe her lips.

'From people in your position, Mrs Murdock, I don't necessarily have to have a retainer.'

'Mr Marlowe,' she said, 'I'm a strong-minded woman. But don't let me scare you. Because if you can be scared by me, you won't be much use to me.'

I nodded and let that one drift with the tide.

She laughed suddenly and then she belched. It was a nice light belch, nothing showy, and performed with easy unconcern. 'My asthma,' she said carelessly. 'I drink this wine as medicine. That's why I'm not offering you any.'

I swung a leg over my knee. I hoped that wouldn't hurt her asthma.

'Money,' she said, 'is not really important. A woman in my position is always overcharged and gets to expect it. I hope you will be worth your fee. Here is the situation. Something of considerable value has been stolen from me. I want it back, but I want more than that. I don't want anybody arrested. The thief happens to be a member of my family–by marriage.'

She turned the wine-glass with her thick fingers and smiled faintly in the dim light of the shadowed room. 'My daughter-in-law,' she said. 'A charming girl–tough as an oak board.'

She looked at me with a sudden gleam in her eyes.

'I have a damn fool of a son,' she said. 'But I'm very fond of him. About a year ago he made an idiotic marriage, without my consent. This was foolish of him because he is quite incapable of earning a living and he has no money except what I give him, and I am not generous with money. The lady he chose, or who chose him, was a night-club singer. Her name, appropriately enough, was Linda Conquest. They have lived here in this house. We didn't quarrel because I don't allow people to quarrel with me in my own house, but there has not been good feeling between us. I have paid their expenses, given each of them a car, made the lady a sufficient but not gaudy allowance for clothes and so on. No doubt she found the life rather dull. No doubt she found my son dull. I find him dull myself. At any rate, she moved out, very abruptly, a week or so ago, without leaving a forwarding address or saying good-bye.'

She coughed, fumbled for a handkerchief, and blew her nose.

'What was taken,' she went on, 'was a coin. A rare gold coin called a Brasher Doubloon. It was the pride of my husband's collection. I care nothing for such things, but he did. I have kept the collection intact since he died four years ago. It is upstairs, in a locked fireproof room, in a set of fireproof cases. It is insured, but I have not reported the loss yet. I don't want to, if I can help it. I'm quite sure Linda took it. The coin is said to be worth over ten thousand dollars. It's a mint specimen.'

'But pretty hard to sell,' I said.

'Perhaps. I don't know. I didn't miss the coin until yesterday. I should not have missed it then, as I never go near the collection, except that a man

in Los Angeles named Morningstar, called up, said he was a dealer, and was
the Murdock Brasher, as he called it, for sale? My son happened to take the
call. He said he didn't believe it was for sale, it never had been, but that if
Mr Morningstar would call some other time, he could probably talk to me.
It was not convenient then, as I was resting. The man said he would do that.
My son reported the conversation to Miss Davis, who reported it to me. I
had her call the man back. I was faintly curious.'

She sipped some more port, flopped her handkerchief about and grunted.

'Why were you curious, Mrs Murdock?' I asked, just to be saying
something.

'If the man was a dealer of any repute, he would know that the coin was
not for sale. My husband, Jasper Murdock, provided in his will that no part
of his collection might be sold, loaned or hypothecated during my lifetime.
Nor removed from this house, except in case of damage to the house
necessitating removal, and then only by action of the trustees. My
husband'—she smiled grimly—'seemed to feel that I ought to have taken
more interest in his little pieces of metal while he was alive.'

It was a nice day outside, the sun shining, the flowers blooming, the birds
singing. Cars went by on the street with a distant comfortable sound. In the
dim room with the hard-faced woman and the winy smell everything
seemed a little unreal. I tossed my foot up and down over my knee and
waited.

'I spoke to Mr Morningstar. His full name is Elisha Morningstar and he
has offices in the Belfont Building on Ninth Street in downtown Los
Angeles. I told him the Murdock collection was not for sale, never had
been, and, so far as I was concerned, never would be, and that I was
surprised that he didn't know that. He hemmed and hawed and then asked
me if he might examine the coin. I said certainly not. He thanked me rather
dryly and hung up. He sounded like an old man. So I went upstairs to
examine the coin myself, something I had not done in a year. It was gone
from its place in one of the locked fireproof cases.'

I said nothing. She refilled her glass and played a tattoo with her thick
fingers on the arm of the chaise-longue. 'What I thought then you can
probably guess.'

I said: 'The part about Mr Morningstar, maybe. Somebody had offered
the coin to him for sale and he had known or suspected where it came from.
The coin must be very rare.'

'What they call a mint specimen is very rare indeed. Yes, I had the same
idea.'

'How would it be stolen?' I asked.

'By anyone in this house, very easily. The keys are in my bag, and my bag
lies around here and there. It would be a very simple matter to get hold of
the keys. Difficult for an outsider, but anybody in the house could have
stolen it.'

'I see. How do you establish that your daughter-in-law took it, Mrs
Murdock?'

'I don't—in a strictly evidential sense. But I'm quite sure of it. The
servants are three women who have been here many, many years—long
before I married Mr Murdock, which was only seven years ago. The
gardener never comes in the house. I have no chauffeur, because either my
son or my secretary drives me. My son didn't take it, first because he is not

the kind of fool that steals from his mother, and second, if he had taken it, he could easily have prevented me from speaking to the coin dealer, Morningstar. Miss Davis—ridiculous. Just not the type at all. Too mousy. No, Mr Marlowe, Linda is the sort of lady who might do it just for spite, if nothing else. And you know what these night-club people are.'

'All sorts of people—like the rest of us,' I said. 'No signs of a burglar, I suppose? It would take a pretty smooth worker to lift just one valuable coin, so there wouldn't be. Maybe I had better look the room over, though.'

She pushed her jaw at me and muscles in her neck made hard lumps. 'I have just told you, Mr Marlowe, that Mrs Leslie Murdock, my daughter-in-law, took the Brasher Doubloon.'

I stared at her and she stared back. Her eyes were as hard as the bricks in her front walk. I shrugged the stare off and said:

'Assuming that is so, Mrs Murdock, just what do you want done?'

'In the first place I want the coin back. In the second place I want an uncontested divorce for my son. And I don't intend to buy it. I dare say you know how these things are arranged.'

She finished the current instalment of port and laughed rudely.

'I may have heard,' I said. 'You say the lady left no forwarding address. Does that mean you have no idea at all where she went?'

'Exactly that.'

'A disappearance then. Your son might have some ideas he hasn't passed along to you. I'll have to see him.'

The big grey face hardened into even more rugged lines. 'My son knows nothing. He doesn't even know the doubloon has been stolen. I don't want him to know anything. When the time comes I'll handle him. Until then I want him left alone. He will do exactly what I want him to.'

'He hasn't always,' I said.

'His marriage,' she said nastily, 'was a momentary impulse. Afterwards he tried to act like a gentleman. I have no such scruples.'

'It takes three days to have that kind of momentary impulse in California, Mrs Murdock.'

'Young man, do you want this job or don't you?'

'I want it if I'm told the facts and allowed to handle the case as I see fit. I don't want it if you're going to make a lot of rules and regulations for me to trip over.'

She laughed harshly. 'This is a delicate family matter, Mr Marlowe. And it must be handled with delicacy.'

'If you hire me, you'll get all the delicacy I have. If I don't have enough delicacy, maybe you'd better not hire me. For instance, I take it you don't want your daughter-in-law framed. I'm not delicate enough for that.'

She turned the colour of a cold boiled beet and opened her mouth to yell. Then she thought better of it, lifted her port glass and tucked away some more of her medicine.

'You'll do,' she said dryly, 'I wish I had met you two years ago, before he married her.'

I didn't know exactly what this last meant, so I let it ride. She bent over sideways and fumbled with the key on a house telephone and growled into it when she was answered.

There were steps and the little copper-blonde came tripping into the room with her chin low, as if somebody might be going to take a swing at her.

'Make this man a cheque for two hundred and fifty dollars,' the old dragon snarled at her. 'And keep your mouth shut about it.

The girl flushed all the way to her neck. 'You know I never talk about your affairs, Mrs Murdock,' she bleated. 'You know I don't. I wouldn't dream of it, I—'

She turned with her head down and ran out of the room. As she closed the door I looked out at her. Her little lip was trembling but her eyes were mad.

'I'll need a photo of the lady and some information,' I said when the door was shut again.

'Look in the desk drawer.' Her rings flashed in the dimness as her thick grey finger pointed.

I went over and opened the single drawer of the reed desk and took out the photo that lay all alone in the bottom of the drawer, face up, looking at me with cool dark eyes. I sat down again with the photo and looked it over. Dark hair parted loosely in the middle and drawn back loosely over a solid piece of forehead. A wide cool go-to-hell mouth with very kissable lips. Nice nose, not too small, not too large. Good bone all over the face. The expression of the face lacked something. Once the something might have been called breeding, but these days I didn't know what to call it. The face looked too wise and too guarded for its age. Too many passes had been made at it and it had grown a little too smart in dodging them. And behind this expression of wiseness there was the look of simplicity of the little girl who still believes in Santa Claus.

I nodded over the photo and slipped it into my pocket, thinking I was getting too much out of it to get out of a mere photo, and in a very poor light at that.

The door opened and the little girl in the linen dress came in with a three-decker cheque book and a fountain-pen and made a desk of her arm for Mrs Murdock to sign. She straightened up with a smile and Mrs Murdock made a sharp gesture towards me and the little girl tore the cheque out and gave it to me. She hovered inside the door waiting. Nothing was said to her, so she went out softly again and closed the door.

I shook the cheque dry, folded it and sat holding it. 'What can you tell me about Linda?'

'Practically nothing. Before she married my son she shared an apartment with a girl name Lois Magic—charming names these people choose for themselves—who is an entertainer of some sort. They worked at a place called the Idle Valley Club, out Ventura Boulevard way. My son Leslie knows it far too well. I know nothing about Linda's family or origins. She said once she was born in Sioux Falls. I suppose she had parents. I was not interested enough to find out.'

Like hell she wasn't. I could see her digging with both hands, digging hard, and getting herself a double handful of gravel.

'You don't know Miss Magic's address?'

'No. I never did know.'

'Would your son be likely to know—or Miss Davis?'

'I'll ask my son when he comes in. I don't think so. You can ask Miss Davis. I'm sure she doesn't.'

'I see. You don't know of any other friends of Linda's?'

'No.'

'It's possible that your son is still in touch with her, Mrs Murdock—without telling you.'

She started to get purple again. I held my hand up and dragged a soothing smile over my face. 'After all he has been married to her a year,' I said. 'He must know something about her.'

'You leave my son out of this,' she snarled.

I shrugged and made a disappointed sound with my lips. 'Very well. She took her car, I suppose. The one you gave her?'

'A steel-grey Mercury, 1940 model, a coupé. Miss Davis can give you the licence number, if you want that. I don't know whether she took it.'

'Would you know what money and clothes and jewels she had with her?'

'Not much money. She might have had a couple of hundred dollars, at most.' A fat sneer made deep lines around her nose and mouth. 'Unless, of course, she has found a new friend.'

'There's that,' I said. 'Jewellery?'

'An emerald and diamond ring of no very great value, a platinum Longines watch with rubies in the mounting, a very good cloudy amber necklace which I was foolish enough to give her myself. It has a diamond clasp with twenty-six small diamonds in the shape of a playing-card diamond. She had other things, of course. I never paid much attention to them. She dressed well but not strikingly. Thank God for a few small mercies.'

She refilled her glass and drank and did some more of her semi-social belching.

'That's all you can tell me, Mrs Murdock?'

'Isn't it enough?'

'Not nearly enough, but I'll have to be satisfied for the time being. If I find she did not steal the coin, that ends the investigation as far as I'm concerned. Correct?'

'We'll talk it over,' she said roughly. 'She stole it all right. And I don't intend to let her get away with it. Paste that in your hat, young man. And I hope you are even half as rough as you like to act, because these night-club girls are apt to have some very nasty friends.'

I was still holding the folded cheque by one corner down between my knees. I got my wallet out and put it away and stood up, reaching my hat off the floor.

'I like them nasty,' I said. 'The nasty ones have very simple minds. I'll report to you when there is anything to report, Mrs Murdock. I think I'll tackle this coin dealer first. He sounds like a lead.'

She let me get to the door before she growled at my back: 'You don't like me very well, do you?'

I turned to grin back at her with my hand on the knob. 'Does anybody?'

She threw her head back and opened her mouth wide and roared with laughter. In the middle of the laughter I opened the door and went out and shut the door on the rough mannish sound. I went back along the hall and knocked on the secretary's half-open door, then pushed it open and looked in.

She had her arms folded on her desk and her face down on the folded arms. She was sobbing. She screwed her head around and looked up at me with tear-stained eyes. I shut the door and went over beside her and put an arm around her thin shoulders.

'Cheer up,' I said. 'You ought to feel sorry for her. She thinks she's tough and she's breaking her back trying to live up to it.'

The little girl jumped erect, away from my arm. 'Don't touch me,' she said breathlessly. 'Please. I never let men touch me. And don't say such awful things about Mrs Murdock.'

Her face was all pink and wet with tears. Without her glasses her eyes were very lovely.

I stuck my long-waiting cigarette into my mouth and lit it.

'I–I didn't mean to be rude,' she snuffled. 'But she does humiliate me so. And I only want to do my best for her.' She snuffled some more and got a man's handkerchief out of her desk and shook it out and wiped her eyes with it. I saw on the hanging-down corner the initials L.M. embroidered in purple. I stared at it and blew cigarette smoke towards the corner of the room, away from her hair. 'Is there something you want?' she asked.

'I want the licence number of Mrs Leslie Murdock's car.'

'It's 2X1111, a grey Mercury convertible, 1940 model.'

'She told me it was a coupé.'

'That's Mr Leslie's car. They're the same make and year and colour. Linda didn't take the car.'

'Oh. What do you know about a Miss Lois Magic?'

'I only saw her once. She used to share an apartment with Linda. She came here with a Mr–a Mr Vannier.'

'Who's he?'

She looked down at her desk. 'I–she just came with him. I don't know him.'

'Okay, what does Miss Lois Magic look like?'

'She's a tall, handsome blonde. Very–very appealing.'

'You mean sexy?'

'Well—' she blushed furiously, 'in a nice well-bred sort of way, if you know what I mean.'

'I know what you mean,' I said, 'but I never got anywhere with it.'

'I can believe that,' she said tartly.

'Know where Miss Magic lives?'

She shook her head, no. She folded the big handkerchief very carefully and put it in the drawer of her desk, the one where the gun was.

'You can swipe another one when that's dirty,' I said.

She leaned back in her chair and put her small neat hands on her desk and looked at me levelly.

'I wouldn't carry that tough-guy manner too far, if I were you, Mr Marlowe. Not with me, at any rate.'

'No?'

'No. And I can't answer any more questions without specific instructions. My position here is very confidential.'

'I'm not tough,' I said. 'Just virile.'

She picked up a pencil and made a mark on a pad. She smiled faintly up at me, all composure again.

'Perhaps I don't like virile men,' she said.

'You're a screwball,' I said, 'if ever I met one. Good-bye.'

I went out of her office, shut the door firmly, and walked back along the empty halls through the big silent sunken funereal living-room and out of the front door.

The sun danced on the warm lawn outside. I put my dark glasses on and went over and patted the little Negro on the head again.

'Brother, it's even worse than I expected,' I told him.

The stumble stones were hot through the soles of my shoes. I got into the car and started it and pulled away from the kerb.

A very small sand-coloured coupé pulled away from the kerb behind me. I didn't think anything of it. The man driving it wore a dark porkpie type straw hat with a gay print band and dark glasses were over his eyes, as over mine.

I drove back towards the city. A dozen blocks later, at a traffic stop, the sand-coloured coupé was still behind me. I shrugged and just for the fun of it circled a few blocks. The coupé held its position. I swung into a street lined with immense pepper trees, dragged my car around in a fast U-turn and stopped against the kerbing.

The coupé came carefully around the corner. The blond head under the cocoa straw hat with the tropical print band didn't even turn my way. The coupé sailed on and I drove back to the Arroyo Seco and on towards Hollywood. I looked carefully several times, but I didn't spot the coupé again.

3

I had an office in the Cahuenga Building, sixth floor, two small rooms at the back. One I left open for a patient client to sit in, if I had a patient client. There was a buzzer on the door which I could switch on and off from my private thinking parlour.

I looked into the reception-room. It was empty of everything but the smell of dust. I threw up another window, unlocked the communicating door and went into the room beyond. Three hard chairs and a swivel chair, flat desk with a glass top, five green filing-cases, three of them full of nothing, a calendar and a framed licence bond on the wall, a phone, a washbowl in a stained wood cupboard, a hat-rack, a carpet that was just something on the floor, and two open windows with net curtains that puckered in and out like the lips of a toothless old man sleeping.

The same stuff I had had last year, and the year before that. Not beautiful, not gay, but better than a tent on the beach.

I hung my hat and coat on the hat-rack, washed my face and hands in cold water, lit a cigarette and hoisted the phone book on to the desk. Elisha Morningstar was listed at 824 Belfont Building, 422 West Ninth Street. I wrote that down and the phone number that went with it and had my hand on the instrument when I remembered that I hadn't switched on the buzzer of the reception room. I reached over the side of the desk and clicked it on and caught it right in stride. Somebody had just opened the door of the outer office.

I turned my pad face down on the desk and went over to see who it was. It was a slim tall self-satisfied looking number in a tropical worsted suit of slate-blue, black and white shoes, a dull ivory-coloured shirt and a tie and display handkerchief the colour of jacaranda bloom. He was holding a long black cigarette-holder in a peeled back white pigskin glove and he was wrinkling his nose at the dead magazines on the library table and the chairs and the rusty floor covering and the general air of not much money being made.

As I opened the communicating door he made a quarter turn and stared at me out of a pair of rather dreamy pale eyes set close to a narrow nose. His skin was sun-flushed, his reddish hair was brushed back hard over a narrow skull, and the thin line of his moustache was much redder than his hair.

He looked me over without haste and without much pleasure. He blew some smoke delicately and spoke through it with a faint sneer.

'You're Marlowe?'

I nodded.

'I'm a little disappointed,' he said. 'I rather expected something with dirty fingernails.'

'Come inside,' I said, 'and you can be witty sitting down.'

I held the door for him and he strolled past me flicking cigarette-ash on the floor with the middle nail of his free hand. He sat down on the customer's side of the desk, took off the glove from his right hand and folded this with the other already off and laid them on the desk. He tapped the cigarette-end out of the long black holder, prodded the ash with a match until it stopped smoking, fitted another cigarette and lit it with a broad mahogany-coloured match. He leaned back in his chair with a smile of a bored aristocrat.

'All set?' I inquired. 'Pulse and respiration normal? You wouldn't like a cold towel on your head or anything?'

He didn't curl his lip because it had been curled when he came in. 'A private detective,' he said. 'I never met one. A shifty business, one gathers. Keyhole peeping, raking up scandal, that sort of thing.'

'You here on business,' I asked him, 'or just slumming?'

His smile was as faint as a fat lady at a firemen's ball.

'The name is Murdock. That probably means a little something to you.'

'You certainly made nice time over here,' I said, and started to fill a pipe.

He watched me fill the pipe. He said slowly: 'I understand my mother has employed you on a job of some sort. She has given you a cheque.'

I finished filling the pipe, put a match to it, got it drawing and leaned back to blow smoke over my right shoulder towards the open window. I didn't say anything.

He leaned forward a little more and said earnestly: 'I know being cagey is all part of your trade, but I am not guessing. A little worm told me, a simple garden worm, often trodden on, but still somehow surviving—like myself. I happened to be not far behind you. Does that help to clear things up?'

'Yeah,' I said. 'Supposing it made any difference to me.'

'You are hired to find my wife, I gather.'

I made a snorting sound and grinned at him over the pipe bowl.

'Marlowe,' he said, even more earnestly, 'I'll try hard, but I don't think I am going to like you.'

'I'm screaming,' I said. 'With rage and pain.'

'And if you will pardon a homely phrase, your tough guy act stinks.'

'Coming from you, that's bitter.'

He leaned back again and brooded at me with pale eyes. He fussed around in the chair, trying to get comfortable. A lot of people had tried to get comfortable in that chair. I ought to try it myself sometime. Maybe it was losing business for me.

'Why should my mother want Linda found?' he asked slowly. 'She hated her guts. I mean my mother hated Linda's guts. Linda was quite decent to my mother. What do you think of her?'

'Your mother?'

'Of course. You haven't met Linda, have you?'

'That secretary of your mother's has her job hanging by a frayed thread. She talks out of turn.'

He shook his head sharply. 'Mother won't know. Anyhow, Mother couldn't do without Merle. She has to have somebody to bully. She might yell at her or even slap her face, but she couldn't do without her. What did you think of her?'

'Kind of cute–in an old-world sort of way.'

He frowned. 'I mean Mother. Merle's just a simple little girl, I know.'

'Your powers of observation startle me,' I said.

He looked surprised. He almost forgot to fingernail the ash of his cigarette. But not quite. He was careful not to get any of it in the ashtray, however.

'About my mother,' he said impatiently.

'A grand old war-horse,' I said. 'A heart of gold and the gold buried good and deep.'

'But why does she want Linda found? I can't understand it. Spending money on it, too. My mother hates to spend money. She thinks money is part of her skin. Why does she want Linda found?'

'Search me,' I said. 'Who said she did?'

'Why, you implied so. And Merle—'

'Merle's just romantic. She made it up. Hell, she blows her nose in a man's handkerchief. Probably one of yours.'

He blushed. 'That's silly. Look, Marlowe. Please, be reasonable and give me an idea what it's all about. I haven't much money, I'm afraid, but would a couple of hundred—'

'I ought to bop you,' I said. 'Besides, I'm not supposed to talk to you. Orders.'

'Why, for heaven's sake?'

'Don't ask me things I don't know. I can't tell you the answers. And don't ask me things I do know, because I won't tell you the answers. Where have you been all your life? If a man in my line of work is handed a job, does he go around answering questions about it to anyone that gets curious?'

'There must be a lot of electricity in the air,' he said nastily, 'for a man in your line of work to turn down two hundred dollars.'

There was nothing in that for me, either. I picked his broad mahogany match out of the tray and looked at it. It had thin yellow edges and there was white printing on it. ROSEMONT. H. RICHARDS '3–the rest was burnt off. I doubled the match and squeezed the halves together and tossed it in the waste basket.

'I love my wife,' he said suddenly, and showed me the hard white edges of his teeth. 'A corny touch, but it's true.'

'The Lombardos are still doing all right.'

He kept his lips pulled back from his teeth and talked through them at me. 'She doesn't love me. I know of no particular reason why she should. Things have been strained between us. She was used to a fast-moving sort of life. With us, well, it has been pretty dull. We haven't quarrelled. Linda's the cool type. But she hasn't really had a lot of fun being married to me.'

'You're just too modest,' I said.

His eyes glinted, but he kept his smooth manner pretty well in place.

'Not good, Marlowe. Not even fresh. Look, you have the air of a decent sort of guy. I know my mother is not putting out two hundred and fifty bucks just to be breezy. Maybe it's not Linda. Maybe it's something else. Maybe—' he stopped and then said this very slowly, watching my eyes, 'maybe it's Morny.'

'Maybe it is,' I said cheerfully.

He picked his gloves up and slapped the desk with them and put them down again. 'I'm in a spot there all right,' he said. 'But I didn't think she knew about it. Morny must have called her up. He promised not to.'

This was easy. I said: 'How much are you into him for?'

It wasn't so easy. He got suspicious again. 'If he called her up, he would have told her. And she would have told you,' he said thinly.

'Maybe it isn't Morny,' I said, beginning to want to drink very badly. 'Maybe the cook is with child by the iceman. But if it was Morny, how much?'

'Twelve thousand,' he said, looking down and flushing.

'Threats?'

He nodded.

'Tell him to go fly a kite,' I said. 'What kind of lad is he? Tough?'

He looked up again, his face being brave. 'I suppose he is. I suppose they all are. He used to be a screen heavy. Good-looking in a flashy way, a chaser. But don't get any ideas. Linda just worked there, like the waiters and the band. And if you are looking for her, you'll have a hard time finding her.'

I sneered at him politely.

'Why would I have a hard time finding her? She's not buried in the backyard, I hope.'

He stood up with a flash of anger in his pale eyes. Standing there leaning over the desk a little he whipped his right hand up in a neat enough gesture and brought out a small automatic, about .25 calibre, with a walnut grip. It looked like the brother of the one I had seen in the drawer of Merle's desk. The muzzle looked vicious enough pointing at me. I didn't move.

'If anybody tries to push Linda around, he'll have to push me around first,' he said tightly.

'That oughtn't to be too hard. Better get more gun—unless you're just thinking of bees.'

He put the little gun back in his inside-pocket. He gave me a straight hard look and picked his gloves up and started for the door.

'It's a waste of time talking to you,' he said. 'All you do is wisecrack.'

I said: 'Wait a minute,' and got up and went around the desk. 'It might be a good idea for you not to mention this interview to your mother, if only for the little girl's sake.'

He nodded. 'For the amount of information I got, it doesn't seem worth mentioning.'

'That straight goods about your owing Morny twelve grand?'

He looked down, then up, and then down again. He said: 'Anybody who could get into Alex Morny for twelve grand would have to be a lot smarter than I am.'

I was quite close to him. I said: 'As a matter of fact, I don't even think you are worried about your wife. I think you know where she is. She didn't run away from you at all. She just ran away from your mother.'

He lifted his eyes and drew one glove on. He didn't say anything.

'Perhaps she'll get a job,' I said. 'And make enough money to support you.'

He looked down at the floor again, turned his body to the right a little and the gloved fist made a tight unrelaxed arc through the air upwards. I moved my jaw out of the way and caught his wrist and pushed it slowly back against his chest, leaning on it. He slid a foot back on the floor and began to breathe hard. It was a slender wrist. My fingers went around it and met.

We stood there looking into each other's eyes. He was breathing like a drunk, his mouth open and his lips pulled back. Small round spots of bright red flamed on his cheeks. He tried to jerk his wrist away, but I put so much weight on him that he had to take another short step back to brace himself. Our faces were now only inches apart.

'How come your old man didn't leave you some money?' I sneered. 'Or did you blow it all?'

He spoke between his teeth, still trying to jerk loose. 'If it's any of your rotten business and you mean Jasper Murdock, he wasn't my father. He didn't like me and he didn't leave me a cent. My father was a man named Horace Bright who lost his money in the crash and jumped out of his office window.'

'You milk easy,' I said, 'but you give pretty thin milk. I'm sorry for what I said about your wife supporting you. I just wanted to get your goat.'

I dropped his wrist and stepped back. He still breathed hard and heavily. His eyes on mine were angry, but he kept his voice down.

'Well, you got it. If you're satisfied, I'll be on my way.'

'I was doing you a favour,' I said. 'A gun toter oughtn't to insult so easily. Better ditch it.'

'That's my business,' he said. 'I'm sorry I took a swing at you. It probably wouldn't have hurt much, if it had connected.'

'That's all right.'

He opened the door and went on out. His steps died along the corridor. Another screwball. I tapped my teeth with a knuckle in time to the sound of his steps as long as I could hear them. Then I went back to the desk, looked at my pad, and lifted the phone.

4

After the bell had rung three times at the other end of the line a light childish sort of girl's voice filtered itself through a bank of gum and said: 'Good morning. Mr Morningstar's office.'

'Is the old gentleman in?'

'Who is calling, please?'

'Marlowe.'

'Does he know you, Mr Marlowe?'

'Ask him if he wants to buy any early American gold coins.'

'Just a minute, please.'

There was a pause suitable to an elderly party in an inner office having his attention called to the fact that somebody on the telephone wanted to talk to him. Then the phone clicked and a man spoke. He had a dry voice. You might even call it parched.

'This is Mr Morningstar.'

'I'm told you called Mrs Murdock in Pasadena, Mr Morningstar. About a certain coin.'

'About a certain coin,' he repeated. 'Indeed. Well?'

'My understanding is that you wished to buy the coin in question from the Murdock collection.'

'Indeed? And who are you, sir?'

'Philip Marlowe. A private detective. I'm working for Mrs Murdock.'

'Indeed,' he said for the third time. He cleared his throat carefully. 'And what did you wish to talk to me about, Mr Marlowe?'

'About this coin.'

'But I was informed it was not for sale.'

'I still want to talk to you about it. In person.'

'Do you mean she has changed her mind about selling?'

'No.'

'Then I'm afraid I don't understand what you want, Mr Marlowe. What have we to talk about?' He sounded sly now.

I took the ace out of my sleeve and played it with a languid grace. 'The point is, Mr Morningstar, that at the time you called up you already knew the coin wasn't for sale.'

'Interesting,' he said slowly. 'How?'

'You're in the business, you couldn't help knowing. It's a matter of public record that the Murdock collection cannot be sold during Mrs Murdock's lifetime.'

'Ah,' he said. 'Ah.' There was a silence. Then, 'At three o'clock,' he said, not sharp, but quick. 'I shall be glad to see you here in my office. You probably know where it is. Will that suit you?'

'I'll be there,' I said.

I hung up and lit my pipe again and sat there looking at the wall. My face was stiff with thoughts, or with something that made my face stiff. I took Linda Murdock's photo out of my pocket, stared at it for a while, decided that the face was pretty commonplace after all, locked the photo away in my desk. I picked Murdock's second match out of my ashtray and looked it over. The lettering on this one read: Top Row W.D. Wright '36.

I dropped it back in the tray, wondering what made this important. Maybe it was a clue.

I got Mrs Murdock's cheque out of my wallet, endorsed it, made out a deposit slip and a cheque for cash, got my bankbook out of the desk, and folded the lot under a rubber band and put them in my pocket.

Lois Magic was not listed in the phone book.

I got the classified section up on the desk and made a list of the half-dozen theatrical agencies that showed in the largest type and called them. They all had bright cheerful voices and wanted to ask a lot of questions, but they either didn't know or didn't care to tell anything about a Miss Lois Magic, said to be an entertainer.

I threw the list in the waste-basket and called Kenny Haste, a crime reporter on the *Chronicle*.

'What do you know about Alex Morny?' I asked him when we were through wisecracking at each other.

'Runs a plushy night-club and gambling joint in Idle Valley, about two miles off the highway back towards the hills. Used to be in pictures. Lousy actor. Seems to have plenty of protection. I never heard of him shooting anybody on the public square at high noon. Or at any other time for that matter. But I wouldn't like to bet on it.'

'Dangerous?'

'I'd say he might be, if necessary. All those boys have been to picture shows and know how night-club bosses are supposed to act. He has a bodyguard who is quite a character. His name's Eddie Prue, he's about six feet five inches tall and thin as an honest alibi. He has a frozen eye, the result of a war wound.'

'Is Morny dangerous to women?'

'Don't be Victorian, old top. Women don't call it danger.'

'Do you know a girl named Lois Magic, said to be an entertainer. A tall gaudy blonde, I hear.'

'No. Sounds as though I might like to.'

'Don't be cute. Do you know anybody named Vannier? None of these people are in the phone book.'

'Nope. But I could ask Gertie Arbogast, if you want to call back. He knows all the night-club aristocrats. And heels.'

'Thanks, Kenny. I'll do that. Half an hour?'

He said that would be fine, and we hung up. I locked the office and left.

At the end of the corridor, in the angle of the wall, a youngish blond man in a brown suit and a cocoa-coloured straw hat with a brown and yellow tropical print band was reading the evening paper with his back to the wall. As I passed him he yawned and tucked the paper under his arm and straightened up.

He got into the elevator with me. He could hardly keep his eyes open he was so tired. I went out on the street and walked a block to the bank to deposit my cheque and draw out a little folding money for expenses. From there I went to the Tigertail Lounge and sat in a shallow booth and drank a martini and ate a sandwich. The man in the brown suit posted himself at the end of the bar and drank Coca-Colas and looked bored and piled pennies in front of him, carefully smoothing the edges. He had his dark glasses on again. That made him invisible.

I dragged my sandwich out as long as I could and then strolled back to the telephone booth at the inner end of the bar. The man in the brown suit turned his head quickly and then covered the motion by lifting his glass. I dialled the *Chronicle* office again.

'Okay,' Kenny Haste said. 'Gertie Arbogast says Morny married your gaudy blonde not very long ago. Lois Magic. He doesn't know Vannier. He says Morny bought a place out beyond Bel-Air, a white house on Stillwood Crescent Drive, about five blocks north of Sunset. Gertie says Morny took it over from a busted flush named Arthur Blake Popham who got caught in a mail fraud rap. Popham's initials are still on the gates. And probably on the toilet paper, Gertie says. He was that kind of a guy. That's all we seem to know.'

'Nobody could ask more. Many thanks, Kenny.'

I hung up, stepped out of the booth, met the dark glasses above the brown suit under the cocoa straw hat and watched them turn quickly away.

I spun around and went back through a swing door into the kitchen and through that to the alley and along the alley a quarter block to the parking lot where I had put my car.

No sand-coloured coupé succeeded in getting behind me as I drove off, in the general direction of Bel-Air.

5

Stillwood Crescent Drive curved leisurely north from Sunset Boulevard, well beyond the Bel-Air Country Club golf-course. The road was lined with walled and fenced estates. Some had high walls, some had low walls, some had ornamental iron fences, some were a bit old-fashioned and got along with tall hedges. The street had no sidewalk. Nobody walked in that neighbourhood, not even the postman.

The afternoon was hot, but not like Pasadena. There was a drowsy smell of flowers and sun, a swishing of lawn sprinklers gentle behind hedges and walls, the clear ratchety sound of lawnmowers moving delicately over serene and confident lawns.

I drove up the hill slowly, looking for monograms on gates. Arthur Blake Popham was the name. A.B.P. would be the initials. I found them almost at the top, gilt on a black shield, the gates folded back on a black composition driveway.

It was a glaring white house that had the air of being brand new, but the landscaping was well advanced. It was modest enough for the neighbourhood, not more than fourteen rooms and probably only one swimming pool. Its wall was low, made of brick with the concrete all oozed out between and set that way and painted over white. On top of the wall a low iron railing painted black. The name A.P.Morny was stencilled on the large silver-coloured postbox at the service entrance.

I parked my car on the street and walked up the black driveway to a side door of glittering white shot with patches of colour from the stained-glass canopy over it. I hammered on a large brass knocker. Back along the side of the house a chauffeur was washing off a Cadillac.

The door opened and a hard-eyed Filipino in a white coat curled his lip at me. I gave him a card.

'Mrs Morny,' I said.

He shut the door. Time passed, as it always does when I go calling. The swish of water on the Cadillac had a cool sound. The chauffeur was a little runt in breeches and leggings and a sweat-stained shirt. He looked like an overgrown jockey and he made the same kind of hissing noise as he worked on the car that a groom makes rubbing down a horse.

A red-throated humming-bird went into a scarlet bush beside the door, shook the long tubular blooms around a little, and zoomed off so fast he simply disappeared in the air.

The door opened, the Filipino poked my card at me. I didn't take it.

'What you want?'

It was a tight crackling voice, like someone tiptoeing across a lot of eggshells.

'Want to see Mrs Morny.'

'She's not at home.'

'Didn't you know that when I gave you the card?'

He opened his fingers and let the card flutter to the ground. He grinned, showing me a lot of cut-rate dental work.

'I know when she tell me.'

He shut the door in my face, not gently.

I picked the card up and walked along the side of the house to where the chauffeur was squirting water on the Cadillac sedan and rubbing the dirt off with a big sponge. He had red-rimmed eyes and a bang of corn-coloured hair. A cigarette hung exhausted at the corner of his lower lip.

He gave me the quick side glance of a man who is minding his own business with difficulty, I said:

'Where's the boss?'

The cigarette jiggled in his mouth. The water went on swishing gently on the paint.

'Ask at the house, Jack.'

'I done asked. They done shut the door in mah face.'

'You're breaking my heart, Jack.'

'How about Mrs Morny?'

'Same answer, Jack. I just work here. Selling something?'

I held my card so that he could read it. It was a business card this time. He put the sponge down on the running-board, and the hose on the cement. He stepped around the water to wipe his hands on a towel that hung at the side of the garage doors. He fished a match out of his pants, struck it and tilted his head back to light the dead butt that was stuck in his face.

His foxy little eyes flicked around this way and that and he moved behind the car, with a jerk of the head. I went over near him.

'How's the little old expense account?' he asked in a small careful voice.

'Fat with inactivity.'

'For five I could start thinking.'

'I wouldn't want to make it that tough for you.'

'For ten I could sing like four canaries and a steel guitar.'

'I don't like these plushy orchestrations,' I said.

He cocked his head sideways. 'Talk English, Jack.'

'I don't want you to lose your job, son. All I want to know is whether Mrs Morny is home. Does that rate more than a buck?'

'Don't worry about my job, Jack. I'm solid.'

'With Morny—or somebody else?'

'You want that for the same buck?'

'Two bucks.'

He eyed me over. 'You ain't working for him, are you?'

'Sure.'

'You're a liar.'

'Sure.'

'Gimme the two bucks,' he snapped.

I gave him two dollars.

'She's in the backyard with a friend,' he said. 'A nice friend. You got a friend that don't work and a husband that works, you're all set, see?' He leered.

'You'll be all set in an irrigation ditch one of these days.'

'Not me, Jack. I'm wise. I know how to play 'em. I monkeyed around these kind of people all my life.'

He rubbed the two dollar bills between his palms, blew on them, folded them longways and wideways and tucked them in the watch pocket of his breeches.

'That was just the soup,' he said. 'Now for five more—'

A rather large blond cocker spaniel tore around the Cadillac, skidded a little on the wet concrete, took off neatly, hit me in the stomach and thighs with all four paws, licked my face, dropped to the ground, ran around my legs, sat down between them, let his tongue out all the way and started to pant.

I stepped over him and braced myself against the side of the car and got my handkerchief out.

A male voice called: 'Here, Heathcliff. Here, Heathcliff.' Steps sounded on a hard walk.

'That's Heathcliff?' the chauffeur said sourly.

'Heathcliff?'

'Cripes, that's what they call the dog, Jack.'

'*Wuthering Heights*?' I asked.

'Now you're double-talking again,' he sneered. 'Look out–company.'

He picked up the sponge and the hose and went back to washing the car. I moved away from him. The cocker spaniel immediately moved between my legs again, almost tripping me.

'Here, Heathcliff,' the male voice called out louder, and a man came into view through the opening of a latticed tunnel covered with climbing roses.

Tall, dark, with a clear olive skin, brilliant black eyes, gleaming white teeth. Sideburns. A narrow black moustache. Sideburns too long, much too long. White shirt with embroidered initials on the pocket, white slacks, white shoes. A wrist-watch that curved half-way around a lean dark wrist, held on by a gold chain. A yellow scarf around a bronzed slender neck.

He saw the dog squatted beneath my legs and didn't like it. He snapped long fingers and snapped a clear hard voice:

'Here, Heathcliff. Come here at once!'

The dog breathed hard and didn't move, except to lean a little closer to my right leg.

'Who are you?' the man asked, staring me down.

I held out my card. Olive fingers took the card. The dog quietly backed out from between my legs, edged around the front of the car, and faded silently into the distance.

'Marlowe,' the man said. 'Marlowe, eh? What's this? A detective? What do you want?'

'Want to see Mrs Morny.'

He looked me up and down, brilliant black eyes sweeping slowly and the silky fringes of long eyelashes following them.

'Weren't you told she was not in?'

'Yeah, but I didn't believe it. Are you Mr Morny?'

'No.'

'That's Mr Vannier,' the chauffeur said behind my back, in the drawled, over-polite voice of deliberate insolence. 'Mr Vannier's a friend of the family. He comes here quite a lot.'

Vannier looked past my shoulder, his eyes furious. The chauffeur came around the car and spat the cigarette-stub out of his mouth with casual contempt.

'I told the shamus the boss wasn't here, Mr Vannier.'

'I see.'

'I told him Mrs Morny and you was here. Did I do wrong?'

Vannier said: 'You could have minded your own business.'

The chauffeur said: 'I wonder why the hell I didn't think of that.'

Vannier said: 'Get out before I break your dirty little neck for you.'

The chauffeur eyed him quietly and then went back into the gloom of the garage and started to whistle. Vannier moved his hot angry eyes over to me and snapped:

'You were told Mrs Morny was not in, but it didn't take. Is that it? In other words the information failed to satisfy you.'

'If we have to have other words,' I said, 'those might do.'

'I see. Could you bring yourself to say what point you wish to discuss with Mrs Morny?'

'I'd prefer to explain that to Mrs Morny herself.'

'The implication is that she doesn't care to see you.'

Behind the car the chauffeur said: 'Watch his right, Jack. It might have a knife in it.'

Vannier's olive skin turned the colour of dried seaweed. He turned on his heel and rapped at me in a stifled voice: 'Follow me.'

He went along the brick path under the tunnel of roses and through a white gate at the end. Beyond was a walled-in garden containing flower-beds crammed with showy annuals, a badminton court, a nice stretch of greensward, and a small tiled pool glittering angrily in the sun. Beside the pool there was a flagged space set with blue and white garden furniture, low tables with composition tops, reclining chairs with footrests and enormous cushions, and over all a blue and white umbrella as big as a small tent.

A long-limbed languorous type of showgirl blonde lay at her ease in one of the chairs, with her feet raised on a padded rest and a tall misted glass at her elbow, near a silver ice bucket and a Scotch bottle. She looked at us lazily as we came over the grass. From thirty feet away she looked like a lot of class. From ten feet away she looked like something made up to be seen from thirty feet away. Her mouth was too wide, her eyes were too blue, her make-up was too vivid, the thin arch of her eyebrows was almost fantastic in its curve and spread, and the mascara was so thick on her eyelashes that they looked like miniature iron railings.

She wore white duck slacks, blue and white open-laced sandals over bare feet and crimson lake toenails, a white silk blouse and a necklace of green stones that were not square-cut emeralds. Her hair was as artificial as a night-club lobby.

On the chair beside her there was a white straw garden hat with a brim the size of a spare tyre and a white satin chin-strap. On the brim of the hat lay a pair of green sun-glasses with lenses the size of doughnuts.

Vannier marched over to her and snapped out: 'You've got to can that nasty little red-eyed driver of yours, but quick. Otherwise I'm liable to break his neck any minute. I can't go near him without getting insulted.'

The blonde coughed lightly, flicked a handkerchief around without doing anything with it, and said:

'Sit down and rest your sex appeal. Who's your friend?'

Vannier looked for my card, found he was holding it in his hand and threw it on her lap. She picked it up languidly, ran her eyes over it, ran them over me, sighed and tapped her teeth with her fingernails.

'Big, isn't he? Too much for you to handle, I guess.'

Vannier looked at me nastily. 'All right, get it over with, whatever it is.'

'Do I talk to her?' I asked. 'Or do I talk to you and have you put it in English?'

The blonde laughed. A silvery ripple of laughter that held the unspoiled naturalness of a bubble dance. A small tongue played roguishly along her lips.

Vannier sat down and lit a gold-tipped cigarette and I stood there looking at them.

I said: 'I'm looking for a friend of yours, Mrs Morny. I understand that she shared an apartment with you about a year ago. Her name is Linda Conquest.'

Vannier flicked his eyes up, down, up, down. He turned his head and looked across the pool. The cocker spaniel named Heathcliff sat over there looking at us with the white of one eye.

Vannier snapped his fingers. 'Here, Heathcliff! Here, Heathcliff! Come here, sir!'

The blonde said: 'Shut up. The dog hates your guts. Give your vanity a rest, for heaven's sake.'

Vannier snapped: 'Don't talk like that to me.'

The blonde giggled and petted his face with her eyes.

I said: 'I'm looking for a girl named Linda Conquest, Mrs Morny.'

The blonde looked at me and said: 'So you said. I was just thinking. I don't think I've seen her in six months. She got married.'

'You haven't seen her in six months?'

'That's what I said, big boy. What do you want to know for?'

'Just a private inquiry I'm making.'

'About what?'

'About a confidential matter,' I said.

'Just think,' the blonde said brightly. 'He's making a private inquiry about a confidential matter. You hear that, Lou? Busting in on total strangers that don't want to see him is quite all right, though, isn't it, Lou? On account of he's making a private inquiry about a confidential matter.'

'Then you don't know where she is, Mrs Morny?'

'Didn't I say so?' Her voice rose a couple of notches.

'No. You said you didn't think you had seen her in six months. Not quite the same thing.'

'Who told you I shared an apartment with her?' the blonde snapped.

'I never reveal a source of information, Mrs Morny.'

'Sweetheart, you're fussy enough to be a dance director. I should tell you everything, you should tell me nothing.'

'The position is quite different,' I said. 'I'm a hired hand obeying instructions. The lady has no reason to hide out, has she?'

'Who's looking for her?'

'Her folks.'

'Guess again. She doesn't have any folks.'

'You must know her pretty well, if you know that,' I said.

'Maybe I did once. That don't prove I do now.'

'Okay,' I said. 'The answer is you know, but you won't tell.'

'The answer,' Vannier said suddenly, 'is that you're not wanted here and the sooner you get out the better we like it.'

I kept on looking at Mrs Morny. She winked at me and said to Vannier: 'Don't get so hostile, darling. You have a lot of charm, but you have small bones. You're not built for the rough work. That right, big boy?'

I said: 'I hadn't thought about it, Mrs Morny. Do you think Mr Morny could help me—or would?'

She shook her head. 'How would I know? You could try. If he don't like you, he has guys around that can bounce you.'

'I think you could tell me yourself, if you wanted to.'

'How are you going to make me want to?' Her eyes were inviting.

'With all these people around,' I said, 'how can I?'

'That's a thought,' she said, and sipped from her glass, watching me over it.

Vannier stood up very slowly. His face was white. He put his hand inside his shirt and said slowly, between his teeth: 'Get out, mug. While you can still walk.'

I looked at him in surprise. 'Where's your refinement?' I asked him. 'And don't tell me you wear a gun with your garden clothes.'

The blonde laughed, showing a fine strong set of teeth. Vannier thrust his hand under his left arm inside the shirt and set his lips. His black eyes were sharp and blank at the same time, like a snake's eyes.

'You heard me,' he said, almost softly. 'And don't write me off too quick. I'd plug you as soon as I'd strike a match. And fix it afterwards.'

I looked at the blonde. Her eyes were bright and her mouth looked sensual and eager, watching us.

I turned and walked away across the grass. About halfway across it I looked back at them. Vannier stood in exactly the same position, his hand inside his shirt. The blonde's eyes were still wide and her lips parted, but the shadow of the umbrella had dimmed her expression and at that distance it might have been either fear or pleased anticipation.

I went on over the grass, through the white gate and along the brick path under the rose arbour. I reached the end of it, turned, walked quietly back to the gate and took another look at them. I didn't know what there would be to see or what I cared about it when I saw it.

What I saw was Vannier practically sprawled on top of the blonde, kissing her.

I shook my head and went back along the walk.

The red-eyed chauffeur was still at work on the Cadillac. He had finished the wash job and was wiping off the glass and nickel with a large chamois. I went around and stood beside him.

'How you come out?' he asked me out of the side of his mouth.

'Badly. They tramped all over me,' I said.

He nodded and went on making the hissing noise of a groom rubbing down a horse.

'You better watch your step. The guy's heeled,' I said. 'Or pretends to be.'

The chauffeur laughed shortly. 'Under that suit? Nix.'

'Who is this guy Vannier? What does he do?'

The chauffeur straightened up, put the chamois over the sill of a window and wiped his hands on the towel that was now stuck in his waistband.

'Women, my guess would be,' he said.

'Isn't it a bit dangerous—playing with this particular woman?'

'I'd say it was,' he agreed. 'Different guys got different ideas of danger. It would scare me.'

'Where does he live?'

'Sherman Oaks. She goes over there. She'll go once too often.'

'Ever run across a girl named Linda Conquest? Tall, dark, handsome, used to be a singer with a band?'

'For two bucks, Jack, you expect a lot of service.'

'I could build it up to five.'

He shook his head. 'I don't know the party. Not by that name. All kinds of dames come here, mostly pretty flashy. I don't get introduced.' He grinned.

I got my wallet out and put three ones in his little damp paw. I added a business card.

'I like small close-built men,' I said. 'They never seem to be afraid of anything. Come and see me some time.'

'I might at that, Jack. Thanks. Linda Conquest, huh? I'll keep my ear-flaps off.'

'So long,' I said. 'The name?'

'They call me Shifty. I never knew why.'

'So long, Shifty.'

'So long. Gat under his arm—in them clothes? Not a chance.'

'I don't know,' I said. 'He made the motion. I'm not hired to gunfight with strangers.'

'Hell, that shirt he's wearing only got two buttons at the top. I noticed. Take him a week to pull a rod from under that.' But he sounded faintly worried.

'I guess he was just bluffing,' I agreed. 'If you hear mention of Linda Conquest, I'll be glad to talk business with you.'

'Okay, Jack.'

I went back along the black driveway. He stood there scratching his chin.

6

I drove along the block looking for a place to park so that I could run up to the office for a moment before going on downtown.

A chauffeur-driven Packard edged out from the kerb in front of a cigar store about thirty feet from the entrance to my building. I slid in the space, locked the car and stepped out. It was only then that I noticed the car in front of which I had parked was a familiar-looking sand-coloured coupé. It didn't have to be the same one. There were thousands of them. Nobody was in it. Nobody was near it that wore a cocoa straw hat with a brown and yellow band.

I went around to the street side and looked at the steering-post. No licence holder. I wrote the licence plate number down on the back of an envelope, just in case, and went on into my building. He wasn't in the lobby, or in the corridor upstairs.

I went into the office, looked on the floor for mail, didn't find any, bought myself a short drink out of the office bottle and left. I didn't have any time to spare to get downtown before three o'clock.

The sand-coloured coupé was still parked, still empty. I got into mine and started up and moved out into the traffic stream.

I was below Sunset on Vine before he picked me up. I kept on going, grinning and wondering where he had hid. Perhaps in the car parked behind his own. I hadn't thought of that.

I drove south to Third and all the way downtown on Third. The sand-coloured coupé kept half a block behind me all the way. I moved over to Seventh and Grand, parked near Seventh and Olive, stopped to buy cigarettes I didn't need, and then walked east along Seventh without looking behind me. At Spring I went into the Hotel Metropole, strolled over to the big horseshoe cigar counter to light one of my cigarettes and then sat down in one of the old brown leather chairs in the lobby.

A blond man in a brown suit, dark glasses and the now familiar hat, came into the lobby and moved unobtrusively among the potted palms and the stucco arches to the cigar counter. He bought a package of cigarettes and broke it open standing there, using the time to lean his back against the counter and give the lobby the benefit of his eagle eye.

He picked up his change and went over and sat down with his back to a pillar. He tipped his hat down over his dark glasses and seemed to go to sleep with an unlighted cigarette between his lips.

I got up and wandered over and dropped into the chair beside him. I looked at him sideways. He didn't move. Seen at close quarters his face seemed young and pink and plump and the blond beard on his chin was very carelessly shaved. Behind the dark glasses his eyelashes flicked up and down rapidly. A hand on his knee tightened and pulled the cloth into wrinkles. There was a wart on his cheek just below the right eyelid.

I struck a match and held the flame to his cigarette. 'Light?'

'Oh—thanks,' he said, very surprised. He drew breath in until the cigarette tip glowed. I shook the match out, tossed it into the sand jar at my elbow and waited. He looked at me sideways several times before he spoke.

'Haven't I seen you somewhere before?'

'Over on Dresden Avenue in Pasadena. This morning.'

I could see his cheeks get pinker than they had been. He sighed.

'I must be lousy,' he said.

'Boy, you stink,' I agreed.

'Maybe it's the hat,' he said.

'That hat helps,' I said. 'But you don't really need it.'

'It's a pretty tough dollar in this town,' he said sadly. 'You can't do it on foot, you ruin yourself with taxi fares if you use taxis, and if you use your own car, it's always where you can't get to it fast enough. You have to stay too close.'

'But you don't have to climb in a guy's pocket,' I said. 'Did you want something with me or are you just practising?'

'I figured I'd find out if you were smart enough to be worth talking to.'

'I'm very smart,' I said. 'It would be a shame not to talk to me.'

He looked carefully around the back of his chair and on both sides of where we were sitting and then drew a small pigskin wallet out. He handed me a nice fresh card from it. It read: George Anson Phillips. Confidential Investigations. 212, Seneger Building, 1924 North Wilcox Avenue, Hollywood. A Glenview telephone number. In the upper left-hand corner there was an open eye with an eyebrow arched in surprise and very long eyelashes.

'You can't do that,' I said, pointing to the eye. 'That's the Pinkertons'. You'll be stealing their business.'

'Oh, hell,' he said, 'what little I get wouldn't bother them.'

I snapped the card on my fingernail and bit down hard on my teeth and slipped the card into my pocket.

'You want one of mine—or have you completed your file on me?'

'Oh I know all about you,' he said. 'I was deputy at Ventura the time you were working on the Gregson case.'

Gregson was a con man from Oklahoma City who was followed all over the United States for two years by one of his victims until he got so jittery that he shot up a service station attendant who mistook him for an acquaintance. It seemed a long time ago to me.

I said: 'Go on from there.'

'I remembered your name when I saw it on your registration this a.m. So when I lost you on the way into town I just looked you up. I was going to come in and talk, but it would have been a violation of confidence. This way I kind of can't help myself.'

Another screwball. That made three in one day, not counting Mrs Murdock, who might turn out to be a screwball, too.

I waited while he took his dark glasses off and polished them and put them on again and gave the neighbourhood the once over again. Then he said:

'I figured we could, maybe, make a deal. Pool our resources, as they say. I saw the guy go into your office, so I figured he had hired you.'

'You know who he was?'

'I'm working on him,' he said, and his voice sounded flat and discouraged. 'And where I am getting is no place at all.'

'What did he do to you?'

'Well, I'm working for his wife.'

'Divorce?'

He looked all around him carefully and said in a small voice: 'So she says. But I wonder.'

'They both want one,' I said. 'Each trying to get something on the other. Comical, isn't it?'

'My end I don't like so well. A guy is tailing me around some of the time. A very tall guy with a funny eye. I shake him but after a while I see him again. A very tall guy. Like a lamppost.'

A very tall man with a funny eye. I smoked thoughtfully.

'Anything to do with you,' the blond man asked me a little anxiously.

I shook my head and threw my cigarette into the sand jar. 'Never saw him that I know of.' I looked at my strap watch. 'We better get together and talk this thing over properly, but I can't do it now. I have an appointment.'

'I'd like to,' he said. 'Very much.'

'Let's then. My office, my apartment, or your office, or where?'

He scratched his badly shaved chin with a well-chewed thumbnail.

'My apartment,' he said at last. 'It's not in the phone book. Give me that card a minute.'

He turned it over on his palm when I gave it to him and wrote slowly with a small metal pencil, moving his tongue along his lips. He was getting younger every minute. He didn't seem much more than twenty by now, but he had to be because the Gregson case had been six years back.

He put his pencil away and handed me back the card. The address he had written on it was 204 Florence Apartments, 128 Court Street.

I looked at him curiously. 'Court Street on Bunker Hill?'

He nodded, flushing all over his blond skin. 'Not too good,' he said quickly. 'I haven't been in the chips lately. Do you mind?'

'No, why would I?'

I stood up and held a hand out. He shook it and dropped it and I pushed it down into my hip pocket and rubbed the palm against the handkerchief I had there. Looking at his face more closely I saw there was a line of moisture across his upper lip and more of it along the side of his nose. It was not as hot as all that.

I started to move off and then I turned back to lean down close to his face and say: 'Almost anybody can pull my leg, but just to make sure, she's a tall blonde with careless eyes, huh?'

'I wouldn't call them careless,' he said.

I held my face together while I said: 'And just between the two of us this divorce stuff is a lot of hooey. It's something else entirely, isn't it?'

'Yes,' he said softly, 'and something I don't like more every minute I think about it. Here.'

He pulled something out of his pocket and dropped it into my hand. It was a flat key.

'No need for you to wait around in the hall, if I happen to be out. I have two of them. What time would you think you would come?'

'About four-thirty, the way it looks now. You sure you want to give me this key?'

'Why, we're in the same racket,' he said, looking up at me innocently, or as innocently as he could look through a pair of dark glasses.

At the edge of the lobby I looked back. He sat there peacefully, with the half-smoked cigarette dead between his lips and the gaudy brown and yellow band on his hat looking as quiet as a cigarette advertisement on the back page of the *Saturday Evening Post*.

We were in the same racket. So I wouldn't chisel him. Just like that. I could have the key to his apartment and go in and make myself at home. I could wear his slippers and drink his liquor and lift up his carpet and count the thousand-dollar bills under it. We were in the same racket.

7

The Belfont Building was eight stories of nothing in particular that had got itself pinched off between a large green and chromium cut-rate suit emporium and a three-storey and basement garage that made a noise like lion cages at feeding time. The small dark narrow lobby was as dirty as a chicken yard. The building directory had a lot of vacant space on it. Only one of the names meant anything to me and I knew that one already. Opposite the directory a large sign tilted against the fake marble wall said: *Space for Renting Suitable for Cigar Stand. Apply Room* 316.

There were two open-grille elevators but only one seemed to be running and that not busy. An old man sat inside it slack-jawed and watery-eyed on a piece of folded burlap on top of a wooden stool. He looked as if he had been sitting there since the Civil War and had come out of that badly.

I got in with him and said 'eight', and he wrestled the doors shut and cranked his buggy and we dragged upwards lurching. The old man breathed hard, as if he was carrying the elevator on his back.

I got out at my floor and started along the hallway and behind me the old man leaned out of the car and blew his nose with his fingers into a carton full of floor sweepings.

Elisha Morningstar's office was at the back, opposite the fire-door. Two rooms, both doors lettered in flaked black paint on pebbled glass. *Elisha Morningstar. Numismatist.* The one farther back said: *Entrance.*

I turned the knob and went into a small narrow room with two windows, a shabby typewriter desk, closed, a number of wall cases of tarnished coins in tilted slots with yellowed typewritten labels under them, two brown filing-cases at the back against the wall, no curtains at the windows, and a dust-grey floor carpet so threadbare that you wouldn't notice the rips in it unless you tripped over one.

An inner wooden door was open at the back across from the filing-cases, behind the little typewriter desk. Through the door came the small sounds a man makes when he isn't doing anything at all. Then the dry voice of Elisha Morningstar called out:

'Come in, please. Come in.'

I went along and in. The inner office was just as small but had a lot more stuff in it. A green safe almost blocked off the front half. Beyond this a heavy old mahogany table against the entrance door held some dark books, some flabby old magazines, and a lot of dust. In the back wall a window was open a few inches, without effect on the musty smell. There was a hatrack with a greasy black felt hat on it. There were three long-legged tables with glass tops and more coins under the glass tops. There was a heavy dark leather-topped desk midway of the room. It had the usual desk stuff on it, and in addition a pair of jeweller's scales under a glass dome and two large nickel-framed magnifying-glasses and a jeweller's eyepiece lying on a buff scratch pad, beside a cracked yellow silk handkerchief spotted with ink.

In the swivel chair at the desk sat an elderly party in a dark grey suit with high lapels and too many buttons down the front. He had some stringy white hair that grew long enough to tickle his ears. A pale grey bald patch loomed high up in the middle of it, like a rock above timberline. Fuzz grew out of his ears, far enough to catch a moth.

He had sharp black eyes which had a pouch under each eye, brownish purple in colour and traced with a network of wrinkles and veins. His cheeks were shiny and his short sharp nose looked as if it had hung over a lot of quick ones in its time. A Hoover collar which no decent laundry would have allowed on the premises nudged his Adam's apple and a black string tie poked a small hard knot out of the bottom of the collar, like a mouse getting ready to come out of a mousehole.

He said: 'My young lady had to go to the dentist. You are Mr Marlowe?'
I nodded.

'Pray, be seated.' He waved a thin hand at the chair across the desk. I sat down. 'You have some indentification, I presume?'

I showed it to him. While he read it I smelled him from across the desk. He had a sort of dry musty smell, like a fairly clean Chinaman.

He placed my card face down on top of his desk and folded his hands on it. His sharp black eyes didn't miss anything in my face.

'Well, Mr Marlowe, what can I do for you?'

'Tell me about the Brasher Doubloon.'

'Ah, yes,' he said. 'The Brasher Doubloon. An interesting coin.' He lifted his hands off the desk and made a steeple of the fingers, like an old-time family lawyer getting set for a little tangled grammar. 'In some ways the most interesting and valuable of all early American coins. As no doubt you know.'

'What I don't know about early American coins you could almost crowd into the Rose Bowl.'

'Is that so?' he said. 'Is that so? Do you want me to tell you?'

'What I'm here for, Mr Morningstar.'

'It is a gold coin, roughly equivalent to a twenty-dollar gold piece, and about the size of a half-dollar. Almost exactly. It was made for the State of New York in the year 1787. It was not minted. There were no mints until 1793, when the first mint was opened in Philadelphia. The Brasher Doubloon was coined probably by the pressure moulding process and its maker was a private goldsmith named Ephraim Brasher, or Brashear. Where the name survives it is usually spelled Brashear, but not on the coin. I don't know why.'

I got a cigarette into my mouth and lit it. I thought it might do something to the musty smell. 'What's the pressure moulding process?'

'The two halves of the mould were engraved in steel, in *intaglio*, of course. These halves were then mounted in lead. Gold blanks were pressed between them in a coin press. Then the edges were trimmed for weight and smoothed. The coin was not milled. There were no milling machines in 1787.'

'Kind of a slow process,' I said.

He nodded his peaked white head. 'Quite. And, since the surface-hardening of steel without distortion could not be accomplished at that time, the dies wore and had to be remade from time to time. With consequent slight variations in design which would be visible under strong magnification. In fact, it would be safe to say no two of the coins would be identical, judged by modern methods of microscopic examination. Am I clear?'

'Yeah,' I said. 'Up to a point. How many of these coins are there and what are they worth?'

He undid the steeple of fingers and put his hands back on the desk top and parted them gently up and down.

'I don't know how many there are. Nobody knows. A few hundred, a thousand, perhaps more. But of these very few indeed are uncirculated specimens in what is called mint condition. The value varies from a couple of thousand on up. I should say that at the present time, since the devaluation of the dollar, an uncirculated specimen, carefully handled by a reputable dealer, might easily bring ten thousand dollars, or even more. It would have to have a history, of course.'

I said: 'Ah,' and let smoke out of my lungs slowly and waved it away with the flat of my hand, away from the old party across the desk from me. He looked like a non-smoker. 'And without a history and not so carefully handled—how much?'

He shrugged. 'There would be the implication that the coin was illegally acquired. Stolen, or obtained by fraud. Of course it might not be so. Rare coins do turn up in odd places at odd times. In old strong boxes, in the secret drawers of desks in old New England houses. Not often, I grant you. But it happens. I know of a very valuable coin that fell out of the stuffing of a horsehair sofa which had been restored by an antique dealer. The sofa had been in the same room in the same house in Fall River, Massachusetts, for ninety years. Nobody knew how the coin got there. But generally speaking, the implication of theft would be strong. Particularly in this part of the country.'

He looked at the corner of the ceiling with an absent stare. I looked at him with a not so absent stare. He looked like a man who could be trusted with a secret—if it was his own secret.

He brought his eyes down to my level slowly and said: 'Five dollars, please.'

I said: 'Huh?'

'Five dollars, please.'

'What for?'

'Don't be absurd, Mr Marlowe. Everything I have told you is available in the public library. In Fosdyke's *Register*, in particular. You choose to come here and take up my time relating it to you. For this my charge is five dollars.'

'And suppose I don't pay it,' I said.

He leaned back and closed his eyes. A very faint smile twitched at the corners of his lips. 'You will pay it,' he said.

I paid it. I took the five out of my wallet and got up to lean over the desk and spread it out right in front of him, carefully. I stroked the bill with my fingertips, as if it was a kitten.

'Five dollars, Mr Morningstar,' I said.

He opened his eyes and looked at the bill. He smiled.

'And now,' I said, 'let's talk about the Brasher Doubloon that somebody tried to sell you.'

He opened his eyes a little wider. 'Oh, did somebody try to sell me a Brasher Doubloon? Now why would they do that?'

'They needed the money,' I said. 'And they didn't want too many questions asked. They knew or found out that you were in the business and that the building where you had your office was a shabby dump where anything could happen. They knew your office was at the end of a corridor and that you were an elderly man who would probably not make any false moves—out of regard for your health.'

'They seem to have known a great deal,' Elisha Morningstar said dryly.

'They knew what they had to know in order to transact their business. Just like you and me. And none of it was hard to find out.'

He stuck his little finger in his ear and worked it around and brought it out with a little dark wax on it. He wiped it off casually on his coat.

'And you assume all this from the mere fact that I called up Mrs Murdock and asked if her Brasher Doubloon was for sale?'

'Sure. She had the same idea herself. It's reasonable. Like I said over the phone to you, you would know that coin was not for sale. If you knew anything about the business at all. And I can see that you do.'

He bowed, about an inch. He didn't quite smile but he looked about as pleased as a man in a Hoover collar ever looks.

'You would be offered this coin for sale,' I said, 'in suspicious circumstances. You would want to buy it, if you could get it cheap and had the money to handle it. But you would want to know where it came from. And even if you were quite sure it was stolen, you could still buy it, if you could get it cheap enough.'

'Oh, I could, could I?' He looked amused, but not in a large way.

'Sure you could—if you are a reputable dealer. I'll assume you are. By buying the coin—cheap—you would be protecting the owner or his insurance carrier from complete loss. They'd be glad to pay you back your outlay. It's done all the time.'

'Then the Murdock Brasher has been stolen,' he said abruptly.

'Don't quote me,' I said. 'It's a secret.'

He almost picked his nose this time. He just caught himself. He picked a hair out of one nostril instead, with a quick jerk and a wince. He held it up and looked at it. Looking at me past it he said:

'And how much will your principal pay for the return of the coin?'

I leaned over the desk and gave him my shady leer. 'One grand. What did you pay?'

'I think you are a very smart young man,' he said. Then he screwed his face up and his chin wobbled and his chest began to bounce in and out and a sound came out of him like a convalescent rooster learning to crow again after a long illness.

He was laughing.

It stopped after a while. His face came all smooth again and his eyes, opened, black and sharp and shrewd.

'Eight hundred dollars,' he said. 'Eight hundred dollars for an un-circulated specimen of the Brasher Doubloon.' He chortled.

'Fine. Got it with you? That leaves you two hundred dollars. Fair enough. A quick turnover, a reasonable profit and no trouble for anybody.'

'It is not in my office,' he said. 'Do you take me for a fool?' He reached an ancient silver watch out of his vest on a black fob. He screwed up his eyes to look at it. 'Let us say eleven in the morning,' he said. 'Come back with your money. The coin may or may not be here, but if I am satisfied with your behaviour, I will arrange matters.'

'That is satisfactory,' I said, and stood up. 'I have to get the money anyhow.'

'Have it in used bills,' he said almost dreamily. 'Used twenties will do. An occasional fifty will do no harm.'

I grinned and started for the door. Half-way there I turned around and went back to lean both hands on the desk and push my face over it.

'What did she look like?'

He looked blank.

'The girl that sold you the coin.'

He looked blanker.

'Okay,' I said. 'It wasn't a girl. She had help. It was a man. What did the man look like?'

He pursed his lips and made another steeple with his fingers. 'He was a middle-aged man, heavy set, about five feet seven inches tall and weighing around one hundred and seventy pounds. He said his name was Smith. He wore a blue suit, black shoes, a green tie and shirt, no hat. There was a brown bordered handkerchief in his outer pocket. His hair was dark brown sprinkled with grey. There was a bald patch about the size of a dollar on the crown of his head and a scar about two inches long running down the side of his jaw. On the left side, I think. Yes, on the left side.'

'Not bad,' I said. 'What about the hole in his right sock?'

'I omitted to take his shoes off.'

'Darn careless of you,' I said.

He didn't say anything. We just stared at each other, half curious, half hostile, like new neighbours. Then suddenly he went into his laugh again.

The five-dollar bill I had given him was still lying on his side of the desk. I flicked a hand across and took it.

'You won't want this now,' I said. 'Since we started talking in thousands.'

He stopped laughing very suddenly. Then he shrugged.

'At eleven a.m.,' he said. 'And no tricks, Mr Marlowe. Don't think I don't know how to protect myself.'

'I hope you do,' I said, 'because what you are handling is dynamite.'

I left him and tramped across the empty outer office and opened the door and let it shut, staying inside. There ought to be footsteps outside in the corridor, but his transom was closed and I hadn't made much noise coming on crepe rubber soles. I hoped he would remember that. I sneaked back across the threadbare carpet and edged in behind the door, between the door and the little closed typewriter desk. A kid trick, but once in a while it will work, especially after a lot of smart conversation, full of worldliness and sly wit. Like a sucker play in football. And if it didn't work this time, we would just be there sneering at each other again.

It worked. Nothing happened for a while except that a nose was blown. Then all by himself in there he went into his sick rooster laugh again. Then a throat was cleared. Then a swivel chair squeaked, and feet walked.

A dingy white head poked into the room, about two inches past the end of the door. It hung there suspended and I went into a state of suspended animation. Then the head was drawn back and four unclean fingernails came around the edge of the door and pulled. The door closed, clicked, was shut.

I started breathing again and put my ear to the wooden panel.

The swivel-chair squeaked once more. The threshing sound of a telephone being dialled. I lunged across to the instrument on the little typewriter desk and lifted it. At the other end of the line the bell had started to ring. It rang six times. Then a man's voice said: 'Yeah?'

'The Florence Apartments?'

'Yeah.'

'I'd like to speak to Mr Anson in Apartment two-o-four.'

'Hold the wire. I'll see if he's in.'

Mr Morningstar and I held the wire. Noise came over it, the blaring sound of a loud radio broadcasting a baseball game. It was not close to the telephone, but it was noisy enough.

Then I could hear the hollow sound of steps coming nearer and the harsh rattle of the telephone receiver being picked up and the voice said:

'Not in. Any message?'

'I'll call later,' Mr Morningstar said.

I hung up fast and did a rapid glide across the floor to the entrance door and opened it very silently, like snow falling, and let it close the same way, taking its weight at the last moment, so that the click of the catch would not have been heard three feet away.

I breathed hard and tight going down the hall, listening to myself. I pushed the elevator button. Then I got out the card which Mr George Anson Phillips had given me in the lobby of the Hotel Metropole. I didn't look at it in any real sense. I didn't have to look at it to recall that it referred to Apartment 204, Florence Apartments, 128 Court Street. I just stood there flicking it with a fingernail while the old elevator came heaving up in the shaft, straining like a gravel truck on a hairpin turn.

The time was three-fifty.

8

Bunker Hill is old town, lost town, shabby town, crook town. Once, very long ago, it was the choice residential district of the city, and there are still standing a few of the jigsaw Gothic mansions with wide porches and walls covered with round-end shingles and full corner bay windows with spindle turrets. They are all rooming houses now, their parquetry floors are scratched and worn through the once glossy finish and the wide sweeping staircases are dark with time and with cheap varnish laid on over generations of dirt. In the tall rooms hagged landladies bicker with shifty tenants. On the wide cool front porches, reaching their cracked shoes into the sun and staring at nothing, sit the old men with faces like lost battles.

In and around the old houses there are flyblown restaurants and Italian fruit-stands and cheap apartment houses and little candy stores where you can buy even nastier things than their candy. And there are ratty hotels where nobody except people named Smith and Jones sign the register and where the night clerk is half watchdog and half pander.

Out of the apartment houses come women who should be young but have faces like stale beer; men with pulled-down hats and quick eyes that look the street over behind the cupped hand that shields the match flame; worn intellectuals with cigarette coughs and no money in the bank; fly cops with granite faces and unwavering eyes; cokies and coke peddlers; people who look like nothing in particular and know it, and once in a while even men that actually go to work. But they come out early, when the wide cracked sidewalks are empty and still have dew on them.

I was earlier than four-thirty getting over there, but not much. I parked at the end of the street, where the funicular railway comes struggling up the yellow clay bank from Hill Street, and walked along Court Street to the Florence Apartments. It was dark brick in front, three stories, the lower windows at sidewalk level and masked by rusted screens and dingy net curtains. The entrance door had a glass panel and enough of the name left to be read. I opened it and went down three brass-bound steps into a hallway you could touch on both sides without stretching. Dim doors painted with numbers in dim paint. An alcove at the foot of the stairs with a pay telephone. A sign: *Manager Apt. 106.* At the back of the hallway a screen-door and in the alley beyond it four tall battered garbage pails in a line, with a dance of flies in the sunlit air above them.

I went up the stairs. The radio I had heard over the telephone was still blatting the baseball game. I read numbers and went up front. Apartment 204 was on the right side and the baseball game was right across the hall from it. I knocked, got no answer and knocked louder. Behind my back three Dodgers struck out against a welter of synthetic crowd noise. I knocked a third time and looked out of the front hall window while I felt in my pocket for the key George Anson Phillips had given me.

Across the street was an Italian funeral home, neat and quiet and reticent, white painted brick, flush with the sidewalk. Pietro Palermo Funeral Parlours. The thin green script of a neon sign lay across its façade, with a chaste air. A tall man in dark clothes came out of the front door and leaned against the white wall. He looked very handsome. He had dark skin and a handsome head of iron-grey hair brushed back from his forehead. He got out what looked at that distance to be a silver or platinum and black enamel cigarette case, opened it languidly with two long brown fingers and selected a gold-tipped cigarette. He put the case away and lit the cigarette with a pocket lighter that seemed to match the case. He put that away and folded his arms and stared at nothing with half-closed eyes. From the tip of his motionless cigarette a thin wisp of smoke rose straight up past his face, as thin and straight as the smoke of a dying campfire at dawn.

Another batter struck out or flew out behind my back in the recreated ball game. I turned from watching the tall Italian, put the key into the door of Apartment 204 and went in.

A square room with a brown carpet, very little furniture and that not inviting. The wall bed with the usual distorting mirror faced me as I opened the door and made me look like a two-time loser streaking home from a reefer party. There was a birchwood easy-chair with some hard-looking upholstery beside it in the form of a davenport. A table before the window held a lamp with a shirred paper shade. There was a door on either side of the bed.

The door to the left led into a small kitchenette with a brown woodstone sink and a three-burner stove and an old electric icebox that clicked and began to throb in torment just as I pushed the door open. On the woodstone drainboard stood the remains of somebody's breakfast, mud at the bottom of a cup, a burnt crust of bread, crumbs on a board, a yellow slime of melted butter down the slope of a saucer, a smeared knife and a granite coffee-pot that smelled like sacks in a hot barn.

I went back around the wall bed and through the other door. It gave on a short hallway with an open space for clothes and a built-in dresser. On the dresser was a comb and a black brush with a few blond hairs in its black bristles. Also a can of talcum, a small flashlight with a cracked lens, a pad of writing-paper, a bank pen, a bottle of ink on a blotter, cigarettes and matches in a glass ashtray that contained half a dozen stubs.

In the drawers of the dresser were about what one suitcase would hold in the way of socks and underclothes and handkerchiefs. There was a dark grey suit on a hanger, not new but still good, and a pair of rather dusty black brogues on the floor under it.

I pushed the bathroom door. It opened about a foot and then stuck. My nose twitched and I could feel my lips stiffen and I smelled the harsh, sharp bitter smell from beyond the door. I leaned against it. It gave a little but came back, as though somebody was holding it against me. I poked my head through the opening.

The floor of the bathroom was too short for him, so his knees were poked up and hung outwards slackly and his head was pressed against the woodstone baseboard at the other end, not tilted up, but jammed tight. His brown suit was rumpled a little and his dark glasses stuck out of his breast-pocket at an unsafe angle. As if that mattered. His right hand was thrown across his stomach, his left hand lay on the floor, palm up, the fingers curled a little. There was a blood-caked bruise on the right side of his head, in the blond hair. His open mouth was full of shiny crimson blood.

The door was stopped by his leg. I pushed hard and edged around it and got in. I bent down to push two fingers into the side of his neck against the big artery. No artery throbbed there, or even whispered. Nothing at all. The skin was icy. It wouldn't have been icy. I just thought it was. I straightened up and leaned my back against the door and made hard fists in my pockets and smelled the cordite fumes. The baseball game was still going on, but through two closed doors it sounded remote.

I stood and looked down at him. Nothing in that, Marlowe, nothing at all. Nothing for you here, nothing. You didn't even know him. Get out, get out fast.

I pulled away from the door and pulled it open and went back through the hall into the living-room. A face in the mirror looked at me. A strained, leering face. I turned away from it quickly and took out the flat key George Anson Phillips had given me and rubbed it between my moist palms and laid it down beside the lamp.

I smeared the doorknob opening the door and the outside knob closing the door. The Dodgers were ahead seven to three, the first half of the eighth. A lady who sounded well on with her drinking was singing 'Frankie and Johnny', the roundhouse version, in a voice that even whisky had failed to improve. A deep man's voice growled to her to shut up and she kept on singing and there was a hard quick movement across the floor and a smack and a yelp and she stopped singing and the baseball game went right on.

I put the cigarette in my mouth and lit it and went back down the stairs and stood in the half dark of the hall angle looking at the little sign that read: *Manager, Apt. 106.*

I was a fool even to look at it. I looked at it for a long minute, biting the cigarette hard between my teeth.

I turned and walked down the hallway towards the back. A small enamelled plate on a door said: *Manager*. I knocked on the door.

9

A chair was pushed back, feet shuffled, the door opened.

'You the manager?'

'Yeah.' It was the same voice I had heard over the telephone. Talking to Elisha Morningstar.

He held an empty, smeared glass in his hand. It looked as if somebody had been keeping goldfish in it. He was a lanky man with carroty short hair growing down to a point on his forehead. He had a long narrow head packed with shabby cunning. Greenish eyes stared under orange eyebrows. His ears were large and might have flapped in a high wind. He had a long nose that would be into things. The whole face was a trained face, a face that would know how to keep a secret, a face that held the effortless composure of a corpse in the morgue.

He wore his vest open, no coat, a woven hair watchguard, and round blue sleeve garters with metal clasps.

I said: 'Mr Anson?'

'Two-o-four.'

'He's not in.'

'What should I do—lay an egg?'

'Neat,' I said. 'You have them all the time, or is this your birthday?'

'Beat it,' he said. 'Drift.' He started to close the door. He opened it again to say: 'Take the air. Scram. Push off.' Having made his meaning clear he started to close the door again.

I leaned against the door. He leaned against it on his side. That brought our faces close together. 'Five bucks,' I said.

It rocked him. He opened the door very suddenly and I had to take a quick step forward in order not to butt his chin with my head.

'Come in,' he said.

A living-room with a wall-bed, everything strictly to specifications, even to the shirred paper lampshade and the glass ashtray. This room was painted egg-yolk yellow. All it needed was a few fat black spiders painted on the yellow to be anybody's bilious attack.

'Sit down,' he said, shutting the door.

I sat down. We looked at each other with the clear innocent eyes of a couple of used-car salesmen.

'Beer?' he said.

'Thanks.'

He opened two cans, filled the smeared glass he had been holding, and reached for another like it. I said I would drink out of the can. He handed me the can.

'A dime,' he said.

I gave him a dime.

He dropped it into his vest and went on looking at me. He pulled a chair over and sat in it and spread his bony upjutting knees and let his empty hand drop between them.

'I ain't interested in your five bucks,' he said.

'That's fine,' I said. 'I wasn't really thinking of giving it to you.'

'A wisey,' he said. 'What gives? We run a nice respectable place here. No funny stuff gets pulled.'

'Quiet, too,' I said. 'Upstairs you could almost hear an eagle scream.'

His smile was wide, about three-quarters of an inch. 'I don't amuse easy,' he said.

'Just like Queen Victoria,' I said.

'I don't get it.'

'I don't expect miracles,' I said. The meaningless talk had a sort of cold bracing effect on me, making a mood with a hard, gritty edge.

I got my wallet out and selected a card from it. It wasn't my card. It read: *James B. Pollock, Indemnity Company, Field Agent.* I tried to remember what James B. Pollock looked like and where I had met him. I couldn't. I handed the carroty man the card.

He read it and scratched the end of his nose with one of the corners. 'Wrong john?' he asked, keeping his green eyes plastered to my face.

'Jewellery,' I said, and waved a hand.

He thought this over. While he thought it over I tried to make up my mind whether it worried him at all. It didn't seem to.

'We get one once in a while,' he conceded. 'You can't help it. He didn't look like it to me, though. Soft looking.'

'Maybe I got a bum steer,' I said. I described George Anson Phillips to him, George Anson Phillips alive, in his brown suit and his dark glasses and his cocoa straw hat with the brown and yellow print band. I wondered what had happened to the hat. It hadn't been up there. He must have got rid of it, thinking it was too conspicuous. His blond head was almost, but not quite, as bad.

'That sounds like him?'

The carroty man took his time making up his mind. Finally he nodded yes, green eyes, watching me carefully, lean hard hand holding the card up to his mouth and running the card along his teeth like a stick along the palings of a picket fence.

'I didn't figure him for no crook,' he said. 'But, hell, they come all sizes and shapes. Only been here a month. If he looked like a wrong gee, wouldn't have been here at all.'

I did a good job of not laughing in his face. 'What say we frisk the apartment while he's out?'

He shook his head. 'Mr Palermo wouldn't like it.'

'Mr Palermo?'

'He's the owner. Across the street. Owns the funeral parlours. Owns this building and a lot of other buildings. Practically owns the district, if you know what I mean.' He gave me a twitch of the lip and a flutter of the right eyelid. 'Gets the vote out. Not a guy to crowd.'

'Well, while he's getting the vote out or playing with a stiff or whatever he's doing at the moment, let's go up and frisk the apartment.'

'Don't get me sore at you,' the carroty man said briefly.

'That would bother me like two per cent of nothing at all,' I said. 'Let's go up and frisk the apartment.' I threw my empty beer can at the waste basket and watched it bounce back and roll half-way across the room.

The carroty man stood up suddenly and spread his feet apart and dusted his hands together and took hold of his lower lip with his teeth.

'You said something about five,' he shrugged.

'That was hours ago,' I said. 'I thought better of it. Let's go up and frisk the apartment.'

'Say that just once more—' his right hand slid towards his hip.

'If you're thinking of pulling a gun, Mr Palermo wouldn't like it,' I said.

'To hell with Mr Palermo,' he snarled, in a voice suddenly furious, out of a face suddenly charged with dark blood.

'Mr Palermo will be glad to know that's how you feel about him,' I said.

'Look,' the carroty man said very slowly, dropping his head to his side and leaning forward from the hips and pushing his face at me as hard as he could. 'Look. I was sitting here having myself a beer or two. Maybe three. Maybe nine. What the hell? I wasn't bothering anybody. It was a nice day. It looked like it might be a nice evening—then you came in.' He waved a hand violently.

'Let's go up and frisk the apartment,' I said.

He threw both fists forward in tight lumps. At the end of the motion he threw his hands wide open, straining the fingers as far as they would go. His nose twitched sharply.

'If it wasn't for the job,' he said.

I opened my mouth. 'Don't say it!' he yelled.

He put a hat on, but no coat, opened a drawer and took out a bunch of keys, walked past me to open the door and stood in it, jerking his chin at me. His face still looked a little wild.

We went out into the hall and along it and up the stairs. The ball game was over and dance music had taken its place. Very loud dance music. The carroty man selected one of his keys and put it in the lock of Apartment 204. Against the booming of the dance band behind us in the apartment across the way a woman's voice suddenly screamed hysterically.

The carroty man withdrew the key and bared his teeth at me. He walked across the narrow hallway and banged on the opposite door. He had to knock hard and long before any attention was paid. Then the door was jerked open and a sharp-faced blonde in scarlet slacks and a green pullover stared out with sultry eyes, one of which was puffed and the other had been socked several days ago. She also had a bruise on her throat and her hand held a tall cool glass of amber fluid.

'Pipe down, but soon,' the carroty man said. 'Too much racket. I don't aim to ask you again. Next time I call some law.'

The girl looked back over her shoulder and screamed against the noise of the radio: 'Hey, Del! The guy says to pipe down! You wanna sock him?'

A chair squeaked, the radio noise died abruptly and a thick, bitter-eyed dark man appeared behind the blonde, yanked her out of the way with one hand and pushed his face at us. He needed a shave. He was wearing trousers, street shoes and an undershirt.

He settled his feet in the doorway, whistled a little breath in through his nose and said:

'Buzz off. I just come in from lunch. I had a lousy lunch. I wouldn't want nobody to push muscle at me.' He was very drunk, but in a hard practised sort of way.

The carroty man said: 'You heard me, Mr Hench. Dim that radio and stop the rough-house in here. And make it sudden.'

The man addressed as Hench said: 'Listen, pickle-puss—' and heaved forward with his right foot in a hard stamp.

The carroty man's left foot didn't wait to be stamped on. The lean body moved back quickly and the thrown bunch of keys hit the floor behind, and clanked against the door of Apartment 204. The carroty man's right hand made a sweeping movement and came up with a woven leather blackjack.

Hench said: 'Yah!' and took two big handfuls of air in his two hairy hands, closed the hands into fists and swung hard at nothing.

The carroty man hit him on top of his head and the girl screamed again and threw a glass of liquor in her boy friend's face. Whether because it was safe to do it now or because she made an honest mistake, I couldn't tell.

Hench turned blindly with his face dripping, stumbled and ran across the floor in a lurch that threatened to land him on his nose at every step. The bed was down and tumbled. Hench made the bed on one knee and plunged a hand under the pillow.

I said: 'Look out—gun.'

'I can fade that, too,' the carroty man said between his teeth and slid his right hand, empty now, under his open vest.

Hench was down on both knees. He came up on one and turned and there was a short black gun in his right hand and he was staring down at it, not holding it by the grip at all, holding it flat on his palm.

'Drop it!' the carroty man's voice said tightly and he went on into the room.

The blonde promptly jumped on his back and wound her long green arms around his neck, yelling lustily. The carroty man staggered and swore and waved his gun around.

'Get him, Del!' the blonde screamed. 'Get him good!'

Hench, one hand on the bed and one foot on the floor, both knees doubled, right hand holding the black gun flat on his palm, eyes staring down at it, pushed himself slowly to his feet and growled deep in his throat.

'This ain't my gun.'

I relieved the carroty man of the gun that was not doing him any good and stepped around him, leaving him to shake the blonde off his back as best he could. A door banged down the hallway and steps came along towards us.

I said: 'Drop it, Hench.'

He looked up at me, puzzled dark eyes suddenly sober.

'It ain't my gun,' he said and held it out flat. 'Mine's a Colt .32—belly gun.'

I took the gun off his hand. He made no effort to stop me. He sat down on the bed, rubbed the top of his head slowly, and screwed his face up in difficulty. 'Where the hell—' his voice trailed off and he shook his head and winced.

I sniffed the gun. It had been fired. I sprang the magazine out and counted the bullets through the small holes in the side. There were six.

With one in the magazine, that made seven. The gun was a Colt .32 automatic, eight shot. It had been fired. If it had not been reloaded, one shot had been fired from it.

The carroty man had the blonde off his back now. He had thrown her into a chair and was wiping a scratch on his cheek. His green eyes were baleful.

'Better get some law,' I said. 'A shot has been fired from this gun and it's about time you found out there's a dead man in the apartment across the hall.'

Hench looked up at me stupidly and said in a quiet, reasonable voice: 'Brother, that simply ain't my gun.'

The blonde sobbed in a rather theatrical manner and showed me an open mouth twisted with misery and ham-acting. The carroty man went softly out of the door.

IO

'Shot in the throat with a medium-calibre gun and a soft-nosed bullet,' Detective-Lieutenant Jesse Breeze said. 'A gun like this and bullets like is in here.' He danced the gun on his hand, the gun Hench had said was not his gun. 'Bullet ranged upwards and probably hit the back of the skull. Still inside his head. The man's dead about two hours. Hands and face cold, but body still warm. No rigor. Was sapped with something hard before being shot. Likely with a gun butt. All that mean anything to you boys and girls?'

The newspaper he was sitting on rustled. He took his hat off and mopped his face and the top of his almost bald head. A fringe of light-coloured hair around the crown was damp and dark with sweat. He put his hat back on, a flat-crowned panama, burned dark by the sun. Not this year's hat, and probably not last year's.

He was a big man, rather paunchy, wearing brown and white shoes and sloppy socks and white trousers with thin black stripes, an open-neck shirt showing some ginger-coloured hair at the top of his chest, and a rough sky-blue sports-coat not wider at the shoulders than a two-car garage. He would be about fifty years old and the only thing about him that very much suggested cop was the calm unwinking, unwavering stare of his prominent pale-blue eyes, a stare that had no thought of being rude, but that anybody but a cop would feel to be rude. Below his eyes across the top of his cheeks and the bridge of his nose there was a wide path of freckles, like a mine-field on a war map.

We were sitting in Hench's apartment and the door was shut. Hench had his shirt on and he was absently tying a tie with thick blunt fingers that trembled. The girl was lying on the bed. She had a green wrap-around thing twisted about her head, a purse by her side and a short squirrel coat across her feet. Her mouth was a little open and her face was drained and shocked.

Hench said thickly: 'If the idea is the guy was shot with the gun under the pillow, okay. Seems like he might have been. It ain't my gun and nothing you boys can think up is going to make me say it's my gun.'

'Assuming that to be so,' Breeze said, 'how come? Somebody swiped your gun and left this one. When, how, what kind of gun was yours?'

'We went out about three-thirty or so to get something to eat at the hashhouse around the corner,' Hench said. 'You can check that. We must have left the door unlocked. We were kind of hitting the bottle a little. I guess we were pretty noisy. We had the ball game going on the radio. I guess we shut it off when we went out. I'm not sure. You remember?' He looked at the girl lying white-faced and silent on the bed. 'You remember, sweet?'

The girl didn't look at him or answer him.

'She's pooped,' Hench said. 'I had a gun, a Colt .32, same calibre as that, but a belly gun. A revolver, not an automatic. There's a piece broken off the rubber grip. A Jew named Morris gave it to me three, four years ago. We worked together in a bar. I don't have no permit, but I don't carry the gun neither.'

Breeze said: 'Hitting the hooch like you birds been and having a gun under the pillow sooner or later somebody was going to get shot. You ought to know that.'

'Hell, we didn't even know the guy,' Hench said. His tie was tied now, very badly. He was cold sober and very shaky. He stood up and picked a coat off the end of the bed and put it on and sat down again. I watched his fingers tremble lighting a cigarette. 'We don't know his name. We don't know anything about him. I see him maybe two, three times in the hall, but he don't even speak to me. It's the same guy, I guess. I ain't even sure of that.'

'It's the fellow that lived there,' Breeze said. 'Let me see now, this ball game is a studio re-broadcast, huh?'

'Goes on at three,' Hench said. 'Three to say four-thirty, or sometimes later. We went out about the last half the third. We was gone about an innings and a half, maybe two. Twenty minutes to half an hour. Not more.'

'I guess he was shot just before you went out,' Breeze said. 'The radio would kill the noise of the gun near enough. You must of left your door unlocked. Or even open.'

'Could be,' Hench said wearily. 'You remember, honey?'

Again the girl on the bed refused to answer him or even look at him.

Breeze said: 'You left your door open or unlocked. The killer heard you go out. He got into your apartment, wanting to ditch his gun, saw the bed down, walked across and slipped his gun under the pillow, and then imagine his surprise. He found another gun there waiting for him. So he took it along. Now if he meant to ditch his gun, why not do it where he did his killing? Why take the risk of going to another apartment to do it? Why the fancy pants?'

I was sitting in the corner of the davenport by the window. I put in my nickel's worth, saying: 'Suppose he had locked himself out of Phillip's apartment before he thought of ditching the gun? Suppose, coming out of the shock of his murder, he found himself in the hall still holding the murder gun. He would want to ditch it fast. Then if Hench's door was open and he had heard them go out along the hall—'

Breeze looked at me briefly and grunted: 'I'm not saying it isn't so. I'm just considering.' He turned his attention back to Hench. 'So now, if this turns out to be the gun that killed Anson, we got to try and trace *your* gun. While we do that we got to have you and the young lady handy. You understand that, of course?'

Hench said: 'You don't have any boys that can bounce me hard enough to make me tell it different.'

'We can always try,' Breeze said mildly. 'And we might just as well get started.'

He stood up, turned and swept the crumpled newspapers off the chair on to the floor. He went over to the door, then turned and stood looking at the girl in the bed. 'You all right, sister, or should I call for a matron?'

The girl on the bed didn't answer him.

Hench said: 'I need a drink. I need a drink bad.'

'Not while I'm watching you,' Breeze said, and went out of the door.

Hench moved across the room and put the neck of a bottle into his mouth and gurgled liquor. He lowered the bottle, looked at what was left in it and went over to the girl. He pushed her shoulder.

'Wake up and have a drink,' he growled at her.

The girl stared at the ceiling. She didn't answer him or show that she had heard him.

'Let her alone,' I said. 'Shock.'

Hench finished what was in the bottle, put the empty bottle down carefully and looked at the girl again, then turned his back on her and stood frowning at the floor. 'Jeeze, I wish I could remember better,' he said under his breath.

Breeze came back into the room with a young fresh-faced plain-clothes detective. 'This is Lieutenant Spangler,' he said. 'He'll take you down. Get going, huh?'

Hench went back to the bed and shook the girl's shoulder. 'Get on up, babe. We gotta take a ride.'

The girl turned her eyes without turning her head, and looked at him slowly. She lifted her shoulders off the bed and put a hand under her and swung her legs over the side and stood up, stamping her right foot, as if it was numb.

'Tough, kid—but you know how it is,' Hench said.

The girl put a hand to her mouth and bit the knuckle of her little finger, looking at him blankly. Then she swung the hand suddenly and hit him in the face as hard as she could. Then she half ran out of the door.

Hench didn't move a muscle for a long moment. There was a confused noise of men talking outside, a confused noise of cars down below in the street. Hench shrugged and cocked his heavy shoulders back and swept a slow look around the room, as if he didn't expect to see it again very soon, or at all. Then he went out past the young, fresh-faced detective.

The detective went out. The door closed. The confused noise outside was dimmed a little and Breeze and I sat looking at each other heavily.

I I

After a while Breeze got tired of looking at me and dug a cigar out of his pocket. He slit the cellophane band with a knife and trimmed the end of the cigar and lit it carefully, turning it around in the flame, and holding the burning match away from it while he stared thoughtfully at nothing and drew on the cigar and made sure it was burning the way he wanted it to burn.

Then he shook the match out very slowly and reached over to lay it on the sill of the open window. Then he looked at me some more.

'You and me,' he said, 'are going to get along.'

'That's fine,' I said.

'You don't think so,' he said. 'But we are. But not because I took any sudden fancy to you. It's the way I work. Everything in the clear. Everything sensible. Everything quiet. Not like that dame. That's the kind of dame that spends her life looking for trouble and when she finds it, it's the fault of the first guy she can get her fingernails into.'

'He gave her a couple of shiners,' I said. 'That wouldn't make her love him too much.'

'I can see,' Breeze said, 'that you know a lot about dames.'

'Not knowing a lot about them has helped me in my business,' I said. 'I'm open-minded.'

He nodded and examined the end of his cigar. He took a piece of paper out of his pocket and read from it. 'Delmar B. Hench, 45, bartender, unemployed. Maybelle Masters, 26, dancer. That's all I know about them. I've got a hunch there ain't a lot more to know.'

'You don't think he shot Anson?' I asked.

Breeze looked at me without pleasure. 'Brother, I just got here.' He took a card out of his pocket and read from that. 'James B. Pollock, Reliance Indemnity Company, Field Agent. What's the idea?'

'In a neighbourhood like this it's bad form to use your own name,' I said. 'Anson didn't either.'

'What's the matter with the neighbourhood?'

'Practically everything,' I said.

'What I would like to know,' Breeze said, 'is what you know about the dead guy?'

'I told you already.'

'Tell me again. People tell me so much stuff I get it all mixed up.'

'I know what it says on his card, that his name is George Anson Phillips, that he claimed to be a private detective. He was outside my office when I went to lunch. He followed me downtown, into the lobby of the Hotel Metropole. I led him there. I spoke to him and he admitted he had been following me and said it was because he wanted to find out if I was smart enough to do business with. That's a lot of baloney, of course. He probably hadn't quite made up his mind what to do and was waiting for something to decide him. He was on a job—he said—he had got leery of and he wanted to join up with somebody, perhaps somebody with a little more experience than he had, if he had any at all. He didn't act as if he had.'

Breeze said: 'And the only reason he picked on you is that six years ago you worked on a case in Ventura while he was a deputy up there.'

I said: 'That's my story.'

'But you don't have to get stuck with it,' Breeze said calmly. 'You can always give us a better one.'

'It's good enough,' I said. 'I mean it's good enough in the sense that it's bad enough to be true.'

He nodded his big slow head.

'What's your idea of all this?' he asked.

'Have you investigated Phillip's office address?'

He shook his head, no.

'My idea is you will find out he was hired because he was simple. He was hired to take this apartment here under a wrong name, and to do something that turned out to be not what he liked. He was scared. He wanted a friend, he wanted help. The fact that he picked me after so long a time and such little knowledge of me showed he didn't know many people in the detective business.'

Breeze got his handkerchief out and mopped his head and face again. 'But it don't begin to show why he had to follow you around like a lost pup instead of walking right up to your office door and in.'

'No,' I said, 'it doesn't.'

'Can you explain that?'

'No. Not really.'

'Well, how would you try to explain it?'

'I've already explained it in the only way I know how. He was undecided whether to speak to me or not. He was waiting for something to decide him. I decided by speaking to him.'

Breeze said: 'That is a very simple explanation. It is so simple it stinks.'

'You may be right,' I said.

'And as a result of this little hotel lobby conversation this guy, a total stranger to you, asks you to his apartment and hands you his key. Because he wants to talk to you.'

I said, 'Yes.'

'Why couldn't he talk to you then?'

'I had an appointment,' I said.

'Business?'

I nodded.

'I see. What you working on?'

I shook my head and didn't answer.

'This is murder,' Breeze said. 'You're going to have to tell me.'

I shook my head again. He flushed a little.

'Look, he said tightly, 'you got to.'

'I'm sorry, Breeze,' I said. 'But so far as things have gone, I'm not convinced of that.'

'Of course you know I can throw you in the can as a material witness,' he said casually.

'On what grounds?'

'On the grounds that you are the one who found the body, that you gave a false name to the manager here, and that you don't give a satisfactory account of your relations with the dead guy.'

I said: 'Are you going to do it?'

He smiled bleakly. 'You got a lawyer?'

'I know several lawyers. I don't have a lawyer on a retainer basis.'

'How many of the commissioners do you know personally?'

'None. That is, I've spoken to three of them, but they might not remember me.'

'But you have good contacts in the mayor's office and so on?'

'Tell me about them,' I said. 'I'd like to know.'

'Look, buddy,' he said earnestly, 'you must have got some friends somewhere. Surely.'

'I've got a good friend in the Sheriff's office, but I'd rather leave him out of it.'

He lifted his eyebrows. 'Why? Maybe you're going to need friends. A good word from a cop we know to be right might go a long way.'

'He's just a personal friend,' I said. 'I don't ride around on his back. If I get in trouble, it won't do him any good.'

'How about the Homicide Bureau?'

'There's Randall,' I said. 'If he's still working out of Central Homicide. I had a little time with him on a case once. But he doesn't like me too well.'

Breeze sighed and moved his feet on the floor, rustling the newspapers he had pushed down out of the chair.

'Is all this on the level—or are you just being smart? I mean about all the important guys you don't know?'

'It's on the level,' I said. 'But the way I am using it is smart.'

'It ain't smart to say so right out.'

'I think it is.'

He put a big freckled hand over the whole lower part of his face and squeezed. When he took the hand away there were round red marks on his cheeks from the pressure of thumb and fingers. I watched the marks fade.

'Why don't you go on home and let a man work?' he asked crossly.

I got up and nodded and went towards the door. Breeze said to my back: 'Gimme your home address.'

I gave it to him. He wrote it down. 'So long,' he said drearily; 'don't leave town. We'll want a statement—maybe tonight.'

I went out. There were two uniformed cops outside on the landing. The door across the way was open and a fingerprint man was still working inside. Downstairs I met two more cops in the hallway, one at each end of it. I didn't see the carroty manager. I went out the front door. There was an ambulance pulling away from the kerb. A knot of people hung around on both sides of the street, not as many as would accumulate in some neighbourhoods.

I pushed along the sidewalk. A man grabbed me by the arm and said: 'What's the damage, Jack?'

I shook his arm off without speaking or looking at his face and went on down the street to where my car was.

12

It was a quarter to seven when I let myself into the office and clicked the light on and picked a piece of paper off the floor. It was a notice from the Green Feather Messenger Service saying that a package was held awaiting my call and would be delivered upon request at any hour of the day or night. I put it on the desk, peeled my coat off, and opened the windows. I got a half-bottle of Old Taylor out of the deep drawer of the desk and drank a short drink, rolling it around on my tongue. Then I sat there holding the neck of the cool bottle and wondering how it would feel to be a homicide dick and find bodies lying around and not mind at all, not have to sneak out wiping doorknobs, not have to ponder how much I could tell without hurting a client and how little I could tell without too badly hurting myself. I decided I wouldn't like it.

I pulled the phone over and looked at the number on the slip and called it. They said my package could be sent right over. I said I would wait for it.

It was getting dark outside now. The rushing sound of the traffic had died a little and the air from the open window, not yet cool from the night, had that tired end-of-the-day smell of dust, automobile exhaust, sunlight rising from hot walls and sidewalks, the remote smell of food in a thousand restaurants, and perhaps, drifting from the residential hills above Hollywood—if you had a nose like a hunting dog—a touch of that peculiar tomcat smell that eucalyptus trees give off in warm weather.

I sat there smoking. Ten minutes later the door was knocked on and I opened it to a boy in a uniform cap who took my signature and gave me a small square package, not more than two and half inches wide, if that. I gave the boy a dime and listened to him whistling his way back to the elevators.

The label had my name and address printed on it in ink, in a quite fair imitation of typed letters, larger and thinner than pica. I cut the string that tied the label to the box and unwound the thin brown paper. Inside was a thin cheap cardboard box pasted over with brown paper and stamped *Made in Japan* with a rubber stamp. It would be the kind of box you would get in a Jap store to hold some small carved animal or a small piece of jade. The lid fitted down all the way and tightly. I pulled it off and saw tissue paper and cotton-wool.

Separating these I was looking at a gold coin about the size of a half-dollar, bright and shining as if it had just come from the mint.

The side facing me showed a spread eagle with a shield for a breast and the initials E.B. punched into the left wing. Around these was a circle of beading, between the beading and the smooth unmilled edge of the coin, the legend E PLURIBUS UNUM. At the bottom was the date 1787.

I turned the coin over on my palm. It was heavy and cold and my palm felt moist under it. The outer side showed a sun rising or setting behind a sharp peak of mountain, then a double circle of what looked like oak leaves, then more Latin, NOVA EBORACA COLUMBIA EXCELSIOR. At the bottom of this side, in smaller capitals, the name BRASHER.

I was looking at the Brasher Doubloon.

There was nothing else in the box or in the paper, nothing on the paper. The hand-written printing meant nothing to me. I didn't know anybody who used it.

I filled an empty tobacco-pouch half full, wrapped the coin up in tissue-paper, snapped a rubber band around it and tucked it into the tobacco in the pouch and put more in on top. I closed the zipper and put the pouch in my pocket. I locked the paper and string and box and label up in a filing cabinet, sat down again and dialled Elisha Morningstar's number on the phone. The bell rang eight times at the other end of the line. It was not answered. I hardly expected that. I hung up again, looked Elisha Morningstar up in the book and saw that he had no listing residence phone in Los Angeles or the outlying towns that were in the phone book.

I got a shoulder holster out of the desk and strapped it on and slipped a Colt .38 automatic into it, put on hat and coat, shut the windows again, put the whisky away, clicked the lights off and had the office door unlatched when the phone rang.

The ringing bell had a sinister sound, for no reason of itself, but because of the ears to which it rang. I stood there braced and tense, lips tightly drawn back in a half grin. Beyond the closed window the neon lights glowed. The dead air didn't move. Outside the corridor was still. The bell rang in darkness, steady and strong.

I went back and leaned on the desk and answered. There was a click and a droning on the wire and beyond that nothing. I depressed the connexion and stood there in the dark, leaning over, holding the phone with one hand and holding the flat riser on the pedestal down with the other. I didn't know what I was waiting for.

The phone rang again. I made a sound in my throat and put it to my ear again, not saying anything at all.

So we were there silent, both of us, miles apart maybe, each one holding a telephone and breathing and listening and hearing nothing, not even the breathing.

Then after what seemed a very long time there was the quiet remote whisper of a voice saying dimly, without any tone:

'Too bad for you, Marlowe.'

Then the click again and the droning on the wire and I hung up and went across the office and out.

13

I drove west on Sunset, fiddled around a few blocks without making up my mind whether anyone was trying to follow me, then parked near a drug-store and went into its phone booth. I dropped my nickel and asked the O-operator for a Pasadena number. She told me how much money to put in.

The voice which answered the phone was angular and cold. 'Mrs Murdock's residence.'

'Philip Marlowe here. Mrs Murdock, please.'

I was told to wait. A soft but very clear voice said: 'Mr Marlowe? Mrs Murdock is resting now. Can you tell me what it is?'

'You oughtn't to have told him.'

'I—who—?'

'That loopy guy whose handkerchief you cry into.'

'How dare you?'

'That's fine,' I said. 'Now let me talk to Mrs Murdock. I have to.'

'Very well. I'll try.' The soft clear voice went away and I waited a long wait. They would have to lift her up on the pillows and drag the port bottle out of her hard grey paw and feed her the telephone. A throat was cleared suddenly over the wire. It sounded like a freight train going through a tunnel.

'This is Mrs Murdock.'

'Could you identify the property we were talking about this morning, Mrs Murdock? I mean, could you pick it out from others just like it?'

'Well—are there others just like it?'

'There must be. Dozens, hundreds for all I know. Anyhow, dozens. Of course, I don't know where they are.'

She coughed. 'I don't really know much about it. I suppose I couldn't identify it then. But in the circumstances—'

'That's what I'm getting at, Mrs Murdock. The identification would seem to depend on tracing the history of the article back to you. At least to be convincing.'

'Yes. I suppose it would. Why? Do you know where it is?'

'Morningstar claims to have seen it. He says it was offered to him for sale—just as you suspected. He wouldn't buy. The seller was not a woman, he says. That doesn't mean a thing, because he gave me a detailed description of the party which was either made up or was a description of somebody he knew more than casually. So the seller may have been a woman.'

'I see. It's not important now.'

'Not important?'

'No. Have you anything else to report?'

'Another question to ask. Do you know a youngish blond fellow named George Anson Phillips? Rather heavy set, wearing a brown suit and a dark porkpie hat with a gay band. Wearing that today. Claimed to be a private detective.'

'I do not. Why should I?'

'I don't know. He enters the picture somewhere. I think he was the one who tried to sell the article. Morningstar tried to call him up after I left. I snuck back into his office and overheard.'

'You what?'

'I snuck.'

'Please do not be witty, Mr Marlowe. Anything else?'

'Yes, I agreed to pay Morningstar one thousand dollars for the return of the—the article. He said he could get it for eight hundred. . . .'

'And where were you going to get the money, may I ask?'

'Well, I was just talking. This Morningstar is a downy bird. That's the kind of language he understands. And then again you might have wanted to pay it. I wouldn't want to persuade you. You could always go to the police. But if for any reason you didn't want to go to the police, it might be the only way you could get it back—buying it back.'

I would probably have gone on like that for a long time, not knowing just what I was trying to say, if she hadn't stopped me with a noise like a seal barking.

'This is all very unnecessary now, Mr Marlowe. I have decided to drop the matter. The coin has been returned to me.'

'Hold the wire a minute,' I said.

I put the phone down on the shelf and opened the booth door and stuck my head out, filling my chest with what they were using for air in the drugstore. Nobody was paying any attention to me. Up front the druggist, in a pale-blue smock, was chatting across the cigar counter. The counter boy was polishing glasses at the fountain. Two girls in slacks were playing the pinball machine. A tall, narrow party in a black shirt and a pale yellow scarf was fumbling magazines at the rack. He didn't look like a gunman.

I pulled the booth shut and picked up the phone and said: 'A rat was gnawing my foot. It's all right now. You got it back, you said. Just like that. How?'

'I hope you are not too disappointed,' she said in her uncompromising baritone. 'The circumstances are a little difficult. I may decide to explain and I may not. You may call at the house to-morrow morning. Since I do not wish to proceed in the investigation, you will keep the retainer as payment in full.'

'Let me get this straight,' I said. 'You actually got the coin back—not a promise of it, merely?'

'Certainly not. And I'm getting tired. So, if you—'

'One moment, Mrs Murdock. It isn't going to be as simple as all that. Things have happened.'

'In the morning you may tell me about them,' she said sharply, and hung up.

I pushed out of the booth and lit a cigarette with thick awkward fingers. I went back along the store. The druggist was alone now. He was sharpening a pencil with a small knife, very intent, frowning.

'That's a nice sharp pencil you have there,' I told him.

He looked up, surprised. The girls at the pinball machine looked at me, surprised. I went over and looked at myself in the mirror behind the counter. I looked surprised.

I sat down on one of the stools and said: 'A double Scotch, straight.'

The counter man looked surprised. 'Sorry, this isn't a bar, sir. You can buy a bottle at the liquor counter.'

'So it is,' I said. 'I mean, so it isn't. I've had a shock. I'm a little dazed. Give me a cup of coffee, weak, and a very thin ham sandwich on stale bread. No, I better not eat yet, either. Good-bye.'

I got down off the stool and walked to the door in a silence that was as loud as a ton of coal going down a chute. The man in the black shirt and yellow scarf was sneering at me over the *New Republic*.

'You ought to lay off the fluff and get your teeth into something solid, like a pulp magazine,' I told him, just to be friendly.

I went on out. Behind me somebody said: 'Hollywood's full of them.'

14

The wind had risen and had a dry taut feeling, tossing the tops of trees, and making the swung arc-light up the side street cast shadows like crawling lava. I turned the car and drove east again.

The hock shop was on Santa Monica, near Wilcox, a quiet old-fashioned little place, washed gently by the lapping waves of time. In the front window there was everything you could think of, from a set of trout flies in a thin wooden box to a portable organ, from a folding baby carriage to a portrait camera with a four-inch lens, from a mother-of-pearl lorgnette in a faded plush case to a single action Frontier Colt, .44 calibre, the model they still make for Western peace officers whose grandfathers taught them how to file the trigger and shoot by fanning the hammer back.

I went into the shop and a bell jangled over my head and somebody shuffled and blew his nose far at the back and steps came. An old Jew in a tall black skull-cap came along behind the counter, smiling at me over cut-out glasses.

I got my tobacco-pouch out, got the Brasher Doubloon out of that and laid it on the counter. The window in front was clear glass and I felt naked. No panelled cubicles with hand-carved spittoons and doors that locked themselves as you closed them.

The Jew took the coin and lifted it on his hand. 'Gold, is it? A gold hoarder you are, maybe,' he said, twinkling.

'Twenty-five dollars,' I said. 'The wife and the kiddies are hungry.'

'Oi, that is terrible. Gold, it feels, by the weight. Only gold and, maybe, platinum it could be.' He weighed it casually on a pair of small scales. 'Gold it is,' he said. 'So ten dollars you are wanting?'

'Twenty-five dollars.'

'For twenty-five dollars what would I do with it? Sell it, maybe? For fifteen dollars worth of gold is maybe in it. Okay. Fifteen dollars.'

'You got a good safe?'

'Mister, in this business are the best safes money can buy. Nothing to worry about here. It is fifteen dollars, is it?'

'Make out the ticket.'

He wrote it out partly with his pen and partly with his tongue. I gave my true name and address. Bristol Apartments, 1624 North Bristol Avenue, Hollywood.

'You are living in that district and you are borrowing fifteen dollars,' the Jew said sadly, and tore off my half of the ticket and counted out the money.

I walked down to the corner drug-store and bought an envelope and borrowed a pen and mailed the pawn-ticket to myself.

I was hungry and hollow inside. I went over to Vine to eat, and after that I drove downtown again. The wind was still rising and it was drier than ever. The steering-wheel had a gritty feeling under my fingers and the inside of my nostrils felt tight and drawn.

The lights were on here and there in the tall buildings. The green and chromium clothier's store on the corner of Ninth and Hill was a blaze of light. In the Belfont Building a few windows glowed here and there, but not many. The same old plough-horse sat in the elevator on his piece of folded burlap, looking straight in front of him, blank-eyed, almost gathered to history.

I said: 'I don't suppose you know where I can get in touch with the building superintendent?'

He turned his head slowly and looked past my shoulder. 'I hear how in Noo York they got elevators that just whiz. Go thirty floors at a time. High speed. That's in Noo York.'

'The hell with New York,' I said. 'I like it here.'

'Must take a good man to run them fast babies.'

'Don't kid yourself, dad. All those cuties do is push buttons, say "Good morning, Mr Whoosis", and look at their beauty spots in the car mirror. Now you take a Model T job like this—it takes a man to run it. Satisfied?'

'I work twelve hours a day,' he said. 'And glad to get it.'

'Don't let the union hear you.'

'You know what the union can do?' I shook my head. He told me. Then he lowered his eyes until they almost looked at me. 'Didn't I see you before somewhere?'

'About the building super,' I said gently.

'Year ago he broke his glasses,' the old man said. 'I could of laughed. Almost did.'

'Yes. Where could I get in touch with him this time of the evening?'

He looked at me a little more directly.

'Oh, the building super? He's home, ain't he?'

'Sure. Probably. Or gone to the pictures. But where is home? What's his name?'

'You want something?'

'Yes.' I squeezed a fist in my pocket and tried to keep from yelling. 'I want the address of one of the tenants. The tenant I want the address of isn't in the phone book—at his home. I mean where he lives when he's not in his office. You know, home.' I took my hands out and made a shape in the air, writing the letters slowly, h-o-m-e.

The old man said: 'Which one?' It was so direct that it jarred me.

'Mr Morningstar.'

'He ain't home. Still in his office.'

'Are you sure?'

'Sure I'm sure. I don't notice people much. But he's old like me and I notice him. He ain't been down yet.'

I got into the car and said: 'Eight.'

He wrestled the doors shut and we ground our way up. He didn't look at me any more. When the car stopped and I got out he didn't speak or look at me again. He just sat there blank-eyed, hunched on the burlap and the wooden stool. As I turned the angle of the corridor he was still sitting there. And the vague expression was back on his face.

At the end of the corridor two doors were alight. They were the only two in sight that were. I stopped outside to light a cigarette and listen, but I didn't hear any sound of activity. I opened the door marked *Entrance* and stepped into the narrow office with the small closed typewriter desk. The wooden door was still ajar. I walked along to it and knocked on the wood and said: 'Mr Morningstar.'

No answer. Silence. Not even a sound of breathing. The hair moved on the back of my neck. I stepped around the door. The ceiling light glowed down on the glass cover of the jeweller's scales, on the old polished wood around the leather desk top, down the side of the desk, on a square-toed, elastic-sided black shoe, with a white cotton sock above it.

The shoe was at the wrong angle, pointing to the corner of the ceiling. The rest of the leg was behind the corner of the big safe. I seemed to be wading through mud as I went on into the room.

He lay crumpled on his back. Very lonely, very dead.

The safe door was wide open and keys hung in the lock of the inner compartment. A metal drawer was pulled out. It was empty now. There may have been money in it once.

Nothing else in the room seemed to be different.

The old man's pocket had been pulled out, but I didn't touch him except to bend over and put the back of my hand against his livid, violet-coloured face. It was like touching a frog's belly. Blood had oozed from the side of his forehead where he had been hit. But there was no powder smell on the air at this time, and the violet colour of his skin showed that he had died of a heart stoppage, due to shock and fear, probably. That didn't make it any less murder.

I left the lights burning, wiped the doorknobs, and walked down the fire stairs to the sixth floor. I read the names on the doors going along, for no reason at all. *H.R. Teager, Dental Laboratories, L. Pridview, Public Accountant, Dalton and Rees Typewriting Service, Dr E.J. Blaskowitz,* and underneath the name in small letters: *Chiropractic Physician.*

The elevator came growling up and the old man didn't look at me. His face was as empty as my brain.

I called the Receiving Hospital from the corner, giving no name.

15

The chessmen, red and white bone, were lined up ready to go and had that sharp, competent and complicated look they always have at the beginning of a game. It was ten o'clock in the evening, I was home at the apartment. I had a pipe in my mouth, a drink at my elbow and nothing on my mind except two murders and the mystery of how Mrs Elizabeth Bright Murdock had got her Brasher Doubloon back while I still had it in my pocket.

I opened a little paper-bound book of tournament games published in Leipzig, picked out a dashing-looking Queen's Gambit, moved the white pawn to Queen's four, and the bell rang at the door.

I stepped around the table and picked the Colt .38 off the drop-leaf of the oak desk and went over to the door holding it down beside my right leg.

'Who is it?'

'Breeze.'

I went back to the desk to lay the gun down again before I opened the door. Breeze stood there looking just as big and sloppy as ever, but a little more tired. The young, fresh-faced dick named Spangler was with him.

They rode me back into the room without seeming to and Spangler shut the door. His bright young eyes flicked this way and that while Breeze let his older and harder ones stay on my face for a long moment, then he walked around me to the davenport.

'Look around,' he said out of the corner of his mouth.

Spangler left the door and crossed the room to the dinette, looked in there, recrossed and went into the hall. The bathroom door squeaked, his steps went farther along.

Breeze took his hat off and mopped his semi-bald dome. Doors opened and closed distantly. Closets. Spangler came back.

'Nobody here,' he said.

Breeze nodded and sat down, placing his panama beside him.

Spangler saw the gun lying on the desk. He said: 'Mind if I look?'

I said: 'Phooey on both of you.'

Spangler walked to the gun and held the muzzle to his nose, sniffing. He broke the magazine out, ejected the shell in the chamber, picked it up and pressed it into the magazine. He laid the magazine on the desk and held the gun so that light went into the open bottom of the breech. Holding it that way he squinted down the barrel.

'A little dust,' he said. 'Not much.'

'What did you expect?' I said. 'Rubies?'

He ignored me, looking at Breeze and added: 'I'd say this gun has not been fired within twenty-four hours. I'm sure of it.'

Breeze nodded and chewed his lips and explored my face with his eyes. Spangler put the gun together neatly and laid it aside and went and sat down. He put a cigarette between his lips and lit it and blew smoke contentedly.

'We know damn well it wasn't a long .38 anyway,' he said. 'One of those things will shoot through a wall. No chance of the slug staying inside a man's head.'

'Just what are you guys talking about?' I asked.

Breeze said: 'The usual thing in our business. Murder. Have a chair. Relax. I thought I heard voices in here. Maybe it was the next apartment.'

'Maybe,' I said.

'You always have a gun lying around on your desk?'

'Except when it's under my pillow,' I said. 'Or under my arm. Or in the drawer of the desk. Or somewhere I can't just remember where I happened to put it. That help you any?'

'We didn't come here to get tough, Marlowe.'

'That's fine,' I said. 'So you prowl my apartment and handle my property without asking my permission. What do you do when you get tough—knock me down and kick me in the face?'

'Aw hell,' he said and grinned. I grinned back. We all grinned. Then Breeze said: 'Use your phone?'

I pointed to it. He dialled a number and talked to someone named Morrison, saying: 'Breeze at'—he looked down at the base of the phone and read the number off—'any time now. Marlowe is the name that goes with it. Sure. Five or ten minutes is okay.'

He hung up and went to the davenport.

'I bet you can't guess why we're here.'

'I'm always expecting the brothers to drop in,' I said.

'Murder ain't funny, Marlowe.'

'Who said it was?'

'Don't you kind of act as if it was?'

'I wasn't aware of it.'

He looked at Spangler and shrugged. Then he looked at the floor. Then he lifted his eyes slowly, as if they were heavy, and looked at me again. I was sitting down by the chess table now.

'You play a lot of chess?' he asked, looking at the chessmen.

'Not a lot. Once in a while I fool around with a game here, thinking things out.'

'Don't it take two guys to play chess?'

'I play over tournament games that have been recorded and published. There's a whole literature about chess. Once in a while I work out problems. They're not chess, properly speaking. What are we talking about chess for? Drink?'

'Not right now,' Breeze said. 'I talked to Randall about you. He remembers you very well, in connexion with a case down at the beach.' He moved his feet on the carpet, as if they were very tired. His solid old face was lined and grey with fatigue. 'He said you wouldn't murder anybody. He says you are a nice guy, on the level.'

'That was friendly of him,' I said.

'He says you make good coffee and you get up kind of late in the mornings and are apt to run to a very bright line of chatter and that we should believe anything you say, provided we can check it by five independent witnesses.'

'To hell with him,' I said.

Breeze nodded exactly as though I had just said what he wanted me to say. He wasn't smiling and he wasn't tough, just a big solid man working at his job. Spangler had his head back on the chair and his eyes half closed and was watching the smoke from the cigarette.

'Randall says we should look out for you. He says you are not as smart as you think you are, but that you are a guy things happen to, and a guy like that could be a lot more trouble than a very smart guy. That's what he says, you understand. You look all right to me. I like everything in the clear. That's why I'm telling you.'

I said it was nice of him.

The phone rang. I looked at Breeze, but he didn't move, so I reached for it and answered it. It was a girl's voice. I thought it was vaguely familiar, but I couldn't place it.

'Is this Mr Philip Marlowe?'

'Yes.'

'Mr Marlowe, I'm in trouble, very great trouble. I want to see you very badly. When can I see you?'

I said: 'You mean to-night? Who am I talking to?'

'My name is Gladys Crane. I live at the Hotel Normandy on Rampart. When can you—'

'You mean you want me to come over there to-night?' I asked, thinking about the voice, trying to place it.

'I—' The phone clicked and the line was dead. I sat there holding it, frowning at it, looking across it at Breeze. His face was quietly empty of interest.

'Some girl says she's in trouble,' I said. 'Connexion broken.' I held the plunger down on the base of the phone waiting for it to ring again. The two cops completely silent and motionless. Too silent, too motionless.

The bell rang again and I let the plunger up and said: 'You want to talk to Breeze, don't you?'

'Yeah.' It was a man's voice and it sounded a little surprised.

'Go on, be tricky,' I said, and got up from the chair and went out to the kitchen. I heard Breeze talking very briefly, then the sound of the phone being returned to the cradle.

I got a bottle of Four Roses out of the kitchen closet and three glasses. I got ice and ginger-ale from the ice-box and mixed three highballs and carried them in on a tray and sat the tray down on the cocktail table in front of the davenport where Breeze was sitting. I took two of the glasses, handed one to Spangler, and took the other to my chair.

Spangler held the glass uncertainly, pinching his lower lip between thumb and finger, looking at Breeze to see whether he would accept the drink.

Breeze looked at me very steadily. Then he sighed. Then he picked the

glass up and tasted it and sighed again and shook his head sideways with a
half smile; the way a man does when you give him a drink and he needs it
very badly and it is just right and the first swallow is like a peek into a
cleaner, sunnier, brighter world.

'I guess you catch on pretty fast, Mr Marlowe,' he said, and leaned back
on the davenport completely relaxed. 'I guess now we can do some business
together.'

'Not that way,' I said.

'Huh?' He bent his eyebrows together. Spangler leaned forward in his
chair and looked bright and attentive.

'Having stray broads call me up and give me a song and dance so you can
say they said they recognized my voice somewhere, sometime.'

'The girl's name is Gladys Crane,' Breeze said.

'So she told me. I never heard of her.'

'Okay,' Breeze said. 'Okay.' He showed me the flat of his freckled hand.
'We're not trying to pull anything that's not legitimate. We only hope you
ain't either.'

'Ain't either what?'

'Ain't either trying to pull anything not legitimate. Such as holding out
on us.'

'Just why shouldn't I hold out on you, if I feel like it?' I asked. 'You're not
paying my salary.'

'Look, don't get tough, Marlowe.'

'I'm not tough. I don't have any idea of being tough. I know enough
about cops not to get tough with them. Go ahead and speak your piece and
don't try to pull any more phonies like that telephone call.'

'We're on a murder case,' Breeze said. 'We have to try to run it the best
we can. You found the body. You had talked to the guy. He had asked you to
come to his apartment. He gave you his key. You said you didn't know what
he wanted to see you about. We figured that maybe with time to think back
you could have remembered.'

'In other words I was lying the first time,' I said.

Breeze smiled a tired smile. 'You been around enough to know that
people always lie in murder cases.'

'The trouble with that is how are you going to know when I stop lying?'

'When what you say begins to make sense, we'll be satisfied.'

I looked at Spangler. He was leaning forward so far he was almost out of
his chair. He looked as if he was going to jump. I couldn't think of any
reason why he should jump, so I thought he must be excited. I looked back
at Breeze. He was about as excited as a hole in the wall. He had one of his
cellophane-wrapped cigars between his thick fingers and he was slitting the
cellophane with a penknife. I watched him get the wrapping off and trim the
cigar end with the blade and put the knife away, first wiping the blade
carefully on his trousers. I watched him strike a wooden match and light the
cigar carefully, turning it around in the flame, then hold the match away
from the cigar, still burning, and draw on the cigar till he decided it was
properly lighted. Then he shook the match out and laid it down beside the
crumpled cellophane on the glass top of the cocktail table. Then he leaned
back and pulled up one leg of his trousers and smoked peacefully. Every
motion had been exactly as it had been when he lit a cigar in Hench's
apartment, and exactly as it always would be whenever he lit a cigar. He was

that kind of man, and that made him dangerous. Not as dangerous as a brilliant man, but much more dangerous than a quick excitable one like Spangler.

'I never saw Phillips before to-day,' I said. 'I don't count that he said he saw me up in Ventura once, because I don't remember him. I met him just the way I told you. He tailed me around and I braced him. He wanted to talk to me, he gave me his key, I went to his apartment, used the key to let myself in when he didn't answer—as he had told me to do. He was dead. The police were called and through a set of events or incidents that had nothing to do with me, a gun was found under Hench's pillow. A gun that had been fired. I told you this and it's true.'

Breeze said: 'When you found him you went down to the apartment manager, guy named Passmore, and got him to go up with you without telling him anybody was dead. You gave Passmore a phony card and talked about jewellery.'

I nodded. 'With people like Passmore and apartment houses like that one, it pays to be a little on the cagey side. I was interested in Phillips. I thought Passmore might tell me something about him, if he didn't know he was dead, that he wouldn't be likely to tell me if he knew the cops were going to bounce in on him in a brief space of time. That's all there was to that.'

Breeze drank a little of his drink and smoked a little of his cigar and said: 'What I'd like to get in the clear is this. Everything you just told us might be strictly the truth, and yet you might not be telling us the truth. If you get what I mean.'

'Like what?' I asked, getting perfectly well what he meant.

He tapped on his knee and watched me with a quiet up from under look. Not hostile, not even suspicious. Just a quiet man doing his job.

'Like this. You're on a job. We don't know what it is. Phillips was playing at being a private dick. He was on a job. He trailed you around. How can we know, unless you tell us, that his job and your job don't tie in somewhere? And if they do, that's our business. Right?'

'That's one way to look at it,' I said. 'But it's not the only way, and it's not my way.'

'Don't forget this is a murder case, Marlowe.'

'I'm not. But don't you forget I've been around this town a long time, more than fifteen years. I've seen a lot of murder cases come and go. Some have been solved, some couldn't be solved, and some could have been solved that were not solved. And one or two or three of them have been solved wrong. Somebody was paid to take a rap, and the chances are it was known or strongly suspected. And winked at. But skip that. It happens, but not often. Consider a case like the Cassidy case. I guess you remember it, don't you?'

Breeze looked at his watch. 'I'm tired,' he said. 'Let's forget the Cassidy case. Let's stick to the Phillips case.'

I shook my head. 'I'm going to make a point, and it's an important point. Just look at the Cassidy case. Cassidy was a very rich man, a multi-millionaire. He had a grown-up son. One night the cops were called to his home and young Cassidy was on his back on the floor with blood all over his face and a bullet-hole in the side of his head. His secretary was lying on *his* back in an adjoining bathroom, with his head against the second bathroom door, leading to a hall, and a cigarette burned out between the fingers of his left hand, just a short burned-out stub that had scorched the skin between his fingers. A gun was lying by his right hand. He was shot in the head, not a contact wound. A lot of drinking had been done. Four hours had elapsed since the deaths and the family doctor had been there for three of them. Now, what did you do with the Cassidy case?'

Breeze sighed. 'Murder and suicide during a drinking spree. The secretary went haywire and shot young Cassidy. I read it in the papers or something. Is that what you want me to say?'

'You read it in the papers,' I said, 'but it wasn't so. What's more, you knew it wasn't so and the D.A. knew it wasn't so and the D.A.'s investigators were pulled off the case within a matter of hours. There was no inquest. But every crime reporter in town and every cop on every homicide detail knew it was Cassidy that did the shooting, that it was Cassidy that was crazy drunk, that it was the secretary who tried to handle him and couldn't and at last tried to get away from him, but wasn't quick enough. Cassidy's was a contact wound and the secretary's was not. The secretary was left-handed and he had a cigarette in his left hand when he was shot. Even if you are right-handed, you don't change a cigarette over to your other hand and shoot a man while casually holding the cigarette. They might do that on *Gang Busters*, but rich men's secretaries don't do it. And what were the family and the family doctor doing during the four hours they didn't call the cops? Fixing it so there would only be a superficial investigation. And why were no tests of the hands made for nitrates? Because you didn't want the truth. Cassidy was too big. But this was a murder case, too, wasn't it?'

'The guys were both dead,' Breeze said. 'What the hell difference did it make who shot who?'

'Did you ever stop to think,' I asked, 'that Cassidy's secretary might have had a mother or a sister or a sweetheart–or all three? That they had their pride and their faith and their love for a kid who was made out to be a drunken paranoiac because his boss's father had a hundred million dollars?'

Breeze lifted his glass slowly and finished his drink slowly and put it down slowly and turned the glass slowly on the glass top of the cocktail table. Spangler sat rigid, all shining eyes and lips parted in a sort of rigid half smile.

Breeze said: 'Make your point.'

I said: 'Until you guys own your own souls you don't own mine. Until you guys can be trusted every time and always, in all times and conditions, to seek the truth out and find it and let the chips fall where they may–until that time comes, I have a right to listen to my conscience, and protect my client the best way I can. Until I'm sure you won't do him more harm than you'll do the truth good. Or until I'm hauled before somebody that can make me talk.'

Breeze said: 'You sound to me just a little like a guy who is trying to hold his conscience down.'

'Hell,' I said. 'Let's have another drink. And then you can tell me about that girl you had me talk to on the phone.'

He grinned: 'That was a dame that lives next door to Phillips. She heard a guy talking to him at the door one evening. She works days as an usherette. So we thought maybe, she ought to hear your voice. Think nothing of it.'

'What kind of voice was it?'

'Kind of a mean voice. She said she didn't like it.'

'I guess that's what made you think of me,' I said.

I picked up the three glasses and went out to the kitchen with them.

16

When I got there I had forgotten which glass was which, so I rinsed them all out and dried them and was starting to make more drinks when Spangler strolled out and stood just behind my shoulder.

'It's all right,' I said. 'I'm not using any cyanide this evening.'

'Don't get too foxy with the old guy,' he said quietly to the back of my neck. 'He knows more angles than you think.'

'Nice of you,' I said.

'Say, I'd like to read up on that Cassidy case,' he said. 'Sounds interesting. Must have been before my time.'

'It was a long time ago,' I said. 'And it never happened. I was just kidding.' I put the glasses on the tray and carried them back to the living-room and set them around. I took mine over to my chair behind the chess table.

'Another phony,' I said. 'Your sidekick sneaks out to the kitchen and gives me advice behind your back about how careful I ought to keep on account of the angles you know that I don't think you know. He has just the right face for it. Friendly and open and an easy blusher.'

Spangler sat down on the edge of his chair and blushed. Breeze looked at him casually, without meaning.

'What did you find out about Phillips?' I asked.

'Yes,' Breeze said. 'Phillips. Well, George Anson Phillips is a kind of pathetic case. He thought he was a detective, but it looks as if he couldn't get anybody to agree with him. I talked to the sheriff at Ventura. He said George was a nice kid, maybe a little too nice to make a good cop, even if he had any brains. George did what they said and he would do it pretty well, provided they told him which foot to start on and how many steps to take which way and little things like that. But he didn't develop much, if you get what I mean. He was the sort of cop who would be likely to hang a pinch on a chicken thief, if he saw the guy steal the chicken and the guy fell down running away and hit his head on a post or something and knocked himself out. Otherwise it might get a little tough and George would have to go back to the office for instructions. Well, it wore the sheriff down after a while and he let George go.'

Breeze drank some more of his drink and scratched his chin with a thumbnail like the blade of a shovel.

'After that George worked in a general store at Simi for a man named Sutcliff. It was a credit business with little books for each customer and George would have trouble with the books. He would forget to write the stuff down or write it in the wrong book and some of the customers would straighten him out and some would let George forget. So Sutcliff thought maybe George would do better at something else, and he came to Los

Angeles. He had come into a little money, not much, but enough for him to get a licence and put up a bond and get himself a piece of an office. I was over there. What he had was desk room with another guy who claims he is selling Christmas cards. Name of Marsh. If George had a customer, the arrangement was Marsh would go for a walk. Marsh says he didn't know where George lived and George didn't have any customers. That is, no business came into the office that Marsh knows about. But George put an advertisement in the paper and he might have got a customer out of that. I guess he did, because about a week ago Marsh found a note on his desk that George would be out of town for a few days. That's the last he heard of him. So George went over to Court Street and took an apartment under the name of Anson and got bumped off. And that's all we know about George so far. Kind of a pathetic case.'

He looked at me with a level, uncurious gaze and raised his glass to his lips.

'What about this advertisement?'

Breeze put the glass down and dug a thin piece of paper out of his wallet and put it down on the cocktail table. I went over and picked it up and read it. It said:

Why worry? Why be doubtful or confused? Why be gnawed by suspicion? Consult cool, careful, confidential, discreet investigator. George Anson Phillips. Glenview 9521.

I put it down on the glass again.

'It ain't any worse than lots of business personals,' Breeze said. 'It don't seem to be aimed at the carriage trade.'

Spangler said: 'The girl in the office wrote it for him. She said she could hardly keep from laughing, but George thought it was swell. The Hollywood Boulevard office of the *Chronicle*.'

'You checked that fast,' I said.

'We don't have any trouble getting information,' Breeze said. 'Except maybe from you.'

'What about Hench?'

'Nothing about Hench. Him and the girl were having a liquor party. They would drink a little and sing a little and scrap a little and listen to the radio and go out to eat once in a while, when they thought of it. I guess it had been going on for days. Just as well we stopped it. The girl has two bad eyes. The next round Hench might have broken her neck. The world is full of bums like Hench—and his girl.'

'What about the gun Hench said wasn't his?'

'It's the right gun. We don't have the slug yet, but we have the shell. It was under George's body and it checks. We had a couple more fired and compared the ejector marks and the firing-pin dents.'

'You believe someone planted it under Hench's pillow?'

'Sure. Why would Hench shoot Phillips? He didn't know him.'

'How do you know that?'

'I know it,' Breeze said, spreading his hands. 'Look, there are things you know because you have them down in black and white. And there are things you know because they are reasonable and have to be so. You don't shoot somebody and then make a lot of racket calling attention to yourself, and all the time you have the gun under your pillow. The girl was with Hench all day. If Hench shot somebody, she would have some idea. She doesn't have any such idea. She would spill, if she had. What is Hench to her? A guy to play around with, no more. Look, forget Hench. The guy who did the shooting hears the loud radio and knows it will cover a shot. But all the same he saps Phillips and drags him into the bathroom and shuts the door before he shoots him. He's not drunk. He's minding his own business, and careful. He goes out, shuts the bathroom door, the radio stops. Hench and the girl go out to eat. Just happens that way.'

'How do you know the radio stopped?'

'I was told,' Breeze said calmly. 'Other people live in that dump. Take it the radio stopped and they went out. Not quiet. The killer steps out of the apartment and Hench's door is open. That must be because otherwise he wouldn't think anything about Hench's door.'

'People don't leave their doors open in apartment houses. Especially in districts like that.'

'Drunks do. Drunks are careless. Their minds don't focus well. And they only think of one thing at a time. The door was open—just a little maybe, but open. The killer went in and ditched his gun on the bed and found another gun there. He took that away, just to make it look worse for Hench.'

'You can check the gun,' I said.

'Hench's gun? We'll try to, but Hench says he doesn't know the number. If we find it, we might do something there. I doubt it. The gun we have we will try to check, but you know how those things are. You get just so far along and you think it is going to open up for you, and then the trail dies out cold. A dead end. Anything else you can think of that we might know that might be a help to you in your business?'

'I'm getting tired,' I said. 'My imagination isn't working very well.'

'You were doing fine a while back,' Breeze said. 'On the Cassidy case.'

I didn't say anything. I filled my pipe up again but it was too hot to light. I laid it on the edge of the table to cool off.

'It's God truth,' Breeze said slowly, 'that I don't know what to make of you. I can't see you deliberately covering up on any murder. And neither can I see you knowing as little about all this as you pretend to know.'

I didn't say anything, again.

Breeze leaned over to revolve his cigar butt in the tray until he had killed the fire. He finished his drink, put on his hat and stood up.

'How long you expect to stay dummied up?' he asked.

'I don't know.'

'Let me help you out. I give you till to-morrow noon, a little better than twelve hours. I won't get my post-mortem report before that anyway. I give you till then to talk things over with your party and decide to come clean.'

'And after that?'

'After that I see the Captain of Detectives and tell him a private eye named Philip Marlowe is withholding information which I need in a murder investigation, or I'm pretty sure he is. And what about it? I figure he'll pull you in fast enough to singe your breeches.'

I said: 'Oh-huh. Did you go through Phillip's desk?'

'Sure. A very neat young feller. Nothing in it at all, except a little kind of diary. Nothing in that either, except about how he went to the beach or took some girl to the pictures and she didn't warm up much. Or how he sat in the office and no business come in. One time he got a little sore about his laundry and wrote a whole page. Mostly it was just three or four lines. There was only one thing about. It was all done in a kind of printing.'

I said: 'Printing?'

'Yeah, printing in pen and ink. Not big block caps like people trying to disguise things. Just neat fast little printing as if the guy could write that way as fast and easy as any way.'

'He didn't write like that on the card he gave me,' I said.

Breeze thought about that for a moment. Then he nodded. 'True. Maybe it was this way. There wasn't any name in the diary either, in the front. Maybe the printing was just a little game he played with himself.'

'Like Pepys's shorthand,' I said.

'What was that?'

'A diary a man wrote in a private shorthand, a long time ago.'

Breeze looked at Spangler, who was standing up in front of his chair, tipping the last few drops of his glass.

'We better beat it,' Breeze said. 'This guy is warming up for another Cassidy case.'

Spangler put his glass down and they both went over to the door. Breeze shuffled a foot and looked at me sideways, with his hand on the doorknob.

'You know any tall blondes?'

'I'd have to think,' I said. 'I hope so. How tall?'

'Just tall. I don't know how tall that is. Except that it would be tall to a guy who is tall himself. A wop named Palermo owns that apartment house on Court Street. We went across to see him in his funeral parlours. He owns them too. He says he saw a tall blonde come out of the apartment house about three-thirty. The manager, Passmore, don't place anybody in the joint that he would call a tall blonde. The wop says she was a looker. I give some weight to what he says because he gave us a good description of you. He didn't see this tall blonde go in, just saw her come out. She was wearing slacks and a sports jacket and a wrap-around. But she had light blonde hair and plenty of it under the wrap-around.'

'Nothing comes to me,' I said. 'But I just remembered something else. I wrote the licence number of Phillip's car down on the back of an envelope. That will give you his former address, probably. I'll get it.'

They stood there while I went to get it out of my coat in the bedroom. I handed the piece of envelope to Breeze and he read what was on it and tucked it into his billfold.

'So you just thought of this, huh?'

'That's right.'

'Well, well,' he said. 'Well, well.'

The two of them went along the hallway towards the elevator, shaking their heads.

I shut the door and went back to my almost untasted second drink. It was flat. I carried it to the kitchen and hardened it up from the bottle and stood there holding it and looking out of the window at the eucalyptus trees tossing their limber tops against the bluish dark sky. The wind seemed to have risen again. It thumped at the north window and there was a heavy slow pounding noise on the wall of the building, like a thick wire banging the stucco between insulators.

I tasted my drink and wished I hadn't wasted the fresh whisky on it. I poured it down the sink and got a fresh glass and drank some ice water.

Twelve hours to tie up a situation which I didn't even begin to understand. Either that or turn up a client and let the cops go to work on her and her whole family. Hire Marlowe and get your house full of law. Why worry? Why be doubtful and confused? Why be gnawed by suspicion? Consult cock-eyed, careless, clubfooted, dissipated investigator, Philip Marlowe, Glenview 7537. See me and you meet the best cops in town. Why despair? Why be lonely? Call Marlowe and watch the wagon come.

This didn't get me anywhere either. I went back to the living-room and put a match to the pipe that had cooled off now on the edge of the chess table. I drew the smoke in slowly, but it still tasted like the smell of hot rubber. I put it away and stood in the middle of the floor, pulling my lower lip out and letting it snap back against my teeth.

The telephone rang. I picked it up and growled into it.

'Marlowe?'

The voice was a harsh low whisper. It was a harsh low whisper I had heard before.

'All right,' I said. 'Talk it up whoever you are. Whose pocket have I got my hand in now?'

'Maybe you're a smart guy,' the harsh whisper said. 'Maybe you would like to do yourself some good.'

'How much good?'

'Say about five C's worth of good.'

'That's grand,' I said. 'Doing what?'

'Keeping your nose clean,' the voice said. 'Want to talk about it?'

'Where, when and who to?'

'Idle Valley Club. Morny. Any time you get here.'

'Who are you?'

A dim chuckle came over the wire. 'Just ask at the gate for Eddie Prue.' The phone clicked dead. I hung it up.

It was near eleven-thirty when I backed my car out of the garage and drove towards Cahuenga Pass.

17

About twenty miles north of the pass a wide boulevard with flowering moss in the parkways turned towards the foothills. It ran for five blocks and died—without a house in its entire length. From its end a curving asphalt road dived into the hills. This was Idle Valley.

Around the shoulder of the first hill there was a low white building with a tiled roof beside the road. It had a roofed porch and a floodlighted sign on it read: *Idle Valley Patrol*. Open gates were folded back on the shoulders of the road, in the middle of which a square white sign standing on its point said STOP in letters sprinkled with reflector buttons. Another floodlight blistered the space of road in front of the sign.

I stopped. A uniformed man with a star and a strapped-on gun in a woven leather holster looked at my car, then at a board on a post.

He came over to the car. 'Good evening. I don't have your car. This is a private road. Visiting?'

'Going to the club.'

'Which one?'

'Idle Valley Club.'

'Eighty-seven seventy-seven. That's what we call it here. You mean Mr Morny's place?'

'Right.'

'You're not a member, I guess.'

'No.'

'I have to check you in. To somebody who is a member or to somebody who lives in the valley. All private property here, you know.'

'No gate crashers, huh?'

He smiled. 'No gate crashers.'

'The name is Philip Marlowe,' I said. 'Calling on Eddie Prue.'

'Prue?'

'He's Mr Morny's secretary. Or something.'

'Just a minute, please.'

He went to the door of the building, and spoke. Another uniformed man inside plugged in on a PBX. A car came up behind me and honked. The clack of the typewriter came from the open door of the patrol office. The man who had spoken to me looked at the honking car and waved it in. It slid around me and scooted off into the dark, a green long open convertible sedan with three dizzy-looking dames in the front seat, all cigarettes and arched eyebrows and go-to-hell expressions. The car flashed around a curve and was gone.

The uniformed man came back to me and put a hand on the car door. 'Okay, Mr Marlowe. Check with the officer at the club, please. A mile ahead on your right. There's a lighted parking lot and the number on the wall. Just the number. Eighty-seven seventy-seven. Check with the officer there, please.'

I said: 'Why would I do that?'

He was very calm, very polite, and very firm. 'We have to know exactly where you go. There's a great deal to protect in Idle Valley.'

'Suppose I don't check with him?'

'You kidding me?' His voice hardened.

'No. I just wanted to know.'

'A couple of cruisers would start looking for you.'

'How many are you in the patrol?'

'Sorry,' he said. 'About a mile ahead on the right, Mr Marlowe.'

I looked at the gun strapped to his hip, the special badge pinned to his shirt. 'And they call this a democracy,' I said.

He looked behind him and then spat on the ground and put a hand on the sill of the car door. 'Maybe you got company,' he said. 'I knew a fellow belonged to the John Reed Club. Over in Boyle Heights, it was.'

'Tovarich,' I said.

'The trouble with revolutions,' he said, 'is that they get in the hands of the wrong people.'

'Check,' I said.

'On the other hand,' he said, 'could they be any wronger than the bunch of rich phonies that live around here?'

'Maybe you'll be living in here yourself some day,' I said.

He spat again. 'I wouldn't live in here if they paid me fifty thousand a year and let me sleep in chiffon pyjamas with a string of matched pink pearls around my neck.'

'I'd hate to make you the offer,' I said.

'You make me the offer any time,' he said. 'Day or night. Just make me the offer and see what it gets you.'

'Well, I'll run along now and check with the officer of the club,' I said.

'Tell him to go spit up his left trousers leg,' he said. 'Tell him I said so.'

'I'll do that,' I said.

A car came up behind and honked. I drove on. Half a block of dark limousine blew me off the road with its horn and went past me making a noise like dead leaves falling.

The wind was quiet out here and the valley moonlight was so sharp that the black shadows looked as if they had been cut with an engraving tool.

Around the curve the whole valley spread out before me. A thousand white houses built up and down the hills, ten thousand lighted windows and the stars hanging down over them politely, not getting too close, on account of the patrol.

The wall of the club building that faced the road was white and blank, with no entrance door, no windows on the lower floor. The number was small but bright in violet-coloured neon. 8777. Nothing else. To the side, under rows of hooded, downward-shining lights, were even rows of cars, set out in the white lined slots on the smooth black asphalt. Attendants in crisp clean uniforms moved in the lights.

The road went around to the back. A deep concrete porch there, with an overhanging canopy of glass, and chromium, but very dim lights. I got out of the car and received a check with the licence number on it, carried it over to a small desk where a uniformed man sat and dumped it in front of him.

'Philip Marlowe,' I said. 'Visitor.'

'Thank you, Mr Marlowe.' He wrote the name and number down, handed me back my check and picked up a telephone.

A Negro, in a white linen double-breasted guards' uniform, gold epaulettes, a cap with a broad gold band, opened the door to me.

The lobby looked like a high-budget musical. A lot of light and glitter, a lot of scenery, a lot of clothes, a lot of sound, an all-star cast, and a plot with all the originality and drive of a split fingernail. Under the beautiful soft indirect lighting the wall seemed to go up for ever, and to be lost in soft lascivious stars that really twinkled. You could just manage to walk on the carpet without waders. At the back was a free-arched stairway with a chromium and white enamel gangway going up in wide shallow carpeted steps. At the entrance to the dining-room a chubby captain of waiters stood negligently with a two-inch satin stripe on his pants and a bunch of gold-plated menus under his arm. He had the sort of face that can turn from a polite simper to a cold-blooded fury almost without moving a muscle.

The bar entrance was to the left. It was dusky and quiet and a bartender moved moth-like against the faint glitter of piled glassware. A tall handsome blonde, in a dress that looked like sea-water sifted over with gold dust, came out of the Ladies' Room touching up her lips and turned towards the arch, humming.

The sound of rhumba music came through the archway and she nodded her gold head in time to it, smiling. A short fat man with a red face and glittering eyes waited for her with a white wrap over his arm. He dug his thick fingers into her bare arm and leered up at her.

A check girl in peach-bloom Chinese pyjamas came over to take my hat and disapprove of my clothes. She had eyes like strange sins.

A cigarette girl came down the gangway. She wore an egret plume in her hair, enough clothes to hide behind a toothpick, one of her long beautiful naked legs was silver, and one was gold. She had the utterly disdainful expression of a dame who makes her dates by long distance.

I went into the bar and sank into a leather bar seat packed with down. Glasses tinkled gently, lights glowed softly, there were quiet voices whispering of love, or ten per cent, or whatever they whisper about in a place like that.

A tall, fine-looking man in a grey suit cut by an angel suddenly stood up from a small table by the wall and walked over to the bar and started to curse one of the barmen. He cursed him in a loud clear voice for a long minute, calling him about nine names that are not usually mentioned by tall, fine-looking men in well-cut grey suits. Everybody stopped talking and looked at him quietly. His voice cut through the muted rhumba music like a shovel through snow.

The barman stood perfectly still, looking at the man. The barman had curly hair and a clear warm skin and wide-set careful eyes. He didn't move or speak. The tall man stopped talking and stalked out of the bar. Everybody watched him out except the barman.

The barman moved slowly along the bar to the end where I sat and looking away from me, with nothing in his face but pallor. Then he turned to me and said:

'Yes, sir?'

'I want to talk to a fellow named Eddie Prue.'

'So?'

'He works here,' I said.

'Works here doing what?' His voice was perfectly level and as dry as dry sand.

'I understand he's the guy that walks behind the boss. If you know what I mean.'

'Oh, Eddie Prue.' He moved one lip slowly over the other and made small tight circles on the bar with his bar cloth. 'Your name?'

'Marlowe.'

'Marlowe. Drink while waiting?'

'A dry martini will do.'

'A martini. Dry, Veddy, veddy dry.'

'Okay.'

'Will you eat it with a spoon or a knife and fork?'

'Cut it in strips,' I said. 'I'll just nibble it.'

'On your way to school,' he said. 'Should I put the olive in a bag for you?'

'Sock me on the nose with it,' I said. 'If it will make you feel any better.'

'Thank you, sir,' he said. 'A dry martini.'

He took three steps away from me and then came back and leaned across the bar and said: 'I made a mistake in a drink. The gentleman was telling me about it.'

'I heard him.'

'He was telling me about it as gentlemen tell you about things like that. As big shot directors like to point out to you your little errors. And you heard him.'

'Yeah,' I said, wondering how long this was going to go on.

'He made himself heard—the gentleman did. So I came over here and practically insult you.'

'I got the idea,' I said.

He held up one of his fingers and looked at it thoughtfully.

'Just like that,' he said. 'A perfect stranger.'

'It's my big brown eyes,' I said. 'They have that gentle look.'

'Thanks, chum,' he said, and quietly went away.

I saw him talking into a phone at the end of the bar. Then I saw him working with a shaker. When he came back with the drink he was all right again.

<h1 style="text-align:center">18</h1>

I carried the drink over to a small table against the wall and sat down there and lit a cigarette. Five minutes went by. The music that was coming through the fret had changed in tempo without my noticing it. A girl was singing. She had a rich deep down around the ankles contralto that was pleasant to listen to. She was singing 'Dark Eyes' and the band behind her seemed to be falling asleep.

There was a heavy round of applause and some whistling when she ended.

A man at the next table said to his girl: 'They got Linda Conquest back with the band. I heard she got married to some rich guy in Pasadena, but it didn't take.'

The girl said: 'Nice voice. If you like female crooners.'

I started to get up but a shadow fell across my table and a man was standing there.

A great long gallows of a man with a ravaged face and a haggard frozen right eye that had a clotted iris and the steady look of blindness. He was so tall that he had to stoop to put his hand on the back of the chair across the table from me. He stood there sizing me up without saying anything and I sat there sipping the last of my drink and listening to the contralto voice singing another song. The customers seemed to like corny music in there. Perhaps they were all tired out trying to be ahead of the minute in the place where they worked.

'I'm Prue,' the man said in his harsh whisper.

'So I gathered. You want to talk to me, I want to talk to you, and I want to talk to the girl that just sang.'

'Let's go.'

There was a locked door at the back end of the bar. Prue unlocked it and held it for me and went through that and up a flight of carpeted steps to the left. A long straight hallway with several closed doors. At the end of it a bright star cross-wired by the mesh of a screen. Prue knocked on a door near the screen and opened it and stood aside for me to pass him.

It was a cosy sort of office, not too large. There was a built-in upholstered corner seat by the french windows and a man in a white dinner-jacket was standing with his back to the room, looking out. He had grey hair. There was a large black and chromium safe, some filing-cases, a large globe in a stand, a small built-in bar, and the usual broad heavy executive desk with the usual high-backed padded leather chair behind it.

I looked at the ornaments on the desk. Everything standard and all copper. A copper lamp, pen set and pencil tray, a glass and copper ashtray with a copper elephant on the rim, a copper letter-opener, a copper thermos bottle on a copper tray, copper corners on the blotter holder. There was a spray of almost copper-coloured sweet peas in a copper vase.

It seemed like a lot of copper.

The man at the window turned around and showed me that he was going on fifty and had soft ash-grey hair and plenty of it, and a heavy handsome face with nothing unusual about it except a short puckered scar in his left cheek that had almost the effect of a deep dimple. I remembered the dimple. I would have forgotten the man. I remembered that I had seen him in pictures a long time ago, at least ten years ago. I didn't remember the pictures or what they were about or what he did in them, but I remembered the dark heavy handsome face and the puckered scar. His hair had been dark then.

He walked over to his desk and sat down and picked up his letter-opener and poked at the ball of his thumb with the point. He looked at me with no expression and said: 'You're Marlowe?'

I nodded.

'Sit down.' I sat down. Eddie Prue sat in a chair against the wall and tilted the front legs off the door.

'I don't like peepers,' Morny said.

I shrugged.

'I don't like them for a lot of reasons,' he said. 'I don't like them in any way or at any time. I don't like them when they bother my friends. I don't like them when they bust in on my wife.'

I didn't say anything.

'I don't like them when they question my driver or when they get tough with my guests,' he said.

I didn't say anything.

'In short,' he said. 'I just don't like them.'

'I'm beginning to get what you mean,' I said.

He flushed and his eyes glittered. 'On the other hand,' he said, 'just at the moment I might have a use for you. It might pay you to play ball with me. It might be a good idea. It might pay you to keep your nose clean.'

'How much might it pay me?' I asked.

'It might pay you in time and health.'

'I seem to have heard this record somewhere,' I said. 'I just can't put a name to it.'

He laid the letter-opener down and swung open a door in the desk and got a cut-glass decanter out. He poured liquid out of it in a glass and drank it and put the stopper back in the decanter and put the decanter back in the desk.

'In my business,' he said, 'tough boys come a dime a dozen. And would-be tough boys come a nickel a gross. Just mind your business and I'll mind my business and we won't have any trouble.' He lit a cigarette. His hand shook a little.

I looked across the room at the tall man sitting tilted against the wall, like a loafer in a country store. He just sat there without motion, his long arms hanging, his lined grey face full of nothing.

'Somebody said something about some money,' I said to Morny. 'What's that for? I know what the bawling out is for. That's you trying to make yourself think you can scare me.'

'Talk like that to me,' Morny said, 'and you are liable to be wearing lead buttons on your vest.'

'Just think,' I said. 'Poor old Marlowe with lead buttons on his vest.'

Eddie Prue made a dry sound in his throat that might have been a chuckle.

'And as for me minding my own business and not minding yours,' I said, 'it might be that my business and your business would get a little mixed up together. Through no fault of mine.'

'It better not,' Morny said. 'In what way?' He lifted his eyes quickly and dropped them again.

'Well, for instance, your hard boy here calling me up on the phone and trying to scare me to death. And later in the evening calling me up and talking about five C's and how it would do me some good to drive out here and talk to you. And, for instance, that same hard boy or somebody who looks just like him—which is a little unlikely—following around after a fellow in my business who happened to get shot this afternoon, on Court Street on Bunker Hill.'

Morny lifted his cigarette away from his lips and narrowed his eyes to look at the tip. Every motion, every gesture, right out of the catalogue.

'Who got shot?'

'A fellow named Phillips, a youngish blond kid. You wouldn't like him. He was a peeper.' I described Phillips to him.

'I never heard of him,' Morny said.

'And also, for instance, a tall blonde who didn't live there was seen coming out of the apartment house just after he was killed,' I said.

'What tall blonde?' His voice had changed a little. There was urgency in it.

'I don't know that. She was seen and the man who saw her could identify her, if he saw her again. Of course, she need not have anything to do with Phillips.'

'This man Phillips was a shamus?'

I nodded. 'I told you that twice.'

'Why was he killed, and how?'

'He was sapped and shot in his apartment. We don't know why he was killed. If we knew that, we would likely know who killed him. It seems to be that kind of a situation.'

'Who is "we"?'

'The police and myself. I found him dead. So I had to stick around.'

Prue let the front legs of his chair down on the carpet very quietly and looked at me. His good eye had a sleepy expression I didn't like.

Morny said: 'You told the cops what?'

I said: 'Very little. I gather from your opening remarks to me here that you know I am looking for Linda Conquest. Mrs Leslie Murdock. I've found her. She's singing here. I don't know why there should have been any secret about it. It seems to me that your wife or Mr Vannier might have told me. But they didn't.'

'What my wife would tell a peeper,' Morny said, 'you could put in a gnat's eye.'

'No doubt she had her reasons,' I said. 'However that's not very important now. In fact, it's not very important that I see Miss Conquest. Just the same I'd like to talk to her a little. If you don't mind.'

'Suppose I mind,' Morny said.

'I guess I would like to talk to her, anyway,' I said. I got a cigarette out of my pocket and rolled it around my fingers and admired his thick and still-dark eyebrows. They had a fine shape, an elegant curve.

Prue chuckled. Morny looked at him and frowned and looked back at me, keeping the frown on his face.

'I asked you what you told the cops,' he said.

'I told them as little as I could. This man Phillips asked me to come and see him. He implied he was too deep in a job he didn't like, and needed help. When I got there he was dead. I told the police that. They didn't think it was quite the whole story. It probably isn't. I have until to-morrow noon to fill it out. So I'm trying to fill it out.'

'You wasted your time coming here,' Morny said.

'I got the idea that I was asked to come here.'

'You can go to hell back any time you want to,' Morny said. 'Or you can do a little job for me—for five hundred dollars. Either way you leave Eddie and me out of any conversations you might have with the police.'

'What's the nature of the job?'

'You were at my house this morning. You ought to have an idea.'

'I don't do divorce business,' I said.

His face turned white. 'I love my wife,' he said. 'We've only been married eight months. I don't want any divorce. She's a swell girl and she knows what time it is, as a rule. But I think she's playing with a wrong number at the moment.'

'Wrong in what way?'

'I don't know. That's what I want found out.'

'Let me get this straight,' I said. 'Are you hiring me on a job—or off a job I already have?'

Prue chuckled again against the wall.

Morny poured himself some more brandy and tossed it quickly down his throat. Colour came back into his face. He didn't answer me.

'And let me get another thing straight,' I said. 'You don't mind your wife playing around, but you don't want her playing with somebody called Vannier. Is that it?'

'I trust her heart,' he said slowly. 'But I don't trust her judgement. Put it that way.'

'And you want me to get something on this man Vannier?'

'I want to find out what he is up to.'

'Oh. Is he up to something?'

'I think he is. I don't know what.'

'You think he is—or you want to think he is?'

He stared at me levelly for a moment, then he pulled the middle drawer of his desk out, reached in and tossed a folded paper across to me. I picked it up and unfolded it. It was a carbon copy of a grey billhead. *Cal-Western Dental Supply Company*, and an address. The bill was for *30 lb. Kerr's Crystobolite* $15.75, and *25 lb. White's Albastone*, $7.75, plus tax. It was made out to *H.R. Teager, Will Call*, and stamped *Paid* with a rubber stamp. It was signed for in the corner: *L.G. Vannier*.

I put it down on the desk.

'That fell out of his pocket one night when he was here,' Morny said. 'About ten days ago. Eddie put one of his big feet on it and Vannier didn't notice he had dropped it.'

I looked at Prue, then at Morny, then at my thumb. 'Is this supposed to mean something to me?'

'I thought you were a smart detective. I figured you could find out.'

I looked at the paper again, folded it and put it in my pocket. 'I'm assuming you wouldn't give it to me unless it meant something,' I said.

Morny went to the black and chromium safe against the wall and opened it. He came back with five new bills spread out in his fingers like a poker hand. He smoothed them edge to edge, riffled them lightly, and tossed them on the desk in front of me.

'There's your five C's,' he said. 'Take Vannier out of my wife's life and there will be the same again for you. I don't care how you do it and I don't want to know anything about how you do it. Just do it.'

I poked at the crisp new bills with a hungry finger. Then I pushed them away. 'You can pay me when—and if—I deliver,' I said. 'I'll take my payment to-night in a short interview with Miss Conquest.'

Morny didn't touch the money. He lifted the square bottle and poured himself another drink. This time he poured one for me and pushed it across the desk.

'And as for this Phillips murder,' I said, 'Eddie here was following Phillips a little. You want to tell me why?'

'No.'

'The trouble with a case like this is that the information might come from somebody else. When a murder gets into the papers you never know what will come out. If it does, you'll blame me.'

He looked at me steadily and said: 'I don't think so. I was a bit tough when you came in, but you shape up pretty good. I'll take a chance.'

'Thanks,' I said. 'Would you mind telling me why you had Eddie call me up and give me the shakes?'

He looked down and tapped on the desk. 'Linda's an old friend of mine. Young Murdock was out here this afternoon to see her. He told her you were working for old lady Murdock. She told me. I didn't know what the job was. You say you don't take divorce business, so it couldn't be that the old lady hired you to fix anything like that up.' He raised his eyes on the last words and stared at me.

I stared back at him and waited.

'I guess I'm just a fellow who likes his friends,' he said. 'And doesn't want them bothered by dicks.'

'Murdock owes you some money, doesn't he?'

He frowned. 'I don't discuss things like that.'

He finished his drink, nodded and stood up. 'I'll send Linda up to talk to you. Pick your money up.'

He went to the door and out. Eddie Prue unwound his long body and stood up and gave me a dim grey smile that meant nothing and wandered off after Morny.'

I lit another cigarette and looked at the dental supply company's bill again. Something squirmed at the back of my mind, dimly. I walked to the window and stood looking out across the valley. A car was winding up a hill towards a big house with a tower that was half glass brick with light behind it. The headlights of the car moved across it and turned in towards a garage. The lights went out and the valley seemed darker.

It was very quiet and quite cool now. The dance band seemed to be somewhere under my feet. It was muffled, and the tune was indistinguishable.

Linda Conquest came in through the open door behind me and shut it and stood looking at me with a cold light in her eyes.

19

She looked like her photo and not like it. She had the wide cool mouth, the short nose, the wide cool eyes, the dark hair parted in the middle and the broad white line between the parting. She was wearing a white coat over her dress, with the collar turned up. She had her hands in the pockets of the coat and a cigarette in her mouth.

She looked older, her eyes were harder, and her lips seemed to have forgotten to smile. They would smile when she was singing, in that staged artificial smile. But in repose they were thin and tight and angry.

She moved over to the desk and stood looking down, as if counting the copper ornaments. She saw the cut-glass decanter, took the stopper out, poured herself a drink and tossed it down with a quick flip of the wrist.

'You're a man named Marlowe?' she asked, looking at me. She put her hips against the end of the desk and crossed her ankles.

I said I was a man named Marlowe.

'By and large,' she said, 'I am quite sure I am not going to like you one damned little bit. So speak your piece and drift away.'

'What I like about this place is everything runs so true to type,' I said. 'The cop on the gate, the shine on the door, the cigarette and check girls, the fat greasy sensual Jew with the tall stately bored showgirl, the well-dressed, drunk and horribly rude director cursing the barman, the silent guy with the gun, the night-club owner with the soft grey hair and the B-picture mannerisms, and now you—the tall dark torcher with the negligent sneer, the husky voice, the hard-boiled vocabulary.'

She said: 'Is that so?' and fitted her cigarette between her lips and drew slowly on it. 'And what about the wise-cracking snooper with the last year's gags and the come-hither smile?'

'And what gives me the right to talk to you at all?' I said.

'I'll bite. What does?'

'She wants it back. Quickly. It has to be fast or there will be trouble.'

'I thought—' she started to say and stopped cold. I watched her remove the sudden trace of interest from her face by monkeying with her cigarette and bending her face over it. 'She wants what back, Mr Marlowe?'

'The Brasher Doubloon.'

She looked up at me and nodded, remembering–letting me see her remembering.

'Oh, the Brasher Doubloon.'

'I bet you completely forgot it,' I said.

'Well, no. I've seen it a number of times,' she said. 'She wants it back, you said. Do you mean she thinks I took it?'

'Yeah. Just that.'

'She's a dirty old liar,' Linda Conquest said.

'What you think doesn't make you a liar,' I said. 'It only sometimes makes you mistaken. Is she wrong?'

'Why would I take her silly old coin?'

'Well–it's worth a lot of money. She thinks you might need money. I gather she was not too generous.'

She laughed, a tight sneering little laugh. 'No,' she said. 'Mrs Elizabeth Bright Murdock would not rate as very generous.'

'Maybe you just took it for spite, kind of,' I said hopefully.

'Maybe I ought to slap your face.' She killed her cigarette in Morny's copper goldfish bowl, speared the crushed stub absently with the letter-opener and dropped it into the waste-basket.

'Passing on from that to perhaps more important matters,' I said, 'will you give him a divorce?'

'For twenty-five grand,' she said, not looking at me. 'I should be glad to.'

'You're not in love with the guy, huh?'

'You're breaking my heart, Marlowe.'

'He's in love with you,' I said. 'After all, you did marry him.'

She looked at me lazily. 'Mister, don't think I didn't pay for that mistake.' She lit another cigarette. 'But a girl has to live. And it isn't always as easy as it looks. And so a girl can make a mistake, marry the wrong guy and the wrong family, looking for something that isn't there. Security, or whatever.'

'But not needing any love to do it,' I said.

'I don't want to be too cynical, Marlowe. But you'd be surprised how many girls marry to find a home, especially girls whose arm muscles are all tired out fighting off the kind of optimists that come into these gin and glitter joints.'

'You had a home and you gave it up.'

'It got to be too dear. That port-sodden old fake made the bargain too tough. How do you like her for a client?'

'I've had worse.'

She picked a shred of tobacco off her lips. 'You notice what she's doing to that girl?'

'Merle? I noticed she bullied her.'

'It isn't just that. She has her cutting out dolls. The girl had a shock of some kind and the old brute has used the effect of it to dominate the girl completely. In company she yells at her but in private she's apt to be stroking her hair and whispering in her ear. And the kid sort of shivers.'

'I didn't quite get all that,' I said.

'The kid's in love with Leslie, but she doesn't know it. Emotionally she's about ten years old. Something funny is going to happen in that family one of these days. I'm glad I won't be there.'

I said: 'You're a smart girl, Linda. And you're tough and you're wise. I suppose when you married him you thought you could get your hands on plenty.'

She curled her lip. 'I thought it would at least be a vacation. It wasn't even that. That's a smart, ruthless woman, Marlowe. Whatever she's got you doing, it's not what she says. She's up to something. Watch your step.'

'Would she kill a couple of men?'

She laughed.

'No kidding,' I said. 'A couple of men have been killed and one of them at least is connected with rare coins.'

'I don't get it,' she looked at me levelly. 'Murdered, you mean?'

I nodded.

'You tell Morny all that?'

'About one of them.'

'You tell the cops?'

'About one of them. The same one.'

She moved her eyes over my face. We stared at each other. She looked a little pale, or just tired. I thought she had grown a little paler than before.

'You're making that up,' she said between her teeth.

I grinned and nodded. She seemed to relax then.

'About the Brasher Doubloon?' I said. 'You didn't take it. Okay. About the divorce, what?'

'That's none of your affair.'

'I agree. Well, thanks for talking to me. Do you know a fellow named Vannier?'

'Yes.' Her face froze hard now. 'Not well. He's a friend of Lois.'

'A very good friend.'

'One of these days he's apt to turn out to be a small quiet funeral, too.'

'Hints,' I said, 'have sort of been thrown in that direction. There's something about the guy. Every time his name comes up the party freezes.'

She stared at me and said nothing. I thought that an idea was stirring at the back of her eyes, but if so it didn't come out. She said quietly:

'Morny will sure as hell kill him, if he doesn't lay off Lois.'

'Go on with you. Lois flops at the drop of a hat. Anybody can see that.'

'Perhaps Alex is the one person who can't see it.'

'Vannier hasn't anything to do with my job, anyway. He has no connexion with the Murdocks.'

She lifted a corner of her lip at me and said: 'No? Let me tell you something. No reason why I should. I'm just a great big open-hearted kid. Vannier knows Elizabeth Bright Murdock and well. He never came to the house but once while I was there, but he called on the phone plenty of times. I caught some of the calls. He always asked for Merle.'

'Well—that's funny,' I said. 'Merle, huh?'

She bent to crush out her cigarette and again she speared the stub and dropped it into the waste-basket.

'I'm very tired,' she said suddenly. 'Please go away.'

I stood there for a moment, looking at her and wondering. Then I said: 'Good night, and thanks. Good luck.'

I went out and left her standing there with her hands in the pockets of the white coat, her head bent and her eyes looking at the floor.

It was two o'clock when I got back to Hollywood and put the car away and went upstairs to my apartment. The wind was all gone but the air still had that dryness and lightness of the desert. The air in the apartment was dead and Breeze's cigar butt had made it a little worse than dead. I opened windows and flushed the place through while I undressed and stripped the pockets of my suit.

Out of them with other things came the dental supply company's bill. It still looked like a bill to one H.R.Teager for 30 lb. of crystobolite and 25 lb. of albastone.

I dragged the phone book up on the desk in the living-room and looked up Teager. Then the confused memory clicked into place. His address was 422 West Ninth Street. The address of the Belfont Building was 422 West Ninth Street.

H.R.Teager Dental Laboratories had been one of the names on doors on the sixth floor of the Belfont Building when I did my backstairs crawl away from the office of Elisha Morningstar.

But even the Pinkertons have to sleep, and Marlowe needed far, far more sleep than the Pinkertons. I went to bed.

20

It was just as hot in Pasadena as the day before and the big dark red brick house on Dresden Avenue looked just as cool and the little painted Negro waiting by the hitching block looked just as sad. The same butterfly landed on the same hydrangea bush—or it looked like the same one—the same heavy scent of summer lay on the morning, and the same middle-aged sourpuss with the frontier voice opened to my ring.

She led me along the same hallways to the same sunless sunroom. In it Mrs Elizabeth Bright Murdock sat in the same reed chaise-longue and as I came into the room she was pouring herself a slug from what looked like the same port bottle but was more probably a grandchild.

The maid shut the door, I sat down and put my hat on the floor, just like yesterday, and Mrs Murdock gave me the same hard level stare and said:

'Well?'

'Things are bad,' I said. 'The cops are after me.'

She looked as flustered as a side of beef. 'Indeed. I thought you were more competent than that.'

I brushed it off. 'When I left here yesterday morning a man followed me in a coupé. I don't know what he was doing here or how he got here. I suppose he followed me here, but I feel doubtful about that. I shook him off, but he turned up again in the hall outside my office. He followed me again, so I invited him to explain why and he said he knew who I was and he needed help and asked me to come to his apartment on Bunker Hill and talk to him. I went, after I had seen Mr Morningstar, and found the man shot to death on the floor of his bathroom.'

Mrs Murdock sipped a little port. Her hand might have shaken a little, but the light in the room was too dim for me to be sure. She cleared her throat.

'Go on.'

'His name is George Anson Phillips. A young, blond fellow, rather dumb. He claimed to be a private detective.'

'I never heard of him,' Mrs Murdock said coldly. 'I never saw him to my knowledge and I don't know anything about him. Did you think I employed him to follow you?'

'I didn't know what to think. He talked about pooling our resources and he gave me the impression that he was working for some member of your family. He didn't say so in so many words.'

'He wasn't. You can be quite definite on that.' The baritone voice was as steady as a rock.

'I don't think you know quite as much about your family as you think you do, Mrs Murdock.'

'I know you have been questioning my son—contrary to my orders,' she said coldly.

'I didn't question him. He questioned me. Or tried to.'

'We'll go into that later,' she said harshly. 'What about this man you found shot? You are involved with the police on account of him?'

'Naturally. They want to know why he followed me, what I was working on, why he spoke to me, why he asked me to come to his apartment and why I went. But that is only the half of it.'

She finished her port and poured herself another glass.

'How's your asthma?' I asked.

'Bad,' she said. 'Get on with your story.'

'I saw Morningstar. I told you about that over the phone. He pretended not to have the Brasher Doubloon, but admitted it had been offered to him and said he could get it. As I told you. Then you told me it had been returned to you, so that was that.'

I waited, thinking she would tell me some story about how the coin had been returned, but she just stared at me bleakly over the wine-glass.

'So, as I had made a sort of arrangement with Mr Morningstar to pay him a thousand dollars for the coin—'

'You had no authority to do anything like that,' she barked.

I nodded, agreeing with her.

'Maybe I was kidding him a little,' I said. 'And I know I was kidding myself. Anyway, after what you told me over the phone I tried to get in touch with him to tell him the deal was off. He's not in the phone book except at his office. I went to his office. This was quite late. The elevator man said he was still in his office. He was lying on his back on the floor, dead. Killed by a blow on the head and shock, apparently. Old men die easily. The blow might not have been intended to kill him. I called the Receiving Hospital, but didn't give my name.'

'That was wise of you,' she said.

'Was it? It was considerate of me, but I don't think I'd call it wise. I want to be nice, Mrs Murdock. You understand that in your rough way, I hope. But two murders happened in the matter of hours and both bodies were found by me. And both the victims were connected—in some manner—with your Brasher Doubloon.'

'I don't understand. This other, younger man also?'

'Yes. Didn't I tell you over the phone? I thought I did.' I wrinkled my brow, thinking back. I knew I had.

She said calmly: 'It's possible. I wasn't paying a great deal of attention to what you said. You see, the doubloon had already been returned. And you sounded a little drunk.'

'I wasn't drunk. I might have felt a little shock, but I wasn't drunk. You take all this very calmly.'

'What do you want me to do?'

I took a deep breath. 'I'm connected with one murder already, by having found the body and reported it. I may presently be connected with another, by having found the body and not reporting it. Which is much more serious for me. Even as far as it goes, I have until noon to-day to disclose the name of my client.'

'That,' she said, still much too calm for my taste, 'would be a breach of confidence. You are not going to do that, I'm sure.'

'I wish you'd leave that damn port alone and make some effort to understand the position,' I snapped at her.

She looked vaguely surprised and pushed her glass away—about four inches away.

'This fellow Phillips,' I said, 'had a licence as a private detective. How did I happen to find him dead? Because he followed me and I spoke to him and he asked me to come to his apartment. And when I got there he was dead. The police know all this. They may even believe it. But they don't believe the connexion between Phillips and me is quite that much of a coincidence. They think there is a deeper connexion between Phillips and me and they insist on knowing what I am doing, who I am working for. Is that clear?'

'You'll find a way out of all that,' she said. 'I expect it to cost me a little more money, of course.'

I felt myself getting pinched around the nose. My mouth felt dry. I needed air. I took another deep breath and another dive into the tub of blubber that was sitting across the room from me on the reed chaise-longue, looking as unperturbed as a bank president refusing a loan.

'I'm working for you,' I said, 'now, this week, to-day. Next week I'll be working for somebody else, I hope. And the week after that for still somebody else. In order to do that I have to be on reasonably good terms with the police. They don't have to love me, but they have to be fairly sure I am not cheating on them. Assume Phillips knew nothing about the Brasher Doubloon. Assume, even, that he knew about it, but that his death had nothing to do with it. I still have to tell the cops what I know about him. And they have to question anybody they want to question. Can't you understand that?'

'Doesn't the law give you the right to protect a client?' she snapped. 'If it doesn't, what is the use of anyone's hiring a detective?'

I got up and walked around my chair and sat down again. I leaned forward and took hold of my kneecaps and squeezed them until my knuckles glistened.

'The law, whatever it is, is a matter of give-and-take, Mrs Murdock. Like most other things. Even if I had the legal right to stay clammed-up—refuse to talk—and got away with it once, that would be the end of my business. I'd be a guy marked for trouble. One way or another they would get me. I value your business, Mrs Murdock, but not enough to cut my throat for you and bleed in your lap.'

She reached for her glass and emptied it.

'You seem to have made a nice mess of the whole thing,' she said. 'You didn't find my daughter-in-law and you didn't find my Brasher Doubloon. But you found a couple of dead men that I have nothing to do with and you have neatly arranged matters so that I must tell the police all my private and personal business in order to protect you from your own incompetence. That's what I see. If I am wrong, pray correct me.'

She poured some more wine and gulped it too fast and went into a paroxysm of coughing. Her shaking hand slid the glass on to the table, slopping the wine. She threw herself forward in her seat and got purple in the face.

I jumped up and went over and landed one on her beefy back that would have shaken the City Hall.

She let out a long strangled wail and drew her breath in rackingly and stopped coughing. I pressed one of the keys on her dictaphone-box and when somebody answered, metallic and loud, through the metal disk, I said: 'Bring Mrs Murdock a glass of water, quick!' and then let the key up again.

I sat down again and watched her pull herself together. When her breath was coming evenly and without effort, I said: 'You're not tough. You just think you're tough. You been living too long with people that are scared of you. Wait'll you meet up with some law. Those boys are professionals. You're just a spoiled amateur.'

The door opened and the maid came in with a pitcher of ice-water and a glass. She put them down on the table and went out.

I poured Mrs Murdock a glass of water and put it in her hand.

'Sip it, don't drink it. You won't like the taste of it, but it won't hurt you.'

She sipped, then drank half of the glass, then put the glass down and wiped her lips.

'To think,' she said raspingly, 'that out of all the snoopers for hire I could have employed, I had to pick out a man who would bully me in my own house.'

'That's not getting you anywhere, either,' I said. 'We don't have a lot of time. What's our story to the police going to be?'

'The police mean nothing to me. Absolutely nothing. And if you give them my name, I shall regard it as a thoroughly disgusting breach of faith.'

That put me back where we started.

'Murder changes everything, Mrs Murdock. You can't dummy up on a murder case. We'll have to tell them why you employed me and what to do. They won't publish it in the papers, you know. That is, they won't if they believe it. They certainly won't believe you hired me to investigate Elisha Morningstar just because he called up and wanted to buy the doubloon. They may not find out that you couldn't have sold the coin, if you wanted to, because they might not think of that angle. But they won't believe you hired a private detective just to investigate a possible purchaser. Why should you?'

'That's my business, isn't it?'

'No. You can't fob the cops off that way. You have to satisfy them that you are being frank and open and have nothing to hide. As long as they think you are hiding something they never let up. Give them a reasonable and plausible story and they go away cheerful. And the most reasonable and plausible story is always the truth. Any objection to telling it?'

'Every possible objection,' she said. 'But it doesn't seem to make much difference. Do you have to tell them that I suspected my daughter-in-law of stealing the coin and that I was wrong?'

'It would be better.'

'And that it has been returned and how?'

'It would be better.'

'That is going to humiliate me very much.'

I shrugged.

'You're a callous brute,' she said. 'You're a cold-blooded fish. I don't like you. I deeply regret ever having met you.'

'Mutual,' I said.

She reached a thick finger to a key and barked into the talking-box. 'Merle. Ask my son to come in here at once. And I think you may as well come in with him.'

She released the key, pressed her broad fingers together and let her hands drop heavily to her thighs. Her bleak eyes went up to the ceiling.

Her voice was quiet and sad, saying: 'My son took the coin, Mr Marlowe. My son. My own son.'

I didn't say anything. We sat there glaring at each other. In a couple of minutes they both came in and she barked at them to sit down.

21

Leslie Murdock was wearing a greenish slack suit and his hair looked damp, as if he had just been taking a shower. He sat hunched forward, looking at the white buck shoes on his feet, and turning a ring on his finger. He didn't have his long black cigarette-holder and he looked a little lonely without it. Even his moustache seemed to droop a little more than it had in my office.

Merle Davis looked just the same as the day before. Probably she always looked the same. Her copper-blonde hair was dragged down just as tight, her shell-rimmed glasses looked just as large and empty, her eyes behind them just as vague. She was even wearing the same one-piece linen dress with short sleeves and no ornament of any kind, not even earrings.

I had the curious feeling of re-living something that had already happened.

Mrs Murdock sipped her port and said quietly:

'All right, son. Tell Mr Marlowe about the doubloon. I'm afraid he has to be told.'

Murdock looked up at me quietly and then dropped his eyes again. His mouth twitched. When he spoke his voice had the toneless quality, a flat tired sound, like a man making a confession after an exhausting battle with his conscience.

'As I told you yesterday in your office, I owe Morny a lot of money. Twelve thousand dollars. I denied it afterwards, but it's true. I do owe it. I didn't want mother to know. He was pressing me pretty hard for payment. I suppose I knew I would have to tell her in the end, but I was weak enough to want to put it off. I took the doubloon, using her keys one afternoon when she was asleep and Merle was out. I gave it to Morny and he agreed to hold it as security because I explained to him that he couldn't get anything like twelve thousand dollars for it unless he could give its history and show that it was legitimately in his possession.'

He stopped talking and looked up at me to see how I was taking it. Mrs Murdock had her eyes on my face, practically puttied there. The little girl was looking at Murdock with her lips parted and an expression of suffering on her face.

Murdock went on. 'Morny gave me a receipt, in which he agreed to hold the coin as collateral and not to convert it without notice and demand. Something like that. I don't profess to know how legal it was. When this man Morningstar called up and asked about the coin I immediately became suspicious that Morny either was trying to sell it or that he was at least thinking of selling it and was trying to get a valuation on it from somebody who knew about rare coins. I was badly scared.'

He looked up and made a sort of face at me. Maybe it was the face of somebody being badly scared. Then he took his handkerchief out and wiped his forehead and sat holding it between his hands.

'When Merle told me mother had employed a detective—Merle ought not to have told me, but mother has promised not to scold her for it.' He looked at his mother. The old warhorse clamped her jaws and looked grim. The little girl had her eyes still on his face and didn't seem to be very worried about the scolding. He went on: 'Then I was sure she had missed the doubloon and had hired you on that account. I didn't really believe she had hired you to find Linda. I knew where Linda was all the time. I went to your office to see what I could find out. I didn't find out very much. I went to see Morny yesterday afternoon and told him about it. At first he laughed in my face, but when I told him that even my mother couldn't sell the coin without violating the terms of Jasper Murdock's will and that she would certainly set the police on him when I told her where the coin was, then he loosened up. He got up and went to the safe and got the coin out and handed it to me without a word. I gave him back his receipt and he tore it up. So I brought the coin home and told mother about it.'

He stopped talking and wiped his face again. The little girl's eyes moved up and down with the motions of his hand.

In the silence that followed I said: 'Did Morny threaten you?'

He shook his head. 'He said he wanted his money and he needed it and I had better get busy and dig it up. But he wasn't threatening. He was very decent, really. In the circumstances.'

'Where was this?'

'At the Idle Valley Club, in his private office.'

'Was Eddie Prue there?'

The little girl tore her eyes away from his face and looked at me. Mrs Murdock said thickly: 'Who is Eddie Prue?'

'Morny's bodyguard,' I said. 'I didn't waste *all* my time yesterday, Mrs Murdock.' I looked at her son, waiting.

He said: 'No, I didn't see him. I know him by sight, of course. You would only have to see him once to remember him. But he wasn't around yesterday.'

I said: 'Is that all?'

He looked at his mother. She said harshly: 'Isn't it enough?'

'Maybe,' I said. 'Where is the coin now?'

'Where would you expect it to be?' she snapped.

I almost told her, just to see her jump. But I managed to hold it in. I said: 'That seems to take care of that, then.'

Mrs Murdock said heavily: 'Kiss your mother, son, and run along.'

He got up dutifully and went over and kissed her on the forehead. She patted his hand. He went out of the room with his head down and quietly shut the door. I said to Merle: 'I think you had better have him dictate that to you just the way he told it and make a copy of it and get him to sign it.'

She looked startled. The old woman snarled:

'She certainly won't do anything of the sort. Go back to your work, Merle. I wanted you to hear this. But if I ever again catch you violating my confidence, you know what will happen.'

The little girl stood up and smiled at her with shining eyes. 'Oh, yes, Mrs Murdock. I never will. Never. You can trust me.'

'I hope so,' the old dragon growled. 'Get out.'

Merle went out softly.

Two big tears formed themselves in Mrs Murdock's eyes and slowly made their way down the elephant hide of her cheeks, reached the corners of her fleshy nose and slid down her lip. She scrabbled around for her handkerchief, wiped them off and then wiped her eyes. She put the handkerchief away, reached for her wine and said placidly:

'I'm very fond of my son, Mr Marlowe. Very fond. This grieves me deeply. Do you think he will have to tell this story to the police?'

'I hope not,' I said. 'He'll have a hell of a time getting them to believe it.'

Her mouth snapped open and her teeth glinted at me in the dim light. She closed her lips and pressed them tight, scowling at me with her head lowered.

'Just what do you mean by that?' she snapped.

'Just what I said. The story doesn't ring true. It has a fabricated, over-simple sound. Did he make it up himself or did you think it up and teach it to him?'

'Mr Marlowe,' she said in a deadly voice, 'you are treading on very thin ice.'

I waved a hand. 'Aren't we all? All right, suppose it's true. Morny will deny it, and we'll be right back where we started. Morny will have to deny it, because otherwise it would tie him to a couple of murders.'

'Is there anything so unlikely about that being the exact situation?' she blared.

'Why should Morny, a man with backing, protection and some influence, tie himself to a couple of small murders in order to avoid tying himself to something trifling, like selling a pledge? It doesn't make sense to me.'

She stared, saying nothing. I grinned at her, because for the first time she was going to like something I said.

'I found your daughter-in-law, Mrs Murdock. It's a little strange to me that your son, who seems so well under your control, didn't tell you where she was.'

'I didn't ask him,' she said in a curiously quiet voice, for her.

'She's back where she started, singing with the band at the Idle Valley Club. I talked to her. She's a pretty hard sort of girl in a way. She doesn't like you very well. I don't find it impossible to think that she took the coin all right, partly from spite. And I find it slightly less impossible to believe that Leslie knew it or found it out and cooked up that yarn to protect her. He says he's very much in love with her.'

She smiled. It wasn't a beautiful smile, being on slightly the wrong kind of face. But it was a smile.

'Yes,' she said gently. 'Yes. Poor Leslie. He would do just that. And in that case'—she stopped and her smile widened until it was almost ecstatic—'in that case my dear daughter-in-law may be involved in murder.'

I watched her enjoying the idea for a quarter of a minute. 'And you'd just love that,' I said.

She nodded, still smiling, getting the idea she liked before she got the rudeness in my voice. Then her face stiffened and her lips came together hard. Between them and her teeth she said:

'I don't like your tone. I don't like your tone at all.'

'I don't blame you,' I said. 'I don't like it myself. I don't like anything. I don't like this house or you or the air of repression in the joint, or the squeezed down face of the little girl or that twerp of a son you have, or this case or the truth I'm not told about it and the lies I am told about it and—'

She started yelling then, noise out of a splotched furious face, eyes tossing with fury, sharp with hate:

'Get out! Get out of this house at once! Don't delay one instant! Get out!'

I stood up and reached my hat off the carpet and said:

'I'll be glad to.'

I gave her a sort of tired leer and picked my way to the door and opened it and went out. I shut it quietly, holding the knob with a stiff hand and clicking the lock gently into place.

For no reason at all.

22

Steps gibbered along after me and my name was called and I kept on going until I was in the middle of the living-room. Then I stopped and turned and let her catch up with me, out of breath, her eyes trying to pop through her glasses and her shining copper-blonde hair catching funny little lights from the high windows.

'Mr Marlowe! Please! Please, don't go away. She wants you. She really does!'

'I'll be darned. You've got Sub-deb Bright on your mouth this morning. Looks all right, too.'

She grabbed my sleeve. 'Please!'

'The hell with her,' I said. 'Tell her to jump in the lake. Marlowe can get sore, too. Tell her to jump in two lakes, if one won't hold her. Not clever, but quick.'

I looked down at the hand on my sleeve and patted it. She drew it away swiftly and her eyes looked shocked.

'Please, Mr Marlowe. She's in trouble. She needs you.'

'I'm in trouble, too,' I growled. 'I'm up to my earflaps in trouble. What are you crying about?'

'Oh, I'm really fond of her. I know she's rough and blustery, but her heart is pure gold.'

'To hell with her heart, too,' I said. 'I don't expect to get intimate enough with her for that to make any difference. She's a fat-faced old liar. I've had enough of her. I think she's in trouble all right, but I'm not in the excavating business. I have to get told things.'

'Oh, I'm sure if you would only be patient—'

I put my arm around her shoulders, without thinking. She jumped about three feet and her eyes blazed with panic.

We stood there staring at each other, making breath noises, me with my mouth open as it too frequently is, she with her lips pressed tight and her little pale nostrils quivering. Her face was as pale as the unhandy make-up would let it be.

'Look,' I said slowly, 'did something happen to you when you were a little girl?'

She nodded, very quickly.

'A man scared you or something like that?'

She nodded again. She took her lower lip between her little white teeth.

'And you've been like this ever since?'

She just stood there, looking white.

'Look,' I said, 'I won't do anything to you that will scare you. Not ever.'

Her eyes melted with tears.

'If I touched you,' I said, 'it was just like touching a chair or a door. It didn't mean anything. Is that clear?'

'Yes.' She got a word out at last. Panic still twitched in the depths of her eyes, behind the tears. 'Yes.'

'That take cares of me,' I said. 'I'm all adjusted. Nothing to worry about in me any more. Now take Leslie. He has his mind on other things. You know he's all right—in the way we mean. Right?'

'Oh, yes,' she said. 'Yes, indeed.' Leslie was aces. With her. With me he was a handful of bird gravel.

'Now take the old wine barrel,' I said. 'She's rough and she's tough and she thinks she can eat walls and spit bricks, and she bawls you out, but she's fundamentally decent to you, isn't she?'

'Oh, she is, Mr Marlowe. I was trying to tell you—'

'Sure. Now why don't you get over it? Is he still around—this other one that hurt you?'

She put her hand to her mouth and gnawed the fleshy part at the base of the thumb, looking at me over it, as if it was a balcony.

'He's dead,' she said. 'He fell out of a—out of a—a window.'

I stopped her with my big right hand. 'Oh, that guy. I heard about him. Forget it, can't you?'

'No,' she said, shaking her head seriously behind the hand. 'I can't. I can't seem to forget it at all. Mrs Murdock is always telling me to forget it. She talks to me for the longest times telling me to forget it. But I just can't.'

'It would be a darn sight better,' I snarled, 'if she would keep her fat mouth shut about it for the longest times. She just keeps it alive.'

She looked surprised and rather hurt at that. 'Oh, that isn't all,' she said. 'I was his secretary. She was his wife. He was her first husband. Naturally she doesn't forget it either. How could she?'

I scratched my ear. That seemed sort of noncommittal. There was nothing much in her expression now except that I didn't really think she realized that I was there. I was a voice coming out of somewhere, but rather impersonal. Almost a voice in her own head.

Then I had one of my funny and often unreliable hunches. 'Look,' I said, 'is there someone you meet that has that effect on you? Some one person more than another?'

She looked all round the room. I looked with her. Nobody was under a chair or peeking at us through a door or a window.

'Why do I have to tell you?' she breathed.

'You don't. It's just how you feel about it.'

'Will you promise not to tell anybody—anybody in the whole world, not even Mrs Murdock?'

'Her last of all,' I said. 'I promise.'

She opened her mouth and put a funny little confiding smile on her face, and then it went wrong. Her throat froze up. She made a croaking noise. Her teeth actually rattled.

I wanted to give her a good hard squeeze but I was afraid to touch her. We stood. Nothing happened. We stood. I was about as much use as a humming-bird's spare egg would have been.

Then she turned and ran. I heard her steps going along the hall. I heard a door close.

I went after her along the hall and reached the door. She was sobbing behind it. I stood there and listened to the sobbing.

There was nothing I could do about it. I wondered if there was anything anybody could do about it.

I went back to the glass porch and knocked on the door and opened it and put my head in. Mrs Murdock sat just as I had left her. She didn't seem to have moved at all.

'Who's scaring the life out of that little girl?' I asked her.

'Get out of my house,' she said between her fat lips.

I didn't move. Then she laughed at me hoarsely.

'Do you regard yourself as a clever man, Mr Marlowe?'

'Well, I'm not dripping with it,' I said.

'Suppose you find out for yourself.'

'At your expense?'

She shrugged her heavy shoulders. 'Possibly. It depends. Who knows?'

'You haven't bought a thing,' I said. 'I'm still going to have to talk to the police.'

'I haven't bought anything,' she said, 'and I haven't paid for anything. Except the return of the coin. I'm satisfied to accept that for the money I have already given you. Now go away. You bore me. Unspeakably.'

I shut the door and went back. No sobbing behind the door. Very still. I went on.

I let myself out of the house. I stood there, listening to the sunshine burn the grass. A car started up in back and a grey Mercury came drifting along the drive at the side of the house. Mr Leslie Murdock was driving it. When he saw me he stopped.

He got out of the car and walked quickly over to me. He was nicely dressed; cream-coloured gabardine now, all fresh clothes, slacks, black and white shoes, with polished black toes, a sports coat of very small black and white check, black and white handkerchief, cream shirt, no tie. He had a pair of green sun-glasses on his nose.

He stood close to me and said in a low timid sort of voice: 'I guess you think I'm an awful heel.'

'On account of that story you told about the doubloon?'

'Yes.'

'That didn't affect my way of thinking about you in the least,' I said.

'Well—'

'Just what do you want me to say?'

He moved his smoothly tailored shoulders in a deprecatory shrug. His silly little reddish-brown moustache glittered in the sun.

'I suppose I like to be liked,' he said.

'I'm sorry, Murdock. I like your being that devoted to your wife. If that's what it is.'

'Oh. Didn't you think I was telling the truth? I mean, did you think I was saying all that just to protect her?'

'There was that possibility.'

'I see.' He put a cigarette into the long black holder, which he took from behind his display handkerchief. 'Well—I guess I can take it that you don't like me.' The dim movement of his eyes was visible behind the green lenses, fish moving in a deep pool.

'It's a silly subject,' I said. 'And damned unimportant. To both of us.'

He put a match to the cigarette and inhaled. 'I see,' he said quietly. 'Pardon me for being crude enough to bring it up.'

He turned on his heel and walked back to his car and got in. I watched him drive away before I moved. Then I went over and patted the little painted Negro boy on the head a couple of times before I left.

'Son,' I said to him, 'you're the only person around this house that's not nuts.'

23

The police loudspeaker-box on the wall grunted and a voice said: 'K.G.P.L. Testing.' A click and it went dead.

Detective-Lieutenant Jesse Breeze stretched his arms high in the air and yawned and said: 'Couple of hours late, ain't you?'

I said: 'Yes. But I left a message for you that I would be. I had to go to the dentist.'

'Sit down.'

He had a small littered desk across one corner of the room. He sat in the angle behind it, with a tall bare window to his left and a wall with a large calendar about eye height to his right. The days that had gone to dust were crossed off carefully in soft black pencil, so that Breeze glancing at the calendar always knew exactly what day it was.

Spangler was sitting sideways at a smaller and much neater desk. It had a green blotter and an onyx pen set and a small brass calendar and an abalone shell full of ashes and matches and cigarette-stubs. Spangler was flipping a handful of bank pens at the felt back of a seat cushion on end against the wall, like a Mexican knife-thrower flipping knives at a target. He wasn't getting anywhere with it. The pens refused to stick.

The room had that remote, heartless, not quite dirty, not quite clean, not quite human smell that such rooms always have. Give a police department a brand new building and in three months all its rooms will smell like that. There must be something symbolic in it.

A New York police reporter wrote once that when you pass in beyond the green lights of the precinct station you pass clear out of this world into a place beyond the law.

I sat down. Breeze got a cellophane-wrapped cigar out of his pocket and the routine with it started. I watched it detail by detail, unvarying, precise. He drew in smoke, shook his match out, laid it gently in the black glass ashtray, and said: 'Hi, Spangler.'

Spangler turned his head and Breeze turned his head. They grinned at each other. Breeze poked the cigar at me.

'Watch him sweat,' he said.

Spangler had to move his feet to turn far enough around to watch me sweat. If I was sweating, I didn't know it.

'You boys are as cute as a couple of lost golf-balls,' I said. 'How in the world do you do it?'

'Skip the wisecracks,' Breeze said. 'Had a busy little morning?'

'Fair,' I said.

He was still grinning. Spangler was still grinning. Whatever it was Breeze was tasting he hated to swallow it.

Finally he cleared his throat, straightened his big freckled face out, turned his head enough so that he was not looking at me but could still see me and said in a vague empty sort of voice:

'Hench confessed.'

Spangler swung clear around to look at me. He leaned forward on the edge of his chair and his lips were parted in an ecstatic half-smile that was almost indecent.

I said: 'What did you use on him—a pickaxe?'

'Nope.'

They were both silent, staring at me.

'A wop,' Breeze said.

'A what?'

'Boy, are you glad?' Breeze said.

'You are going to tell me or are you just going to sit there looking fat and complacent and watch me being glad?'

'We like to watch a guy being glad,' Breeze said. 'We don't often get a chance.'

I put a cigarette in my mouth and jiggled it up and down.

'We used a wop on him,' Breeze said. 'A wop named Palermo.'

'Oh. You know something?'

'What?' Breeze asked.

'I just thought of what is the matter with policeman's dialogue.'

'What?'

'They think every line is a punch line.'

'And every pinch is a good pinch,' Breeze said calmly. 'You want to know—or you want to just wisecrack?'

'I want to know.'

'Was like this, then. Hench was drunk. I mean he was drunk deep inside, not just on the surface. Screwy drunk. He'd been living on it for weeks. He's practically quit eating and sleeping. Just liquor. He'd got to the point where liquor wasn't making him drunk, it was keeping him sober. It was the last hold he had on the real world. When a guy gets like that and you take his liquor away and don't give him anything to hold him down, he's a lost cuckoo.'

I didn't say anything. Spangler still had the same erotic leer on his young face. Breeze tapped the side of his cigar and no ash fell off and he put it back in his mouth and went on.

'He's a psycho case, but we don't want any psycho case made out of our pinch. We make that clear. We want a guy that don't have any psycho record.'

'I thought you were sure Hench was innocent.'

Breeze nodded vaguely. 'That was last night. Or maybe I was kidding a little. Anyway in the night, bang, Hench is bugs. So they drag him over to the hospital ward and shoot him full of hop. The jail doc. does. That's between you and me. No hop in the record. Get the idea?'

'All too clearly,' I said.

'Yeah.' He looked vaguely suspicious of the remark, but he was too full of his subject to waste time on it. 'Well, this a.m. he is fine. Hop still working, the guy is pale but peaceful. We go see him. How you doing, kid? Anything you need? Any little thing at all? Be glad to get it for you. They treating you nice in here? You know the line.'

'I do,' I said. 'I know the line.'

Spangler licked his lips in a nasty way.

'So after a while he opens his trap just enough to say "Palermo". Palermo is the name of the wop across the street that owns the funeral home and the apartment house and stuff. You remember? Yeah, you remember. On account of he said something about a tall blonde. All hooey. Them wops got tall blondes on the brain. In sets of twelve. But this Palermo is important. I asked around. He gets the vote out up there. He's a guy that can't be pushed around. Well, I don't aim to push him around. I say to Hench, "You mean Palermo's a friend of yours?" He says, "Get Palermo." So we come back here to the hutch and phone Palermo and Palermo says he will be right down. Okay. He is here very soon. We talk like this: Hench wants to see you, Mr Palermo. I wouldn't know why. He's a poor guy, Palermo says. A nice guy. I think he's okay. He wanta see me, that'sa fine. I see him. I see him alone. Without any coppers. I say, Okay, Mr Palermo, and we go over to the hospital ward and Palermo talks to Hench and nobody listens. After a while Palermo comes out and he says, Okay, copper. He make the confess. I pay the lawyer, maybe. I like the poor guy. Just like that. He goes away.'

I didn't say anything. There was a pause. The loudspeaker on the wall put out a bulletin and Breeze cocked his head and listened to ten or twelve words and then ignored it.

'So we go in with a steno and Hench gives us the dope. Phillips made a pass at Hench's girl. That was day before yesterday, out in the hall. Hench was in the room and he saw it, but Phillips got into his apartment and shut the door before Hench could get out. But Hench was sore. He socked the girl in the eye. But that didn't satisfy him. He got to brooding, the way a drunk will brood. He says to himself, that guy can't make a pass at my girl.

I'm the boy that will give him something to remember me by. So he keeps an eye open for Phillips. Yesterday afternoon he sees Phillips go into his apartment. He tells the girl to go for a walk. She don't want to go for a walk, so Hench socks her in the other eye. She goes for a walk. Hench knocks on Phillips's door and Phillips opens it. Hench is a little surprised at that, but I told him Phillips was expecting you. Anyway, the door opens and Hench goes in and tells Phillips how he feels and what he is going to do and Phillips is scared and pulls a gun. Hench hits him with a sap. Phillips falls down and Hench ain't satisfied. You hit a guy with a sap and he falls down and what have you? No satisfaction, no revenge. Hench picks the gun off the floor and he is very drunk there being dissatisfied and Phillips grabs for his ankle. Hench doesn't know why he did what he did then. He's all fuzzy in the head. He drags Phillips into the bathroom and gives him the business with his own gun. You like it?'

'I love it,' I said. 'But what is the satisfaction in it for Hench?'

'Well, you know how a drunk is. Anyway, he gives him the business. Well it ain't Hench's gun, you see, but he can't make a suicide out of it. There wouldn't be any satisfaction for him in that. So Hench takes the gun away and puts it under his pillow and takes his own gun out and ditches it. He won't tell us where. Probably passes it to some tough guy in the neighbourhood. Then he finds the girl and they eat.'

'That was a lovely touch,' I said. 'Putting the gun under his pillow. I'd never in the world have thought of that.'

Breeze leaned back in his chair and looked at the ceiling. Spangler, the big part of the entertainment over, swung around in his chair and picked up a couple of bank pens and threw one at the cushion.

'Look at it this way,' Breeze said. 'What was the effect of that stunt? Look how Hench did it. He was drunk, but he was smart. He found that gun and showed it before Phillips was found dead. First we get the idea that a gun is under Hench's pillow that killed a guy—been fired anyway—and then we get the stiff. We believed Hench's story. It seemed reasonable. Why would we think any man would be such a sap as to do what Hench did? It doesn't make any sense. So we believed somebody put the gun under Hench's pillow and took Hench's gun away and ditched it. And suppose Hench ditched the death gun instead of his own, would he have been any better off? Things being what they were we would be bound to suspect him. And that way he wouldn't have started our minds thinking any particular way about him. The way he did he got us thinking he was a harmless drunk that went out and left his door open and somebody ditched a gun on him.'

He waited, with his mouth a little open and the cigar in front of it, held up by a hard freckled hand, and his pale blue eyes full of dim satisfaction.

'Well,' I said, 'if he was going to confess anyway, it wouldn't have made very much difference. Will he cop a plea?'

'Sure. I think so. I figure Palermo could get him off with manslaughter. Naturally, I'm not sure.'

'Why would Palermo want to get him off with anything?'

'He kind of likes Hench. And Palermo is a guy we can't push around.'

I said: 'I see.' I stood up. Spangler looked at me sideways along glistening eyes. 'What about the girl?'

'Won't say a word. She's smart. We can't do anything to her. Nice neat little job all around. You wouldn't kick would you? Whatever your business is, it's still your business. Get me?'

'And the girl is a tall blonde,' I said. 'Not of the freshest, but still a tall blonde. Although only one. Maybe Palermo doesn't mind.'

'Hell, I never thought of that,' Breeze said. He thought about it and shook it off. 'Nothing in that, Marlowe. Not enough class.'

'Cleaned up and sober, you never can tell,' I said. 'Class is a thing that has a way of dissolving rapidly in alcohol. That all you want with me?'

'Guess so.' He slanted the cigar up and aimed it at my eye. 'Not that I wouldn't like to hear your story. But I don't figure I have an absolute right to insist on it the way things are.'

'That's white of you, Breeze,' I said. 'And you, too, Spangler. A lot of the good things in life to both of you.'

They watched me go out, both with their mouths a little open.

I rode down to the big marble lobby and went and got my car out of the official parking lot.

24

Mr Pietro Palermo was sitting in a room which, except for a mahogany roll-up desk, a sacred triptych in gilt frames and a large ebony and ivory crucifixion, looked exactly like a Victorian parlour. It contained a horseshoe sofa and chairs with carved mahogany frames and antimacassars of fine lace. There was an ormolu clock on the grey-green marble mantel, a grandfather clock ticking lazily in the corner, and some wax flowers under a glass dome on an oval table with a marble top and curved elegant legs. The carpet was thick and full of gentle sprays of flowers. There was even a cabinet for bric-à-brac and there was plenty of bric-à-brac in it, little cups of fine china, little figurines in glass and porcelain, odds and ends of ivory and dark rosewood, painted saucers, an early American set of swan salt-cellars, stuff like that.

Long lace curtains hung across the windows, but the room faced south and there was plenty of light. Across the street I could see the windows of the apartment where George Anson Phillips had been killed. The street between was sunny and silent.

The tall Italian with the dark skin and the handsome head of iron grey hair read my card and said:

'I got business in twelve minutes. What you want, Meester Marlowe?'

'I'm the man that found the dead man across the street yesterday. He was a friend of mine.'

His cold black eyes looked me over silently. 'That'sa not what you tell Luke.'

'Luke?'

'He manage the joint for me.'

'I don't talk much to strangers, Mr Palermo.'

'That'sa good. You talk to me, huh?'

'You're a man of standing, an important man. I can talk to you. You saw me yesterday. You described me to the police. Very accurately, they said.'

'Si. I see much,' he said without emotion.

'You saw a tall blonde woman come out of there yesterday.'

He studied me. 'Not yesterday. Wasa two three days ago. I tell the coppers yesterday.' He snapped his long dark fingers. 'The coppers, bah!'

'Did you see any strangers yesterday, Mr Palermo?'

'Is back way in and out,' he said. 'Is stair from second floor also.' He looked at his wrist-watch.

'Nothing there then,' I said. 'This morning you saw Hench.'

He lifted his eyes and ran them lazily over my face.

'The coppers tell you that, huh?'

'They told me you got Hench to confess. They said he was a friend of yours. How good a friend they didn't know, of course.'

'Hench make the confess, huh?' He smiled, a sudden brilliant smile.

'Only Hench didn't do the killing,' I said.

'No?'

'No.'

'That'sa interesting. Go on, Meester Marlowe.'

'The confession is a lot of baloney. You got him to make it for some reason of your own.'

He stood up and went to the door and called out: 'Tony.'

He sat down again. A short, tough-looking wop came into the room, looked at me and sat down against the wall in a straight chair.

'Tony, thees man a Meester Marlowe. Look, take the card.'

Tony came to get the card and sat down with it. 'You look at thees man very good, Tony. Not forget him, huh?'

Tony said: 'Leave it to me, Mr Palermo.'

Palermo said: 'Was a friend to you, huh? A good friend, huh?'

'Yes.'

'That'sa bad. Yeah. That'sa bad. I tell you something. A man's friend is a man's friend. So I tell you. But you don' tell anybody else. Not the damn coppers, huh?'

'No.'

'That'sa promire- Meester Marlowe. That'sa something not to forget. You not forget?'

'I won't forget.'

'Tony, he not forget you. Get the idea?'

'I gave you my word. What you tell me is between us here.'

'That'sa fine. Okay. I come of large family. Many sisters and brothers. One brother very bad. Almost so bad as Tony.'

Tony grinned.

'Okay, thees brother live very quiet. Across the street. Gotta move. Okay, the coppers fill the joint up. Not so good. Ask too many questions. Not good for business, not good for thees bad brother. You get the idea?'

'Yes,' I said. 'I get the idea.'

'Okay, thees Hench no good, but poor guy, drunk, no job. Pay no rent, but I got lotsa money. So I say, Look, Hench, you make the confess. You sick man. Two three weeks sick. You go into court. I have a lawyer for you. You say to hell with the confess. I was drunk. The damn coppers are stuck. The judge he turn you loose and you come back to me and I take care of you. Okay? So Hench say okay, make the confess. That's all.'

I said: 'And after two or three weeks the bad brother is a long way from here and the trail is cold and the cops will likely just write the Phillips killing off as unsolved. Is that it?'

'Si.' He smiled again. A brilliant warm smile, like the kiss of death.

'That takes care of Hench, Mr Palermo,' I said. 'But it doesn't help me much about my friend.'

He shook his head and looked at his watch again. I stood up. Tony stood up. He wasn't going to do anything, but it's better to be standing up. You move faster.

'The trouble with you birds,' I said, 'is you make mystery of nothing. You have to give the password before you bite a piece of bread. If I went down to headquarters and told the boys anything you have told me, they would laugh in my face. And I would be laughing with them.'

'Tony don't laugh much,' Palermo said.

'The earth is full of people who don't laugh much, Mr Palermo,' I said. 'You ought to know. You put a lot of them where they are.'

'Is my business,' he said, shrugging enormously.

'I'll keep my promise,' I said. 'But in case you should get to doubting that, don't try to make any business for yourself out of me. Because in my part of town I'm a pretty good man and if the business got made out of Tony instead, it would be strictly on the house. No profit.'

Palermo laughed. 'That'sa good,' he said. 'One funeral—on the house. Okay.'

He stood up and held his hand out, a fine strong warm hand.

25

In the lobby of the Belfont Building, in the single elevator that had light in it, on the piece of folded burlap, the same watery-eyed relic sat motionless, giving his imitation of the forgotten man. I got in with him and said: 'Six.'

The elevator lurched into motion and pounded its way upstairs. It stopped at six, I got out, and the old man leaned out of the car to spit and said in a dull voice:

'What's cookin'?'

I turned around all in one piece, like a dummy on a revolving platform. I stared at him.

He said: 'You got a grey suit on to-day.'

'So I have,' I said. 'Yes.'

'Looks nice,' he said. 'I like the blue you was wearing yesterday, too.'

'Go on,' I said. 'Give out.'

'You rode up to eight,' he said. 'Twice. Second time was late. You got back on at six. Shortly after that the boys in blue came bustlin' in.'

'Any of them up there now?'

He shook his head. His face was like a vacant lot. 'I ain't told them anything,' he said. 'Too late to mention it now. They'd eat my ass off.'

I said: 'Why?'

'Why I ain't told them? The hell with them. You talked to me civil. Damn few people do that. Hell, I know you didn't have nothing to do with that killing.'

'I played you wrong,' I said. 'Very wrong.' I got a card out and gave it to him. He fished a pair of metal-framed glasses out of his pocket, perched them on his nose and held the card a foot away from them. He read it slowly, moving his lips, looked at me over the glasses, handed me back the card.

'Better keep it,' he said. 'Case I get careless and drop it. Mighty interestin' life yours, I guess.'

'Yes and no. What was the name?'

'Grandy. Just call me Pop. Who killed him?'

'I don't know. Did you notice anybody going up there or coming down—anybody that seemed out of place in this building, or strange to you?'

'I don't notice much,' he said. 'I just happened to notice you.'

'A tall blonde, for instance, or a slender man with sideburns, about thirty-five years old.'

'Nope.'

'Everybody going up or down about then would ride in your car.'

He nodded his worn head. 'Less they used the fire stairs. They come out in the alley, bar-lock door. Party would have to come in this way, but there's stairs back of the elevator to the second floor. From there they can get to the fire stairs. Nothing to it.'

I nodded. 'Mr Grandy, could you use a five-dollar bill—not as a bribe in any sense, but as a token of esteem from a sincere friend?'

'Son, I could use a five-dollar bill so rough Abe Lincoln's whiskers would be all lathered up with sweat.'

I gave him one. I looked at it before I passed it over. It was Lincoln on the five, all right.

He tucked it small and put it away deep in his pocket. 'That's right nice of you,' he said. 'I hope to hell you don't think I was fishin'.'

I shook my head and went along the corridor, reading the names again. *Dr E.J.Blaskowitz, Chiropractic Physician. Dalton and Rees Typewriting Service. L.Pridview, Public Accountant.* Four blank doors. *Moss Mailing Company.* Two more blank doors. *H.R.Teager, Dental Laboratories.* In the same relative position as the Morningstar office two floors above, but the rooms were cut up differently. Teager had only one door and there was more wall space between his door and the next one.

The knob didn't turn. I knocked. There was no answer. I knocked harder, with the same result. I went back to the elevator. It was still at the sixth floor. Pop Grandy watched me come as if he had never seen me before.

'Know anything about H.R.Teager?' I asked him.

He thought. 'Heavy-set, oldish, sloppy clothes, dirty fingernails, like mine. Come to think I didn't see him in to-day.'

'Do you think the super would let me into his office to look around?'

'Pretty nosey, the super is. I wouldn't recommend it.'

He turned his head very slowly and looked up the side of the car. Over his head on a big metal ring a key was hanging. A pass-key. Pop Grandy turned his head back to normal position, stood up off his stool and said: 'Right now I gotta go to the can.'

He went. When the door had closed behind him I took the key off the cage wall and went back along to the Office of H.R.Teager, unlocked it and went in.

Inside was a small windowless ante-room on the furnishings of which a great deal of expense had been spared. Two chairs, a smoking-stand from a cut-rate drugstore, a standing lamp from the basement of some borax emporium, a flat stained wood table with some old picture magazines on it. The door closed behind me on the door-closer and the place went dark except for what little light came through the pebbled glass panel. I pulled the chain switch of the lamp and went over to the inner door in a wall that cut across the room. It was marked: *H.R.Teager. Private.* It was not locked.

Inside it there was a square office with two uncurtained east windows and very dusty sills. There was a swivel-chair and two straight chairs, both plain hard stained wood, and there was a squarish flat-topped desk. There was nothing on the top of it except an old blotter and a cheap pen set and a round glass ashtray with cigar ash in it. The drawers of the desk contained some dusty paper linings, a few wire clips, rubber bands, worn-down pencils, rusty pen points, used blotter, four uncancelled two-cent stamps, and some printed letterheads, envelopes and bill forms.

The wire paper-basket was full of junk. I almost wasted ten minutes going through it rather carefully. At the end of that time I knew what I was pretty sure of already: that H.R.Teager carried on a small business as a dental technician doing laboratory work for a number of dentists in unprosperous sections of the city, the kind of dentists who have shabby offices on second floor walk-ups over stores, who lack both the skill and the equipment to do their own laboratory work, and who like to send it out to men like themselves, rather than to the big efficient hard-boiled laboratories who wouldn't give them any credit.

I did find one thing. Teager's home address at 1354B Toberman Street on the receipted part of a gas bill.

I straightened up, dumped the stuff back into the basket and went over to the wooden door marked *Laboratory*. It had a new Yale lock on it and the pass-key didn't fit it. That was that. I switched off the lamp in the outer office and left.

The elevator was downstairs again. I rang for it and when it came up I sidled in around Pop Grandy, hiding the key, and hung it up over his head. The ring tinkled against the cage. He grinned.

'He's gone,' I said. 'Must have left last night. Must have been carrying a lot of stuff. His desk is cleaned out.'

Pop Grandy nodded. 'Carried two suitcases. I wouldn't notice that, though. Most always does carry a suitcase. I figure he picks up and delivers his work.'

'Work such as what?' I asked as the car growled down. Just to be saying something.

'Such as makin' teeth that don't fit,' Pop Grandy said. 'For poor old bastards like me.'

'You wouldn't notice,' I said, as the doors struggled open on the lobby. 'You wouldn't notice the colour of a humming-bird's eye at fifty feet. Not much you wouldn't.'

He grinned. 'What's he done?'

'I'm going over to his house and find out,' I said. 'I think most likely he's taken a cruise to nowhere.'

'I'd shift places with him,' Pop Grandy said. 'Even if he only got to Frisco and got pinched there, I'd shift places with him.'

26

Toberman Street. A wide dusty street, off Pico. No. 1354B was an upstairs flat, south, in a yellow and white frame building. The entrance door was on the porch, beside another marked 1352B. The entrances to the downstairs flats were at right angles, facing each other across the width of the porch. I kept on ringing the bell, even after I was sure that nobody would answer it. In a neighbourhood like that there is always an expert window-peeker.

Sure enough the door of 1354A was pulled open and a small bright-eyed woman looked out at me. Her dark hair had been washed and waved and was an intricate mass of bobby pins.

'You want Mrs Teager?' she shrilled.

'Mr or Mrs.'

'They gone away last night on their vacation. They loaded up and gone away late. They had me stop the milk and the paper. They didn't have much time. Kind of sudden, it was.'

'Thanks. What kind of car do they drive?'

The heart-rending dialogue of some love serial came out of the room behind her and hit me in the face like a wet dish-towel.

The bright-eyed woman said: 'You a friend of theirs?' In her voice suspicion was as thick as the ham in her radio.

'Never mind,' I said in a tough voice. 'All we want is our money. Lots of ways to find out what car they were driving.'

The woman cocked her head, listening. 'That's Beula May,' she told me with a sad smile. 'She won't go to the dance with Doctor Myers. I was scared she wouldn't.'

'Aw hell,' I said, and went back to my car and drove on home to Hollywood.

The office was empty. I unlocked my inner room and threw the windows up and sat down.

Another day drawing to its end, the air dull and tired, the heavy growl of homing traffic on the boulevard, and Marlowe in his office nibbling a drink and sorting the day's mail. Four advertisements; two bills; a handsome coloured postcard from a hotel in Santa Rosa where I had stayed for four days last year, working on a case; a long, badly typed letter from a man named Peabody in Sausalito, the general and slightly cloudy drift of which was that a sample of the handwriting of a suspected person would, when exposed to the searching Peabody examination, reveal the inner emotional characteristics of the individual, classified according to both the Freudian and Jung systems.

There was a stamped addressed envelope inside. As I tore the stamp off and threw the letter and envelope away I had a vision of a pathetic old rooster in long hair, black felt hat and black bow tie, rocking on a rickety porch in front of a lettered window, with the smell of ham hocks and cabbage coming out of the door at his elbow.

I sighed, retrieved the envelope, wrote its name and address on a fresh one, folded a dollar bill into a sheet of paper and wrote on it: 'This is positively the last contribution.' I signed my name, sealed the envelope, stuck a stamp on it and poured another drink.

I filled and lit my pipe and sat there smoking. Nobody came in, nobody called, nothing happened, nobody cared whether I died or went to El Paso.

Little by little the roar of the traffic quieted down. The sky lost its glare. Over in the west it would be red. An early neon light showed a block away, diagonally over roofs. The ventilator churned dully in the wall of the coffee shop down the alley. A truck filled and backed and growled its way out on to the boulevard.

Finally the telephone rang. I answered it and the voice said: 'Mr Marlowe? This is Mr Shaw. At the Bristol.'

'Yes, Mr Shaw. How are you?'

'I'm very well, thanks, Mr Marlowe. I hope you are the same. There's a young lady here asking to be let into your apartment. I don't know why.'

'Me neither, Mr Shaw. I didn't order anything like that. Does she give a name?'

'Oh yes. Quite. Her name is Davis. Miss Merle Davis. She is—what shall I say?—quite verging on the hysterical.'

'Let her in,' I said, rapidly. 'I'll be there in ten minutes. She's the secretary of a client. It's a business matter entirely.'

'Quite. Oh yes. Shall I—er—remain with her?'

'Whatever you think,' I said and hung up.

Passing the open door of the wash cabinet I saw a stiff excited face in the glass.

27

As I turned the key in my door and opened it Shaw was already standing up from the davenport. He was a tall man with glasses and a high-domed bald head that made his ears look as it they had slipped down on his head. He had the fixed smile of polite idiocy on his face.

The girl sat in my easy-chair behind the chess table. She wasn't doing anything, just sitting there.

'Ah, there you are, Mr Marlowe,' Shaw chirped. 'Yes. Quite. Miss Davis and I have been having such an interesting little conversation. I was telling her I originally came from England. She hasn't—er—told me where she came from.' He was half-way to the door saying this.

'Very kind of you, Mr Shaw,' I said.

'Not at all,' he chirped. 'Not at all. I'll just run along now. My dinner, possibly—'

'It's very nice of you,' I said. 'I appreciate it.'

He nodded and was gone. The unnatural brightness of his smile seemed to linger in the air after the door closed like the smile of a Cheshire cat.

I said: 'Hello, there.'

She said: 'Hello.' Her voice was quite calm, quite serious. She was wearing a brownish linen coat and skirt, a broad-brimmed low-crowned straw hat with a brown velvet band that exactly matched the colour of her shoes and the leather trimming on the edges of her linen envelope bag. The hat was tilted rather daringly, for her. She was not wearing her glasses.

Except for her face she would have looked all right. In the first place her eyes were quite mad. There was white showing all around the iris and they had a sort of fixed look. When they moved the movement was so stiff that you could almost hear something creak. Her mouth was in a tight line at the corners, but the middle part of her upper lip kept lifting off her teeth, upwards and outwards as if fine threads attached to the edge of the lip were pulling it. It would go up so far that it didn't seem possible, and then the entire lower part of her face would go into a spasm and when the spasm was over her mouth would be tight shut, and then the process would slowly start all over again. In addition to this there was something wrong with her neck, so that very slowly her head was drawn down around to the left about forty-five degrees. It would stop there, her neck would twitch, and her head would slide back the way it had come.

The combination of these two movements, taken with the immobility of her body, the tight-clasped hands in her lap, and the fixed stare of her eyes, was enough to start anybody's nerves backfiring.

There was a can of tobacco on the desk, between which and her chair was the chess table with the chessmen in their box. I got the pipe out of my pocket and went over to fill it at the can of tobacco. That put me just on the other side of the chess table from her. Her bag was lying on the edge of the table, in front of her and a little to one side. She jumped a little when I went over there, but after that she was just like before. She even made an effort to smile.

I filled the pipe and struck a paper match and lit it and stood there holding the match after I had blown it out.

'You're not wearing your glasses,' I said.

She spoke. Her voice was quiet, composed. 'Oh, I only wear them around the house and for reading. They're in my bag.'

'You're in the house now,' I said. 'You ought to be wearing them.'

I reached casually for the bag. She didn't move. She didn't watch my hands. Her eyes were on my face. I turned my body a little as I opened the bag. I fished the glass case out and slid it across the table.

'Put them on,' I said.

'Oh, yes, I'll put them on,' she said. 'But I'll have to take my hat off, I think . . .'

'Yes, take your hat off,' I said.

She took her hat off and held it on her knees. Then she remembered about the glasses and forgot about the hat. The hat fell on the floor while she reached for the glasses. She put them on. That helped her appearance a lot, I thought.

While she was doing this I got the gun out of her bag and slid it into my hip pocket. I didn't think she saw me. It looked like the same Colt .25 automatic with the walnut grip that I had seen in the top right-hand drawer of her desk the day before.

I went back to the davenport and sat down and said: 'Well, here we are. What do we do now? Are you hungry?'

'I've been over to Mr Vannier's house,' she said.

'Oh.'

'He lives in Sherman Oaks. At the end of Escamillo Drive. At the very end.'

'Quite, probably,' I said without meaning, and tried to blow a smoke ring, but didn't make it. A nerve in my cheek was trying to twang like a wire. I didn't like it.

'Yes,' she said in her composed voice, with her upper lip still doing the hoist and flop movement and her chin still swinging around at anchor and back again. 'It's very quiet there. Mr Vannier has been living there three years now. Before that he lived in the Hollywood hills, on Diamond Street. Another man lived with him there, but they didn't get along very well, Mr Vannier said.'

'I feel as if I could understand that, too,' I said. 'How long have you known Mr Vannier?'

'I've known him eight years. I haven't known him very well. I have had to take him a—a parcel now and then. He liked to have me bring it myself.'

I tried again with a smoke ring. Nope.

'Of course,' she said, 'I never liked him very well. I was afraid he would—I was afraid he—'

'But he didn't,' I said.

For the first time her face got a human natural expression—surprise.

'No,' she said. 'He didn't. That is, he didn't really. But he had his pyjamas on.'

'Taking it easy,' I said. 'Lying around all afternoon with his pyjamas on. Well, some guys have all the luck, don't they?'

'Well you have to know something,' she said seriously. 'Something that makes people pay you money. Mrs Murdock has been wonderful to me, hasn't she?'

'She certainly has,' I said. 'How much were you taking him to-day?'

'Only five hundred dollars. Mrs Murdock said that was all she could spare, and she couldn't really spare that. She said it would have to stop. It couldn't go on. Mr Vannier would always promise to stop, but he never did.'

'It's a way they have,' I said.

'So there was only one thing to do. I've known that for years, really. It was all my fault and Mrs Murdock has been so wonderful to me. It couldn't make me any worse than I was already, could it?'

I put my hand up and rubbed my cheek hard, to quiet the nerve. She forgot that I hadn't answered her and went on again.

'So I did it,' she said. 'He was there in his pyjamas, with a glass beside him. He was leering at me. He didn't even get up to let me in. But there was a key in the front door. Somebody had left a key there. It was—it was—' her voice jammed in her throat.

'It was a key in the front door,' I said. 'So you were able to get in.'

'Yes.' She nodded and almost smiled again. 'There wasn't anything to it, really. I don't even remember hearing the noise. But there must have been a noise, of course. Quite a loud noise.'

'I suppose so,' I said.

'I went over quite close to him, so I couldn't miss,' she said.

'And what did Mr Vannier do?'

'He didn't do anything at all. He just leered, sort of. Well, that's all there is to it. I didn't like to go back to Mrs Murdock and make any more trouble for her. And for Leslie.' Her voice hushed on the name, and hung suspended, and a little shiver rippled over her body. 'So I came here,' she said. 'And when you didn't answer the bell, I found the office and asked the manager to let me in and wait for you. I knew you would know what to do.'

'And what did you touch in the house while you were there?' I asked. 'Can you remember at all? I mean, beside the front door. Did you just go in at the door and come out without touching anything in the house?'

She thought and her face stopped moving. 'Oh, I remember one thing,' she said. 'I put the light out. Before I left. It was a lamp. One of these lamps that shine upwards, with big bulbs. I put that out.'

I nodded and smiled at her. Marlowe, one smile, cheerful.

'What time was this—how long ago?'

'Oh, just before I came over here. I drove. I had Mrs Murdock's car. The one you asked about yesterday. I forget to tell you that she didn't take it when she went away. Or did I? No, I remember now I did tell you.'

'Let's see,' I said. 'Half an hour to drive here, anyway. You've been here close to an hour. That would be about five-thirty when you left Mr Vannier's house. And you put the light off.'

'That's right.' she nodded again, quite brightly. Pleased at remembering. 'I put the light out.'

'Would you care for a drink?' I asked her.

'Oh, no.' She shook her head quite vigorously. 'I never drink anything at all.'

'Would you mind if I had one?'

'Certainly not. Why should I?'

I stood up, gave her a studying look. Her lip was still going up and her head was still going round, and I thought not so far. It was like a rhythm which is dying down.

It was difficult to know how far to go with this. It might be that the more she talked, the better. Nobody knows very much about the time of absorption of a shock.

I said: 'Where is your home?'

'Why—I live with Mrs Murdock. In Pasadena.'

'I mean, your real home. Where your folks are.'

'My parents live in Wichita,' she said. 'But I don't go there—ever. I write once in a while, but I haven't seen them for years.'

'What does your father do?'

'He has a dog and cat hospital. He's a veterinarian. I hope they won't have to know. They didn't about the other time. Mrs Murdock kept it from everybody.'

'Maybe they won't have to know,' I said. 'I'll get my drink.'

I went out around the back of her chair to the kitchen and poured it and I made it a drink that was a drink. I put it down in a lump and took the little gun off my hip and saw that the safety was on. I smelled the muzzle, broke out the magazine. There was a cartridge in the chamber, but it was one of those guns that won't fire when the magazine is out. I held it so that I could look into the breech. The cartridge in there was the wrong size and was crooked against the breech block. It looked like a .32. The cartridges in the magazine were the right size, .25's. I fitted the gun together again and went back to the living-room.

I hadn't heard a sound. She had just slid forward in a pile in front of the chair, on top of her nice hat. She was as cold as a mackerel.

I spread her out a little and took her glasses off and made sure she hadn't swallowed her tongue. I wedged my folded handkerchief into the corner of her mouth so that she wouldn't bite her tongue when she came out of it. I went to the phone and called Carl Moss.

'Phil Marlowe, Doc. Any more patients or are you through?'

'All through,' he said. 'Leaving. Trouble?'

'I'm home,' I said, 'Four-o-eight Bristol Apartments, if you don't remember. I've got a girl here who has pulled a faint. I'm not afraid of the faint, I'm afraid she may be nuts when she comes out of it.'

'Don't give her any liquor,' he said. 'I'm on my way.'

I hung up and knelt down beside her. I began to rub her temples. She opened her eyes. The lips started to lift. I pulled the handkerchief out of her mouth. She looked up at me and said: 'I've been over to Mr Vannier's house. He lives in Sherman Oaks. I—'

'Do you mind if I lift you up and put you on the davenport? You know me–Marlowe, the big boob that goes around asking all the wrong questions.'

'Hello,' she said.

I lifted her. She went stiff on me, but she didn't say anything. I put her on the davenport and tucked her skirt down over her legs and put a pillow under her head and picked her hat up. It was as flat as a flounder. I did what I could to straighten it out and laid it aside on the desk.

She watched me sideways, doing this.

'Did you call the police?' she asked softly.

'Not yet,' I said. 'I've been too busy.'

She looked surprised. I wasn't quite sure, but I thought she looked a little hurt, too.

I opened up her bag and turned my back to her to slip the gun back into it. While I was doing that I took a look at what else was in the bag. The usual oddments, a couple of handkerchiefs, lipstick, a silver and red enamel compact with powder in it, a couple of tissues, a purse with some hard money and a few dollar bills, no cigarettes, no matches, no tickets for the theatre.

I pulled open the zipper pocket at the back. That held her driver's licence and a flat packet of bills, ten fifties. I rifled them. None of them brand new. Tucked into the rubber band that held them was a folded paper. I took it out and opened it and read it. It was neatly typewritten, dated that day. It was a common receipt form and it would, when signed, acknowledge the receipt of $500. 'Payment on Account.'

It didn't seem as if it would ever be signed now. I slipped money and receipt into my pocket. I closed the bag and looked over at the davenport.

She was looking at the ceiling and doing that with her face again. I went into my bedroom and got a blanket to throw over her.

Then I went into the kitchen for another drink.

28

Dr Carl Moss was a big burly Jew with a Hitler moustache, pop eyes and the calmness of a glacier. He put his hat and bag on a chair and went over and stood looking down at the girl on the davenport inscrutably.

'I'm Dr Moss,' he said. 'How are you?'

She said: 'Aren't you the police?'

He bent down and felt her pulse and then stood there watching her breathing. 'Where does it hurt, Miss—'

'Davis,' I said. 'Miss Merle Davis.'

'Miss Davis.'

'Nothing hurts me,' she said, staring up at him. 'I–I don't even know why I'm lying here like this. I thought you were the police. You see, I killed a man.'

'Well, that's a normal human impulse,' he said. 'I've killed dozens.' He didn't smile.

She lifted her lip and moved her head round for him.

'You know you don't have to do that,' he said, quite gently. 'You feel a twitch of the nerves here and there and you proceed to build it up and dramatize it. You can control it, if you want to.'

'Can I?' she whispered.

'If you want to,' he said. 'You don't have to. It doesn't make any difference to me either way. Nothing pains at all, eh?'

'No.' She shook her head.

He patted her shoulder and walked out of the kitchen. I went after him. He leaned his hips against the sink and gave me a cool stare. 'What's the story?'

'She's the secretary of a client. A Mrs Murdock in Pasadena. The client is rather a brute. About eight years ago a man made a hard press at Merle. How hard I don't know. Then–I don't mean immediately–but around that time he fell out of a window or jumped. Since then she can't have a man touch her–not in the most casual way, I mean.'

'Uh-huh.' His pop eyes continued to read my face. 'Does she think he jumped out of the window on her account?'

'I don't know. Mrs Murdock is the man's widow. She married again and her second husband is dead too. Merle has stayed with her. The old woman treats her like a rough parent treats a naughty child.'

'I see. Regressive.'

'What's that?'

'Emotional shock, and the subconscious attempt to escape back to childhood. If Mrs Murdock scolds her a good deal, but not too much, that would increase the tendency. Identification of childhood subordination with childhood protection.'

'Do we have to go into that stuff?' I growled.

He grinned at me calmly. 'Look, pal. The girl's obviously a neurotic. It's party induced and partly deliberate. I mean to say that she really enjoys a lot of it. Even if she doesn't realize that she enjoys it. However, that's not of immediate importance. What's this about killing a man?'

'A man named Vannier who lives in Sherman Oaks. There seems to be some blackmail angle. Merle had to take him his money, from time to time. She was afraid of him. I've seen the guy. A nasty type. She went over there this afternoon and she says she shot him.'

'Why?'

'She says she didn't like the way he leered at her.'

'Shot him with what?'

'She had a gun in her bag. Don't ask me why. I don't know. But if she shot him, it wasn't with that. The gun's got a wrong cartridge in the breech. It can't be fired as it is. Also it hasn't been fired.'

'This is too deep for me,' he said. 'I'm just a doctor. What did you want me to do with her?'

'Also,' I said, ignoring the question, 'she said the lamp was turned on and it was about five-thirty of a nice summery afternoon. And the guy was wearing his sleeping-suit and there was a key in the lock of the front door. And he didn't get up to let her in. He just sort of sat there sort of leering.'

He nodded and said: 'Oh.' He pushed a cigarette between his heavy lips and lit it. 'If you expect me to tell you whether she really thinks she shot him, I can't do it. From your description I gather that the man is shot. That's so?'

'Brother, I haven't been there. But that much seems pretty clear.'

'If she thinks she shot him and isn't just acting–and, God, how these types do act!–that indicates it was not a new idea to her. You say she carried a gun. So perhaps it wasn't. She may have a guilt complex. Wants to be punished, wants to expiate some real or imaginary crime. Again I ask what do you want me to do with her? She's not sick, she's not loony.'

'She's not going back to Pasadena.'

'Oh.' He looked at me curiously. 'Any family?'

'In Wichita. Father's a vet. I'll call him, but she'll have to stay here to-night.'

'I don't know about that. Does she trust you enough to spend the night in your apartment?'

'She came here of her own free will, and not socially. So I guess she does.'

He shrugged and fingered the sidewall of his coarse black moustache. 'Well, I'll give her some nembutal and we'll put her to bed. And you can walk the floor wrestling with your conscience.'

'I have to go out,' I said. 'I have to go over there and see what has happened. And she can't stay here alone. And no man, not even a doctor, is going to put her to bed. Get a nurse. I'll sleep somewhere else.'

'Phil Marlowe,' he said. 'The shop-soiled Galahad. Okay. I'll stick around until the nurse comes.'

He went back into the living-room and telephoned the Nurses' Registry. Then he telephoned his wife. While he was telephoning, Merle sat up on the davenport and clasped her hands primly in her lap.

'I don't see why the lamp was on,' she said. 'It wasn't dark in the house at all. Not that dark.'

I said: 'What's your dad's first name?'

'Dr Wilbur Davis. Why?'

'Wouldn't you like something to eat?'

At the telephone Carl Moss said to me: 'To-morrow will do for that. This is probably just a lull.' He finished his call, hung up, went to his bag and came back with a couple of yellow capsules in his hand on a fragment of cotton. He got a glass of water, handed her the capsules and said: 'Swallow.'

'I'm not sick, am I?' she said, looking up at him.

'Swallow, my child, swallow.'

She took them and put them in her mouth and took the glass of water and drank.

I put my hat on and left.

On the way down in the elevator I remembered that there hadn't been any keys in her bag, so I stopped at the lobby floor and went out through the lobby to the Bristol Avenue side. The car was not hard to find. It was parked crookedly about two feet from the kerb. It was a grey Mercury convertible and its licence number was 2X1111. I remembered that this was the number of Linda Murdock's car.

A leather keyholder hung in the lock. I got in the car, started the engine, saw that there was plenty of gas, and drove it away. It was a nice eager little car. Over Cahuenga Pass it had the wings of a bird.

29

Escamillo Drive made three jogs in four blocks, for no reason that I could see. It was very narrow, averaged about five houses to a block and was overhung by a section of shaggy brown foothill on which nothing lived at this season except sage and manzanita. In its fifth and last block, Escamillo Drive did a neat little curve to the left, hit the base of the hill hard, and died without a whimper. In this last block were three houses, two on the opposite entering corners, one at the dead end. This was Vannier's. My spotlight showed the key still in the door.

It was a narrow English type bungalow with a high roof, leaded front windows, a garage to the side, and a trailer parked beside the garage. The early moon lay quietly on its small lawn. A large oak tree grew almost on the front porch. There was no light in the house now, none visible from the front at least.

From the lay of the land a light in the living-room in the daytime did not seem utterly improbable. It would be a dark house except in the morning. As a love-nest the place had its points, but as a residence for a blackmailer I didn't give it very high marks. Sudden death can come to you anywhere, but Vannier had made it too easy.

I turned into his driveway, backed to get myself pointed out of the dead end, and then drove down to the corner and parked there. I walked back in the street because there was no sidewalk. The front door was made of iron-bound oak planks, bevelled where they joined. There was a thumb latch instead of a knob. The head of the flat key projected from the lock. I rang the bell, and it rang with that remote sound of a bell ringing at night in an empty house. I walked round the oak tree and poked the light of my pencil flash between the leaves of the garage door. There was a car in there. I went back round the house and looked at a small flowerless yard, walled in by a low wall of fieldstone. Three more oak trees, a table and a couple of all-metal chairs under one of them. A rubbish burner at the back. I shone my light into the trailer before I went back to the front. There didn't seem to be anybody in the trailer. Its door was locked.

I opened the front door, leaving the key in the lock. I wasn't going to work any dipsy-doodle in this place. Whatever was, was. I just wanted to make sure. I felt round on the wall inside the door for a light switch, found one and tilted it up. Pale flame bulbs in pairs in wall brackets went on all around the room, showing me the big lamp Merle had spoken of, as well as other things. I went over to switch the lamp on, then back to switch the wall lights off. The lamp had a big bulb inverted in a porcelain glass bowl. You could get three different intensities of light. I clicked the button switch around until I had all there was.

The room ran from front to back, with a door at the back and an arch up front to the right. Inside that was a small dining-room. Curtains were half-drawn across the arch, heavy pale green brocade curtains, far from new. The fireplace was in the middle of the left wall, bookshelves opposite and on both sides of it, not built in. Two davenports angled across the corners of the room and there was one gold chair, one pink chair, one brown chair, one brown and gold jacquard chair with footstool.

Yellow pyjama legs were on the footstool, bare ankles, feet in dark green morocco leather slippers. My eyes ran up from the feet, slowly, carefully. A dark green figured silk robe, tied with a tasselled belt. Open above the belt showing a monogram on the pocket of the pyjamas. A handkerchief neat in the pocket, two stiff points of white linen. A yellow neck, the face turned sideways, pointed at a mirror on the wall. I walked round and looked in the mirror. The face leered all right.

The left arm and hand lay between a knee and the side of the chair, the right arm hung outside the chair, the ends of the fingers touching the rug. Touching also the butt of a small revolver, about .32 calibre, a belly gun, with practically no barrel. The right side of the face was against the back of the chair, but the right shoulder was dark brown with blood and there was some on the right sleeve. Also on the chair. A lot of it on the chair.

I didn't think his head had taken that position naturally. Some sensitive soul had not liked the right side of it.

I lifted my foot and gently pushed the footstool sideways a few inches. The heels of the slippers moved reluctantly over the jacquard surface, not with it. The man was as stiff as a board. So I reached down and touched his ankle. Ice was never half as cold.

On a table at his right elbow was half a dead drink, an ashtray full of butts and ash. Three of the butts had lipstick on them. Bright Chinese-red lipstick. What a blonde would use.

There was another ashtray beside another chair. Matches in it and a lot of ash, but no stubs.

On the air of the room a rather heavy perfume struggled with the smell of death, and lost. Although defeated, it was still there.

I poked through the rest of the house, putting lights on and off. Two bedrooms, one furnished in light wood, one in red maple. The light one seemed to be a spare. A nice bathroom with tan and mulberry tiling and a stall shower with a glass door. The kitchen was small. There were a lot of bottles on the sink. Lots of bottles, lots of glass, lots of fingerprints, lots of evidence. Or not, as the case might be.

I went back to the living-room and stood in the middle of the floor breathing with my mouth as far as possible and wondering what the score would be when I turned this one in. Turn this one in and report that I was the fellow who had found Morningstar and run away. The score would be low, very low. Marlowe, three murders. Marlowe practically knee-deep in dead men. And no reasonable, logical, friendly account of himself whatsoever. But that wasn't the worst of it. The minute I opened up I would cease to be a free agent. I would be through with doing whatever it was I was doing and with finding out whatever it was I was finding out.

Carl Moss might be willing to protect Merle with the mantle of Aesculapius, up to a point. Or he might think it would do her more good in the long run to get it all off her chest, whatever it was.

I wandered back to the jacquard chair and set my teeth and grabbed enough of his hair to pull the head away from the chair back. The bullet had gone in at the temple. The set-up could be for suicide. But people like Louis Vannier do not commit suicide. A blackmailer, even a scared blackmailer, has a sense of power, and loves it.

I let the head go back where it wanted to go and leaned down to scrub my hand on the nap of the rug. Leaning down I saw the corner of a picture frame under the lower shelf of the table at Vannier's elbow. I went round and reached for it with a handkerchief.

The glass was cracked across. It had fallen off the wall. I could see the small nail. I could make a guess how it had happened. Somebody standing at Vannier's right, even leaning over him, somebody he knew and had no fear of, had suddenly pulled a gun and shot him in the right temple. And then, startled by the blood or the recoil of the shot, the killer had jumped back against the wall and knocked the picture down. It had landed on a corner and jumped under the table. And the killer had been too careful to touch it, or too scared.

I looked at it. It was a small picture, not interesting at all. A guy in doublet and hose, with lace at his sleeve ends, and one of those round puffy velvet hats with a feather, leaning far out of a window and apparently calling out to somebody downstairs. Downstairs not being in the picture. It was a colour reproduction of something that had never been needed in the first place.

I looked round the room. There were other pictures, a couple of rather nice water-colours, some engravings—very old-fashioned this year, engravings, or are they? Half a dozen in all. Well, perhaps the guy liked the picture, so what? A man leaning out of a high window. A long time ago.

I looked at Vannier. He wouldn't help me at all. A man leaning out of a high window, a long time ago.

The touch of the idea at first was so light that I almost missed it and passed on. A touch of a feather, hardly that. The touch of a snowflake. A high window, a man leaning out—a long time ago.

It snapped in place. It was so hot it sizzled. Out of a high window a long time ago—eight years ago—a man leaning—too far—a man falling—to his death. A man named Horace Bright.

'Mr Vannier,' I said with a little touch of admiration, 'you played that rather neatly.'

I turned the picture over. On the back dates and amounts of money were written. Dates over almost eight years, amounts mostly of $500, a few $750s, two for $1,000. There was a running total in small figures. It was $11,100. Mr Vannier had not received the latest payment. He had been dead when it arrived. It was not a lot of money, spread over eight years. Mr Vannier's customer had bargained hard.

The cardboard back was fastened into the frame with steel gramophone needles. Two of them had fallen out. I worked the cardboard loose and tore it a little getting it loose. There was a white envelope between the back and the picture. Sealed, blank. I tore it open. It contained two square photographs and a negative. The photos were just the same. They showed a man leaning far out of a window with his mouth open yelling. His hands were on the brick edges of the window-frame. There was a woman's face behind his shoulder.

He was a thinnish dark-haired man. His face was not very clear, nor the face of the woman behind him. He was leaning out of a window and yelling or calling out.

There I was holding the photograph and looking at it. And so far as I could see, it didn't mean a thing. I knew it had to. I just didn't know why. But I kept on looking at it. And in a little while something was wrong. It was a very small thing, but it was vital. The position of the man's hands, lined against the corner of the wall where it was cut out to make the window-frame. The hands were not holding anything, they were not touching anything. It was the inside of his wrists that lined against the angle of the bricks. The hands were in air.

The man was not leaning. He was falling.

I put the stuff back in the envelope and folded the cardboard back and stuffed that into my pocket also. I hid frame, glass and picture in the linen closet under towels.

All this had taken too long. A car stopped outside the house. Feet came up the walk.

I dodged behind the curtains in the archway.

30

The front door opened and then quietly closed.

There was a silence, hanging in the air like a man's breath in frosty air, and then a thick scream, ending in a wail of despair.

Then a man's voice, tight with fury, saying: 'Not bad, not good. Try again.'

The woman's voice said: 'My God, it's Louis! He's dead!'

The man's voice said: 'I may be wrong, but I still think it stinks.'

'My God! He's dead, Alex. Do something–for God's sake–*do* something!'

'Yeah,' the hard, tight voice of Alex Morny said. 'I ought to. I ought to make you look just like him. With blood and everything. I ought to make you just as dead, just as cold, just as rotten. No, I don't have to do that. You're that already. Just as rotten. Eight months married and cheating on me with a piece of merchandise like that. My God! What did I ever think of to put in with a chippy like you?'

He was almost yelling at the end of it.

The woman made another wailing noise.

'Quit stalling,' Morny said bitterly. 'What do you think I brought you over here for? You're not kidding anybody. You've been watched for weeks. You were here last night. I've been here already to-day. I've seen what there is to see. Your lipstick on cigarettes, your glass that you drank out of. I can see you now, sitting on the arm of his chair, rubbing his greasy hair, and then feeding him a slug while he was still purring. Why?'

'Oh, Alex—darling—don't say such awful things.'

'Early Lillian Gish,' Morny said. 'Very early Lillian Gish. Skip the agony, Toots. I have to know how to handle this. What the hell you think I'm here for? I don't give one little flash in hell about you any more. Not any more, Toots, not any more, my precious darling angel blonde mankiller. But I do care about myself and my reputation and my business. For instance, did you wipe the gun off?'

Silence. Then the sound of a blow. The woman wailed. She was hurt, terribly hurt. Hurt in the depths of her soul. She made it rather good.

'Look, angel,' Morny snarled. 'Don't feed me the ham. I've been in pictures. I'm a connoisseur of ham. Skip it. You're going to tell me how this was done if I have to drag you around the room by your hair. Now—did you wipe off the gun?'

Suddenly she laughed. An unnatural laugh, but clear and with a nice tinkle to it. Then she stopped laughing, just as suddenly.

Her voice said: 'Yes.'

'And the glass you were using?'

'Yes.' Very quiet now, very cool.

'And you put his prints on the gun?'

'Yes.'

He thought in the silence. 'Probably won't fool them,' he said. 'It's almost impossible to get a dead man's prints on a gun in a convincing way. However. What else did you wipe off.'

'N-nothing. Oh, Alex. Please don't be so brutal.'

'Stop it. *Stop it!* Show me how you did it, how you were standing, how you held the gun.'

She didn't move.

'Never mind about the prints,' Morny said. 'I'll put better ones on. Much better ones.'

She moved slowly across the opening of the curtains and I saw her. She was wearing pale-green gabardine slacks, a fawn-coloured leisure jacket with stitching on it, a scarlet turban with a gold snake in it. Her face was smeared with tears.

'Pick it up,' Morny yelled at her. 'Show me!'

She bent beside the chair and came up with the gun in her hand and her teeth bared. She pointed the gun across the opening in the curtains, towards the space of room where the door was.

Morny didn't move, didn't make a sound.

The blonde's hand began to shake and the gun did a queer up and down dance in the air. Her mouth trembled and her arm fell.

'I can't do it,' she breathed. 'I ought to shoot you but I can't.'

The hand opened and the gun thudded to the floor.

Morny went swiftly past the break in the curtains, pushed her out of the way and with his foot pushed the gun back to about where it had been.

'You couldn't do it,' he said thickly. 'You couldn't do it. Now watch.'

He whipped a handkerchief out and bent to pick the gun up again. He pressed something and the gate fell open. He reached his right hand into his pocket and rolled a cartridge in his fingers, moving his fingertips on the metal, pushed the cartridge into a cylinder. He repeated the performance four times more, snapped the gate shut, then opened it and spun it a little to set it in a certain spot. He placed the gun down on the floor, withdrew his hand and handkerchief and straightened up.

'You couldn't shoot me,' he sneered, 'because there was nothing in the gun but one empty cartridge. Now it's loaded again. The cylinders are in the right place. One shot has been fired. And your fingerprints are on the gun.'

The blonde was very still, looking at him with haggard eyes.

'I forgot to tell you,' he said softly. '*I* wiped the gun off. I thought it would be so much nicer to be *sure* your prints were on it. I was pretty sure they were–but I felt as if I would like to be *quite* sure. Get it?'

The girl sat quietly: 'You're going to turn me in?'

His back was towards me. Dark clothes. Felt hat pulled low. So I couldn't see his face. But I could just about see the leer with which he said:

'Yes, angel, I am going to turn you in.'

'I see,' she said, and looked at him levelly. There was a sudden grave dignity in her over-emphasized chorus-girl's face.

'I'm going to turn you in, angel,' he said slowly, spacing his words as if he enjoyed the act. 'Some people are going to be sorry for me and some people are going to laugh at me. But it's not going to do my business any harm. Not a bit of harm. That's one nice thing about a business like mine. A little notoriety won't hurt it at all.'

'So I'm just publicity value to you, now,' she said. 'Apart, of course, from the danger that you might have been suspected yourself.'

'Just so,' he said. 'Just so.'

'How about my motive?' she asked, still calm, still level-eyed and so gravely contemptuous that he didn't get the expression at all.

'I don't know,' he said. 'I don't care. You were up to something with him. Eddie tailed you downtown to a street on Bunker Hill where you met a blond guy in a brown suit. You gave him something. Eddie dropped you and tailed the guy to an apartment house near there. He tried to tail him some more, but he had a hunch the guy spotted him, and he had to drop it. I don't know what it was all about. I know one thing, though. In that apartment house a young guy named Phillips was shot yesterday. Would you know anything about that, my sweet?'

The blonde said: 'I wouldn't know anything about it. I don't know anybody named Phillips and strangely enough I didn't just run up and shoot anybody out of sheer girlish fun.'

'But you shot Vannier, my dear,' Morny said almost gently.

'Oh, yes,' she drawled. 'Of course. We were wondering what my motive was. You get it figured out yet?'

'You can work that out with the johns,' he snapped. 'Call it a lover's quarrel. Call it anything you like.'

'Perhaps,' she said, 'when he was drunk he looked just a little like you. Perhaps that was the motive.'

He said: 'Ah,' and sucked his breath in.

'Better-looking,' she said. 'Younger, with less belly. But with the same god-damned self-satisfied smirk.'

'Ah,' Morny said, and he was suffering.

'Would that do?' she asked him softly.

He stepped forward and swung a fist. It caught her on the side of the face and she went down and sat on the floor, a long leg straight out in front of her, one hand to her jaw, her very blue eyes looking up at him.

'Maybe you oughtn't to have done that,' she said. 'Maybe I won't go through with it, now.'

'You'll go through with it, all right. You won't have any choice. You'll get off easy enough. Christ, I know that. With your looks. But you'll go through with it, angel. Your fingerprints are on that gun.'

She got to her feet slowly, still with the hand to her jaw.

Then she smiled. 'I knew he was dead,' she said. 'That is my key in the door. I'm quite willing to go downtown and say I shot him. But don't lay your smooth white paw on me again—if you want my story. Yes. I'm quite willing to go to the cops. I'll feel a lot safer with them than I feel with you.'

Morny turned and I saw the hard white leer of his face and the scar dimple in his cheek twitching. He walked past the opening in the curtain. The front door opened again. The blonde stood still a moment, looked back over her shoulder at the corpse, shuddered slightly, and passed out of my line of vision.

The door closed. Steps on the walk. Then car doors opening and closing. The motor throbbed, and the car went away.

31

After a long time I moved out from my hiding-place and stood looking around the living-room again. I went over and picked the gun up and wiped it off very carefully and put it down again. I picked the three rouge-stained cigarette-stubs out of the tray on the table and carried them into the bathroom and flushed them down the toilet. Then I looked around for the second glass with her fingerprints on it. There wasn't any second glass. The one that was half full of a dead drink I took to the kitchen and rinsed out and wiped on a dish-towel.

Then the nasty part. I kneeled on the rug by his chair and picked up the gun and reached for the trailing bone-stiff hand. The prints would not be good, but they would be prints and they would not be Lois Morny's. The gun had a checked rubber grip, with a piece broken off on the left side below the screw. No prints on that. An index print on the right side of the barrel, two fingers on the trigger guard, a thumbprint on the flat piece on the left side, behind the chambers. Good enough.

I took one more look around the living-room.

I put the lamp down to a lower light. It still glared too much on the dead yellow face. I opened the front door, pulled the key out and wiped it off and pushed it back into the lock. I shut the door and wiped the thumb-latch off and went my way down the block to the Mercury.

I drove back to Hollywood and locked the car up and started along the sidewalk past the other parked cars to the entrance of the Bristol.

A harsh whisper spoke to me out of darkness, out of a car. It spoke my name. Eddie Prue's long blank face hung somewhere up near the roof of a small Packard, behind its wheel. He was alone in it. I leaned on the door of the car and looked in at him.

'How you making out, shamus?'

I tossed a match down and blew smoke at his face. I said: 'Who dropped that dental supply company's bill you gave me last night? Vannier, or somebody else?'

'Vannier.'

'What was I supposed to do with it—guess the life history of a man named Teager?'

'I don't go for dumb guys,' Eddie Prue said.

I said: 'Why would he have it in his pocket to drop? And if he did drop it, why wouldn't you just hand it back to him? In other words, seeing that I'm a dumb guy, explain to me why a bill for dental supplies should get anybody all excited and start trying to hire private detectives. Especially gents like Alex Morny, who don't like private detectives.'

'Morny's a good head,' Eddie Prue said coldly.

'He's the fellow for whom they coined the phrase, "as ignorant as an actor".'

'Skip that. Don't you know what they use that dental stuff for?'

'Yeah. I found out. They use albastone for making moulds of teeth and cavities. It's very hard, very fine grain and retains any amount of fine detail. The other stuff, crystobolite, is used to cook out the wax in an invested wax model. It's used because it stands a great deal of heat without distortion. Tell me you don't know what I'm talking about.'

'I guess you know how they make gold inlays,' Eddie Prue said. 'I guess you do, huh?'

'I spent two of my hours learning to-day. I'm an expert. What does it get me?'

He was silent for a little while, and then he said: 'You ever read the paper?'

'Once in a while.'

'It couldn't be you read where an old guy named Morningstar was bumped off in the Belfont Building on Ninth Street, just two floors above where this H. R. Teager had his office. It couldn't be you read that, could it?'

I didn't answer him. He looked at me for a moment longer, then he put his hand forward to the dash and pushed the starter-button. The motor of his car caught and he started to ease in the clutch.

'Nobody could be as dumb as you act,' he said softly. 'Nobody ain't. Good night to you.'

The car moved away from the kerb and drifted down the hill towards Franklin. I was grinning into the distance as it disappeared.

I went up to the apartment and unlocked the door and pushed it open a few inches and then knocked gently. There was movement in the room. The door was pulled open by a strong-looking girl with a black stripe on the cap of her white nurse's uniform.

'I'm Marlowe. I live here.'

'Come in, Mr Marlowe. Dr Moss told me.'

I shut the door quietly and we spoke in low voices. 'How is she?' I asked.

'She's asleep. She was already drowsy when I got here. I'm Miss Lymington. I don't know very much about her except that her temperature is normal and her pulse still rather fast, but going down. A mental disturbance, I gather.'

'She found a man murdered,' I said. 'It shot her full of holes. Is she hard enough asleep so that I could go in and get a few things to take to the hotel?'

'Oh, yes. If you're quiet. She probably won't wake. If she does, it won't matter.'

I went over and put some money on the desk. 'There's coffee and bacon and eggs and bread and tomato juice and oranges and liquor here,' I said. 'Anything else you'll have to phone for.'

'I've already investigated your supplies,' she said, smiling.

'We have all we need until after breakfast to-morrow. Is she going to stay here?'

'That's up to Dr Moss. I think she'll be going home as soon as she is fit for it. Home being quite a long way off, in Wichita.'

'I'm only a nurse,' she said. 'But I don't think there is anything the matter with her that a good night's sleep won't cure.'

'A good night's sleep and a change of company,' I said, but that didn't mean anything to Miss Lymington.

I went along the hallway and peeked into the bedroom. They had put a pair of my pyjamas on her. She lay almost on her back with one arm outside the bedclothes. The sleeve of the pyjama coat was turned up six inches or more. The small hand below the end of the sleeve was in a tight fist. Her face looked drawn and white and quite peaceful. I poked about in the closet and got a suitcase and put some junk in it. As I started back out I looked at Merle again. Her eyes opened and looked straight up at the ceiling. Then they moved just enough to see me and a faint little smile tugged at the corners of her lips.

'Hello.' It was a weak spent little voice, a voice that knew its owner was in bed and had a nurse and everything.

'Hello.'

I went around near her and stood looking down, with my polished smile on my clear-cut features.

'I'm all right,' she whispered. 'I'm fine. Aren't I?'

'Sure.'

'Is this your bed I'm in?'

'That's all right. It won't bite you.'

'I'm not afraid,' she said. A hand came sliding towards me and lay palm up, waiting to be held. I held it. 'I'm not afraid of you. No woman would ever be afraid of you, would she?'

'Coming from you,' I said, 'I guess that's meant to be a compliment.'

Her eyes smiled, then got grave again. 'I lied to you,' she said softly. 'I–I didn't shoot anybody.'

'I know. I was over there. Forget it. Don't think about it.'

'People are always telling you to forget unpleasant things. But you never do. It's so kind of silly to tell you to, I mean.'

'Okay,' I said, pretending to be hurt. 'I'm silly. How about making some more sleep?'

She turned her head until she was looking into my eyes. I sat on the edge of the bed, holding her hand.

'Will the police come here?' she asked.

'No. And try not to be disappointed.'

She frowned. 'You must think I'm an awful fool.'

'Well–maybe.'

A couple of tears formed in her eyes and slid out at the corners and rolled gently down her cheeks.

'Does Mrs Murdock know where I am?'

'Not yet. I'm going over to tell her.'

'Will you have to tell her–everything?'

'Yeah, why not?'

She turned her head away from me. 'She'll understand,' her voice said softly. 'She knows the awful thing I did eight years ago. The frightful terrible thing.'

'Sure,' I said. 'That's why she's been paying Vannier money all this time.'

'Oh, dear,' she said, and brought her other hand out from under the bedclothes and pulled away the other I was holding so that she could squeeze them tightly together. 'I wish you hadn't had to know that. I wish you hadn't. Nobody ever knew but Mrs Murdock. My parents never knew. I wish you hadn't.'

The nurse came in at the door and looked at me severely.

'I don't think she ought to be talking like this, Mr Marlowe. I think you should leave now.'

'Look, Miss Lymington, I've known this little girl two days. You've only known her two hours. This is doing her a lot of good.'

'It might bring on another–er–spasm,' she said severely, avoiding my eyes.

'Well, if she has to have it, isn't it better for her to have it now, while you're here, and get it over with? Go on out to the kitchen and buy yourself a drink.'

'I never drink on duty,' she said coldly. 'Besides, somebody might smell my breath.'

'You're working for me now. All my employees are required to get liquored up from time to time. Besides, if you had a good dinner and were to eat a couple of the Chasers in the kitchen cabinet, nobody would smell your breath.'

She gave me a quick grin and went back out of the room. Merle had been listening to this as if it was a frivolous interruption to a very serious play. Rather annoyed.

'I want to tell you all about it,' she said breathlessly. 'I—'

I reached over and put a paw over her two locked hands. 'Skip it. I know. Marlowe knows everything–except how to make a decent living. It doesn't amount to beans. Now you're going back to sleep and to-morrow I'm going to take you on the way back to Wichita–to visit your parents.

At Mrs Murdock' expense.'

'Why, that's wonderful of her,' she cried, her eyes opening wide and shining. 'But she's always been wonderful to me.'

I got up off the bed. 'She's a wonderful woman,' I said, grinning down at her. 'Wonderful. I'm going over there now and we're going to have a perfectly lovely talk over the teacups. And if you don't go to sleep right now, I won't let you confess to any more murders.'

'You're horrid,' she said. 'I don't like you.' She turned her head away and put her arms back under the bedclothes and shut her eyes.

I went towards the door. At the door I swung round and looked back quickly. She had one eye open, watching me. I gave her a leer and it snapped shut in a hurry.

I went back to the living-room, gave Miss Lymington what was left of my leer, and went out with my suitcase.

I drove over to Santa Monica Boulevard. The hock-shop was still open. The old Jew in the tall black skull-cap seemed surprised that I was able to redeem my pledge so soon. I told him that was the way it was in Hollywood.

He got the envelope out of the safe and tore it open and took my money and pawnticket and slipped the shining gold coin out on his palm'

'So valuable this is I am hating to give it back to you,' he said. 'The workmanship, you understand, the workmanship is beautiful.'

'And the gold in it must be worth all of twenty dollars,' I said.

He shrugged and smiled and I put the coin in my pocket and said good night to him.

32

The moonlight lay like a white sheet on the front lawn except under the deodar where there was the thick darkness of black velvet. Lights in two lower windows were lit and in one upstairs room visible from the front. I walked across the stumblestones and rang the bell.

I didn't look at the little painted Negro by the hitching-block. I didn't pat his head to-night. The joke seemed to have worn thin.

A white-haired, red-faced woman I hadn't seen before opened the door and I said: 'I'm Philip Marlowe. I'd like to see Mrs Murdock. Mrs Elizabeth Murdock.'

She looked doubtful. 'I think she's gone to bed,' she said. 'I don't think you can see her.'

'It's only nine o'clock.'

'Mrs Murdock goes to bed early.' She started to close the door.

She was a nice old thing and I hated to give the door the heavy shoulder. I just leaned against it.

'It's about Miss Davis,' I said. 'It's important. Could you tell her that?'

'I'll see.'

I stepped back and let her shut the door.

A mocking-bird sang in a dark tree nearby. A car tore down the street much too fast and skidded round the next corner. The thin shreds of a girl's laughter came back along the dark street as if the car had spilled them out in its rush.

The door opened after a while and the woman said: 'You can come in.'

I followed her across the big empty entrance room. A single dim light burned in one lamp, hardly reaching to the opposite wall. The place was too still, and the air needed freshening. We went along the hall to the end and up a flight of stairs with a carved handrail and newel post. Another hall at the top, a door open towards the back.

I was shown in at the open door and the door was closed behind me. It was a big sitting-room with a lot of chintz, a blue and silver wallpaper, a couch, a blue carpet and french windows open on a balcony. There was an awning over the balcony.

Mrs Murdock was sitting in a padded wing chair with a card-table in front of her. She was wearing a quilted robe and her hair looked a little fluffed out. She was playing solitaire. She had the pack in her left hand and she put a card down and moved another one before she looked up at me.

Then she said: 'Well?'

I went over by the card-table and looked down at the game. It was Canfield.

'Merle's at my apartment,' I said. 'She threw an ingbing.'

Without looking up she said: 'And just what is an ing-bing, Mr Marlowe?'

She moved another card, then two more quickly.

'A case of the vapours, they used to call it,' I said. 'Ever catch yourself cheating at that game?'

'It's no fun if you cheat,' she said gruffly. 'And very little if you don't. · What's this about Merle? She has never stayed out like this before. I was getting worried about her.'

I pulled a slipper chair over and sat down across the table from her. It put me too low down. I got up and got a better chair and sat on that.

'No need to worry about her,' I said. 'I got a doctor and a nurse. She's asleep. She was over to see Vannier.'

She laid the pack of cards down and folded her big grey hands on the edge of the table and looked at me stolidly.

'Mr Marlowe,' she said, 'you and I had better have something out. I made a mistake calling you in the first place. That was my dislike of being played for a sucker, as you would say, by a hard-boiled little animal like Linda. But it would have been much better, if I had not raised the point at all. The loss of the doubloon would have been much easier to bear than you are. Even if I had never got it back.'

'But you did get it back,' I said.

She nodded. Her eyes stayed on my face. 'Yes. I got it back. You heard how.'

'I didn't believe it.'

'Neither did I,' she said calmly. 'My fool of a son was simply taking the blame for Linda. An attitude I find childish.'

'You have a sort of knack,' I said, 'of getting yourselves surrounded with people who take such attitudes.'

She picked her cards up again and reached down to put a black ten on a red jack, both cards that were already in the layout. Then she reached sideways to a small heavy table on which was her port. She drank some, put the glass down and gave me a hard, level stare.

'I have a feeling that you are going to be insolent, Mr Marlowe.'

I shook my head. 'Not insolent. Just frank. I haven't done so badly for you, Mrs Murdock. You did get the doubloon back. I kept the police away from you—so far. I didn't do anything on the divorce, but I found Linda—your son knew where she was all the time—and I don't think you'll have any trouble with her. She knows she made a mistake marrying Leslie. However, if you don't think you got value—'

She made a humph noise and played another card. She got the ace of diamonds up to the top line. 'The ace of clubs is buried, darn it. I'm not going to get it out in time.'

'Kind of slide it out,' I said, 'when you're not looking.'

'Hadn't you better,' she said very quietly, 'get on with telling me about Merle? And don't gloat too much, if you have found out a few family secrets, Mr Marlowe.'

'I'm not gloating about anything. You sent Merle to Vannier's place this afternoon, with five hundred dollars.'

'And if I did?' She poured some of her port and sipped, eyeing me steadily over the glass.

'When did he ask for it?'

'Yesterday. I couldn't get it out of the bank until to-day. What happened?'

'Vannier's been blackmailing you for about eight years, hasn't he? On account of something that happened on 26 April 1953?'

A sort of panic twitched in the depths of her eyes, but very far back, very dim, and somehow as though it had been there for a long time and had just peeped out at me for a second.

'Merle told me a few things,' I said. 'Your son told me how his father died. I looked up the records and the papers to-day. Accidental death. There had been an accident in the street under his office and a lot of people were craning out of windows. He just craned out too far. There was some talk of suicide because he was broke and had fifty thousand life insurance for his family. But the coroner was nice and slid past that.'

'Well?' she said. It was a cold hard voice, neither a croak nor a gasp. A cold, hard, utterly composed voice.

'Merle was Horace Bright's secretary. A queer little girl in a way, over-timid, not sophisticated, a little-girl mentality, likes to dramatize herself, very old-fashioned ideas about men, all that sort of thing. I figure he got high one time and made a pass at her and scared her out of her socks.'

'Yes?' Another cold hard monosyllable prodding me like a gun-barrel.

'She brooded and got a little murderous inside. She got a chance and passed right back at him. While he was leaning out of a window. Anything in it?'

'Speak plainly, Mr Marlowe. I can stand plain talk.'

'Good grief, how plain do you want it? She pushed her employer out of a window. Murdered him, in two words. And got away with it. With your help.'

She looked down at the left hand clenched over her cards. She nodded. Her chin moved a short inch, down, up.

'Did Vannier have any evidence?' I asked. 'Or did he just happen to see what happened and put the bite on you and you paid him a little now and then to avoid scandal—and because you were really very fond of Merle?'

She played another card before she answered me. Steady as a rock.

'He talked about a photograph,' she said. 'But I never believed it. He couldn't have taken one. And if he had taken one, he would have shown it to me—sooner or later.'

I said: 'No, I don't think so. It would have been a very fluky shot, even if he happened to have the camera in his hand, on account of the doings down below in the street. But I can see he might not have dared to show it. You're a pretty hard woman, in some ways. He might have been afraid you would have him taken care of. I mean that's how it might look to him, a crook. How much have you paid him?'

'That's none—' she started to say, then stopped and shrugged her big shoulders. A powerful woman, strong, rugged, ruthless, and able to take it. She thought. 'Eleven thousand one hundred dollars, not counting the five hundred I sent him this afternoon.'

'Ah. It was pretty darn nice of you, Mrs Murdock. Considering everything.'

She moved a hand vaguely, made another shrug. 'It was my husband's fault,' she said. 'He was drunk, vile. I don't think he really hurt her, but, as you say, he frightened her out of her wits. I—I can't blame her too much. She has blamed herself enough all these years.'

'She had to take the money to Vannier in person?'

'That was her idea of penance. A strange penance.'

I nodded. 'I guess that would be in character. Later you married Jasper Murdock and you kept Merle with you and took care of her. Anybody else know?'

'Nobody. Only Vannier. Surely he wouldn't tell anybody.'

'No. I hardly think so. Well, it's all over now. Vannier is through.'

She lifted her eyes slowly and gave me a long level gaze. Her grey head was a rock on top of a hill. She put the cards down at last and clasped her hands tightly on the edge of the table. Her knuckles glistened.

I said: 'Merle came to my apartment when I was out. She asked the manager to let her in. He phoned me and I said yes. I got over there quickly. She told me she had shot Vannier.'

Her breath was a faint swift whisper in the stillness of the room.

'She had a gun in her bag. God knows why. Some idea of protecting herself against men, I suppose. But somebody—Leslie, I should guess—had fixed it to be harmless by jamming a wrong size cartridge in the breech. She told me she had killed Vannier and fainted. I got a doctor friend of mine. I went over to Vannier's house. There was a key in the door. He was dead in a chair, long dead, cold, stiff. Dead long before Merle went there. She didn't shoot him. Her telling me that was just drama. The doctor explained it after a fashion, but I won't bore you with it. I guess you understand all right.'

She said: 'Yes. I think I understand. And now?'

'She's in bed, in my apartment. There's a nurse there. I phoned Merle's father long-distance. He wants her to come home. That all right with you?'

She just stared.

'He doesn't know anything,' I said quickly. 'Not this or the other time. I'm sure of that. He just wants her to come home. I thought I'd take her. It seems to be my responsibility now. I'll need that last five hundred that Vannier didn't get—for expenses.'

'And how much more?' she asked brutally.

'Don't say that. You know better.'

'Who killed Vannier?'

'Looks like he committed suicide. A gun at his right hand. Temple contact wound. Morny and his wife were there while I was. I hid. Morny's trying to pin it on his wife. She was playing games with Vannier. So she probably thinks he did it, or had it done. But it shapes up like suicide. The cops will be there by now. I don't know what they will make of it. We just have to sit tight and wait it out.'

'Men like Vannier,' she said grimly, 'don't commit suicide.'

'That's like saying girls like Merle don't push people out of windows. It doesn't mean anything.'

We stared at each other, with that inner hostility that had been there from the first. After a moment I pushed my chair back and went over to the french windows. I opened the screen and stepped out on to the porch. The night was all around, soft and quiet. The white moonlight was cold and clear, like the justice we dream of but don't find.

The trees down below cast heavy shadows under the moon. In the middle of the garden there was a sort of garden within a garden. I caught the glint of an ornamental pool. A lawn swing beside it. Somebody was lying in the lawn swing and a cigarette-tip glowed as I looked down.

I went back into the room. Mrs Murdock was playing solitaire again. I went over to the table and looked down.

'You got the ace of clubs out,' I said.

'I cheated,' she said without looking up.

'There was one thing I wanted to ask you,' I said. 'This doubloon business is still cloudy, on account of a couple of murders which don't seem to make sense now that you have the coin back. What I wondered was if there was anything about the Murdock Brasher that might identify it to an expert—to a man like old Morningstar.'

She thought, sitting still, not looking up. 'Yes. There might be. The coinmaker's initials E.B. are on the left wing of the eagle. Usually, I'm told, they are on the right wing. That's the only thing I can think of.'

I said: 'I think that might be enough. You did actually get the coin back, didn't you? I mean that wasn't just something said to stop my ferreting around?'

She looked up swiftly and then down. 'It's in the strong room at this moment. If you can find my son, he will show it to you.'

'Well, I'll say good night. Please have Merle's clothes packed and sent to my apartment in the morning.'

Her head snapped up again and her eyes glared. 'You're pretty high-handed about all this, young man.'

'Have them packed,' I said. 'And send them. You don't need Merle any more—now that Vannier is dead.'

Our eyes locked hard and held locked for a long moment. A queer stiff smile moved the corners of her lips. Then her head went down and her right hand took the top card off the pack held in her left hand and turned it and her eyes looked at it and she added it to the pile of unplayed cards below the layout, and then turned the next card, quietly, calmly, in a hand as steady as a stone pier in a light breeze.

I went across the room and out, closed the door softly, went along the hall, down the stairs, along the lower hall past the sun-room and Merle's little office, and out into the cheerless, stuffy, unused living-room that made me feel like an embalmed corpse just to be in it.

The french doors at the back opened and Leslie Murdock stepped in and stopped, staring at me.

33

His slack suit was rumpled and also his hair. His little reddish moustache looked just as ineffectual as ever. The shadows under his eyes were almost pits.

He was carrying his long black cigarette-holder, empty, and tapping it against the heel of his left hand as he stood, not liking me, not wanting to meet me, not wanting to talk to me.

'Good evening,' he said stiffly. 'Leaving?'

'Not quite yet. I want to talk to you.'

'I don't think we have anything to talk about. And I'm tired of talking.'

'Oh, yes we have. A man named Vannier.'

'Vannier? I hardly know the man. I've seen him around. What I know I don't like.'

'You know him a little better than that,' I said.

He came forward into the room and sat down in one of the I-dare-you-to-sit-in-me chairs and leaned forward to cup his chin in his right hand and look at the floor.

'All right,' he said wearily. 'Get on with it. I have a feeling you are going to be very brilliant. Remorseless flow of logic and intuition and all that rot. Just like a detective in a book.'

'Sure. Taking the evidence piece by piece, putting it all together in a neat pattern, sneaking in an odd bit I had on my hip here and there, analysing the motives and characters and making them out to be quite different from what anybody—or I myself for that matter—thought them to be up to this golden moment—and finally making a sort of world-weary pounce on the least promising suspect.'

He lifted his eyes and almost smiled. 'Who thereupon turns as pale as paper, froths at the mouth, and pulls a gun out of his right ear.'

I sat down near him and got a cigarette out. 'That's right. We ought to play it together some time. You got a gun?'

'Not with me. I have one. You know that.'

'Have it with you last night when you called on Vannier?'

He shrugged and bared his teeth. 'Oh. Did I call on Vannier last night?'

'I think so. Deduction. You smoke Benson & Hedges Virginia cigarettes. They leave a firm ash that keeps its shape. An ashtray at his house had enough of those little grey rolls to account for at least two cigarettes. But no stubs in the tray. Because you smoke them in a holder and a stub from a holder looks different. So you removed the stubs. Like it?'

'No.' His voice was quiet. He looked down at the floor again.

'That's an example of deduction. A bad one. For there might not have been any stubs, but if there had been and they had been removed, it might have been because they had lipstick on them. Of a certain shade that would at least indicate the colouring of the smoker. And your wife has a quaint habit of throwing her stubs into the waste-bucket.'

'Leave Linda out of this,' he said coldly.

'Your mother still thinks Linda took the doubloon and that your story about taking it to give to Alex Morny was just a cover-up to protect her.'

'I said leave Linda out of it.' The tapping of the black holder against his teeth had a sharp quick sound, like a telegraph key.

I'm willing to,' I said. 'But I didn't believe your story for a different reason. This.' I took the doubloon out and held it on my hand under his eyes.

He stared at it tightly. His mouth set.

'This morning when you were telling your story this was hocked on Santa Monica Boulevard for safe keeping. It was sent to me by a would-be detective named George Phillips. A simple sort of fellow who allowed himself to get into a bad spot through poor judgement and over-eagerness for a job. A thickset blond fellow in a brown suit, wearing dark glasses and a rather gay hat. Driving a sand-coloured Pontiac, almost new. You might have seen him hanging about in the hall outside my office yesterday morning. He had been following me around and before that he might have been following you around.'

He looked genuinely surprised. 'Why would he do that?'

I lit my cigarette and dropped the match in a jade ashtray that looked as if it had never been used as an ashtray.

'I said he might have. I'm not sure he did. He might have just been watching this house. He picked me up here and I don't think he followed me here.' I still had the coin on my hand. I looked down at it, turned it over by tossing it, looked at the initials E.B. stamped into the left wing, and put it away. 'He might have been watching the house because he had been hired to peddle a rare coin to an old coin dealer named Morningstar. And the old coin dealer somehow suspected where the coin came from, and told Phillips, or hinted to him, and that the coin was stolen. Incidentally, he was wrong about that. If your Brasher Doubloon is really at this moment upstairs, then the coin Phillips was hired to peddle was not a stolen coin. It was a counterfeit.'

His shoulders gave a quick little jerk, as if he was cold. Otherwise he didn't move or change position.

'I'm afraid it's getting to be one of those long stories after all,' I said, rather gently. 'I'm sorry. I'd better organize it a little better. It's not a pretty story, because it has two murders in it, maybe three. A man named Vannier and a man named Teager had an idea. Teager is a dental technician in the Belfont Buildings, old Morningstar's building. The idea was to counterfeit a rare and valuable gold coin, not too rare to be marketable, but rare enough to be worth a lot of money. The method they thought of was about what a dental technician uses to make a gold inlay. Requiring the same materials, the same apparatus, the same skill. That is, to reproduce a model exactly, in gold, by making a matrix in a hard white fine cement called albastone, then making a replica of the model in that matrix in moulding-wax, complete in the finest detail, then investing the wax, as they call it, in another kind of cement called crystobolite, which has the property of standing great heat without distortion. A small opening is left from the wax to outside by attaching a steel pin which is withdrawn when the cement sets. Then the crystobolite casting is cooked over a flame until the wax boils out through this small opening, leaving a hollow mould of the original model. This is clamped against a crucible on a centrifuge and molten gold is shot into it by centrifugal force from the crucible. Then the crystobolite, still hot, is held under cold water and it disintegrates, leaving the gold core with a gold pin attached, repressting the small opening. This is trimmed off, the casting is cleaned in acid and polished and you have, in this case, a brand new Brasher Doubloon, made of solid gold and exactly the same as the original. You get the idea?'

He nodded and moved a hand wearily across his head.

'The amount of skill this would take,' I went on, 'would be just what a dental technician would have. The process would be of no use for a current coinage, if we had a gold coinage, because the material and labour would cost more than the coin would be worth. But for a gold coin that was valuable through being rare, it would be fine. So that's what they did. But they had to have a model. That's where you came in. You took the doubloon all right, but not to give to Morny. You took it to give to Vannier. Right?'

He stared at the floor and didn't speak.

'Loosen up,' I said. 'In the circumstances it's nothing very awful. I suppose he promised you money, because you needed it to pay off gambling debts and your mother is close. But he had a stronger hold over you than that.'

He looked up quickly then, his face very white, a kind of horror in his eyes.

'How did you know that?' he almost whispered.

'I found out. Some I was told, some I researched, some I guessed. I'll get to that later. Now Vannier and his pal have made a doubloon and they want to try it out. They wanted to know their merchandise would stand up under inspection by a man supposed to know rare coins. So Vannier had the idea of hiring a sucker and getting him to try to sell the counterfeit to old Morningstar, cheap enough so the old guy would think it was stolen. They picked George Phillips for their sucker, through a silly ad. he was running in the paper for business. I think Lois Morny was Vannier's contact with Phillips, at first, anyway. I don't think she was in the racket. She was seen to give Phillips a small package. This package may have contained the doubloon Phillips was to try to sell. But when he showed it to old Morningstar he ran into a snag. The old man knew his coin collections and his rare coins. He probably thought the coin was genuine enough–it would take a lot of testing to show it wasn't–but the way the maker's initials were stamped on the coin was unusual and suggested to him that the coin might be the Murdock Brasher. He called up here and tried to find out. That made your mother suspicious and the coin was found to be missing and she suspected Linda, whom she hates, and hired me to get it back and put the squeeze on Linda for a divorce, without alimony.'

'I don't want a divorce,' Murdock said hotly. 'I never had any such idea. She had no right—' he stopped and made a despairing gesture and a kind of sobbing sound.

'Okay, I know that. Well, old Morningstar threw a scare into Phillips, who wasn't crooked, just dumb. He managed to get Phillips's phone number out of him. I heard the old man call that number, eavesdropping in his office after he thought I had left. I had just offered to buy the doubloon back for a thousand dollars and Morningstar had taken up the offer, thinking he could get the coin from Phillips, make himself some money and everything lovely. Meantime Phillips was watching this house, perhaps to see if any cops were coming and going. He saw me, saw my car, got my name off the registration and it just happened he knew who I was.

'He followed me around trying to make up his mind to ask me for help until I braced him in a downtown hotel and he mumbled about knowing me from a case in Ventura when he was a deputy up there, and about being in a spot he didn't like and about being followed around by a tall guy with a funny eye. That was Eddie Prue, Morny's side-winder. Morny knew his wife was playing games with Vannier and had her shadowed. Prue saw her make contact with Phillips near where he lived on Court Street, Bunker Hill, and then followed Phillips until he thought Phillips had spotted him, which he had. And Prue, or somebody working for Morny, may have seen me go to Phillips's apartment on Court Street. Because he tried to scare me over the phone and later asked me to come and see Morny.'

I got rid of my cigarette-stub in the jade ashtray, looked at the bleak, unhappy face of the man sitting opposite me, and ploughed on. It was heavy going, and the sound of my voice was beginning to sicken me.

'Now we come back to you. When Merle told you your mother had hired a dick, that threw a scare into *you*. You figured she had missed the doubloon and you came steaming up to my office and tried to pump me. Very debonair, very sarcastic at first, very solicitous for your wife, but very worried. I don't know what you think you found out, but you got in touch with Vannier. You now had to get the coin back to your mother in a hurry, with some kind of story. You met Vannier somewhere and he gave you a doubloon. Chances are it's another counterfeit. He would be likely to hang on to the real one. Now Vannier sees his racket in danger of blowing up before it gets started. Morningstar has called your mother and I have been hired. Morningstar has spotted something. Vannier goes down to Phillips's apartment, sneaks in the back way and has it out with Phillips, trying to find out where he stands.

'Phillips doesn't tell him he has already sent the counterfeit doubloon to me, addressing it in a kind of printing afterwards found in a diary in his office. I infer that from the fact Vannier didn't try to get it back from me. I don't know what Phillips told Vannier, of course, but the chances are he told him the job was crooked, that he knew where the coin came from, and that he was going to the police or to Mrs Murdock. And Vannier pulled a gun, knocked him on the head and shot him. He searched him and the apartment and didn't find the doubloon. So he went to Morningstar. Morningstar didn't have the counterfeit doubloon either, but Vannier probably thought he had. He cracked the old man's skull with a gun-butt and went through the safe, perhaps found some money, perhaps found nothing, at any rate left the appearance of a stick-up behind him. Then Mr Vannier breezed on home, still rather annoyed because he hadn't found the doubloon, but with the satisfaction of a good afternoon's work under his vest. A couple of nice neat murders. That left you.'

34

Murdock flicked a strained look at me, then his eyes went to the black cigarette-holder he still had clenched in his hand. He tucked it in his shirt pocket, stood up suddenly, ground the heels of his hands together and sat down again. He got a handkerchief out and mopped his face.

'Why me?' he asked in a thick strained voice.

'You knew too much. Perhaps you knew about Phillips, perhaps not. Depends how deep you were in it. But you knew about Morningstar. The scheme had gone wrong and Morningstar had been murdered. Vannier couldn't just sit back and hope you wouldn't hear about that. He had to shut your mouth, very, very tight. But he didn't have to kill you to do it. In fact, killing you would be a bad move. It would break his hold on your mother. She's a cold, ruthless, grasping woman, but hurting you would make a wildcat of her. She wouldn't care what happened.'

Murdock lifted his eyes. He tried to make them blank with astonishment. He only made them dull and shocked.

'My mother—what—?'

'Don't kid me any more than you have to,' I said. 'I'm tired to death of being kidded by the Murdock family. Merle came to my apartment this evening. She's there now. She had been over to Vannier's house to bring him some money. Blackmail money. Money that had been paid to him off and on for eight years. I know why.'

He didn't move. His hands were rigid with strain on his knees. His eyes had almost disappeared into the back of his head. They were doomed eyes.

Merle found Vannier dead. She came to me and said she had killed him. Let's not go into why she thinks she ought to confess to other people's murders. I went over there and he had been dead since last night. He was as stiff as a wax dummy. There was a gun lying on the floor by his right hand. It was a gun I had heard described, a gun that belonged to a man named Hench, in an apartment across the hall from Phillips's apartment. Somebody ditched the gun that killed Phillips and took Hench's gun. Hench and his girl were drunk and left their apartment open. It's not proved that it was Hench's gun, but it will be. If it is Hench's gun, and Vannier committed suicide, it ties Vannier to the death of Phillips. Lois Morny also ties him to Phillips, in another way. If Vannier didn't commit suicide—and I don't believe he did—it might still tie him to Phillips. Or it might tie somebody else to Phillips, somebody who also killed Vannier. There are reasons why I don't like that idea.'

Murdock's head came up. He said: 'No?' in a suddenly clear voice. There was a new expression on his face, something bright and shining and at the same time just a little silly. The expression of a weak man being proud.

I said: 'I think you killed Vannier.'

He didn't move and the bright shining expression stayed on his face.

'You went over there last night. He sent for you. He told you he was in a jam and that if the law caught up with him, he would see that you were in the jam with him. Didn't he say something like that?'

'Yes,' Murdock said quietly. 'Something exactly like that. He was drunk and a bit high and he seemed to have a sense of power. He gloated, almost. He said if they got him in the gas chamber I would be sitting right beside him. But that wasn't all he said.'

'No. He didn't want to sit in the gas chamber and he didn't at the time see any very good reason why he should, if you kept your mouth good and tight. So he played his trump card. His first hold on you, what made you take the doubloon and give it to him, even if he did promise you money as well, was something about Merle and your father. I know about it. Your mother told me what little I hadn't put together already. That was his first hold and it was pretty strong. Because it would let you justify yourself. But last night he wanted something still stronger. So he told you the truth and said he had proof.'

He shivered, but the light clear proud look managed to stay on his face.

'I pulled a gun on him,' he said, almost in a happy voice. 'After all, she is my mother.'

'Nobody can take that away from you.'

He stood up, very straight, very tall. 'I went over to the chair he sat in and reached down and put the gun against his face. He had a gun in the pocket of his robe. He tried to get it, but he didn't get it in time. I took it away from him. I put my gun back in my pocket. I put the muzzle of the other gun against the side of his head and told him I would kill him, if he didn't produce his proof and give it to me. He began to sweat and babble that he was just kidding me. I clicked back the hammer on the gun to scare him some more.'

He stopped and held a hand out in front of him. The hand shook but as he stared down at it it got steady. He dropped it to his side and looked me in the eye.

'The gun must have been filed or had a very light action. It went off. I jumped back against the wall and knocked a picture down. I jumped from surprise that the gun went off, but it kept the blood off me. I wiped the gun off and put his fingers around it and then put it down on the floor close to his hand. He was dead at once. He hardly bled except the first spurt. It was an accident.'

'Why spoil it?' I half-sneered. 'Why not make it a nice clean honest murder?'

'That's what happened. I can't prove it, of course. But I think I might have killed him anyway. What about the police?'

I stood up and shrugged my shoulders. I felt tired, spent, drawn out and sapped. My throat was sore from yapping and my brain ached from trying to keep my thoughts orderly.

'I don't know about the police,' I said. 'They and I are not very good friends, on account of they think I am holding out on them. And God knows they are right. They may get to you. If you weren't seen, if you didn't leave any fingerprints around, and even if you did, if they don't have any other reason to suspect you and get your fingerprints to check, then they may never think of you. If they find out about the doubloon and that it was the Murdock Brasher, I don't know where you stand. It all depends on how well you stand up to them.'

'Except for mother's sake,' he said, 'I don't very much care. I've always been a flop.'

'And on the other hand,' I said, ignoring the feeble talk, 'if the gun really has a very light action and you get a good lawyer and tell an honest story and so on, no jury will convict you. Juries don't like blackmailers.'

'That's too bad,' he said. 'because I am not in a position to use that defence. I don't know anything about blackmail. Vannier showed me where I could make some money, and I needed it badly.'

I said: 'Uh-huh. If they get you where you need the blackmail dope, you'll use it all right. Your old lady will make you. If it's her neck or yours, she'll spill.'

'It's horrible,' he said. 'Horrible to say that.'

'You were lucky about that gun. All the people we know have been playing with it, wiping prints off and putting them on. I even put a set on myself just to be fashionable. It's tricky when the hand is stiff. But I had to do it. Morny was over there having his wife put hers on. He thinks she killed Vannier, so she probably thinks he did.'

He just stared at me. I chewed my lip. It felt as stiff as a piece of glass.

'Well, I guess I'll just be running along now,' I said.

'You mean you are going to let me get away with it?' His voice was getting a little supercilious again.

'I'm not going to turn you in, if that's what you mean. Beyond that I guarantee nothing. If I'm involved in it, I'll have to face up to the situation. There's no question of morality involved. I'm not a cop nor a common informer nor an officer of the court. You say it was an accident. Okay, it was an accident. I wasn't a witness. I haven't any proof either way. I've been working for your mother and whatever right to my silence that gives her, she can have. I don't like her, I don't like you. I don't like this house. I didn't particularly like your wife. But I like Merle. She's kind of silly and morbid, but she's kind of sweet, too. And I know what has been done to her in this damn family for the past eight years. And I know she didn't push anybody out of any window. Does that explain matters?'

He gobbled, but nothing came that was coherent.

'I'm taking Merle home,' I said. 'I asked your mother to send her clothes to my apartment in the morning. In case she kind of forgets, being busy with her solitaire game, would you see that that is done?'

He nodded dumbly. Then he said in a queer small voice: 'You are going—just like that? I haven't—I haven't even thanked you. A man I hardly know, taking risks for me—I don't know what to say.'

'I'm going the way I always go,' I said. 'With an airy smile and a quick flip of the wrist. And with a deep and heartfelt hope that I won't be seeing you in the fishbowl. Good night.'

I turned my back on him and went to the door and out. I shut the door with a quiet, firm click of the lock. A nice, smooth exit, in spite of all the nastiness. For the last time I went over and patted the little Negro on the head and then walked across the long lawn by the moon-drenched shrubs and the deodar tree to the street and my car.

I drove back to Hollywood, bought a pint of good liquor, checked in at the Plaza, and sat on the side of the bed staring at my feet and lapping the whisky out of the bottle.

Just like any common bedroom drunk.

When I had enough of it to make my brain fuzzy enough to stop thinking, I undressed and got into bed, and after a while, but not soon enough, I went to sleep.

35

It was three o'clock in the afternoon and there were five pieces of luggage inside the apartment door, side by side on the carpet. There was my yellow cowhide, well scraped on both sides from being pushed around in the boots of cars. There were two pieces of airplane luggage, both marked L.M. There was an old black imitation walrus thing marked M.D. and there was one of these little leatherette overnight cases which you can buy in drugstores for a dollar forty-nine.

Dr Carl Moss had just gone out of the door cursing me because he had kept his afternoon class of hypochondriacs waiting. The sweetish smell of his Fatima poisoned the air for me. I was turning over in what was left of my mind what he had said when I asked him how long it would take Merle to get well.

'It depends what you mean by well. She'll always be high on nerves and low on animal emotion. She'll always breathe thin air and smell snow. She'd have made a perfect man. The religious dream, with its narrowness, its stylized emotions and its grim purity, would have been a perfect release for her. As it is, she will probably turn out to be one of these acid-faced virgins that sit behind little desks in public libraries and stamp dates in books.'

'She's not that bad,' I had said, but he had just grinned at me with his wise Jew face and gone out of the door. 'And besides, how do you know they are virgins?' I added to the closed door, but that didn't get me any farther.

I lit a cigarette and wandered over to the window and after a while she came through the doorway from the bedroom part of the apartment and stood there looking at me with her eyes dark-ringed and a pale composed little face without any make-up except on the lips.

'Put some rouge on your cheeks,' I told her. 'You look like the snow maiden after a hard night with the fishing fleet.'

She went back and put some rouge on her cheeks. When she came back again she looked at the luggage and said softly: 'Leslie lent me two of his suitcases.'

I said: 'Yeah,' and looked her over. She looked very nice. She had a pair of long-waisted, rust-coloured slacks on, and Bata shoes and a brown and white print shirt and an orange scarf. She didn't have her glasses on. Her large clear cobalt eyes had a slightly dopey look, but not more than you would expect. Her hair was dragged down tight, but I couldn't do anything much about that.

'I've been a terrible nuisance,' she said. 'I'm terribly sorry.'

'Nonsense. I talked to your father and mother both. They're tickled to death. They've only seen you twice in over eight years and they feel as if they had almost lost you.'

'I'll love seeing them for a while,' she said, looking down at the carpet. 'It's very kind of Mrs Murdock to let me go. She's never been able to spare me for long.' She moved her legs as if she wondered what to do with them in slacks, although they were her slacks and she must have had to face the problem before. She finally put her knees close together and clasped her hands on top of them.

'Any little talking we might have to do,' I said, 'or anything you might want to say to me, let's get it over with now. Because I'm not driving half-way across the United States with a nervous breakdown in the seat behind me.'

She bit a knuckle and sneaked a couple of quick looks at me around the side of the knuckle. 'Last night'–she said, and stopped and coloured.

'Let's use a little of the old acid,' I said. 'Last night you told me you killed Vannier and then you told me you didn't. I know you didn't. That's settled.'

She dropped her knuckles, looked at me levelly, quiet, composed and the hands on her knees now not straining at all.

'Vannier was dead a long time before you got there. You went there to give him some money from Mrs Murdock.'

'No–for me,' she said. 'Although, of course, it was Mrs Murdock's money. I owe her more than I'll ever be able to repay. Of course, she doesn't give me much salary, but that would hardly—'

I said roughly: 'Her not giving you much salary is a characteristic touch and your owing her more than you can ever repay is more truth than poetry. It would take the Yankee outfield with two bats each to give her what she has coming from you. However, that's unimportant now. Vannier committed suicide because he had got caught out in a crooked job. That's flat and final. The way you behaved was more or less an act. You got a severe nervous shock seeing his leering dead face in a mirror and that shock merged into another one a long time ago and you just dramatized it in your screwy little way.'

She looked at me shyly and nodded her copper-blonde head, as if in agreement.

'And you didn't push Horace Bright out of any window,' I said.

Her face jumped then and turned startlingly pale. 'I–I—' her hand went to her mouth and stayed there and her shocked eyes looked at me over it.

'I wouldn't be doing this,' I said, 'if Dr Moss hadn't said it would be all right and we might as well hand it to you now. I think, maybe, you think you killed Horace Bright. You had a motive and an opportunity and just for a second I think you might have had the impulse to take advantage of the opportunity. But it wouldn't be in your nature. At the last minute you would hold back. But at that last minute probably something snapped and you pulled a faint. He did actually fall, of course, but you were not the one that pushed him.'

I held it a moment and watched the hand drop down again to join the other one and the two of them twine together and pull hard on each other.

'You were made to think you had pushed him,' I said. 'It was done with care, deliberation and the sort of quiet ruthlessness you only find in a certain kind of woman dealing with another woman. You wouldn't think of jealousy to look at Mrs Murdock now–but if that was a motive, she had it. She had a better one–fifty thousand dollars' life insurance–all that was left from a ruined fortune. She had the strange wild possessive love for her son such women have. She's cold, bitter, unscrupulous, and she used you without mercy or pity, as insurance, in case Vannier ever blew his top. You were just a scapegoat to her. If you want to come out of this pallid sub-emotional life you have been living, you have got to realize and believe what I am telling you. I know it's tough.'

'It's utterly impossible,' she said quietly, looking at the bridge of my nose. 'Mrs Murdock has been wonderful to me always. It's true I never remembered very well–but you shouldn't say such awful things about people.'

I got out the white envelope that had been in the back of Vannier's picture. Two prints in it and a negative. I stood in front of her and put a print on her lap.

'Okay, look at it. Vannier took it from across the street.'

She looked at it. 'Why, that's Mr Bright,' she said. 'It's not a very good picture, is it? And that's Mrs Murdock–Mrs Bright she was then–right behind him. Mr Bright looks mad.' She looked up at me with a sort of mild curiosity.

'If he looks mad there,' I said, 'you ought to have seen him a few seconds later, when he bounced.'

'When he what?'

'Look,' I said, and there was a kind of desperation in my voice now, 'that is a snapshot of Mrs Elizabeth Bright Murdock giving her first husband the heave out of his office window. He's falling. Look at the position of his hands. He's screaming with fear. She is behind him and her face is hard with rage–or something. Don't you get it at all? This is what Vannier has had for proof all these years. The Murdocks never saw it, never really believed it existed. But it did. I found it last night, by a fluke of the same sort that was involved in the taking of the picture. Which is a fair sort of justice. Do you begin to understand?'

She looked at the photo again and laid it aside. 'Mrs Murdock has always been lovely to me,' she said.

'She made you the goat,' I said, in the quietly strained voice of a stage manager at a bad rehearsal. 'She's a smart, tough, patient woman. She knows her complexes. She'll even spend a dollar to keep a dollar, which is what few of her type will do. I hand it to her. I'd like to hand it to her with an elephant gun, but my polite breeding restrains me.'

'Well,' she said, 'that's that.' And I could see she had heard one word in three and hadn't believed what she had heard. 'You must never show this to Mrs Murdock. It would upset her terribly.'

I got up and took the photo out of her hand and tore it into small pieces and dropped them in the waste-basket.

'Maybe you'll be sorry I did that,' I told her, not telling her I had another and the negative. 'Maybe some night–three months–three years from now–you will wake up in the night and realize I have been telling you the truth. And, maybe, then you will wish you could look at that photograph again. And, maybe, I am wrong about this, too. Maybe you would be very disappointed to find out you hadn't really killed anybody. That's fine. Either way it's fine. Now we are going downstairs and get in my car and we are going to drive to Wichita to visit your parents. And I don't think you are going back to Mrs Murdock, but it may well be that I am wrong about that, too. But we are not going to talk about this any more. Not any more.'

'I haven't any money,' she said.

'You have five hundred dollars that Mrs Murdock sent you. I have it in my pocket.'

'That's really awfully kind of her,' she said.

'Oh hell and fireflies,' I said and went out to the kitchen and gobbled a quick drink, before we started. It didn't do me any good. It just made me want to climb up the wall and gnaw my way across the ceiling.

36

I was gone ten days. Merle's parents were vague, kind, patient people, living in an old frame house in a quiet shady street. They cried when I told them as much of the story as I thought they should know. They said they were glad to have her back and they would take good care of her and they blamed themselves a lot, and I let them do it.

When I left, Merle was wearing a bungalow apron and rolling pie-crust. She came to the door wiping her hands on the apron and kissed me on the mouth and began to cry and ran back into the house, leaving the doorway empty until her mother came into the space with a broad homely smile on her face to watch me drive away.

I had a funny feeling as I saw the house disappear, as though I had written a poem and it was very good and I had lost it and would never remember it again.

I called Lieutenant Breeze when I got back and went down to ask him how the Phillips case was coming. They had cracked it very neatly, with the right mixture of brains and luck you always have to have. The Mornys never went to the police after all, but somebody called and told about a shot in Vannier's house and hung up quickly. The fingerprint man didn't like the prints on the gun too well, so they checked Vannier's hand for powder nitrates. When they found them they decided it was suicide after all. Then a dick named Lackey working out of Central Homicide thought to work on the gun a little and he found that a description of it had been distributed, and a gun like it was wanted in connexion with the Phillips killing. Hench identified it, but better than that they found a half-print of his thumb on the side of the trigger, which, not ordinarily being pulled back, had not been wiped off completely.

With that much in hand and a better set of Vannier's prints than I could make, they went over Phillips's apartment again and also over Hench's. They found Vannier's left hand on Hench's bed and one of his fingers on the underside of the toilet flush lever in Phillips's place. Then they got to work in the neighbourhood with photographs of Vannier, and proved he had been along the alley twice and on a side street at least three times. Curiously, nobody in the apartment house had seen him, or would admit it.

All they lacked now was a motive. Teager obligingly gave them that by getting himself pinched in Salt Lake City trying to peddle a Brasher Doubloon to a coin dealer who thought it was genuine but stolen. He had a dozen of them at his hotel, and one of them turned out to be genuine. He told them the whole story and showed a minute mark that he had used to identify the genuine coin. He didn't know where Vannier got it and they never found out because there was enough in the papers to make the owner come forward, if it had been stolen. And the owner never did. And the police didn't care any more about Vannier once they were convinced he had done murder. They left it at suicide, although they had a few doubts.

They let Teager go after a while, because they didn't think he had any idea of murder being done and all they had on him was attempted fraud. He had bought the gold legally and counterfeiting an obsolete New York State coin didn't come under the federal counterfeiting laws. Utah refused to bother with him.

They never believed Hench's confession. Breeze said he just used it for a squeeze on me, in case I was holding out. He knew I couldn't keep quiet if I had proof that Hench was innocent. It didn't do Hench any good, either. They put him in the line-up and pinned five liquor-store hold-ups on him and a wop named Gaetano Prisco, in one of which a man was shot dead. I never heard whether Prisco was a relative of Palermo's, but they never caught him, anyway.

'Like it?' Breeze asked me, when he had told me all this, or all that had then happened.

'Two points not clear,' I said. 'Why did Teager run away and why did Phillips live on Court Street under a phony name?'

'Teager ran away because the elevator man told him old Morningstar had been murdered and he smelled a hook-up. Phillips was using the name of Anson because the finance company was after his car and he was practically broke and getting desperate. That explains why a nice young boob like him could get roped in to something that must have looked shady from the start.'

I nodded and agreed that could be so.

Breeze walked to his door with me. He put a hard hand on my shoulder and squeezed.

'Remember that Cassidy case you were howling about to Spangler and me that night in your apartment?'

'Yes.'

'You told Spangler there wasn't any Cassidy case. There was—under another name. I worked on it.'

He took his hand off my shoulder and opened the door for me and grinned straight into my eyes.

'On account of the Cassidy case,' he said, 'and the way it made me feel, I sometimes give a guy a break he could perhaps not really deserve. A little something paid back out of the dirty millions to a working stiff—like me—or like you. Be good.'

It was night. I went home and put my old house clothes on and set the chessmen out and mixed a drink and played over another Capablanca. It went fifty-nine moves. Beautiful, cold, remorseless chess, almost creepy in its silent implacability.

When it was done I listened at the open window for a while and smelled the night. Then I carried my glass out to the kitchen and rinsed it and filled it with ice water and stood at the sink sipping it and looking at my face in the mirror.

'You and Capablanca,' I said.

The Lady
in the Lake

Raymond CHANDLER

I

The Treloar Building was, and is, on Olive Street, near Sixth, on the west side. The sidewalk in front of it had been built of black and white rubber blocks. They were taking them up now to give to the government, and a hatless pale man with a face like a building superintendent was watching the work and looking as if it was breaking his heart.

I went past him through an arcade of speciality shops into a vast black and gold lobby. The Gillerlain Company was on the seventh floor, in front, behind swinging double plate-glass doors bound in platinum. Their reception-room had Chinese rugs, dull silver walls, angular but elaborate furniture, sharp shiny bits of abstract sculpture on pedestals and a tall display in a triangular showcase in the corner. On tiers and steps and islands and promontories of shining mirror-glass it seemed to contain every fancy bottle and box that has ever been designed. There were creams and powders and soaps and toilet waters for every season and every occasion. There were perfumes in tall thin bottles that looked as if a breath would blow them over and perfumes in little pastel phials tied with ducky satin bows, like little girls at a dancing class. The cream of the crop seemed to be something very small and simple in a squat amber bottle. It was in the middle at eye height, had a lot of space to itself, and was labelled *Gillerlain Regal, The Champagne of Perfumes*. It was definitely the stuff to get. One drop of that in the hollow of your throat and the matched pink pearls started falling on you like summer rain.

A neat little blonde sat off in a far corner at a small PBX, behind a railing and well out of harm's way. At a flat desk in line with the doors was a tall, lean, dark-haired lovely whose name, according to the titled embossed plaque on her desk, was Miss Adrienne Fromsett.

She wore a steel-grey business suit and under the jacket a dark blue shirt and a man's tie of lighter shade. The edges of the folded handkerchief in the breast pocket looked sharp enough to slice bread. She wore a linked bracelet and no other jewellery. Her dark hair was parted and fell in loose but not unstudied waves. She had a smooth ivory skin and rather severe eyebrows and large dark eyes that looked as if they might warm up at the right time and in the right place.

I put my plain card, the one without the tommy gun in the corner, on her desk and asked to see Mr Derace Kingsley.

She looked at the card and said: 'Have you an appointment?'

'No appointment.'

'It is very difficult to see Mr Kingsley without an appointment.'

That wasn't anything I could argue about.

'What is the nature of your business, Mr Marlowe?'

'Personal.'

'I see. Does Mr Kingsley know you, Mr Marlowe?'

'I don't think so. He may have heard my name. You might say I'm from Lieutenant M'Gee.'

'And does Mr Kingsley know Lieutenant M'Gee?'

She put my card beside a pile of freshly typed letterheads. She leaned back and put one arm on the desk and tapped lightly with a small gold pencil.

I grinned at her. The little blonde at the PBX cocked a shell-like ear and smiled a small fluffy smile. She looked playful and eager, but not quite sure of herself, like a new kitten in a house where they don't care much about kittens.

'I'm hoping he does,' I said. 'But maybe the best way to find out is to ask him.'

She initialled three letters rapidly, to keep from throwing her pen set at me. She spoke again without looking up.

'Mr Kingsley is in conference. I'll send your card in when I have an opportunity.'

I thanked her and went and sat in a chromium and leather chair that was a lot more comfortable than it looked. Time passed and silence descended on the scene. Nobody came in or went out. Miss Fromsett's elegant hand moved over her papers and the muted peep of the kitten at the PBX was audible at moments, and the little click of the plugs going in and out.

I lit a cigarette and dragged a smoking stand beside the chair. The minutes went by on tiptoe, with their fingers to their lips. I looked the place over. You can't tell anything about an outfit like that. They might be making millions, and they might have the sheriff in the back room, with his chair tilted against the safe.

Half an hour and three or four cigarettes later a door opened behind Miss Fromsett's desk and two men came out backwards, laughing. A third held the door for them and helped them laugh. They all shook hands heartily and the two men went across the office and out. The third man dropped the grin off his face and looked as if he had never grinned in his life. He was a tall bird in a grey suit and he didn't want any nonsense.

'Any calls?' he asked in a sharp bossy voice.

Miss Fromsett said softly: 'A Mr Marlowe to see you. From Lieutenant M'Gee. His business is personal.'

'Never heard of him,' the tall man barked. He took my card, didn't even glance at me, and went back into his office. His door closed on the pneumatic closer and made a sound like 'phooey'. Miss Fromsett gave me a sweet sad smile and I gave it back to her in the form of an obscene leer. I ate another cigarette and more time staggered by. I was getting to be very fond of the Gillerlain Company.

Ten minutes later the same door opened again and the big shot came out with his hat on and sneered that he was going to get a hair-cut. He started off across the Chinese rug in a swinging athletic stride, made about half the distance to the door and then did a sharp cutback and came over to where I was sitting.

'You want to see me?' he barked.

He was about six feet two and not much of it soft. His eyes were stone grey with flecks of cold light in them. He filled a large size in smooth grey flannel with a narrow chalk stripe, and filled it elegantly. His manner said he was very tough to get along with.

I stood up. 'If you're Mr Derace Kingsley.'

'Who the hell did you think I was?'

I let him have that trick and gave him my other card, the one with the business on it. He clamped it in his paw and scowled down at it.

'Who's M'Gee?' he snapped.

'He's just a fellow I know.'

'I'm fascinated,' he said, glancing back at Miss Fromsett. She liked it. She liked it very much. 'Anything else you would care to let drop about him?'

'Well, they call him Violets M'Gee,' I said. 'On account of he chews little throat pastilles that smell of violets. He's a big man with soft silvery hair and a cute little mouth made to kiss babies with. When last seen he was wearing a neat blue suit, wide-toed brown shoes, grey homburg hat, and he was smoking opium in a short briar pipe.'

'I don't like your manner,' Kingsley said in a voice you could have cracked a brazil nut on.

'That's all right,' I said. 'I'm not selling it.'

He reared back as if I had hung a week-old mackerel under his nose. After a moment he turned his back on me and said over his shoulder:

'I'll give you exactly three minutes. God knows why.'

He burned the carpet back past Miss Fromsett's desk to his door, yanked it open and let it swing to in my face. Miss Fromsett liked that too, but I thought there was a little sly laughter behind her eyes now.

2

The private office was everything a private office should be. It was long and dim and quiet and air-conditioned and its windows were shut and its grey venetian blinds half-closed to keep out the July glare. Grey drapes matched the grey carpeting. There was a large black and silver safe in the corner and a low row of low filing cases that exactly matched it. On the wall there was a huge tinted photograph of an elderly party with a chiselled beak and whiskers and a wing collar. The Adam's apple that edged through his wing collar looked harder than most people's chins. The plate underneath the photograph read: *Mr Matthew Gillerlain, 1860–1934.*

Derace Kingsley marched briskly behind about eight hundred dollars' worth of executive desk and planted his backside in a tall leather chair. He reached himself a panatela out of a copper and mahogany box and trimmed it and lit it with a fat copper desk lighter. He took his time about it. It didn't matter about my time. When he had finished this, he leaned back and blew a little smoke and said:

'I'm a business man. I don't fool around. You're a licensed detective, your card says. Show me something to prove it.'

I got my wallet out and handed him things to prove it. He looked at them and threw them back across the desk. The celluloid holder with the photostat of my licence in it fell to the floor. He didn't bother to apologize.

'I don't know M'Gee,' he said. 'I know Sheriff Petersen. I asked for the name of a reliable man to do a job. I suppose you are the man.'

'M'Gee is in the Hollywood sub-station of the sheriff's office,' I said. 'You can check on that.'

'Not necessary. I guess you might do, but don't get flip with me. And remember when I hire a man he's my man. He does exactly what I tell him and he keeps his mouth shut. Or he goes out fast. Is that clear? I hope I'm not too tough for you.'

'Why not leave that an open question?' I said.

He frowned. He said sharply: 'What do you charge?'

'Twenty-five a day and expenses. Eight cents a mile for my car.'

'Absurd,' he said. 'Far too much. Fifteen a day flat. That's plenty. I'll pay the mileage, within reason, the way things are now. But no joyriding.'

I blew a little grey cloud of cigarette smoke and fanned it with my hand. I said nothing. He seemed a little surprised that I said nothing.

He leaned over the desk and pointed with his cigar. 'I haven't hired you yet,' he said, 'but if I do, the job is absolutely confidential. No talking it over with your cop friends. Is that understood?'

'Just what do you want done, Mr Kingsley?'

'What do you care? You do all kinds of detective work, don't you?'

'Not all kinds. Only the fairly honest kinds.'

He stared at me level-eyed, his jaw tight. His grey eyes had an opaque look.

'For one thing I don't do divorce business,' I said. 'And I get a hundred down as a retainer–from strangers.'

'Well, well,' he said, in a voice suddenly soft. 'Well, well.'

'And as for your being too tough for me,' I said, 'most of the clients start out either by weeping down my shirt or bawling me out to show who's boss. But usually they end up very reasonable–if they're still alive.'

'Well, well,' he said again, in the same soft voice, and went on staring at me. 'Do you lose very many of them?' he asked.

'Not if they treat me right,' I said.

'Have a cigar,' he said.

I took a cigar and put it in my pocket.

'I want you to find my wife,' he said. 'She's been missing for a month.'

'Okay,' I said. 'I'll find your wife.'

He patted his desk with both hands. He stared at me solidly. 'I think you will at that,' he said. Then he grinned. 'I haven't been called down like that in four years,' he said.

I didn't say anything.

'Damn it all,' he said, 'I liked it. I liked it fine.' He ran a hand through his thick dark hair. 'She's been gone a whole month,' he said. 'From a cabin we have in the mountains. Near Puma Point. Do you know Puma Point?'

I said I knew Puma Point.

'Our place is three miles from the village,' he said, 'partly over a private road. It's on a private lake. Little Fawn Lake. There's a dam three of us put up to improve the property. I own the tract with two other men. It's quite large, but undeveloped and won't be developed now for some time, of course. My friends have cabins, I have a cabin and a man named Bill Chess lives with his wife in another cabin rent-free and looks after the place. He's a disabled veteran with a pension. That's all there is up there. My wife went up the middle of May, came down twice for week-ends, was due down the

12th of June for a party and never showed up. I haven't seen her since.'

'What have you done about it?' I asked.

'Nothing. Not a thing. I haven't even been up there.' He waited, wanting me to ask why.

I said: 'Why?'

He pushed his chair back to get a locked drawer open. He took out a folded paper and passed it over. I unfolded it and saw it was a postal telegraph form. The wire had been filed at El Paso on June 14th, at 9.19 a.m. It was addressed to Derace Kingsley, 965 Carson Drive, Beverly Hills, and read:

AM CROSSING TO GET MEXICAN DIVORCE STOP WILL MARRY CHRIS STOP GOOD LUCK AND GOODBYE CRYSTAL

I put this down on my side of the desk and he was handing me a large and very clear snapshot on glazed paper which showed a man and a woman sitting on the sand under a beach umbrella. The man wore trunks and the woman what looked like a very daring sharkskin bathing suit. She was a slim blonde, young and shapely and smiling. The man was a hefty dark handsome lad with fine shoulders and legs, sleek dark hair and white teeth. Six feet of a standard type of home-wrecker. Arms to hold you close and all his brains in his face. He was holding a pair of dark glasses in his hand and smiling at the camera with a practised and easy smile.

'That's Crystal,' Kingsley said, 'and that's Chris Lavery. She can have him and he can have her and to hell with them both.'

I put the photo down on the telegram. 'All right, what's the catch?' I asked him.

'There's no telephone up there,' he said, 'and there was nothing important about the affair she was coming down for. So I got the wire before I gave much thought to it. The wire surprised me only mildly. Crystal and I have been washed up for years. She lives her life and I live mine. She has her own money and plenty of it. About twenty thousand a year from a family holding corporation that owns valuable oil leases in Texas. She plays around and I knew Lavery was one of her playmates. I might have been a little surprised that she would actually marry him, because the man is nothing but a professional chaser. But the picture looked all right so far, you understand?'

'And then?'

'Nothing for two weeks. Then the Prescott Hotel in San Bernardino got in touch with me and said a Packard Clipper registered to Crystal Grace Kingsley at my address was unclaimed in their garage and what about it. I told them to keep it and I sent them a cheque. There was nothing much in that either. I figured she was still out of the state and that if they had gone in a car at all, they had gone in Lavery's car. The day before yesterday, however, I met Lavery in front of the Athletic Club down on the corner here. He said he didn't know where Crystal was.'

Kingsley gave me a quick look and reached a bottle and two tinted glasses up on the desk. He poured a couple of drinks and pushed one over. He held his against the light and said slowly:

'Lavery said he hadn't gone away with her, hadn't seen her in two months, hadn't had any communication with her of any kind.'

I said, 'You believed him?'

He nodded, frowning, and drank his drink and pushed the glass to one side. I tasted mine. It was Scotch. Not very good Scotch.

'If I believed him—' Kingsley said, 'and I was probably wrong to do it—it wasn't because he's a fellow you have to believe. Far from it. It's because he's a no-good son of a bitch who thinks it is smart to lay his friends' wives and brag about it. I feel he would have been tickled pink to stick it into me and break it off that he had got my wife to run away with him and leave me flat. I know these tomcats and I know this one too well. He rode a route for us for a while and he was in trouble all the time. He couldn't keep his hands off the office help. And apart from all that there was this wire from El Paso and I told him about it, and why would he think it worth while to lie about it?'

'She might have tossed him out on his can,' I said. 'That would have hurt him in his deep place—his Casanova complex.'

Kingsley brightened up a little, but not very much. He shook his head. 'I still more than half-way believe him,' he said. 'You'll have to prove me wrong. That's part of why I wanted you. But there's another and very worrying angle. I have a good job here, but a job is all it is. I can't stand scandal. I'd be out of here in a hurry if my wife got mixed up with the police.'

'Police?'

'Among her other activities,' Kingsley said grimly, 'my wife occasionally finds time to lift things in department stores. I think it's just a sort of delusion of grandeur she gets when she has been hitting the bottle too hard, but it happens, and we have had some pretty nasty scenes in managers' offices. So far I've been able to keep them from filing charges, but if something like that happened in a strange city where nobody knew her'—he lifted his hands and let them fall with a smack on the desk—'well, it might be a prison matter, mightn't it?'

'Has she ever been finger-printed?'

'She has never been arrested,' he said.

'That's not what I mean. Sometimes in large department stores they make it a condition of dropping shoplifting charges that you give them your prints. It scares the amateurs and builds up a file of kleptomaniacs in their protective association. When the prints come in a certain number of times they call time on you.'

'Nothing like that has happened to my knowledge,' he said.

'Well, I think we might almost throw the shoplifting angle out of this for the time being,' I said. 'If she got arrested, she would get searched. Even if the cops let her use a Jane Doe name on the police blotter, they would be likely to get in touch with you. Also she would start yelling for help when she found herself in a jam.' I tapped the blue-and-white telegraph form. 'And this is a month old. If what you are thinking about happened around that time, the case would have been settled by now. If it was a first offence, she would get off with a scolding and a suspended sentence.'

He poured himself another drink to help him with his worrying. 'You're making me feel better,' he said.

'There are too many other things that could have happened,' I said. 'That she did go away with Lavery and they split up. That she went away with some other man and the wire is a gag. That she went away alone or with a woman. That she drank herself over the edge and is holed up in some private sanatorium taking a cure. That she got into some jam we have no idea of. That she met foul play.'

'Good God, don't say that,' Kingsley exclaimed.

'Why not? You've got to consider it. I get a very vague idea of Mrs Kingsley—that she is young, pretty, reckless, and wild. That she drinks and does dangerous things when she drinks. That she is a sucker for the men and might take up with a stranger who might turn out to be a crook. Does that fit?'

He nodded. 'Every word of it.'

'How much money would she have with her?'

'She liked to carry enough. She has her own bank and her own bank account. She could have any amount of money.'

'Any children?'

'No children.'

'Do you have the management of her affairs?'

He shook his head. 'She hasn't any—excepting depositing cheques and drawing out money and spending it. She never invests a nickel. And her money certainly never does me any good, if that's what you are thinking.' He paused and then said: 'Don't think I haven't tried. I'm human and it's not fun to watch twenty thousand a year go down the drain and nothing to show for it but hangovers and boy friends of the class of Chris Lavery.'

'How are you with her bank? Could you get a detail of the cheques she has drawn for the past couple of months?'

'They wouldn't tell me. I tried to get some information of the sort once, when I had an idea she was being blackmailed. All I got was ice.'

'We can get it,' I said, 'and we may have to. It will mean going to the Missing Persons Bureau. You wouldn't like that?'

'If I had liked that, I wouldn't have called you,' he said.

I nodded, gathered my exhibits together and put them away in my pockets. 'There are more angles to this than I can even see now,' I said, 'but I'll start by talking to Lavery and then taking a run up to Little Fawn Lake and asking questions there. I'll need Lavery's address and a note to your man in charge at the mountain place.'

He got a letterhead out of his desk and wrote and passed it over. I read: 'Dear Bill: This will introduce Mr Philip Marlowe who wishes to look over the property. Please show him my cabin and assist him in every way. Yrs Derace Kingsley.'

I folded this up and put it in the envelope he had addressed while I was reading it. 'How about the other cabins up there?' I asked.

'Nobody up this year so far. One man's in government service in Washington and the other is at Fort Leavenworth. Their wives are with them.'

'Now Lavery's address,' I said.

He looked at a point well above the top of my head. 'In Bay City. I could find the house but I forget the address. Miss Fromsett can give it to you, I think. She needn't know why you want it. She probably will. And you want a hundred dollars, you said.'

'That's all right,' I said. 'That's just something I said when you were tramping on me.'

He grinned. I stood up and hesitated by the desk looking at him. After a moment I said: 'You're not holding anything back, are you—anything important?'

He looked at his thumb. 'No. I'm not holding anything back. I'm worried and I want to know where she is. I'm damn worried. If you get anything at all, call me any time, day or night.'

I said I would do that, and we shook hands and I went back down the long cool office and out to where Miss Fromsett sat elegantly at her desk.

'Mr Kingsley thinks you can give me Chris Lavery's address,' I told her and watched her face.

She reached very slowly for a brown leather address book and turned the leaves. Her voice was tight and cold when she spoke.

'The address we have is 623 Altair Street, in Bay City. Telephone Bay City 12523. Mr Lavery has not been with us for more than a year. He may have moved.'

I thanked her and went on to the door. From there I glanced back at her. She was sitting very still, with her hands clasped on her desk, staring into space. A couple of red spots burned in her cheeks. Her eyes were remote and bitter.

I got the impression that Mr Chris Lavery was not a pleasant thought to her.

3

Altair Street lay on the edge of the V forming the inner end of a deep canyon. To the north was the cool blue sweep of the bay out to the point about Malibu. To the south the beach town of Bay City was spread out on a bluff above the coast highway.

It was a short street, not more than three or four blocks, and ended in a tall iron fence enclosing a large estate. Beyond the gilded spikes of the fence I could see trees and shrubs and a glimpse of lawn and part of a curving driveway, but the house was out of sight. On the inland side of Altair Street the houses were well kept and fairly large, but the few scattered bungalows on the edge of the canyon were nothing much. In the short half-block ended by the iron fence were only two houses, on opposite sides of the street and almost directly across from each other. The smaller was number 623.

I drove past it, turned the car in the paved half-circle at the end of the street and came back to park in front of the lot next to Lavery's place. His house was built downwards, one of those clinging vine effects, with the front door a little below street level, the patio on the roof, the bedrooms in the basement, and a garage like the corner pocket on a pool table. A crimson bougainvillea was rustling against the front wall and the flat stones of the front walk were edged with Korean moss. The door was narrow, grilled and topped by a lancet arch. Below the grille there was an iron knocker. I hammered on it.

Nothing happened. I pushed the bell at the side of the door and heard it ring inside not very far off and waited and nothing happened. I worked on the knocker again. Still nothing. I went back up the walk and along to the garage and lifted the door far enough to see that a car with white side-walled tyres was inside. I went back to the front door.

A neat black Cadillac coupé came out of the garage across the way, backed, turned and came along past Lavery's house, slowed, and a thin man in dark glasses looked at me sharply, as if I hadn't any business to be there. I gave him my steely glare and he went on his way.

I went down Lavery's walk again and did some more hammering on his knocker. This time I got results. The judas window opened and I was looking at a handsome bright-eyed number through the bars of the grille.

'You make a hell of a lot of noise,' a voice said.

'Mr Lavery?'

He said he was Mr Lavery and what about it. I poked a card through the grille. A large brown hand took the card. The bright brown eyes came back and the voice said: 'So sorry. Not needing any detectives to-day, please.'

'I'm working for Derace Kingsley.'

'The hell with both of you,' he said, and banged the judas window.

I leaned on the bell beside the door and got a cigarette out with my free hand and had just struck the match on the woodwork beside the door when it was yanked open and a big guy in bathing trunks, beach sandals and a white terrycloth bathrobe started to come out at me.

I took my thumb off the bell and grinned at him. 'What's the matter?' I asked him. 'Scared?'

'Ring that bell again,' he said, 'and I'll throw you clear across the street.'

'Don't be childish,' I told him. 'You know perfectly well I'm going to talk to you and you're going to talk to me.'

I got the blue-and-white telegram out of my pocket and held it in front of his bright brown eyes. He read it morosely, chewed his lips and growled:

'Oh for Chrissake, come on in then.'

He held the door wide and I went in past him, into a dim pleasant room with an apricot Chinese rug that looked expensive, deep-sided chairs, a number of white drum lamps, a big Capehart in the corner, a long and very wide davenport in pale tan mohair shot with dark brown, and a fireplace with a copper screen and an overmantel in white wood. A fire was laid behind the screen and partly masked by a large spray of manzanita bloom. The bloom was turning yellow in places but was still pretty. There was a bottle of Vat 69 and glasses on a tray and a copper icebucket on a low round burl walnut table with a glass top. The room went clear to the back of the house and ended in a flat arch through which showed three narrow windows and the top few feet of the white iron railing of the staircase going down.

Lavery swung the door shut and sat on the davenport. He grabbed a cigarette out of a hammered silver box and lit it and looked at me irritably. I sat down opposite him and looked him over. He had everything in the way of good looks the snapshot had indicated. He had a terrific torso and magnificent thighs. His eyes were chestnut brown and the whites of them slightly grey-white. His hair was rather long and curled a little over his temples. His brown skin showed no signs of dissipation. He was a nice piece of beef, but to me that was all he was. I could understand that women would think he was something to yell for.

'Why not tell us where she is?' I said. 'We'll find out eventually anyway, and if you tell us now we won't be bothering you.'

'It would take more than a private dick to bother me,' he said.

'No, it wouldn't. A private dick can bother anybody. He's persistent and used to snubs. He's paid for his time and he would just as soon use it to bother you as any other way.'

'Look,' he said, leaning forward and pointing his cigarette at me. 'I know what that wire says, but it's the bunk. I didn't go to El Paso with Crystal Kingsley. I haven't seen her in a long time—long before the date of the wire. I haven't had any contact with her. I told Kingsley that.'

'He didn't have to believe you.'

'Why would I lie to him?' He looked surprised.

'Why wouldn't you?'

'Look,' he said earnestly, 'it might seem so to you, but you don't know her. Kingsley has no strings on her. If he doesn't like the way she behaves he has a remedy. These proprietary husbands make me sick.'

'If you didn't go to El Paso with her,' I said, 'why did she send this telegram?'

'I haven't the faintest idea.'

'You can do better than that,' I said. I pointed to the spray of manzanita in the fireplace. 'You pick that up at Little Fawn Lake?'

'The hills around here are full of manzanita,' he said contemptuously.

'It doesn't bloom like that down here.'

He laughed. 'I was up there the third week in May. If you have to know. I suppose you can find out. That's the last time I saw her.'

'You didn't have any idea of marrying her?'

He blew smoke and said through it: 'I've thought of it, yes. She has money. Money is always useful. But it would be too tough a way to make it.'

I nodded, but didn't say anything. He looked at the manzanita spray in the fireplace and leaned back to blow smoke in the air and show me the strong brown line of his throat. After a moment, when I still didn't say anything, he began to get restless. He glanced down at the card I had given him and said:

'So you hire yourself out to dig up dirt? Doing well at it?'

'Nothing to brag about. A dollar here, a dollar there.'

'And all of them pretty slimy,' he said.

'Look, Mr Lavery, we don't have to get into a fight. Kingsley thinks you know where his wife is, but won't tell him. Either out of meanness or motives of delicacy.'

'Which way would he like it?' the handsome brown-faced man sneered.

'He doesn't care, as long as he gets the information. He doesn't care a great deal what you and she do together or where you go or whether she divorces him or not. He just wants to feel sure that everything is all right and that she isn't in trouble of any kind.'

Lavery looked interested. 'Trouble? What kind of trouble?' He licked the word around on his brown lips, tasting it.

'Maybe you won't know the kind of trouble he is thinking of.'

'Tell me,' he pleaded sarcastically. 'I'd just love to hear about some kind of trouble I didn't know about.'

'You're doing fine,' I told him. 'No time to talk business, but always time for a wisecrack. If you think we might try to get a hook into you because you crossed a state line with her, forget it.'

'Go climb up your thumb, wise guy. You'd have to prove I paid the freight, or it wouldn't mean anything.'

'This wire has to mean something,' I said stubbornly. It seemed to me that I had said it before, several times.

'It's probably just a gag. She's full of little tricks like that. All of them silly, and some of them vicious.'

'I don't see any point in this one.'

He flicked cigarette ash carelessly at the glass-top table. He gave me a quick up from under look and immediately looked away.

'I stood her up,' he said slowly. 'It might be her idea of a way to get back at me. I was supposed to run up there one week-end. I didn't go. I was—sick of her.'

I said: 'Uh-huh,' and gave him a long steady stare. 'I don't like that so well. I'd like it better if you did go to El Paso with her and had a fight and split up. Could you tell it that way?'

He flushed solidly behind the sunburn.

'God damn it,' he said, 'I told you I didn't go anywhere with her. Not anywhere. Can't you remember that?'

'I'll remember it when I believe it.'

He leaned over to stub out his cigarette. He stood up with an easy movement, not hurried at all, pulled the belt of his robe tight, and moved out to the end of the davenport.

'All right,' he said in a clear tight voice. 'Out you go. Take the air. I've had enough of your third-degree tripe. You're wasting my time and your own—if it's worth anything.'

I stood up and grinned at him. 'Not a lot, but for what it's worth I'm being paid for it. It couldn't be, for instance, that you ran into a little unpleasantness in some departmental store—say at the stocking or jewellery counter.'

He looked at me very carefully, drawing his eyebrows down at the corners and making his mouth small.

'I don't get it,' he said, but there was thought behind his voice.

'That's all I wanted to know,' I said. 'And thanks for listening. By the way, what line of business are you in—since you left Kingsley?'

'What the hell business is it of yours?'

'None. But of course I can always find out,' I said, and moved a little way towards the door, not very far.

'At the moment I'm not doing anything,' he said coldly. 'I expect a commission in the Navy almost any day.'

'You ought to do well at that,' I said.

'Yeah. So long, snooper. And don't bother to come back. I won't be at home.'

I went over to the door and pulled it open. It stuck on the lower sill, from the beach moisture. When I had it open, I looked back at him. He was standing there narrow-eyed, full of muted thunder.

'I may have to come back,' I said. 'But it won't be just to swop gags. It will be because I find something out that needs talking over.'

'So you still think I'm lying,' he said savagely.

'I think you have something on your mind. I've looked at too many faces not to know. It may not be any of my business. If it is, you're likely to have to throw me out again.'

'A pleasure,' he said. 'And next time bring somebody to drive you home. In case you land on your fanny and knock your brains out.'

Then without any rhyme or reason that I could see, he spat on the rug in front of his feet.

It jarred me. It was like watching the veneer peel off and leave a tough kid in an alley. Or like hearing an apparently refined woman start expressing herself in four-letter words.

'So long, beautiful hunk,' I said, and left him standing there. I closed the door, had to jerk it to get it shut, and went up the path to the street. I stood on the sidewalk looking at the house across the way.

4

It was a wide shallow house with rose stucco walls faded out to a pleasant pastel shade and trimmed with dull green at the window frames. The roof was of green tiles, round rough ones. There was a deeply inset front door framed in a mosaic of multi-coloured pieces of tiling and a small flower garden in front, behind a low stucco wall topped by an iron railing which the beach moisture had begun to corrode. Outside the wall to the left was the three-car garage, with a door opening inside the yard and a concrete path going from there to a side door of the house.

Set into the gate post was a bronze tablet which read: 'Albert S. Almore, M.D.'

While I was standing there staring across the street, the black Cadillac I had already seen came purring around the corner and then down the block. It slowed and started to sweep outwards to get turning space to go into the garage, decided my car was in the way of that, and went on to the end of the road and turned in the widened-out space in front of the ornamental iron railing. It came back slowly and went into the empty third of the garage across the way.

The thin man in sun-glasses went along the sidewalk to the house, carrying a double-handled doctor's bag. Halfway along he slowed down to stare across at me. I went along towards my car. At the house he used a key and as he opened the door he looked across at me again.

I got into the Chrysler and sat there smoking and trying to make up my mind whether it was worth while hiring somebody to pull a tail on Lavery. I decided it wasn't, not the way things looked so far.

Curtains moved at a lower window close to the side door Dr Almore had gone in at. A thin hand held them aside and I caught the glint of light on glasses. They were held aside for quite some time, before they fell together again.

I looked along the street at Lavery's house. From this angle I could see that his service porch gave on a flight of painted wooden steps to a sloping concrete walk and a flight of concrete steps ending in the paved alley below.

I looked across at Dr Almore's house again, wondering idly if he knew Lavery and how well. He probably knew him, since theirs were the only two houses in the block. But being a doctor, he wouldn't tell me anything about him. As I looked, the curtains which had been lifted apart were now completely drawn aside.

The middle segment of the triple window they had masked had no screen. Behind it, Dr Almore stood staring across my way, with a sharp frown on his thin face. I shook cigarette ash out of the window and he turned abruptly and sat down at a desk. His double-handled bag was on the desk in front of him. He sat rigidly, drumming on the desk beside the bag. His hand reached for the telephone, touched it and came away again. He lit a cigarette and shook the match violently, then strode to the window and stared out at me some more.

This was interesting, if at all, only because he was a doctor. Doctors, as a rule, are the least curious of men. While they are still internes they hear enough secrets to last them a lifetime. Dr Almore seemed interested in me. More than interested, bothered.

I reached down to turn the ignition key, then Lavery's front door opened and I took my hand away and leaned back again. Lavery came briskly up the walk of his house, shot a glance down the street and turned to go into his garage. He was dressed as I had seen him. He had a rough towel and a steamer rug over his arm. I heard the garage door lift up, then the car door open and shut, then the grind and cough of the starting car. It backed up the steep incline to the street, white steamy exhaust pouring from its rear end. It was a cute little blue convertible, with the top folded down and Lavery's sleek dark head just rising above it. He was now wearing a natty pair of sun-goggles with very wide white sidebows. The convertible swooped off down the block and danced around the corner.

There was nothing in that for me. Mr Christopher Lavery was bound for the edge of the broad Pacific, to lie in the sun and let the girls see what they didn't necessarily have to go on missing.

I gave my attention back to Dr Almore. He was on the telephone now, not talking, holding it to his ear, smoking and waiting. Then he leaned forward as you do when the voice comes back, listened, hung up and wrote something on a pad in front of him. Then a heavy book with yellow sides appeared on his desk and he opened it just about in the middle. While he was doing this he gave one quick look out of the window, straight at the Chrysler.

He found his place in the book, leaned down over it and quick puffs of smoke appeared in the air over the pages. He wrote something else, put the book away, and grabbed for the telephone again. He dialled, waited, began to speak quickly, pushing his head down and making gestures in the air with his cigarette.

He finished his call and hung up. He leaned back and sat there brooding, staring down at his desk, but not forgetting to look out of the window every half-minute. He was waiting, and I waited with him, for no reason at all. Doctors make many phone calls, talk to many people. Doctors look out of their front windows, doctors frown, doctors show nervousness, doctors have things on their mind and show the strain. Doctors are just people, born to sorrow, fighting the long grim fight like the rest of us.

But there was something about the way this one behaved that intrigued me. I looked at my watch, decided it was time to get something to eat, lit another cigarette and didn't move.

It took about five minutes. Then a green sedan whisked around the corner and bore down the block. It coasted to a stop in front of Dr Almore's house and its tall buggy-whip aerial quivered. A big man with dusty blond hair got out and went up to Dr Almore's front door. He rang the bell and leaned down to strike a match on the step. His head came around and he stared across the street exactly at where I was sitting.

The door opened and he went into the house. An invisible hand gathered the curtains at Dr Almore's study window and blanked the room. I sat there, and stared at the sun-darkened lining of the curtains. More time trickled by.

The front door opened again and the big man loafed casually down the steps and through the gate. He snapped his cigarette end off into the distance and rumpled his hair. He shrugged once, pinched the end of his chin, and walked diagonally across the street. His steps in the quiet were leisurely and distinct. Dr Almore's curtains moved apart again behind him. Dr Almore stood in his window and watched.

A large freckled hand appeared on the sill of the car door at my elbow. A large face, deeply lined, hung above it. The man had eyes of metallic blue. He looked at me solidly and spoke in a deep harsh voice.

'Waiting for somebody?' he asked.

'I don't know,' I said. 'Am I?'

'I'll ask the questions.'

'Well, I'll be damned,' I said. 'So that's the answer to the pantomime.'

'What pantomime?' He gave me a hard level unfriendly stare from his very blue eyes.

I pointed across the street with my cigarette. 'Nervous Nellie and the telephone. Calling the cops, after first getting my name from the Auto Club, probably, then looking it up in the city directory. What goes on?'

'Let me see your driver's licence.'

I gave him back his stare. 'You fellows ever flash a buzzer—or is acting tough all the identification you need?'

'If I have to get tough, fellow, you'll know it.'

I leaned down and turned my ignition key and pressed the starter. The motor caught and idled down.

'Cut that motor,' he said savagely, and put his foot on the running-board.

I cut the motor again and leaned back and looked at him.

'God damn it,' he said, 'do you want me to drag you out of there and bounce you on the pavement?'

I got my wallet out and handed it to him. He drew the celluloid pocket out and looked at my driver's licence, then turned the pocket over and looked at the photostat of my other licence on the back. He rammed it contemptuously back into the wallet and handed me the wallet. I put it away. His hand dipped and came up with a blue-and-gold police badge.

'Degarmo, detective-lieutenant,' he said in his heavy brutal voice.

'Pleased to meet you, lieutenant.'

'Skip it. Now tell why you're down here casing Almore's place.'

'I'm not casing Almore's place, as you put it, lieutenant. I never heard of Dr Almore and I don't know of any reason why I should want to case his house.'

He turned his head to spit. I was meeting the spitting boys to-day.

'What's your grift then? We don't like peepers down here. We don't have one in town.'

'Is that so?'

'Yeah, that's so. So come on, talk it up. Unless you want to ride down to the clubhouse and sweat it out under the bright lights.'

I didn't answer him.

'Her folks hire you?' he asked suddenly.

I shook my head.

'The last boy that tried it ended up on the road gang, sweetheart.'

'I bet it's good,' I said, 'if only I could guess. Tried what?'

'Tried to put the bite on him,' he said thinly.

'Too bad I don't know how,' I said. 'He looks like an easy man to bite.'

'That line of talk don't buy you anything,' he said.

'All right,' I said. 'Let's put it this way. I don't know Dr Almore, never heard of him, and I'm not interested in him. I'm down here visiting a friend and looking at the view. If I'm doing anything else, it doesn't happen to be any of your business. If you don't like that, the best thing to do is to take it down to headquarters and see the day captain.'

He moved a foot heavily on the running-board and looked doubtful. 'Straight goods?' he asked slowly.

'Straight goods.'

'Aw hell, the guy's screwy,' he said suddenly and looked back over his shoulder at the house. 'He ought to see a doctor.' He laughed, without any amusement in the laugh. He took his foot off my running-board and rumpled his wiry hair.

'Go on–beat it,' he said. 'Stay off our reservation, and you won't make any enemies.'

I pressed the starter again. When the motor was idling gently I said: 'How's Al Norgaard these days?'

He stared at me. 'You knew Al?'

'Yeah. He and I worked on a case down here a couple of years ago–when Wax was chief of police.'

'Al's in the military police. Wish I was,' he said bitterly. He started to walk away and then swung sharply on his heel. 'Go on, beat it before I change my mind,' he snapped.

He walked heavily across the street and through Dr Almore's front gate again.

I let the clutch in and drove away. On the way back to the city, I listened to my thoughts. They moved fitfully in and out, like Dr Almore's thin nervous hands pulling at the edges of his curtains.

Back in Los Angeles I ate lunch and went up to my office in the Cahuenga Building to see what mail there was. I called Kingsley from there.

'I saw Lavery,' I told him. 'He told me just enough dirt to sound frank. I tried to needle him a little, but nothing came of it. I still like the idea that they quarrelled and split up and that he hopes to fix it up with her yet.'

'Then he must know where she is,' Kingsley said.

'He might, but it doesn't follow. By the way, a rather curious thing happened to me on Lavery's street. There are only two houses. The other belongs to a Dr Almore.' I told him briefly about the rather curious thing.

He was silent for a moment at the end and then he said: 'Is this Dr Albert Almore?'

'Yes.'

'He was Crystal's doctor for a time. He came to the house several times when she was–well, when she had been overdrinking. I thought him a little too quick with a hypodermic needle. His wife–let me see, there was something about his wife. Oh yes, she committed suicide.'

I said, 'When?'

'I don't remember. Quite a long time now. I never knew them socially. What are you going to do now?'

I told him I was going up to Puma Lake, although it was a little late in the day to start.

He said I would have plenty of time and that they had an hour more of daylight in the mountains.

I said that was fine and we hung up.

5

San Bernardino baked and shimmered in the afternoon heat. The air was hot enough to blister my tongue. I drove through it gasping, stopped long enough to buy a pint of liquor in case I fainted before I got to the mountains, and started up the long grade to Crestline. In fifteen miles the road climbed five thousand feet, but even then it was far from cool. Thirty miles of mountain driving brought me to the tall pines and a place called Bubbling Springs. It had a clapboard store and a gas pump, but it felt like paradise. From there on it was cool all the way.

The Puma Lake dam had an armed sentry at each end and one in the middle. The first one I came to had me close all the windows of the car before crossing over the dam. About a hundred yards from the dam a rope with cork floats barred the pleasure boats from coming any closer. Beyond these details the war did not seem to have done anything much to Puma Lake.

Canoes paddled about on the blue water and rowing-boats with outboard motors put-putted and speedboats showing off like fresh kids made wide swathes of foam and turned on a dime and girls in them shrieked and dragged their hands in the water. Jounced around in the wake of the speedboats people who had paid two dollars for a fishing licence were trying to get a dime of it back in tired-tasting fish.

The road skimmed along a high granite outcrop and dropped to meadows of coarse grass in which grew what was left of the wild irises and white and purple lupin and bugle flowers and columbine and pennyroyal and desert paint brush. Tall yellow pines probed at the clear blue sky. The road dropped again to lake level and the landscape began to be full of girls in gaudy slacks and snoods and peasant handkerchiefs and rat rolls and fat-soled sandals and fat white thighs. People on bicycles wobbled cautiously over the highway and now and then an anxious-looking bird thumped past on a power-scooter.

A mile from the village the highway was joined by another lesser road which curved back into the mountains. A rough wooden sign under the highway sign said: *Little Fawn Lake 1¾ miles.* I took it. Scattered cabins were perched along the slopes for the first mile and then nothing. Presently another very narrow road debouched from this one and another rough wood sign said: *Little Fawn Lake. Private Road. No Trespassing.*

I turned the Chrysler into this and crawled carefully around huge bare granite rocks and past a little waterfall and through a maze of black oak-trees and ironwood and manzanita and silence. A blue-jay squawked on a branch and a squirrel scolded at me and beat one paw angrily on the pine cone it was holding. A scarlet-topped woodpecker stopped probing in the bark long enough to look at me with one beady eye and then dodge behind the tree trunk to look at me with the other one. I came to a five-barred gate and another sign.

Beyond the gate the road wound for a couple of hundred yards through trees and then suddenly below me was a small oval lake deep in trees and rocks and wild grass, like a drop of dew caught in a curled leaf. At the near end of it was a rough concrete dam with a rope hand-rail across the top and an old millwheel at the side. Near that stood a small cabin of native pine with the bark on it.

Across the lake the long way by the road and the short way by the top of the dam a large redwood cabin overhung the water and farther along, each well separated from the others, were two other cabins. All three were shut up and quiet, with drawn curtains. The big one had orange-yellow venetian blinds and a twelve-paned window facing on the lake.

At the far end of the lake from the dam was what looked like a small pier and band pavilion. A warped wooden sign on it was painted in large white letters: *Camp Kilkare*. I couldn't see any sense in that in these surroundings, so I got out of the car and started down towards the nearest cabin. Somewhere behind it an axe thudded.

I pounded on the cabin door. The axe stopped. A man's voice yelled from somewhere. I sat down on a rock and lit a cigarette. Steps came around the corner of the cabin, uneven steps. A man with a harsh face and a swarthy skin came into view carrying a double-bitted axe.

He was heavily built and not very tall and he limped as he walked, giving his right leg a little kick out with each step and swinging the foot in a shallow arc. He had a dark unshaven chin and steady blue eyes and grizzled hair that curled over his ears and needed cutting badly. He wore blue denim pants and a blue shirt open on a brown muscular neck. A cigarette hung from the corner of his mouth. He spoke in a tight tough city voice.

'Yeah?'

'Mr Bill Chess?'

'That's me.'

I stood up and got Kingsley's note of introduction out of my pocket and handed it to him. He squinted at the note, then clumped into the cabin and came back with glasses perched on his nose. He read the note carefully and then again. He put it in his shirt pocket, buttoned the flap of the pocket and put his hand out.

'Pleased to meet you, Mr Marlowe.'

We shook hands. He had a hand like a wood rasp.

'You want to see Kingsley's cabin, huh? Glad to show you. He ain't selling for Chrissake?' He eyed me steadily and jerked a thumb across the lake.

'He might,' I said. 'Everything's for sale in California.'

'Ain't that the truth? That's his—the redwood job. Lined with knotty pine, composition roof, stone foundations and porches, full bath and shower, venetian blinds all around, big fireplace, oil-stove in the big bedroom—and brother, you need it in the spring and autumn—Pilgrim combination gas and wood range, everything first class. Cost about eight thousand and that's money for a mountain cabin. And private reservoir in the hills for water.'

'How about electric light and telephone?' I asked, just to be friendly.

'Electric light, sure. No phone. You couldn't get one now. If you could, it would cost plenty to string the lines out here.'

He looked at me with steady blue eyes and I looked at him. In spite of his weathered appearance he looked like a drinker. He had the thickened and glossy skin, the too noticeable veins, the bright glitter in the eyes.

I said: 'Anybody living there now?'

'Nope. Mrs Kingsley was here a few weeks back. She went down the hill. Back any day, I guess. Didn't he say?'

I looked surprised. 'Why? Does she go with the cabin?'

He scowled and then put his head back and burst out laughing. The roar of his laughter was like a tractor backfiring. It blasted the woodland silence to shreds.

'Jesus, if that ain't a kick in the pants!' he gasped. 'Does she go with the—' He put out another bellow and then his mouth shut tight as a trap.

'Yeah, it's a swell cabin,' he said, eyeing me carefully.

'The beds comfortable?' I asked.

He leaned forward and smiled. 'Maybe you'd like a face full of knuckles,' he said.

I stared at him with my mouth open. 'That one went by me too fast,' I said. 'I never laid an eye on it.'

'How would I know if the beds are comfortable?' he snarled, bending down a little so that he could reach me with a hard right, if it worked out that way.

'I don't know why you wouldn't know,' I said. 'I won't press the point. I can find out for myself.'

'Yah,' he said bitterly, 'think I can't smell a dick when I meet one? I played hit and run with them in every state in the Union. Nuts to you, pal. And nuts to Kingsley. So he hires himself a dick to come up here and see am I wearing his pyjamas, huh? Listen, Jack, I might have a stiff leg and all, but the women I could get—'

I put a hand out, hoping he wouldn't pull it off and throw it in the lake.

'You're slipping your clutch,' I told him. 'I didn't come up here to inquire into your love life. I never saw Mrs Kingsley. I never saw Mr Kingsley until this morning. What the hell's the matter with you?'

He dropped his eyes and rubbed the back of his hand viciously across his mouth, as if he wanted to hurt himself. Then he held the hand in front of his eyes and squeezed it into a hard fist and opened it again and stared at the fingers. They were shaking a little.

'Sorry, Mr Marlowe,' he said slowly. 'I was out on the roof last night and I've got a hangover like seven Swedes. I've been up here alone for a month and it's got me talking to myself. A thing happened to me.'

'Anything a drink would help?'

His eyes focused sharply on me and glinted. 'You got one?'

I pulled the pint of rye out of my pocket and held it so that he could see the green label over the cap.

'I don't deserve it,' he said. 'God damn it, I don't. Wait till I get a couple of glasses or would you come into the cabin?'

'I like it out here. I'm enjoying the view.'

He swung his stiff leg and went into his cabin and came back carrying a couple of small cheese glasses. He sat down on the rock beside me, smelling of dried perspiration.

I tore the metal cap off the bottle and poured him a stiff drink and a light one for myself. We touched glasses and drank. He rolled the liquor on his tongue and a bleak smile put a little sunshine into his face.

'Man, that's from the right bottle,' he said. 'I wonder what made me sound off like that. I guess a guy gets the blues up here all alone. No company, no real friends, no wife.' He paused and added with a sideways look. 'Especially no wife.'

I kept my eyes on the blue water of the tiny lake. Under an overhanging rock a fish surfaced in a lance of light and a circle of widening ripples. A light breeze moved the tops of the pines with a noise like a gentle surf.

'She left me,' he said slowly. 'She left me a month ago. Friday the 12th of June. A day I'll remember.'

I stiffened, but not too much to pour more whisky into his empty glass. Friday the 12th of June was the day Mrs Crystal Kingsley was supposed to have come into town for a party.

'But you don't want to hear about that,' he said. And in his faded blue eyes was the deep yearning to talk about it, as plain as anything could possibly be.

'It's none of my business,' I said. 'But if it would make you feel any better—'

He nodded sharply. 'Two guys will meet on a park bench,' he said, 'and start talking about God. Did you ever notice that? Guys that wouldn't talk about God to their best friend.'

'I know that,' I said.

He drank and looked across the lake. 'She was one swell kid,' he said softly. 'A little sharp in the tongue sometimes, but one swell kid. It was love at first sight with me and Muriel. I met her in a joint in Riverside, a year and three months ago. Not the kind of joint where a guy would expect to meet a girl like Muriel, but that's how it happened. We got married. I loved her. I knew I was well off. And I was too much of a skunk to play ball with her.'

I moved a little to show him I was still there, but I didn't say anything for fear of breaking the spell. I sat with my drink untouched in my hand. I like to drink, but not when people are using me for a diary.

He went on sadly: 'But you know how it is with marriage–any marriage. After a while a guy like me, a common no-good guy like me, he wants to feel a leg. Some other leg. Maybe it's lousy, but that's the way it is.'

He looked at me and I said I had heard the idea expressed.

He tossed his second drink off. I passed him the bottle. A blue-jay went up a pine-tree hopping from branch to branch without moving his wings or even pausing to balance.

'Yeah,' Bill Chess said. 'All these hillbillies are half-crazy and I'm getting that way too. Here I am sitting pretty, no rent to pay, a good pension cheque every month, half my bonus money in war bonds, I'm married to as neat a little blonde as ever you clapped an eye on and all the time I'm nuts and I don't know it. I go for *that*.' He pointed hard at the redwood cabin across the lake. It was turning the colour of ox blood in the late afternoon light. 'Right in the front yard,' he said, 'right under the windows, and a showy little tart that means no more to me than a blade of grass. Jesus, what a sap a guy can be.'

He drank his third drink and steadied the bottle on a rock. He fished a cigarette out of his shirt, fired a match on his thumb-nail and puffed rapidly. I breathed with my mouth open, as silent as a burglar behind a curtain.

'Hell,' he said at last, 'you'd think if I had to jump off the dock I'd go a little ways from home and pick me a change in types at least. But little roundheels over there ain't even that. She's a blonde like Muriel, same size and weight, same type, almost the same colour eyes. But, brother, how different from then on in. Pretty, sure, but no prettier to anybody and not half so pretty to me. Well, I'm over there burning trash that morning and minding my own business, as much as I ever mind it. And she comes to the back door of the cabin in peekaboo pyjamas so thin you can see the pink of her nipples against the cloth. And she says in her lazy, no-good voice: "Have a drink, Bill. Don't work so hard on such a beautiful morning." And me, I like a drink too well and I go to the kitchen door and take it. And then I take another and then I take another and then I'm in the house. And the closer I get to her the more bedroom her eyes are.'

He paused and swept me with a hard level look.

'You asked me if the beds over there were comfortable and I got sore. You didn't mean a thing. I was just too full remembering. Yeah—the bed I was in was comfortable.'

He stopped talking and I let his words hang in the air. They fell slowly and after them was silence. He leaned to pick the bottle off the rock and stare at it. He seemed to fight with it in his mind. The whisky won the fight, as it always does. He took a long savage drink out of the bottle and then screwed the cap on tightly, as if that meant something. He picked up a stone and flicked it into the water.

'I came back across the dam,' he said slowly, in a voice already thick with alcohol. 'I'm as smooth as a new piston head. I'm getting away with something. Us boys can be so wrong about those little things, can't we? I'm not getting away with anything at all. Not anything at all. I listen to Muriel telling me and she don't even raise her voice. But she tells me things about myself I didn't even imagine. Oh yeah, I'm getting away with it lovely.'

'So she left you,' I said, when he fell silent.

'That night. I wasn't even here. I felt too mean to stay even half-sober. I hopped into my Ford and went over to the north side of the lake and holed up with a couple of no-goods like myself and got good and stinking. Not that it did me any good. Along about 4 a.m. I got back home and Muriel had gone, packed up and gone, nothing left but a note on the bureau and some cold cream on the pillow.'

He pulled a dog-eared piece of paper out of a shabby old wallet and passed it over. It was written in pencil on blue-lined paper from a note-book. It read:

'I'm sorry, Bill, but I'd rather be dead than live with you any longer. Muriel.'

I handed it back. 'What about over there?' I asked, pointing across the lake with a glance.

Bill Chess picked up a flat stone and tried to skip it across the water, but it refused to skip.

'Nothing over there,' he said. 'She packed up and went down the same night. I didn't see her again. I don't want to see her again. I haven't heard a word from Muriel in the whole month, not a single word. I don't have any idea at all where she's at. With some other guy, maybe. I hope he treats her better than I did.'

He stood up and took keys out of his pocket and shook them. 'So if you want to go across and look at Kingsley's cabin, there isn't a thing to stop you. And thanks for listening to the soap opera. And thanks for the liquor. Here.' He picked the bottle up and handed me what was left of the pint.

6

We went down the slope to the bank of the lake and the narrow top of the dam. Bill Chess swung his stiff leg in front of me, holding on to the rope hand-rail set in iron stanchions. At one point water washed over the concrete in a lazy swirl.

'I'll let some out through the wheel in the morning,' he said over his shoulder. 'That's all the darn thing is good for. Some movie outfit put it up three years ago. They made a picture up here. That little pier down at the other end is some more of their work. Most of what they built is torn down and hauled away, but Kingsley had them leave the pier and the millwheel. Kind of gives the place a touch of colour.'

I followed him up a flight of heavy wooden steps to the porch of the Kingsley cabin. He unlocked the door and we went into hushed warmth. The closed-up room was almost hot. The light filtering through the slatted blinds made narrow bars across the floor. The living-room was long and cheerful and had Indian rugs, padded mountain furniture with metal-strapped joints, chintz curtains, a plain hardwood floor, plenty of lamps and a little built-in bar with round stools in one corner. The room was neat and clean and had no look of having been left at short notice.

We went into the bedrooms. Two of them had twin beds and one a large double bed with a cream-coloured spread having a design in plum-coloured wool stitched over it. This was the master bedroom, Bill Chess said. On a dresser of varnished wood there were toilet articles and accessories in jade-green enamel and stainless steel, and an assortment of cosmetic oddments. A couple of cold cream jars had the wavy gold brand of the Gillerlain Company on them. One whole side of the room consisted of closets with sliding doors. I slid one open and peeked inside. It seemed to be full of women's clothes of the sort they wear at resorts. Bill Chess watched me sourly while I pawed them over. I slid the door shut and pulled open a deep shoe drawer underneath. It contained at least half a dozen pairs of new-looking shoes. I heaved the drawer shut and straightened up.

Bill Chess was planted squarely in front of me, with his chin pushed out and his hard hands in knots on his hips.

'So what did you want to look at the lady's clothes for?' he asked in an angry voice.

'Reasons,' I said. 'For instance, Mrs Kingsley didn't go home when she left here. Her husband hasn't seen her since. He does not know where she is.'

He dropped his fists and twisted them slowly at his sides. 'Dick it is,' he snarled. 'The first guess is always right. I had myself about talked out of it. Boy, did I open up to you. Nellie with her hair in her lap. Boy, am I a smart little egg!'

'I can respect a confidence as well as the next fellow,' I said, and walked around him into the kitchen.

There was a big green-and-white combination range, a sink of lacquered yellow pine, an automatic water-heater in the service porch, and opening off the other side of the kitchen a cheerful breakfast-room with many windows and an expansive plastic breakfast set. The shelves were gay with coloured dishes and glasses and a set of pewter serving-dishes.

Everything was in apple-pie order. There were no dirty cups or plates on the drain-board, no smeared glasses or empty liquor bottles hanging around. There were no ants and no flies. Whatever loose living Mrs Derace Kingsley indulged in she managed without leaving the usual Greenwich Village slop behind her.

I went back to the living-room and out on the front porch again and waited for Bill Chess to lock up. When he had done that and turned to me with his scowl well in place I said:

'I didn't ask you to take your heart out and squeeze it for me, but I didn't try to stop you either. Kingsley doesn't have to know his wife made a pass at you, unless there's a lot more behind all this than I can see now.'

'The hell with you,' he said, and the scowl stayed right where it was.

'All right, the hell with me. Would there be any chance your wife and Kingsley's wife went away together?'

'I don't get it,' he said.

'After you went to drown your troubles they could have had a fight and made up and cried down each other's necks. Then Mrs Kingsley might have taken your wife down the hill. She had to have something to ride in, didn't she?'

It sounded silly, but he took it seriously enough.

'Nope. Muriel didn't cry down anybody's neck. They left the weeps out of Muriel. And if she did want to cry on a shoulder, she wouldn't have picked little roundheels. And as for transportation, she has a Ford of her own. She couldn't drive mine easily on account of the way the controls are switched over for my stiff leg.'

'It was just a passing thought,' I said.

'If any more like it pass you, let them go right on,' he said.

'For a guy that takes his long wavy hair down in front of complete strangers, you're pretty damn touchy,' I said.

He took a step towards me. 'Want to make something of it?'

'Look, pal,' I said. 'I'm working hard to think you are a fundamentally good egg. Help me out a little, can't you?'

He breathed hard for a moment and then dropped his hands and spread them helplessly.

'Boy, can I brighten up anybody's afternoon,' he sighed. 'Want to walk back around the lake?'

'Sure, if your leg will stand it.'

'Stood it plenty of times before.'

We started off side by side, as friendly as puppies again. It would probably last all of fifty yards. The roadway, barely wide enough to pass a car, hung above the level of the lake and dodged between high rocks. About half-way to the far end another smaller cabin was built on a rock foundation. The third was well beyond the end of the lake, on a patch of almost level ground. Both were closed up and had that long-empty look.

Bill Chess said after a minute or two: 'That straight, good little round heels lammed off?'

'So it seems.'

'You are a real dick or just a shamus?'

'Just a shamus.'

'She go with some guy?'

'I should think it likely.'

'Sure she did. It's a cinch. Kingsley ought to be able to guess that. She had plenty of friends.'

'Up here?'

He didn't answer me.

'Was one of them named Lavery?'

'I wouldn't know,' he said.

'There's no secret about this one,' I said. 'She sent a wire from El Paso saying she and Lavery were going to Mexico.' I dug the wire out of my pocket and held it out. He fumbled his glasses loose from his shirt and stopped to read it. He handed the paper back and put his glasses away again and stared out over the blue water.

'That's a little confidence for you to hold against some of what you gave me,' I said.

'Lavery was up here once,' he said slowly.

'He admits he saw her a couple of months ago, probably up here. He claims he hasn't seen her since. We don't know whether to believe him. There's no reason why we should and no reason why we shouldn't.'

'She isn't with him now, then?'

'He says not.'

'I wouldn't think she would fuss with little details like getting married,' he said soberly. 'A Florida honeymoon would be more in her line.'

'But you can't give me any positive information? You didn't see her go or hear anything that sounded authentic?'

'Nope,' he said. 'And if I did, I doubt if I would tell. I'm dirty, but not that kind of dirty.'

'Well, thanks for trying,' I said.

'I don't owe you any favours,' he said. 'The hell with you and every other God-damn snooper.'

'Here we go again,' I said.

We had come to the end of the lake now. I left him standing there and walked out on the little pier. I leaned on the wooden railing at the end of it and saw that what had looked like a band pavilion was nothing but two pieces of propped-up wall meeting at a flat angle towards the dam. About two feet deep of overhanging roof was stuck on the wall, like a coping. Bill Chess came up behind me and leaned on the railing at my side.

'Not that I don't thank you for the liquor,' he said.

'Yeah. Any fish in the lake?'

'Some smart old bastards of trout. No fresh stock. I don't go for fish much myself. I don't bother with them. Sorry I got tough again.'

I grinned and leaned on the railing and stared down into the deep, still water. It was green when you looked down into it. There was a swirl of movement down there and a swift greenish form moved in the water.

'There's Granpa,' Bill Chess said. 'Look at the size of that old bastard. He ought to be ashamed of himself getting so fat.'

Down below the water there was what looked like an underwater flooring. I couldn't see the sense of that. I asked him.

'Used to be a boat landing before the dam was raised. That lifted the water level so far the old landing was six feet under.'

A flat-bottomed boat dangled on a frayed rope tied to a post of the pier. It lay in the water almost without motion, but not quite. The air was peaceful and calm and sunny and held a quiet you don't get in cities. I could have stayed there for hours doing nothing but forgetting all about Derace Kingsley and his wife and her boy friends.

There was a hard movement at my side and Bill Chess said, 'Look there!' in a voice that growled like mountain thunder.

His hard fingers dug into the flesh of my arm until I started to get mad. He was bending far out over the railing, staring down like a loon, his face as white as the weather tan would let it get. I looked down with him into the water at the edge of the submerged staging.

Languidly at the edge of this green and sunken shelf of wood something waved out from the darkness, hesitated, waved back again out of sight under the flooring.

The something had looked far too much like a human arm.

Bill Chess straightened his body rigidly. He turned without a sound and clumped back along the pier. He bent to a loose pile of stones and heaved. His panting breath reached me. He got a big one free and lifted it breast high and started back out on the pier with it. It must have weighed a hundred pounds. His neck muscles stood out like ropes under canvas under his taut brown skin. His teeth were clamped tight and his breath hissed between them.

He reached the end of the pier and steadied himself and lifted the rock high. He held it a moment poised, his eyes staring down now, measuring. His mouth made a vague, distressful sound and his body lurched forward hard against the quivering rail and the heavy stone smashed down into the water.

The splash it made went over both of us. The rock fell straight and true and struck on the edge of the submerged planking, almost exactly where we had seen the thing wave in and out.

For a moment the water was a confused boiling, then the ripples widened off into the distance, coming smaller and smaller with a trace of froth at the middle, and there was a dim sound as of wood breaking under water, a sound that seemed to come to us a long time after it should have been audible. An ancient rotted plank popped suddenly through the surface, stuck out a full foot of its jagged end, and fell back with a flat slap and floated off.

The depths cleared again. Something moved in them that was not a board. It rose slowly, with an infinitely careless languor, a long dark twisted something that rolled lazily in the water as it rose. It broke surface casually, lightly, without haste. I saw wool, sodden and black, a leather jerkin blacker than ink, a pair of slacks. I saw shoes and something that bulged nastily between the shoes and the cuffs of the slacks. I saw a wave of dark blonde hair straighten out in the water and hold still for a brief instant as if with a calculated effect, and then swirl into a tangle again.

The thing rolled over once more and an arm flapped up barely above the skin of the water and the arm ended in a bloated hand that was the hand of a freak. Then the face came. A swollen pulpy grey white mass without features, without eyes, without mouth. A blotch of grey dough, a nightmare with human hair on it.

A heavy necklace of green stones showed on what had been a neck, half-embedded, large rough green stones with something that glittered joining them together.

Bill Chess held the hand-rail and his knuckles were polished bones.

'Muriel!' his voice said croakingly. 'Sweet Christ, it's Muriel!'

His voice seemed to come to me from a long way off, over a hill, through a thick silent growth of trees.

7

Behind the window of the board shack one end of a counter was piled with dusty folders. The glass upper half of the door was lettered in flaked black paint. *Chief of Police. Fire Chief. Town Constable. Chamber of Commerce.* In the lower corners a USO card and a Red Cross emblem were fastened to the glass.

I went in. There was a pot-bellied stove in the corner and a roll-top desk in the other corner behind the counter. There was a large blue print map of the district on the wall and beside that a board with four hooks on it, one of which supported a frayed and much-mended mackinaw. On the counter beside the dusty folders lay the usual sprung pen, exhausted blotter and smeared bottle of gummy ink. The end wall beside the desk was covered with telephone numbers written in hard-bitten figures that would last as long as the wood and looked as if they had been written by a child.

A man sat at the desk in a wooden armchair whose legs were anchored to flat boards, fore and aft, like skis. A spittoon big enough to coil a hose in was leaning against the man's right leg. He had a sweat-stained Stetson on the back of his head and his large hairless hands were clasped comfortably over his stomach, above the waistband of a pair of khaki pants that had been scrubbed thin years ago. His shirt matched the pants except that it was even more faded. It was buttoned tight to the man's thick neck and undecorated by a tie. His hair was mousy brown except at the temples, where it was the colour of old snow. He sat more on his left hip than his right, because there was a hip holster down inside his right hip pocket, and a half-foot of forty-five gun reared up and bored into his solid back. The star on his left breast had a bent point.

He had large ears and friendly eyes and his jaws munched slowly and he looked as dangerous as a squirrel and much less nervous. I liked everything about him. I leaned on the counter and looked at him and he looked at me and nodded and loosed half a pint of tobacco juice down his right leg into the spittoon. It made a nasty sound of something falling into water.

I lit a cigarette and looked round for an ash-tray.

'Try the floor, son,' the large friendly man said.

'Are you Sheriff Patton?'

'Constable and deputy-sheriff. What law we got to have around here I'm it. Come election anyways. There's a couple of good boys running against me this time and I might get whupped. Job pays eighty a month, cabin, firewood and electricity. That ain't hay in these little old mountains.'

'Nobody's going to whip you,' I said. 'You're going to get a lot of publicity.'

'That so?' he asked indifferently and ruined the spittoon again.

'That is, if your jurisdiction extends over to Little Fawn Lake.'

'Kingsley's place. Sure. Something bothering over there, son?'

'There's a dead woman in the lake.'

That shook him to the core. He unclasped his hands and scratched one ear. He got to his feet by grasping the arms of his chair and deftly kicking it back from under him. Standing up he was a big man and hard. The fat was just cheerfulness.

'Anybody I know?' he inquired uneasily.

'Muriel Chess. I guess you know her. Bill Chess's wife.'

'Yep, I know Bill Chess.' His voice hardened a little.

'Looks like suicide. She left a note which sounded as if she was just going away. But it could be a suicide note just as well. She's not nice to look at. Been in the water a long time, about a month judging by the circumstances.'

He scratched his other ear. 'What circumstances would that be?' His eyes were searching my face now, slowly and calmly, but searching. He didn't seem in any hurry to blow his whistle.

'They had a fight a month ago. Bill went over to the north shore of the lake and was gone some hours. When he got home she was gone. He never saw her again.'

'I see. Who are you, son?'

'My name is Marlowe. I'm up from L.A. to look at the property. I had a note from Kingsley to Bill Chess. He took me around the lake and we went out on that little pier the movie people built. We were leaning on the rail and looking down into the water and something that looked like an arm waved out under the submerged flooring, the old boat landing. Bill dropped a heavy rock in and the body popped up.'

Patton looked at me without moving a muscle.

'Look, sheriff, hadn't we better run over there? The man's half-crazy with shock and he's there all alone.'

'How much liquor has he got?'

'Very little when I left. I had a pint, but we drank most of it talking.'

He moved over to the roll-top desk and unlocked a drawer. He brought up three or four bottles and held them against the light.

'This baby's near full,' he said, patting one of them. 'Mount Vernon. That ought to hold him. County don't allow me no money for emergency liquor, so I just have to seize a little here and there. Don't use it myself. Never could understand folks letting theirselves get gummed up with it.'

He put the bottle on his left hip and locked the desk up and lifted the flap in the counter. He fixed a card against the inside of the glass door panel.

I looked at the card as we went out. It read: *Back in Twenty Minutes—Maybe.*

'I'll run down and get Doc Hollis,' he said. 'Be right back and pick you up. That your car?'

'Yes.'

'You can follow along then, as I come back by.'

He got into a car which had a siren on it, two red spotlights, two fog-lights, a red and white fire plate, a new air-raid horn on top, three axes, two heavy coils of rope and a fire-extinguisher in the back seat, extra petrol and oil and water-cans in a frame on the running-board, and extra spare tyre roped to the one on the rack, the stuffing coming out of the upholstery in dingy wads, and half an inch of dust over what was left of the paint.

Behind the right-hand lower corner of the windshield there was a white card printed in block capitals. It read:

VOTERS, ATTENTION! KEEP JIM PATTON CONSTABLE. HE IS TOO OLD TO GO TO WORK

He turned the car and went off down the street in a swirl of white dust.

8

He stopped in front of a white frame building across the road from the stage depot. He went into the white building and presently came out with a man who got into the back seat with the axes and the rope. The official car came back up the street and I fell in behind it. We sifted along the main stem through the slacks and shorts and French sailor jerseys and knotted bandannas and knobby knees and scarlet lips. Beyond the village we went up a dusty hill and stopped at a cabin. Patton touched the siren gently and a man in faded blue overalls opened the cabin door.

'Get in, Andy. Business.'

The man in blue overalls nodded morosely and ducked back into the cabin. He came back out wearing an oyster-grey lion-hunter's hat and got in under the wheel of Patton's car while Patton slid over. He was about thirty, dark, lithe, and had the slightly dirty and lightly underfed look of the native.

We drove out to Little Fawn Lake with me eating enough dust to make a batch of mud pies. At the five-barred gate Patton got out and let us through and we went on down to the lake. Patton got out again and went to the edge of the water and looked along towards the little pier. Bill Chess was sitting naked on the floor of the pier, with his head in his hands. There was something stretched out on the wet planks beside him.

'We can ride a ways more,' Patton said.

The two cars went on to the end of the lake and all four of us trooped down to the pier behind Bill Chess's back. The doctor stopped to cough rackingly into a handkerchief and look thoughtfully at the handkerchief. He was an angular bug-eyed man with a sad sick face.

The thing that had been a woman lay face down on the boards with a rope under the arms. Bill Chess's clothes lay to one side. His stiff leg, flat and scarred at the knee, was stretched out in front of him, the other leg bent up and his forehead resting against it. He didn't move or look up as we came down behind him.

Patton took the pint bottle of Mount Vernon off his hip and unscrewed the top and handed it.

'Drink hearty, Bill.'

There was a horrible, sickening smell in the air. Bill Chess didn't seem to notice it, nor Patton nor the doctor. The man called Andy got a dusty brown blanket out of the car and threw it over the body. Then without a word he went and vomited under a pine-tree.

Bill Chess drank a long drink and sat holding the bottle against his bare bent knee. He began to talk in a stiff wooden voice, not looking at anybody, not talking to anybody in particular. He told about the quarrel and what happened after it, but not why it had happened. He didn't mention Mrs Kingsley even in the most casual way. He said that after I left him he had got a rope and stripped and gone down into the water and got the thing out. He had dragged it ashore and then got it up on his back and carried it out on the pier. He didn't know why. He had gone back into the water again then. He didn't have to tell us why.

Patton put a cut of tobacco into his mouth and chewed on it silently, his calm eyes full of nothing. Then he shut his teeth tight and leaned down to pull the blanket off the body. He turned the body over carefully, as if it might come to pieces. The late afternoon sun winked on the necklace of large green stones that were partly embedded in the swollen neck. They were roughly carved and lustreless, like soapstone or false jade. A gilt chain with an eagle clasp set with small brilliants joined the ends. Patton straightened his broad back and blew his nose on a tan handkerchief.

'What you say, Doc?'

'About what?' the bug-eyed man snarled.

'Cause and time of death.'

'Don't be a damn fool, Jim Patton.'

'Can't tell nothing, huh?'

'By looking at that? Good God!'

Patton sighed. 'Looks drowned all right,' he admitted. 'But you can't always tell. There's been cases where a victim would be knifed or poisoned or something, and they would soak him in the water to make things look different.'

'You get many like that up here?' the doctor inquired nastily.

'Only honest to God murder I ever had up here,' Patton said, watching Bill Chess out of the corner of his eye, 'Was old Dad Meacham over on the north shore. He had a shack in Sheedy Canyon, did a little panning in summer on an old placer claim he had back in the valley near Belltop. Folks didn't see him around for a while in late fall, then come a heavy snow and his roof caved in to one side. So we was over there trying to prop her up a bit, figuring Dad had gone down the hill for the winter without telling anybody, the way them old prospectors do things. Well by gum, old Dad never went down the hill at all. There he was in bed with most of a kindling axe in the back of his head. We never did find out who done it. Somebody figured he had a little bag of gold hid away from the summer's panning.'

He looked thoughtfully at Andy. The man in the lion-hunter's hat was feeling a tooth in his mouth. He said:

''Course we know who done it. Guy Pope done it. Only Guy was dead nine days of pneumonia before we found Dad Meacham.'

'Eleven days,' Patton said.

'Nine,' the man in the lion-hunter's hat said.

'Was all of six years ago, Andy. Have it your own way, son. How you figure Guy Pope done it?'

'We found about three ounces of small nuggets in Guy's cabin along with some dust. Never was anything bigger'n sand on Guy's claim. Dad had nuggets all of a penny-weight, plenty of times.'

'Well, that's the way it goes,' Patton said, and smiled at me in a vague manner. 'Fellow always forgets something, don't he? No matter how careful he is.'

'Cop stuff,' Bill Chess said disgustedly and put his pants on and sat down again to put on his shoes and shirt. When he had them on he stood up and reached down for the bottle and took a good drink and laid the bottle carefully on the planks. He thrust his hairy wrists out towards Patton.

'That's the way you guys feel about it, put the cuffs on and get it over,' he said in a savage voice.

Patton ignored him and went over to the railing and looked down. 'Funny place for a body to be,' he said. 'No current here to mention, but what there is would be towards the dam.'

Bill Chess lowered his wrists and said quietly: 'She did it herself, you darn fool. Muriel was a fine swimmer. She dived down in and swum under the boards there and just breathed water in. Had to. No other way.'

'I wouldn't quite say that, Bill,' Patton answered him mildly. His eyes were as blank as new plates.

Andy shook his head. Patton looked at him with a sly grin. 'Crabbin' again, Andy?'

'Was nine days, I tell you. I just counted back,' the man in the lion-hunter's hat said morosely.

The doctor threw his arms up and walked away, with one hand to his head. He coughed into his handkerchief again, and again looked into the handkerchief with passionate attention.

Patton winked at me and spat over the railing. 'Let's get on to this one, Andy.'

'You ever try to drag a body six feet under water?'

'Nope, can't say I ever did, Andy. Any reason it couldn't be done with a rope?'

Andy shrugged. 'If a rope was used, it will show on the corpse. If you got to give yourself away like that, why bother to cover up at all?'

'Question of time,' Patton said. 'Fellow has his arrangements to make.'

Bill Chess snarled at them and reached down for the whisky. Looking at their solemn mountain faces I couldn't tell what they were really thinking.

Patton said absently: 'Something was said about a note.'

Bill Chess rummaged in his wallet and drew the folded piece of ruled paper loose. Patton took it and read it slowly.

'Don't seem to have any date,' he observed.

Bill Chess shook his head sombrely. 'No. She left a month ago. June 12th.'

'Left you once before, didn't she?'

'Yeah.' Bill Chess stared at him fixedly. 'I got drunk and stayed with a chippy. Just before the first snow last December. She was gone a week and came back all prettied up. Said she just had to get away for a while and had been staying with a girl she used to work with in L.A.'

'What was the name of this party?' Patton asked.

'Never told me and I never asked her. What Muriel did was all silk with me.'

'Sure. Note left that time, Bill?' Patton asked smoothly.

'No.'

'This note here looks middling old,' Patton said, holding it up.

'I carried it a month,' Bill Chess growled. 'Who told you she left me before?'

'I forget,' Patton said. 'You know how it is in a place like this. Not much folks don't notice. Except maybe in summer time where there's a lot of strangers about.'

Nobody said anything for a while and then Patton said absently: 'June 12th you say she left? Or you thought she left? Did you say the folks across the lake were up here then?'

Bill Chess looked at me and his face darkened again. 'Ask this snoopy guy—if he didn't already spill his guts to you.'

Patton didn't look at me at all. He looked at the line of mountains far beyond the lake. He said gently: 'Mr Marlowe here didn't tell me anything at all, Bill, except how the body come up out of the water and who it was. And that Muriel went away, as you thought, and left a note you showed him. I don't guess there's anything wrong in that, is there?'

There was another silence and Bill Chess stared down at the blanket-covered corpse a few feet away from him. He clenched his hands and a thick tear ran down his cheek.

'Mrs Kingsley was here,' he said. 'She went down the hill that same day. Nobody was in the other cabins. Perrys and Farquhars ain't been up at all this year.'

Patton nodded and was silent. A kind of charged emptiness hung in the air, as if something that had not been said was plain to all of them and didn't need saying.

Then Bill Chess said wildly: 'Take me in, you sons of bitches! Sure I did it! I drowned her. She was my girl and I loved her. I'm a heel, always was a heel, always will be a heel, but just the same I loved her. Maybe you guys wouldn't understand that. Just don't bother to try. Take me in, damn you!'

Nobody said anything at all.

Bill Chess looked down at his hard brown fist. He swung it up viciously and hit himself in the face with all his strength.

'You rotten son of a bitch,' he breathed in a harsh whisper.

His nose began to bleed slowly. He stood and the blood ran down his lip, down the side of his mouth, to the point of his chin. A drop fell sluggishly to his shirt.

Patton said quietly: 'Got to take you down the hill for questioning, Bill. You know that. We ain't accusing you of anything, but the folks down there have got to talk to you.'

Bill Chess said heavily: 'Can I change my clothes?'

'Sure. You go with him, Andy. And see what you can find to kind of wrap up what he got here.'

They went off along the path at the edge of the lake. The doctor cleared his throat and looked out over the water and sighed.

'You'll want to send the corpse down in my ambulance, Jim, won't you?'

Patton shook his head. 'Nope. This is a poor county, Doc. I figure the lady can ride cheaper than what you get for that ambulance.'

The doctor walked away from him angrily, saying over his shoulder: 'Let me know if you want me to pay for the funeral.'

'That ain't no way to talk,' Patton sighed.

9

The Indian Head Hotel was a brown building on a corner across from the new dance hall. I parked in front of it and used its rest-room to wash my face and hands and comb the pine needles out of my hair, before I went into the dining-drinking parlour that adjoined the lobby. The whole place was full to overflowing with males in leisure jackets and liquor breaths and females in high-pitched laughs, ox-blood finger-nails and dirty knuckles. The manager of the joint, a low budget tough guy in shirtsleeves and a mangled cigar, was prowling the room with watchful eyes. At the cash desk a pale-haired man was fighting to get the war news on a small radio that was as full of static as the mashed potatoes were full of water. In the deep back corner of the room, a hillbilly orchestra of five pieces, dressed in ill-fitting white jackets and purple shirts, was trying to make itself heard above the brawl at the bar and smiling glassily into the fog of cigarette smoke and the blur of alcoholic voices. At Puma Point summer, that lovely season, was in full swing.

I gobbled what they called the regular dinner, drank a brandy to sit on its chest and hold it down, and went out on to the main street. It was still broad daylight but some of the neon signs had been turned on, and the evening reeled with the cheerful din of motor horns, children screaming, bowls rattling, skeeballs clunking, .22s snapping merrily in shooting-galleries, juke boxes playing like crazy, and behind all this out on the lake the hard barking roar of the speedboats going nowhere at all and acting as though they were racing with death.

In my Chrysler a thin, serious-looking, brown-haired girl in dark slacks was sitting smoking a cigarette and talking to a dude ranch cowboy who sat on my running-board. I walked around the car and got into it. The cowboy strolled away hitching his jeans up. The girl didn't move.

'I'm Birdie Keppel,' she said cheerfully. 'I'm the beautician here daytimes and evenings I work on the *Puma Point Banner*. Excuse me sitting in your car.'

'That's all right,' I said. 'You want to just sit or you want me to drive you somewhere?'

'You can drive down the road a piece where it's quieter, Mr Marlowe. If you're obliging enough to talk to me.'

'Pretty good grapevine you've got up here,' I said and started the car.

I drove down past the post office to a corner where a blue-and-white arrow marked *Telephone* pointed down a narrow road towards the lake. I turned down that, drove down past the telephone office, which was a log cabin with a tiny railed lawn in front of it, passed another small cabin and pulled up in front of a huge oak-tree that flung its branches all the way across the road and a good fifty feet beyond it.

'This do, Miss Keppel?'

'Mrs. But just call me Birdie. Everybody does. This is fine. Pleased to meet you, Mr Marlowe. I see you come from Hollywood, that sinful city.'

She put a firm brown hand out and I shook it. Clamping bobbie pins into fat blondes had given her a grip like a pair of iceman's tongs.

'I was talking to Doc Hollis,' she said, 'about poor Muriel Chess. I thought you could give me some details. I understand you found the body.'

'Bill Chess found it really. I was just with him. You talk to Jim Patton?'

'Not yet. He went down the hill. Anyway, I don't think Jim would tell me much.'

'He's up for re-election,' I said. 'And you're a newspaper woman.'

'Jim's no politician, Mr Marlowe, and I could hardly call myself a newspaper woman. This little paper we get out up here is a pretty amateurish proposition.'

'Well, what do you want to know?' I offered her a cigarette and lit it for her.

'You might just tell me the story.'

'I came up here with a letter from Derace Kingsley to look at his property. Bill Chess showed me around, got talking to me, told me his wife had moved out on him and showed me the note she left. I had a bottle along and he punished it. He was feeling pretty blue. The liquor loosened him up, but he was lonely and aching to talk anyway. That's how it happened. I didn't know him. Coming back around the end of the lake we went out on the pier and Bill spotted an arm waving out from under the planking down in the water. It turned out to belong to what was left of Muriel Chess. I guess that's all.'

'I understand from Doc Hollis she had been in the water a long time. Pretty badly decomposed and all that.'

'Yes. Probably the whole month he thought she had been gone. There's no reason to think otherwise. The note's a suicide note.'

'Any doubt about that, Mr Marlowe?'

I looked at her sideways. Thoughtful dark eyes looked out at me under fluffed-out brown hair. The dusk had begun to fall now, very slowly. It was no more than a slight change in the quality of the light.

'I guess the police always have doubts in these cases,' I said.

'How about you?'

'My opinion doesn't go for anything.'

'But for what it's worth?'

'I only met Bill Chess this afternoon,' I said. 'He struck me as a quick-tempered lad and from his own account he's no saint. But he seems to have been in love with his wife. And I can't see him hanging around there for a month knowing she was rotting down in the water under that pier. Coming out of his cabin in the sunlight and looking along that soft blue water and seeing in his mind what was under it and what was happening to it. And knowing he put it there.'

'No more can I,' Birdie Keppel said softly. 'No more could anybody. And yet we know in our minds that such things have happened and will happen again. Are you in the real-estate business, Mr Marlowe?'

'No.'

'What line of business are you in, if I may ask?'

'I'd rather not say.'

'That's almost as good as saying,' she said. 'Besides, Doc Hollis heard you tell Jim Patton your full name. And we have an L.A. city directory in our office. I haven't mentioned it to anyone.'

'That's nice of you,' I said.

'And what's more, I won't,' she said. 'If you don't want me to.'

'What does it cost me?'

'Nothing,' she said. 'Nothing at all. I don't claim to be a very good newspaper woman. And we wouldn't print anything that would embarrass Jim Patton. Jim's the salt of the earth. But it does open up, doesn't it?'

'Don't draw any wrong conclusions,' I said. 'I had no interest in Bill Chess whatever.'

'No interest in Muriel Chess?'

'Why should I have any interest in Muriel Chess?'

She snuffed her cigarette out carefully into the ash-tray under the dashboard. 'Have it your own way,' she said. 'But here's a little item you might like to think about, if you don't know it already. There was a Los Angeles copper named De Soto up here about six weeks back, a big roughneck with damn poor manners. We didn't like him and we didn't open up to him much. I mean the three of us in the *Banner* office didn't. He had a photograph with him and he was looking for a woman called Mildred Haviland, he said. On police business. It was an ordinary photograph, an enlarged snapshot, not a police photo. He said he had information the woman was staying up here. The photo looked a good deal like Muriel Chess. The hair seemed to be reddish and in a very different style than she has worn it here, and the eyebrows were all plucked to narrow arches, and that changes a woman a good deal. But it did look a good deal like Bill Chess's wife.'

I drummed on the door of the car and after a moment I said, 'What did you tell him?'

'We didn't tell him anything. First off, we couldn't be sure. Second, we didn't like his manner. Third, even if we had been sure and had liked his manner, we likely would not have sicked him on to her. Why would we? Everybody's done something to be sorry for. Take me. I was married once—to a professor of classical languages at Redlands University.' She laughed lightly.

'You might have got yourself a story,' I said.

'Sure. But up here we're just people.'

'Did this man De Soto see Jim Patton?'

'Sure, he must have. Jim didn't mention it.'

'Did he show you his badge?'

She thought and then shook her head. 'I don't recall that he did. We just took him for granted, from what he said. He certainly acted like a tough city cop.'

'To me that's a little against his being one. Did anybody tell Muriel about this guy?'

She hesitated, looking quietly out through the windshield for a long moment before she turned her head and nodded.

'I did. Wasn't any of my damn business, was it?'

'What did she say?'

'She didn't say anything. She gave a funny little embarrassed laugh, as if I had been making a bad joke. Then she walked away. But I did get the impression that there was a queer look in her eyes, just for an instant. You still not interested in Muriel Chess, Mr Marlowe?'

'Why should I be? I never heard of her until I came up here this afternoon. Honest. And I never heard of anybody named Mildred Haviland either. Drive you back to town?'

'Oh no, thanks. I'll walk. It's only a few steps. Much obliged to you. I kind of hope Bill doesn't get into a jam. Especially a nasty jam like this.'

She got out of the car and hung on one foot, then tossed her head and laughed. 'They say I'm a pretty good beauty operator,' she said. 'I hope I am. As an interviewer I'm terrible. Good night.'

I said good night and she walked off into the evening. I sat there watching her until she reached the main street and turned out of sight. Then I got out of the Chrysler and went over towards the telephone company's little rustic building.

10

A tame doe deer with a leather dog collar on wandered across the road in front of me. I patted her rough hairy neck and went into the telephone office. A small girl in slacks sat at a small desk working on the books. She got me the rate to Beverly Hills and the change for the coin box. The booth was outside, against the front wall of the building.

'I hope you like it up here,' she said. 'It's very quiet, very restful.'

I shut myself into the booth. For ninety cents I could talk to Derace Kingsley for five minutes. He was at home and the call came through quickly but the connexion was full of mountain static.

'Find anything up there?' he asked me in a three-highball voice. He sounded tough and confident again.

'I've found too much,' I said. 'And not at all what we want. Are you alone?'

'What does that matter?'

'It doesn't matter to me. But I know what I'm going to say. You don't.'

'Well, get on with it, whatever it is,' he said.

'I had a long talk with Bill Chess. He was lonely. His wife had left him—a month ago. They had a fight and he went out and got drunk and when he came back she was gone. She left a note saying she would rather be dead than live with him any more.'

'I guess Bill drinks too much,' Kingsley's voice said from very far off.

'When he got back, both the women had gone. He has no idea where Mrs Kingsley went. Lavery was up here in May, but not since. Lavery admitted that much himself. Lavery could, of course, have come up again while Bill was out getting drunk, but there wouldn't be a lot of point to that and there would be two cars to drive down the hill. And I thought that possibly Mrs K. and Muriel Chess might have gone away together, only Muriel also had a car of her own. But that idea, little as it was worth, has been thrown out by another development. Muriel Chess didn't go away at all. She went down into your little private lake. She came back up to-day. I was there.'

'Good God!' Kingsley sounded properly horrified. 'You mean she drowned herself?'

'Perhaps. The note she left could be a suicide note. It would read as well that way as the other The body was stuck down under that old submerged landing below the pier. Bill was the one who spotted an arm moving down there while we were standing on the pier looking down into the water. He got her out. They've arrested him. The poor guy's pretty badly broken up.'

'Good God!' Kingsley said again. 'I should think he would be. Does it look as if he—' He paused as the operator came in on the line and demanded another forty-five cents. I put in two quarters and the line cleared.

'Look as if he what?'

Suddenly very clear, Kingsley's voice said: 'Look as if he murdered her?'

I said: 'Very much. Jim Patton, the constable up here, doesn't like the note not being dated. It seems she left him once before over some woman. Patton sort of suspects Bill might have saved up an old note. Anyhow they've taken Bill down to San Bernardino for questioning and they've taken the body down to be post-mortemed.'

'And what do you think?' he asked slowly.

'Well, Bill found the body himself. He didn't have to take me around by that pier. She might have stayed down in the water very much longer, or for ever. The note could be old because Bill had carried it in his wallet and handled it from time to time, brooding over it. It could just as easily be undated this time as another time. I'd say notes like that are undated more often than not. The people who write them are apt to be in a hurry and not concerned with dates.'

'The body must be pretty far gone. What can they find out now?'

'I don't know how well equipped they are. They can find out if she died by drowning, I guess. And whether there are any marks of violence that wouldn't be erased by water and decomposition. They could tell if she had been shot or stabbed. If the hyoid bone in the throat was broken, they could assume she was throttled. The main thing for us is that I'll have to tell why I came up here. I'll have to testify at an inquest.'

'That's bad,' Kingsley growled. 'Very bad. What do you plan to do now?'

'On my way home I'll stop at the Prescott Hotel and see if I can pick up anything there. Were your wife and Muriel Chess friendly?'

'I guess so. Crystal's easy enough to get along with most of the time. I hardly knew Muriel Chess.'

'Did you ever know anybody named Mildred Haviland?'

'What?'

I repeated the name.

'No,' he said. 'Is there any reason why I should?'

'Every question I ask you ask another right back,' I said. 'No, there isn't any reason why you should know Mildred Haviland. Especially if you hardly knew Muriel Chess. I'll call you in the morning.'

'Do that,' he said, and hesitated. 'I'm sorry you had to walk into such a mess,' he added, and then hesitated again and said good night and hung up.

The bell rang again immediately and the long-distance operator told me sharply I had put in five cents too much money. I said the sort of thing I would be likely to put into an opening like that. She didn't like it.

I stepped out of the booth and gathered some air into my lungs. The tame doe with the leather collar was standing in the gap in the fence at the end of the walk. I tried to push her out of the way, but she just leaned against me and wouldn't push. So I stepped over the fence and went back to the Chrysler and drove back to the village.

There was a hanging light in Patton's headquarters but the shack was empty and his 'Back in Twenty Minutes' sign was still against the inside of the glass part of the door. I kept on going down to the boat-landing and beyond to the edge of a deserted swimming-beach. A few put-puts and speedboats were still fooling around on the silky water. Across the lake tiny yellow lights began to show in toy cabins perched on miniature slopes. A single bright star glowed low in the north-east above the ridge of the mountains. A robin sat on the spike top of a hundred-foot pine and waited for it to be dark enough for him to sing his good-night song.

In a little while it was dark enough and he sang and went away into the invisible depths of sky. I snapped my cigarette into the motionless water a few feet away and climbed back into the car and started back in the direction of Little Fawn Lake.

11

The gate across the private road was padlocked. I put the Chrysler between two pine-trees and climbed the gate and pussy-footed along the side of the road until the glimmer of the little lake bloomed suddenly at my feet. Bill Chess's cabin was dark. The three cabins on the other side were abrupt shadows against the pale granite outcrop. Water gleamed white where it trickled across the top of the dam, and fell almost soundlessly along the sloping outer face to the brook below. I listened, and heard no other sound at all.

The front door of the Chess cabin was locked. I padded along to the back and found a brute of a padlock hanging at that. I went along the walls feeling window screens. They were all fastened. One window higher up was screenless, a small double cottage window half-way down the north wall. This was locked too. I stood still and did some more listening. There was no breeze and the trees were as quiet as their shadows.

I tried a knife blade between the two halves of the small window. No soap. The catch refused to budge. I leaned against the wall and thought and then suddenly I picked up a large stone and smacked it against the place where the two frames met in the middle. The catch pulled out of dry wood with a tearing noise. The window swung back into darkness. I heaved up on the sill and wangled a cramped leg over and edged through the opening. I rolled and let myself down into the room. I turned, grunting a little from the exertion at that altitude, and listened again.

A blazing flash beam hit me square in the eyes.

A very calm voice said: 'I'd rest right there, son. You must be all tuckered out.'

The flash pinned me against the wall like a squashed fly. Then a light switch clicked and a table lamp glowed. The flash went out. Jim Patton was sitting in an old brown Morris chair beside the table. A fringed brown scarf hung over the end of the table and touched his thick knee. He wore the same clothes he had worn that afternoon, with the addition of a leather jerkin which must have been new once, say about the time of Grover Cleveland's first term. His hands were empty except for the flash. His eyes were empty. His jaws moved in gentle rhythm.

'What's on your mind, son—besides breaking and entering?'

I poked a chair out and straddled it and leaned my arms on the back and looked around the cabin.

'I had an idea,' I said. 'It looked pretty good for a while, but I guess I can learn to forget it.'

The cabin was larger than it had seemed from outside. The part I was in was the living-room. It contained a few articles of modest furniture, a rag rug on the pineboard floor, a round table against the end wall and two chairs set against it. Through an open door the corner of a big black cookstove showed.

Patton nodded and his eyes studied me without rancour. 'I heard a car coming,' he said. 'I knew it had to be coming here. You walk right nice though. I didn't hear you walk worth a darn. I've been a mite curious about you, son.'

I said nothing.

'I hope you don't mind me callin' you "son",' he said. 'I hadn't ought to be so familiar, but I got myself into the habit and I can't seem to shake it. Anybody that don't have a long white beard and arthritis is "son" to me.'

I said he could call me anything that came to mind. I wasn't sensitive.

He grinned. 'There's a mess of detectives in the L.A. phone book,' he said. 'But only one of them is called Marlowe.'

'What made you look?'

'I guess you might call it lowdown curiosity. Added to which Bill Chess told me you was some sort of dick. You didn't bother to tell me yourself.'

'I'd have got around to it,' I said. 'I'm sorry it bothered you.'

'It didn't bother me none. I don't bother at all easy. You got any identification with you?'

I got my wallet out and showed him this and that.

'Well, you got a good build on you for the work,' he said, satisfied. 'And your face don't tell a lot of stories. I guess you was aiming to search the cabin.'

'Yeah.'

'I already pawed around considerable myself. Just got back and come straight here. That is, I stopped by my shack a minute and then come. I don't figure I could let you search the place, though.' He scratched his ear. 'That is, dum if I know whether I could or not. You telling who hired you?'

'Derace Kingsley. To trace his wife. She skipped out on him a month ago. She started from here. So I started from here. She's supposed to have gone away with a man. The man denies it. I thought maybe something up here might give me a lead.'

'And did anything?'

'No. She's traced pretty definitely as far as San Bernardino and then El Paso. There the trail ends. But I've only just started.'

Patton stood up and unlocked the cabin door. The spicy smell of the pines surged in. He spat outdoors and sat down again and rumpled the mousy brown hair under his Stetson. His head with the hat off had the indecent look of heads that are seldom without hats.

'You didn't have no interest in Bill Chess at all?'

'None whatever.'

'I guess you fellows do a lot of divorce business,' he said. 'Kind of smelly work, to my notion.'

I let that ride.

'Kingsley wouldn't have asked help from the police to find his wife, would he?'

'Hardly,' I said. 'He knows her too well.'

'None of what you've been saying don't hardly explain your wanting to search Bill's cabin,' he said judiciously.

'I'm just a great guy to poke around.'

'Hell,' he said, 'you can do better than that.'

'Say I am interested in Bill Chess then. But only because he's in trouble and rather a pathetic case—in spite of being a good deal of a heel. If he murdered his wife, there's something here to point that way. If he didn't, there's something to point that way too.'

He held his head sideways, like a watchful bird. 'As for instance what kind of thing?'

'Clothes, personal jewellery, toilet articles, whatever a woman takes with her when she goes away, not intending to come back.'

He leaned back slowly. 'But she didn't go away, son.'

'Then the stuff should be still here. But if it was still here, Bill would have noticed she hadn't taken it. He would know she hadn't gone away.'

'By gum, I don't like it either way,' he said.

'But if he murdered her,' I said, 'then he would have to get rid of the things she ought to have taken with her, if she had gone away.'

'And how do you figure he would do that, son?' The yellow lamplight made bronze of one side of his face.

'I understand she had a Ford car of her own. Except for that I'd expect him to burn what he could burn and bury what he could not burn out in the woods. Sinking it in the lake might be dangerous. But he couldn't burn or bury her car. Could he drive it?'

Patton looked surprised. 'Sure. He can't bend his right leg at the knee, so he couldn't use the foot-brake very handy. But he could get by with the hand-brake. All that's different on Bill's own Ford is the brake pedal is set over on the left side of the post, close to the clutch, so he can shove them both down with one foot.'

I shook ash from my cigarette into a small blue jar that had once contained a pound of orange honey, according to the small gilt label on it.

'Getting rid of the car would be his big problem,' I said. 'Wherever he took it he would have to get back, and he would rather not be seen coming back. And if he simply abandoned it on a street, say, down in San Bernardino, it would be found and identified very quickly. He wouldn't want that either. The best stunt would be to unload it on a hot car dealer, but he probably doesn't know one. So the chances are he hid it in the woods within walking distance of here. And walking distance for him would not be very far.'

'For a fellow that claims not to be interested, you're doing some pretty close figuring on all this,' Patton said dryly. 'So now you've got the car hid out in the woods. What then?'

'He has to consider the possibility of its being found. The woods are lonely, but rangers and woodcutters get around in them from time to time. If the car is found, it would be better for Muriel's stuff to be found in it. That would give him a couple of outs—neither one very brilliant but both at least possible. One, that she was murdered by some unknown party who fixed things to implicate Bill when and if the murder was discovered. Two, that Muriel did actually commit suicide, but fixed things so that he would be blamed. A revenge suicide.'

Patton thought all this over with calm and care. He went to the door to unload again. He sat down and rumpled his hair again. He looked at me with solid scepticism.

'The first one's possible like you say,' he admitted. 'But only just, and I don't have anybody in mind for the job. There's that little matter of the note to be got over.'

I shook my head. 'Say Bill already had the note from another time. Say she went away, as he thought, without leaving a note. After a month had gone by without any word from her he might be just worried and uncertain enough to show the note, feeling it might be some protection to him in case anything had happened to her. He didn't say any of this, but he could have had it in his mind.'

Patton shook his head. He didn't like it. Neither did I. He said slowly: 'As to your other notion, it's just plain crazy. Killing yourself and fixing things so as somebody else would get accused of murdering you don't fit in with my simple ideas of human nature at all.'

'Then your ideas of human nature are too simple,' I said. 'Because it has been done, and when it has been done, it has nearly always been done by a woman.'

'Nope,' he said, 'I'm a man fifty-seven years old and I've seen a lot of crazy people, but I don't go for that worth a peanut shell. What I like is that she did plan to go away and did write the note, but he caught her before she got clear and saw red and finished her off. Then he would have to do all them things we been talking about.'

'I never met her,' I said. 'So I wouldn't have any idea what she would be likely to do. Bill said he met her in a place in Riverside something over a year ago. She may have had a long and complicated history before that. What kind of girl was she?'

'A mighty cute little blonde when she fixed herself up. She kind of let herself go with Bill. A quiet girl, with a face that kept its secrets. Bill says she had a temper, but I never seen any of it. I seen plenty of nasty temper in him.'

'And did you think she looked like the photo of somebody called Mildred Haviland?'

His jaws stopped munching and his mouth became almost primly tight. Very slowly he started chewing again.

'By gum,' he said, 'I'll be mighty careful to look under the bed before I crawl in to-night. To make sure you ain't there. Where did you get that information?'

'A nice little girl called Birdie Keppel told me. She was interviewing me in the course of her spare-time newspaper job. She happened to mention that an L.A. cop named De Soto was showing the photo around.'

Patton smacked his thick knee and hunched his shoulders forward.

'I done wrong there,' he said soberly. 'I made one of my mistakes. This big bruiser showed his picture to darn near everybody in town before he showed it to me. That made me kind of sore. It looked some like Muriel, but not enough to be sure by any manner of means. I asked him what she was wanted for. He said it was police business. I said I was in that way of business myself, in an ignorant countrified kind of way. He said his instructions were to locate the lady and that was all he knew. Maybe he did wrong to take me up short like that. So I guess I done wrong to tell him I didn't know anybody that looked like his little picture.'

The big calm man smiled vaguely at the corner of the ceiling, then brought his eyes down and looked at me steadily.

'I'll thank you to respect this confidence, Mr Marlowe. You done right nicely in your figuring too. You ever happen to go over to Coon Lake?'

'Never heard of it.'

'Back about a mile,' he said, pointing over his shoulder with a thumb, 'there's a little narrow wood road turns over west. You can just drive in and miss the trees. It climbs about five hundred feet in another mile and comes out by Coon Lake. Pretty little place. Folks go up there to picnic once in a while, but not often. It's hard on tyres. There's two three small shallow lakes full of reeds. There's snow up there even now in the shady places. There's a bunch of old hand-hewn log cabins that's been falling down ever since I recall, and there's a big broken-down frame building that Montclair University used to use for a summer camp maybe years back. They ain't used it in a very long time. This building sits back from the lakes in heavy timber. Round at the back of it there's a wash-house with an old rusty boiler and along of that there's a big woodshed with a sliding door hung on rollers. It was built for a garage, but they kept their wood in it and they locked it up out of season. Wood's one of the few things people will steal up here, but folks who might steal it off a pile wouldn't break a lock to get it. I guess you know what I found in that woodshed.'

'I thought you went down to San Bernardino.'

'Changed my mind. Didn't seem right to let Bill ride down there with his wife's body in the back of the car. So I sent it down in Doc's ambulance and I sent Andy down with Bill. I figured I kind of ought to look around a little more before I put things up to the sheriff and the coroner.'

'Muriel's car was in the woodshed?'

'Yep. And two unlocked suit-cases in the car. Packed with clothes and packed kind of hasty, I thought. Women's clothes. The point is, son, no stranger would have known about that place.'

I agreed with him. He put his hand into the slanting side pocket of his jerkin and brought out a small twist of tissue paper. He opened it up on his palm and held the hand out flat.

'Take a look at this.'

I went over and looked. What lay on the tissue was a thin gold chain with a tiny lock hardly larger than a link of the chain. The gold had been snipped through, leaving the lock intact. The chain seemed to be about seven inches long. There was white powder sticking to both chain and paper.

'Where would you guess I found that?' Patton asked.

I picked the chain up and tried to fit the cut ends together. They didn't fit. I made no comment on that, but moistened a finger and touched the powder and tasted it.

'In a can or box of confectioner's sugar,' I said. 'The chain is an anklet. Some women never take them off, like wedding-rings. Whoever took this one off didn't have the key.'

'What do you make of it?'

'Nothing much,' I said. 'There wouldn't be any point in Bill cutting it off Muriel's ankle and leaving that green necklace on her neck. There wouldn't be any point in Muriel cutting it off herself—assuming she had lost the key—and hiding it to be found. A search thorough enough to find it wouldn't be made unless her body was found first. If Bill cut it off, he would have thrown it into the lake. But if Muriel wanted to keep it and yet hide it from Bill, there's some sense in the place where it was hidden.'

Patton looked puzzled this time. 'Why is that?'

'Because it's a woman's hiding-place. Confectioner's sugar is used to make cake icing. A man would never look there. Pretty clever of you to find it, sheriff.'

He grinned a little sheepishly. 'Hell, I knocked the box over and some of the sugar spilled,' he said. 'Without that I don't guess I ever would have found it.' He rolled the paper up again and slipped it back into his pocket. He stood up with an air of finality.

'You staying up here or going back to town, Mr Marlowe?'

'Back to town. Until you want me for the inquest. I suppose you will.'

'That's up to the coroner, of course. If you'll kind of shut that window you bust in, I'll put this lamp out and lock up.'

I did what he said and he snapped his flash on and put out the lamp. We went out and he felt the cabin door to make sure the lock had caught. He closed the screen softly and stood looking across the moonlit lake.

'I don't figure Bill meant to kill her,' he said sadly. 'He could choke a girl to death without meaning to at all. He has mighty strong hands. Once done, he has to use what brains God gave him to cover up what he done. I feel real bad about it, but that don't alter the facts and the probabilities. It's simple and natural and the simple and natural things usually turn out to be right.'

I said: 'I should think he would have run away. I don't see how he could stand it to stay here.'

Patton spat into the black velvet shadow of a manzanita bush. He said slowly: 'He had a government pension and he would have to run away from that too. And most men can stand what they've got to stand, when it steps up and looks them straight in the eye. Like they're doing all over the world right now. Well, good night to you. I'm going to walk down to that little pier again and stand there awhile in the moonlight and feel bad. A night like this, and we got to think about murders.'

He moved quietly off into the shadows and became one of them himself. I stood there until he was out of sight and then went back to the locked gate and climbed over it. I got into the car and drove back down the road looking for a place to hide.

12

Three hundred yards from the gate a narrow track, sifted over with brown oak leaves from last autumn, curved around a granite boulder and disappeared. I followed it around and bumped along the stones of the outcrop for fifty or sixty feet, then swung the car around a tree and set it pointing back the way it had come. I cut the lights and switched off the motor and sat there waiting.

Half an hour passed. Without tobacco it seemed a long time. Then far off I heard a car motor start up and grow louder and the white beam of headlights passed below me on the road. The sound faded into the distance and a faint dry tang of dust hung in the air for a while after it was gone.

I got out of my car and walked back to the gate and to the Chess cabin. A hard push opened the sprung window this time. I climbed in again and let myself down to the floor and poked the flash I had brought across the room to the table lamp. I switched the lamp on and listened a moment, heard nothing and went out to the kitchen. I switched on a hanging bulb over the sink.

The wood-box beside the stove was neatly piled with split wood. There were no dirty dishes in the sink, no foul-smelling pots on the stove. Bill Chess, lonely or not, kept his house in good order. A door opened from the kitchen into the bedroom, and from that a very narrow door led into a tiny bathroom which had evidently been built on to the cabin fairly recently. The clean celotex lining showed that. The bathroom told me nothing.

The bedroom contained a double bed, a pinewood dresser with a round mirror on the wall above it, a bureau, two straight chairs and a tin waste-basket. There were two oval rag rugs on the floor, one on each side of the bed. On the walls Bill Chess had tacked up a set of war maps from the *National Geographic*. There was a silly-looking red-and-white flounce on the dressing-table.

I poked around in the drawers. An imitation leather trinket-box with an assortment of gaudy costume jewellery had not been taken away. There was the usual stuff women use on their faces and finger-nails and eyebrows, and it seemed to me that there was too much of it. But that was just guessing. The bureau contained both man's and woman's clothes, not a great deal of either. Bill Chess had a very noisy check shirt with starched matching collar, among other things. Underneath a sheet of blue tissue paper in one corner I found something I didn't like. A seemingly brand-new peach-coloured silk slip trimmed with lace. Silk slips were not being left behind that year, not by any woman in her senses.

This looked bad for Bill Chess. I wondered what Patton had thought of it.

I went back to the kitchen and prowled the open shelves above and beside the sink. They were thick with cans and jars of household staples. The confectioner's sugar was in a square brown box with a torn corner. Patton had made an attempt to clean up what was spilled. Near the sugar were salt, borax, baking-soda, cornstarch, brown sugar and so on. Something might be hidden in any of them.

Something that had been clipped from a chain anklet whose cut ends did not fit together.

I shut my eyes and poked a finger out at random and it came to rest on the baking-soda. I got a newspaper from the back of the wood-box and spread it out and dumped the soda out of the box. I stirred it around with a spoon. There seemed to be an indecent lot of baking-soda, but that was all there was. I funnelled it back into the box and tried the borax. Nothing but borax. Third time lucky. I tried the cornstarch. It made too much fine dust, and there was nothing but cornstarch.

The sound of distant steps froze me to the ankles. I reached up and yanked the light out and dodged back into the living-room and reached for the lamp switch. Much too late to be of any use, of course. The steps sounded again, soft and cautious. The hackles rose on my neck.

I waited in the dark, with the flash in my left hand. A deadly long two minutes crept by. I spent some of the time breathing, but not all.

It wouldn't be Patton. He would walk up to the door and open it and tell me off. The careful quiet steps seemed to move this way and that, a movement, a long pause, another movement, another long pause. I sneaked across to the door and twisted the knob silently. I yanked the door wide and stabbed out with the flash.

It made golden lamps of a pair of eyes. There was a leaping movement and a quick thudding of hoofs back among the trees. It was only an inquisitive deer.

I closed the door again and followed my flashlight beam back into the kitchen. The small round glow rested squarely on the box of confectioner's sugar.

I put the light on again, lifted the box down and emptied it on the newspaper.

Patton hadn't gone deep enough. Having found one thing by accident he had assumed that was all there was. He hadn't seemed to notice that there ought to be something else.

Another twist of white tissue showed in the fine white powdered sugar. I shook it clean and unwound it. It contained a tiny gold heart, no larger than a woman's little finger-nail.

I spooned the sugar back into the box and put the box back on the shelf and crumpled the piece of newspaper into the stove. I went back to the living-room and turned the table lamp on. Under that brighter light the tiny engraving on the back of the little gold heart could just be read without a magnifying-glass.

It was in script. It read: 'Al to Mildred. June 28th, 1938. With all my love.'

Al to Mildred. Al somebody to Mildred Haviland. Mildred Haviland was Muriel Chess. Muriel Chess was dead—two weeks after a cop named De Soto had been looking for her.

I stood there, holding it, wondering what it had to do with me. Wondering, and not having the faintest glimmer of an idea.

I wrapped it up again and left the cabin and drove back to the village.

Patton was in his office telephoning when I got around there. The door was locked. I had to wait while he talked. After a while he hung up and came to unlock the door.

I walked in past him and put the twist of tissue paper on his counter and opened it up.

'You didn't go deep enough into the powdered sugar,' I said.

He looked at the little gold heart, looked at me, went around behind the counter and got a cheap magnifying-glass off his desk. He studied the back of the heart. He put the glass down and frowned at me.

'Might have known if you wanted to search that cabin, you was going to do it,' he said gruffly. 'I ain't going to have trouble with you, am I, son?'

'You ought to have noticed that the cut ends of the chain didn't fit,' I told him.

He looked at me sadly. 'Son, I don't have your eyes.' He pushed the little heart around with his square blunt finger. He stared at me and said nothing.

I said: 'If you were thinking that anklet meant something Bill could have been jealous about, so was I—provided he ever saw it. But strictly on the cuff I'm willing to bet he never did see it and that he never heard of Mildred Haviland.'

Patton said slowly: 'Looks like maybe I owe this De Soto party an apology, don't it?'

'If you ever see him,' I said.

He gave me another long empty stare and I gave it right back to him. 'Don't tell me, son,' he said. 'Let me guess all for myself that you got a brand-new idea about it.'

'Yeah. Bill didn't murder his wife.'

'No?'

'No. She was murdered by somebody out of her past. Somebody who had lost track of her and then found it again and found her married to another man and didn't like it. Somebody who knew the country up here—as hundreds of people do who don't live here—and knew a good place to hide the car and the clothes. Somebody who hated and could dissimulate. Who persuaded her to go away with him and when everything was ready and the note was written, took her around the throat and gave her what he thought was coming to her and put her in the lake and went his way. Like it?'

'Well,' he said judiciously, 'it does make things kind of complicated, don't you think? But there ain't anything impossible about it. Not one bit impossible.'

'When you get tired of it, let me know. I'll have something else,' I said.

'I'll just be doggone sure you will,' he said, and for the first time since I had met him he laughed.

I said good night again and went out, leaving him there moving his mind around with the ponderous energy of a homesteader digging up a stump.

13

At somewhere around eleven I got down to the bottom of the grade and parked in one of the diagonal slots at the side of the Prescott Hotel in San Bernardino. I pulled an overnight bag out of the boot and had taken three steps with it when a bellhop in braided pants and a white shirt and black bow-tie yanked it out of my hand.

The clerk on duty was an egg-headed man with no interest in me or in anything else. He wore parts of a white linen suit and he yawned as he handed me the desk pen and looked off into the distance as if remembering his childhood.

The hop and I rode a four by four elevator to the second floor and walked a couple of blocks around corners. As we walked it got hotter and hotter. The hop unlocked a door into a boy's-size room with one window on an air-shaft. The air-conditioner inlet up in the corner of the ceiling was about the size of a woman's handkerchief. The bit of ribbon tied to it fluttered weakly, just to show that something was moving.

The hop was tall and thin and yellow and not young and as cool as a slice of chicken in aspic. He moved his gum around in his face, put my bag on a chair, looked up at the grating and then stood looking at me. He had eyes the colour of a drink of water.

'Maybe I ought to have asked for one of the dollar rooms,' I said. 'This one seems a mite close-fitting.'

'I reckon you're lucky to get one at all. This town's bulgin' at the seams.'

'Bring us up some ginger ale and glasses and ice,' I said.

'Us?'

'That is, if you happen to be a drinking man.'

'I reckon I might take a chance this late.'

He went out. I took off my coat, tie, shirt and undershirt and walked around in the warm draught from the open door. The draught smelled of hot iron. I went into the bathroom sideways—it was that kind of bathroom—and doused myself with tepid cold water. I was breathing a little more freely when the tall languid hop returned with a tray. He shut the door and I brought out a bottle of rye. He mixed a couple of drinks and we made the usual insincere smiles over them and drank. The perspiration started from the back of my neck down my spine and was halfway to my socks before I put the glass down. But I felt better all the same. I sat on the bed and looked at the hop.

'How long can you stay?'

'Doing what?'

'Remembering.'

'I ain't a damn bit of use at it,' he said.

'I have money to spend,' I said, 'in my own peculiar way.' I got my wallet unstuck from the lower part of my back and spread tired-looking dollar bills along the bed.

'I beg yore pardon,' the hop said. 'I reckon you might be a dick.'

'Don't be silly,' I said. 'You never saw a dick playing solitaire with his own money. You might call me investigator.'

'I'm interested,' he said. 'The likker makes my mind work.'

I gave him a dollar bill. 'Try that on your mind. And can I call you Big Tex from Houston?'

'Amarillo,' he said. 'Not that it matters. And how do you like my Texas drawl? It makes me sick, but I find people go for it.'

'Stay with it,' I said. 'It never lost anybody a dollar yet.'

He grinned and tucked the folded dollar neatly into the watch pocket of his pants.

'What were you doing on Friday, June 12th?' I asked him. 'Late afternoon or evening. It was a Friday.'

He sipped his drink and thought, shaking the ice around gently and drinking past his gum. 'I was right here, six to twelve shift,' he said.

'A woman, slim, pretty blonde, checked in here and stayed until time for the night train to El Paso. I think she must have taken that because she was in El Paso Sunday morning. She came here driving a Packard Clipper registered to Crystal Grace Kingsley, 965 Carson Drive, Beverly Hills. She may have registered as that, or under some other name, and she may not have registered at all. Her car is still in the hotel garage. I'd like to talk to the boys that checked her in and out. That wins another dollar—just thinking about it.'

I separated another dollar from my exhibit and it went into his pocket with a sound like caterpillars fighting.

'Can do,' he said calmly.

He put his glass down and left the room, closing the door. I finished my drink and made another. I went into the bathroom and used some more warm water on my torso. While I was doing this the telephone on the wall tinkled and I wedged myself into the minute space between the bathroom door and the bed to answer it.

The Texas voice said: 'That was Sonny. He was inducted last week. Another boy we call Les checked her out. He's here.'

'Okay. Shoot him up, will you?'

I was playing with my second drink and thinking about the third when a knock came and I opened the door to a small, green-eyed rat with a tight, girlish mouth.

He came in almost dancing and stood looking at me with a faint sneer.

'Drink?'

'Sure,' he said coldly. He poured himself a large one, and added a whisper of ginger ale, put the mixture down in one long swallow, tucked a cigarette between his smooth little lips and snapped a match alight while it was coming up from his pocket. He blew smoke and went on staring at me. The corner of his eye caught the money on the bed, without looking directly at it. Over the pocket of his shirt, instead of a number, the word *Captain* was stitched.

'You Les?' I asked him.

'No.' He paused. 'We don't like dicks here,' he added. 'We don't have one of our own and we don't care to bother with dicks that are working for other people.'

'Thanks,' I said. 'That will be all.'

'Huh?' The small mouth twisted unpleasantly.

'Beat it,' I said.

'I thought you wanted to see me,' he sneered.

'You're the bell captain?'

'Check.'

'I wanted to buy you a drink. I wanted to give you a buck. Here.' I held it out to him. 'Thanks for coming up.'

He took the dollar and pocketed it, without a word of thanks. He hung there, smoke trailing from his nose, his eyes tight and mean.

'What I say here goes,' he said.

'It goes as far as you can push it,' I said. 'And that couldn't be very far.

You had your drink and you had your graft. Now you can scram out.'

He turned with a swift tight shrug and slipped out of the room noiselessly.

Four minutes passed, then another knock, very light. The tall boy came in grinning. I walked away from him and sat on the bed again.

'You didn't take to Les, I reckon?'

'Not a great deal. Is he satisfied?'

'I reckon so. You know what captains are. They have to have their cut. Maybe you better call me Les, Mr Marlowe.'

'So you checked her out.'

'No, that was all a stall. She never checked in at the desk. But I remember the Packard. She gave me a dollar to put it away for her and to look after her stuff until train time. She ate dinner here. A dollar gets you remembered in this town. And there's been talk about the car bein' left so long.'

'What was she like to look at?'

'She wore a black and white outfit, mostly white, and a panama hat with a black and white band. She was a neat blonde lady like you said. Later on she took a hack to the station. I put her bags into it for her. They had initials on them but I'm sorry I can't remember the initials.'

'I'm glad you can't,' I said. 'It would be too good. Have a drink. How old would she be?'

He rinsed the other glass and mixed a civilized drink for himself.

'It's mighty hard to tell a woman's age these days,' he said. 'I reckon she was about thirty, or a little more or a little less.'

I dug in my coat for the snapshot of Crystal and Lavery on the beach and handed it to him.

He looked at it steadily and held it away from his eyes, then close.

'You won't have to swear to it in court,' I said.

He nodded. 'I wouldn't want to. These small blondes are so much of a pattern that a change of clothes or light or make-up makes them all alike or all different.' He hesitated, staring at the snapshot.

'What's worrying you?' I asked.

'I'm thinking about the gent in this snap. He enter into it at all?'

'Go on with that,' I said.

'I think this fellow spoke to her in the lobby, and had dinner with her. A tall good-lookin' jasper, built like a fast light-heavy. He went in the hack with her too.'

'Quite sure about that?'

He looked at the money on the bed.

'Okay, how much does it cost?' I asked wearily.

He stiffened, laid the snapshot down and drew the two folded bills from his pocket and tossed them on the bed.

'I thank you for the drink,' he said, 'and to hell with you.' He started for the door.

'Oh, sit down and don't be so touchy,' I growled.

He sat down and looked at me stiff-eyed.

'And don't be so damn southern,' I said. 'I've been kneedeep in hotel hops for a lot of years. If I've met one who wouldn't pull a gag, that's fine. But you can't expect me to expect to meet one that wouldn't pull a gag.'

He grinned slowly and nodded quickly. He picked the snapshot up again and looked at me over it.

'This gent takes a solid photo,' he said. 'Much more so than the lady. But there was another little item that made me remember him. I got the impression the lady didn't quite like him walking up to her so openly in the lobby.'

I thought that over and decided it didn't mean anything much. He might have been late or have missed some earlier appointment. I said:

'There's a reason for that. Did you notice what jewellery the lady was wearing? Rings, ear-pendants, anything that looked conspicuous or valuable?'

He hadn't noticed, he said.

'Was her hair long or short, straight or waved or curly, natural blonde or bleached?'

He laughed. 'Hell, you can't tell that last point, Mr Marlowe. Even when it's natural they want it lighter. As to the rest, my recollection is it was rather long, like they're wearing it now and turned in a little at the bottom and rather straight. But I could be wrong.' He looked at the snapshot again. 'She has it bound back here. You can't tell a thing.'

'That's right,' I said. 'And the only reason I asked you was to make sure that you didn't over-observe. The guy that sees too much detail is just as unreliable a witness as the guy that doesn't see any. He's nearly always making half of it up. You check just about right, considering the circumstances. Thanks very much.'

I gave him back his two dollars and a five to keep them company. He thanked me, finished his drink and left softly. I finished mine and washed off again and decided I would rather drive home than sleep in that hole. I put my shirt and coat on again and went downstairs with my bag.

The red-headed rat of a captain was the only hop in the lobby. I carried my bag over to the desk and he didn't move to take it off my hands. The egg-headed clerk separated me from two dollars without even looking at me.

'Two bucks to spend the night in this manhole,' I said, 'when for free I could have a nice airy ashcan.'

The clerk yawned, got a delayed reaction and said brightly: 'It gets quite cool here about three in the morning. From then on until eight, or even nine, it's quite pleasant.'

I wiped the back of my neck and staggered out to the car. Even the seat of the car was hot at midnight.

I got home about two-forty-five and Hollywood was an ice-box. Even Pasadena had felt cool.

14

I dreamed I was far down in the depths of icy green water with a corpse under my arm. The corpse had long blonde hair that kept floating around in front of my face. An enormous fish with bulging eyes and a bloated body and scales shining with putrescence swam around leering like an elderly roué. Just as I was about to burst from lack of air, the corpse came alive under my arm and got away from me and then I was fighting with the fish and the corpse was rolling over and over in the water, spinning its long hair.

I woke up with a mouth full of sheet and both hands hooked on the head-frame of the bed and pulling hard. The muscles ached when I let go and lowered them. I got up and walked the room and lit a cigarette, feeling the carpet with bare toes. When I had finished the cigarette, I went back to bed.

It was nine o'clock when I woke up again. The sun was on my face. The room was hot. I showered and shaved and partly dressed and made the morning toast and eggs and coffee in the dinette. While I was finishing up there was a knock at the apartment door.

I went to open it with my mouth full of toast. It was a lean serious-looking man in a severe grey suit.

'Floyd Greer, lieutenant, Central Detective Bureau,' he said and walked into the room.

He put out a dry hand and I shook it. He sat down on the edge of a chair, the way they do, and turned his hat in his hands and looked at me with the quiet stare they have.

'We got a call from San Bernardino about that business up at Puma Lake. Drowned woman. Seems you were on hand when the body was discovered.'

I nodded and said, 'Have some coffee?'

'No, thanks. I had breakfast two hours ago.'

I got my coffee and sat down across the room from him.

'They asked us to look you up,' he said. 'Give them a line on you.'

'Sure.'

'So we did that. Seems like you have a clean bill of health so far as we are concerned. Kind of coincidence a man in your line would be around when the body was found.'

'I'm like that,' I said. 'Lucky.'

'So I just thought I'd drop around and say howdy.'

'That's fine. Glad to know you, lieutenant.'

'Kind of a coincidence,' he said again, nodding. 'You up there on business, so to speak?'

'If I was,' I said, 'my business had nothing to do with the girl who was drowned, so far as I know.'

'But you couldn't be sure?'

'Until you've finished with a case, you can't ever be quite sure what its ramifications are, can you?'

'That's right.' He circled his hat brim through his fingers again, like a bashful cowboy. There was nothing bashful about his eyes. 'I'd like to feel sure that if these ramifications you speak of happened to take in this drowned woman's affairs, you would put us wise.'

'I hope you can rely on that,' I said.

He bulged his lower lip with his tongue. 'We'd like a little more than a hope. At the present time you don't care to say?'

'At the present time I don't know anything that Patton doesn't know.'

'Who's he?'

'The constable up at Puma Point.'

The lean serious man smiled tolerantly. He cracked a knuckle and after a pause said: 'The San Berdoo D.A. will likely want to talk to you—before the inquest. But that won't be very soon. Right now they're trying to get a set of prints. We lent them a technical man.'

'That will be tough. The body's pretty far gone.'

'It's done all the time,' he said. 'They worked out the system back in New York where they're all the time pulling in floaters. They cut patches of skin off the fingers and harden them in a tanning solution and make stamps. It works well enough as a rule.'

'You think this woman had a record of some kind?'

'Why, we always take prints of a corpse,' he said. 'You ought to know that.'

I said: 'I didn't know the lady. If you thought I did and that was why I was up there, there's nothing in it.'

'But you wouldn't care to say just why you *were* up there,' he persisted.

'So you think I'm lying to you,' I said.

He spun his hat on a bony forefinger. 'You got me wrong, Mr Marlowe. We don't think anything at all. What we do is investigate and find out. This stuff is just routine. You ought to know that. You been around long enough.' He stood up and put his hat on. 'You might let me know if you have to leave town. I'd be obliged.'

I said I would and went to the door with him. He went out with a duck of his head and a sad half-smile. I watched him drift languidly down the hall and punch the elevator button.

I went back out to the dinette to see if there was any more coffee. There was about two-thirds of a cup. I added cream and sugar and carried my cup over to the telephone. I dialled Police Headquarters downtown and asked for the Detective Bureau and then for Lieutenant Floyd Greer.

The voice said: 'Lieutenant Greer is not in the office. Anybody else do?'

'De Soto in?'

'Who?'

I repeated the name.

'What's his rank and department?'

'Plain clothes something or other.'

'Hold the line.'

I waited. The burring male voice came back after a while and said: 'What's the gag? We don't have a De Soto on the roster. Who's this talking?'

I hung up, finished my coffee and dialled the number of Derace Kingsley's office. The smooth and cool Miss Fromsett said he had just come in and put me through without a murmur.

'Well,' he said, loud and forceful at the beginning of a fresh day, 'what did you find out at the hotel?'

'She was there all right. And Lavery met her there. The hop who gave me the dope brought Lavery into it himself, without any prompting from me. He had dinner with her and went with her in a cab to the railroad station.'

'Well, I ought to have known he was lying,' Kingsley said slowly. 'I got the impression he was surprised when I told him about the telegram from El Paso. I was just letting my impressions get too sharp. Anything else?'

'Not there. I had a cop calling on me this morning, giving me the usual looking over and warning not to leave town without letting him know. Trying to find out why I went to Puma Point. I didn't tell him as he wasn't even aware of Jim Patton's existence, it's evident that Patton didn't tell anybody.'

'Jim would do his best to be decent about it,' Kingsley said. 'Why were you asking me last night about some name—Mildred something or other?'

I told him, making it brief. I told him about Muriel Chess's car and clothes being found and where.

'That looks bad for Bill,' he said. 'I know Coon Lake myself, but it would never have occurred to me to use that old woodshed—or even that there was an old woodshed. It not only looks bad, it looks premeditated.'

'I disagree with that. Assuming he knew the country well enough it wouldn't take him any time to search his mind for a likely hiding-place. He was very restricted as to distance.'

'Maybe. What do you plan to do now?' he asked.

'Go up against Lavery again, of course.'

He agreed that that was the thing to do. He added: 'This other, tragic as it is, is really no business of ours, is it?'

'Not unless your wife knew something about it.'

His voice sounded sharply, saying: 'Look here, Marlowe, I think I can understand your detective instinct to tie everything that happens into one compact knot, but don't let it run away with you. Life isn't like that at all—not life as I have known it. Better leave the affairs of the Chess family to the police and keep your brains working on the Kingsley family.'

'Okay,' I said.

'I don't mean to be domineering,' he said.

I laughed heartily, said good-bye, and hung up. I finished dressing and went down to the basement for the Chrysler. I started for Bay City again.

15

I drove past the intersection of Altair Street to where the cross street continued to the edge of the canyon and ended in a semicircular parking place with a sidewalk and a white wooden guard fence around it. I sat there in the car a little while, thinking, looking out to sea and admiring the blue-grey fall of the foothills towards the ocean. I was trying to make up my mind whether to try handling Lavery with a feather or go on using the back of my hand and the edge of my tongue. I decided I could lose nothing by the soft approach. If that didn't produce for me—and I didn't think it would—nature could take its course and we could bust up the furniture.

The paved alley that ran along half-way down the hill below the houses on the outer edge was empty. Below that, on the next hillside street, a couple of kids were throwing a boomerang up the slope and chasing it with the usual amount of elbowing and mutual insult. Farther down still a house was enclosed in trees and a red brick wall. There was a glimpse of washing on the line in the backyard and two pigeons strutted along the slope of the roof bobbing their heads. A blue and tan bus trundled along the street in front of the brick house and stopped and a very old man got off with slow care and settled himself firmly on the ground and tapped with a heavy cane before he started to crawl back up the slope.

The air was clearer than yesterday. The morning was full of peace. I left the car where it was and walked along Altair Street to No. 623.

The venetian blinds were down across the front windows and the place had a sleepy look. I stepped down over the Korean moss and punched the bell and saw that the door was not quite shut. It had dropped in its frame, as most of our doors do, and the spring bolt hung a little on the lower edge of the lock plate. I remembered that it had wanted to stick the day before, when I was leaving.

I gave the door a little push and it moved inward with a light click. The room beyond was dim, but there was some light from west windows. Nobody answered my ring. I didn't ring again. I pushed the door a little wider and stepped inside.

The room had a hushed warm smell, the smell of late morning in a house not yet opened up. The bottle of Vat 69 on the round table by the davenport was almost empty and another full bottle waited beside it. The copper ice-bucket had a little water in the bottom. Two glasses had been used, and half a siphon of carbonated water.

I fixed the door about as I had found it and stood there and listened. If Lavery was away I thought I would take a chance and frisk the joint. I didn't have anything much on him, but it was probably enough to keep him from calling the cops.

In the silence time passed. It passed in the dry whirr of the electric clock on the mantel, in the far-off toot of an auto horn on Aster Drive, in the hornet drone of a plane over the foothills across the canyon, in the sudden lurch and growl of the electric refrigerator in the kitchen.

I went farther into the room and stood peering around and listening and hearing nothing except those fixed sounds belonging to the house and having nothing to do with the humans in it. I started along the rug towards the archway at the back.

A hand in a glove appeared on the slope of the white metal railing, at the edge of the archway, where the stairs went down. It appeared and stopped.

It moved and a woman's hat showed, then her head. The woman came quietly up the stairs. She came all the way up, turned through the arch and still didn't seem to see me. She was a slender woman of uncertain age, with untidy brown hair, a scarlet mess of a mouth, too much rouge on her cheekbones, shadowed eyes. She wore a blue tweed suit that looked like the dickens with a purple hat that was doing its best to hang on to the side of her head.

She saw me and didn't stop or change expression in the slightest degree. She came slowly on into the room, holding her right hand away from her body. Her left hand wore the brown glove I had seen on the railing. The right-hand glove that matched it was wrapped around the butt of a small automatic.

She stopped then and her body arched back and a quick distressful sound came out of her mouth. Then she giggled, a high nervous giggle. She pointed the gun at me, and came steadily on.

I kept on looking at the gun and not screaming.

The woman came close. When she was close enough to be confidential she pointed the gun at my stomach and said:

'All I wanted was my rent. The place seems well taken care of. Nothing broken. He has always been a good tidy careful tenant. I just didn't want him to get too far behind in the rent.'

A fellow with a kind of strained and unhappy voice said politely: 'How far behind is he?'

'Three months,' she said. 'Two hundred and forty dollars. Eighty dollars is very reasonable for a place as well furnished as this. I've had a little trouble collecting before, but it always came out very well. He promised me a cheque this morning. Over the telephone. I mean he promised to give it to me this morning.'

'Over the telephone,' I said. 'This morning.'

I shuffled around a bit in an inconspicuous sort of way. The idea was to get close enough to make a side swipe at the gun, knock it outwards and then jump in fast before she could bring it back in line. I've never had a lot of luck with the technique, but you have to try it once in a while. This looked like the time to try it.

I made about six inches, but not nearly enough for a first down. I said: 'And you're the owner?' I didn't look at the gun directly. I had a faint, a very faint hope that she didn't know she was pointing it at me.

'Why, certainly. I'm Mrs Fallbrook. Who did you think I was?'

'Well, I thought you might be the owner,' I said. 'You talking about the rent and all. But I didn't know your name.' Another eight inches. Nice smooth work. It would be a shame to have it wasted.

'And who are you, if I may inquire?'

'I just came about the car payment,' I said. 'The door was open just a teeny weensy bit and I kind of shoved in. I don't know why.'

I made a face like a man from the finance company coming about the car payment. Kind of tough, but ready to break into a sunny smile.

'You mean Mr Lavery is behind in his car payments?' she asked, looking worried.

'A little. Not a great deal,' I said soothingly.

I was all set now. I had the reach and I ought to have the speed. All it needed was a clean sharp sweep inside the gun and outward. I started to take my left foot out of the rug.

'You know,' she said, 'it's funny about this gun. I found it on the stairs. Nasty oily things, aren't they? And the stair carpet is a very nice grey chenille. Quite expensive.'

And she handed me the gun.

My hand went out for it, as stiff as an eggshell, almost as brittle. I took the gun. She sniffed with distaste at the glove which had been wrapped around the butt. She went on talking in exactly the same tone of cockeyed reasonableness. My knees cracked, relaxing.

'Well, of course, it's much easier for you,' she said. 'About the car, I mean. You can just take it away, if you have to. But taking a house with nice furniture in it isn't so easy. It takes time and money to evict a tenant. There is apt to be bitterness and things get damaged, sometimes on purpose. The rug on this floor cost over two hundred dollars, second-hand. It's only a jute rug, but it has a lovely colouring, don't you think? You'd never know it was only jute, second-hand. But that's silly too because they're always second-hand after you've used them. And I walked over here too, to save my tyres for the government. I could have taken a bus part way, but the darn things never come along except going in the wrong direction.'

I hardly heard what she said. It was like surf breaking beyond a point, out of sight. The gun had my interest.

I broke the magazine out. It was empty. I turned the gun and looked into the breech. That was empty too. I sniffed the muzzle. It reeked.

I dropped the gun into my pocket. A six-shot .25-calibre automatic.

Emptied out. Shot empty, and not too long ago. But not in the last half-hour either.

'Has it been fired?' Mrs Fallbrook inquired pleasantly. 'I certainly hope not.'

'Any reason why it should have been fired?' I asked her. The voice was steady, but the brain was still bouncing.

'Well, it was lying on the stairs,' she said. 'After all, people do fire them.'

'How true that is,' I said. 'But Mr Lavery probably had a hole in his pocket. He isn't home, is he?'

'Oh no.' She shook her head and looked disappointed. 'And I don't think it's very nice of him. He promised me the cheque and I walked over—'

'When was it you phoned him?' I asked.

'Why, yesterday evening.' She frowned, not liking so many questions.

'He must have been called away,' I said.

She stared at a spot between my big brown eyes.

'Look, Mrs Fallbrook,' I said. 'Let's not kid around any more, Mrs Fallbrook. Not that I don't love it. And not that I like to say this. But you didn't shoot him, did you—on account of he owed you three months' rent?'

She sat down very slowly on the edge of a chair and worked the tip of her tongue along the scarlet slash of her mouth.

'Why, what a perfectly horrid suggestion,' she said angrily. 'I don't think you are nice at all. Didn't you say the gun had not been fired?'

'All guns have been fired sometime. All guns have been loaded sometime. This one is not loaded now.'

'Well, then—' she made an impatient gesture and sniffed at her oily glove.

'Okay, my idea was wrong. Just a gag anyway. Mr Lavery was out and you went through the house. Being the owner, you have a key. Is that correct?'

'I didn't mean to be interfering,' she said, biting a finger. 'Perhaps I ought not to have done it. But I have a right to see how things are kept.'

'Well, you looked. And you're sure he's not here?'

'I didn't look under the beds or in the icebox,' she said coldly. 'I called out from the top of the stairs when he didn't answer my ring. Then I went down to the lower hall and called out again. I even peeped into the bedroom.' She lowered her eyes as if bashfully and twisted a hand on her knee.

'Well, that's that,' I said.

She nodded brightly. 'Yes, that's that. And what did you say your name was?'

'Vance,' I said. 'Philo Vance.'

'And what company are you employed with, Mr Vance?'

'I'm out of work right now,' I said. 'Until the police commissioner gets in a jam again.'

She looked startled. 'But you said you came about a car payment.'

'That's just part-time work,' I said. 'A fill-in job.'

She rose to her feet and looked at me steadily. Her voice was cold saying: 'Then in that case I think you had better leave now.'

I said: 'I thought I might take a look around first, if you don't mind. There might be something you missed.'

'I don't think that is necessary,' she said. 'This is my house. I'll thank you to leave now, Mr Vance.'

I said: 'And if I don't leave, you'll get somebody who will. Take a chair again, Mrs Fallbrook. I'll just glance through. This gun, you know, is kind of queer.'

'But I told you I found it lying on the stairs,' she said angrily. 'I don't know anything else about it. I don't know anything about guns at all. I—I never shot one in my life.' She opened a large blue bag and pulled a handkerchief out of it and sniffled.

'That's your story,' I said. 'I don't have to get stuck with it.'

She put her left hand to me with a pathetic gesture, like the erring wife in *East Lynne*.

'Oh, I shouldn't have done!' she cried. 'It was horrid of me. I know it was. Mr Lavery will be furious.'

'What you shouldn't have done,' I said, 'was let me find out the gun was empty. Up to then you were holding everything in the deck.'

She stamped her foot. That was all the scene lacked. That made it perfect.

'Why, you perfectly loathsome man,' she squawked. 'Don't you dare touch me! Don't you take a single step towards me! I won't stay in this house another minute with you. How *dare* you be so insulting—'

She caught her voice and snapped it in mid-air like a rubber band. Then she put her head down, purple hat and all, and ran for the door. As she passed me she put a hand out as if to stiff-arm me, but she wasn't near enough and I didn't move. She jerked the door wide and charged out through it and up the walk to the street. The door came slowly shut and I heard her rapid steps above the sound of its closing.

I ran a finger-nail along my teeth and punched the point of my jaw with a knuckle, listening. I didn't hear anything anywhere to listen to. A six-shot automatic, fired empty.

'Something,' I said out loud, 'is all wrong with this scene.'

The house seemed now to be abnormally still. I went along the apricot rug and through the archway to the head of the stairs. I stood there for another moment and listened again.

I shrugged and went quietly down the stairs.

16

The lower hall had a door at each end and two in the middle side by side. One of these was a linen closet and the other was locked. I went along to the end and looked in at a spare bedroom with drawn blinds and no sign of being used. I went back to the other end of the hall and stepped into a second bedroom with a wide bed, a café-au-lait rug, angular furniture in light wood, a box mirror over the dressing-table and a long fluorescent lamp over the mirror. In the corner a crystal greyhound stood on a mirror-top table and beside him a crystal box with cigarettes in it.

Face powder was spilled around on the dressing-table. There was a smear of dark lipstick on a towel hanging over the waste basket. On the bed were pillows side by side, with depressions in them that could have been made by heads. A woman's handkerchief peeped from under one pillow. A pair of sheer black pyjamas lay across the foot of the bed. A rather too emphatic trace of chypre hung in the air.

I wondered what Mrs Fallbrook had thought of all this.

I turned around and looked at myself in the long mirror of a closet door. The door was painted white and had a crystal knob. I turned the knob in my handkerchief and looked inside. The cedar-lined closet was fairly full of man's clothes. There was a nice friendly smell of tweed. The closet was not entirely full of man's clothes.

There was also a woman's black and white tailored suit, mostly white, black and white shoes under it, a panama with a black and white rolled band on a shelf above it. There were other woman's clothes, but I didn't examine them.

I shut the closet door and went out of the bedroom, holding my handkerchief ready for more doorknobs.

The door next the linen closet, the locked door, had to be the bathroom. I shook it, but it went on being locked. I bent down and saw there was a short, slit-shaped opening in the middle of the knob. I knew then that the door was fastened by pushing a button in the middle of the knob inside, and that the slit-like opening was for a metal key without wards that would spring the lock open in case somebody fainted in the bathroom, or the kids locked themselves in and got sassy.

The key for this ought to be kept on the top shelf of the linen closet but it wasn't. I tried my knife blade, but that was too thin. I went back to the bedroom and got a flat nail-file off the dresser. That worked. I opened the bathroom door.

A man's sand-coloured pyjamas were tossed over a painted hamper. A pair of heelless green slippers lay on the floor. There was a safety-razor on the edge of the washbowl and a tube of cream with the cap off. The bathroom window was shut, and there was a pungent smell in the air that was not quite like any other smell.

Three empty shells lay bright and coppery on the nile-green tiles of the bathroom floor, and there was a nice clean hole in the frosted pane of the window. To the left and a little above the window were two scarred places in the plaster where the white showed behind the paint and where something, such as a bullet, had gone in.

The shower curtain was green and white oiled silk and it hung on shiny chromium rings and it was drawn across the shower opening. I slid it aside, the rings making a thin scraping noise, which for some reason sounded indecently loud.

I felt my neck creak a little as I bent down. He was there all right—there wasn't anywhere else for him to be. He was huddled in the corner under the two shining faucets, and water dripped slowly on his chest from the chromium showerhead.

His knees were drawn up but slack. The two holes in his naked chest were dark blue and both of them were close enough to his heart to have killed him. The blood seemed to have been washed away.

His eyes had a curiously bright and expectant look, as if he smelled the morning coffee and would be coming right out.

Nice efficient work. You have just finished shaving and stripped for the shower and you are leaning in against the shower curtain and adjusting the temperature of the water. The door opens behind you and somebody comes in. The somebody appears to have been a woman. She has a gun. You look at the gun and she shoots it.

She misses with three shots. It seems impossible, at such short range, but there it is. Maybe it happens all the time. I've been around so little.

You haven't anywhere to go. You could lunge at her and take a chance, if you were that kind of fellow, and if you were braced for it. But leaning in over the shower faucets, holding the curtains closed, you are off balance. Also you are apt to be somewhat petrified with panic, if you are at all like other people.

That is where you go. You go into it as far as you can, but a shower stall is a small place and the tiled wall stops you. You are backed up against the last wall there is now. You are all out of space, and you are all out of living. And then there are two more shots, possibly three, and you slide down the wall, and your eyes are not even frightened any more now. They are just the empty eyes of the dead.

She reaches in and turns the shower off. She sets the lock of the bathroom door. On her way out of the house she throws the empty gun on the stair carpet. She should worry. It is probably your gun.

Is that right? It had better be right.

I bent and pulled at his arm. Ice couldn't have been any colder or any stiffer. I went out of the bathroom, leaving it unlocked. No need to lock it now. It only makes work for the cops.

I went into the bedroom and pulled the handkerchief out from under the pillow. It was a minute piece of linen rag with a scalloped edge embroidered in red. Two small initials were stitched in the corner, in red. *A.F.*

'Adrienne Fromsett,' I said. I laughed. It was a rather ghoulish laugh.

I shook the handkerchief to get some of the chypre out of it and folded it up in a tissue and put it in a pocket. I went back upstairs to the living-room and poked around in the desk against the wall. The desk contained no interesting letters, phone numbers or provocative match-folders. Or if it did, I didn't find them.

I looked at the phone. It was on a small table against the wall beside the fireplace. It had a long cord so that Mr Lavery could be lying on his back on the davenport, a cigarette between his smooth brown lips, a tall cool one at the table at his side, and plenty of time for a nice long cosy conversation with a lady friend. An easy, languid, flirtatious, kidding, not too subtle and not too blunt conversation, of the sort he would be apt to enjoy.

All that wasted too. I went away from the telephone to the door and set the lock so I could come in again and shut the door tight, pulling it hard over the sill until the lock clicked. I went up the walk and stood in the sunlight looking across the street at Dr Almore's house.

Nobody yelled or ran out of the door. Nobody blew a police whistle. Everything was quiet and sunny and calm. No cause for excitement whatever. It's only Marlowe, finding another body. He does it rather well by now. Murder-a-day Marlowe, they call him. They have the meat wagon following him around to follow up on the business he finds.

A nice enough fellow, in an ingenious sort of way.

I walked back to the intersection and got into my car and started it and backed it and drove away from there.

17

The bellhop at the Athletic Club was back in three minutes with a nod for me to come with him. We rode up to the fourth floor and went around a corner and he showed me a half-open door.

'Around to the left, sir. As quietly as you can. A few of the members are sleeping.'

I went into the club library. It contained books behind glass doors and magazines on a long central table and a lighted portrait of the club's founder. But its real business seemed to be sleeping. Outward-jutting book-cases cut the room into a number of small alcoves and in the alcoves were high-backed leather chairs of an incredible size and softness. In a number of the chairs old boys were snoozing peacefully, their faces violet with high blood pressure, thin racking snores coming out of their pinched noses.

I climbed over a few feet and stole around to the left. Derace Kingsley was in the very last alcove in the far end of the room. He had two chairs arranged side by side, facing into the corner. His big dark head just showed over the top of one of them. I slipped into the empty one and gave him a quick nod.

'Keep your voice down,' he said. 'This room is for after-luncheon naps. Now what is it? When I employed you it was to save me trouble, not to add trouble to what I already had. You made me break an important engagement.'

'I know,' I said, and put my face close to his. He smelled of highballs, in a nice way. 'She shot him.'

His eyebrows jumped and his face got that stony look. His teeth clamped tight. He breathed softly and twisted a large hand on his kneecap.

'Go on,' he said, in a voice the size of a marble.

I looked back over the top of my chair. The nearest old geezer was sound asleep and blowing the dusty fuzz in his nostrils back and forth as he breathed.

'No answer at Lavery's place,' I said. 'Door slightly open. But I noticed yesterday it sticks on the sill. Pushed it open. Room dark, two glasses with drinks having been in them. House very still. In a moment a slim dark woman calling herself Mrs Fallbrook, landlady, came up the stairs with her glove wrapped around a gun. Said she had found it on the stairs. Said she came to collect her three months' back rent. Used her key to get in. Inference is she took the chance to snoop around and look the house over. Took the gun from her and found it had been fired recently, but didn't tell her so. She said Lavery was not home. Got rid of her by making her mad and she departed in high dudgeon. She may call the police, but it's much more likely she will just go out and hunt butterflies and forget the whole thing—except the rent.'

I paused. Kingsley's head was turned towards me and his jaw muscles bulged with the way his teeth were clamped. His eyes looked sick.

'I went downstairs. Signs of a woman having spent the night. Pyjamas, face powder, perfume, and so on. Bathroom locked, but got it open. Three empty shells on the floor, two shots in the wall, one in the window. Lavery in the shower stall, naked and dead.'

'My God!' Kingsley whispered. 'Do you mean to say he had a woman with him last night and she shot him this morning in the bathroom?'

'Just what did you think I was trying to say?' I asked.

'Keep your voice down,' he groaned. 'It's a shock, naturally. Why in the bathroom?'

'Keep your own voice down,' I said. 'Why not in the bathroom? Could you think of a place where a man would be more completely off guard?'

He said: 'You don't know that a woman shot him. I mean, you're not sure, are you?'

'No,' I said. 'That's true. It might have been somebody who used a small gun and emptied it carelessly to look like a woman's work. The bathroom is downhill, facing outwards on space and I don't think shots down there would be easily heard by anyone not in the house. The woman who spent the night might have left—or there need not have been any woman at all. The appearances could have been faked. *You* might have shot him.'

'What would I want to shoot him for?' he almost bleated, squeezing both kneecaps hard. 'I'm a civilized man.'

That didn't seem to be worth an argument either. I said: 'Does your wife own a gun?'

He turned a drawn miserable face to me and said hollowly: 'Good God, man, you can't really think that!'

'Well, does she?'

He got the words out in small gritty pieces. 'Yes—she does. A small automatic.'

'You buy it locally?'

'I—I didn't buy it at all. I took it away from a drunk at a party in San Francisco a couple of years ago. He was waving it around, with an idea that that was very funny. I never gave it back to him.' He pinched his jaw hard until his knuckles whitened. 'He probably doesn't even remember how or when he lost it. He was that kind of a drunk.'

'This is working out almost too neatly,' I said. 'Could you recognize this gun?'

He thought hard, pushing his jaw out and half-closing his eyes. I looked back over the chairs again. One of the elderly snoozers had waked himself up with a snort that almost blew him out of his chair. He coughed, scratched his nose with a thin dried-up hand, and fumbled a gold watch out of his vest. He peered at it bleakly, put it away, and went to sleep again.

I reached in my pocket and put the gun in Kingsley's hand. He stared down at it miserably.

'I don't know,' he said slowly. 'It's like it, but I can't tell.'

'There's a serial number on the side,' I said.

'Nobody remembers the serial numbers of guns.'

'I was hoping you wouldn't,' I said. 'It would have worried me very much.'

His hand closed around the gun and he put it down beside him in the chair.

'The dirty rat,' he said softly. 'I suppose he ditched her.'

'I don't get it,' I said. 'The motive was inadequate for you, on account of you're a civilized man. But it was adequate for her.'

'It's not the same motive,' he snapped. 'And women are more impetuous than men.'

'Like cats are more impetuous than dogs.'

'How?'

'Some women are more impetuous than some men. That's all that means. We'll have to have a better motive, if you want your wife to have done it.'

He turned his head enough to give me a level stare in which there was no amusement. White crescents were bitten into the corners of his mouth.

'This doesn't seem to me a very good spot for the light touch,' he said. 'We can't let the police have this gun. Crystal had a permit and the gun was registered. So they will know the number, even if I don't. We can't let them have it.'

'But Mrs Fallbrook knows I had the gun.'

He shook his head stubbornly. 'We'll have to chance that. Yes, I know you're taking a risk. I intend to make it worth your while. If the set-up were possible for suicide, I'd say put the gun back. But the way you tell it, it isn't.'

'No. He'd have to have missed himself with the first three shots. But I can't cover up a murder, even for a ten-dollar bonus. The gun will have to go back.'

'I was thinking of more money than that,' he said quietly. 'I was thinking of five hundred dollars.'

'Just what did you expect to buy with it?'

He leaned close to me. His eyes were serious and bleak, but not hard. 'Is there anything in Lavery's place, apart from the gun, that might indicate Crystal has been there lately?'

'A black and white dress and a hat like the bellhop in Bernardino described on her. There may be a dozen things I don't know about. There almost certainly will be fingerprints. You say she was never printed, but that doesn't mean they won't get her prints to check. Her bedroom at home will be full of them. So will the cabin at Little Fawn Lake. And her car.'

'We ought to get the car—' he started to say. I stopped him.

'No use. Too many other places. What kind of perfume does she use?'

He looked blank for an instant. 'Oh—Gillerlain Regal, the Champagne of Perfumes,' he said woodenly. 'A Chanel number once in a while.'

'What's this stuff of yours like?'

'A kind of chypre. Sandalwood chypre.'

'The bedroom reeks with it,' I said. 'It smelled like cheap stuff to me. But I'm no judge.'

'Cheap?' he said, stung to the quick. 'My God, cheap? We get thirty dollars an ounce for it.'

'Well, this stuff smelled more like three dollars a gallon.'

He put his hands down hard on his knees and shook his head.

'I'm talking about money,' he said. 'Five hundred dollars. A cheque for it right now.'

I let the remark fall to the ground, eddying like a soiled feather. One of the old boys behind us stumbled to his feet and groped his way wearily out of the room.

Kingsley said gravely: 'I hired you to protect me from scandal, and, of course, to protect my wife, if she needed it. Through no fault of yours the chance to avoid scandal is pretty well shot. It's a question of my wife's neck now. I don't believe she shot Lavery. I have no reason for that belief. None at all. I just feel the conviction. She may even have been there last night, this gun may even be her gun. It doesn't prove she killed him. She would be as careless with the gun as with anything else. Anybody could have got hold of it.'

'The cops down there won't work very hard to believe that,' I said. 'If the one I met is a fair specimen, they'll just pick the first head they see and start swinging with their blackjacks. And hers will certainly be the first head they see when they look the situation over.'

He ground the heels of his hands together. His misery had a theatrical flavour, as real misery so often has.

'I'll go along with you up to a point,' I said. 'The set-up down there is almost too good, at first sight. She leaves clothes there she has been seen wearing and which can probably be traced. She leaves the gun on the stairs. It's hard to think she would be as dumb as that.'

'You give me a little heart,' Kingsley said wearily.

'But none of that means anything,' I said. 'Because we are looking at it from the angle of calculation, and people who commit crimes of passion or hatred just commit them and walk out. Everything I have heard indicates that she is a reckless, foolish woman. There's no sign of planning in any of the scene down there. There's every sign of a complete lack of planning. But even if there wasn't a thing down there to point to your wife, the cops would tie her up to Lavery. They will investigate his background, his friends, his women. Her name is bound to crop up somewhere along the line, and when it does, the fact that she has been out of sight for a month will make them sit up and rub their horny palms with glee. And of course they'll trace the gun, and if it's her gun—'

His hand dived for the gun in the chair beside him.

'Nope,' I said. 'They'll have to have the gun. Marlowe may be a very smart guy and very fond of you personally, but he can't risk the suppression of such vital evidence as the gun that killed a man. Whatever I do has to be on the basis that your wife is an obvious suspect, but that the obviousness can be wrong.'

He groaned and put his big hand out with the gun in it. I took it and put it away. Then I took it out again and said: 'Lend me your handkerchief. I don't want to use mine. I might be searched.'

He handed me a stiff white handkerchief and I wiped the gun off carefully all over and dropped it into my pocket. I handed him back the handkerchief.

'My prints are all right,' I said. 'But I don't want yours on it. Here's the only thing I can do. Go back down there and replace the gun and call the law. Ride it out with them and let the chips fall where they have to. The story will have to come out. What I was doing down there and why. At the worst they'll find her and prove she killed him. At the best they'll find her a lot quicker than I can and let me use my energies proving that she didn't kill him, which means, in effect, proving that someone else did. Are you game for that?'

He nodded slowly. He said: 'Yes—and the five hundred stands. For showing Crystal didn't kill him.'

'I don't expect to earn it,' I said. 'You may as well understand that now. How well did Miss Fromsett know Lavery? Out of office hours?'

His face tightened up like a charleyhorse. His fists went into hard lumps on his thighs. He said nothing.

'She looked kind of queer when I asked her for his address yesterday morning,' I said.

He let a breath out slowly.

'Like a bad taste in the mouth,' I said. 'Like a romance that fouled out. Am I too blunt?'

His nostrils quivered a little and his breath made noise in them for a moment. Then he relaxed and said quietly:

'She–she knew him rather well–at one time. She's a girl who would do about what she pleased in that way. Lavery was, I guess, a fascinating bird–to women.'

'I'll have to talk to her,' I said.

'Why?' he asked shortly. Red patches showed in his cheeks.

'Never mind why. It's my business to ask all sorts of questions of all sorts of people.'

'Talk to her then,' he said tightly. 'As a matter of fact she knew the Almores. She knew Almore's wife, the one who killed herself. Lavery knew her too. Could that have any possible connexion with this business?'

'I don't know. You're in love with her, aren't you?'

'I'd marry her to-morrow if I could,' he said stiffly.

I nodded and stood up. I looked back along the room. It was almost empty now. At the far end a couple of elderly relics were still blowing bubbles. The rest of the soft-chair boys had staggered back to whatever it was they did when they were conscious.

'There's just one thing,' I said, looking down at Kingsley. 'Cops get very hostile when there is a delay in calling them after a murder. There's been delay this time and there will be more. I'd like to go down there as if it was the first visit to-day. I think I can make it that way, if I leave the Fallbrook woman out.'

'Fallbrook?' He hardly knew what I was talking about. 'Who the hell–oh yes, I remember.'

'Well, don't remember. I'm almost certain they'll never hear a peep from her. She's not the kind to have anything to do with the police of her own free will.'

'I understand,' he said.

'Be sure you handle it right then. Questions will be asked you *before* you are told Lavery is dead, before I'm allowed to get in touch with you–so far as they know. Don't fall into any traps. If you do, I won't be able to find anything out. I'll be in the clink.'

'You could call me from the house down there–before you call the police,' he said reasonably.

'I know. But the fact that I don't will be in my favour. And they'll check the phone calls, it's one of the first things they do. And if I call you from anywhere else, I might just as well admit that I came up here to see you.'

'I understand,' he said again. 'You can trust me to handle it.'

We shook hands and I left him standing there.

18

The Athletic Club was on a corner across the street and half a block down from the Treloar Building. I crossed and walked north to the entrance. They had finished laying rose-coloured concrete where the rubber sidewalk had been. It was fenced around, leaving a narrow gangway in and out of the building. The space was clotted with office help going in from lunch.

The Gillerlain Company's reception-room looked even emptier than the day before. The same fluffy little blonde was tucked in behind the PBX in the corner. She gave me a quick smile and I gave her the gunman's salute, a stiff forefinger pointing at her, the three lower fingers tucked back under it, and the thumb wiggling up and down like a western gun-fighter fanning his hammer. She laughed heartily, without making a sound. This was more fun than she had had in a week.

I pointed to Miss Fromsett's empty desk and the little blonde nodded and pushed a plug in and spoke. A door opened and Miss Fromsett swayed elegantly out to her desk and sat down and gave me her cool expectant eyes.

'Yes, Mr Marlowe? Mr Kingsley is not in, I'm afraid.'

'I just came from him. Where do we talk?'

'Talk?'

'I have something to show you.'

'Oh, yes?' She looked me over thoughtfully. A lot of guys had probably tried to show her things, including etchings. At another time I wouldn't have been above taking a flutter at it myself.

'Business,' I said. 'Mr Kingsley's business.'

She stood up and opened the gate in the railing. 'We may as well go into his office then.'

We went in. She held the door for me. As I passed her I sniffed. Sandalwood. I said:

'Gillerlain Regal, the Champagne of Perfumes?'

She smiled faintly, holding the door. 'On my salary?'

'I didn't say anything about your salary. You don't look like a girl who has to buy her own perfume.'

'Yes, that's what it is,' she said. 'And if you want to know, I detest wearing perfume in the office. He makes me.'

We went down the long dim office and she took a chair at the end of the desk. I sat where I had sat the day before. We looked at each other. She was wearing tan to-day, with a ruffled jabot at her throat. She looked a little warmer, but still no prairie fire.

I offered her one of Kingsley's cigarettes. She took it, took a light from his lighter, and leaned back.

'We needn't waste time being cagey,' I said. 'You know by now who I am and what I am doing. If you didn't know yesterday morning, it's only because he loves to play big shot.'

She looked down at the hand that lay on her knee, then lifted her eyes and smiled almost shyly.

'He's a great guy,' she said. 'In spite of the heavy executive act he likes to put on. He's the only guy that gets fooled by it after all. And if you only knew what he has stood from that little tramp—' She waved her cigarette. 'Well, perhaps I'd better leave that out. What was it you wanted to see me about?'

'Kingsley said you knew the Almores.'

'I knew Mrs Almore. That is, I met her a couple of times.'

'Where?'

'At a friend's house. Why?'

'At Lavery's house?'

'You're not going to be insolent, are you, Mr Marlowe?'

'I don't know what your definition of that would be. I'm going to talk business as if it was business, not international diplomacy.'

'Very well.' She nodded slightly. 'At Chris Lavery's house, yes. I used to go there—once in a while. He had cocktail parties.'

'Then Lavery knew the Almores—or Mrs Almore.'

She flushed very slightly. 'Yes. Quite well.'

'And a lot of other women—quite well, too. I don't doubt that. Did Mrs Kingsley know her too?'

'Yes, better than I did. They called each other by their first names. Mrs Almore is dead, you know. She committed suicide, about a year and a half ago.'

'Any doubt about that?'

She raised her eyebrows, but the expression looked artificial to me, as if it just went with the question I asked, as a matter of form.

She said: 'Have you any particular reason for asking that question in that particular way? I mean, has it anything to do with—with what you are doing?'

'I didn't think so. I still don't know that it has. But yesterday Dr Almore called a cop just because I looked at his house. After he had found out from my car licence who I was. The cop got pretty tough with me, just for being there. He didn't know what I was doing and I didn't tell him I had been calling on Lavery. But Dr Almore must have known that. He had seen me in front of Lavery's house. Now why would he think it necessary to call a cop? And why would the cop think it smart to say that the last fellow who tried to put the bite on Almore ended up on the road gang? And why would the cop ask me if her folks—meaning Mrs Almore's folks, I suppose—had hired me? If you can answer any of those questions, I might know whether it's any of my business.'

She thought about it for a moment, giving me one quick glance while she was thinking, and then looking away again.

'I only met Mrs Almore twice,' she said slowly. 'But I think I can answer your questions—all of them. The last time I met her was at Lavery's place, as I said, and there were quite a lot of people there. There was a lot of drinking and loud talk. The women were not with their husbands and the men were not with their wives, if any. There was a man there named Brownwell who was very tight. He's in the Navy now, I heard. He was ribbing Mrs Almore about her husband's practice. The idea seemed to be that he was one of those doctors who run around all night with a case of loaded hypodermic needles, keeping the local fast set from having pink elephants for breakfast. Florence Almore said she didn't care how her husband got his money as long as he got plenty of it and she had the spending of it. She was tight too, and not a very nice person sober, I should imagine. One of these slinky glittering females who laugh too much and sprawl all over their chairs, showing a great deal of leg. A very light blonde with high colour and indecently large baby-blue eyes. Well, Brownwell told her not to worry, it would always be a good racket. In and out of the patient's house in fifteen minutes and anywhere from ten to fifty bucks a trip. But one thing bothered him, he said, however a doctor could get hold of so much dope without underworld contacts. He asked Mrs Almore if they had many nice gangsters to dinner at their house. She threw a glass of liquor in his face.'

I grinned, but Miss Fromsett didn't. She crushed her cigarette out in Kingsley's big copper and glass tray and looked at me soberly.

'Fair enough,' I said. 'Who wouldn't, unless he had a large hard fist to throw?'

'Yes. A few weeks later, Florence Almore was found dead in the garage late at night. The door of the garage was shut and the car motor was running.' She stopped and moistened her lips slightly. 'It was Chris Lavery who found her. Coming home at God knows what o'clock in the morning. She was lying on the concrete floor in pyjamas, with her head under a blanket which was also over the exhaust pipe of the car. Dr Almore was out. There was nothing about the affair in the papers, except that she had died suddenly. It was well hushed up.'

She lifted her clasped hands a little and then let them fall slowly into her lap again. I said:

'Was something wrong with it, then?'

'People thought so, but they always do. Some time later I heard what purported to be the lowdown. I meet this man Brownwell on Vine Street and he asked me to have a drink with him. I didn't like him, but I had half an hour to kill. We sat at the back of Levy's bar and he asked me if I remembered the babe who threw the drink in his face. I said I did. The conversation then went something very like this. I remember it very well.

'Brownwell said: "Our pal Chris Lavery is sitting pretty, if he ever runs out of girl friends he can touch for dough."

'I said: "I don't think I understand."

'He said: "Hell, maybe you don't want to. The night the Almore woman died she was over at Lou Condy's place losing her shirt at roulette. She got into a tantrum and said the wheels were crooked and made a scene. Condy practically had to drag her into his office. He got hold of Dr Almore through the Physicians' Exchange and after a while the doc came over. He shot her with one of his busy little needles. Then he went away, leaving Condy to get her home. It seems he had a very urgent case. So Condy took her home and the doc's office nurse showed up, having been called by the doc, and Condy carried her upstairs and the nurse put her to bed. Condy went back to his chips. So she had to be carried to bed and yet the same night she got up and walked down to the family garage and finished herself off with monoxide. What do you think of that?" Brownwell was asking me.

'I said: "I don't know anything about it. How do you?"

'He said: "I know a reporter on the rag they call a newspaper down there. There was no inquest and no autopsy. If any tests were made, nothing was told about them. They don't have a regular coroner down there. The undertakers take turns at being acting coroner, a week at a time. They're pretty well subservient to the political gang naturally. It's easy to fix a thing like that in a small town, if anybody with any pull wants it fixed. And Condy had plenty at that time. He didn't want the publicity of an investigation and neither did the doctor."'

Miss Fromsett stopped talking and waited for me to say something. When I didn't, she went on: 'I suppose you know what all this means to Brownwell?'

'Sure. Almore finished her off and then he and Condy between them bought a fix. It has been done in cleaner little cities than Bay City ever tried to be. But that isn't all the story, is it?'

'No. It seems Mrs Almore's parents hired a private detective. He was a man who ran a night watchman service down there and he was actually the second man on the scene that night, after Chris Brownwell said he must have had something in the way of information, but he never got a chance to use it. They arrested him for drunk driving and he got a jail sentence.'

I said: 'Is that all?'

She nodded. 'And if you think I remember it too well, it's part of my job to remember conversations.'

'What I was thinking was that it doesn't have to add up to very much. I don't see where it has to touch Lavery, even if he was the one who found her. Your gossipy friend Brownwell seems to think what happened gave somebody a chance to blackmail the doctor. But there would have to be some evidence, especially when you're trying to put the bite on a man who has already cleared himself with the law.'

Miss Fromsett said: 'I think so too. And I'd like to think blackmail was one of the nasty little tricks Chris Lavery didn't quite run to. I think that's all I can tell you, Mr Marlowe. And I ought to be outside.'

She started to get up. I said: 'It's not quite all. I have something to show you.'

I got the little perfumed rag that had been under Lavery's pillow out of my pocket and leaned over to drop it on the desk in front of her.

19

She looked at the handkerchief, looked at me, picked up a pencil and pushed the little piece of linen around with the eraser end.

'What's on it?' she asked. 'Flyspray?'

'Some kind of sandalwood, I thought.'

'A cheap synthetic. Repulsive is a mild word for it. And why did you want me to look at this handkerchief, Mr Marlowe?' She leaned back again and stared at me with level cool eyes.

'I found it in Chris Lavery's house, under the pillow on his bed. It has initials on it.'

She unfolded the handkerchief without touching it by using the rubber tip of the pencil. Her face got a little grim and taut.

'It has two letters embroidered on it,' she said in a cold angry voice. 'They happen to be the same letters as my initials. Is that what you mean?'

'Right,' I said. 'He probably knows half a dozen women with the same initials.'

'So you're going to be nasty after all,' she said quietly.

'Is it your handkerchief—or isn't it?'

She hesitated. She reached out to the desk and very quietly got herself another cigarette and lit it with a match. She shook the match slowly, watching the small flame creep along the wood.

'Yes, it's mine,' she said, 'I must have dropped it there. It's a long time ago. And I assure you I didn't put it under a pillow on his bed. Is that what you wanted to know?'

I didn't say anything, and she added: 'He must have lent it to some woman who—who would like this kind of perfume.'

'I get a mental picture of the woman,' I said. 'And she doesn't quite go with Lavery.'

Her upper lip curled a little. It was a long upper lip. I like long upper lips.

'I think,' she said, 'you ought to do a little more work on your mental picture of Chris Lavery. Any touch of refinement you may have noticed is purely coincidental.'

'That's not a nice thing to say about a dead man,' I said.

For a moment she just sat there and looked at me as if I hadn't said anything and she was waiting for me to say something. Then a slow shudder started at her throat and passed over her whole body. Her hands clenched and the cigarette bent into a crook. She looked down at it and threw it into the ash-tray with a quick jerk of her arm.

'He was shot in his shower,' I said. 'And it looks as if it was done by some woman who spent the night there. He had just been shaving. The woman left a gun on the stairs and this handkerchief on the bed.'

She moved very slightly in her chair. Her eyes were perfectly empty now. Her face was as cold as a carving.

'And did you expect me to be able to give you information about that?' she asked me bitterly.

'Look, Miss Fromsett, I'd like to be smooth and distant and subtle about all this too. I'd like to play this sort of game just once the way somebody like you would like it to be played. But nobody will let me—not the clients, nor the cops, nor the people I play against. However hard I try to be nice I always end up with my nose in the dirt and my thumb feeling for somebody's eye.'

She nodded as if she had only barely heard me. 'When was he shot?' she asked, and then shuddered slightly again.

'This morning, I suppose. Not long after he got up. I said he had just shaved and was going to take a shower.'

'That,' she said, 'would probably have been quite late. I've been here since eight-thirty.'

'I didn't think you shot him.'

'Awfully kind of you,' she said. 'But it is my handkerchief, isn't it? Although not my perfume. But I don't suppose policemen are very sensitive to quality in perfume—or in anything else.'

'No—and that goes for private detectives too,' I said. 'Are you enjoying this a lot?'

'God,' she said, and put the back of her hand hard against her mouth.

'He was shot at five or six times,' I said. 'And missed all but twice. He was cornered in the shower-stall. It was a pretty grim scene, I should think. There was a lot of hate on one side of it. Or a pretty cold-blooded mind.'

'He was quite easy to hate,' she said emptily. 'And poisonously easy to love. Women—even decent women—make such ghastly mistakes about men.'

'All you're telling me is that you once thought you loved him, but not any more, and that you didn't shoot him.'

'Yes.' Her voice was light and dry now, like the perfume she didn't like to wear at the office. 'I'm sure you'll respect the confidence.' She laughed shortly and bitterly. 'Dead,' she said. 'The poor, egotistical, cheap, nasty, handsome, treacherous guy. Dead and cold and done with. No, Mr Marlowe, I didn't shoot him.'

I waited, letting her work it out of her. After a moment she said quietly: 'Does Mr Kingsley know?'

I nodded.

'And the police, of course.'

'Not yet. At least not from me. I found him. The house door wasn't quite shut. I went in. I found him.'

She picked the pencil up and poked at the handkerchief again. 'Does Mr Kingsley know about this scented rag?'

'Nobody knows about that, except you and me, and whoever put it there.'

'Nice of you,' she said dryly. 'And nice of you to think what you thought.'

'You have a certain quality of aloofness and dignity that I like,' I said. 'But don't run it into the ground. What would you expect me to think? Do I pull the hankie out from under the pillow and sniff it and hold it out and say, "Well, well, Miss Adrienne Fromsett's initials and all. Miss Fromsett must have known Lavery, perhaps very intimately. Let's say, just for the book, as intimately as my nasty little mind can conceive. And that would be pretty damn intimately. But this is cheap synthetic sandalwood and Miss Fromsett wouldn't use cheap scent. And this was under Lavery's pillow and Miss Fromsett just never keeps her hankies under a man's pillow. Therefore this has absolutely nothing to do with Miss Fromsett. It's just an optical delusion.'

'Oh, shut up,' she said.

I grinned.

'What kind of girl do you think I am?' she snapped.

'I came in too late to tell you.'

She flushed, but delicately and all over her face this time. Then, 'Have you any idea who did it?'

'Ideas, but that's all they are. I'm afraid the police are going to find it simple. Some of Mrs Kingsley's clothes are hanging in Lavery's closet. And when they know the whole story—including what happened at Little Fawn Lake yesterday—I'm afraid they'll just reach for the handcuffs. They have to find her first. But that won't be so hard for them.'

'Crystal Kingsley,' she said emptily. 'So he couldn't be spared even that.'

I said: 'It doesn't have to be. It could be an entirely different motivation, something we know nothing about. It could have been somebody like Dr Almore.'

She looked up quickly, then shook her head. 'It could be,' I insisted. 'We don't know anything against it. He was pretty nervous yesterday, for a man who has nothing to be afraid of. But, of course, it isn't only the guilty who are afraid.'

I stood up and tapped on the edge of the desk looking down at her. She had a lovely neck. She pointed to the handkerchief.

'What about that?' she asked dully.

'If it was mine, I'd wash that cheap scent out of it.'

'It has to mean something, doesn't it? It might mean a lot.'

I laughed. 'I don't think it means anything at all. Women are always leaving their handkerchiefs around. A fellow like Lavery would collect them and keep them in a drawer with a sandalwood sachet. Somebody would find the stock and take one out to use. Or he would lend them, enjoying the reactions to the other girl's initials. I'd say he was that kind of a heel. Goodbye, Miss Fromsett, and thanks for talking to me.'

I started to go, then I stopped and asked her: 'Did you hear the name of the reporter down there who gave Brownwell all his information?'

She shook her head.

'Or the name of Mrs Almore's parents?'

'Not that either. But I could probably find that out for you. I'd be glad to try.'

'How?'

'Those things are usually printed in death notices, aren't they? There is pretty sure to have been a death notice in the Los Angeles papers.'

'That would be very nice of you,' I said. I ran a finger along the edge of the desk and looked at her sideways. Pale ivory skin, dark and lovely eyes, hair as light as hair can be and eyes as dark as night can be.

I walked back down the room and out. The little blonde at the PBX looked at me expectantly, her small red lips parted, waiting for more fun.

I didn't have any more. I went out.

20

No police cars stood in front of Lavery's house, nobody hung around on the sidewalk and when I pushed the front door open there was no smell of cigar or cigarette smoke inside. The sun had gone away from the windows and a fly buzzed softly over one of the liquor glasses. I went down to the end and hung over the railing that led downstairs. Nothing moved in Mr Lavery's house. Nothing made sound except very faintly down below in the bathroom the quiet trickle of water dripping on a dead man's shoulder.

I went to the telephone and looked up the number of the police department in the directory. I dialled and while I was waiting for an answer, I took the little automatic out of my pocket and laid it on the table beside the telephone.

When the male voice said: 'Bay City police—Smoot talking,' I said: 'There's been a shooting at 623 Altair Street. Man named Lavery lives there. He's dead.'

'Six-two-three Altair. Who are you?'

'The name is Marlowe.'

'You there in the house?'

'Right.'

'Don't touch anything at all.'

I hung up, sat down on the davenport and waited.

Not very long. A siren whined far off, growing louder with great surges of sound. Tyres screamed at a corner, and the siren wail died to a metallic growl, then the silence, and the tyres screamed again in front of the house. The Bay City police conserving rubber. Steps hit the sidewalk and I went over to the front door and opened it.

Two uniformed cops barged into the room. They were the usual large size and they had the usual weathered faces and suspicious eyes. One of them had a carnation tucked under his cap, behind his right ear. The other one was older, a little grey and grim. They stood and looked at me warily, then the older one said briefly:

'All right, where is it?'

'Downstairs in the bathroom, behind the shower curtain.'

'You stay here with him, Eddie.'

He went rapidly along the room and disappeared. The other one looked at me steadily and said out of the corner of his mouth:

'Don't make any false moves, buddy.'

I sat down on the davenport again. The cop ranged the room with his eyes. There were sounds below stairs, feet walking. The cop with me suddenly spotted the gun lying on the telephone table. He charged at it violently, like a downfield blocker.

'This the death gun?' he almost shouted.

'I should imagine so. It's been fired.'

'Ha!' He leaned over the gun, baring his teeth at me, and put his hand to his holster. His finger tickled the flap off the stud and he grasped the butt of the black revolver.

'You should what?' he barked.

'I should imagine so.'

'That's very good,' he sneered. 'That's very good indeed.'

'It's not that good,' I said.

He reeled back a little. His eyes were being careful of me. 'What you shoot him for?' he growled.

'I've wondered and wondered.'

'Oh, a wisenheimer.'

'Let's just sit down and wait for the homicide boys,' I said. 'I'm reserving my defence.'

'Don't give me none of that,' he said.

'I'm not giving you any of anything. If I had shot him, I wouldn't be here. I wouldn't have called up. You wouldn't have found the gun. Don't work so hard on the case. You won't be on it more than ten minutes.'

His eyes looked hurt. He took his cap off and the carnation dropped to the floor. He bent and picked it up and twirled it between his fingers, then dropped it behind the fire screen.

'Better not do that,' I told him. 'They might think it's a clue and waste a lot of time on it.'

'Aw hell.' He bent over the screen and retrieved the carnation and put it in his pocket. 'You know all the answers, don't you, buddy?'

The other cop came back up the stairs, looking grave. He stood in the middle of the floor and looked at his wristwatch and made a note in a notebook and then looked out of the front windows, holding the venetian blinds to one side to do it.

The one who had stayed with me said: 'Can I look now?'

'Let it lie, Eddie. Nothing in it for us. You call the coroner?'

'I thought Homicide would do that.'

'Yeah, that's right. Captain Webber will be on it and he likes to do everything himself.' He looked at me and said: 'You're a man named Marlowe?'

I said I was a man named Marlowe.

'He's a wise guy, knows all the answers,' Eddie said.

The older one looked at me absently, looked at Eddie absently, spotted the gun lying on the telephone table and looked at that not at all absently.

'Yeah, that's the death gun,' Eddie said. 'I ain't touched it.'

The other nodded. 'The boys are not so fast to-day. What's your line, mister? Friend of his?' He made a thumb towards the floor.

'Saw him yesterday for the first time. I'm a private operative from L.A.'

'Oh.' He looked at me very sharply. The other cop looked at me with deep suspicion.

'Cripes, that means everything will be all balled up,' he said.

That was the first sensible remark he had made. I grinned at him affectionately.

The older cop looked out of the front window again. 'That's the Almore place across the street, Eddie,' he said.

Eddie went and looked with him. 'Sure is,' he said. 'You can read the plate. Say, this guy downstairs might be the guy—'

'Shut up,' the other one said and dropped the venetian blind. They both turned around and stared at me woodenly.

A car came down the block and stopped and a door slammed and more steps came down the walk. The older of the prowl-car boys opened the door to two men in plain clothes, one of whom I already knew.

21

The one who came first was a small man for a cop, middle-aged, thin-faced, with a permanently tired expression. His nose was sharp and bent a little to one side, as if somebody had given it the elbow one time when it was into something. His blue pork-pie hat was set very square on his head and chalk-white hair showed under it. He wore a dull brown suit and his hands were in the side pockets of the jacket, with the thumbs outside the seam.

The man behind him was Degarmo, the big cop with the dusty blond hair and the metallic blue eyes and the savage, lined face who had not liked my being in front of Dr Almore's house.

The two uniformed men looked at the small man and touched their caps.

'The body's in the basement, Captain Webber. Been shot twice after a couple of misses, looks like. Dead quite some time. This party's name is

Marlowe. He's a private eye from Los Angeles. I didn't question him beyond that.'

'Quite right,' Webber said sharply. He had a suspicious voice. He passed a suspicious eye over my face and nodded briefly. 'I'm Captain Webber,' he said. 'This is Lieutenant Degarmo. We'll look at the body first.'

He went along the room. Degarmo looked at me as if he had never seen me before and followed him. They went downstairs, the older of the two prowl men with them. The cop called Eddie and I stared each other down for a while.

I said: 'This is right across the street from Dr Almore's place, isn't it?'

All the expression went out of his face. There hadn't been much to go. 'Yeah. So what?'

'So nothing,' I said.

He was silent. The voices came up from below, blurred and indistinct. The cop cocked his ear and said in a more friendly tone: 'You remember that one?'

'A little.'

He laughed. 'They killed that one pretty,' he said. 'They wrapped it up and hid it in back of the shelf. The top shelf in the bathroom closet. The one you can't reach without standing on a chair.'

'So they did,' I said. 'I wonder why.'

The cop looked at me sternly. 'There was good reasons, pal. Don't think there wasn't. You know this Lavery well?'

'Not well.'

'On to him for something?'

'Working on him a little,' I said. 'You knew him?'

The cop called Eddie shook his head. 'Nope, I just remembered it was a guy from this house found Almore's wife in the garage that night.'

'Lavery may not have been here then,' I said.

'How long's he been here?'

'I don't know,' I said.

'Would be about a year and a half,' the cop said, musingly. 'The L.A. papers give it any play?'

'Paragraph on the Home Counties page,' I said, just to be moving my mouth.

He scratched his ear and listened. Steps were coming back up the stairs. The cop's face went blank and he moved away from me and straightened up.

Captain Webber hurried over to the telephone and dialled the number and spoke, then held the phone away from his ear and looked back over his shoulder.

'Who's deputy coroner this week, Al?'

'Ed Garland,' the big lieutenant said woodenly.

'Call Ed Garland,' Webber said into the phone. 'Have him come over right away. And tell the flash squad to step on it.'

He put the phone down and barked sharply: 'Who handled this gun?'

I said: 'I did.'

He came over and teetered on his heels in front of me and pushed his small sharp chin up at me. He held the gun delicately on a handkerchief in his hand.

'Don't you know enough not to handle a weapon found at the scene of a crime?'

'Certainly,' I said. 'But when I handled it I didn't know there had been a crime. I didn't know the gun had been fired. It was lying on the stairs and I thought it had been dropped.'

'A likely story,' Webber said bitterly. 'You get a lot of that sort of thing in your business?'

'A lot of what sort of thing?'

He kept his hard stare on me and didn't answer.

I said: 'How would it be for me to tell you my story as it happened?'

He bridled at me like a cockerel. 'Suppose you answer my questions exactly as I choose to put them.'

I didn't say anything to that. Webber swivelled sharply and said to the two uniformed men: 'You boys can get back to your car and check in with the despatcher.'

They saluted and went out, closing the door softly until it stuck, then getting as mad at it as anybody else. Webber listened until their car went away. Then he put the bleak and callous eye on me once more.

'Let me see your identification.'

I handed him my wallet and he rooted in it. Degarmo sat in a chair and crossed his legs and stared up blankly at the ceiling. He got a match out of his pocket and chewed the end of it. Webber gave me back my wallet. I put it away.

'People in your line make a lot of trouble,' he said.

'Not necessarily,' I said.

He raised his voice. It had been sharp enough before. 'I said they make a lot of trouble, and a lot of trouble is what I meant. But get this straight. You're not going to make any in Bay City.'

I didn't answer him. He jabbed a forefinger at me.

'You're from the big town,' he said. 'You think you're tough and you think you're wise. Don't worry. We can handle you. We're a small place, but we're very compact. We don't have any political tug-of-war down here. We work on the straight line and we work fast. Don't worry about us, mister.'

'I'm not worrying,' I said. 'I don't have anything to worry about. I'm just trying to make a nice clean dollar.'

'And don't give me any of the flip talk,' Webber said. 'I don't like it.'

Degarmo brought his eyes down from the ceiling and curled a forefinger to stare at the nail. He spoke in a heavy bored voice.

'Look, chief, the fellow downstairs is called Lavery. He's dead. I knew him a little. He was a chaser.'

'What of it?' Webber snapped, not looking away from me.

'The whole set-up indicates a dame,' Degarmo said. 'You know what these private eyes work at. Divorce stuff. Suppose we'd let him tie into it, instead of just trying to scare him dumb.'

'If I'm scaring him,' Webber said, 'I'd like to know it. I don't see any signs of it.'

He walked over to the front window and yanked the venetian blind up. Light poured into the room almost dazzlingly, after the long dimness. He came back bouncing on his heels and poked a thin hard finger at me and said:

'Talk.'

I said, 'I'm working for a Los Angeles business man who can't take a lot of loud publicity. That's why he hired me. A month ago his wife ran off and later a telegram came which indicated she had gone with Lavery. But my client met Lavery in town a couple of days ago and he denied it. The client believed him enough to get worried. It seems the lady is pretty reckless. She might have taken up with some bad company and got into a jam. I came down to see Lavery and he denied to me that he had gone with her. I half believed him but later I got reasonable proof that he had been with her in a San Bernardino hotel the night she was believed to have left the mountain cabin where she had been staying. With that in my pocket I came down to tackle Lavery again. No answer to the bell, the door was slightly open. I came inside, looked around, found the gun and searched the house. I found him. Just the way he is now.'

'You had no right to search the house,' Webber said coldly.

'Of course not,' I agreed. 'But I wouldn't be likely to pass up the chance either.'

'The name of this man you're working for?'

'Kingsley.' I gave him the Beverly Hills address. 'He manages a cosmetic company in the Treloar Building on Olive. The Gillerlain Company.'

Webber looked at Degarmo. Degarmo wrote lazily on an envelope. Webber looked back at me and said: 'What else?'

'I went up to this mountain cabin where the lady had been staying. It's at a place called Little Fawn Lake, near Puma Point, forty-six miles into the mountains from San Bernardino.'

I looked at Degarmo. He was writing slowly. His hand stopped a moment and seemed to hang in the air stiffly, then it dropped to the envelope and wrote again. I went on:

'About a month ago the wife of the caretaker at Kingsley's place up there had a fight with him and left, as everybody thought. Yesterday she was found drowned in the lake.'

Webber almost closed his eyes and rocked on his heels. Almost softly he asked: 'Why are you telling me this? Are you implying a connexion?'

'There's a connexion in time. Lavery had been up there. I don't know of any other connexion, but I thought I'd better mention it.'

Degarmo was sitting very still, looking at the floor in front of him. His face was tight and he looked even more savage than usual. Webber said:

'This woman that was drowned? Suicide?'

'Suicide or murder. She left a good-bye note. But her husband has been arrested on suspicion. The name is Chess. Bill and Muriel Chess, his wife.'

'I don't want any part of that,' Webber said sharply. 'Let's confine ourselves to what went on here.'

'Nothing went on here,' I said, looking at Degarmo. 'I've been down here twice. The first time I talked to Lavery and didn't get anywhere. The second time I didn't talk to him and didn't get anywhere.'

Webber said slowly: 'I'm going to ask you a question and I want an honest answer. You won't want to give it, but now will be as good a time as later. You know I'll get it eventually. The question is this. You have looked through the house and I imagine pretty thoroughly. Have you seen anything that suggests to you that this Kingsley woman has been here?'

'That's not a fair question,' I said. 'It calls for a conclusion of the witness.'

'I want an answer to it,' he said grimly. 'This isn't a court of law.'

'The answer is yes,' I said. 'There are women's clothes hanging in a closet downstairs that have been described to me as being worn by Mrs Kingsley at San Bernardino the night she met Lavery there. The description was not exact though. A black and white suit, mostly white, and a panama hat with a rolled black and white band.'

Degarmo snapped a finger against the envelope he was holding. 'You must be a great guy for a client to have working for him,' he said. 'That puts the woman right in this house where a murder has been committed and she is the woman he's supposed to have gone away with. I don't think we'll have to look far for the killer, chief.'

Webber was staring at me fixedly, with little or no expression on his face but a kind of tight watchfulness. He nodded absently to what Degarmo had said.

I said: 'I'm assuming you fellows are not a pack of damn fools. The clothes are tailored and easy to trace. I've saved you an hour by telling you, perhaps even no more than a phone call.'

'Anything else?' Webber asked quietly.

Before I could answer, a car stopped outside the house, and then another. Webber skipped over to open the door. Three men came in, a short, curly-haired man and a large ox-like man, both carrying heavy black leather cases. Behind them a tall thin man in a dark-grey suit and black tie. He had very bright eyes and a poker face.

Webber pointed a finger at the curly-haired man and said: 'Downstairs in the bathroom, Busoni. I want a lot of prints from all over the house, particularly any that seem to be made by a woman. It will be a long job.'

'I do all the work,' Busoni grunted. He and the ox-like man went along the room and down the stairs.

'We have a corpse for you, Garland,' Webber said to the third man. 'Let's go down and look at him. You've ordered the wagon?'

The bright-eyed man nodded briefly and he and Webber went downstairs after the other two.

Degarmo put the envelope and pencil away. He stared at me woodenly.

I said: 'Am I supposed to talk about our conversation yesterday—or is that a private transaction?'

'Talk about it all you like,' he said. 'It's our job to protect the citizen.'

'You talk about it,' I said. 'I'd like to know more about the Almore case.'

He flushed slowly and his eyes got mean. 'You said you didn't know Almore.'

'I didn't yesterday, or know anything about him. Since then I've learned that Lavery knew Mrs Almore, that she committed suicide, that Lavery found her dead, and that Lavery has at least been suspected of blackmailing him—or of being in a position to blackmail him. Also both your prowl-car boys seemed interested in the fact that Almore's house was across the street from here. And one of them remarked that the case had been killed pretty, or words to that effect.'

Degarmo said in a slow deadly tone: 'I'll have the badge off the son of a bitch. All they do is flap their mouths. God damn empty-headed bastards.'

'Then there's nothing in it,' I said.

He looked at his cigarette. 'Nothing in what?'

'Nothing in the idea that Almore murdered his wife, and had enough pull to get it fixed.'

Degarmo came to his feet and walked over to lean down at me. 'Say that again,' he said softly.

I said it again.

He hit me across the face with his open hand. It jerked my head around hard. My face felt hot and large.

'Say it again,' he said softly.

I said it again. His hand swept and knocked my head to one side again.

'Say it again.'

'Nope. Third time lucky. You might miss.' I put a hand up and rubbed my cheek.

He stood leaning down, his lips drawn back over his teeth, a hard animal glare in his very blue eyes.

'Any time you talk like that to a cop,' he said, 'you know what you got coming. Try it on again and it won't be the flat of a hand I'll use on you.'

I bit hard on my lips and rubbed my cheek.

'Poke your big nose into our business and you'll wake up in an alley with the cats looking at you,' he said.

I didn't say anything. He went and sat down again, breathing hard. I stopped rubbing my face and held my hand out and worked the fingers slowly, to get the hard clench out of them.

'I'll remember that,' I said. 'Both ways.'

22

It was early evening when I got back to Hollywood and up to the office. The building had emptied out and the corridors were silent. Doors were open and the cleaning women were inside with their vacuum cleaners and their dry mops and dusters.

I unlocked the door to mine and picked up an envelope that lay in front of the mail slot and dropped it on the desk without looking at it. I ran the windows up and leaned out, looking at the early neon lights glowing, smelling the warm, foody air that drifted up from the alley ventilator of the coffee shop next door.

I peeled off my coat and tie and sat down at the desk and got the office bottle out of the deep drawer and bought myself a drink. It didn't do any good. I had another, with the same result.

By now Webber would have seen Kingsley. There would be a general alarm out for his wife, already, or very soon. The thing looked cut and dried to them. A nasty affair between two rather nasty people, too much loving, too much drinking, too much proximity ending in a savage hatred and a murderous impulse and death.

I thought this was all a little too simple.

I reached for the envelope and tore it open. It had no stamp. It read: 'Mr Marlowe: Florence Almore's parents are a Mr and Mrs Eustace Grayson, at present residing at the Rossmore Arms, 640 South Oxford Avenue. I checked this by calling the listed phone number. Yrs ADRIENNE FROMSETT.'

An elegant handwriting, like the elegant hand that wrote it. I pushed it to one side and had another drink. I began to feel a little less savage. I pushed things around on the desk. My hands felt thick and hot and awkward. I ran a finger across the corner of the desk and looked at the streak made by the wiping off of the dust. I looked at the dust on my finger and wiped that off. I looked at my watch. I looked at the wall. I looked at nothing.

I put the liquor bottle away and went over to the washbowl to rinse the glass out. When I had done that I washed my hands and bathed my face in cold water and looked at it. The flush was gone from the left cheek, but it looked a little swollen. Not very much, but enough to make me tighten up again. I brushed my hair and looked at the grey in it. There was getting to be plenty of grey in it. The face under the hair had a sick look. I didn't like the face at all.

I went back to the desk and read Miss Fromsett's note again. I smoothed it out on the glass and sniffed it and smoothed it out some more and folded it and put it in my coat pocket.

I sat very still and listened to the evening grow quiet outside the open windows. And very slowly I grew quiet with it.

23

The Rossmore Arms was a gloomy pile of dark red brick built around a huge forecourt. It had a plush-lined lobby containing silence, tubbed plants, a bored canary in a cage as big as a dog-house, a smell of old carpet dust and the cloying fragrance of gardenias long ago.

The Graysons were on the fifth floor in front, in the north wing. They were sitting together in a room which seemed to be deliberately twenty years out of date. It had fat overstuffed furniture and brass doorknobs, shaped like eggs, a huge wall mirror in a gilt frame, a marble-topped table in the window and dark red plush side drapes by the windows. It smelled of tobacco smoke and behind that the air was telling me they had had lamb chops and broccoli for dinner.

Grayson's wife was a plump woman who might once have had big baby-blue eyes. They were faded out now and dimmed by glasses and slightly protuberant. She had kinky white hair. She sat darning socks with her thick ankles crossed, her feet just reaching the floor, and a big wicker sewing basket in her lap.

Grayson was a long, stooped, yellow-faced man with high shoulders, bristly eyebrows and almost no chin. The upper part of his face meant business. The lower part was just saying good-bye. He wore bifocals and he had been gnawing fretfully at the evening paper. I had looked him up in the city directory. He was a C.P.A. and looked it every inch. He even had ink on his fingers and there were four pencils in the pocket of his open vest.

He read my card carefully for the seventh time and looked me up and down and said slowly:

'What is it you want to see us about, Mr Marlowe?'

'I'm interested in a man named Lavery. He lives across the street from Dr Almore. Your daughter was the wife of Dr Almore. Lavery is the man who found your daughter the night she—died.'

They both pointed like bird dogs when I deliberately hesitated on the last word. Grayson looked at his wife and she shook her head.

'We don't care to talk about that,' Grayson said promptly. 'It is much too painful to us.'

I waited a moment and looked gloomy with them. Then I said: 'I don't blame you. I don't want to make you. I'd like to get in touch with the man you hired to look into it, though.'

They looked at each other again. Mrs Grayson didn't shake her head this time.

Grayson asked: 'Why?'

'I'd better tell you a little of my story.' I told them what I had been hired to do, not mentioning Kingsley by name. I told them the incident with Degarmo outside Almore's house the day before. They pointed again on that.

Grayson said sharply: 'Am I to understand that you were unknown to Dr Almore, had not approached him in any way, and that he nevertheless called a police officer because you were outside his house?'

I said: 'That's right. Had been outside for at least an hour though. That is, my car had.'

'That's very queer,' Grayson said.

'I'd say that was one very nervous man,' I said. 'And Degarmo asked me if her folks—meaning your daughter's folks—had hired me. Looks as if he didn't feel safe yet, wouldn't you say?'

'Safe about what?' He didn't look at me saying this. He re-lit his pipe, slowly, then tamped the tobacco down with the end of a big metal pencil and lit it again.

I shrugged and didn't answer. He looked at me quickly and looked away. Mrs Grayson didn't look at me, but her nostrils quivered.

'How did he know who you were?' Grayson asked suddenly.

'Made a note of the car licence, called the Auto Club, looked up the name in the directory. At least that's what I'd have done and I saw him through his window making some of the motions.'

'So he has the police working for him,' Grayson said.

'Not necessarily. If they made a mistake that time, they wouldn't want it found out now.'

'Mistake!' He laughed almost shrilly.

'Okay,' I said. 'The subject is painful but a little fresh air won't hurt it. You've always thought he murdered her, haven't you? That's why you hired this dick—detective.'

Mrs Grayson looked up with quick eyes and ducked her head down and rolled up another pair of mended socks.

Grayson said nothing.

I said: 'Was there any evidence, or was it just that you didn't like him?'

'There was evidence,' Grayson said bitterly, and with a sudden clearness of voice, as if he had decided to talk about it after all. 'There must have been. We were told there was. But we never got it. The police took care of that.'

'I heard they had this fellow arrested and sent up for drunk driving.'

'You heard right.'

'But he never told you what he had to go on?'

'No.'

'I don't like that,' I said. 'That sounds a little as if this fellow hadn't made up his mind whether to use his information for your benefit or keep it and put a squeeze on the doctor.'

Grayson looked at his wife again. She said quietly: 'Mr Talley didn't impress me that way. He was a quiet unassuming little man. But you can't always judge, I know.'

I said: 'So Talley was his name. That was one of the things I hoped you would tell me.'

'And what were the others?' Grayson asked.

'How can I find Talley—and what it was that laid the groundwork of suspicion in your minds. It must have been there, or you wouldn't have hired Talley without a better showing from him that *he* had grounds.'

Grayson smiled very thinly and primly. He reached for his little chin and rubbed it with one long yellow finger.

Mrs Grayson said: 'Dope.'

'She means that literally,' Grayson said at once, as if the single word had been a green light. 'Almore was, and no doubt is, a dope doctor. Our daughter made that clear to us. In his hearing too. He didn't like it.'

'Just what do you mean by a dope doctor, Mr Grayson?'

'I mean a doctor whose practice is largely with people who are living on the raw edge of nervous collapse, from drink and dissipation. People who have to be given sedatives and narcotics all the time. The stage comes when an ethical physician refuses to treat them any more, outside a sanatorium. But not the Dr Almores. *They* will keep on as long as the money comes in, as long as the patient remains alive and reasonably sane, even if he or she becomes a hopeless addict in the process. A lucrative practice,' he said primly, 'and I imagine a dangerous one to the doctor.'

'No doubt of that,' I said. 'But there's a lot of money in it. Do you know a man named Condy?'

'No. We know who he was. Florence suspected he was a source of Almore's narcotic supply.'

I said: 'Could be. He probably wouldn't want to write himself too many prescriptions. Did you know Lavery?'

'We never saw him. We knew who he was.'

'Ever occur to you that Lavery might have been blackmailing Almore?'

It was a new idea to him. He ran his hand over the top of his head and brought it down over his face and dropped it to his bony knee. He shook his head.

'No. Why should it?'

'He was first to the body,' I said. 'Whatever looked wrong to Talley must have been equally visible to Lavery.'

'Is Lavery that kind of man?'

'I don't know. He has no visible means of support, no job. He gets around a lot, especially with women.'

'It's an idea,' Grayson said. 'And those things can be handled very discreetly.' He smiled wryly. 'I have come across traces of them in my work. Unsecured loans, long outstanding. Investments on the face of them worthless made by men who would not be likely to make worthless investments. Bad debts that should obviously be charged off and have not been, for fear of inviting scrutiny from the income-tax people. Oh yes, those things can easily be arranged.'

I looked at Mrs Grayson. Her hands had never stopped working. She had a dozen pairs of darned socks finished. Grayson's long bony feet would be hard on socks.

'What's happened to Talley? Was he framed?'

'I dont think there's any doubt about it. His wife was very bitter. She said he had been given a doped drink in a bar and he had been drinking with a policeman. She said a police car was waiting across the street for him to start driving and that he was picked up at once. Also that he was given only the most perfunctory examination at the jail.'

'That doesn't mean too much. That's what he told her after he was arrested. He'd tell her something like that automatically.'

'Well, I hate to think the police are not honest,' Grayson said. 'But these things are done, and everybody knows it.'

I said: 'If they made an honest mistake about your daughter's death, they would hate to have Talley show them up. It might mean several lost jobs. If they thought what he was really after was blackmail, they wouldn't be too fussy about how they took care of him. Where is Talley now? What it all boils down to is that if there was any solid clue, he either had it or was on the track of it and knew what he was looking for.'

Grayson said: 'We don't know where he is. He got six months, but that expired long ago.'

'How about his wife?'

He looked at his own wife. She said briefly: '1618½ Westmore Street, Bay City. Eustace and I sent her a little money. She was badly off.'

I made a note of the address and leaned back in my chair and said:

'Somebody shot Lavery this morning in his bathroom.'

Mrs Grayson's pudgy hands became still on the edges of the basket. Grayson sat with his mouth open, holding his pipe in front of it. He made a noise of clearing his throat softly, as if in the presence of the dead. Nothing ever moved slower than his old black pipe going back between his teeth.

'Of course it would be too much to expect,' he said and let it hang in the air and blew a little pale smoke at it, and then added, 'that Dr Almore had any connexion with that.'

'I'd like to think he had,' I said. 'He certainly lives at a handy distance. The police think my client's wife shot him. They have a good case too, when they find her. But if Almore had anything to do with it, it must surely arise out of your daughter's death. That's why I'm trying to find out something about that.'

Grayson said: 'A man who has done one murder wouldn't have more than twenty-five per cent of the hesitation in doing another.' He spoke as if he had given the matter considerable study.

I said: 'Yeah, maybe. What was supposed to be the motive for the first one?'

'Florence was wild,' he said sadly. 'A wild and difficult girl. She was wasteful and extravagant, always picking up new and rather doubtful friends, talking too much and too loudly, and generally acting the fool. A wife like that can be very dangerous to a man like Albert S. Almore. But I don't believe that was the prime motive, was it, Lettie?'

He looked at his wife, but she didn't look at him. She jabbed a darning-needle into a round ball of wool and said nothing.

Grayson sighed and went on: 'We had reason to believe he was carrying on with his office nurse and that Florence had threatened him with a public scandal. He couldn't have anything like that, could he? One kind of scandal might too easily lead to another.'

I said: 'How did he do the murder?'

'With morphine, of course. He always had it, he always used it. He was an expert in the use of it. Then when she was in a deep coma he would have placed her in the garage and started the car motor. There was no autopsy, you know. But if there had been, it was known that she had been given a hypodermic injection that night.'

I nodded and he leaned back satisfied and ran his hand over his head and down his face and let it fall slowly to his bony knee. He seemed to have given a lot of study to this angle too.

I looked at them. A couple of elderly people sitting there quietly, poisoning their minds with hate, a year and a half after it had happened. They would like it if Almore had shot Lavery. They would love it. It would warm them clear down to their ankles.

After a pause I said: 'You're believing a lot of this because you want to. It's always possible that she committed suicide, and that the cover-up was partly to protect Condy's gambling club and partly to prevent Almore having to be questioned at a public hearing.'

'Rubbish,' Grayson said sharply. 'He murdered her all right. She was in bed, asleep.'

'You don't know that. She might have been taking dope herself. She might have established a tolerance for it. The effect wouldn't last long in that case. She might have got up in the middle of the night and looked at herself in the glass and seen devils pointing at her. These things happen.'

'I think you have taken up enough of our time,' Grayson said.

I stood up. I thanked them both and made a yard towards the door and said: 'You didn't do anything more about it after Talley was arrested?'

'Saw an assistant district attorney named Leach,' Grayson grunted. 'Got exactly nowhere. He saw nothing to justify his office in interfering. Wasn't even interested in the narcotic angle. But Condy's place was closed up about a month later. That might have come out of it somehow.'

'That was probably the Bay City cops throwing a little smoke. You'd find Condy somewhere else, if you knew where to look. With all his original equipment intact.'

I started for the door again and Grayson hoisted himself out of his chair and dragged across the room after me. There was a flush on his yellow face.

'I didn't mean to be rude,' he said. 'I guess Lettie and I oughtn't to brood about this business the way we do.'

'I think you've both been very patient,' I said. 'Was there anybody else involved in all this that we haven't mentioned by name?'

He shook his head, then looked back at his wife. Her hands were motionless holding the current sock on the darning-egg. Her head was tilted a little to one side. Her attitude was of listening, but not to us.

I said: 'The way I got the story, Dr Almore's office nurse put Mrs Almore to bed that night. Would that be the one he was supposed to be playing around with?'

Mrs Grayson said sharply: 'Wait a minute. We never saw the girl. But she had a pretty name. Just give me a minute.'

We gave her a minute. 'Mildred something,' she said, and snapped her teeth.

I took a deep breath. 'Would it be Mildred Haviland, Mrs Grayson?'

She smiled brightly and nodded. 'Of course, Mildred Haviland. Don't you remember, Eustace?'

He didn't remember. He looked at us like a horse that has got into the wrong stable. He opened the door and said: 'What does it matter?'

'And you said Talley was a small man,' I bored on. 'He wouldn't for instance be a big loud bruiser with an overbearing manner?'

'Oh no,' Mrs Grayson said. 'Mr Talley is a man of not more than medium height, middle-aged, with brownish hair and a very quiet voice. He had a sort of worried expression. I mean, he looked as if he always had it.'

'Looks as if he needed it,' I said.

Grayson put his bony hand out and I shook it. It felt like shaking hands with a towel-rack.

'If you get him,' he said and clamped his mouth hard on his pipe stem, 'call back with a bill. If you get Almore, I mean, of course.'

I said I knew he meant Almore, but that there wouldn't be any bill.

I went back along the silent hallway. The self-operating elevator was carpeted in red plush. It had an elderly perfume in it, like three widows drinking tea.

24

The house on Westmore Street was a small frame bungalow behind a larger house. There was no number visible on the smaller house, but the one in front showed a stencilled 1618 beside the door, with a dim light behind the stencil. A narrow concrete path led along under windows to the house at the back. It had a tiny porch with a single chair on it. I stepped up on the porch and rang the bell.

It buzzed not very far off. The front door was open behind the screen but there was no light. From the darkness a querulous voice said:

'What is it?'

I spoke into the darkness. 'Mr Talley in?'

The voice became flat and without tone. 'Who wants him?'

'A friend.'

The woman sitting inside in the darkness made a vague sound in her throat which might have been amusement. Or she might just have been clearing her throat.

'All right,' she said. 'How much is this one?'

'It's not a bill, Mrs Talley. I suppose you are Mrs Talley?'

'Oh, go away and let me alone,' the voice said. 'Mr Talley isn't here. He hasn't been here. He won't be here.'

I put my nose against the screen and tried to peer into the room. I could see the vague outlines of its furniture. From where the voice came from also showed the shape of a couch. A woman was lying on it. She seemed to be lying on her back and looking up at the ceiling. She was quite motionless.

'I'm sick,' the voice said. 'I've had enough trouble. Go away and leave me be.'

I said: 'I've just come from talking to the Graysons.'

There was a little silence, but no movement, then a sigh. 'I never heard of them.'

I leaned against the frame of the screen door and looked back along the narrow walk to the street. There was a car across the way with parking lights burning. There were other cars along the block.

I said: 'Yes, you have, Mrs Talley. I'm working for them. They're still in there pitching. How about you? Don't you want something back?'

The voice said: 'I want to be let alone.'

'I want information,' I said. 'I'm going to get it. Quietly, if I can. Loud, if it can't be quiet.'

The voice said: 'Another copper, eh?'

'You know I'm not a copper, Mrs Talley. The Graysons wouldn't talk to a copper. Call them up and ask them.'

'I never heard of them,' the voice said. 'I don't have a phone, if I knew them. Go away, copper. I'm sick. I've been sick for a month.'

'My name is Marlowe,' I said. 'Philip Marlowe. I'm a private eye in Los Angeles. I've been talking to the Graysons. I've got something, but I want to talk to your husband.'

The woman on the couch let out a dim laugh which barely reached across the room. 'You've got something,' she said. 'That sounds familiar. My God it does! You've got something. George Talley had something too–once.'

'He can have it again,' I said, 'if he plays his cards right.'

'If that's what it takes,' she said, 'you can scratch him off right now.'

I leaned against the door-frame and scratched my chin instead. Somebody back on the street had clicked a flash-light on. I didn't know why. It went off again. It seemed to be near my car.

The pale blur of face on the couch moved and disappeared. Hair took its place. The woman had turned her face to the wall.

'I'm tired,' she said, her voice now muffled by talking at the wall. 'I'm so damn tired. Beat it, mister. Be nice and go away.'

'Would a little money help any?'

'Can't you smell the cigar smoke?'

I sniffed. I didn't smell any cigar smoke. I said, 'No.'

'They've been here. They were here two hours. God, I'm tired of it all. Go away.'

'Look, Mrs Talley—'

She rolled on the couch and the blur of her face showed again. I could almost see her eyes, not quite.

'Look yourself,' she said. 'I don't know you. I don't want to know you. I have nothing to tell you. I wouldn't tell it, if I had. I live here, mister, if you call it living. Anyway, it's the nearest I can get to living. I want a little peace and quiet. Now you get out and leave me alone.'

'Let me in the house,' I said. 'We can talk this over. I think I can show you—'

She rolled suddenly on the couch again and feet struck the floor. A tight anger came into her voice.

'If you don't get out,' she said, 'I'm going to start yelling my head off. Right now. Now!'

'Okay!' I said quickly. 'I'll stick my card in the door. So you won't forget my name. You might change your mind.'

I got the card out and wedged it into the crack of the screen door. I said: 'Well, good night, Mrs Talley.'

No answer. Her eyes were looking across the room at me, faintly luminous in the dark. I went down off the porch and back along the narrow walk to the street.

Across the way a motor purled gently in the car with the parking lights on. Motors purl gently in thousands of cars on thousands of streets, everywhere.

I got into the Chrysler and started it up.

25

Westmore was a north and south street on the wrong side of town. I drove north. At the next corner I bumped over disused interurban tracks and on into a block of junk yards. Behind wooden fences the decomposing carcases of old automobiles lay in grotesque designs, like a modern battlefield. Piles of rusted parts looked lumpy under the moon. Roof-high piles, with alleys between them.

Headlights glowed in my rear view mirror. They got larger. I stepped on the gas and reached keys out of my pocket and unlocked the glove compartment. I took a .38 out and laid it on the car seat close to my leg.

Beyond the junk yards there was a brickfield. The tall chimney of the kiln was smokeless, far off over waste land. Piles of dark bricks, a low wooden building with a sign on it, emptiness, no one moving, no light.

The car behind me gained. The low whine of a lightly touched siren growled through the night. The sound loafed over the fringes of a neglected golf course to the east, across the brickyard to the west. I speeded up a bit more, but it wasn't any use. The car behind me came up fast and a huge red spotlight suddenly glared all over the road.

The car came up level and started to cut in. I stood the Chrysler on its nose, swung out behind the police car, and made a U turn with half an inch to spare. I gunned the motor the other way. Behind me sounded the rough clashing of gears, the howl of an infuriated motor, and the red spotlight swept for what seemed miles over the brickyard.

It wasn't any use. They were behind me and coming fast again. I didn't have any idea of getting away. I wanted to get back where there were houses and people to come out and watch and perhaps to remember.

I didn't make it. The police car heaved up alongside again and a hard voice yelled:

'Pull over, or we'll blast a hole in you!'

I pulled over to the kerb and set the brake. I put the gun back in the glove compartment and snapped it shut. The police car jumped on its springs just in front of my left front fender. A fat man slammed out of it roaring.

'Don't you know a police siren when you hear one? Get out of that car!'

I got out of the car and stood beside it in the moonlight. The fat man had a gun in his hand.

'Gimme your licence!' he barked in a voice as hard as the blade of a shovel.

I took it out and held it out. The other cop in the car slid out from under the wheel and came around beside me and took what I was holding out. He put a flash on it and read.

'Name of Marlowe,' he said. 'Hell, the guy's a shamus. Just think of that, Cooney.'

Cooney said: 'Is that all? Guess I won't need this.' He tucked the gun back in his holster and buttoned the leader flap down over it. 'Guess I can handle this with my little flippers,' he said. 'Guess I can at that.'

The other one said: 'Doing fifty-five. Been drinking, I wouldn't wonder.'

'Smell the bastard's breath,' Cooney said.

The other one leaned forward with a polite leer. 'Could I smell the breath, shamus?'

I let him smell the breath.

'Well,' he said judiciously, 'he ain't staggering. I got to admit that.'

''S a cold night for summer. Buy the boy a drink, Officer Dobbs.'

'Now that's a sweet idea,' Dobbs said. He went to the car and got a half-pint bottle out of it. He held it up. It was a third full. 'No really solid drinking here,' he said. He held the bottle out. 'With our compliments, pal.'

'Suppose I don't want a drink,' I said.

'Don't say that,' Cooney whined. 'We might get the idea you wanted feet-prints on your stomach.'

I took the bottle and unscrewed the cap and sniffed. The liquor in the bottle smelled like whisky. Just whisky.

'You can't work the same gag all the time,' I said.

Cooney said: 'Time is eight twenty-seven. Write it down, Officer Dobbs.'

Dobbs went to the car and leaned in to make a note on his report. I held the bottle up and said to Cooney: 'You insist that I drink this?'

'Naw. You could have me jump on your belly instead.'

I tilted the bottle, locked my throat, and filled my mouth with whisky. Cooney lunged forward and sank a fist in my stomach. I sprayed the whisky and bent over choking. I dropped the bottle.

I bent to get it and saw Cooney's fat knee rising at my face. I stepped to one side and straightened and slammed him on the nose with everything I had. His left hand went to his face and his voice howled and his right hand jumped to his gun holster. Dobbs ran at me from the side and his arm swung low. The blackjack hit me behind the left knee, the leg went dead and I sat down hard on the ground, gritting my teeth and spitting whisky.

Cooney took his hand away from his face full of blood.

'Jesus,' he cracked in a thick horrible voice. 'This is blood, my blood.' He let out a wild roar and swung his foot at my face.

I rolled far enough to catch it on my shoulder. It was bad enough taking it there.

Dobbs pushed between us and said: 'We got enough, Charlie. Better not get it all gummed up.'

Cooney stepped backwards three shuffling steps and sat down on the running-board of the police car and held his face. He groped for a handkerchief and used it gently on his nose.

'Just gimme a minute,' he said through the handkerchief. 'Just a minute, pal. Just one little minute.'

Dobbs said, 'Pipe down. We got enough. That's the way it's going to be.' He swung the blackjack slowly beside his leg. Cooney got up off the running-board and staggered forward. Dobbs put a hand against his chest and pushed him gently. Cooney tried to knock the hand out of his way.

'I gotta see blood,' he croaked. 'I gotta see more blood.'

Dobbs said sharply, 'Nothing doing. Pipe down. We got all we wanted.'

Cooney turned and moved heavily away to the other side of the police car. He leaned against it, muttering through his handkerchief. Dobbs said to me:

'Up on the feet, boy friend.'

I got up and rubbed behind my knee. The nerve of the leg was jumping like an angry monkey.

'Get in the car,' Dobbs said. 'Our car.'

I went over and climbed into the police car.

Dobbs said: 'You drive the other heap, Charlie.'

'I'll tear every God-damn fender off'n it,' Cooney roared.

Dobbs picked the whisky bottle off the ground, threw it over the fence, and slid into the car beside me. He pressed the starter.

'This is going to cost you,' he said. 'You hadn't ought to have socked him.'

I said: 'Just why not?'

'He's a good guy,' Dobbs said. 'A little loud.'

'But not funny,' I said. 'Not at all funny.'

'Don't tell him,' Dobbs said. The police car began to move. 'You'd hurt his feelings.'

Cooney slammed into the Chrysler and started it and clashed the gears as if he was trying to strip them. Dobbs tooled the police car smoothly around and started north again along the brickyard.

'You'll like our new jail,' he said.

'What will the charge be?'

He thought a moment, guiding the car with a gentle hand and watching in the mirror to see that Cooney followed along behind.

'Speeding,' he said. 'Resisting arrest. H.B.D. H.B.D. is police slang for "had been drinking".'

'How about being slammed in the belly, kicked in the shoulder, forced to drink liquor under threat of bodily harm, threatened with a gun and struck with a blackjack while unarmed? Couldn't you make a little something more out of that?'

'Aw, forget it,' he said wearily. 'You think this sort of thing is my idea of a good time?'

'I thought they cleaned this town up,' I said. 'I thought they had it so that a decent man could walk the streets at night without wearing a bullet-proof vest.'

'They cleaned it up some,' he said. 'They wouldn't want it too clean. They might scare away a dirty dollar.'

'Better not talk like that,' I said. 'You'll lose your union card.'

He laughed. 'The hell with them,' he said. 'I'll be in the army in two weeks.'

The incident was over for him. It meant nothing. He took it as a matter of course. He wasn't even bitter about it.

26

The cell block was almost brand-new. The battleship-grey paint on the steel walls and door still had the fresh gloss of newness disfigured in two or three places by squirted tobacco juice. The overhead light was sunk in the ceiling behind a heavy frosted panel. There were two bunks on one side of the cell and a man snored in the top bunk, with a dark-grey blanket wrapped around him. Since he was asleep that early and didn't smell of whisky or gin and had chosen the top berth where he would be out of the way, I judged he was an old lodger.

I sat on the lower bunk. They had tapped me for a gun but they hadn't stripped my pockets. I got out a cigarette and rubbed the hot swelling behind my knee. The pain radiated all the way to the ankle. The whisky I had coughed on my coat front had a rank smell. I held the cloth up and breathed smoke into it. The smoke floated up around the flat square of lighted glass in the ceiling. The jail seemed very quiet. A woman was making a shrill racket somewhere very far off in another part of the jail. My part was as peaceful as a church.

The woman was screaming, wherever she was. The screaming had a thin, sharp, unreal sound, something like the screaming of coyotes in the moonlight, but it didn't have the rising keening note of the coyote. After a while the sound stopped.

I smoked two cigarettes through and dropped the butts into the small toilet in the corner. The man in the upper berth still snored. All I could see of him was damp greasy hair sticking out over the edge of the blanket. He slept on his stomach. He slept well. He was one of the best.

I sat down on the bunk again. It was made of flat steel slats with a thin hard mattress over them. Two dark-grey blankets were folded on it quite neatly. It was a very nice jail. It was on the twelfth floor of the new city hall. It was a very nice city hall. Bay City was a very nice place. People lived there and thought so. If I lived there, I would probably think so. I would see the nice blue bay and the cliffs and the yacht harbour and the quiet streets of houses, old houses brooding under old trees and new houses with sharp green lawns and wire fences and staked saplings set into the parkway in front of them. I knew a girl who lived on Twenty-fifth Street. It was a nice street. She was a nice girl. She liked Bay City.

She wouldn't think about the Mexican and Negro slums stretched out on the dismal flats south of the old interurban tracks. Nor of the waterfront dives along the flat shore south of the cliffs, the sweaty little dance halls on the pike, the marijuana joints, the narrow fox faces watching over the tops of newspapers in far too quiet hotel lobbies, nor the pickpockets and grifters and con men and drunk rollers and pimps and queans on the board walk.

I went over to stand by the door. There was nobody stirring across the way. The lights in the cell block were bleak and silent. Business in the jail was rotten.

I looked at my watch. Nine fifty-four. Time to go home and get your slippers on and play over a game of chess. Time for a tall cool drink and a long quiet pipe. Time to sit with your feet up and think of nothing. Time to start yawning over your magazine. Time to be a human being, a householder, a man with nothing to do but rest and suck in the night air and rebuild the brain for to-morrow.

A man in the blue-grey jail uniform came along between the cells reading numbers. He stopped in front of mine and unlocked the door and gave me the hard stare they think they have to wear on their pans for ever and for ever and for ever. I'm a cop, brother, I'm tough, watch your step, brother, or we'll fix you up so you'll crawl on your hands and knees, brother, snap out of it, brother, let's get a load of the truth, brother, let's go, and let's not forget we're tough guys, we're cops, and we do what we like with punks like you.

'Out,' he said.

I stepped out of the cell and he relocked the door and jerked his thumb and we went along to a wide steel gate and he unlocked that and we went through and he relocked it and the keys tinkled pleasantly on the big steel ring, and after a while we went through a steel door that was painted like wood on the outside and battleship-grey on the inside.

Degarmo was standing there by the counter talking to the desk sergeant. He turned his metallic blue eyes on me and said: 'How you doing?'

'Fine.'

'Like our jail?'

'I like your jail fine.'

'Captain Webber wants to talk to you.'

'That's fine,' I said.

'Don't you know any words but fine?'

'Not right now,' I said. 'Not in here.'

'You're limping a little,' he said. 'You trip over something?'

'Yeah,' I said. 'I tripped over a blackjack. It jumped up and bit me behind the left knee.'

'That's too bad,' Degarmo said, blank-eyed. 'Get your stuff from the property clerk.'

'I've got it,' I said. 'It wasn't taken away from me.'

'Well, that's fine,' he said.

'It sure is,' I said. 'It's fine.'

The desk sergeant lifted his shaggy head and gave us both a long stare. 'You ought to see Cooney's little Irish nose,' he said. 'If you want to see something fine. It's spread over his face like syrup on a waffle.'

Degarmo said absently: 'What's the matter? He get in a fight?'

'I wouldn't know,' the desk sergeant said. 'Maybe it was the same blackjack that jumped up and bit him.'

'For a desk sergeant you talk too much,' Degarmo said.

'A desk sergeant always talks too God damn much,' the desk sergeant said. 'Maybe that's why he isn't a lieutenant on homicide.'

'You see how we are here,' Degarmo said. 'Just one great big happy family.'

'With beaming smiles on our faces,' the desk sergeant said, 'and our arms spread wide in welcome, and a rock in each hand.'

Degarmo jerked his head at me and we went out.

27

Captain Webber pushed his sharp bent nose across the desk at me and said: 'Sit down.'

I sat down in a round-backed wooden armchair and eased my left leg away from the sharp edge of the seat. It was a large neat corner office. Degarmo sat at the end of the desk and crossed his legs and rubbed his ankle thoughtfully, and looked out of a window.

Webber went on: 'You asked for trouble, and you got it. You were doing fifty-five miles an hour in a residential zone and you attempted to get away from a police car that signalled you to stop with its siren and red spotlight. You were abusive when stopped and you struck an officer in the face.'

I said nothing. Webber picked a match off his desk and broke it in half and threw the pieces over his shoulder.

'Or are they lying—as usual?' he asked.

'I didn't see their report,' I said. 'I was probably doing fifty-five in a residential district, or anyhow within city limits. The police car was parked outside a house I visited. It followed me when I drove away and I didn't at that time know it was a police car. It had no good reason to follow me and I didn't like the look of it. I went a little fast, but all I was trying to do was get to a better-lighted part of town.'

Degarmo moved his eyes to give a bleak meaningless stare. Webber snapped his teeth impatiently.

He said: 'After you knew it was a police car you made a half-turn in the middle of the block and still tried to get away. Is that right?'

I said: 'Yes. It's going to take a little frank talk to explain that.'

'I'm not afraid of a little frank talk,' Webber said. 'I tend to kind of specialize in frank talk.'

I said: 'These cops that picked me up were parked in front of the house where George Talley's wife lives. They were there before I got there. George Talley is the man who used to be a private detective down here. I wanted to see him. Degarmo knows why I wanted to see him.'

Degarmo picked a match out of his pocket and chewed on the soft end of it quietly. He nodded, without expression. Webber didn't look at him.

I said: 'You are a stupid man, Degarmo. Everything you do is stupid, and done in a stupid way. When you went up against me yesterday in front of Almore's house you had to get tough when there was nothing to get tough about. You had to make me curious when I had nothing to be curious about. You even had to drop hints which showed me how I could satisfy that curiosity, if it became important. All you had to do to protect your friends was to keep your mouth shut until I made a move. I never would have made one, and you would have saved all this.'

Webber said: 'What the devil has all this got to do with your being arrested in the twelve hundred block on Westmore Street?'

'It has to do with the Almore case,' I said. 'George Talley worked on the Almore case—until he was pinched for drunk-driving.'

'Well, I never worked on the Almore case,' Webber snapped. 'I don't know who stuck the first knife into Julius Caesar either. Stick to the point, can't you?'

'I am sticking to the point. Degarmo knows about the Almore case and he doesn't like it talked about. Even your prowl-car boys know about it. Cooney and Dobbs had no reason to follow me unless it was because I visited the wife of a man who had worked on the Almore case. I wasn't doing fifty-five miles an hour when they started to follow me. I tried to get away from them because I had a good idea I might get beaten up for going there. Degarmo had given me that idea.'

Webber looked quickly at Degarmo. Degarmo's hard blue eyes looked across the room at the wall in front of him.

I said: 'And I didn't bust Cooney in the nose until after he had forced me to drink whisky and then hit me in the stomach when I drank it, so that I would spill it down my coat front and smell of it. This can't be the first time you have heard of that trick, captain.'

Webber broke another match. He leaned back and looked at his small tight knuckles. He looked again at Degarmo and said: 'If you got made chief of police to-day, you might let me in on it.'

Degarmo said: 'Hell, the shamus just got a couple of playful taps. Kind of kidding. If a guy can't take a joke—'

Webber said: 'You put Cooney and Dobbs over there?'

'Well—yes, I did,' Degarmo said. 'I don't see why we have to put up with these snoopers coming into our town and stirring up a lot of dead leaves just to promote themselves a job and work a couple of old suckers for a big fee. Guys like that need a good sharp lesson.'

'Is that how it looks to you?' Webber asked.

'That's exactly how it looks to me,' Degarmo said.

'I wonder what fellows like you need,' Webber said. 'Right now I think you need a little air. Would you please take it, lieutenant?'

Degarmo opened his mouth slowly. 'You mean you want me to breeze on out?'

Webber leaned forward suddenly and his sharp little chin seemed to cut the air like the forefoot of a cruiser. 'Would you be so kind?'

Degarmo stood up slowly, a dark flush staining his cheek-bones. He leaned a hard hand flat on the desk and looked at Webber. There was a little charged silence. He said:

'Okay, captain. But you're playing this wrong.'

Webber didn't answer him. Degarmo walked to the door and out. Webber waited for the door to close before he spoke.

'Is it your line that you can tie this Almore business a year and a half ago to the shooting in Lavery's place to-day? Or is it just a smoke-screen you're lying down because you know damn well Kingsley's wife shot Lavery?'

I said: 'It was tied to Lavery before he was shot. In a rough sort of way, perhaps only with a granny knot. But enough to make a man think.'

'I've been into this matter a little more thoroughly than you might think,' Webber said coldly. 'Although I never had anything personally to do with the death of Almore's wife and I wasn't chief of detectives at that time. If you didn't even know Almore yesterday morning, you must have heard a lot about him since.'

I told him exactly what I had heard, both from Miss Fromsett and from the Graysons.

'Then it's your theory that Lavery may have blackmailed Dr Almore?' he asked at the end. 'And that that may have something to do with the murder?'

'It's not a theory. It's no more than a possibility. I wouldn't be doing a job if I ignored it. The relations, if any, between Lavery and Almore might have been deep and dangerous or just the merest acquaintance, or not even that. For all I positively know they may never even have spoken to each other. But if there was nothing funny about the Almore case, why get so tough with anybody who shows an interest in it? It could be coincidence that George Talley was hooked for drunk-driving just when he was working on it. It could be coincidence that Almore called a cop because I stared at his house, and that Lavery was shot before I could talk to him a second time. But it's no coincidence that two of your men were watching Talley's home to-night, ready, willing and able to make trouble for me, if I went there.'

'I grant you that,' Webber said. 'And I'm not done with that incident. Do you want to file charges?'

'Life's too short for me to be filing charges of assault against police officers,' I said.

He winced a little. 'Then we'll wash all that out and charge it to experience,' he said. 'And as I understand you were not even booked, you're free to go home any time you want to. And if I were you, I'd leave Captain Webber to deal with the Lavery case and with any remote connexion it might turn out to have with the Almore case.'

I said: 'And with any remote connexion it might have with a woman named Muriel Chess being found drowned in a mountain lake near Puma Point yesterday?'

He raised his little eyebrows. 'You think that?'

'Only you might not know her as Muriel Chess. Supposing that you knew her at all you might have known her as Mildred Haviland, who used to be Dr Almore's office nurse. Who put Mrs Almore to bed the night she was found dead in the garage, and who, if there was any hanky-panky about that, might know who it was, and be bribed or scared into leaving town shortly thereafter.'

Webber picked up two matches and broke them. His small bleak eyes were fixed on my face. He said nothing.

'And at that point,' I said, 'you run into a real basic coincidence, the only one I'm willing to admit in the whole picture. For this Mildred Haviland met a man named Bill Chess in a Riverside beer parlour and for reasons of her own married him and went to live with him at Little Fawn Lake. And Little Fawn Lake was the property of a man whose wife was intimate with Lavery, who had found Mrs Almore's body. That's what I call a real coincidence. It can't be anything else, but it's basic, fundamental. Everything else flows from it.'

Webber got up from his desk and went over to the water-cooler and drank two paper cups of water. He crushed the cups slowly in his hand and twisted them into a ball and dropped the ball into a brown metal basket under the cooler. He walked to the windows and stood looking out over the bay. This was before the dim-out went into effect, and there were many lights in the yacht harbour.

He came slowly back to the desk and sat down. He reached up and pinched his nose. He was making up his mind about something.

He said slowly: 'I can't see what the hell sense there is in trying to mix that up with something that happened a year and a half later.'

'Okay,' I said, 'and thanks for giving me so much of your time.' I got up to go.

'Your leg feel pretty bad?' he asked, as I leaned down to rub it.

'Bad enough, but it's getting better.'

'Police business,' he said almost gently, 'is a hell of a problem. It's a good deal like politics. It asks for the highest type of men, and there's nothing in it to attract the highest type of men. So we have to work with what we get—and we get things like this.'

'I know,' I said. 'I've always known that. I'm not bitter about it. Good night, Captain Webber.'

'Wait a minute,' he said. 'Sit down a minute. If we've got to have the Almore case in this, let's drag it out into the open and look at it.'

'It's about time somebody did that,' I said. I sat down again.

28

Webber said quietly: 'I suppose some people think we're just a bunch of crooks down here. I suppose they think a fellow kills his wife and then calls me up on the phone and says: "Hi, Cap, I got a little murder down here cluttering up the front-room. And I've got five hundred iron men that are not working." And then I say: "Fine. Hold everything and I'll be right down with a blanket."'

'Not quite that bad,' I said.

'What did you want to see Talley about when you went to his house to-night?'

'He had some line on Florence Almore's death. Her parents hired him to follow it up, but he never told them what it was.'

'And you thought he would tell you?' Webber asked sarcastically.

'All I could do was try.'

'Or was it just that Degarmo getting tough with you made you feel like getting tough right back at him?'

'There might be a little of that in it too,' I said.

'Talley was a petty blackmailer,' Webber said contemptuously. 'On more than one occasion. Anyway, to get rid of him was good enough. So I'll tell you what it was he had. He had a slipper he had stolen from Florence Almore's foot.'

'A slipper?'

He smiled faintly. 'Just a slipper. It was later found hidden in his house. It was a green velvet dancing-pump with some little stones set into the heel. It was custom-made, by a man in Hollywood who makes theatrical footwear and such. Now ask me what was important about this slipper.'

'What was important about it, captain?'

'She had two pair of them, exactly alike, made on the same order. It seems that is not unusual. In case one of them gets scuffed or some drunken ox tries to walk up a lady's leg.' He paused and smiled thinly. 'It seems that one pair had never been worn.'

'I think I'm beginning to get it,' I said.

He leaned back and tapped the arms of his chair. He waited.

'The walk from the side door of the house to the garage is rough concrete,' I said. 'Fairly rough. Suppose she didn't walk it, but was carried. And suppose whoever carried her put her slippers on—and got one that had not been worn.'

'Yes?'

'And suppose Talley noticed this while Lavery was telephoning to the doctor, who was out on his rounds. So he took the unworn slipper, regarding it as evidence that Florence Almore had been murdered.'

Webber nodded his head. 'It was evidence if he left it where it was, for the police to find it. After he took it, it was just evidence that he was a rat.'

'Was a monoxide test made of her blood?'

He put his hands flat on his desk and looked down at them. 'Yes,' he said. 'And there was monoxide all right. Also the investigating officers were satisfied with appearances. There was no sign of violence. They were satisfied that Dr Almore had not murdered his wife. Perhaps they were wrong. I think the investigation was a little superficial.'

'And who was in charge of it?' I asked.

'I think you know the answer to that.'

'When the police came, didn't they notice that a slipper was missing?'

'When the police came there was no slipper missing. You must remember that Dr Almore was back at his home, in response to Lavery's call, before the police were called. All we know about the missing shoe is from Talley himself. He might have taken the unworn shoe from the house. The side door was unlocked. The maids were asleep. The objection to that is that he wouldn't have been likely to know there was an unworn slipper to take. I wouldn't put it past him to think of it. He's a sharp sneaky little devil. But I can't fix the necessary knowledge on him.'

We sat there and looked at each other, thinking about it.

'Unless,' Webber said slowly, 'we can suppose that this nurse of Almore's was involved with Talley in a scheme to put the bite on Almore. It's possible. There are things in favour of it. There are more things against it. What reasons have you for claiming that the girl drowned up in the mountains was this nurse?'

'Two reasons, neither one conclusive separately, but pretty powerful taken together. A tough guy who looked and acted like Degarmo was up there a few weeks ago showing a photograph of Mildred Haviland that looked something like Muriel Chess. Different hair and eyebrows and so on, but a fair resemblance. Nobody helped him much. He called himself De Soto and said he was a Los Angeles cop. There isn't any Los Angeles cop named De Soto. When Muriel Chess heard about it, she looked scared. If it was Degarmo, that's easily established. The other reason is that a golden anklet with a heart on it was hidden in a box of powdered sugar in the Chess cabin. It was found after her death, after her husband had been arrested. On the back of the heart was engraved: "*Al to Mildred. June 28th.*

1938. With all my love.'''

'It could have been some other Al and some other Mildred,' Webber said.

'You don't really believe that, captain.'

He leaned forward and made a hole in the air with his forefinger. 'What do you want to make of all this exactly?'

'I want to make it that Kingsley's wife didn't shoot Lavery. That his death had something to do with the Almore business. And with Mildred Haviland. And possibly with Dr Almore. I want to make it that Kingsley's wife disappeared because something happened that gave her a bad fright, that she may or may not have guilty knowledge, but that she hasn't murdered anybody. There's five hundred dollars in it for me, if I can determine that. It's legitimate to try.'

He nodded. 'Certainly it is. And I'm the man that would help you, if I could see any grounds for it. We haven't found the woman, but the time has been very short. But I can't help you put something on one of my boys.'

I said: 'I heard you call Degarmo Al. But I was thinking of Almore. His name's Albert.'

Webber looked at his thumb. 'But he was never married to the girl,' he said quietly. 'Degarmo was. I can tell you she led him a pretty dance. A lot of what seems bad in him is the result of it.'

I sat very still. After a moment I said: 'I'm beginning to see things I didn't know existed. What kind of a girl was she?'

'Smart, smooth and no good. She had a way with men. She could make them crawl over her shoes. The big boob would tear your head off right now, if you said anything against her. She divorced him, but that didn't end it for him.'

'Does he know she is dead?'

Webber sat quiet for a long moment before he said: 'Not from anything he has said. But how could he help it, if it's the same girl?'

'He never found her in the mountains—so far as we know.' I stood up and leaned down on the desk. 'Look, captain, you're not kidding me, are you?'

'No. Not one damn bit. Some men are like that and some women can make them like it. If you think Degarmo went up there looking for her because he wanted to hurt her, you're as wet as a bar towel.'

'I never quite thought that,' I said. 'It would be possible, provided Degarmo knew the country up there pretty well. Whoever murdered the girl did.'

'This is all between us,' he said. 'I'd like you to keep it that way.'

I nodded, but I didn't promise him. I said good night again and left. He looked after me as I went down the room. He looked hurt and sad.

The Chrysler was in the police lot at the side of the building with the keys in the ignition and none of the fenders smashed. Cooney hadn't made good on his threat. I drove back to Hollywood and went up to my apartment in the Bristol. It was late, almost midnight.

The green and ivory hallway was empty of all sound except that a telephone bell was ringing in one of the apartments. It rang insistently and got louder as I came near to my door. I unlocked the door. It was my telephone.

I walked across the room in darkness to where the phone stood on the ledge of an oak desk against the side wall. It must have rung at least ten times before I got to it.

I lifted it out of the cradle and answered, and it was Derace Kingsley on the line.

His voice sounded tight and brittle and strained. 'Good Lord, where in hell have you been?' he snapped. 'I've been trying to reach you for hours.'

'All right. I'm here now,' I said. 'What is it?'

'I've heard from her.'

I held the telephone very tight and drew my breath in slowly and let it out slowly. 'Go ahead,' I said.

'I'm not far away. I'll be over there in five or six minutes. Be prepared to move.'

He hung up.

I stood there holding the telephone half-way between my ear and the cradle. Then I put it down very slowly and looked at the hand that had held it. It was half-open and clenched stiff, as if it was still holding the instrument.

29

The discreet midnight tapping sounded on the door and I went over and opened it. Kingsley looked as big as a horse in a creamy Shetland sports coat with a green and yellow scarf around the neck inside the loosely turned-up collar. A dark reddish-brown snapbrim hat was pulled low on his forehead and under its brim his eyes looked like the eyes of a sick animal.

Miss Fromsett was with him. She was wearing slacks and sandals and a dark-green coat and no hat and her hair had a wicked lustre. In her ears hung ear-drops made of a pair of tiny artificial gardenia blooms, hanging one above the other, two on each ear. Gillerlain Regal, the Champagne of Perfumes, came in at the door with her.

I shut the door and indicated the furniture and said: 'A drink will probably help.'

Miss Fromsett sat in an armchair and crossed her legs and looked around for cigarettes. She found one and lit it with a long casual flourish and smiled bleakly at a corner of the ceiling.

Kingsley stood in the middle of the floor trying to bite his chin. I went out to the dinette and mixed three drinks and brought them in and handed them. I went over to the chair by the chess table with mine.

Kingsley said: 'What have you been doing and what's the matter with the leg?'

I said: 'A cop kicked me. A present from the Bay City police department. It's a regular service they give down there. As to where I've been—in jail for drunk-driving. And from the expression on your face, I think I may be right back there soon.'

'I don't know what you're talking about,' he said shortly. 'I haven't the foggiest idea. This is no time to kid around.'

'All right, don't,' I said. 'What did you hear and where is she?'

He sat down with his drink and flexed the fingers of his right hand and put it inside his coat. It came out with an envelope, a long one.

'You have to take this to her,' he said. 'Five hundred dollars. She wanted more, but this is all I could raise. I cashed a cheque at a night-club. It wasn't easy. She has to get out of town.'

I said: 'Out of what town?'

'Bay City somewhere. I don't know where. She'll meet you at a place called the Peacock Lounge, on Arguello Boulevard, at Eighth Street, or near it.'

I looked at Miss Fromsett. She was still looking at the corner of the ceiling as if she had just come along for the ride.

Kingsley tossed the envelope across and it fell on the chess table. I looked inside it. It was money all right. That much of his story made sense. I let it lie on the small polished table with its inlaid squares of brown and pale gold.

I said: 'What's the matter with her drawing her own money? Any hotel would clear a cheque for her. Most of them would cash one. Has her bank account got lockjaw or something?'

'That's no way to talk,' Kingsley said heavily. 'She's in trouble. I don't know how she knows she's in trouble. Unless a pick-up order has been broadcast. Has it?'

I said I didn't know. I hadn't had much time to listen to police calls. I had been too busy listening to live policemen. Kingsley said: 'Well, she won't risk cashing a cheque now. It was all right before. But not now.' He lifted his eyes slowly and gave me one of the emptiest stares I had ever seen.

'All right, we can't make sense where there isn't any,' I said. 'So she's in Bay City. Did you talk to her?'

'No. Miss Fromsett talked to her. She called the office. It was just after hours but that cop from the beach, Captain Webber, was with me. Miss Fromsett naturally didn't want her to talk at all then. She told her to call back. She wouldn't give any number we could call.'

I looked at Miss Fromsett. She brought her glance down from the ceiling and pointed it at the top of my head. There was nothing in her eyes at all. They were like drawn curtains.

Kingsley went on: 'I didn't want to talk to her. She didn't want to talk to me. I don't want to see her. I guess there's no doubt she shot Lavery. Webber seemed quite sure of it.'

'That doesn't mean anything,' I said. 'What he says and what he thinks don't even have to be on the same map. I don't like her knowing the cops were after her. It's a long time since anybody listened to the police short-wave for amusement. So she called back later. And then?'

'It was almost half-past six,' Kingsley said. 'We had to sit there in the office and wait for her to call. You tell him.' He turned his head to the girl.

Miss Fromsett said: 'I took the call in Mr Kingsley's office. He was sitting right beside me, but he didn't speak. She said to send the money down to the Peacock place and asked who would bring it.'

'Did she sound scared?'

'Not in the least. Completely calm. I might say, icily calm. She had it all worked out. She realized somebody would have to bring the money she might not know. She seemed to know Derry—Mr Kingsley wouldn't bring it.'

'Call him Derry,' I said. 'I'll be able to guess who you mean.'

She smiled faintly. 'She will go into this Peacock Lounge every hour about fifteen minutes past the hour. I–I guess I assumed you would be the one to go. I described you to her. And you're to wear Derry's scarf. I described that. He keeps some clothes at the office and this was among them. It's distinctive enough.'

It was all of that. It was an affair of fat green kidneys laid down on an egg-yolk background. It would be almost as distinctive as if I went in there wheeling a red, white and blue wheelbarrow.

'For a blimp brain she's doing all right,' I said.

'This is no time to fool around,' Kingsley put in sharply.

'You said that before,' I told him. 'You've got a hell of a crust assuming I'll go down there and take a getaway stake to somebody I know the police are looking for.'

He twisted a hand on his knee and his face twisted into a crooked grin.

'I admit it's a bit thick,' he said. 'Well, how about it?'

'It makes accessories after the fact out of all three of us. That might not be too tough for her husband and his confidential secretary to talk out of, but what they would do to me would be nobody's dream of a vacation.'

'I'm going to make it worth your while,' he said. 'And we wouldn't be accessories if she hasn't done anything.'

'I'm willing to suppose it,' I said. 'Otherwise I wouldn't be talking to you. And in addition to that, if I decide she did do any murder, I'm going to turn her over to the police.'

'She won't talk to you,' he said.

I reached for the envelope and put it in my pocket. 'She will, if she wants this.' I looked at my strap watch. 'If I start right away, I might make the one-fifteen deadline. They must know her by heart in that bar after all these hours. That makes it nice too.'

'She's dyed her hair dark brown,' Miss Fromsett said. 'That ought to help a little.'

I said: 'It doesn't help me to think she is just an innocent wayfarer.' I finished my drink and stood up. Kingsley swallowed his at a gulp and stood up and got the scarf off his neck and handed it to me.

'What did you do to get the police on your neck down there?' he asked.

'I was using some information Miss Fromsett very kindly got for me. And that led to my looking for a man named Talley who worked on the Almore case. And that led to the clink. They had the house staked. Talley was the dick the Graysons hired,' I added, looking at the tall dark girl. 'You'll probably be able to explain to him what it's all about. It doesn't matter anyway. I haven't time to go into it now. You two want to wait here?'

Kingsley shook his head. 'We'll go to my place and wait for a call from you.'

Miss Fromsett stood up and yawned. 'No. I'm tired, Derry. I'm going home and going to bed.'

'You'll come with me,' he said sharply. 'You've got to keep me from going nuts.'

'Where do you live, Miss Fromsett?' I asked.

'Bryson Tower on Sunset Place. Apartment 716. Why?' She gave me a speculative look.

'I might want to reach you some time.'

Kingsley's face looked bleakly irritated, but his eyes still were the eyes of a sick animal. I wound his scarf around my neck and went out to the dinette to switch off the light. When I came back they were both standing by the door. Kingsley had his arm around her shoulders. She looked very tired and rather bored.

'Well, I certainly hope—' he started to stay, then took a quick step and put his hand out. 'You're a pretty level guy, Marlowe.'

'Go on, beat it,' I said. 'Go away. Go far away.'

He gave a queer look and they went out.

I waited until I heard the elevator come up and stop, and the doors open and close again, and the elevator start down. Then I went out myself and took the stairs down to the basement garage and got the Chrysler awake again.

30

The Peacock Lounge was a narrow front next to a gift shop in whose window a tray of small crystal animals shimmered in the street light. The Peacock had a glass brick front and soft light glowed out around the stained-glass peacock that was set into the brick. I went in around a Chinese screen and looked along the bar and then sat at the outer edge of a small booth. The light was amber, the leather was Chinese red and the booths had polished plastic tables. In one booth four soldiers were drinking beer moodily, a little glassy in the eyes and obviously bored even with drinking beer. Across from them a party of two girls and two flashy-looking men were making the only noise in the place. I saw nobody that looked like my idea of Crystal Kingsley.

A wizened waiter with evil eyes and a face like a gnawed bone put a napkin with a printed peacock on it down on the table in front of me and gave me a bacardi cocktail. I sipped it and looked at the amber face of the bar clock. It was just past one-fifteen.

One of the men with the two girls got up suddenly and stalked along to the door and went out. The voice of the other man said:

'What did you have to insult the guy for?'

A girl's tinny voice said: 'Insult him? I like that. He propositioned me.'

The man's voice said complainingly: 'Well, you didn't have to insult him, did you?'

One of the soldiers suddenly laughed deep in his chest and then wiped the laugh off his face with a brown hand and drank a little more beer. I rubbed the back of my knee. It was hot and swollen still but the paralysed feeling had gone away.

A tiny, white-faced Mexican boy with enormous black eyes came in with morning papers and scuttled along the booths trying to make a few sales before the barman threw him out. I bought a paper and looked through it to see if there were any interesting murders. There were not.

I folded it and looked up as a slim, brown-haired girl in coal-black slacks and a yellow shirt and a long grey coat came out of somewhere and passed the booth without looking at me. I tried to make up my mind whether her face was familiar or just such a standard type of lean, rather hard, prettiness that I must have seen it ten thousand times. She went out of the street door around the screen. Two minutes later the little Mexican boy came back in, shot a quick look at the barman, and scuttled over to stand in front of me.

'Mister,' he said, his great big eyes shining with mischief. Then he made a beckoning sign and scuttled out again.

I finished my drink and went after him. The girl in the grey coat and yellow shirt and black slacks was standing in front of the gift shop, looking in at the window. Her eyes moved as I went out. I went and stood beside her.

She looked at me again. Her face was white and tired. Her hair looked darker than dark brown. She looked away and spoke to the window.

'Give me the money, please.' A little mist formed on the plate-glass from her breath.

I said: 'I'd have to know who you are.'

'You know who I am,' she said softly. 'How much did you bring?'

'Five hundred.'

'It's not enough,' she said. 'Not nearly enough. Give it to me quickly. I've been waiting half of eternity for somebody to get here.'

'Where can we talk?'

'We don't have to talk. Just give me the money and go the other way.'

'It's not that simple. I'm doing this at quite a risk. I'm at least going to have the satisfaction of knowing what goes on and where I stand.'

'Damn you,' she said acidly. 'Why couldn't he come himself? I don't want to talk. I want to get away as soon as I can.'

'You didn't want him to come himself. He understood that you didn't even want to talk to him on the phone.'

'That's right,' she said quickly and tossed her head.

'But you've got to talk to me,' I said. 'I'm not as easy as he is. Either to me or to the law. There's no way out of it. I'm a private detective and I have to have some protection too.'

'Well, isn't he charming,' she said. 'Private detective and all.' Her voice held a low sneer.

'He did the best he knew how. It wasn't easy for him to know what to do.'

'What do you want to talk about?'

'You, and what you've been doing and where you've been and what you expect to do. Things like that. Little things, but important.'

She breathed on the glass of the shop window and waited while the mist of her breath disappeared.

'I think it would be much better,' she said in the same cool empty voice, 'for you to give me the money and let me work things out for myself.'

'No.'

She gave me another sharp sideways glance. She shrugged the shoulders of the grey coat impatiently.

'Very well, if it has to be that way. I'm at the Granada, two blocks north on Eighth. Apartment 618. Give me ten minutes. I'd rather go in alone.'

'I have a car.'

'I'd rather go alone.' She turned quickly and walked away.

She walked back to the corner and crossed the boulevard and disappeared along the block under a line of pepper trees. I went and sat in the Chrysler and gave her the ten minutes before I started it.

The Granada was an ugly grey building on a corner. The plate-glass entrance-door was level with the street. I drove around the corner and saw a milky globe with 'Garage' painted on it. The entrance to the garage was down a ramp into the hard rubber-smelling silence of parked cars in rows. A lanky Negro came out of a glassed-in office and looked the Chrysler over.

'How much to leave this here a short time? I'm going upstairs.'

He gave me a shady leer. 'Kinda late, boss. She needs a good dustin' too. Be a dollar.'

'What goes on here?'

'Be a dollar,' he said woodenly.

I got out. He gave me a ticket. I gave him the dollar. Without my asking him he said the elevator was in back of the office, by the men's room.

I rode up to the sixth floor and looked at numbers on doors and listened to stillness and smelled beach air coming in at the ends of corridors. The place seemed decent enough. There would be a few happy ladies in any apartment house. That would explain the lanky Negro's dollar. A great judge of character, that boy.

I came to the door of Apartment 618 and stood outside it a moment and then knocked softly.

31

She still had the grey coat on. She stood back from the door and I went past her into a square room with twin wall beds and a minimum of uninteresting furniture. A small lamp on a window-table made a dim yellowish light. The window behind it was open.

The girl said: 'Sit down and talk then.'

She closed the door and went to sit in a gloomy Boston rocker across the room. I sat down on a thick davenport. There was a dull-green curtain hanging across an open door space at one end of the davenport. That would lead to dressing-room and bathroom. There was a closed door at the other end. That would be the kitchenette. That would be all there was.

The girl crossed her ankles and leaned her head back against the chair and looked at me under long beaded lashes. Her eyebrows were thin and arched and as brown as her hair. It was a quiet, secret face. It didn't look like the face of a woman who would waste a lot of motion.

'I got a rather different idea of you,' I said, 'from Kingsley.'

Her lips twisted a little. She said nothing.

'From Lavery too,' I said. 'It just goes to show that we talk different languages to different people.'

'I haven't time for this sort of talk,' she said. 'What is it you have to know?'

'He hired me to find you. I've been working on it. I supposed you would know that.'

'Yes. His office sweetie told me that over the phone. She told me you would be a man named Marlowe. She told me about the scarf.'

I took the scarf off my neck and folded it up and slipped it into a pocket. I said:

'So I know a little about your movements. Not very much. I know you left your car at the Prescott Hotel in San Bernardino and that you met Lavery there. I know you sent a wire from El Paso. What did you do then?'

'All I want from you is the money he sent. I don't see that my movements are any of your business.'

'I don't have to argue about that,' I said. 'It's a question of whether you want the money.'

'Well, we went to El Paso,' she said, in a tired voice. 'I thought of marrying him then. So I sent that wire. You saw the wire?'

'Yes.'

'Well, I changed my mind. I asked him to go home and leave me. He made a scene.'

'Did he go home and leave you?'

'Yes. Why not?'

'What did you do then?'

'I went to Santa Barbara and stayed there a few days. Over a week, in fact. Then to Pasadena. Same thing. Then to Hollywood. Then I came down here. That's all.'

'You were alone all this time?'

She hesitated a little and then said: 'Yes.'

'Not with Lavery—any part of it?'

'Not after he went home.'

'What was the idea?'

'Idea of what?' Her voice was a little sharp.

'Idea of going these places and not sending any word. Didn't you know he would be very anxious?'

'Oh, you mean my husband,' she said coolly. 'I don't think I worried much about him. He'd think I was in Mexico, wouldn't he? As for the idea of it all—well, I just had to think things out. My life had got to be a hopeless tangle. I had to be somewhere quite alone and try to straighten myself out.'

'Before that,' I said, 'you spent a month at Little Fawn Lake trying to straighten it out and not getting anywhere. Is that it?'

She looked down at her shoes and then up at me and nodded earnestly. The wavy brown hair surged forward along her cheeks. She put her left hand up and pushed it back and then rubbed her temple with one finger.

'I seemed to need a new place,' she said. 'Not necessarily an interesting place. Just a strange place. Without associations. A place where I would be very much alone. Like an hotel.'

'How are you getting on with it?'

'Not very well. But I'm not going back to Derace Kingsley. Does he want me to?'

'I don't know. Why did you come down here to the town where Lavery was?'

She bit a knuckle and looked at me over her hand.

'I wanted to see him again. He's all mixed up in my mind. I'm in love with him and yet—well, I suppose in a way I am. But I don't think I want to marry him. Does that make sense?'

'That part of it makes sense. But staying away from home in a lot of crummy hotels doesn't. You've lived your own life for years, as I understand it.'

'I had to be alone to—to think things out,' she said a little desperately and bit the knuckle again, hard. 'Won't you please give me the money and go away?'

'Sure. Right away. But wasn't there any other reason for your going away from Little Fawn Lake just then? Anything connected with Muriel Chess, for instance?'

She looked surprised. But anyone can look surprised. 'Good heavens, what would there be? That frozen-faced little drip—what is she to me?'

'I thought you might have had a fight with her—about Bill.'

'Bill? Bill Chess?' She seemed even more surprised. Almost too surprised.

'Bill claims you made a pass at him.'

She put her head back and let out a tinny and unreal laugh. 'Good heavens, that muddy-faced boozer?' Her face sobered suddenly. 'What's happened? Why all the mystery?'

'He might be a muddy-faced boozer,' I said. 'The police think he's a murderer too. Of his wife. She's been found drowned in the lake. After a month.'

She moistened her lips and held her head on one side, staring at me fixedly. There was a quiet little silence. The damp breath of the Pacific slid into the room around us.

'I'm not too surprised,' she said slowly. 'So it came to that in the end. They fought terribly at times. Did you think that had something to do with my leaving?'

I nodded. 'There was a chance of it.'

'It didn't have anything to do with it at all,' she said seriously, and shook her head back and forth. 'It was just the way I told you. Nothing else.'

'Muriel's dead,' I said. 'Drowned in the lake. You don't get much of a boot out of that, do you?'

'I hardly knew the girl,' she said. 'Really. She kept to herself. After all—'

'I don't suppose you knew she had once worked in Dr Almore's office?'

She looked completely puzzled now. 'I was never in Dr Almore's office,' she said slowly. 'He made a few house calls a long time ago. I—what are you talking about?'

'Muriel Chess was really a girl called Mildred Haviland, who had been Dr Almore's office nurse.'

'That's a queer coincidence,' she said wonderingly. 'I knew Bill met her in Riverside. I didn't know how or under what circumstances or where she came from. Dr Almore's office, eh? It doesn't have to mean anything, does it?'

I said, 'No. I guess it's a genuine coincidence. They do happen. But you see why I had to talk to you. Muriel being found drowned and you having gone away and Muriel being Mildred Haviland who was connected with Dr Almore at one time—as Lavery was also, in a different way. And, of course, Lavery lives across the street from Dr Almore. Did he, Lavery, seem to know Muriel from somewhere else?'

She thought about it, biting her lower lip gently. 'He saw her up there,' she said finally. 'He didn't act as if he had ever seen her before.'

'And he would have,' I said. 'Being the kind of guy he was.'

'I don't think Chris had anything to do with Dr Almore,' she said. 'He knew Dr Almore's wife. I don't think he knew the doctor at all. So he probably wouldn't know Dr Almore's office nurse.'

'Well, I guess there's nothing in all this to help me,' I said. 'But you can see why I had to talk to you. I guess I can give you the money now.'

I got the envelope out and stood up to drop it on her knee. She let it lie there. I sat down again.

'You do this character very well,' I said. 'This confused innocence with an undertone of hardness and bitterness. People have made a bad mistake about you. They have been thinking of you as a reckless little idiot with no brains and no control. They have been very wrong.'

She stared at me, lifting her eyebrows. She said nothing. Then a small smile lifted the corners of her mouth. She reached for the envelope, tapped it on her knee, and laid it aside on the table. She stared at me all the time.

'You did the Fallbrook character very well too,' I said. 'Looking back on it, I think it was a shade overdone. But at the time it had me going all right. That purple hat that would have been all right on blonde hair but looked like hell on straggly brown, that messed-up make-up that looked as if it had been put on in the dark by somebody with a sprained wrist, the jittery screwball manner. All very good. And when you put the gun in my hand like that—I fell like a brick.'

She snickered and put her hands in the deep pockets of her coat. Her heels tapped on the floor.

'But why did you go back at all?' I asked. 'Why take such a risk in broad daylight, in the middle of the morning?'

'So you think I shot Chris Lavery?' she said quietly.

'I don't think it. I know it.'

'Why did I go back? Is that what you want to know?'

'I don't really care,' I said.

She laughed. A sharp cold laugh. 'He had all my money,' she said. 'He had stripped my purse. He had it all, even silver. That's why I went back. There wasn't any risk at all. I know how he lived. It was really safer to go back. To take in the milk and the newspaper, for instance. People lose their heads in these situations. I don't, I didn't see why I should. It's so very much safer not to.'

'I see,' I said. 'Then, of course, you shot him the night before. I ought to have thought of that, not that it matters. He had been shaving. But guys with dark beards and lady friends sometimes shave the last thing at night, don't they?'

'It has been heard of,' she said almost gaily. 'And just what are you going to do about it?'

'You're a cold-blooded little bitch if ever I saw one,' I said. 'Do about it? Turn you over to the police, naturally. It will be a pleasure.'

'I don't think so.' She threw the words out, almost with a lilt. 'You wondered why I gave you the empty gun. Why not? I had another one in my bag. Like this.'

Her right hand came up from her coat pocket and she pointed it at me.

I grinned. It may not have been the heartiest grin in the world, but it was a grin.

'I've never liked this scene,' I said. 'Detective confronts murderer. Murderer produces gun, points same at detective. Murderer tells detective the whole sad story, with the idea of shooting him at the end of it. Thus wasting a lot of valuable time, even if in the end murderer did shoot detective. Only murderer never does. Something always happens to prevent it. The gods don't like this scene either. They always manage to spoil it.'

'But this time,' she said softly and got up and moved towards me softly across the carpet, 'suppose we make it a little different. Suppose I don't tell you anything and nothing happens and I do shoot you?'

'I still wouldn't like the scene,' I said.

'You don't seem to be afraid,' she said, and slowly licked her lips, coming towards me very gently without any sound of footfalls on the carpet.

'I'm not afraid,' I lied. 'It's too late at night, too still, and the window is open and the gun would make too much noise. It's too long a journey down to the street and you're not good with guns. You would probably miss me. You missed Lavery three times.'

'Stand up,' she said.

I stood up.

'I'm going to be too close to miss,' she said. She pushed the gun against my chest. 'Like this. I really can't miss now, can I? Now be very still. Hold your hands up by your shoulders and then don't move at all. If you move at all, the gun will go off.'

I put my hands up beside my shoulders. I looked down at the gun. My tongue felt a little thick, but I could still wave it.

Her probing left hand didn't find a gun on me. It dropped and she bit her lip, staring at me. The gun bored into my chest. 'You'll have to turn around now,' she said, polite as a tailor at a fitting.

'There's something a little off key about everything you do,' I said. 'You're definitely not good with guns. You're much too close to me, and I hate to bring this up—but there's that old business of the safety-catch not being off. You've overlooked that too.'

So she started to do two things at once. To take a long step backwards and to feel with her thumb for the safety-catch, without taking her eyes off my face. Two very simple things, needing only a second to do. But she didn't like my telling her. She didn't like my thought riding over hers. The minute confusion of it jarred her.

She let out a small choked sound and I dropped my right hand and yanked her face hard against my chest. My left hand smashed down on her right wrist, the heel of my hand against the base of her thumb. The gun jerked out of her hand to the floor. Her face writhed against my chest and I think she was trying to scream.

Then she tried to kick me and lost what little balance she had left. Her hands came up to claw at me. I caught her wrist and began to twist it behind her back. She was very strong, but I was very much stronger. So she decided to go limp and let her whole weight sag against the hand that was holding her head. I couldn't hold her up with one hand. She started to go down and I had to bend down with her.

There were vague sounds of our scuffling on the floor by the davenport, and hard breathing, and if a floorboard creaked I didn't hear it. I thought a curtain-ring checked sharply on a rod. I wasn't sure and I had no time to consider the question. A figure loomed up suddenly on my left, just behind, and out of range of clear vision. I knew there was a man there and that he was a big man.

That was all I knew. The scene exploded into fire and darkness. I didn't even remember being slugged. Fire and darkness and just before the darkness a sharp flash of nausea.

32

I smelled of gin. Not just casually, as if I had taken four or five drinks of a winter morning to get out of bed on, but as if the Pacific Ocean was pure gin and I had nosedived off the boat deck. The gin was in my hair and eyebrows, on my chin and under my chin. It was on my shirt. I smelled like dead toads.

My coat was off and I was lying flat on my back beside the davenport on somebody's carpet and I was looking at a framed picture. The frame was of cheap soft wood varnished and the picture showed part of an enormously high pale-yellow viaduct across which a shiny black locomotive was dragging a Prussian-blue train. Through one lofty arch of the viaduct a wide yellow beach showed and was dotted with sprawled bathers and striped beach umbrellas. Three girls walked close up, with paper parasols, one girl in cerise, one in pale blue, one in green. Beyond the beach a curving bay was bluer than any bay has any right to be. It was drenched with sunshine and flecked and dotted with aching white sails. Beyond the inland curve of the bay three ranges of hills rose in three precisely opposed colours, gold and terracotta and lavender.

Across the bottom of the picture was printed in large capitals, SEE THE FRENCH RIVIERA BY THE BLUE TRAIN.

It was a fine time to bring that up.

I reached up wearily and felt the back of my head. It felt pulpy. A shoot of pain from the touch went clear to the soles of my feet. I groaned, and made a grunt out of the groan, from professional pride—what was left of it. I rolled over slowly and carefully and looked at the foot of a pulled-down wall-bed; one twin, the other being still up in the wall. The flourish of design on the painted wood was familiar. The picture had hung over the davenport and I hadn't even looked at it.

When I rolled a square gin bottle rolled off my chest and hit the floor. It was water white, and empty. It didn't seem possible there could be so much gin in just one bottle.

I got my knees under me and stayed on all fours for a while, sniffing like a dog who can't finish his dinner, but hates to leave it. I moved my head around on my neck. It hurt. I moved it around some more and it still hurt, so I climbed up on my feet and discovered I didn't have any shoes on.

The shoes were lying against the baseboard, looking as dissipated as shoes ever looked. I put them on wearily. I was an old man now. I was going down the last long hill. I still had a tooth though. I felt it with my tongue. It didn't seem to taste of gin.

'It will all come back to you,' I said. 'Some day it will all come back to you. And you won't like it.'

There was the lamp on the table by the open window. There was the fat green davenport. There was the doorway with the green curtain across it.

Never sit with your back to a green curtain. It always turns out badly. Something always happens. Who had I said that to? A girl with a gun. A girl with a clear, empty face and dark-brown hair that had been blonde.

I looked around for her. She was still there. She was lying on the pulled-down twin bed.

She was wearing a pair of tan stockings and nothing else. Her hair was tumbled. There were dark bruises on her throat. Her mouth was open and a swollen tongue filled it to overflowing. Her eyes bulged and the whites of them were not white.

Across her naked belly four angry scratches leered crimson red against the whiteness of flesh. Deep angry scratches, gouged out by four bitter finger-nails.

On the davenport there were tumbled clothes, mostly hers. My coat was there also. I disentangled it and put it on. Something crackled under my hand in the tumbled clothes. I drew out a long envelope with money still in it. I put it in my pocket. Marlowe, five hundred dollars. I hoped it was all there. There didn't seem much else to hope for.

I stepped on the balls of my feet softly, as if walking on very thin ice. I bent down to rub behind my knee and wondered which hurt most, my knee, or my head when I bent down to rub the knee.

Heavy feet came along the hallway and there was a hard mutter of voices. The feet stopped. A hard fist knocked on the door.

I stood there leering at the door, with my lips drawn back tight against my teeth. I waited for somebody to open the door and walk in. The knob was tried, but nobody walked in. The knocking began again, stopped, the voices muttered again. The steps went away. I wondered how long it would take to get the manager with a passkey. Not very long.

Not nearly long enough for Marlowe to get home from the French Riviera.

I went to the green curtain and brushed it aside and looked down a short dark hallway into a bathroom. I went in there and put the light on. Two wash rugs on the floor, a bath mat folded over the edge of the tub, a pebbled glass window at the corner of the tub. I shut the bathroom door and stood on the edge of the tub and eased the window up. This was the sixth floor. There was no screen. I put my head out and looked into darkness and a narrow glimpse of a street with trees. I looked sideways and saw that the bathroom window of the next apartment was not more than three feet away. A well-nourished mountain goat could make it without any trouble at all.

The question was whether a battered private detective could make it, and if so, what the harvest would be.

Behind me a rather remote and muffled voice seemed to be chanting the policeman's litany: 'Open it up or we'll kick it in.' I sneered back at the voice. They wouldn't kick it in because kicking in a door is hard on the feet. Policemen are kind to their feet. Their feet are about all they are kind to.

I grabbed a towel off the rack and pulled the two halves of the window down and eased out on the sill. i swung half of me over to the next sill, holding on to the frame of the open window. I could just reach to push the next window down, if it was unlocked. It wasn't unlocked. I got my foot over there and kicked the glass over the catch. It made a noise that ought to have been heard in Reno. I wrapped the towel around my left hand and reached in to turn the catch. Down on the street a car went by, but nobody yelled at me.

I pushed the broken window down and climbed across to the other sill. The towel fell out of my hand and fluttered down into the darkness to a strip of grass far below, between the two wings of the building.

I climbed in at the window of the other bathroom.

33

I climbed down into darkness and groped through darkness to a door and opened it and listened. Filtered moonlight coming through north windows showed a bedroom with twin beds, made up and empty. Not wall beds. This was a larger apartment. I moved past the beds to another door and into a living-room. Both rooms were closed up and smelled musty. I felt my way to a lamp and switched it on. I ran a finger along the wood of a table edge. There was a light film of dust, such as accumulates in the cleanest room when it is left shut up.

The room contained a library dining-table, an armchair radio, a book-rack built like a hod, a big bookcase full of novels with their jackets still on them, a dark wood highboy with a siphon and a cut-glass bottle of liquor and four striped glasses upside down on an Indian brass tray. Beside this paired photographs in a double silver frame, a youngish middle-aged man and woman, with round healthy faces and cheerful eyes. They looked out at me as if they didn't mind my being there at all.

I sniffed the liquor, which was Scotch, and used some of it. It made my head feel worse but it made the rest of me feel better. I put a light on in the bedroom and poked into closets. One of them had a man's clothes, tailor-made, plenty of them. The tailor's label inside a coat pocket declared the owner's name to be H.G. Talbot. I went to the bureau and poked around and found a soft blue shirt that looked a little small for me. I carried it into the bathroom and stripped mine off and washed my face and chest and wiped my hair off with a wet towel and put the blue shirt on. I used plenty of Mr Talbot's rather insistent hair tonic on my hair and used his brush and comb to tidy it up. By that time I smelled of gin only remotely, if at all.

The top button of the shirt wouldn't meet its buttonhole, so I poked into the bureau again and found a dark-blue crêpe tie and strung it around my neck. I got my coat back on and looked at myself in the mirror. I looked slightly too neat for that hour of the night, even for as careful a man as Mr Talbot's clothes indicated him to be. Too neat and too sober.

I rumbled my hair a little and pulled the tie loose, and went back to the whisky decanter and did what I could about being too sober. I lit one of Mr Talbot's cigarettes and hoped that Mr and Mrs Talbot, wherever they were, were having a much better time than I was. I hoped I would live long enough to come and visit them.

I went to the living-room door, the one giving on the hallway, and opened it and leaned in the opening smoking. I didn't think it was going to work. But I didn't think waiting there for them to follow my trail through the window was going to work any better.

A man coughed a little way down the hall and I poked my head out farther and he was looking at me. He came towards me briskly, a small sharp man in a neatly pressed police uniform. He had reddish hair and red-gold eyes.

I yawned and said languidly: 'What goes on, officer?'

He stared at me thoughtfully. 'Little trouble next door to you. Hear anything?'

'I thought I heard knocking. I just got home a little while ago.'

'Little late,' he said.

'That's a matter of opinion,' I said. 'Trouble next door, eh?'

'A dame,' he said. 'Know her?'

'I think I've seen her.'

'Yeah,' he said. 'You ought to see her now—' He put his hands to his throat and bulged his eyes out and gurgled unpleasantly. 'Like that,' he said. 'You didn't hear nothing, huh?'

'Nothing I noticed—except the knocking.'

'Yeah. What was the name?'

'Talbot.'

'Just a minute, Mr Talbot. Wait there just a minute.'

He went along the hallway and leaned into an open doorway through which light streamed out. 'Oh, Lieutenant,' he said. 'The man next door is on deck.'

A tall man came out of the doorway and stood looking along the hall straight at me. A tall man with rusty hair and very blue, eyes. Degarmo. That made it perfect.

'Here's the guy lives next door,' the small neat cop said helpfully. 'His name's Talbot.'

Degarmo looked straight at me, but nothing in his acid blue eyes showed that he had ever seen me before. He came quietly along the hall and put a hard hand against my chest and pushed me back into the room. When he had me half a dozen feet from the door he said over his shoulder:

'Come in here and shut the door, Shorty.'

The small cop came in and shut the door.

'Quite a gag,' Degarmo said lazily. 'Put a gun on him, Shorty.'

Shorty flicked his black belt holster open and had his .38 in his hand like a flash. He licked his lips.

'Oh boy,' he said softly, whistling a little. 'Oh boy. How'd you know, Lieutenant?'

'Know what?' Degarmo asked, keeping his eyes fixed on mine. 'What were you thinking of doing, pal—going down to get a paper—to find out if she was dead?'

'Oh boy,' Shorty said. 'A sex-killer. He pulled the girl's clothes off and choked her with his hands, Lieutenant. How'd you know?'

Degarmo didn't answer him. He just stood there, rocking a little on his heels, his face empty and granite-hard.

'Yah, he's the killer, sure,' Shorty said suddenly. 'Sniff the air in here, Lieutenant. The place ain't been aired out for days. And look at the dust on those bookshelves. And the clock on the mantel's stopped, Lieutenant. He come in through the—lemme look a minute, can I, Lieutenant?'

He ran out of the room into the bedroom. I heard him fumbling around. Degarmo stood woodenly.

Shorty came back. 'Come in at the bathroom window. There's broken glass in the tub. And something stinks of gin in there something awful. You remember how that apartment smelled of gin when we went in? Here's a shirt, Lieutenant. Smells like it was washed in gin.'

He held the shirt up. It perfumed the air rapidly. Degarmo looked at it vaguely and then stepped forward and yanked my coat open and looked at the shirt I was wearing.

'I know what he done,' Shorty said. 'He stole one of the guy's shirts that lives here. You see what he done, Lieutenant?'

'Yeah.' Degarmo held his hand against my chest and let it fall slowly. They were talking about me as if I was a piece of wood.

'Frisk him, Shorty.'

Shorty ran around me feeling here and there for a gun. 'Nothing on him,' he said.

'Let's get him out the back way,' Degarmo said. 'It's our pinch, if we make it before Webber gets here. That lug Reed couldn't find a moth in a shoe-box.'

'You ain't even detailed on the case,' Shorty said doubtfully. 'Didn't I hear you was suspended or something?'

'What can I lose,' Degarmo asked, 'if I'm suspended?'

'I can lose this here uniform,' Shorty said.

Degarmo looked at him wearily. The small cop blushed and his bright red-gold eyes were anxious.

'Okay, Shorty. Go and tell Reed.'

The small cop licked his lip. 'You say the word, Lieutenant, and I'm with you. I don't have to know you got suspended.'

'We'll take him down ourselves, just the two of us,' Degarmo said.

'Yeah, sure.'

Degarmo put his finger against my chin. 'A sex-killer,' he said quietly. 'Well, I'll be damned.' He smiled at me thinly, moving only the extreme corners of his wide brutal mouth.

34

We went out of the apartment and along the hall the other way from Apartment 618. Light streamed from the still open door. Two men in plain clothes now stood outside it smoking cigarettes inside their cupped hands, as if a wind was blowing. There was a sound of wrangling voices from the apartment.

We went around the bend of the hall and came to the elevator. Degarmo opened the fire door beyond the elevator shaft and we went down echoing concrete steps, floor after floor. At the lobby floor Degarmo stopped and held his hand on the doorknob and listened. He looked back over his shoulder.

'You got a car?' he asked me.

'In the basement garage.'

'That's an idea.'

We went on down the steps and came out into the shadowy basement.

The lanky Negro came out of the little office and I gave him my car check. He looked furtively at the police uniform on Shorty. He said nothing. He pointed to the Chrysler.

Degarmo climbed under the wheel of the Chrysler. I got in beside him and Shorty got into the back seat. We went up the ramp and out into the damp cool night air. A big car with twin red spotlights was charging towards us from a couple of blocks away.

Degarmo spat out of the car window and yanked the Chrysler the other way. 'That will be Webber,' he said. 'Late for the funeral again. We sure skinned his nose on that one, Shorty.'

'I don't like it to well, Lieutenant. I don't, honest.'

'Keep the chin up, kid. You might get back on homicide.'

'I'd rather wear buttons and eat,' Shorty said. The courage was oozing out of him fast.

Degarmo drove the car hard for ten blocks and then slowed a little. Shorty said uneasily:

'I guess you know what you're doing, Lieutenant, but this ain't the way to the Hall.'

'That's right,' Degarmo said. 'It never was, was it?'

He let the car slow down to a crawl and then turned into a residential street of small exact houses squatting behind small exact lawns. He braked the car gently and coasted over to the kerb and stopped about the middle of the block. He threw an arm over the back of the seat and turned his head to look back at Shorty.

'You think this guy killed her, Shorty?'

'I'm listening,' Shorty said in a tight voice.

'Got a flash?'

'No.'

I said: 'There's one in the car pocket on the left side.'

Shorty fumbled around and metal clicked and the white beam of the flashlight came on. Degarmo said:

'Take a look at the back of this guy's head.'

The beam moved and settled. I heard the small man's breathing behind me and felt it on my neck. Something felt for and touched the bump on my head. I grunted. The light went off and the darkness of the street rushed in again.

Shorty said: 'I guess maybe he was sapped, Lieutenant. I don't get it.'

'So was the girl,' Degarmo said. 'It didn't show much but it's there. She was sapped so she could have her clothes pulled off and be clawed up before she was killed. So the scatches would bleed. Then she was throttled. And none of this made any noise. Why would it? And there's no telephone in that apartment. Who reported it, Shorty?'

'How the hell would I know? A guy called up and said a woman had been murdered in 618 Granada Apartments on Eighth. Reed was still looking for a cameraman when you come in. The desk said a guy with a thick voice, likely disguised. Didn't give any name at all.'

'All right then,' Degarmo said. 'If you had murdered the girl, how would you get out of there?'

'I'd walk out,' Shorty said. 'Why not? Hey,' he barked at me suddenly, 'why didn't you?'

I didn't answer him. Degarmo said tonelessly: 'You wouldn't climb out of a bathroom window six floors up and then bust in another bathroom window into a strange apartment where people would likely be sleeping, would you? You wouldn't pretend to be the guy that lived there and you wouldn't throw away a lot of your time by calling the police, would you? Hell, that girl could have laid there for a week. You wouldn't throw away the chance of a start like that, would you, Shorty?'

'I don't guess I would,' Shorty said cautiously. 'I don't guess I would call up at all. But you know these sex fiends do funny things, Lieutenant. They ain't normal like us. And this guy could have had help and the other guy could have knocked him out to put him in the middle.'

'Don't tell me you thought that last bit up all by yourself,' Degarmo grunted. 'So here we sit, and the fellow that knows all the answers is sitting here with us and not saying a word.' He turned his head and stared at me. 'What were you doing there?'

'I can't remember,' I said. 'The crack on the head seems to have blanked me out.'

'We'll help you to remember,' Degarmo said. 'We'll take you up back in the hills a few miles where you can be quiet and look at the stars and remember. You'll remember all right.'

Shorty said: 'That ain't no way to talk, Lieutenant. Why don't we just go back to the Hall and play this the way it says in the rule book?'

'To hell with the rule book,' Degarmo said. 'I like this guy. I want to have one long sweet talk with him. He just needs a little coaxing, Shorty. He's just bashful.'

'I don't want any part of it,' Shorty said.

'What you want to do, Shorty?'

'I want to go back to the Hall.'

'Nobody's stopping you, kid. You want to walk?'

Shorty was silent for a moment. 'That's right,' he said at last, quietly. 'I want to walk.' He opened the car door and stepped out on to the kerbing. 'And I guess you know I have to report all this, Lieutenant?'

'Right,' Degarmo said. 'Tell Webber I was asking for him. Next time he buys a hamburger, tell him to turn down an empty plate for me.'

'That don't make any sense to me,' the small cop said. He slammed the car door shut. Degarmo let the clutch in and gunned the motor and hit forty in the first block and a half. In the third block he hit fifty. He slowed down at the boulevard and turned east and began to cruise along at a legal speed. A few late cars drifted by both ways, but for the most part the world lay in the cold silence of early morning.

After a little while we passed the city limits and Degarmo spoke. 'Let's hear you talk,' he said quietly. 'Maybe we can work this out.'

The car topped a long rise and dipped down to where the boulevard wound through the park-like grounds of the veterans' hospital. The tall triple electroliers had haloes from the beach fog that had drifted in during the night. I began to talk.

'Kingsley came over to my apartment to-night and said he had heard from his wife over the phone. She wanted some money quick. The idea was I was to take it to her and get her out of whatever trouble she was in. My idea was a little different. She was told how to identify me and I was to be at the Peacock Lounge at Eighth and Arguello at fifteen minutes past the hour. Any hour.'

Degarmo said slowly: 'She had to breeze and that meant she had something to breeze from, such as murder.' He lifted his hands lightly and let them fall on the wheel again.

'I went down there, hours after she had called. I had been told her hair was dyed brown. She passed me going out of the bar, but I didn't know her. I had never seen her in the flesh. All I had seen was what looked like a pretty good snapshot, but could be that and still not a very good likeness. She sent a Mexican kid in to call me out. She wanted the money and no conversation. I wanted her story. Finally she saw she would have to talk a little and told me she was at the Granada. She made me wait ten minutes before I followed her over.'

Degarmo said: 'Time to fix up a plant.'

'There was a plant all right, but I'm not sure she was in on it. She didn't want me to come up there, didn't want to talk. Yet she ought to have known I would insist on some explanation before I gave up the money, so her reluctance could have been just an act, to make me feel that I was controlling the situation. She could act all right. I found that out. Anyhow I went and we talked. Nothing she said made very much sense until we talked about Lavery getting shot. Then she made too much sense too quick. I told her I was going to turn her over to the police.'

Westwood Village, dark except for one all-night service station and a few distant windows in apartment houses, slid away to the north of us.

'So she pulled a gun,' I said. 'I think she meant to use it, but she got too close to me and I got a headlock on her. While we were wrestling around, somebody came out from behind a green curtain and slugged me. When I came out of that the murder was done.'

Degarmo said slowly: 'You get any kind of a look at who slugged you?'

'No. I felt or half-saw he was a man and a big one. And this lying on the davenport, mixed in with clothes.' I reached Kingsley's yellow-and-green scarf out of my pocket and draped it over his knee. 'I saw Kingsley wearing this earlier this evening,' I said.

Degarmo looked down at the scarf. He lifted it under the dashlight. 'You wouldn't forget that too quick,' he said. 'It steps right up and smacks you in the eye. Kingsley, huh? Well, I'm damned. What happened then?'

'Knocking on the door. Me still woozy in the head, not too bright and a bit panicked. I had been flooded with gin and my shoes and coat stripped off and maybe I looked and smelled a little like somebody who would yank a woman's clothes off and strangle her. So I got out through the bathroom window, cleaned myself up as well as I could, and the rest you know.'

Degarmo said: 'Why didn't you lie dormy in the place you climbed into?'

'What was the use? I guess even a Bay City cop would have found the way I had gone in a little while. If I had any chance at all, it was to walk out before that was discovered. If nobody was there who knew me, I had a fair chance of getting out of the building.'

'I don't think so,' Degarmo said. 'But I can see where you didn't lose much trying. What's your idea of the motivation here?'

'Why did Kingsley kill her—if he did? That's not hard. She had been cheating on him, making him a lot of trouble, endangering his job and now she had killed a man. Also, she had money and Kingsley wanted to marry another woman. He might have been afraid that with money to spend she could beat the rap and be left laughing at him. If she didn't beat the rap, and got sent up, her money would be just as thoroughly beyond his reach. He'd have to divorce her to get rid of her. There's plenty of motive for murder in all that. Also he saw a chance to make me the goat. It wouldn't stick, but it would make confusion and delay. If murderers didn't think they could get away with their murders, very few would be committed.'

Degarmo said: 'All the same it could be somebody else, somebody who isn't in the picture at all. Even if he went down there to see her, it could still be somebody else. Somebody else could have killed Lavery too.'

'If you like it that way.'

He turned his head. 'I don't like it any way at all. But if I crack the case, I'll get by with a reprimand from the police board. If I don't crack it, I'll be thumbing a ride out of town. You said I was dumb. Okay, I'm dumb. Where does Kingsley live? One thing I know is how to make people talk.'

'Nine-six-five Carson Drive, Beverly Hills. About five blocks on you turn north to the foothills. It's on the left side, just below Sunset. I've never been there, but I know how the block numbers run.'

He handed me the yellow-and-green scarf. 'Tuck that back into your pocket until we want to spring it on him.'

35

It was a two-storeyed white house with a dark roof. Bright moonlight lay against its wall like a fresh coat of paint. There were wrought-iron grilles against the lower halves of the front windows. A level lawn swept up to the front door which was set diagonally into the angle of a jutting wall. All the visible windows were dark.

Degarmo got out of the car and walked along the parkway and looked back along the drive to the garage. He moved down the driveway and the corner of the house hid him. I heard the sound of a garage door going up, then the thud as it was lowered again. He reappeared at the corner of the house, shook his head at me, and walked across the grass to the front door. He leaned his thumb on the bell and juggled a cigarette out of his pocket with one hand and put it between his lips.

He turned away from the door to light it and the flare of the match cut deep lines into his face. After a while there was light on the fan over the door. The peephole in the door swung back. I saw Degarmo holding up his shield. Slowly and as if unwillingly the door was opened. He went in.

He was gone four or five minutes. Light went on behind various windows, then off again. Then he came out of the house and while he was walking back to the car the light went off in the fan and the whole house was again as dark as we had found it.

He stood beside the car smoking and looking off down the curve of the street.

'One small car in the garage,' he said. 'The cook says it's hers. No sign of Kingsley. They say they haven't seen him since this morning. I looked in all the rooms. I guess they told the truth. Webber and a print man were there

late this afternoon and the dusting-powder is still all over the main
bedroom. Webber would be getting prints to check against what we
found in Lavery's house. He didn't tell me what he got. Where would
he be—Kingsley?'

'Anywhere,' I said. 'On the road, in an hotel, in a Turkish bath getting
the kinks out of his nerves. But we'll have to try his girl-friend first. Her
name is Fromsett and she lives at the Bryson Tower on Sunset Place. That's
away downtown, near Bullock's Wilshire.'

'She does what?' Degarmo asked, getting in under the wheel.

'She holds the fort in his office and holds his hand out of office hours.
She's no office cutie, though. She has brains and style.'

'This situation is going to use all she has,' Degarmo said. He drove down
to Wilshire and we turned east again.

Twenty-five minutes brought us to the Bryson Tower, a white stucco
palace with fretted lanterns in the forecourt and tall date-palms. The
entrance was in an L, up marble steps, through a Moorish archway, and
over a lobby that was too big and a carpet that was too blue. Blue Ali Baba
oil jars were dotted around, big enough to keep tigers in. There was a desk
and a night clerk with one of those moustaches that get stuck under your
finger-nail.

Degarmo lunged past the desk towards an open elevator beside which a
tired old man sat on a stool waiting for a customer. The clerk snapped at
Degarmo's back like a terrier.

'One moment, please. Whom did you wish to see?'

Degarmo spun on his heel and looked at me wonderingly. 'Did he say
"whom"?'

'Yeah, but don't hit him,' I said. 'There is such a word.'

Degarmo licked his lips. 'I knew there was,' he said. 'I often wondered
where they kept it. Look, buddy,' he said to the clerk, 'we want up seven-
sixteen. Any objections?'

'Certainly I have,' the clerk said coldly. 'We don't announce guests
at'—he lifted his arm and turned it neatly to look at the narrow oblong watch
on the inside of his wrist—'at twenty-three minutes past four in the
morning.'

'That's what I thought,' Degarmo said. 'So I wasn't going to bother you.
You get the idea?' He took his shield out of his pocket and held it so that
the light glinted on the gold and the blue enamel. 'I'm a police lieutenant.'

The clerk shrugged. 'Very well. I hope there isn't going to be any trouble.
I'd better announce you then. What names?'

'Lieutenant Degarmo and Mr Marlowe.'

'Apartment 716. That will be Miss Fromsett. One moment.'

He went behind a glass screen and we heard him talking on the phone
after a longish pause. He came back and nodded.

'Miss Fromsett is in. She will receive you.'

'That's certainly a load off my mind,' Degarmo said. 'And don't bother to
call your house-peeper and send him up to the scatter. I'm allergic to house-
peepers.'

The clerk gave a small cold smile and we got into the elevator.

The seventh floor was cool and quiet. The corridor seemed a mile long.
We came at last to a door with 716 on it in gilt numbers in a circle of gilt
leaves. There was an ivory button beside the door. Degarmo pushed it and

chimes rang inside the door and it was opened.

Miss Fromsett wore a quilted blue robe over her pyjamas. On her feet were small tufted slippers with high heels. Her dark hair was fluffed out engagingly and the cold cream had been wiped from her face and just enough make-up applied.

We went past her into a rather narrow room with several handsome oval mirrors and grey period furniture upholstered in blue damask. It didn't look like apartment-house furniture. She sat down on a slender love seat and leaned back and waited calmly for somebody to say something.

I said: 'This is Lieutenant Degarmo of the Bay City police. We're looking for Kingsley. He's not at his house. We thought you might be able to give us an idea where to find him.'

She spoke to me without looking at me. 'Is it that urgent?'

'Yes. Something has happened.'

'What has happened?'

Degarmo said bluntly: 'We just want to know where Kingsley is, sister. We don't have time to build up a scene.'

The girl looked at him with complete absence of expression. She looked back at me and said:

'I think you had better tell me, Mr Marlowe.'

'I went down there with money,' I said. 'I met her as arranged. I went to her apartment to talk to her. While there I was slugged by a man who was hidden behind a curtain. I didn't see the man. When I came out of it she had been murdered.'

'Murdered?'

I said: 'Murdered.'

She closed her fine eyes and the corners of her lovely mouth drew in. Then she stood up with a quick shrug and went over to a small, marble-topped table with spindly legs. She took a cigarette out of a small embossed silver box and lit it, staring emptily down at the table. The match in her hand was waved more and more slowly until it stopped, still burning, and she dropped it into a tray. She turned and put her back to the table.

'I suppose I ought to scream or something,' she said. 'I don't seem to have any feeling about it at all.'

Degarmo said: 'We don't feel so interested in your feelings right now. What we want to know is where Kingsley is. You can tell us or not tell us. Either way you can skip the attitudes. Just make your mind up.'

She said to me quietly: 'The lieutenant here is a Bay City officer?'

I nodded. She turned at him slowly, with a lovely contemptuous dignity. 'In that case,' she said, 'he has no more right in my apartment than any other loud-mouthed bum that might try to toss his weight around.'

Degarmo looked at her bleakly. He grinned and walked across the room and stretched his long legs from a deep downy chair. He waved his hand at me.

'Okay, you work on her. I can get all the co-operation I need from the L.A. boys, but by the time I had things explained to them, it would be a week from next Tuesday.'

I said: 'Miss Fromsett, if you know where he is, or where he started to go, please tell us. You can understand that he has to be found.'

She said calmly, 'Why?'

Degarmo put his head back and laughed. 'This babe is good,' he said.

'Maybe she thinks we should keep it a secret from him that his wife has been knocked off.'

'She's better than you think,' I told him. His face sobered and he bit his thumb. He looked her up and down insolently.

She said: 'Is it just because he has to be told?'

I took the yellow-and-green scarf out of my pocket and shook it out loose and held it in front of her.

'This was found in the apartment where she was murdered. I think you have seen it.'

She looked at the scarf and she looked at me, and in neither of the glances was there any meaning. She said: 'You ask for a great deal of confidence, Mr Marlowe. Considering that you haven't been such a very smart detective after all.'

'I ask for it,' I said, 'and I expect to get it. And how smart I've been is something you don't really know anything about.'

'This is cute,' Degarmo put in. 'You two make a nice team. All you need is acrobats to follow you. But right now—'

She cut through his voice as if he didn't exist. 'How was she murdered?'

'She was strangled and stripped naked and scratched up.'

'Derry wouldn't have done anything like that,' she said quietly.

Degarmo made a noise with his lips. 'Nobody ever knows what anybody else will do, sister. A cop knows that much.'

She still didn't look at him. In the same level tone she asked: 'Do you want to know where we went after we left your apartment and whether he brought me home—things like that?'

'Yes.'

'Because if he did, he wouldn't have had time to go down to the beach and kill her? Is that it?'

I said, 'That's a good part of it.'

'He didn't bring me home,' she said slowly. 'I took a taxi on Hollywood Boulevard, not more than five minutes after we left your place. I didn't see him again. I supposed he went home.'

Degarmo said: 'Usually the bim tries to give her boy-friend a bit more alibi than that. But it takes all kinds, don't it?'

Miss Fromsett said to me: 'He wanted to bring me home, but it was a long way out of his way and we were both tired. The reason I am telling you this is because I know it doesn't matter in the least. If I thought it did, I wouldn't tell you.'

'So he did have time,' I said.

She shook her head. 'I don't know. I don't know how much time was needed. I don't know how he could have known where to go. Not from me, not from her through me. She didn't tell me.' Her dark eyes were on mine, searching, probing. 'Is this the kind of confidence you ask for?'

I folded the scarf up and put it back in my pocket. 'We want to know where he is now.'

'I can't tell you because I have no idea.' Her eyes had followed the scarf down to my pocket. They stayed there. 'You say you were slugged. You mean knocked unconscious?'

'Yes. By somebody who was hidden out behind a curtain. We still fall for it. She pulled a gun on me and I was busy trying to take it away from her. There's no doubt she shot Lavery.'

Degarmo stood up suddenly: 'You're making yourself a nice smooth scene, fellow,' he growled. 'But you're not getting anywhere. Let's blow.'

I said: 'Wait a minute. I'm not finished. Suppose he had something on his mind, Miss Fromsett, something that was eating pretty deep into him. That was how he looked tonight. Suppose he knew more about all this than we realized—or than I realized—and knew things were coming to a head. He would want to go somewhere quietly and try to figure out what to do. Don't you think he might?'

I stopped and waited, looking sideways at Degarmo's impatience. After a moment the girl said tonelessly: 'He wouldn't run away or hide, because it wasn't anything he could run away and hide from. But he might want a time to himself to think.'

'In a strange place, in an hotel,' I said, thinking of the story that had been told me in the Granada. 'Or in a much quieter place than that.'

I looked around for the telephone.

'It's in my bedroom,' Miss Fromsett said, knowing at once what I was looking for.

I went down the room and through the door at the end. Degarmo was right behind me. The bedroom was ivory and ashes of roses. There was a big bed with no footboard and a pillow with the rounded hollow of a head. Toilet articles glistened on a built-in dresser with panelled mirrors on the wall above it. An open door showed mulberry bathroom tiles. The phone was on a night table by the bed.

I sat down on the edge of the bed and patted the place where Miss Fromsett's head had been and lifted the phone and dialled long distance. When the operator answered I asked for Constable Jim Patton at Puma Point, person to person, very urgent. I put the phone back in the cradle and lit a cigarette. Degarmo glowered down at me, standing with his legs apart, tough and tireless and ready to be nasty. 'What now?' he grunted.

'Wait and see.'

'Who's running this show?'

'Your asking me shows that. I am—unless you want the Los Angeles police to run it.'

He scratched a match on his thumb-nail and watched it burn and tried to blow it out with a long steady breath that just bent the flame over. He got rid of that match and put another between his teeth and chewed on it. The phone rang in a moment.

'Ready with your Puma Point call.'

Patton's sleepy voice came on the line. 'Yes? This is Patton at Puma Point.'

'This is Marlowe in Los Angeles,' I said. 'Remember me?'

'Sure I remember you, son. I ain't only half awake though.'

'Do me a favour,' I said. 'Although I don't know why you should. Go or send over to Little Fawn Lake and see if Kingsley is there. Don't let him see you. You can spot his car outside the cabin or maybe see lights. And see that he stays put. Call me back as soon as you know. I'm coming up. Can you do that?'

Patton said: 'I got no reason to stop him if he wants to leave.'

'I'll have a Bay City police officer with me who wants to question him about a murder. Not your murder, another one.'

There was a drumming silence along the wire. Patton said; 'You ain't just bein' tricky, are you, son?'

'No. Call me back at Tunbridge 2722.'

'Should likely take me half an hour,' he said.

I hung up. Degarmo was grinning now. 'This babe flash you a signal I couldn't read?'

I stood up off the bed. 'No. I'm just trying to read his mind. He's no cold killer. Whatever fire there was is all burned out of him by now. I thought he might go to the quietest and most remote place he knows—just to get a grip of himself. In a few hours he'll probably turn himself in. It would look better for you if you got to him before he did that.'

'Unless he puts a slug in his head,' Degarmo said coldly. 'Guys like him are very apt to do that.'

'You can't stop him until you find him.'

'That's right.'

We went back into the living-room. Miss Fromsett poked her head out of her kitchenette and said she was making coffee, and did we want any. We had some coffee and sat around looking like people seeing friends off at the railroad station.

The call from Patton came through in about twenty-five minutes. There was light in the Kingsley cabin and a car was parked beside it.

36

We ate some breakfast at Alhambra and I had the tank filled. We drove out Highway 70 and started moving past the trucks into the rolling ranch country. I was driving. Degarmo sat moodily in the corner, his hands deep in his pockets.

I watched the fat straight rows of orange trees spin by like the spokes of a wheel. I listened to the whine of the tyres on the pavement and I felt tired and stale from lack of sleep and too much emotion.

We reached the long slope south of San Dimas that goes up to a ridge and drops down into Pomona. This is the ultimate end of the fog belt, and the beginning of that semi-desert region where the sun is as light and dry as old sherry in the morning, as hot as a blast-furnace at noon, and drops like an angry brick at nightfall.

Degarmo stuck a match in the corner of his mouth and said almost sneeringly:

'Webber gave me hell last night. He said he was talking to you and what about.'

I said nothing. He looked at me and looked away again. He waved a hand outwards. 'I wouldn't live in this damn country if they gave it to me. The air's stale before it gets up in the morning.'

'We'll be coming to Ontario in a minute. We'll switch over to Foothill Boulevard and you'll see five miles of the finest grevillea trees in the world.'

'I wouldn't know one from a fireplug,' Degarmo said.

We came to the centre of town and turned north on Euclid, along the splendid parkway. Degarmo sneered at the grevillea trees.

After a while he said: 'That was my girl that drowned in the lake up there. I haven't been right in the head since I heard about it. All I can see is red. If I could get my hands on that guy Chess—'

'You made enough trouble,' I said, 'letting her get away with murdering Almore's wife.'

I stared straight ahead through the windshield. I knew his head moved and his eyes froze on me. I didn't know what his hands were doing. I didn't know what expression was on his face. After a long time his words came. They came through tight teeth and edgeways, and they scraped a little as they came out.

'You a little crazy or something?'

'No,' I said. 'Neither are you. You know as well as anybody could know anything that Florence Almore didn't get up out of bed and walk down to that garage. You know she was carried. You know that was why Talley stole her slipper, the slipper that had never walked on a concrete path. You knew that Almore gave his wife a shot in the arm at Condy's place and that it was just enough and not any too much. He knew his shots in the arm the way you know how to rough up a bum that hasn't any money or any place to sleep. You know that Almore didn't murder his wife with morphine and that if he wanted to murder her, morphine would be the last thing in the world he would use. But you know that somebody else did, and that Almore carried her down to the garage and put her there—technically still alive to breathe in some monoxide, but medically just as dead as though she had stopped breathing. You know all that.'

Degarmo said softly: 'Brother, how did you ever manage to live so long?'

I said: 'By not falling for too many gags and not getting too much afraid of professional hard guys. Only a heel would have done what Almore did, only a heel and a badly scared man who had things on his soul that wouldn't stand daylight. Technically he may even have been guilty of murder. I don't think the point has ever been settled. Certainly he would have a hell of a time proving that she was in such a deep coma that she was beyond any possibility of help. But as a practical matter of who killed her, you know the girl killed her.'

Degarmo laughed. It was a grating unpleasant laugh, not only mirthless, but meaningless.

We reached Foothill Boulevard and turned east again. I thought it was still cool, but Degarmo was sweating. He couldn't take his coat off because of the gun under his arm.

I said: 'The girl, Mildred Haviland, was playing house with Almore and his wife knew it. She had threatened him. I got that from her parents. The girl, Mildred Haviland, knew all about morphine and where to get all of it she needed and how much to use. She was alone in the house with Florence Almore, after she put her to bed. She was in a perfect spot to load a needle with four or five grains and shoot it into an unconscious woman through the same puncture Almore had already made. She would die, perhaps while Almore was still out of the house, and he would come home and find her dead. The problem would be his. He would have to solve it. Nobody would believe anybody else had doped his wife to death. Nobody that didn't know all the circumstances. But you knew. I'd have to think you much more of a damn fool than I think you are to believe you didn't know. You covered the girl up. You were in love with her still. You scared her out of town, out of danger, out of reach, but you covered up for her. You let the murder ride. She had you that way. Why did you go up to the mountains looking for her?'

'And how did I know where to look?' he said harshly. 'It wouldn't bother you to add an explanation of that, would it?'

'Not at all,' I said. 'She got sick of Bill Chess and his boozing and his tempers and his down-at-heels living. But she had to have money to make a break. She thought she was safe now, that she had something on Almore that was safe to use. So she wrote him for money. He sent you up to talk to her. She didn't tell Almore what her present name was or any details or where or how she was living. A letter addressed to Mildred Haviland at Puma Point would reach her. All she had to do was ask for it. But no letter came and nobody connected her with Mildred Haviland. All you had was an old photo and your usual bad manners, and they didn't get you anywhere with those people.'

Degarmo said gratingly: 'Who told you she tried to get money from Almore?'

'Nobody. I had to think of something to fit what happened. If Lavery or Mrs Kingsley had known who Muriel Chess had been, and had tipped it off, you would have known where to find her and what name she was using. You didn't know those things. Therefore the lead had to come from the only person up there who knew who she was, and that was herself. So I assume she wrote to Almore.'

'Okay,' he said at last. 'Let's forget it. It doesn't make any difference any more now. If I'm in a jam, that's my business. I'd do it again, in the same circumstances.'

'That's all right,' I said. 'I'm not planning to put the bite on anybody myself. Not even on you. I'm telling you this mostly so you won't try to hang any murders on Kingsley that don't belong to him. If there is one that does, let it hang.'

'Is that why you're telling me?' he asked.

'Yeah.'

'I thought maybe it was because you hated my guts,' he said.

'I'm all done with hating you,' I said. 'It's all washed out of me. I hate people hard, but I don't hate them very long.'

We were going through the grape country now, the open sandy grape country along the scarred flanks of the foothills. We came in a little to San Bernardino and I kept on through it without stopping.

37

At Crestline, elevation 5,000 feet, it had not yet started to warm up. We stopped for a beer. When we got back into the car, Degarmo took the gun from his under-arm holster and looked it over. It was a .38 Smith and Wesson on a .44 frame, a wicked weapon with a kick like a .45 and a much greater effective range.

'You won't need that,' I said. 'He's big and strong, but he's not that kind of tough.'

He put the gun back under his arm and grunted. We didn't talk any more now. We had no more to talk about. We rolled around the curves and along the sharp sheer edges walled with white guard rails and in some places with walls of field stone and heavy iron chains. We climbed through the tall oaks and on to the altitudes where the oaks are not so tall and the pines are taller and taller. We came at last to the dam at the end of Puma Lake.

I stopped the car and the sentry threw his piece across his body and stepped up to the window.

'Close all the windows of your car before proceeding across the dam, please.'

I reached back to wind up the rear window on my side. Degarmo held his shield up. 'Forget it, buddy. I'm a police officer,' he said with his usual tact.

The sentry gave him a solid expressionless stare. 'Close all windows, please,' he said in the same tone he had used before.

'Nuts to you,' Degarmo said. 'Nuts to you, soldier boy.'

'It's an order,' the sentry said. His jaw muscles bulged very slightly. His dull greyish eyes stared at Degarmo. 'And I didn't write the order, mister. Up with the windows.'

'Suppose I told you to go jump in the lake,' Degarmo sneered.

The sentry said: 'I might do it. I scare easily.' He patted the breech of his rifle with a leathery hand.

Degarmo turned and closed the windows on his side. We drove across the dam. There was a sentry in the middle and one at the far end. The first one must have flashed them some kind of signal. They looked at us with steady watchful eyes, without friendliness.

I drove on through the piled masses of granite and down through the meadows of coarse grass where cows grazed. The same gaudy slacks and short shorts and peasant handkerchiefs as yesterday, the same light breeze and golden sun and clear blue sky, the same smell of pine needles, the same cool softness of a mountain summer. But yesterday was a hundred years ago, something crystallized in time, like a fly in amber.

I turned off on the road to Little Fawn Lake and wound around the huge rocks and past the little gurgling waterfall. The gate into Kingsley's property was open and Patton's car was standing in the road pointing towards the lake, which was invisible from that point. There was nobody in it. The card sign on the windshield still read, '*Keep Jim Patton Constable. He Is Too Old To Go To Work*'.

Close to it and pointed the other way was a small battered coupé. Inside the coupé a lion-hunter's hat. I stopped my car behind Patton's and locked it and got out. Andy got out of the coupé and stood staring at us woodenly.

I said: 'This is Lieutenant Degarmo of the Bay City police.'

Andy said: 'Jim's just over the ridge. He's waiting for you. He ain't had any breakfast.'

We walked up the road to the ridge as Andy got back into his coupé. Beyond it the road dropped to the tiny blue lake. Kingsley's cabin across the water seemed to be without life.

'That's the lake,' I said.

Degarmo looked down at it silently. His shoulders moved in a heavy shrug. 'Let's go get the bastard,' was all he said.

We went on and Patton stood up from behind a rock. He was wearing the same old Stetson and khaki pants and shirt buttoned to his thick neck. The star on his left breast still had a bent point. His jaws moved slowly, munching.

'Nice to see you again,' he said, not looking at me, but at Degarmo.

He put his hand out and shook Degarmo's hard paw. 'Last time I seen you, Lieutenant, you was wearing another name. Kind of undercover, I guess you'd call it. I guess I didn't treat you right neither. I apologize. Guess I know who that photo of yours was all the time.'

Degarmo nodded and said nothing.

'Likely if I'd of been on my toes and played the game right, a lot of trouble would have been saved,' Patton said. 'Maybe a life would have been saved. I feel kind of bad about it, but then again I ain't a fellow that feels too bad about anything very long. Suppose we sit down here and you tell me what it is we're supposed to be doing now.'

Degarmo said: 'Kingsley's wife was murdered in Bay City last night. I have to talk to him about it.'

'You mean you suspect him?' Patton asked.

'And how,' Degarmo grunted.

Patton rubbed his neck and looked across the lake. 'He ain't showed outside the cabin at all. Likely he's still asleep. Early this morning I snuck around the cabin. There was a radio goin' then and I heard sounds like a man would make playing with a bottle and a glass. I stayed away from him. Was that right?'

'We'll go over there now,' Degarmo said.

'You got a gun Lieutenant?'

Degarmo patted under his left arm. Patton looked at me. I shook my head, no gun.

'Kingsley might have one, too,' Patton said. 'I don't hanker after no fast shooting around here, Lieutenant. It wouldn't do me no good to have a gun-fight. We don't have that kind of community up here. You look to me like a fellow who would jack his gun out kind of fast.'

'I've got plenty of swift, if that's what you mean,' Degarmo said. 'But I want this guy talking.'

Patton looked at Degarmo, looked at me, looked back at Degarmo and spat tobacco juice in a long stream to one side.

'I ain't heard enough to even approach him,' he said stubbornly.

So we sat down on the ground and told him the story. He listened silently, not blinking an eye. At the end he said to me: 'You got a funny way of working for people, seems to me. Personally I think you boys are plumb misinformed. We'll go over and see. I'll go in first—in case you would know what you are talking about and Kingsley would have a gun and would be a little desperate. I got a big belly. Makes a nice target.'

We stood up off the ground and started around the lake the long way. When we came to the little pier I said:

'Did they autopsy her yet, Sheriff?'

Patton nodded. 'She drowned all right. They say they're satisfied that's how she died. She wasn't knifed or shot or had her head cracked in or anything. There's marks on the body, but too many to mean anything. And it ain't a very nice body to work with.'

Degarmo looked white and angry.

'I guess I oughtn't to have said that, Lieutenant,' Patton added mildly. 'Kind of tough to take. Seeing you knew the lady pretty well.'

Degarmo said: 'Let's get it over and do what we have to do.'

We went on along the shore of the lake and came to Kingsley's cabin. We went up the heavy steps. Patton went quietly across the porch to the door. He tried the screen. It was not hooked. He opened it and tried the door. That was unlocked also. He held the door shut, with the knob turned in his hand, and Degarmo took hold of the screen and pulled it wide. Patton opened the door and we walked into the room.

Derace Kingsley lay back in a deep chair by the cold fireplace with his eyes closed. There was an empty glass and an almost empty whisky bottle on the table beside him. The room smelled of whisky. A dish near the bottle was choked with cigarette-stubs. Two crushed empty packs lay on top of the stubs.

All the windows in the room were shut. It was already close and hot in there. Kingsley was wearing a sweater and his face was flushed and heavy. He snored and his hands hung lax outside the arms of the chair, the finger-tips touching the floor.

Patton moved to within a few feet of him and stood looking silently down at him for a long moment before he spoke.

'Mr Kingsley,' he said then, in a calm, steady voice, 'we got to talk to you a little.'

38

Kingsley moved with a kind of jerk, and opened his eyes and moved them without moving his head. He looked at Patton, then at Degarmo, lastly at me. His eyes were heavy, but the light sharpened in them. He sat up slowly in the chair and rubbed his hands up and down the sides of his face.

'I was asleep,' he said. 'Fell asleep a couple of hours ago. I was as drunk as a skunk, I guess. Anyway, much drunker than I like to be.' He dropped his hands and let them hang.

Patton said: 'This is Lieutenant Degarmo of the Bay City police. He has to talk to you.'

Kingsley looked briefly at Degarmo and his eyes came around to stare at me. His voice when he spoke again sounded sober and quiet and tired to death.

'So you let them get her?' he said.

I said: 'I would have, but I didn't.'

Kingsley thought about that, looking at Degarmo. Patton had left the front door open. He pulled the brown venetian blinds up at two front windows and pulled the windows up. He sat in a chair near one of them and clasped his hands over his stomach. Degarmo stood glowering down at Kingsley.

'Your wife is dead, Kingsley,' he said brutally. 'If it's any news to you.'

Kingsley stared at him and moistened his lips.

'Takes it easy, don't he?' Degarmo said. 'Show him the scarf.'

I took the yellow-and-green scarf out and dangled it. Degarmo jerked a thumb. 'Yours?'

Kingsley nodded. He moistened his lips again.

'Careless of you to leave it behind you,' Degarmo said. He was breathing a little hard. His nose was pinched and deep lines ran from his nostrils to the corners of his mouth.

Kingsley said very quietly: 'Leave it behind me where?' He had barely glanced at the scarf. He hadn't looked at all at me.

'In the Granada Apartments, on Eighth Street, in Bay City. Apartment 618. Am I telling you something?'

Kingsley now very slowly lifted his eyes to meet mine. 'Is that where she was?' he breathed.

I nodded. 'She didn't want me to go there. I wouldn't give her the money until she talked to me. She admitted she killed Lavery. She pulled a gun and planned to give me the same treatment. Somebody came from behind the curtain and knocked me out without letting me see him. When I came to she was dead.' I told him how she was dead and how she looked. I told him what I had done and what had been done to me.

He listened without moving a muscle of his face. When I had done talking he made a vague gesture towards the scarf. 'What has that got to do with it?'

'The lieutenant regards it as evidence that you were the party hidden out in the apartment.'

Kingsley thought that over. He didn't seem to get the implications of it very quickly. He leaned back in the chair and rested his head against the back. 'Go on,' he said at length. 'I suppose you know what you're talking about. I'm quite sure I don't.'

Degarmo said: 'All right, play dumb. See what it gets you. You could begin by accounting for your time last night after you dropped your biddy at her apartment house.'

Kingsley said evenly: 'If you mean Miss Fromsett, I didn't. She went home in a taxi. I was going home myself, but I didn't. I came up here instead. I thought the trip and the night air and the quiet might help me to get straightened out.'

'Just think of that,' Degarmo jeered. 'Straightened out from what, if I might ask?'

'Straightened out from all the worry I had been having.'

'Hell,' Degarmo said, 'a little thing like strangling your wife and clawing her belly wouldn't worry you that much, would it?'

'Son, you hadn't ought to say things like that,' Patton put in from the background. 'That ain't no way to talk. You ain't produced anything yet that sounds like evidence.'

'No?' Degarmo swung his hard head at him. 'What about this scarf, fatty? Isn't that evidence?'

'You didn't fit it in to anything—not that I heard,' Patton said peacefully. 'And I ain't fat, either, just well covered.'

Degarmo swung away from him disgustedly. He jabbed his finger at Kingsley.

'I suppose you didn't go down to Bay City at all?' he said harshly.

'No. Why should I? Marlowe was taking care of that. And I don't see why you are making a point of the scarf. Marlowe was wearing it.'

Degarmo stood rooted savage. He turned very slowly and gave me his bleak angry stare.

'I don't get this,' he said. 'Honest, I don't. It wouldn't be that somebody is kidding me, would it? Somebody like you?'

I said: 'All I told about the scarf was that it was in the apartment and that I had seen Kingsley wearing it earlier in the evening. That seemed to be all you wanted. I might have added that I had later worn the scarf myself, so the girl I was to meet could identify me that much easier.'

Degarmo backed away from Kingsley and leaned against the wall at the end of the fireplace. He pulled his lower lip out with thumb and forefinger of his left hand. His right hand hung lax at his side, the fingers slightly curved.

I said: 'I told you all I had ever seen of Mrs Kingsley was a snapshot. One of us had to be sure of being able to identify the other. The scarf seemed obvious enough for identification. As a matter of fact I had seen her once before, although I didn't know it when I went to meet her. But I didn't recognize her at once.' I turned to Kingsley. 'Mrs Fallbrook,' I said.

'I thought you said Mrs Fallbrook was the owner of the house,' he answered slowly.

'That's what she said at the time. That's what I believed at the time. Why wouldn't I?'

Degarmo made a sound in his throat. His eyes were a little crazy. I told him about Mrs Fallbrook and her purple hat and her fluttery manner and the empty gun she had been holding and how she gave it to me.

When I stopped, he said very carefully: 'I didn't hear you tell Webber any of that.'

'I didn't tell him. I didn't want to admit I had already been in the house three hours before. That I had gone to talk it over with Kingsley before I reported it to the police.'

'That's something we're going to love you for,' Degarmo said with a cold grin. 'Jesus, what a sucker I've been. How much you paying this shamus to cover up your murders for you, Kingsley?'

'His usual rates,' Kingsley told him emptily. 'And a five hundred dollar bonus if he can prove my wife didn't murder Lavery.'

'Too bad he can't earn that,' Degarmo sneered.

'Don't be silly,' I said. 'I've already earned it.'

There was a silence in the room. One of those charged silences which seem about to split apart with a peal of thunder. It didn't. It remained, hung heavy and solid, like a wall. Kingsley moved a little in his chair, and after a long moment, he nodded his head.

'Nobody could possibly know that better than you know it, Degarmo,' I said.

Patton had as much expression on his face as a chunk of wood. He watched Degarmo quietly. He didn't look at Kingsley at all. Degarmo looked at a point between my eyes, but not as if that was anything in the room with him. Rather as if he was looking at something very far away, like a mountain across a valley.

After what seemed a very long time, Degarmo said quietly: 'I don't see why. I don't know anything about Kingsley's wife. To the best of my knowledge I never laid eyes on her—until last night.'

He lowered his eyelids a little and watched me broodingly. He knew perfectly well what I was going to say. I said it anyway.

'And you never saw her last night. Because she had already been dead for over a month. Because she had been drowned in Little Fawn Lake. Because the woman you saw dead in the Granada Apartments was Mildred Haviland, and Mildred Haviland was Muriel Chess. And since Mrs Kingsley was dead long before Lavery was shot, it follows that Mrs Kingsley did not shoot him.'

Kingsley clenched his fists on the arms of his chair, but he made no sound, no sound at all.

39

There was another heavy silence. Patton broke it by saying in his careful slow voice: 'That's kind of a wild statement, ain't it? Don't you kind of think Bill Chess would know his own wife?'

I said: 'After a month in the water? With his wife's clothes on her and some of his wife's trinkets? With water-soaked blonde hair like his wife's hair and almost no recognizable face? Why would he even have a doubt about it? She left a note that might be a suicide note. She was gone away. They had quarrelled. Her clothes and car had gone away. During the month she was gone, he had heard nothing from her. He had no idea where she had gone. And then this corpse comes up out of the water with Muriel's clothes on it. A blonde woman about his wife's size. Of course there would be differences and if any substitution had been suspected, they would have been found and checked. But there was no reason to suspect any such thing. Crystal Kingsley was still alive. She had gone off with Lavery. She had left her car in San Bernardino. She had sent a wire to her husband from El Paso. She was all taken care of, so far as Bill Chess was concerned. He had no thoughts about her at all. She didn't enter the picture anywhere for him. Why should she?'

Patton said: 'I ought to of thought of it myself. But if I had, it would be one of those ideas a fellow would throw away almost as quick as he thought of it. It would look too kind of far-fetched.'

'Superficially, yes,' I said. 'But only superficially. Suppose the body had not come up out of the lake for a year, or not at all, unless the lake was dragged for it. Muriel Chess was gone and nobody was going to spend much time looking for her. We might never have heard of her again. Mrs Kingsley was a different proposition. She had money and connexions and an anxious husband. She would be searched for, as she was, eventually. But not very soon, unless something happened to start suspicion. It might have been a matter of months before anything was found out. The lake might have been dragged, but if a search along her trail seemed to indicate that she had actually left the lake and gone down the hill, even as far as San Bernardino, and the train from there east, then the lake might never have been dragged. And even if it was and the body was found, there was rather better than an even chance that the body would not be correctly identified. Bill Chess was arrested for his wife's murder. For all I know he might even have been convicted of it, and that would have been that, as far as the body in the lake was concerned. Crystal Kingsley would still be missing, and it would be an unsolved mystery. Eventually it would be assumed that something had happened to her and that she was no longer alive. But nobody would know where or when or how it had happened. If it hadn't been for Lavery, we might not be here talking about it now. Lavery is the key to the whole thing. He was in the Prescott Hotel in San Bernardino the night Crystal Kingsley was supposed to have left here. He saw a woman there who had Crystal Kingsley's car, who was wearing Crystal Kingsley's clothes, and of course he knew who she was. But he didn't have to know there was anything wrong. He didn't have to know they were Crystal Kingsley's clothes or that the woman had put Crystal Kingsley's car in the hotel garage. All he had to know was that he met Muriel Chess. Muriel took care of the rest.'

I stopped and waited for somebody to say anything. Nobody did. Patton sat immovable in his chair, his plump, hairless hands clasped comfortably across his stomach. Kingsley leaned his head back and he had his eyes half-closed and he was not moving. Degarmo leaned against the wall by the fireplace, taut and white-faced and cold, a big, hard, solemn man whose thoughts were deeply hidden.

I went on talking.

'If Muriel Chess impersonated Crystal Kingsley, she murdered her. That's elementary. All right, let's look at it. We know who she was and what kind of woman she was. She had already murdered before she met and married Bill Chess. She had been Dr Almore's office nurse and his little pal and she had murdered Dr Almore's wife in such a neat way that Almore had to cover up for her. And she had been married to a man in the Bay City police who also was sucker enough to cover up for her. She got the men that way, she could make them jump through hoops. I didn't know her long enough to see why, but her record proves it. What she was able to do with Lavery proves it. Very well, she killed people who got in her way, and Kingsley's wife got in her way too. I hadn't meant to talk about this, but it doesn't matter much now. Crystal Kingsley could make the men do a little jumping through hoops too. She made Bill Chess jump and Bill Chess's wife wasn't the girl to take that and smile. Also, she was sick to death of her life up here—she must have been—and she wanted to get away. But she needed money. She had tried to get if from Almore, and that sent Degarmo up here looking for her. That scared her a little. Degarmo is the sort of fellow you are never quite sure of. She was right not to be sure of him, wasn't she, Degarmo?'

Degarmo moved his foot on the ground. 'The sands are running against you, fellow,' he said grimly. 'Speak your little piece while you can.'

'Mildred didn't positively have to have Crystal Kingsley's car and clothes and credentials and what not, but they helped. What money she had must have helped a great deal, and Kingsley says she liked to have a good deal of money with her. Also she must have had jewellery which could eventually be turned into money. All this made killing her a rational as well as an agreeable thing to do. That disposes of motive, and we come to means and opportunity.

'The opportunity was made to order for her. She had quarrelled with Bill and he had gone off to get drunk. She knew her Bill and how drunk he could get and how long he would stay away. She needed time. Time was of the essence. She had to assume that there was time. Otherwise the whole thing flopped. She had to pack her own clothes and take them in her car to Coon Lake and hide them there, because they had to be gone. She had to walk

back. She had to murder Crystal Kingsley and dress her in Muriel's clothes
and get her down in the lake. All that took time. As to the murder itself, I
imagine she got her drunk or knocked her on the head and drowned her in
the bathtub in this cabin. That would be logic and simple too. She was a
nurse, she knew how to handle things like bodies. She knew how to
swim—we have it from Bill that she was a fine swimmer. And a drowned
body will sink. All she had to do was guide it down into the deep water
where she wanted it. There is nothing in all this beyond the powers of one
woman who could swim. She did it, she dressed in Crystal Kingsley's
clothes, packed what else of hers she wanted, got into Crystal Kingsley's car
and departed. And at San Bernardino she ran into her first snag—Lavery.

'Lavery knew her as Muriel Chess. We have no evidence and no reason
whatever to assume that he knew her as anything else. He had seen her up
here and he was probably on his way up here again when he met her. She
wouldn't want that. All he would find would be a locked-up cabin, but he
might get talking to Bill and it was part of her plan that Bill should not know
positively that she had ever left Little Fawn Lake. So that when, and if, the
body was found, he would identify it. So she put her hooks into Lavery at
once, and that wouldn't be too hard. If there is one thing we know for
certain about Lavery, it is that he couldn't keep his hands off the women.
The more of them, the better. He would be easy for a smart girl like Mildred
Haviland. So she played him and took him away with her. She took him to
El Paso and there sent a wire he knew nothing about. Finally she played him
back to Bay City. She probably couldn't help that. He wanted to go home
and she couldn't let him get too far from her. Because Lavery was
dangerous to her. Lavery alone could destroy all the indications that Crystal
Kingsley had actually left Little Fawn Lake. When the search for Crystal
Kingsley eventually began, it had to come to Lavery, and at that moment
Lavery's life wasn't worth a plugged nickel. His first denials might not be
believed, as they were not, but when he opened up with the whole story,
that would be believed, because it could be checked. So the search began
and immediately Lavery was shot dead in his bathroom, the very night after
I went down to talk to him. That's about all there is to it, except why she
went back to the house the next morning. That's just one of those things
that murderers seem to do. She said he had taken her money, but I don't
believe it. I think more likely she got to thinking he had some of his own
hidden away, or that she had better edit the job with a cool head and make
sure it was all in order and pointing the right way; or perhaps it was just
what she said, and to take in the paper and the milk. Anything is possible.
She went back and I found her there and she put on an act that left me with
both feet in my mouth.'

Patton said: 'Who killed her, son? I gather you don't like Kingsley for
that little job.'

I looked at Kingsley and said: 'You didn't talk to her on the phone, you
said. What about Miss Fromsett? Did she think she was talking to your
wife?'

Kingsley shook his head. 'I doubt it. It would be pretty hard to fool her
that way. All she said was that she seemed very changed and subdued. I had
no suspicion then. I didn't have any until I got up here. When I walked into
this cabin last night, I felt there was something wrong. It was too clean and
neat and orderly. Crystal didn't leave things that way. There would have

been clothes all over the bedrooom, cigarette-stubs all over the house, bottles and glasses all over the kitchen. There would have been unwashed dishes and ants and flies. I thought Bill's wife might have cleaned up, and then I remembered that Bill's wife wouldn't have, not on that particular day. She had been too busy quarrelling with Bill and being murdered, or committing suicide, whichever it was. I thought about all this in a confused sort of way, but I don't claim I actually made anything of it.'

Patton got up from his chair and went out on the porch. He came back wiping his lips with his tan handkerchief. He sat down again, and eased himself over on his left hip, on account of the hip holster on the other side. He looked thoughtfully at Degarmo. Degarmo stood against the wall, hard and rigid, a stone man. His right hand still hung down at his side, with the fingers curled.

Patton said: 'I still ain't heard who killed Muriel. Is that part of the show or is that something that still has to be worked out?'

I said: 'Somebody who thought she needed killing, somebody who had loved her and hated her, somebody who was too much of a cop to let her get away with any more murders, but not enough of a cop to pull her in and let the whole story come out. Somebody like Degarmo.'

40

Degarmo straightened away from the wall and smiled bleakly. His right hand made a hard clean movement and was holding a gun. He held it with a lax wrist, so that it pointed down at the floor in front of him. He spoke to me without looking at me.

'I don't think you have a gun,' he said. 'Patton has a gun but I don't think he can get it out fast enough to do him any good. Maybe you have a little evidence to go with that last guess. Or wouldn't that be important enough for you to bother with?'

'A little evidence,' I said. 'Not very much. But it will grow. Somebody stood behind that green curtain in the Granada for more than half an hour and stood as silently as only a cop on a stake-out knows how to stand. Somebody who had a blackjack. Somebody who knew I had been hit with one without looking at the back of my head. You told Shorty, remember? Somebody who knew the dead girl had been hit with one, too, although it wouldn't have showed and he wouldn't have been likely at that time to have handled the body enough to find out. Somebody who stripped her and raked her body with scratches in the kind of sadistic hate a man like you might feel for a woman who had made a small private hell for him. Somebody who has blood and cuticle under his finger-nails right now, plenty enough for a chemist to work on. I bet you won't let Patton look at the finger-nails of your right hand, Degarmo.'

Degarmo lifted the gun a little and smiled. A wide white smile.

'And just how did I know where to find her?' he asked.

'Almore saw her—coming out of, or going into, Lavery's house. That's what made him so nervous, that's why he called you when he saw me hanging around. As to how exactly you trailed her to the apartment, I don't know. I don't see anything difficult about it. You could have hid out in Almore's house and followed her, or followed Lavery. All that would be routine work for a copper.'

Degarmo nodded and stood silent for a moment, thinking. His face was grim, but his metallic blue eyes held a light that was almost amusement. The room was hot and heavy with a disaster that could no longer be mended. He seemed to feel it less than any of us.

'I want to get out of here,' he said at last. 'Not very far, maybe, but no hick cop is going to put the arm on me. Any objections?'

Patton said quietly: 'Can't be done, son. You know I got to take you. None of this ain't proved, but I can't just let you walk out.'

'You have a nice fat belly, Patton. I'm a good shot. How do you figure to take me?'

'I been trying to figure,' Patton said and rumpled his hair under his pushed-back hat. 'I ain't got very far with it. I don't want no holes in my belly. But I can't let you make a monkey of me in my own territory either.'

'Let him go,' I said. 'He can't get out of these mountains. That's why I brought him up here.'

Patton said soberly: 'Somebody might get hurt taking him. That wouldn't be right. If it's anybody, it's got to be me.'

Degarmo grinned. 'You're a nice boy, Patton,' he said. 'Look, I'll put the gun back under my arm and we'll start from scratch. I'm good enough for that too.'

He tucked the gun under his arm. He stood with his arms hanging, his chin pushed forward a little, watching. Patton chewed softly, with his pale eyes on Degarmo's vivid eyes.

'I'm sitting down,' he complained. 'I ain't as fast as you anyways. I just don't like to look yellow.' He looked at me sadly. 'Why the hell did you have to bring this up here? It ain't any part of my troubles. Now look at the jam I'm in.' He sounded hurt and confused and rather feeble.

Degarmo put his head back a little and laughed. While he was still laughing, his right hand jumped for his gun again.

I didn't see Patton move at all. The room throbbed with the roar of his frontier Colt.

Degarmo's arm shot straight out to one side and the heavy Smith and Wesson was torn out of his hand and thudded against the knotty pine wall behind him. He shook his numbed right hand and looked down at it with wonder in his eyes.

Patton stood up slowly. He walked slowly across the room and kicked the revolver under a chair. He looked at Degarmo sadly. Degarmo was sucking a little blood off his knuckles.

'You give me a break,' Patton said sadly. 'You hadn't ought ever to give a man like me a break. I been a shooter more years than you been alive, son.'

Degarmo nodded to him and straightened his back and started for the door.

'Don't do that,' Patton told him calmly.

Degarmo kept on going. He reached the door and pushed on the screen. He looked back at Patton and his face was very white now.'

'I'm going out of here,' he said. 'There's only one way you can stop me. So long, fatty.'

Patton didn't move a muscle.

Degarmo went out through the door. His feet made heavy sounds on the porch and then on the steps. I went to the front window and looked out. Patton still hadn't moved. Degarmo came down off the steps and started across the top of the little dam.

'He's crossing the dam,' I said. 'Has Andy got a gun?'

'I don't figure he'd use one if he had,' Patton said calmly. 'He don't know any reason why he should.'

'Well, I'll be damned,' I said.

Patton sighed. 'He hadn't ought to have given me a break like that,' he said. 'Had me cold. I got to give it back to him. Kind of puny too. Won't do him a lot of good.'

'He's a killer,' I said.

'He ain't that kind of killer,' Patton said. 'You lock your car?'

I nodded. 'Andy's coming down to the other end of the dam,' I said. 'Degarmo has stopped him. He's speaking to him.'

'He'll take Andy's car maybe,' Patton said sadly.

'Well, I'll be damned,' I said again. I looked back at Kingsley. He had his head in his hands and he was staring at the floor. I turned back to the window. Degarmo was out of sight beyond the rise. Andy was half-way across the dam, coming slowly, looking back over his shoulder now and then. The sound of a starting car came distinctly. Andy looked up at the cabin, then turned back and started to run back along the dam.

The sound of the motor died away. When it was quite gone, Patton said: 'Well, I guess we better go back to the office and do some telephoning.'

Kingsley got up suddenly and went out to the kitchen and came back with a bottle of whisky. He poured himself a stiff drink and drank it standing. He waved a hand at it and walked heavily out of the room. I heard bed-springs creak.

Patton and I went quietly out of the cabin.

41

Patton had just finished putting his calls through to block the highways when a call came through from the sergeant in charge of the guard detail at Puma Lake dam. We went out and got into Patton's car and Andy drove very fast along the lake road through the village and along the lake shore back to the big dam at the end. We were waved across the dam to where the sergeant was waiting in a jeep beside the headquarters hut.

The sergeant waved his arm and started the jeep and we followed him a couple of hundred feet along the highway to where a few soldiers stood on the edge of the canyon looking down. Several cars had stopped there and a cluster of people was grouped near the soldiers. The sergeant got out of the jeep and Patton and Andy and I climbed out of the official car and went over by the sergeant.

'Guy didn't stop for the sentry,' the sergeant said, and there was bitterness in his voice. 'Damn near knocked him off the road. The sentry in the middle of the bridge had to jump fast to get missed. The one at this end had enough. He called the guy to halt. Guy kept going.'

The sergeant chewed his gum and looked down into the canyon.

'Orders are to shoot in a case like that,' he said. 'The sentry shot.' He pointed down to the grooves in the shoulder at the edge of the drop. 'This is where he went off.'

A hundred feet down in the canyon a small coupé was smashed against the side of a huge granite boulder. It was almost upside down, leaning a little. There were three men down there. They had moved the car enough to lift something out.

Something that had been a man.

The Long Goodbye

Raymond CHANDLER

I

The first time I laid eyes on Terry Lennox he was drunk in a Rolls-Royce
Silver Wraith outside the terrace of The Dancers. The parking lot attendant
had brought the car out and he was still holding the door open because
Terry Lennox's left foot was still dangling outside, as if he had forgotten he
had one. He had a young-looking face but his hair was bone white. You
could tell by his eyes that he was plastered to the hairline, but otherwise he
looked like any other nice young guy in a dinner jacket who had been
spending too much money in a joint that exists for that purpose and for no
other.

There was a girl beside him. Her hair was a lovely shade of dark red and
she had a distant smile on her lips and over her shoulders she had a blue
mink that almost made the Rolls-Royce look like just another automobile. It
didn't quite. Nothing can.

The attendant was the usual half-tough character in a white coat with the
name of the restaurant stitched across the front of it in red. He was getting
fed up.

'Look, mister,' he said with an edge to his voice, 'would you mind a whole
lot pulling your leg into the car so I can kind of shut the door? Or should I
open it all the way so you can fall out?'

The girl gave him a look which ought to have stuck at least four inches out
of his back. It didn't bother him enough to give him the shakes. At The
Dancers they get the sort of people that disillusion you about what a lot of
golfing money can do for the personality.

A low-slung foreign speedster with no top drifted into the parking lot and
a man got out of it and used the dash lighter on a long cigarette. He was
wearing a pullover check shirt, yellow slacks, and riding boots. He strolled
off trailing clouds of incense, not even bothering to look towards the Rolls-
Royce. He probably thought it was corny. At the foot of the steps up to the
terrace he paused to stick a monocle in his eye.

The girl said with a nice burst of charm: 'I have a wonderful idea darling.
Why don't we just take the cab to your place and get your convertible out?
It's such a wonderful night for a run up the coast to Montecito. I know some
people there who are throwing a dance around the pool.'

The white-haired lad said politely: 'Awfully sorry, but I don't have it any
more. I was compelled to sell it.' From his voice and articulation you
wouldn't have known he had had anything stronger than orange juice to
drink.

'Sold it, darling? How do you mean?' She slid away from him along the
seat but her voice slid away a lot farther than that.

'I mean I had to,' he said. 'For eating money.'

'Oh I see.' A slice of spumoni wouldn't have melted on her now.

The attendant had the white-haired boy right where he could reach him—in a low income bracket. 'Look, buster,' he said, 'I've got to put a car away. See you some more some other time—maybe.'

He let the door swing open. The drunk promptly slid off the seat and landed on the blacktop on the seat of his pants. So I went over and dropped my nickel. I guess it's always a mistake to interfere with a drunk. Even if he knows and likes you he is always liable to haul off and poke you in the teeth. I got him under the arms and got him up on his feet.

'Thank you so very much,' he said politely.

The girl slid under the wheel. 'He gets so goddam English when he's loaded,' she said in a stainless-steel voice. 'Thanks for catching him.'

'I'll get him in the back of the car,' I said.

'I'm terribly sorry. I'm late for an engagement.' She let the clutch in and the Rolls started to glide. 'He's just a lost dog,' she added with a cool smile. 'Perhaps you can find a home for him. He's housebroken—more or less.'

And the Rolls ticked down the entrance driveway on to Sunset Boulevard, made a right turn, and was gone. I was looking after her when the attendant came back. And I was still holding the man up and he was now sound asleep.

'Well, that's one way of doing it,' I told the white coat.

'Sure,' he said cynically. 'Why waste it on a lush? Them curves and all.'

'You know him?'

'I heard the dame call him Terry. Otherwise I don't know him from a cow's caboose. But I only been here two weeks.'

'Get my car, will you?' I gave him the ticket.

By the time he brought my Olds over I felt as if I was holding up a sack of lead. The white coat helped me get him into the front seat. The customer opened an eye and thanked us and went to sleep again.

'He's the politest drunk I ever met,' I said to the white coat.

'They come all sizes and shapes and all kinds of manners,' he said. 'And they're all bums. Looks like this one had a plastic job one time.'

'Yeah.' I gave him a dollar and he thanked me. He was right about the plastic job. The right side of my new friend's face was frozen and whitish and seamed with thin, fine scars. The skin had a glossy look along the scars. A plastic job and a pretty drastic one.

'Watcha aim to do with him?'

'Take him home and sober him up enough to tell me where he lives.'

The white coat grinned at me. 'Okay, sucker. If it was me, I'd just drop him in the gutter and keep going. Them booze hounds just make a man a lot of trouble for no fun. I got a philosophy about them things. The way the competition is nowadays a guy has to save his strength to protect hisself in the clinches.'

'I can see you've made a big success out of it,' I said.

He looked puzzled and then he started to get mad, but by that time I was in the car and moving.

He was partly right of course. Terry Lennox made me plenty of trouble. But after all that's my line of work.

I was living that year in a house on Yucca Avenue in the Laurel Canyon district. It was a small hillside house on a dead-end street with a long flight of redwood steps to the front door and a grove of eucalyptus trees across the way. It was furnished, and it belonged to a woman who had gone to Idaho to live with her widowed daughter for a while. The rent was low, partly because the owner wanted to be able to come back on short notice, and partly because of the steps. She was getting too old to face them every time she came home.

I got the drunk up them somehow. He was eager to help but his legs were rubber and he kept falling asleep in the middle of an apologetic sentence. I got the door unlocked and dragged him inside and spread him on the long couch, threw a rug over him and let him go back to sleep. He snored like a grampus for an hour. Then he came awake all of a sudden and wanted to go to the bathroom. When he came back he looked at me peeringly, squinting his eyes, and wanted to know where the hell he was. I told him. He said his name was Terry Lennox and that he lived in an apartment in Westwood and no one was waiting up for him. His voice was clear and unslurred.

He said he could handle a cup of black coffee. When I brought it he sipped it carefully, holding the saucer close under the cup.

'How come I'm here,' he asked, looking around.

'You squiffed out at The Dancers in a Rolls. Your girl friend ditched you.'

'Quite,' he said. 'No doubt she was entirely justified.'

'You English?'

'I've lived there. I wasn't born there. If I might call a taxi. I'll take myself off.'

'You've got one waiting.'

He made the steps on his own going down. He didn't say much on the way to Westwood, except that it was very kind of me and he was sorry to be such a nuisance. He had probably said it so often and to so many people that it was automatic.

His apartment was small and stuffy and impersonal. He might have moved in that afternoon. On a coffee table in front of a hard green davenport there was a half-empty Scotch bottle and melted ice in a bowl and three empty fizzwater bottles and two glasses and a glass ashtray loaded with stubs with and without lipstick. There wasn't a photograph or a personal article of any kind in the place. It might have been a hotel room rented for a meeting or a farewell, for a few drinks and a talk, for a roll in the hay. It didn't look like a place where anyone lived.

He offered me a drink. I said no thanks. I didn't sit down. When I left he thanked me some more, but not as if I had climbed a mountain for him, nor as if it was nothing at all. He was a little shaky and a little shy but polite as hell. He stood in the open door until the automatic elevator came up and I got into it. Whatever he didn't have he had manners.

He hadn't mentioned the girl again. Also, he hadn't mentioned that he had no job and no prospects and that almost his last dollar had gone into paying the check at The Dancers for a bit of high-class fluff that couldn't stick around long enough to make sure he didn't get tossed in the sneezer by some prowl car boys or rolled by a tough hackie and dumped out in a vacant lot.

On the way down in the elevator I had an impulse to go back up and take the Scotch bottle away from him. But it wasn't any of my business and it never does any good anyway. They always find a way to get it if they have to have it.

I drove home chewing my lip. I'm supposed to be tough but there was something about the guy that got to me. I didn't know what it was unless it was the white hair and the scarred face and the clear voice and the politeness. Maybe that was enough. There was no reason why I should ever see him again. He was just a lost dog, like the girl said.

2

It was the week after Thanksgiving when I saw him again. The stores along Hollywood Boulevard were already beginning to fill up with overpriced Christmas junk, and the daily papers were beginning to scream about how terrible it would be if you didn't get your Christmas shopping done early. It would be terrible anyway; it always is.

It was about three blocks from my office building that I saw a cop car double-parked and the two buttons in it staring at something over by a shop window on the sidewalk. The something was Terry Lennox—or what was left of him—and that little was not too attractive.

He was leaning against a store front. He had to lean against something. He shirt was dirty and open at the neck and partly outside his jacket and partly not. He hadn't shaved for four or five days. His nose was pinched. His skin was so pale that the long thin scars hardly showed. And his eyes were like holes poked in a snow bank. It was pretty obvious that the buttons in the prowl car were about ready to drop the hook on him, so I went over there fast and took hold of his arm.

'Straighten up and walk,' I said, putting on the tough. I winked at him from the side. 'Can you make it? Are you stinko?'

He looked me over vaguely and then smiled his little one-sided smile. 'I have been,' he breathed. 'Right now I guess I'm just a little—empty.'

'Okay, but make with the feet. You're half-way into the drunk tank already.'

He made the effort and let me walk him through the sidewalk loafers to the edge of the kerb. There was a taxi stand there and I yanked open the door.

'He goes first,' the hackie said, jerking a thumb at the cab ahead. He swung his head around and saw Terry. 'If at all,' he added.

'This is an emergency. My friend is sick.'

'Yeah,' the hackie said. 'He could get sick somewhere else.'

'Five bucks,' I said, 'and let's see that beautiful smile.'

'Oh well,' he said, and stuck a magazine with a Martian on the cover behind his mirror. I reached in and got the door open. I got Terry Lennox in and the shadow of the prowl car blocked the far window. A grey-haired cop got out and came over. I went around the taxi and met him.

'Just a minute, Mac. What have we got here? Is the gentleman in the soiled laundry a real close friend of yours?'

'Close enough for me to know he needs a friend. He's not drunk.'

'For financial reasons, no doubt,' the cop said. He put his hand out and I put my licence in it. He looked at it and handed it back. 'Oh no,' he said. 'A P.I. picking up a client.' His voice changed and got tough. 'That tells a little something about you, Mr Marlowe. What about him?'

'His name's Terry Lennox. He works in pictures.'

'That's nice,' the cop said sarcastically. He leaned into the taxi and stared at Terry back in the corner. 'I'd say he didn't work too lately. I'd say he didn't sleep indoors too lately. I'd even say he was a wag and so maybe we ought to take him in.'

'Your arrest record can't be that low,' I said. 'Not in Hollywood.'

He was still looking in at Terry. 'What's your friend's name, buddy?'

'Philip Marlowe,' Terry said slowly. 'He lives on Yucca Avenue, Laurel Canyon.'

The cop pulled his head out of the window space. He turned, and made a gesture with his hand. 'You could of just told him.'

'I could have, but I didn't.'

He stared at me for a second or two. 'I'll buy it this time,' he said. 'But get him off the street.' He got into the police car and the police car went away.

I got into the taxi and we went the three odd blocks to my parking lot and shifted to my car. I held out the five spot to the hackie. He gave me a stiff look and shook his head.

'Just what's on the meter, Jack, or an even buck if you feel like it. I been down and out myself. In Frisco. Nobody picked me up in no taxi either. There's one stony-hearted town.'

'San Francisco,' I said mechanically.'

'I call it Frisco,' he said. 'The hell with them minority groups. Thanks.' He took the dollar and went away.

We went to a drive-in where they made hamburgers that didn't taste like something the dog wouldn't eat. I fed Terry Lennox a couple and a bottle of beer and drove him home. The steps were still tough on him but he grinned and panted and made the climb. An hour later he was shaved and bathed and he looked human again. We sat down over a couple of very mild drinks.

'Lucky you remembered my name,' I said.

'I made a point of it,' he said. 'I looked you up too. Could I do less?'

'So why not give me a ring? I live here all the time. I have an office as well.'

'Why should I bother you?'

'Looks like you had to bother somebody. Looks like you don't have many friends.'

'Oh I have friends,' he said, 'of a sort.' He turned his glass on the table top. 'Asking for help doesn't come easy—especially when it's all your own fault.' He looked up with a tired smile. 'Maybe I can quit drinking one of these days. They all say that, don't they?'

'It takes about three years.'

'Three years?' He looked shocked.

'Usually it does. It's a different world. You have to get used to a paler set of colours, a quieter lot of sounds. You have to allow for relapses. All the people you used to know well will get to be just a little strange. You won't even like most of them, and they won't like you too well.'

'That wouldn't be much of a change,' he said. He turned and looked at the clock. 'I have a two-hundred dollar suitcase checked at the Hollywood bus station. If I could bail it out I could buy a cheap one and pawn the one that's checked for enough to get to Vegas on the bus. I can get a job there.'

I didn't say anything. I just nodded and sat there nursing my drink.

'You're thinking that idea might have come to me a little sooner,' he said quietly.

'I'm thinking there's something behind all this that's none of my business. Is the job for sure or just a hope?'

'It's for sure. Fellow I knew very well in the army runs a big club there, the Terrapin Club. He's part racketeer, of course, they all are—but the other part is a nice guy.'

'I can manage the bus fare and something over. But I'd just as soon it bought something that would stay bought for a while. Better talk to him on the phone.'

'Thank you, but it's not necessary. Randy Starr won't let me down. He never has. And the suitcase will pawn for fifty dollars. I know from experience.'

'Look,' I said, 'I'd put up what you need. I'm no big soft-hearted slob. So you take what's offered and be good. I want you out of my hair because I've got a feeling about you.'

'Really?' He looked down into his glass. He was only sipping the stuff. 'We've only met twice and you've been more than white to me both times. What sort of feeling?'

'A feeling that next time I'll find you in worse trouble than I can get you out of. I don't know just why I have the feeling, but I have it.'

He touched the right side of his face gently with two finger-tips. 'Maybe it's this. It does make me look a little sinister, I suppose. But it's an honourable wound—or anyhow the result of one.'

'It's not that. That doesn't bother me at all. I'm a private dick. You're a problem that I don't have to solve. But the problem is there. Call it a hunch. If you want to be extra polite, call it a sense of character. Maybe that girl didn't walk out on you at The Dancers just because you were drunk. Maybe she had a feeling too.'

He smiled faintly. 'I was married to her once. Her name is Sylvia Lennox. I married her for her money.'

I stood up scowling at him. 'I'll fix you some scrambled eggs. You need food.'

'Wait a minute, Marlowe. You're wondering why if I was down and out and Sylvia had plenty I couldn't ask her for a few bucks. Did you ever hear of pride?'

'You're killing me, Lennox.'

'Am I? My kind of pride is different. It's the pride of a man who has nothing else. I'm sorry if I annoy you.'

I went out to my kitchen and cooked some Canadian bacon and scrambled eggs and coffee and toast. We ate in the breakfast nook. The house belonged to the period that always had one.

I said I had to go to the office and would pick up his suitcase on the way back. He gave me the check ticket. His face now had a little colour and the eyes were not so far back in his head that you had to grope for them.

Before I went out I put the whisky bottle on the table in front of the couch. 'Use your pride on that,' I said. 'And call Vegas, if only as a favour to me.'

He just smiled and shrugged his shoulders. I was still sore going down the steps. I didn't know why, any more than I knew why a man would starve and walk the streets rather than pawn his wardrobe. Whatever his rules were he played by them.

The suitcase was the damnedest thing you ever saw. It was bleached pigskin and when new had been a pale cream colour. The fittings were gold. It was English made and if you could buy it here at all, it would cost more like eight hundred than two.

I planked it down in front of him. I looked at the bottle on the cocktail table. He hadn't touched it. He was as sober as I was. He was smoking, but not liking that very well.

'I called Randy,' he said. 'He was sore because I hadn't called him before.'

'It takes a stranger to help you,' I said. 'A present from Sylvia?' I pointed at the suitcase.

He looked out of the window. 'No. That was given to me in England, long before I met her. Very long ago indeed. I'd like to leave it with you, if you could lend me an old one.'

I got five double sawbucks out of my wallet and dropped them in front of him. 'I don't need security.'

'That wasn't the idea at all. You're no pawnbroker. I just don't want it with me in Vegas. And I don't need this much money.'

'Okay. You keep the money and I'll keep the suitcase. But this house is easy to burgle.'

'It wouldn't matter,' he said indifferently. 'It wouldn't matter at all.'

He changed his clothes and we ate dinner at Musso's about five-thirty. No drinks. He caught the bus on Cahuenga and I drove home thinking about this and that. His empty suitcase was on my bed where he had unpacked it and put his stuff in a light-weight job of mine. He had a gold key which was in one of the locks. I locked the suitcase up empty and tied the key to the handle and put it on the high shelf on my clothes closet. It didn't feel quite empty, but what was in it was no business of mine.

It was a quiet night and the house seemed emptier than usual. I set out the chessmen and played a French defence against Steinitz. He beat me in forty-four moves, but I had him sweating a couple of times.

The phone rang at nine-thirty and the voice that spoke was one I had heard before.

'Is this Mr Philip Marlowe?'

'Yeah, I'm Marlowe.'

'This is Sylvia Lennox, Mr Marlowe. We met very briefly in front of The Dancers one night last month. I heard afterwards that you had been kind enough to see that Terry got home.'

'I did that.'

'I suppose you know that we are not married any more, but I've been a little worried about him. He gave up the apartment he had in Westwood and nobody seems to know where he is.'

'I noticed how worried you were the night we met.'

'Look, Mr Marlowe. I've been married to the man. I'm not very sympathetic to drunks. Perhaps I was a little unfeeling and perhaps I had something rather important to do. You're a private detective and this can be put on a professional basis, if you prefer it.'

'It doesn't have to be put on any basis at all, Mrs Lennox. He's on a bus going to Las Vegas. He has a friend there who will give him a job.'

She brightened up very suddenly. 'Oh–to Las Vegas? How sentimental of him. That's where we were married.'

'I guess he forgot,' I said, 'or he would have gone somewhere else.'

Instead of hanging up on me she laughed. It was a cute little laugh. 'Are you always as rude as this to your clients?'

'You're not a client, Mrs Lennox.'

'I might be some day. Who knows? Let's say to your lady friends, then.'

'Same answer. The guy was down and out, starving, dirty, without a bean. You could have found him if it had been worth your time. He didn't want anything from you then and he probably doesn't want anything from you now.'

'That,' she said coolly, 'is something you couldn't possibly know anything about. Good night.' And she hung up.

She was dead right, of course, and I was dead wrong. But I didn't feel wrong. I just felt sore. If she had called up half an hour earlier I might have been sore enough to beat the hell out of Steinitz—except that he had been dead for fifty years and the chess game was out of a book.

3

Three days before Christmas I got a cashier's cheque on a Las Vegas bank for $100. A note written on hotel paper came with it. He thanked me, wished me a Merry Christmas and all kinds of luck, and said he hoped to see me again soon. The kick was in a postscript. 'Sylvia and I are starting a second honeymoon. She says please don't be sore at her for wanting to try again.'

I caught the rest of it in one of those snob columns in the society section of the paper. I don't read them often, only when I run out of things I dislike.

'Your correspondent is all fluttery at the news that Terry and Sylvia Lennox had rehitched at Las Vegas, the dears. She's the younger daughter of multimillionaire Harlan Potter of San Francisco and Pebble Beach, of course. Sylvia is having Marcel and Jeanne Duhaux redecorate the entire mansion in Encino from basement to roof in the most devastatingly *dernier cri*. Curt Westerheym, Sylvia's last but one, my dears, gave her the little eighteen-room shack for a wedding present, you may remember. And whatever happened to Curt, you ask? Or do you? St Tropez has the answer, and permanently, I hear. Also a certain very, *very* blue-blooded French duchess with two perfectly adorable children. And what does Harlan Potter think of the remarriage, you may also ask? One can only guess. Mr Potter is one person who but *never* gives an interview. How exclusive can you get, darlings?'

I threw the paper into the corner and turned on the TV set. After the society page dog vomit even the wrestlers looked good. But the facts were probably right. On the society page they better be.

I had a mental picture of the kind of eighteen-room shack that would go with a few of the Potter millions, and to mention decorations by Duhaux in the latest sub-phallic symbolism. But I had no mental picture at all of Terry Lennox loafing around one of the swimming pools in Bermuda shorts and phoning the butler by R/T to ice the champagne and get the grouse atoasting. There was no reason why I should have. If the guy wanted to be somebody's woolly bear, it was no skin off my teeth. I just didn't want to see him again. But I knew I would–if only on account of his goddam gold-plated pigskin suitcase.

It was five o'clock of a wet March evening when he walked into my down-at-heels brain emporium. He looked changed. Older, very sober and severe, and beautifully calm. He looked like a guy who had learned to roll with a punch. He wore an oyster-white raincoat and gloves and no hat, and his white hair was as smooth as a bird's breast.

'Let's go to some quiet bar and have a drink,' he said, as if he had been in ten minutes before. 'If you have the time, that is.'

We didn't shake hands. We never did. Englishmen don't shake hands all the time like Americans and although he wasn't English he had some of the mannerisms.

I said: 'Let's go by my place and pick up your fancy suitcase. It kind of worries me.'

He shook his head. 'It would be kind of you to keep it for me.'

'Why?'

'I just feel that way. Do you mind? It's a sort of link with a time when I wasn't a no-good waster.'

'Nuts to that,' I said. 'But it's your business.'

'If it bothers you because you think it might be stolen—'

'That's your business too. Let's go get that drink.'

We went to Victor's. He drove me in a rust-coloured Jowette Jupiter with a flimsy canvas rain top under which there was only just room for the two of us. It had pale leather upholstery and what looked like silver fittings. I'm not too fussy about cars, but the damn thing did make my mouth water a little. He said it would do sixty-five in second. It had a squatty little gear shift that barely came up to his knee.

'Four speeds,' he said. 'They haven't invented an automatic shift that will work for one of these jobs yet. You don't really need one. You can start it in third even uphill and that's as high as you can shift in traffic anyway.'

'Wedding present?'

'Just a casual "I happened to see this gadget in a window" sort of present. I'm a very pampered guy.'

'Nice,' I said. 'If there's no price tag.'

He glanced at me quickly and then put his eyes back on the wet pavement. Double wipers swished gently over the little wind-screen. 'Price tag? There's always a price tag, chum. You think I'm not happy maybe?'

'Sorry. I was out of line.'

'I'm rich. Who the hell wants to be happy?' There was a bitterness in his voice that was new to me.

'How's your drinking?'

'Perfectly elegant, old top. For some strange reason I seem to be able to handle the stuff. But you never know, do you?'

'Perhaps you were never really drunk.'

We sat in a corner of the bar at Victor's and drank gimlets. 'They don't know how to make them here,' he said. 'What they call a gimlet is just some lime or lemon juice and gin with a dash of sugar and bitters. A real gimlet is half gin and half Rose's Lime Juice and nothing else. It beats martinis hollow.'

'I was never fussy about drinks. How did you get on with Randy Starr?
Down my street he's called a tough number.'

He leaned back and looked thoughtful. 'I guess he is. I guess they all are.
But it doesn't show on him. I could name you a couple of lads in the same
racket in Hollywood that act the part. Randy doesn't bother. In Las Vegas
he's a legitimate business man. You look him up next time you're there.
He'll be your pal.'

'Not too likely. I don't like hoodlums.'

'That's just a word, Marlowe. We have that kind of world. Two wars gave
it to us and we are going to keep it. Randy and I and another fellow were in a
jam once. It made a sort of bond between us.'

'Then why didn't you ask him for help when you needed it?'

He drank up his drink and signalled the waiter. 'Because he couldn't
refuse.'

The waiter brought fresh drinks and I said: 'That's just talk to me. If by
any chance the guy owed you something, think of *his* end. He'd like a chance
to pay something back.'

He shook his head slowly. 'I know you're right. Of course I did ask him
for a job. But I worked at it while I had it. As for asking favours or handouts,
no.'

'But you'll take them from a stranger.'

He looked me straight in the eye. 'The stranger can keep going and
pretend not to hear.'

We had three gimlets, not doubles, and it didn't do a thing to him. That
much would just get a real souse started. So I guess maybe he was cured at
that.

Then he drove me back to the office.

'We have dinner at eight-fifteen,' he said. 'Only millionaires can afford it.
Only millionaire's servants will stand for it nowadays. Lots of lovely people
coming.'

From then on it got to be a sort of habit with him to drop in around five
o'clock. We didn't always go to the same bar, but oftener to Victor's than
anywhere else. It may have had some association for him that I didn't know
about. He never drank too much, and that surprised him.

'It must be something like the tertian ague,' he said. 'When it hits you it's
bad. When you don't have it, it's as though you never did have it.'

'What I don't get is why a guy with your privileges would want to drink
with a down-at-heel private eye.'

'Are you being modest?'

'Nope. I'm just puzzled. I'm a reasonably friendly type but we don't live
in the same world. I don't even know where you hang out except that it's
Encino. I should guess your home life is adequate.'

'I don't have any home life.'

We were drinking gimlets again. The place was almost empty. There was
the usual light scattering of compulsive drinkers getting tuned up at the bar
on the stools, the kind that reach very slowly for the first one and watch their
hands so they won't knock anything over.

'I don't get that. Am I supposed to?'

'Big production, no story, as they say around the movie lots. I guess
Sylvia is happy enough though not necessarily with me. In our circle that's

not too important. There's always something to do if you don't have to work or consider the cost. It's no real fun but the rich don't know that. They never had any. They never want anything very hard except maybe somebody else's wife and that's a pretty pale desire compared with the way a plumber's wife wants new curtains for the living-room.'

I didn't say anything. I let him carry the ball.

'Mostly I just kill time,' he said, 'and it dies hard. A little tennis, a little golf, a little swimming and horseback riding, and the exquisite pleasure of watching Sylvia's friends trying to hold out to lunch time before they start killing their hangovers.'

'The night you went to Vegas she said she didn't like drunks.'

He grinned crookedly. I was getting so used to his scarred face that I only noticed it when some change of expression emphasized its one-sided woodenness.

'She meant drunks without money. With money they are just heavy drinkers. If they vomit in the lanai, that's for the butler to handle.'

'You didn't have to have it the way it is.'

He finished his drink at a gulp and stood up. 'I've got to run, Marlowe. Besides I'm boring you and God knows I'm boring myself.'

'You're not boring me. I'm a trained listener. Sooner or later I may figure out why you like being a kept poodle.'

He touched his scars gently with a fingertip. He had a remote little smile. 'You should wonder why she wants me around, not why I want to be there, waiting patiently on my satin cushion to have my head patted.'

'You like satin cushions,' I said, as I stood up to leave with him. 'You like silk sheets and bells to ring and the butler to come with his deferential smile.'

'Could be. I was raised in an orphanage in Salt Lake City.'

We went out into the tired evening and he said he wanted to walk. We had come in my car, and for once I had been fast enough to grab the check. I watched him out of sight. The light from a store window caught the gleam of his white hair for a moment as he faded into the light mist.

I liked him better drunk, down and out, hungry and beaten and proud. Or did I? Maybe I just liked being top man. His reasons for things were hard to figure. In my business there's a time to ask questions and a time to let your man simmer until he boils over. Every good cop knows that. It's a good deal like chess or boxing. Some people you have to crowd and keep off balance. Some you just box and they will end up beating themselves.

He would have told me the story of his life if I had asked him. But I never even asked him how he got his face smashed. If I had and he told me, it just possibly might have saved a couple of lives. Just possibly, no more.

4

The last time we had a drink in a bar was in May and it was earlier than usual, just after four o'clock. He looked tired and thinner but he looked around with a slow smile of pleasure.

'I like bars just after they open for the evening. When the air inside is still cool and clean and everything is shiny and the bar-keep is giving himself that last look in the mirror to see if his tie is straight and his hair is smooth. I like the neat bottles on the bar back and the lovely shining glasses and the anticipation. I like to watch the man mix the first one of the evening and put it down on a crisp mat and put the little folded napkin beside it. I like to taste it slowly. The first quiet drink of the evening in a quiet bar–that's wonderful.'

I agreed with him.

'Alcohol is like love,' he said. 'The first kiss is magic, the second is intimate, the third is routine. After that you take the girl's clothes off.'

'Is that bad?' I asked him.

'It's excitement of a high order, but it's an impure emotion–impure in the aesthetic sense. I'm not sneering at sex. It's necessary and it doesn't have to be ugly. But it always has to be managed. Making it glamorous is a billion-dollar industry and it costs every cent of it.'

He looked around and yawned. 'I haven't been sleeping well. It's nice in here. But after a while the lushes will fill the place up and talk loud and laugh and the goddam women will start waving their hands and screwing up their faces and tinkling their goddam bracelets and making up with the packaged charm which will later on in the evening have a slight but unmistakable odour of sweat.'

'Take it easy,' I said. 'So they're human, they sweat, they get dirty, they have to go to the bathroom. What did you expect–golden butterflies hovering in a rosy mist?'

He emptied his glass and held it upside down and watched a slow drop form on the rim and then tremble and fall.

'I'm sorry for her,' he said slowly. 'She's such an absolute bitch. Could be I'm fond of her too in a remote sort of way. Some day she'll need me and I'll be the only guy around not holding a chisel. Likely enough then I'll flunk out.'

I just looked at him. 'You do a great job of selling yourself,' I said after a moment.

'Yeah, I know. I'm a weak character, without guts or ambition. I caught the brass ring and it shocked me to find out it wasn't gold. A guy like me has one big moment in his life, one perfect swing on the high trapeze. Then he spends the rest of his time trying not to fall off the sidewalk into the gutter.'

'What's this in favour of?' I got out a pipe and started to fill it.

'She's scared. She's scared stiff.'

'What of?'

'I don't know. We don't talk much any more. Maybe of the old man. Harlan Potter is a cold-hearted son of a bitch. All Victorian dignity on the outside. Inside he's as ruthless as a Gestapo thug. Sylvia is a tramp. He knows it and he hates it and there's nothing he can do about it. But he waits and he watches and if Sylvia ever gets into a big mess of scandal he'll break her in half and bury the two halves a thousand miles apart.'

'You're her husband.'

He lifted the empty glass and brought it down hard on the edge of the table. It smashed with a sharp ping. The barman stared, but didn't say anything.

'Like that, chum. Like that. Oh sure, I'm her husband. That's what the record says. I'm the three white steps and the big green front door and the brass knocker you rap one long and two short and the maid lets you into the hundred-dollar whore-house.'

I stood up and dropped some money on the table. 'You talk too damn much,' I said, 'and it's too damn much about you. See you later.'

I walked out, leaving him sitting there shocked and white-faced as well as I could tell by the kind of light they have in bars. He called something after me, but I kept going.

Ten minutes later I was sorry. But ten minutes later I was somewhere else. He didn't come to the office any more. Not at all, not once. I had got to him where it hurt.

I didn't see him again for a month. When I did it was five o'clock in the morning and just beginning to get light. The persistent ringing of the doorbell yanked me out of bed. I ploughed down the hall and across the living-room and opened up. He stood there looking as if he hadn't slept for a week. He had a light topcoat on with the collar turned up and he seemed to be shivering. A dark felt hat was pulled down over his eyes.

He had a gun in his hand.

5

The gun wasn't pointed at me, he was just holding it. It was a medium-calibre automatic, foreign made, certainly not a Colt or a Savage. With the white face and the scars and the turned-up collar and the pulled-down hat and the gun, he could have stepped right out of an old-fashioned kick-'em-in-the-teeth gangster movie.

'You're driving me to Tijuana to get a plane at ten-fifteen,' he said. 'I have a passport and visa and I'm all set except for transportation. For certain reasons I can't take a train or a bus or a plane from L.A. Would five hundred bucks be a reasonable taxi fare?'

I stood in the doorway and didn't move to let him in. 'Five hundred plus the gat?' I asked.

He looked down at it rather absently. Then he dropped it into his pocket. 'It might be a protection,' he said, 'for you. Not for me.'

'Come on in then.' I stood to one side and he came in with an exhausted lunge and fell into a chair.

The living-room was still dark, because of the heavy growth of shrubbery the owner had allowed to mask the windows. I put a lamp on and mooched a cigarette. I lit it. I stared down at him. I rumpled my hair which was already rumpled. I put the old tired grin on to my face.

'What's the hell's the matter with me—sleeping such a lovely morning away? Ten-fifteen, huh? Well, there's plenty of time. Let's go out to the kitchen and I'll brew some coffee.'

'I'm in a great deal of trouble, shamus.' Shamus, it was the first time he had called me that. But it kind of went with his style of entry, the way he was dressed, the gun and all.

'It's going to be a peach of a day. Light breeze. You can hear those tough old eucalyptus trees across the street whispering to each other. Talking about old times in Australia when the wallabies hopped about underneath the branches and the koala bears rode piggy back on each other. Yes, I got the general idea you were in some trouble. Let's talk about it after I've had a couple of cups of coffee. I'm always a little light-headed when I first wake up. Let us confer with Mr Huggins and Mr Young.'

'Look, Marlowe, this is not the time—'

'Fear nothing, old boy. Mr Huggins and Mr Young are two of the best. They make Huggins-Young Coffee for me. It's their life work, their pride and joy. One of these days I'm going to see that they get the recognition they deserve. So far all they're making is money. You couldn't expect that to satisfy them.'

I left him with that bright chatter and went out to the kitchen at the back. I turned the hot water on and got the coffee-maker down off the shelf. I wet the rod and measured the stuff into the top and by that time the water was steaming. I filled the lower half of the dingus and set it on the flame. I set the upper part on top and gave it a twist so it would bind.

By that time he had come in after me. He leaned in the doorway a moment and then edged across to the breakfast nook and slid into the seat. He was still shaking. I got a bottle of Old Grand-dad off the shelf and poured him a shot in a big glass. I knew he would need a big glass. Even with that he had to use both hands to get it to his mouth. He swallowed, put the glass down with a thud, and hit the back of the seat with a jar.

'Almost passed out,' he muttered. 'Seems like I've been up for a week. Didn't sleep at all last night.'

The coffee-maker was almost ready to bubble. I turned the flame low and watched the water rise. It hung a little at the bottom of the glass tube. I turned the flame up just enough to get it over the hump and then turned it low again quickly. I stirred the coffee and covered it. I set my timer for three minutes. Very methodical guy, Marlowe. Nothing must interfere with his coffee technique. Not even a gun in the hand of a desperate character.

I poured him another slug. 'Just sit there,' I said. 'Don't say a word. Just sit.'

He handled the second slug with one hand. I did a fast wash-up in the bathroom and the bell of the timer went just as I got back. I cut the flame and set the coffee-maker on a straw mat on the table. Why do I go into such detail! Because the charged atmosphere made every little thing stand out as a performance, a movement distinct and vastly important. It was one of those hypersensitive moments when all your automatic movements, however long established, however habitual, become separate acts of will. You are like a man learning to walk after polio. You take nothing for granted, absolutely nothing at all.

The coffee was all down and the air rushed in with its usual fuss and the coffee bubbled and then became quiet. I removed the top of the maker and set it on the drainboard in the socket of the cover.

I poured two cups and added a slug to his. 'Black for you, Terry.' I added two lumps of sugar and some cream to mine, I was coming out of it by now. I wasn't conscious of how I opened the fridge and got the cream carton.

I sat down across from him. He hadn't moved. He was propped in the corner of the nook, rigid. Then without warning his head came down on the table and he was sobbing.

He didn't pay any attention when I reached across and dug the gun out of his pocket. It was a Mauser 7.65, a beauty. I sniffed it. Not fired. I sprang the magazine loose. It was full. Nothing in the breech.

He lifted his head and saw the coffee and drank some slowly, not looking at me. 'I didn't shoot anybody,' he said.

'Well—not recently anyhow. And the gun would have had to be cleaned. I hardly think you shot anybody with this.'

'I'll tell you about it,' he said.

'Wait just a minute.' I drank my coffee as quickly as the heat would let me. I refilled my cup. 'It's like this,' I said. 'Be very careful what you tell me. If you really want me to ride you down to Tijuana, there are two things I must not be told. One—are you listening?'

He nodded very slightly. He was looking blank-eyed at the wall over my head. The scars were very livid this morning. His skin was almost dead white but the scars seemed to shine out of it just the same.

'One,' I repeated slowly, 'if you have committed a crime or anything the law calls a crime—a serious crime, I mean—I can't be told about it. Two, if you have essential knowledge that such a crime has been committed, I can't be told about that either. Not if you want me to drive you to Tijuana. That clear?'

He looked me in the eye. His eyes focused, but they were lifeless. He had the coffee inside him. He had no colour, but he was ready. I poured him some more and loaded it in the same way.

'I told you I was in a jam,' he said.

'I heard you. I don't want to know what kind of jam. I have a living to earn, a licence to protect.'

'I could hold the gun on you,' he said.

I grinned and pushed the gun across the table. He looked down at it but didn't touch it.

'Not to Tijuana you couldn't hold it on me, Terry. Not across the border, not up the steps into a plane. I'm a man who occasionally has business with guns. We'll forget about the gun. I'd look great telling the cops I was so scared I just had to do what you told me to. Supposing, of course, which I don't know, that there was anything to tell the cops.'

'Listen,' he said, 'it will be noon or even later before anybody knocks at the door. The help knows better than to disturb her when she sleeps late. But by about noon her maid would knock and go in. She wouldn't be in her room.'

I sipped my coffee and said nothing.

'The maid would see that her bed hadn't been slept in,' he went on. 'Then she would think of another place to look. There's a big guest house pretty far back from the main house. It has its own driveway and garage and so on. Sylvia spent the night there. The maid would eventually find her there.'

I frowned. 'I've got to be very careful what questions I ask you, Terry. Couldn't she have spent the night away from home?'

'Her clothes would be thrown all over her room. She never hangs anything up. The maid would know she had put a robe over her pyjamas and gone out that way. So it would only be to the guest house.'

'Not necessarily,' I said.

'It would be to the guest house. Hell, do you think they don't know what goes on in the guest house? Servants always know.'

'Pass it,' I said.

He ran a finger down the side of his good cheek hard enough to leave a red streak. 'And in the guest house,' he went on slowly, 'the maid would find—'

'Sylvia dead drunk, paralysed, spifflicated, iced to the eyebrows,' I said harshly.

'Oh.' He thought about it. Big think. 'Of course,' he added, 'that's how it would be. Sylvia is not a souse. When she does get over the edge it's pretty drastic.'

'That's the end of the story,' I said. 'Or almost. Let me improvise. The last time we drank together I was a bit rough with you, walked out, if you recall. You irritated the hell out of me. Thinking it over afterwards I could see that you were just trying to sneer yourself out of a feeling of disaster. You say you have a passport and a visa. It takes a little time to get a visa to Mexico. They don't let just anybody in. So you've been planning to blow for some time. I was wondering how long you would stick.'

'I guess I felt some vague kind of obligation to be around, some idea she might need me for something more than a front to keep the old man from nosing around too hard. By the way, I tried to call you in the middle of the night.'

'I sleep hard. I didn't hear.'

'Then I went to a Turkish bath place. I stayed a couple of hours, had a steam bath, a plunge, a needle shower, a rub-down, and made a couple of phone calls from there. I left the car at La Brea and Fountain. I walked from there. Nobody saw me turn into your street.'

'Do these phone calls concern me?'

'One was to Harlan Potter. The old man flew down to Pasadena yesterday, some business. He hadn't been to the house. I had a lot of trouble getting him. But he finally talked to me. I told him I was sorry, but I was leaving.' He was looking a little sideways when he said this, towards the window over the sink and the tecoma bush that fretted against the screen.

'How did he take it?'

'He was sorry. He wished me luck. Asked if I needed any money.' Terry laughed harshly. 'Money. Those are the first five letters of his alphabet. I said I had plenty. Then I called Sylvia's sister. Much the same story there. That's all.'

'I want to ask this,' I said. 'Did you ever find her with a man in that guest house?'

He shook his head. 'I never tried. It would not have been difficult. It never has been.'

'Your coffee's getting cold.'

'I don't want any more.'

'Lots of men, huh? But you went back and married her again. I realize that she's quite a dish, but all the same—'

'I told you I was no good. Hell, why did I leave her the first time? Why after that did I get stinking every time I saw her? Why did I roll in the gutter rather than ask her for money? She's been married five times, not including me. Any one of them would go back at the crook of her finger. And not just for a million bucks.'

'She's quite a dish,' I said. I looked at my watch. 'Just why does it have to be ten-fifteen in Tijuana?'

'There's always space on that flight. Nobody from L.A. wants to ride a

DC-3 over mountains when he can take a Connie and make it in seven hours to Mexico City. And the Connies don't stop where I want to go.'

I stood up and leaned against the sink. 'Now let's add it up and don't interrupt me. You came to me this morning in a highly emotional condition and wanted to be driven to Tijuana to catch an early plane. You had a gun in your pocket, but I needn't have seen it. You told me you had stood things as long as you could but last night you blew up. You found your wife dead drunk and a man had been with her. You got out and went to a Turkish bath to pass the time until morning and you phoned your wife's two closest relatives and told them what you were doing. Where you went was none of my business. You had the necessary documents to enter Mexico. How you went was none of my business either. We are friends and I did what you asked me without much thought. Why wouldn't I? You're not paying me anything. You had your car but you felt too upset to drive yourself. That's your business too. You're an emotional guy and you got yourself a bad wound in the war. I think I ought to pick up your car and shove it in a garage somewhere for storage.'

He reached into his clothes and pushed a leather key-holder across the table.

'How does it sound?' he asked.

'Depends who's listening. I haven't finished. You took nothing but the clothes you stood up in and some money you had from your father-in-law. You left everything she had given you including that beautiful piece of machinery you parked at La Brea and Fountain. You want to go away as clean as it was possible for you to go and still go. All right. I'll buy it. Now I shave and get dressed.'

'Why are you doing it, Marlowe?'

'Buy yourself a drink while I shave.'

I walked out and left him sitting there hunched in the corner of the nook. He still had his hat and light topcoat on. But he looked a lot more alive.

I went into the bathroom and shaved. I was back in the bedroom knotting my tie when he came and stood in the doorway. 'I washed the cups just in case,' he said. 'But I got thinking. Maybe it would be better if you called the police.'

'Call them yourself. I haven't anything to tell them.'

'You want me to?'

I turned around sharply and gave him a hard stare. 'God damn it!' I almost yelled at him. 'Can't you for Chrissake just leave it lay?'

'I'm sorry.'

'Sure you're sorry. Guys like you are always sorry, and always too late.'

He turned and walked back along the hall to the living-room.

I finished dressing and locked up the back part of the house. When I got to the living-room he had fallen asleep in a chair, his head on one side, his face drained of colour, his whole body slack with exhaustion. He looked pitiful. When I touched his shoulder he came awake slowly as if it was a long way from where he was to where I was.

When I had his attention I said: 'What about a suitcase? I still got that white pigskin job on the top shelf in my closet.'

'It's empty,' he said without interest. 'Also it's too conspicuous.'

'You'd be more conspicuous without any baggage.'

I walked back to the bedroom and stood up on the steps in the clothes

closet and pulled the white pigskin job down off the high shelf. The square
ceiling trap was right over my head, so I pushed that up and reached in as far
as I could and dropped his leather key-holder behind one of the dusty tie
beams or whatever they were.

I climbed down with the suitcase, dusted it off and shoved some things
into it, a pair of pyjamas never worn, tooth-paste, an extra toothbrush, a
couple of cheap towels and washcloths, a package of cotton handkerchiefs, a
fifteen-cent tube of shaving cream, and one of those razors they give with a
package of blades. Nothing used, nothing marked, nothing conspicuous,
except that his own stuff would be better. I added a pint of bourbon still in
its wrapping paper. I locked the suitcase and left the key in one of the locks
and carried it up front. He had gone to sleep again. I opened the door
without waking him and carried the suitcase down to the garage and put it in
the convertible behind the front seat. I got the car out and locked the garage
and went up the steps to wake him. I finished locking up and we left.

I drove fast but not fast enough to get tagged. We hardly spoke on the way
down. We didn't stop to eat either. There wasn't that much time.

The border people had nothing to say to us. Up on the windy mesa where
the Tijuana Airport is I parked close to the office and just sat while Terry
got his ticket. The propellers of the DC-3 were already turning over slowly,
just enough to keep warm. A tall dreamboat of a pilot in a grey uniform was
chatting with a group of four people. One was about six feet four and carried
a gun case. There was a girl in slacks beside him, and a smallish middle-aged
man and a grey-haired woman so tall that she made him look puny. Three or
four obvious Mexicans were standing around as well. That seemed to be the
load. The steps were at the door but nobody seemed anxious to get in. Then
a Mexican flight steward came down the steps and stood waiting. There
didn't seem to be any loudspeaker equipment. The Mexicans climbed into
the plane but the pilot was still chatting with the Americans.

There was a big Packard parked next to me. I got out and took a gander at
the licence on the post. Maybe some day I'll learn to mind my own business.
As I pulled my head out I saw the tall woman staring in my direction.

Then Terry came across the dusty gravel.

'I'm all set,' he said. 'This is where I say good-bye.'

He put his hand out. I shook it. He looked pretty good now, just tired,
just tired as all hell.

I lifted the pigskin suitcase out of the Olds and put it down on the gravel.
He stared at it angrily.

'I told you I didn't want it,' he said snappishly.

'There's a nice pint of hooch in it, Terry. Also some pyjamas and stuff.
And it's all anonymous. If you don't want it, check it. Or throw it away.'

'I have reasons,' he said stiffly.

'So have I.'

He smiled suddenly. He picked up the suitcase and squeezed my arm
with his free hand. 'Okay, pal. You're the boss. And remember, if things get
tough, you have a blank cheque. You don't owe me a thing. We had a few
drinks together and got to be friendly and I talked too much about me. I left
five C notes in your coffee can. Don't be sore at me.'

'I'd rather you hadn't.'

'I'll never spend half of what I have.'

'Good luck, Terry.'

The two Americans were going up the steps into the plane. A squatty guy with a wide-dark face came out of the door of the office building and waved and pointed.

'Climb aboard,' I said. 'I know you didn't kill her. That's why I'm here.'

He braced himself. His whole body got stiff. He turned slowly, then looked back.

'I'm sorry,' he said quietly. 'But you're wrong about that. I'm going to walk quite slowly to the plane. You have plenty of time to stop me.'

He walked. I watched him. The guy in the doorway of the office was waiting, but not too impatient. Mexicans seldom are. He reached down and patted the pigskin suitcase and grinned at Terry. Then he stood aside and Terry went through the door. In a little while Terry came out through the door on the other side, where the customs people are when you're coming in. He walked, still slowly, across the gravel to the steps. He stopped there and looked towards me. He didn't signal or wave. Neither did I. Then he went up into the plane, and the steps were pulled back.

I got into the Olds and started it and backed and turned and moved half-way across the parking space. The tall woman and the short man were still out on the field. The woman had a handkerchief out to wave. The plane began to taxi down to the end of the field, raising plenty of dust. It turned at the far end and the motors revved up in a thundering roar. It began to move forward, picking up speed slowly.

The dust rose in clouds behind it. Then it was airborne. I watched it lift slowly into the gusty air and fade off into the naked blue sky to the south-east.

Then I left. Nobody at the border gate looked at me as if my face meant as much as the hands on a clock.

6

It's a long drag from Tijuana and one of the dullest drives in the state. Tijuana is nothing; all they want there is the buck. The kid who sidles over to your car and looks at you with big wistful eyes and says, 'One dime, please, mister,' will try to sell you his sister in the next sentence. Tijuana is not Mexico. No border town is anything but a border town, just as no waterfront is anything but a waterfront. San Diego? One of the most beautiful harbours in the world and nothing in it but navy and a few fishing boats. At night it is fairyland. The swell is as gentle as an old lady singing hymns. But Marlowe has to get home and count the spoons.

The road north is as monotonous as a sailor's chanty. You go through a town, down a hill, along a stretch of beach, through a town, down a hill, along a stretch of beach.

It was two o'clock when I got back and they were waiting for me in a dark sedan with no police tags, no red light, only the double antenna, and not only police cars have those. I was half-way up the steps before they came out of it and yelled at me, the usual couple in the usual suits, with the usual stony leisure of movement, as if the world was waiting hushed and silent for them to tell it what to do.

'Your name Marlowe? We want to talk to you.'

He let me see the glint of a badge. For all I caught of it he might have been Pest Control. He was grey-blond and looked sticky. His partner was tall, good-looking, neat, and had a precise nastiness about him, a goon with an education. They had watching and waiting eyes, patient and careful eyes, cool, disdainful eyes, cops' eyes. They get them at the passing-out parade at the police school.

'Sergeant Green, Central Homicide. This is Detective Dayton.'

I went on up and unlocked the door. You don't shake hands with big city cops. That close is too close.

They sat in the living-room. I opened the windows and the breeze whispered. Green did the talking.

'Man named Terry Lennox. Know him, huh?'

'We have a drink together once in a while. He lives in Encino, married money. I've never been where he lives.'

'Once in a while,' Green said. 'How often would that be?'

'It's a vague expression. I meant it that way. It could be once a week or once in two months.'

'Met his wife?'

'Once, very briefly, before they were married.'

'You saw him last when and where?'

I took a pipe off the end table and filled it. Green leaned forward close to me. The tall lad sat farther back holding a ballpoint poised over a red-edged pad.

'This is where I say, "What's this all about?" and you say, "We ask the questions."'

'So you just answer them, huh?'

I lit the pipe. The tobacco was a little too moist. It took me some time to light it properly and three matches.

'I got time,' Green said, 'but I already used up a lot of it waiting around. So snap it up, mister. We know who you are. And you know we ain't here to work up an appetite.'

'I was just thinking,' I said. 'We used to go to Victor's fairly often, and not so often to The Green Lantern and The Bull and Bear—that's the place down at the end of the Strip that tries to look like an English inn—'

'Quit stalling.'

'Who's dead?' I asked.

Detective Dayton spoke up. He had a hard, mature, don't-try-to-fool-with-me voice. 'Just answer the questions, Marlowe. We are conducting a routine investigation. That's all you need to know.'

Maybe I was tired and irritable. Maybe I felt a little guilty. I could learn to hate this guy without even knowing him. I could just look at him across the width of a cafeteria and want to kick his teeth in.

'Shove it, Jack,' I said. 'Keep that guff for the juvenile bureau. It's a horse laugh even to them.'

Green chuckled. Nothing changed in Dayton's face that you could put a finger on but he suddenly looked ten years older and twenty years nastier. The breath going through his nose whistled faintly.

'He passed the bar examination,' Green said. 'You can't fool around with Dayton.'

I got up slowly and went over to the bookshelves. I took down the bound copy of the California Penal Code. I held it out to Dayton.

'Would you kindly find me the section that says I have to answer the questions?'

He was holding himself very still. He was going to slug me and we both knew it. But he was going to wait for the break. Which meant that he didn't trust Green to back him up if he got out of line.

He said: 'Every citizen has to co-operate with the police. In all ways, even by physical action, and especially by answering any questions of a non-incriminating nature the police think it necessary to ask.' His voice saying this was hard and bright and smooth.

'It works out that way,' I said. 'Mostly by a process of direct or indirect intimidation. In law no such obligation exists. Nobody has to tell the police anything, any time, anywhere.'

'Aw shut up,' Green said impatiently. 'You're crawfishing and you know it. Sit down. Lennox's wife has been murdered. In a guest house at their place in Encino. Lennox has skipped out. Anyway he can't be found. So we're looking for a suspect in a murder case. That satisfy you?'

I threw the book in a chair and went back to the couch across the table from Green. 'So why come to me?' I asked. 'I've never been near the house. I told you that.'

Green patted his thighs, up and down, up and down. He grinned at me quietly. Dayton was motionless in the chair. His eyes ate me.

'On account of your phone number was written on a pad in his room during the past twenty-four hours,' Green said. 'It's a date pad and yesterday was torn off but you could see the impression on today's page. We don't know when he called you up. We don't know where he went or why or when. But we got to ask, natch.'

'Why in the guest house?' I asked, not expecting him to answer, but he did.

He blushed a little. 'Seems she went there pretty often. At night. Had visitors. The help can see down through the trees where the lights show. Cars come and go, sometimes late, sometimes very late. Too much is enough, huh. Don't kid yourself. Lennox is our boy. He went down that way about one in the a.m. The butler happened to see. He came back alone, maybe twenty minutes later. After that nothing. The lights stayed on. This morning no Lennox. The butler goes down by the guest house. The dame is as naked as a mermaid on the bed and let me tell you he don't recognize her by her face. She practically ain't got one. Beat to pieces with a bronze statuette of a monkey.'

'Terry Lennox wouldn't do anything like that,' I said. 'Sure she cheated on him. Old stuff. She always had. They'd been divorced and remarried. I don't suppose it made him happy but why should he go crazy over it now?'

'Nobody knows that answer,' Green said patiently. 'It happens all the time. Men and women both. A guy takes it and takes it and takes it. Then he don't. He probably don't know why himself, why at that particular instant he goes berserk. Only he does, and somebody's dead. So we got business to do. So we ask you one simple question. So quit horsing around or we take you in.'

'He's not going to tell you, Sergeant,' Dayton said acidly. 'He read that law book. Like a lot of people read a law book he thinks the law is in it.'

'You make the notes,' Green said, 'and leave your brains alone. If you're real good we'll let you sing "Mother Machree" at the police smoker.'

'The hell with you, Sarge, if I may say so with proper respect for your rank.'

'Let's you and him fight,' I said to Green. 'I'll catch him when he drops.'

Dayton laid his note pad and ballpoint aside very carefully. He stood up with a bright gleam in his eyes. He walked over and stood in front of me.

'On your feet, bright boy. Just because I went to college don't make me take any guff from a nit like you.'

I started to get up. I was still off balance when he hit me. He hooked me with a neat left and crossed it. Bells rang, but not for dinner. I sat down and shook my head. Dayton was still there. He was smiling now.

'Let's try again,' he said. 'You weren't set that time. It wasn't really kosher.'

I looked at Green. He was looking at his thumb as if studying a hangnail. I didn't move or speak, waiting for him to look up. If I stood up again, Dayton would slug me again. He might slug me again anyhow. But if I stood up and he slugged me, I would take him to pieces, because the blows proved he was strictly a boxer. He put them in the right place but it would take a lot of them to wear me down.

Green said almost absently: 'Smart work, Billy boy. You gave the man exactly what he wanted. Clam juice.'

Then he looked up and said mildly: 'Once more, for the record, Marlowe. Last time you saw Terry Lennox, where and how and what was talked about, and where did you come from just now. Yes—or no?'

Dayton was standing loosely, nicely balanced. There was a soft, sweet sheen in his eyes.

'How about the other guy?' I asked, ignoring him.

'What other guy was that?'

'In the hay, in the guest house. No clothes on. You're not saying she had to go down there to play solitaire.'

'That comes later—when we get the husband.'

'Fine. If it's not too much trouble when you already have a patsy.'

'You don't talk, we take you in, Marlowe.'

'As a material witness?'

'As a material my foot. As a suspect. Suspicion of accessory after the fact of murder. Helping a suspect escape. My guess is you took the guy somewhere. And right now a guess is all I need. The skipper is tough these days. He knows the rule book but he gets absent-minded. This could be a misery for you. One way or another we get a statement from you. The harder it is to get, the surer we are we need it.'

'That's a lot of crap to him,' Dayton said. 'He knows the book.'

'It's a lot of crap to everybody,' Green said calmly. 'But it still works. Come on, Marlowe. I'm blowing the whistle on you.'

'Okay,' I said. 'Blow it. Terry Lennox was my friend. I've got a reasonable amount of sentiment invested in him. Enough not to spoil it just because a cop says come through. You've got a case against him, maybe far more than I hear from you. Motive, opportunity, and the fact that he skipped out. The motive is old stuff, long neutralized, almost part of the deal. I don't admire that kind of deal, but that's the kind of guy he is—a little weak and very gentle. The rest of it means nothing except that if he knew she was dead he knew he was a sitting duck for you. At the inquest if they have one and if they call me, I'll have to answer questions. I don't have to answer yours. I can see you're a nice guy, Green. Just as I can see your partner is just another goddam badge-flasher with a power complex. If you want to get me in a real jam, let him hit me again. I'll break his goddam pencil for him.'

Green stood up and looked at me sadly. Dayton hadn't moved. He was a one-shot tough guy. He had to have time out to pat his back.

'I'll use the phone,' Green said. 'But I know what answer I'll get. You're a sick chicken, Marlowe. A very sick chicken. Get the hell outa my way.' This last to Dayton. Dayton turned and went back and picked up his pad.

Green crossed to the phone and lifted it slowly, his plain face creased with the long, slow, thankless grind. That's the trouble with cops. You're all set to hate their guts and then you meet one that goes human on you.

The Captain said to bring me in, and rough.

They put handcuffs on me. They didn't search the house, which seemed careless of them. Possibly they figured I would be too experienced to have anything there that could be dangerous to me. In which they were wrong. An expert search would have turned up the car keys. And when the car was found, as it would be sooner or later, they would fit the keys to it and know he had been in my company.

Actually, as it turned out, that meant nothing. The car was never found by any police. It was stolen some time in the night, driven most probably to El Paso, fitted with new keys and forged papers, and put on the market eventually in Mexico City. The procedure is routine. Mostly the money comes back in the form of heroin. Part of the good-neighbour policy, as the hoodlums see it.

7

The homicide skipper that year was Captain Gregorius, a type of copper that is getting rarer but by no means extinct, the kind that solves crimes with the bright light, the soft sap, the kick in the kidneys, the knee to the groin, the fist to the solar plexus, the night stick to the base of the spine. Six months later he was indicted for perjury before a grand jury, booted without trial, and later stamped to death by a big stallion on his ranch in Wyoming.

Right now I was his raw meat. He sat behind his desk with his coat off and his sleeves rolled almost to his shoulders. He was as bald as a brick and getting heavy around the waist like all hard-muscled men in middle age. His eyes were fish grey. His big nose was a network of burst capillaries. He was drinking coffee and not quietly. His blunt, strong hands had hairs thick on their backs. Grizzled tufts stuck out of his ears. He pawed something on his desk and looked at Green.

Green said: 'All we got on him is he won't tell us nothing, skipper. The phone number makes us look him up. He's out riding and don't say where. He knows Lennox pretty well and don't say when he saw him last.'

'Thinks he's tough,' Gregorius said indifferently. 'We could change that.' He said it as if he didn't care one way or another. He probably didn't. Nobody was tough on him. 'Point is the D.A. smells a lot of headlines on this one. Can't blame him, seeing who the girl's old man is. I guess we better pick this fellow's nose for him.'

He looked at me as if I was a cigarette stub, or an empty chair. Just something in his line of vision, without interest for him.

Dayton said respectfully: 'It's pretty obvious that his whole attitude was designed to create a situation where he could refuse to talk. He quoted law at us and needled me into socking him. I was out of line there, Captain.'

Gregorius eyed him bleakly. 'You must needle easy if this punk can do it. Who took the cuffs off?'

Green said he did. 'Put them back on,' Gregorius said. 'Tight. Give him something to brace him up.'

Green put the cuffs back on or started to. 'Behind the back,' Gregorius barked. Green cuffed my hands behind my back. I was sitting in a hard chair.

'Tighter,' Gregorius said. 'Make them bite.'

Green made them tighter. My hands started to feel numb.

Gregorius looked at me sadly. 'You can talk now. Make it snappy.'

I didn't answer him. He leaned back and grinned. His hand went out slowly for his coffee cup and went around it. He leaned forward a little. The cup jerked but I beat it by going sideways out of the chair. I landed hard on my shoulders, rolled over, and got up slowly. My hands were quite numb now. They didn't feel anything. The arms above the cuffs were beginning to ache.

Green helped me back into the chair. The wet smear of the coffee was over the back and some of the seat, but most of it was on the floor.

'He don't like coffee,' Gregorius said. 'He's a swifty. He moves fast. Good reflexes.'

Nobody said anything. Gregorius looked me over with fish eyes.

'In here, mister, a dick licence don't mean any more than a calling card. Now let's have your statement, verbal at first. We'll take it down later. Make it complete. Let's have, say, a full account of your movements since ten p.m. last night. I mean full. This office is investigating a murder and the prime suspect is missing. You connect with him. Guy catches his wife cheating and beats her head to raw flesh and bone and blood-soaked hair. Our old friend the bronze statuette. Not original but it works. You think any goddam private eye is going to quote law at me over this, mister, you got a hell of a tough time coming your way. There ain't a police force in the country could do its job with a law book. You got information and I want it. You could of said no and I could of not believed you. But you didn't even say no. You're not dummying up on me, my friend. Not six cents' worth. Let's go.'

'Would you take the cuffs off, Captain?' I asked. 'I mean if I made a statement?'

'I might. Make it short.'

'If I told you I hadn't seen Lennox within the last twenty-four hours, hadn't talked to him and had no idea where he might be—would that satisfy you, Captain?'

'It might—if I believed it.'

'If I told you I had seen him and where and when, but had no idea he had murdered anyone or that any crime had been committed, and further had no idea where he might be at the moment, that wouldn't satisfy you at all, would it?'

'With more detail I might listen. Things like where, when, what he looked like, what was talked about, where he was headed. It might grow into something.'

'With your treatment,' I said, 'it would probably grow into making me an accessory.'

His jaw muscles bulged. His eyes were dirty ice. 'So?'

'I don't know,' I said. 'I need legal advice. I'd like to co-operate. How would it be if we had somebody from the D.A.'s office here?'

He let out a short raucous laugh. It was over very soon. He got up slowly and walked around the desk. He leaned down close to me, one big hand on the wood, and smiled. Then without change of expression he hit me on the side of the neck with a fist like a piece of iron.

The blow travelled eight or ten inches, no more. It nearly took my head off. Bile seeped into my mouth. I tasted blood mixed with it. I heard nothing but a roaring in my head. He leaned over me still smiling, his left hand still on the desk. His voice seemed to come from a long way off.

'I used to be tough but I'm getting old. You take a good punch, mister, and that's all you get from me. We got boys over at the City jail that ought to be working in the stockyards. Maybe we hadn't ought to have them because they ain't nice, clean powder-puff punchers like Dayton here. They don't have four kids and a rose garden like Green. They live for different amusements. It takes all kinds and labour's scarce. You got any more funny little ideas about what you might say, if you bothered to say it?'

'Not with the cuffs on, Captain.' It hurt even to say that much.

He leaned further towards me and I smelled his sweat and the gas of corruption. Then he straightened and went back around the desk and planted his solid buttocks in his chair. He picked up a three-cornered ruler and ran his thumb along one edge as if it was a knife. He looked at Green.

'What are you waiting for, Sergeant?'

'Orders.' Green ground out the word as if he hated the sound of his own voice.

'You got to be told? You're an experienced man, it says in the records. I want a detailed statement of this man's movements for the past twenty-four hours. Maybe longer, but that much at first. I want to know what he did every minute of the time. I want it signed and witnessed and checked. I want it in two hours. Then I want him back here clean, tidy, and unmarked. And one thing more, Sergeant—'

He paused and gave Green a stare that would have frozen a fresh-baked potato.

'—next time I ask a suspect a few civil questions I don't want you standing there looking as if I had torn his ear off.'

'Yes sir.' Green turned to me. 'Let's go,' he said gruffly.

Gregorius bared his teeth at me. They needed cleaning—badly. 'Let's have the exit line, chum.'

'Yes, sir,' I said politely. 'You probably didn't intend it, but you've done me a favour. With an assist from Detective Dayton. You've solved a problem for me. No man likes to betray a friend but I wouldn't betray an enemy into your hands. You're not only a gorilla, you're an incompetent. You don't know how to operate a simple investigation. I was balanced on a knife edge and you could have swung me either way. But you had to abuse me, throw coffee in my face, and use your fists on me when I was in a spot where all I could do was take it. From now on I wouldn't tell you the time by the clock on your own wall.'

For some reason he sat there perfectly still and let me say it. Then he grinned. 'You're just a little old cop-hater, friend. That's all you are, shamus, just a little old cop-hater.'

'There are places where cops are not hated, Captain. But in those places you wouldn't be a cop.'

He took that too. I guess he could afford it. He'd probably taken worse many times. Then the phone rang on his desk. He looked at it and gestured. Dayton stepped smartly around the desk and lifted the receiver.

'Captain Gregorius's office. Detective Dayton speaking.'

He listed. A tiny frown drew his handsome eyebrows together. He said softly: 'One moment, please, sir.'

He held the phone out to Gregorius. 'Commissioner Allbright, sir.'

Gregorius scowled. 'Yeah? What's that snotty bastard want?' He took the phone, held it a moment and smoothed his face out. 'Gregorius, Commissioner.'

He listened. 'Yeah, he's here in my office, Commissioner. I been asking him a few questions. Not co-operative. Not co-operative at all . . . How's that again?' A sudden ferocious scowl twisted his face into dark knots. The blood darkened his forehead. But his voice didn't change in tone by a fraction. 'If that's a direct order, it ought to come through the Chief of Detectives, Commissioner . . . Sure, I'll act on it until it's confirmed. Sure . . . Hell, no. Nobody laid a glove on him . . . Yes, sir. Right away.'

He put the phone back in its cradle. I thought his hand shook a little. His eyes moved up and across my face and then to Green. 'Take the cuffs off,' he said tonelessly.

Green unlocked the cuffs. I rubbed my hands together, waiting for the pins and needles of circulation.

'Book him in the County jail, Gregorius said slowly. 'Suspicion of murder. The D.A. has glommed the case right out of our hands. Lovely system we got around here.'

Nobody moved. Green was close to me, breathing hard. Gregorius looked up at Dayton.

'Watcha waiting for, cream puff? An ice cream cone maybe?'

Dayton almost choked. 'You didn't give me any orders, skipper.'

'Say sir to me, damn you! I'm skipper to sergeants and better. Not to you, kiddo. Not to you. Out.'

'Yes, sir.' Dayton walked quickly to the door and went out. Gregorius heaved himself to his feet and moved to the window and stood with his back to the room.

'Come on, let's drift,' Green muttered in my ear.

'Get him out of here before I kick his face in,' Gregorius said to the window.

Green went to the door and opened it. I started through. Gregorius barked suddenly. 'Hold it! Shut that door!'

Green shut it and leaned his back to it.

'Come here you!' Gregorius barked at me.

I didn't move. I stood and looked at him. Green didn't move either. There was a grim pause. Then very slowly Gregorius walked across the room and stood facing me toe to toe. He put his big, hard hands in his pockets. He rocked on his heels.

'Never laid a glove on him,' he said under his breath, as if talking to himself. His eyes were remote and expressionless. His mouth worked convulsively.

Then he spat in my face.

He stepped back. 'That will be all, thank you.'

He turned and went back to the window. Green opened the door again.

I went through it reaching for my handkerchief.

8

Cell No. 3 in the felony tank has two bunks, Pullman style, but the tank was not very full and I had the cell to myself. In the felony tank they treat you pretty well. You get two blankets, neither dirty nor clean, and a lumpy mattress two inches thick which goes over criss-crossed metal slats. There is a flush toilet, a washbasin, paper towels, and gritty grey soap. The cell block is clean and doesn't smell of disinfectant. The trusties do the work. The supply of trusties is always ample.

The jail deputies look you over and they have wise eyes. Unless you are drunk or a psycho or act like one you get to keep your matches and cigarettes. Until preliminary you wear your own clothes. After that you wear the jail denims, no tie, no belt, no shoelaces. You sit on the bunk and wait. There is nothing else to do.

In the drunk tank it is not so good. No bunk, no chair, no blankets, no nothing. You lie on the concrete floor. You sit on the toilet and vomit in your own lap. That is the depth of misery. I've seen it.

Although it was still daylight the lights were on in the ceiling. Inside the steel door of the cell block was a basket of steel bars around the Judas window. The lights were controlled from outside the steel door. They went out at nine p.m. Nobody came through the door or said anything. You might be in the middle of a sentence in a newspaper or magazine. Without any sound of a click or any warning–darkness. And there you were until the summer dawn with nothing to do but sleep if you could, smoke if you had anything to smoke, and think if you had anything to think about that didn't make you feel worse than not thinking at all.

In jail a man has no personality. He is a minor disposal problem and a few entries on reports. Nobody cares who loves or hates him, what he looks like, what he did with his life. Nobody reacts to him unless he gives trouble. Nobody abuses him. All that is asked of him is that he go quietly to the right cell and remain quiet when he gets there. There is nothing to fight against, nothing to be mad at. The jailers are quiet men without animosity or sadism. All this stuff you read about men yelling and screaming, beating against the bars, running spoons along them, guards rushing in with clubs—all that is for the big house. A good jail is one of the quietest places in the world. You could walk through the average cell block at night and look in through the bars and see a huddle of brown blanket, or a head of hair, or a pair of eyes looking at nothing. You might hear a snore. Once in a long while you might hear a nightmare. The life in a jail is in suspension, without purpose or meaning. In another cell you might see a man who cannot sleep or even try to sleep. He is sitting on the edge of his bunk doing nothing. He looks at you or doesn't. You look at him. He says nothing and you say nothing. There is nothing to communicate.

In the corner of the cell block there may be a second steel door that leads to the show-up box. One of its walls is wire mesh painted black. On the back wall are ruled lines for height. Overhead are floodlights. You go in there in the morning as a rule, just before the night captain goes off duty. You stand against the measuring lines and the lights glare at you and there is no light behind the wire mesh. But plenty of people are out there; cops, detectives, citizens who have been robbed or assaulted or swindled or kicked out of their cars at gun point or conned out of their life savings. You don't see or hear them. You hear the voice of the night captain. You receive him loud and clear. He puts you through your paces as if you were a performing dog. He is tired and cynical and competent. He is the stage manager of a play that has had the longest run in history, but it no longer interests him.

'All right, you. Stand straight. Pull your belly in. Pull your chin in. Keep your shoulders back. Hold your head level. Look straight front. Turn left. Turn right. Face front again and hold your hands out. Palms up. Palms down. Pull your sleeves back. No visible scars. Hair dark brown, some grey. Eyes brown. Height six feet, one-half inch. Weight about one-ninety. Name, Philip Marlowe. Occupation, private detective. Well, well, nice to see you, Marlowe. That's all. Next man.'

Much obliged, Captain. Thanks for the time. You forgot to have me open my mouth. I have some nice inlays and one very high-class porcelain jacket crown. Eighty-seven dollars' worth of porcelain jacket crown. You forgot to look inside my nose too, Captain. A lot of scar tissues in there for you. Septum operation and was that guy a butcher! Two hours of it in those days. I hear they do it in twenty minutes now. I got it playing football, Captain, a slight miscalculation in an attempt to block a punt. I blocked the guy's foot instead—after he kicked the ball. Fifteen yards penalty, and that's about how much stiff bloody tape they pulled out of my nose an inch at a time the day after the operation. I'm not bragging, Captain. I'm just telling you. It's the little things that count.

On the third day a deputy unlocked my cell in the middle of the morning.

'Your lawyer's here. Kill the butt—and not on the floor.'

I flushed it down the toilet. He took me to the conference room. A tall, pale, dark-haired man was standing there looking out of the window. There was a fat brown brief-case on the table. He turned. He waited for the door to close. Then he sat down near his brief-case on the far side of a scarred oak table that came out of the Ark. Noah bought it second-hand. The lawyer opened a hammered-silver cigarette case and put it in front of him and looked me over.

'Sit down, Marlowe. Care for a cigarette? My name is Endicott. Sewell Endicott. I've been instructed to represent you without cost or expense to you. I guess you'd like to get out of here, wouldn't you?'

I sat down and took one of the cigarettes. He held a lighter for me.

'Nice to see you again, Mr Endicott. We've met before—while you were D.A.'

He nodded. 'I don't remember, but it's quite possible.' He smiled faintly. 'That position was not quite in my line. I guess I don't have enough tiger in me.'

'Who sent you?'

'I'm not at liberty to say. If you accept me as your attorney, the fee will be taken care of.'

'I guess that mean's they've got him.'

He just stared at me. I puffed at the cigarette. It was one of those things with filters in them. It tasted like a high fog strained through cotton wool.

'If you mean Lennox,' he said, 'and of course you do, no—they haven't got him.'

'Why the mystery, Mr Endicott? About who sent you.'

'My principal wishes to remain anonymous. That is the privilege of my principal. Do you accept me?'

'I don't know,' I said. 'If they haven't got Terry, why are they holding me? Nobody has asked me anything, nobody has been near me.'

He frowned and looked down at his long white delicate fingers. 'District Attorney Springer has taken personal charge of this matter. He may have been too busy to question you yet. But you are entitled to arraignment and a preliminary hearing. I can get you out on bail on a habeas corpus proceeding. You probably know what the law is.'

'I'm booked on suspicion of murder.'

He shrugged impatiently. 'That's just a catch-all. You could have been booked in transit to Pittsburgh, or any one of a dozen charges. What they probably mean is accessory after the fact. You took Lennox somewhere, didn't you?'

I didn't answer. I dropped the tasteless cigarette on the floor and stepped on it. Endicott shrugged again and frowned.

'Assume you did then, just for the sake of argument. To make you an accessory they have to prove intent. In this case that would mean knowledge that a crime had been committed and that Lennox was a fugitive. It's bailable in any case. Of course what you really are is a material witness. But a man can't be held in prison as a material witness in this state except by court order. He's not a material witness unless a judge so declares. But the law enforcement people can always find a way to do what they want to do.'

'Yeah,' I said. 'A detective named Dayton slugged me. A homicide captain named Gregorius threw a cup of coffee at me, hit me in the neck hard enough to bust an artery—you can see it's still swollen, and when a call from Police Commissioner Allbright kept him from turning me over to the wrecking crew, he spat in my face. You're quite right, Mr Endicott. The law boys can always do what they want to do.'

He looked at his wrist-watch rather pointedly. 'You want out on bail or don't you?'

'Thanks. I don't think I do. A guy out on bail is already half guilty in the public mind. If he gets off later on, he had a smart lawyer.'

'That's silly,' he said impatiently.

'Okay, it's silly. I'm silly. Otherwise I wouldn't be here. If you're in touch with Lennox, tell him to quit bothering about me. I'm not in here for

him. I'm in here for me. No complaints. It's part of the deal. I'm in a
business where people come to me with troubles. Big troubles, little
troubles, but always troubles they don't want to take to the cops. How long
would they come if any bruiser with a police shield could hold me upside
down and drain my guts?'

'I see your point,' he said slowly. 'But let me correct you on one point. I
am not in touch with Lennox. I scarcely know him. I'm an officer of the
court, as all lawyers are. If I knew where Lennox was, I couldn't conceal the
information from the District Attorney. The most I could do would be to
agree to surrender him at a specified time and place after I had had an
interview with him.'

'Nobody else would bother to send you here to help me.'

'Are you calling me a liar?' He reached down to rub out his cigarette stub
on the underside of the table.

'I seem to remember that you're a Virginian, Mr Endicott. In this
country we have a sort of historical fixation about Virginians. We think of
them as the flower of southern chivalry and honour.'

He smiled. 'That was nicely said. I only wish it was true. But we're
wasting time. If you had had a grain of sense you'd have told the police you
hadn't seen Lennox for a week. It didn't have to be true. Under oath you
could always have told the real story. There's no law against lying to the
cops. They expect it. They feel much happier when you lie to them than
when you refuse to talk to them. That's a direct challenge to their authority.
What do you expect to gain by it?'

I didn't answer. I didn't really have an answer. He stood up and reached
for his hat and snapped his cigarette case shut and put it in his pocket.

'You had to play the big scene,' he said coldly. 'Stand on your rights, talk
about the law. How ingenuous can a man get, Marlowe? A man like you who
is supposed to know his way around. The law isn't justice. It's a very
imperfect mechanism. If you press exactly the right buttons and are also
lucky, justice may show up in the answer. A mechanism is all the law ever
was ever intended to be. I guess you're not in any mood to be helped. So I'll
take myself off. You can reach me if you change your mind.'

'I'll stick it out for a day or two longer. If they catch Terry they won't care
how he got away. All they'll care about is the circus they can make of the
trial. The murder of Mr Harlan Potter's daughter is headline material all
over the country. A crowd pleaser like Springer could ride himself right into
Attorney-General on that show, and from there into the governor's chair
and from there—' I stopped talking and let the rest of it float in the air.

Endicott smiled a slow derisive smile. 'I don't think you know very much
about Mr Harlan Potter,' he said.

'And if they don't get Lennox, they won't want to know how he got away,
Mr Endicott. They'll just want to forget the whole thing fast.'

'Got it all figured out, haven't you, Marlowe?'

'I've had the time. All I know about Mr Harlan Potter is that he is
supposed to be worth a hundred million bucks, and that he owns nine or ten
newspapers. How's the publicity going?'

'The publicity?' His voice was ice-cold saying it.

'Yeah. Nobody's interviewed me from the press. I expected to make a big
noise in the papers out of this. Get lots of business. Private eye goes to jail
rather than split on a pal.'

He walked to the door and turned with his hand on the knob. 'You amuse me, Marlowe. You're childish in some ways. True, a hundred million dollars can buy a great deal of publicity. It can also, my friend, if shrewdly employed, buy a great deal of silence.'

He opened the door and went out. Then a deputy came in and took me back to Cell No. 3 in the felony block.

'Guess you won't be with us long, if you've got Endicott,' he said pleasantly as he locked me in. I said I hoped he was right.

9

The deputy on the early night shift was a big blond guy with meaty shoulders and a friendly grin. He was middle-aged and had long since outlived both pity and anger. He wanted to put in eight easy hours and he looked as if almost anything would be easy down his street. He unlocked my door.

'Company for you. Guy from the D.A.'s office. No sleep, huh?'

'It's a little early for me. What time is it?'

'Ten-fourteen.' He stood in the doorway and looked over the cell. One blanket was spread on the lower bunk, one was folded for a pillow. There were a couple of used paper towels in the trash bucket and a small wad of toilet paper on the edge of the wash basin. He nodded approval. 'Anything personal in here?'

'Just me.'

He left the cell door open. We walked along a quiet corridor to the elevator and rode down to the booking desk. A fat man in a grey suit stood by the desk smoking a corncob. His fingernails were dirty and he smelled.

'I'm Spranklin from the D.A.'s office,' he told me in a tough voice. 'Mr Grenz wants you upstairs.' He reached behind his hip and came up with a pair of bracelets. 'Let's try these for size.'

The jail deputy and the booking clerk grinned at him with deep enjoyment. 'What's the matter, Sprank? Afraid he'll mug you in the elevator?'

'I don't want no trouble,' he growled. 'Had a guy break from me once. They ate my ass off. Let's go, boy.'

The booking clerk pushed a form at him and he signed it with a flourish. 'I never take no unnecessary chances,' he said. 'Man never knows who he's up against in this town.'

A prowl car cop brought in a drunk with a bloody ear. We went towards the elevator. 'You're in trouble, boy,' Spranklin told me in the elevator. 'Heap bad trouble.' It seemed to give him a vague satisfaction. 'A guy can get hisself in a lot of trouble in this town.'

The elevator man turned his head and winked at me. I grinned.

'Don't try nothing, boy,' Spranklin told me severely. 'I shot a man once. Tried to break. They ate my ass off.'

'You get it coming and going, don't you?'

He thought it over. 'Yeah,' he said. 'Either way they eat your ass off. It's a tough town. No respect.'

We got out and went in through the double doors of the D.A.'s office. The switchboard was dead, with lines plugged in for the night. There was nobody in the waiting chairs. Lights were on in a couple of offices. Spranklin opened the door of a small, lighted room which contained a desk, a filing case, a hard chair or two, and a thick-set man with a hard chin and stupid eyes. His face was red and he was just pushing something into the drawer of his desk.

'You could knock,' he barked at Spranklin.

'Sorry, Mr Grenz,' Spranklin bumbled. 'I was thinkin' about the prisoner.'

He pushed me into the office. 'Should I take the cuffs off, Mr Grenz?'

'I don't know what the hell you put them on for,' Grenz said sourly. He watched Spranklin unlock the cuffs on my wrists. He had the key on a bunch the size of a grapefruit and it troubled him to find it.

'Okay, scram,' Grenz said. 'Wait outside to take him back.'

'I'm kind of off duty, Mr Grenz.'

'You're off duty when I say you're off duty.'

Spranklin flushed and edged his fat bottom out through the door. Grenz looked after him savagely, then when the door closed he moved the same look to me. I pulled a chair over and sat down.

'I didn't tell you to sit down,' Grenz barked.

I got a loose cigarette out of my pocket and stuck it in my mouth. 'And I didn't say you could smoke,' Grenz roared.

'I'm allowed to smoke in the cell block. Why not here?'

'Because this is my office. I make the rules here.' A raw smell of whisky floated across the desk.

'Take another quick one,' I said. 'It'll calm you down. You got kind of interrupted when we came in.'

His back hit the back of the chair hard. His face went dark red. I struck a match and lit my cigarette.

After a long minute Grenz said softly: 'Okay, tough boy. Quite a man, aren't you? You know something? They're all sizes and shapes when they come in here, but they all go out the same size–small. And the same shape–bent.'

'What did you want to see me about, Mr Grenz? And don't mind me if you feel like hitting that bottle. I'm a fellow that will take a snort myself, if I'm tired and nervous and overworked.'

'You don't seem much impressed by the jam you're in.'

'I don't figure I'm in any jam.'

'We'll see about that. Meantime I want a very full statement from you.' He flicked a finger at a recording set on a stand beside his desk. 'We'll take it now and have it transcribed tomorrow. If the Chief Deputy is satisfied with your statement, he may release you on your own undertaking not to leave town. Let's go.' He switched on the recorder. His voice was cold, decisive, and as nasty as he knew how to make it. But his right hand kept edging towards the desk drawer. He was too young to have veins in his nose, but he had them, and the whites of his eyes were a bad colour.

'I get so tired of it,' I said.

'Tired of what?' he snapped.

'Hard little men in hard little offices talking hard little words that don't mean a goddam thing. I've had fifty-six hours in the felony block. Nobody pushed me around, nobody tried to prove he was tough. They didn't have to. They had it on ice for when they needed it. And why was I in there? I was booked on suspicion. What the hell kind of legal system lets a man be shoved in a felony tank because some cop didn't get an answer to some question? What evidence did he have? A telephone number on a pad. And what was he trying to prove by locking me up? Not a damn thing except that he had the power to do it. Now you're on the same pitch—trying to make me feel what a lot of power you generate in this cigar box you call your office. You send this scared baby-sitter over late at night to bring me here. You think maybe sitting alone with my thoughts for fifty-six hours has made me gruel out of my brains? You think I'm going to cry in your lap and ask you to stroke my head because I'm so awful goddam lonely in the great big jail? Come off it, Grenz. Take your drink and get human; I'm willing to assume you are just doing your job. But take the brass knuckles off before you start. If you're big enough you don't need them, and if you need them you're not big enough to push me around.'

He sat there and listened and looked at me. Then he grinned sourly. 'Nice speech,' he said. 'Now you've got the crap out of your system, let's get that statement. You want to answer specific questions, or just tell it your own way?'

'I was talking to the birds,' I said. 'Just to hear the breeze blow. I'm not making any statement. You're a lawyer and you know I don't have to.'

'That's right,' he said coolly. 'I know the law. I know police work. I'm offering you a chance to clear yourself. If you don't want it, that's jake with me too. I can arraign you tomorrow morning at ten a.m. and have you set for a preliminary hearing. You may get bail, although I'll fight it, but if you do, it will be stiff. It'll cost you plenty. That's one way we can do it.'

He looked down at a paper on his desk, read it, and turned it face down.

'On what charge?' I asked him.

'Section Thirty-two. Accessory after the fact. A felony. It rates up to a five spot in Quentin.'

'Better catch Lennox first,' I said carefully. Grenz had something and I sensed it in his manner. I didn't know how much, but he had something all right.

He leaned back in his chair and picked up a pen and twirled it slowly between his palms. Then he smiled. He was enjoying himself.

'Lennox is a hard man to hide, Marlowe. With most people you need a photo and a good clear photo. Not with a guy that has scars all over one side of his face. Not to mention white hair, and not over thirty-five years old. We got four witnesses, maybe more.'

'Witnesses to what?' I was tasting something bitter in my mouth, like the bile I had tasted after Captain Gregorius slugged me. That reminded me my neck was still sore and swollen. I rubbed it gently.

'Don't be a chump, Marlowe. A San Diego superior court judge and his wife happened to be seeing their son and daughter-in-law off on that plane. All four saw Lennox and the judge's wife saw the car he came in and who came with him. You don't have a prayer?'

'That's nice,' I said. 'How did you get to them?'

'Special bulletin on radio and TV. A full description was all it took. The judge called in.'

'Sounds good,' I said judicially. 'But it takes a little more than that,

Grenz. You have to catch him and prove he committed a murder. Then you have to prove I knew it.'

He snapped a finger at the back of the telegram. 'I think I will take that drink,' he said. 'Been working nights too much.' He opened the drawer and put a bottle and a shot glass on the desk. He poured it full to the brim and knocked it back in a lump. 'Better,' he said. 'Much better. Sorry I can't offer you one while you're in custody.' He corked the bottle and pushed it away from him, but not out of reach. 'Oh yeah, we got to prove something, you said. Well, it could be we already got a confession, chum. Too bad, huh?'

A small but very cold finger moved the whole length of my spine, like an icy insect crawling.

'So why do you need a statement from me?'

He grinned. 'We like a tidy record. Lennox will be brought back and tried. We need everything we can get. It's not so much what we want from you, as what we might be willing to let you get away with—if you co-operate.'

I stared at him. He did a little paper-fiddling. He moved around in his chair, looked at his bottle, and had to use up a lot of will-power not grabbing for it. 'Maybe you'd like the whole libretto,' he said suddenly with an off-key leer. 'Well, smart guy, just to show you I'm not kidding here it is.'

I leaned across his desk and he thought I was reaching for his bottle. He grabbed it away and put it back in the drawer. I just wanted to drop a stub in his ashtray. I leaned back again and lit another pill. He spoke rapidly.

'Lennox got off the plane at Mazatlan, an airline junction point and a town of about thirty-five thousand. He disappeared for two or three hours. Then a tall man with black hair and a dark skin and what might have been a lot of knife scars booked to Torreon under the name of Silvano Rodriguez. His Spanish was good but not good enough for a man of his name. He was too tall for a Mexican with such a dark skin. The pilot turned in a report on him. The cops were too slow at Torreon. Mex cops are no balls of fire. What they do best is shoot people. By the time they got going the man had chartered a plane and gone on to a little mountain town called Otatoclan, a small-time summer resort with a lake. The pilot of the charter plane had trained as a combat pilot in Texas. He spoke good English. Lennox pretended not to catch what he said.'

'If it *was* Lennox,' I put in.

'Wait a while, chum. It was Lennox all right. Okay, he gets off at Otatoclan and registers at the hotel there, this time as Mario de Cerva. He was wearing a gun, a Mauser 7.65, which doesn't mean too much in Mexico, of course. But the charter pilot thought the guy didn't seem kosher, so he had a word with the local law. They put Lennox under surveillance. They did some checking with Mexico City and then they moved in.'

Grenz picked up a ruler and sighted along it, a meaningless gesture which kept him from looking at me.

I said. 'Uh-huh. Smart boy, your charter pilot, and nice to his customers. The story stinks.'

He looked up at me suddenly. 'What we want,' he said dryly, 'is a quick trial, a plea of second degree, which we will accept. There are some angles we'd rather not go into. After all, the family is pretty influential.'

'Meaning Harlan Potter.'

He nodded briefly. 'For my money the whole idea is all wet. Springer could have a field day with it. It's got everything. Sex, scandal, money, beautiful unfaithful wife, wounded war-hero husband—I suppose that's where he got the scars—hell, it would be front page stuff for weeks. Every rag in the country would eat it up. So we shuffle it off to a fast fade.' He shrugged. 'Okay, if the chief wants it that way, it's up to him. Do I get that statement?' He turned to the recording machine which had been humming away softly all this time, with the light showing in front.

'Turn it off,' I said.

He swung around and gave me a vicious look. 'You like it in jail?'

'It's not too bad. You don't meet the best people, but who the hell wants to? Be reasonable, Grenz. You're trying to make a fink out of me. Maybe I'm obstinate, or even sentimental, but I'm practical too. Suppose you had to hire a private eye—yeah, yeah, I know how you would hate the idea—but just suppose you were where it was your only way out. Would you want one that finked on his friends?'

He stared at me with hate.

'A couple more points. Doesn't it strike you that Lennox's evasion tactics were just a little too transparent? If he wanted to be caught, he didn't have to go to all that trouble. If he didn't want to be caught, he had brains enough not to disguise himself as a Mexican in Mexico.'

'Meaning what?' Grenz was snarling at me now.

'Meaning you could just be filling me up with a lot of hooey you made up, that there wasn't any Rodriguez with dyed hair and there wasn't any Mario de Cerva at Otatoclan, and you don't know any more about where Lennox is than where Blackbeard the Pirate buried his treasure.'

He got his bottle out again. He poured himself a shot and drank it down quickly, as before. He relaxed slowly. He turned in his chair and switched off the recording machine.

'I'd like to have tried you,' he said gratingly. 'You're the kind of wise guy I like to work over. This rap will be hanging over you for a long, long time, cutie. You'll walk with it and eat with it and sleep with it. And next time you step out of line we'll murder you with it. Right now I got to do something that turns my guts inside out.'

He pawed on his desk and pulled the face-down paper to him, turned it over, and signed it. You can always tell when a man his writing his own name. He has a special way of moving. Then he stood up and marched around the desk and threw the door of his shoe box open and yelled for Spranklin.

The fat man came in with his B.O. Grenz gave him the paper.

'I've just signed your release order,' he said. 'I'm a public servant and sometimes I have unpleasant duties. Would you care to know why I signed it?'

I stood up. 'If you want to tell me.'

'The Lennox case is closed, mister. There ain't any Lennox case. He wrote out a full confession this afternoon in his hotel room and shot himself. In Otatoclan, just like I said.'

I stood there looking at nothing. Out of the corner of my eye I saw Grenz back away slowly as if he thought I might be going to slug him. I must have looked pretty nasty for a moment. Then he was behind his desk again and Spranklin had grabbed on to my arm.

'Come on, move,' he said in a whining kind of voice. 'Man likes to get home nights once in a while.'

I went out with him and closed the door. I closed it quietly as if in a room where someone had just died.

<hr />

10

<hr />

I dug out the carbon of my property slip and turned it over and receipted on the original. I put my belongings back in my pockets. There was a man draped over the end of the booking desk and as I turned away he straightened up and spoke to me. He was about six feet four inches tall and as thin as a wire.

'Need a ride home?'

In the bleak light he looked young-old, tired, and cynical, but he didn't look like a grifter. 'For how much?'

'For free. I'm Lonnie Morgan of the *Journal*. I'm knocking off.'

'Oh, police beat,' I said.

'Just this week. The City Hall is my regular beat.'

We walked out of the building and found his car in the parking lot. I looked up at the sky. There were stars but there was too much glare. It was a cool, pleasant night. I breathed it in. Then I got into his car and he drove away from there.

'I live way out in Laurel Canyon,' I said. 'Just drop me anywhere.'

'They ride you in,' he said, 'but they don't worry how you get home. This case interests me, in a repulsive sort of way.'

'It seems there isn't any case,' I said. 'Terry Lennox shot himself this afternoon. So they say. So they say.'

'Very convenient,' Lonnie Morgan said, staring ahead through the windshield. His car drifted quietly along quiet streets. 'It helps them build their wall.'

'What wall?'

'Somebody's building a wall around the Lennox case, Marlowe. You're smart enough to see that, aren't you? It's not getting the kind of play it rates. The D.A. left town tonight for Washington. Some kind of convention. He walked out on the sweetest hunk of publicity he's had in years. Why?'

'No use to ask me. I've been in cold storage.'

'Because somebody made it worth his while, that's why. I don't mean anything crude like a wad of dough. Somebody promised him something important to him and there's only one man connected with the case in a position to do that. The girl's father.'

I leaned my head back in a corner of the car. 'Sounds a little unlikely,' I said. 'What about the press? Harlan Potter owns a few papers, but what about the competition?'

He gave me a brief amused glance and then concentrated on his driving. 'Ever been a newspaper man?'

'No.'

'Newspapers are owned and published by rich men. Rich men all belong to the same club. Sure, there's competition—hard, tough competition for circulation, for newsbeats, for exclusive stories. Just so long as it doesn't damage the prestige and privilege and position of the owners. If it does, down comes the lid. The lid, my friend, is down on the Lennox case. The Lennox case, my friend, properly built up, could have sold a hell of a lot of papers. It has everything. The trial would have drawn feature writers from all over the country. But there ain't going to be no trial. On account of Lennox checked out before it could get moving. Like I said–very convenient–for Harlan Potter and his family.'

I straightened up and gave him a hard stare.

'You calling the whole thing a fix?'

He twisted his mouth sardonically. 'Could just be Lennox had some help committing suicide. Resisting arrest a little. Mexican cops have very itchy trigger fingers. If you want to lay a little bet, I'll give you nice odds that nobody gets to count the bullet holes.'

'I think you're wrong,' I said. 'I knew Terry Lennox pretty well. He wrote himself off a long time ago. If they brought him back alive, he would have let them have it their way. He'd have copped a manslaughter plea.'

Lonnie Morgan shook his head. I knew what he was going to say and he said it. 'Not a chance. If he had shot her or cracked her skull, maybe yes. But there was too much brutality. Her face was beaten to a pulp. Second degree murder would be the best he could get, and even that would raise a stink.'

I said: 'You could be right.'

He looked at me again. 'You say you knew the guy. Do you go for the set-up?'

'I'm tired. I'm not in a thinking mood tonight.'

There was a long pause. Then Lonnie Morgan said quietly: 'If I was a real bright guy instead of a hack newspaper man, I'd think maybe he didn't kill her at all.'

'It's a thought.'

He stuck a cigarette in his mouth and lit it by scratching a match on the dashboard. He smoked silently with a fixed frown on his thin face. We reached Laurel Canyon and I told him where to turn off the boulevard and where to turn again into my street. His car churned up the hill and stopped at the foot of my redwood steps.

I got out. 'Thanks for the ride, Morgan. Care for a drink?'

'I'll take a rain check. I figure you'd rather be alone.'

'I've got lots of time to be alone. Too damn much.'

'You've got a friend to say good-bye to,' he said. 'He must have been that if you let them toss you into the can on his account.'

'Who said I did that?'

He smiled faintly. 'Just because I can't print it don't mean I didn't know it, chum. So long. See you around.'

I shut the car door and he turned and drove off down the hill. When his tail lights vanished around the corner I climbed the steps, picked up newspapers, and let myself into the empty house. I put all the lamps on and opened all the windows. The place was stuffy.

I made some coffee and drank it and took the five C notes out of the coffee can. They were rolled tight and pushed down into the coffee at the side. I walked up and down with a cup of coffee in my hand, turned the TV on, turned it off, sat, stood, and sat again. I read through the papers that had piled up on the front steps. The Lennox case started out big, but by that morning it was a Part Two item. There was a photo of Sylvia, but none of Terry. There was a snap of me that I didn't know existed. 'L.A Private Detective Held for Questioning.' There was a large photo of the Lennox home in Encino. It was pseudo-English with a lot of peaked roof and it would have cost a hundred bucks to wash the windows. It stood on a knoll in a big two acres, which is a lot of real estate for the Los Angeles area. There was a photo of the guest house, which was a miniature of the main building. It was hedged in with trees. Both photos had obviously been taken from some distance off and then blown up and trimmed. There was no photo of what the papers called the 'death room'.

I had seen all this stuff before, in jail, but I read it and looked at it again with different eyes. It told me nothing except that a rich and beautiful girl had been murdered and the press had been pretty thoroughly excluded. So influence had started to work very early. The crime beat boys must have gnashed their teeth and gnashed them in vain. It figured. If Terry talked to his father-in-law in Pasadena the very night she was killed, there would have been a dozen guards on the estate before the police were even notified.

But there was something that didn't figure at all—the way she had been beaten up. Nobody could sell me that Terry had done that.

I put the lamps out and sat by an open window. Outside in a bush a mocking bird ran through a few trills and admired himself before settling down for the night.

My neck itched, so I shaved and showered and went to bed and lay on my back listening, as if far off in the night I might hear a voice, the kind of calm and patient voice that makes everything clear. I didn't hear it and I knew I wasn't going to. Nobody was going to explain the Lennox case to me. No explanation was necessary. The murderer had confessed and he was dead. There wouldn't even be an inquest.

As Lonnie Morgan of the *Journal* had remarked—very convenient. If Terry Lennox had killed his wife, that was fine. There was no need to try him and bring out all the unpleasant details. If he hadn't killed her, that was fine too. A dead man is the best fall guy in the world. He never talks back.

11

In the morning I shaved again and dressed and drove downtown in the usual way and parked in the usual place, and if the parking lot attendant happened to know that I was an important public character he did a top job in hiding it. I went upstairs and along the corridor and got keys out to unlock my door. A dark, smooth-looking guy watched me.

'You Marlowe?'

'So?'

'Stick around,' he said. 'A guy wants to see you.' He unplastered his back from the wall and strolled off languidly.

I stepped inside the office and picked up the mail. There was more of it on the desk where the night cleaning woman had put it. I slit the envelopes after I opened windows and threw away what I didn't want, which was practically all of it. I switched on the buzzer to the other door and filled a pipe and lit it and then just sat there waiting for somebody to scream for help.

I thought about Terry Lennox in a detached sort of way. He was already receding into the distance, white hair and scarred face and weak charm and his peculiar brand of pride. I didn't judge him or analyse him, just as I had never asked him questions about how he got wounded or how he ever happened to get himself married to anyone like Sylvia. He was like somebody you meet on board ship and get to know very well and never really know at all. He was gone like the same fellow when he says good-bye at the pier and let's keep in touch, old man, and you know you won't and he won't. Likely enough you'll never even see the guy again. If you do he will be an entirely different person, just another Rotarian in a club car. How's business? Oh, not too bad. You look good. So do you. I've put on too much weight. Don't we all? Remember that trip in the *Franconia* (or whatever it was)? Oh sure, swell trip, wasn't it?

The hell it was a swell trip. You were bored stiff. You only talked to the guy because there wasn't anybody around that interested you. Maybe it was like that with Terry Lennox and me. No, not quite. I owned a piece of him. I had invested time and money in him, and three days in the ice-house, not to mention a slug on the jaw and a punch in the neck that I felt every time I swallowed. Now he was dead and I couldn't even give him back his five hundred bucks. That made me sore. It is always the little things that make you sore.

The door buzzer and the telephone rang at the same time. I answered the phone first because the buzzer meant only that somebody had walked into my pint-size waiting-room.

'Is this Mr Marlowe? Mr Endicott is calling you. One moment please.'

He came on the line. 'This is Sewell Endicott,' he said, as if he didn't know his goddam secretary had already fed me his name.

'Good morning, Mr Endicott.'

'Glad to hear they turned you loose. I think possibly you had the right idea not to build any resistance.'

'It wasn't an idea. It was just mulishness.'

'I doubt if you'll hear any more about it. But if you do and need help, let me hear from you.'

'Why would I? The man is dead. They'd have a hell of a time proving he ever came near me. Then they'd have to prove I had guilty knowledge. And then they'd have to prove he had committed a crime or was a fugitive.'

He cleared his throat. 'Perhaps,' he said carefully, 'you haven't been told he left a full confession.'

'I was told, Mr Endicott. I'm talking to a lawyer. Would I be out of line in suggesting that the confession would have to be proved too, both as to genuineness and as to veracity?'

'I'm afraid I have no time for a legal discussion,' he said sharply. 'I'm flying to Mexico with a rather melancholy duty to perform. You can probably guess what it is?'

'Uh-huh. Depends who you're representing. You didn't tell me, remember?'

'I remember very well. Well, good-bye, Marlowe. My offer of help is still good. But let me also offer you a little advice. Don't be too certain you're in the clear. You're in a pretty vulnerable business.'

He hung up. I put the phone back in its cradle carefully. I sat for a moment with my hand on it, scowling. Then I wiped the scowl off my face and got up to open the communicating door into my waiting-room.

A man was sitting by the window ruffling a magazine. He wore a bluish-grey suit with an almost invisible pale blue check. On his crossed feet were black moccasin type ties, the kind with two eyelets that are almost as comfortable as strollers and don't wear your socks out every time you walk a block. His white handkerchief was folded square and the end of a pair of sunglasses showed behind it. He had thick, dark, wavy hair. He was tanned very dark. He looked up with bird-bright eyes and smiled under a hair-line moustache. His tie was a dark maroon tied in a pointed bow over a sparkling white shirt.

He threw the magazine aside. 'The crap these rags go for,' he said. 'I been reading a piece about Costello. Yeah, they know all about Costello. Like I know all about Helen of Troy.'

'What can I do for you?'

He looked me over hurriedly. 'Tarzan on a big red scooter,' he said.

'What?'

'You, Marlowe. Tarzan on a big red scooter. They rough you up much?'

'Here and there. What makes it your business?'

'After Allbright talked to Gregorius?'

'No. Not after that.'

He nodded shortly. 'You got a crust asking Allbright to use ammunition on that slob.'

'I asked you what made it your business. Incidentally I don't know Commissioner Allbright and I didn't ask him to do anything. Why would he do anything for me?'

He stared at me morosely. He stood up slowly, graceful as a panther. He walked across the room and looked into my office. He jerked his head at me and went in. He was a guy who owned the place where he happened to be. I went in after him and shut the door. He stood by the desk looking round, amused.

'You're small-time,' he said. 'Very small-time.'

I went behind my desk and waited.

'How much you make in a month, Marlowe?'

I let it ride, and lit my pipe.

'Seven-fifty would be tops,' he said.

I dropped a burnt match into a tray and puffed tobacco smoke.

'You're a piker, Marlowe. You're a peanut grifter. You're so little it takes a magnifying glass to see you.'

I didn't say anything at all.

'You got cheap emotions. You're cheap all over. You pal around with a guy, eat a few drinks, talk a few gags, slip him a little dough when he's strapped, and you're sold out to him. Just like some school kid that read Frank Merriwell. You got no guts, no brains, no connexions, no savvy, so you throw out a phony attitude and expect people to cry over you. Tarzan on a big red scooter.' He smiled a small weary smile. 'In my book you're a nickel's worth of nothing.'

He leaned across the desk and flicked me across the face back-handed,

casually and contemptuously, not meaning to hurt me, and the small smile
stayed on his face. Then, when I didn't even move for that, he sat down
slowly and leaned an elbow on the desk and cupped his brown chin in his
brown hand. The bird-bright eyes stared at me without anything in them
but brightness.

'Know who I am, cheapie?'

'Your name's Menendez. The boys call you Mendy. You operate on the
Strip?'

'Yeah? How did I get so big?'

'I wouldn't know. You probably started out as a pimp in a Mexican
whorehouse.'

He took a gold cigarette case out of his pocket and lit a brown cigarette
with a gold lighter. He blew acrid smoke and nodded. He put the gold
cigarette case on the desk and caressed it with his fingertips.

'I'm a big bad man, Marlowe. I make lots of dough. I got to make lots of
dough to juice the guys I got to juice in order to make lots of dough to juice
the guys I got to juice. I got a place in Bel-Air that cost ninety grand and I
already spent more than that to fix it up. I got a lovely platinum blonde wife
and two kids in private schools back east. My wife's got a hundred and fifty
grand in rocks and another seventy-five in furs and clothes. I got a butler,
two maids, a cook, a chauffeur, not counting the monkey that walks behind
me. Everywhere I go I'm a darling. The best of everything, the best food,
the best drinks, the best clothes, the best hotel suites. I got a place in Florida
and a seagoing yacht with a crew of five men. I got a Bentley, two Cadillacs,
a Chrysler station wagon, and an MG for my boy. Couple of years my girl
gets one too. What you got?'

'Not much,' I said. 'This year I have a house to live in—all to myself.'

'No woman?'

'Just me. In addition to that I have what you see here and twelve hundred
dollars in the bank and a few thousand in bonds. That answer your
question?'

'What's the most you ever made on a single job?'

'Eight-fifty.'

'Jesus, how cheap can a guy get?'

'Stop hamming and tell me what you want.'

He killed his cigarette half-smoked and immediately lit another. He
leaned back in his chair. His lip curled at me.

'We were three guys in a foxhole eating,' he said. 'It was cold as hell, snow
all around. We ate out of cans. Cold food. A little shelling, more mortar fire.
We are blue with the cold, and I mean blue, Randy Starr and me and this
Terry Lennox. A mortar shell plops right in the middle of us and for some
reason it don't go off. Those Jerries have a lot of tricks. They got a twisted
sense of humour. Sometimes you think it's a dud and three seconds later it
ain't a dud. Terry grabs it and he's out of the foxhole before Randy and me
can even start to get unstuck. But I mean quick, brother. Like a good ball
handler. He throws himself face down and throws the thing away from him
and it goes off in the air. Most of it goes over his head but a hunk gets the
side of his face. Right then the krauts mount an attack and the next thing we
know we ain't there any more.'

Menendez stopped talking and gave me the bright steady glare of his dark
eyes.

'Thanks for telling me,' I said.

'You take a good ribbing, Marlowe. You're okay. Randy and me talked things over and we decided that what happened to Terry Lennox was enough to screw up any guy's brains. For a long time we figured he was dead but he wasn't. The krauts got him. They worked him over for about a year and a half. They did a good job but they hurt him too much. It cost us money to find out, and it cost us money to find him. But we made plenty in the black market after the war. We could afford it. All Terry gets out of saving our lives is half a new face, white hair, and a bad case of nerves. Back east he hits the bottle, gets picked up here and there, kind of goes to pieces. There's something on his mind but we never know what. The next thing we know he's married to this rich dame and riding high. He unmarries her, hits bottom again, marries her again, and she gets dead. Randy and me can't do a thing for him. He won't let us except for that short job in Vegas. And when he gets in a real jam he don't come to us, he goes to a cheapie like you, a guy that cops can push around. So then *he* gets dead, and without telling us good-bye, and without giving us a chance to pay off. I got connexions in Mexico that could have buried him for ever. I could have got him out of the country faster than a card sharp can stack a deck. But he goes crying to you. It makes me sore. A cheapie, a guy cops can push around.'

'The cops can push anybody around. What do you want me to do about it?'

'Just lay off,' Menendez said tightly.

'Lay off what?'

'Trying to make yourself dough or publicity out of the Lennox case. It's finished, wrapped up. Terry's dead and we don't want him bothered any more. The guy suffered too much.'

'A hoodlum with sentiment,' I said. 'That slays me.'

'Watch your lip, cheapie. Watch your lip. Mendy Menendez don't argue with guys. He tells them. Find yourself another way to grab a buck. Get me?'

He stood up. The interview was finished. He picked up his gloves. They were snow-white pigskin. They didn't look as if he had ever had them on. A dressy type, Mr Menendez. But very tough behind it all.

'I'm not looking for publicity,' I said. 'And nobody's offered me any dough. Why would they and for what?'

'Don't kid me, Marlowe. You didn't spend three days in the freezer just because you're a sweetheart. You got paid off. I ain't saying who by but I got a notion. And the party I'm thinking about has plenty more of the stuff. The Lennox case is closed and it stays closed even if—' he stopped dead and flipped his gloves at the desk edge.

'Even if Terry didn't kill her,' I said.

His surprise was as thin as the gold on a week-end wedding ring. 'I'd like to go along with you on that, cheapie. But it don't make any sense. But if it did make sense—and Terry wanted it the way it is—then that's how it stays.'

I didn't say anything. After a moment he grinned slowly. 'Tarzan on a big red scooter,' he drawled. 'A tough guy. Lets me come in here and walk all over him. A guy that gets hired for nickels and dimes and gets pushed around by anybody. No dough, no family, no prospects, no nothing. See you around, cheapie.'

I sat still with my jaws clamped, staring at the glitter of his gold cigarette case on the desk corner. I felt old and tired. I got up slowly and reached for the case.

'You forgot this,' I said, going around the desk.

'I got half a dozen of them,' he sneered.

When I was near enough to him I held it out. His hand reached for it casually. 'How about half a dozen of these?' I asked him and hit him as hard as I could in the middle of his belly.

He doubled up mewling. The cigarette case fell to the floor. He backed against the wall and his hands jerked back and forth convulsively. His breath fought to get in his lungs. He was sweating. Very slowly and with an intense effort he straightened up and we were eye to eye again. I reached out and ran a finger along the bone of his jaw. He held still for it. Finally he worked a smile on to his brown face.

'I didn't think you had it in you,' he said.

'Next time bring a gun—or don't call me cheapie.'

'I got a guy to carry the gun.'

'Bring him with you. You'll need him.'

'You're a hard guy to get sore, Marlowe.'

I moved the gold cigarette case to one side with my foot and bent and picked it up and handed it to him. He took it and dropped it into his pocket.

'I couldn't figure you,' I said. 'Why it was worth your time to come up here and ride me. Then it got monotonous. All tough guys are monotonous. Like playing cards with a deck that's all aces. You've got everything and you've got nothing. You're just sitting there looking at yourself. No wonder Terry didn't come to you for help. It would be like borrowing money from a whore.'

He pressed delicately on his stomach with two fingers. 'I'm sorry you said that, cheapie. You could crack wise once too often.'

He walked to the door and opened it. Outside the bodyguard straightened from the opposite wall and turned. Menendez jerked his head. The bodyguard came into the office and stood there looking me over without expression.

'Take a good look at him, Chick,' Menendez said. 'Make sure you know him just in case. You and him might have business one of these days.'

'I already saw him, Chief,' the smooth, dark, tight-lipped guy said in the tight-lipped voice they all affect. 'He wouldn't bother me none.'

'Don't let him hit you in the guts,' Menendez said with a sour grin. 'His right hook ain't funny.'

The bodyguard just sneered at me. 'He wouldn't get that close.'

'Well, so long, cheapie,' Menendez told me and went out.

'See you around,' the bodyguard told me coolly. 'The name's Chick Agostino. I guess you'll know me.'

'Like a dirty newspaper,' I said. 'Remind me not to step on your face.'

His jaw muscles bulged. Then he turned suddenly and went out after his boss.

The door closed slowly on the pneumatic gadget. I listened but I didn't hear their steps going down the hall. They walked as softly as cats. Just to make sure, I opened the door again after a minute and looked out. But the hall was quite empty.

I went back to my desk and sat down and spent a little time wondering why a fairly important local racketeer like Menendez would think it worth his time to come in person to my office and warn me to keep my nose clean, just minutes after I had received a similar though differently expressed warning from Sewell Endicott.

I didn't get anywhere with that, so I thought I might as well make it a perfect score. I lifted the phone and put in a call to the Terrapin Club at Las Vegas, person to person, Philip Marlowe calling Mr Randy Starr. No soap. Mr Starr was out of town, and would I talk to anyone else? I would not. I didn't even want to talk to Starr very badly. It was just a passing fancy. He was too far away to hit me.

After that nothing happened for three days. Nobody slugged me or shot at me or called me up on the phone and warned me to keep my nose clean. Nobody hired me to find the wandering daughter, the erring wife, the lost pearl necklace, or the missing will. I just sat there and looked at the wall. The Lennox case died almost as suddenly as it had been born. There was a brief inquest to which I was not summoned. It was held at an odd hour, without previous announcement and without a jury. The coroner entered his own verdict, which was that the death of Sylvia Potter Westerheym di Giorgio Lennox had been caused with homicidal intent by her husband, Terence William Lennox, since deceased outside the jurisdiction of the coroner's office. Presumably a confession was read into the record. Presumably it was verified enough to satisfy the coroner.

The body was released for burial. It was flown north and buried in the family vault. The press was not invited. Nobody gave any interviews, least of all Mr Harlan Potter, who never gave interviews. He was about as hard to see as the Dalai Lama. Guys with a hundred million dollars live a peculiar life, behind a screen of servants, bodyguards, secretaries, lawyers, and tame executives. Presumably they eat, sleep, get their hair cut, and wear clothes. But you never know for sure. Everything you read or hear about them has been processed by a public relations gang of guys who are paid big money to create and maintain a usable personality, something simple and clean and sharp, like a sterilized needle. It doesn't have to be true. It just has to be consistent with the known facts, and the known facts you could count on your fingers.

Late afternoon of the third day the telephone rang and I was talking to a man who said his name was Howard Spencer, that he was a representative of a New York publishing house in California on a brief business trip, that he had a problem he would like to discuss with me and would I meet him in the bar of the Ritz-Beverly Hotel at eleven a.m. the next morning.

I asked him what sort of problem.

'Rather a delicate one,' he said, 'but entirely ethical. If we don't agree, I shall expect to pay you for your time, naturally.'

'Thank you, Mr Spencer, but that won't be necessary. Did someone I know recommend me to you?'

'Someone who knows about you—including your recent brush with the law, Mr Marlowe. I might say that that was what interested me. My business, however, has nothing to do with that tragic affair. It's just that—well, let's discuss it over a drink, rather than over the telephone.'

'You sure you want to mix it with a guy who has been in the cooler?'

He laughed. His laugh and his voice were both pleasant. He talked the way New Yorkers used to talk before they learned to talk Flatbush.

'From my point of view, Mr Marlowe, that is a recommendation. Not, let me add, the fact that you were, as you put it, in the cooler, but the fact, shall I say, that you appear to be extremely reticent, even under pressure.'

He was a guy who talked with commas, like a heavy novel. Over the phone anyway.

'Okay, Mr Spencer, I'll be there in the morning.'

He thanked me and hung up. I wondered who could have given me the plug. I thought it might be Sewell Endicott and called him to find out. But he had been out of town all week, and still was. It didn't matter much. Even in my business you occasionally get a satisfied customer. And I needed a job because I needed the money—or thought I did, until I got home that night and found the letter with a portrait of Madison in it.

12

The letter was in the red and white birdhouse mail box at the foot of my steps. A woodpecker on top of the box attached to the swing arm was raised and even at that I might not have looked inside because I never got mail at the house. But the woodpecker had lost the point of his beak quite recently. The wood was fresh broken. Some smart kid shooting off his atom gun.

The letter had Correo Aereo on it and a flock of Mexican stamps, and writing that I might or might not have recognized if Mexico hadn't been on my mind pretty constantly lately. I couldn't read the postmark. It was hand-stamped and the ink pad was pretty far gone. The letter was thick. I climbed my steps and sat down in the living-room to read it. The evening seemed very silent. Perhaps a letter from a dead man brings its own silence with it.

It began without date and without preamble.

'I'm sitting beside a second-floor window in a room in a not-too-clean hotel in a town called Otatoclan, a mountain town with a lake. There's a mail box just below the window and when the mozo comes in with some coffee I've ordered he is going to mail the letter for me and hold it up so that I can see it before he puts it in the slot. When he does that he gets a hundred-peso note, which is a hell of a lot of money for him.

'Why all the finagling? There's a swarthy character with pointed shoes and a dirty shirt outside the door watching it. He's waiting for something, I don't know what, but he won't let me out. It doesn't matter too much as long as the letter gets posted. I want you to have this money because I don't need it and the local gendarmerie would swipe it for sure. It is not intended to buy anything. Call it an apology for making you so much trouble and a token of esteem for a pretty decent guy. I've done everything wrong as usual, but I still have the gun. My hunch is that you have probably made up your mind on a certain point. I might have killed her and perhaps I did, but I never could have done the other thing. That kind of brutality is not in my line. So something is very sour. But it doesn't matter, not in the least. The main thing now is to save an unnecessary and useless scandal. Her father and her sister never did me any harm. They have their lives to live and I'm up to here in disgust with mine. Sylvia didn't make a bum out of me, I was one already. I can't give you any very clear answer about why she married me. I suppose it was just a whim. At least she died young and beautiful. They say lust makes a man old, but keeps a woman young. They say a lot of nonsense. They say the rich can always protect themselves and that in their world it is always summer. I've lived with them and they are bored and lonely people.

'I have written a confession. I feel a little sick and more than a little scared. You read about these situations in books, but you don't read the truth. When it happens to you, when all you have left is the gun in your pocket, when you are cornered in a dirty little hotel in a strange country, and have only one way out—believe me, pal, there is nothing elevating or dramatic about it. It is just plain nasty and sordid and grey and grim.

'So forget it and me. But first drink a gimlet for me at Victor's. And the next time you make coffee, pour me a cup, and put some bourbon in it and light me a cigarette and put it beside the cup. And after that forget the whole thing. Terry Lennox over and out. And so good-bye.

'A knock at the door. I guess it will be the mozo with the coffee. If it isn't, there will be some shooting. I like Mexicans, as a rule, but I don't like their jails. So long. Terry.'

That was all. I refolded the letter and put it back in the envelope. It had been the mozo with the coffee all right. Otherwise I would never have had the letter. Not with a portrait of Madison in it. A portrait of Madison is a $5,000 bill.

It lay in front of me green and crisp on the table top. I had never seen one before. Lots of people who work in banks haven't either. Very likely characters like Randy Starr and Menendez wear them for folding money. If you went to a bank and asked for one, they wouldn't have it. They'd have to get it for you from the Federal Reserve. It might take several days. There are only about a thousand of them in circulation in the whole U.S.A. Mine had a nice glow around it. It created a little private sunshine all its own.

I sat there and looked at it for a long time. At last I put it away in my letter-case and went out to the kitchen to make that coffee. I did what he asked me to, sentimental or not. I poured two cups and added some bourbon to his and set it down on the side of the table where he had sat the morning I took him to the plane. I lit a cigarette for him and set it in an ashtray beside the cup. I watched the steam rise from the coffee and the thin thread of smoke rise from the cigarette. Outside in the tecoma a bird was gussing around, talking to himself in low chirps, with an occasional brief flutter of wings.

Then the coffee didn't steam any more and the cigarette stopped smoking and was just a dead butt on the edge of an ashtray. I dropped it into the garbage can under the sink. I poured the coffee out and washed the cup and put it away.

That was that. It didn't seem quite enough to do for five thousand dollars.

I went to a late movie after a while. It meant nothing. I hardly saw what went on. It was just noise and big faces. When I got home again I set out a very dull Ruy Lopez and that didn't mean anything either. So I went to bed.

But not to sleep. At three a.m. I was walking the floor and listening to Katchaturian working in a tractor factory. He called it a violin concerto. I called it a loose fan belt and the hell with it.

A white night for me is as rare as a fat postman. If it hadn't been for Mr

Howard Spencer at the Ritz-Beverly I would have killed a bottle and knocked myself out. And the next time I saw a polite character drunk in a Rolls-Royce Silver Wraith, I would depart rapidly in several directions. There is no trap so deadly as the trap you set for yourself.

13

At eleven o'clock I was sitting in the third booth on the right-hand side as you go in from the dining-room annexe. I had my back against the wall and I could see anyone who came in or went out. It was a clear morning, no smog, no high fog even, and the sun dazzled the surface of the swimming-pool which began just outside the plate-glass wall of the bar and stretched to the far end of the dining-room. A girl in a white sharkskin suit and a luscious figure was climbing the ladder to the high board. I watched the band of white that showed between the tan of her thighs and the suit. I watched it carnally. Then she was out of sight, cut off by the deep overhang of the roof. A moment later I saw her flash down in a one and a half. Spray came high enough to catch the sun and make rainbows that were almost as pretty as the girl. Then she came up the ladder and unstrapped her white helmet and shook her bleach job loose. She wobbled her bottom over to a small white table and sat down beside a lumberjack in white drill pants and dark glasses and a tan so evenly dark that he couldn't have been anything but the hired man around the pool. He reached over and patted her thigh. She opened a mouth like a fire-bucket and laughed. That terminated my interest in her. I couldn't hear the laugh but the hole in her face when she unzipped her teeth was all I needed.

The bar was pretty empty. Three booths down a couple of sharpies were selling each other pieces of Twentieth Century Fox, using double arm gestures instead of money. They had a telephone on the table between them and every two or three minutes they would play the match game to see who called Zanuck with a hot idea. They were young, dark, eager, and full of vitality. They put as much muscular activity into a telephone conversation as I would put into carrying a fat man up four flights of stairs.

There was a sad fellow over on a bar stool talking to the bartender, who was polishing a glass and listening with that plastic smile people wear when they are trying not to scream. The customer was middle-aged, handsomely dressed, and drunk. He wanted to talk and he couldn't have stopped even if he hadn't really wanted to talk. He was polite and friendly and when I heard him he didn't seem to slur his words much, but you knew that he got up on the bottle and only let go of it when he fell asleep at night. He would be like that for the rest of his life and that was what his life was. You would never know how he got that way because even if he told you it would not be the truth. At the very best a distorted memory of the truth as he knew it. There is a sad man like that in every quiet bar in the world.

I looked at my watch and this high-powered publisher man was already twenty minutes late. I would wait half an hour and then I would leave. It never pays to let the customer make all the rules. If he can push you around, he will assume other people can too, and that is not what he hires you for. And right now I didn't need the work badly enough to let some fathead from back East use me for a horse-holder, some executive character in a panelled office on the eighty-fifth floor with a row of push-buttons and an intercom and a secretary in a Hattie Carnegie Career Girl's special and a pair of those big, beautiful, promising eyes. This was the kind of operator who would tell you to be there at nine sharp and if you weren't sitting quietly with a pleased smile on your pan when he floated in two hours later on a double Gibson, he would have a paroxysm of outraged executive ability which would necessitate five weeks at Acapulco before he got back the hop on his high hard one.

The old bar waiter came drifting by and glanced softly at my weak Scotch and water. I shook my head and he bobbed his white thatch, and right then a dream walked in. It seemed to me for an instant that there was no sound in the bar, that the sharpies stopped sharping and the drunk on the stool stopped burbling away, and it was like just after the conductor taps on his music stand and raises his arms and holds them poised.

She was slim and quite tall in a white linen tailor-made with a black and white polka-dotted scarf around her throat. Her hair was the pale gold of a fairy princess. There was a small hat on it into which the pale gold hair nestled like a bird in its nest. Her eyes were cornflower blue, a rare colour, and the lashes were long and almost too pale. She reached the table across the way and was pulling off a white gauntleted glove and the old waiter had the table pulled out in a way no waiter will ever pull a table out for me. She sat down and slipped the gloves under the strap of her bag and thanked him with a smile so gentle, so exquisitely pure, that he was damn near paralysed by it. She said something to him in a very low voice. He hurried away, bending forward. There was a guy who really had a mission in life.

I stared. She caught me staring. She lifted her glance half an inch and I wasn't there any more. But wherever I was I was holding my breath.

There are blondes and blondes and it is almost a joke word nowadays. All blondes have their points, except perhaps the metallic ones who are as blonde as a Zulu under the bleach and as to disposition as soft as a sidewalk. There is the small cute blonde who cheeps and twitters, and the big statuesque blonde who straight-arms you with an ice-blue glare. There is the blonde who gives you the up-from-under look and smells lovely and shimmers and hangs on your arm and is always very, very tired when you take her home. She makes that helpless gesture and has that goddamned headache and you would like to slug her except that you are glad you found about the headache before you invested too much time and money and hope in her. Because the headache will always be there, a weapon that never wears out and is as deadly as the bravo's rapier or Lucrezia's poison vial.

There is the soft and willing and alcoholic blonde who doesn't care what she wears as long as it is mink or where she goes as long as it is the Starlight Roof and there is plenty of dry champagne. There is the small perky blonde who is a little pale and wants to pay her own way and is full of sunshine and common sense and knows judo from the ground up and can toss a truck driver over her shoulder without missing more than one sentence out of the editorial in the *Saturday Review*. There is the pale, pale blonde with anaemia of some non-fatal but incurable type. She is very languid and very shadowy and she speaks softly out of nowhere and you can't lay a finger on her because in the first place you don't want to and in the second place she is reading *The Waste Land* or Dante in the original, or Kafka or Kierkegaard or studying Provençal. She adores music and when the New York Philharmonic is playing Hindemith she can tell you which one of the six bass viols came in a quarter of a beat too late. I hear Toscanini can also. That makes two of them.

And lastly there is the gorgeous show piece who will outlast three kingpin racketeers and then marry a couple of millionaires at a million a head and end up with a pale rose villa at Cap d'Antibes, an Alfa Romeo town car complete with pilot and co-pilot, and a stable of shopworn aristocrats, all of whom she will treat with the affectionate absent-mindedness of an elderly duke saying good night to his butler.

The dream across the way was none of these, not even of that kind of world. She was unclassifiable, as remote and clear as mountain water, as elusive as its colour. I was still staring when a voice close to my elbow said:

'I'm shockingly late. I apologize. You must blame it on this. My name's Howard Spencer. You're Marlowe, of course.'

I turned my head and looked at him. He was middle-aged, rather plump, dressed as if he didn't give any thought to it, but well shaved and with thin hair smoothed back carefully over a head that was wide between the ears. He wore a flashy double-breasted vest, the sort of thing you hardly ever see in California except perhaps on a visiting Bostonian. His glasses were rimless and he was patting a shabby old dog of a brief-case which was evidently the 'this'.

'Three brand-new book-length manuscripts. Fiction. It would be embarrassing to lose them before we have a chance to reject them.' He made a signal to the old waiter who had just stepped back from placing a tall green something or other in front of the dream. 'I have a weakness for gin and orange. A silly sort of drink really. Will you join me? Good.'

I nodded and the old waiter drifted away.

Pointing to the brief-case I said: 'How do you know you are going to reject them?'

'If they were any good, they wouldn't be dropped at my hotel by the writers in person. Some New York agent would have them.'

'Then why take them at all?'

'Partly not to hurt feelings. Partly the thousand to one chance all publishers live for. But mostly you're at a cocktail party and get introduced to all sorts of people, and some of them have novels written and you are just liquored up enough to be benevolent and full of love for the human race, so you say you'd love to see the script. It is then dropped at your hotel with such sickening speed that you are forced to go through the motions of reading it. But I don't suppose you are much interested in publishers and their problems.'

The waiter brought the drinks. Spencer grabbed for his and took a healthy swig. He wasn't noticing the golden girl across the way. I had all his attention. He was a good contact man.

'If it's part of the job,' I said, 'I can read a book once in a while.'

'One of our most important authors lives around here,' he said casually. 'Maybe you've read his stuff. Roger Wade.'

'Uh-huh.'

'I see your point.' He smiled sadly. 'You don't care for historical romances. But they sell brutally.'

'I don't have any point, Mr Spencer. I looked at one of his books once. I thought it was tripe. Is that the wrong thing for me to say?'

He grinned. 'Oh no. There are many people who agree with you. But the point is at the moment that he's an automatic best-seller. And every publisher has to have a couple with the way costs are now.'

I looked across at the golden girl. She had finished her limeade or whatever it was and was glancing at a microscopic wristwatch. The bar was filling up a little, but not yet noisy. The two sharpies were still waving their hands and the solo drinker on the bar stool had a couple of pals with him. I looked back at Howard Spencer.

'Something to do with your problem?' I asked him. 'This fellow Wade, I mean.'

He nodded. He was giving me a careful once-over. 'Tell me a little about yourself, Mr Marlowe. That is, if you don't find the request objectionable.'

'What sort of thing? I'm a licensed private investigator and have been for quite a while. I'm a lone wolf, unmarried, getting middle-aged, and not rich. I've been in jail more than once and I don't do divorce business. I like liquor and women and chess and a few other things. The cops don't like me too well, but I know a couple I get along with. I'm a native son, born in Santa Rosa, both parents dead, no brothers or sisters, and when I get knocked off in a dark alley sometime, if it happens, as it could to anyone in my business, and to plenty of people in any business or no business at all these days, nobody will feel that the bottom has dropped out of his or her life.'

'I see,' he said. 'But all that doesn't exactly tell me what I want to know.'

I finished the gin and orange. I didn't like it. I grinned at him. 'I left out one item, Mr Spencer. I have a portrait of Madison in my pocket.'

'A portrait of Madison? I'm afraid I don't—'

'A five thousand dollar bill,' I said. 'Always carry it. My lucky piece.'

'Good God,' he said in a hushed voice. 'Isn't that terribly dangerous?'

'Who was it said that beyond a certain point all dangers are equal?'

'I think it was Walter Bagehot. He was talking about a steeplejack.' Then he grinned. 'Sorry, but I *am* a publisher. You're all right, Marlowe. I'll take a chance on you. If I didn't you would tell me to go to hell. Right?'

I grinned back at him. He called the waiter and ordered another pair of drinks.

'Here it is,' he said carefully. 'We are in bad trouble over Roger Wade. He can't finish a book. He's losing his grip and there's something behind it. The man seems to be going to pieces. Wild fits of drinking and temper. Every once in a while he disappears for days on end. Not very long ago he threw his wife downstairs and put her in the hospital with five broken ribs. There's no trouble between them in the usual sense, none at all. The man just goes nuts when he drinks.' Spencer leaned back and looked at me gloomily. 'We have to have that book finished. We need it badly. To a certain extent my job depends on it. But we need more than that. We want to save a very able writer who is capable of much better things than he has ever done. Something is very wrong. This trip he won't even see me. I realize this sounds like a job for a psychiatrist. Mrs Wade disagrees. She is convinced that he is perfectly sane but that something is worrying him to death. A blackmailer, for instance. The Wades have been married five years.

Something from his past may have caught up with him. It might even be—just a wild guess—a fatal hit-and-run accident and someone has the goods on him. We don't know what it is. We want to know. And we are willing to pay well to correct the trouble. If it turns out to be a medical matter, well—that's that. If not, there has to be an answer. And in the meantime Mrs Wade has to be protected. He might kill her the next time. You never know.'

The second round of drinks came. I left mine untouched and watched him gobble half of his in one swallow. I lit a cigarette and just stared at him.

'You don't want a detective,' I said. 'You want a magician. What the hell could I do? If I happened to be there at exactly the right time, and if he isn't too tough for me to handle, I might knock him out and put him to bed. But I'd have to *be* there. It's a hundred to one against. You know that.'

'He's about your size,' Spencer said, 'but he's not in your condition. And you could be there all the time.'

'Hardly. And drunks are cunning. He'd be certain to pick a time when I wasn't around to throw his wingding. I'm not in the market for a male nurse.'

'A male nurse wouldn't be any use. Roger Wade is not the kind of man to accept one. He is a very talented guy who has been jarred loose from his self-control. He has made too much money writing junk for half-wits. But the only salvation for a writer is to write. If there is anything good in him, it will come out.'

'Okay, I'm sold on him,' I said wearily. 'He's terrific. Also he's damn dangerous. He has a guilty secret and he tries to drown it in alcohol. It's not my kind of problem, Mr Spencer.'

'I see.' He looked at his wristwatch with a worried frown that knotted his face and made it look older and smaller. 'Well, you can't blame me for trying.'

He reached for his fat brief-case. I looked across at the golden girl. She was getting ready to leave. The white-haired waiter was hovering over her with the check. She gave him some money and a lovely smile and he looked as if he had shaken hands with God. She touched up her lips and put her white gauntlets on and the waiter pulled the table half-way across the room for her to stroll out.

I glanced at Spencer. He was frowning down at the empty glass on the table edge. He had the brief-case on his knees.

'Look,' I said. 'I'll go see the man and try to size him up, if you want me to. I'll talk to his wife. But my guess is he'll throw me out of the house.'

A voice that was not Spencer's said: 'No, Mr Marlowe, I don't think he would do that. On the contrary I think he might like you.'

I looked up into the pair of violet eyes. She was standing at the end of the table. I got up and canted myself against the back of the booth in that awkward way you have to stand when you can't slide out.

'Please don't get up,' she said in a voice like the stuff they use to line summer clouds with. 'I know I owe you an apology, but it seemed important for me to have a chance to observe you before I introduced myself. I am Eileen Wade.'

Spencer said grumpily: 'He's not interested, Eileen.'

She smiled gently: 'I disagree.'

I pulled myself together. I had been standing there off balance with my mouth open and me breathing through it like a sweet girl graduate. This was really a dish. Seen close up she was almost paralysing.

'I didn't say I wasn't interested, Mrs Wade. What I said or meant to say was that I didn't think I could do any good, and it might be a hell of a mistake for me to try. It might do a lot of harm.'

She was very serious now. The smile had gone. 'You are deciding too soon. You can't judge people by what they do. If you judge them at all, it must be by what they are.'

I nodded, vaguely. Because that was exactly the way I had thought about Terry Lennox. On the facts he was no bargain, except for that one brief flash of glory in the foxhole—if Menendez told the truth about that—but the facts didn't tell the whole story by any means. He had been a man it was impossible to dislike. How many do you meet in a lifetime that you can say that about?

'And you have to know them for that,' she added gently. 'Good-bye, Mr Marlowe. If you should change your mind—' She opened her bag quickly and gave me a card. 'And thank you for being here.'

She nodded to Spencer and walked away. I watched her out of the bar, down the glassed-in annex to the dining-room. She carried herself beautifully. I watched her turn under the archway that led to the lobby. I saw the last flicker of her white linen skirt as she turned the corner. Then I eased myself down into the booth and grabbed the gin and orange.

Spencer was watching me. There was something hard in his eyes.

'Nice work,' I said, 'but you ought to have looked at her once in a while. A dream like that doesn't sit across the room from you for twenty minutes without your even noticing.'

'Stupid of me, wasn't it?' He was trying to smile, but he didn't really want to. He didn't like the way I had looked at her. 'People have such queer ideas about private detectives. When you think of having one in your home—'

'Don't think of having one in your home,' I said. 'Anyhow, think up another story first. You can do better than trying to make me believe anybody, drunk or sober, would throw that gorgeous downstairs and break five ribs for her.'

He reddened. His hands tightened on the brief-case. 'You think I'm a liar?'

'What's the difference? You've made your play. You're a little hot for the lady yourself, maybe.'

He stood up suddenly. 'I don't like your tone,' he said. 'I'm not sure I like *you*. Do me a favour and forget the whole idea. I think this ought to pay you for your time.'

He threw twenty on the table, and then added some ones for the waiter. He stood a moment staring down at me. His eyes were bright and his face was still red. 'I'm married and have four children,' he said abruptly.

'Congratulations.'

He made a swift noise in his throat and turned and went. He went pretty fast. I watched him for a while and then I didn't. I drank the rest of my drink and got out my cigarettes and shook one loose and stuck it in my mouth and lit it. The old waiter came up and looked at the money.

'Can I get you anything else, sir?'

'Nope. The dough is all yours.'

He picked it up slowly. 'This is a twenty-dollar bill, sir. The gentleman made a mistake.'

'He can read. The dough is all yours, I said.'

'I'm sure I'm very grateful. If you are quite sure, sir—'

'Quite sure.'

He bobbed his head and went away, still looking worried. The bar was filling up. A couple of streamlined demi-virgins went by carolling and waving. They knew the two hotshots in the booth farther on. The air began to be spattered with darlings and crimson fingernails.

I smoked half of my cigarette, scowling at nothing, and then got up to leave. I turned to reach back for my cigarettes and something bumped into me hard from behind. It was just what I needed. I swung round and I was looking at the profile of a broad-beamed crowd-pleaser in an overdraped Oxford flannel. He had the outstretched arm of the popular character and the two-by-six grin of the guy who never loses a sale.

I took hold of the outstretched arm and spun him around. 'What's the matter, Jack? Don't they make the aisles wide enough for your personality?'

He shook his arm loose and got tough. 'Don't get fancy, buster. I might loosen your jaw for you.'

'Ha, ha,' I said. 'You might play centre field for the Yankees and hit a home run with a breadstick.'

He doubled a meaty fist.

'Darling, think of your manicure,' I told him.

He controlled his emotions. 'Nuts to you, wise guy,' he sneered. 'Some other time, when I have less on my mind.'

'Could there be less?'

'G'wan, beat it,' he snarled. 'One more crack and you'll need new bridgework.'

I grinned at him. 'Call me up, Jack. But with better dialogue.'

His expression changed. He laughed. 'You in pictures, chum?'

'Only the kind they pin up in the post office.'

'See you in the mug book,' he said, and walked away, still grinning.

It was all very silly, but it got rid of the feeling. I went along the annex and across the lobby of the hotel to the main entrance. I paused inside to put on my sunglasses. It wasn't until I got into my car that I remembered to look at the card Eileen Wade had given me. It was an engraved card, but not a formal calling card, because it had an address and a telephone number on it. Mrs Roger Stearns Wade, 1247 Idle Valley Road. Tel. Idle Valley 5-6324.

I knew a good deal about Idle Valley, and I knew it had changed a great deal from the days when they had the gatehouse at the entrance and the private police force, and the gambling casino on the lake, and the fifty-dollar joy girls. Quiet money had taken over the tract after the casino was closed out. Quiet money had made it a subdivider's dream. A club owned the lake and the lake frontage and if they didn't want you in the club, you didn't get to play in the water. It was exclusive in the only remaining sense of the word that doesn't mean merely expensive.

I belonged in Idle Valley like a pearl onion on a banana split.

Howard Spencer called me up late in the afternoon. He had got over his mad and wanted to say he was sorry and he hadn't handled the situation very well, and had I perhaps any second thoughts.

'I'll go see him if he asks me to. Not otherwise.'

'I see. There would be a subdivider bonus—'

'Look, Mr Spencer,' I said impatiently, 'you can't hire destiny. If Mrs Wade is afraid of the guy, she can move out. That's *her* problem. Nobody could protect her twenty-four hours a day from her own husband. There isn't that much protection in the world. But that's not all you want. You want to know why and how and when the guy jumped the rails, and then fix it so that he doesn't do it again—at least until he finishes that book. And that's up to him. If he wants to write the damn book bad enough, he'll lay off the hooch until he does it. You want too damn much.'

'They all go together,' he said. 'It's all one problem. But I guess I understand. It's a little over-subtle for your kind of operation. Well, good-bye. I'm flying back to New York tonight.'

'Have a smooth trip.'

He thanked me and hung up. I forgot to tell him I had given his twenty to the waiter. I thought of calling back to tell him, then I thought he was miserable enough already.

I closed the office and started off in the direction of Victor's to drink a gimlet, as Terry had asked me to in his letter. I changed my mind. I wasn't feeling sentimental enough. I went to Lowry's and had a martini and some prime ribs and Yorkshire pudding instead.

When I got home I turned on the TV set and looked at the fights. They were no good, just a bunch of dancing masters who ought to have been working for Arthur Murray. All they did was jab and bob up and down and feint one another off balance. Not one of them could hit hard enough to wake his grandmother out of a light doze. The crowd was booing and the referee kept clapping his hands for action, but they went right on swaying and jittering and jabbing long lefts. I turned to another channel and looked at a crime show. The action took place in a clothes closet and the faces were tired and over-familiar and not beautiful. The dialogue was stuff even Monogram wouldn't have used. The dick had a coloured houseboy for comic relief. He didn't need it, he was plenty comical all by himself. And the commercials would have sickened a goat raised on barbed wire and broken beer bottles.

I cut if off and smoked a long, cool, tightly packed cigarette. It was kind to my throat. It was made of fine tobacco. I forgot to notice what brand it was. I was about ready to hit the hay when Detective-Sergeant Green of homicide called me up.

'Thought you might like to know they buried your friend Lennox a couple of days ago right in that Mexican town where he died. A lawyer representing the family went down there and attended to it. You were pretty lucky this time, Marlowe. Next time you think of helping a pal skip the country, don't.'

'How many bullet holes did he have in him?'

'What's that?' he barked. Then he was silent for a space. Then he said rather too carefully: 'One, I should say. It's usually enough when it blows a guy's head off. The lawyer is bringing back a set of prints and whatever was in his pockets. Anything more you'd like to know?'

'Yeah, but you can't tell me. I'd like to know who killed Lennox's wife.'

'Cripes, didn't Grenz tell you he left a full confession? It was in the papers, anyway. Don't you read the papers any more?'

'Thanks for calling me, Sergeant. It was real kind of you.'

'Look, Marlowe,' he said raspingly. 'You got any funny ideas about this case, you could buy yourself a lot of grief talking about them. The case is closed, finalized, and laid away in mothballs. Damn lucky for you it is. Accessory after the fact is good for five years in this state. And let me tell you something else. I've been a cop a long time and one thing I've learned for sure is it ain't always what you do that gets you sent up. It's what it can be made to look like when it comes into court. Good night.'

He hung up in my ear. I replaced the phone, thinking that an honest cop with a bad conscience always acts tough. So does a dishonest cop. So does almost anyone, including me.

14

Next morning the bell rang as I was wiping the talcum off an earlobe. When I got to the door and opened up I looked into a pair of violet-blue eyes. She was in brown linen this time, with a pimento-coloured scarf, and no earrings or hat. She looked a little pale, but not as though anyone had been throwing her downstairs. She gave me a hesitant little smile.

'I know I shouldn't have come here to bother you, Mr Marlowe. You probably haven't even had breakfast. But I had a reluctance to go to your office and I hate telephoning about personal matters.'

'Sure. Come in, Mrs Wade. Would you go for a cup of coffee?'

She came into the living-room and sat on the davenport without looking at anything. She balanced her bag on her lap and sat with her feet close together. She looked rather prim. I opened windows and pulled up venetian blinds and lifted a dirty ashtray off the cocktail table in front of her.

'Thank you. Black coffee, please. No sugar.'

I went out to the kitchen and spread a paper napkin on a green metal tray. It looked as cheesy as a celluloid collar. I crumpled it up and got out one of those fringed things that come in sets with little triangular napkins. They came with the house, like most of the furniture. I set out two Desert Rose coffee cups and filled them and carried the tray in.

She sipped. 'This is very nice,' she said. 'You make good coffee.'

'Last time anyone drank coffee with me was just before I went to jail,' I said. 'I guess you knew I'd been in the cooler, Mrs Wade.'

She nodded. 'Of course. You were suspected of having helped him escape, wasn't it?'

'They didn't say. They found my telephone number on a pad in his room. They asked me questions I didn't answer—mostly because of the way they were asked. But I don't suppose you are interested in that.'

She put her cup down carefully and leaned back and smiled at me. I offered her a cigarette.

'I don't smoke, thank you. Of course I'm interested. A neighbour of ours knew the Lennoxes. He must have been insane. He doesn't sound at all like that kind of man.'

I filled a bulldog pipe and lit it. 'I guess so,' I said. 'He must have been.

He was badly wounded in the war. But he's dead and it's all done with. And I don't think you came here to talk about that.'

She shook her head slowly. 'He was a friend of yours, Mr Marlowe. You must have a pretty strong opinion. And I think you are a pretty determined man.'

I tamped the tobacco in my pipe and lit it again. I took my time and stared at her over the pipe bowl while I was doing it.

'Look, Mrs Wade,' I said finally. 'My opinion means nothing. It happens every day. The most unlikely people commit the most unlikely crimes. Nice old ladies poison whole families. Clean-cut kids commit multiple hold-ups and shootings. Bank managers with spotless records going back twenty years are found out to be long-term embezzlers. And successful and popular and supposedly happy novelists get drunk and put their wives in the hospital. We know damn little about what makes even our best friends tick.'

I thought it would burn her up, but she didn't do much more than press her lips together and narrow her eyes.

'Howard Spencer shouldn't have told you that,' she said. 'It was my own fault. I didn't know enough to keep away from him. I've learned since that the one thing you can never do to a man who is drinking too much is to try to stop him. You probably know that much better than I do.'

'You certainly can't stop him with words,' I said. 'If you're lucky, and *if* you have the strength, you can sometimes keep him from hurting himself or someone else. Even that takes luck.'

She reached quietly for her coffee cup and saucer. Her hands were lovely, like the rest of her. The nails were beautifully shaped and polished and only very slightly tinted.

'Did Howard tell you he hadn't seen my husband this time?'

'Yeah.'

She finished her coffee and put the cup carefully back on the tray. She fiddled with the spoon for a few seconds. Then she spoke without looking up at me.

'He didn't tell you why, because he didn't know. I am very fond of Howard but he is the managing type, wants to take charge of everything. He thinks he is very executive.'

I waited, not saying anything. There was another silence. She looked at me quickly then looked away again. Very softly she said: 'My husband has been missing for three days. I don't know where he is. I came here to ask you to find him and bring him home. Oh, it has happened before. One time he drove himself all the way to Portland and got sick in a hotel there and had to get a doctor to sober him up. It's a wonder how he ever got that far without getting into trouble. He hadn't eaten anything for three days. Another time he was in a Turkish bath in Long Beach, one of those Swedish places where they give high colonics. And the last time it was some sort of small private and probably not very reputable sanatorium. This was less than three weeks ago. He wouldn't tell me the name of it or where it was, just said he had been taking a cure and was all right. But he looked deadly pale and weak. I got a brief glimpse of the man who brought him home. A tall man dressed in the sort of over-elaborate cowboy outfit you would only see on the stage or in a Technicolor musical film. He let Roger out in the driveway and backed out and drove away at once.'

'Could have been a dude ranch,' I said. 'Some of these tame cowpunchers spend every dime they make on a fancy outfit like that. The women go crazy over them. That's what they're there for.'

She opened her bag and took out a folded paper. 'I've brought you a cheque for five hundred dollars, Mr Marlowe. Will you accept it as a retainer?'

She put the folded cheque down on the table. I looked at it, but didn't touch it. 'Why?' I asked her. 'You say he has been gone three days. It takes three or four to sober a man up and get some food into him. Won't he come back the way he did before? Or does something make this time different?'

'He can't stand much more of it, Mr Marlowe. It will kill him. The intervals are getting shorter. I'm badly worried. I'm more than worried, I'm scared. It's unnatural. We've been married for five years. Roger was always a drinker, but not a psychopathic drinker. Something is all wrong. I want him found. I didn't sleep more than an hour last night.'

'Any idea *why* he drinks?'

The violet eyes were looking at me steadily. She seemed a bit fragile this morning, but certainly not helpless. She bit her lower lip and shook her head. 'Unless it's me,' she said at last, almost in a whisper. 'Men fall out of love with their wives.'

'I'm only an amateur psychologist, Mrs Wade. A man in my racket has to be a little of that. I'd say it's more likely he has fallen out of love with the kind of stuff he writes.'

'It's quite possible,' she said quietly. 'I imagine all writers have spells like that. It's true that he can't seem to finish a book he is working on. But it isn't as if he had to finish it for the rent money. I don't think that is quite enough reason.'

'What sort of guy is he sober?'

She smiled. 'Well, I'm rather prejudiced. I think he is a very nice guy indeed.'

'And how is he drunk?'

'Horrible. Bright and hard and cruel. He thinks he is being witty when he is only being nasty.'

'You left out violent.'

She raised her tawny eyebrows. 'Just once, Mr Marlowe. And too much has been made of that. I'd never have told Howard Spencer. Roger told him himself.'

I got up and walked around in the room. It was going to be a hot day. It already was hot. I turned the blinds on one of the windows to keep the sun out. Then I gave it to her straight.

'I looked him up in *Who's Who* yesterday afternoon. He's forty-two years old, yours is his only marriage, no children. His people are New Englanders, he went to Andover and Princeton. He has a war record and a good one. He has written twelve of these fat sex and sword-play historical novels and every damn one of them has been on the best-seller lists. He must have made plenty of the folding. If he had fallen out of love with his wife, he sounds like the type who would say so and get a divorce. If he was haring around with another woman, you would probably know about it, and anyway he wouldn't have to get drunk just to prove he felt bad. If you've been married five years, then he was thirty-seven when that happened. I'd say he knew most of what there is to know about women by that time. I say most, because nobody ever knows all of it.'

I stopped and looked at her and she smiled at me. I wasn't hurting her feelings. I went on:

'Howard Spencer suggested–on what grounds I have no idea–that what's the matter with Roger Wade is something that happened a long time ago before you were married and that it has caught up with him now, and is hitting him harder than he can take. Spencer thought of blackmail. Would you know?'

She shook her head slowly. 'If you mean would I know if Roger has been paying out a lot of money to someone–no, I wouldn't know that. I don't meddle with his book-keeping affairs. He could give away a lot of money without my knowing it.'

'Okay then. Not knowing Mr Wade I can't have much idea how he would react to having the bite put on him. If he has a violent temper, he might break somebody's neck. If the secret, whatever it is, might damage his social or professional standing or even, to take an extreme case, made the law boys drop around, he might pay off–for a while anyhow. But none of this gets us anywhere. You want him found, you're worried, you're more than worried. So how do I go about finding him. I don't want your money, Mrs Wade. Not now, anyway.'

She reached into her bag again and came up with a couple of pieces of yellow paper. They looked like second sheets, folded, and one of them looked crumpled. She smoothed them out and handed them to me.

'One I found on his desk,' she said. 'It was very late, or rather early in the morning. I knew he had been drinking and I knew he hadn't come upstairs. About two o'clock I went down to see if he was all right–or comparatively all right, passed out on the floor or the couch or something. He was gone. The other paper was in the waste-basket or rather caught on the edge, so that it hadn't fallen in.'

I looked at the first piece, the one not crumpled. There was a short typewritten paragraph on it, no more. It read: 'I do not care to be in love with myself and there is no longer anyone else for me to be in love with. Signed: Roger (F. Scott Fitzgerald) Wade. P.S. This is why I never finished The Last Tycoon.'

'That mean anything to you, Mrs Wade?'

'Just attitudinizing. He says Fitzgerald is the best drunken writer since Coleridge, who took dope. Notice the typing, Mr Marlowe. Clear, even, and no mistakes.'

'I did. Most people can't even write their names properly when soused.' I opened the crumpled paper. More typing, also without errors or unevenness. This one read: 'I do not like you, Dr V. But right now you're the man for me.'

She spoke while I was still looking at it. 'I have no idea who Dr V. is. We don't know any doctor with a name beginning that way. I suppose he is the one who has that place where Roger was the last time.'

'When the cowpoke brought him home? Your husband didn't mention any names at all–even place-names?'

She shook her head. 'Nothing. I've looked in the directory. There are dozens of doctors of one sort or another whose names begin with V. Also, it may not be his surname.'

'Quite likely he's not even a doctor,' I said. 'That brings up the question of ready cash. A legitimate man would take a cheque, but a quack wouldn't.

It might turn into evidence. And a guy like that wouldn't be cheap. Room and board at his house would come high. Not to mention the needle.'

She looked puzzled. 'The needle.'

'All the shady ones use dope on their clients. Easiest way to handle them. Knock them out for ten or twelve hours and when they come out of it, they're good boys. But using narcotics without a licence can get you room and board with Uncle Sam. And that comes very high indeed.'

'I see. Roger probably would have several hundred dollars. He always keeps that much in his desk. I don't know why. I suppose it's just a whim. There's none there now.'

'Okay,' I said. 'I'll try to find Dr V. I don't know just how, but I'll do my best. Take the cheque with you, Mrs Wade.'

'But why? Aren't you entitled—'

'Later on, thanks. And I'd rather have it from Mr Wade. He's not going to like what I do in any case.'

'But if he's sick and helpless—'

'He could have called his own doctor or asked you to. He didn't. That means he didn't want to.'

She put the cheque back in her bag and stood up. She looked very forlorn. 'Our doctor refused to treat him,' she said bitterly.'

'There are hundreds of doctors, Mrs Wade. Any one of them would handle him once. Most of them would stay with him for some time. Medicine is a pretty competitive affair nowadays.'

'I see. Of course you must be right.' She walked slowly to the door and I walked with her. I opened it.

'You could have called a doctor on your own. Why didn't you?'

She faced me squarely. Her eyes were bright. There might have been a hint of tears in them. A lovely dish and no mistake.

'Because I love my husband, Mr Marlowe. I'd do anything in the world to help him. But I know what sort of man he is too. If I called a doctor every time he took too many drinks, I wouldn't have a husband very long. You can't treat a grown man like a child with a sore throat.'

'You can if he's a drunk. Often you damn well have to.'

She was standing close to me. I smelt her perfume. Or thought I did. It hadn't been put on with a spray gun. Perhaps it was just the summer day.

'Suppose there is something shameful in his past,' she said, dragging the words out one by one as if each of them had a bitter taste. 'Even something criminal. It would make no difference to me. But I'm not going to be the means of its being found out.'

'But it's all right if Howard Spencer hires me to find out?'

She smiled very slowly. 'Do you really think I expected you to give Howard any answer but the one you did—a man who went to jail rather than betray a friend?'

'Thanks for the plug, but that wasn't why I got jugged.'

She nodded after a moment of silence, said good-bye, and started down the redwood steps. I watched her into her car, a slim, grey Jaguar, very new looking. She drove it up to the end of the street and swung around in the turning circle there. Her glove waved at me as she went by down the hill. The little car whisked around the corner and was gone.

There was a red oleander bush against part of the front wall of the house. I heard a flutter in it and a baby mocking-bird started cheeping anxiously. I spotted him hanging on to one of the top branches, flapping his wings as if he was having trouble keeping his balance. From the cypress trees at the corner of the wall there was a single harsh warning chirp. The cheeping stopped at once and the little fat bird was silent.

I went inside and shut the door and left him to his flying lesson. Birds have to learn too.

15

No matter how smart you think you are, you have to have a place to start from; a name, an address, a neighbourhood, a background, an atmosphere, a point of reference of some sort. All I had was typing on a crumpled yellow page that said, 'I do not like you, Dr V. But right now you're the man for me.' With that I could pin-point the Pacific Ocean, spend a month wading through the lists of half a dozen country medical associations, and end up with the big round O. In our town quacks breed like guinea pigs. There are eight counties within a hundred miles of the City Hall and in every town in every single one of them there are doctors, some genuine medical men, some just mail-order mechanics with a licence to cut corns or jump up and down on your spine. Of the real doctors some are prosperous and some poor, some ethical, others not sure they can afford it. A well-heeled patient with incipient D.T.s could be money from home to plenty of old geezers who have fallen behind in the vitamin and antibiotic trade. But without a clue there was no place to start. I didn't have the clue and Eileen Wade either didn't have it or didn't know she had it. And even if I found somebody that fitted and had the right initial, he might turn out to be a myth, so far as Roger Wade was concerned. The jingle might be something that just happened to run through his head while he was getting himself stewed up. Just as the Scott Fitzgerald allusion might be merely an off-beat way of saying good-bye.

In a situation like that the small man tries to pick the big man's brains. So I called up a man I knew in the Carne Organization, a flossy agency in Beverly Hills that specialized in protection for the carriage trade–protection meaning almost anything with one foot inside the law. The man's name was George Peters and he said he could give me ten minutes if I made it fast.

They had half the second floor of one of these candy pink four-storeyed buildings where the elevator doors open all by themselves with an electric eye, where the corridors are cool and quiet, and the parking lot has a name on every stall, and the druggist off the front lobby has a sprained wrist from filling bottles of sleeping pills.

The door was French grey outside with raised metal lettering, as clean and sharp as a new knife. THE CARNE ORGANIZATION, INC. GERALD C. CARNE, PRESIDENT. Below and smaller: ENTRANCE. It might have been an investment trust.

Inside was a small and ugly reception-room, but the ugliness was deliberate and expensive. The furniture was scarlet and dark green, the walls were a flat Brunswick green, and the pictures hung on them were framed in a green about three shades darker than that. The pictures were guys in red coats on big horses that were just crazy to jump over high fences. There were two frameless mirrors tinted a slight but disgusting shade of rose pink. The magazines on the table of polished primavera were of the latest issue and each one was enclosed in a clear plastic cover. The fellow who decorated that room was not a man to let the colours scare him. He probably wore a pimento shirt, mulberry slacks, zebra shoes, and vermilion drawers with his initials on them in a nice friendly Mandarin orange.

The whole thing was just window-dressing. The clients of the Carne Organization were charged a minimum of one hundred fish per diem and they expected service in their homes. They didn't go sit in no waiting-rooms. Carne was an ex-colonel of military police, a big pink and white guy as hard as a board. He had offered me a job once, but I never got desperate enough to take it. There are one hundred and ninety ways of being a bastard and Carne knew all of them.

A rubbed glass partition slid open and a receptionist looked out at me. She had an iron smile and eyes that could count the money in your hip wallet.

'Good morning. May I help you?'

'George Peters, please. My name is Marlowe.'

She put a green leather book on the ledge. 'Is he expecting you, Mr Marlowe? I don't see your name on the appointment list.'

'It's a personal matter. I just talked to him on the phone.'

'I see. How do you spell your name, Mr Marlowe? And your first name, please?'

I told her. She wrote it down on a long narrow form, then slipped the edge under a clock punch.

'Who's that supposed to impress?' I asked her.

'We are very particular about details here,' she said coldly. 'Colonel Carne says you never know when the most trivial fact may turn out to be vital.'

'Or the other way around,' I said, but she didn't get it. When she had finished her book work she looked up and said:

'I will announce you to Mr Peters.'

I told her that made me very happy. A minute later a door in the panelling opened and Peters beckoned me into a battleship-grey corridor lined with little offices that looked like cells. His office had sound proofing on the ceiling, a grey steel desk with two matching chairs, a grey dictating machine on a grey stand, a telephone and pen set of the same colour as the walls and floor. There were a couple of framed photographs on the walls, one of Carne in uniform, with his snowdrop helmet on, and one of Carne as a civilian seated behind a desk and looking inscrutable. Also framed on the wall was a small inspirational legend in steely letters on a grey background. It read:

A CARNE OPERATIVE DRESSES, SPEAKS, AND BEHAVES LIKE A GENTLEMAN AT ALL TIMES AND IN ALL PLACES. THERE ARE NO EXCEPTIONS TO THIS RULE.

Peters crossed the room in two long steps and pushed one of the pictures aside. Set into the grey wall behind it was a grey microphone pick-up. He pulled it out, unclipped a wire, and pushed it back in place. He moved the picture in front of it again.

'Right now I'd be out of a job,' he said, 'except that the son of a bitch is out fixing a drunk-driving rap for some actor. All the mike switches are in his office. He has the whole joint wired. The other morning I suggested to him that he have a microfilm camera installed with infra-red light behind a diaphanous mirror in the reception-room. He didn't like the idea too well. Maybe because somebody else had it.'

He sat down in one of the hard grey chairs. I stared at him. He was a gawky, long-legged man with a bony face and receding hair. His skin had the worn, weathered look of a man who has been out of doors a great deal, in all kinds of weather. He had deep-set eyes and an upper lip almost as long as his nose. When he grinned the bottom half of his face disappeared into two enormous ditches that ran from his nostrils to the ends of his wide mouth.

'How can you take it?' I asked him.

'Sit down, pal. Breathe quietly, keep your voice down and remember that a Carne operative is to a cheap shamus like you what Toscanini is to an organ grinder's monkey.' He paused and grinned. 'I take it because I don't give a damn. It's good money and any time Carne starts acting like he thought I was doing time in that maximum security prison he ran in England during the war, I'll pick up my cheque and blow. What's your trouble? I hear you had it rough a while back.'

'No complaints about that. I'd like to look at your file on the barred-window boys. I know you have one. Eddie Dowst told me after he quit here.'

He nodded. 'Eddie was just a mite too sensitive for the Carne Organization. The file you mention is top secret. In no circumstances must any confidential information be disclosed to outsiders. I'll get it at once.'

He went out and I stared at the grey waste-basket and the grey linoleum and the grey leather corners of the desk blotter. Peters came back with a grey cardboard file in his hand. He put it down and opened it.

'For Chrissake, haven't you got anything in this place that isn't grey?'

'The school colours, my lad. The spirit of the organization. Yeah, I have something that isn't grey.'

He pulled a desk drawer open and took out a cigar about eight inches long.

'An Upmann Thirty,' he said. 'Presented to me by an elderly gent from England who has been forty years in California and still says "wireless". Sober he is just an old swish with a good deal of superficial charm, which is all right with me, because most people don't have any, superficial or otherwise, including Carne. He has as much charm as a steel puddler's underpants. Not sober, the client has a strange habit of writing cheques on banks which never heard of him. He always makes good and with my fond help he has so far stayed out of the icebox. He gave me this. Should we smoke it together, like a couple of Indian chiefs planning a massacre?'

'I can't smoke cigars.'

Peters looked at the huge cigar sadly. 'Same here,' he said. 'I thought of giving it to Carne. But it's not really a one-man cigar, even when the one man is Carne.' He frowned. 'You know something? I'm talking too much about Carne. I must be edgy.' He dropped the cigar back in the drawer and looked at the open file. 'Just what do we want from this?'

'I'm looking for a well-heeled alcoholic with expensive tastes and money to gratify them. So far he hasn't gone in for cheque-bouncing. I haven't heard so anyway. He has a streak of violence and his wife is worried about him. She thinks he's hid out in some sobering-up joint but she can't be sure. The only clue we have is a jingle mentioning a Doctor V. Just the initial. My man is gone three days now.'

Peters stared at me thoughtfully. 'That's not too long,' he said. 'What's to worry about?'

'If I find him first, I get paid.'

He looked at me some more and shook his head. 'I don't get it, but that's okay. We'll see.' He began to turn the pages of the file. 'It's not too easy,' he said. 'These people come and go. A single letter ain't much of a lead.' He pulled a page out of the folder, turned some more pages, pulled another, and finally a third. 'Three of them here,' he said. 'Dr Amos Varley, an osteopath. Big place in Altadena. Makes or used to make night calls for fifty bucks. Two registered nurses. Was in a hassle with the State Narcotics people a couple of years back, and turned in his prescription book. This information is not really up to date.'

I wrote down the name and address in Altadena.

'Then we have Dr Lester Vukanich. Ear, Nose, and Throat, Stockwell Building, on Hollywood Boulevard. This one's a dilly. Office practice mostly, and seems to sort of specialize in chronic sinus infections. Rather a neat routine. You go in and complain of a sinus headache and he washes out your antrums for you. First of course he has to anaesthetize with novocain. But if he likes your looks it don't have to be novocain. Catch?'

'Sure.' I wrote that down.

'This is good,' Peters went on, reading some more. 'Obviously his trouble would be supplies. So our Dr Vukanich does a lot of fishing off Ensenada and flies down in his own plane.'

'I wouldn't think he'd last long if he brings the dope in himself,' I said.

Peters thought about that and shook his head. 'I don't think I agree. He could last for ever if he's not too greedy. His only real danger is a discontented customer—pardon me, I mean patient—but he probably knows how to handle that. He's had fifteen years in the same office.'

'Where the hell do you get this stuff?' I asked him.

'We're an organization, my boy. Not a lone wolf like you. Some we get from the clients themselves, some we get from the inside. Carne's not afraid to spend money. He's a good mixer when he wants to be.'

'He'd love this conversation.'

'Screw him. Our last offering today is a man named Verringer. The operative who filed on him is long gone. Seems a lady poet suicided at Verringer's ranch in Sepulveda Canyon one time. He runs a sort of art colony for writers and such who want seclusion and a congenial atmosphere. Rates moderate. He sounds legit. He calls himself doctor, but doesn't practice medicine. Could be a Ph.D. Frankly, I don't know why he's in here. Unless there was something about this suicide.' He picked up a newspaper clipping pasted to a blank sheet. 'Yeah, overdose of morphine. No suggestion Verringer knew anything about it.'

'I like Verringer,' I said. 'I like him very much.'

Peters closed the file and slapped it. 'You haven't seen this,' he said. He got up and left the room. When he came back I was standing up to leave. I started to thank him, but he shook it off.

'Look,' he said, 'there must be hundreds of places where your man could be.'

I said I knew that.

'And by the way, I heard something about your friend Lennox that might interest you. One of our boys ran across a fellow in New York five or six years ago that answers the description exactly. But the guy's name was not Lennox, he says. It was Marston. Of course he could be wrong. The guy was drunk all the time, so you couldn't really be sure.'

I said: 'I doubt if it was the same man. Why would he change his name? He had a war record that could be checked.'

'I didn't know that. Our man's in Seattle right now. You can talk to him when he gets back, if it means anything to you. His name is Ashterfelt.'

'Thanks for everything, George. It was a pretty long ten minutes.'

'I might need *your* help some day.'

'The Carne Organization,' I said, 'never needs anything from anybody.'

He made a rude gesture with his thumb. I left him in his metallic grey cell and departed through the waiting-room. It looked fine now. The loud colours made sense after the cell block.

16

Back from the highway at the bottom of Sepulveda Canyon were two square yellow gateposts. A five-barred gate hung open from one of them. Over the entrance was a sign hung on wire: PRIVATE ROAD. NO ADMITTANCE. The air was warm and quiet and full of the tomcat smell of eucalyptus trees.

I turned in and followed a gravelled road round the shoulder of a hill, up a gentle slope, over a ridge, and down the other side into a shadow valley. It was hot in the valley, ten or fifteen degrees hotter than on the highway. I could see now that the gravelled road ended in a loop around some grass edged with stones that had been lime-washed. Off to my left there was an empty swimming-pool, and nothing ever looks emptier than an empty swimming-pool. Around three sides of it there was what remained of a lawn dotted with redwood lounging chairs with badly faded pads on them. The pads had been of many colours, blue, green, yellow, orange, rust-red. Their edge bindings had come loose in spots, the buttons had popped, and the pads were bloated where this had happened. On the fourth side there was the high wire fence of a tennis court. The diving board over the empty pool looked knee-sprung and tired. Its matting covering hung in shreds and its metal fittings were flaked with rust.

I came to the turning loop and stopped in front of a redwood building with a shake roof and a wide front porch. The entrance had double screen doors. Large black flies dozed on the screens. Paths led off among the evergreen and always dusty California oaks and among the oaks there were rustic cabins scattered loosely over the side of the hill, some almost completely hidden. Those I could see had that desolate out-of-season look. Their doors were shut, their windows were blanked by drawn curtains of monks-cloth or something of that order. You could almost feel the thick dust on their sills.

I switched off the ignition and sat there with my hands on the wheel listening. There was no sound. The place seemed to be as dead as Pharaoh, except that the doors behind the double screens were open and something moved in the dimness of the room beyond. Then I heard a light accurate whistling and a man's figure showed against the screen, pushed it open, and strolled down the steps. He was something to see.

He wore a flat black gaucho hat with the woven strap under his chin. He wore a white silk shirt, spotlessly clean, open at the throat, with tight wristlets and loose puffed sleeves above. Around his neck a black fringed scarf was knotted unevenly so that one end was short and the other dropped almost to his waist. He wore a wide black sash and black pants, skin tight at the hips, coal black, and stitched with gold thread down the side to where they were slashed and belled out loosely with gold buttons along both sides of the slash. On his feet he wore patent-leather dancing pumps.

He stopped at the foot of the steps and looked at me, still whistling. He was as lithe as a whip. He had the largest and emptiest smoke-coloured eyes I had ever seen, under long, silky lashes. His features were delicate and perfect without being weak. His nose was straight and almost but not quite thin, his mouth was a handsome pout, there was a dimple in his chin, and his small ears nestled gracefully against his head. His skin had that heavy pallor which the sun never touches.

He struck an attitude with his left hand on a hip and his right made a graceful curve in the air.

'Greetings,' he said. 'Lovely day, isn't it?'

'Pretty hot in here for me.'

'I like it hot.' The statement was flat and final and closed the discussion. What I liked was beneath his notice. He sat down on a step, produced a long file from somewhere, and began to file his fingernails. 'You from the bank?' he asked without looking up.

'I'm looking for Doctor Verringer.'

He stopped working with the file and looked off into the warm distance. 'Who's he?' he asked with no possible interest.

'He owns the place. Laconic as hell aren't you? As if you didn't know.'

He went back to his file and finger-nails. 'You got told wrong, sweetie. The bank owns the place. They done foreclosed it or it's in escrow or something. I forget the details.'

He looked up at me with the expression of a man to whom details mean nothing. I got out of the Olds and leaned against the hot door, then I moved away from that to where there was some air.

'Which bank would that be?'

'You don't know, you don't come from there. You don't come from there, you don't have any business here. Hit the trail, sweetie. Buzz off but fast.'

'I have to find Dr Verringer.'

'The joint's not operating, sweetie. Like it says on the sign, this is a private road. Some gopher forgot to lock the gate.'

'You the caretaker?'

'Sort of. Don't ask any more questions, sweetie. My temper's not reliable.'

'What do you do when you get mad—dance a tango with a ground squirrel?'

He stood up suddenly and gracefully. He smiled a minute, an empty smile. 'Looks like I got to toss you back in your little old convertible,' he said.

'Later. Where would I find Dr Verringer about now?'

He pocketed his file in his shirt and something else took its place in his right hand. A brief motion and he had a fist with shining brass knuckles on it. The skin over his cheekbones was tighter and there was a flame deep in his large smoky eyes.

He strolled towards me. I stepped back to get more room. He went on whistling but the whistle was high and shrill.

'We don't have to fight,' I told him. 'We don't have anything to fight about. And you might split those lovely britches.'

He was as quick as a flash. He came at me with a smooth leap and his left hand snaked out very fast. I expected a jab and moved my head well enough but what he wanted was my right wrist and he got it. He had a grip too. He jerked me off balance and the hand with the brass knucks came around in a looping bolo punch. A crack on the back of the head with those and I would be a sick man. If I pulled he would catch me on the side of the face or on the upper arm below the point of the shoulder. It would have been a dead arm or a dead face, whichever it happened to be. In a spot like that there is only one thing to do.

I went with the pull. In passing I blocked his left foot from behind, grabbed his shirt, and heard it tear. Something hit me on the back of the neck, but it wasn't the metal. I spun to the left and he went over sideways and landed catlike and was on his feet again before I had any kind of balance. He was grinning now. He was delighted with everything. He loved his work. He came for me fast.

A strong beefy voice yelled from somewhere: 'Earl! Stop that at once! At once, do you hear me?'

The gaucho boy stopped. There was a sort of sick grin on his face. He made a quick motion and the brass knucks disappeared into the wide sash around the top of his pants.

I turned and looked at a solid chunk of man in a Hawaiian shirt hurrying towards us down one of the paths, waving his arms. He came up breathing a little fast.

'Are you crazy Earl?'

'Don't ever say that, Doc,' Earl said softly. Then he smiled, turned away, and went to sit on the steps of the house. He took off the flat crowned hat, produced a comb, and began to comb his thick dark hair with an absent expression. In a second or two he started to whistle softly.

The heavy man in the loud shirt stood and looked at me. I stood and looked at him.

'What's going on here?' he growled. 'Who are you, sir?'

'Name's Marlowe. I was asking for Dr Verringer. The lad you call Earl wanted to play games. I figure it's too hot.'

'I am Dr Verringer,' he said with dignity. He turned his head. 'Go in the house, Earl.'

Earl stood up slowly. He gave Dr Verringer a thoughtful, studying look, his large smoky eyes blank of expression. Then he went up the steps and pulled the screen door open. A cloud of flies buzzed angrily and then settled on the screen again as the door closed.

'Marlowe?' Dr Verringer gave me his attention again. 'And what can I do for you, Mr Marlowe?'

'Earl says you are out of business here.'

'That is correct. I am just waiting for certain legal formalities before moving out. Earl and I are alone here.'

'I'm disappointed,' I said, looking disappointed. 'I thought you had a man named Wade staying with you.'

He hoisted a couple of eyebrows that would have interested a Fuller Brush man. 'Wade? I might possibly know somebody of that name–it's a common enough name–but why should he be staying with me?'

'Taking the cure.'

He frowned. When a guy has eyebrows like that he can really do you a frown. 'I am a medical man, sir, but no longer in practice. What sort of cure did you have in mind?'

'The guy's a wino. He goes off his rocker from time to time and disappears. Sometimes he comes home under his own power, sometimes he gets brought home, and sometimes he takes a bit of finding.' I got a business card out and handed it to him.

He read it with no pleasure.

'What goes with Earl?' I asked him. 'He thinks he's Valentino or something?'

He made with the eyebrows again. They fascinated me. Parts of them curled off all by themselves as much as an inch and a half. He shrugged his meaty shoulders.

'Earl is quite harmless, Mr Marlowe. He is–at times–a little dreamy. Lives in a play world, shall we say?'

'You say it, Doc. From where I stand he plays rough.'

'Tut, tut, Mr Marlowe. You exaggerate surely. Earl likes to dress himself up. He is childlike in that respect.'

'You mean he's a nut,' I said. 'This place is some kind of sanatorium, isn't it? Or was?'

'Certainly not. When it was in operation it was an artists' colony. I provided meals, lodging, facilities for exercise and entertainment, and above all, seclusion. And for moderate fees. Artists, as you probably know, are seldom wealthy people. In the term artists I of course include writers, musicians, and so on. It was a rewarding occupation for me–while it lasted.'

He looked sad when he said this. The eyebrows drooped at the outer corners to match his mouth. Give them a little more growth and they would be *in* his mouth.

'I know that,' I said. 'It's in the file. Also the suicide you had here a while back. A dope case, wasn't it?'

He stopped drooping and bristled. 'What file?' he asked sharply.

'We've got a file on what we call the barred window boys, Doctor. Places where you can't jump out of when the French fits take over. Small private sanatoriums or what have you that treat alcoholics and dopers and mild cases of mania.'

'Such places must be licensed by law,' Dr Verringer said harshly.

'Yeah. In theory anyway. Sometimes they kind of forget about that.'

He drew himself up stiffly. The guy had a kind of dignity, at that. 'The suggestion is insulting, Mr Marlowe. I have no knowledge of why my name should be on any such list as you mention. I must ask you to leave.'

'Let's get back to Wade. Could he be here under another name, maybe?'

'There is no one here but Earl and myself. We are quite alone. Now if you will excuse me—'

'I'd like to look around.'

Sometimes you can get them mad enough to say something off-key. But not Dr Verringer. He remained dignified. His eyebrows went all the way with him. I looked towards the house. From inside there came a sound of music, dance music. And very faintly the snapping of fingers.

'I bet he's in there dancing,' I said. 'That's a tango. I bet you he's dancing all by himself in there. Some kid.'

'Are you going to leave, Mr Marlowe? Or shall I have to ask Earl to assist me in putting you off my property?'

'Okay, I'll leave. No hard feelings, Doctor. There were only three names beginning with V and you seemed the most promising of them. That's the only real clue we had–Dr V. He scrawled it on a piece of paper before he left. Doctor V.'

'There must be dozens,' Dr Verringer said evenly.

'Oh, sure. But not dozens in our file of the barred window boys. Thanks for the time, Doctor. Earl bothers me a little.'

I turned and went over to my car and got into it. By the time I had the door shut Dr Verringer was beside me. He leaned in with a pleasant expression.

'We need not quarrel, Mr Marlowe. I realize that in your occupation you often have to be rather intrusive. Just what bothers you about Earl?'

'He's so obviously phoney. Where you find one thing phoney you're apt to expect others. The guy's a manic-depressive, isn't he? Right now he's on the upswing.'

He stared at me in silence. He looked grave and polite. 'Many interesting and talented people have stayed with me, Mr Marlowe. Not all of them were as level-headed as you may be. Talented people are often neurotic. But I have no facilities for the care of lunatics or alcoholics, even if I had the taste for that sort of work. I have no staff except Earl, and he is hardly the type to care for the sick.'

'Just what would you say he is the type for, Doctor? Apart from bubble-dancing and stuff?'

He leaned on the door. His voice got low and confidential. 'Earl's parents were dear friends of mine, Mr Marlowe. Someone has to look after Earl and they are no longer with us. Earl has to live a quiet life, away from the noise and temptations of the city. He is unstable but fundamentally harmless. I control him with absolute ease, as you saw.'

'You've got a lot of courage,' I said.

He sighed. His eyebrows waved gently, like the antennae of some suspicious insect. 'It has been a sacrifice,' he said. 'A rather heavy one. I thought Earl could help me with my work here. He plays beautiful tennis, swims and dives like a champion, and can dance all night. Almost always he is amiability itself. But from time to time there were–incidents.' He waved a broad hand as if pushing painful memories into the background. 'In the end it was either give up Earl or give up my place here.'

He held both hands palms up, spread them apart, turned them over, and let them fall to his sides. His eyes looked moist with unshed tears.

'I sold out,' he said. 'This peaceful little valley will become a real estate development. There will be sidewalks and lamp-posts and children with scooters and blatting radios. There will even'—he heaved a forlorn sigh—'be Television.' He waved his hand in a sweeping gesture. 'I hope they will spare the trees,' he said, 'but I'm afraid they won't. Along the ridges there will be television aerials instead. But Earl and I will be far away, I trust.'

'Good-bye, Doctor. My heart bleeds for you.'

He put out his hand. It was moist but very firm. 'I appreciate your sympathy and understanding, Mr Marlowe. And I regret I am unable to help you in your quest for Mr Slade.'

'Wade,' I said.

'Pardon me, Wade, of course. Good-bye and good luck, sir.'

I started up and drove back along the gravelled road by the way I had come. I felt sad, but not quite as sad as Dr Verringer would have liked me to feel.

I came out through the gates and drove far enough around the curve of the highway to park out of sight of the entrance. I got out and walked back along the edge of the paving to where I could just see the gates from the barbed-wire boundary fence. I stood there under a eucalyptus and waited.

Five minutes or so passed. Then a car came down the private road churning gravel. It stopped out of sight from where I was. I pulled back still farther into the brush. I heard a creaking noise then the click of a heavy catch and the rattle of a chain. The car motor revved up and the car went back up the road.

When the sound of it had died I went back to my Olds and did a U-turn to face back towards town. As I drove past the entrance to Dr Verringer's private road I saw that the gate was fastened with a padlocked chain. No more visitors today, thank you.

17

I drove the twenty-odd miles back to town and ate lunch. While I ate I felt more and more silly over the whole deal. You just don't find people the way I was going about it. You meet interesting characters like Earl and Dr Verringer, but you don't meet the man you are looking for. You waste tyres, gasoline, words, and nervous energy in a game with no pay-off. You're not even betting table limit four ways on Black 28. With three names that started with V I had as much chance of paging my man as I had of breaking Nick the Greek in a crap game.

Anyway the first one is always wrong, a dead end, a promising lead that blows up in your face with no music. But he shouldn't have said Slade instead of Wade. He was an intelligent man. He wouldn't forget that easy, and if he did he would just forget.

Maybe, and maybe not. It had not been a long acquaintance. Over my coffee I thought about Dr Vukanich and Varley. Yes or no? They would kill most of the afternoon. By then I could call the Wade mansion in Idle Valley and be told the head of the household had returned to his domicile and all was gleaming bright for the time being.

Dr Vukanich was easy. He was only half a dozen blocks down the line. But Dr Varley was away to hell and gone in the Altadena hills, a long, hot, boring drive. Yes or no?

The final answer was yes. For three good reasons. One was that you can never know too much about the shadow line and the people who walk it. The second was that anything I could add to the file Peters had got out for me was just that much thanks and good will. The third reason was that I didn't have anything else to do.

I paid my check, left my car where it was, and walked the north side of the street to the Stockwell Building. It was an antique with a cigar counter in the entrance and a manually operated elevator that lurched and hated to level off. The corridor of the sixth floor was narrow and the door had frosted glass panels. It was older and much dirtier than my own building. It was loaded with doctors, dentists and Christian Science practitioners not doing too good, the kind of lawyers you hope the other fellow has, the kind of doctors and dentists who just scrape along. Not too skillful, not too clean, not too much on the ball, three dollars and please pay the nurse; tired, discouraged men who know just exactly were they stand, what kind of patients they can get and how much money they can be squeezed into paying. Please Do Not Ask For Credit. Doctor is In, Doctor is Out. That's a pretty shaky molar you have there, Mrs Kazinski. Now if you want this new acrylic filling, every bit as good as a gold inlay, I can do it for you for fourteen dollars. Novocain will be two dollars extra, if you wish it. Doctor is In, Doctor is Out. That will be Three Dollars. Please Pay the Nurse.

In a building like that there will always be a few guys making real money, but they don't look it. They fit into the shabby background, which is protective colouring for them. Shyster lawyers who are partners in a bail bond racket on the side (only about two per cent of all forfeited bail bonds are ever collected). Abortionists posing as anything you like that explains their furnishings. Dope pushers posing as urologists, dermatologists, or any branch of medicine in which the treatment can be frequent, and the regular use of local anaesthetics is normal.

Dr Lester Vukanich had a small and ill-furnished waiting-room in which there were a dozen people, all uncomfortable. They looked like anybody else. They had no signs on them. Anyway you can't tell a doper well under control from a vegetarian book-keeper. I had to wait three-quarters of an hour. The patients went in through two doors. An active ear, nose, and throat man can handle four sufferers at once, if he has enough room.

Finally I got in. I got to sit in a brown leather chair beside a table covered with a white towel on which was a set of tools. A sterilizing cabinet bubbled against the wall. Dr Vukanich came in briskly with his white smock and his round mirror strapped to his forehead. He sat down in front of me on a stool.

'A sinus headache, is it? Very severe?' He looked at a folder the nurse had given him.

I said it was awful. Blinding. Especially when I first got up in the morning. He nodded sagely.

'Characteristic,' he said, and fitted a glass cap over a thing that looked like a fountain pen.

He pushed it into my mouth. 'Close the lips but not the teeth, please.' While he said it he reached out and switched off the light. There was no window. A ventilating fan purred somewhere.

Dr Vukanich withdrew his glass tube and put the lights back up. He looked at me carefully.

'No congestion at all, Mr Marlowe. If you have a headache, it is not from a sinus condition. I'd hazard a guess that you never had sinus trouble in your life. You had a septum operation sometime in the past, I see.'

'Yes, Doctor. Got a kick playing football.'

He nodded. 'There is a slight shelf of bone which should have been cut away. Hardly enough to interfere with breathing, however.'

He leaned back on the stool and held his knee. 'Just what did you expect me to do for you?' he asked. He was a thin-faced man with an uninteresting pallor. He looked like a tubercular white rat.

'I wanted to talk to you about a friend of mine. He's in bad shape. He's a writer. Plenty of dough, but bad nerves. Needs help. He lives on the sauce for days on end. He needs that little extra something. His own doctor won't co-operate any more.'

'Exactly what do you mean by co-operate?' Dr Vukanich asked.

'All the guy needs is an occasional shot to calm him down. I thought maybe we could work something out. The money would be solid.'

'Sorry, Mr Marlowe. It is not my sort of problem.' He stood up. 'Rather a crude approach, if I may say so. Your friend may consult me, if he chooses. But he'd better have something wrong with him that requires treatment. That will be ten dollars, Mr Marlowe.'

'Come off it, Doc. You're on the list.'

Dr Vukanich leaned against the wall and lit a cigarette. He was giving me time. He blew smoke and looked at it. I gave him one of my cards to look at instead. He looked at it.

'What list would that be?' he inquired.

'The barred window boys. I figured you might know my friend already. His name's Wade. I figure you might have him stashed away somewhere in a little white room. The guy is missing from home.'

'You are an ass,' Dr Vukanich told me. 'I don't go in for penny rate stuff like four-day liquor cures. They cure nothing in any case. I have no little white rooms and I am not acquainted with the friend you mention—even if he exists. That will be ten dollars—cash—right now. Or would you rather I called the police and made a complaint that you solicited me for narcotics?'

'That would be dandy,' I said. 'Let's.'

'Get out of here, you cheap grifter.'

I stood up off the chair. 'I guess I made a mistake, Doctor. The last time the guy broke parole he holed up with a doctor whose name began with a V. It was strictly an under-cover operation. They fetched him late at night and brought him back the same way when he was over the jumps. Didn't even wait long enough to see him go in the house. So when he hops the coop again and don't come back for quite a piece, naturally we check over our files for a lead. We come up with three doctors whose names begin with V.'

'Interesting,' he said with a bleak smile. He was still giving me time. 'What is the basis of your selection?'

I stared at him. His right hand was moving softly up and down the upper part of his left arm on the inside of it. His face was covered with a light sweat.

'Sorry, Doctor. We operate very confidential.'

'Excuse me a moment. I have another patient that—'

He left the rest of it hanging in the air and went out. While he was gone a nurse poked her head through the doorway, looked at me briefly, and withdrew.

Then Dr Vukanich came back in strolling happily. He was smiling and relaxed. His eyes were bright.

'What? Are you still here?' He looked very surprised or pretended to. 'I thought our little visit had been brought to an end.'

'I'm leaving. I thought you wanted me to wait.'

He chuckled. 'You know something, Mr Marlowe? We live in extraordinary times. For a mere five hundred dollars I could have you put in the hospital with several broken bones. Comical, isn't it?'

'Hilarious,' I said. 'Shoot yourself in the vein, don't you, Doc? Boy, do you brighten up!'

I started out. '*Hasta luego, amigo,*' he chirped. 'Don't forget my ten bucks. Pay the nurse.'

He moved to an intercom and was speaking into it as I left. In the waiting-room the same twelve people or twelve just like them were being uncomfortable. The nurse was right on the job.

'That will be ten dollars, please, Mr Marlowe. This office requires immediate cash payment.'

I stepped among the crowded feet to the floor. She hounded out of her chair and ran around the desk. I pulled the door open.

'What happens when you don't get it?' I asked her.

'You'll find out what happens,' she said angrily.

'Sure. You're just doing your job. So am I. Take a gander at the card I left and you'll see what my job is.'

I went on out. The waiting patients looked at me with disapproving eyes. That was no way to treat Doctor.

18

Dr Amos Varley was a very different proposition. He had a big old house in a big old garden with big old oak trees shading it. It was a massive frame structure with elaborate scrollwork along the overhang of the porches and the white porch railings had turned and fluted uprights like the legs of an old-fashioned grand piano. A few frail elderly people sat in long chairs on the porches with rugs tucked around them.

The entrance doors were double and had stained-glass panels. The hall inside was wide and cool and the parquet floor was polished and without a single rug. Altadena is a hot place in summer. It is pushed back against the hills and the breeze jumps clear over it. Eight years ago people knew how to build houses for this climate.

A nurse in crisp white took my card and after a wait Dr Amos Varley condescended to see me. He was a big, bald-headed guy with a cheery smile. His long white coat was spotless, he walked noiselessly on crêpe rubber soles.

'What can I do for you, Mr Marlowe?' He had a rich, soft voice to soothe the pain and comfort the anxious heart. Doctor is here, there is nothing to worry about, everything will be fine. He had that bedside manner, thick, honeyed layers of it. He was wonderful—and he was as tough as armour plate.

'Doctor, I am looking for a man named Wade, a well-to-do alcoholic who has disappeared from his home. His past history suggests that he is holed up in some discreet joint that can handle him with skill. My only lead is a reference to Dr V. You're my third Dr V. And I'm getting discouraged.'

He smiled benignly. 'Only your third, Mr Marlowe? Surely there must be a hundred doctors in and around the Los Angeles area whose names begin with V.'

'Sure, but not many of them would have rooms with barred windows. I noticed a few upstairs here, on the side of the house.'

'Old people,' Dr Varley said sadly, but it was a rich full sadness. 'Lonely old people, depressed and unhappy old people, Mr Marlowe. Sometimes—' he made an expressive gesture with his hand, a curving motion outwards, a pause, then a gentle falling, like a dead leaf fluttering to the ground. 'I don't treat alcoholics here,' he added precisely. 'Now if you will excuse me—'

'Sorry Doctor. You just happened to be on our list. Probably a mistake. Something about a run-in with the narcotics people a couple of years ago.'

'Is that so?' He looked puzzled, then the light broke. 'Ah, yes, an assistant I was unwise enough to employ. For a very short time. He abused my confidence badly. Yes, indeed.'

'Not the way I heard it,' I said. 'I guess I heard it wrong.'

'And how did you hear it, Mr Marlowe?' He was still giving me the full treatment with his smile and his mellow tones.

'That you had to turn in your narcotics prescription book.'

That got to him a little. He didn't quite scowl but he peeled off a few layers of the charm. His blue eyes had a chilly glint. 'And the source of this fantastic information?'

'A large detective agency that has had facilities for building files on that sort of thing.'

'A collection of cheap blackmailers, no doubt.'

'Not cheap, Doctor. Their base rate is a hundred dollars a day. It's run by a former colonel of military police. No nickel grabber, Doctor. He rates way up.'

'I shall give him a piece of my mind,' Dr Varley said with cool distaste. 'His name?' The sun had set in Dr Varley's manner. It was getting to be a chilly evening.

'Confidential, Doctor. But don't give it a thought. All in the day's work. Name of Wade doesn't ring a bell at all, huh?'

'I believe you know your way out, Mr Marlowe.'

The door of a small elevator opened behind him. A nurse pushed a wheel chair out. The chair contained what was left of a broken old man. His eyes were closed, his skin had a bluish tinge. He was well wrapped up. The nurse wheeled him silently across the polished floor and out of a side door. Dr Varley said softly:

'Old people. Sick old people. Lonely old people. Do not come back, Mr Marlowe. You might annoy me. When annoyed I can be rather unpleasant. I might say *very* unpleasant.'

'Okay by me, Doctor. Thanks for the time. Nice little dying-in home you got here.'

'What was that?' He took a step towards me and peeled off the remaining layers of honey. The soft lines of his face set themselves into hard ridges.

'What's the matter?' I asked him. 'I can see my man wouldn't be here. I wouldn't look for anybody here that wasn't too frail to fight back. Sick old people. Lonely old people. You said it yourself, Doctor. Unwanted old people, but with money and hungry heirs. Most of them probably judged incompetent by the court.'

'I am getting annoyed,' Dr Varley said.

'Light food, light sedation, firm treatment. Put them out in the sun, put them back in the bed. Bar some of the windows in case there's a little spunk left. They love you, Doctor, one and all. They die holding your hand and seeing the sadness in your eyes. It's genuine, too.'

'It certainly is,' he said in a low throaty growl. His hands were fists now. I ought to knock it off. But he had begun to nauseate me.

'Sure it is,' I said. 'Nobody likes to lose a good paying customer. Especially one you don't even have to please.'

'Somebody has to do it,' he said. 'Somebody has to care for these sad old people, Mr Marlowe.'

'Somebody has to clean out cesspools. Come to think of it that's a clean honest job. So long, Dr Varley. When my job makes me feel dirty I'll think of you. It will cheer me up no end.'

'You filthy louse,' Dr Varley said between his wide white teeth. 'I ought to break your back. Mine is an honourable branch of an honourable profession.'

'Yeah.' I looked at him wearily. 'I know it is. Only it smells of death.'

He didn't slug me, so I walked away from him and out. I looked back from the wide double doors. He hadn't moved. He had a job to do, putting back the layers of honey.

19

I drove back to Hollywood feeling like a short length of chewed string. It was too early to eat, and too hot. I turned on the fan in my office. It didn't make the air any cooler, just a little more lively. Outside on the boulevard the traffic brawled endlessly. Inside my head thoughts stuck together like flies on fly paper.

Three shots, three misses. All I had been doing was seeing too many doctors.

I called the Wade home. A Mexican sort of accent answered and said that Mrs Wade was not at home. I asked for Mr Wade. The voice said Mr Wade was not at home either. I left my name. He seemed to catch it without any trouble. He said he was the houseboy.

I called George Peters at the Carne Organization. Maybe he knew some more doctors. He wasn't in. I left a phoney name and a right telephone number. An hour crawled by like a sick cockroach. I was a grain of sand on the desert of oblivion. I was a two-gun cowpoke fresh out of bullets. Three shots, three misses. I hate it when they come in threes. You call on Mr A. Nothing. You call on Mr B. Nothing. You call on Mr C. More of the same. A week later you find out it should have been Mr D. Only you didn't know he existed and by the time you found out the client had changed his mind and killed the investigation.

Drs Vukanich and Varley were scratched. Varley had it too rich to fool with hooch cases. Vukanich was a punk, a high-wire performer who hit the main line in his own office. The help must know. At least some of the patients must know. All it took to finish him was one sore head and one telephone call. Wade wouldn't have gone within blocks of him, drunk or sober. He might not be the brightest guy in the world—plenty of successful people are far from mental giants—but he couldn't be dumb enough to fool with Vukanich.

The only possible was Dr Verringer. He had the space and the seclusion. He probably had the patients. But Sepulveda Canyon was a long way from Idle Valley. Where was the point of contact, how did they know each other, and if Verringer owned that property and had a buyer for it, he was half-way to being pretty well heeled. That gave me an idea. I called a man I knew in a title company to find out the status of the property. No answer. The title company had closed for the day.

I closed for the day too, and drove over to La Cienaga to Rudy's Bar-B-Q, gave my name to the master of ceremonies and waited for the big moment on a bar stool with a whisky sour in front of me and Marek Weber's waltz music in my ears. After a while I got in past the velvet rope and ate one of Rudy's 'world-famous' Salisbury steaks, which is hamburger on a slab of burnt wood, ringed with browned-over mashed potato, supported by fried onion rings and one of those mixed-up salads which men will eat with complete docility in restaurants, although they would probably start yelling if their wives tried to feed them one at home.

After that I drove home. As I opened the front door the phone started to ring.

'This is Eileen Wade, Mr Marlowe. You wanted me to call you.'

'Just to find out if anything had happened at your end. I have been seeing doctors all day and have made no friends.'

'No, I'm sorry. He still hasn't showed up. I can't help being rather anxious. Then you have nothing to tell me, I suppose.' Her voice was low and dispirited.

'It's a big crowded county, Mrs Wade.'

'It will be four whole days tonight.'

'Sure, but that's not too long.'

'For me it is.' She was silent for a while. 'I've been doing a lot of thinking, trying to remember something,' she went on. 'There must be something, some kind of hint or memory. Roger talks a great deal about all sorts of things.'

'Does the name Verringer mean anything to you, Mrs Wade?'

'No, I'm afraid not. Should it?'

'You mentioned that Mr Wade was brought home one time by a tall man dressed in a cowboy outfit. Would you recognize this tall man if you saw him again, Mrs Wade?'

'I suppose I might,' she said hesitantly, 'if the conditions were the same. But I only caught the merest glimpse of him. Was his name Verringer?'

'No, Mrs Wade. Verringer is a heavily built, middle-aged man who runs, or more accurately has run, some kind of guest ranch in Sepulveda Canyon. He has a dressed-up fancy boy named Earl working for him. And Verringer calls himself a doctor.'

'That's wonderful,' she said warmly. 'Don't you feel that you're on the right track?'

'I could be wetter than a drowned kitten. I'll call you when I know. I just wanted to make sure Roger hadn't come home and that you hadn't recalled anything definite.'

'I'm afraid I haven't been of much help to you,' she said sadly. 'Please call me at any time, no matter how late it is.'

I said I would do that and we hung up. I took a gun and a three-cell flashlight with me this time. The gun was a tough little short-barrelled .32 with flat-point cartridges. Dr Verringer's boy Earl might have other toys than brass knuckles. If he had, he was plenty goofy enough to play with them.

I hit the highway again and drove as fast as I dared. It was a moonless night, and would be getting dark by the time I reached the entrance to Dr Verringer's estate. Darkness was what I needed.

The gates were still locked with the chain and padlock. I drove on past and parked well off the highway. There was still some light under the trees but it wouldn't last long. I climbed the gate and went up the side of the hill looking for a hiking path. Far back in the valley I thought I heard a quail. A mourning dove exclaimed against the miseries of life. There wasn't any hiking path or I couldn't find one, so I went back to the road and walked along the edge of the gravel. The eucalyptus trees gave way to the oaks and I crossed the ridge and far off I could see a few lights. It took me three-quarters of an hour to work up behind the swimming-pool and the tennis courts to a spot where I could look down on the main building at the end of the road. It was lighted up and I could hear music coming from it. And farther off in the trees another cabin showed light. There were small dark cabins dotted all over the place in the trees. I went along a path now and suddenly a floodlight went on at the back of the main cabin. I stopped dead. The floodlight was not looking for anything. It pointed straight down and made a wide pool of light on the back porch and the ground beyond. Then a door banged open and Earl came out. Then I knew I was in the right place.

Earl was a cowpoke tonight, and it had been a cowpoke who brought Roger Wade home the time before. Earl was spinning a rope. He wore a dark shirt stitched with white and a polka-dot scarf knotted loosely around his neck. He wore a wide leather belt with a load of silver on it and a pair of tooled leather holsters with ivory-handled guns in them. He wore elegant riding pants and boots cross-stitched in white and glistening new. On the back of his head was a white sombrero and what looked like a woven silver cord hanging loosely down his shirt, the ends not fastened.

He stood there alone under the white floodlight, spinning his rope around him, stepping in and out of it, an actor without an audience, a tall, slender, handsome dude wrangler putting on a show all by himself and loving every minute of it. Two-Gun Earl, the Terror of Chochise County. He belonged on one of those guest ranches that are so all-fired horsey the telephone girl wears riding boots to work.

All at once he heard a sound, or pretended to. The rope dropped, his hands swept the two guns from the holsters and the crook of his thumbs was over the hammers as they came level. He peered into the darkness. I didn't dare move. The damn guns could be loaded. But the floodlight had blinded him and he didn't see anything. He slipped his guns back in the holsters, picked up the rope and gathered it loosely, went back into the house. The light went off, and so did I.

I moved around through the trees and got close to the small lighted cabin on the slope. No sound came from it. I reached a screened window and looked in. The light came from a lamp on a night table beside a bed. A man lay flat on his back in the bed, his body relaxed, his arms in pyjama sleeves outside the covers, his eyes wide open and staring at the ceiling. He looked big. His face was partly shadowed, but I could see that he was pale and that he needed a shave and had needed one for just about the right length of time. The spread fingers of his hands lay motionless on the outside of the bed. He looked as if he hadn't moved for hours.

I heard steps coming along the path at the far side of the cabin. A screen door creaked and then the solid shape of Dr Verringer showed in the doorway. He was carrying what looked like a large glass of tomato juice. He switched on a standing lamp. His Hawaiian shirt gleamed yellowly. The man in the bed didn't even look at him.

Dr Verringer put the glass down on the night table and pulled a chair close and sat down. He reached for one of the wrists and felt a pulse. 'How are you feeling now, Mr Wade?' His voice was kindly and solicitous.

The man on the bed didn't answer him or look at him. He went on staring at the ceiling.

'Come, come, Mr Wade. Let us not be moody. Your pulse is only slightly faster than normal. You are weak, but otherwise—'

'Tejjy,' the man on the bed said suddenly, 'tell the man that if he knows how I am, the son of a bitch needn't bother to ask me.' He had a nice clear voice, but the tone was bitter.

'Who is Tejjy?' Dr Verringer asked patiently.

'My mouthpiece. She's up there in the corner.'

Dr Verringer looked up. 'I see a small spider,' he said. 'Stop acting, Mr Wade. It is not necessary with me.'

'*Tegenaria domestica*, the common jumping spider, pal. I like spiders. They practically never wear Hawaiian shirts.'

Dr Verringer moistened his lips. 'I have no time for playfulness, Mr Wade.'

'Nothing playful about Tejjy.' Wade turned his head slowly, as if it weighed very heavy, and stared at Dr Verringer contemptuously. 'Tejjy is dead serious. She creeps up on you. When you're not looking she makes a quick, silent hop. After a while she's near enough. She makes the last jump. You get sucked dry, Doctor. Very dry. Tejjy doesn't eat you. She just sucks the juice until there's nothing left but the skin. If you plan to wear that shirt much longer, Doctor, I'd say it couldn't happen too soon.'

Dr Verringer leaned back in the chair. 'I need five thousand dollars,' he said calmly. 'How soon could that happen?'

'You got six hundred and fifty bucks,' Wade said nastily. 'As well as my loose change. How the hell much does it cost in this bordello?'

'Chicken feed,' Dr Verringer said. 'I told you my rates had gone up.'

'You didn't say they had moved to Mount Wilson.'

'Don't fence with me, Wade,' Dr Verringer said curtly. 'You are in no position to get funny. Also you have betrayed my confidence.'

'I didn't know you had any.'

Dr Verringer tapped slowly on the arms of the chair. 'You called me up in the middle of the night,' he said. 'You were in a desperate condition. You said you would kill yourself if I didn't come. I didn't want to do it and you know why. I have no licence to practise medicine in this state. I am trying to get rid of this property without losing it all. I have Earl to look after and he was about due for a bad spell. I told you it would cost you a lot of money. You still insisted and I went. I want five thousand dollars.'

'I was foul with strong drink,' Wade said. 'You can't hold a man to that kind of bargain. You're damn well paid already.'

'Also,' Dr Verringer said slowly, 'you mentioned my name to your wife. You told her I was coming for you.'

Wade looked surprised. 'I didn't do anything of the sort,' he said. 'I didn't even see her. She was asleep.'

'Some other time then. A private detective has been here asking about you. He couldn't possibly have known where to come, unless he was told. I stalled him off, but he may come back. You have to go home, Mr Wade. But first I want my five thousand dollars.'

'You're not the brightest guy in the world, are you, Doc? If my wife knew where I was, why would she need a detective? She could have come herself—supposing she cared that much. She could have brought Candy, our houseboy. Candy would cut your Blue Boy into thin strips while Blue Boy was making up his mind what picture he was starring in today.'

'You have a nasty tongue, Wade. And a nasty mind.'

'I have a nasty five thousand bucks, too, Doc. Try and get it.'

'You will write me a cheque,' Dr Verringer said firmly. 'Now, at once. Then you will get dressed and Earl will take you home.'

'A cheque?' Wade was almost laughing. 'Sure I'll give you a cheque. Fine. How will you cash it?'

Dr Verringer smiled quietly. 'You think you will stop payment, Mr Wade. But you won't. I assure you that you won't.'

'You fat crook!' Wade yelled at him.

Dr Verringer shook his head. 'In some things, yes. Not in all. I am a mixed character like most people. Earl will drive you home.'

'Nix. That lad makes my skin crawl,' Wade said.

Dr Verringer stood up gently and reached over and patted the shoulder of the man on the bed. 'To me Earl is quite harmless, Mr Wade. I have ways of controlling him.'

'Name one,' a new voice said, and Earl came through the door in his Roy Rogers outfit. Dr Verringer turned, smiling.

'Keep that psycho away from me,' Wade yelled, showing fear for the first time.

Earl put his hands upon his ornamented belt. His face was deadpan. A light whistling noise came from between his teeth. He moved slowly into the room.

'You shouldn't have said that,' Dr Verringer said quickly, and turned towards Earl. 'All right, Earl. I'll handle Mr Wade myself. I'll help him get dressed while you bring the car up here as close to the cabin as possible. Mr Wade is quite weak.'

'And he's going to be a lot weaker,' Earl said in a whistling kind of voice. 'Out of the way, fatso.'

'Now, Earl—' he reached out and grabbed the handsome young man's arm, 'you don't want to go back to Camarillo, do you? One word from me and—'

That was as far as he got. Earl jerked his arm loose and his right hand came up with a flash of metal. The armoured fist crashed against Dr Verringer's jaw. He went down as if shot through the heart. The fall shook the cabin. I started running.

I reached the door and yanked it open. Earl spun round, leaning forward a little, staring at me without recognition. There was a bubbling sound behind his lips. He started for me fast.

I jerked the gun out and showed it to him. It meant nothing. Either his own guns were not loaded or he had forgotten all about them. The brass knuckles were all he needed. He kept coming.

I fired through the open window across the bed. The crash of the gun in the small room seemed much louder than it should have been. Earl stopped dead. His head slewed around and he looked at the hole in the window screen. He looked back at me. Slowly his face came alive and he grinned.

'Wha' happen?' he asked brightly.

'Get rid of the knucks,' I said, watching his eyes.

He looked surprisedly down at his hand. He slipped the mauler off and threw it casually in the corner.

'Now the gun belt,' I said. 'Don't touch the guns, just the buckle.'

'They're not loaded,' he said, smiling. 'Hell, they're not even guns, just stage money.'

'The belt. Hurry it.'

He looked at the short-barrelled .32. 'That a real one? Oh, sure it is. The screen. Yeah, the screen.'

The man on the bed wasn't on the bed any more. He was behind Earl. He reached swiftly and pulled one of the bright guns loose. Earl didn't like this. His face showed it.

'Lay off him,' I said angrily. 'Put that back where you got it.'

'He's right,' Wade said. 'They're cap guns.' He backed away and put the shiny pistol on the table. 'Christ, I'm weak as a broken arm.'

'Take the belt off,' I said for the third time. When you start something with a type like Earl you have to finish it. Keep it simple and don't change your mind.

He did it at last, quite amiably. Then, holding the belt, he walked over to the table and got his other gun and put it in the holster and put the belt right back on again. I let him do it. It wasn't until then that he saw Dr Verringer crumpled on the floor against the wall. He made a sound of concern, went quickly across the room into the bathroom, and came back with a glass jug of water. He dumped the water on Dr Verringer's head. Dr Verringer sputtered and rolled over. Then he groaned. Then he clapped a hand to his jaw. Then he started to get up. Earl helped him.

'Sorry, Doc. I must have just let fly without seeing who it was.'

'It's all right, nothing broken,' Verringer said, waving him away. 'Get the car up here, Earl. And don't forget the key for the padlock down below.'

'Car up here, sure. Right away. Key for the padlock. I got it. Right away, Doc.'

He went out of the room whistling.

Wade was sitting on the side of the bed, looking shaky. 'You the dick he was talking about?' he asked me. 'How did you find me?'

'Just asking around from people who know about these things,' I said. 'If you want to get home, you might get clothes on.'

Dr Verringer was leaning against the wall, massaging his jaw. 'I'll help him,' he said thickly. 'All I do is help people and all they do is kick me in the teeth.'

'I know just how you feel,' I said.

I went out and left them to work at it.

20

The car was close by when they came out, but Earl was gone. He had stopped the car, cut the lights, and walked back towards the big cabin without saying anything to me. He was still whistling, groping for some half-remembered tune.

Wade climbed carefully into the back seat and I got in beside him. Dr Verringer drove. If his jaw hurt badly and his head ached, he didn't show it or mention it. We went over the ridge and down to the end of the gravelled drive. Earl had already been down and unlocked the gate and pulled it open. I told Verringer where my car was and he pulled up close to it. Wade got into it and sat silent, staring at nothing. Verringer got out and went round beside him. He spoke to Wade gently.

'About my five thousand dollars, Mr Wade. The cheque you promised me.'

Wade slid down and rested his head on the back of the seat. 'I'll think about it.'

'You promised it. I need it.'

'Duress, the word is, Verringer, a threat of harm. I have protection now.'

'I fed and washed you,' Verringer persisted. 'I came in the night. I protected you, I cured you—for the time being, at least.'

'Not five grand worth,' Wade sneered. 'You got plenty out of my pockets.'

Verringer wouldn't let go. 'I have a promise of a connexion in Cuba, Mr Wade. You are a rich man. You should help others in their need. I have Earl to look after. To avail myself of this opportunity I need the money. I will pay it back in full.'

I began to squirm. I wanted to smoke, but I was afraid it would make Wade sick.

'Like hell you'd pay it back,' Wade said wearily. 'You won't live long enough. One of these nights Blue Boy will kill you in your sleep.'

Verringer stepped back. I couldn't see his expression, but his voice hardened. 'There are more unpleasant ways to die,' he said. 'I think yours will be one of them.'

He walked back to his car and got into it. He drove in through his gates and was gone. I backed and turned and headed towards the city. After a mile or two Wade muttered: 'Why should I give that fat slob five thousand dollars?'

'No reason at all.'

'Then why do I feel like a bastard for not giving it to him?'

'No reason at all.'

He turned his head just enough to look at me. 'He handled me like a baby,' Wade said. 'He hardly left me alone for fear Earl would come in and beat me up. He took every dime I had in my pockets.'

'You probably told him to.'

'You on his side?'

'Skip it,' I said. 'This is just a job to me.'

Silence for a couple of miles more. We went past the fringe of one of the outlying suburbs. Wade spoke again.

'Maybe I'll give it to him. He's broke. The property is foreclosed. He won't get a dime out of it. All on account of that psycho. Why does he do it?'

'I wouldn't know.'

'I'm a writer,' Wade said. 'I'm supposed to understand what makes people tick. I don't understand one damn thing about anybody.'

I turned over the pass and after a climb the lights of the valley spread out endlessly in front of us. We dipped down to the highway north and west that goes to Ventura. After a while we passed through Encino. I stopped for a light and looked up towards the lights high on the hill where the big houses were. In one of them the Lennoxes had lived. We went on.

'The turn off is pretty close now,' Wade said. 'Or do you know it.'

'I know it.'

'By the way, you haven't told me your name.'

'Philip Marlowe.'

'Nice name.' His voice changed abruptly, saying: 'Wait a minute. You the guy that was mixed up with Lennox?'

'Yeah.'

He was staring at me in the darkness of the car. We passed the last buildings on the main drag of Encino.

'I knew her,' Wade said. 'A little. Him I never saw. Queer business, that. The law boys gave you the rough edge, didn't they?'

I didn't answer him.

'Maybe you don't like to talk about it,' he said.

'Could be. Why would it interest you?'

'Hell, I'm a writer. It must be quite a story.'

'Take tonight off. You must be feeling pretty weak.'

'Okay, Marlowe. Okay. You don't like me. I get it.'

We reached the turn-off and I swung the car into it and towards the low hills and the gap between them that was Idle Valley.

'I don't either like you or dislike you,' I said. 'I don't know you. Your wife asked me to find you and bring you home. When I deliver you at your house I'm through. Why she picked on me I couldn't say. Like I said, it's just a job.'

We turned the flank of a hill and hit a wider more firmly paved road. He said his house was a mile farther on, on the right side. He told me the number, which I already knew. For a guy in his shape he was a pretty persistent talker.

'How much is she paying you?' he asked.

'We didn't discuss it.'

'Whatever it is, it's not enough. I owe you a lot of thanks. You did a great job, chum. I wasn't worth the trouble.'

'That's just the way you feel tonight.'

He laughed. 'You know something, Marlowe? I could get to like you. You're a bit of a bastard–like me.'

We reached the house. It was a two-storey overall shingle house with a small pillared portico and a long lawn from the entrance to a thick row of shrubs inside the white fence. There was a light in the portico. I pulled into the driveway and stopped close to the garage.

'Can you make it without help?'

'Of course.' He got out of the car. 'Aren't you coming in for a drink or something?'

'Not tonight, thanks; I'll wait here until you're in the house.'

He stood there breathing hard. 'Okay,' he said shortly.

He turned and walked carefully along a flagged path to the front door. He held on to a white pillar for a moment, then tried the door. It opened, he went in. The door stayed open and light washed across the green lawn. There was a sudden flutter of voices. I started backing from the driveway, following the back-up light. Somebody called out.

I looked and saw Eileen Wade standing in the open doorway. I kept going and she started to run. So I had to stop. I cut the lights and got out of the car. When she came up I said:

'I ought to have called you, but I was afraid to leave him.'

'Of course. Did you have a lot of trouble?'

'Well–a little more than ringing a doorbell.'

'Please come in the house and tell me all about it.'

'He should be in bed. By tomorrow he'll be as good as new.'

'Candy will put him to bed,' she said. 'He won't drink tonight, if that's what you are thinking of.'

'Never occurred to me. Good night, Mrs Wade.'

'You must be tired. Don't you want a drink yourself?'

I lit a cigarette. It seemed like a couple of weeks since I had tasted tobacco. I drank in the smoke.

'May I have just one puff?'

'Sure. I thought you didn't smoke.'

'I don't often.' She came close to me and I handed her the cigarette. She drew on it and coughed. She handed it back laughing. 'Strictly an amateur, as you see.'

'So you knew Sylvia Lennox,' I said. 'Was that why you wanted to hire me?'

'I knew who?' She sounded puzzled.

'Sylvia Lennox.' I had the cigarette back now. I was eating it pretty fast.

'Oh,' she said, startled. 'That girl that was–murdered. No, I didn't know her personally. I knew who she was. Didn't I tell you that?'

'Sorry, I'd forgotten just what you did tell me.'

She was still standing there quietly, close to me, slim and tall in a white dress of some sort. The light from the open door touched the fringe of her hair and made it glow softly.

'Why did you ask me if that had anything to do with my wanting to, as you put it, hire you?' When I didn't answer at once she added, 'Did Roger tell you he knew her?'

'He said something about the case when I told him my name. He didn't connect me with it immediately, then he did. He talked so damn much I don't remember half of what he said.'

'I see. I must go in, Mr Marlowe, and see if my husband needs anything. And if you won't come in—'

'I'll leave this with you,' I said.

I took hold of her and pulled her towards me and tilted her head back. I kissed her hard on the lips. She didn't fight me and she didn't respond. She pulled herself away quietly and stood there looking at me.

'You shouldn't have done that,' she said. 'That was wrong. You're too nice a person.'

'Sure. Very wrong,' I agreed. 'But I've been such a nice faithful well-behaved gun dog all day long, I got charmed into one of the silliest ventures I ever tackled, and damned if it didn't turn out just as though somebody had written a script for it. You know something? I believe you knew where he was all along–or at least knew the name of Dr Verringer. You just wanted to get me involved with him, tangled up with him so I'd feel a sense of responsibility to look after him. Or am I crazy?'

'Of course you're not crazy,' she said coldly. 'That is the most outrageous nonsense I ever listened to.' She started to turn away.

'Wait a minute,' I said. 'That kiss won't leave a scar. You just think it will. And don't tell me I'm too nice a person. I'd rather be a heel.'

She looked back. 'Why?'

'If I hadn't been a nice guy to Terry Lennox, he would still be alive.'

'Yes?' she said quietly. 'How can you be so sure? Good night, Mr Marlowe. And thank you so very much for almost everything.'

She walked back along the edge of the grass. I watched her into the house. The door closed. The porch light went off. I waved at nothing and drove away.

21

Next morning I got up late on account of the big fee I had earned the night before. I drank an extra cup of coffee, smoked an extra cigarette, ate an extra slice of Canadian bacon, and for the three hundredth time I swore I would never again use an electric razor. That made the day normal. I hit the office about ten, picked up some odds and ends of mail, slit the envelopes, and let the stuff lie on the desk. I opened the windows wide to let out the smell of dust and dinginess that collected in the night and hung in the still air, in the corners of the room, in the slats of the venetian blinds. A dead moth was spread-eagled on a corner of the desk. On the window-sill a bee with tattered wings was crawling along the woodwork, buzzing in a tired remote sort of way, as if she knew it wasn't any use, she was finished, she had flown too many missions and would never get back to the hive again.

I knew it was going to be one of those crazy days. Everyone has them. Days when nobody rolls in but the loose wheels, the dingoes who park their brains with their gum, the squirrels who can't find their nuts, the mechanics who always have a gear wheel left over.

The first was a big, blond roughneck named Kuissenen or something Finnish like that. He jammed his massive bottom in the customer's chair and planted two wide, horny hands on my desk and said he was a power-shovel operator, that he lived in Culver City, and the goddam woman who lived next door to him was trying to poison his dog. Every morning before he let the dog out for a run in the backyard he had to search the place from fence to fence for meatballs thrown over the potato vine from next door. He'd found nine of them so far and they were loaded with a greenish powder he knew was an arsenic weedkiller.

'How much to watch out and catch her at it?' He stared at me as unblinkingly as a fish in a tank.

'Why not do it yourself?'

'I got to work for a living, mister. I'm losing four twenty-five an hour just coming up here to ask.'

'Try the police?'

'I try the police. They might get around to it some time next year. Right now they're busy sucking up to MGM.'

'S.P.C.A.? The Tailwaggers?'

'What's them?'

I told him about the Tailwaggers. He was far from interested. He knew about S.P.C.A. The S.P.C.A. could take a running jump. They couldn't see nothing smaller than a horse.

'It says on the door you're an investigator,' he said truculently. 'Okay, go the hell out and investigate. Fifty bucks if you catch her.'

'Sorry,' I said. 'I'm tied up. Spending a couple of weeks hiding in a gopher hole in your back-yard would be out of my line anyway–even for fifty bucks.'

He stood up glowering. 'Big shot,' he said. 'Don't need the dough, huh? Can't be bothered saving the life of a itty-bitty dog. Nuts to you, big shot.'

'I've got troubles too, Mr Kuissenen.'

'I'll twist her goddam neck if I catch her,' he said, and I didn't doubt he could have done it. He could have twisted the hind leg off an elephant. 'That's what makes it I want somebody else. Just because the little tyke barks when a car goes by the house. Sour-faced old bitch.'

He started for the door. 'Are you sure it's the dog she's trying to poison?' I asked his back.

'Sure I'm sure.' He was half-way to the door before the nickel dropped. He swung around fast then. 'Say that again, buster.'

I just shook my head. I didn't want to fight him. He might hit me on the head with my desk. He snorted and went out, almost taking the door with him.

The next cookie in the dish was a woman, not old, not young, not clean, not too dirty, obviously poor, shabby, querulous, and stupid. The girl she roomed with–in her set any woman who works is a girl–was taking money out of her purse. A dollar here, four bits there, but it added up. She figured she was out close to twenty dollars in all. She couldn't afford it. She couldn't afford to move either. She couldn't afford a detective. She thought I ought to be willing to throw a scare into the room-mate just on the telephone like, not mentioning any names.

It took her twenty minutes or more to tell me this. She kneaded her bag incessantly while telling it.

'Anybody you know could do that,' I said.

'Yeah, but you bein' a dick and all.'

'I don't have a licence to threaten people I know nothing about.'

'I'm goin' to tell her I been in to see you. I don't have to say it's her. Just that you're workin' on it.'

'I wouldn't if I were you. If you mention my name she may call me up. If she does that, I'll tell her the facts.'

She stood up and slammed her shabby bag against her stomach. 'You're no gentleman,' she said shrilly.

'Where does it say I have to be?'

She went out mumbling.

After lunch I had Mr Simpson W. Edelweiss. He had a card to prove it. He was manager of a sewing machine agency. He was a small tired-looking man about forty-eight to fifty, small hands and feet, wearing a brown suit with sleeves too long, and a stiff white collar behind a purple tie with black diamonds on it. He sat on the edge of the chair without fidgeting and looked at me out of sad black eyes. His hair was black too and thick and rough without a sign of grey in it that I could see. He had a clipped moustache with a reddish tone. He could have passed for thirty-five if you didn't look at the backs of his hands.

'Call me Simp,' he said. 'Everybody else does. I got it coming. I'm a Jewish man married to a Gentile woman, twenty-four years of age, beautiful. She run away a couple of times before.'

He got out a photo of her and showed it to me. She might have been beautiful to him. To me she was a big, sloppy-looking cow of a woman with a weak mouth.

'What's your trouble, Mr Edelweiss? I don't do divorce business.' I tried to give him back the photo. He waved it away. 'The client is always mister to me,' I added. 'Until he has told me a few dozen lies anyway.'

He smiled. 'Lies I got no use for. It's not a divorce matter. I just want Mabel back again. But she don't come back until I find her. Maybe it's a kind of game with her.'

He told me about her, patiently, without rancour. She drank, she played around, she wasn't a very good wife by his standards, but he could have been brought up too strict. She had a heart as big as a house, he said, and he loved her. He didn't kid himself he was any dreamboat, just a steady worker bringing home the pay-cheque. They had a joint bank account. She had drawn it all out, but he was prepared for that. He had a pretty good idea who she had lit out with, and if he was right the man would clean her out and leave her stranded.

'Name of Kerrigan,' he said. 'Monro Kerrigan. I don't aim to knock the Catholics. There is plenty of bad Jews too. This Kerrigan is a barber when he works. I ain't knocking barbers either. But a lot of them are drifters and horse players. Not real steady.'

'Won't you hear from her when she is cleaned out?'

'She gets awful ashamed. She might hurt herself.'

'It's a "Missing Persons" job, Mr Edelweiss. You should go down and make a report.'

'No. I'm not knocking the police, but I don't want it that way. Mabel would be humiliated.'

The world seemed to be full of people Mr Edelweiss was not knocking. He put some money on the desk.

'Two hundred dollars,' he said. 'Down payment. I'd rather do it my way.'

'It will happen again,' I said.

'Sure.' He shrugged and spread his hands gently. 'But twenty-four years old and me almost fifty. How could it be different? She'll settle down after a while. Trouble is, no kids. She can't have kids. A Jew likes to have a family. So Mabel knows that. She's humiliated.'

'You're a very forgiving man, Mr Edelweiss.'

'Well, I ain't a Christian,' he said. 'And I'm not knocking Christians, you understand. But with me it's a real. I don't just say it. I do it. Oh, I almost forgot the most important.'

He got out a picture postcard and pushed it across the desk after the money. 'From Honolulu she sends it. Money goes fast in Honolulu. One of my uncles had a jewellery business there. Retired now. Lives in Seattle.'

I picked the photo up again. 'I'll have to farm this one out,' I told him. 'And I'll have to have this copied.'

'I could hear you saying that, Mr Marlowe, before I got here. So I come prepared.' He took out an envelope and it contained five more prints. 'I got Kerrigan too, but only a snapshot.' He went into another pocket and gave me another envelope. I looked at Kerrigan. He had a smooth dishonest face that did not surprise me. Three copies of Kerrigan.

Mr Simpson W. Edelweiss gave me another card which had his name, his residence, his telephone number. He said he hoped it would not cost too much but that he would respond at once to any demand for further funds and he hoped to hear from me.

'Two hundred ought to pretty near do it if she's still in Honolulu,' I said. 'What I need now is a detailed physical description of both parties that I can put into a telegram. Height, weight, age, colouring, any noticeable scars or other identifying marks, what clothes she was wearing and had with her, and how much money was in the account she cleaned out. If you've been through this before, Mr Edelweiss, you will know what I want.'

'I got a peculiar feeling about this Kerrigan. Uneasy.'

I spent another half-hour milking him and writing things down. Then he stood up quietly, shook hands quietly, bowed, and left the office quietly.

'Tell Mabel everything is fine,' he said as he went out.

It turned out to be routine. I sent a wire to an agency in Honolulu and followed it with an airmail containing the photos and whatever information I had left out of the wire. They found her working as a chambermaid's helper in a luxury hotel, scrubbing bathtubs and bathroom floors and so on. Kerrigan had done just what Mr Edelweiss expected, cleaned her out while she was asleep and skipped, leaving her stuck with the hotel bill. She pawned a ring which Kerrigan couldn't have taken without violence, and got enough out of it to pay the hotel but not enough to buy her way home. So Edelweiss hopped a plane and went after her.

He was too good for her. I sent him a bill for twenty dollars and the cost of a long telegram. The Honolulu agency grabbed the two hundred. With a portrait of Madison in my office safe I could afford to be underpriced.

So passed a day in the life of a P.I. Not exactly a typical day but not totally untypical either. What makes a man stay in it nobody knows. You don't get rich, you don't often have much fun. Sometimes you get beaten up or shot at or tossed into the jailhouse. Once in a long while you get dead. Every other month you decide to give it up and find some sensible occupation while you still walk without shaking your head. Then the door buzzer rings and you open the inner door to the waiting-room and there stands a new face with a new problem, a new load of grief, and a small piece of money.

'Come in, Mr Thingummy. What can I do for you?'

There must be a reason.

Three days later in the shank of the afternoon Eileen Wade called me up, and asked me to come round to the house for a drink the next evening. They were having a few friends in for cocktails. Roger would like to see me and thank me adequately. And would I please send in a bill?

'You don't owe me anything, Mrs Wade. What little I did I got paid for.'

'I must have looked very silly acting Victorian about it,' she said. 'A kiss doesn't seem to mean much nowadays. You will come, won't you?'

'I guess so. Against my better judgement.'

'Roger is quite well again. He's working.'

'Good.'

'You sound very solemn today. I guess you take life pretty seriously.'

'Now and then. Why?'

She laughed very gently and said good-bye and hung up. I sat there for a while taking life seriously. Then I tried to think of something so that I could have a great big laugh. Neither way worked, so I got Terry Lennox's letter of farewell out of the safe and re-read it. It reminded me that I had never gone to Victor's for that gimlet he asked me to drink for him. It was just about the right time of day for the bar to be quiet, the way he would have liked it himself, if he had been around to go with me. I thought of him with a vague sadness and with a puckering bitterness too. When I got to Victor's I almost kept going. Almost, but not quite. I had too much of his money. He had made a fool of me but he had paid well for the privilege.

22

It was so quiet in Victor's that you almost heard the temperature drop as you came in at the door. On a bar stool a woman in a black tailor-made, which couldn't at that time of year have been anything but some synthetic fabric like orlon, was sitting alone with a pale greenish coloured drink in front of her and smoking a cigarette in a long jade holder. She had that fine-drawn, intense look that is sometimes neurotic, sometimes sex-hungry, and sometimes just the result of drastic dieting.

I sat down two stools away and the barkeep nodded to me, but didn't smile.

'A gimlet,' I said. 'No bitters.'

He put the little napkin in front of me and kept looking at me. 'You know something,' he said in a pleased voice. 'I heard you and your friend talking one night and I got me in a bottle of that Rose's Lime Juice. Then you didn't come back any more and I only opened it tonight.'

'My friend left town,' I said. 'A double if it's all right with you. And thanks for taking the trouble.'

He went away. The woman in black gave me a quick glance, then looked down into her glass. 'So few people drink them around here,' she said so quietly that I didn't realize at first she was speaking to me. Then she looked my way again. She had very large dark eyes. She had the reddest fingernails I had ever seen. But she didn't look like a pick-up and there was no trace of come-on in her voice. 'Gimlets, I mean.'

'A fellow taught me to like them,' I said.

'He must be English.'

'Why?'

'The lime juice. It's as English as boiled fish with that awful anchovy sauce that looks as if the cook had bled into it. That's how they got called limeys. The English—not the fish.'

'I thought it was more a tropical drink, hot weather stuff. Malaya or some place like that.'

'You might be right.' She turned away again.

The bartender set the drink in front of me. With the lime juice it has a sort of pale-greenish-yellowish, misty look. I tasted it. It was both sweet and sharp at the same time. The woman in black watched me. Then she lifted her own glass towards me. We both drank. Then I knew hers was the same drink.

The next move was routine, so I didn't make it. I just sat there. 'He wasn't English,' I said after a moment. 'I guess maybe he had been there during the war. We used to come in here once in a while, early like now. Before the mob started boiling.'

'It's a pleasant hour,' she said. 'In a bar almost the only pleasant hour.' She emptied her glass. 'Perhaps I knew your friend,' she said. 'What was his name?'

I didn't answer her right away. I lit a cigarette and watched her tap the stub of hers out of the jade holder and fit another in its place. I reached across with a lighter. 'Lennox,' I said.

She thanked me for the light and gave me a brief searching glance. Then she nodded. 'Yes, I knew him very well. Perhaps a little too well.'

The barkeep drifted over and glanced at my glass. 'A couple more of the same,' I said. 'In a booth.'

I got down off the stool and stood waiting. She might or might not blow me down. I didn't particularly care. Once in a while in this much too sex-conscious country a man and a woman can meet and talk without dragging bedrooms into it. This could be it, or she could just think I was on the make. If so, the hell with her.

She hesitated, but not for long. She gathered up a pair of black gloves and a black suede bag with a gold frame and clasp and walked across into a corner booth and sat down without a word. I sat down across the small table.

'My name is Marlowe.'

'Mine is Linda Loring,' she said calmly. 'A bit of a sentimentalist, aren't you, Mr Marlowe?'

'Because I came here to drink a gimlet? How about yourself?'

'I might have a taste for them.'

'So might I. But it would be a little too much coincidence.'

She smiled at me vaguely. She had emerald ear-rings and an emerald lapel pin. They looked like real stones because of the way they were cut—flat with bevelled edges. And even in the dim light of a bar they had an inner glow.

'So you're the man,' she said.

The bar waiter brought the drinks over and set them down. When he went away I said: 'I'm a fellow who knew Terry Lennox, liked him, and had an occasional drink with him. It was kind of a side deal, an accidental friendship. I never went to his home or knew his wife. I saw her once in a parking lot.'

'There was a little more to it than that, wasn't there?'

She reached for her glass. She had an emerald ring set in a nest of diamonds. Beside it a thin platinum band said she was married. I put her in the seond half of the thirties, early in the second half.

'Maybe,' I said. 'The guy bothered me. He still does. How about you?'

She leaned on an elbow and looked up at me without any particular expression. 'I said I knew him rather too well. Too well to think it mattered much what happened to him. He had a rich wife who gave him all the luxuries. All she asked in return was to be left alone.'

'Seems reasonable,' I said.

'Don't be sarcastic, Mr Marlowe. Some women are like that. They can't help it. It wasn't as if he didn't know in the beginning. If he had to get proud, the door was open. He didn't have to kill her.'

'I agree with you.'

She straightened up and looked hard at me. Her lip curled. 'So he ran away and, if what I hear is true, you helped him. I suppose you feel proud about that.'

'Not me,' I said. 'I just did it for the money.'

'That is not amusing, Mr Marlowe. Frankly I don't know why I sit here drinking with you.'

'That's easily changed, Mrs Loring.' I reached for my glass and dropped the contents down the hatch. 'I thought perhaps you could tell me something about Terry that I didn't know. I'm not interested in speculating why Terry Lennox beat his wife's face to a bloody sponge.'

'That's a pretty brutal way to put it,' she said angrily.

'You don't like the words? Neither do I. And I wouldn't be here drinking a gimlet if I believed he did anything of the sort.'

She stared. After a moment she said slowly: 'He killed himself and left a full confession. What more do you want?'

'He had a gun,' I said. 'In Mexico that might be enough excuse for some jittery cop to pour lead into him. Plenty of American police have done their killings the same way—some of them through doors that didn't open fast enough to suit them. As for the confession, I haven't seen it.'

'No doubt the Mexican police faked it,' she said tartly.

'They wouldn't know how, not in a little place like Otatoclan. No, the confession is probably real enough, but it doesn't prove he killed his wife. Not to me anyway. All it proves to me is that he didn't see any way out. In a spot like that a certain sort of man—you can call him weak or soft or sentimental if it amuses you—might decide to save some other people from a lot of very painful publicity.'

'That's fantastic,' she said. 'A man doesn't kill himself or deliberately get himself killed to save a little scandal. Sylvia was already dead. As for her sister and her father—they could take care of themselves very efficiently. People with enough money, Mr Marlowe, can always protect themselves.'

'Okay, I'm wrong about the motive. Maybe I'm wrong all down the line. A minute ago you were mad at me. You want me to leave now—so you can drink *your* gimlet?'

Suddenly she smiled. 'I'm sorry. I'm beginning to think you are sincere. What I thought then was that you were trying to justify yourself, for more than Terry. I don't think you are, somehow.'

'I'm not. I did something foolish and I got the works for it. Up to a point anyway. I don't deny that his confession saved me a lot worse. If they had brought him back and tried him, I guess they would have hung one on me too. The least it would have cost me would have been far more money than I could afford.'

'Not to mention your licence,' she said dryly.

'Maybe. There was a time when any cop with a hangover could get me busted. It's a little different now. You get a hearing before a commission of the state licensing authority. Those people are not too crazy about the city police.'

She tasted her drink and said slowly: 'All things considered, don't you think it was best the way it was? No trial, no sensational headlines, no mud-slinging just to sell newspapers without the slightest regard for truth or fair play or for the feelings of innocent people.'

'Didn't I just say so? And you said it was fantastic.'

She leaned back and put her head against the upper curve of the padding on the back of the booth. 'Fantastic that Terry Lennox should have killed himself just to achieve that. Not fantastic that it was better for all parties that there should be no trial.'

'I need another drink,' I said, and waved at the waiter. 'I feel an icy breath on the back of my neck. Could you by any chance be related to the Potter family, Mrs Loring?'

'Sylvia Lennox was my sister,' she said simply.'I thought you would know.'

The waiter drifted over and I gave him an urgent message. Mrs Loring shook her head and said she didn't want anything more. When the waiter took off I said:

'With the hush old man Potter—excuse me, Mr Harlan Potter—put on this affair, I would be lucky to know for sure that Terry's wife even had a sister.'

'Surely, you exaggerate. My father is hardly that powerful, Mr Marlowe—and certainly not that ruthless. I'll admit he does have very old-fashioned ideas about his personal privacy. He never gives interviews even to his own newspapers. He is never photographed, he never makes speeches, he travels mostly by car or in his own plane with his own crew. But he is quite human for all that. He liked Terry. He said Terry was a gentleman twenty-four hours a day instead of for the fifteen minutes between the time the guests arrive and the time they feel their first cocktail.'

'He slipped a little at the end. Terry did.'

The waiter trotted up with my third gimlet. I tried it for flavour and then sat there with a finger on the edge of the round base of the glass.

'Terry's death was quite a blow to him, Mr Marlowe. And you're getting sarcastic again. Please don't. Father knew it would all look far too neat to some people. He would much rather Terry had just disappeared. If Terry had asked him for help, I think he would have given it.'

'Oh no, Mrs Loring. His own daughter had been murdered.'

She made an irritable motion and eyed me coldly.

'This is going to sound pretty blunt, I'm afraid. Father had written my sister off long ago. When they met he barely spoke to her. If he expressed himself, which he hasn't and won't, I feel sure he would be just as doubtful about Terry as you are. But once Terry was dead, what did it matter? They could have been killed in a plane crash or a fire or a highway accident. If she had to die, it was the best possible time for her to die. In another ten years she would have been a sex-ridden hag like some of these frightful women you see at Hollywood parties, or used to a few years back. The dregs of the international set.'

All of a sudden I got mad, for no good reason. I stood up and looked over the booth. The next one was still empty. In the one beyond a guy was reading a paper all by himself, quietly. I sat down with a bump, pushed my glass out of the way and leaned across the table. I had sense enough to keep my voice down.

'For hell's sake, Mrs Loring, what are you trying to sell me? That Harlan Potter is such a sweet, lovely character he wouldn't dream of using his influence on a political D.A. to drop the blanket on a murder investigation so that the murder was never really investigated at all? That he had doubts about Terry's guilt but didn't let anyone lift a finger to find out who was really the killer? That he didn't use the political power of his newspapers and his bank account and the nine hundred guys who would trip over their chins trying to guess what he wanted done before he knew himself? That he didn't arrange it so that a tame lawyer and nobody else, nobody from the D.A.'s office or the city cops, went down to Mexico to make sure Terry actually had put a slug in his head instead of being knocked off by some Indian with a hot gun just for kicks? Your old man is worth a hundred million bucks, Mrs Loring. I wouldn't know just how he got it, but I know damn well he didn't get it without building himself a pretty far-reaching organization. He's no softie. He's a hard, tough man. You've got to be in these days to make that kind of money. And you do business with some funny people. You may not meet them or shake hands with them, but they are there on the fringe doing business with you.'

'You're a fool,' she said angrily. 'I've had enough of you.'

'Oh sure. I don't make the kind of music you like to hear. Let me tell you something. Terry talked to your old man the night Sylvia died. What about? What did your old man say to him? "Just run on down to Mexico and shoot yourself, old boy. Let's keep this in the family. I know my daughter is a tramp and that any one of a dozen drunken bastards might have blown his top and pushed her pretty face down her throat for her. But that's incidental, old boy. The guy will be sorry when he sobers up. You've had it soft and now is the time you pay back. What we want is to keep the fair Potter name as sweet as mountain lilac. She married you because she needed a front. She needs it worse than ever now she's dead. And you're it. If you can get lost and stay lost, fine. But if you get found, you check out. See you in the morgue."'

'Do you really think,' the woman in black asked with dry ice in her voice, 'that my father talks like that?'

I leaned back and laughed unpleasantly. 'We could polish up the dialogue a little if that helps.'

She gathered her stuff together and slid along the seat. 'I'd like to give you a word of warning,' she said slowly and very carefully, 'a very simple word of warning. If you think my father is that kind of man and if you go around broadcasting the kind of thoughts you have just expressed to me, your career in this city in your business or in any business is apt to be extremely short and terminated very suddenly.'

'Perfect, Mrs Loring. Perfect. I get it from the law, I get it from the hoodlum element, I get it from the carriage trade. The words change, but the meaning is the same. Lay off. I came in here to drink a gimlet because a man asked me to. Now look at me. I'm practically in the boneyard.'

She stood up and nodded briefly. 'Three gimlets. Doubles. Perhaps you're drunk.'

I dropped too much money on the table and stood up beside her. 'You had one and a half, Mrs Loring. Why even that much? Did a man ask you too, or was it all your own idea? Your own tongue got a little loose.'

'Who knows, Mr Marlowe? Who knows? Who really knows anything? There's a man over there at the bar watching us. Would it be anyone you know?'

I looked around, surprised that she had noticed. A lean dark character sat on the end stool nearest the door.

'His name is Chick Agostino,' I said. 'He's a gun toter for a gambling boy named Menendez. Let's knock him down and jump on him.'

'You certainly are drunk,' she said quickly and started to walk. I went after her. The man on the stool swung around and looked to his front. When I came abreast I stepped up behind him and reached in under both his arms quickly. Maybe I *was* a little drunk.

He swung around angrily and slid off the stool. 'Watch it, kiddo,' he snarled. Out of the corner of my eye I saw that she had stopped just inside the door to glance back.

'No guns, Mr Agostino? How reckless of you. It's almost dark. What if you should run into a tough midget?'

'Scram!' he said savagely.

'Aw, you stole that line from the *New Yorker*.'

His mouth worked but he didn't move. I left him and followed Mrs Loring out through the door into the space under the awning. A grey-haired chauffeur stood there talking to the kid from the parking lot. He touched his cap and went off and came back with a flossy Cadillac limousine. He opened the door and Mrs Loring got in. He shut the door as though he was putting down the lid of a jewel box. He went around the car to the driver's seat.

She ran the window down and looked out at me, half smiling. 'Good night, Mr Marlowe. It's been nice—or has it?'

'We had quite a fight.'

'You mean you had—and mostly with yourself.'

'It usually is. Good night, Mrs Loring. You don't live around here, do you?'

'Not exactly. I live in Idle Valley. At the far end of the lake. My husband is a doctor.'

'Would you happen to know any people named Wade?'

She frowned. 'Yes, I know the Wades. Why?'

'Why do I ask? They're the only people in Idle Valley that I know.'

'I see. Well, good night again, Mr Marlowe.'

She leaned back in the seat and the Cadillac purred politely and slid away into the traffic along the Strip.

Turning, I almost bumped into Chick Agostino.

'Who's the doll?' he sneered. 'And next time you crack wise, be missing.'

'Nobody that would want to know you,' I said.

'Okay, bright boy. I got the licence number. Mendy likes to know little things like that.'

The door of a car banged open and a man about seven feet high and four feet wide jumped out of it, took one look at Agostino, then one long stride, and grabbed him by the throat with one hand.

'How many times I gotta tell you cheap hoods not to hang around where I eat?' he roared.

He shook Agostino and hurled him across the sidewalk against the wall. Chick crumpled up, coughing.

'Next time,' the enormous man yelled. 'I sure as hell put the blast on you, and believe me, boy, you'll be holding a gun when they pick you up.'

Chick shook his head and said nothing. The big man gave me a raking glance and grinned. 'Nice night,' he said and strolled into Victor's.

I watched Chick straighten himself out and regain some of his composure. 'Who's your buddy?' I asked him.

'Big Willie Magoon,' he said thickly. 'A vice squad bimbo. He thinks he's tough.'

'You mean he isn't sure?' I asked him politely.

He looked at me emptily and walked away. I got my car out of the lot and drove home. In Hollywood anything can happen, anything at all.

23

A low-slung Jaguar swept around the hill in front of me and slowed down so as not to bathe me in the granite dust from the half-mile of neglected paving at the entrance to Idle Valley. It seemed they wanted it left that way to discourage the Sunday drivers, spoilt by drifting along on super-highways. I caught a glimpse of a bright scarf and a pair of sun goggles. A hand waved at me casually, neighbour to neighbour. Then the dust slid across the road and added itself to the white film already well spread over the scrub and sunbaked grass. Then I was around the outcrop and the paving started up in proper shape and everything was smooth and cared for. Live oaks clustered towards the road, as if they were curious to see who went by, and sparrows with rosy heads hopped about pecking at things only a sparrow would think worth pecking at.

Then there were a few cottonwoods but no eucalyptus. Then a thick

growth of Carolina poplars screening a white house. Then a girl walking a
horse along the shoulder of the road. She had trousers on and a loud shirt
and she was chewing on a twig. The horse looked hot but not lathered and
the girl was crooning to him gently. Beyond a field-stone wall a gardener
was guiding a power lawnmower over a huge undulating lawn that ended far
back in the portico of a Williamsburg Colonial mansion, the large *de luxe*
size. Somewhere someone was playing left-handed exercises on a grand
piano.

Then all this wheeled away and the glisten of the lake showed hot and
bright and I began to watch numbers on gate-posts. I had seen the Wades'
house only once and in the dark. It wasn't as big as it had looked by night.
The driveway was full of cars, so I parked on the side of the road and walked
in. A Mexican butler in a white coat opened the door for me. He was a
slender, neat, good-looking Mexican and his coat fitted him elegantly and
he looked like a Mexican who was getting fifty a week and not killing himself
with hard work.

He said: '*Buenas tardes señor*,' and grinned as if he had put one over. '*Su
nombre de usted, por favor?*'

'Marlowe,' I said, 'and who are you trying to upstage, Candy? We talked
on the phone, remember?'

He grinned and I went in. It was the same old cocktail party, everybody
talking too loud, nobody listening, everybody hanging on for dear life to a
mug of the juice, eyes very bright, cheeks flushed or pale and sweaty
according to the amount of alcohol consumed and the capacity of the
individual to handle it. Then Eileen Wade materialized beside me in a pale
blue something which did her no harm. She had a glass in her hand but it
didn't look as if it was more than a prop.

'I'm so glad you could come,' she said gravely. 'Roger wants to see you in
his study. He hates cocktail parties. He's working.'

'With this racket going on?'

'It never seems to bother him. Candy will get you a drink—or if you'd
rather go to the bar—'

'I'll do that,' I said. 'Sorry about the other night.'

She smiled. 'I think you apologized already. It was nothing.'

'The hell it was nothing.'

She kept the smile long enough to nod and turn and walk away. I spotted
the bar over in the corner by some very large french doors. It was one of
those things you push around. I was half-way across the room, trying not to
bump anybody, when a voice said: 'Oh, Mr Marlowe.'

I turned and saw Mrs Loring on a couch beside a prissy-looking man in
rimless cheaters with a smear on his chin that might have been a goatee. She
had a drink in her hand and looked bored. He sat still with his arms folded
and scowled.

I went over there. She smiled at me and gave me her hand. 'This is my
husband, Dr Loring. Mr Philip Marlowe, Edward.'

The guy with the goatee gave me a brief look and a still briefer nod.
He didn't move otherwise. He seemed to be saving his energy for better
things.

'Edward is very tired,' Linda Loring said. 'Edward is always very tired.'

'Doctors often are,' I said. 'Can I get you a drink, Mrs Loring. Or you,
Doctor?'

'She's had enough,' the man said without looking at either of us. 'I don't drink. The more I see of people who do, the more glad I am that I don't.'

'Come back, little Sheba,' Mrs Loring said dreamily.

He swung around and did a take. I got away from there and made it to the bar. In the company of her husband Linda Loring seemed like a different person. There was an edge to her voice and a sneer in her expression which she hadn't used on me even when she was angry.

Candy was behind the bar. He asked me what I would drink.

'Nothing right now, thanks. Mr Wade wants to see me.'

'*Es muy occupado, señor*. Very busy.'

I didn't think I was going to like Candy. When I just looked at him he added: 'But I go see. *De pronto, señor.*'

He threaded his way delicately through the mob and was back in no time at all. 'Okay, chum, let's go,' he said cheerfully.

I followed him across the room the long way of the house. He opened a door, I went through, he shut it behind me, and a lot of the noise was dimmed. It was a corner room, big and cool and quiet, with french doors and roses outside and an air-conditioner set in a window to one side. I could see the lake, and I could see Wade lying flat out on a long, blond leather couch. A big bleached wood desk had a typewriter on it and there was a pile of yellow paper beside the typewriter.

'Good of you to come, Marlowe,' he said lazily. 'Park yourself. Did you have a drink or two?'

'Not yet.' I sat down and looked at him. He still looked a bit pale and pinched. 'How's the working going?'

'Fine, except that I get tired too quick. Pity a four-day drunk is so painful to get over. I often do my best work after one. In my racket it's so easy to tighten up and get all stiff and wooden. Then the stuff is no good. When it's good it comes easy. Anything you have read or heard to the contrary is a lot of mish-mash.'

'Depends who the writer, is, maybe,' I said. 'It didn't come easy to Flaubert, and his stuff is good.'

'Okay,' Wade said, sitting up. 'So you have read Flaubert, and that makes you an intellectual, a critic, a savant of the literary world.' He rubbed his forehead. 'I'm on the wagon and I hate it. I hate everybody with a drink in his hand. I've got to go out there and smile at those creeps. Every damn one of them knows I'm an alcoholic. So they wonder what I'm running away from. Some Freudian bastard has made that a commonplace. Every ten-year-old knows it by now. If I had a ten-year-old kid, which God forbid, the brat would be asking me, "What are you running away from when you get drunk, daddy?"'

'The way I got it, all this was rather recent,' I said.

'It's got worse, but I was always a hard man with a bottle. When you're young and in hard condition you can absorb a lot of punishment. When you are pushing forty you don't snap back the same way.'

I leaned back and lit a cigarette. 'What did you want to see me about?'

'What do *you* think I'm running away from, Marlowe?'

'No idea. I don't have enough information. Besides, everybody is running away from something.'

'Not everybody gets drunk. What are *you* running away from? Your youth or a guilty conscience or the knowledge that you're a small-time operator in a small-time business?'

'I get it,' I said. 'You need somebody to insult. Fire away, chum. When it begins to hurt I'll let you know.'

He grinned and rumpled his thick curly hair. He speared his chest with a forefinger. 'You're looking right at a small-time operator in a small-time business, Marlowe. All writers are punks and I am one of the punkest. I've written twelve best-sellers, and if I ever finish that stack of magoozlum on the desk there I may possibly have written thirteen. And not a damn one of them worth the powder to blow it to hell. I have a lovely home in a highly restricted neighbourhood that belongs to a highly restricted multi-millionaire. I have a lovely wife who loves me and a lovely publisher who loves me and I love me the best of all. I'm an egotistical son of a bitch, a literary prostitute or pimp—choose your own word—and an all-round heel. So what can you do for me?'

'Well, what?'

'Why don't you get sore?'

'Nothing to get sore about. I'm just listening to you hate yourself. It's boring but it doesn't hurt my feelings.'

He laughed roughly. 'I like you,' he said. 'Let's have a drink.'

'Not in here, chum. Not you and me alone. I don't care to watch you take the first one. Nobody can stop you and I don't guess anyone would try. But I don't have to help.'

He stood up. 'We don't have to drink in here. Let's go outside and glance at a choice selection of the sort of people you get to know when you make enough lousy money to live where they live.'

'Look,' I said. 'Shove it. Knock it off. They're no different from anybody else.'

'Yeah,' he said tightly, 'but they ought to be. If they're not, what use are they? They're the class of the county and they're no better than a bunch of truckdrivers full of cheap whisky. Not as good.'

'Knock it off,' I said again. 'You want to get boiled, get boiled. But don't take it out on a crowd that can get boiled without having to lie up with Dr Verringer or get loose in the head and throw their wives down the stairs.'

'Yeah,' he said, and he was suddenly calm and thoughtful. 'You pass the test, chum. How about coming to live here for a while? You could do me a lot of good just being here.'

'I don't see how.'

'But I do. Just by being here. Would a thousand a month interest you? I'm dangerous when I'm drunk. I don't want to be dangerous and I don't want to be drunk.'

'I couldn't stop you.'

'Try it for three months. I'd finish the damn book and then go far off for a while. Lie up some place in the Swiss mountains and get clean.'

'The book, huh? Do you have to have the money?'

'No. I just have to finish something I started. If I don't I'm through. I'm asking you as a friend. You did more than that for Lennox.'

I stood up and walked over close to him and gave him a hard stare. 'I got Lennox killed, mister. I got him killed.'

'Phooey. Don't go soft on me, Marlowe.' He put the edge of his hand against his throat. 'I'm up to here in the soft babies.'

'Soft?' I asked. 'Or just kind?'

He stepped back and stumbled against the edge of the couch, but didn't lose his balance.

'The hell with you,' he said smoothly. 'No deal. I don't blame you, of course. There's something I want to know, that I have to know. You don't know what it is and I'm not sure I know myself. All I'm positive of is that there is something, and I have to know it.'

'About who? Your wife?'

He moved his lips one over the other. 'I think it's about me,' he said. 'Let's go get that drink.'

He walked to the door and threw it open and we went out.

If he had been trying to make me uncomfortable, he had done a first-class job.

24

When he opened the door the buzz from the living-room exploded into our faces. It seemed louder than before, if possible. About two drinks louder. Wade said hello here and there and people seemed glad to see him. But by that time they would have been glad to see Pittsburgh Phil with his custom-built ice-pick. Life was just one great big vaudeville show.

On the way to the bar we came face to face with Dr Loring and his wife. The doctor stood up and stepped forward to face Wade. He had a look on his face that was almost sick with hatred.

'Nice to see you, Doctor,' Wade said amiably. 'Hi, Linda. Where have you been keeping yourself lately? No, I guess that was a stupid question. I—'

'Mr Wade,' Loring said in a voice that had a tremor to it, 'I have something to say to you. Something very simple, and I hope very conclusive. Stay away from my wife.'

Wade looked at him curiously. 'Doctor, you're tired. And you don't have a drink. Let me get you one.'

'I don't drink, Mr Wade. As you very well know. I am here for one purpose and I have expressed that purpose.'

'Well, I guess I get your point,' Wade said, still amiable. 'And since you are a guest in my house, I have nothing to say except that I think you are a little off the beam.'

There had been a drop in the talk near by. The boys and girls were all ears. Big production. Dr Loring took a pair of gloves out of his pocket, straightened them, took hold of one by the finger end, and swung it hard against Wade's face.

Wade didn't bat an eye. 'Pistols and coffee at dawn?' he asked quietly.

I looked at Linda Loring. She was flushed with anger. She stood up slowly and faced the doctor.

'Dear God, what a ham you are, darling. Stop acting like a damn fool, will you, darling? Or would you rather stick around until somebody slaps *your* face?'

Loring swung around to her and raised the gloves. Wade stepped in front of him. 'Take it easy, Doc. Around here we only hit our wives in private.'

'If you are speaking for yourself, I am well aware of it,' Loring sneered. 'And I don't need lessons in manners from you.'

'I only take promising pupils,' Wade said. 'Sorry you have to leave so soon.' He raised his voice. 'Candy! *Que de Doctor Loring salga de aqui en el acto!*' He swung back to Loring. 'In case you don't speak Spanish, Doctor, that means the door is over there.' He pointed.

Loring stared at him without moving. 'I have warned you, Mr Wade,' he said icily. 'And a number of people have heard me. I shall not warn you again.'

'Don't,' Wade said curtly. 'But if you do, make it on neutral territory. Gives me a little more freedom of action. Sorry, Linda. But you married him.' He rubbed his cheek gently where the heavy end of the glove had hit him. Linda Loring was smiling bitterly. She shrugged.

'We are leaving,' Loring said. 'Come, Linda.'

She sat down again and reached for her glass. She gave her husband a glance of quiet contempt. 'You are,' she said. 'You have a number of calls to make, remember.'

'You are leaving with me,' he said furiously.

She turned her back on him. He reached suddenly and took hold of her arm. Wade took him by the shoulder and spun him around.

'Take it easy, Doc. You can't win them all.'

'Take your hand off me!'

'Sure, just relax,' Wade said. 'I have a good idea, Doctor. Why don't you see a good doctor?'

Somebody laughed loudly. Loring tensed like an animal all set to spring. Wade sensed it and neatly turned his back and moved away. Which left Dr Loring holding the bag. If he went after Wade, he would look sillier than he looked now. There was nothing for him to do but leave, and he did it. He marched quickly across the room staring straight in front of him to where Candy was holding the door open. He went out. Candy shut the door, wooden-faced, and went back to the bar. I went over there and asked for some Scotch. I didn't see where Wade went to. He just disappeared. I didn't see Eileen either. I turned my back on the room and let them sizzle while I drank my Scotch.

A small girl with mud-coloured hair and a band around her forehead popped up beside me and put a glass on the bar and bleated. Candy nodded and made her another drink.

The small girl turned to me. 'Are you interested in Communism?' she asked me. She was glassy-eyed and she was running a small red tongue along her lips as if looking for a crumb of chocolate. 'I think everyone ought to be,' she went on. 'But when you ask any of the men here they just want to paw you.'

I nodded and looked over my glass at her snub nose and sun-coarsened skin.

'Not that I mind too much if it's done nicely,' she told me, reaching for the fresh drink. She showed me her molars while she inhaled half of it.

'Don't rely on me,' I said.

'What's your name?'

'Marlowe.'

'With an "e" or not?'

'With.'

'Ah, Marlowe,' she intoned. 'Such a sad beautiful name.' She put her glass down damn nearly empty and closed her eyes and threw her head back and her arms out, almost hitting me in the eye. Her voice throbbed with emotion, saying:

> *'Was this the face that launch'd a thousand ships*
> *And burnt the topless towers of Ilium?*
> *Sweet Helen, make me immortal with a kiss.'*

She opened her eyes, grabbed her glass and winked at me. 'You were pretty good in there, chum. Been writing any poetry lately?'

'Not very much.'

'You can kiss me if you like,' she said coyly.

A guy in a shantung jacket and an open-neck shirt came up behind her and grinned at me over the top of her head. He had short red hair and a face like a collapsed lung. He was as ugly a guy as I ever saw. He patted the top of the little girl's head.

'Come on, Kitten. Time to go home.'

She rounded on him furiously. 'You mean you got to water those goddamned begonias again?' she yelled.

'Aw listen, Kitten—'

'Take your hands off me, you goddamned rapist,' she screamed and threw the rest of her drink in his face. The rest wasn't more than a teaspoonful and two lumps of ice.

'For Chrissake, baby, I'm your husband,' he yelled back, grabbing for a handkerchief and mopping his face. 'Get it? Your husband.'

She sobbed violently and threw herself into his arms. I stepped around them and got out of there. Every cocktail party is the same, even the dialogue.

The house was leaking guests out into the evening air now. Voices were fading, cars were starting, good-byes were bouncing around like rubber balls. I went to the french windows and out on to a flagged terrace. The ground sloped towards the lake which was as motionless as a sleeping cat. There was a short wooden pier down there with a row-boat tied to it by a white painter. Towards the far shore, which wasn't very far, a black water-hen was doing lazy curves, like a skater. They didn't seem to cause as much as a shallow ripple.

I stretched out on a padded aluminium chaise and lit a pipe and smoked peacefully and wondered what the hell I was doing there. Roger Wade seemed to have enough control to handle himself if he really wanted to. He had done all right with Loring. I wouldn't have been too surprised if he had hung one on Loring's sharp little chin. He would have been out of line by the rules, but Loring was much farther out of line.

If the rules mean anything at all any more, they mean that you don't pick a roomful of people as the spot to threaten a man and hit him across the face with a glove when your wife is standing right beside you and you are practically accusing her of a little double time. For a man still shaky from a hard bout with the hard stuff Wade had done all right. He had done more than all right. Of course I hadn't seen him drunk. I didn't know what he would be like drunk. I didn't even know that he was an alcoholic. There's a big difference. A man who drinks too much on occasion is still the same man as he was sober. An alcoholic, a real alcoholic, is not the same man at all. You can't predict anything about him for sure except that he will be someone you never met before.

Light steps sounded behind me and Eileen Wade came across the terrace and sat down beside me on the edge of a chaise.

'Well, what did you think?' she asked quietly.

'About the gentleman with the loose gloves?'

'Oh, no.' She frowned. Then she laughed. 'I hate people who make stagey scenes like that. Not that he isn't a fine doctor. He has played that scene with half the men in the valley. Linda Loring is no tramp. She doesn't look like one, talk like one, or behave like one. I don't know what makes Dr Loring behave as if she was.'

'Maybe he's a reformed drunk,' I said. 'A lot of them grow pretty puritanical.'

'It's possible,' she said, and looked towards the lake. 'This is a very peaceful place. One would think a writer would be happy here—if a writer is ever happy anywhere.' She turned to look at me. 'So you won't be persuaded to do what Roger asked.'

'There's no point in it, Mrs Wade. Nothing I could do. I've said all this before. I couldn't be sure of being around at the right time. I'd have to be around *all* the time. That's impossible, even if I had nothing else to do. If he went wild, for example, it would happen in a flash. And I haven't seen any indication that he does get wild. He seems pretty solid to me.'

She looked down at her hands. 'If he could finish his book, I think things would be much better.'

'I can't help him do that.'

She looked up and put her hands on the edge of the chaise beside her. She leaned forward a little. 'You can if he thinks you can. That's the whole point. Is it that you would find it distasteful to be a guest in our house and be paid for it?'

'He needs a psychiatrist, Mrs Wade. If you know one that isn't a quack.'

She looked startled. 'A psychiatrist? Why?'

I knocked the ashes out of my pipe and sat holding it, waiting for the bowl to get cooler before I put it away.

'You want an amateur opinion, here it is. He thinks he has a secret buried in his mind and he can't get at it. It may be a guilty secret about himself, it may be about someone else. He thinks that's what makes him drink, because he can't get at this thing. He probably thinks whatever happened, happened while he was drunk and he ought to find it wherever people go when they're drunk—really bad drunk, the way he gets. That's a job for a psychiatrist. So far, so good. If that is wrong, then he gets drunk because he wants to or can't help it, and the idea about the secret is just his excuse. He can't write his book, or anyway can't finish it. Because he gets drunk. That is, the assumption seems to be that he can't finish his book because he knocks himself out by drinking. It could be the other way around.'

'Oh, no,' she said. 'No. Roger has a great deal of talent. I feel quite sure that his best work is still to come.'

'I told you it was an amateur opinion. You said the other morning that he might have fallen out of love with his wife. That's something else that could go the other way around.'

She looked towards the house, then turned so that she had her back to it. I looked the same way. Wade was standing inside the doors, looking out at us. As I watched he moved behind the bar and reached for a bottle.

'There's no use interfering,' she said quickly. 'I never do. Never. I suppose you're right, Mr Marlowe. There just isn't anything to do but let him work it out of his system.'

The pipe was cool now and I put it away. 'Since we're groping around in the back of the drawer, how about that other way around?'

'I love my husband,' she said simply. 'Not as a young girl loves, perhaps. But I love him. A woman is only a young girl once. The man I loved then is dead. He died in the war. His name, strangely enough, had the same initials as yours. It doesn't matter now—except that sometimes I can't quite believe that he is dead. His body was never found. But that happened to many men.'

She gave me a searching look. 'Sometimes—not often, of course—when I go into a quiet cocktail lounge or the lobby of a good hotel at a dead hour, or along the deck of a liner early in the morning or very late at night, I think I may see him waiting for me in some shadowy corner.' She paused and dropped her eyes. 'It's very silly. I'm ashamed of it. We were very much in love—the wild, mysterious, improbable kind of love that never comes but once.'

She stopped talking and sat there in half a trance looking out over the lake. I looked back at the house again. Wade was standing just inside the open french doors with a glass in his hand. I looked back at Eileen. For her I wasn't there any more. I got up and went into the house. Wade stood there with the drink and the drink looked pretty heavy. And his eyes looked wrong.

'How you making out with my wife, Marlowe?' It was said with a twist of the mouth.

'No passes, if you mean it that way.'

'That's exactly the way I mean it. You got to kiss her the other night. Probably fancy yourself as a fast worker, but you're wasting your time, bud. Even if you had the right kind of polish.'

I tried to move around him but he blocked me with a solid shoulder. 'Don't hurry away, old man. We like you around. We get so few private dicks in our house.'

'I'm the one too many,' I said.

He hoisted the glass and drank from it. When he lowered it he leered at me.

'You ought to give yourself a little more time to build resistance,' I told him. 'Empty words, huh?'

'Okay, coach. Some little character builder, aren't you? You ought to have more sense than to try educating a drunk. Drunks don't educate, my friend. They disintegrate. And part of the process is a lot of fun.' He drank from the glass again, leaving it nearly empty. 'And part of it is damned awful. But if I may quote the scintillating words of the good Dr Loring, a bastardly bastard with a little black bag, stay away from my wife, Marlowe. Sure you go for her. They all do. You'd like to sleep with her. They all would. You'd like to share her dreams and sniff the rose of her memories. Maybe I would too. But there is nothing to share, chum—nothing, nothing, nothing. You're all alone in the dark.'

He finished his drink and turned the glass upside down.

'Empty like that, Marlowe. Nothing there at all. I'm the guy that knows.'

He put the glass on the edge of the bar and walked stiffly to the foot of the stairs. He made about a dozen steps up, holding on to the rail, and stopped and leaned against it. He looked down at me with a sour grin.

'Forgive the corny sarcasm, Marlowe. You're a nice guy. I wouldn't want anything to happen to you.'

'Anything like what?'

'Perhaps she didn't get around yet to that haunting magic of her first love, the guy that went missing in Norway. You wouldn't want to be missing, would you, chum? You're my own special private eye. You find me when I'm lost in the savage splendour of Sepulveda Canyon.' He moved the palm of his hand in a circular motion on the polished wood banister. 'It would hurt me to the quick if you got lost yourself. Like that character who hitched up with the limeys. He got so lost a man sometimes wonders if he ever existed. You figure she could have maybe just invented him to have a toy to play with?'

'How would I know?'

He looked down at me. There were deep lines between his eyes now and his mouth was twisted with bitterness.

'How would anybody know? Maybe she don't know herself. Baby's tired. Baby been playing too long with broken toys. Baby wants to go bye-bye.'

He went on up the stairs. I stood there until Candy came in and started tidying up around the bar, putting glasses on a tray, examining bottles to see what was left, paying no attention to me. Or so I thought. Then he said:

'*Señor*. One good drink left. Pity to waste him.' He held up a bottle.

'You drink it.'

'*Gracias, señor, no me gusta. Un vaso de cerveza, no más.* A glass of beer is my limit.'

'Wise man.'

'One lush in the house is enough,' he said, staring at me. 'I speak good English, not?'

'Sure, fine.'

'But I think Spanish. Sometimes I think with a knife. The boss is my guy. He don't need any help, hombre. I take care of him, see.'

'A great job you're doing, punk.'

'*Hijo de la flauta,*' he said between his white teeth. He picked up a loaded tray and swung it up on the edge of his shoulder and the flat of hand, bus boy style.

I walked to the door and let myself out, wondering how an expression meaning 'son of a flute' had come to be an insult in Spanish. I didn't wonder very long. I had too many other things to wonder about. Something more than alcohol was the matter with the Wade family. Alcohol was no more than a disguised reaction.

Later that night, between nine-thirty and ten, I called the Wades' number. After eight rings I hung up, but I had only just taken my hand off the instrument when it started to ring me. It was Eileen Wade.

'Someone just rang here,' she said. 'I had a sort of hunch it might be you. I was getting ready to take a shower.'

'It was me, but it wasn't important, Mrs Wade. He seemed a little woolly-headed when I left—Roger did. I guess maybe I feel a little responsibility for him by now.'

'He's quite all right,' she said. 'Fast asleep in bed. I think Dr Loring upset him more than he showed. No doubt he talked a lot of nonsense to you.'

'He said he was tired and wanted to go to bed. Pretty sensible, I thought.'

'If that is all he said, yes. Well, good night and thank you for calling, Mr Marlowe.'

'I didn't say it was all he said. I said he said it.'

There was a pause, then: 'Everyone gets fantastic ideas once in a while. Don't take Roger too seriously, Mr Marlowe. After all his imagination is rather highly developed. Naturally it would be. He shouldn't have had anything to drink so soon after the last time. Please try to forget all about it. I suppose he was rude to you among other things.'

'He wasn't rude to me. He made quite a lot of sense. Your husband is a guy who can take a long, hard look at himself and see what is there. It's not a very common gift. Most people go through life using up half their energy trying to protect a dignity they never had. Good night, Mrs Wade.'

She hung up and I set out the chess board. I filled a pipe, paraded the chessmen, and inspected them for French shaves and loose buttons, and played a championship tournament game between Gortchakoff and Meninkin, seventy-two moves to a draw, a prize specimen of the irresistible force meeting the immovable object, a battle without armour, a war without blood, and as elaborate a waste of human intelligence as you could find anywhere outside an advertising agency.

25

Nothing happened for a week except that I went about my business which just then didn't happen to be very much business. One morning George Peters of the Carne Organization called me up and told me he had happened to be down Sepulveda Canyon way and he had looked in on Dr Verringer's place just out of curiosity. But Dr Verringer was no longer there. Half a dozen teams of surveyors were mapping the tract for a subdivision. Those he spoke to had never even heard of Dr Verringer.

'The poor sucker got closed out on a trust deal,' Peters said. 'I checked. They gave him a grand for a quit claim just to save time and expense, and now somebody is going to make a million bucks a year, out of cutting the place up for residential property. That's the difference between crime and business. For business you gotta have capital. Sometimes I think it's the only difference.'

'A properly cynical remark,' I said, 'but big-time crime takes capital too.'

'And where does it come from, chum? Not from guys that hold up liquor stores. So long. See you soon.'

It was ten minutes to eleven on a Thursday night when Wade called me up. His voice was thick, almost gurgling, but I recognized it somehow. And I could hear short, hard, rapid breathing over the telephone.

'I'm in bad shape, Marlowe. Very bad. I'm slipping my anchor. Could you make it out here in a hurry?'

'Sure—but let me talk to Mrs Wade a minute.'

He didn't answer. There was a crashing sound, then a dead silence, then in a short while a kind of banging around. I yelled something into the phone without getting any answer. Time passed. Finally the light click of the receiver being replaced and the buzz of an open line.

In five minutes I was on the way. I made it in slightly over half an hour and I still don't know how. I went over the pass on wings and hit Ventura Boulevard with the light against me and made a left turn anyhow and dodged between trucks and generally made a damn fool of myself. I went through Encino at close to sixty with a spotlight on the outer edge of the parked cars so that it would freeze anyone with a notion to step out suddenly. I had the kind of luck you only get when you don't care. No cops, no sirens, no red flashers. Just visions of what might be happening in the Wade residence and not very pleasant visions. She was alone in the house with a drunken maniac, she was lying at the bottom of the stairs with her neck broken, she was behind a locked door and somebody was howling outside and trying to break it in, she was running down a moonlit road barefoot and a big buck Negro with a meat cleaver was chasing her.

It wasn't like that at all. When I swung the Olds into their driveway lights were on all over the house and she was standing in the open doorway with a cigarette in her mouth. I got out and walked over the flagstones to her. She had slacks on and a shirt with an open collar. She looked at me calmly. If there was any excitement around there I had brought it with me.

The first thing I said was as lousy as the rest of my behaviour. 'I thought you didn't smoke.'

'What? No, I don't usually.' She took the cigarette out and dropped it and stepped on it. 'Once in a long while. He called Dr Verringer.'

It was a remote placid voice, a voice heard at night over water. Completely relaxed.

'He couldn't,' I said. 'Dr Verringer doesn't live there any more. He called me.'

'Oh really? I just heard him telephoning and asking someone to come in a hurry. I thought it must be Dr Verringer.'

'Where is he now?'

'He fell down,' she said. 'He must have tipped the chair too far back. He's done it before. He cut his head on something. There's a little blood, not much.'

'Well, that's fine,' I said. 'We wouldn't want a whole lot of blood. Where is he now, I asked you.'

She looked at me solemnly. Then she pointed. 'Out there somewhere. By the edge of the road or in the bushes along the fence.'

I leaned forward and peered at her. 'Chrissake, didn't you look?' I decided by this time that she was in shock. Then I looked back across the lawn. I didn't see anything but there was heavy shadow near the fence.

'No, I didn't look,' she said quite calmly. 'You find him I've had all of it I can take. I've had more than I can take. You find him.'

She turned and walked back into the house, leaving the door open. She didn't walk very far. About a yard inside the door she just crumpled to the floor and lay there. I scooped her up and spread her out in one of two big davenports that faced each other across a long, blond cocktail table. I felt her pulse. It didn't seem very weak or unsteady. Her eyes were closed and the lids were blue. I left her there and went back out.

He was there all right, just as she had said. He was lying on his side in the shadow of the hibiscus. He had a fast, thumping pulse and his breathing was unnatural. Something on the back of his head was sticky. I spoke to him and shook him a little. I slapped his face a couple of times. He mumbled but didn't come to. I dragged him up into a sitting position and dragged one of his arms over my shoulder and heaved him up with my back turned to him and grabbed for a leg. I lost. He was as heavy as a block of cement. We both sat down on the grass and I took a short breather and tried again. Finally I got him hoisted into a fireman's lift position and ploughed across the lawn in the direction of the open front door. It seemed about the same distance as a round trip to Siam. The two steps of the porch were ten feet high. I staggered over to the couch and went down on my knees and rolled him off. When I straightened up again my spine felt as if it was cracked in at least three places.

Eileen Wade wasn't there any more. I had the room to myself. I was too bushed at the moment to care where anybody was. I sat down and looked at him and waited for some breath. Then I looked at his head. It was smeared with blood. His hair was sticky with it. It didn't look very bad but you never know with a head wound.

Then Eileen Wade was standing beside me, quietly looking down at him with that same remote expression.

'I'm sorry I fainted,' she said. 'I don't know why.'

'I guess we'd better call a doctor.'

'I telephoned Dr Loring. He is my doctor, you know. He didn't want to come.'

'Try somebody else then.'

'Oh, he's coming,' she said. 'He didn't want to. But he's coming as soon as he can manage.'

'Where's Candy?'

'This is his day off. Thursday. The cook and Candy have Thursdays off. It's the usual thing around here. Can you get him up to bed?'

'Not without help. Better get a rug or blanket. It's a warm night, but cases like this get pneumonia very easily.'

She said she would get a rug. I thought it was damn nice of her. But I wasn't thinking very intelligently. I was too bushed from carrying him.

We spread a steamer rug over him and in fifteen minutes Dr Loring came, complete with starched collar and rimless cheaters and the expression of a man who has been asked to clean up after the dog got sick.

He examined Wade's head. 'A superficial cut and bruises,' he said. 'No chance of concussion. I should say his breath would indicate his condition rather obviously.'

He reached for his hat. He picked up his bag.

'Keep him warm,' he said. 'You might bathe his head gently and get rid of the blood. He'll sleep it off.'

'I can't get him upstairs alone, Doctor,' I said.

'Then leave him where he is.' He looked at me without interest. 'Good night, Mrs Wade. As you know, I don't treat alcoholics. Even if I did, your husband would not be one of my patients. I'm sure you understand that.'

'Nobody's asking you to treat him,' I said. 'I'm asking for some help to get him into his bedroom so that I can undress him.'

'And just who are you?' Dr Loring asked me freezingly.

'My name's Marlowe. I was here a week ago. Your wife introduced me.'

'Interesting,' he said. 'In what connexion do you know my wife?'

'What the hell does that matter? All I want is—'

'I'm not interested in what you want,' he cut in on me. He turned to Eileen, nodded briefly, and started out. I got between him and the door and put my back to it.

'Just a minute, Doc. Must be a long time since you glanced at that little piece of prose called the Hippocratic Oath. This man called me on the phone and I live some way off. He sounded bad and I broke every traffic law in the state getting over here. I found him lying out on the ground and I carried him in here and believe me he isn't any bunch of feathers. The houseboy is away and there's nobody here to help me upstairs with Wade. How does it look to you?'

'Get out of my way,' he said between his teeth. 'Or I shall call the sheriff's sub-station and have them send over a deputy. As a professional man—'

'As a professional man you're a handful of flea dirt,' I said, and moved out of his way.

He turned red—slowly but distinctly. He choked on his own bile. Then he opened the door and went out. He shut it carefully. As he pulled it shut he looked in at me. It was as nasty a look as I ever got and as nasty a face as I ever saw.

When I turned away from the door Eileen was smiling.

'What's funny?' I snarled.

'You. You don't care what you say to people, do you? Don't you know who Dr Loring is?'

'Yeah—and I know what he is.'

She glanced at her wristwatch. 'Candy ought to be home by now,' she said. 'I'll go and see. He has a room behind the garage.'

She went out through an archway and I sat down and looked at Wade. The great big writer man went on snoring. His face was sweaty but I left the rug over him. In a minute or two Eileen came back and she had Candy with her.

16

The Mex had on a black and white checked sport shirt, heavily pleated black slacks without a belt, two-tone black and white buckskin shoes, spotlessly clean. His thick black hair was brushed straight back and shining with some kind of hair oil or cream.

'*Señor*,' he said, and sketched a brief, sarcastic bow.

'Help Mr Marlowe carry my husband upstairs, Candy. He fell and hurt himself a little. I'm sorry to trouble you.'

'*De nada, señora*,' Candy said, smiling.

'I think I'll say good night,' she said to me. 'I'm tired out. Candy will get you anything you want.'

She went slowly up the stairs. Candy and I watched her.

'Some doll,' he said confidently. 'You stay the night?'

'Hardly.'

'*Es lástima*. She is very lonely, that one.'

'Get that gleam out of your eyes, kid. Let's put this to bed.'

He looked sadly at Wade snoring on the couch. '*Pobrecito*,' he murmured as if he meant it. '*Borracho como una cuba*.'

'He may be drunk but he sure ain't little,' I said. 'You take the feet.'

We carried him and even for two he was as heavy as a lead coffin. At the top of the stairs we went along an open balcony past a closed door. Candy pointed to it with his chin.

'*La señora*,' he whispered. 'You knock very light maybe she let you in.'

I didn't say anything because I needed him. We went on with the carcass and turned in at another door and dumped him on the bed. Then I took hold of Candy's arm high up near the shoulder where dug-in fingers can hurt. I made mine hurt him. He winced a little and then his face set hard.

'What's your name, *cholo*?'

'Take your hand off me,' he snapped. 'And don't call me a *cholo*. I'm no wetback. My name is Juan Garcia de Soto y Sotomayor. I am Chileno.'

'Okay, Don Juan. Just don't get out of line around here. Keep your nose and mouth clean when you talk about the people you work for.'

He jerked loose and stepped back, his black eyes hot with anger. His hand slipped inside his shirt and came out with a long thin knife. He balanced it by the point on the heel of his hand, hardly even glancing at it. Then he dropped the hand and caught the handle of the knife while it hung in the air. It was done very fast and without any apparent effort. His hand went up to shoulder height, then snapped forward and the knife sailed through the air and hung quivering in the wood of the window frame.

'*Cuidado, señor!*' he said with a sharp sneer. 'And keep your paws to yourself. Nobody fools with me.'

He walked lithely across the room and plucked the knife out of the wood, tossed it in the air, spun on his toes, and caught it behind him. With a snap it disappeared under his shirt.

'Neat,' I said, 'but just a little on the gaudy side.'

He strolled up to me, smiling derisively.

'And it might get you a broken elbow,' I said. 'Like this.'

I took hold of his right wrist, jerked him off balance, swung to one side and a little behind him, and brought my bent forearm up under the back of his elbow joint. I bore down on it, using my forearm as a fulcrum.

'One hard jerk,' I said, 'and your elbow joint cracks. A crack is enough. You'd be out of commission as a knife thrower for several months. Make the jerk a little harder and you'd be through permanently. Take Mr Wade's shoes off.'

I let go of him and he grinned at me. 'Good trick,' he said. 'I will remember.'

He turned to Wade and reached for one of his shoes, then stopped. There was a smear of blood on the pillow.

'Who cut the boss?'

'Not me, chum. He fell and cut his head on something. It's only a shallow cut. The doctor has been here.'

Candy let out his breath slowly. 'You see him fall?'

'Before I got here. You like this guy, don't you?'

He didn't answer me. He took the shoes off. We got Wade undressed little by little and Candy dug out a pair of green and silver pyjamas. We got Wade into those and got him inside the bed and well covered up. He was still sweaty and still snoring. Candy looked down at him sadly, shaking his sleek head from side to side, slowly.

'Somebody's got to take care of him,' he said. 'I go change my clothes.'

'Get some sleep. I'll take care of him. I can call you if I need you.'

He faced me. 'You better take care of him good,' he said in a quiet voice. 'Very good.'

He went out of the room. I went into the bathroom and got a wet washcloth and a heavy towel. I turned Wade over a little and spread the towel on the pillow and washed the blood off his head gently so as not to start the bleeding again. Then I could see a sharp, shallow cut about two inches long. It was nothing. Dr Loring had been right that much. It wouldn't have hurt to stitch it but it probably was not really necessary. I found a pair of scissors and cut the hair away enough so that I could put on a strip of adhesive. Then I turned him on his back and washed his face. I guess that was a mistake.

He opened his eyes. They were vague and unfocused at first, then they cleared and he saw me standing beside the bed. His hand moved and went up to his head and felt the adhesive. His lips mumbled something, then his voice cleared up also.

'Who hit me? You?' His hand felt for the adhesive.

'Nobody hit you. You took a fall.'

'Took a fall? When? Where?'

'Wherever you telephoned from. You called me. I heard you fall. Over the wire.'

'I called you?' He grinned slowly. 'Always available, aren't you, fella? What time is it?'

'After one a.m.'

'Where's Eileen?'

'Gone to bed. She had it rough.'

He thought that over silently. His eyes were full of pain. 'Did I—' He stopped and winced.

'You didn't touch her as far as I know. If that's what you mean. You just wandered outdoors and passed out near the fence. Quit talking. Go to sleep.'

'Sleep,' he said quietly and slowly, like a child reciting its lesson. 'What would that be?'

'Maybe a pill would help. Got any?'

'In the drawer. Night table.'

I opened it and found a plastic bottle with red capsules in it. Seconal, 1½ grains. Prescription by Dr Loring. That nice Dr Loring. Mrs Roger Wade's prescription.

I shook two of them loose and put the bottle back and poured a glass of water from a Thermos jug on the night table. He said one capsule would be enough. He took it and drank some water and lay back and stared at the ceiling again. Time passed. I sat in a chair and watched him. He didn't seem to get sleepy. Then he said slowly:

'I remember something. Do me a favour, Marlowe. I wrote some crazy stuff I don't want Eileen to see. It's on top of the typewriter under the cover.

Tear it up for me.'

'Sure. That all you remember?'

'Eileen is all right? Positive about that?'

'Yes. She's just tired. Let it ride, Wade. Stop thinking. I shouldn't have asked you.'

'Stop thinking, the man says.' His voice was a little drowsy now. He was talking as if to himself. 'Stop thinking, stop dreaming, stop loving, stop hating. Good night, sweet prince. I'll take that other pill.'

I gave it to him with some more water. He lay back again, this time with his head turned so that he could see me. 'Look, Marlowe, I wrote some stuff I don't want Eileen—'

'You told me already. I'll attend to it when you go to sleep.'

'Oh. Thanks. Nice to have you around. Very nice.'

Another longish pause. His eyelids were getting heavy.

'Ever kill a man, Marlowe?'

'Yes.'

'Nasty feeling, isn't it?'

'Some people like it.'

His eyes went shut all the way. Then they opened again, but they looked vague. 'How could they?'

I didn't answer. The eyelids came down again, very gradually, like a slow curtain in the theatre. He began to snore. I waited a little longer. Then I dimmed the light in the room and went out.

27

I stopped outside Eileen's door and listened. I didn't hear any sound of movement inside, so I didn't knock. If she wanted to know how he was, it was up to her. Downstairs the living-room looked bright and empty. I put out some of the lights. From over near the front door I looked up at the balcony. The middle part of the living-room rose to the full height of the house walls and was crossed by open beams that also supported the balcony. The balcony was wide and edged on two sides by a solid railing which looked to be about three and a half feet high. The top and the uprights were cut square to match the cross beams. The dining-room was through a square arch closed off by double louvered doors. Above it I guessed there were servants' quarters. This part of the second floor was walled off so there would be another stairway reaching it from the kitchen part of the house. Wade's room was in the corner of his study. I could see the light from his open door reflected against the high ceiling and I could see the top foot of his doorway.

I cut all the lights except in one standing lamp and crossed to the study. The door was shut but two lamps were lit, a standing lamp at the end of the leather couch and a cowled desk lamp. The typewriter was on a heavy stand under this and beside it on the desk there was a disorderly mess of yellow paper. I sat in a padded chair and studied the layout. What I wanted to know was how he had cut his head. I sat in his desk-chair with the phone at my left hand. The spring was set very weak. If I tilted back and went over, my head may have caught the corner of the desk. I moistened my handkerchief and rubbed the wood. No blood, nothing there. There was a lot of stuff on the desk, including a row of books between bronze elephants, and an old-fashioned square glass inkwell. I tried that without result. Not much point to it anyway, because if someone else had slugged him, the weapon didn't have to be in the room. And there wasn't anyone else to do it. I stood up and switched on the cornice lights. They reached into the shadowy corners and of course the answer was simple enough after all. A square metal waste-basket was lying on its side over against the wall, with paper spilt. It couldn't have walked there, so it had been thrown or kicked. I tried its sharp corners with my moistened handkerchief. I got the red-brown smear of blood this time. No mystery at all. Wade had fallen over and struck his head on the sharp corner of the waste-bucket—a glancing blow most likely—picked himself up and booted the damn thing across the room. Easy.

Then he would have another quick drink. The drinking liquor was on the cocktail table in front of the couch. An empty bottle, another three-quarters full, a Thermos jug of water and a silver bowl containing water which had been ice cubes. There was only one glass and it was the large economy size.

Having taken his drink he felt a little better. He noticed the phone off the hook in a bleary sort of way and very likely didn't remember any more what he had been doing with it. So he just walked across and put it back in its cradle. The time had been just about right. There is something compulsive about a telephone. The gadget-ridden man of our age loves it, loathes it, and is afraid of it. But he always treats it with respect, even when he is drunk. The telephone is a fetish.

Any normal man would have said hello into the mouthpiece before hanging up, just to be sure. But not necessarily a man who was bleary with drink and had just taken a fall. It didn't matter anyhow. His wife might have done it, she might have heard the fall and the bang as the waste-basket bounced against the wall and come into the study. About that time the last drink would kick him in the face and he would stagger out of the house and across the front lawn and pass out where I had found him. Somebody was coming for him. By this time he didn't know who it was. Maybe the good Dr Verringer.

So far, so good. So what would his wife do? She couldn't handle him or reason with him and she might well be afraid to try. So she would call somebody to come and help. The servants were out, so it would have to be done by the telephone. Well, she *had* called somebody. She had called that nice Dr Loring. I'd just assumed she called him after I got there. She hadn't said so.

From here on it didn't quite add up. You'd expect her to look for him and find him and make sure he wasn't hurt. It wouldn't hurt him to lie out on the ground on a warm summer night for a while. She couldn't move him. It had taken all I had to do that. But you wouldn't expect to find her standing in the open doorway smoking a cigarette, not knowing except very vaguely where he was. Or would you? I didn't know what she had been through with him, how dangerous he was in that condition, how much afraid she might be to go near him. 'I've had all of it I can take,' she had said to me when I arrived. 'You find him.' Then she had gone inside and pulled a faint.

It still bothered me, but I had to leave it at that. I had to assume that when she had been up against the situation often enough to know there was nothing she could do about it except to let it ride, then that would be what she would do. Just that. Let it ride. Let him lie out there on the ground until somebody came around with the physical equipment to handle him.

It still bothered me. It bothered me also that she had checked out and gone into her own room while Candy and I got him upstairs to bed. She said she loved the guy. He was her husband, they had been married for five years, he was a very nice guy indeed when sober–these were her own words. Drunk he was something else, something to stay away from because he was dangerous. All right, forget it. But somehow it still bothered me. If she was really scared, she wouldn't have been standing there in the open door smoking a cigarette. If she was just bitter and withdrawn and disgusted, she wouldn't have fainted.

There was something else. Another woman, perhaps. Then she had only just found out. Linda Loring? Maybe. Dr Loring thought so and said so in a very public manner.

I stopped thinking about it and took the cover off the typewriter. The stuff was there, several loose sheets of typed yellow paper that I was supposed to destroy so Eileen wouldn't see them. I took them over to the couch and decided I deserved a drink to go with the reading-matter. There was a half-bath off the study. I rinsed the tall glass out and poured a libation and sat down with it to read. And what I read was really wild. Like this:

28

'The moon's four days off the full and there's a square patch of moonlight on the wall and it's looking at me like a big blind milky eye, a wall eye. Joke. Goddam silly simile. Writers. Everything has to be like something else. My head is as fluffy as whipped cream but not as sweet. More similes. I could vomit just thinking about the lousy racket. I could vomit anyway. I probably will. Don't push me. Give me time. The worms in my solar plexus crawl and crawl and crawl. I would be better off in bed but there would be a dark animal underneath the bed and the dark animal would crawl around rustling and bump himself and bump the underside of the bed, then I would let out a yell that wouldn't make any sound except to me. A dream yell, a yell in a nightmare. There is nothing to be afraid of and I am not afraid because there is nothing to be afraid of, but just the same I was lying like that once in bed and the dark animal was doing it to me, bumping himself against the underside of the bed, and I had an orgasm. That disgusted me more than any other of the nasty things I have done.

'I'm dirty. I need a shave. My hands are shaking. I'm sweating. I smell foul to myself. The shirt under my arms is wet and on the chest and back. The sleeves are wet in the folds of the elbows. The glass on the table is empty. It would take both hands to pour the stuff now. I could get one out of the bottle maybe to brace me. The taste of the stuff is sickening. And it wouldn't get me anywhere. In the end I won't be able to sleep even and the

whole world will moan in the horror of tortured nerves. Good stuff, huh,
Wade? More.

'It's all right for the first two or three days and then it is negative. You
suffer and you take a drink and for a little while it is better, but the price
keeps getting higher and higher and what you get for it is less and less and
then there is always the point where you get nothing but nausea. Then you
call Verringer. All right, Verringer, here I come. There isn't any Verringer
any more. He's gone to Cuba or he is dead. The queen has killed him. Poor
old Verringer, what a fate, to die in bed with a queen—that kind of queen.
Come on, Wade, let's get up and go places. Places where we haven't ever
been and aren't ever going back to when we have been. Does this sentence
make sense? No. Okay, I'm not asking any money for it. A short pause here
for a long commercial.

'Well, I did it. I got up. What a man. I went over to the couch and here I
am kneeling beside the couch with my hands down on it and face in my
hands, crying. Then I prayed and despised myself for praying. Grade
Three drunk despising himself. What the hell are you praying to, you fool?
If a well man prays, that's faith. A sick man prays and he is just scared. Nuts
to prayer. This is the world you made and you make it all by yourself and
what little outside help you got—well, you made that too. Stop praying, you
jerk. Get up on your feet and take that drink. It's too late for anything else
now.

'Well, I took it. Both hands. Poured it in the glass to. Hardly spilled a
drop. Now if I can hold it without vomiting. Better add some water. Now
lift it slow. Easy, not too much at a time. It gets warm. It gets hot. If I could
stop sweating. The glass is empty. It's down on the table again.

'There's a haze over the moonlight but I set that glass down in spite of it,
carefully, carefully, like a spray of roses in a tall thin vase. The roses nod
their heads with dew. Maybe I'm a rose. Brother, have I got dew. Now to
get upstairs. Maybe a short one straight for the journey. No? Okay,
whatever you say. Take it upstairs when I get there. If I get there,
something to look forward to. If I make it upstairs I am entitled to
compensation. A token of regard from me to me. I have such a beautiful love
for myself—and the sweet part of it—no rivals.

'Double space. Been up and came down. Didn't like it upstairs. The
altitude makes my heart flutter. But I keep hitting these typewriter keys.
What a magician is the subconscious. If only it would work regular hours.
There was moonlight upstairs too. Probably the same moon. No variety
about the moon. It comes and goes like the milkman and the moon's milk is
always the same. The milk's moon is always—hold it, chum. You've got your
feet crossed. This is no time to get involved in the case history of the moon.
You got enough case history to take care of the whole damn valley.

'She was sleeping on her side without sound. Her knees drawn up. Too
still I thought. You always make some sound when you sleep. Maybe not
sleep, maybe just trying to sleep. If I went closer I would know. Might fall
down too. One of her eyes opened—or did it? She looked at me or did she?
No. Would have sat up and said, Are you sick, darling? Yes, I am sick,
darling. But don't give it a thought, darling, because this sick is my sick and
not your sick, and let you sleep still and lovely and never remember and no
slime from me to you and nothing come near you that is grim and grey and
ugly.

'You're a louse, Wade. Three adjectives, you lousy writer. Can't you even stream of consciousness you louse without getting it in three adjectives for Chrissake? I came downstairs again holding on to the rail. My guts lurched with the steps and I held them together with a promise. I made the main floor and I made the study and I made the couch and I waited for my heart to slow down. The bottle is handy. One thing you can say about Wade's arrangements the bottle is always handy. Nobody hides it, nobody locks it up. Nobody says, don't you think you've had enough, darling? You'll make youself sick, darling. Nobody says that. Just sleep on side softly like roses.

'I gave Candy too much money. Mistake. Should have started him with a bag of peanuts and worked up to a banana. Then a little real change, slow and easy, always keep him eager. You give him a big slug of the stuff to begin with and pretty soon he has a stake. He can live in Mexico for a month, live high wide and nasty, on what it costs here for a day. So when he gets that stake, what does he do? Well, does a man ever have enough money, if he thinks he can get more? Maybe it's all right. Maybe I ought to kill the shiny-eyed bastard. A good man died for me once, why not a cockroach in a white jacket?

'Forget Candy. There's always a way to blunt a needle. The other I shall never forget. It's carved on my liver in green fire.

'Better telephone. Losing control. Feel them jumping, jumping, jumping. Better call someone quick before the pink things crawl on my face. Better call, call, call. Call Sioux City Sue. Hello, Operator, give me Long Distance. Hello, Long Distance, get me Sioux City Sue. What's her number? No have number, just name, Operator. You'll find her walking along Tenth Street, on the shady side, under the tall corn trees with their spreading ears . . . All right, Operator, all right. Just cancel the whole programme and let me tell you something, I mean, ask you something. Who's going to pay for all those snazzy parties Gifford is throwing in London, if you cancel my long distance call? Yeah, you think your job is solid. You think. Here, I better talk to Gifford direct. Get him on the line. His valet just brought in his tea. If he can't talk we'll send over somebody that can.

'Now what did I write that for? What was I trying not to think about? Telephone. Better telephone now. Getting very bad, very very—'

That was all. I folded the sheets up small and pushed them down into my inside breast pocket behind the note case. I went over to the french doors and opened them wide and stepped out on to the terrace. The moonlight was a little spoiled. But it was summer in Idle Valley and summer is never quite spoiled. I stood there looking at the motionless, colourless lake and thought and wondered. Then I heard a shot.

29

On the balcony two lighted doors were open now—Eileen's and his. Her room was empty. There was a sound of struggling from his and I came through the door in a jump to find her bending over the bed wrestling with him. The black gleam of a gun shot up into the air, two hands, a large male hand and a woman's small hand were both holding it, neither by the butt. Roger was sitting up in bed and leaning forward pushing. She was in a pale blue housecoat, one of those quilted things, her hair was all over her face, and now she had both hands on the gun and with a quick jerk she got it away from him. I was surprised that she had the strength, even dopey as he was. He fell back glaring and panting and she stepped away and bumped into me.

She stood there leaning against me, holding the gun with both hands pressed hard against her body. She was racked with panting sobs. I reached around her body and put my hand on the gun.

She spun around as if it took that to realize I was there. Her eyes widened and her body sagged against me. She let go of the gun. It was a heavy, clumsy weapon, a Webley double-action hammerless. The barrel was warm. I held her with one arm, dropped the gun in my pocket, and looked past her head at him. Nobody said anything.

Then he opened his eyes and that weary smile played on his lips. 'Nobody hurt,' he muttered. 'Just a wild shot into the ceiling.'

I felt her go stiff. Then she pulled away. Her eyes were focused and clear. I let her go.

'Roger,' she said in a voice not much more than a sick whisper, 'did it have to be that?'

He stared owlishly, licked his lip, and said nothing. She went and leaned against the dressing-table. Her hand moved mechanically and threw her hair back from her face. She shuddered once from head to foot, shaking her head from side to side. 'Roger,' she whispered again. 'Poor Roger. Poor miserable Roger.'

He was staring straight up at the ceiling now. 'I had a nightmare,' he said slowly. 'Somebody with a knife was leaning over the bed. I don't know who. Looked a little like Candy. Couldn't have been Candy.'

'Of course not, darling,' she said softly. She left the dressing-table and sat down on the side of the bed. She put her hand out and began to stroke his forehead. 'Candy has gone to bed long ago. And why would Candy have a knife?'

'He's a Mex. They all have knives,' Roger said in the same remote impersonal voice. 'They like knives. And he doesn't like me.'

'Nobody likes you,' I said brutally.

She turned her head swiftly. 'Please—please don't talk like that. He didn't know. He had a dream—'

'Where was the gun?' I growled, watching her, not paying any attention to him.

'Night table. In the drawer.' He turned his head and met my stare. There hadn't been any gun in the drawer, and he knew I knew it. The pills had been in there and some odds and ends, but no gun.

'Or under the pillow,' he added. 'I'm vague about it. I shot once'—he lifted a heavy hand and pointed—'up there.'

I looked up. There seemed to be a hole in the ceiling plaster all right. I went where I could look up at it. Yes, the kind of hole a bullet might make. From that gun it would go on through, into the attic. I went back close to the bed and stood looking down at him, giving him the hard eye.

'Nuts. You meant to kill yourself. You didn't have any nightmare. You were swimming in a sea of self-pity. You didn't have any gun in the drawer or under your pillow either. You got up and got the gun and got back into bed and there you were all ready to wipe out the whole messy business. But I don't think you had the nerve. You fired a shot not meant to hit any-thing. And your wife came running—that's what you wanted. Just pity and sympathy, pal. Nothing else. Even the struggle was mostly fake. She couldn't take a gun away from you if you didn't want her to.'

'I'm sick,' he said. 'But you could be right. Does it matter?'

'It matters like this. They'd put you in the psycho ward, and believe me, the people who run that place are about as sympathetic as Georgia chain gang guards.'

Eileen stood up solemnly. 'That's enough,' she said sharply. 'He is sick, and you know it.'

'He wants to be sick. I'm just reminding him of what it would cost him.'

'This is not the time to tell him.'

'Go on back to your room.'

Her blue eyes flashed. 'How dare you—'

'Go on back to your room. Unless you want me to call the police. These things are supposed to be reported.'

He almost grinned. 'Yeah, call the police,' he said, 'like you did on Terry Lennox.'

I didn't pay any attention to that. I was still watching her. She looked exhausted now, and frail, and very beautiful. The moment of flashing anger was gone. I put a hand out and touched her arm. 'It's all right,' I said. 'He won't do it again. Go back to bed.'

She gave him a long look and went out of the room. When the open door was empty of her I sat down on the side of the bed where she had been sitting.

'More pills?'

'No thanks. It doesn't matter whether I sleep. I feel a lot better.'

'Did I hit right about that shot? It was just a crazy bit of acting?'

'More or less,' he turned his head away. 'I guess I was lightheaded.'

'Nobody can stop you from killing yourself, if you really want to. I realize that. So do you.'

'Yes.' He was still looking away. 'Did you do what I asked you—that stuff in the typewriter.'

'Uh-huh. I'm surprised you remember. It's pretty crazy writing. Funny thing, it's clearly typed.'

'I can always do that—drunk or sober—up to a point anyway.'

'Don't worry about Candy,' I said. 'You're wrong about his not liking you. And I was wrong to say nobody did. I was trying to jar Eileen, make her mad.'

'Why?'

'She pulled one faint already tonight.'

He shook his head slightly. 'Eileen never faints.'

'Then it was a phoney.'

He didn't like that either.'

'What did you mean—a good man died for you?' I asked.

He frowned, thinking about it. 'Just rubbish. I told you I had a dream—'

'I'm talking about that guff you typed out.'

He looked at me now, turning his head on the pillow as if it had enormous weight. 'Another dream.'

'I'll try again. What's Candy got on you?'

'Shove it, Jack,' he said and closed his eyes.

I got up and closed the door. 'You can't run for ever, Wade. Candy could be a blackmailer, sure. Easy. He could even be nice about it—like you and lift your dough at the same time. What is it—a woman?'

'You believe that fool, Loring,' he said with his eyes closed.

'Not exactly. What about the sister—the one that's dead?'

It was a wild pitch in a sense but it happened to split the plate. His eyes snapped wide open. A bubble of saliva showed on his lips.

'Is that—why you're here?' he asked slowly, and in a whispering voice.

'You know better. I was invited. You invited me.'

His head rolled back and forth on the pillow. In spite of the seconal he was eaten up by his nerves. His face was covered with sweat.

'I'm not the first loving husband who has been an adulterer. Leave me alone, damn you. Leave me alone.'

I went into the bathroom and got a face towel and wiped his face off. I grinned at him sneeringly. I was the heel to end all heels. Wait until the man is down, then kick him and kick him again. He's weak. He can't resist or kick back.

'One of these days we'll get together on it,' I said.

'I'm not crazy,' he said.

'You just hope you're not crazy.'

'I've been living in hell.'

'Oh sure. That's obvious. The interesting point is why. Here—take this.' I had another seconal out of the night table and another glass of water. He got up on one elbow and grabbed for the glass and missed it by a good four inches. I put it in his hand. He managed to drink and swallow his pill. Then he lay back flat and deflated, his face drained of emotion. His nose had that pinched look. He could almost have been a dead man. He wasn't throwing anybody down any stairs tonight. Most likely not any night.

When his eyelids got heavy I went out of the room. The weight of the Webley was against my hip, dragging at my pocket. I started back downstairs again. Eileen's door was open. Her room was dark but there was enough light from the moon to frame her standing just inside the door. She called out something that sounded like a name, but it wasn't my name. I stepped close to her.

'Keep your voice down,' I said. 'He's gone back to sleep.'

'I always knew you would come back,' she said softly. 'Even after ten years.'

I peered at her. One of us was goofy.

'Shut the door,' she said in the same caressing voice. 'All these years I have kept myself for you.'

I turned and shut the door. It seemed like a good idea at the moment. When I faced her she was already falling towards me. So I caught her. I damn well had to. She pressed herself hard against me and her hair brushed my face. Her mouth came up to be kissed. She was trembling. Her lips opened and her teeth opened and her tongue darted. Then her hands dropped and jerked at something and the robe she was wearing came open, and underneath it she was as naked as September Morn but a darn sight less coy.

'Put me on the bed,' she breathed.

I did that. Putting my arms around her I touched her bare skin, soft skin, soft, yielding flesh. I lifted her and carried her arms around my neck. She was making some kind of a whistling noise in her throat. Then she threshed about and moaned. This was murder. I was as erotic as a stallion. I was losing control. You don't get that sort of invitation from that sort of woman very often anywhere.

Candy saved me. There was a thin squeak and I swung around to see the doorknob moving. I jerked loose and jumped for the door. I got it open and barged out through it and the Mex was tearing along the hall and down the stairs. Half-way down he stopped and turned and leered at me. Then he was gone.

I went back to the door and shut it—from the outside this time. Some kind of weird noises were coming from the woman on the bed, but that's all they were now. Weird noises. The spell was broken.

I went down the stairs fast and crossed into the study and grabbed the bottle of Scotch and tilted it. When I couldn't swallow any more I leaned against the wall and panted and let the stuff burn in me until the fumes reached my brain.

It was a long time since dinner. It was a long time since anything that was normal. The whisky hit me hard and fast and I kept guzzling it until the room started to get hazy and the furniture was all in the wrong places and the lamplight was like wildfire or summer lightning. Then I was flat out on the leather couch, trying to balance the bottle on my chest. It seemed to be empty. It rolled away and thumped on the floor.

That was the last incident of which I took any precise notice.

30

A shaft of sunlight tickled one of my ankles. I opened my eyes and saw the crown of a tree moving gently against a hazed blue sky. I rolled over and leather touched my cheek. An axe split my head. I sat up. There was a rug over me. I threw that off and got my feet on the floor. I scowled at a clock. The clock said a minute short of six-thirty.

I got up on my feet and it took character. It took will power. It took a lot out of me, and there wasn't as much to spare as there once had been. The hard, heavy years had worked me over.

I ploughed across to the half-bath and stripped off my tie and shirt and sloshed cold water in my face with both hands and sloshed it on my head. When I was dripping wet I towelled myself off savagely. I put my shirt and tie back on and reached for my jacket and the gun in the pocket banged against the wall. I took it out and swung the cylinder away from the frame and tipped the cartridges into my hand, five full, one just a blackened shell. Then I thought, what's the use, there are always more of them. So I put them back where they had been before and carried the gun into the study and put it away in one of the drawers of the desk.

When I looked up Candy was standing in the doorway, spick and span in his white coat, his hair brushed back and shining black, his eyes bitter.

'You want some coffee?'

'Thanks.'

'I put the lamps out. The boss is okay. Asleep. I shut his door. Why you get drunk?'

'I had to.'

He sneered at me. 'Didn't make her, huh? Got tossed out on your can, shamus.'

'Have it your own way.'

'You ain't tough this morning, shamus. You ain't tough at all.'

'Get the goddam coffee,' I yelled at him.

'Hijo de la puta!'

In one jump I had him by the arm. He didn't move. He just looked at me contemptuously. I laughed and let go of his arm.

'You're right, Candy. I'm not tough at all.'

He turned and went out. In no time at all he was back with a silver tray and a small silver pot of coffee on it and sugar and cream and a neat triangular napkin. He set it down on the cocktail table and removed the empty bottle and the rest of the drinking materials. He picked another bottle off the floor.

'Fresh. Just made,' he said, and went out.

I drank two cups black. Then I tried a cigarette. It was all right. I still belonged to the human race. Then Candy was back in the room again.

'You want breakfast?' he asked morosely.

'No, thanks.'

'Okay, scram out of here. We don't want you around.'

'Who's we?'

He lifted the lid of a box and helped himself to a cigarette. He lit it and blew smoke at me insolently.

'I take care of the boss,' he said.

'You making it pay?'

He frowned, then nodded. 'Oh yes. Good money.'

'How much on the side—for not spilling what you know?'

He went back to Spanish. *'No entendido.'*

'You understand all right. How much you shake him for? I bet it's not more than a couple of yards.'

'What's that? Couple of yards?'

'Two hundred bucks.'

He grinned. 'You give me couple of yards, shamus. So I don't tell the boss you come out of her room last night.'

'That would buy a whole busload of wetbacks like you.'

He shrugged that off. 'The boss gets pretty rough when he blows his top. Better pay up, shamus.'

'Pachuco stuff,' I said contemptuously. 'All you're touching is the small money. Lots of men play around when they're lit. Anyhow she knows all about it. You don't have anything to sell.'

There was a gleam in his eye. 'Just don't come round any more, tough boy.'

'I'm leaving.'

I stood up and walked around the table. He moved enough to keep facing towards me. I watched his hand but he evidently wasn't wearing a knife this morning. When I was close enough I slapped a hand across his face.

'I don't get called a son of a whore by the help, greaseball. I've got business here and I come around whenever I feel like it. Watch your lip from now on. You might get pistol-whipped. That pretty face of yours would never look the same again.'

He didn't react at all, not even to the slap. That and being called a greaseball must have been deadly insults to him. But this time he just stood there wooden-faced, motionless. Then without a word he picked up the coffee-tray and carried it out.

'Thanks for the coffee,' I said to his back.

He kept going. When he was gone I felt the bristles on my chin, shook myself, and decided to be on my way. I had had a skinful of the Wade family.

As I crossed the living-room Eileen was coming down the stairs in white slacks and open-toed sandals and a pale blue shirt. She looked at me with complete surprise. 'I didn't know you were here, Mr Marlowe,' she said, as though she hadn't seen me for a week, and at that time I had just dropped in for tea.

'I put his gun in the desk,' I said.

'Gun?' Then it seemed to dawn on her. 'Oh, last night was a little hectic, wasn't it? But I thought you had gone home.'

I walked over closer to her. She had a thin gold chain around her neck and some kind of fancy pendant in gold and blue on white enamel. The blue enamelled part looked like a pair of wings, but not spread out. Against these there was a broad white enamel and gold dagger that pierced a scroll. I couldn't read the words. It was some kind of military emblem.

'I got drunk,' I said. 'Deliberately and not elegantly. I was a little lonely.'

'You didn't have to be,' she said, and her eyes were as clear as water. There wasn't a trace of guile in them.

'A matter of opinion,' I said. 'I'm leaving now and I'm not sure I'll be back. You heard what I said about the gun?'

'You put it in his desk. It might be a good idea to put it somewhere else. But he didn't really mean to shoot himself, did he?'

'I can't answer that. But next time he might.'

She shook her head. 'I don't think so. I really don't. You were a wonderful help last night, Mr Marlowe. I don't know how to thank you.'

'You made a pretty good try.'

She got pink. Then she laughed. 'I had a very curious dream in the night,' she said slowly, looking off over my shoulder. 'Someone I used to know was here in the house. Someone who has been dead for ten years.' Her fingers went up and touched the gold and enamel pendant. 'That's why I am wearing this today. He gave it to me.'

'I had a curious dream myself,' I said. 'But I'm not telling mine. Let me know how Roger gets on and if there is anything I can do.'

She lowered her eyes and looked into mine. 'You said you were not coming back.'

'I said I wasn't sure. I may have to come back. I hope I won't. There is something very wrong in this house. And only part of it came out of a bottle.'

She stared at me, frowning. 'What does that mean?'

'I think you know what I'm talking about.'

She thought it over carefully. Her fingers were still touching the pendant gently. She let out a slow patient sigh. 'There's always another woman,' she said quietly. 'At some time or other. It's not necessarily fatal. We're talking at cross purposes, aren't we? We are not even talking about the same thing, perhaps.'

'Could be,' I said. She was still standing on the steps, the third step from the bottom. She still had her fingers on the pendant. She still looked like a golden dream. 'Especially if you have in mind that the other woman is Linda Loring.'

She dropped her hand from the pendant and came down one more step of the stairs.

'Dr Loring seems to agree with me,' she said indifferently. 'He must have some source of information.'

'You said he had played that scene with half the males in the valley.'

'Did I? Well—it was the conventional sort of thing to say at the time.' She came down another step.

'I haven't shaved,' I said.

That startled her. Then she laughed. 'Oh, I wasn't expecting you to make love to me.'

'Just what did you expect of me, Mrs Wade—in the beginning, when you first persuaded me to go hunting? Why me—what have I got to offer?'

'You kept faith,' she said quietly. 'When it couldn't have been very easy.'

'I'm touched. But I don't think that was the reason.'

She came down the last step and then she was looking up at me. 'Then what was the reason?'

'Or if it was—it was a damn poor reason. Just about the worst reason in the world.'

She frowned a tiny frown. 'Why?'

'Because what I did—this keeping faith—is something even a fool doesn't do twice.'

'You know,' she said lightly, 'this is getting to be a very enigmatic conversation.'

'You're a very enigmatic person, Mrs Wade. So long and good luck and if you really care anything about Roger, you'd better find him the right kind of doctor—and quick.'

She laughed again. 'Oh, that was a mild attack last night. You ought to see him in a bad one. He'll be up and working by this afternoon.'

'Like hell he will.'

'But believe me he will. I know him so well.'

I gave her the last shot right in the teeth and it sounded pretty nasty.

'You don't really want to save him, do you? You just want to look as if you are trying to save him.'

'That,' she said deliberately, 'was a very beastly thing to say to me.'

She stepped past me and walked through the dining-room doors and then the big room was empty and I crossed to the front door and let myself out. It was a perfect summer morning in that bright secluded valley. It was too far from the city to get any smog and cut off by the low mountains from the dampness of the ocean. It was going to be hot later, but in a nice refined exclusive sort of way, nothing brutal like the heat of the desert, not sticky and rank like the heat of the city. Idle Valley was a perfect place to live.

Perfect. Nice people with nice homes, nice cars, nice horses, nice dogs, possibly even nice children.

But all a man named Marlowe wanted from it was out. And fast.

31

I went home and showered and shaved and changed clothes and began to feel clean again. I cooked some breakfast, ate it, washed up, swept the kitchen and the service porch, filled a pipe, and called the phone answering service. I shot a blank. Why go to the office? There would be nothing there but another dead moth and another layer of dust. In the safe would be my portrait of Madison. I could go down and play with that, and with the five crisp hundred-dollar bills that still smelt of coffee. I could do that, but I didn't want to. Something inside me had gone sour. None of it really belonged to me. What was it supposed to buy? How much loyalty can a dead man use? Phooey. I was looking at life through the mists of a hangover.

It was the kind of morning that seems to go on for ever. I was flat and tired and dull and the passing minutes seemed to fall into a void, with a soft whirring sound, like spent rockets. Birds chirped in the shrubbery outside and the cars went up and down Laurel Canyon Boulevard endlessly. Usually I wouldn't even hear them. But I was brooding and irritable and mean and over-sensitive. I decided to kill the hangover.

Ordinarily I was not a morning drinker. The Southern California climate is too soft for it. You don't metabolize fast enough. But I mixed a tall cold one this time and sat in an easy-chair with my shirt open and pecked at a magazine, reading a crazy story about a guy that had two lives and two psychiatrists, one was human and one was some kind of insect in a hive. The guy kept going from one to the other and the whole thing was as crazy as a crumpet, but funny in an off-beat sort of way. I was handling the drink carefully, a sip at a time, watching myself.

It was about noon when the telephone rang and the voice said:

'This is Linda Loring. I called your office and your phone service told me to try your home. I'd like to see you.'

'Why?'

'I'd rather explain that in person. You go to your office from time to time, I suppose.'

'Yeah. From time to time. Is there any money in it?'

'I hadn't thought of it that way. But I have no objection, if you want to be paid. I could be at your office in about an hour.'

'Goody.'

'What's the matter with you?' she asked sharply.

'Hangover. But I'm not paralysed. I'll be there. Unless you'd rather come here.'

'Your office would suit me better.'

'I've got a nice quiet place here. Dead-end street, no near neighbours.'

'The implication does not attract me—if I understand you.'

'Nobody understands me, Mrs Loring. I'm enigmatic. Okay, I'll struggle down to the coop.'

'Thank you so much.' She hung up.

I was slow getting down there because I stopped on the way for a sandwich. I aired out the office and switched on the buzzer and poked my head through the communicating door and she was there already, sitting in the same chair where Mendy Menendez had sat and looking through what could have been the same magazine. She had a tan gabardine suit on today and she looked pretty elegant. She put the magazine aside, gave me a serious look, and said:

'Your Boston fern needs watering. I think it needs repotting too. Too many air roots.'

I held the door open for her. The hell with the Boston fern. When she was inside and I had let the door swing shut I held the customer's chair for her and she gave the office the usual once-over. I got around to my side of the desk.

'Your establishment isn't exactly palatial,' she said. 'Don't you even have a secretary?'

'It's a sordid life, but I'm used to it.'

'And I shouldn't think very lucrative,' she said.

'Oh I don't know. Depends. Want to see a portrait of Madison?'

'A what?'

'A five-thousand-dollar bill. Retainer. I've got it in the safe.' I got up and started over there. I spun the knob and opened it and unlocked a drawer inside, opened an envelope, and dropped it in front of her. She stared at it in something like amazement.

'Don't let the office fool you,' I said. 'I worked for an old boy one time that would cash in at about twenty millions. Even your old man would say hello to him. His office was no better than mine, except he was a bit deaf and had that sound-proofing stuff on the ceiling. On the floor brown linoleum, no carpet.'

She picked the portrait of Madison up and pulled it between her fingers and turned it over. She put it down again.

'You got this from Terry, didn't you?'

'Gosh, you know everything, don't you, Mrs Loring?'

She pushed the bill away from her, frowning. 'He had one. He carried it on him ever since he and Sylvia were married the second time. He called it his mad money. It was not found on his body.'

'There could be other reasons for that.'

'I know. But how many people carry a five-thousand-dollar bill around with them? How many who could afford to give you that much money would give it to you in this form?'

It wasn't worth answering. I just nodded. She went on brusquely:

'And what were you supposed to do for it, Mr Marlowe? Or would you tell me? On that last ride down to Tijuana he had plenty of time to talk. You made it very clear the other evening that you didn't believe his confession. Did he give you a list of his wife's lovers so that you might find a murderer among them?'

I didn't answer that either, but for different reasons.

'And would the name of Roger Wade appear on the list by any chance?' she asked harshly. 'If Terry didn't kill his wife, the murderer would have to be some violent and irresponsible man, a lunatic or a savage drunk. Only that sort of man could, to use your own repulsive phrase, beat her face into a bloody sponge. Is that why you are making yourself so very useful to the Wades—a regular mother's helper who comes on call to nurse him when he is drunk, to find him when he is lost, to bring him home when he is helpless?'

'Let me set you right on a couple of points, Mrs Loring. Terry may or may not have given me that beautiful piece of engraving. But he gave me no list and mentioned no names. There was nothing he asked me to do except what you seem to feel sure I did do, drive him to Tijuana. My getting involved with the Wades was the work of a New York publisher who is desperate to have Roger Wade finish his book, which involves him being fairly sober, which in turn involves finding out if there is any special trouble that makes him get drunk. If there is and it can be found out, then the next step would be an effort to remove it. I say effort, because the chances are you couldn't do it. But you could try.'

'I could tell you in one simple sentence why he gets drunk,' she said contemptuously. 'That anaemic blonde showpiece he's married to.'

'Oh I don't know,' I said. 'I wouldn't call her anaemic.'

'Really? How interesting.' Her eyes glittered.

I picked up my portrait of Madison. 'Don't chew too long on that one, Mrs Loring. I am not sleeping with the lady. Sorry to disappoint you.'

I went over to the safe and put my money away in the locked compartment. I shut the safe and spun the dial.

'On second thoughts,' she said to my back, 'I doubt very much that anyone is sleeping with her.'

I went back and sat on the corner of the desk. 'You're getting bitchy, Mrs Loring. Why? Are you carrying a torch for our alcoholic friend?'

'I hate remarks like that,' she said bitingly. 'I hate them. I suppose that idiotic scene my husband made makes you think you have the right to insult me. No, I am not carrying a torch for Roger Wade. I never did—even when he was a sober man who behaved himself. Still less now that he is what he is.'

I flopped into my chair, reached for a matchbox, and stared at her. She looked at her watch.

'You people with a lot of money are really something,' I said. 'You think anything you choose to say, however nasty, is perfectly all right. You can make sneering remarks about Wade and his wife to a man you hardly know, but if I hand you back a little change, that's an insult. Okay, let's play it low down. Any drunk will eventually turn up with a loose woman. Wade is a drunk, but you're not a loose woman. That's just a casual suggestion your high-bred husband drops to brighten up a cocktail party. He doesn't mean it, he's just saying it for laughs. So we rule you out, and look for a loose women elsewhere. How far do we have to look, Mrs Loring—to find one that would involve you enough to bring you down here trading sneers with me? It had to be somebody rather special, doesn't it—otherwise why should you care?'

She sat perfectly silent, just looking. A long half minute went by. The corners of her mouth were white and her hands were rigid on her gaberdine bag that matched her suit.

'You haven't exactly wasted your time, have you?' she said at last. 'How convenient that this publisher should have thought of employing you! So Terry named no names to you! Not a name. But it really didn't matter, did it, Mr Marlowe? Your instinct was unerring. May I ask what you propose to do next?'

'Nothing.'

'Why, what a waste of talent! How can you reconcile it with your obligation to your portrait of Madison? Surely there must be something you can do.'

'Just between the two of us,' I said, 'you're getting pretty corny. So Wade knew your sister. Thanks for telling me, however indirectly. I already guessed it. So what? He's just one of what was most likely a fairly rich collection. Let's leave it there. And let's get around to why you wanted to see me. That kind of got lost in the shuffle, didn't it?'

She stood up. She glanced at her watch once more. 'I have a car downstairs. Could I prevail upon you to drive home with me and drink a cup of tea?'

'Go on,' I said. 'Let's have it.'

'Do I sound so suspicious? I have a guest who would like to make your acquaintance.

'The old man?'

'I don't call him that,' she said evenly.

I stood up and leaned across the desk. 'Honey, you're awful cute sometimes. You really are. Is it all right if I carry a gun?'

'Surely you're not afraid of an old man.' She wrinkled her lip at me.

'Why not? I'll bet you are—plenty.'

She sighed. 'Yes, I'm afraid I am. I always have been. He can be rather terrifying.'

'Maybe I'd better take two guns,' I said, then wished I hadn't.

32

It was the damnedest-looking house I ever saw. It was a square, grey box three storeys high, with a mansard roof, steeply sloped and broken by twenty or thirty double dormer windows with a lot of wedding-cake decorations around them and between them. The entrance had double stone pillars on each side but the cream of the joint was an outside spiral staircase with a stone railing, topped by a tower room from which there must have been a view the whole length of the lake.

The motor yard was paved with stone. What the place really seemed to need was a half-mile of poplar-lined driveway and a deer park and a wild garden and a terrace on three levels and a few hundred roses outside the library window and a long green vista from every window ending in forest and silence and quiet emptiness. What it had was a wall of fieldstone around a comfortable ten or fifteen acres, which is a fair hunk of real estate in our crowded little county. The driveway was lined with a cypress hedge trimmed round. There were all sorts of ornamental trees in clumps here and there and they didn't look like California trees. Imported stuff. Whoever built that place was trying to drag the Atlantic seaboard over the Rockies. He was trying hard, but he hadn't made it.

Amos, the middle-aged coloured chauffeur, stopped the Caddy gently in front of the pillared entrance, hopped out, and came around to hold the door open for Mrs Loring. I got out first and helped him hold it. I helped her get out. She had hardly spoken to me since we got into the car in front of my building. She looked tired and nervous. Maybe this idiotic hunk of architecture depressed her. It would have depressed a laughing jackass and made it coo like a mourning dove.

'Who built this place?' I asked her. 'And who was he mad at?'

She finally smiled. 'Hadn't you seen it before?'

'Never been this far into the valley.'

She walked me over to the other side of the driveway and pointed up. 'The man who built it jumped out of that tower-room and landed about where you are standing. He was a French count named La Tourelle and, unlike most French counts, he had a lot of money. His wife was Ramona Desborough who was not exactly threadbare herself. In the silent picture days she made thirty thousand a week. La Tourelle built this place for their home. It's supposed to be a miniature of the Château de Blois. You know that, of course.'

'Like the back of my hand,' I said. 'I remember now. It was one of those Sunday paper stories once. She left him and he killed himself. There was some kind of queer will too, wasn't there?'

She nodded. 'He left his ex-wife a few millions for car-fare and tied up the rest in a trust. The estate was to be kept on just as it was. Nothing was to be changed, the dining-table was to be laid in style every night, and nobody was to be allowed inside the grounds except the servants and the lawyers. The will was broken, of course. Eventually the estate was carved up to some extent and when I married Dr Loring my father gave it to me for a wedding present. It must have cost him a fortune merely to make it fit to live in again. I loathe it. I always have.'

'You don't have to stay here, do you?'

She shrugged in a tired sort of way. 'Part of the time, at least. One of his daughters has to show him some sign of stability. Dr Loring likes it here.'

'He would. Any guy who could make the kind of scene he made at Wade's house ought to wear spats with his pyjamas.'

She arched her eyebrows. 'Why, thank you for taking such an interest, Mr Marlowe. But I think enough has been said on that subject. Shall we go in? My father doesn't like to be kept waiting.'

We crossed the driveway again and went up the stone steps and half of the big double doors swung open noiselessly and an expensive and very snooty-looking character stood aside for us to enter. The hallway was bigger than all the floor space in the house I was living in. It had a tessellated floor and there seemed to be stained-glass windows at the back, and if there had been any light coming through them I might have been able to see what else was there. From the hallway we went through some more double carved doors into a dim room that couldn't have been less than seventy feet long. A man was sitting there waiting, silent. He stared at us coldly.

'Am I late, father?' Mrs Loring asked hurriedly. 'This is Mr Philip Marlowe. Mr Harlan Potter.'

The man just looked at me and moved his chin down about half an inch.

'Ring for tea,' he said. 'Sit down, Mr Marlowe.'

I sat down and looked at him. He looked at me like an entomologist looking at a beetle. Nobody said anything. There was complete silence until the tea came. It was put down on a huge silver tray on a Chinese table. Linda sat at the table and poured.

'Two cups,' Harlan Potter said. 'You can have your tea in another room, Linda.'

'Yes, Father. How do you like your tea, Mr Marlowe?'

'Any way at all,' I said. My voice seemed to echo off into the distance and get small and lonely.

She gave the old man a cup and then gave me a cup. Then she stood up silently and went out of the room. I watched her go. I took a sip of tea and got a cigarette out.

'Don't smoke, please. I am subject to asthma.'

I put the cigarette back in the pack. I stared at him. I don't know how it feels to be worth a hundred millions or so, but he didn't look as if he was having any fun. He was an enormous man, all of six feet five and built to scale. He wore a grey tweed suit with no padding. His shoulders didn't need any. He wore a white shirt and a dark tie and no display handkerchief. A spectacle case showed in the outside breast pocket. It was black, like his shoes. His hair was black too, no grey at all. It was brushed sideways across his skull in a MacArthur sweep. And I had a hunch there was nothing under it but bare skull. His eyebrows were thick and black. His voice seemed to come from a long way off. He drank his tea as if he hated it.

'It will save time, Mr Marlowe, if I put my position before you. I believe you are interfering in my affairs. If I am correct, I propose to stop it.'

'I don't know enough about your affairs to interfere in them, Mr Potter.'

'I disagree.'

He drank some more tea and put the cup aside. He leaned back in the big chair he was sitting in and took me to pieces with his hard grey eyes.

'I know who you are, naturally. And how you make your living—if you make one—and how you became involved with Terry Lennox. It has been reported to me that you helped Terry get out of the country, that you have doubts about his guilt, and that you have since made contact with a man who was known to my dead daughter. For what purpose has not been explained to me. Explain it.'

'If the man has a name,' I said, 'name it.'

He smiled very slightly but not as if he was falling for me. 'Wade. Roger Wade. Some sort of writer, I believe. A writer, they tell me, of rather prurient books which I should not be interested to read. I further understand that this man is a dangerous alcoholic. That may have given you a strange notion.'

'Maybe you had better let me have my own notions, Mr Potter. They are not important, naturally, but they're all I have. First, I do not believe Terry killed his wife, because of the way it was done and because I don't think he was that kind of man. Second, I didn't make contact with Wade. I was asked to live in his house and do what I could to keep him sober while he finished a job of writing. Third, if he is a dangerous alcoholic, I haven't seen any sign of it. Fourth, my first contact was at the request of his New York publisher and I didn't at that time have any idea that Roger Wade even knew your daughter. Fifth, I refused this offer of employment and then Mrs Wade asked me to find her husband who was away somewhere taking a cure. I found him and took him home.'

'Very methodical,' he said dryly.

'I'm not finished being methodical, Mr Potter. Sixth—I think that's the correct number—you or someone on your instructions sent a lawyer named Sewell Endicott to get me out of jail. He didn't say who sent him, but there wasn't anyone else in the picture. Seventh, when I got out of jail a hoodlum named Mendy Menendez pushed me around and warned me to keep my nose clean and gave me a song and dance about how Terry had saved his life and the life of a gambler at Las Vegas named Randy Starr. The story could be true for all I know. Menendez pretended to be sore that Terry hadn't asked him for help getting to Mexico and had asked a punk like me instead. He, Menendez, could have done it two ways from the jack by lifting one finger, and done it much better.'

'Surely,' Harlan Potter said with a bleak smile, 'you are not under the impression that I number Mr Menendez and Mr Starr among my acquaintances.'

'I wouldn't know, Mr Potter. A man doesn't make your kind of money in any way I can understand. The next person to warn me off the court-house lawn was your daughter, Mrs Loring. We met by accident at a bar and we spoke because we were both drinking gimlets, Terry's favourite drink, but an uncommon one around here. I didn't know who she was until she told me. I told her a little of how I felt about Terry and she gave me the idea that I would have a short, unhappy career if I got you mad. Are you mad, Mr Potter?'

'When I am,' he said coldly, 'you will not have to ask me. You will be in no uncertainty about it.'

'What I thought. I've been kind of expecting the goon squad to drop around, but they haven't shown so far. I haven't been bothered by the cops either. I could have been. I could have been given a rough time. I think all you wanted, Mr Potter, was quiet. Just what have I done to disturb you?'

He grinned. It was a sour kind of grin, but it was a grin. He put his long, yellow fingers together and crossed a leg over his knee and leaned back comfortably.

'A pretty good pitch, Mr Marlowe, and I have let you make it. Now you listen to me. You are exactly right in thinking all I want is quiet. It's quite possible that your connexion with the Wades may be incidental, accidental, and coincidental. Let it remain so. I am a family man in an age when it means almost nothing. One of my daughters married a Bostonian prig and the other made a number of foolish marriages, the last being with a complaisant pauper who allowed her to live a worthless and immoral life until he suddenly and for no good reason lost his self-control and murdered her. You think that impossible to accept because of the brutality with which it was done. You are wrong. He shot her with a Mauser automatic, the very gun he took with him to Mexico. And after he shot her he did what he did in order to cover the bullet wound. I admit the brutality of this, but remember the man had been in a war, had been badly wounded, had suffered a great deal and seen others suffer. He may not have intended to kill her. There may have been some sort of scuffle, since the gun belonged to my daughter. It was a small but powerful gun, 7.65 mm. calibre, a model called P.P.K. The bullet went completely through her head and lodged in the wall behind a chintz curtain. It was not found immediately and the fact was not published at all. Now let us consider the situation.' He broke off and stared at me. 'Are you very badly in need of a cigarette?'

'Sorry, Mr Potter. I took it out without thinking. Force of habit.' I put the cigarette back for the second time.

'Terry had just killed his wife. He had ample motive from the rather limited police point of view. But he also had an excellent defence—that it was her gun in her possession and that he tried to take it away from her and failed and she shot herself with it. A good trial lawyer could have done a lot with that. He would probably have been acquitted. If he had called me up then, I would have helped him. But by making the murder a brutal affair to cover the traces of the bullet, he made it impossible. He had to run away and even that he did clumsily.'

'He certainly did, Mr Potter. But he called you up in Pasadena first, didn't he? He told me he did.'

The big man nodded. 'I told him to disappear and I would still see what I could do. I didn't want to know where he was. That was imperative. I could not hide a criminal.'

'Sounds good, Mr Potter.'

'Do I detect a note of sarcasm? No matter. When I learned the details there was nothing to be done. I could not permit the sort of trial that kind of killing would result in. To be frank, I was very glad when I learned that he had shot himself in Mexico and left a confession.'

'I can understand that, Mr Potter.'

He beetled his eyebrows at me. 'Be careful, young man. I don't like irony. Can you understand now that I cannot tolerate any further investigation of any sort by any person? And why I have used all my influence to make what investigation there was as brief as possible and as little publicized as possible?'

'Sure—if you're convinced he killed her.'

'Of course he killed her. With what intent is another matter. It is no longer important. I am not a public character and I do not intend to be. I have always gone to a great deal of trouble to avoid any kind of publicity. I have influence but I don't abuse it. The District Attorney of Los Angeles County is an ambitious man who has too much good sense to wreck his career for the notoriety of the moment. I see a glint in your eye, Marlowe. Get rid of it. We live in what is called a democracy, rule by the majority of the people. A fine deal if it could be made to work. The people elect, but the party machines nominate, and the party machines to be effective must spend a great deal of money. Somebody has to give it to them, and that somebody whether it be an individual, a financial group, a trade union, or what have you expects some consideration in return. What I and people of my kind expect is to be allowed to live our lives in decent privacy. I own newspapers, but I don't like them. I regard them as a constant menace to whatever privacy we have left. Their constant yelping about a free press means, with a few honourable exceptions, freedom to peddle scandal, crime, sex, sensationalism, hate, innuendo, and the political and financial uses of propaganda. A newspaper is a business out to make money through advertising revenue. That is predicated on its circulation and you know what the circulation depends on.'

I got up and walked around my chair. He eyed me with cold attention. I sat down again. I needed a little luck. Hell, I needed it in carload lots.

'Okay, Mr Potter, what goes from here?'

He wasn't listening. He was frowning at his own thoughts. 'There's a peculiar thing about money,' he went on. 'In large quantities it tends to have a life of its own, even a conscience of its own. The power of money becomes very difficult to control. Man has always been a venal animal. The growth of population, the huge cost of wars, the incessant pressure of confiscatory taxation–all these things make him more and more venal. The average man is tired and scared, and a tired, scared man can't afford ideals. He has to buy food for his family. In our time we have seen a shocking decline in both public and private morals. You can't expect quality from people whose lives are a subjection to a lack of quality. You can't have quality with mass production. You don't want it because it lasts too long. So you substitute styling, which is a commercial swindle intended to produce artificial obsolescence. Mass production couldn't sell its goods next year unless it made what it sold this year look unfashionable a year from now. We have the whitest kitchens and the most shining bathrooms in the world. But in the lovely white kitchen the average American housewife can't produce a meal fit to eat, and the lovely shining bathroom is mostly a receptacle for deodorants, laxatives, sleeping pills, and the products of that confidence racket called the cosmetic industry. We make the finest packages in the world, Mr Marlowe. The stuff inside is mostly junk.'

He took out a large white handkerchief and touched his temples with it. I was sitting there with my mouth open, wondering what made the guy tick. He hated everything.

'It's a little too warm for me in these parts,' he said. 'I'm used to a cooler climate. I'm beginning to sound like an editorial that has forgotten the point it wanted to make.'

'I got your point all right, Mr Potter. You don't like the way the world is going so you use what power you have to close off a private corner to live in as near as possible to the way you remember people lived fifty years ago before the age of mass production. You've got a hundred million dollars and all it has bought you is a pain in the neck.'

He pulled the handkerchief taut by two opposite corners, then crumpled it into a ball, and stuffed it in a pocket.

'And then?' he asked shortly.

'That's all there is, there isn't any more. You don't care who murdered your daughter, Mr Potter. You wrote her off as a bad job long ago. Even if Terry Lennox didn't kill her, and the real murderer is still walking around free, you don't care. You wouldn't want him caught, because that would revive the scandal and there would have to be a trial and his defence would blow your privacy as high as the Empire State Building. Unless, of course, he was obliging enough to commit suicide, before there was any trial. Preferably in Tahiti or Guatemala or the middle of the Sahara Desert. Anywhere the County would hate the expense of sending a man to verify what had happened.'

He smiled suddenly, a big rugged smile with a reasonable amount of friendliness in it.

'What do you want from me, Marlowe?'

'If you mean how much money, nothing. I didn't ask myself here. I was brought. I told the truth about how I met Roger Wade. But he did know your daughter and he does have a record of violence, although I haven't seen any of it. Last night the guy tried to shoot himself. He's a haunted man. He has a massive guilt complex. If I happened to be looking for a good suspect, he might do. I realize he's only one of many, but he happens to be the only one I've met.'

He stood up and standing up he was really big. Tough too. He came over and stood in front of me.

'A telephone call, Mr Marlowe, would deprive you of your licence. Don't fence with me. I won't put up with it.'

'Two telephone calls and I'd wake up kissing the gutter—with the back of my head missing.'

He laughed harshly. 'I don't operate that way. I suppose in your quaint line of business it is natural for you to think so. I've given you too much of my time. I'll ring for the butler to show you out.'

'Not necessary,' I said, and stood up myself. 'I came here and got told. Thanks for the time.'

He held his hand out. 'Thank you for coming. I think you're a pretty honest sort of fellow. Don't be a hero, young man. There's no percentage in it.'

I shook hands with him. He had a grip like a pipe wrench. He smiled at me benignantly now. He was Mr Big, the winner, everything under control.

'One of these days I might be able to throw some business your way,' he said. 'And don't go away thinking that I buy politicians or law enforcement officers. I don't have to. Good-bye, Mr Marlowe. And thank you again for coming.'

He stood there and watched me out of the room. I had my hand on the front door when Linda Loring popped out of a shadow somewhere.

'Well?' she asked me quietly. 'How did you get on with Father?'

'Fine. He explained civilization to me. I mean how it looks to him. He's going to let it go for a little while longer. But it better be careful and not interfere with his private life. If it does, he's apt to make a phone call to God and cancel the order.'

'You're hopeless,' she said.

'Me? I'm hopeless? Lady, take a look at your old man. Compared with him I'm a blue-eyed baby with a brand-new rattle.'

I went on out and Amos had the Caddy there waiting. He drove me back to Hollywood. I offered him a buck but he wouldn't take it. I offered to buy him the poems of T.S.Eliot. He said he already had them.

———
33
———

A week went by and I heard nothing from the Wades. The weather was hot and sticky and the acid sting of the smog had crept as far west as Beverly Hills. From the top of Mulholland Drive you could see it levelled out all over the city, a groundlike mist. When you were in it you could taste it and smell it and it made your eyes smart. Everybody was griping about it. In Pasadena, where the stuffy millionaires holed up after Beverly Hills was spoiled for them by the movie crowd, the city fathers screamed with rage. Everything was the fault of the smog. If the canary wouldn't sing, if the milkman was late, if the Pekinese had fleas, if an old coot in a starched collar had a heart attack on the way to church, that was the smog. Where I lived it was usually clear in the early morning and nearly always at night. Once in a while a whole day would be clear, nobody quite knew why.

It was on a day like that—it happened to be a Thursday—that Roger Wade called me up. 'How are you? This is Wade.' He sounded fine.

'Fine, and you?'

'Sober, I'm afraid. Scratching a hard buck. We ought to have a talk. And I think I owe you some dough.'

'Nope.'

'Well, how about lunch today? Could you make it here somewhere around one?'

'I guess so. How's Candy?'

'Candy?' He sounded puzzled. He must have blacked out plenty that night. 'Oh, he helped you put me to bed that night.'

'Yeah. He's a helpful little guy—in spots. And Mrs Wade?'

'She's fine too. She's in town shopping today.'

We hung up and I sat and rocked in my swivel chair. I ought to have asked him how the book was going. Maybe you always ought to ask a writer how the book is going. And then again maybe he gets damned tired of that question.

I had another call in a little while, a strange voice.

'This is Roy Ashterfelt. George Peters told me to call you up, Marlowe.'

'Oh yes, thanks. You're the fellow that knew Terry Lennox in New York. Called himself Marston then.'

'That's right. He was sure on the sauce. But it's the same guy all right. You couldn't very well mistake him. Out here I saw him in Chasen's one night with his wife. I was with a client. The client knew them. Can't tell you the client's name, I'm afraid.'

'I understand. It's not very important now, I guess. What was his first name?'

'Wait a minute while I bite my thumb. Oh yeah, Paul. Paul Marston. And there was one thing more, if it interests you. He was wearing a British Army Service badge. Their version of the ruptured duck.'

'I see. What happened to him?'

'I don't know. I came west. Next time I saw him he was here too—married to Harlan Potter's somewhat wild daughter. But you know all that.'

'They're both dead now. But thanks for telling me.'

'Not at all. Glad to help. Does it mean anything to you?'

'Not a thing,' I said, and I was a liar. 'I never asked him about himself. He told me once he had been brought up in an orphanage. Isn't it just possible you made a mistake?'

'With that white hair and that scarred face, brother? Not a chance. I won't say I never forget a face, but not that one.'

'Did he see you?'

'If he did, he didn't let on. Hardly expect him to in the circumstances. Anyhow he might not have remembered me. Like I said he was always pretty well lit back in New York.'

I thanked him some more and he said it was a pleasure and we hung up.

I thought about it for a while. The noise of the traffic outside the building on the boulevard made an unmusical *obbligato* to my thinking. It was too loud. I got up and shut the lower part of the window and called Detective-Sergeant Green at Homicide. He was obliging enough to be in.

'Look,' I said, after the preliminaries, 'I heard something about Terry Lennox that puzzles me. A fellow I know used to know him in New York under another name. You check his war record?'

'You guys never learn,' Green said harshly. 'You just never learn to stay on your own side of the street. That matter is closed, locked up, weighted with lead, and dropped in the ocean. Get it?'

'I spent part of an afternoon with Harlan Potter last week. At his daughter's house in Idle Valley. Want to check?'

'Doing what?' he asked sourly. 'Supposing I believe you.'

'Talking things over. I was invited. He likes me. Incidentally, he told me the girl was shot with a Mauser 7.65 mm., Model P.P.K. That news to you?'

'Go on.'

'Her own gun, chum. Makes a little difference, maybe. But don't get me wrong. I'm not looking into any dark corners. This is a personal matter. Where did he get that wound?'

Green was silent. I heard a door close in the background. Then he said quietly: 'Probably in a knife fight south of the border.'

'Aw hell, Green, you had his prints. You sent them to Washington like always. You got a report back—like always. All I asked was something about his service record.'

'Who said he had one?'

'Well, Mendy Menendez for one. Seems Lennox saved his life one time and that's how he got the wound. He was captured by the Germans and they gave him the face he had.'

'Menendez, huh? You believe that son of a bitch? You got a hole in your head. Lennox didn't have any war record. Didn't have any record of any kind under any name. You satisfied?'

'If you say so,' I said. 'But I don't see why Menendez would bother to come up here and tell me a yarn and warn me to keep my nose clean on account of Lennox was a pal of him and Randy Starr in Vegas and they didn't want anybody fooling around. After all Lennox was already dead.'

'Who knows what a hoodlum figures?' Green asked bitterly. 'Or why? Maybe Lennox was in a racket with them before he married all that money and got respectable. He was a floor manager at Starr's place in Vegas for a while. That's where he met the girl. A smile and a bow and a dinner jacket. Keep the customers happy and keep and eye on the house players. I guess he had class for the job.'

'He had charm,' I said. 'They don't use it in the police business. Much obliged, Sergeant. How is Captain Gregorius these days?'

'Retirement leave. Don't you read the papers?'

'Not the crime news, Sergeant. Too sordid.'

I started to say good-bye but he chopped me off. 'What did Mr Money want with you?'

'We just had a cup of tea together. A social call. He said he might put some business my way. He also hinted—just hinted, not in so many words—that any cop that looked cross-eyed at me would be facing a grimy future.'

'He don't run the police department,' Green said.

'He admits it. Doesn't even buy commissioners or D.A.s, he said. They just kind of curl up in his lap when he's having a doze.'

'Go to hell,' Green said and hung up in my ear.

A difficult thing, being a cop. You never know whose stomach it's safe to jump up and down on.

34

The stretch of broken-paved road from the highway to the curve of the hill was dancing in the noon heat and the scrub that dotted the parched land on both sides of it was flour-white with granite dust by this time. The weedy smell was almost nauseating. A thin, hot, acrid breeze was blowing. I had my coat off and my sleeves rolled up, but the door was too hot to rest an arm on. A tethered horse dozed wearily under a clump of live oaks. A brown Mexican sat on the ground and ate something out of a newspaper. A tumbleweed rolled lazily across the road and came to rest against a piece of granite outcrop, and a lizard that had been there an instant before disappeared without seeming to move at all.

Then I was around the hill on the blacktop and in another country. In five minutes I turned into the driveway of the Wades' house, parked and walked across the flagstones, and rang the bell. Wade answered the door himself, in a brown and white checked shirt with short sleeves, pale blue denim slacks, and house slippers. He looked tanned and he looked good. There was an ink stain on his hand and a smear of cigarette ash on one side of his nose.

He led the way into his study and parked himself behind his desk. On it there was a thick pile of yellow typescript. I put my coat on a chair and sat on the couch.

'Thanks for coming, Marlowe. Drink?'

I got that look on my face you get when a drunk asks you to have a drink. I could feel it. He grinned.

'I'll have a coke,' he said.

'You pick up fast,' I said. 'I don't think I want a drink right now. I'll take a coke with you.'

He pressed something with his foot and after a while Candy came. He looked surly. He had a blue shirt on and an orange scarf and no white coat. Two-tone black and white shoes, elegant high-waisted gabardine pants.

Wade ordered the cokes. Candy gave me a hard stare and went away.

'Book?' I said, pointing to the stack of paper.

'Yeah. Stinks.'

'I don't believe it. How far along?'

'About two-thirds of the way—for what's it's worth. Which is damn little. You know how a writer can tell when he's washed up?'

'Don't know anything about writers.' I filled my pipe.

'When he starts reading his old stuff for inspiration. That's absolute. I've got five hundred pages of typescript here, well over a hundred thousand words. My books run long. The public like long books. The damnfool public thinks if there's a lot of pages there must be a lot of gold. I don't dare read it over. And I can't remember half of what's in it. I'm just plain scared to look at my own work.'

'You look good yourself,' I said. 'From the other night I wouldn't have believed it. You're got more guts than you think you have.'

'What I need right now is more than guts. Something you don't get by wishing for it. A belief in yourself. I'm a spoiled writer who doesn't believe any more. I have a beautiful home, a beautiful wife, and a beautiful sales record. But all I really want is to get drunk and forget.'

He leaned his chin in his cupped hands and stared across the desk.

'Eileen said I tried to shoot myself. Was it that bad?'

'You don't remember?'

He shook his head. 'Not a damn thing except that I fell down and cut my head. And after a while I was in bed. And you were there. Did Eileen call you?'

'Yeah. Didn't she say?'

'She hasn't been talking to me very much this last week. I guess she's had it. Up to here.' He put the edge of one hand against his neck just under his chin. 'That show Loring put on here didn't help any.'

'Mrs Wade said it meant nothing.'

'Well, she would, wouldn't she? It happened to be the truth, but I don't suppose she believed it when she said it. The guy is just abnormally jealous. You have a drink or two with his wife in the corner and laugh a little and kiss her good-bye and right off he assumes you are sleeping with her. One reason being that he isn't.'

'What I like about Idle Valley,' I said, 'is that everybody is living just a comfortable, normal life.'

He frowned and then the door opened and Candy came in with two cokes and glasses and poured the cokes. He set one in front of me without looking at me.

'Lunch in half an hour,' Wade said, 'and where's the white coat?'

'This is my day off,' Candy said, deadpan. 'I ain't the cook, boss.'

'Cold cuts or sandwiches and beer will do,' Wade said. 'The cook's off today, Candy. I've got a friend to lunch.'

'You think he is your friend?' Candy sneered. 'Better ask your wife.'

Wade leaned back in his chair and smiled at him. 'Watch your lip, little man. You've got it soft here. I don't often ask a favour of you, do I?'

Candy looked down at the floor. After a moment he looked up and grinned. 'Okay, boss. I put the white coat on. I get the lunch, I guess.'

He turned softly and went out. Wade watched the door close. Then he shrugged and looked at me.

'We used to call them servants. Now we called them domestic help. I wonder how long it will be before we have to give them breakfast in bed. I'm paying the guy too much money. He's spoiled.'

'Wages—or something on the side?'

'Such as what?' he asked sharply.

I got up and handed him some folded yellow sheets. 'You'd better read it. Evidently you don't remember asking me to tear it up. It was in your typewriter, under the cover.'

He unfolded the yellow pages and leaned back to read them. The glass of coke fizzed unnoticed on the desk in front of him. He read slowly, frowning.

When he came to the end he refolded the sheets and ran a finger along the edge.

'Did Eileen see this?' he asked carefully.

'I wouldn't know. She might have.'

'Pretty wild, isn't it?'

'I liked it. Especially the part about a good man dying for you.'

He opened the paper again and tore it into long strips viciously and dumped the strips into his waste-basket.

'I suppose a drunk will write or say or do anything,' he said slowly. 'It's meaningless to me. Candy's not blackmailing me. He likes me.'

'Maybe you'd better get drunk again. You might remember what you meant. You might remember a lot of things. We've been through this before—that night when the gun went off. I suppose the seconal blanked you out too. You sounded sober enough. But now you pretend not to remember writing that stuff I just gave you. No wonder you can't write your book, Wade. It's a wonder you can stay alive.'

He reached sideways and opened a drawer of his desk. His hand fumbled in it and came up with a three-decker cheque-book. He opened it and reached for a pen.

'I owe you a thousand dollars,' he said quietly. He wrote in the book. Then on the counterfoil. He tore the cheque out, came around the desk with it, and dropped it in front of me. 'Is that all right?'

I leaned back and looked up at him and didn't touch the cheque and didn't answer him. His face was tight and drawn. His eyes were deep and empty.

'I suppose you think I killed her and let Lennox take the rap,' he said slowly. 'She was a tramp all right. But you don't beat a woman's head in just because she's a tramp. Candy knows I went there sometimes. The funny part of it is I don't think he would tell. I could be wrong, but I don't think so.'

'Wouldn't matter if he did,' I said. 'Harlan Potter's friends wouldn't listen to him. Also, she wasn't killed with that bronze thing. She was shot through the head with her own gun.'

'She maybe had a gun,' he said almost dreamily. 'But I didn't know she had been shot. It wasn't published.'

'Didn't know or didn't remember?' I asked him. 'No, it wasn't published.'

'What are you trying to do to me, Marlowe?' His voice was still dreamy, almost gentle. 'What do you want me to do? Tell my wife? Tell the police? What good would it do?'

'You said a good man died for you.'

'All I meant was that if there had been any real investigation I might have been identified as one—but only one—of the possible suspects. It would have finished me in several ways.'

'I didn't come here to accuse you of a murder, Wade. What's eating you is that you're not sure yourself. You have a record of violence to your wife. You black out when you're drunk. It's no argument to say you don't beat a woman's head in just because she's a tramp. That is exactly what somebody did do. And the guy who got credit for the job seemed to me a lot less likely than you.'

He walked to the open french windows and stood looking out at the

shimmer of heat over the lake. He didn't answer me. He hadn't moved or
spoken a couple of minutes later when there was a light knock at the door
and Candy came in wheeling a tea wagon, with a crisp white cloth, silver-
covered dishes, a pot of coffee, and two bottles of beer.

'Open the beer, boss?' he asked Wade's back.

'Bring me a bottle of whisky.' Wade didn't turn around.

'Sorry, boss. No whisky.'

Wade spun around and yelled at him, but Candy didn't budge. He looked
down at the cheque lying on the cocktail table and his head twisted as he
read it. Then he looked up at me and hissed something between his teeth.
Then he looked at Wade.

'I go now. This my day off.'

He turned and went. Wade laughed.

'So I get it myself,' he said sharply, and went.

I lifted one of the covers and saw some neatly trimmed three-cornered
sandwiches. I took one and poured some beer and ate the sandwich standing
up. Wade came back with a bottle and a glass. He sat down on the couch and
poured a stiff jolt and sucked it down. There was the sound of a car going
away from the house, probably Candy leaving by the service driveway. I
took another sandwich.

'Sit down and make yourself comfortable,' Wade said. 'We have all
afternoon to kill.' He had a glow on already. His voice was vibrant and
cheerful. 'You don't like me, do you, Marlowe?'

'That question has already been asked and answered.'

'Know something? You're a pretty ruthless son of a bitch. You'd do
anything to find what you want. You'd even make love to my wife while I
was helplessly drunk in the next room.'

'You believe everything that knife-thrower tells you?'

He poured some more whisky into his glass and held it up against the
light. 'Not everything, no. A pretty colour whisky is, isn't it? To drown in a
golden flood—that's not so bad. "To cease upon the midnight with no pain."
How does that go on? Oh, sorry, you wouldn't know. Too literary. You're
some kind of a dick, aren't you? Mind telling me why you're here?'

He drank some more whisky and grinned at me. Then he spotted the
cheque lying on the table. He reached for it and read it over his glass.

'Seems to be made out to somebody named Marlowe. I wonder why,
what for? Seems I signed it. Foolish of me. I'm a gullible chap.'

'Stop acting,' I said roughly. 'Where's your wife?'

He looked up politely. 'My wife will be home in due course. No doubt by
that time I shall be passed out and she can entertain you at her leisure. The
house will be yours.'

'Where's the gun?' I asked suddenly.

He looked blank. I told him I had put it in his desk. 'Not there now, I'm
sure,' he said. 'You may search if it pleases you. Just don't steal any rubber
bands.'

I went to the desk and frisked it. No gun. That was something. Probably
Eileen had hidden it.

'Look, Wade, I asked you where your wife was. I think she ought to come
home. Not for my benefit, friend, but yours. Somebody has to look out for
you, and I'll be goddamned if it's going to be me.'

He stared vaguely. He was still holding the cheque. He put his glass down and tore the cheque across, then again and again, and let the pieces fall to the floor.

'Evidently the amount was too small,' he said. 'Your services come very high. Even a thousand dollars *and* my wife fail to satisfy you. Too bad, but I can't go any higher. Except on this.' He patted the bottle.

'I'm leaving,' I said.

'But why? You wanted me to remember. Well—here in the bottle is my memory. Stick around, pal. When I get lit enough I'll tell you about all the women I have murdered.'

'All right, Wade. I'll stick around for a while. But not in here. If you need me, just smash a chair against the wall.'

I went out and left the door open. I walked across the big living-room and out to the patio and pulled one of the chaises into the shadow of the overhang and stretched out on it. Across the lake there was a blue haze against the hills. The ocean breeze had begun to filter through the low mountains to the west. It wiped the air clean and it wiped away just enough of the heat. Idle Valley was having a perfect summer. Somebody had planned it that way. Paradise Incorporated, and also Highly Restricted. Only the nicest people. Absolutely no Central Europeans. Just the cream, the top-drawer crowd, the lovely, lovely people. Like the Lorings and the Wades. Pure gold.

35

I lay there for half an hour trying to make up my mind what to do. Part of me wanted to let him get good and drunk and see if anything came out. I didn't think anything much would happen to him in his own study in his own house. He might fall down again but it would be a long time. The guy had capacity. And somehow a drunk never hurts himself very badly. He might get back his mood of guilt. More likely, this time he would just go to sleep.

The other part of me wanted to get out and stay out, but this was the part I never listened to. Because if I ever had I would have stayed in the town where I was born and worked in the hardware store and married the boss's daughter and had five kids and read them the funny paper on Sunday morning and smacked their heads when they got out of line and squabbled with the wife about how much spending money they were to get and what programmes they could have on the radio or TV set. I might even have got rich—small-town rich, an eight-room house, two cars in the garage, chicken every Sunday, and the *Reader's Digest* on the living-room table, the wife with a cast-iron permanent and me with a brain like a sack of Portland cement. You take it, friend. I'll take the big, sordid, dirty, crooked city.

I got up and went back to the study. He was just sitting there staring at nothing, the Scotch bottle more than half empty, a loose frown on his face and a dull glitter in his eyes. He looked at me like a horse looking over a fence.

'What d'you want?'

'Nothing. You all right?'

'Don't bother me. I have a little man on my shoulder telling me stories.'

I got another sandwich off the tea wagon and another glass of beer. I munched the sandwich and drank the beer, leaning against his desk.

'Know something?' he asked suddenly, and his voice suddenly seemed much more clear. 'I had a male secretary once. Used to dictate to him. Let him go. He bothered me sitting there waiting for me to create. Mistake. Ought to have kept him. Word would have got around I was a homo. The clever boys that write book reviews because they can't write anything else would have caught on and started giving me the build-up. Have to take care of their own, you know. They're all queers, every damn one of them. The queer is the artistic arbiter of our age, chum. The pervert is the top guy now.'

'That so? Always been around, hasn't he?'

He wasn't looking at me. He was just talking. But he heard what I said.

'Sure, thousands of years. And especially in all the great ages of art. Athens, Rome, the Renaissance, the Elizabethan Age, the Romantic Movement in France—loaded with them. Queers all over the place. Ever read *The Golden Bough*? No, too long for you. Shorter version though. Ought to read it. Proves our sexual habits are pure convention—like wearing a black tie with a dinner jacket. Me, I'm a sex writer, but with frills and straight.'

He looked up at me and sneered. 'You know something? I'm a liar. My heroes are eight feet tall and my heroines have calluses on their bottoms from lying in bed with their knees up. Lace and ruffles, swords and coaches, elegance and leisure, duels and gallant death. All lies. They used perfume instead of soap, their teeth rotted because they never cleaned them, their fingernails smelled of stale gravy. The nobility of France urinated against the walls in the marble corridors of Versailles, and when you finally got several sets of underclothes off the lovely marquise the first thing you noticed was that she needed a bath. I ought to write it that way.'

'Why don't you?'

He chuckled. 'Sure, and live in a five-room house in Compton—if I was that lucky.' He reached down and patted the whisky bottle. 'You're lonely, pal. You need company.'

He got up and walked fairly steadily out of the room. I waited, thinking about nothing. A speedboat came racketing down the lake. When it came in sight I could see that it was high out of the water on its step and towing a surfboard with a husky, sunburnt lad on it. I went over to the french doors and watched it make a sweeping turn. Too fast, the speedboat almost turned over. The surfboard rider danced on one foot trying to hold his balance, then went shooting off into the water. The speedboat drifted to a stop and the man in the water came up to it in a lazy crawl, then went back along the tow rope and rolled himself on to the surfboard.

Wade came back with another bottle of whisky. The speedboat picked up and went off into the distance. Wade put his fresh bottle down beside the other. He sat down and brooded.

'Christ, you're not going to drink all that, are you?'

He squinted his eyes at me. 'Take off, buster. Go on home and mop the kitchen floor or something. You're in my light.' His voice was thick again. He had taken a couple in the kitchen, as usual.

'If you want me, holler.'

'I couldn't get low enough to want you.'

'Yeah, thanks. I'll be around until Mrs Wade comes home. Ever hear of anybody named Paul Marston?'

His head came up slowly. His eyes focused, but with effort, I could see him fighting for control. He won the fight–for the moment. His face became expressionless.

'Never did,' he said carefully, speaking very slowly. 'Who's he?'

The next time I looked in on him he was asleep, with his mouth open, his hair damp with sweat, and reeking of Scotch. His lips were pulled back from his teeth in a loose grimace and the furred surface of his tongue looked dry.

One of the whisky bottles was empty. A glass on the table had about two inches in it and the other bottle was about three-quarters full. I put the empty on the tea wagon and rolled it out of the room, then went back to close the french doors and turn the slats of the blinds. The speedboat might come back and wake him. I shut the study door.

I wheeled the tea wagon out to the kitchen, which was blue and white and large and airy and empty. I was still hungry. I ate another sandwich and drank what was left of the beer, then poured a cup of coffee and drank that. The beer was flat but the coffee was still hot. Then I went back to the patio. It was quite a long time before the speedboat came tearing down the lake again. It was almost four o'clock when I heard its distant roar swell into an ear-splitting howl of noise. There ought to be a law. Probably was and the guy in the speedboat didn't give a damn. He enjoyed making a nuisance of himself, like other people I was meeting. I walked down to the edge of the lake.

He made it this time. The driver slowed just enough on the turn and the brown lad on the surfboard leaned far out against the centrifugal pull. The surfboard was almost out of the water, but one edge stayed in and then the speedboat straightened out and the surfboard still had a rider and they went back the way they had come and that was that. The waves stirred up by the boat came charging in towards the shore of the lake at my feet. They slapped hard against the piles of the short landing and jumped the tied boat up and down. They were still lapping it around when I turned back to the house.

As I reached the patio I heard a bell chiming from the direction of the kitchen. When it sounded again I decided that only the front door would have chimes. I crossed to it and opened it.

Eileen Wade was standing there looking away from the house. As she turned she said: 'I'm sorry, I forgot my key.' Then she saw me. 'Oh–I thought it was Roger or Candy.'

'Candy isn't here. It's Thursday.'

She came in and I shut the door. She put a bag down on the table between the two davenports. She looked cool and also distant. She pulled off a pair of white pigskin gloves.

'Is anything wrong?'

'Well, there's a little drinking being done. Not bad. He's asleep on the couch in his study.'

'He called you?'

'Yes, but not for that. He asked me to lunch. I'm afraid he didn't have any himself.'

'Oh.' She sat down slowly on a davenport. 'You know, I completely forgot it was Thursday. The cook's away too. How stupid.'

'Candy got the lunch before he left. I guess I'll blow now. I hope my car wasn't in your way.'

She smiled. 'No. There was plenty of room. Won't you have some tea? I'm going to have some.'

'All right.' I didn't know why I said that. I didn't want any tea. I just said it.

She slipped off a linen jacket. She hadn't worn a hat. 'I'll just look in and see if Roger is all right.'

I watched her cross to the study and open it. She stood there a moment and closed the door and came back.

'He's still asleep. Very soundly. I have to go upstairs for a moment. I'll be right down.'

I watched her pick up her jacket and gloves and bag and go up the stairs and into her room. The door closed. I crossed to the study with the idea of removing the bottle of hooch. If he was still asleep, he wouldn't need it.

36

The shutting of the french doors had made the room stuffy and the turning off of the venetian blinds had made it dim. There was an acrid smell on the air and there was too heavy a silence. It was not more than sixteen feet from the door to the couch and I didn't need more than half of that to know a dead man lay on that couch.

He was on his side with his face to the back of the couch, one arm crooked under him and the forearm of the other lying almost across his eyes. Between his chest and the back of the couch there was a pool of blood and in that pool lay the Webley Hammerless. The side of his face was a smeared mask.

I bent over him, peering at the edge of the wide-open eye, the bare and gaudy arm, at the inner curve of which I could see the puffed and blackened hole in his head from which the blood oozed still.

I left him like that. His wrist was warm but there was no doubt he was quite dead. I looked around for some kind of note or scribble. There was nothing but the pile of script on the desk. They don't leave notes. The typewriter was uncovered on its stand. There was nothing in that. Otherwise everything looked natural enough. Suicides prepare themselves in all sorts of ways, some with liquor, some with elaborate champagne dinners. Some in evening clothes, some in no clothes. People have killed themselves on the tops of walls, in ditches, in bathrooms, in the water, over the water, on the water. They have hanged themselves in barns and gassed themselves in garages. This one looked simple. I hadn't heard the shot but it must have gone off when I was down by the lake watching the surfboard rider make his turn. There was plenty of noise. Why that should have mattered to Roger Wade I don't know. Perhaps it hadn't. The final impulse had coincided with the run of the speedboat. I didn't like it, but nobody cared what I liked.

The torn strips of the cheque were still on the floor but I left them. The torn strips of that stuff he had written that other night were in the waste-basket. These I did not leave. I picked them out and made sure I had them all and stuffed them into my pocket. The basket was almost empty, which made it easy. No use wondering where the gun had been. There were too many places to hide it in. It could have been in a chair or in the couch, under one of the cushions. It could have been on the floor, behind the books, anywhere.

I went out and shut the door. I listened. From the kitchen, sounds. I went out there. Eileen had a blue apron on and the kettle was just beginning to whistle. She turned the flame down and gave me a brief, impersonal glance.

'How do you like your tea, Mr Marlowe?'

'Just out of the pot as it comes.'

I leaned against the wall and got a cigarette out just to have something to do with my fingers. I pinched and squeezed it and broke it in half and threw one half on the floor. Her eyes followed it down. I bent and picked it up. I squeezed the two halves together into a little ball.

She made the tea. 'I always take cream and sugar,' she said over her shoulder. 'Strange, when I drink my coffee black. I learned tea drinking in England. They were using saccharine instead of sugar. When the war came they had no cream, of course.'

'You lived in England?'

'I worked there. I stayed all through the Blitz. I met a man—but I told you about that.'

'Where did you meet Roger?'

'In New York.'

'Married there?'

She swung around, frowning. 'No, we were not married in New York. Why?'

'Just talking while the tea draws.'

She looked out of the window over the sink. She could see down to the lake from there. She leaned against the edge of the drainboard and her fingers fiddled with a folded tea towel.

'It has to be stopped,' she said, 'and I don't know how. Perhaps he'll have to be committed to an institution. Somehow I can't quite see myself doing that. I'd have to sign something, wouldn't I?'

She turned around when she asked that.

'He could do it himself,' I said. 'That is, he could have up to now.'

The tea timer rang its bell. She turned back to the sink and poured the tea from one pot into another. Then she put the fresh pot on the tray she had already fixed up with cups. I went over and got the tray and carried it to the table between the two davenports in the living-room. She sat down opposite me and poured two cups. I reached for mine and set it down in front of me for it to cool. I watched her fix hers with two lumps of sugar and the cream. She tasted it.

'What did you mean by that last remark?' she asked suddenly. 'That he could have up to now—committed himself to some institution, you meant, didn't you?'

'I guess it was a wild pitch. Did you hide the gun I told you about? You know, the morning after he made that play upstairs.'

'Hide it?' she repeated, frowning. 'No. I never do anything like that. I don't believe in it. Why are you asking?'

'And you forgot your house keys today?'

'I told you I did.'

'But not the garage key. Usually in this kind of house the outside keys are mastered.'

'I don't need a key for the garage,' she said sharply. 'It opens by a switch. There's a relay switch inside the front door you push up as you go out. Then another switch beside the garage operates that door. Often we leave the garage open. Or Candy goes out and closes it.'

'I see.'

'You are making some rather strange remarks,' she said with acid in her voice. 'You did the other morning.'

'I've had some rather strange experiences in this house. Guns going off in the night, drunks lying out on the front lawn, and doctors coming that won't do anything. Lovely women wrapping their arms around me and talking as if they thought I was someone else. Mexican houseboys throwing knives. It's a pity about that gun. But you don't really love your husband, do you? I guess I said that before too.'

She stood up slowly. She was as calm as a custard, but her violet eyes didn't seem quite the same colour, nor of quite the same softness. Then her mouth began to tremble.

'Is—is something—wrong in there?' she asked very slowly, and looked towards the study.

I barely had time to nod before she was running. She was at the door in a flash. She threw it open and darted in. If I expected a wild scream I was fooled. I didn't hear anything. I felt lousy. I ought to have kept her out and eased into that corny routine about bad news, prepare yourself, won't you sit down. I'm afraid something serious has happened. Blah, blah, blah. And when you have worked your way through it you haven't saved anybody a thing. Often enough you have made it worse.

I got up and followed her into the study. She was kneeling beside the couch with his head pulled against her breast, smearing herself with his blood. She wasn't making a sound of any kind. Her eyes were shut. She was rocking back and forth on her knees as far as she could, holding him tight.

I went back out and found a telephone and a book. I called the sheriff's sub-station that seemed to be nearest. Didn't matter, they'd relay it by radio in any case. Then I went out to the kitchen and turned the water on and fed the strips of yellow paper from my pocket down the electric garbage grinder. I dumped the tea leaves from the other pot after it. In a matter of seconds the stuff was gone. I shut off the water and switched off the motor. I went back to the living-room and opened the front door and stepped outside.

There must have been a deputy cruising close by because he was there in about six minutes. When I took him into the study she was still kneeling by the couch. He went over to her at once.

'I'm sorry, ma'am. I understand how you must feel, but you shouldn't be touching anything.'

She turned her head, then scrambled to her feet. 'It's my husband. He's been shot.'

He took his cap off and put it on the desk. He reached for the telephone.

'His name is Roger Wade,' she said in a high brittle voice. 'He's the famous novelist.'

'I know who he is, ma'am,' the deputy said and dialled.

She looked down at the front of her blouse. 'May I go upstairs and change this?'

'Sure.' He nodded to her and spoke into the phone, then hung up and turned. 'You say he's been shot. That mean somebody else shot him?'

'I think this man murdered him,' she said without looking at me, and went quickly out of the room.

The deputy looked at me. He got a notebook out. He wrote something in it. 'I better have your name,' he said casually, 'and address. You the one called in?'

'Yes.' I told him my name and address.

'Just take it easy until Lieutenant Ohls gets here.'

'Bernie Ohls?'

'Yeah. You know him?'

'Sure. I've known him a long time. He used to work out of the D.A.'s office.'

'Not lately,' the deputy said. 'He's Assistant Chief of Homicide, working out of the L.A. Sheriff's Office. You a friend of the family, Mr Marlowe?'

'Mrs Wade didn't make it sound that way.'

He shrugged and half-smiled. 'Just take it easy, Mr Marlowe. Not carrying a gun, are you?'

'Not today.'

'I better make sure.' He did. He looked towards the couch then. 'In spots like this you can't expect the wife to make much sense. We better wait outside.'

37

Ohls was a medium-sized thick man with short-cropped faded, blond hair and faded blue eyes. He had stiff white eyebrows and in the days before he stopped wearing a hat you were always a little surprised when he took it off—there was so much more head than you expected. He was a hard, tough cop with a grim outlook on life but a very decent guy underneath. He ought to have made captain years ago. He had passed the examination among the top three half a dozen times. But the Sheriff didn't like him and he didn't like the Sheriff.

He came down the stairs rubbing the side of his jaw. Flashlights had been going off in the study for a long time. Men had gone in and out. I had just sat in the living-room with a plain-clothes dick and waited.

Ohls sat down on the edge of a chair and dangled his hands. He was chewing on an unlit cigarette. He looked at me broodingly.

'Remember the old days when they had a gatehouse and a private police force in Idle Valley?'

I nodded. 'And gambling also.'

'Sure. You can't stop it. This whole Valley is still private property. Like Arrowhead used to be, and Emerald Bay. Long time since I was on a case with no reporters jumping around. Somebody must have whispered in Sheriff Peterson's ear. They kept if off the teletype.'

'Real considerate of them,' I said. 'How is Mrs Wade?'

'Too relaxed. She must of grabbed some pills. There's half a dozen kinds up there—even demerol. That's bad stuff. Your friends don't have a lot of luck lately, do they? They get dead.'

I didn't have anything to say to that.

'Gunshot suicides always interest me,' Ohls said loosely. 'So easy to fake. The wife says you killed him. Why would she say that?'

'She doesn't mean it literally.'

'Nobody else was here. She says you knew where the gun was, knew he was getting drunk, knew he had fired off the gun the other night when she had to fight with him to get the gun away from him. You were there that night too. Don't seem to help much, do you?'

'I searched his desk this afternoon. No gun. I'd told her where it was and to put it away. She says now she didn't believe in that sort of thing.'

'Just when would "now" be?' Ohls asked gruffly.

'After she came home and before I phoned the sub-station.'

'You searched the desk. Why?' Ohls lifted his hands and put them on his knees. He was looking at me indifferently, as if he didn't care what I said.

'He was getting drunk. I thought it just as well to have the gun somewhere else. But he didn't try to kill himself the other night. It was just show-off.'

Ohls nodded. He took the chewed cigarette out of his mouth, dropped it into a tray, and put a fresh one in place of it.

'I quit smoking,' he said. 'Got me coughing too much. But the goddam things still ride me. Can't feel right without one in my mouth. You supposed to watch the guy when he's alone?'

'Certainly not. He asked me to come out and have lunch. We talked and he was kind of depressed about his writing not going well. He decided to hit the bottle. Think I should have taken it away from him?'

'I'm not thinking yet. I'm just trying to get a picture. How much drinking did you do?'

'Beer.'

'It's your tough luck you were here, Marlowe. What was the cheque for? The one he wrote and signed and tore up?'

'They all wanted me to come and live here and keep him in line. All means himself, his wife, and his publisher, a man named Howard Spencer. He's in New York, I guess. You can check with him. I turned it down. Afterwards she came to me and said her husband was off on a toot and she was worried and would I find him and bring him home. I did that. Next thing I knew I was carrying him in off his front lawn and putting him to bed. I didn't want any part of it, Bernie. It just kind of grew up around me.'

'Nothing to do with the Lennox case, huh?'

'Aw, for Pete's sake. There isn't any Lennox case.'

'How true,' Ohls said dryly. He squeezed his kneecaps. A man came in at the front door and spoke to the other dick, then came across to Ohls.

'There's a Dr Loring outside, Lieutenant. Says he was called. He's the lady's doctor.'

'Let him in.'

The dick went back and Dr Loring came in with his neat black bag. He was cool and elegant in a tropical worsted suit. He went past me without looking at me.

'Upstairs?' he asked Ohls.

'Yeah–in her room.' Ohls stood up. 'What you give her that demerol for, Doc?'

Dr Loring frowned at him. 'I prescribe for my patient as I think proper,' he said coldly. 'I am not required to explain why. Who says I gave Mrs Wade demerol?'

'I do. The bottle's up there with your name on it. She's got a regular drugstore in her bathroom. Maybe you don't know it, Doc, but we have a pretty complete exhibit of the little pills downtown. Bluejays, redbirds, yellow jackets, goofballs, and all the rest of the list. Demerol's about the worst of the lot. That's the stuff Goering lived on, I heard somewhere. Took eighteen a day when they caught him. Took the army doctors three months to cut him down.'

'I don't know what these words mean,' Dr Loring said frigidly.

'You don't? Pity. Bluejays are sodium amytal. Redbirds are seconal. Yellow jackets are nembutal. Goofballs are one of the barbiturates laced with benzedrine. Demerol is a synthetic narcotic that is very habit-forming. You just hand 'em out, huh? Is the lady suffering from something serious?'

'A drunken husband can be a very serious complaint indeed for a sensitive woman,' Dr Loring said.

'You didn't get around to him, huh? Pity. Mrs Wade's upstairs, Doc. Thanks for the time.'

'You are impertinent, sir. I shall report you.'

'Yeah, do that,' Ohls said. 'But before you report me, do something else. Keep the lady clear in her head. I've got questions to ask.'

'I shall do exactly what I think best for her condition. Do you know who I am, by any chance? And just to make matters clear, Mr Wade was not my patient. I don't treat alcoholics.'

'Just their wives, huh?' Ohls snarled at him. 'Yeah, I know who you are, Doc. I'm bleeding internally with panic. The name is Ohls. Lieutenant Ohls.'

Dr Loring went on up the stairs. Ohls sat down again and grinned at me.

'You got to be diplomatic with this kind of people,' he said.

A man came out of the study and came up to Ohls. A thin serious-looking man with glasses and a brainy forehead.

'Lieutenant.'

'Shoot.'

'The wound is contact, typically suicidal, with a good deal of distension from gas pressure. The eyes are exophthalmic from the same cause. I don't think there will be any prints on the outside of the gun. It's been bled on too freely.'

'Could it be homicide if the guy was asleep or passed out drunk?' Ohls asked him.

'Of course, but there's no indication of it. The gun's a Webley Hammerless. Typically, this gun takes a very stiff pull to cock it, but a very light pull to discharge it. The recoil explains the position of the gun. I see nothing against suicide so far. I expect a high figure on alcoholic concentration. If it's high enough'–the man stopped and shrugged meaningly–'I might be inclined to doubt suicide.'

'Thanks. Somebody call the coroner?'

The man nodded and went away. Ohls yawned and looked at his watch.

Then he looked at me.

'You want to blow?'

'Sure, if you'll let me. I thought I was a suspect.'

'We might oblige you later on. Stick around where you can be found, that's all. You were a dick once, you know how they go. Some you got to work fast before the evidence gets away from you. This one is just the opposite. If it was homicide, who wanted him dead? His wife? She wasn't here. You? Fine, you had the house to yourself and knew where the gun was. A perfect set-up. Everything but a motive, and we might perhaps give some weight to your experience. I figure if you wanted to kill a guy, you could maybe do it a little less obviously.'

'Thanks, Bernie. I could at that.'

'The help wasn't here. They're out. So it must have been somebody that just happened to drop by. That somebody had to know where Wade's gun was, had to find him drunk enough to be asleep or passed out, and had to pull the trigger when that speedboat was making enough noise to drown the shot, and had to get away before you came back into the house. That I don't buy on any knowledge I have now. The only person who had the means and opportunity was the one guy who wouldn't have used them—for the simple reason he was the one guy who had them.'

I stood up to go. 'Okay, Bernie. I'll be home all evening.'

'There's just one thing,' Ohls said musingly. 'This man Wade was a big-time writer. Lots of dough, lots of reputation. I don't go for his sort of crap myself. You might find nicer people than his characters in a whorehouse. That's a matter of taste and none of my business as a cop. With all this money he had a beautiful home in one of the best places to live in in the county. He had a beautiful wife, lots of friends, and no troubles at all. What I want to know is what made all that so tough that he had to pull a trigger? Sure as hell something did. If you know, you better get ready to lay it on the line. See you.'

I went to the door. The man on the door looked back at Ohls, got the sign, and let me out. I got into my car and had to edge over on the lawn to get around the various official cars that jammed the driveway. At the gate another deputy looked me over but didn't say anything. I slipped my dark glasses on and drove back towards the main highway. The road was empty and peaceful. The afternoon sun beat down on the manicured lawns and the large, roomy, expensive houses behind them.

A man not unknown to the world had died in a pool of blood in a house in Idle Valley, but the lazy quiet had not been disturbed. So far as the newspapers were concerned it might have happened in Tibet.

At a turn of the road the walls of two estates came down to the shoulder and a dark green sheriff's car was parked there. A deputy got out and held up his hand. I stopped. He came to the window.

'May I see your driver's licence, please?'

I took out my wallet and handed it to him open.

'Just the licence, please. I'm not allowed to touch your wallet.'

I took it out and gave it to him. 'What's the trouble?'

He glanced into my car and handed me back my licence.

'No trouble,' he said. 'Just a routine check. Sorry to have troubled you.'

He waved me on and went back to the parked car. Just like a cop. They never tell you why they are doing anything. That way you don't find out they don't know themselves.

I drove home, bought myself a couple of cold drinks, went out to dinner, came back, opened the windows and my shirt, and waited for something to happen. I waited a long time. It was nine o'clock when Bernie Ohls called up and told me to come in and not stop on the way to pick any flowers.

38

They had Candy in a hard chair against the wall of the sheriff's ante-room. He hated me with his eyes as I went by him into the big square room where Sheriff Petersen held court in the middle of a collection of testimonials from a grateful public to his twenty years of faithful public service. The walls were loaded with photographs of horses and Sheriff Petersen made a personal appearance in every photograph. The corners of his carved desk were horses' heads. His inkwell was a mounted, polished horse's hoof and his pens were planted in the mate to it filled with white sand. A gold plate on each of these said something or other about a date. In the middle of a spotless desk blotter lay a bag of Bull Durham and a pack of brown cigarette papers. Petersen rolled his own. He could roll one with one hand on horseback and often did, especially when leading a parade on a big white horse with a Mexican saddle loaded with beautiful Mexican silverwork. On horseback he wore a flat-crowned Mexican sombrero. He rode beautifully and his horse always knew exactly when to be quiet, when to act up so that the Sheriff with his calm, inscrutable smile could bring the horse back under control with one hand. The Sheriff had a good act. He had a handsome hawk-like profile, getting a little saggy under the chin by now, but he knew how to hold his head so it wouldn't show too much. He put a lot of hard work into having his picture taken. He was in his middle fifties and his father, a Dane, had left him a lot of money. The Sheriff didn't look like a Dane, because his hair was dark and his skin was brown and he had the impassive poise of a cigar store Indian and about the same kind of brains. But nobody had ever called him a crook. There had been crooks in his department and they had fooled him as well as they had fooled the public, but none of the crookedness rubbed off on Sheriff Petersen. He just went right on getting elected without even trying, riding white horses at the head of parades, and questioning suspects in front of cameras. That's what the captions said. As a matter of fact he never questioned anybody. He wouldn't have known how. He just sat at his desk looking sternly at the suspect, showing his profile to the camera. The flash bulbs would go off, the camera men would thank the Sheriff deferentially, and the suspect would be removed not having opened his mouth, and the Sheriff would go home to his ranch in the San Fernando Valley. There he could always be reached. If you couldn't reach him in person, you could talk to one of his horses.

Once in a while, come election time, some misguided politician would try to get Sheriff Petersen's job, and would be apt to call him things like The Guy With The Built-In Profile or The Ham That Smokes Itself, but it didn't get him anywhere. Sheriff Petersen just went right on getting re-elected, a living testimonial to the fact that you can hold an important public office for ever in our country with no qualifications for it but a clean nose, a photogenic face, and a close mouth. If on top of that you look good on a horse, you are unbeatable.

As Ohls and I went in Sheriff Petersen was standing behind his desk and the camera boys were filing out by another door. The Sheriff had his white stetson on. He was rolling a cigarette. He was all set to go home. He looked at me sternly.

'Who's this?' he asked in a rich baritone voice.

'Name's Philip Marlowe, Chief,' Ohls said. 'Only person in the house when Wade shot himself. You want a picture?'

The Sheriff studied me. 'I don't think so,' he said, and turned to a big, tired-looking man with iron-grey hair. 'If you need me, I'll be at the ranch, Captain Hernandez.'

'Yes, sir.'

Petersen lit his cigarette with a kitchen match. He lit it on his thumbnail. No lighters for Sheriff Petersen. He was strictly a roll-your-own-and-light-'em-with-one-hand-type.

He said good night and went out. A deadpan character with hard black eyes went with him, his personal bodyguard. The door closed. When he was gone Captain Hernandez moved to the desk and sat in the Sheriff's enormous chair and a stenotype operator in the corner moved his stand out from the wall to get elbow room. Ohls sat at the end of the desk and looked amused.

'All right, Marlowe,' Hernandez said briskly. 'Let's have it.'

'How come I don't get my photo taken?'

'You heard what the Sheriff said.'

'Yeah, but why?' I whined.

Ohls laughed. 'You know damn well why.'

'You mean on account of I'm tall, dark, and handsome and somebody might look at me?'

'Cut it,' Hernandez said coldly. 'Let's get on with your statement. Start from the beginning.'

I gave it to them from the beginning: my interview with Howard Spencer, my meeting with Eileen Wade, her asking me to find Roger, my finding him, her asking me to the house, what Wade asked me to do and how I found him passed out near the hibiscus bushes, and the rest of it. The stenotype operator took it down. Nobody interrupted me. All of it was true. The truth and nothing but the truth. But not quite all the truth. What I left out was my business.

'Nice,' Hernandez said at the end. 'But not quite complete.' This was a cool, competent, dangerous guy, this Hernandez. Somebody in the Sheriff's Office had to be. 'The night Wade shot off the gun in his bedroom you went into Mrs Wade's room and were in there for some time with the door shut. What were you doing in there?'

'She called me in and asked me how he was.'

'Why shut the door?'

'Wade was half asleep and I didn't want to make any noise. Also the houseboy was hanging around with his ear out. Also she asked me to shut the door. I didn't realize it was going to be important.'

'How long were you in there?'

'I don't know. Three minutes maybe.'

'I suggest you were in there a couple of hours,' Hernandez said coldly. 'Do I make myself clear?'

I looked at Ohls. Ohls didn't look at anything. He was chewing on an unlighted cigarette as usual.

'You are misinformed, Captain.'

'We'll see. After you left the room you went downstairs to the study and spent the night on the couch. Perhaps I should say the rest of the night.'

'It was ten minutes to eleven when he called me at home. It was long past two o'clock when I went into the study for the last time that night. Call it the rest of the night if you like.'

'Get the house boy in here,' Hernandez said.

Ohls went out and came back with Candy. They put Candy in a chair. Hernandez asked him a few questions to establish who he was and so on. Then he said:

'All right, Candy—we'll call you that for convenience—after you helped Marlowe put Roger Wade to bed, what happened?'

I knew what was coming more or less. Candy told his story in a quiet, savage voice with very little accent. It seemed as if he could turn that on and off at will. His story was that he had hung around downstairs in case he was wanted again, part of the time in the kitchen where he got himself some food, part of the time in the living-room. While in the living-room sitting in a chair near the front door he had seen Eileen Wade standing in the door of her room and he had seen her take her clothes off. He had seen her put a robe on with nothing under it and he had seen me go into her room and I had shut the door and stayed in there a long time, a couple of hours, he thought. He had gone up the stairs and listened. He had heard the bed springs making sounds. He had heard whisperings. He made his meaning very obvious. When he had finished he gave me a corrosive look and his mouth was twisted tight with hatred.

'Take him out,' Hernandez said.

'Just a minute,' I said. 'I want to question him.'

'I ask the questions here,' Hernandez said sharply.

'You don't know how, Captain. You weren't there. He's lying and he knows it and I know it.'

Hernandez leaned back and picked up one of the Sheriff's pens. He bent the handle of the pen. It was long and pointed and made of stiffened horsehair. When he let go of the point it sprang back.

'Shoot,' he said at last.

I faced Candy. 'Where were you when you saw Mrs Wade take her clothes off?'

'I was sitting down in a chair near the front door,' he said in a surly tone.

'Between the front door and the two facing davenports?'

'What I said.'

'Where was Mrs Wade?'

'Just inside the door of her room. The door was open.'

'What light was there in the living-room?'

'One lamp. Tall lamp what they call a bridge lamp.'

'What light was on the balcony?'

'No light. Light in her bedroom.'

'What kind of light in her bedroom?'

'Not much light. Night table lamp, maybe.'

'Not a ceiling light?'

'No.'

'After she took her clothes off–standing just inside the door of her room, you said–she put on a robe. What kind of robe?'

'Blue robe. Long thing like a housecoat. She tie it with a sash.'

'So if you hadn't actually seen her take her clothes off you wouldn't know what she had on under the robe?'

He shrugged. He looked vaguely worried. '*Si.* That's right. But I see her take her clothes off.'

'You're a liar. There isn't any place in the living-room from which you could see her take her clothes off right bang in her doorway, much less inside her room. She would have to come out to the edge of the balcony. If she had done that she would have seen you.'

He glared at me. I turned to Ohls. 'You've seen the house. Captain Hernandez hasn't–or has he?'

Ohls shook his head slightly. Hernandez frowned and said nothing.

'There is no spot in that living-room, Captain Hernandez, from which he could see even the top of Mrs Wade's head–even if he was standing up–and he said he was sitting down–provided she was as far back as her own doorway or inside it. I'm four inches taller than he is and I could only see the top foot of an open door when I was standing just inside the front door of the house. She would have to come out to the edge of the balcony for him to see what he says he saw. Why would she do that? Why would she undress in her doorway even? There's no sense to it.'

Hernandez just looked at me. Then he looked at Candy. 'How about the time element?' he asked softly, speaking to me.

'That's his word against mine. I'm talking about what can be proved.'

Hernandez spat Spanish at Candy too fast for me to understand. Candy just stared at him sulkily.

'Take him out,' Hernandez said.

Ohls jerked a thumb and opened the door. Candy went out. Hernandez brought out a box of cigarettes, stuck one on his lip, and lit it with a gold lighter.

Ohls came back into the room. Hernandez said calmly: 'I just told him that if there was an inquest and he told that story on the stand, he'd find himself doing a one to three up in Q for perjury. Didn't seem to impress him much. It's obvious what's eating him. An old-fashioned case of hot pants. If he'd been around and we had any reason to suspect murder, he'd make a pretty good pigeon–except that he would have used a knife. I got the impression earlier that he felt pretty bad about Wade's death. Any questions you want to ask, Ohls?'

Ohls shook his head. Hernandez looked at me and said: 'Come back in the morning and sign your statement. We'll have it typed out by then. We ought to have a P.M. report by ten o'clock, preliminary anyway. Anything you don't like about this set-up, Marlowe?'

'Would you mind rephrasing the question? The way you put it suggests there might be something I do like about it.'

'Okay,' he said wearily. 'Take off. I'm going home.'

I stood up.

'Of course I never did believe that stuff Candy pulled on us,' he said. 'Just used it for a corkscrew. No hard feelings, I hope.'

'No feelings at all, Captain. No feelings at all.'

They watched me go out and didn't say good night. I walked down the long corridor to the Hill Street entrance and got into my car and drove home.

No feelings at all was exactly right. I was as hollow and empty as the spaces between the stars. When I got home I mixed a stiff one and stood by the open window in the living-room and sipped it and listened to the ground swell of the traffic on Laurel Canyon Boulevard and looked at the glare of the big, angry city hanging over the shoulder of the hills through which the boulevard had been cut. Far off the banshee wail of police or fire sirens rose and fell, never for very long completely silent. Twenty-four hours a day somebody is running, somebody else is trying to catch him. Out there in the night of a thousand crimes people were dying, being maimed, cut by flying glass, crushed against steering wheels or under heavy car tyres. People were being beaten, robbed, strangled, raped, and murdered. People were hungry, sick, bored, desperate with loneliness or remorse or fear, angry, cruel, feverish, shaken by sobs. A city no worse than others, a city rich and vigorous and full of pride, a city lost and beaten and full of emptiness.

It all depends on where you sit and what your own private score is. I didn't have one. I didn't care.

I finished the drink and went to bed.

39

The inquest was a flop. The Coroner sailed into it before the medical evidence was complete, for fear the publicity would die on him. He needn't have worried. The death of a writer—even a loud writer—is not news for long, and that summer there was too much to compete. A king abdicated and another was assassinated. In one week three large passenger planes crashed. The head man of a big wire service was shot to pieces in Chicago in his own automobile. Twenty-four convicts were burnt to death in a prison fire. The Coroner of Los Angeles County was out of luck. He was missing the good things in life.

As I left the stand I saw Candy. He had a bright, malicious grin on his face—I had no idea why—and as usual he was dressed just a little too well, in a cocoa-brown gabardine suit with a white nylon shirt and a midnight blue bow tie. On the witness stand he was quiet and made a good impression. Yes, the boss had been pretty drunk lately a lot of times. Yes, he had helped put him to bed the night the gun went off upstairs. Yes, the boss had demanded whisky before he, Candy, left on the last day, but he had refused to get it. No, he didn't know anything about Mr Wade's literary work, but he knew the boss had been discouraged. He kept throwing it away and then getting it out of the waste-basket again. No, he had never heard Mr Wade quarrelling with anyone. And so on. The Coroner milked him but it was thin stuff. Somebody had done a good coaching job on Candy.

Eileen Wade wore black and white. She was pale and spoke in a low, clear voice which even the amplifier could not spoil. The Coroner handled her with two pairs of velvet gloves. He talked to her as if he had trouble keeping the sobs out of his voice. When she left the stand he stood up and bowed and she gave him a faint fugitive smile that nearly made him choke on his saliva.

She almost passed me without a glance on the way out, then at the last moment turned her head a couple of inches and nodded very slightly, as if I was somebody she must have met somewhere a long time ago, but couldn't quite place in her memory.

Outside on the steps, when it was all over, I ran into Ohls. He was watching the traffic down below, or pretending to.

'Nice job,' he said without turning his head. 'Congratulations.'

'You did all right on Candy.'

'Not me, kid. The D.A. decided the sexy stuff was irrelevant.'

'What sexy stuff was that?'

He looked at me then. 'Ha, ha, ha,' he said. 'And I don't mean you.' Then his expression got remote. 'I been looking at them for too many years. It wearies a man. This one came out of the special bottle. Old private stock. Strictly for the carriage trade. So long, sucker. Call me when you start wearing twenty-dollar shirts. I'll drop around and hold your coat for you.'

People eddied around us going up and down the steps. We just stood there. Ohls took a cigarette out of his pocket and looked at it and dropped it on the concrete and ground it to nothing with his heel.

'Wasteful,' I said.

'Only a cigarette, pal. It's not a life. After a while maybe you marry the girl, huh?'

'Shove it.'

He laughed sourly. 'I been talking to the right people about the wrong things,' he said acidly. 'Any objection?'

'No objection, Lieutenant,' I said, and went on down the steps. He said something behind me but I kept going.

I went over to a cornbeef joint on Flower. It suited my mood. A rude sign over the entrance said: 'Men only. Dogs and Women Not Admitted.' The service inside was equally polished. The waiter who tossed your food at you needed a shave and deducted his tip without being invited. The food was simple but very good and they had a brown Swedish beer which could hit as hard as a martini.

When I got back to the office the phone was ringing. Ohls said: 'I'm coming by your place. I've got things to say.'

He must have been at or near the Hollywood sub-station because he was in the office inside twenty minutes. He planted himself in the customer's chair and crossed his legs and growled:

'I was out of line. Sorry. Forget it.'

'Why forget it? Let's open up the wound.'

'Suits me. Under the hat, though. To some people you're a wrong gee. I never knew you to do anything too crooked.'

'What was the crack about twenty-dollar shirts?'

'Aw hell, I was just sore,' Ohls said. 'I was thinking of old man Potter. Like he told a secretary to tell a lawyer to tell District Attorney Springer to tell Captain Hernandez you were a personal friend of his.'

'He wouldn't take the trouble.'

'You met him. He gave you time.'

'I met him, period. I didn't like him, but perhaps it was only envy. He sent for me to give me some advice. He's big and he's tough and I don't know what else. I don't figure he's a crook.'

'There ain't no clean way to make a hundred million bucks,' Ohls said. 'Maybe the head man thinks his hands are clean but somewhere along the line guys got pushed to the wall, nice little businesses got the ground cut from under them and had to sell out for nickels, decent people lost their jobs, stocks got rigged on the market, proxies got bought up like a pennyweight of old gold, and the five per centers and the big law firms got paid hundred grand fees for beating some law the people wanted but the rich guys didn't, on accout of it cut into their profits. Big money is big power and big power gets used wrong. It's the system. Maybe it's the best we can get, but it still ain't my Ivory Soap deal.'

'You sound like a Red,' I said, just to needle him.

'I wouldn't know,' he said contemptuously. 'I ain't been investigated yet. You liked the suicide verdict, didn't you?'

'What else could it be?'

'Nothing else, I guess.' He put his hard blunt hands on the desk and looked at the big brown freckles on the backs of them. 'I'm getting old. Keratosis, they call those brown spots. You don't get them until you're past fifty. I'm an old cop and an old cop is an old bastard. I don't like a few things about this Wade death.'

'Such as?' I leaned back and watched the tight sun wrinkles around his eyes.

'You get so you can smell a wrong set-up, even when you know you can't do a damn thing about it. Then you just sit and talk like now. I don't like that he left no note.'

'He was drunk. Probably just a sudden crazy impulse.'

Ohls lifted his pale eyes and dropped his hands off the desk. 'I went through his desk. He wrote letters to himself. He wrote and wrote and wrote. Drunk or sober he hit that typewriter. Some of it is wild, some of it kind of funny, and some of it is sad. The guy had something on his mind. He wrote all around it but he never quite touched it. That guy would have left a two-page letter if he knocked himself off.'

'He was drunk,' I said again.

'With him that didn't matter,' Ohls said wearily. 'The next thing I don't like is he did it there in that room and left his wife to find him. Okay, he was drunk. I still don't like it. The next thing I don't like is he pulled the trigger just when the noise of that speedboat could drown out the shot. What difference would it make to him? More coincidence, huh? More coincidence still that the wife forgot her door keys on the help's day off and had to ring the bell to get into the house.'

'She could have walked around to the back,' I said.

'Yeah, I know. What I'm talking about is a situation. Nobody to answer the door for you, and she said on the stand she didn't know you were there. Wade wouldn't have heard the bell if he had been alive and working in his study. His door is sound-proofed. The help was away. That was Thursday. That she forgot. Like she forgot her keys.'

'You're forgetting something yourself, Bernie. My car was in the driveway. So she knew I was there–or that somebody was there–before she rang the bell.'

He grinned. 'I forgot that, didn't I? All right, here's the picture. You were down at the lake, the speedboat was making all that racket–incidentally it was a couple of guys from Lake Arrowhead just visiting, had their boat on a trailer–Wade was asleep in his study or passed out, somebody took the gun out of his desk already, and she knew you had put it there because you told her that other time. Now suppose she didn't forget her keys, that she goes into the house, looks across and sees you down at the water, looks into the study and sees Wade asleep, knows where the gun is, gets it, waits for the right moment, plugs him, drops the gun where it was found, goes back outside the house, waits a little while for the speedboat to go away, and then rings the doorbell and waits for you to open it. Any objections?'

'With what motive?'

'Yeah,' he said sourly. 'That knocks it. If she wanted to slough the guy, it was easy. She had him over a barrel, habitual drunk, record of violence to her. Plenty alimony, nice fat property settlement. No motive at all. Anyhow the timing was too neat. Five minutes earlier and she couldn't have done it, unless you were in on it.'

I started to say something but he put his hand up. 'Take it easy. I'm not accusing anybody, just speculating. Five minutes later and you get the same answer. She had ten minutes to pull it off.'

'Ten minutes,' I said irritably, 'that couldn't possibly have been foreseen, much less planned.'

He leaned back in the chair and sighed. 'I know. You've got all the answers. I've got all the answers. And I still don't like it. What the hell were you doing with these people anyway? The guy writes you a cheque for a grand, then tears it up. Got mad at you, you say. You didn't want it, anyway, wouldn't have taken it, you say. Maybe. Did he think you were sleeping with his wife?'

'Lay off, Bernie.'

'I didn't ask were you, I asked did he think you were.'

'Same answer.'

'Okay, try this. What did the Mex have on him?'

'Nothing that I know of.'

'The Mex has too much money. Over fifteen hundred in the bank, all kinds of clothes, a brand-new Chevvy.'

'Maybe he peddles dope,' I said.

Ohls pushed himself up out of the chair and scowled down at me.

'You're an awful lucky boy, Marlowe. Twice you've slid out from under a heavy one. You could get over-confident. You were pretty helpful to those people and you didn't make a dime. You were pretty helpful to a guy named Lennox too, the way I hear it. And you didn't make a dime out of that one either. What do you do for eating money, pal? You got a lot saved up so you don't have to work any more?'

I stood up and walked around the desk and faced him. 'I'm a romantic, Bernie. I hear voices crying in the night and I go see what's the matter. You don't make a dime that way. You got sense, you shut your windows and turn up more sound on the TV set. Or you shove down on the gas and get far away from there. Stay out of other people's troubles. All it can get you is the smear. The last time I saw Terry Lennox we had a cup of coffee together that I made myself here in this house, and we smoked a cigarette. So when I heard he was dead I went out to the kitchen and made some coffee and poured a cup for him and lit a cigarette for him, and when the coffee was cold and the cigarette was burned down I said good night to him. You don't make a dime that way. *You* wouldn't do it. That's why you're a good cop and I'm a private eye. Eileen Wade is worried about her husband, so I go out and find him and bring him home. Another time he's in trouble and calls me up and I go out and carry him in off the lawn and put him to bed, and I don't make a dime out of it. No percentage at all. No nothing, except sometimes I get my faced pushed in or get tossed in the can or get threatened by some fast money boy like Mendy Menendez. But no money, not a dime. I've got a five-thousand-dollar bill in my safe but I'll never spend a nickel of it. Because there was something wrong with the way I got it. I played with it a little at first and I still get it out once in a while and look at it. But that's all—not a dime of spending money.'

'Must be a phoney,' Ohls said dryly, 'except they don't make them that big. So what's your point with all this yap?'

'No point. I told you I was a romantic.'

'I heard you. And you don't make a dime at it. I heard that too.'

'But I can always tell a cop to go to hell. Go to hell, Bernie.'

'You wouldn't tell me to go to hell if I had you in the back room under the light, chum.'

'Maybe we'll find out about that some day.'

He walked to the door and yanked it open. 'You know something, kid? You think you're cute but you're just stupid. You're a shadow on the wall. I've got twenty years on the cops without a mark against me. I know when I'm being kidded and I know when a guy is holding out on me. The wise guy never fools anybody but himself. Take it from me, chum. I know.'

He pulled his head back out of the doorway and let the door close. His heels hammered down the corridor. I could still hear them when the phone on my desk started to sound. The voice said in that clear professional voice:

'New York is calling Mr Philip Marlowe.'

'I'm Philip Marlowe.'

'Thank you. One moment, please, Mr Marlowe. Here is your party.'

The next voice I knew. 'Howard Spencer, Mr Marlowe. We've heard about Roger Wade. It was a pretty hard blow. We haven't the full details, but your name seems to be involved.'

'I was there when it happened. He just got drunk and shot himself. Mrs Wade came home a little later. The servants were away—Thursday's the day off.'

'You were alone with him?'

'I wasn't with him. I was outside the house, just hanging around waiting for his wife to come home.'

'I see. Well, I suppose there will be an inquest.'

'It's all over, Mr Spencer. Suicide. And remarkably little publicity.'

'Really? That's curious.' He didn't exactly sound disappointed—more like puzzled and surprised. 'He was so well known. I should have thought—well, never mind what I thought. I guess I'd better fly out there, but I can't make it before the end of next week. I'll send a wire to Mrs Wade.

There may be something I could do for her—and also about the book. I mean there may be enough of it so that we could get someone to finish it. I assume you did take the job after all.'

'No. Although he asked me to himself. I told him right out I couldn't stop him from drinking.'

'Apparently you didn't even try.'

'Look, Mr Spencer, you don't know the first damn thing about this situation. Why not wait until you do before jumping to conclusions? Not that I don't blame myself a little. I guess that's inevitable when something like this happens, and you're the guy on the spot.'

'Of course,' he said. 'I'm sorry I made that remark. Most uncalled for. Will Eileen Wade be at her home now—or wouldn't you know?'

'I wouldn't know, Mr Spencer. Why don't you just call her up?'

'I hardly think she would want to speak to anyone yet,' he said slowly.

'Why not? She talked to the Coroner and never batted an eye.'

He cleared his throat. 'You don't sound exactly sympathetic.'

'Roger Wade is dead, Spencer. He was a bit of a bastard and maybe a bit of a genius too. That's over my head. He was an egotistical drunk and he hated his own guts. He made me a lot of trouble and in the end a lot of grief. Why the hell should I be sympathetic?'

'I was talking about Mrs Wade,' he said shortly.

'So was I.'

'I'll call you when I get in,' he said abruptly. 'Good-bye.'

He hung up. I hung up. I stared at the telephone for a couple of minutes without moving. Then I got the phone book up on the desk and looked for a number.

40

I called Sewell Endicott's office. Somebody said he was in court and would not be available until late in the afternoon. Would I care to leave my name? No.

I dialled the number of Mendy Menendez's joint on the Strip. It was called El Tapado this year, not a bad name either. In American Spanish that means buried treasure among other things. It had been called other names in the past, quite a few other names. One year it was just a blue neon number on a blank high wall facing south on the Strip, with its back against the hill and a driveway curving around one side out of sight of the street. Very exclusive. Nobody knew much about it except vice cops and mobsters and people who could afford thirty bucks for a good dinner and any amount up to fifty grand in the big quiet room upstairs.

I got a woman who didn't know from nothing. Then I got a captain with a Mex accent.

'You wish to speak to Mr Menendez? Who is calling?'

'No names, *amigo*. Private matter.'

'*Un momento, por favor.*'

There was a longish wait. I got a hard boy this time. He sounded as if he was talking through the slit in an armoured car. It was probably just the slit in his face.

'Talk it up. Who wants him?'

'The name's Marlowe.'

'Who's Marlowe?'

'This Chick Agostino?'

'No, this ain't Chick. Come on, let's have the pass-word.'

'Go fry your face.'

There was a chuckle. 'Hold the line.'

Finally another voice said: 'Hello, cheapie. What's the time by you?'

'You alone?'

'You can talk, cheapie. I been looking over some acts for the floor show.'

'You could cut your throat for one.'

'What would I do for an encore?'

I laughed. He laughed. 'Been keeping your nose clean?' he asked.

'Haven't you heard? I got to be friends with another guy who suicided. They're going to call me the "Kiss-of-Death-Kid" from now on.'

'That's funny, huh?'

'No, it isn't funny. Also the other afternoon I had tea with Harlan Potter.'

'Nice going. I never drink the stuff myself.'

'He said for you to be nice to me.'

'I never met the guy and I don't figure to.'

'He casts a long shadow. All I want is a little information, Mendy. Like about Paul Marston.'

'Never heard of him.'

'You said that too quick. Paul Marston was the name Terry Lennox used one time in New York before he came west.'

'So?'

'His prints were checked through the F.B.I. files. No record. That means he never served in the Armed Forces.'

'So?'

'Do I have to draw you a picture? Either that foxhole yarn of yours was all spaghetti or it happened somewhere else.'

'I didn't say where it happened, cheapie. Take a kind word and forget the whole thing. You got told, you better stay told.'

'Oh sure. I do something you don't like and I'm swimming to Catalina with a streetcar on my back. Don't try to scare me, Mendy. I've been up against the pros. You ever been in England?'

'Be smart, cheapie. Things can happen to a guy in this town. Things can happen to big strong boys like Big Willie Magoon. Take a look at the evening paper.'

'I'll get one if you say so. It might even have my picture in it. What about Magoon?'

'Like I said—things can happen. I wouldn't know how except what I read. Seems Magoon tried to shake down four boys in a car with Nevada plates. Was parked right by his house. Nevada plates with big numbers like they don't have. Must have been some kind of a rib. Only Magoon ain't feeling funny, what with both arms in casts, and his jaw wired in three places, and one leg in high traction. Magoon ain't tough any more. It could happen to you.'

'He bothered you, huh? I saw him bounce your boy Chick off the wall in front of Victor's. Should I ring up a friend in the Sheriff's office and tell him?'

'You do that, cheapie,' he said very slowly. 'You do that.'

'And I'll mention that at the time I was just through having a drink with Harlan Potter's daughter. Corroborative evidence, in a sense, don't you think? You figure to smash her up too?'

'Listen to me careful, cheapie—'

'Were you ever in England, Mendy? You and Randy Starr and Paul Marston or Terry Lennox or whatever his name was? In the British Army perhaps? Had a little racket in Soho and got hot and figured the Army was a cooling-off spot?'

'Hold the line.'

I held it. Nothing happened except that I waited and my arm got tired. I switched the receiver to the other side. Finally he came back.

'Now listen careful, Marlowe. You stir up that Lennox case and you're dead. Terry was a pal and I got feelings too. So you got feelings. I'll go along with you just this far. It was a commando outfit. It was British. It happened in Norway, one of those islands off the coast. They got a million of them. November 1942. Now will you lie down and rest that tired brain of yours?'

'Thank you, Mendy. I will do that. Your secret is safe with me. I'm not telling it to anybody but the people I know.'

'Buy yourself a paper, cheapie. Read and remember. Big tough Willie Magoon. Beat up in front of his own house. Boy, was he surprised when he came out of the ether!'

He hung up. I went downstairs and bought a paper and it was just as Menendez had said. There was a picture of Big Willie Magoon in his hospital bed. You could see half his face and one eye. The rest of him was bandages. Seriously but not critically injured. The boys had been very careful about that. They wanted him to live. After all he was a cop. In our town the mobs don't kill a cop. They leave that to the juveniles. And a live cop who has been put through the meat grinder is a much better advertisement. He gets well eventually and goes back to work. But from that time on something is missing—the last inch of steel that makes all the difference. He's a walking lesson that it is a mistake to push the racket boys too hard—especially if you are on the vice squad and eating at the best places and driving a Cadillac.

I sat there and brooded about it for a while and then I dialled the number of the Carne Organization and asked for George Peters. He was out. I left my name and said it was urgent. He was expected in about five-thirty.

I went over to the Hollywood Public Library and asked questions in the reference room, but couldn't find what I wanted. So I had to go back for my Olds and drove downtown to the Main Library. I found it there, in a smallish, red-bound book published in England. I copied what I wanted from it and drove home. I called the Carne Organization again. Peters was still out, so I asked the girl to re-route the call to me at home.

I put the chessboard on the coffee table and set out a problem called The Sphinx. It is printed on the end-papers of a book on chess by Blackburn, the English chess wizard, probably the most dynamic chess player who ever lived, although he wouldn't get to first base in the cold war type of chess they play nowadays. The Sphinx is an eleven-mover and it justifies its name. Chess problems seldom run to more than four or five moves. Beyond that the difficulty of solving them rises in almost geometrical progression. An eleven-mover is sheer unadulterated torture.

Once in a long while when I feel mean enough I set it out and look for a new way to solve it. It's a nice quiet way to go crazy. You don't even scream, but you come awfully close.

George Peters called me at five-forty. We exchanged pleasantries and condolences.

'You've got yourself in another jam, I see,' he said cheerfully. 'Why don't you try some quiet business like embalming?'

'Takes too long to learn. Listen, I want to become a client of your agency, if it doesn't cost too much.'

'Depends what you want done, old boy. And you'd have to talk to Carne.'

'No.'

'Well, tell me.'

'London is full of guys like me, but I wouldn't know one from the other. They call them private inquiry agents. Your outfit would have connexions. I'd just have to pick a name at random and probably get hornswoggled. I want some information that should be easy enough to get, and I want it quick. Must have it before the end of next week.'

'Spill.'

'I want to know something about the war service of Terry Lennox or Paul Marston, whatever name he used. He was in the Commandos over there. He was captured wounded in November 1942 in a raid on some Norwegian island. I want to know what outfit he was posted from and what happened to him. The War Office will have all that. It's not secret information, or I wouldn't think so. Let's say a question of inheritance is involved.'

'You don't need a P.I. for that. You could get it direct. Write them a letter.'

'Shove it, George. I might get an answer in three months. I want one in five days.'

'You have a thought there, pal. Anything else?'

'One thing more. They keep all their vital records over there in a place they call Somerset House. I want to know if he figures there in any connexion—birth, marriage, naturalization, anything at all.'

'Why?'

'What do you mean, why? Who's paying the bill?'

'Suppose the names don't show?'

'Then I'm stuck. If they do, I want certified copies of anything your man turns up. How much you soaking me?'

'I'll have to ask Carne. He may thumb it out altogether. We don't want the kind of publicity you get. If he lets me handle it, and you agree not to mention the connexion, I'd say three hundred bucks. Those guys over there don't get much by dollar standards. He might hit us for ten guineas, less than thirty bucks. On top of that any expenses he might have. Say fifty bucks and Carne wouldn't open a file for less than two-fifty.'

'Professional rates.'

'Ha, ha. He never heard of them.'

'Call me, George. Want to eat dinner?'

'Romanoff's?'

'All right,' I growled, 'if they'll give me a reservation—which I doubt.'

'We can have Carne's table. I happen to know he's dining privately. He's a regular at Romanoff's. It pays off in the upper brackets of the business. Carne is a pretty big boy in this town.'

'Yeah, sure. I know somebody—and know him personally—who could lose Carne under his little fingernail.'

'Good work, kid. I always knew you would come through in the clutch. See you about seven o'clock in the bar at Romanoff's. Tell the head thief you're waiting for Colonel Carne. He'll clear a space around you so you don't get elbowed by any riff-raff like screenwriters or television actors.'

'See you at seven,' I said.

We hung up and I went back to the chess board. But The Sphinx didn't seem to interest me any more. In a little while Peters called me back and said it was all right with Carne provided the name of their agency was not connected with any of my problems. Peters said he would get a night letter off to London at once.

41

Howard Spencer called me on the following Friday morning. He was at the Ritz-Beverly and suggested I drop over for a drink in the bar.

'Better make it in your room,' I said.

'Very well, if you prefer it. Room 828. I've just talked to Eileen Wade. She seems quite resigned. She has read the script Roger left and says she thinks it can be finished off very easily. It will be a good deal shorter than his other books, but that is balanced by the publicity value. I guess you think we publishers are a pretty callous bunch. Eileen will be home all afternoon. Naturally she wants to see me and I want to see her.'

'I'll be over in half an hour, Mr Spencer.'

He had a nice roomy suite on the west side of the hotel. The living-room had tall windows opening on a narrow, iron-railed balcony. The furniture was upholstered in some candy-striped material and that with the heavily flowered design of the carpet gave it an old-fashioned air, except that everything you could put a drink down on had a plate-glass top and there were nineteen ashtrays spotted around. A hotel room is a pretty sharp indication of the manners of the guests. The Ritz-Beverly wasn't expecting them to have any.

Spencer shook hands.

'Sit down,' he said. 'What will you drink?'

'Anything or nothing. I don't have to have a drink.'

'I fancy a glass of Amontillado. California is poor drinking country in the summer. In New York you can handle four times as much for one half the hangover.'

'I'll take a rye-whisky sour.'

He went to the phone and ordered. Then he sat down on one of the candy-striped chairs and took off his rimless glasses to polish them on a handkerchief. He put them back on, adjusted them carefully, and looked at me.

'I take it you have something on your mind. That's why you wanted to see me up here rather than in the bar.'

'I'll drive you out to Idle Valley. I'd like to see Mrs Wade too.'

He looked a little uncomfortable. 'I'm not sure she wants to see you,' he said.

'I know she doesn't. I can get in on your ticket.'

'That would not be very diplomatic of me, would it?'

'She tell you she didn't want to see me?'

'Not exactly, not in so many words.' He cleared his throat. 'I get the impression that she blames you for Roger's death.'

'Yeah. She said that right out—to the deputy who came the afternoon he died. She probably said it to the Sheriff's homicide lieutenant that investigated the death. She didn't say it to the Coroner, however.'

He leaned back and scratched the inside of his hand with a finger, slowly. It was just a sort of doodling gesture.

'What good would it do for you to see her, Marlowe? It was a pretty dreadful experience for her. I imagine her whole life had been pretty dreadful for some time. Why make her live it over? Do you expect to convince her that you didn't miss out a little?'

'She told the deputy I killed him.'

'She couldn't have meant that literally. Otherwise—'

The door buzzer rang. He got up to go to the door and open it. The room service waiter came in with the drinks and put them down with as much flourish as if he was serving a seven-course dinner. Spencer signed the check and gave him four bits. The guy went away. Spencer picked up his glass of sherry and walked away as if he didn't want to hand me my drink. I let it stay where it was.

'Otherwise what?' I asked him.

'Otherwise she *would* have said something to the Coroner, wouldn't she?' He frowned at me. 'I think we are talking nonsense. Just what did you want to see me about?'

'You wanted to see me.'

'Only,' he said coldly, 'because when I talked to you from New York you said I was jumping to conclusions. That implied to me that you had something to explain. Well, what is it?'

'I'd like to explain it in front of Mrs Wade.'

'I don't care for the idea. I think you had better make your own arrangements. I have a great regard for Eileen Wade. As a business man I'd like to salvage Roger's work if it can be done. If Eileen feels about you as you suggest I can't be the means of getting you into her house. Be reasonable.'

'That's all right,' I said. 'Forget it. I can get to see her without any trouble. I just thought I'd like to have somebody along with me as a witness.'

'Witness to what?' he almost snapped at me.

'You'll hear it in front of her or you won't hear it at all.'

'Then I won't hear it at all.'

I stood up. 'You're probably doing the right thing, Spencer. You want that book of Wade's—if it can be used. And you want to be a nice guy. Both laudable ambitions. I don't share either of them. The best of luck to you and good-bye.'

He stood up suddenly and started towards me. 'Now just a minute, Marlowe. I don't know what's on your mind but you seem to take it hard. Is there some mystery about Roger Wade's death?'

'No mystery at all. He was shot through the head with a Webley Hammerless revolver. Didn't you see a report of the inquest?'

'Certainly.' He was standing close to me now and he looked bothered. 'What was in the eastern papers and a couple of days later a much fuller account in the Los Angeles paper. He was alone in the house, although you were not far away. The servants were away. Candy and the cook, and Eileen had been uptown shopping and arrived home just after it happened. At the moment it happened a very noisy motor-boat on the lake drowned the sound of the shot, so that even you didn't hear it.'

'That's correct,' I said. 'Then the motor-boat went away, and I walked back from the lake edge up to the house, heard the doorbell ringing and opened it to find Eileen Wade had forgotten her keys. Roger was already dead. She looked into the study from the doorway, thought he was asleep on the couch, went out to the kitchen to make some tea. A little later than she did I also looked into the study, noticed there was no sound of breathing, and found out why. In due course I called the law.'

'I see no mystery,' Spencer said quietly, all the sharpness gone from his voice. 'It was Roger's own gun, and only the week before he had shot it off in his own room. You found Eileen struggling to get it away from him. His state of mind, his behaviour, his depression over his work—all that was brought out.'

'She told you the stuff is good. Why would he be depressed over it?'

'That's just her opinion, you know. It may be very bad. Or he may have thought it worse than it was. Go on. I'm not a fool. I can see there is more.'

'The homicide dick who investigated the case is an old friend of mine. He's a bulldog and a bloodhound and an old wise cop. He doesn't like a few things. Why did Roger leave no note—when he was a writing fool? Why did he shoot himself in such a way as to leave the shock of discovery to his wife? Why did he bother to pick the moment when I couldn't hear the gun go off? Why did she forget her house keys so that she had to be let into the house? Why did she leave him alone on the day the help got off? Remember, she said she didn't know I would be there. If she did, those two cancel out.'

'My God,' Spencer bleated, 'are you telling me the damnfool cop suspects Eileen?'

'He would if he could think of a motive.'

'That's ridiculous. Why not suspect you? You had all afternoon. There could have been only a few minutes when she could have done it—and she had forgotten her house keys.'

'What motive could I have?'

He reached back and grabbed my whisky sour and swallowed it whole. He put the glass down carefully and got a handkerchief out and wiped his lips and his fingers where the chilled glass had moistened them. He put the handkerchief away. He stared at me.

'Is the investigation still going on?'

'Couldn't say. One thing is sure. They know by now whether he had drunk enough hooch to pass him out. If he had, there may still be trouble.'

'And you want to talk to her,' he said slowly, 'in the presence of a witness.'

'That's right.'

'That means only one of two things to me, Marlowe. Either you are badly scared or you think she ought to be.'

I nodded.

'Which one?' he asked grimly.

'I'm not scared.'

He looked at his watch. 'I hope to God you're crazy.'

We looked at each other in silence.

42

North through Coldwater Canyon it began to get hot. When we topped the rise and started to wind down towards the San Fernando Valley it was breathless and blazing. I looked sideways at Spencer. He had a vest on, but the heat didn't seem to bother him. He had something else to bother him a lot more. He looked straight ahead through the wind-shield and said nothing. The Valley had a thick layer of smog nuzzling down on it. From above it looked like a ground mist and then we were in it and it jerked Spencer out of his silence.

'My God, I thought Southern California had a climate,' he said. 'What are they doing—burning old truck tyres?'

'It'll be all right in Idle Valley,' I told him soothingly. 'They get an ocean breeze in there.'

'I'm glad they get something besides drunk,' he said. 'From what I've seen of the local crowd in the rich suburbs I think Roger Wade made a tragic mistake in coming out here to live. A writer needs stimulation—and not the kind they bottle. There's nothing around here but one great big suntanned hangover. I'm referring to the upper crust people of course.'

I turned off and slowed down for the dusty stretch to the entrance of Idle Valley, then hit the paving again and in a little while the ocean breeze made itself felt, drifting down through the gap in the hills at the far end of the lake. High sprinklers revolved over the big, smooth lawns and the water made a swishing sound as it licked at the grass. By this time most of the well-heeled people were away somewhere else. You could tell by the shuttered look of the houses and the way the gardener's truck was parked smack in the middle of the driveway. Then we reached the Wades' place and I swung through the gateposts and stopped behind Eileen's Jaguar. Spencer got out and marched solidly across the flagstones to the portico of the house. He rang the bell and the door opened almost at once. Candy was there in the white jacket and the dark, good-looking face and the sharp black eyes. Everything was in order.

Spencer went in. Candy gave me a brief look and neatly shut the door in my face. I waited and nothing happened. I leaned on the bell and heard the chimes. The door swung wide and Candy came out snarling.

'Beat it! Turn blue. You want a knife in the belly?'

'I came to see Mrs Wade.'

'She don't want any part of you.'

'Out of my way, peasant. I got business here.'

'Candy!' It was her voice, and it was sharp.

He gave me a final scowl and backed into the house. I went in and shut the

door. She was standing at the end of one of the facing davenports, and
Spencer was standing beside her. She looked like a million. She had white
slacks on, very high-waisted, and a white sport shirt with half sleeves, and a
lilac-coloured handkerchief budding from the pocket over her left breast.

'Candy is getting rather dictatorial lately, she said to Spencer. 'It's good
to see you, Howard. And so nice of you to come all this way. I didn't realize
you were bringing someone with you.'

'Marlowe drove me out,' Spencer said. 'Also he wanted to see you.'

'I can't imagine why,' she said coolly. Finally she looked at me, but not as
if not seeing me for a week had left an emptiness in her life. 'Well?'

'It's going to take a little time,' I said.

She sat down slowly. I sat down on the other davenport. Spencer was
frowning. He took his glasses off and polished them. That gave him a chance
to frown more naturally. Then he sat on the other end of the davenport from
me.

'I was sure you would come in time for lunch,' she told him, smiling.

'Not today, thanks.'

'No? Well, of course if you are too busy. Then you just want to see that
script.'

'If I may.'

'Of course. Candy! Oh, he's gone. It's on the desk in Roger's study. I'll
get it.'

Spencer stood up. 'May I get it?'

Without waiting for an answer he started across the room. Ten feet
behind her he stopped and gave me a strained look. Then he went on. I just
sat there and waited until her head came around and her eyes gave me a cool
impersonal stare.

'What was it you wanted to see me about?' she asked curtly.

'This and that. I see you are wearing that pendant again.'

'I often wear it. It was given to me by a very dear friend a long time ago.'

'Yeah. You told me. It's a British military badge of some sort, isn't it?'

She held it out at the end of the thin chain. 'It's a jeweller's reproduction
of one. Smaller than the original and in gold and enamel.'

Spencer came back across the room and sat down again and put a thick
pile of yellow paper on the corner of the cocktail table in front of him. He
glanced at it idly, then his eyes were watching Eileen.

'Could I look at it a little closer?' I asked her.

She pulled the chain around until she could unfasten the clasp. She
handed the pendant to me, or rather she dropped it in my hand. Then she
folded her hands in her lap and just looked curious. 'Why are you so
interested? It's the badge of a regiment called the Artists Rifles, a
Territorial Regiment. The man who gave it to me was lost soon afterwards.
At Andalsnes in Norway, in the spring of that terrible year–1940.' She
smiled and made a brief gesture with one hand. 'He was in love with me.'

'Eileen was in London all through the Blitz,' Spencer said in an empty
voice. 'She couldn't get away.'

We both ignored Spencer. 'And you were in love with him,' I said.

She looked down and then raised her head and our glances locked. 'It was
a long time ago,' she said. 'And there was a war. Strange things happen.'

'There was a little more to it than that, Mrs Wade. I guess you forgot how
much you opened up about him. "The wild mysterious improbable kind of

love that never comes but once." I'm quoting you. In a way you're still in love with him. It's darn nice of me to have the same initials. I suppose that had something to do with your picking me out.'

'His name was nothing like yours,' she said coldly. 'And he is dead, dead, dead.'

I held the gold and enamel pendant out to Spencer. He took it reluctantly. 'I've seen it before,' he muttered.

'Check me on the design,' I said. 'It consists of a broad dagger in white enamel with a gold edge. The dagger points downwards and the flat of the blade crosses in front of a pair of upward-curling blue enamel wings. Then it crosses in back of a scroll. On the scroll are the words: WHO CARES WINS.'

'That seems to be correct,' he said. 'What makes it important?'

'She says it's a badge of the Artists Rifles, a Territorial outfit. She says it was given to her by a man who was in that outfit and was lost in the Norwegian campaign with the British Army in the spring of 1940 at Andalsnes.'

I had their attention. Spencer watched me steadily. I wasn't talking to the birds and he knew it. Eileen knew it too. Her tawny eyebrows were crimped in a puzzled frown which could have been genuine. It was also unfriendly.

'This is a sleeve badge,' I said. 'It came into existence because the Artists Rifles were made over or attached or seconded or whatever the correct term is into a Special Air Service Outfit. They had originally been a Territorial Regiment of infantry. This badge didn't even exist until 1947. Therefore nobody gave it to Mrs Wade in 1940. Also, no Artists Rifles were landed at Andalsnes in Norway in 1940. Sherwood Foresters and Leicestershires, yes. Both Territorial. Artists Rifles, no. Am I being nasty?'

Spencer put the pendant down on the coffee table and pushed it slowly across until it was in front of Eileen. He said nothing.

'Do you think I wouldn't know?' Eileen asked me contemptuously.

'Do you think the British War Office wouldn't know?' I asked her right back.

'Obviously there must be some mistake,' Spencer said mildly.

I swung around and gave him a hard stare. 'That's one way of putting it.'

'Another way of putting it is that I am a liar,' Eileen Wade said icily. 'I never knew anyone named Paul Marston, never loved him or he me. He never gave me a reproduction of his regimental badge, he was never missing in action, he never existed. I bought this badge myself in a shop in New York where they specialize in imported British luxuries, things like leather goods, hand-made brogues, regimental and school ties and cricket blazers, knick-knacks with coats of arms on them, and so on. Would an explanation like that satisfy you, Mr Marlowe?'

'The last part would. Not the first. No doubt somebody told you it was an Artists Rifles badge and forgot to mention what kind, or didn't know. But you did know Paul Marston and he did serve in that outfit, and he was missing in action in Norway. But it didn't happen in 1940, Mrs Wade. It happened in 1942 and he was in the Commandos then, and it wasn't at Andalsnes, but on a little island off the coast where the Commando boys pulled a fast raid.'

'I see no need to be so hostile about it,' Spencer said in an executive sort of voice. He was fooling with the yellow sheets in front of him now. I didn't know whether he was trying to stooge for me or was just sore. He picked up a slab of yellow script and weighed it on his hand.

'You going to buy that stuff by the pound?' I asked him.

He looked startled, then he smiled a small difficult smile.

'Eileen had a pretty rough time in London,' he said. 'Things get confused in one's memory.'

I took a folded paper out of my pocket. 'Sure,' I said. 'Like who you got married to. This is a certified copy of a marriage certificate. The original came from Caxton Hall Register Office. The date of the marriage is August 1942. The parties named are Paul Edward Marston and Eileen Victoria Sampsell. In a sense Mrs Wade is right. There was no such person as Paul Edward Marston. It was a fake name because in the army you have to get permission to get married. The man faked his identity. In the army he had another name. I have his whole army history. It's a wonder to me that people never seem to realize that all you have to do is ask.'

Spencer was very quiet now. He leaned back and stared. But not at me. He stared at Eileen. She looked back at him with one of those faint, half-deprecatory, half-seductive smiles women are so good at.

'But he was dead, Howard. Long before I met Roger. What could it possibly matter? Roger knew all about it. I never stopped using my unmarried name. In the circumstances I had to. It was on my passport. Then after he was killed in action—' she stopped and drew a slow breath and let her hand fall slowly and softly to her knee. 'All finished, all done for, all lost.'

'You're sure Roger knew?' he asked her slowly.

'He knew something,' I said. 'The name Paul Marston had a meaning for him. I asked him once and he got a funny look in his eyes. But he didn't tell me why.'

She ignored that and spoke to Spencer.

'Why, of course Roger knew all about it.' Now she was smiling at Spencer patiently as if he was being a little slow on the take. The tricks they have.

'Then why lie about the dates?' Spencer asked dryly. 'Why say the man was lost in 1940 when he was lost in 1942? Why wear a badge that he couldn't have given you and make a point of saying that he did give it to you?'

'Perhaps I was lost in a dream,' she said softly. 'Or a nightmare, more accurately. A lot of my friends were killed in the bombing. When you said good night in those days you tried not to make it sound like good-bye. But that's what it often was. And when you said good-bye to a soldier—it was worse. It's always the kind and gentle ones that get killed.'

He didn't say anything. I didn't say anything. She looked down at the pendant lying on the table in front of her. She picked it up and fitted it to the chain around her neck again and leaned back composedly.

'I know I haven't any right to cross-examine you, Eileen,' Spencer said slowly. 'Let's forget it. Marlowe made a big thing out of the badge and the marriage certificate and so on. Just for a moment I guess he had me wondering.'

'Mr Marlowe,' she told him quietly, 'makes a big thing out of trifles. But when it comes to a really big thing—like saving a man's life—he is out by the lake watching a silly speedboat.'

'And you never saw Paul Marston again,' I said.

'How could I when he was dead?'

'You didn't know he was dead. There was no report of his death from the Red Cross. He might have been taken prisoner.'

She shuddered suddenly. 'In October 1942,' she said slowly, 'Hitler issued an order that all Commando prisoners were to be turned over to the Gestapo. I think we all know what that meant. Torture and a nameless death in some Gestapo dungeon.' She shuddered again. Then she blazed at me: 'You're a horrible man. You want me to live that over again, to punish me for a trivial lie. Suppose someone you loved had been caught by those people and you knew what happened, what must have happened to him or her? Is it so strange that I tried to build another kind of memory—even a false one?'

'I need a drink,' Spencer said. 'I need a drink badly. May I have one?'

She clapped her hands and Candy drifted up from nowhere as he always did. He bowed to Spencer.

'What you like to drink, Señor Spencer?'

'Straight Scotch, and plenty of it,' Spencer said.

Candy went over in the corner and pulled the bar out from the wall. He got a bottle up on it and poured a stiff jolt into a glass. He came back and set it down in front of Spencer. He started to leave again.

'Perhaps, Candy,' Eileen said quietly, 'Mr Marlowe would like a drink too.'

He stopped and looked at her, his face dark and stubborn.

'No, thanks,' I said. 'No drink for me.'

Candy made a snorting sound and walked off. There was another silence. Spencer put down half of his drink. He lit a cigarette. He spoke to me without looking at me.

'I'm sure Mrs Wade or Candy could drive me back to Beverly Hills. Or can I get a cab. I take it you've said your piece.'

I refolded the certified copy of the marriage licence. I put it back in my pocket.

'Sure that's the way you want it?' I asked him.

'That's the way everybody wants it.'

'Good,' I stood up. 'I guess I was a fool to try to play it this way. Being a big-time publisher and having the brains to go with it—if it takes any—you might have assumed I didn't come out here just to play the heavy. I didn't revive ancient history or spend my own money to get the facts just to twist them around somebody's neck. I didn't investigate Paul Marston because the Gestapo murdered him, because Mrs Wade was wearing the wrong badge, because she got mixed up on her dates, because she married him in one of those quickie wartime marriages. When I started investigating him I didn't know any of those things. All I knew was his name. Now how do you suppose I knew that?'

'No doubt somebody told you,' Spencer said curtly.

'Correct, Mr Spencer. Somebody who knew him in New York after the war and later on saw him out here in Chasen's with his wife.'

'Marston is a pretty common name,' Spencer said and sipped his whisky. He turned his head sideways and his right eyelid drooped a fraction of an inch. So I sat down again. 'Even Paul Marston would hardly be unique. There are nineteen Howard Spencers in the Greater New York area telephone directories, for instance. And four of them are just plain Howard Spencer with no middle initial.'

'Yeah. How many Paul Marstons would you say had had one side of their faces smashed by a delayed-action mortar shell and showed the scars and marks of the plastic surgery that repaired the damage?'

Spencer's mouth fell open. He made some kind of heavy breathing sound. He got out a handkerchief and tapped his temples with it.

'How many Paul Marstons would you say had saved the lives of a couple of tough gamblers named Mendy Menendez and Randy Starr on that same occasion? They're still around, they've got good memories. They can talk when it suits them. Why ham it up any more, Spencer? Paul Marston and Terry Lennox were the same man. It can be proved beyond any shadow of a doubt.'

I didn't expect anyone to jump six feet into the air and scream and nobody did. But there is a kind of silence that is almost as loud as a shout. I had it. I had it all around me, thick and hard. In the kitchen I could hear water run. Outside on the road I could hear the dull thump of a folded newspaper hit the driveway, then the light, inaccurate whistling of a boy wheeling away on his bicycle.

I felt a tiny sting on the back of my neck. I jerked away from it and swung around. Candy was standing there with his knife in his hand. His dark face was wooden but there was something in his eyes I hadn't seen before.

'You are tired, *amigo*,' he said softly. 'I fix you a drink, no?'

'Bourbon on the rocks, thanks,' I said.

'*De pronto, señor.*'

He snapped the knife shut, dropped it into the side pocket of his white jacket, and went softly away.

Then at last I looked at Eileen. She sat leaning forward, her hands clasped tightly. The downward tilt of her face hid her expression if she had any. And when she spoke her voice had the lucid emptiness of that mechanical voice on the telephone that tells you the time, and if you keep listening, which people don't because they have no reason to, it will keep on telling you the passing seconds for ever, without the slightest change of inflection.

'I saw him once, Howard. Just once. I didn't speak to him at all. Nor he to me. He was terriby changed. His hair was white and his face—it wasn't quite the same face. But of course I knew him, and of course he knew me. We looked at each other. That was all. Then he was gone out of the room and the next day he was gone from her house. It was at the Lorings I saw him—and her. One afternoon, late. You were there, Howard. And Roger was there. I suppose you saw him too.'

'We were introduced,' Spencer said. 'I knew who he was married to.'

'Linda Loring told me he just disappeared. He gave no reason. There was no quarrel. Then after a while that woman divorced him. And still later I heard she found him again. He was down and out. And they were married again. Heaven knows why. I suppose he had no money and it didn't matter to him any more. He knew that I was married to Roger. We were lost to each other.'

'Why?' Spencer asked.

Candy put my drink in front of me without a word. He looked at Spencer and Spencer shook his head. Candy drifted away. Nobody paid any attention to him. He was like the prop man in a Chinese play, the fellow that moves things around on the stage and the actors and audience alike behave as if he wasn't there.

'Why?' she repeated. 'Oh, you wouldn't understand. What we had was lost. It could never be recovered. The Gestapo didn't get him after all. There must have been *some* decent Nazis who didn't obey Hitler's order about the Commandos. So he survived, he came back. I used to pretend to myself that I would find him again, but as he had been, eager, young, and unspoiled. But to find him married to that red-headed whore—that was disgusting. I already knew about her and Roger. I have no doubt Paul did too. So did Linda Loring, who is a bit of a tramp herself, but not completely so. They all are in that set. You ask me why I didn't leave Roger and go back to Paul. After he had been in her arms and Roger had been in those same willing arms? No thank you. I need a little more inspiration than that. Roger I could forgive. He drank, he didn't know what he was doing. He worried about his work and he hated himself because he was just a mercenary hack. He was a weak man, unreconciled, frustrated, but understandable. He was just a husband. Paul was either much more or he was nothing. In the end he was nothing.'

I took a swig of my drink. Spencer had finished his. He was scratching at the material of the davenport. He had forgotten the pile of paper in front of him, the unfinished novel of the very much finished popular author.

'I wouldn't say he was nothing,' I said.

She lifted her eyes and looked at me vaguely and dropped them again.

'Less than nothing,' she said, with a new note of sarcasm in her voice. 'He knew what she was, he married her. Then because she was what he knew she was he killed her. And then ran away and killed himself.'

'He didn't kill her,' I said, 'and you know it.'

She came upright with a smooth motion and stared at me blankly. Spencer let out a noise of some kind.

'Roger killed her,' I said, 'and you also know that.'

'Did he tell you?' she asked quietly.

'He didn't have to. He did give me a couple of hints. He would have told me or someone in time. It was tearing him to pieces not to.'

She shook her head slightly. 'No, Mr Marlowe. That was not why he was tearing himself to pieces. Roger didn't know he had killed her. He had blacked out completely. He knew something was wrong and he tried to bring it to the surface, but he couldn't. The shock had destroyed his memory of it. Perhaps it would have come back and perhaps in the last moments of his life it did come back. But not until then. Not until then,'

Spencer said in a sort of growl: 'That sort of thing just doesn't happen, Eileen.'

'Oh yes it does,' I said. 'I know of two well-established instances. One was a blackout drunk who killed a woman he picked up in a bar. He strangled her with a scarf she was wearing fastened with a fancy clasp. She went home with him and what went on then is not known except that she got dead and when the law caught up with him he was wearing the fancy clasp on his own tie and he didn't have the faintest idea where he got it.'

'Never?' Spencer said. 'Or just at the time?'

'He never admitted it. And he's not around any more to be asked. They gassed him. The other case was a head wound. He was living with a rich pervert, the kind that collects first editions and does fancy cooking and has a very expensive secret library behind a panel in the wall. The two of them had a fight. They fought all over the house, from room to room, the place was a shambles and the rich guy eventually got the low score. The killer, when they caught him, had dozens of bruises on him and a broken finger. All he knew for sure was that he had a headache and he couldn't find his way back to Pasadena. He kept circling around and stopping to ask directions at the same service station. The guy at the service station decided he was nuts and called the cops. Next time around they were waiting for him.'

'I don't believe that about Roger,' Spencer said. 'He was no more psycho than I am.'

'He blacked out when he was drunk,' I said.

'I was there. I saw him do it,' Eileen said calmly.

I grinned at Spencer. It was some kind of grin, not the cheery kind probably, but I could feel my face doing its best.

'She's going to tell us about it,' I told him. 'Just listen. She's going to tell us. She can't help herself now.'

'Yes, that is true,' she said gravely. 'There are things no one likes to tell about an enemy, much less about one's own husband. And I have to tell them publicly on a witness stand, you are not going to enjoy it, Howard. Your fine, talented, ever so popular and lucrative author is going to look pretty cheap. Sexy as all get out, wasn't he? On paper, that is. And how the poor fool tried to live up to it! All that woman was to him was a trophy. I spied on them. I should be ashamed of that. One has to say these things. I am ashamed of nothing. I saw the whole nasty scene. The guest house she used for her amours happens to be a nice secluded affair with its own garage and entrance on a side street, a dead end, shaded by big trees. The time came, as it must to people like Roger, when he was no longer a satisfactory lover. Just a little too drunk. He tried to leave but she came out after him screaming and stark naked, waving some kind of small statuette. She used language of a depth of filth and depravity I couldn't attempt to describe. Then she tried to hit him with the statuette. You are both men and you must know that nothing shocks a man quite so much as to hear a supposedly refined woman use the language of the gutter and the public urinal. He was drunk, he had had sudden spells of violence, and he had one then. He tore the statuette out of her hand. You can guess the rest.'

'There must have been a lot of blood,' I said.

'Blood?' She laughed bitterly. 'You should have seen him when he got home. When I ran for my car to get away he was standing there looking down at her. Then he bent and picked her up in his arms and carried her into the guest house. I knew then that the shock had partially sobered him. He got home in about an hour. He was very quiet. It shook him when he saw me waiting. But he wasn't drunk them. He was dazed. There was blood on his face, on his hair, all over the front of his coat. I got him into the lavatory off the study and got him stripped and cleaned off enough to get him upstairs into the shower. I put him to bed. I got an old suitcase and went downstairs and gathered up the bloody clothes and put them in the suitcase. I cleaned the basin and the floor and then I took a wet towel out and made sure his car was clean. I put it away and got mine out. I drove to the Chatsworth Reservoir and you can guess what I did with the suitcase full of bloody clothes and towels.'

She stopped. Spencer was scratching at the palm of his left hand. She gave him a quick glance and went on.

'While I was away he got up and drank a lot of whisky. And the next morning he didn't remember a single thing. That is, he didn't say a word about it or behave as if he had anything on his mind but a hangover. And I said nothing.'

'He must have missed the clothes,' I said.

She nodded. 'I think he did eventually–but he didn't say so. Everything seemed to happen at once about that time. The papers were full of it, then Paul was missing, and then he was dead in Mexico. How was I to know what would happen? Roger was my husband. He had done an awful thing, but she was an awful woman. And he hadn't known what he was doing. Then almost as suddenly as it began the papers dropped it. Linda's father must have had something to do with that. Roger read the papers, of course, and he made just the sort of comments one would expect from an innocent bystander who had just happened to know the people involved.'

'Weren't you afraid?' Spencer asked her quietly.

'I was sick with fear, Howard. If he remembered, he would probably kill me. He was a good actor–most writers are–and perhaps he already knew and was just waiting for a chance. But I couldn't be sure. He might–he just might–have forgotten the whole thing permanently. And Paul was dead.'

'If he never mentioned the clothes that you had dumped in the reservoir, that proved he suspected something,' I said. 'And remember, in that stuff he left in the typewriter the other time–the time he shot the gun off upstairs and I found you trying to get it away from him–he said a good man died for him.'

'He said that?' Her eyes widened just the right amount.

'He wrote it–on the typewriter. I destroyed it, he asked me to. I supposed you had already seen it.'

'I never read anything he wrote in his study.'

'You read the note he left the time Verringer took him away. You even dug something out of the waste-basket.'

'That was different,' she said coolly. 'I was looking for a clue to where he might have gone.'

'Okay,' I said and leaned back. 'Is there any more?'

She shook her head slowly, with a deep sadness. 'I suppose not. At the very last, the afternoon he killed himself, he may have remembered. We'll never know. Do we want to know?'

Spencer cleared his throat. 'What was Marlowe supposed to do in all this? It was your idea to get him here. You talked me into that, you know.'

'I was terribly afraid. I was afraid of Roger and I was afraid *for* him. Mr Marlowe was Paul's friend, almost the last person to see him who knew him. Paul might have told him something. I had to be sure. If he was dangerous, I wanted him on my side. If he found out the truth, there might still be some way to save Roger.'

Suddenly and for no reason that I could see Spencer got tough. He leaned forward and pushed out his jaw.

'Let me get this straight, Eileen. Here was a private detective who was already in bad with the police. They'd had him in jail. He was supposed to have helped Paul–I call him that because you do–jump the country to Mexico. That's a felony, if Paul was a murderer. So if he found out the truth and could clear himself, he would just sit on his hands and do nothing. Was that your idea?'

'I was afraid, Howard. Can't you understand that? I was living in the house with a murderer who might be a maniac. I was alone with him a large part of the time.'

'I understand that,' Spencer said, still tough. 'But Marlowe didn't take it on, and you were still alone. Then Roger fired the gun off and for a week after that you were alone. Then Roger killed himself and very conveniently it was Marlowe who was alone that time.'

'That is true,' she said. 'What of it? Could I help it?'

'All right,' Spencer said. 'Is it just possible you thought Marlowe might find the truth and with the background of the gun going off once already just kind of hand it to Roger and say something like, "Look, old man, you're a murderer and I know it and your wife knows it. She's a fine woman. She has suffered enough. Not to mention Sylvia Lennox's husband. Why not do the decent thing and pull the trigger and everybody will assume it was a case of too much wild drinking? So I'll stroll down by the lake and smoke a cigarette, old man. Good luck and good-bye. Oh, here's the gun. It's loaded and it's all yours."'

'You're getting horrible, Howard. I didn't think anything of the sort.'

'You told the deputy Marlowe had killed Roger. What was that supposed to mean?'

She looked at me briefly, almost shyly. 'I was very wrong to say that. I didn't know what I was saying.'

'Maybe you thought Marlowe had shot him,' Spencer suggested calmly.

Her eyes narrowed. 'Oh no, Howard. Why? Why would he do that? That's an abominable suggestion.'

'Why?' Spencer wanted to know. 'What's abominable about it? The police had the same idea. And Candy gave them a motive. He said Marlowe was in your room for two hours the night Roger shot a hole in the ceiling—after Roger had been put to sleep with pills.'

She flushed to the roots of her hair. She stared at him dumbly.

'And you didn't have any clothes on,' Spencer said brutally. 'That's what Candy told them.'

'But at the inquest—' she began to say in a shattered kind of voice. Spencer cut her off.

'The police didn't believe Candy. So he didn't tell it at the inquest.'

'Oh.' It was a sigh of relief.

'Also,' Spencer went on coldly, 'the police suspected you. They still do. All they need is a motive. Looks to me like they might be able to put one together now.'

She was up on her feet. 'I think you had both better leave my house,' she said angrily. 'The sooner, the better.'

'Well, did you or didn't you?' Spencer asked calmly, not moving except to reach for his glass and find it empty.

'Did I or didn't I what?'

'Shoot Roger?'

She was standing there staring at him. The flush had gone. Her face was white and tight and angry.

'I'm just giving you the sort of thing you'd get in court.'

'I was out. I had forgotten my keys. I had to ring to get into the house. He was dead when I got home. All that is known. What has got into you, for God's sake?'

He took a handkerchief out and wiped his lips. 'Eileen, I've stayed in this house twenty times. I've never known that front door to be locked during the day-time. I don't say you shot him. I just asked you. And don't tell me it was impossible. The way things worked out it was easy.'

'I shot my own husband?' she asked slowly and wonderingly.

'Assuming,' Spencer said in the same indifferent voice, 'that he *was* your husband. You had another when you married him.'

'Thank you, Howard. Thank you very much. Roger's last book, his swan song, is there in front of you. Take it and go. And I think you had better call the police and tell them what you think. It will be a charming ending to our friendship. Most charming. Good-bye, Howard. I am very tired and I have a headache. I'm going to my room and lie down. As for Mr Marlowe–and I suppose he put you up to all this–I can only say to him that if he didn't kill Roger in a literal sense, he certainly drove him to his death.'

She turned to walk away. I said sharply: 'Mrs Wade, just a moment. Let's finish the job. No sense in being bitter. We are all trying to do the right thing. That suitcase you threw into the Chatsworth Reservoir–was it heavy?'

She turned and stared at me. 'It was an old one, I said. Yes, it was very heavy.'

'How did you get it over the high wire fence around the reservoir?'

'What? The fence?' She made a helpless gesture. 'I suppose in emergencies one has an abnormal strength to do what has to be done. Somehow or other I did it. That's all.'

'There isn't any fence,' I said.

'Isn't any fence?' She repeated it dully, as if it didn't mean anything.

'And there was no blood on Roger's clothes. And Sylvia Lennox wasn't killed outside the guest house, but inside it on the bed. And there was practically no blood, because she was already dead–shot dead with a gun–and when the statuette was used to beat her face to a pulp, it was beating a dead woman. And the dead, Mrs Wade, bleed very little.'

She curled her lip at me contemptuously. 'I suppose you were there,' she said scornfully.

Then she went away from us.

We watched her go. She went upstairs slowly, moving with calm elegance. She disappeared into her room and the door closed softly but firmly behind her. Silence.

'What was that about the wire fence?' Spencer asked me vaguely. He was moving his head back and forth. He was flushed and sweating. He was taking it gamely but it wasn't easy for him to take.

'Just a gag,' I said. 'I've never been close enough to the Chatsworth Reservoir to know what it looks like. Maybe it has a fence around it, maybe not.'

'I see,' he said unhappily. 'But the point is she didn't know either.'

'Of course not. She killed both of them.'

43

Then something moved softly and Candy was standing at the end of the couch looking at me. He had his switch knife in his hand. He pressed the button and the blade shot out. He pressed the button and the blade went back into the handle. There was a sleek glitter in his dark eyes.

'*Millon de perdones, Señor,*' he said. 'I was wrong about you. She killed the boss I think—' he stopped and the blade shot out again.

'No.' I stood up and held my hand out. 'Give me the knife, Candy. You're just a nice Mexican houseboy. They'd hang it on to you and love it. Just the kind of smoke screen that would make them grin with delight. You don't know what I'm talking about. But I do. They fouled it up so bad that they couldn't straighten it out now if they wanted to. And they don't want to. They'd blast a confession out of you so quick you wouldn't even have time to tell them your full name. And you'd be sitting on your fanny up in San Quentin with a life sentence three weeks from Tuesday.'

'I tell you before I am not a Mexican. I am Chileno from Vina del Mar near Valparaiso.'

'The knife, Candy. I know all that. You're free, You've got money saved. You've probably got eight brothers and sisters back home. Be smart and go back where you come from. This job here is dead.'

'Lots of jobs,' he said quietly. Then he reached out and dropped the knife into my hand. 'For you I do this.'

I dropped the knife into my pocket. He glanced up towards the balcony. '*La señora*—what do we do now?'

'Nothing. We do nothing at all. The *señora* is very tired. She has been living under a great strain. She doesn't want to be disturbed.'

'We've got to call the police,' Spencer said grittily.

'Why?'

'Oh my God, Marlowe—we have to.'

'Tomorrow. Pick up your pile of unfinished novel and let's go.'

'We've got to call the police. There is such a thing as law.'

'We don't have to do anything of the sort. We haven't enough evidence to swat a fly with. Let the law enforcement people do their own dirty work. Let the lawyers work it out. They write the laws for other lawyers to dissect in front of other lawyers called judges so that other judges can say the first judges were wrong and the Supreme Court can say the second lot were wrong. Sure there's such a thing as law. We're up to our necks in it. About all it does is make business for lawyers. How long do you think the big-shot mobsters would last if the lawyers didn't show them how to operate?'

Spencer said angrily: 'That has nothing to do with it. A man was killed in this house. He happened to be an author and a very successful and important one, but that has nothing to do with it either. He was a man and you and I know who killed him. There's such a thing as justice.'

'Tomorrow.'

'You're just as bad as she is if you let her get away with it. I'm beginning to wonder about you a little, Marlowe. You could have saved his life if you had been on your toes. In a sense you did let her get away with it. And for all I know this whole performance this afternoon has been just that—a performance.'

'That's right. A disguised love scene. You could see Eileen is crazy about me. When things quieten down we may get married. She ought to be pretty well fixed. I haven't made a buck out of the Wade family yet. I'm getting impatient.'

He took his glasses off and polished them. He wiped perspiration from the hollows under his eyes, replaced the glasses and looked at the floor.

'I'm sorry,' he said. 'I've taken a pretty stiff pinch this afternoon. It was bad enough to know Roger had killed himself. But this other version makes me fell degraded—just knowing about it.' He looked up at me. 'Can I trust you?'

'To do what?'

'The right thing—whatever it is.' He reached down and picked up the pile of yellow script and tucked it under his arm. 'No, forget it. I guess you know what you are doing. I'm a pretty good publisher but this is out of my line. I guess what I really am is just a goddam stuffed shirt.'

He walked past me and Candy stepped out of his way, then went quickly to the front door and held it open. Spencer went out past him with a brief nod. I followed. I stopped beside Candy and looked into his dark shining eyes.

'No tricks, *amigo*,' I said.

'The *señora* is very tired,' he said quietly. 'She has gone to her room. She will not be disturbed. I know nothing, *señor. No me acuerdo de nada . . . A sus ordenes, señor.*'

I took the knife out of my pocket and held it out to him. He smiled.

'Nobody trusts me, but I trust you, Candy.'

'*Lo mismo, señor. Muchas gracias.*'

Spencer was already in the car. I got in and started it and backed down the driveway and drove him back to Beverly Hills. I let him out at the side entrance of the hotel.

'I've been thinking all the way back,' he said as he got out. 'She must be a little insane. I guess they'd never convict her.'

'They won't even try,' I said. 'But she doesn't know that.'

He struggled with the batch of yellow paper under his arm, got it straightened out, and nodded to me. I watched him heave open the door and go on in. I eased up on the brake and the Olds slid out from the white kerb, and that was the last I saw of Howard Spencer.

I got home late and tired and depressed. It was one of those nights when the air is heavy and the night noises seem muffled and far away. There was a high, misty, indifferent moon. I walked the floor, played a few records and hardly heard them. I seemed to hear a steady ticking somewhere, but there wasn't anything in the house to tick. The ticking was in my head. I was a one-man death watch.

I thought of the first time I had seen Eileen Wade and the second and the third and the fourth. But after that something in her got out of drawing. She no longer seemed quite real. A murderer is always unreal once you know he is a murderer. There are people who kill out of hate or fear or greed. There are the cunning killers who plan and expect to get away with it. There are the angry killers who do not think at all. And there are the killers who are in love with death, to whom murder is a remote kind of suicide. In a sense they are all insane, but not in the way Spencer meant it.

It was almost daylight when I finally went to bed.

The jangle of the telephone dragged me up out of a black well of sleep. I rolled over on the bed, fumbled for slippers and realized that I hadn't been asleep for more than a couple of hours. I felt like a half-digested meal eaten in a greasy spoon joint. My eyes were stuck together and my mouth was full of sand. I heaved up on the feet and lumbered into the living-room and pulled the phone off the cradle and said into it: 'Hold the line.'

I put the phone down and went into the bathroom and hit myself in the face with some cold water. Outside the window something went snip, snip, snip. I looked out vaguely and saw a brown, expressionless face. It was the once-a-week Jap gardener I called Hard-Hearted Harry. He was trimming the tecoma—the way a Japanese gardener trims your tecoma. You ask him four times and he says, 'next week', and then he comes by at six o'clock in the morning and trims it outside your bedroom window.

I rubbed my face dry and went back to the telephone.

'Yeah?'

'This is Candy, *Señor*.'

'Good morning, Candy.'

'*La señora es muerta.*'

Dead. What a cold, black, noiseless word it is in any language. The lady is dead.

'Nothing you did, I hope.'

'I think the medicine. It is called demerol. I think forty, fifty in the bottle. Empty now. No dinner last night. This morning I climb up on the ladder and look in the window. Dressed just like yesterday afternoon. I break the screen open. *La señora es muerta. Fria como agua de nieve.*'

Cold as ice-water. 'You call anybody?'

'*Si. El Doctor Loring.* He call the cops. Not here yet.'

'Dr Loring, huh? Just the man to come too late.'

'I don't show him the letter,' Candy said.

'Letter to who?'

'Señor Spencer.'

'Give it to the police, Candy. Don't let Dr Loring have it. Just the police. And one more thing, Candy. Don't hide anything, don't tell them any lies. We were there. Tell the truth. This time the truth and all the truth.'

There was a little pause. Then he said: '*Si.* I catch. *Hasta la vista, amigo.*' He hung up.

I dialled the Ritz-Beverly and asked for Howard Spencer.

'One moment, please. I'll give you the desk.'

A man's voice said: 'Desk speaking. May I help you?'

'I asked for Howard Spencer. I know it's early, but it's urgent.'

'Mr Spencer checked out last evening. He took the eight o'clock plane to New York.'

'Oh, sorry. I didn't know.'

I went out to the kitchen to make coffee—yards of coffee. Rich, strong, bitter, boiling hot, ruthless, depraved. The life-blood of tired men.

It was a couple of hours later that Bernie Ohls called me.

'Okay, wise guy,' he said. 'Get down here and suffer.'

44

It was like the other time except that it was day and we were in Captain Hernandez's office and the Sheriff was up in Santa Barbara opening Fiesta Week. Captain Hernandez was there and Bernie Ohls and a man from the Coroner's office and Dr Loring, who looked as if he had been caught performing an abortion, and a man named Lawford, a Deputy from the D.A.'s office, a tall, gaunt, expressionless man whose brother was vaguely rumoured to be a boss of the numbers racket in the Central Avenue district.

Hernandez had some handwritten sheets of note-paper in front of him, flesh-pink paper, deckle-edged, and written on with green ink.

'This is informal,' Hernandez said, when everybody was as comfortable as you can get in hard chairs. 'No stenotype or recording equipment. Say what you like. Dr Weiss represents the Coroner who will decide whether an inquest is necessary. Dr Weiss?'

He was fat, cheerful, and looked competent. 'I think no inquest,' he said. 'There is every surface indication of narcotic poisoning. When the ambulance arrived the woman was still breathing very faintly and she was in a deep coma and all the reflexes were negative. At that stage you don't save one in a hundred. Her skin was cold and respiration would not be noticed without close examination. The houseboy thought she was dead. She died approximately an hour after that. I understand the lady was subject to occasional violent attacks of bronchial asthma. The demerol was prescribed by Dr Loring as an emergency measure.'

'Any information or deduction about the amount of demerol taken, Dr Weiss?'

'A fatal dose,' he said, smiling faintly. 'There is no quick way of determining that without knowing the medical history, the acquired or natural tolerance. According to her confession she took twenty-three hundred milligrams, four or five times the minimal lethal dose for a non-addict.' He looked questioningly at Dr Loring.

'Mrs Wade was not an addict,' Dr Loring said coldly. 'The prescribed dose would be one or two fifty-milligram tablets. Three or four during a twenty-four hour period would be the most I'd permit.'

'But you gave her fifty at a whack,' Captain Hernandez said. 'A pretty dangerous drug to have around in that quantity, don't you think? How bad was this bronchial asthma, Doctor?'

Dr Loring smiled contemptuously. 'It was intermittent, like all asthma. It never amounted to what we term *status asthmaticus,* an attack so severe that the patient seems in danger of suffocating.'

'Any comment, Dr Weiss?'

'Well,' Dr Weiss said slowly, 'assuming the note didn't exist and assuming we had no other evidence of how much of the stuff she took, it could be an accidental overdose. The safety margin isn't very wide. We'll know for sure tomorrow. You don't want to suppress the note, Hernandez, for Pete's sake?'

Hernandez scowled down at his desk. 'I was just wondering. I didn't know narcotics were standard treatment for asthma. Guy learns something every day.'

Loring flushed. 'An emergency measure, I said, Captain. A doctor can't be everywhere at once. The onset of an asthmatic flare-up can be very sudden.'

Hernandez gave him a brief glance and turned to Lawford. 'What happens to your office, if I give this letter to the press?'

The D.A.'s Deputy glanced at me emptily. 'What's this guy doing here, Hernandez?'

'I invited him.'

'How do you know he won't repeat everything said in here to some reporter?'

'Yeah, he's a great talker. You found that out. The time you had him pinched.'

Lawford grinned, then cleared his throat. 'I've read that purported confession,' he said carefully. 'And I don't believe a word of it. You've got a background of emotional exhaustion, bereavement, some use of drugs, the strain of wartime life in England under bombing, this clandestine marriage, the man coming back here, and so on. Undoubtedly she developed a feeling of guilt and tried to purge herself of it by a sort of transference.'

He stopped and looked around, but all he saw was faces with no expression. 'I can't speak for the D.A. but my own feeling is that your confession would be no grounds to seek an indictment even if the woman had lived.'

'And having already believed one confession you wouldn't care to believe another that contradicted the first one,' Hernandez said caustically.

'Take it easy, Hernandez. Any law-enforcement agency has to consider public relations. If the papers printed that confession we'd be in trouble. That's for sure. We've got enough eager beaver reformer groups around just waiting for that kind of chance to stick a knife into us. We've got a Grand Jury that's already jittery about the working over your vice squad lieutenant got last week.'

Hernandez said 'Okay, it's your baby. Sign the receipt for me.'

He shuffled the pink deckle-edged pages together and Lawford leaned down to sign a form. He picked up the pink pages, folded them, put them in his breast pocket, and walked out.

Dr Weiss stood up. He was tough, good-natured, unimpressed. 'We had the last inquest on the Wade family too quick,' he said. 'I guess we won't bother to have this one at all.'

He nodded to Ohls and Hernandez, shook hands formally with Loring, and went out. Loring stood up to go, then hesitated.

'I take it that I may inform a certain interested party that there will be no further investigation of this matter?' he said stiffly.

'Sorry to have kept you away from your patients so long. Doctor.'

'You haven't answered my question,' Loring said sharply. 'I'd better warn you—'

'Get lost, Jack,' Hernandez said.

Dr Loring almost staggered with shock. Then he turned and fumbled his way rapidly out of the room. The door closed and it was a half-minute before anybody said anything. Hernandez shook himself and lit a cigarette. Then he looked at me.

'Well?' he said.

'Well what?'

'What are you waiting for?'

'This is the end, then? Finished? Kaput?'

'Tell him, Bernie.'

'Yeah, sure it's the end,' Ohls said. 'I was all set to pull her in for questioning. Wade didn't shoot himself. Too much alcohol in his brain. But like I told you, where was the motive? Her confession could be wrong in details, but it proves she spied on him. She knew the layout of the guest house in Encino. The Lennox frail had taken both her men from her. What happened in the guest house is just what you want to imagine. One question you forgot to ask Spencer. Did Wade own a Mauser P.P.K.? Yeah, he owned a small Mauser automatic. We talked to Spencer already today on the phone. Wade was a blackout drunk. The poor unfortunate bastard either thought he had killed Sylvia Lennox or he actually had killed her or else he had some reason to know his wife had. Either way he was going to lay it on the line eventually. Sure, he'd been hitting the hooch long before, but he was a he-guy married to a beautiful nothing. The Mex knows all about it. The little bastard knows damn near everything. That was a dream girl. Some of her was here and now, but a lot of her was there and then. If she ever got hot pants, it wasn't for her husband. Get what I'm talking about?'

I didn't answer him.

'Damn near made her yourself, didn't you?'

I gave him the same no answer.

Ohls and Hernandez both grinned sourly. 'Us guys aren't exactly brainless,' Ohls said. 'We knew there was something in that story about her taking her clothes off. You out-talked him and he let you. He was hurt and confused and he liked Wade and he wanted to be sure. When he got sure he'd have used his knife. This was a personal matter with him. He never snitched on Wade. Wade's wife did, and she deliberately fouled up the issue just to confuse Wade. It all adds. In the end I guess she was scared of him. And Wade never threw her down any stairs. That was an accident. She tripped and the guy tried to catch her. Candy saw that too.'

'None of it explains why she wanted me around.'

'I could think of reasons. One of them is old stuff. Every cop has run into it a hundred times. You were the loose end, the guy that helped Lennox escape, his friend, and probably to some extent his confidant. What did he know and what did he tell you? He took the gun that had killed her and he knew it had been fired. She could have thought he did it for her. That made her think he knew she had used it. When he killed himself she was sure. But what about you? You were still the loose end. She wanted to milk you, and she had the charm to use, and a situation ready-made for an excuse to get next to you. And if she needed a fall guy, you were it. You might say she was collecting fall guys.'

'You're imputing too much knowledge to her,' I said.

Ohls broke a cigarette in half and started chewing on one half. The other half he stuck behind his ear.

'Another reason is she wanted a man, a big, strong guy that could crush her in his arms and make her dream again.'

'She hated me,' I said. 'I don't buy that one.'

'Of course,' Hernandez put in dryly. 'You turned her down. But she would have got over that. And then you blew the whole thing up in her face with Spencer listening in.'

'You two characters been seeing any psychiatrists lately?'

'Hell,' Ohls said, 'hadn't you heard? We got them in our hair all the time these days. We've got two of them on the staff. This ain't police business any more. It's getting to be a branch of the medical racket. They're in and out of jail, the courts, the interrogation rooms. They write reports fifteen pages long on why some punk of a juvenile held up a liquor store or raped a schoolgirl or peddled tea to the senior class. Ten years from now guys like Marty and me will be doing Rohrschach tests and word associations instead of chin-ups and target practice. When we go out on a case we'll carry little black bags with portable lie detectors and bottles of truth serum. Too bad we didn't grab the four hard monkeys that poured it on Big Willie Magoon. We might have been able to unmaladjust them and make them love their mothers.'

'Okay for me to blow?'

'What are you not convinced about?' Hernandez asked, snapping a rubber band.

'I'm convinced. The case is dead. She's dead, they're all dead. A nice smooth routine all round. Nothing to do but go home and forget it ever happened. So I'll do that.'

Ohls reached the half-cigarette from behind his ear, looked at it as if wondering how it got there, and tossed it over his shoulder.

'What are you crying about?' Hernandez said. 'If she hadn't been fresh out of guns she might have made it a perfect score.'

'Also,' Ohls said grimly, 'the telephone was working yesterday.'

'Oh sure,' I said. 'You'd have some running and what you would have found would have been a mixed-up story that admitted nothing but a few silly lies. This morning you have what I suppose is a full confession. You haven't let me read it, but you wouldn't have called in the D.A. if it was just a love note. If any real solid work had been done on the Lennox case at the time, somebody would have dug up his war record and where he got wounded and all the rest of it. Somewhere along the line a connexion with the Wades would have turned up. Roger Wade knew who Paul Marston was. So did another P.I. I happened to get in touch with.'

'It's possible,' Hernandez admitted, 'but that isn't how police investigations work. You don't fool around with an open-shut case, even if there's no heat on to get it finalized and forgotten. I've investigated hundreds of homicides. Some are all of a piece, neat, tidy, and according to the book. Most of them make sense here, don't make sense there. But when you get motive, means, opportunity, flight, a written confession, and a suicide immediately afterwards, you leave it lay. No police department in the world has the men or the time to question the obvious. The only thing against Lennox being a killer was that somebody thought he was a nice guy who wouldn't have done it and that there were others who could equally well have done it. But the others didn't take it on the lam, didn't confess, didn't blow their brains out. He did. And as for being a nice guy I figure sixty to seventy per cent of all the killers that end up in the gas chamber or the hot seat or on the end of a rope are people the neighbours thought were just as harmless as a Fuller Brush salesman. Just as harmless and quiet and well bred as Mrs Roger Wade. You want to read what she wrote in that letter? Okay, read it. I've got to go down the hall.'

He stood up and pulled a drawer open and put a folder on the top of the desk. 'There are five photostats in here, Marlowe. Don't let me catch you looking at them.'

He started for the door and then turned his head and said to Ohls: 'You want to talk to Peshorek with me?'

Ohls nodded and followed him out. When I was alone in the office I lifted the cover of the file folder and looked at the white on black photostats. Then touching only the edges I counted them. There were six, each of several pages clipped together. I took one and rolled it up and slipped it into my pocket. Then I read over the next one in the pile. When I had finished I sat down and waited. In about ten minutes Hernandez came back alone. He sat down behind his desk again, tallied the photostats in the file folder, and put the file back in his desk.'

He raised his eyes and looked at me without any expression. 'Satisfied?'

'Lawford know you have those?'

'Not from me. Not from Bernie. Bernie made them himself. Why?'

'What would happen if one got loose?'

He smiled unpleasantly. 'It won't. But if it did, it wouldn't be anybody in the Sheriff's office. The D.A. has photostat equipment too.'

'You don't like District Attorney Springer too well, do you, Captain?'

He looked surprised. 'Me? I like everybody, even you. Get the hell out of here. I've got work to do.'

I stood up to go. He said suddenly: 'You carry a gun these days?'

'Part of the time.'

'Big Willie Magoon carried two. I wonder why he didn't use them.'

'I guess he figured he had everybody scared.'

'That could be it,' Hernandez said casually. He picked up a rubber band and stretched it between his thumbs. He stretched it farther and farther. Finally with a snap it broke. He rubbed his thumb where the loose end had snapped back against it. 'Anything can be stretched too far,' he said. 'No matter how tough he looks. See you around.'

I went out of the door and got out of the building fast. Once a patsy, always a patsy.

45

Back in my dog house on the sixth floor of the Cahuenga Building I went through my regular double play with the morning mail. Mail slot to desk to waste-basket, Tinker to Evers to Chance. I blew a clear space on the top of the desk and unrolled the photostat on it. I had rolled it so as not to make creases.

I read it over again. It was detailed enough and reasonable enough to satisfy any open mind. Eileen Wade had killed Terry's wife in a fit of jealous fury, and later, when the opportunity was set up, she had killed Roger because she was sure he knew. The gun fired into the ceiling of his room that night had been part of the set-up. The unanswered and for ever unanswerable question was why Roger Wade had stood still and let her put it over. He must have known how it would end. So he had written himself off and didn't care. Words were his business, he had words for almost everything, but none for this.

'I have forty-six demerol tablets left from my last prescription,' she wrote. 'I now intend to take them all and lie down on the bed. The door is locked. In a very short time I shall be beyond saving. This, Howard, is to be understood. What I write is in the presence of death. Every word is true. I have no regrets—except possibly that I could not have found them together and killed them together. I have no regrets for Paul whom you have heard called Terry Lennox. He was the empty shell of the man I loved and married. He meant nothing to me. When I saw him that afternoon for the only time after he came back from the war—at first I didn't even know him. Then I did and he knew me at once. He should have died young in the snow of Norway, my lover that I gave to death. He came back a friend of gamblers, the husband of a rich whore, a spoiled and ruined man, and probably some kind of a crook in his past life. Time makes everything mean and shabby and wrinkled. The tragedy of life, Howard, is not that the beautiful things die young, but that they grow old and mean. It will not happen to me. Good-bye, Howard.'

I put the photostat in the desk and locked it up. It was time for lunch but I wasn't in the mood. I got the office bottle out of the deep drawer and poured a slug and then got the phone book off the hook at the desk and looked up the number of the *Journal*. I dialled it and asked the girl for Lonnie Morgan.

'Mr Morgan doesn't come in until around four o'clock. You might try the Press Room at the City Hall.'

I called that. And I got him. He remembered me well enough. 'You've been a pretty busy guy, I heard.'

'I've got something for you, if you want it. I don't think you want it.'

'Yeah? Such as?'

'A photostat of a confession of two murders.'

'Where are you?'

I told him. He wanted more information. I wouldn't give him any over the phone. He said he wasn't on a crime beat. I said he was still a newspaper man and on the only independent paper in the city. He still wanted to argue.

'Where did you get this whatever it is? How do I know it's worth my time?'

'The D.A.'s office has the original. They won't release it. It breaks open a couple of things they hid behind the ice-box.'

'I'll call you. I have to check with the brass.'

We hung up. I went down to the drugstore and ate a chicken salad sandwich and drank some coffee. The coffee was over-strained and the sandwich was as full of rich flavour as a piece torn off an old shirt. Americans will eat anything if it is toasted and held together with a couple of toothpicks and has lettuce sticking out of the sides, preferably a little wilted.

At three-thirty or so Lonnie Morgan came in to see me. He was the same long, thin, wiry piece of tired and expressionless humanity as he had been the night he drove me home from the jailhouse. He shook hands listlessly and rooted in a crumpled pack of cigarettes.

'Mr Sherman—that's the Managing Editor—said I could look you up and see what you have.'

'It's off the record unless you agree to my terms.' I unlocked the desk and handed him the photostat. He read the four pages rapidly and then again more slowly He looked very excited—about as excited as a mortician at a cheap funeral.

'Gimme the phone.'

I pushed it across the desk. He dialled, waited, and said: 'This is Morgan. Let me talk to Mr Sherman.' He waited and got some other female and then got his party and asked him to ring back on another line.

He hung up and sat holding the telephone in his lap with the forefinger pressing the button down. It rang again and he lifted the receiver to his ear.

'Here it is, Mr Sherman.'

He read slowly and distinctly. At the end there was a pause. Then, 'One moment, sir.' He lowered the phone and glanced across the desk. 'He wants to know how you got hold of this.'

I reached across the desk and took the photostat away from him. 'Tell him it's none of his goddam business how I got hold of it. Where is something else. The stamp on the back of the pages shows that.'

'Mr Sherman, it's apparently an offical document of the Los Angeles Sheriff's office. I guess we could check its authenticity easy enough. Also, there's a price.'

He listened some more and then said: 'Yes, sir. Right here.' He pushed the phone across the desk. 'Wants to talk to you.'

It was a brusque authoritative voice. 'Mr Marlowe, what are your terms? And remember the *Journal* is the only paper in Los Angeles which would even consider touching this matter.'

'You didn't do much on the Lennox case, Mr Sherman.'

'I realize that. But at that time it was purely a question of scandal for scandal's sake. There was no question of who was guilty. What we have now, if your document is genuine, is something quite different. What are your terms?'

'You print the confession in full in the form of a photographic reproduction. Or you don't print it at all.'

'It will be verified. You understand that.'

'I don't see how, Mr Sherman. If you asked the D.A. he will either deny it or give it to every paper in town. He'd have to. If you ask the Sheriff's office they will put it up to the D.A.'

'Don't worry about that, Mr Marlowe. We have ways. How about your terms?'

'I just told you.'

'Oh. You don't expect to be paid?'

'Not with money.'

'Well, you know your own business, I suppose. May I have Morgan again?'

I gave the phone back to Lonnie Morgan.

He spoke briefly and hung up. 'He agrees,' he said. 'I take that photostat and he checks it. He'll do what you say. Reduced to half size it will take about half of page 1A.'

I gave him back the photostat. He held it and pulled at the tip of his long nose. 'Mind my saying I think you're a damn fool?'

'I agree with you.'

'You can still change your mind.'

'Nope. Remember that night you drove me home from the City Bastille? You said I had a friend to say good-bye to. I've never really said good-bye to him. If you publish this photostat, that will be it. It's been a long time—a long, long time.'

'Okay, chum.' He grinned crookedly. 'But I think you're a damn fool. Do I have to tell you why?'

'Tell me anyway.'

'I know more about you than you think. That's the frustrating part of newspaper work. You always know so many things you can't use. You get cynical. If this confession is printed in the *Journal*, a lot of people will be sore. The D.A., the Coroner, the Sheriff's crowd, an influential and powerful private citizen named Potter, and a couple of toughies called Menendez and Starr. You'll probably end up in the hospital or in jail again.'

'I don't think so.'

'Think what you like, pal. I'm telling you what I think. The D.A. will be sore because he dropped a blanket on the Lennox case. Even if the suicide and confession of Lennox made him look justified, a lot of people will want to know how Lennox, an innocent man, came to make a confession, how he got dead, did he really commit suicide or was he helped, why was there no investigation into the circumstances, and how come the whole thing died so fast. Also, if he has the original of this photostat he will think he has been double-crossed by the Sheriff's people.'

'You don't have to print the identifying stamp on the back.'

'We won't. We're pals with the Sheriff. We think he's a straight guy. We don't blame him because he can't stop guys like Menendez. Nobody can stop gambling as long as it's legal in all forms in some places and legal in some forms in all places. You stole this from the Sheriff's office. I don't know how you got away with it. Want to tell me?'

'No.'

'Okay. The Coroner will be sore because he buggered up the Wade suicide. The D.A. helped him with that too. Harlan Potter will be sore because something is reopened that he used a lot of power to close up. Menendez and Starr will be sore for reasons I'm not sure of, but I know you got warned off. And when those boys get sore at somebody he gets hurt. You're apt to get the treatment Big Willie Magoon got.'

'Magoon was probably getting too heavy for his job.'

'Why?' Morgan drawled. 'Because those boys have to make it stick. If they take the trouble to tell you to lay off, you lay off. If you don't and they let you get away with it they look weak. The hard boys that run the business, the big wheels, the board of directors, don't have any use for weak people. They're dangerous. And then there's Chris Mady.'

'He just about runs Nevada, I heard.'

'You heard right, chum. Mady is a nice guy but he knows what's right for Nevada. The rich hoodlums that operate in Reno and Vegas are very careful not to annoy Mr Mady. If they did, their taxes would go up fast and their police co-operation would go down the same way. Then the top guys back East would decide some changes were necessary. An operator who can't get along with Chris Mady ain't operating correctly. Get him the hell out of there and put somebody else in. Getting him out of there means only one thing to them. Out in a wooden box.'

'They never heard of me,' I said.

Morgan frowned and whipped an arm up and down in a meaningless gesture. 'They don't have to. Mady's estate on the Nevada side of Tahoe is right next to Harlan Potter's estate. Could be they say hello once in a while. Could be some character that is on Mady's payroll hears from another guy on Potter's payroll that a punk named Marlowe is buzzing too loud about things that are not any of his business. Could be that this passing remark gets passed on down to where the phone rings in some apartment in L.A. and a guy with large muscles gets a hint to go out and exercise himself and two or three of his friends. If somebody wants you knocked off or smashed, the muscle men don't have to have it explained why. It's mere routine to them. No hard feelings at all. Just sit still while we break your arm. You want this back?'

He held out the photostat.

'You know what I want,' I said.

Morgan stood up slowly and put the photostat in his inside pocket. 'I could be wrong,' he said. 'You may know more about it than I do. I wouldn't know how a man like Harlan Potter looks at things.'

'With a scowl,' I said. 'I've met him. But he wouldn't operate with a goon squad. He couldn't reconcile it with his opinion of how he wants to live.'

'For my money,' Morgan said sharply, 'stopping a murder investigation with a phone call and stopping it by knocking off the witnesses is just a question of method. And both methods stink in the nostrils of civilization. See you around–I hope.'

He drifted out of the office like something blown by the wind.

46

I drove out to Victor's with the idea of drinking a gimlet and sitting around until the evening edition of the morning papers was on the street. But the bar was crowded and it wasn't any fun. When the barkeep I knew got around to me he called me by name.

'You like a dash of bitters in it, don't you?'

'Not usually. Just for tonight two dashes of bitters.'

'I haven't seen your friend lately. The one with the green ice.'

'Neither have I.'

He went away and came back with the drink. I pecked at it to make it last, because I didn't feel like getting a glow on. Either I would get really stiff or stay sober. After a while I had another of the same. It was just past six when the kid with the papers came into the bar. One of the barkeeps yelled at him to beat it, but he managed one quick round of the customers before a waiter got hold of him and threw him out. I was one of the customers. I opened up the *Journal* and glanced at page 1 A. They had made it. It was all there. They had reversed the photostat by making it black on white and by reducing it in size they had fitted it into the top half of the page. There was a short brusque editorial on another page. There was a half-column by Lonnie Morgan with a by-line, on still another page.

I finished my drink and left and went to another place to eat dinner and then drove home.

Lonnie Morgan's piece was a straightforward factual recapitulation of the facts and happenings involved in the Lennox case and the 'suicide' of Roger Wade—the facts as they had been published. It added nothing, deduced nothing, imputed nothing. It was clear, concise, businesslike reporting. The editorial was something else. It asked questions—the kind a newspaper asks of public officials when they are caught with jam on their faces.

About nine-thirty the telephone rang and Bernie Ohls said he would drop by on his way home.

'Seen the *Journal*?' he asked coyly, and hung up without waiting for an answer.

When he got there he grunted about the steps and said he would drink a cup of coffee if I had one. I said I would make some. While I made it he wandered around the house and made himself very much at home.

'You live pretty lonely for a guy that could get himself disliked,' he said. 'What's over the hill in back?'

'Another street. Why?'

'Just asking. Your shrubbery needs pruning.'

I carried some coffee into the living-room and he parked himself and sipped it. He lit one of my cigarettes and puffed at it for a minute or two, then put it out. 'Getting so I don't care for the stuff,' he said. 'Maybe it's the TV commercials. They make you hate everything they try to sell. God, they must think the public is a half-wit. Every time some jerk in a white coat with a stethoscope hanging around his neck holds up some toothpaste or a pack of cigarettes or a bottle of beer or a mouthwash or a jar of shampoo or a little box of something that makes a fat wrestler smell like mountain lilac I always make a note of never to buy any. Hell, I wouldn't buy the product even if I liked it. You read the *Journal*, huh?'

'A friend of mine tipped me off. A reporter.'

'You got friends?' he asked wonderingly. 'Didn't tell you how they got hold of the material, did he?'

'No. And in this state he doesn't have to tell you.'

'Springer is hopping mad. Lawford, the deputy D.A. that got the letter this morning, claims he took it straight to his boss, but it makes a guy wonder. What the *Journal* printed looks like a straight reproduction from the original.'

I sipped coffee and said nothing.

'Serves him right,' Ohls went on. 'Springer ought to have handled it himself. Personally I don't figure it was Lawford that leaked. He's a politician too.' He stared at me woodenly.

'What are you here for, Bernie? You don't like me. We used to be friends—as much as anybody can be friends with a tough cop. But it soured a little.'

He leaned forward and smiled—a little wolfishly. 'No cop likes it when a private citizen does police work behind his back. If you had connected up Wade and the Lennox frail for me the time Wade got dead I'd have made out. If you had connected up Mrs Wade and this Terry Lennox I'd have had her in the palm of my hand—alive. If you had come clean from the start Wade might be still alive. Not to mention Lennox. You figure you're a pretty smart monkey, don't you?'

'What would you like me to say?'

'Nothing. It's too late. I told you a wise guy never fools anybody but himself. I told you straight and clear. So it didn't take. Right now it might be smart for you to leave town. Nobody likes you and a couple of guys that don't like people do something about it. I had the word from a stoolie.'

'I'm not that important, Bernie. Let's stop snarling at each other. Until Wade was dead you didn't even enter the case. After that it didn't seem to matter to you and to the Coroner or to the D.A. or to anybody. Maybe I did some things wrong. But the truth came out. You could have had her yesterday afternoon—with what?'

'With what you had to tell us about her.'

'Me? With the police work I did behind your back?'

He stood up abruptly. His face was red. 'Okay, wise guy. She'd have been alive. We could have booked her on suspicion. You *wanted* her dead, you punk, and you know it.'

'I wanted her to take a good, long, quiet look at herself. What she did about it was her business. I wanted to clear an innocent man. I didn't give a good goddam how I did it and I don't now. I'll be around when you feel like doing something about me.'

'The hard boys will take care of you, buster. I won't have to bother. You think you're not important enough to bother them. As a P.I. named Marlowe, check. You're not. As a guy who was told where to get off and blew a raspberry in their faces publicly in a newspaper, that's different. That hurts their pride.'

'That's pitiful,' I said. 'Just thinking about it makes me bleed internally, to use your own expression.'

He went across to the door and opened it. He stood looking down the redwood steps and at the trees on the hill across the way and up the slope at the end of the street.

'Nice and quiet here,' he said. 'Just quiet enough.'

He went on down the steps and got into his car and left. Cops never say good-bye. They're always hoping to see you again in the line-up.

47

For a short time the next day things looked like getting lively. District-Attorney Springer called an early press conference and delivered a statement. He was the big, florid, black-browed, prematurely grey-haired type that always does so well in politics.

'I have read the document which purports to be a confession by the unfortunate and unhappy woman who recently took her life, a document which may or may not be genuine, but which, if genuine, is obviously the product of a disordered mind. I am willing to assume that the *Journal* published this document in good faith, in spite of its many absurdities and inconsistencies, and these I shall not bore you with enumerating. If Eileen Wade wrote these words, and my office in conjunction with the staff of my respected coadjutor, Sheriff Petersen, will soon determine whether or no she did, then I say to you that she did not write them with a clear head nor with a steady hand. It is only a matter of weeks since the unfortunate lady found her husband wallowing in his own blood, spilled by his own hand. Imagine the shock, the despair, the utter loneliness which must have followed so sharp a disaster! And now she has joined him in the bitterness of death. Is anything to be gained by disturbing the ashes of the dead? Anything, my friends, beyond the sale of a few copies of a newspaper which is badly in need of circulation? Nothing, my friends, nothing. Let us leave it at that. Like Ophelia in that great dramatic masterpiece called *Hamlet*, by the immortal William Shakespeare, Eileen Wade wore her rue with a difference. My political enemies would like to make much of that difference, but my friends and fellow voters will not be deceived. They know that this office has long stood for wise and mature law-enforcement, for justice tempered with mercy, for solid, stable, and conservative government. The *Journal* stands for I know not what, and for what it stands I do not much or greatly care. Let the enlightened public judge for itself.'

The *Journal* printed this guff in its early edition (it was a round-the-clock newspaper) and Henry Sherman, the Managing Editor, came right back at Springer with a signed comment.

'Mr District-Attorney Springer was in good form this morning. He is a fine figure of a man and he speaks with a rich baritone voice that is a pleasure to listen to. He did not bore us with any facts. Any time Mr Springer cares to have the authenticity of the document in question proved to him, the *Journal* will be most happy to oblige. We do not expect Mr Springer to take any action to reopen cases which have been officially closed with his sanction or under his direction, just as we do not expect Mr Springer to stand on his head on the tower of the City Hall. As Mr Springer so aptly phrases it, is anything to be gained by disturbing the ashes of the dead? Or, as the *Journal* would prefer to phrase it less elegantly, is anything to be gained by finding out who committed a murder when the murderess is already dead? Nothing, of course, but justice and truth.

'On behalf of the late William Shakespeare, the *Journal* wishes to thank Mr Springer for his favourable mention of *Hamlet*, and for his substantially, although not exactly correct allusion to Ophelia. "You must wear your rue with a difference" was not said of Ophelia but by her, and just what she meant has never been very clear to our less erudite minds. But let that pass. It sounds well and helps to confuse the issue. Perhaps we may be permitted to quote, also from that officially approved dramatic production known as *Hamlet*, a good thing that happened to be said by a bad man:

'"And where the offence is let the great axe fall."'

Lonnie Morgan called me up about noon and asked me how I liked it. I told him I didn't think it would do Springer any harm.

'Only with the eggheads,' Lonnie Morgan said, 'and they already had his number. I meant what about you?'

'Nothing about me. I'm just sitting here waiting for a soft buck to rub itself against my cheek.'

'That wasn't exactly what I meant.'

'I'm still healthy. Quit trying to scare me. I got what I wanted. If Lennox was still alive he could walk right up to Springer and spit in his eye.'

'You did it for him. And by this time Springer knows that. They got a hundred ways to frame a guy they don't like. I don't figure what made it worth your time. Lennox wasn't that much man.'

'What's that got to do with it?'

He was silent for a moment. Then he said: 'Sorry, Marlowe. Shut my big mouth. Good luck.'

We hung up after the usual good-byes.

About two in the afternoon Linda Loring called me. 'No names, please,' she said. 'I've just flown in from that big lake up north. Somebody up there is boiling over something that was in the *Journal* last night. My almost ex-husband got it right between the eyes. The poor man was weeping when I left. He flew up to report.'

'What do you mean, almost ex-husband?'

'Don't be stupid. For once father approves. Paris is an excellent place to get a quiet divorce. So I shall soon be leaving to go there. And if you have any sense left you could do worse than spend a little of that fancy engraving you showed me going a long way off yourself.'

'What's it got to do with me?'

'That's the second stupid question you've asked. You're not fooling anyone but yourself, Marlowe. Do you know how they shoot tigers?'

'How would I?'

'They tie a goat to a stake and then hide out in a blind. It's apt to be rough on the goat. I like you. I'm sure I don't know why, but I do. I hate the idea of your being the goat. You tried so hard to do the right thing—as you saw it.'

'Nice of you,' I said. 'If I stick my neck out and it gets chopped, it's still my neck.'

'Don't be a hero, you fool,' she said sharply. 'Just because someone we knew chose to be a fall guy, you don't have to imitate him.'

'I'll buy you a drink if you're going to be around long enough.'

'Buy me one in Paris. Paris is lovely in the fall.'

'I'd like to do that too. I hear it was even better in the spring. Never having been there I wouldn't know.'

'The way you're going you never will.'

'Good-bye, Linda. I hope you find what you want.'

'Good-bye,' she said coldly. 'I always find what I want. But when I find it, I don't want it any more.'

She hung up. The rest of the day was a blank. I ate dinner and left the Olds at an all-night garage to have the brake linings checked. I took a can home. The street was as empty as usual. In the wooden mailbox was a free soap coupon. I went up the steps slowly. It was a soft night with a little haze in the air. The trees on the hill hardly moved. No breeze. I unlocked the door and pushed it part way open and then stopped. The door was about ten inches open from the frame. It was dark inside, there was no sound. But I had the feeling that the room beyond was not empty. Perhaps a spring squeaked faintly or I caught the gleam of a white jacket across the room. Perhaps on a warm, still night like this one the room beyond the door was not warm enough, not still enough. Perhaps there was a drifting smell of man on the air. And perhaps I was just on edge.

I stepped sideways off the porch on to the ground and leaned down against the shrubbery. Nothing happened. No light went on inside, there was no movement anywhere that I heard. I had a gun in a belt holster on the left side, butt forward, a short-barrelled Police .38. I jerked it out and it got me nowhere. The silence continued. I decided I was a damn fool. I straightened up and lifted a foot to go back to the front door, and then a car turned the corner and came fast up the hill and stopped almost without sound at the foot of my steps. It was a big black sedan with the lines of a Cadillac. It could have been Linda Loring's car, except for two things. Nobody opened a door and the windows on my side were all shut. I waited and listened, crouched against the bush and there was nothing to listen to and nothing to wait for. Just a dark car motionless at the foot of my redwood steps, with the windows closed. If its motor was still running I couldn't hear it. Then a big red spotlight clicked on and the beam struck twenty feet beyond the corner of the house. And then very slowly the big car backed until the spotlight could swing across the front of the house, across the hood and up.

Policemen don't drive Cadillacs. Cadillacs with red spotlights belong to the big boys, mayors and police commissioners, perhaps District Attorneys. Perhaps hoodlums.

The spotlight traversed. I went down flat, but it found me just the same. It held on me. Nothing else. Still the car door didn't open, still the house was silent and without light.

Then a siren growled in low pitch just for a second or two and stopped. And then at last the house was full of lights and a man in a white dinner jacket came out to the head of the steps and looked along the wall and the shrubbery.

'Come on in, cheapie,' Menendez said with a chuckle. 'You've got company.'

I could have shot him with no trouble at all. Then he stepped back and it was too late—even if I could have done it. Then a window went down at the back of the car and I could hear the thud as it opened. Then a machine pistol went off and fired a short burst into the slope of the bank thirty feet away from me.

'Come on in, cheapie,' Menendez said again from the doorway. 'There just ain't anywhere else to go.'

So I straightened up and went and the spotlight followed me accurately. I put the gun back in the holster on my belt. I stepped up on to the small redwood landing and went in through the door and stopped just inside. A man was sitting across the room with his legs crossed and a gun resting sideways on his thigh. He looked rangy and tough and his skin had that dried-out look of people who live in sun-bleached climates. He was wearing a dark brown gabardine-type windbreaker and the zipper was open almost to his waist. He was looking at me and neither his eyes nor the gun moved. He was as calm as an adobe wall in the moonlight.

48

I looked at him too long. There was a brief half-seen move at my side and a numbing pain in the point of my shoulder. My whole arm went dead to the finger-tips. I turned and looked at a big mean-looking Mexican. He wasn't grinning, he was just watching me. The forty-five in his brown hand dropped to his side. He had a moustache and his head bulged with oily black hair brushed up and back and over and down. There was a dirty sombrero on the back of his head and the leather chin strap hung loose in two strands down the front of a stitched shirt that smelled of sweat. There is nothing tougher than a tough Mexican, just as there is nothing gentler than a gentle Mexican, nothing more honest than an honest Mexican and above all nothing sadder than a sad Mexican. This guy was one of the hard boys. They don't come any harder anywhere.

I rubbed my arm. It tingled a little but the ache was still there and the numbness. If I had tried to pull a gun I should probably have dropped it.

Menendez held his hand out towards the slugger. Without seeming to look he tossed the gun and Menendez caught it. He stood in front of me now and his face glistened. 'Where would you like it, cheapie?' His black eyes danced.

I just looked at him. There is no answer to a question like that.

'I asked you a question, cheapie.'

I wet my lips and asked one back. 'What happened to Agostino? I thought he was your gun handler.'

'Chick went soft,' he said gently.

'He was always soft—like his boss.'

The man in the chair flicked his eyes. He almost but not quite smiled. The tough boy who had paralysed my arm neither moved nor spoke. I knew he was breathing. I could smell that.

'Somebody bump into your arm, cheapie?'

'I tripped over an enchilada.'

Negligently, not quite looking at me even, he slashed me across the face with the gun barrel.

'Don't get gay with me, cheapie. You're out of time for all that. You got told and you got told nice. When I take the trouble to call around personally and tell a character to lay off—he lays off. Or else he lays down and don't get up.'

I could feel a trickle of blood down my cheek. I could feel the full numbing ache of the blow in my cheekbone. It spread until my whole head ached. It hadn't been a hard blow, but the thing he used was hard. I could still talk and nobody tried to stop me.

'How come you do your own slugging, Mendy? I thought that was coolie labour for the sort of boys that beat up Big Willie Magoon.'

'It's the personal touch,' he said softly, 'on account of I had personal reasons for telling you. The Magoon job was strictly business. He got to thinking he could push me around—me that bought his clothes and his cars and stocked his safe deposit box and paid off the trust deed on his house. These vice squad babies are all the same. I even paid school bills for his kid. You'd think the bastard would have some gratitude. So what does he do? He walks into my private office and slaps me around in front of the help.'

'On account of why?' I asked him, in the vague hope of getting him mad at somebody else.

'On account of some lacquered chippie said we used loaded dice. Seems like the bim was one of his sleepy time gals. I had her put out of the club—with every dime she brought in with her.'

'Seems understandable,' I said. 'Magoon ought to know no professional gambler plays crooked games. He doesn't have to. But what have I done to you?'

He hit me again, thoughtfully. 'You made me look bad. In my racket you don't tell a guy twice. Not even a hard number. He goes out and does it, or you ain't got control. You ain't got control, you ain't got business.'

'I've got a hunch that there's a little more to it than that,' I said. 'Excuse me if I reach for a handkerchief.'

The gun watched me while I got one out and touched the blood on my face.

'A two-bit peeper,' Menendez said slowly, 'figures he can make a monkey out of Mendy Menendez. He can get me laughed at. He can get me the big razzoo—me, Menendez. I ought to use a knife on you, cheapie. I ought to cut you into slices of raw meat.'

'Lennox was your pal,' I said, and watched his eyes. 'He got dead. He got buried like a dog without even a name over the dirt where they put his body. And I had a little something to do with proving him innocent. So that makes you look bad, huh? He saved your life and he lost his, and that didn't mean anything to you. All that means anything to you is playing the big shot. You didn't give a hoot in hell for anybody but yourself. You're not big, you're just loud.'

His face froze and he swung his arm back to slug me a third time with the power behind it. His arm was still going back when I took a half-step forward and kicked him in the pit of the stomach.

I didn't think, I didn't plan, I didn't figure my chances or whether I had any. I just got enough of his yap and I ached and bled and maybe I was just a little punch drunk by this time.

He jack-knifed, gasping, and the gun fell out of his hand. He groped for it wildly, making strained sounds deep in his throat. I put a knee into his face. He screeched.

The man in the chair laughed. That staggered me. Then he stood up and the gun in his hand came up with him.

'Don't kill him,' he said mildly. 'We want to use him for live bait.'

Then there was movement in the shadow of the hall and Ohls came through the door, blank-eyed, expressionless, and utterly calm. He looked down at Menendez. Menendez was kneeling with his head on the floor.

'Soft,' Ohls said. 'Soft as mush.'

'He's not soft,' I said. 'He's hurt. Any man can be hurt. Was Big Willie Magoon soft?'

Ohls looked at me. The other man looked at me. The tough Mex at the door hadn't made a sound.

'Take that goddam cigarette out of your face,' I snarled at Ohls. 'Either smoke it or leave it alone. I'm sick of watching you. I'm sick of you, period. I'm sick of cops.'

He looked surprised. Then he grinned.

'That was a plant, kiddo,' he said cheerfully. 'You hurt bad? Did the nasty mans hit your facey-wacey? Well, for my money you had it coming and it was damn useful that you had.' He looked down at Mendy. Mendy had his knees under him. He was climbing out of a well, a few inches at a time. He breathed gaspingly.

'What a talkative lad he is,' Ohls said, 'when he doesn't have three shysters with him to button his lip.'

He jerked Menendez to his feet. Mendy's nose was bleeding. He fumbled the handkerchief out of his white dinner-jacket and held it to his nose. He said no word.

'You got crossed up, sweetheart,' Ohls told him carefully. 'I ain't grieving a whole lot over Magoon. He had it coming. But he was a cop and punks like you lay off cops—always and for ever.'

Menendez lowered the handkerchief and looked at Ohls. He looked at me. He looked at the man who had been sitting in the chair. He turned slowly and looked at the tough Mex by the door. They all looked at him. There was nothing in their faces. Then a knife shot into view from nowhere and Mendy lunged for Ohls. Ohls side-stepped and took him by the throat with one hand and chopped the knife out of hand with ease, almost indifferently. Ohls spread his feet and straightened his back and bent his legs slightly and lifted Menendez clear off the floor with one hand holding his neck. He walked him across the floor and pinned him against the wall. He let him down, but didn't let go of his throat.

'Touch me with one finger and I'll kill you,' Ohls said. 'One finger.' Then he dropped his hands.

Mendy smiled at him scornfully, looked at his handkerchief and refolded it to hide the blood. He held it to his nose again. He looked down at the gun he had used to hit me. The man from the chair said loosely: 'Not loaded, even if you could grab it.'

'A cross,' Mendy said to Ohls. 'I heard you the first time.'

'You ordered three muscles,' Ohls said. 'What you got was three deputies from Nevada. Somebody in Vegas don't like the way you forget to clear them. The somebody wants to talk to you. You can go along with the deputies or you can go downstairs with me and get hung on the back of the door by a pair of handcuffs. There's a couple of boys down there would like to see you close up.'

'God help Nevada,' Mendy said quietly, looking around again at the tough Mex by the door. Then he crossed himself quickly and walked out of the front door. The tough Mex followed him. Then the other one, the dried-out desert type, picked up the gun and the knife and went out too. He shut the door. Ohls waited motionless. There was a sound of doors banging shut, then a car went off into the night.

'You sure those mugs were deputies?' I asked Ohls.

He turned as if surprised to see me there. 'They had stars,' he said shortly.

'Nice work, Bernie. Very nice. Think he'll get to Vegas alive, you cold-hearted son of a bitch?'

I went to the bathroom and ran cold water and held a soaked towel against my throbbing cheek. I looked at myself in the glass. The cheek was puffed out of shape and bluish and there were jagged wounds on it from the force of the gun barrel hitting against the cheekbone. There was a discoloration under my left eye too. I wasn't going to be beautiful for a few days.

Then Ohls reflection showed behind me in the mirror. He was rolling his damn unlighted cigarette along his lips, like a cat teasing a half-dead mouse, trying to get it to run away just once more.

'Next time don't try to outguess the cops,' he said gruffly. 'You think we let you steal that photostat just for laughs? We had a hunch Mendy would come gunning for you. We put it up to Starr cold. We told him we couldn't stop gambling in the county, but we could make it tough enough to cut way into the take. No mobster beats up a cop, not even a bad cop, and gets away with it in our territory. Starr convinced us he had nothing to do with it, that the outfit was sore about it and Menendez was going to get told. So when Mendy called for a squad of out-of-town hard boys to come and give you the treatment, Starr sent him three guys he knew, in one of his own cars, at his own expense. Starr is a police commissioner in Vegas.'

I turned around and looked at Ohls. 'The coyotes out in the desert will get fed tonight. Congratulations. Cop business is wonderful, uplifting, idealistic work, Bernie. The only thing wrong with cop business is the cops that are in it.'

'Too bad for you, hero,' he said with a sudden cold savagery. 'I could hardly help laughing when you walked into your own parlour to take your beating. I got a rise out of that, kiddo. It was a dirty job and it had to be done dirty. To make these characters talk you got to give them a sense of power. You ain't hurt bad, but we had to let them hurt you some.'

'So sorry,' I said. 'So very sorry you had to suffer like that.'

He shoved his taut face at me. 'I hate gamblers,' he said in a rough voice, 'I hate them the way I hate dope pushers. They pander to a disease that is every bit as corrupting as dope. You think those places in Reno and Vegas are just for harmless fun? Nuts, they're for the little guy, the something-for-nothing sucker, the lad that stops off with his pay envelope in his pocket and loses the week-end grocery money. The rich gambler loses forty grand and laughs it off and comes back for more. But the rich gambler don't make the big racket, pal. The big steal is in dimes and quarters and half dollars and once in a while a buck or even a five-spot. The big racket money comes in like water from the pipe in your bathroom, a steady stream that never stops flowing. Any time anybody wants to knock off a professional gambler that's for me. I like it. And any time a state government takes money from gambling and calls it taxes, that government is helping to keep the mobs in business. The barber or the beauty parlour girl puts two bucks on the nose. That's for the Syndicate, that's what really makes the profits. The people want an honest police force, do they? What for? To protect the guys with courtesy cards? We got legal horse tracks in this state, we got them all year round. They operate honest and the state gets its cut, and for every dollar laid at the track there's fifty laid with the bookies. There's eight or nine races on a card and in half of them, the little ones nobody notices, the fix can be in any time somebody says so. There's only one way a jock can win a race, but there's twenty ways he can lose one, with a steward at every eighth pole watching, and not able to do a damn thing about it if the jock knows his stuff. That's legal gambling, pal, clean honest business, state approved. So it's right, is it? Not by my book, it ain't. Because it's gambling and it breeds gamblers, and when you add it all up there's only one kind of gambling—the wrong kind.'

'Feel better?' I asked him, putting some white iodine on my wounds.

'I'm an old tired beat-up cop. All I feel is sore.'

I turned around and stared at him. 'You're a damn good cop, Bernie, but just the same you're all wet. In one way cops are all the same. They all blame the wrong things. If a guy loses his pay-cheque at a crap table, stop gambling. If he gets drunk, stop liquor. If he kills somebody in a car crash, stop making automobiles. If he gets pinched with a girl in a hotel room, stop sexual intercourse. If he falls downstairs, stop building houses.'

'Aw shut up!'

'Sure, shut me up. I'm just a private citizen. Get off it, Bernie. We don't have mobs and crime syndicates and goon squads because we have crooked politicians and their stooges in the City Hall and the legislatures. Crime isn't a disease, it's a symptom. Cops are like a doctor that gives you aspirin for a brain tumour, except that the cop would rather cure it with a blackjack. We're a big, rough, rich, wild people and crime is the price we pay for it, and organized crime is the price we pay for organization. We'll have it with us a long time. Organized crime is just the dirty side of the sharp dollar.'

'What's the clean side?'

'I never saw it. Maybe Harlan Potter could tell you. Let's have a drink.'

'You looked pretty good walking in that door,' Ohls said.

'You looked better when Mendy pulled the knife on you.'

'Shake,' he said, and put his hand out.

We had a drink and he left by the back door, which he had jimmied to get in, having dropped by the night before for scouting purposes. Back doors are a soft touch if they open out and are old enough for the wood to have dried and shrunk. You knock the pins out of the hinges and the rest is easy. Ohls showed me a dent in the frame when he left to go back over the hill to where he had left his car on the next street. He could have opened the front door almost as easily but that would have broken the lock. It would have shown up too much.

I watched him climb through the trees with the beam of a torch in front of him and disappear over the rises. I locked the door and mixed another mild drink and went back to the living-room and sat down. I looked at my watch. It was still early. It only seemed a long time since I had come home.

I went to the phone and dialled the operator and gave her the Lorings' phone number. The butler asked who was calling, then went to see if Mrs Loring was in. She was.

'I was the goat all right,' I said, 'but they caught the tiger alive. I'm bruised up a little.'

'You must tell me about it sometime.' She sounded about as far away as if she had got to Paris already.'

'I could tell you over a drink—if you had time.'

'Tonight? Oh, I'm packing my things to move out. I'm afraid that would be impossible.'

'Yes, I can see that. Well, I just thought you might like to know. It was kind of you to warn me. It had nothing at all to do with your old man.'

'Are you sure?'

'Positive.'

'Oh. Just a minute.' She was gone for a time, then she came back and sounded warmer. 'Perhaps I could fit a drink in. Where?'

'Anywhere you say. I haven't a car tonight, but I can get a cab.'

'Nonsense. I'll pick you up, but it will be an hour or longer. What is the address there?'

I told her and she hung up and I put the porch light on and then stood in the open door inhaling the night. It had got much cooler.

I went back in and tried to phone Lonnie Morgan but couldn't reach him. Then just for the hell of it I put in a call to the Terrapin Club at Las Vegas, Mr Randy Starr. He probably wouldn't take it. But he did. He had a quiet, competent, man-of-affairs voice.

'Nice to hear from you, Marlowe. Any friend of Terry's is a friend of mine. What can I do for you?'

'Mendy is on his way.'

'On his way where?'

'To Vegas, with the three goons you sent after him in a big black Caddy with a red spotlight and siren. Yours, I presume?'

He laughed. 'In Vegas, as some newspaper guy said, we use Cadillacs for trailers. What's this all about?'

'Mendy staked out here in my house with a couple of hard boys. His idea was to beat me up–putting it low–for a piece in the paper he seemed to think was my fault.'

'Was it your fault?'

'I don't own any newspapers, Mr Starr.'

'I don't own any hard boys in Cadillacs, Mr Marlowe.'

'They were deputies maybe.'

'I couldn't say. Anything else?'

'He pistol-whipped me. I kicked him in the stomach and used my knee on his nose. He seemed dissatisfied. All the same I hope he gets to Vegas alive.'

'I'm sure he will, if he started this way. I'm afraid I'll have to cut this conversation short now.'

'Just a second, Starr. Were you in that caper at Otatoclan–or did Mendy work it alone?'

'Come again?'

'Don't kid, Starr. Mendy wasn't sore at me for why he said–not to the point of staking out in my house and giving me the treatment he gave Big Willie Magoon. Not enough motive. He warned me to keep my nose clean and not to dig into the Lennox case. But I did, because it just happened to work out that way. So he did what I've just told you. So there was a better reason.'

'I see,' he said slowly and still mildly and quietly. 'You think there was something not quite kosher about how Terry got dead? That he didn't shoot himself, for instance, but someone did?'

'I think the details would help. He wrote a confession which was false. He wrote a letter to me which got mailed. A waiter or hop in the hotel was going to sneak it out and mail it for him. He was holed up in the hotel and couldn't get out. There was a big bill in the letter and the letter was finished just as a knock came at his door. I'd like to know who came into the room.'

'Why?'

'If it had been a bellhop or a waiter, Terry would have added a line to the letter and said so. If it was a cop, the letter wouldn't have been mailed. So who was it—and why did Terry write that confession?'

'No idea, Marlowe. No idea at all.'

'Sorry I bothered you, Mr Starr.'

'No bother, glad to hear from you. I'll ask Mendy if he has any ideas.'

'Yeah—if you ever see him again—alive. If you don't—find out anyway. Or somebody else will.'

'You?' His voice hardened now, but it was still quiet.

'No, Mr Starr. Not me. Somebody that could blow you out of Vegas without taking a long breath. Believe me, Mr Starr. Just believe me. This is strictly on the level.'

'I'll see Mendy alive. Don't worry about that, Marlowe.'

'I figured you knew all about that. Good night, Mr Starr.'

49

When the car stopped out front and the door opened I went out and stood at the top of the steps to call down. But the middle-aged coloured driver was holding the door for her to get out. Then he followed her up the steps carrying a small overnight case. So I just waited.

She reached the top and turned to the driver: 'Mr Marlowe will drive me to my hotel, Amos. Thank you for everything. I'll call you in the morning.'

'Yes, Mrs Loring. May I ask Mr Marlowe a question?'

'Certainly, Amos.'

He put the overnight case down inside the door and she went in past me and left us.

'"I grow old . . . I grow old . . . I shall wear the bottoms of my trousers rolled." What does that mean, Mr Marlowe?'

'Not a bloody thing. It just sounds good.'

He smiled. 'That is from "The Love Song of J. Alfred Prufrock". Here's another one. "In the room the women come and go Talking of Michelangelo." Does that suggest anything to you, sir?'

'Yeah—it suggests to me that the guy didn't know very much about women.'

'My sentiments exactly, sir. Nonetheless I admire T. S. Eliot very much.'

'Did you say "nonetheless"?'

'Why, yes I did, Mr Marlowe. Is that correct?'

'No, but don't say it in front of a millionaire. He might think you were giving him the hotfoot.'

He smiled sadly. 'I shouldn't dream of it. Have you had an accident, sir?'

'Nope. It was planned that way. Good night, Amos.'

'Good night, sir.'

He went back down the steps and I went back into the house. Linda Loring was standing in the middle of the living-room looking around her.

'Amos is a graduate of Howard University,' she said. 'You don't live in a very safe place—for such an unsafe man, do you?'

'There aren't any safe places.'

'Your poor face. Who did that to you?'

'Mendy Menendez.'

'What did you do to him?'

'Nothing much. Kicked him a time or two. He walked into a trap. He's on his way to Nevada in the company of three or four tough Nevada deputies. Forget him.'

She sat down on the davenport.

'What would you like to drink?' I asked. I got a cigarette box and held it out to her. She said she didn't want to smoke. She said anything would do to drink.

'I thought of champagne,' I said. 'I haven't any ice-bucket, but it's cold. I've been saving it for years. Two bottles. Cordon Rouge. I guess it's good. I'm no judge.'

'Saving it for what?' she asked.

'For you.'

She smiled, but she was still staring at my face. 'You're all cut.' She reached her fingers up and touched my cheek lightly. 'Saving it for me? That's not very likely. It's only a couple of months since we met.'

'Then I was saving it until we met. I'll go get it.' I picked up her overnight bag and started across the room with it.

'Just where are you going with that?' she asked sharply.

'It's an overnight bag, isn't it?'

'Put it down and come back here.'

I did that. Her eyes were bright and at the same time they were sleepy.

'This is something new,' she said slowly. 'Something quite new.'

'In what way?'

'You've never laid a finger on me. No passes, no suggestive remarks, no pawing, no nothing. I thought you were tough, sarcastic, mean, and cold.'

'I guess I am—at times.'

'Now I'm here and I suppose without preamble, after we have had a reasonable quantity of champagne you plan to grab me and throw me on the bed. Is that it?'

'Frankly,' I said, 'some such idea did stir at the back of my mind.'

'I'm flattered, but suppose I don't want it that way? I like you. I like you very much. But it doesn't follow that I want to go to bed with you. Aren't you rather jumping to conclusions—just because I happened to bring an overnight bag with me?'

'Could be I made an error,' I said. I went and got her overnight bag and put it back by the front door. 'I'll get the champagne.'

'I didn't mean to hurt your feelings. Perhaps you would rather save the champagne for some more auspicious occasion.'

'It's only two bottles,' I said. 'A really auspicious occasion would call for a dozen.'

'Oh, I see,' she said, suddenly angry. 'I'm just to be a fill-in until someone more beautiful and attractive comes along. Thank you so very much. Now you've hurt my feelings, but I suppose it's something to know that I'm safe here. If you think a bottle of champagne will make a loose woman out of me, I can assure you that you are very much mistaken.'

'I admitted the mistake already.'

'The fact that I told you I was going to divorce my husband and that I had Amos drop me by here with an overnight bag doesn't make me as easy as all that,' she said, still angry.

'Damn the overnight bag!' I growled. 'The hell with the overnight bag! Mention it again and I'll throw the damn thing down the front steps. I asked you to have a drink. I'm going out to the kitchen to get the drink. That's all. I hadn't the least idea of getting you drunk. You don't want to go to bed with me. I understand perfectly. No reason why you should. But we can still have a glass or two of champagne, can't we? This doesn't have to be a wrangle about who is going to get seduced and when and where and on how much champagne.'

'You don't have to lose your temper,' she said, flushing.

'That's just another gambit,' I snarled. 'I know fifty of them and I hate them all. They're phoney and they all have a sort of leer at the edges.'

She got up and came over close to me and ran the tips of her fingers gently over the cuts and swollen places on my face. 'I'm sorry. I'm a tired and disappointed woman. Please be kind to me. I'm no bargain to anyone.'

'You're not tired and you're no more disappointed than most people are. By all the rules you ought to be the same sort of shallow, spoiled, promiscuous brat your sister was. By some miracle you're not. You've got all the honesty and a large part of the guts in your family. You don't need anyone to be kind to you.'

I turned and walked out of the room down the hall to the kitchen and got one of the bottles of champagne out of the ice-box and popped the cork and filled a couple of shallow goblets quickly and drank one down. The sting of it brought tears to my eyes, but I emptied the glass. I filled it again. Then I put the whole works on a tray and carted it into the living-room.

She wasn't there. The overnight bag wasn't there. I put the tray down and opened the front door. I hadn't heard any sound of its opening and she had no car. I hadn't heard any sound at all.

Then she spoke from behind me. 'Idiot, did you think I was going to run away?'

I shut the door and turned. She had loosened her hair and she had tufted slippers on her bare feet and a silk robe the colour of a sunset in a Japanese print. She came towards me slowly with a sort of unexpectedly shy smile. I held a glass out to her. She took it, took a couple of sips of the champagne, and handed it back.

'It's very nice,' she said. Then, very quietly and without a trace of acting or affectation, she came into my arms and pressed her mouth against mine and opened her lips and her teeth. The tip of her tongue touched mine. After a long time she pulled her head back but kept her arms around my neck. She was starry-eyed.

'I meant to all the time,' she said. 'I just had to be difficult. I don't know why. Just nerves perhaps. I'm not really a loose woman at all. Is that a pity?'

'If I had thought you were I'd have made a pass at you the first time I met you in the bar at Victor's.'

She shook her head slowly and smiled. 'I don't think so. That's why I am here.'

'Perhaps not that night,' I said. 'That night belonged to something else.'

'Perhaps you don't ever make passes at women in bars.'

'Not often. The light's too dim.'

'But a lot of women go to bars just to have passes made at them.'

'A lot of women get up in the morning with the same idea.'

'But liquor is an aphrodisiac—up to a point.'

'Doctors recommend it.'

'Who said anything about doctors? I want my champagne.'

I kissed her some more. It was light, pleasant work.

'I want to kiss your poor cheek,' she said, and did. 'It's burning hot,' she said.

'The rest of me is freezing.'

'It is not. I want my champagne.'

'Why?'

'It'll get flat if we don't drink it. Besides I like the taste of it.'

'All right.'

'Do you love me very much? Or will you if I go to bed with you?'

'Possibly.'

'You don't have to go to bed with me, you know. I don't absolutely insist on it.'

'Thank you.'

'I want my champagne.'

'How much money have you got?'

'Altogether? How would I know? About eight million dollars.'

'I've decided to go to bed with you.'

'Mercenary,' she said.

'I paid for the champagne.'

'The hell with the champagne,' she said.

50

An hour later she stretched out a bare arm and tickled my ear and said:

'Would you consider marrying me?'

'It wouldn't last six months.'

'Well, for God's sake,' she said, 'suppose it didn't. Wouldn't it be worth it? What do you expect from life—full coverage against all possible risks?'

'I'm forty-two years old. I'm spoiled by independence. You're spoiled a little—not too much—by money.'

'I'm thirty-six. It's no disgrace to have money and no disgrace to marry it. Most of those who have it don't deserve it and don't know how to behave with it. But it won't be long. We'll have another war and at the end of that nobody will have any money—except the crooks and the chisellers. We'll all be taxed to nothing, the rest of us.'

I stroked her hair and wound some of it around my finger. 'You may be right.'

'We could fly to Paris and have a wonderful time.' She raised herself on an elbow and looked down at me. I could see the shine of her eyes but I couldn't read her expression. 'Do you have something against marriage?'

'For two people in a hundred it's wonderful. The rest just work at it. After twenty years all the guy has left is a work bench in the garage. American girls are terrific. American wives take in too damn much territory. Besides—'

'I want some champagne.'

'Besides,' I said, 'it would be just an incident to you. The first divorce is the only tough one. After that it's merely a problem in economics. No problem to you. Ten years from now you might pass me on the street and wonder where the hell you had seen me before. If you noticed me at all.'

'You self-sufficient, self-satisfied, self-confident, untouchable bastard. I want some champagne.'

'This way you will remember me.'

'Conceited too. A mass of conceit. Slightly bruised at the moment. You think I'll remember you? No matter how many men I marry or sleep with, you think I'll remember you? Why should I?'

'Sorry. I overstated my case. I'll get you some champagne.'

'Aren't we sweet and reasonable?' she said sarcastically. 'I'm a rich woman, darling, and I shall be infinitely richer. I could buy you the world if it were worth buying. What have you now? An empty house to come home to, with not even a dog or cat, a small stuffy office to sit in and wait. Even if I divorced you I'd never let you go back to that.'

'How would you stop me? I'm no Terry Lennox.'

'Please. Don't let's talk about him. Nor about that golden icicle, the Wade woman. Nor about her poor drunken, sunken husband. Do you want to be the only man who turned me down? What kind of pride is that? I've paid you the greatest compliment I know how to pay. I've asked you to marry me.'

'You paid me a greater compliment.'

She began to cry. 'You fool, you utter fool!' Her cheeks were wet. I could feel the tears on them. 'Suppose it lasted six months or a year or two years. What would you have lost except the dust on your office desk and the dirt on your venetian blinds and the loneliness of a pretty empty kind of life?'

'You still want some champagne?'

'All right.'

I pulled her close and she cried against my shoulder. She wasn't in love with me and we both knew it. She wasn't crying over me. It was just time for her to shed a few tears.

Then she pulled away and I got out of bed and she went into the bathroom to fix her face. I got the champagne. When she came back she was smiling.

'I'm sorry I blubbered,' she said. 'In six months from now I won't even remember your name. Bring it into the living-room. I want to see lights.'

I did what she said. She sat on the davenport as before. I put the champagne in front of her. She looked at the glass but didn't touch it.

'I'll introduce myself,' I said. 'We'll have a drink together.'

'Like tonight?'

'It won't ever be like tonight again.'

She raised her glass of champagne, drank a little of it slowly, turned her body on the davenport, and threw the rest in my face. Then she began to cry again. I got a handkerchief out and wiped my face off and wiped hers for her.

'I don't know why I did that,' she said. 'But for God's sake don't say I'm a woman and a woman never knows why she does anything.'

I poured some more champagne into her glass and laughed at her. She drank it slowly and then turned the other way and fell across my knees.

'I'm tired,' she said. 'You'll have to carry me this time.'

After a while she went to sleep.

In the morning she was still asleep when I got up and made coffee. I showered and shaved and dressed. She woke up then. We had breakfast together. I called a cab and carried her overnight bag down the steps.

We said good-bye. I watched the cab out of sight. I went back up the steps and into the bedroom and pulled the bed to pieces and remade it. There was a long dark hair on one of the pillows. There was a lump of lead at the pit of my stomach.

The French have a phrase for it. The bastards have a phrase for everything and they are always right.

To say good-bye is to die a little.

51

Sewell Endicott said he was working late and I could drop around in the evening about seven-thirty.

He had a corner office with a blue carpet, a red mahogany desk with carved corners, very old and obviously very valuable, the usual glass-front bookshelves of mustard-yellow legal books, the usual cartoons by Spy of famous English judges, and a large portrait of Justice Oliver Wendell Holmes on the south wall, alone. Endicott's chair was quilted in black leather. Near him was an open roll-top desk jammed with papers. It was an office no decorator had had a chance to pansy up.

He was in his shirtsleeves and he looked tired, but he had that kind of face. He was smoking one of his tasteless cigarettes. Ashes from it had fallen on his loosened tie. His limp black hair was all over the place.

He stared at me silently after I sat down. Then he said: 'You're a stubborn son of a bitch, if ever I met one. Don't tell me you're still digging into that mess.'

'Something worries me a little. Would it be all right now if I assumed you were representing Mr Harlan Potter when you came to see me in the birdcage?'

He nodded. I touched the side of my face gently with my finger-tips. It was all healed up and the swelling was gone, but one of the blows must have damaged a nerve. Part of the cheek was still numb. I couldn't let it alone. It would get all right in time.

'And that when you went to Otatoclan you were temporarily deputized as a member of the D.A.'s staff?'

'Yes, but don't rub it in, Marlowe. It was a valuable connexion. Perhaps I gave it too much weight.'

'Still is, I hope.'

He shook his head. 'No. That's finished. Mr Potter does his legal business through San Francisco, New York, and Washington firms.'

'I guess he hates my guts—if he thinks about it.'

Endicott smiled. 'Curiously enough, he put all the blame on his son-in-law, Dr Loring. A man like Harlan Potter has to blame somebody. He couldn't possibly be wrong himself. He felt that if Loring hadn't been feeding the woman dangerous drugs, none of it would have happened.'

'He's wrong. You saw Terry Lennox's body in Otatoclan, didn't you?'

'I did indeed. In the back of a cabinet-maker's shop. They have no proper mortuary there. He was making the coffin too. The body was ice-cold. I saw the wound in the temple. There's no question of identity, if you had any ideas along those lines.'

'No, Mr Endicott. I didn't, because in his case it could hardly be possible. He was disguised a little though, wasn't he?'

'Face and hands darkened, hair dyed black. But the scars were still obvious. And the finger-prints, of course, were easily checked from things he had handled at home.'

'What kind of police force do they have down there?'

'Primitive. The *jefe* could just about read and write. But he knew about finger-prints. It was hot weather, you know. Quite hot.' He frowned and took his cigarette out of his mouth and dropped it negligently into an enormous black basalt sort of receptacle. 'They had to get ice from the hotel,' he added. 'Plenty of ice.' He looked at me again. 'No embalming there. Things have to move fast.'

'You speak Spanish, Mr Endicott?'

'Only a few words. The hotel manager interpreted.' He smiled. 'A well-dressed smoothie, that fellow. Looked tough, but he was very polite and helpful. It was all over in no time.'

'I had a letter from Terry. I guess Mr Potter would know about it. I told his daughter, Mrs Loring. I showed it to her. There was a portrait of Madison in it.'

'A what?'

'Five-thousand-dollar bill.'

He raised his eyebrows. 'Really. Well, he could certainly afford it. His wife gave him a cool quarter of a million the second time they were married. I've an idea he meant to go to Mexico to live anyhow–quite apart from what happened. I don't know what happened to the money. I wasn't in on that.'

'Here's the letter, Mr Endicott, if you care to read it.'

I took it out and gave it to him. He read it carefully, the way lawyers read everything. He put it down on the desk and leaned back staring at nothing.

'A little literary, isn't it?' he said quietly. 'I wonder why he did it?'

'Killed himself, confessed, or wrote me the letter?'

'Confessed and killed himself, of course,' Endicott said sharply. 'The letter is understandable. At least you got a reasonable recompense for what you did for him–and since.'

'The mailbox bothers me,' I said. 'Where he says there was a mailbox on the street under his window and the hotel waiter was going to hold his letter up before he mailed it, so Terry could see that it was mailed.'

Something in Endicott's eyes went to sleep. 'Why?' he asked indifferently. He picked another of his filtered cigarettes out of a square box. I held my lighter across the desk for him.

'They wouldn't have one in a place like Otatoclan,' I said.

'Go on.'

'I didn't get it at first. Then I looked the place up. It's a mere village.

Population say ten or twelve hundred. One street partly paved. The *jefe* has a Model A Ford as an official car. The post office is in the corner of a store, the chanceria, the butcher shop. One hotel, a couple of cantinas, no good roads, a small airfield. There's hunting around there in the mountains—lots of it. Hence the airfield. Only decent way to get there.'

'Go on. I know about the hunting.'

'So there's a mailbox on the street. Like there's a racecourse and a dog-track and a golf-course and a *jai alai fronton* and park with a coloured fountain and a bandstand.'

'Then he made a mistake,' Endicott said coldly. 'Perhaps it was something that looked like a mailbox to him—say a trash receptacle.'

I stood up. I reached for the letter and refolded it and put it back in my pocket.

'A trash receptacle,' I said. 'Sure, that's it. Painted with the Mexican colours, green, white, red, and a sign on it stencilled in large clear print: KEEP OUR CITY CLEAN. In Spanish, of course. And lying around it seven mangy dogs.'

'Don't get cute, Marlowe.'

'Sorry if I let my brains show. Another small point I have already raised with Randy Starr. How come the letter got mailed at all? According to the letter the method was prearranged. So somebody told him about the mailbox. So somebody lied. So somebody mailed the letter with five grand in it just the same. Intriguing, don't you agree?'

He puffed smoke and watched it float away.

'What's your conclusion—and why bring Starr in on it?'

'Starr and a heel named Menendez, now removed from our midst, were pals of Terry in the British Army. They are wrong gees in a way—I should say in almost every way—but they still have room for personal pride and so on. There was a cover-up here engineered for obvious reasons. There was another sort of cover-up in Otatoclan, for entirely different reasons.'

'What's your conclusion?' he asked me again and much more sharply.

'What's yours?'

He didn't answer me. So I thanked him for his time and left.

He was frowning as I opened the door, but I thought it was an honest frown of puzzlement. Or maybe he was trying to remember how it looked outside the hotel and whether there was a mailbox there.

It was another wheel to start turning—no more. It turned for a solid month before anything came up.

Then on a certain Friday morning I found a stranger waiting for me in my office. He was a well-dressed Mexican or Sud-americano of some sort. He sat by the open window smoking a brown cigarette that smelled strong. He was tall and very slender and very elegant, with a neat dark moustache and dark hair, rather longer than we wear it, and a fawn-coloured suit of some loosely-woven material. He wore those green sun-glasses. He stood up politely.

'Señor Marlowe?'

'What can I do for you?'

He handed me a folded paper. '*Un aviso de parte del Señor Starr en Las Vegas, señor. Habla Ud. español?*'

'Yeah, but not fast. English would be better.'

'English then,' he said. 'It is all the same to me.'

I took the paper and read it. 'This introduces Cisco Maioranos, a friend of mine. I think he can fix you up. S.'

'Let's go inside, Señor Maioranos,' I said.

I held the door open for him. He smelled of perfume as he went by. His eyebrows were awfully damned dainty too. But he probably wasn't as dainty as he looked because there were knife scars on both sides of his face.

52

He sat down in the customer's chair and crossed his knees. 'You wish certain information about Señor Lennox, I am told.'

'The last scene only.'

'I was there at the time, *señor*. I had a position in the hotel.' He shrugged. 'Unimportant and of course temporary. I was the day clerk.' He spoke perfect English but with a Spanish rhythm. Spanish–American Spanish that is–has a definite rise and fall which to an American ear seems to have nothing to do with the meaning. It's like the swell of the ocean.

'You don't look the type,' I said.

'One has difficulties.'

'Who mailed the letter to me?'

He held out a box of cigarettes. 'Try one of these.'

I shook my head. 'Too strong for me. Colombian cigarettes I like. Cuban cigarettes are murder.'

He smiled faintly, lit another pill himself, and blew smoke. The guy was so goddam elegant he was beginning to annoy me.

'I know about the letter, *señor*. The *mozo* was afraid to go up to the room of this Señor Lennox after the *guarda* was posted. The cop or dick, as you say. So I myself took the letter to the *correo*. After the shooting, you understand.'

'You ought to have looked inside. It had a large piece of money in it.'

'The letter was sealed,' he said coldly. '*El honor no se mueve de lado como les congrejos*. That is, honour does not move sideways like a crab, *señor*.'

'My apologies. Please continue.'

'Señor Lennox had a hundred-peso note in his left hand when I went into the room and shut the door in the face of the *guarda*. In his right hand was a pistol. On the table before him was the letter. Also another paper which I did not read. I refused the note.'

'Too much money,' I said, but he didn't react to the sarcasm.

'He insisted. So I took the note finally and gave it to the *mozo* later. I took the letter out under the napkin on the tray from the previous service of coffee. The dick looked hard at me. But he said nothing. I was half-way down the stairs when I heard the shot. Very quickly I hid the letter and ran back upstairs. The dick was trying to kick the door open. I used my key. Señor Lennox was dead.'

He moved his finger-tips gently along the edge of the desk and sighed. 'The rest no doubt you know.'

'Was the hotel full?'

'Not full, no. There were half a dozen guests.'

'Americans?'

'Two *Americanos del Norte*. Hunters.'

'Real Gringos or just transplanted Mexicans?'

He drew a finger-tip slowly along the fawn-coloured cloth above his knee. 'I think one of them could well have been of Spanish origin. He spoke border Spanish. Very inelegant.'

'They go near Lennox's room at all?'

He lifted his head sharply but the green cheaters didn't do a thing for me. 'Why should they, *señor?*'

I nodded. 'Well, it was damn nice of you to come in here and tell me about it, Señor Maioranos. Tell Randy I'm ever so grateful, will you?'

'*No hay de que, señor*. It is nothing.'

'And later on, if he has time, he could send me somebody who knows what he is talking about.'

'*Señor?*' His voice was soft, but icy. 'You doubt my word?'

'You guys are always talking about honour. Honour is the cloak of thieves—sometimes. Don't get mad. Sit quiet and let me tell it another way.'

He leaned back superciliously.

'I'm only guessing, mind. I could be wrong. But I could be right too. These two Americanos were there for a purpose. They came in on a plane. They pretended to be hunters. One of them was named Menendez, a gambler. He registered under some other name or not. I wouldn't know. Lennox knew they were there. He knew why. He wrote me that letter because he had a guilty conscience. He had played me for a sucker and he was too nice a guy for that to rest easy on him. He put the bill—five thousand dollars it was—in the letter because he had a lot of money and he knew I hadn't. He also put in a little off-beat hint which might or might not register. He was the kind of guy who always wants to do the right thing but somehow winds up doing something else. You say you took the letter to the *correo*. Why didn't you mail it in the box in front of the hotel?'

'The box, *señor?*'

'The mailbox. The *cajón cartero*, you call it, I think.'

He smiled. 'Otatoclan is not Mexico City, *señor*. It is a very primitive place. A street mailbox in Otatoclan? No one there would understand what it was for. No one would collect letters from it.'

I said: 'Oh. Well, skip it. You did not take any coffee on any tray up to Señor Lennox's room, Señor Maioranos. You did not go into the room past the dick. But the two Americanos did go in. The dick was fixed, of course. So were several other people. One of the Americanos slugged Lennox from behind. Then he took the Mauser pistol and opened up one of the cartridges and took out the bullet and put the cartridge back in the breech. Then he put this gun to Lennox's temple and pulled the trigger. It made a nasty-looking wound, but it did not kill him. Then he was carried out on a stretcher covered up and well hidden. Then when the American lawyer arrived, Lennox was doped and packed in ice and kept in a dark corner of the *carpinteria* where the man was making a coffin. The American lawyer saw Lennox there, he was ice cold, in a deep stupor, and there was a bloody blackened wound in his temple. He looked plenty dead. The next day the coffin was buried with stones in it. The American lawyer went home with the finger-prints and some kind of document which was a piece of cheese. How do you like that, Señor Maioranos?'

He shrugged. 'It would be possible, *señor*. It would require money and influence. It would be possible, perhaps, if this Señor Menendez was closely related to important people in Otatoclan, the *alcalde,* the hotel proprietor, and so on.'

'Well, that's possible, too. It's a good idea. It would explain why they picked a remote little place like Otatoclan.'

He smiled quickly. 'Then Señor Lennox may still be alive, no?'

'Sure. The suicide had to be some kind of fake to back up the confession. It had to be good enough to fool a lawyer who had been a District Attorney, but it would make a very sick monkey out of the current D.A. if it back-fired. This Menendez is not as tough as he thinks he is, but he was tough enough to pistol-whip me for not keeping my nose clean. So he had to have reasons. If the fake got exposed, Mendendez would be right in the middle of an international stink. The Mexicans don't like crooked police work any more than we do.'

'All that is possible, *señor,* as I very well know. But you accused me of lying. You said I did not go into the room where Señor Lennox was and get his letter.'

'You were already in there, chum—writing the letter.'

He reached up and took the dark glasses off. Nobody can change the colour of a man's eyes.

'I suppose it's a bit too early for a gimlet,' he said.

53

They had done a wonderful job on him in Mexico City, but why not? Their doctors, technicians, hospitals, painters, architects, are as good as ours. Sometimes a little better. A Mexican cop invented the paraffin test for powder nitrates. They couldn't make Terry's face perfect, but they had done plenty. They had even changed his nose, taken out some bone and made it look flatter, less Nordic. They couldn't eliminate every trace of a scar, so they had put a couple on the other side of his face too. Knife scars are not uncommon in Latin countries.

'They even did a nerve graft up here,' he said, and touched what had been the bad side of his face.

'How close did I come?'

'Close enough. A few details wrong, but they are not important. It was a quick deal and some of it was improvised and I didn't know myself just what was going to happen. I was told to do certain things and to leave a clear trail. Mendy didn't like my writing to you, but I held out for that. He undersold you a little. He never noticed the bit about the mailbox.'

'You knew who killed Sylvia?'

He didn't answer me directly. 'It's pretty tough to turn a woman in for murder—even if she never meant much to you.'

'It's a tough world. Was Harlan Potter in on all this?'

He smiled again. 'Would he be likely to let anyone know that? My guess is not. My guess is he thinks I am dead. Who would tell him otherwise—unless you did?'

'What I'd tell him you could fold into a blade of grass. How's Mendy these days—or is he?'

'He's doing all right. In Acapulco. He slipped by because of Randy. But the boys don't go for rough work on cops. Mendy's not as bad as you think. He has a heart.'

'So has a snake.'

'Well, what about that gimlet?'

I got up without answering him and went to the safe. I spun the knob and got out the envelope with the portrait of Madison on it and the five C notes that smelled of coffee. I dumped the lot out on the desk and then picked up the five C notes.

'These I keep. I spent all of it on expenses and research. The portrait of Madison I enjoyed playing with. It's all yours now.'

I spread it on the edge of the desk in front of him. He looked at it but didn't touch it.

'It's yours to keep,' he said. 'I've got plenty. You could have let things lie.'

'I know. After she killed her husband and got away with it she might have gone on to better things. He was of no real importance, of course. Just a human being with blood and a brain and emotions. He knew what happened too and he tried pretty hard to live with it. He wrote books. You may have heard of him.'

'Look, I couldn't very well help what I did,' he said slowly. 'I didn't want anyone to get hurt. I wouldn't have had a dog's chance up here. A man can't figure every angle that quick. I was scared and I ran. What should I have done?'

'I don't know.'

'She had a mad streak. She might have killed him anyway.'

'Yeah, she might.'

'Well, thaw out a little. Let's go have a drink somewhere where it's cool and quiet.'

'No time right now, Señor Maioranos.'

'We were pretty good friends once,' he said unhappily.

'Were we? I forget. That was two other fellows, seems to me. You permanently in Mexico?'

'Oh yes. I'm not here legally even. I never was. I told you I was born in Salt Lake City. I was born in Montreal. I'll be a Mexican national pretty soon now. All it takes is a good lawyer. I've always liked Mexico. It wouldn't be much risk going to Victor's for that gimlet.'

'Pick up your money, Señor Maioranos. It has too much blood on it.'

'You're a poor man.'

'How would you know?'

He picked the bill up and stretched it between his thin fingers and slipped it casually into an inside pocket. He bit his lip with the very white teeth you can have when you have a brown skin.

'I couldn't tell you any more than I did that morning you drove me to Tijuana. I gave you a chance to call the law and turn me in.'

'I'm not sore at you. You're just that kind of guy. For a long time I couldn't figure you at all. You had nice ways and nice qualities, but there was something wrong. You had standards and you lived up to them, but they were personal. They had no relation to any kind of ethics or scruples. You were a nice guy because you had a nice nature. But you were just as happy with mugs or hoodlums as with honest men. Provided the hoodlums spoke fairly good English and had fairly acceptable table manners. You're a moral defeatist. I think maybe the war did it and again I think maybe you were born that way.'

'I don't get it,' he said. 'I really don't. I'm trying to pay you back and you won't let me. I couldn't have told you any more than I did. You wouldn't have stood for it.'

'That's as nice a thing as was ever said to me.'

'I'm glad you like something about me. I got in a bad jam. I happened to know the sort of people who know how to deal with bad jams. They owed me for an incident that happened long ago in the war. Probably the only time in my life I ever did the right thing quick like a mouse. And when I needed them, they delivered. And for free. You're not the only guy in the world that has no price tag, Marlowe.'

He leaned across the desk and snapped at one of my cigarettes. There was an uneven flush on his face under the deep tan. The scars showed up against it. I watched him spring a fancy gas cartridge lighter loose from a pocket and light the cigarette. I got a whiff of perfume from him.

'You bought a lot of me, Terry. For a smile and a nod and a wave of the hand and a few quiet drinks in a quiet bar here and there. It was nice while it lasted. So long, *amigo*. I won't say good-bye. I said it to you when it meant something. I said it when it was sad and lonely and final.'

'I came back too late,' he said. 'These plastic jobs take time.'

'You wouldn't have come at all if I hadn't smoked you out.'

There was suddenly a glint of tears in his eyes. He put his dark glasses back on quickly.

'I wasn't sure about it,' he said. 'I hadn't made up my mind. They didn't want me to tell you anything. I just hadn't made up my mind.'

'Don't worry about it, Terry. There's always somebody around to do it for you.'

'I was in the Commandos, bud. They don't take you if you're just a piece of fluff. I got badly hurt and it wasn't any fun with those Nazi doctors. It did something to me.'

'I know all that, Terry. You're a very sweet guy in a lot of ways. I'm not judging you. I never did. It's just that you're not here any more. You're long gone. You've got nice clothes and perfume and you're as elegant as a fifty-dollar whore.'

'That's just an act,' he said almost desperately.

'You get a kick out of it, don't you?'

His mouth dropped in a sour smile. He shrugged an expressive Latin shrug.

'Of course. An act is all there is. There isn't anything else. In here'—he tapped his chest with the lighter—'there isn't anything. I've had it, Marlowe. I had it long ago. Well—I guess that winds things up.'

He stood up. I stood up. He put out a lean hand. I shook it.

'So long, Señor Maioranos. Nice to have known you—however briefly.'

'Good-bye.'

He turned and walked across the floor and out. I watched the door close. I listened to his steps going away down the imitation marble corridor. After a while they got faint, then they got silent. I kept on listening anyway. What for? Did I want him to stop suddenly and turn and come back and talk me out of the way I felt? Well, he didn't. That was the last I saw of him.

I never saw any of them again—except the cops. No way has yet been invented to say good-bye to them.

Playback

Raymond CHANDLER

PLAYBACK

To Jean and Helga
without whom this book would never have been
written

I

The voice on the telephone seemed to be sharp and peremptory, but I didn't hear too well what it said—partly because I was only half-awake and partly because I was holding the receiver upside down. I fumbled it around and grunted.

'Did you hear me! I said I was Clyde Umney, the lawyer.'

'Clyde Umney, the lawyer. I thought we had several of them.'

'You're Marlowe, aren't you?'

'Yeah. I guess so.' I looked at my wristwatch. It was 6.30 a.m., not my best hour.

'Don't get fresh with me, young man.'

'Sorry, Mr Umney. But I'm not a young man. I'm old, tired, and full of no coffee. What can I do for you, sir?'

'I want you to meet the Super Chief at eight o'clock, identify a girl among the passengers, follow her until she checks in somewhere, and then report to me. Is that clear?'

'No.'

'Why not?' he snapped.

'I don't know enough to be sure I could accept the case.'

'I'm Clyde Um—'

'Don't,' I interrupted. 'I might get hysterical. Just tell me the basic facts. Perhaps another investigator would suit you better. I never was an FBI man.'

'Oh. My secretary, Miss Vermilyea, will be at your office in half an hour. She will have the necessary information for you. She is very efficient. I hope you are.'

'I'm more efficient when I've had breakfast. Have her come here, would you?'

'Where is here?'

I gave him the address of my place on Yucca Avenue, and told him how she would find it.

'Very well,' he said grudgingly, 'but I want one thing very clear. The girl is not to know she is being followed. This is very important. I am acting for a very influential firm of Washington attorneys. Miss Vermilyea will advance you some expense money and pay you a retainer of $250. I expect a high degree of efficiency. And let's not waste time talking.'

'I'll do the best I can, Mr Umney.'

He hung up. I struggled out of bed, showered, shaved, and was nuzzling my third cup of coffee when the door bell rang.

'I'm Miss Vermilyea, Mr Umney's secretary,' she said in a rather chintzy voice.

'Please come in.'

She was quite a doll. She wore a white belted raincoat, no hat, a well-cherished head of platinum hair, bootees to match the raincoat, a folding plastic umbrella, a pair of blue-grey eyes that looked at me as if I had said a dirty word. I helped her off with her raincoat. She smelled very nice. She had a pair of legs—so far as I could determine—that were not painful to look at. She wore night-sheer stockings. I stared at them rather intently, especially when she crossed her legs and held out a cigarette to be lighted.

'Christian Dior,' she said, reading my rather open mind. 'I never wear anything else. A light, please.'

'You're wearing a lot more today,' I said, snapping a lighter for her.

'I don't greatly care for passes this early in the morning.'

'What time would suit you, Miss Vermilyea?'

She smiled rather acidly, inventoried her hand-bag, and tossed me a manila envelope. 'I think you'll find everything you need in this.'

'Well—not quite everything.'

'Get on with it, you goof. I've heard all about you. Why do you think Mr Umney chose you? He didn't. I did. And stop looking at my legs.'

I opened the envelope. It contained another sealed envelope and two cheques made out to me. One, for $250, was marked 'Retainer, as an advance against fees for professional services'. The other was for $200 and was marked 'Advance to Philip Marlowe for necessary expenses'.

'You will account for the expenses to me, in exact detail,' Miss Vermilyea said. 'And buy your own drinks.'

The other envelope I didn't open—not yet. 'What makes Umney think I'll take a case I know nothing about?'

'You'll take it. You're not asked to do anything wrong. You have my word for that.'

'What else do I have?'

'Oh, we might discuss that over a drink some rainy evening, when I'm not too busy.'

'You've sold me.'

I opened the other envelope. It contained a photograph of a girl. The pose suggested a natural ease, or a lot of experience in being photographed. It showed darkish hair which might possibly have been red, a wide, clear forehead, serious eyes, high cheekbones, nervous nostrils, and a mouth which was not giving anything away. It was a fine-drawn, almost a taut face, and not a happy one. 'Turn it over,' Miss Vermilyea said.

On the back there was clearly typed material.

'Name: Eleanor King. Height five feet four inches. Age about 29. Hair dark reddish-brown, thick, with a natural wave. Erect carriage, low, distinct voice, well-dressed but not overdressed. Conservative make-up. No visible scars. Characteristic mannerisms: habit of moving her eyes without moving her head when entering a room. Scratches palm of right hand when tense. Left-handed but adept in concealing it. Plays fast tennis, swims and dives beautifully, holds her liquor. No convictions, but prints on file.'

'Been in the coop,' I said, looking up at Miss Vermilyea.

'I have no information beyond what is there. Just follow your instructions.'

'No name, Miss Vermilyea. At twenty-nine a dish like this would almost certainly have been married. There's no mention of a wedding ring or any other jewels. That makes me wonder.'

She glanced at her watch. 'Better do your wondering at the Union Station. You haven't much time.' She stood up. I helped her on with her white raincoat and opened the door.

'You came in your own car?'

'Yes.' She went half-way out and turned. 'There's one thing I like about you. You don't paw. And you have nice manners—in a way.'

'It's rotten technique—to paw.'

'And there's one thing I don't like about you. Guess what it is.'

'Sorry. No idea—except that some people hate me for being alive.'

'I didn't mean that.'

I followed her down the steps and opened her car door for her. It was a cheap job, a Fleetwood Cadillac. She nodded briefly and slid down the hill.

I went back up and loaded a few things into an overnight bag, just in case.

2

There was nothing to it. The Super Chief was on time, as it almost always is, and the subject was as easy to spot as a kangaroo in a dinner jacket. She wasn't carrying anything but a paperback which she dumped in the first trash can she came to. She sat down and looked at the floor. An unhappy girl, if ever I saw one. After a while she got up and went to the book rack. She left it without picking anything out, glanced at the big clock on the wall, and shut herself in a telephone booth. She talked to someone after putting a handful of silver into the slot. Her expression didn't change at all. She hung up and went to the magazine rack, picked up a *New Yorker*, looked at her watch again, and sat down to read.

She was wearing a midnight blue tailor-made suit with a white blouse showing at the neck and a big sapphire blue lapel pin which would probably have matched her earrings, if I could see her ears. Her hair was a dusky red. She looked like her photograph, but a little taller than I expected. Her dark blue ribbon hat had a short veil hanging from it. She was wearing gloves.

After a while she moved across the arches outside of which the taxis wait. She looked left at the coffee shop, turned and went into the main waiting-room, glanced at the drugstore and news-stand, the information booth, and the people sitting on the clean wooden benches. Some of the ticket windows were open, some not. She wasn't interested in them. She sat down again and looked up at the big clock. She pulled off her right glove and set her wrist watch, a small plain platinum toy without jewels. Mentally I put Miss Vermilyea beside her. She didn't look soft or prissy, or prudish, but she made the Vermilyea look like a pick-up.

She didn't stay long sitting down this time, either. She got up and strolled. She went out into the patio and came back and went into the drugstore and stayed some time at the paper-book rack. Two things were obvious. If anyone was going to meet her, the date hadn't been for train time. She looked like a girl waiting between trains. She went into the coffee shop. She sat down at one of the plastic-top tables, read the menu, and then started to read her book. A waitress came with the inevitable glass of ice water, and the menu. The subject gave an order. The waitress went away, the subject went on reading her book. It was about nine-fifteen.

I went out through the arches to where a redcap was waiting by the taxi starter. 'You work the Super Chief?' I asked him.

'Yeah. Part of it.' He glanced without too deep interest at the buck I was teasing with my fingers.

'I was expecting someone on the Washington–San Diego through car. Anybody get off?'

'You mean get off permanent, baggage and all?'

I nodded.

He thought about it, studying me with intelligent chestnut eyes. 'One passenger got off,' he said at last. 'What your friend look like?'

I described a man. Someone who looked something like Edward Arnold. The redcap shook his head.

'Can't help you, mister. What got off don't look like that at all. Your friend is probably still on the train. They don't have to get off the through car. She gets hitched on to Seventy-Four. Leaves here eleven-thirty. The train ain't made up yet.'

'Thanks,' I said, and gave him the dollar. The subject's baggage was still on the train, which was all I wanted to know.

I went back to the coffee shop and looked in through the glass wall.

Subject was reading her paperback and toying with coffee and a snail. I moved over to a phone booth and called a garage I knew well and asked them to send somebody for my car if I didn't call again by noon. They'd done this often enough to have a spare key on hand. I went out to the car and got my overnight bag out of it and into a two-bit locker. In the enormous waiting-room, I bought a round trip to San Diego and trotted back to the coffee shop once again.

Subject was in place, but no longer alone. A guy was across the table from her smiling and talking, and one look was enough to show that she knew him and regretted it. He was California from the tips of his port wine loafers to the buttoned and tieless brown and yellow check shirt inside his rough cream sports jacket. He was about six feet one, slender, with a thin conceited face and too many teeth. He was twisting a piece of paper in his hand.

The yellow handkerchief in his outside breast pocket sprayed out like a small bunch of daffodils. And one thing was as clear as distilled water. The girl didn't want him there.

He went on talking and twitching the paper. Finally he shrugged and got up from his chair. He reached over and ran a fingertip down her cheek. She jerked back. Then he opened the twisted paper and laid it carefully down in front of her. He waited, smiling.

Her eyes went down to it very, very slowly. Her eyes held on it. Her hand moved to take it, but his was quicker. He put it away in his pocket, still smiling. Then he took out one of those pocket notebooks with perforated pages, and wrote something with a clip pen and tore the sheet out and put that down in front of her. That she could have. She took it, read it, and put it in her purse. At last she looked at him. And at last she smiled at him. My guess was that it took quite an effort. He reached across to pat her hand, then walked away from the table and out.

He shut himself in a phone booth, dialled, and talked for quite a while. He came out, found himself a redcap and went with the redcap to a locker. Out came a light oyster-white suitcase and a matching overnight case. The redcap carried them through the doors to the parking lot and followed him to a sleek two-toned Buick Roadmaster, the solid top convertible type that isn't convertible. The redcap put the stuff in behind the tipped seat, took his money, went away. The guy in the sports coat and yellow handkerchief got in and backed his car out and then stopped long enough to put on dark glasses and light a cigarette. After that he was gone. I wrote down the licence number and went back into the station.

The next hour was three hours long. The girl left the coffee shop and read her book in the waiting-room. Her mind wasn't on it. She kept turning back to see what she had read. Part of the time she didn't read at all, just held the book and looked at nothing. I had an early morning edition of the evening paper and behind it I watched her and added up what I had in my head. None of it was solid fact. It just helped to pass the time.

The guy who had sat at the table with her had come off the train, since he had baggage. It could have been her train and he could have been the passenger that got off her car. Her attitude made it pretty clear that she didn't want him around, and his that that was too bad but if she would glance at his piece of paper she would change her mind. And apparently she did. Since this happened after they got off the train when it could have happened more quietly before, then it followed that he didn't have his piece of paper on the train.

At this point the girl got up abruptly and went to the news-stand and came back with a packet of cigarettes. She tore it open and lit one. She smoked awkwardly as if she wasn't used to it, and while she smoked her attitude seemed to change, to become more flashy and hard, as if she was deliberately vulgarizing herself for some purpose. I looked at the wall clock. Ten-forty-seven. I went on with my thinking.

The twist of paper had looked like a newspaper clipping. She had tried to grab it, he hadn't let her. Then he had written some words on a piece of blank paper and given them to her and she had looked at him and smiled. Conclusion: the dreamboat had something on her and she had to pretend to like it.

Next point was that earlier on he had left the station and gone somewhere, perhaps to get his car, perhaps to get the clipping, perhaps anything you like. That meant he wasn't afraid that she would run out on him, and that reinforced the idea that he hadn't at that time disclosed everything he was holding up his sleeve but had disclosed some of it. Could be he wasn't sure himself. Had to check. But now having shown her his hole card he had gone off in a Buick with his baggage. Therefore he was no longer afraid of losing her. Whatever held them together was strong enough to keep on holding them.

At eleven-five I tossed all this out of the window and started with a fresh premise. I got nowhere. At eleven-ten the public address system said Number Seventy-Four on Track Eleven was now ready to receive passengers for Santa Ana, Oceanside, Del Mar, and San Diego. A bunch of people left the waiting-room, including the girl. Another bunch was already going through the gate. I watched her through and went back to the phone booths. I dropped my dime and dialled the number of Clyde Umney's office.

Miss Vermilyea answered by giving the phone number only.

'This is Marlowe. Mr Umney in?'

Her voice was formal saying: 'I'm sorry, Mr Umney is in court. May I take a message?'

'Am in contact and leaving by train for San Diego, or some intermediate stop. Can't tell which yet.'

'Thank you. Anything else?'

'Yeah, the sun's shining and our friend is no more on the lam than you are. She ate breakfast in the coffee shop which has a glass wall towards the concourse. She sat in the waiting-room with a hundred and fifty other people. And she could have stayed on the train out of sight.'

'I have all that, thank you. I'll get it to Mr Umney as soon as possible. You have no firm opinion then?'

'I have one firm opinion. That you're holding out on me.'

Her voice changed abruptly. Somebody must have left the office. 'Listen, chum, you were hired to do a job. Better do it and do it right. Clyde Umney draws a lot of water in this town.'

'Who wants water, beautiful? I take mine straight with a beer chaser. I might make sweeter music if I was encouraged.'

'You'll get paid, shamus—if you do a job. Not otherwise. Is that clear?'

'That's the nicest thing you ever said to me, sweetheart. Good-bye now.'

'Listen Marlowe,' she said with sudden urgency. 'I didn't mean to be rough with you. This is very important to Clyde Umney. If he doesn't come through, he might lose a very valuable connexion. I was just sounding off.'

'I liked it, Vermilyea. It did things to my subconscious. I'll call in when I can.'

I hung up, went through the gate, down the ramp, walked about from here to Ventura to get to Track Eleven, and climbed aboard a coach that was already full of the drifting cigarette smoke that is so kind to your throat and nearly always leaves you with one good lung. I filled and lit a pipe and added to the general frowst.

The train pulled out, dawdled interminably through the yards and the back stretches of east L.A., picked up a little speed and made its first stop at Santa Ana. Subject did not get off. At Oceanside and Del Mar the same. At San Diego I hopped off quickly, chartered a cab, and then waited eight minutes outside the old Spanish station for the redcaps to come out with the baggage. Then the girl came out too.

She didn't take a cab. She crossed the street and rounded the corner to a U-Drive outfit and after a longish interval came out again looking disappointed. No driver's licence, no U-Drive. You'd think she would have known that.

She took a cab this time and it did a U-turn and started north. Mine did the same. I had a little difficulty with my driver about the tail job.

'That's something you read about in books, mister. We don't do it in Dago.'

I passed him a fin and the four by two and half photostat of my licence. He looked them over, both of them. He looked off up the block.

'Okay, but I report it,' he said. 'The dispatcher may report it to the Police Business Office. That's the way it is here, chum.'

'Sounds like the kind of city I ought to live in,' I said. 'And you've lost the tail. He turned left two blocks ahead.'

The driver handed me back my wallet. 'Lost my left eye,' he said tensely. 'What you think a two-way radiophone is for?' He picked it up and talked into it.

He turned left at Ash Street to Highway 101 and we merged with the traffic and kept going at a peaceable forty. I stared at the back of his head.

'You don't have a worry in the world,' the driver told me over his shoulder. 'This five is on top of the fare, huh?'

'Right. And why don't I have a worry in the world?'

'The passenger's going to Esmeralda. That's twelve miles north of here on the ocean front. Destination, unless changed *en route*—and if it is I'll get told—a motel joint called the Rancho Descansado. That's Spanish for relax, take it easy.'

'Hell, I didn't need a cab at all,' I said.

'You got to pay for the service, mister. We ain't buying groceries giving it away.'

'You Mexican?'

'We don't call ourselves that, mister. We call ourselves Spanish-Americans. Born and raised in the U.S.A. Some of us don't hardly speak Spanish any more.'

'*Es gran lástima*,' I said. '*Una lengua muchissima hermosa.*'

He turned his head and grinned. '*Tiene Vd. razón, amigo. Estoy muy bien de acuerdo.*'

We went on to Torrance Beach, through there and swung out towards the point. From time to time the hackie talked into his radiophone. He turned his head enough to speak to me again.

'You want to keep out of sight?'

'What about the other driver? Will he tell his passenger she's being tailed?'

'He ain't been told hisself. That's why I asked you.'

'Pass him and get there ahead, if you can. That's five more on the top.'

'A cinch. He won't even see me. I can rib him later on over a bottle of Tecate.'

We went through a small shopping centre, then the road widened and the houses on one side looked expensive and not new, while the houses on the other side looked very new and still not cheap. The road narrowed again and we were in a twenty-five-mile zone. My driver cut to the right, wound through some narrow streets, jumped a stop sign, and before I had had time to size up where we were going, we were sliding down into a canyon with the Pacific glinting off to the left beyond a wide, shallow beach with two lifeguard stations on open metal towers. At the bottom of the canyon the driver started to turn in through the gates, but I stopped him. A large sign, gold script on a green background, said: 'El Rancho Descansado'.

'Get out of sight,' I said. 'I want to make sure.'

He swung back on the highway, drove fast down beyond the end of the stucco wall, then cut into a narrow winding road on the far side and stopped. A gnarled eucalyptus with a divided trunk hung over us. I got out of the cab, put dark glasses on, strolled down to the highway, and leaned against a bright red jeep with the name of a service station painted on it. A cab came down the hill and turned into the Rancho Descansado. Three minutes passed. The cab came out empty and turned back up the hill. I went back to my driver.

'Cab No. 423,' I said. 'That check?'

'That's your pigeon. What now?'

'We wait. What's the layout over there?'

'Bungalows with car ports. Some single, some double. Office in a small one down front. Rates pretty steep in season. This is slack time around here. Half price probably and plenty of room.'

'We wait five minutes. Then I check in, drop my suitcase, and look for a car to rent.'

He said that was easy. In Esmeralda there were three places that rented cars, time and mileage, any make you wanted.

We waited the five minutes. It was now just past three o'clock. I was empty enough to steal the dog's dinner.

I paid my driver off, watched him leave, and went across the highway and into the office.

3

I leaned a polite elbow on the counter and looked across at the happy-faced young guy in the polka-dotted bow tie. I looked from him to the girl at the small PBX against the side wall. She was an out-doorsy type with shiny make-up and a horse's tail of medium blonde hair sticking out at the back of her noddle. But she had nice large soft eyes and when they looked at the clerk they glistened. I looked back at him and choked back a snarl. The girl at the PBX swung her horse tail in an arc and put the eye on me also.

'I'd be glad to show you what we have vacant, Mr Marlowe,' the young guy said politely. 'You can register later, if you decide to stay here. About how long would you be likely to want accommodation?'

'Only as long as she does,' I said. 'The girl in the blue suit. She just registered. Using what name I wouldn't know.'

He and the PBX girl stared at me. Both their faces had the same expression of distrust mixed with curiosity. There are a hundred ways of playing this scene. But this was a new one for me. In no city hotel in the world would it work. It might work here. Mostly because I didn't give a damn.

'You don't like that, do you?' I said.

He shook his head slightly. 'At least you're frank about it.'

'I'm tired of being cagey. I'm worn out with it. Did you notice her ring finger?'

'Why no, I didn't.' He looked at the PBX girl. She shook her head and kept her eyes on my face.

'No wedding ring,' I said. 'Not any more. All gone. All broken up. All the years–ah, the hell with it. I've followed her all the way from–well, never mind where. She won't even speak to me. What am I doing here? Making a damn fool of myself.' I turned away quickly and blew my nose. I had their attention. 'I'd better go somewhere else,' I said, turning back.

'You want to make it up and she won't,' the PBX girl said quietly.

'Yes.'

'I'm sympathetic,' the young guy said. 'But you know how it is Mr

Marlowe. A hotel has to be very careful. These situations can lead to anything—even shootings.'

'Shootings?' I looked at him with wonder. 'Good God, what sort of people do that?'

He leaned both arms on the desk. 'Just what would you like to do, Mr Marlowe?'

'I'd like to be near her—in case she needs me. I wouldn't speak to her. I wouldn't even knock at her door. But she would know I was there and she'd know why. I'd be waiting. I'll always be waiting.'

The girl loved it now. I was up to my neck in the soft corn. I took a deep, slow breath and shot for the grand prize. 'And I don't somehow like the look of the guy who brought her here,' I said.

'Nobody brought her here—except a cab driver,' the clerk said. But he knew what I meant all right.

The PBX girl half smiled. 'He doesn't mean that, Jack. He means the reservation.'

Jack said, 'I kind of gathered as much, Lucille. I'm not so dumb.' Suddenly he brought a card out from the desk and put it down in front of me. A registration card. Across the corner diagonally was written the name Larry Mitchell. In a very different writing in the proper places: (Miss) Betty Mayfield, West Chatham, New York. Then in the top left-hand corner in the same writing as Larry Mitchell a date, a time, a price, a number.

'You're very kind,' I said. 'So she's gone back to her maiden name. It's legal, of course.'

'Any name is legal, if there's no intent to defraud. You would like to be next door to her?'

I widened my eyes. Maybe they glistened a little. Nobody ever tried harder to make them glisten.

'Look,' I said, 'it's damn nice of you. But you can't do it. I'm not going to make any trouble, but you can't be sure. It's your job if I pulled anything.'

'Okay,' he said. 'I've got to learn some day. You look all right to me. Just don't tell anybody.' He took the pen from its cup and held it out. I signed my name with an address on East Sixty-First Street, New York City.

Jack looked at it. 'That's near Central Park, isn't it?' he asked idly.

'Three blocks and a bit,' I said. 'Between Lexington and Third Avenue.'

He nodded. He knew where it was. I was in. He reached for a key.

'I'd like to leave my suitcase here', I said, 'and go get something to eat and maybe rent a car, if I can. You could have it put in the room for me?'

Sure. He could do that for me easy. He took me outside and pointed up through a grove of saplings. The cottages were all over shingled, white with green roofs. They had porches with railings. He showed me mine through the trees. I thanked him. He started back in and I said, 'Look, there's one thing. She may check out when she knows.'

He smiled. 'Of course. Nothing we can do about that, Mr Marlowe. Lots of our guests only stay a night or two—except in summer. We don't expect to be filled up this time of year.'

He went on into the office cottage and I heard the girl say to him: 'He's kind of cute, Jack—but you shouldn't have done it.'

I heard his answer too. 'I hate that guy Mitchell—even if he is a pal of the owner.'

4

The room was bearable. It had the usual concrete couch, chairs without cushions, a small desk against the front wall, a walk-in closet with a built-in chest, a bathroom with a Hollywood bath and neon shaving lights beside the mirror over the basin, a small kitchenette with a refrigerator and a white stove, a three-burner electric. In a wall cupboard over the sink enough dishes and stuff. I got some ice cubes and made myself a drink with the bottle from my suitcase, sipped it, and sat in a chair listening, leaving the windows shut and the venetian blinds dark. I heard nothing next door, then I heard the toilet flush. Subject was in residence. I finished the drink, killed a cigarette, and studied the wall heater on the party wall. It consisted of two long frosted bulbs in a metal box. It didn't look as if it would throw out much heat, but in the closet there was a plug-in fan heater with a thermostat and a three-way plug, which made it 220 volts. I slipped off the chromium grille guard of the wall heater and twisted out the frosted bulbs. I got a doctor's stethoscope out of my suitcase and held it against the metal backing and listened. If there was another similar heater back against it in the next room, and there almost certainly would be, all I had between the two rooms was a metal panel and some insulation, probably a bare minimum of that.

I heard nothing for a few minutes, then I heard a telephone being dialled. The reception was perfect. A woman's voice said: 'Esmeralda 4–1499, please.'

It was a cool, contained voice, medium pitch, very little expression in it except that it sounded tired. It was the first time I had heard her voice in all the hours I had been following her.

There was a longish pause, then she said: 'Mr Larry Mitchell please.'

Another pause, but shorter. Then: 'This is Betty Mayfield, at the Rancho Descansado.' She pronounced the 'a' in Descansado wrong. Then, 'Betty Mayfield, I said. Please don't be stupid. Do you want me to spell it for you?'

The other end had things to say. She listened. After a while she said: 'Apartment 12C. You ought to know. You made the reservation. . . . Oh, I see. . . . Well, all right. I'll be here.'

She hung up. Silence. Complete silence. Then the voice in there said slowly and emptily: 'Betty Mayfield, Betty Mayfield, Betty Mayfield. Poor Betty. You were a nice girl once–long ago.'

I was sitting on the floor on one of the striped cushions with my back to the wall. I got up carefully, laid the stethoscope down on the cushion and went to lie on the day bed. After a while he would arrive. She was in there waiting for him, because she had to. She'd had to come there for the same reason. I wanted to know what it was.

He must have been wearing crêpe soles because I didn't hear anything until the buzzer sounded next door. Also, he hadn't driven his car up to the cottage. I got down on the floor and went to work with the stethoscope.

She opened the door, he came in and I could imagine the smile on his face as he said: 'Hello, Betty. Betty Mayfield is the name, I believe. I like it.'

'It was my name originally.' She closed the door.

He chuckled. 'I suppose you were wise to change it. But how about the initials on your luggage?'

I didn't like his voice any better than his smile. It was high and cheerful, and almost bubbly with sly good humour. There was not quite a sneer in it, but close enough. It made me clamp my teeth.

'I suppose,' she said dryly, 'that was the first thing you noticed.'

'No, baby. *You* were the first thing I noticed. The mark of a wedding ring but no wedding ring was the second. The initials were only the third.'

'Don't call me "baby", you cheap blackmailer,' she said with a sudden muted fury.

It didn't faze him in the least. 'I may be a blackmailer, honey, but'—another conceited chuckle—'I'm certainly not cheap.'

She walked, probably away from him. 'Do you want a drink? I see you have a bottle with you.'

'It might make me lascivious.'

'There's only one thing about you I'm afraid of, Mr Mitchell,' the girl said coolly. 'Your big loose mouth. You talk too much and you like yourself too well. We'd better understand each other. I like Esmeralda. I've been here before and I always wanted to come back. It's nothing but sheer bad luck that you live here and that you were on the train that was taking me here. It was the worst kind of luck that you should have recognized me. But that's all it is—bad luck.'

'Good luck for me, honey,' he drawled.

'Perhaps,' she said, 'if you don't put too much pressure on it. If you do, it's liable to blow up in your face.'

There was a brief silence. I could see them in my imagination, staring at each other. His smile might be getting a little nervous, but not much.

'All I've got to do', he said quietly, 'is pick up the phone and call the San Diego papers. You want publicity? I can arrange it for you.'

'I came here to get rid of it,' she said bitterly.

He laughed. 'Sure, by an old coot of a judge falling to pieces with senile decay, and in the only State in the Union—and I've checked on that—where it could happen after the jury said otherwise. You've changed your name twice. If your story got printed out here—and it's a pretty good story, honey—I guess you'd have to change your name again—and start travelling a little more. Gets kind of tiresome, doesn't it?'

'That's why I'm here,' she said. 'That's why you're here. How much do you want? I realize it will be only a down payment.'

'Have I said anything about money?'

'You will,' she said. 'And keep your voice down.'

'The cottage is all yours, honey. I walked around it before I came in. Doors closed, windows shut, blinds drawn, car ports empty. I can check with the office, if you're nervous. I've got friends around here—people you need to know, people who can make life pleasant for you. Socially this is a tough town to break into. And it's a damn dull town if you're on the outside looking in.'

'How did *you* get in, Mr Mitchell?'

'My old man is a big shot in Toronto. We don't get on and he won't have me around home. But he's still my old man and he's still the real thing, even if he does pay me to stay away.'

She didn't answer him. Her steps went away. I heard her in the kitchen making the usual sounds connected with getting ice out of a tray of cubes. The water ran, the steps came back.

'I'd like one myself,' she said. 'Perhaps I've been rude to you. I'm tired.'

'Sure,' he said equably. 'You're tired.' A pause. 'Well, here's to when you're not tired. Say about seven-thirty this evening at The Glass Room. I'll pick you up. Nice place for dinner. Dancing. Quiet. Exclusive, if that means anything any more. Belongs to the Beach Club. They don't have a table unless they know you. I'm among friends there.'

'Expensive?' she asked.

'A little. Oh yes—and that reminds me. Until my monthly cheque comes in, you could let me have a couple of dollars.' He laughed. 'I'm surprised at myself. I did mention money after all.'

'A couple of dollars?'

'A couple of hundred would be better.'

'Sixty dollars is all I have—until I can open an account or cash some travellers' cheques.'

'You can do that at the office, baby.'

'So I can. Here's fifty. I don't want to spoil you, Mr Mitchell.'

'Call me Larry. Be human.'

'Should I?' Her voice had changed. There was a hint of invitation in it. I could imagine the slow smile of pleasure on his face. Then I guessed from the silence that he had grabbed her and she had let him. Finally her voice was a little muffled, saying:

'That's enough, Larry. Be nice now and run along. I'll be ready at seven-thirty.'

'One more for the road.'

In a moment the door opened and he said something I didn't catch. I got up and went to the window and took a careful look through the slats of the blind. A floodlight was turned on in one of the tall trees. Under it I saw him stroll off up the slope and disappear. I went back to the heater panel and for a while I heard nothing and wasn't sure what I was listening for. But I knew soon enough.

There was quick movement back and forth, the sound of drawers being pulled open, the snap of a lock, the bump of a lifted lid against something.

She was packing up to leave.

I screwed the long, frosted bulbs back into the heater and replaced the grille and put the stethoscope back in my suitcase. The evening was getting chilly. I slipped my jacket on and stood in the middle of the floor. It was getting dark and no light on. I just stood there and thought it over. I could go to the phone and make a report and by that time she could be on her way in another cab to another train or plane to another destination. She could go anywhere she liked, but there would always be a dick to meet the train if it meant enough to the big, important people back in Washington. There would always be a Larry Mitchell or a reporter with a good memory. There would always be the little oddness to be noticed and there would always be somebody to notice it. You can't run away from yourself.

I was doing a cheap, sneaky job for people I didn't like, but—that's what you hire out for, chum. They pay the bills, you dig the dirt. Only this time

I could taste it. She didn't look like a tramp and she didn't look like a crook. Which meant only that she could be both with more success than if she had.

5

I opened the door and went along to the next and pushed the little buzzer. Nothing moved inside. There was no sound of steps. Then came the click of a chain set in the groove and the door opened a couple of inches on light and emptiness. The voice said from behind the door: 'Who is it?'

'Could I borrow a cup of sugar?'

'I haven't any sugar.'

'Well how about a couple of dollars until my cheque comes in?'

More silence. Then the door opened to the limit of the chain and her faced edged into the opening and shaded eyes stared out at me. They were just pools in the dark. The floodlight set high in the tree glinted on them obliquely.

'Who are you?'

'I'm your next-door neighbour. I was having a nap, and voices woke me. The voices spoke words. I was intrigued.'

'Go somewhere else and be intrigued.'

'I could do that, Mrs King—pardon me, Miss Mayfield—but I'm not sure you'd want me to.'

She didn't move and her eyes didn't waver. I shook a cigarette out of a packet and tried to push up the top of my Zippo with my thumb and rotate the wheel. You should be able to do it one-handed. You can too, but it's an awkward process. I made it at last and got the cigarette going, yawned, and blew smoke out through my nose.

'What do you do for an encore?' she asked.

'To be strictly kosher I should call L.A. and tell the party who sent me. Maybe I could be talked out of it.'

'God,' she said fervently, 'two of them in one afternoon. How lucky can a girl get?'

'I don't know,' I said. 'I don't know anything. I think I've been played for a sucker, but I'm not sure.'

'Wait a minute.' She shut the door in my face. She wasn't gone long. The chain came out of the groove inside and the door came open.

I went in slowly and she stepped back and away from me. 'How much did you hear? And shut the door, please.'

I shut it with my shoulder and leaned against it.

'The tag end of a rather nasty conversation. The walls here are as thin as a hoofer's wallet.'

'You in show business?'

'Just the opposite of show business. I'm in the hide-and-seek business. My name is Philip Marlowe. You've seen me before.'

'Have I?' She walked away from me in little cautious steps and went over by her open suitcase. She leaned against the arm of a chair. 'Where?'

'Union Station in L.A. We waited between trains, you and I. I was interested in you. I was interested in what went on between you and Mr Mitchell—that's his name, isn't it? I didn't hear anything and I didn't see much because I was outside the coffee shop.'

'So what interested you, you great big lovable something or other?'

'I've just told you part of it. The other thing that interested me was how you changed after your talk with him. I watched you work at it. It was very deliberate. You made yourself over into just another flip, hard-boiled modern cutie. Why?'

'What was I before?'

'A nice quiet, well-bred girl.'

'That was the act,' she said. 'The other was my natural personality. Which goes with something else.' She brought a small automatic up from her side.

I looked at it. 'Oh guns,' I said. 'Don't scare me with guns. I've lived with them all my life. I teethed on an old Derringer, single-shot, the kind the river-boat gamblers used to carry. As I got older I graduated to a light-weight sporting rifle, then a .303 target rifle and so on. I once made a bull at nine hundred yards with open sights. In case you don't know, the whole target looks the size of a postage stamp at nine hundred yards.'

'A fascinating career,' she said.

'Guns never settle anything,' I said. 'They are just a fast curtain to a bad second act.'

She smiled faintly and transferred the gun to her left hand. With her right she grabbed the edge of her blouse at the collar line and with a quick decisive motion tore it to the waist.

'Next,' she said, 'but there's no hurry about it, I turn the gun in my hand like this'—she put it back in her right hand, but held it by the barrel—'I slam myself on the cheekbone with the butt. I do a beautiful bruise.'

'And after that,' I said, 'you get the gun into its proper position and release the safety catch and pull the trigger, just about the time I get through the lead column in the Sports Section.'

'You wouldn't get half-way across the room.'

I crossed my legs and leaned back and lifted the green glass ashtray from the table beside the chair and balanced it on my knee and held the cigarette I was smoking between the first and second fingers of my right hand.

'I wouldn't get any of the way across the room. I'd be sitting here like this, quite comfortable and relaxed.'

'But slightly dead,' she said. 'I'm a good shot and it isn't nine hundred yards.'

'Then you try to sell the cops your account of how I tried to attack you and you defended yourself.'

She tossed the gun into her suitcase and laughed. It sounded like a genuine laugh with real amusement in it.

'Sorry,' she said. 'You sitting there with your legs crossed and a hole in your head and me trying to explain how I shot you to defend my honour—the picture makes me a little light-headed.'

She dropped into a chair and leaned forward with her chin cupped in a hand, the elbow propped on her knee, her face taut and drained, her dark red hair framing it too luxuriantly, so that her face looked smaller than it should have.

'Just what are you doing to me, Mr Marlowe? Or is it the other way around—what can I do for you in return for you not doing anything at all?'

'Who is Eleanor King? What was she in Washington, D.C.? Why did she change her name somewhere along the way and have the initials taken off her bag? Odds and ends like that are what you could tell me. You probably won't.'

'Oh, I don't know. The porter took the initials off my things. I told him I had had a very unhappy marriage and was divorced and had been given the right to resume my unmarried name. Which is Elizabeth or Betty Mayfield. That could all be true, couldn't it?'

'Yeah. But it doesn't explain Mitchell.'

She leaned back and relaxed. Her eyes stayed watchful. 'Just an acquaintance I made along the way. He was on the train.'

I nodded. 'But he came down here in his own car. He made the reservation here for you. He's not liked by the people here, but apparently he is a friend of someone with a lot of influence.'

'An acquaintanceship on a train or a ship sometimes develops very quickly,' she said.

'So it seems. He even touched you for a loan. Very fast work. And I got the impression you didn't care for him too well.'

'Well,' she said. 'So what? But as a matter of fact I'm crazy about him.' She turned her hand over and looked down at it. 'Who hired you, Mr Marlowe, and for what?'

'A Los Angeles lawyer, acting on instructions from back East. I was to follow you and check you in somewhere. Which I did. But now you're getting ready to move out. I'm going to have to start over again.'

'But with me knowing you're there,' she said shrewdly. 'So you'll have a much harder job of it. You're a private detective of some sort, I gather.'

I said I was. I had killed my cigarette some time back. I put the ashtray back on the table and stood up.

'Harder for me, but there are lots of others, Miss Mayfield.'

'Oh, I'm sure there are, and all such nice little men. Some of them are even fairly clean.'

'The cops are not looking for you. They'd have had you easily. It was known about your train. I even got a photo of you and a description. But Mitchell can make you do just what he wants. Money isn't all he'll want.'

I thought she flushed a little, but the light didn't strike her face directly. 'Perhaps so,' she said. 'And perhaps I don't mind.'

'You mind.'

She stood up suddenly and came near me. 'You're in a business that doesn't pay fortunes, aren't you?'

I nodded. We were very close now.

'Then what would it be worth to you to walk out of here and forget you ever saw me?'

'I'd walk out of here for free. As for the rest, I have to make a report.'

'How much?' She said it as if she meant it. 'I can afford a substantial retainer. That's what you call it, I've heard. A much nicer word than blackmail.'

'It doesn't mean the same thing.'

'It could. Believe me, it can mean just that—even with some lawyers and doctors. I happen to know.'

'Tough break, huh?'

'Far from it, shamus. I'm the luckiest girl in the world. I'm alive.'

'I'm on the other side. Don't give it away.'

'Well, what do you know,' she drawled. 'A dick with scruples. Tell it to the seagulls, buster. On me it's just confetti. Run along now, Mr PI Marlowe, and make that little old phone call you're so anxious about. I'm not restraining you.'

She started for the door, but I caught her by the wrist and spun her around. The torn blouse didn't reveal any startling nakedness, merely some skin and part of a brassière. You'd see more on the beach, far more, but you wouldn't see it through a torn blouse.

I must have been leering a little, because she suddenly curled her fingers and tried to claw me.

'I'm no bitch in heat,' she said between tight teeth. 'Take your paws off me.'

I got the other wrist and started to pull her closer. She tried to knee me in the groin, but she was already too close. Then she went limp and pulled her head back and closed her eyes. Her lips opened with a sardonic twist to them. It was a cool evening, maybe even cold down by the water. But it wasn't cold where I was.

After a while she said with a sighing voice that she had to dress for dinner. I said: 'Uh-huh.'

After another pause she said it was a long time since a man had unhooked her brassière. We did a slow turn in the direction of one of the twin day beds. They had pink and silver covers on them. The little odd things you notice.

Her eyes were open and quizzical. I studied them one at a time because I was too close to see them together. They seemed well matched.

'Honey,' she said softly, 'you're awful sweet, but I just don't have the time.'

I closed her mouth for her. It seems that a key slid into the door from the outside, but I wasn't paying too close attention. The lock clicked, the door opened, and Mr Larry Mitchell walked in.

We broke apart. I turned and he looked at me droopy-eyed, six feet one, and tough and wiry.

'I thought to check at the office,' he said, almost absently. '12B was rented this afternoon, very soon after this was occupied. I got faintly curious, because there are a lot of vacancies here at the moment. So I borrowed the other key. And who is this hunk of beef, baby?'

'She told you not to call her "baby", remember?'

If that meant anything to him, he didn't show it. He swung a knotted fist gently at his side.

The girl said: 'He's a private eye named Marlowe. Somebody hired him to follow me.'

'Did he have to follow you as close as all that? I seem to be intruding on a beautiful friendship.'

She jerked away from me and grabbed the gun out of her suitcase. 'What we've been talking is money,' she told him.

'Always a mistake,' Mitchell said. His colour was high and his eyes too bright. 'Especially in that position. You won't need the gun, honey.'

He poked at me with a straight right, very fast and well sprung. I stepped

inside it, fast, cool, and clever. But the right wasn't his meal ticket. He was a
lefty, too. I ought to have noticed that at the Union Station in L.A. Trained
observer, never miss a detail. I missed him with a right hook and he didn't
miss with his left.

It snapped my head back. I went off balance just long enough for him to
lunge sideways and lift the gun out of the girl's hand. It seemed to dance
through the air and nestle in his left hand.

'Just relax,' he said. 'I know it sounds corny, but I could drill you and get
away with it. I really could.'

'Okay,' I said thickly. 'For fifty bucks a day I don't get shot. That costs
seventy-five.'

'Please turn around. It would amuse me to look at your wallet.'

I lunged for him, gun and all. Only panic could have made him shoot and
he was on his home field and nothing to panic about. But it may be that the
girl wasn't so sure. Dimly at the extreme edge of vision I saw her reach for
the whisky bottle on the table.

I caught Mitchell on the side of the neck. His mouth yapped. He hit me
somewhere, but it wasn't important. Mine was the better punch, but it
didn't win the wristwatch, because at that moment an army mule kicked me
square on the back of my brain. I went zooming out over a dark sea and
exploded in a sheet of flame.

6

The first sensation was that if anybody spoke harshly to me I should burst
out crying. The second that the room was too small for my head. The front
of the head was a long way from the back, the sides were an enormous
distance apart, in spite of which a dull throbbing beat from temple to
temple. Distance means nothing nowadays.

The third sensation was that somewhere not far off an insistent whining
noise went on. The fourth and last was that ice water was running down my
back. The cover of a day bed proved that I had been lying on my face, if I
still had one. I rolled over gently and sat up and a rattling noise ended in a
thump. What rattled and thumped was a knotted towel full of melting ice
cubes. Somebody who loved me very much had put them on the back of my
head. Somebody who loved me less had bashed in the back of my skull. It
could have been the same person. People have moods.

I got up on my feet and lunged for my hip. The wallet was there in the left
pocket, but the flap was unbuttoned. I went through it. Nothing was gone.
It had yielded its information, but that was no secret any more. My suitcase
stood open on the stand at the foot of the day bed. So I was home in my own
quarters.

I reached a mirror and looked at the face. It seemed familiar. I went to the
door and opened it. The whining noise was louder. Right in front of me was
a fattish man leaning against the railing. He was a middle-sized fat man and
the fat didn't look flabby. He wore glasses and large ears under a dull grey
felt hat. The collar of his top-coat was turned up. His hands were in the

pockets of his coat. The hair that showed at the sides of his head was battleship grey. He looked durable. Most fat men do. The light from the open door behind me bounced back from his glasses. He had a small pipe in his mouth, the kind they call a toy bulldog. I was still foggy but something about him bothered me.

'Nice evening,' he said.

'You want something?'

'Looking for a man. You're not him.'

'I'm alone in here.'

'Right,' he said. 'Thanks.' He turned his back on me and leaned his stomach against the railing of the porch.

I went along the porch to the whining noise. The door of 12c was wide open and the lights were on and the noise was a vacuum cleaner being operated by a woman in a green uniform.

I went in and looked the place over. The woman switched off the vacuum and stared at me. 'Something you wanted?'

'Where's Miss Mayfield?'

She shook her head.

'The lady who had this apartment,' I said.

'Oh, that one. She checked out. Half an hour ago.' She switched the vacuum on again. 'Better ask at the office,' she yelled through the noise. 'This apartment is on change.'

I reached back and shut the door. I followed the black snake of the vacuum cord over to the wall and yanked the plug out. The woman in the green uniform stared at me angrily. I went over and handed her a dollar bill. She looked less angry.

'Just want to phone,' I said.

'Ain't you got a phone in your room?'

'Stop thinking,' I said. 'A dollar's worth.'

I went to the phone and lifted it. A girl's voice said: 'Office. Your order, please.'

'This is Marlowe. I'm very unhappy.'

'What? . . . Oh yes, Mr Marlowe. What can we do for you?'

'She's gone. I never even got to talk to her.'

'Oh, I'm sorry, Mr Marlowe,' she sounded as if she meant it. 'Yes, she left. We couldn't very well—'

'She say where to?'

'She just paid up and left, sir. Quite suddenly. No forwarding address at all.'

'With Mitchell?'

'I'm sorry, sir. I didn't see anyone with her.'

'You must have seen something. How did she leave?'

'In a taxi. I'm afraid—'

'All right. Thank you.' I went back to my own apartment.

The middle-sized fat man was sitting comfortably in a chair with his knees crossed.

'Nice of you to drop in,' I said. 'Anything in particular I could do for you?'

'You could tell me where Larry Mitchell is.'

'Larry Mitchell?' I thought it over carefully. 'Do I know him?'

He opened a wallet and extracted a card. He struggled to his feet and handed it to me. The card read: 'Goble and Green, Investigators, 310 Prudence Building, Kansas City, Missouri.'

'Must be interesting work, Mr Goble.'

'Don't get funny with me, buster. I get annoyed rather easy.'

'Fine. Let's watch you get annoyed. What do you do—bite your moustache?'

'I ain't got no moustache, stupid.'

'You could grow one. I can wait.'

He got up on his feet much more rapidly this time. He looked down at his fist. Suddenly a gun appeared in his hand. 'You ever get pistol-whipped, stupid?'

'Breeze off. You bore me. Mudheads always bore me.'

His hand shook and his face turned red. Then he put the gun back in the shoulder holster and wobbled towards the door.

'You ain't through with me,' he snarled over his shoulder.

I let him have that one. It wasn't worth topping.

7

After a while I went down to the office.

'Well, it didn't work,' I said. 'Does either one of you happen to have noticed the cab driver who took her away?'

'Joe Harms,' the girl said promptly. 'You ought to maybe find him at the stand half-way up Grand. Or you could call the office. A pretty nice guy. He made a pass at me once.'

'And missed by from here to Paso Robles,' the clerk sneered.

'Oh, I don't know. You didn't seem to be there.'

'Yeah,' he sighed. 'You work twenty hours a day trying to put enough together to buy a home. And by the time you have, fifteen other guys have been smooching your girl.'

'Not this one,' I said. 'She's just teasing you. She glows every time she looks at you.'

I went out and left them smiling at each other.

Like most small towns, Esmeralda had one main street from which in both directions its commercial establishments flowed gently for a short block or so and then with hardly a change of mood became streets with houses where people lived. But unlike most small California towns it had no false fronts, no cheesy billboards, no drive-in hamburger joints, no cigar counters or poolrooms, and no street corner toughs to hang around in front of them. The stores on Grand Street were either old and narrow but not tawdry or else well modernized with plate glass and stainless steel fronts and neon lighting in clear crisp colours. Not everybody in Esmeralda was prosperous, not everybody was happy, not everybody drove a Cadillac, a Jaguar, or a Riley, but the percentage of obviously prosperous living was very high, and the stores that sold luxury goods were as neat and expensive-looking as those in Beverly Hills and far less flashy. There was another small difference too. In Esmeralda what was old was also clean and sometimes quaint. In other small towns what is old is just shabby.

I parked midway of the block and the telephone office was right in front of me. It was closed of course, but the entrance was set back and in the alcove which deliberately sacrificed money space to style were two dark green phone booths, like sentry boxes. Across the way was a pale buff taxi, parked diagonally to the kerb in slots painted red. A grey-haired man sat in it reading the paper. I crossed to him.

'You Joe Harms?'

He shook his head. 'He'll be back after a while. You want a cab?'

'No, thanks.'

I walked away from him and looked in at a store window. There was a checked brown and beige sports shirt in the window which reminded me of Larry Mitchell. Walnut brogues, imported tweeds, ties, two or three, and matching shirts for them set out with plenty of room to breathe. Over the store the name of a man who was once a famous athlete. The name was in script, carved and painted in relief against a redwood background.

A telephone jangled and the cab driver got out of the taxi and went across the sidewalk to answer it. He talked, hung up, got in his cab, and backed out of the slot. When he was gone, the street was utterly empty for a minute. Then a couple of cars went by, then a good-looking, well-dressed coloured boy and his prettied-up cutie came strolling the block looking in at the windows and chattering. A Mexican in a green bellhop's uniform drove up in somebody's Chrysler New Yorker—it could be his for all I knew—went into the drugstore and came out with a carton of cigarettes. He drove back towards the hotel.

Another beige cab with the name Esmeralda Cab Company tooled around the corner and drifted into the red slot. A big bruiser with thick glasses got out and checked on the wall phone, then got back into his cab and pulled a magazine out from behind his rear view mirror.

I strolled over to him and he was it. He was coatless and had his sleeves rolled up past the elbows, although this was no Bikini suit weather.

'Yeah. I'm Joe Harms.' He stuck a pill in his kisser and lit it with a Ronson.

'Lucille down at the Rancho Descansado thought maybe you'd give me a little information.' I leaned against his cab and gave him my big warm smile. I might as well have kicked the kerbing.

'Information about what?'

'You picked up a fare this evening from one of their cottages. Number 12C. A tallish girl with reddish hair and a nice shape. Her name's Betty Mayfield but she probably didn't tell you that.'

'Mostly they just tell me where they want to go. Quaint isn't it?' He blew a lungful of smoke at his windshield and watched it flatten out and float around in the cab. 'What's the pitch?'

'Girl friend walked out on me. We had a little argument. All my fault. I'd like to tell her I'm sorry.'

'Girl friend got a home somewhere?'

'A long way from here.'

He knocked ash from his cigarette by flicking his little finger at it still in his mouth.

'Could be she planned it that way. Could be she don't want you to know where she went. Could be you were lucky at that. They can drop the arm on you for shacking up in a hotel in this town. I'll admit it has to be pretty flagrant.'

'Could be I'm a liar,' I said, and got a business card out of my wallet. He read it and handed it back.

'Better,' he said. 'Some better. But it's against the company rules. I'm not driving this hack just to build muscle.'

'A five interest you? Or is that against the rules too?'

'My old man owns the company. He'd be pretty sore if I was on the chisel. Not that I don't like money.'

The phone on the wall jangled. He slid out of the cab and went over to it in about three long strides. I just stood planted, gnawing my lip. He talked and came back and stepped into the cab and was sitting behind the wheel all in one motion.

'Have to blow,' he said. 'Sorry. I'm kind of behind schedule. Just got back from Del Mar. The seven-forty-seven to L.A. makes flag stop there. Most people from here go that way.'

He started his motor and leaned out of the cab to drop his cigarette in the street.

I said, 'Thanks.'

'For what?' He backed out and was gone.

I looked at my watch again. Time and distance checked. It was all of twelve miles to Del Mar. It would take almost an hour to ferry someone to Del Mar and drop him or her off at the railroad station and turn around and come back. He had told me in his own way. There was no point in telling me at all unless it meant something.

I watched him out of sight and then crossed the street to the booths outside the telephone company's office. I left the booth door open and dropped my dime and dialled the big O.

'I'd like to make a collect call to West Los Angeles, please.' I gave her a Bradshaw number. 'Person to person, Mr Clyde Umney. My name is Marlowe and I'm calling from Esmeralda 4–2673, a pay phone.'

She got him a lot quicker than it took me to tell her all that. He came on sharp and quick.

'Marlowe? It's about time you reported in. Well—let's have it.'

'I'm in San Diego. I've lost her. She slipped away while I was taking a nap.'

'I just knew I'd picked a smart cookie,' he said unpleasantly.

'It's not as bad as it sounds, Mr Umney. I have a rough idea where she went.'

'Rough ideas are not good enough for me. When I hire a man I expect him to deliver exactly what I order. And just what do you mean by a rough idea?'

'Would it be possible for you to give me some notion of what this is all about, Mr Umney? I grabbed it off kind of quick on account of meeting the train. Your secretary gave me a lot of personality but very little information. You want me to be happy in my work, don't you, Mr Umney?'

'I gathered that Miss Vermilyea told you all there is to know,' he grumbled. 'I am acting at the request of an important law firm in Washington. Their client desires to remain anonymous for the present. All you have to do is to trace this party to a stopping place, and by stopping place I do not mean a rest room or a hamburger stand. I mean a hotel, apartment house, or perhaps the home of someone she knows. That's all.

How much simpler do you want it?'

'I'm not asking for simplicity, Mr Umney. I'm asking for background material. Who the girl is, where she came from, what she's supposed to have done to make this job necessary.'

'Necessary?' he yapped at me. 'Who the hell are you to decide what is necessary? Find that girl, pin her down, and phone me her address. And if you expect to be paid, you better do it damn quick. I'll give you until ten o'clock tomorrow morning. After that I'll make other arrangements.'

'Okay, Mr Umney.'

'Where are you exactly and what is your telephone number?'

'I'm just kind of wandering around. I got hit on the head with a whisky bottle.'

'Well, that's too bad,' he said acidly. 'I presume you had already emptied the bottle.'

'Oh, it might have been worse, Mr Umney. It might have been *your* head. I'll call you around 10 a.m. at your office. Don't worry about anybody losing anybody. There's two other guys working the same side of the street. One's a local boy named Mitchell and the other is a Kansas City shamus name of Goble. He carries a gun. Well, good night, Mr Umney.'

'Hold it!' he roared. 'Wait a minute! What does that mean—two other operatives?'

'You asking me what it means? I'm the guy that asked you. Looks like you only got a piece of the job.'

'Hold it! Hold it right there!' There was a silence. Then in a steady voice that didn't bluster any more: 'I'll call Washington the first thing in the morning, Marlowe. Excuse me if I sounded off. It begins to look as though I am entitled to a little more information about this project.'

'Yeah.'

'If you make contact again, call me here. At any hour. Any hour at all.'

'Yeah.'

'Good night, then.' He hung up.

I put the phone back on the hook and took a deep breath. My head still ached but the dizziness was gone. I breathed in the cool night air laced with sea fog. I pushed out of the booth and looked across the street. The old guy who had been in the taxi slot when I arrived was back again. I strolled across and asked him how to get to The Glass Room, which was where Mitchell had promised to take Miss Betty Mayfield to dinner—whether she liked it or not. He told me, I thanked him, re-crossed the empty street, and climbed into my rented car, and started back the way I had come.

It was still possible that Miss Mayfield had grabbed the seven-forty-seven for Los Angeles or some way station. It was a lot more likely that she had not. A cab driver taking a fare to the station doesn't stick around to watch the fare get on the train. Larry Mitchell wouldn't be that easy to shake. If he had enough on her to make her come to Esmeralda, he had enough to keep her there. He knew who I was and what I was doing. He didn't know why, because I didn't know myself. If he had half a brain, and I gave him credit for a good deal more, he would have to assume I could trace her movements as far as a taxi took her. The first guess I was working on was that he would have driven to Del Mar, parked his big Buick somewhere in the shadows, and waited for her taxi to drive up and unload. When it turned around and started back, he would pick her up and drive her back to

Esmeralda. The second guess I was working on was that she wouldn't tell him anything he didn't already know. I was a Los Angeles private eye, unknown parties had hired me to follow her, I had done so and then made the mistake of trying to get too close. That would bother him because it suggested he didn't have the field to himself. But if his information, whatever it was, came from a press clipping, he could hardly expect to have it to himself for ever. Anybody with enough interest and enough patience could turn it up in time. Anybody with enough reason to hire a private dick probably knew it already. And that in turn meant that whatever kind of bite he planned to put on Betty Mayfield, financial or amatory or both, would have to be put on fast.

A third of a mile down the canyon a small illuminated sign with an arrow pointing seaward said in script: THE GLASS ROOM. The road wound down between cliffside houses with warm lights in the windows, manicured gardens, stucco walls, and one or two of fieldstone or brick inset with tiles in the Mexican tradition.

I drove down the last curve of the last hill and the smell of raw seaweed filled my nostrils and the fog-veiled lights of The Glass Room swelled to amber brightness and the sound of dance music drifted across the paved parking lot. I parked with the sea growling out of sight almost at my feet. There was no attendant. You just locked your car and went in.

A couple of dozen cars, no more. I looked them over. One hunch at least had paid off. The Buick Roadmaster solid top bore a licence number I had in my pocket. It was parked almost at the entrance and next to it in the very last space near the entrance was a pale green and ivory Cadillac convertible with oyster-white leather seats, a plaid travelling rug thrown over the front seat to keep it dry, and all the gadgets a dealer could think of, including two enormous spotlights with mirrors on them, a radio aerial almost long enough for a tuna boat, a folding chromium luggage rack to help out the boot if you wanted to travel far and in style, a sun visor, a prism reflector to pick up traffic lights obscured by the visor, a radio with enough knobs on it for a control panel, a cigarette lighter into which you dropped your cigarette and it smoked it for you, and various other trifles which made me wonder how long it would be before they installed radar, sound-recording equipment, a bar, and an anti-aircraft battery.

All this I saw by the light of a clip-on flash. I moved it to the licence holder and the name was Clark Brandon, Hotel Casa del Poniente, Esmeralda, California.

8

The entrance lobby was on a balcony which looked down over the bar and a dining-room on two levels. A curving, carpeted staircase led down to the bar. Nobody was upstairs but the hat-check girl and an elderly party in a phone booth whose expression suggested that nobody better fool with him.

I went down the stairs to the bar and tucked myself in a small curved space that commanded a view of the dance floor. One side of the building was an enormous glass window. Outside of it was nothing but fog, but on a clear night with a moon low over the water it would have been sensational. A three-piece Mexican band was making the kind of music a Mexican band always makes. Whatever they play, it all sounds the same. They always sing the same song, and it always has nice open vowels and a drawn-out, sugary lilt, and the guy who sings it always strums on a guitar and has a lot to say about *amor, mi corazôn*, a lady who is 'linda' but very hard to convince, and he always has too long and too oily hair and when he isn't making with the love stuff he looks as if his knife work in an alley would be efficient and economical.

On the dance floor half a dozen couples were throwing themselves around with the reckless abandon of a night watchman with arthritis. Most of them were dancing cheek to cheek, if dancing is the word. The men wore white tuxedos and the girls wore bright eyes, ruby lips, and tennis or golf muscles. One couple was not dancing cheek to cheek. The guy was too drunk to keep time and the girl was too busy not getting her pumps walked on to think of anything else. I needn't have worried about losing Miss Betty Mayfield. She was there and with Mitchell, but far from happy. Mitchell's mouth was open, he was grinning, his face was red and shiny, and his eyes had that glazed look. Betty was holding her head as far as she could get away from him without breaking her neck. It was very obvious that she had had about all of Mr Larry Mitchell that she could take.

A Mexican waiter in a short green jacket and white pants with a green stripe down the side came up and I ordered a double Gibson and asked if I could have a club sandwich where I was. He said, '*Muy bien, señor,*' smiled brightly, and disappeared.

The music stopped, there was desultory clapping. The orchestra was deeply moved, and played another number. A dark-haired head-waiter who looked like a road company Herbert Marshall circulated among the tables, offering his intimate smile and stopping here and there to polish an apple. Then he pulled out a chair and sat down opposite a big, handsome, Irish-type character with grey in his hair and just enough of it. He seemed to be alone. He wore a dark dinner jacket with a maroon carnation in the lapel. He looked like a nice guy if you didn't crowd him. At that distance and in that light I couldn't tell much more, except that if you did crowd him, you had better be big, fast, tough, and in top condition.

The head-waiter leaned forward and said something and they both looked towards Mitchell and the Mayfield girl. The captain seemed concerned, the big guy didn't seem to care much one way or another. The head-waiter got up and left. The big guy fitted a cigarette into a holder and a waiter popped a lighter at him as if he had been waiting all evening for the opportunity. The big guy thanked him without looking up.

My drink came and I grabbed it and drank. The music stopped and stayed stopped. The couples divided and strolled back to their tables. Larry Mitchell still had hold of Betty. He was still grinning. Then he began to pull her close. He put his hand behind her head. She tried to shake him off. He pulled harder and pushed his flushed face down on hers. She struggled but he was too strong for her. He chewed her face some more. She kicked him. He jerked his head up, annoyed.

'Let go of me, you drunken slob,' she said breathlessly but very distinctly.

His face got a nasty look. He grabbed her arms hard enough to bruise her and slowly using his strength he pulled her tight against his body and held her there. People looked hard, but nobody moved.

'Whassa matta, baby, you no love poppa no more?' he inquired loudly and thickly.

I didn't see what she did to him with her knee but I could guess and it hurt him. He pushed her away and his face went savage. Then he hauled off and slapped her across the mouth, forehand and backhand. The red showed on her skin at once. She stood quite still. Then in a voice the whole joint could hear she said clearly and slowly:

'Next time you do that, Mr Mitchell—be sure to wear a bullet-proof vest.'

She turned and walked away. He just stood there. His face had gone glistening white—whether from pain or rage I couldn't tell. The head-waiter walked softly up to him and murmured something with an inquiring lift of the eyebrow.

Mitchell brought his eyes down and looked at the man. Then without a word he walked right through him and the head-waiter had to stagger out of his way. Mitchell followed Betty, and on the way he bumped a man in a chair and didn't stop to apologize. Betty was sitting down now at a table against the glass wall right next to the big dark guy in the dinner jacket. He looked at her. He looked at Mitchell. He took his cigarette holder out of his mouth and looked at that. His face was quite expressionless.

Mitchell reached the table. 'You hurt me, sweetness,' he said thickly but loudly. 'I'm a bad man to hurt. Catch on? Very bad. Want to apologize?'

She stood up, jerked a wrap off the back of the chair and faced him.

'Shall I pay the check, Mr Mitchell—or will you pay it with what you borrowed from me?'

His hand went back for another swing at her face. She didn't move. The guy at the next table did. He came up on his feet in one smooth movement and grabbed Mitchell's wrist.

'Take it easy, Larry. You've got a skin full.' His voice was cool, almost amused.

Mitchell jerked his wrist loose and spun around. 'Stay out of this, Brandon.'

'Delighted, old man. I'm not in it. But you'd better not slug the lady again. They don't often throw people out of here—but it could happen.'

Mitchell laughed angrily. 'Why don't you go spit in your hat, mister?'

The big man said softly, 'Take it easy, Larry, I said. I won't say it again.'

Mitchell glared at him. 'Okay, see you later,' he said in a sulky voice. He started off and stopped. 'Much later,' he added, half turning. Then he went out—unsteadily but quickly, looking at nothing.

Brandon just stood there. The girl just stood there. She looked uncertain about what to do next.

She looked at him. He looked at her. He smiled, just polite and easy-going, no come on. She didn't smile back.

'Anything I could do?' he asked. 'Drop you anywhere?' Then he half turned his head. 'Oh, Carl.'

The head-waiter came up to him quickly.

'No check,' Brandon said. 'You know, in the circumstances—'

'Please,' the girl said sharply. 'I don't want other people paying my bills.'

He shook his head slowly. 'Custom of the house,' he said. 'Nothing to do with me personally. But may I send you a drink?'

She looked at him some more. He had what it took all right. 'Send?' she asked.

He smiled politely. 'Well, bring then—if you care to sit down.'

And this time he pulled out the chair at his own table. And she sat down. And at that moment, not a second before, the head-waiter signalled the orchestra and they began to play another number.

Mr Clark Brandon seemed to be the sort of man who got what he wanted without raising his voice.

After a while my club sandwich came. It was nothing to brag about, but eatable. I ate it. I stuck around for half an hour. Brandon and the girl seemed to be doing all right. They were both quiet. After a while they danced. Then I left and sat in the car outside and smoked. She could have seen me although she didn't show it. I knew Mitchell hadn't. He had turned too quickly up the stairs, he had been too mad to see anything.

About ten-thirty Brandon came out with her and they got into the Cadillac convertible with the top down. I followed it away without trying to hide because the way they went would be the way anybody would go back to the downtown part of Esmeralda. Where they went was to the Casa del Poniente, and Brandon drove down the ramp to the garage.

There was only one thing more to find out. I parked in the side lot and went through the lobby to the house phones.

'Miss Mayfield, please. Betty Mayfield.'

'One moment, please'—slight pause—'Oh yes, she just checked in. I'm ringing the room, sir.'

Another and much longer pause.

'I'm sorry, Miss Mayfield's room does not answer.'

I thanked her and hung up. I beat it out of there fast in case she and Brandon should get off at the lobby.

I went back to my rented chariot, and poked my way along the canyon through the fog to the Rancho Descansado. The cottage where the office was seemed to be locked up and empty. A single hazy light outside showed the position of a night bell. I groped my way up to 12C, tucked the car in the car port, and yawned my way into my room. It was cold and damp and miserable. Someone had been in and taken the striped cover off the day bed and removed the matching pillowcases.

I undressed and put my curly head on the pillow and went to sleep.

9

A tapping sound awoke me. It was very light but it was also persistent. I had the feeling that it had been going on a long time and that it had very gradually penetrated my sleep. I rolled over and listened. Somebody tried the door and then the tapping started again. I glanced at my wristwatch. The faint phosphorescence showed it was past three o'clock. I got up on my feet and moved over to my suitcase and reached down into it for the gun. I went over to the door and opened it a crack.

A dark figure in slacks stood there. Some kind of windbreaker also. And a dark scarf knotted around the head. It was a woman.

'What do you want?'

'Let me in—quickly. Don't put any light on.'

So it was Betty Mayfield. I pulled the door back and she slid in like a wisp of the fog. I shut the door. I reached for my bathrobe and pulled it on.

'Anybody else outside?' I asked. 'There's nobody next door.'

'No. I'm alone.' She leaned against the wall and breathed quickly. I fumbled my pen flash out of my coat and poked a small beam around and found the heater switch. I shone the little light on her face. She blinked away from it and raised a hand. I put the light down on the floor and trailed it over to the windows and shut them both and lowered and turned the blind. Then I went back and switched on the lamp.

She let out a gasp, then said nothing. She was still leaning against the wall. She looked as if she needed a drink. I went out to the kitchenette and poured some whisky into a glass and carried it to her. She waved it away, then changed her mind and grabbed the glass and emptied it.

I sat down and lit a cigarette, the always mechanical reaction that gets so boring when someone else does it. Then I just sat there and looked at her and waited.

Our eyes met across great gulfs of nothing. After a while she reached slowly into the slanted pocket of the windbreaker and pulled out the gun.

'Oh no,' I said. 'Not that again.'

She looked down at the gun. Her lip twitched. She wasn't pointing it anywhere. She pushed herself away from the wall and crossed to lay the gun down at my elbow.

'I've seen it,' I said. 'We're old friends. Last time I saw it Mitchell had it. So?'

'That's why I knocked you out. I was afraid he would shoot you.'

'That would have fouled up all his plans—whatever his plans were.'

'Well, I couldn't be sure. I'm sorry. Sorry I hit you.'

'Thanks for the ice cubes,' I said.

'Aren't you going to look at the gun?'

'I have looked at it.'

'I walked all the way over here from the Casa. I'm staying there now. I—I moved in this afternoon.'

'I know. You took a taxi to the Del Mar station to catch an evening train and then Mitchell picked you up there and drove you back. You had dinner together and danced and there was a little ill-feeling. A man named Clark Brandon took you back to the hotel in his convertible.'

She stared. 'I didn't see you there,' she said finally, in a voice that was thinking of other things.

'I was in the bar. While you were with Mitchell you were too busy getting your face slapped and telling him to wear a bullet-proof vest next time he came around. Then at Brandon's table you sat with your back to me. I left before you did and waited outside.'

'I'm beginning to think you *are* a detective,' she said quietly. Her eyes went to the gun again. 'He never gave it back to me,' she said. 'Of course I couldn't prove that.'

'That means you'd like to be able to.'

'It might help a little. It probably wouldn't help quite enough. Not when they found out about me. I guess you know what I'm talking about.'

'Sit down and stop grinding your teeth.'

She moved slowly to a chair and sat down on the edge and leaned forward. She stared at the floor.

'I know there's something to find out,' I said. 'Because Mitchell found it out. So I could find it out too—if I tried. Anyone could who knows there is something to find. I don't know at this moment. All I was hired to do was to keep in touch and report back.'

She looked up briefly. 'And you've done that?'

'I reported in,' I said after a pause. 'I'd lost contact at the time. I mentioned San Diego. He'd get that from the operator anyway.'

'You'd lost contact,' she repeated dryly. 'He must think a lot of you, whoever he is.' Then she bit her lip. 'I'm sorry. I didn't mean to say that. I'm trying to make up my mind about something.'

'Take your time.' I said. 'It's only twenty past three a.m.'

'Now *you're* sneering.'

I looked towards the wall heater. It didn't show a thing, but there seemed to be a lessening of the chill if no more. I decided I needed a drink. I went out to the kitchenette and got it. I put it down, poured some more, and came back.

She had a small imitation leather folder in her hand now. She showed it to me.

'I have $5,000 in American Express cheques in this—one hundred dollar size. How far would you go for five grand, Marlowe?'

I took a sip of whisky. I thought about it with a judicial expression. 'Assuming a normal rate of expenses, that would buy me full time for several months. That is, if I happened to be for sale.'

She tapped on the chair arm with the folder. I could see that her other hand was almost pulling her kneecap off.

'You're for sale all right,' she said. 'And this would be merely a down payment. I can buy big. I've got more money than you ever dreamed of. My last husband was so rich that it was pitiful. I got a cool half million dollars out of him.'

She put a hard-boiled sneer on her face and gave me plenty of time to get used to it.

'I take it I wouldn't have to murder anybody?'

'You wouldn't have to murder anybody.'

'I don't like the way you say that.'

I looked sideways at the gun that I hadn't so far laid a finger on. She had walked over from the Casa in the middle of the night to bring it to me. I didn't have to touch it. I stared at it. I bent over and sniffed it. I still didn't have to touch it, but I knew I was going to.

'Who's wearing the bullet?' I asked her. The cold in the room had got into my blood. It ran ice water.

'Just one bullet? How did you know?'

I picked up the gun then. I slipped the magazine out, looked at it, slipped it back. It snapped home in the butt.

'Well, it could have been two,' I said. 'There are six in the magazine. This gun holds seven. You could jack one into the chamber and then add another to the magazine. Of course you could fire the whole supply and then put six in the magazine.'

'We're just talking, aren't we?' she said slowly. 'We don't quite want to say it in plain words.'

'All right. Where is he?'

'Lying across a chaise on the balcony of my room. All the rooms on that side have balconies. They have concrete walls across them, and the end walls—between the rooms or suites, that is—are slanted outwards. I guess a steeplejack or a mountain climber might get around one of the end walls, but not carrying a weight. I'm on the twelfth floor. There's nothing any higher but the penthouse floor.' She stopped and frowned, then made a sort of helpless gesture with the hand that had been squeezing her kneecap. 'This is going to sound a little corny,' she went on. 'He could only have got there through my room. And I didn't let him through my room.'

'But you're sure he's dead?'

'Quite sure. Quite dead. Stone cold dead. I don't know when it happened. I didn't hear a sound. Something woke me all right. But it wasn't any sound like a shot. Anyhow he was already cold. So I don't know what woke me. And I didn't get up right away, I just lay there, thinking. I didn't go back to sleep, so after a while I put the light on and got up and walked around and smoked. Then I noticed the fog was gone and it was moonlight. Not down on the ground, but up there on my floor. I could still see fog down below when I went out on the balcony. It was damned cold. The stars seemed enormous. I stood there near the wall for quite a while before I even saw him. I guess that sounds pretty corny too—or pretty unlikely. I can't imagine the police taking it very seriously—even at first. And afterwards—well, just take it this way. I haven't a chance in a million—unless I get help.'

I stood up, tossed down what whisky was left in the glass and walked over to her.

'Let me tell you two or three things. First off, you're not taking this with normal reactions. You're not icy cool, but you're too cool. No panic, no hysteria, no nothing. You're fatalistic. Next, I heard the entire conversation between you and Mitchell this afternoon. I took those bulbs out'—I pointed to the wall heater—'and used a stethoscope against the partition at the back. What Mitchell had on you was a knowledge of who you were, and that knowledge was something that if published could drive you into another switch of names and another dodge to some other town somewhere. You said you were the luckiest girl in the world because you were alive. Now a man is dead on your balcony, shot with your gun, and the man of course is Mitchell. Right?'

She nodded. 'Yes, it's Larry.'

'And you didn't kill him, you say. And the cops would hardly believe that even at first; you say. And later on not at all. My guess is that you've been there before.'

She was still looking up at me. She came slowly to her feet. Our faces were close, we stared hard into each other's eyes. It didn't mean a thing.

'Half a million dollars is a lot of money, Marlowe. You're not too hard to take. There are places in the world where you and I could have a beautiful life. In one of those tall apartment houses along the ocean front in Rio. I don't know how long it would last, but things can always be arranged, don't you think?'

I said: 'What a lot of different girls you are. Now you're making like a moll. When I first saw you, you were a quiet well-bred little lady. You didn't like dreamboats like Mitchell making a pitch at you. Then you bought yourself a packet of cigarettes and smoked one as if you hated it. Then you let him cuddle you—after you got down here. Then you tore your blouse at me ha, ha, ha, cynical as a Park Avenue pet after her butter and egg man goes home. Then you let me cuddle you. Then you cracked me on the head with a whisky bottle. Now you're talking about a beautiful life in Rio. Which one of you would have her head on the next pillow when I woke up in the morning?'

'Five thousand dollars down. And a lot more to come. The police wouldn't give you five toothpicks. If you think different, you have a telephone.'

'What do I do for the five grand?'

She let her breath out slowly as if a crisis was past. 'The hotel is built almost on the edge of the cliff. At the foot of the wall there's only a narrow walk, very narrow. Below the cliffs are rocks and the sea. It's almost high tide. My balcony hangs right over all that.'

I nodded. 'Are there fire stairs?'

'From the garage. They start just beside the basement elevator landing, which is just up two or three steps from the garage floor. But it's a long, hard climb.'

'For five grand I'd climb it in a diver's suit. Did you come out through the lobby?'

'Fire stairs. There's an all-night man in the garage but he was asleep in one of the cars.'

'You said Mitchell is lying on a chaise. Is there a lot of blood?'

She winced. 'I—I didn't notice. I suppose there must be.'

'You didn't notice? You went near enough to find out he was stone cold dead. Where was he shot?'

'Nowhere that I saw. It must have been under him.'

'Where was the gun?'

'It was lying on the floor of the porch—beside his hand.'

'Which hand?'

She widened her eyes slightly. 'Does it matter? I don't know which hand. He's sort of lying across the chaise with his head hanging on one side and his legs on the other. Do we have to keep on talking about it?'

'All right,' I said. 'I don't know a damn thing about the tides and currents around here. He might wash up on the beach tomorrow and he might not show up for two weeks. Assuming, of course, we bring it off. If it's a long time they may not even find out he was shot. Then I guess there's some possibility that he won't be found at all. Not much, but some. There are barracuda in these waters, and other things.'

'You certainly do a thorough job of making it revolting,' she said.

'Well, I had a running start. Also I was thinking if there was any chance of suicide. Then we'd have to put the gun back. He was left-handed, you know. That's why I wanted to know which hand.'

'Oh. Yes, he was left-handed. You're right. But not suicide. Not that smirking, self-satisfied gentleman.'

'Sometimes a man kills the dearest thing he loves, they say. Couldn't it be himself?'

'Not this character,' she said briefly and finally. 'If we are very lucky, they will probably think he fell off the balcony. God knows he was drunk enough. And by that time I'll be in South America. My passport is still valid.'

'In what name is your passport?'

She reached out and drew her fingertips down my cheek. 'You'll know all about me soon enough. Don't be impatient. You'll know all the intimate things about me. Can't you wait a little?'

'Yeah. Start getting intimate with those American Express cheques. We have another hour or two of darkness and more than that of fog. You play with the cheques while I get dressed.'

I reached into my jacket and gave her a fountain pen. She sat down near the light and began to sign them with the second signature. Her tongue peeped out between her teeth. She wrote slowly and carefully. The name she wrote was Elizabeth Mayfield.

So the switch of names had been planned before she left Washington.

While I dressed I wondered if she was really foolish enough to think I'd help her dispose of a body.

I carried the glasses out to the kitchenette and scooped the gun up on the way. I let the swing door close and slipped the gun and the magazine into the tray under the broiler of the stove. I rinsed out the glasses and wiped them off. I went back into the living-room and threw my clothes on. She didn't even look at me.

She went on signing the cheques. When she had finished, I took the folder of cheques and flipped them over one by one, checking the signatures. The big money meant nothing to me. I shoved the folder into my pocket, put the lamp out, and moved to the door. I opened it and she was beside me. She was close beside me.

'Sneak out,' I said. 'I'll pick you up on the highway just above where the fence ends.'

She faced me and leaned a little towards me. 'Can I trust you?' she asked softly.

'Up to a point.'

'You're honest at least. What happens if we don't get away with it? If somebody reported a shot, if he has been found, if we walk in on that and the place is full of policemen?'

I just stood there with my eyes on her face and didn't answer her.

'Just let me guess,' she said very softly and slowly. 'You'll sell me out fast. And you won't have any five thousand dollars. Those cheques will be an old newspaper. You won't dare cash a single one of them.'

I still didn't say anything.

'You son of a bitch.' She didn't raise her voice even a semitone. 'Why did I ever come to you?'

I took her face between my hands and kissed her on the lips. She pulled away.

'Not for that,' she said. 'Certainly not for that. And one more small point. It's terribly small and unimportant, I know. I've had to learn that. From expert teachers. Long, hard, painful lessons and a lot of them. It just happens that I really didn't kill him.'

'Maybe I believe you.'

'Don't bother to try,' she said. 'Nobody else will.'

She turned and slid along the porch and down the steps. She flitted off through the trees. In thirty feet the fog hid her.

I locked up and got into the rent car and drove it down the silent driveway past the closed office with the light over the night bell. The whole place was hard asleep, but trucks were rumbling up through the canyon with building materials and oil and the big closed-up jobs with and without trailers, full of anything and everything that a town needs to live on. The fog lights were on and the trucks were slow and heavy up the hill.

Fifty yards beyond the gate she stepped out of the shadows at the end of the fence and climbed in. I switched on my headlights. Somewhere out on the water a foghorn was moaning. Upstairs in the clear reaches of the sky a formation of jets from North Island went over with a whine and a whoosh and a bang of the shock wave and were gone in less time than it took me to pull the lighter out of the dash and light a cigarette.

The girl sat motionless beside me, looking straight ahead and not speaking. She wasn't seeing the fog or the back of a truck we were coming up behind. She wasn't seeing anything. She was just sitting there frozen in one position, stony with despair, like somebody on the way to be hanged.

Either that or she was the best little scene stealer I had come across in a long, long time.

10

The Casa del Poniente was set on the edge of the cliffs in about seven acres of lawn and flower beds, with a central patio on the sheltered side, tables set out behind a glass screen, and a trellised walk leading through the middle of it to an entrance. There was a bar on one side, a coffee shop on the other, and at each end of the building black-top parking lots partly hidden behind six-foot hedges of flowering shrubs. The parking lots had cars in them. Not everyone bothered to use the basement garage, although the damp salt air down there is hard on chromium.

I parked in a spot near the garage ramp and the sound of the ocean was very close and you could feel the drifting spray and smell it and taste it. We got out and moved over to the garage entrance. A narrow raised walk edged the ramp. A sign hung midway of the entrance said: Descend in Low Gear. Sound Horn. The girl grabbed me by the arm and stopped me.

'I'm going in by the lobby. I'm too tired to climb the stairs.'

'Okay. No law against it. What's the room number?'

'Twelve twenty-four. What do we get if we're caught?'

'Caught doing what?'

'You know what. Putting—putting it over the balcony wall. Or somewhere.'

'I'd get staked out on an anthill. I don't know about you. Depends what else they have on you.'

'How can you talk like that before breakfast?'

She turned and walked away quickly. I started down the ramp. It curved as they all do and then I could see a glassed in cubbyhole of an office with a hanging light in it. A little farther down and I could see that it was empty. I listened for sounds of somebody doing a little work on a car, water in a wash rack, steps, whistling, any little noise to indicate where the night man was and what he was doing. In a basement garage you can hear a very small noise indeed. I heard nothing.

I went on down and was almost level with the upper end of the office. Now by stooping I could see the shallow steps up into the basement elevator lobby. There was a door marked: ELEVATOR. It had glass panels and I could see light beyond it, but little else.

I took three more steps and froze. The night man was looking right at me. He was in a big Packard sedan in the back seat. The light shone on his face and he wore glasses and the light shone hard on the glasses. He was leaning back comfortably in the corner of the car. I stood there and waited for him to move. He didn't move. His head was against the car cushions. His mouth was open. I had to know why he didn't move. He might be just pretending to be asleep until I got out of sight. When that happened he would beat it across to the phone and call the office.

Then I thought that was silly. He wouldn't have come on the job until evening and he couldn't know all the guests by sight. The sidewalk that bordered the ramp was there to walk on. It was almost 4 a.m. In an hour or so it would begin to get light. No hotel prowler would come around that late.

I walked straight over to the Packard and looked in on him. The car was shut up tight, all windows. The man didn't move. I reached for the door handle and tried to open the door without noise. He still didn't move. He looked like a very light-coloured man. He also looked asleep and I could hear him snoring even before I got the door open. Then I got it full in the face—the honeyed reek of well-cured marijuana. The guy was out of circulation, he was in the valley of peace, where time is slowed to a standstill, where the world is all colours and music. And in a couple of hours from now he wouldn't have a job, even if the cops didn't grab him and toss him into the deep freeze.

I shut the car door again and crossed to the glass-panelled door. I went through into a small, bare elevator lobby with a concrete floor and two blank elevator doors and beside them, opening on a heavy door closer, the fire stairs. I pulled that open and started up. I went slowly. Twelve storeys and a basement take a lot of stairs. I counted the fire doors as I passed them because they were not numbered. They were heavy and solid and grey like the concrete of the steps. I was sweating and out of breath when I pulled open the door to the twelfth corridor. I prowled along to Room 1224 and tried the knob. It was locked, but almost at once the door was opened, as if she had been waiting just behind it. I went in past her and flopped into a chair and waited to get some breath back. It was a big, airy room with french windows opening on a balcony. The double bed had been slept in or arranged to look that way. Odds and ends of clothing on chairs, toilet articles on the dresser, luggage. It looked about twenty bucks a day, single.

She turned the night latch in the door. 'Have any trouble?'

'The night man was junked to the eyes. Harmless as a kitten.' I heaved myself out of the chair and started across to the french doors.

'Wait!' she said sharply. I looked back at her. 'It's no use,' she said. 'Nobody could do a thing like that.'

I stood there and waited.

'I'd rather call the police,' she said. 'Whatever it means for me.'

'That's a bright idea,' I said. 'Why ever didn't we think of it before?'

'You'd better leave,' she said. 'There's no need for you to be mixed up in it.'

I didn't say anything. I watched her eyes. She could hardly keep them open. It was either delayed shock or some kind of dope. I didn't know which.

'I swallowed two sleeping pills,' she said, reading my mind. 'I just can't take any more trouble tonight. Go away from here. Please. When I wake I'll call room service. When the waiter comes I'll get him out on the balcony somehow and he'll find—whatever he'll find. And I won't know a damn thing about it.' Her tongue was getting thick. She shook herself and rubbed hard against her temples. 'I'm sorry about the money. You'll have to give it back to me, won't you?'

I went over close to her. 'Because if I don't you'll tell them the whole story?'

'I'll have to,' she said drowsily. 'How can I help it? They'll get it out of me. I'm—I'm too tired to fight any more.'

I took hold of her arm and shook her. Her head wobbled. 'Quite sure you only took two capsules?'

She blinked her eyes open 'Yes. I never take more than two.'

'Then listen. I'm going out there and have a look at him. Then I'm going back to the Rancho. I'm going to keep your money. Also I have your gun. Maybe it can't be traced to me but—Wake up! Listen to me!' Her head was rolling sideways again. She jerked straight and her eyes widened, but they looked dull and withdrawn. 'Listen. If it can't be traced to you, it certainly can't be traced to me. I'm working for a lawyer and my assignment is you. The travellers' cheques and the gun will go right where they belong. And your story to the cops won't be worth a wooden nickel. All it will do is to help to hang you. Understand that?'

'Ye-es,' she said. 'And I don't g-give a damn.'

'That's not you talking. It's the sleeping medicine.'

She sagged forward and I caught her and steered her over to the bed. She flopped on it any old way. I pulled her shoes off and spread a blanket over her and tucked her in. She was asleep at once. She began to snore. I went into the bathroom and groped around and found a bottle of nembutal on the shelf. It was almost full. It had a prescription number and a date on it. The date was a month old, the drugstore was in Baltimore. I dumped the yellow capsules out into my palm and counted them. There were forty-seven and they almost filled the bottle. When they take them to kill themselves, they take them all—except what they spill, and they nearly always spill some. I put the pills back in the bottle and put the bottle in my pocket.

I went back and looked at her again. The room was cold. I turned the radiator on, not too much. And finally at long last I opened the french doors and went out on the balcony. It was as cold as hell out there. The balcony was about twelve by fourteen feet, with a thirty-inch wall across the front and a low iron railing sprouting out of that. You could jump off easy enough, but you couldn't possibly fall off accidentally. There were two aluminium patio chaises with padded cushions, two armchairs of the same type. The dividing wall to the left stuck out the way she had told me. I didn't think even a steeplejack could get around the projection without climbing tackle. The wall at the other end rose sheer to the edge of what must be one of the penthouse terraces.

Nobody was dead on either of the chaises, nor on the floor of the balcony, nor anywhere at all. I examined them for traces of blood. No blood. No blood on the balcony. I went along the safety wall. No blood. No signs of anything having been heaved over. I stood against the wall and held on to the metal railing and leaned out as far as I could lean. I looked straight down the face of the wall to the ground. Shrubs grew close to it, then a narrow strip of lawn, then a flatstone footpath, then another strip of lawn, and then a heavy fence with more shrubs growing against that. I estimated the distance. At that height it wasn't easy, but it must have been at least thirty-five feet. Beyond the fence the sea creamed on some half-submerged rocks.

Larry Mitchell was about half an inch taller than I was but weighed about fifteen pounds less, at a rough guess. The man wasn't born who could heave a hundred and seventy-five pound body over that railing and far enough out to fall into the ocean. It was barely possible that a girl wouldn't realize that, just barely possible, about one-tenth of one per cent possible.

I opened the french door and went through and shut it and crossed to stand beside the bed. She was still sound asleep. She was still snoring. I touched her cheek with the back of my hand. It was moist. She moved a little and mumbled. Then she sighed and settled her head into the pillow. No stertorous breathing, no deep stupor, no coma, and therefore no overdose.

She had told me the truth about one thing, and about damned little else.

I found her bag in the top drawer of the dresser. It had a zipper pocket at the back. I put her folder of travellers' cheques in it and looked through it for information. There was some crisp folding money in the zipper pocket, a Santa Fe time-table, the folder her ticket had been in, and the stub of the railroad ticket and the Pullman reservation. She had had Bedroom E on Car 19, Washington, D.C., to San Diego, California. No letters, nothing to identify her. That would be locked up in the luggage. In the main part of the bag was what a woman carries, a lipstick, a compact, a change purse, some silver, and a few keys on a ring with a tiny bronze tiger hanging from it. A packet of cigarettes that seemed just about full but had been opened. A match book with one match used. Three handkerchiefs with no initials, a packet of emery boards, a cuticle knife, and some kind of eyebrow stuff, a comb in a leather case, a little round jar of nail polish, a tiny address book. I pounced on that. Blank, not used at all. Also in the bag were a pair of sun glasses with spangled rims in a case, no name on the case; a fountain pen, a small gold pencil, and that was all. I put the bag back where I had found it. I went over to the desk for a piece of hotel stationery and an envelope.

I used the hotel pen to write: 'Dear Betty: So sorry I couldn't stay dead. Will explain tomorrow. Larry.'

I sealed the note in the envelope, wrote *Miss Betty Mayfield* on it, and dropped it where it might be if it had been pushed under the door.

I opened the door, went out, shut the door, went back to the fire stairs, then said out loud: 'The hell with it,' and rang for the elevator. It didn't come. I rang again and kept on ringing. Finally it came up and a sleepy-eyed young Mexican opened the doors and yawned at me, then grinned apologetically. I grinned back and said nothing.

There was nobody at the desk, which faced the elevators. The Mexican parked himself in a chair and went back to sleep before I had taken six steps.

Everybody was sleepy but Marlowe. He works around the clock, and doesn't even collect.

I drove back to the Rancho Descansado, saw nobody awake there, looked longingly at the bed, but packed my suitcase—with Betty's gun in the bottom of it—put twelve bucks in an envelope and on the way out put that through the slot in the office door, with my room key.

I drove to San Diego, turned the rent car in, and ate breakfast at a joint across from the station. At seven-fifteen I caught the two-car diesel job that makes the run to L.A. non-stop and pulls in at exactly 10 a.m.

I rode home in a taxi and shaved and showered and ate a second breakfast and glanced through the morning paper. It was near on eleven o'clock when I called the office of Mr Clyde Umney, the lawyer.

He answered himself. Maybe Miss Vermilyea hadn't got up yet.

'This is Marlowe. I'm home. Can I drop around?'

'Did you find her?'

'Yeah. Did you call Washington?'

'Where is she?'

'I'd like to tell you in person. Did you call Washington?'

'I'd like your information first. I have a very busy day ahead.' His voice was brittle and lacked charm.

'I'll be there in half an hour.' I hung up fast and called the place where my Olds was.

I I

There are almost too many offices like Clyde Umney's office. It was panelled in squares of combed plywood set at right angles one to the other to make a checker-board effect. The lighting was indirect, the carpeting wall to wall, the furniture blonde, the chairs comfortable, and the fees probably exorbitant. The metal window frames opened outwards and there was a small but neat parking lot behind the building, and every slot in it had a name painted on a white board. For some reason Clyde Umney's stall was vacant, so I used it. Maybe he had a chauffeur drive him to his office. The building was four storeys high, very new, and occupied entirely by doctors and lawyers.

When I entered, Miss Vermilyea was just fixing herself for a hard day's work by touching up her platinum blonde coiffure. I thought she looked a little the worse for wear. She put away her hand mirror and fed herself a cigarette.

'Well, well. Mr Hard Guy in person. To what may we attribute this honour?'

'Umney's expecting me.'

'*Mister* Umney to you, buster.'

'Boydie-boy to you, sister.'

She got raging in an instant. 'Don't call me "sister", you cheap gumshoe!'

'Then don't call me buster, you very expensive secretary. What are you doing tonight? And don't tell me you're going out with four sailors again.'

The skin around her eyes turned whiter. Her hand crisped into a claw around a paperweight. She just didn't heave it at me. 'You son of a bitch!' she said somewhat pointedly. Then she flipped a switch on her talk box and said to the voice: 'Mr Marlowe is here, Mr Umney.'

Then she leaned back and gave me the look. 'I've got friends who could cut you down so small you'd need a stepladder to put your shoes on.'

'Somebody did a lot of hard work on that one,' I said. 'But hard work's no substitute for talent.'

Suddenly we both burst out laughing. The door opened and Umney stuck his face out. He gestured me in with his chin, but his eyes were on the platinum girl.

I went in and after a moment he closed the door and went behind his enormous semicircular desk, with a green leather top and just piles and piles of important documents on it. He was a dapper man, very carefully dressed, too short in the legs, too long in the nose, too sparse in the hair. He had limpid brown eyes which, for a lawyer, looked very trustful.

'You making a pass at my secretary?' he asked me in a voice that was anything but limpid.

'Nope. We were just exchanging pleasantries.'

I sat down in the customer's chair and looked at him with something approaching politeness.

'She looked pretty mad to me.' He squatted in his executive-vice-president-type chair and made his face tough.

'She's booked up for three weeks,' I said. 'I couldn't wait that long.'

'Just watch your step, Marlowe. Lay off. She's private property. She wouldn't give you the time of day. Besides being a lovely piece of female humanity, she's as smart as a whip.'

'You mean she can type and take dictation as well?'

'As well as what?' He reddened suddenly. 'I've taken enough lip from you. Just watch your step, very carefully. I have enough influence around this town to hang a red light on you. Now let me have your report and make it short and to the point.'

'You talk to Washington yet?'

'Never mind what I did or didn't do. I want your report as of right now. The rest is my business. What's the present location of the King girl?' He reached for a nice sharp pencil and a nice clean pad. Then he dropped the pencil and poured himself a glass of water from a black and silver Thermos jug.

'Let's trade,' I said. 'You tell me why you want her found and I'll tell you where she is.'

'You're my employee,' he snapped. 'I don't have to give you any information whatsoever.' He was still tough but beginning to shred a little around the edge.

'I'm your employee if I want to be, Mr Umney. No cheque has been cashed, no agreement has been made.'

'You accepted the assignment. You took an advance.'

'Miss Vermilyea gave me a cheque for $250 as an advance, and another cheque for $200 for expenses. But I didn't bank them. Here they are.' I took the two cheques out of my pocketbook and laid them on the desk in front of him. 'Better keep them until you make up your mind whether you want an investigator or a yes man, and until I make up my mind whether I was offered a job or was being suckered into a situation I knew nothing about.'

He looked down at the cheques. He wasn't happy. 'You've already had expenses,' he said slowly.

'That's all right, Mr Umney. I had a few dollars saved up–and the expenses are deductible. Also I've had fun.'

'You're pretty stubborn, Marlowe.'

'I guess, but I have to be in my business. Otherwise I wouldn't be in business. I told you the girl was being blackmailed. Your Washington friends must know why. If she's a crook, fine. But I have to get told. And I have an offer you can't match.'

'For more money you are willing to switch sides?' he asked angrily. 'That would be unethical.'

I laughed. 'So I've got ethics now. Maybe we're getting somewhere.'

He took a cigarette out of a box and lit it with a pot-bellied lighter that matched the Thermos and the pen set.

'I still don't like your attitude,' he growled. 'Yesterday I didn't know any more than you did. I took it for granted that a reputable Washington law firm would not ask me to do anything against legal ethics. Since the girl could have been arrested without difficulty, I assumed it was some sort of domestic mix-up, a runaway wife or daughter, or an important but reluctant witness who was already outside the jurisdiction where she could be subpoenaed. That was just guessing. This morning things are a little different.'

He got up and walked to the big window and turned the slats of the blinds enough to keep the sun off his desk. He stood there smoking, looking out, then came back to the desk and sat down again.

'This morning', he went on slowly and with a judicious frown, 'I talked to my Washington associates and I am informed that the girl was confidential secretary to a rich and important man–I'm not told his name–and that she absconded with certain important and dangerous papers from his private files. Papers that might be damaging to him if made public. I'm not told in what way. Perhaps he has been fudging his tax returns. You never know these days.'

'She took this stuff to blackmail him?'

Umney nodded. 'That is the natural assumption. They had no value to her otherwise. The client, Mr A. we will call him, didn't realize that the girl had left until she was already in another state. He then checked his files and found that some of his material was gone. He was reluctant to go to the police. He expects the girl to go far enough away to feel safe and from that point to start negotiations with him for the return of the material at a heavy price. He wants to peg her down somewhere without her knowing it, walk in, and catch her off balance and especially before she contacts some sharp lawyer, of whom I regret to say there are far too many, and with the sharp lawyer works out a scheme that would make her safe from prosecution. Now you tell me someone is blackmailing her. On what grounds?'

'If your story stood up, it could be because he is in a position to spoil her play,' I said. 'Maybe he knows something that could hang a pinch on her without opening up the other box of candy.'

'You say if the story stood up,' he snapped. 'What do you mean by that?'

'It's as full of holes as a sink strainer. You're being fed a line, Mr Umney. Where would a man keep material like the important papers you mention–if he had to keep them at all? Certainly not where a secretary could get them. And unless he missed the stuff before she left, how did he get her followed to the train? Next, although she took a ticket to California, she could have got off anywhere. Therefore she would have to be watched on the train, and if that was done, why did someone need me to pick her up here? Next, this, as you tell it, would be a job for a large agency with nation-wide connexions. It would be idiotic to take a chance on one man. I lost her yesterday. I could lose her again. It takes a bare minimum of six operatives to do a standard tail job in any sizeable place, and that's just what I mean—a bare minimum. In a really big city you'd need a dozen. An operative has to eat and sleep and change his shirt. If he's tailing by car he has to be able to drop a man while he finds a place to park. Department stores and hotels may have half a dozen entrances. But all this girl does is hang around Union Station here for three hours in full view of everybody. And all your friends in Washington do is mail you a picture, call you on the phone, and then go back to watching television.'

'Very clear,' he said. 'Anything else?' His face was deadpan now.

'A little. Why—if she didn't expect to be followed—would she change her name? Why if she did expect to be followed would she make it so easy? I told you two other guys were working the same side of the street. One is a Kansas City private detective named Goble. He was in Esmeralda yesterday. He knew just where to go. Who told him? I had to follow her and bribe a taxi driver to use his R/T outfit to find out where her cab was going so that I wouldn't lose her. So why was I hired?'

'We'll come to that,' Umney said curtly. 'Who was the other party you say was working the same side of the street?'

'A playboy named Mitchell. He lives down there. He met the girl on the train. He made a reservation for her in Esmeralda. They're just like that'—I held up two touching fingers—'except that she hates his guts. He's got something on her and she is afraid of him. What he has on her is a knowledge of who she is, where she came from, what happened to her there, and why she is trying to hide under another name. I overheard enough to know that, but not enough to give me exact information.'

Umney said acidly: 'Of course the girl was covered on the train. Do you think you are dealing with idiots? You were nothing more than a decoy—to determine whether she had any associates. On your reputation—such as it is—I relied on you to grandstand enough to let her get wise to you. I guess you know what an open shadow is.'

'Sure. One that deliberately lets the subject spot him, then shake him, so that another shadow can pick him up when he thinks he is safe.'

'You were it.' He grinned at me contemptuously. 'But you still haven't told me where she is.'

I didn't want to tell him, but I knew I'd have to. I had up to a point accepted the assignment, and giving him back his money was only a move to force some information out of him.

I reached across the desk and picked up the $250 cheque. 'I'll take this as payment in full, expenses included. She is registered as Miss Betty Mayfield at the Casa del Poniente in Esmeralda. She is loaded with money. But of course your expert organization must know all this already.'

I stood up. 'Thanks for the ride, Mr Umney.'

I went out and shut his door. Miss Vermilyea looked up from a magazine.

I heard a faint muffled click from somewhere in her desk.

'I'm sorry I was rude to you,' I said. 'I didn't get enough sleep last night.'

'Forget it. It was a stand-off. With a little practice I might get to like you. You're kind of cute in a low-down sort of way.'

'Thanks,' I said and moved to the door. I wouldn't say she looked exactly wistful, but neither did she look as hard to get as a controlling interest in General Motors.

I turned back and closed the door.

'I guess it's not raining tonight, is it? There was something we might have discussed over a drink, if it had been a rainy night. And if you had not been too busy.'

She gave me a cool, amused look. 'Where?'

'That would be up to you.'

'Should I drop by your place?'

'It would be damn nice of you. That Fleetwood might help my credit standing.'

'I wasn't exactly thinking of that.'

'Neither was I.'

'About six-thirty perhaps. And I'll take good care of my nylons.'

'I was hoping you would.'

Our glances locked. I went out quickly.

12

At half past six the Fleetwood purred to the front door and I had it open when she came up the steps. She was hatless. She wore a flesh-coloured coat with the collar turned up against her platinum hair. She stood in the middle of the living-room and looked around casually. Then she slipped the coat off with a lithe movement and threw it on the davenport and sat down.

'I didn't really think you'd come,' I said.

'No. You're the shy type. You knew darned well I'd come. Scotch and soda, if you have it.'

'I have it.'

I brought the drinks and sat down beside her, but not close enough for it to mean anything. We touched glasses and drank.

'Would you care to go to Romanoffs for dinner?'

'And then what?'

'Where do you live?'

'West Los Angeles. A house on a quiet old street. It happens to belong to me. I asked you, and then what, remember?'

'That would be up to you, naturally.'

'I thought you were a tough guy. You mean I don't have to pay for my dinner?'

'I ought to slap your face for that crack.'

She laughed suddenly and stared at me over the edge of her glass.

'Consider it slapped. We had each other a bit wrong. Romanoffs could wait a while, couldn't it?'

'We could try West Los Angeles first.'

'Why not here?'

'I guess this will make you walk out on me. I had a dream here once, a year and a half ago. There's still a shred of it left. I'd like it to stay in charge.'

She stood up quickly and grabbed her coat. I managed to help her on with it.

'I'm sorry,' I said, 'I should have told you that before.'

She swung around with her face close to mine, but I didn't touch her.

'Sorry that you had a dream and kept it alive? I've had dreams too, but mine died. I didn't have the courage to keep them alive.'

'It's not quite like that. There was a woman. She was rich. She thought she wanted to marry me. It wouldn't have worked. I'll probably never see her again. But I remember.'

'Let's go,' she said quietly. 'And let's leave the memory in charge. I only wish I had one worth remembering.'

On the way down to the Cadillac I didn't touch her either. She drove beautifully. When a woman is a really good driver she is just about perfect.

13

The house was on a curving, quiet street between San Vincente and Sunset Boulevard. It was set far back and had a long driveway and the entrance to the house was at the back with a small patio in front of it. She unlocked the door and switched on lights all over the house and then disappeared without a word. The living-room had nicely-mixed furniture and a feeling of comfort. I stood waiting until she came back with two tall glasses. She had taken her coat off.

'You've been married, of course,' I said.

'It didn't take. I got this house and some money out of it, but I wasn't gunning for anything. He was a nice guy, but we were wrong for each other. He's dead now—plane crash—he was a jet pilot. Happens all the time. I know a place between here and San Diego that is full of girls who were married to jet pilots when they were alive.'

I took a single sip of my drink and put it down.

I lifted her glass out of her hand and put it down too.

'Remember yesterday morning when you told me to stop looking at your legs?'

'I seem to remember.'

'Try and stop me now.'

I took hold of her and she came into my arms without a word. I picked her up and carried her and somehow found the bedroom. I put her down on the bed. I peeled her skirt up until I could see the white thighs above her long, beautiful nylon-clad legs. Suddenly she reached up and pulled my head down against her breast.

'Beast! Could we have a little less light?'

I went to the door and switched the light off in the room. There was still a glow from the hall. When I turned she was standing by the bed as naked as

Aphrodite fresh from the Aegean. She stood there proudly and without either shame or enticement.

'Damn it,' I said. 'When I was young you could undress a girl slowly. Nowadays she's in the bed while you're struggling with your collar button.'

'Well, struggle with your goddam collar button.'

She pulled the bed-covers back and lay on the bed shamelessly nude. She was just a beautiful naked woman completely unashamed of being what she was.

'Satisfied with my legs?' she asked.

I didn't answer.

'Yesterday morning,' she said, half dreamily, 'I said there was something about you I liked—you didn't paw—and something I didn't like. Know what it was?'

'No.'

'That you didn't make me do this then.'

'Your manner hardly encouraged it.'

'You're supposed to be a detective. Please put out all the lights now.'

Then very soon in the dark she was saying, Darling, darling, darling in that very special tone of voice a woman uses only in those special moments. Then a slow, gentle relaxing, a peace, a quietness.

'Still satisfied with my legs?' she asked dreamily.

'No man ever would be. They would haunt him, no matter how many times he made love to you.'

'You bastard. You complete bastard. Come closer.'

She put her head on my shoulder and we were very close now.

'I don't love you,' she said.

'Why would you? But let's not be cynical about it. There are sublime moments—even if they are only moments.'

I felt her tight and warm against me. Her body surged with vitality. Her beautiful arms held me tight.

And again in the darkness that muted cry, and then again the slow quiet peace.

'I hate you,' she said with her mouth against mine. 'Not for this, but because perfection never comes twice and with us it came too soon. And I'll never see you again and I don't want to. It would have to be for ever or not at all.'

'And you acted like a hard-boiled pick-up who had seen too much of the wrong side of life.'

'So did you. And we were both wrong. And it's useless. Kiss me harder.'

Suddenly she was gone from the bed almost without sound or movement.

After a little while the light went on in the hall-way and she stood in the door in a long wrapper.

'Good-bye,' she said calmly. 'I'm calling a taxi for you. Wait out in front for it. You won't see me again.'

'What about Umney?'

'A poor frightened jerk. He needs someone to bolster his ego, to give him a feeling of power and conquest. I give it to him. A woman's body is not so sacred that it can't be used—especially when she has already failed at love.'

She disappeared. I got up and put my clothes on and listened before I went out. I heard nothing. I called out, but there was no answer. When I reached the sidewalk in front of the house the taxi was just pulling up. I looked back. The house seemed completely dark.

No one lived there. It was all a dream. Except that someone had called the taxi. I got into it and was driven home.

14

I left Los Angeles and hit the super-highway that now bypassed Oceanside. I had time to think.

From San Onofre to Oceanside were eighteen miles of divided six-lane super-highway dotted at intervals with the carcasses of wrecked, stripped, and abandoned cars tossed against the high bank to rust until they were hauled away. So I started thinking about why I was going back to Esmeralda. The case was all backwards and it wasn't my case anyway. Usually a PI gets a client who, for too little money, wants too much information. You get it or you don't, depending on circumstances. The same with your fee. But once in a while you get the information and too much else, including a story about a body on a balcony which wasn't there when you went to look. Common sense says go home and forget it, no money coming in. Common sense always speaks too late. Common sense is the guy who tells you you ought to have had your brakes relined last week before you smashed a front end this week. Common sense is the Monday morning quarterback who could have won the ball game if he had been on the team. But he never is. He's high up in the stands with a flask on his hip. Common sense is the little man in a grey suit who never makes a mistake in addition. But it's always somebody else's money he's adding up.

At the turn-off I dipped down into the canyon and ended up at the Rancho Descansado. Jack and Lucille were in their usual positions. I dropped my suitcase and leaned on the desk.

'Did I leave the right change?'

'Yes thanks,' Jack said. 'And now you want the room back, I suppose.'

'If possible.'

'Why didn't you tell us you were a detective?'

'Now, what a question.' I grinned at him. 'Does a detective ever tell anyone he's a detective? You watch TV, don't you?'

'When I get a chance. Not too often here.'

'You can always tell a detective on TV. He never takes his hat off. What do you know about Larry Mitchell?'

'Nothing,' Jack said stiffly. 'He's a friend of Brandon's. Mr Brandon owns this place.'

Lucille said brightly: 'Did you find Joe Harms all right?'

'Yes, thanks.'

'And did you—'

'Uh-huh.'

'Button the lip, kid,' Jack said tersely. He winked at me and pushed the key across the counter. 'Lucille has a dull life, Mr Marlowe. She's stuck here with me and a PBX. And an itty-bitty diamond ring—so small I was ashamed to give it to her. But what can a man do? If he loves a girl, he'd like it to show on her finger.'

Lucille held her left hand up and moved it around to get a flash from the little stone. 'I hate it,' she said. 'I hate it like I hate the sunshine and the summer and the bright stars and the full moon. That's how I hate it.'

I picked up the key and my suitcase and left them. A little more of that and I'd be falling in love with myself. I might even give myself a small, unpretentious diamond ring.

15

The house phone at the Casa del Poniente got no reply from Room 1224. I walked over to the desk. A stiff-looking clerk was sorting letters. They are always sorting letters.

'Miss Mayfield is registered here, isn't she?' I asked.

He put a letter in a box before he answered me. 'Yes, sir. What name shall I say?'

'I know her room number. She doesn't answer. Have you seen her today?'

He gave me a little more of his attention, but I didn't really send him. 'I don't think so.' He glanced over his shoulder. 'Her key is out. Would you care to leave a message?'

'I'm a little worried. She wasn't well last night. She could be up there sick, not able to answer the phone. I'm a friend of hers. Marlowe's the name.'

He looked me over. His eyes were wise eyes. He went behind a screen in the direction of the cashier's office and spoke to somebody. He came back in a short time. He was smiling.

'I don't think Miss Mayfield is ill, Mr Marlowe. She ordered quite a substantial breakfast in her room. And lunch. She has had several telephone calls.'

'Thanks a lot,' I said. 'I'll leave a message. Just my name and that I'll call back later.'

'She might be out in the grounds or down on the beach,' he said. 'We have a warm beach, well sheltered by a breakwater.' He glanced at the clock behind him. 'If she is, she won't be there much longer. It's getting cool by now.'

'Thanks. I'll be back.'

The main part of the lobby was up three steps and through an arch. There were people in it just sitting, the dedicated hotel lounge sitters, usually elderly, usually rich, usually doing nothing but watching with hungry eyes. They spend their lives that way. Two old ladies with severe faces and purplish permanents were struggling with an enormous jigsaw puzzle set out on a specially built king-size card table. Farther along there was a canasta game going—two women, two men. One of the women had enough ice on her to cool the Mojave Desert and enough make-up to paint a steam yacht. Both women had cigarettes in long holders. The men with them looked grey and tired, probably from signing cheques. Farther along, still sitting where they could look out through the glass, a young couple were holding hands. The girl had a diamond and emerald sparkler and a wedding ring which she kept touching with her fingertips. She looked a little dazed.

I went out through the bar and poked around in the gardens. I went along the path that threaded the cliff top and had no trouble picking out the spot I had looked down on the night before from Betty Mayfield's balcony. I could pick it out because of the sharp angle.

The bathing beach and small, curved breakwater were a hundred yards along. Steps led down to it from the cliff. People were lying around on the sand. Some in swim suits or trunks, some just sitting there on rugs. Kids ran around screaming. Betty Mayfield was not on the beach.

I went back into the hotel and sat in the lounge.

I sat and smoked. I went to the news-stand and bought an evening paper and looked through it and threw it away. I strolled by the desk. My note was still in box 1224. I went to the house phones and called Mr Mitchell. No answer. I'm sorry. Mr Mitchell does not answer his telephone.

A woman's voice spoke behind me: 'The clerk said you wanted to see me Mr Marlowe,' she said. 'Are you Mr Marlowe?'

She looked as fresh as a morning rose. She was wearing dark green slacks and saddle shoes and a green windbreaker over a white shirt with a loose Paisley scarf around that. A bandeau on her hair made a nice wind-blown effect.

The bell captain was hanging out his ear six feet away. I said:

'Miss Mayfield?'

'I'm Miss Mayfield.'

'I have the car outside. Do you have time to look at the property?'

She looked at her wristwatch. 'Ye-es, I guess so,' she said. 'I ought to change pretty soon, but—oh, all right.'

'This way, Miss Mayfield.'

She fell in beside me. We walked across the lobby. I was getting to feel quite at home there. Betty Mayfield glanced viciously at the two jigsaw puzzlers.

'I hate hotels,' she said. 'Come back here in fifteen years and you would find the same people sitting in the same chairs.'

'Yes, Miss Mayfield. Do you know anybody named Clyde Umney?'

She shook her head. 'Should I?'

'Helen Vermilyea? Ross Goble?'

She shook her head again.

'Want a drink?'

'Not now, thanks.'

We came out of the bar and went along the walk and I held the door of the Olds for her. I backed out of the slot and pointed it straight up Grand Street towards the hills. She slipped dark glasses with spangled rims on her nose. 'I found the travellers' cheques,' she said. 'You're a queer sort of detective.'

I reached in my pocket and held out her bottle of sleeping pills. 'I was a little scared last night,' I said. 'I counted these but I didn't know how many had been there to start with. You said you took two. I couldn't be sure you wouldn't rouse up enough to gulp a handful.'

She took the bottle and stuffed it into her windbreaker. 'I had quite a few drinks. Alcohol and barbiturates make a bad combination. I sort of passed out. It was nothing else.'

'I wasn't sure. It takes a minimum of thirty-five grains of that stuff to kill. Even then it takes several hours. I was in a tough spot. Your pulse and breathing seemed all right but maybe they wouldn't be later on. If I called a doctor, I might have to do a lot of talking. If you had taken an overdose, the homicide boys would be told, even if you snapped out of it. They investigate all suicide attempts. But if I guessed wrong, you wouldn't be riding with me today. And where would I be then?'

'It's a thought,' she said. 'I can't say I'm going to worry about it terribly. Who are these people you mentioned?'

'Clyde Umney's the lawyer who hired me to follow you—on instructions from a firm of attorneys in Washington, D.C. Helen Vermilyea is his secretary. Ross Goble is a Kansas City private eye who says he is trying to find Mitchell.' I described him to her.

Her face turned stony. 'Mitchell? Why should he be interested in Larry?'

I stopped at the corner of Fourth and Grand for an old coot in a motorized wheel chair to make a left turn at four miles an hour. Esmeralda is full of the damn things.

'Why should he be looking for Larry Mitchell?' she asked bitterly. 'Can't anybody leave anybody else alone?'

'Don't tell me anything,' I said. 'Just keep on asking me questions to which I don't know the answers. It's good for my inferiority complex. I told you I had no more job. So why am I here? That's easy. I'm groping for that five grand in travellers' cheques again.'

'Turn left at the next corner,' she said, 'and we can go up into the hills. There's a wonderful view from up there. And a lot of very fancy homes.'

'The hell with them,' I said.

'It's also very quiet up there.' She picked a cigarette out of the packet clipped to the dash and lit it.

'That's two in two days,' I said. 'You're hitting them hard. I counted your cigarettes last night too. And your matches. I went through your bag. I'm kind of snoopy when I get roped in on a phoney like that one. Especially when the client passes out and leaves me holding the baby.'

She turned her head to stare at me. 'It must have been the dope and the liquor,' she said. 'I must have been a little off base.'

'Over at the Rancho Descansado you were in great shape. You were hard as nails. We were going to take off for Rio and live in luxury. Apparently also in sin. All I had to do was get rid of the body. What a let-down! No body.'

She was still staring at me, but I had to watch my driving. I made a boulevard stop and a left turn. I went along another dead end street with old streetcar tracks still in the paving.

'Turn left up the hill at that sign. That's the high school down there.'

'Who fired the gun and what at?'

She pressed her temples with the heels of her hands. 'I guess *I* must have. I must have been crazy. Where is it?'

'The gun? It's safe. Just in case your dream came true, I might have to produce it.'

We were climbing now. I set the pointer to hold the Olds in third. She watched that with interest. She looked around her at the pale leather seats and the gadgets.

'How can you afford an expensive car like this? You don't make a lot of money, do you?'

'They're all expensive nowadays, even the cheap ones. Fellow might as well have one that can travel. I read somewhere that a dick should always have a plain, dark, inconspicuous car that nobody would notice. The guy had never been to L.A. In L.A. to be conspicuous you would have to drive a flesh-pink Mercedes-Benz with a sun porch on the roof and three pretty girls sun-bathing.'

She giggled.

'Also', I laboured the subject, 'it's good advertising. Maybe I dreamed I was going to Rio. I could sell it there for more than it set me back new. On a freighter it wouldn't cost too much to ferry.'

She sighed. 'Oh, stop teasing me about that. I don't feel funny today.'

'Seen your boy friend around?'

She sat very still. 'Larry?'

'You got others?'

'Well—you might have meant Clark Brandon, although I hardly know him. Larry was pretty drunk last night. No—I haven't seen him. Perhaps he's sleeping it off.'

'Doesn't answer his phone.'

The road forked. One white line curved to the left. I kept straight on, for no particular reason. We passed some old Spanish houses built high on the slope and some very modern houses built downhill on the other side. The road passed these and made a wide turn to the right. The paving here looked new. The road ran out to a point of land and a turning circle. There were two big houses facing each other across the turning circle. They were loaded with glass brick and their seaward windows were green glass. The view was magnificent. I looked at it for all of three seconds. I stopped against the end kerb and cut the motor and sat. We were about a thousand feet up and the whole town was spread out in front of us like a forty-five degree air photo.

'He might be sick,' I said. 'He might have gone out. He might even be dead.'

'I told you—' She began to shake. I took the stub of the cigarette away from her and put it in the ashtray. I ran the car windows up and put an arm around her shoulders and pulled her head down on my shoulder. She was limp, unresisting: but she still shook.

'You're a comfortable man,' she said. 'But don't rush me.'

'There's a pint in the glove compartment. Want a snort?'

'Yes.'

I got it out and managed to pull the metal strip loose with one hand and my teeth. I held the bottle between my knees and got the cap off. I held it to her lips. She sucked some in and shuddered. I re-capped the pint and put it away.

'I hate drinking from the bottle,' she said.

'Yeah. Unrefined. I'm not making love to you, Betty. I'm worried. Anything you want done?'

She was silent for a moment. Then her voice was steady, saying: 'Such as what? You can have those cheques back. They were yours. I gave them to you.'

'Nobody gives anybody five grand like that. It makes no sense. That's why I came back down from L.A. I drove up there early this morning.

Nobody goes all gooey over a character like me and talks about having half a million dollars and offers me a trip to Rio and a nice home complete with all the luxuries. Nobody drunk or sober does that because she dreamed a dead man was lying out on her balcony and would I please hurry around and throw him off into the ocean. Just what did you expect me to do when I got there—hold your hand while you dreamed?'

She pulled away and leaned in the far corner of the car. 'All right, I'm a liar. I've always been a liar.'

I glanced at the rear view mirror. Some kind of a small, dark car had turned into the road behind and stopped. I couldn't see who or what was in it. Then it swung hard right against the kerbing and backed and made off the way it had come. Some fellow took the wrong road and saw it was a dead end.

'While I was on the way up those damn fire stairs,' I went on, 'you swallowed your pills and then faked being awfully terribly sleepy and then after a while you actually did go to sleep—I think. Okay, I went out on the balcony. No stiff. No blood. If there had been, I might have managed to get him over the top of the wall. Hard work, but not impossible, if you know how to lift. But six trained elephants couldn't have thrown him far enough to land in the ocean. It's thirty-five feet to the fence and you'd have to throw him so far out that he would clear the fence. I figure an object as heavy as a man's body would have to be thrown a good fifty feet outwards to clear the fence.'

'I told you I was a liar.'

'But you didn't tell me why. Let's be serious. Suppose a man had been dead on your balcony. What would you expect me to do about it? Carry him down the fire stairs and get him into the car I had and drive off into the woods somewhere and bury him? You do have to take people into your confidence once in a while when bodies are lying around.'

'You took my money,' she said tonelessly. 'You played up to me.'

'That way I might find out who was crazy.'

'You found out. You should be satisfied.'

'I found out nothing—not even who you are.'

She got angry. 'I told you I was out of my mind,' she said in a rushing voice. 'Worry, fear, liquor, pills—why can't you leave me alone? I told you I'd give you back that money. What more do you want?'

'What do I do for it?'

'Just take it.' She was snapping at me now. 'That's all. Take it and go away. Far, far away.'

'I think you need a good lawyer.'

'That's a contradiction in terms,' she sneered. 'If he was good, he wouldn't be a lawyer.'

'Yeah. So you've had some painful experience along those lines. I'll find out in time, either from you or some other way. But I'm still being serious. You're in trouble. Apart from what happened to Mitchell, if anything, you're in enough trouble to justify hiring yourself a lawyer. You changed your name. So you had reasons. Mitchell was putting the bite on you. So *he* had reasons. A firm of Washington attorneys is looking for you. So *they* have reasons. And their client has reasons to have them looking for you.'

I stopped and looked at her as well as I could see her in the freshly darkening evening. Down below, the ocean was getting a lapis lazuli blue

that somehow failed to remind me of Miss Vermilyea's eyes. A flock of
seagulls went south in a fairly compact mass but it wasn't the kind of tight
formation North Island is used to. The evening plane from L.A. came down
the coast with its port and starboard lights showing, and then the winking
light below the fuselage went on and it swung out to sea for a long, lazy turn
into Lindbergh Field.

'So you're just a shill for a crooked lawyer,' she said nastily, and grabbed
for another of my cigarettes.

'I don't think he's very crooked. He just tries too hard. But that's not the
point. You can lose a few bucks to him without screaming. The point is
something called privilege. A licensed investigator doesn't have it. A lawyer
does, provided his concern is with the interests of a client who has retained
him. If the lawyer hires an investigator to work in those interests, then the
investigator has privilege. That's the only way he can get it.'

'You know what you can do with your privilege,' she said. 'Especially as it
was a lawyer that hired you to spy on me.'

I took the cigarette away from her and puffed on it a couple of times and
handed it back.

'It's all right, Betty. I'm no use to you. Forget I tried to be.'

'Nice words, but only because you think I'll pay you more to be of use to
me. You're just another of them. I don't want your damn cigarette either.'
She threw it out of the window. 'Take me back to the hotel.'

I got out of the car and stamped on the cigarette. 'You don't do that in the
California hills,' I told her. 'Not even out of season.' I got back into the car
and turned the key and pushed the starter button. I backed away and made
the turn and drove back up the curve to where the road divided. On the
upper level where the solid white line curved away a small car was parked.
The car was lightless. It could have been empty.

I swung the Olds hard the opposite way from the way I had come, and
flicked my headlights on with the high beam. They swept the car as I
turned. A hat went down over a face, but not quick enough to hide the
glasses, the fat broad face, the out-jutting ears, of Mr Ross Goble of Kansas
City.

The lights went on past and I drove down a long hill with lazy curves. I
didn't know where it went except that all roads around there led to the ocean
sooner or later. At the bottom there was a T-intersection. I swung to the
right and after a few blocks of narrow street I hit the boulevard and made
another right turn. I was now driving back towards the main part of
Esmeralda.

She didn't speak again until I got to the hotel. She jumped out quickly
when I stopped.

'If you'll wait here, I'll get the money.'

'We were tailed,' I said.

'What—?' She stopped dead, with her head half turned.

'Small car. You didn't notice him unless you saw my lights brush him as I
made the turn at the top of the hill.'

'Who was it?' Her voice was tense.

'How would I know? He must have picked us up here, therefore he'll
come back here. Could he be a cop?'

She looked back at me, motionless, frozen. She took a slow step, and then
she rushed at me as if she was going to claw my face. She grabbed me by the

arms and tried to shake me. Her breath came whistling.

'Get me out of here. Get me out of here, for the love of Christ. Anywhere. Hide me. Get me a little peace. Somewhere where I can't be followed, hounded, threatened. He swore he would do it to me. He'd follow me to the ends of the earth, to the remotest islands of the Pacific—'

'To the crest of the highest mountain, to the heart of the loneliest desert,' I said. 'Somebody's been reading a rather old-fashioned book.'

She dropped her arms and let them hang limp at her side.

'You've got as much sympathy as a loan shark.'

'I'll take you nowhere,' I said. 'Whatever it is that's eating you, you're going to stay put and take it.'

I turned and got into the car. When I looked back, she was already half way to the bar entrance, walking with quick strides.

16

If I had any sense, I would pick up my suitcase and go back home and forget all about her. By the time she made up her mind which part she was playing in which act of which play, it would probably be too late for me to do anything about it except maybe get pinched for loitering in the post office.

I waited and smoked a cigarette. Goble and his dirty little jaloppy ought to slow up and slip into a parking lot almost any moment. He couldn't have picked us up anywhere else, and since he knew that much he couldn't have followed us for any reason except to find out where we went.

He didn't show. I finished the cigarette, dropped it overboard, and backed out. As I turned out of the driveway towards the town, I saw his car on the other side of the street, parked left hand to the kerb. I kept going, turned right at the boulevard, and took it easy so he wouldn't blow a gasket trying to keep up. There was a restaurant about a mile along called the Epicure. It had a low roof, and a red brick wall to shield it from the street and it had a bar. The entrance was at the side. I parked and went in. It wasn't doing any business yet. The barkeep was chatting with the captain and the captain didn't even wear a dinner jacket. He had one of those high desks where they keep the reservation book. The book was open and had a list of names in it for later in the evening. But it was early now. I could have a table.

The dining-room was dim, candle-lit, divided by a low wall into two halves. It would have looked crowded with thirty people in it. The captain shoved me in a corner and lit my candle for me. I said I would have a double Gibson. A waiter came up and started to remove the place setting on the far side of the table. I told him to leave it, a friend might join me. I studied the menu, which was almost as large as the dining-room. I could have used a flashlight to read it, if I had been curious. This was about the dimmest joint I was ever in. You could be sitting at the next table from your mother and not recognize her.

The Gibson arrived. I could make out the shape of the glass and there seemed to be something in it. I tasted it and it wasn't too bad. At that moment Goble slid into the chair across from me. In so far as I could see him at all, he looked about the same as he had looked the day before. I went on peering at the menu. They ought to have printed it in braille.

Goble reached across for my glass of ice water and drank. 'How you making out with the girl?' he asked casually.

'Not getting anywhere. Why?'

'Whatcha go up on the hill for?'

'I thought maybe we could neck. She wasn't in the mood. What's your interest? I thought you were looking for some guy named Mitchell.'

'Very funny indeed. Some guy named Mitchell. Never heard of him, I believe you said.'

'I've heard of him since. I've seen him. He was drunk. Very drunk. He damn near got himself thrown out of a place.'

'Very funny,' Goble said, sneering. 'And how did you know his name?'

'On account of somebody called him by it. That would be *too* funny, wouldn't it?'

He sneered. 'I told you to stay out of my way. I know who you are now. I looked you up.'

I lit a cigarette and blew smoke in his face. 'Go fry a stale egg.'

'Tough, huh,' he sneered. 'I've pulled the arms and legs off bigger guys than you.'

'Name two of them.'

He leaned across the table, but the waiter came up.

'I'll have bourbon and plain water,' Goble told him. 'Bonded stuff. None of that bar whisky for me. And don't try to fool me. I'll know. And bottled water. The city water here is terrible.'

The waiter just looked at him.

'I'll have another of these,' I said, pushing my glass.

'What's good tonight?' Goble wanted to know. 'I never bother with these billboards.' He flicked a disdainful finger at the menu.

'The *plat du jour* is meat loaf,' the waiter said nastily.

'Hash with a starched collar,' Goble said. 'Make it meat loaf.'

The waiter looked at me. I said the meat loaf was all right with me. The waiter went away. Goble leaned across the table again, after first taking a quick look behind him and on both sides.

'You're out of luck, friend,' he said cheerfully. 'You didn't get away with it.'

'Too bad,' I said. 'Get away with what?'

'You're bad out of luck, friend. Very bad. The tide was wrong or something. Abalone fisher—one of those guys with frog feet and rubber masks—stuck under a rock.'

'The Abalone fisher stuck under a rock?' A cold, prickly feeling crawled down my back. When the waiter came with the drinks, I had to fight myself not to grab for mine.

'Very funny, friend.'

'Say that again and I'll smash your goddam glasses for you,' I snarled.

He picked up his drink and sipped it, tasted it, thought about it, nodded his head.

'I came out here to make money,' he mused. 'I didn't nowise come out to make trouble. Man can't make money making trouble. Man can make money keeping his nose clean. Get me?'

'Probably a new experience for you,' I said. 'Both ways. What was that about an Abalone fisher?' I kept my voice controlled, but it was an effort.

He leaned back. My eyes were getting used to the dimness now. I could see that his fat face was amused.

'Just kidding,' he said. 'I don't know any Abalone fishers. Only last night I learned how to pronounce the word. Still don't know what the stuff is. But things are kind of funny at that. I can't find Mitchell.'

'He lives at the hotel.' I took some more of my drink, not too much. This was no time to dive into it.

'I know he lives at the hotel, friend. What I don't know is where he is at right now. He ain't in his room. The hotel people ain't seen him around. I thought maybe you and the girl had some ideas about it.'

'The girl is screwy,' I said. 'Leave her out of it. And in Esmeralda they don't say "ain't seen". That Kansas City dialect is an offence against public morals here.'

'Shove it, Mac. When I want to get told how to talk English I won't go to no beat-up California peeper.' He turned his head and yelled: 'Waiter!'

Several faces looked at him with distaste. The waiter showed up after a while and stood there with the same expression as the customers.

'Hit me again,' Goble said, snapped a finger at his glass.

'It is not necessary to yell at me,' the waiter said. He took the glass away.

'When I want service,' Goble yelped at his back, 'service is what I want.'

'I hope you like the taste of wood alcohol,' I told Goble.

'Me and you could get along', Goble said indifferently, 'if you had any brains.'

'And if you had any manners and were six inches taller and had a different face and another name and didn't act like you thought you could lick your weight in frog spawn.'

'Cut the doodads and get back to Mitchell,' he said briskly. 'And to the dish you was trying to fumble up the hill.'

'Mitchell is a man she met on a train. He had the same effect on her that you have on me. He created in her a burning desire to travel in the opposite direction.'

It was a waste of time. The guy was as invulnerable as my great-great-grandfather.

'So,' he sneered, 'Mitchell to her is just a guy she met on a train and didn't like when she got to know him. So she ditched him for you? Convenient you happened to be around.'

The waiter came with the food. He set it out with a flourish. Vegetables, salad, hot rolls in a napkin.

'Coffee?'

I said I'd rather have mine later. Goble said yes and wanted to know where his drink was. The waiter said it was on the way—by slow freight, his tone suggested. Goble tasted his meat loaf and looked surprised. 'Hell, it's good,' he said. 'What with so few customers I thought the place was a bust.'

'Look at your watch,' I said. 'Things don't get moving until much later. It's that kind of town. Also, it's out of season.'

'Much later is right,' he said, munching. 'An awful lot later. Two, three in the a.m. sometimes. People go calling on their friends. You back at the Rancho, friend?'

I looked at him without saying anything.

'Do I have to draw you a picture, friend? I work long hours when I'm on a job.'

I didn't say anything.

He wiped his mouth. 'You kind of stiffened up when I said that about the guy stuck under a rock. Or could I be wrong?'

I didn't answer him.

'Okay, clam up,' Goble sneered. 'I thought maybe we could do a little business together. You got the physique and you take a good punch. But you don't know nothing about nothing. You don't have what it takes in my business. Where I come from you got to have brains to get by. Out here you just got to get sunburned and forget to button your collar.'

'Make me a proposition,' I said between my teeth.

He was a rapid eater even when he talked too much. He pushed his plate away from him, drank some of his coffee, and got a toothpick out of his vest.

'This is a rich town, friend,' he said slowly. 'I've studied it. I've boned up on it. I've talked to guys about it. They tell me it's one of the few spots left in our fair green country where the dough ain't quite enough. In Esmeralda you got to belong, or you're nothing. If you want to belong and get asked around and get friendly with the right people you got to have class. There's a guy here made five million fish in the rackets back in Kansas City. He bought up property, subdivided, built houses, built some of the best properties in town. But he didn't belong to the Beach Club because he didn't get asked. So he bought it. They know who he is, they touch him big when they got a fund-raising drive, he gets service, he pays his bills, he's a good, solid citizen. He throws big parties but the guests come from out of town unless they're moochers, no-goods, the usual trash you always find hopping about where there's money. But the class people of the town? He's just a nigger to them.'

It was a long speech and while he made it he glanced at me casually from time to time, glanced around the room, leaned back comfortably in his chair, and picked at his teeth.

'He must be breaking his heart,' I said. 'How did they find out where his dough came from?'

Goble leaned across the small table. 'A big shot from the Treasury Department comes here for a vacation every spring. Happened to see Mr Money and know all about him. He spread the word. You think it's not breaking his heart? You don't know these hoods that have made theirs and gone respectable. He's bleeding to death inside, friend. He's found something he can't buy with folding money and it's eating him to a shell.'

'How did you find out all this?'

'I'm smart. I get around. I find things out.'

'All except one,' I said.

'Just what's that?'

'You wouldn't know if I told you.'

The waiter came up with Goble's delayed drink and took dishes away. He offered the menu.

'I never eat dessert,' Goble said. 'Scram.'

The waiter looked at the toothpick. He reached over and deftly flicked it out from between Goble's fingers. 'There's a Men's Room here, chum,' he said. He dropped the toothpick into the ashtray and removed the ashtray.

'See what I mean?' Goble said to me. 'Class.'

I told the waiter I would have a chocolate sundae and some coffee. 'And give this gentleman the check,' I added.

'A pleasure,' the waiter said. Goble looked disgusted. The waiter drifted. I leaned across the table and spoke softly.

'You're the biggest liar I've met in two days. And I've met a few beauties. I don't think you have any interest in Mitchell. I don't think you ever saw or heard of him until yesterday when you got the idea of using him as a cover story. You were sent here to watch a girl and I know who sent you—not who hired you, but who had it done. I know why she is being watched and I know how to fix it so that she won't be watched. If you've got any high cards, you'd better play them right away quick. Tomorrow could be too late.'

He pushed his chair back and stood up. He dropped a folded and crimped bill on the table. He looked me over coolly.

'Big mouth, small brain,' he said. 'Save it for Thursday when they set the trash cans out. You don't know from nothing, friend. My guess is you never will.'

He walked off with his head thrust forward belligerently.

I reached across for the folded and crimped bill Goble had dropped on the table. As I expected it was only a dollar. Any guy who would drive a jaloppy that might be able to do forty-five miles an hour downhill would eat in joints where the eighty-five cent dinner was something for a wild Saturday night.

The waiter slid over and dumped the check on me. I paid up and left Goble's dollar in the plate.

'Thanks,' the waiter said. 'That guy's a real close friend of yours, huh?'

'The operative word is close,' I said.

'The guy might be poor,' the waiter said tolerantly. 'One of the choice things about this town is that the people who work here can't afford to live here.'

There were all of twenty people in the place when I left, and the voices were beginning to bounce down off the low ceiling.

17

The ramp down to the garage looked just the same as it had looked at four o'clock in the morning, but there was a swishing of water audible as I rounded the curve. The glassed-in cubicle office was empty. Somewhere somebody was washing a car, but it wouldn't be the attendant. I crossed to the door leading into the elevator lobby and held it open. The buzzer sounded behind me in the office. I let the door close and stood outside it waiting and a lean man in a long white coat came around the corner. He wore glasses, had a skin the colour of cold oatmeal and hollow, tired eyes. There was something Mongolian about his face, something south-of-the-border, something Indian, and something darker than that. His black hair was flat on a narrow skull.

'Your car, sir? What name, please?'

'Mr Mitchell's car in? The two-tone Buick hard-top?'

He didn't answer right away. His eyes went to sleep. He had been asked that question before.

'Mr Mitchell took his car out early this morning.'

'How early?'

He reached for a pencil that was clipped to his pocket over the stitched-on scarlet-script with the hotel name. He took the pencil out and looked at it.

'Just before seven o'clock. I went off at seven.'

'You work a twelve-hour shift? It's only a little past seven now.'

He put the pencil back in his pocket. 'I work an eight-hour shift but we rotate.'

'Oh. Last night you worked eleven to seven.'

'That's right.' He was looking past my shoulder at something far away. 'I'm due off now.'

I got out a packet of cigarettes and offered him one.

He shook his head.

'I'm only allowed to smoke in the office.'

'Or in the back of a Packard sedan.'

His right hand curled, as if around the haft of a knife.

'How's your supply? Needing anything?'

He stared.

'You should have said "Supply of what?"' I told him.

He didn't answer.

'And I would have said I wasn't talking about tobacco,' I went on cheerfully. 'About something cured with honey.'

Our eyes met and locked. Finally he said softly: 'You a pusher?'

'You snapped out of it real nice, if you were in business at 7 a.m. this morning. Looked to me like you would be out of circulation for hours. You must have a clock in your head—like Eddie Arcaro.'

'Eddie Arcaro,' he repeated. 'Oh yes, the jockey. Has a clock in his head, has he?'

'So they say.'

'We might do business,' he said remotely. 'What's your price?'

The buzzer sounded in the office. I had heard the elevator in the shaft subconsciously. The door opened and the couple I had seen holding hands in the lobby came through. The girl had on an evening dress and the boy wore a tux. They stood side by side, looking like two kids who had been caught kissing. The attendant glanced at them and went off and a car started and came back. A nice new Chrysler convertible. The guy handed the girl in carefully, as if she was already pregnant. The attendant stood holding the door. The guy came around the car and thanked him and got in.

'Is it very far to The Glass Room?' he asked diffidently.

'No, sir.' The attendant told them how to get there.

The guy smiled and thanked him and reached in his pocket and gave the attendant a dollar bill.

'You could have your car brought around to the entrance, Mr Preston. All you have to do is call down.'

'Oh, thanks, but this is fine,' the guy said hurriedly. He started carefully up the ramp. The Chrysler purred out of sight and was gone.

'Honeymooners,' I said. 'They're sweet. They just don't want to be stared at.'

The attendant was standing in front of me again with the same flat look in his eyes.

'But there's nothing sweet about us,' I added.

'If you're a cop, let's see the buzzer.'

'You think I'm a cop?'

'You're some kind of nosy bastard.' Nothing he said changed the tone of his voice at all. It was frozen in B Flat. Johnny One-Note.

'I'm all of that,' I agreed. 'I'm a private star. I followed somebody down here last night. You were in a Packard right over there'–I pointed–'and I went over and opened the door and sniffed the weed. I could have driven four Cadillacs out of here and you wouldn't have turned over in bed. But that's your business.'

'The price today,' he said. 'I'm not arguing about last night.'

'Mitchell left by himself?'

He nodded.

'No baggage?'

'Nine pieces. I helped him load it. He checked out. Satisfied?'

'You checked with the office?'

'He had his bill. All paid up and receipted.'

'Sure. And with that amount of baggage a hop came with him naturally.'

'The elevator kid. No hops on until seven-thirty. This was about 1 a.m.'

'Which elevator kid?'

'A Mex kid we call Chico.'

'You're not Mex?'

'I'm part Chinese, part Hawaiian, part Filipino, and part nigger. You'd hate to be me.'

'Just one more question. How in hell do you get away with it? The muggles, I mean.'

He looked around. 'I only smoke when I feel extra special low. What the hell's it to you? What the hell's it to anybody? Maybe I get caught and lose a crummy job. Maybe I get tossed in a cell. Maybe I've been in one all my life, carry it round with me. Satisfied?' He was talking too much. People with unstable nerves are like that. One moment monosyllables, next moment a flood. The low, tired monotone of his voice went on.

'I'm not sore at anybody. I live. I eat. Sometimes I sleep. Come around and see me some time. I live in a flea bag in an old frame cottage on Polton's Lane, which is really an alley. I live right behind the Esmeralda Hardware Company. The toilet's in a shed. I wash in the kitchen, at a tin sink. I sleep on a couch with broken springs. Everything there is twenty years old. This is a rich man's town. Come and see me. I live on a rich man's property.'

'There's a piece missing from your story about Mitchell,' I said.

'Which one?'

'The truth.'

'I'll look under the couch for it. It might be a little dusty.'

There was the rough noise of a car entering the ramp from above. He turned away and I went through the door and rang for the elevator. He was a queer duck, the attendant, very queer. Kind of interesting, though. And kind of sad, too. One of the sad, one of the lost.

The elevator was a long time coming and before it came I had company waiting for it. Six foot three inches of handsome, healthy male named Clark Brandon. He was wearing a leather windbreaker and a heavy roll-collar blue sweater under it, a pair of beat-up Bedford cord breeches, and the kind of high laced boots that field engineers and surveyors wear in rough country. He looked like the boss of a drilling crew. In an hour from now, I had no doubt he would be at The Glass Room in a dinner suit and he would look like the boss of that too, and perhaps he was. Plenty of money, plenty of health, and plenty of time to get the best out of both, and wherever he went he would be the owner.

He glanced at me and waited for me to get into the elevator when it came. The elevator kid saluted him respectfully. He nodded. We both got off at the lobby. Brandon crossed to the desk and got a big smile from the clerk—a new one I hadn't seen before—and the clerk handed him a fistful of letters. Brandon leaned against the end of the counter and tore the envelopes open one by one and dropped them into a waste-basket beside where he was standing. Most of the letters went the same way. There was a rack of travel folders there. I picked one off and lit a cigarette and studied the folder.

Brandon had one letter that interested him. He read it several times. I could see that it was short and handwritten on the hotel stationery, but without looking over his shoulder that was all I could see. He stood holding the letter. Then he reached down into the basket and came up with the envelope. He studied that. He put the letter in his pocket and moved along the desk. He handed the clerk the envelope.

'This was handed in. Did you happen to see who left it? I don't seem to know the party.'

The clerk looked at the envelope and nodded. 'Yes, Mr Brandon, a man left it just after I came on. He was a middle-aged fat man with glasses. Grey suit and topcoat and grey felt hat. Not a local type. A little shabby. A nobody.'

'Did he ask for me?'

'No, sir. Just asked me to put the note in your box. Anything wrong, Mr Brandon?'

'Look like a goof?'

The clerk shook his head. 'He just looked what I said. Like a nobody.'

Brandon chuckled. 'He wants to make me a Mormon bishop for fifty dollars. Some kind of nut, obviously.' He picked the envelope up off the counter and put it in his pocket. He started to turn away, then said: 'Seen Larry Mitchell around?'

'Not since I've been on, Mr Brandon. But that's only a couple of hours.'

'Thanks.'

Brandon walked across to the elevator and got in. It was a different elevator. The operator grinned all over his face and said something to Brandon. Brandon didn't answer him or look at him. The kid looked hurt as he whooshed the doors shut. Brandon was scowling. He was less handsome when he scowled.

I put the travel folder back in the rack and moved over to the desk. The clerk looked at me without interest. His glance said I was not registered there. 'Yes, sir?'

He was a grey-haired man who carried himself well.

'I was just going to ask for Mr Mitchell, but I heard what you said.'

'The house phones are over there.' He pointed with his chin. 'The operator will connect you.'

'I doubt it.'

'Meaning what?'

I pulled my jacket open to get at my letter case. I could see the clerk's eyes freeze on the rounded butt of the gun under my arm. I got the letter case out and pulled a card.

'Would it be convenient for me to see your house man? If you have one.'

He took the card and read it. He looked up. 'Have a seat in the main lobby, Mr Marlowe.'

'Thank you.'

He was on the phone before I had done a complete turn away from the desk. I went through the arch and sat against the wall where I could see the desk. I didn't have very long to wait.

The man had a hard, straight back and a hard, straight face, with the kind of skin that never tans but only reddens and pales out again. His hair was almost pompadour and mostly reddish blond. He stood in the archway and let his eyes take in the lobby slowly. He didn't look at me any longer than at anybody else. Then he came over and sat down in the next chair to me. He wore a brown suit and a brown and yellow bow tie. His clothes fitted him nicely. There were fine blond hairs on his cheeks high up. There was a grace note of grey in his hair.

'My name's Javonen,' he said without looking at me. 'I know yours. Got your card in my pocket. What's your trouble?'

'Man named Mitchell, I'm looking for him. Larry Mitchell.'

'You're looking for him, why?'

'Business. Any reason why I shouldn't look for him?'

'No reason at all. He's out of town. Left early this morning.'

'So I heard. It puzzled me some. He only got home yesterday. On the Super Chief. In L.A. he picked up his car and drove down. Also, he was broke. Had to make a touch for dinner money. He ate dinner at The Glass Room with a girl. He was pretty drunk—or pretended to be. It got him out of paying the check.'

'He can sign his checks there,' Javonen said indifferently. His eyes kept flicking around the lobby as if he expected to see one of the canasta players yank a gun and shoot his partner or one of the old ladies at the big jigsaw puzzle start pulling hair. He had two expressions—hard and harder. 'Mr Mitchell is well known in Esmeralda.'

'Well, but not favourably,' I said.

He turned his head and gave me a bleak stare. 'I'm an assistant manager here, Mr Marlowe. I double as security officer. I can't discuss the reputation of a guest of the hotel with you.'

'You don't have to. I know it. From various sources. I've observed him in action. Last night he put the bite on somebody and got enough to blow town. Taking his baggage with him, is my information.'

'Who gave this information to you?' He looked tough asking that.

I tried to look tough not answering it. 'On top of that I'll give you three guesses,' I said. 'One, his bed wasn't slept in last night. Two, it was reported to the office some time today that his room had been cleaned out. Three, somebody on your night staff won't show for work tonight. Mitchell couldn't get all his stuff out without help.'

Javonen looked at me, then prowled the lobby again with his eyes. 'Got something that proves you are what the card reads? Anyone can have a card printed.'

I got my wallet out and slipped a small photostat of my licence from it and passed it over. He glanced at it and handed it back. I put it away.

'We have our own organization to take care of skip-outs,' he said. 'They happen–in any hotel. We don't need your help. And we don't like guns in the lobby. The clerk saw yours. Somebody else could see it. We had a stick-up attempted here nine months ago. One of the heist guys got dead. I shot him.'

'I read about it in the paper,' I said. 'It scared me for days and days.'

'You read some of it. We lost four or five thousand dollars worth of business the week following. People checked out by the dozen. You get my point?'

'I let the clerk see my gun butt on purpose. I've been asking for Mitchell all day and all I got was the runaround. If the man checked out, why not say so? Nobody had to tell me he had jumped his bill.'

'Nobody said he jumped his bill. His bill, Mr Marlowe, was paid in full. So where does that leave you?'

'Wondering why it was a secret he had checked out.'

He looked contemptuous. 'Nobody said that either. You don't listen good. I said he was out of town on a trip. I said his bill was paid in full. I didn't say how much baggage he took. I didn't say he had given up his room. I didn't say that what he took was all he had. . . . Just what are you trying to make out of all this?'

'Who paid his bill?'

His face got a little red. 'Look, buster, I told you *he* paid it. In person, last night, in full and a week in advance as well. I've been pretty patient with you. Now you tell me something. What's your angle?'

'I don't have one. You've talked me out of it. I wonder why he paid a week in advance.'

Javonen smiled–very slightly. Call it a down payment on a smile. 'Look, Marlowe, I put in five years in Military Intelligence. I can size up a man–like for instance the guy we're talking about. He pays in advance because we feel happier that way. It has a stabilizing influence.'

'He ever pay in advance before?'

'God damn it. . . !'

'Watch yourself,' I cut in. 'The elderly gent with the walking stick is interested in your reactions.'

He looked half-way across the lobby to where a thin, old, bloodless man sat in a very low, round-backed, padded chair, with his chin on gloved hands and the gloved hands on the crook of a stick. He stared unblinkingly in our direction.

'Oh, him,' Javonen said. 'He can't even see this far. He's eighty years old.'

He stood up and faced me. 'Okay, you're clammed,' he said quietly. 'You're a private op, you've got a client and instructions. I'm only interested in protecting the hotel. Leave the gun home next time. If you have questions, come to me. Don't question the help. It gets told around and we don't like it. You wouldn't find the local cops friendly if I suggested you were being troublesome.'

'Can I buy a drink in the bar before I go?'

'Keep your jacket buttoned.'

'Five years in Military Intelligence is a lot of experience,' I said looking up at him admiringly.

'It ought to be enough.' He nodded briefly and strolled away through the arch, back straight, shoulders back, chin in, a hard, lean, well-set-up piece of man. A smooth operator. He had milked me dry—of everything that was printed on my business card.

Then I noticed that the old party in the low chair had lifted a gloved hand off the crook of his stick and was curving a finger at me. I pointed a finger at my chest and looked the question. He nodded, so over I went.

He was old, all right, but a long way from feeble and a long way from dim. His white hair was neatly parted, his nose was long and sharp and veined, his faded-out blue eyes were still keen, but the lids drooped wearily over them. One ear held the plastic button of a hearing aid, greyish-pink like his ear. The suede gloves on his hands had the cuffs turned back. He wore grey spats over polished black shoes. 'Pull up a chair, young man.' His voice was thin and dry and rustled like bamboo leaves.

I sat down beside him. He peered at me and his mouth smiled. 'Our excellent Mr Javonen spent five years in Military Intelligence, as no doubt he told you.'

'Yes, sir. CIC, a branch of it.'

'Military Intelligence is an expression which contains an interior fallacy. So you are curious about how Mr Mitchell paid his bill?'

I stared at him. I looked at the hearing aid. He tapped his breast pocket. 'I was deaf long before they invented these things. As the result of a hunter baulking at a fence. It was my own fault. I lifted him too soon. I was still a young man. I couldn't see myself using an ear trumpet, so I learned to lip-read. It takes a certain amount of practice.'

'What about Mitchell, sir?'

'We'll come to him. Don't be in a hurry.' He looked up and nodded.

A voice said, 'Good evening, Mr Clarendon.' A bellhop went by on his way to the bar. Clarendon followed him with his eyes.

'Don't bother with that one,' he said. 'He's a pimp. I have spent many, many years in lobbies, in lounges, and bars, on porches, terraces, and ornate gardens in hotels all over the world. I have outlived everyone in my family. I shall go on being useless and inquisitive until the day comes when the stretcher carries me off to some nice airy corner room in a hospital. The starched white dragons will minister to me. The bed will be wound up, wound down. Trays will come with that awful loveless hospital food. My pulse and temperature will be taken at frequent intervals and invariably when I am dropping off to sleep. I shall lie there and hear the rustle of the starched skirts, the slurring sound of the rubber shoe soles on the aseptic floor, and see the silent horror of the doctor's smile. After a while they will put the oxygen tent over me and draw the screens around the little white bed and I shall, without even knowing it, do the one thing in the world no man ever has to do twice.'

He turned his head slowly and looked at me. 'Obviously, I talk too much. Your name, sir?'

'Philip Marlowe.'

'I am Henry Clarendon IV. I belong to what used to be called the upper classes. Groton, Harvard, Heidelberg, the Sorbonne. I even spent a year at Uppsala. I cannot clearly remember why. To fit me for a life of leisure, no doubt. So you are a private detective. I do eventually get around to speaking of something other than myself, you see.'

'Yes, sir.'

'You should have come to me for information. But of course you couldn't know that.'

I shook my head. I lit a cigarette, first offering one to Mr Henry Clarendon IV. He refused it with a vague nod.

'However, Mr Marlowe, it is something you should have certainly learned. In every luxury hotel in the world there will be half a dozen elderly idlers of both sexes who sit around and stare like owls. They watch, they listen, they compare notes, they learn everything about everyone. They have nothing else to do, because hotel life is the most deadly of all forms of boredom. And no doubt I'm boring you equally.'

'I'd rather hear about Mr Mitchell, sir. Tonight at least, Mr Clarendon.'

'Of course. I'm egocentric, and absurd, and I prattle like a schoolgirl. You observe that handsome dark-haired woman over there playing canasta? The one with too much jewellery and the heavy gold trim on her glasses?'

He didn't point or even look. But I picked her out. She had an overblown style and she looked just a little hardboiled. She was the one with the ice, the paint.

'Her name is Margo West. She is seven times a divorcée. She has stacks of money and reasonably good looks, but she can't hold a man. She tries too hard. Yet she's not a fool. She would have an affair with a man like Mitchell, she would give him money and pay his bills, but she would never marry him. They had a fight last night. Nevertheless I believe she may have paid his bill. She often has before.'

'I thought he got a cheque from his father in Toronto every month. Not enough to last him, huh?'

Henry Clarendon IV gave me a sardonic smile. 'My dear fellow, Mitchell has no father in Toronto. He gets no monthly cheque. He lives on women. That is why he lives in a hotel like this. There is always some rich and lonely female in a luxury hotel. She may not be beautiful or very young, but she has other charms. In the dull season in Esmeralda, which is from the end of the race meet at Del Mar until the middle of January, the pickings are very lean. Then Mitchell is apt to travel—Majorca or Switzerland if he can make it, to Florida or one of the Caribbean islands if he is not in rich funds. This year he had poor luck. I understand he only got as far as Washington.'

He brushed a glance at me. I stayed deadpan polite, just a nice, youngish guy (by his standards) being polite to an old gentleman who liked to talk.

'Okay,' I said. 'She paid his hotel bill, maybe. But why a week in advance?'

He moved one gloved hand over the other. He tilted his stick and followed it with his body. He stared at the pattern in the carpet. Finally he clicked his teeth. He had solved the problem. He straightened up again.

'That would be severance pay,' he said dryly. 'The final and irrevocable end of the romance. Mrs West, as the English say it, had had it. Also, there was a new arrival in Mitchell's company yesterday, a girl with dark red hair. Chestnut red, not fire red or strawberry red. What I saw of their relationship seemed to me a little peculiar. They were both under some sort of strain.'

'Would Mitchell blackmail a woman?'

He chuckled. 'He would blackmail an infant in a cradle. A man who lives on women always blackmails them, although the word may not be used. He also steals from them when he can get his hands on any of their money. Mitchell forged two cheques with Margo West's name. That ended the affair. No doubt she has the cheques. But she won't do anything about it except keep them.'

'Mr Clarendon, with all due respect, how in hell would you know all these things?'

'She told me. She cried on my shoulder.' He looked towards the handsome, dark-haired woman. 'She does not at the moment look as if I could be telling the truth. Nevertheless I am.'

'And why are you telling it to me?'

His face moved into a rather ghastly grin. 'I have no delicacy. I should like to marry Margo West myself. It would reverse the pattern. Very small things amuse a man of my age. A humming bird, the extraordinary way a strellitzia bloom opens. Why at a certain point in its growth does the bud turn at right angles? Why does the bud split so gradually and why do the flowers emerge always in a certain exact order, so that the sharp, unopened end of the bud looks like a bird's beak and the blue and orange petals make a bird of paradise? What strange deity made such a complicated world when presumably he could have made a simple one? Is he omnipotent? How could he be? There's so much suffering and almost always by the innocent. Why will a mother rabbit trapped in a burrow by a ferret put her babies behind her and allow her throat to be torn out? Why? In two weeks more she would not even recognize them. Do you believe in God, young man?'

It was a long way around, but it seemed I had to travel it. 'If you mean an omniscient and omnipotent God who intended everything exactly the way it is, no.'

'But you should, Mr Marlowe. It is a great comfort. We all come to it in the end because we have to die and become dust. Perhaps for the individual that is all, perhaps not. There are grave difficulties about the after-life. I don't think I should really enjoy a heaven in which I shared lodgings with a Congo pygmy or a Chinese coolie or a Levantine rug peddler or even a Hollywood producer. I'm a snob, I suppose, and the remark is in bad taste. Nor can I imagine a heaven presided over by a benevolent character in a long white beard locally known as God. These are foolish conceptions of very immature minds. But you may not question a man's religious beliefs however idiotic they may be. Of course I have no right to assume that I shall go to heaven. Sounds rather dull, as a matter of fact. On the other hand how can I imagine a hell in which a baby that died before baptism occupies the same degraded position as a hired killer or a Nazi death camp commandant or a member of the Politburo? How strange it is that man's finest aspirations, dirty little animal that he is, his finest actions also, his great and unselfish heroism, his constant daily courage in a harsh world—how strange that these things should be so much finer than his fate on this earth. That has to be somehow made reasonable. Don't tell me that honour is merely a chemical reaction or that a man who deliberately gives his life for another is merely following a behaviour pattern. Is God happy with the poisoned cat dying alone in convulsions behind the billboard? Is God happy that life is cruel and that only the fittest survive? The fittest for what? Oh no, far from it. If God were omnipotent and omniscient in any literal sense, he wouldn't have bothered to make the universe at all. There is no success where there is no possibility of failure, no art without the resistance of the medium. Is it blasphemy to suggest that God has his bad days when nothing goes right, and that God's days are very, very long?'

'You're a wise man, Mr Clarendon. You said something about reversing the pattern.'

He smiled faintly. 'You thought I had lost the place in the overlong book of my words. No, sir, I had not. A woman like Mrs West almost always ends up marrying a series of pseudo-elegant fortune hunters, tango dancers with handsome side-burns, skiing instructors with beautiful blond muscles, faded French and Italian aristocrats, shoddy princelings from the Middle East, each worse than the one before. She might even in her extremity marry a man like Mitchell. If she married me, she would marry an old bore, but at least she would marry a gentleman.'

'Yeah.'

He chuckled. 'The monosyllable indicates a surfeit of Henry Clarendon IV. I don't blame you. Very well, Mr Marlowe, why are you interested in Mitchell? But I suppose you can't tell me.'

'No, sir, I can't. I'm interested in knowing why he left so soon after coming back, who paid his bill for him, and why, if Mrs West or, say, some well-heeled friend like Clark Brandon paid for him, it was necessary to pay a week in advance as well.'

His thin, worn eyebrows curved upwards. 'Brandon could easily guarantee Mitchell's account by lifting the telephone. Mrs West might prefer to give him the money and have him pay the bill himself. But a week in advance? Why would our Javonen tell you that? What does it suggest to you?

'That there's something about Mitchell the hotel doesn't want known. Something that might cause the sort of publicity they hate.'

'Such as?'

'Suicide and murder are the sort of things I mean. That's just by way of example. You've noticed how the name of a big hotel is hardly ever mentioned when one of the guests jumps out of a window? It's always a mid-town or a down-town hotel or a well-known, exclusive hotel –something like that. And if it's rather a high-class place, you never see any cops in the lobby, no matter what happened upstairs.'

His eyes went sideways and mine followed his. The canasta table was breaking up. The dolled-up and well-iced woman called Margo West strolled off towards the bar with one of the men, her cigarette holder sticking out like a bowsprit.

'So?'

'Well,' I said, and I was working hard, 'if Mitchell keeps his room on the records, whatever room he had—'

'Four-eighteen,' Clarendon put in calmly. 'On the ocean side. Fourteen dollars a day out of season, eighteen in season.'

'Not exactly cheap for a guy on his uppers. But he still has it, let's say. So whatever happened, he's just away for a few days. Took his car out, put his luggage in around 7 a.m. this morning. A damn funny time to leave when he was as drunk as a skunk late last night.'

Clarendon leaned back and let his gloved hands hang limp. I could see that he was getting tired. 'If it happened that way, wouldn't the hotel prefer to have you think he had left for good? Then you'd have to search for him somewhere else. That is, if you really are searching for him.'

I met his pale stare. He grinned.

'You're not making very good sense to me, Mr Marlowe. I talk and talk, but not merely to hear the sound of my voice. I don't hear it naturally in any case. Talking gives me an opportunity to study people without seeming altogether rude. I have studied you. My intuition, if such be the correct word, tells me that your interest in Mitchell is rather tangential. Otherwise you would not be so open about it.'

'Uh-huh. Could be,' I said. It was a spot for a paragraph of lucid prose. Henry Clarendon IV would have obliged. I didn't have a damn thing more to say.

'Run along now,' he said. 'I'm tired. I'm going up to my room and lie down a little. A pleasure to have met you, Mr Marlowe.' He got slowly to his feet and steadied himself with the stick. It was an effort. I stood up beside him.

'I never shake hands,' he said. 'My hands are ugly and painful. I wear gloves for that reason. Good evening. If I don't see you again, good luck.'

He went off, walking slowly and keeping his head erect. I could see that walking wasn't any fun for him. The two steps up from the main lobby to the arch were made one at a time, with a pause in between. His right foot always moved first. The cane bore down hard beside his left. He went out through the arch and I watched him move towards an elevator. I decided Mr Henry Clarendon IV was a pretty smooth article.

I strolled along to the bar. Mrs Margo West was sitting in the amber shadows with one of the canasta players. The waiter was just setting drinks before them. I didn't pay too much attention because farther along in a little booth against the wall was someone I knew better. And alone.

She had the same clothes on except that she had taken the bandeau off her hair and it hung loose around her face.

I sat down. The waiter came over and I ordered. He went away. The music from the invisible record player was low and ingratiating.

She smiled a little. 'I'm sorry I lost my temper,' she said. 'I was very rude.'

'Forget it. I had it coming.'

'Were you looking for me in here?'

'Not especially.'

'Were you—oh, I forgot.' She reached for her bag and put it in her lap. She fumbled in it and then passed something rather small across the table, something not small enough for her hand to hide that it was a folder of travellers' cheques. 'I promised you these.'

'No.'

'Take them, you fool! I don't want the waiter to see.'

I took the folder and slipped it into my pocket. I reached into my inside pocket and got out a small receipt book. I entered the counterfoil and then the body of the receipt. 'Received from Miss Betty Mayfield, Hotel Casa del Poniente, Esmeralda, California, the sum of $5,000 in American Express Company travellers' cheques of $100 denomination, countersigned by the owner, and remaining her property, subject to her demand at any time until a fee is arranged with, and an employment accepted by me, the undersigned.'

I signed this rigmarole and held the book for her to see it.

'Read it and sign your name in the lower left-hand corner.'

She took it and held it close to the light.

'You make me tired,' she said. 'Whatever are you trying to spring?'

'That I'm on the level and you think so.'

She took the pen I held out and signed and gave the stuff back to me. I tore out the original and handed it to her. I put the book away.

The waiter came and put my drink down. He didn't wait to be paid. Betty shook her head at him. He went away.

'Why don't you ask me if I have found Larry?'

'All right. Have you found Larry, Mr Marlowe?'

'No. He had skipped the hotel. He had a room on the fourth floor on the same side as your room. Must be fairly nearly under it. He took nine pieces of luggage and beat it in his Buick. The house peeper, whose name is Javonen—he calls himself an assistant manager and security officer—is satisfied that Mitchell paid his bill and even a week in advance for his room. He has no worries. He doesn't like me, of course.'

'Does somebody?'

'You do—five thousand dollars' worth.'

'Oh, you *are* an idiot. Do you think Mitchell will come back?'

'I told you he paid a week in advance.'

She sipped her drink quietly. 'So you did. But that could mean something else.'

'Sure. Just spitballing, for example, I might say it could mean that he didn't pay his bill, but someone else did. And that the someone else wanted time to do something—such as getting rid of that body on your balcony last night. That is, if there was a body.'

'Oh, stop it!'

She finished her drink, killed her cigarette, stood up, and left me with the check. I paid it and went back through the lobby, for no reason that I could think of. Perhaps by pure instinct. And I saw Goble getting into the elevator. He seemed to have a rather strained expression. As he turned he caught my eye, or seemed to, but he gave no sign of knowing me. The elevator went up.

I went out to my car and drove back to the Rancho Descansado. I lay down on the couch and went to sleep. It had been a lot of day. Perhaps if I had a rest and my brain cleared, I might have some faint idea of what I was doing.

18

An hour later I was parked in front of the hardware store. It wasn't the only hardware store in Esmeralda, but it was the only one that backed on the alley called Polton's Lane. I walked east and counted the stores. There were seven of them to the corner, all shining with plate glass and chromium trim. On the corner was a dress shop with mannequins in the windows, scarves and gloves and costume jewellery laid out under the lights. No prices showing. I rounded the corner and went south. Heavy eucalyptus trees grew out of the sidewalk. They branched low down and the trunks looked hard and heavy, quite unlike the tall, brittle stuff that grows around Los Angeles. At the far corner of Polton's Lane there was an automobile agency. I followed its high, blank wall, looking at broken crates, piles of cartons, trash drums, dusty parking spaces, the backyard of elegance. I counted the buildings. It was easy. No questions to ask. A light burned in the small window of a tiny frame cottage that had long ago been somebody's simple home. The cottage had a wooden porch with a broken railing. It had been painted once, but that was in the remote past before the shops swallowed it up. Once it may even have had a garden. The shingles of the roof were warped. The front door was a dirty mustard yellow. The window was shut tight and needed hosing off. Behind part of it hung what remained of an old roller blind. There were two steps up to the porch, but only one had a tread. Behind the cottage and half way to the loading platform of the hardware store there was what had presumably been a privy. But I could see where a water pipe cut through the sagging side. A rich man's improvements on a rich man's property. A one-unit slum.

I stepped over the hollow place where a step should have been and knocked on the door. There was no bell push. Nobody answered. I tried the knob. Nobody had locked the door. I pushed it open and went in. I had that feeling. I was going to find something nasty inside.

A bulb burned in a frayed lamp crooked on its base, the paper shade split. There was a couch with a dirty blanket on it. There was an old cane chair, a Boston rocker, a table covered with a smeared oilcloth. On the table spread out beside a coffee cup was a copy of *El Diario*, a Spanish language newspaper, also a saucer with cigarette stubs, a dirty plate, a tiny radio which emitted music. The music stopped and a man began to rattle off a commercial in Spanish. I turned it off. The silence fell like a bag of feathers. Then the clicking of an alarm clock from beyond a half-open door. Then the clank of a small chain, a fluttering sound, and a cracked voice said rapidly: '*Quién es? Quién es? Quién es?*' This was followed by the angry chattering of monkeys. Then silence again.

From a big cage over in the corner the round, angry eye of a parrot looked at me. He sidled along the perch as far as he could go.

'*Amigo*,' I said.

The parrot let out a screech of insane laughter.

'Watch your language, brother,' I said.

The parrot crabwalked to the other end of the perch and pecked into a white cup and shook oatmeal from his beak contemptuously. In another cup there was water. It was messy with oatmeal.

'I bet you're not even housebroken,' I said.

The parrot stared at me and shuffled. He turned his head and stared at me with his other eye. Then he leaned forward and fluttered his tail feathers and proved me right.

'*Necio!*' he screamed. '*Fuera!*'

Somewhere water dripped from a leaky faucet. The clock ticked. The parrot imitated the ticking amplified.

I said: 'Pretty Polly.'

'*Hijo de la chingada*,' the parrot said.

I sneered at him and pushed the half-open door into what there was of a kitchen. The linoleum on the floor was worn through to the boards in front of the sink. There was a rusty three-burner gas stove, an open shelf with some dishes and the alarm clock, a riveted hot-water tank on a support in the corner, the antique kind that blows up because it has no safety valve. There was a narrow rear door, closed, with a key in the lock, and a single window, locked. There was a light bulb hanging from the ceiling. The ceiling above it was cracked and stained from roof leaks. Behind me the parrot shuffled aimlessly on his perch and once in a while let out a bored croak.

On the zinc drainboard lay a short length of black rubber tubing, and beside that a glass hypodermic syringe with the plunger pushed home. In the sink were three long, thin, empty tubes of glass with tiny corks near them. I had seen such tubes before.

I opened the back door, stepped to the ground, and walked to the converted privy. It had a sloping roof, about eight feet high in front, less than six at the back. It opened outwards, being too small to open the other way. It was locked but the lock was old. It did not resist me much.

The man's scuffed toes almost touched the floor. His head was up in the darkness inches from the two by four that held up the roof. He was hanging by a black wire, probably a piece of electric light wire. The toes of his feet were pointed down as if they reached to stand on tiptoe. The worn cuffs of his khaki denim pants hung below his heels. I touched him enough to know that he was cold enough so that there was no point in cutting him down.

He had made very sure of that. He had stood by the sink in his kitchen and knotted the rubber tube around his arm, then clenched his fist to make the vein stand out, then shot a syringe full of morphine sulphate into his blood stream. Since all three of the tubes were empty, it was a fair guess that one of them had been full. He could not have taken in less than enough. Then he had laid the syringe down and released the knotted tube. It wouldn't be long, not a shot directly into the blood stream. Then he had gone out to his privy and stood on the seat and knotted the wire around his throat. By that time he would be dizzy. He could stand there and wait until his knees went slack and the weight of his body took care of the rest. He would know nothing. He would already be asleep.

I closed the door on him. I didn't go back into the house. As I went along the side towards Polton's Lane, that handsome residential street, the parrot inside the shack heard me and screeched '*Quién es? Quién es? Quién es?*'

Who is it? Nobody, friend. Just a footfall in the night.

I walked softly, going away.

19

I walked softly, in no particular direction, but I knew where I would end up. I always did. At the Casa del Poniente. I climbed back into my car on Grand and circled a few blocks aimlessly, and then I was parked as usual in a slot near the bar entrance. As I got out I looked at the car beside mine. It was Goble's shabby, dark little jalopy. He was as adhesive as a band aid.

At another time I would have been racking my brains for some idea of what he was up to, but now I had a worse problem. I had to go to the police and report the hanging man. But I had no notion what to tell them. Why did I go to his house? Because, if he was telling the truth, he had seen Mitchell leave early in the morning. Why was that of significance? Because I was looking for Mitchell myself. I wanted to have a heart-to-heart talk with him. About what? And from there on I had no answers that would not lead to Betty Mayfield, who she was, where she came from, why she changed her name, what had happened back in Washington, or Virginia or wherever it was, that made her run away.

I had five thousand dollars of her money in travellers' cheques in my pocket, and she wasn't even formally my client. I was stuck, but good.

I walked over to the edge of the cliff and listened to the sound of the surf. I couldn't see anything but the occasional gleam of a wave breaking out beyond the cove. In the cove the waves don't break, they slide in politely, like floorwalkers. There would be a bright moon later, but it hadn't checked in yet.

Someone was standing not far away, doing what I was doing. A woman. I waited for her to move. When she moved I would know whether I knew her. No two people move in just the same way, just as no two sets of fingerprints match exactly.

I lit a cigarette and let the lighter flare in my face, and she was beside me.

'Isn't it about time you stopped following me around?'

'You're my client. I'm trying to protect you. Maybe on my seventieth birthday someone will tell me why.'

'I didn't ask you to protect me. I'm not your client. Why don't you go home—if you have a home—and stop annoying people?'

'You're my client—five thousand dollars' worth. I have to do something for it—even if it's no more than growing a moustache.'

'You're impossible. I gave you the money to let me alone. You're impossible. You're the most impossible man I ever met. And I've met some dillies.'

'What happened to that tall, exclusive apartment house in Rio? Where I was going to lounge around in silk pyjamas and play with your long, lascivious hair, while the butler set out the Wedgwood and the Georgian silver, with that faint dishonest smile and those delicate gestures, like a pansy hair stylist fluttering around a screen star?'

'Oh, shut up!'

'Wasn't a firm offer, huh? Just a passing fancy, or not even that. Just a trick to make me slaughter my sleeping hours and trot around looking for bodies that weren't there.'

'Did anybody ever give you a swift poke in the nose?'

'Frequently, but sometimes I make them miss.'

I grabbed hold of her. She tried to fight me off, but no fingernails. I kissed the top of her head. Suddenly she clung to me and turned her face up.

'All right. Kiss me, if it's any satisfaction to you. I suppose you would rather have this happen where there was a bed.'

'I'm human.'

'Don't kid yourself. You're a dirty, low-down detective. Kiss me.'

I kissed her. With my mouth close to hers I said: 'He hanged himself tonight.'

She jerked away from me violently. 'Who?' she asked in a voice that could hardly speak.

'The night garage attendant here. You may never have seen him. He was on mesca, tea, marijuana. But tonight he shot himself full of morphine and hanged himself in the privy behind his shack in Polton's Lane. That's an alley behind Grant Street.'

She was shaking now. She was hanging on to me as if to keep from falling down. She tried to say something, but her voice was just a croak.

'He was the guy that said he saw Mitchell leave with his nine suitcases early this morning. I wasn't sure I believed him. He told me where he lived and I went over this evening to talk to him some more. And now I have to go to the cops and tell them. And what do I tell them without telling them about Mitchell and from then on about you?'

'Please—please—*please* leave me out of it,' she whispered. 'I'll give you more money. I'll give you all the money you want.'

'For Pete's sake. You've already given me more than I'd keep. It isn't money I want. It's some sort of understanding of what the hell I'm doing and why. You must have heard of professional ethics. Some shreds of them still stick to me. Are you my client?'

'Yes. I give up. They all give up to you in the end, don't they?'

'Far from it. I get pushed around plenty.'

I got the folder of travellers' cheques out of my pocket and put a pencil flash on them and tore out five. I refolded it and handed it to her. 'I've kept five hundred dollars. That makes it legal. Now tell me what it's all about.'

'No. You don't have to tell anybody about that man.'

'Yes, I do. I have to go to the cop house just about now. I have to. And I have no story to tell them that they won't bust open in three minutes. Here, take your goddam cheques—and if you ever push them at me again, I'll smack your bare bottom.'

She grabbed the folder and tore off into the darkness to the hotel. I just stood there and felt like a damn fool. I don't know how long I stood there, but finally I stuffed the five cheques into my pocket and went wearily back to my car and started off to the place where I knew I had to go.

20

A man named Fred Pope who ran a small motel had once told me his views on Esmeralda. He was elderly, talkative, and it always pays to listen. The most unlikely people sometimes drop a fact or two that means a lot in my business.

'I been here thirty years,' he said. 'When I come here I had dry asthma. Now I got wet asthma. I recall when this town was so quiet dogs slept in the middle of the boulevard and you had to stop your car, if you had a car, and get out and push them out of the way. The bastards just sneered at you. Sundays it was like you was already buried. Everything shut up as tight as a bank vault. You could walk down Grand Street and have as much fun as a stiff in the morgue. You couldn't even buy a pack of cigarettes. It was so quiet you could of heard a mouse combin' his whiskers. Me and my old woman—she's been dead fifteen years now—used to play cribbage in a little place we had down on the street that goes along the cliff, and we'd listen in case something exciting would happen—like an old geezer taking a walk and tapping with a cane. I don't know if the Hellwigs wanted it that way or whether old man Hellwig done it out of spite. In them years he didn't live here. He was a big shot in the farm equipment business.'

'More likely', I said, 'he was smart enough to know that a place like Esmeralda would become a valuable investment in time.'

'Maybe,' Fred Pope said. 'Anyhow, he just about created the town. And after a while he come to live here—up on the hill in one of them great big stucco houses with tile roofs. Pretty fancy. He had gardens with terraces and big green lawns and flowering shrubs, and wrought-iron gates —imported from Italy, I heard, and Arizona fieldstone walks, and not just one garden, half a dozen. And enough land to keep the neighbours out of his hair. He drank a couple bottles of hooch a day and I heard he was a pretty rough customer. He had one daughter, Miss Patricia Hellwig. She was the real cream and still is.

'By that time Esmeralda had begun to fill up. At first it was a lot of old women and their husbands, and I'm tellin' you the mortician business was real good with tired old men that died and got planted by their loving widows. The goddam women last too long. Mine didn't.'

He stopped and turned his head away for a moment, before he went on.

'There was a streetcar from San Diego by then, but the town was still quiet—too quiet. Not hardly anybody got born here. Child-bearing was thought kind of too sexy. But the war changed all that. Now we got guys that sweat, and tough school kids in levis and dirty shirts, and artists and country club drunks and them little gifte shoppes that sell you a two-bit highball glass for eight-fifty. We got restaurants and liquor stores, but we still don't have no billboards or poolrooms or drive-ins. Last year they tried to put in a dime-in-the-slot telescope in the park. You ought to of heard the town council scream. They killed it for sure, but the place ain't no bird refuge any more. We got as smart stores as Beverly Hills. And Miss Patricia, she spent her whole life working like a beaver to give things to the town. Hellwig died five years ago. The doctors told him he would have to cut down on the booze or he wouldn't live a year. He cussed them out and said if he couldn't take a drink when he wanted to, morning, noon, or night, he'd be damned if he'd take one at all. He quit—and he was dead in a year.

'The docs had a name for it—they always have—and I guess Miss Hellwig had a name for them. Anyway, they got bumped off the staff of the hospital and that knocked them loose from Esmeralda. It didn't matter a whole lot. We still got about sixty doctors here. The town's full of Hellwigs, some with other names, but all of the family one way or another. Some are rich and some work. I guess Miss Hellwig works harder than most. She's eighty-six now, but tough as a mule. She don't chew tobacco, drink, smoke, swear, or use no make-up. She give the town the hospital, a private school, a library, an art centre, public tennis courts, and God knows what else. And she still gets driven in a thirty-year-old Rolls-Royce that's about as noisy as a Swiss watch. The mayor here is two jumps from a Hellwig, both downhill. I guess she built the municipal centre too, and sold it to the city for a dollar. She's some woman. Of course we got Jews here now, but let me tell you something. A Jew is supposed to give you a sharp deal and steal your nose, if you ain't careful. That's all bunk. A Jew enjoys trading; he likes business, but he's only tough on the surface. Underneath a Jewish businessman is usually real nice to deal with. He's human. If you want cold-blooded skinning, we got a bunch of people in this town now that will cut you down to the bone and add a service charge. They'll take your last dollar from you between your teeth and look at you like you stole it from them.'

21

The cop house was part of a long, modernistic building at the corner of Hellwig and Orcutt. I parked and went into it, still wondering how to tell my story, and still knowing I had to tell it.

The business office was small but very clean, and the duty officer on the desk had two sharp creases in his shirt, and his uniform looked as if it had been pressed ten minutes before. A battery of speakers on the wall was bringing in police and sheriff's reports from all over the country. A tilted plaque on the desk said the duty officer's name was Griddell. He looked at me the way they all look, waiting.

'What can we do for you, sir?' He had a cool, pleasant voice, and that look of discipline you find in the best ones.

'I have to report a death. In a shack behind the hardware store on Grand, on an alley called Polton's Lane, there's a man hanging in a sort of privy. He's dead. No chance to save him.'

'Your name, please?' He was already pressing buttons.

'Philip Marlowe. I'm a Los Angeles private detective.'

'Did you notice the number of this place?'

'It didn't have one that I could see. But it's right smack behind the Esmeralda Hardware Company.'

'Ambulance call, urgent,' he said into his mike. 'Possible suicide in a small house behind the Esmeralda Hardware Store. Man hanging in a privy behind the house.'

He looked at me. 'Do you know his name?'

I shook my head. 'But he was the night garage man at the Casa del Poniente.'

He flicked some sheets of a book. 'We know him. Has a record for marijuana. Can't figure how he held the job, but he may be off it now, and his sort of labour is pretty scarce here.'

A tall sergeant with a granite face came into the office, gave me a quick glance, and went out. A car started.

The duty officer flicked a key on a small PBX. 'Captain, this is Griddell on the desk. A Mr Philip Marlowe has reported a death in Polton's Lane. Ambulance moving. Sergeant Green is on his way. I have two patrol cars in the vicinity.'

He listened for a moment, then looked at me. 'Captain Alessandro would like to speak to you, Mr Marlowe. Down the hall, last door on the right, please.'

He was on the mike again before I was through the swinging door.

The last door on the right had two names on it. Captain Alessandro in a plaque fastened to the wood, and Sergeant Green on a removable panel. The door was half open, so I knocked and went in.

The man at the desk was as immaculate as the desk officer. He was studying a card through a magnifying glass, and a tape recorder beside him was telling some dreary story in a crumpled, unhappy voice. The Captain was about six feet three inches tall and had thick, dark hair and a clear, olive skin. His uniform cap was on the desk near him. He looked up, cut off the tape recorder, and put down the magnifying glass and the card.

'Have a seat, Mr Marlowe.'

I sat down. He looked at me for a moment without speaking. He had rather soft, brown eyes, but his mouth was not soft.

'I understand you know Major Javonen at the Casa.'

'I've met him, Captain. We are not close friends.'

He smiled faintly. 'That's hardly to be expected. He wouldn't enjoy private detectives asking questions in the hotel. He used to be in the CIC. We still call him Major. This is the politest goddam town I was ever in. We are a goddam smooth bunch around here, but we're police just the same. Now about this Ceferino Chang?'

'So that's his name. I didn't know.'

'Yes. We know him. May I ask what you are doing in Esmeralda?'

'I was hired by a Los Angeles attorney named Clyde Umney to meet the Super Chief and follow a certain party until that party came to a stop somewhere. I wasn't told why, but Mr Umney said he was acting for a firm of Washington attorneys and he didn't know why himself. I took the job because there is nothing illegal in following a person, if you don't interfere with that person. The party ended up in Esmeralda. I went back to Los Angeles and tried to find out what it was all about. I couldn't, so I took what I thought was a reasonable fee, $250, and absorbed my own expenses. Mr Umney was not very pleased with me.'

The Captain nodded. 'That doesn't explain why you are here or what you have to do with Ceferino Chang. And since you are not working for Mr Umney, unless you are working for another attorney you have no privilege.'

'Give me a break, if you can, Captain. I found out that the party I was following was being blackmailed, or there was an attempt at blackmail, by a man named Larry Mitchell. He lives or lived at the Casa. I have been trying to get in touch with him, but the only information I have is from Javonen and this Ceferino Chang. Javonen said he checked out, paid his bill, and a week in advance for his room. Chang told me he left at 7 a.m. this morning with nine suitcases. There was something a bit peculiar about Chang's manner, so I wanted to have another talk with him.'

'How did you know where he lived?'

'He told me. He was a bitter man. He said he lived on a rich man's property, and he seemed angry that it wasn't kept up.'

'Not good enough, Marlowe.'

'Okay, I didn't think it was myself. He was on the weed. I pretended to be a pusher. Once in a while in my business a man has to do a good deal of faking.'

'Better. But there's something missing. The name of your client—if you have one.'

'Could it be in confidence?'

'Depends. We never disclose the names of blackmail victims, unless they come out in court. But if this party has committed or been indicted for a crime, or has crossed a state line to escape prosecution, then it would be my duty as an officer of the law to report her present whereabouts and the name she is using.'

'Her? So you know already. Why ask me? I don't know why she ran away. She won't tell me. All I know is she is in trouble and in fear, and that somehow Mitchell knew enough to make her say uncle.'

He made a smooth gesture with his hand and fished a cigarette out of a drawer. He stuck it in his big mouth but didn't light it.

He gave me another steady look.

'Okay, Marlowe, for now I'll let it lay. But if you dig anything up, here is where you bring it.'

I stood up. He stood up too and held his hand out.

'We're not tough. We just have a job to do. Don't get too hostile with Javonen. The guy who owns that hotel draws a lot of water around here.'

'Thanks, Captain. I'll try to be a nice little boy—even to Javonen.'

I went back along the hall. The same officer was on the desk. He nodded to me and I went out into the evening and got into my car. I sat with my hands tight on the steering wheel. I wasn't too used to cops who treated me as if I had a right to be alive. I was sitting there when the desk officer poked his head out of the door and called that Captain Alessandro wanted to see me again.

When I got back to Captain Alessandro's office, he was on the telephone. He nodded me to the customer's chair and went on listening and making quick notes in what looked like the sort of condensed writing that many reporters use. After a while he said: 'Thanks very much. We'll be in touch.'

He leaned back and tapped on his desk and frowned.

'That was a report from the sheriff's sub-station at Escondido. Mitchell's car has been found—apparently abandoned. I thought you might like to know.'

'Thanks, Captain. Where was this?'

'About twenty miles from here, on a country road that leads to Highway 395, but is not the road a man would naturally take to get to 395. It's a place called Los Penasquitos Canyon. Nothing there but outcrop and barren land and a dry river bed. I know the place. This morning a rancher named Gates went by there with a small truck, looking for fieldstone to build a wall. He passed a two-tone Buick hardtop parked off the side of the road. He didn't pay much attention to the Buick, except to notice that it hadn't been in a wreck, so somebody just parked it there.

'Later on in the day, around four, Gates went back to pick up another load of fieldstone. The Buick was still there. This time he stopped and looked it over. No keys in the lock but the car wasn't locked up. No sign of any damage. Just the same Gates wrote down the licence number and the name and address on the registration certificate. When he got back to his ranch he called the sub-station at Escondido. Of course the deputies knew Los Penasquitos Canyon. One of them went over and looked at the car. Clean as a whistle. The deputy managed to trick the trunk open. Empty except for a spare tyre and a few tools. So he went back to Escondido and called in here. I've just been talking to him.'

I lit a cigarette and offered one to Captain Alessandro. He shook his head.

'Got any ideas, Marlowe?'

'No more than you have.'

'Let's hear them anyway.'

'If Mitchell had some good reasons to get lost and had a friend who would pick him up–a friend nobody here knew anything about–he would have stored his car in some garage. That wouldn't have made anyone curious. There wouldn't be anything to make the garage curious. They would be just storing a car. Mitchell's suitcases would already have been in his friend's car.'

'So?'

'So there wasn't any friend. So Mitchell disappeared into thin air–with his nine suitcases–on a very lonely road that was hardly ever used.'

'Go on from there.' His voice was hard now. It had an edge to it. I stood up.

'Don't bully me, Captain Alessandro. I haven't done anything wrong. You've been very human so far. Please don't get the idea that I had anything to do with Mitchell's disappearance. I didn't–and still don't–know what he had on my client. I just know that she is a lonely and frightened and unhappy girl. When I know why, if I do manage to find out, I'll let you know or I won't. If I don't you'll just have to throw the book at me. It wouldn't be the first time it's happened to me. I don't sell out–even to good police officers.'

'Let's hope it doesn't turn out that way, Marlowe. Let's hope.'

'I'm hoping with you, Captain. And thanks for treating me the way you have.'

I walked back down the corridor, nodded to the duty officer on the desk, and climbed back into my car again. I felt twenty years older.

I knew–and I was pretty damn sure Captain Alessandro knew too–that Mitchell wasn't alive, that he hadn't driven his car to Los Penasquitos Canyon, but somebody had driven him there, with Mitchell lying dead on the floor of the back seat.

There was no other possible way to look at it. There are things that are facts, in a statistical sense, on paper, on a tape recorder, in evidence. And there are things that are facts because they have to be facts, because nothing makes any sense otherwise.

22

It is like a sudden scream in the night, but there is no sound. Almost always at night, because the dark hours are the hours of danger. But it has happened to me also in broad daylight–that strange, clarified moment when I suddenly know something I have no reason for knowing. Unless out of the long years and the long tensions, and in the present case, the abrupt certainty that what bullfighters call 'the moment of truth' is here.

There was no other reason, no sensible reason at all. But I parked across from the entrance to the Rancho Descansado, and cut my lights and ignition, and then drifted about fifty yards downhill and pulled the brake back hard.

I walked up to the office. There was the small glow of light over the night bell, but the office was closed. It was only ten-thirty. I walked around to the back and drifted through the trees. I came on two parked cars. One was a Hertz rent car, as anonymous as a nickel in a parking meter, but by bending down I could read the licence number. The car next to it was Goble's little dark jalopy. It didn't seem very long since it was parked by the Casa del Poniente. Now it was here.

I went on through the trees until I was below my room. It was dark, soundless. I went up the few steps very slowly and put my ear to the door. For a little while I heard nothing. Then I heard a strangled sob—a man's sob, not a woman's. Then a thin, low, cackling laugh. Then what seemed to be a hard blow. Then silence.

I went back down the steps and through the trees to my car. I unlocked the trunk and got out a tyre iron. I went back to my room as carefully as before—even more carefully. I listened again. Silence. Nothing. The quiet of the night. I reached out my pocket flash and flicked it once at the window, then slid away from the door. For several minutes nothing happened. Then the door opened a crack.

I hit it hard with my shoulder and smashed it wide open. The man stumbled back and then laughed. I saw the glint of his gun in the faint light. I smashed his wrist with the tyre iron. He screamed. I smashed his other wrist. I heard the gun hit the floor.

I reached back and switched the lights on. I kicked the door shut.

He was a pale-faced redhead with dead eyes. His face was twisted with pain, but his eyes were still dead. Hurt as he was, he was still tough.

'You ain't going to live long, boy,' he said.

'You're not going to live at all. Get out of my way.'

He managed to laugh.

'You've still got legs,' I said. 'Bend them at the knees and lie down—face down—that is, if you want a face.'

He tried to spit at me, but his throat choked. He slid down to his knees, holding his arms out. He was groaning now. Suddenly he crumpled. They're so goddam tough when they hold the stacked deck. And they never know any other kind of deck.

Goble was lying on the bed. His face was a mass of bruises and cuts. His nose was broken. He was unconscious and breathing as if half strangled.

The redhead was still out, and his gun lay on the floor near him. I wrestled his belt off and strapped his ankles together. Then I turned him over and went through his pockets. He had a wallet with $670 in it, a driver's licence in the name of Richard Harvest, and the address of a small hotel in San Diego. His pocketbook contained numbered cheques on about twenty banks, a set of credit cards, but no gun permit.

I left him lying there and went down to the office. I pushed the button of the night bell, and kept on pushing it. After a while a figure came down through the dark. It was Jack in a bathrobe and pyjamas. I still had the tyre iron in my hand.

He looked startled. 'Something the matter, Mr Marlowe?'

'Oh, no. Just a hoodlum in my room waiting to kill me. Just another man beaten to pieces on my bed. Nothing the matter at all. Quite normal around here, perhaps.'

'I'll call the police.'

'That would be awfully damn nice of you, Jack. As you see, I am still alive. You know what you ought to do with this place? Turn it into a pet hospital.'

He unlocked the door and went into the office. When I heard him talking to the police I went back to my room. The redhead had guts. He had managed to get into a sitting position against the wall. His eyes were still dead and his mouth was twisted into a grin.

I went over to the bed. Goble's eyes were open.

'I didn't make it,' he whispered. 'Wasn't as good as I thought I was. Got out of my league.'

'The cops are on the way. How did it happen?'

'I walked into it. No complaints. This guy's a life-taker. I'm lucky. I'm still breathing. Made me drive over here. He cooled me, tied me up, then he was gone for a while.'

'Somebody must have picked him up, Goble. There's a rent car beside yours. If he had that over at the Casa, how did he get back there for it?'

Goble turned his head slowly and looked at me. 'I thought I was a smart cookie. I learned different. All I want is back to Kansas City. The little guys can't beat the big guys—not ever. I guess you saved my life.'

Then the police were there.

First two prowl car boys, nice, cool-looking, serious men in the always immaculate uniforms and the always deadpan faces. Then a big, tough sergeant who said his name was Sergeant Holzminder, and that he was the cruising sergeant on the shift. He looked at the redhead and went over to the bed.

'Call the hospital,' he said briefly, over his shoulder.

One of the cops went out to the car. The Sergeant bent down over Goble. 'Want to tell me?'

'The redhead beat me up. He took my money. Stuck a gun into me at the Casa. Made me drive him here. Then he beat me up.'

'Why?'

Goble made a sighing sound and his head went lax on the pillow. Either he passed out again or faked it. The Sergeant straightened up and turned to me. 'What's your story?'

'I haven't any, Sergeant. The man on the bed had dinner with me tonight. We'd met a couple of times. He said he was a Kansas City PI. I never knew what he was doing here.'

'And this?' The Sergeant made a loose motion towards the redhead, who was still grinning a sort of unnatural epileptic grin.

'I never saw him before. I don't know anything about him, except that he was waiting for me with a gun.'

'That your tyre iron?'

'Yes, Sergeant.'

The other cop came back into the room and nodded to the Sergeant. 'On the way.'

'So you had a tyre iron,' the Sergeant said coldly. 'So why?'

'Let's say I just had a hunch someone was waiting for me here.'

'Let's try it that you didn't have a hunch, that you already knew. And knew a lot more.'

'Let's try it that you don't call me a liar until you know what you're talking about. And let's try it that you don't get so goddam tough just because you have three stripes. And let's try something more. This guy may be a hood, but he still has two broken wrists, and you know what that means, Sergeant? He'll never be able to handle a gun again.'

'So we book you for mayhem.'

'If you say so, Sergeant.'

Then the ambulance came. They carried Goble out first and then the interne put temporary splints on the two wrists of the redhead. They unstrapped his ankles. He looked at me and laughed.

'Next time, pal, I'll think of something original—but you did all right. You really did.'

He went out. The ambulance doors clanged shut and the growling sound of it died. The Sergeant was sitting down now, with his cap off. He was wiping his forehead.

'Let's try again,' he said evenly. 'From the beginning. Like as if we didn't hate each other and were just trying to understand. Could we?'

'Yes, Sergeant. We could. Thanks for giving me the chance.'

23

Eventually I landed back at the cop house. Captain Alessandro had gone. I had to sign a statement for Sergeant Holzminder.

'A tyre iron, huh?' he said musingly. 'Mister, you took an awful chance. He could have shot you four times while you were swinging on him.'

'I don't think so, Sergeant. I bumped him pretty hard with the door. And I didn't take a full swing. Also, maybe he wasn't supposed to shoot me. I don't figure he was in business for himself.'

A little more of that, and they let me go. It was too late to do anything but go to bed, too late to talk to anyone. Just the same I went to the telephone company office and shut myself in one of the two neat, outdoor booths and dialled the Casa del Poniente.

'Miss Mayfield, please. Miss Betty Mayfield. Room 1224.'

'I can't ring a guest at this hour.'

'Why? You got a broken wrist?' I was a real tough boy tonight. 'Do you think I'd call if it wasn't an emergency?'

He rang and she answered in a sleepy voice.

'This is Marlowe. Bad trouble. Do I come there or do you come to my place?'

'What? What kind of trouble?'

'Just take it from me for just this once. Should I pick you up in the parking lot?'

'I'll get dressed. Give me a little time.'

I went out to my car and drove to the Casa. I was smoking my third cigarette and wishing I had a drink when she came quickly and noiselessly up to the car and got in.

'I don't know what this is all about,' she began, but I interrupted her.

'You're the only one that does. And tonight you're going to tell me. And don't bother getting indignant. It won't work again.'

I jerked the car into motion and drove fast through silent streets and then down the hill and into the Rancho Descansado and parked under the trees. She got out without a word and I unlocked my door and put the lights on.

'Drink?'

'All right.'

'Are you doped?'

'Not tonight, if you mean sleeping pills. I was out with Clark and drank quite a lot of champagne. That always makes me sleepy.'

I made a couple of drinks and gave her one. I sat down and leaned my head back.

'Excuse me,' I said. 'I'm a little tired. Once in every two or three days I have to sit down. It's a weakness I've tried to get over, but I'm not as young as I was. Mitchell's dead.'

Her breath caught in her throat and her hand shook. She may have turned pale. I couldn't tell.

'Dead?' she whispered. 'Dead?'

'Oh, come off it. As Lincoln said, you can fool all the detectives some of the time, and some of the detectives all the time, but you can't—'

'Shut up! Shut up right now! Who the hell do you think you are?'

'Just a guy who has tried very hard to get where he could do you some good. A guy with enough experience and enough understanding to know that you were in some kind of jam. And wanted to help you out of it, with no help from you.'

'Mitchell's dead,' she said in a low, breathless voice. 'I didn't mean to be nasty. Where?'

'His car has been found abandoned in a place you wouldn't know. It's about twenty miles inland, on a road that's hardly used. A place called Los Penasquitos Canyon. A place of dead land. Nothing in his car, no suitcases. Just an empty car parked at the side of a road hardly anybody ever uses.'

She looked down at her drink and took a big gulp. 'You said he was dead.'

'It seems like weeks, but it's only hours ago that you came over here and offered me the top half of Rio to get rid of his body.'

'But there wasn't—I mean, I must just have dreamed—'

'Lady, you came over here at three o'clock in the morning in a state of near-shock. You described just where he was and how he was lying on the chaise on your little porch. So I went back with you and climbed the fire stairs, using the infinite caution for which my profession is famous. And no Mitchell, and then you asleep in your little bed with your little sleeping pill cuddled up to you.'

'Get on with your act,' she snapped at me. 'I know how you love it. Why didn't *you* cuddle up to me? I wouldn't have needed a sleeping pill—perhaps.'

'One thing at a time, if you don't mind. And the first thing is that you were telling the truth when you came here. Mitchell *was* dead on your porch. But someone got his body out of there while you were over here making a sucker out of me. And somebody got him down to his car and then packed his suitcases and got them down. All this took time. It took more than time. It took a great big reason. Now who would do a thing like that—just to save you the mild embarrassment of reporting a dead man on your porch?'

'Oh, shut up!' She finished her drink and put the glass aside. 'I'm tired. Do you mind if I lie down on your bed?'

'Not if you take your clothes off.'

'All right—I'll take my clothes off. That's what you've been working up to, isn't it?'

'You might not like that bed. Goble was beaten up on it tonight—by a hired gun named Richard Harvest. He was really brutalized. You remember Goble, don't you? The fat sort of man in the little dark car that followed us up the hill the other night.'

'I don't know anybody named Goble. And I don't know anybody named Richard Harvest. How do you know all this? Why were they here—in your room?'

'The hired gun was waiting for me. After I heard about Mitchell's car I had a hunch. Even generals and other important people have hunches. Why not me? The trick is to know when to act on one. I was lucky tonight—or last night. I acted on the hunch. He had a gun, but I had a tyre iron.'

'What a big, strong, unbeatable man you are,' she said bitterly, 'I don't mind the bed. Do I take my clothes off now?'

I went over and jerked her to her feet and shook her. 'Stop your nonsense, Betty. When I want your beautiful white body, it won't be while you're my client. I want to know what you are afraid of. How the hell can I do anything about it, if I don't know? Only you can tell me.'

She began to sob in my arms.

Women have so few defences, but they certainly perform wonders with those they have.

I held her tight against me. 'You can cry and cry and sob and sob, Betty. Go ahead, I'm patient. If I wasn't that—well, hell, if I wasn't that—'

That was as far as I got. She was pressed tight to me trembling. She lifted her face and dragged my head down until I was kissing her.

'Is there some other woman?' she asked softly, between my teeth.

'There have been.'

'But someone very special?'

'There was once, for a brief moment. But that's a long time ago now.'

'Take me. I'm yours—all of me is yours. Take me.'

24

A banging on the door woke me. I opened my eyes stupidly. She was clinging to me so tightly that I could hardly move. I moved her arms gently until I was free. She was still sound asleep.

I got out of bed and pulled a bathrobe on and went to the door; I didn't open it.

'What's the matter? I was asleep.'

'Captain Alessandro wants you at the office right away. Open the door.'

'Sorry, can't be done. I have to shave and shower and so on.'

'Open the door. This is Sergeant Green.'

'I'm sorry, Sergeant. I just can't. But I'll be along just as soon as I can make it.'

'You got a dame in there?'

'Sergeant, questions like that are out of line. I'll be there.'

I heard his steps go down off the porch. I heard someone laugh. I heard a voice say, 'This guy is really rich. I wonder what he does on his day off.'

I heard the police car going away. I went into the bathroom and showered and shaved and dressed. Betty was still glued to the pillow. I scribbled a note and put it on my pillow. 'The cops want me. I have to go. You know where my car is. Here are the keys.'

I went out softly and locked the door and found the Hertz car. I knew the keys would be in it. Operators like Richard Harvest don't bother about keys. They carry sets of them for all sorts of cars.

Captain Alessandro looked exactly as he had the day before. He would always look like that. There was a man with him, an elderly stony-faced man with nasty eyes.

Captain Alessandro nodded me to the usual chair. A cop in uniform came in and put a cup of coffee in front of me. He gave me a sly grin as he went out.

'This is Mr Henry Kinsolving of Westfield, Carolina, Marlowe. North Carolina. I don't know how he found his way out here, but he did. He says Betty Mayfield murdered his son.'

I didn't say anything. There was nothing for me to say. I sipped the coffee which was too hot, but good otherwise.

'Like to fill us in a little, Mr Kinsolving?'

'Who's this?' He had a voice as sharp as his face.

'A private detective named Philip Marlowe. He operates out of Los Angeles. He is here because Betty Mayfield is his client. It seems that you have rather more drastic ideas about Miss Mayfield than he has.'

'I don't have any ideas about her, Captain,' I said. 'I just like to squeeze her once in a while. It soothes me.'

'You like being soothed by a murderess?' Kinsolving barked at me.

'Well, I didn't know she was a murderess, Mr Kinsolving. It's all news to me. Would you care to explain?'

'The girl who calls herself Betty Mayfield—and that was her maiden name—was the wife of my son, Lee Kinsolving. I never approved of the marriage. It was one of those wartime idiocies. My son received a broken neck in the war and had to wear a brace to protect his spinal column. One night she got it away from him and taunted him until he rushed at her. Unfortunately, he had been drinking rather heavily since he came home, and there had been quarrels. He tripped and fell across the bed. I came into the room and found her trying to put the brace back on his neck. He was already dead.'

I looked at Captain Alessandro. 'Is this being recorded, Captain?'

He nodded. 'Every word.'

'All right, Mr Kinsolving. There's more, I take it.'

'Naturally. I have a great deal of influence in Westfield. I own the bank, the leading newspaper, most of the industry. The people of Westfield are my friends. My daughter-in-law was arrested and tried for murder and the jury brought in a verdict of guilty.'

'The jury were all Westfield people, Mr Kinsolving?'

'They were. Why shouldn't they be?'

'I don't know, sir. But it sounds like a one-man town.'

'Don't get impudent with me, young man.'

'Sorry, sir. Would you finish?'

'We have a peculiar law in our state, and I believe in a few other jurisdictions. Ordinarily the defence attorney makes an automatic motion for a directed verdict of not guilty and it is just as automatically denied. In my state the judge may reserve his ruling until after the verdict. The judge was senile. He reserved his ruling. When the jury brought in a verdict of guilty, he declared in a long speech that the jury had failed to consider the possibility that my son had in a drunken rage removed the brace from his neck in order to terrify his wife. He said that where there was so much bitterness anything was possible, and that the jury had failed to consider the possibility that my daughter-in-law might have been doing exactly what she said she was doing—trying to put the brace back on my son's neck. He voided the verdict and discharged the defendant.

'I told her that she had murdered my son and that I would see to it that she had no place of refuge anywhere on this earth. That is why I am here.'

I looked at the Captain. He looked at nothing. I said: 'Mr Kinsolving, whatever your private convictions, Mrs Lee Kinsolving, whom I know as Betty Mayfield, has been tried and acquitted. You have called her a murderess. That's a slander. We'll settle for a million dollars.'

He laughed almost grotesquely. 'You small-town nobody,' he almost screamed. 'Where I come from you would be thrown into jail as a vagrant.'

'Make it a million and a quarter,' I said. 'I'm not so valuable as your ex-daughter-in-law.'

Kinsolving turned on Captain Alessandro. 'What goes on here?' he barked. 'Are you all a bunch of crooks?'

'You're talking to a police officer, Mr Kinsolving.'

'I don't give a good goddam what you are,' Kinsolving said furiously. 'There are plenty of crooked police.'

'It's a good idea to be sure—before you call them crooked,' Alessandro said, almost with amusement. Then he lit a cigarette and blew smoke and smiled through it.

'Take it easy, Mr Kinsolving. You're a cardiac case. Prognosis unfavourable. Excitement is very bad for you. I studied medicine once. But somehow I became a cop. The war cut me off, I guess.'

Kinsolving stood up. Spittle showed on his chin. He made a strangled sound in his throat. 'You haven't heard the last of this,' he snarled.

Alessandro nodded. 'One of the interesting things about police work is that you never hear the last of anything. There are always too many loose ends. Just what would you like me to do? Arrest someone who has been tried and acquitted, just because you are a big shot in Westfield, Carolina?'

'I told her I'd never give her any peace,' Kinsolving said furiously. 'I'd follow her to the end of the earth. I'd make sure everyone knew just what she was!'

'And what is she, Mr Kinsolving?'

'A murderess that killed my son and was let off by an idiot of a judge—that's what she is!'

Captain Alessandro stood up, all six feet three inches of him. 'Take off, buster,' he said coldly. 'You annoy me. I've met all kinds of punks in my time. Most of them have been poor, stupid backward kids. This is the first time I've come across a great, big, important man who was just as stupid and vicious as a fifteen-year-old delinquent. Maybe you own Westfield,

North Carolina, or think you do. You don't own a cigar butt in my town. Get out before I put the arm on you for interfering with an officer in the performance of his duties.'

Kinsolving almost staggered to the door and groped for the knob, although the door was wide open. Alessandro looked after him. He sat down slowly.

'You were pretty rough, Captain.'

'It's breaking my heart. If anything I said makes him take another look at himself—oh well, hell!'

'Not his kind. Am I free to go?'

'Yes. Goble won't make charges. He'll be on his way back to Kansas City today. We'll dig up something on this Richard Harvest, but what's the use? We put him away for a while, and a hundred just like him are available for the same work.'

'What do I do about Betty Mayfield?'

'I have a vague idea that you've already done it,' he said, deadpan.

'Not until I know what happened to Mitchell.' I was just as deadpan as he was.

'All I know is that he's gone. That doesn't make him police business.'

I stood up. We gave each other those looks. I went out.

25

She was still asleep. My coming in didn't wake her. She slept like a little girl, soundlessly, her face at peace. I watched her for a moment, then lit a cigarette and went out to the kitchen. When I had put coffee on to percolate in the handsome, paper-thin, dime-store aluminium percolator provided by the management, I went back and sat on the bed. The note I had left was still on the pillow with my car keys.

I shook her gently and her eyes opened and blinked.

'What time is it?' she asked stretching her bare arms as far as she could. 'God, I slept like a log.'

'It's time for you to get dressed. I have some coffee brewing. I've been down to the police station—by request. Your father-in-law is in town, Mrs Kinsolving.'

She shot upright and stared at me without breathing.

'He got the brush, but good, from Captain Alessandro. He can't hurt you. Was that what all the fear was about?'

'Did he say—say what happened back in Westfield?'

'That's what he came here to say. He's mad enough to jump down his own throat. And what of it? You didn't, did you? Do what they said?'

'I did not.' Her eyes blazed at me.

'Wouldn't matter, if you had—now. But it wouldn't make me very happy about last night. How did Mitchell get wise?'

'He just happened to be there or somewhere nearby. Good heavens, the papers were full of it for weeks. It wasn't hard for him to recognize me. Didn't they have it in the papers here?'

'They ought to have covered it, if only because of the unusual legal tangle. If they did, I missed it. The coffee ought to be ready now. How do you take it?'

'Black, please. No sugar.'

'Fine. I don't have any cream or sugar. Why did you call yourself Eleanor King? No, don't answer that. I'm stupid. Old man Kinsolving would know your unmarried name.'

I went out to the kitchen and removed the top of the percolator, and poured us both a cup. I carried hers to her. I sat down in a chair with mine. Our eyes met and were strangers again.

She put her cup aside. 'That was good. Would you mind looking the other way while I gather myself together?'

'Sure.' I picked a paperback off the table and made a pretence of reading it. It was about some private eye whose idea of a hot scene was a dead, naked woman hanging from the shower rail with the marks of torture on her. By that time Betty was in the bathroom. I threw the paperback into the waste-basket, not having a garbage can handy at the moment. Then I got to thinking there are two kinds of women you can make love to. Those who give themselves so completely and with such utter abandonment, like Helen Vermilyea, that they don't even think about their bodies. And there are those who are self-conscious and always want to cover up a little. I remembered a girl in a story by Anatole France who insisted on taking her stockings off. Keeping them on made her feel like a whore. She was right.

When Betty came out of the bathroom she looked like a fresh-opened rose, her make-up perfect, her eyes shining, every hair exactly in place.

'Will you take me back to the hotel? I want to speak to Clark.'

'You in love with him?'

'I thought I was in love with you.'

'It was a cry in the night,' I said. 'Let's not try to make it more than it was. There's more coffee out in the kitchen.'

'No, thanks. Not until breakfast. Haven't you ever been in love? I mean enough to want to be with a woman every day, every month, every year?'

'Let's go.'

'How can such a hard man be so gentle?' she asked wonderingly.

'If I wasn't hard, I wouldn't be alive. If I couldn't ever be gentle, I wouldn't deserve to be alive.'

I held her coat for her and we went out to my car. On the way back to the hotel she didn't speak at all. When we got there and I slid into the now familiar parking slot, I took the five folded travellers' cheques out of my pocket and held them out to her.

'Let's hope it's the last time we pass these back and forth,' I said. 'They're wearing out.'

She looked at them, but didn't take them. 'I thought they were for your fee,' she said rather sharply.

'Don't argue, Betty. You know very well that I couldn't take money from you.'

'After last night?'

'After nothing. I just couldn't take it. That's all. I haven't done anything for you. What are you going to do? Where are you going? You're safe now.'

'I've no idea. I'll think of something.'

'Are you in love with Brandon?'

'I might be.'

'He's an ex-racketeer. He hired a gunman to scare Goble off. The gunman was ready to kill me. Could you really love a man like that?'

'A woman loves a man. Not what he is. And he may not have meant it.'

'Good-bye, Betty. I gave it what I had, but it wasn't enough.'

She reached her hand out slowly and took the cheques. 'I think you're crazy. I think you're the craziest man I ever met.' She got out of the car and walked away quickly, as she always did.

26

I gave her time to clear the lobby and go up to her room, and then I went into the lobby myself and asked for Mr Clark Brandon on a house phone. Javonen came by and gave me a hard look, but he didn't say anything.

A man's voice answered. It was his all right.

'Mr Brandon, you don't know me, although we shared an elevator the other morning. My name is Philip Marlowe. I'm a private detective from Los Angeles, and I'm a friend of Miss Mayfield. I'd like to talk to you a little, if you'll give me the time.'

'I seem to have heard something about you, Marlowe. But I'm all set to go out. How about a drink around six this evening?'

'I'd like to get back to Los Angeles, Mr Brandon. I won't keep you long.'

'All right,' he said grudgingly. 'Come on up.'

He opened the door, a big, tall, very muscular man in top condition, neither hard nor soft. He didn't offer to shake hands. He stood aside, and I went in.

'You alone here, Mr Brandon?'

'Sure. Why?'

'I wouldn't want anyone else to hear what I have to say.'

'Well say it and get done.'

He sat in a chair and put his feet upon an ottoman. He flicked a gold lighter at a gold-tipped cigarette. Big deal.

'I first came down here on the instructions of a Los Angeles lawyer to follow Miss Mayfield and find out where she went, and then report back. I didn't know why and the lawyer said he didn't either, but that he was acting for a reputable firm of attorneys in Washington. Washington, D.C.'

'So you followed her. So what?'

'So she made contact with Larry Mitchell, or he with her, and he had a hook of some sort into her.'

'Into a lot of women from time to time,' Brandon said coldly. 'He specialized in it.'

'He doesn't any more, does he?'

He stared at me with cool, blank eyes. 'What's that mean?'

'He doesn't do anything any more. He doesn't exist any more.'

'I heard he left the hotel and went off in his car. What's it to do with me?'

'You didn't ask me how I know he doesn't exist any more.'

'Look, Marlowe.' He flicked ash from his cigarette with a contemptuous gesture. 'It could be that I don't give a damn. Get to what concerns me, or else get out.'

'I also got involved down here, if involved is the word, with a man named Goble who said he was a private eye from Kansas City, and had a card which may or may not have proved it. Goble annoyed me a good deal. He kept following me around. He kept talking about Mitchell. I couldn't figure what he was after. Then one day at the desk you got an anonymous letter. I watched you read it over and over. You asked the clerk who left it. The clerk didn't know. You even picked the empty envelope out of the waste-basket. And when you went up in the elevator you didn't look happy.'

Brandon was beginning to look a little less relaxed. His voice had a sharper edge.

'You could get too nosy, Mr PI. Ever think of that?'

'That's a silly question. How else would I make a living?'

'Better get out of here while you can still walk.'

I laughed at him, and that really burned him. He shot to his feet and came striding over to where I was sitting.

'Listen, boy friend. I'm a pretty big man in this town. I don't get pushed around much by small-time operators like you. Out!'

'You don't want to hear the rest?'

'I said, out!'

I stood up. 'Sorry. I was prepared to settle this with you privately. And don't get the idea that I'm trying to put a bite on you—like Goble. I just don't do those things. But if you toss me out—without hearing me out—I'll have to go to Captain Alessandro. He'll listen.'

He stood glowering for a long moment. Then a curious sort of grin appeared on his face.

'So he'll listen to you. So what? I could get him transferred with one phone call.'

'Oh, no. Not Captain Alessandro. He's not brittle. He got tough with Henry Kinsolving this morning. And Henry Kinsolving isn't a man that's used to having anyone get tough with him, any place, any time. He just about broke Kinsolving in half with a few contemptuous words. You think you could get that guy to lay off? You should live so long.'

'Jesus,' he said, still grinning, 'I used to know guys like you once. I've lived here so long now I must have forgotten they still make them. Okay. I'll listen.'

He went back to the chair and picked another gold-tipped cigarette from a case and lit it. 'Care for one?'

'No thanks. This boy Richard Harvest—I think he was a mistake. Not good enough for the job.'

'Not nearly good enough, Marlowe. Not nearly. Just a cheap sadist. That's what comes of getting out of touch. You lose your judgement. He could have scared Goble silly without laying a finger on him. And then taking him over to your place—what a laugh! What an amateur! Look at him now. No good for anything any more. He'll be selling pencils. Would you care for a drink?'

'I'm not on that kind of terms with you, Brandon. Let me finish. In the middle of the night—the night I made contact with Betty Mayfield, and the night you chased Mitchell out of The Glass Room—and did it very nicely, I might add—Betty came over to my room at the Rancho Descansado. One of your properties, I believe. She said Mitchell was dead on a chaise on her porch. She offered me large things to do something about it. I came back over here and there was no man dead on her porch. The next morning the night garage man told me Mitchell had left in his car with nine suitcases. He'd paid his bill and a week in advance to hold his room. The same day his car was found abandoned in Los Penasquitos Canyon. No suitcases, no Mitchell.'

Brandon stared hard at me, but said nothing.

'Why was Betty Mayfield afraid to tell me what she was afraid of? Because she had been convicted of murder in Westfield, North Carolina, and then the verdict was reversed by the judge, who has that power in that state, and used it. But Henry Kinsolving, the father of the husband she was accused of murdering, told her he would follow her anywhere she went and see that she had no peace. Now she finds a dead man on her porch. And the cops investigate and her whole story comes out. She's frightened and confused. She thinks she couldn't be lucky twice. After all, a jury did convict her.'

Brandon said softly: 'His neck was broken. He fell over the end wall of my terrace. She couldn't have broken his neck. Come out here. I'll show you.'

We went out on to the wide, sunny terrace. Brandon marched to the end wall and I looked down over it and I was looking straight down on a chaise on Betty Mayfield's porch.

'This wall isn't very high,' I said. 'Not high enough to be safe.'

'I agree,' Brandon said calmly. 'Now suppose he was standing like this'—he stood with his back against the wall, and the top of it didn't come very much above the middle of his thighs. And Mitchell had been a tall man too—'and he goads Betty into coming over near enough so that he can grab her, and she pushes him off hard, and over he goes. And he just happens to fall in such a way—by pure chance—that his neck snaps. And that's exactly how her husband died. Do you blame the girl for getting in a panic?'

'I'm not sure I blame anybody, Brandon. Not even you.'

He stepped away from the wall and looked out to sea and was silent for a moment. Then he turned.

'For anything,' I said, 'except that you managed to get rid of Mitchell's body.'

'Now, how in the hell could I do that?'

'You're a fisherman, among other things. I'll bet that right here in this apartment you have a long, strong cord. You're a powerful man. You could get down to Betty's porch, you could put the cord under Mitchell's arms, and you have the strength to lower him to the ground behind the shrubbery. Then, already having his key out of his pocket, you could go to his room and pack up all his stuff, and carry it down to the garage, either in the elevator, or down the fire stairs. That would take three trips. Not too much for you. Then you could drive his car out of the garage. You probably knew the night-man was a doper and that he couldn't talk, if he knew you knew. This was in the small hours of the night. Of course the garage man lied about the time. Then you could drive the car as near as possible to where Mitchell's body was, and dump him into it, and drive off to Los Penasquitos Canyon.'

Brandon laughed bitterly. 'So I am in Los Penasquitos Canyon with a car and a dead man and nine suitcases. How do I get out of there?'

'Helicopter.'

'Who's going to fly it?'

'You. They don't check much on helicopters yet, but they soon will, because they are getting more and more numerous. You could have one brought to you in Los Penasquitos Canyon, having arranged in advance, and you could have had someone come along to pick up the pilot. A man in your position can do almost anything, Brandon.'

'And then what?'

'You loaded Mitchell's body and his suitcases into the helicopter and flew out to sea and set the helicopter hovering close to the water, and then you could dump the body and the suitcases, and drift on back to wherever the helicopter came from. A nice, clean, well-organized job.'

Brandon laughed raucously–too raucously. The laugh had a forced sound.

'You think I'd actually be idiot enough to do all this for a girl I had only just met?'

'Uh-uh. Think again, Brandon. You did it for you. You forget Goble. Goble came from Kansas City. Didn't *you?*'

'What if I did?'

'Nothing. End of the line. But Goble didn't come out here for the ride. And he wasn't looking for Mitchell, unless he already knew him. And between them, they figured they had a gold mine. You were the gold mine. But Mitchell got dead and Goble tried to go it alone, and he was a mouse fighting with a tiger. But would you want to explain how Mitchell fell off your terrace? Would you want an investigation of your background? What so obvious as for the police to think you had thrown Mitchell over the wall? And even if they couldn't prove it, where would you be in Esmeralda from then on?'

He walked slowly to the far end of the terrace and back. He stood in front of me, his expression completely blank.

'I could have you killed, Marlowe. But in some strange way in the years I have lived here, I don't seem to be that kind of a guy any more. So you have me licked. I don't have any defence, except to have you killed. Mitchell was the lowest kind of man, a blackmailer of women. You could be right all along the line, but I wouldn't regret it. And it's just possible, believe me, just possible that I, too, went out on a limb for Betty Mayfield. I don't expect you to believe it, but it *is* possible. Now, let's deal. How much?'

'How much for what?'

'For not going to the cops.'

'I already told you how much. Nothing. I just wanted to know what happened. Was I approximately right?'

'Dead right, Marlowe. Right on the nose. They may get me for it yet.'

'Maybe. Well, I'll take myself out of your hair now. Like I said–I want to get back to Los Angeles. Somebody might offer me a cheap job. I have to live, or do I?'

'Would you shake hands with me?'

'No. You hired a gun. That puts you out of the class of people I shake hands with. I might be dead today, if I hadn't had a hunch.'

'I didn't mean him to kill anyone.'

'You hired him. Good-bye.'

27

I got out of the elevator and Javonen seemed to be waiting for me. 'Come into the bar,' he said. 'I want to talk to you.'

We went into the bar, which was very quiet at that hour. We sat at a corner table. Javonen said quietly: 'You think I'm a bastard, don't you?'

'No. You have a job. I have a job. Mine annoyed you. You didn't trust me. That doesn't make you a bastard.'

'I try to protect the hotel. Who do you try to protect?'

'I never know. Often, when I do know, I don't know how. I just fumble around and make a nuisance of myself. Often I'm pretty inadequate.'

'So I heard—from Captain Alessandro. If it's not too personal, how much do you make on a job like this?'

'Well, this was a little out of the usual line, Major. As a matter of fact, I didn't make anything.'

'The hotel will pay you five thousand dollars—for protecting its interests.'

'The hotel, meaning Mr Clark Brandon.'

'I suppose. He's the boss.'

'It has a sweet sound—five thousand dollars. A very sweet sound. I'll listen to it on my way back to Los Angeles.' I stood up.

'Where do I send the cheque, Marlowe?'

'The Police Relief Fund could be glad to have it. Cops don't make much money. When they get in trouble they have to borrow from the Fund. Yes, I think the Police Relief Fund would be very grateful to you.'

'But not you?'

'You were a major in the CIC. You must have had a lot of chances to graft. But you're still working. I guess I'll be on my way.'

'Listen, Marlowe. You're being a damn fool. I want to tell you—'

'Tell yourself, Javonen. You have a captive audience. And good luck.'

I walked out of the bar and got into my car. I drove to the Descansado and picked up my stuff and stopped at the office to pay my bill. Jack and Lucille were in their usual positions. Lucille smiled at me.

Jack said: 'No bill, Mr Marlowe. I've been instructed. And we offer you our apologies for last night. But they're not worth much, are they?'

'How much would the bill be?'

'Not much. Twelve-fifty maybe.'

I put the money on the counter, Jack looked at it and frowned. 'I said there was no bill, Mr Marlowe.'

'Why not? I occupied the room.'

'Mr Brandon—'

'Some people never learn, do they? Nice to have known you both. I'd like a receipt for this. It's deductible.'

28

I didn't do more than ninety back to Los Angeles. Well, perhaps I hit a hundred for a few seconds now and then. Back on Yucca Avenue I stuck the Olds in the garage and poked at the mailbox. Nothing, as usual. I climbed the long flight of redwood steps and unlocked my door. Everything was the same. The room was stuffy and dull and impersonal as it always was. I opened a couple of windows and mixed a drink in the kitchen. I sat down on the couch and stared at the wall. Wherever I went, whatever I did, this was what I would come back to. A blank wall in a meaningless room in a meaningless house.

I put the drink down on a side table without touching it. Alcohol was no cure for this. Nothing was any cure but the hard inner heart that asked for nothing from anyone.

The telephone started to ring. I picked it up and said emptily: 'Marlowe speaking.'

'Is this Mr Philip Marlowe?'

'Yes.'

'Paris has been trying to reach you, Mr Marlowe. I'll call you back in a little while.'

I put the phone down slowly and I think my hand shook a little. Driving too fast, or not enough sleep.

The call came through in fifteen minutes: 'The party calling you from Paris is on the line, sir. If you have any difficulty, please flash your operator.'

'This is Linda. Linda Loring. You remember me, don't you, darling?'

'How could I forget?'

'How are you?'

'Tired—as usual. Just came off a very trying sort of case. How are you?'

'Lonely. Lonely for you. I've tried to forget you. I haven't been able to. We made beautiful love together.'

'That was a year and a half ago. And for one night. What am I supposed to say?'

'I've been faithful to you. I don't know why. The world is full of men. But I've been faithful to you.'

'I haven't been faithful to you, Linda. I didn't think I'd ever see you again. I didn't know you expected me to be faithful.'

'I didn't. I don't. I'm just trying to say that I love you. I'm asking you to marry me. You said it wouldn't last six months. But why not give it a chance? Who knows—it might last for ever. I'm begging you. What does a woman have to do to get the man she wants?'

'I don't know. I don't even know how she knows she wants him. We live in different worlds. You're a rich woman, used to being pampered. I'm a tired hack with a doubtful future. Your father would probably see to it that I didn't even have that.'

'You're not afraid of my father. You're not afraid of anyone. You're just afraid of marriage. My father knows a man when he sees one. Please, please, please. I'm at the Ritz. I'll send you a plane ticket at once.'

I laughed. 'You'll send *me* a plane ticket? What sort of guy do you think I am? I'll send *you* a plane ticket. And that will give you time to change your mind.'

'But, darling. I don't need you to send me a plane ticket. I have—'

'Sure. You have the money for five hundred plane tickets. But this one will be *my* plane ticket. Take it, or don't come.'

'I'll come, darling. I'll come. Hold me in your arms. Hold me close in your arms. I don't want to own you. Nobody ever will. I just want to love you.'

'I'll be here. I always am.'

'Hold me in your arms.'

The phone clicked, there was a buzzing sound, and then the line went dead.

I reached for my drink. I looked around the empty room—which was no longer empty. There was a voice in it, and a tall, slim, lovely woman. There was a dark head on the pillow in the bedroom. There was that soft, gentle perfume of a woman who presses herself tight against you, whose lips are soft and yielding, whose eyes are half-blind.

The telephone rang again. I said: 'Yes?'

'This is Clyde Umney, the lawyer. I don't seem to have had any sort of satisfactory report from you. I'm not paying you to amuse yourself. I want an accurate and complete account of your activities at once. I demand to know in full detail exactly what you have been doing since you returned to Esmeralda.'

'Having a little quiet fun—at my own expense.'

His voice rose to a sharp crackle. 'I demand a full report from you at once. Otherwise I'll see that you get bounced off your licence.'

'I have a suggestion for you, Mr Umney. Why don't you go kiss a duck?'

There were sounds of strangled fury as I hung up on him. Almost immediately the telephone started to ring again.

I hardly heard it. The air was full of music.

Farewell My Lovely

Raymond CHANDLER

FAREWELL MY LOVELY

I

It was one of the mixed blocks over on Central Avenue, the blocks that are not yet all negro. I had just come out of a three-chair barber shop where an agency thought a relief barber named Dimitrios Aleidis might be working. It was a small matter. His wife said she was willing to spend a little money to have him come home.

I never found him, but Mrs Aleidis never paid me any money either.

It was a warm day, almost the end of March, and I stood outside the barber shop looking up at the jutting neon sign of a second-floor dine and dice emporium called Florian's. A man was looking up at the sign too. He was looking up at the dusty windows with a sort of ecstatic fixity of expression, like a hunky immigrant catching his first sight of the Statue of Liberty. He was a big man but not more than six feet five inches tall and not wider than a beer truck. He was about ten feet away from me. His arms hung loose at his sides and a forgotten cigar smoked behind his enormous fingers.

Slim quiet negroes passed up and down the street and stared at him with darting side glances. He was worth looking at. He wore a shaggy borsalino hat, a rough grey sports coat with white golf balls on it for buttons, a brown shirt, a yellow tie, pleated grey flannel slacks and alligator shoes with white explosions on the toes. From his outer breast pocket cascaded a show handkerchief of the same brilliant yellow as his tie. There were a couple of coloured feathers tucked into the band of his hat, but he didn't really need them. Even on Central Avenue, not the quietest dressed street in the world, he looked about as inconspicuous as a tarantula on a slice of angel food.

His skin was pale and he needed a shave. He would always need a shave. He had curly black hair and heavy eyebrows that almost met over his thick nose. His ears were small and neat for a man of that size and his eyes had a shine close to tears that grey eyes often seem to have. He stood like a statue, and after a long time he smiled.

He moved slowly across the sidewalk to the double swinging doors which shut off the stairs to the second floor. He pushed them open, cast a cool expressionless glance up and down the street, and moved inside. If he had been a smaller man and more quietly dressed, I might have thought he was going to pull a stick-up. But not in those clothes, and not with that hat, and that frame.

The doors swung back outwards and almost settled to a stop. Before they had entirely stopped moving they opened again, violently, outwards. Something sailed across the sidewalk and landed in the gutter between two parked cars. It landed on its hands and knees and made a high keening noise like a cornered rat. It got up slowly, retrieved a hat and stepped back on to the sidewalk. It was a thin, narrow-shouldered brown youth in a lilac coloured suit and a carnation. It had slick black hair. It kept its mouth open and whined for a moment. People stared at it vaguely. Then it settled its hat jauntily, sidled over to the wall and walked silently splay-footed off along the block.

Silence. Traffic resumed. I walked along to the double doors and stood in front of them. They were motionless now. It wasn't any of my business. So I pushed them open and looked in.

A hand I could have sat in came out of the dimness and took hold of my shoulder and squashed it to a pulp. Then the hand moved me through the doors and casually lifted me up a step. The large face looked at me. A deep soft voice said to me, quietly:

'Smokes in here, huh? Tie that for me, pal.'

It was dark in there. It was quiet. From up above came vague sounds of humanity, but we were alone on the stairs. The big man stared at me solemnly and went on wrecking my shoulder with his hand.

'A dinge,' he said. 'I just thrown him out. You seen me throw him out?'

He let go of my shoulder. The bone didn't seem to be broken, but the arm was numb.

'It's that kind of a place,' I said, rubbing my shoulder. 'What did you expect?'

'Don't say that, pal,' the big man purred softly, like four tigers after dinner. 'Velma used to work here. Little Velma.'

He reached for my shoulder again. I tried to dodge him but he was as fast as a cat. He began to chew my muscles up some more with his iron fingers.

'Yeah,' he said. 'Little Velma. I ain't seen her in eight years. You say this here is a dinge joint?'

I croaked that it was.

He lifted me up two more steps. I wrenched myself loose and tried for a little elbow room. I wasn't wearing a gun. Looking for Dimitrios Aleidis hadn't seemed to require it. I doubted if it would do me any good. The big man would probably take it away from me and eat it.

'Go on up and see for yourself,' I said, trying to keep the agony out of my voice.

He let go of me again. He looked at me with a sort of sadness in his grey eyes. 'I'm feelin' good,' he said. 'I wouldn't want anybody to fuss with me. Let's you and me go on up and maybe nibble a couple.'

'They won't serve you. I told you it's a coloured joint.'

'I ain't seen Velma in eight years,' he said in his deep sad voice. 'Eight long years since I said good-bye. She ain't wrote to me in six. But she'll have a reason. She used to work here. Cute she was. Let's you and me go on up, huh?'

'All right,' I yelled. 'I'll go up with you. Just lay off carrying me. Let me walk. I'm fine. I'm all grown up. I go to the bathroom alone and everything. Just don't carry me.'

'Little Velma used to work here,' he said gently. He wasn't listening to me.

We went on up the stairs. He let me walk. My shoulder ached. The back of my neck was wet.

2

Two more swing doors closed off the head of the stairs from whatever was beyond. The big man pushed them open lightly with his thumbs and we went into the room. It was a long narrow room, not very clean, not very bright, not very cheerful. In the corner a group of negroes chanted and chattered in the cone of light over a crap table. There was a bar against the right-hand wall. The rest of the room was mostly small round tables. There were a few customers, men and women, all negroes.

The chanting at the crap table stopped dead and the light over it jerked out. There was a sudden silence as heavy as a waterlogged boat. Eyes looked at us, chestnut-coloured eyes, set in faces that ranged from grey to deep black. Heads turned slowly and the eyes in them glistened and stared in the dead alien silence of another race.

A large, thick-necked negro was leaning against the end of the bar with pink garters on his shirt sleeves and pink and white suspenders crossing his broad back. He had bouncer written all over him. He put his lifted foot down slowly and turned slowly and stared at us, spreading his feet gently and moving a broad tongue along his lips. He had a battered face that looked as if it had been hit by everything but the bucket of a dragline. It was scarred, flattened, thickened, chequered, and welted. It was a face that had nothing to fear. Everything had been done to it that anybody could think of.

The short crinkled hair had a touch of grey. One ear had lost its lobe.

The negro was heavy and wide. He had big heavy legs and they looked a little bowed, which is unusual in a negro. He moved his tongue some more and smiled and moved his body. He came towards us in a loose fighter's crouch. The big man waited for him silently.

The negro with the pink garters on his arms put a massive brown hand against the big man's chest. Large as it was the hand looked like a stud. The big man didn't move. The bouncer smiled gently.

'No white folks, brother. Jes' fo' the coloured people. I'se sorry.'

The big man moved his small sad grey eyes and looked around the room. His cheeks flushed a little. 'Shine box,' he said angrily, under his breath. He raised his voice. 'Where's Velma at?' he asked the bouncer.

The bouncer didn't quite laugh. He studied the big man's clothes, his brown shirt and yellow tie, his rough grey coat and the white golf balls on it. He moved his thick head around delicately and studied all this from various angles. He looked down at the alligator shoes. He chuckled lightly. He seemed amused. I felt a little sorry for him. He spoke softly again.

'Velma you says? No Velma heah, brother. No hooch, no gals, no nothing. Jes' the scram, white boy, jes' the scram.'

'Velma used to work here,' the big man said. He spoke almost dreamily, as if he was all by himself, out in the woods, picking johnny-jump-ups. I got my handkerchief out and wiped the back of my neck again.

The bouncer laughed suddenly. 'Shuah,' he said, throwing a quick look back over his shoulder at his public. 'Velma used to work here. But Velma don't work heah no mo'. She done reti'ed. Haw. Haw.'

'Kind of take your goddamned mitt off my shirt,' the big man said.

The bouncer frowned. He was not used to being talked to like that. He took his hand off the shirt and doubled it into a fist about the size and colour of a large eggplant. He had his job, his reputation for toughness, his public esteem to consider. He considered them for a second and made a mistake. He swung the fist very hard and short with a sudden outward jerk of the elbow and hit the big man on the side of the jaw. A soft sigh went around the room.

It was a good punch. The shoulder dropped and the body swung behind it. There was a lot of weight in that punch and the man who landed it had had plenty of practice. The big man didn't move his head more than an inch. He didn't try to block the punch. He took it, shook himself lightly, made a quiet sound in his throat and took hold of the bouncer by the throat.

The bouncer tried to knee him in the groin. The big man turned him in the air and slid his gaudy shoes apart on the scaly linoleum that covered the floor. He bent the bouncer backwards and shifted his right hand to the bouncer's belt. The belt broke like a piece of butcher's string. The big man put his enormous hand flat against the bouncer's spine and heaved. He threw him clear across the room, spinning and staggering and flailing with his arms. Three men jumped out of the way. The bouncer went over with a table and smacked into the baseboard with a crash that must have been heard in Denver. His legs twitched. Then he lay still.

'Some guys,' the big man said, 'has got wrong ideas about when to get tough.' He turned to me. 'Yeah,' he said. 'Let's you and me nibble one.'

We went over to the bar. The customers, by ones and twos and threes, became quiet shadows that drifted soundless across the floor, soundless through the doors at the head of the stairs. Soundless as shadows on grass. They didn't even let the doors swing.

We leaned against the bar. 'Whisky sour,' the big man said. 'Call yours.'

'Whisky sour,' I said.

We had whisky sours.

The big man licked his whisky sour impassively down the side of the thick squat glass. He stared solemnly at the barman, a thin, worried-looking negro in a white coat who moved as if his feet hurt him.

'*You* know where Velma is?'

'Velma, you says?' the barman whined. 'I ain't seen her 'round heah lately. Not right lately, nossuh.'

'How long you been here?'

'Le's see,' the barman put his towel down and wrinkled his forehead and started to count on his fingers. ''Bout ten months, I reckon. 'Bout a yeah. 'Bout—'

'Make your mind up,' the big man said.

The barman goggled and his Adam's apple flopped around like a headless chicken.

'How long's this coop been a dinge joint?' the big man demanded gruffly.

'Says which?'

The big man made a fist into which his whisky sour glass melted almost out of sight.

'Five years anyway,' I said. 'This fellow wouldn't know anything about a white girl named Velma. Nobody here would.'

The big man looked at me as if I had just hatched out. His whisky sour hadn't seemed to improve his temper.

'Who the hell asked you to stick your face in?' he asked me.

I smiled. I made it a big warm friendly smile. 'I'm the fellow that came in with you. Remember?'

He grinned back then, a flat white grin without meaning. 'Whisky sour,' he told the barman. 'Shake them fleas outa your pants. Service.'

The barman scuttled around, rolling the whites of his eyes. I put my back against the bar and looked at the room. It was now empty, save for the barman, the big man and myself, and the bouncer crushed over against the wall. The bouncer was moving. He was moving slowly as if with great pain and effort. He was crawling softly along the baseboard like a fly with one wing. He was moving behind the tables, wearily, a man suddenly old, suddenly disillusioned. I watched him move. The barman put down two more whisky sours. I turned to the bar. The big man glanced casually over at the crawling bouncer and then paid no further attention to him.

'There ain't nothing left of the joint,' he complained. 'They was a little stage and band and cute little rooms where a guy could have fun. Velma did some warbling. A redhead she was. Cute as lace pants. We was to of been married when they hung the frame on me.'

I took my second whisky sour. I was beginning to have enough of the adventure. 'What frame?' I asked.

'Where you figure I been them eight years I said about?'

'Catching butterflies.'

He prodded his chest with a forefinger like a banana. 'In the caboose. Malloy is the name. They call me Moose Malloy, on account of I'm large. The Great Bend bank job. Forty grand. Solo job. Ain't that something?'

'You going to spend it now?'

He gave me a sharp look. There was a noise behind us. The bouncer was on his feet again, weaving a little. He had his hand on the knob of a dark door over behind the crap table. He got the door open, half fell through. The door clattered shut. A lock clicked.

'Where's that go?' Moose Malloy demanded.

The barman's eyes floated in his head, focused with difficulty on the door through which the bouncer had stumbled.

'Tha—tha's Mistah Montgomery's office, suh. He's the boss. He's got his office back there.'

'He might know,' the big man said. He drank his drink at a gulp. 'He better not crack wise neither. Two more of the same.'

He crossed the room slowly, lightfooted, without a care in the world. His enormous back hid the door. It was locked. He shook it and a piece of the panel flew off to one side. He went through and shut the door behind him.

There was silence. I looked at the barman. The barman looked at me. His eyes became thoughtful. He polished the counter and sighed and leaned down with his right arm.

I reached across the counter and took hold of the arm. It was thin, brittle. I held it and smiled at him.

'What you got down there, bo?'

He licked his lips. He leaned on my arm, and said nothing. Greyness invaded his shining face.

'This guy is tough,' I said. 'And he's liable to go mean. Drinks do that to him. He's looking for a girl he used to know. This place used to be a white establishment. Get the idea?'

The barman licked his lips.

'He's been away a long time,' I said. 'Eight years. He doesn't seem to realize how long that is, although I'd expect him to think it a lifetime. He thinks the people here should know where his girl is. Get the idea?'

The barman said slowly: 'I thought you was with him.'

'I couldn't help myself. He asked me a question down below and then dragged me up. I never saw him before. But I didn't feel like being thrown over any houses. What you got down there?'

'Got me a sawed-off,' the barman said.

'Tsk. That's illegal,' I whispered. 'Listen, you and I are together. Got anything else?'

'Got me a gat,' the barman said. 'In a cigar box. Leggo my arm.'

'That's fine,' I said. 'Now move along a bit. Easy now. Sideways. This isn't the time to pull the artillery.'

'Says you,' the barman sneered, putting his tired weight against my arm. 'Says—'

He stopped. His eyes rolled. His head jerked.

There was a dull flat sound at the back of the place, behind the closed door beyond the crap table. It might have been a slammed door. I didn't think it was. The barman didn't think so either.

The barman froze. His mouth drooled. I listened. No other sound. I started quickly for the end of the counter. I had listened too long.

The door at the back opened with a bang and Moose Malloy came through it with a smooth heavy lunge and stopped dead, his feet planted and a wide pale grin on his face.

A Colt Army .45 looked like a toy pistol in his hand.

'Don't nobody try to fancy pants,' he said cosily. 'Freeze the mitts on the bar.'

The barman and I put our hands on the bar.

Moose Malloy looked the room over with a raking glance. His grin was taut, nailed on. He shifted his feet and moved silently across the room. He looked like a man who could take a bank single-handed–even in those clothes.

He came to the bar. 'Rise up, nigger,' he said softly. The barman put his hands high in the air. The big man stepped to my back and prowled me over carefully with his left hand. His breath was hot on my neck. It went away.

'Mister Montgomery didn't know where Velma was neither,' he said. 'He tried to tell me–with this.' His hard hand patted the gun. I turned slowly and looked at him. 'Yeah,' he said. 'You'll know me. You ain't forgetting me, pal. Just tell them johns not to get careless is all.' He waggled the gun. 'Well, so long, punks. I gotta catch a street car.'

He started towards the head of the stairs.

'You didn't pay for the drinks,' I said.

He stopped and looked at me carefully.

'Maybe you got something there,' he said, 'but I wouldn't squeeze it too hard.'

He moved on, slipped through the double doors, and his steps sounded remotely going down the stairs.

The barman stooped. I jumped around behind the counter and jostled him out of the way. A sawed-off shotgun lay under a towel on a shelf under the bar. Beside it was a cigar box. In the cigar box was a .38 automatic. I took both of them. The barman pressed back against the tier of glasses behind the bar.

I went back around the end of the bar and across the room to the gaping door behind the crap table. There was a hallway behind it, L-shaped, almost lightless. The bouncer lay sprawled on its floor unconscious, with a knife in his hand. I leaned down and pulled the knife loose and threw it down a back stairway. The bouncer breathed stertorously and his hand was limp.

I stepped over him and opened a door marked 'Office' in flaked black paint.

There was a small scarred desk close to a partly boarded-up window. The torso of a man was bolt upright in the chair. The chair had a high back which just reached to the nape of the man's neck. His head was folded back over the high back of the chair so that his nose pointed at the boarded-up window. Just folded, like a handkerchief or a hinge.

A drawer of the desk was open at the man's right. Inside it was a newspaper with a smear of oil in the middle. The gun would have come from there. It had probably seemed like a good idea at the time, but the position of Mr Montgomery's head proved that the idea had been wrong.

There was a telephone on the desk. I laid the sawed-off shotgun down and went over to lock the door before I called the police. I felt safer that way and Mr Montgomery didn't seem to mind.

When the prowl car boys stamped up the stairs, the bouncer and the barman had disappeared and I had the place to myself.

3

A man named Nulty got the case, a lean-jawed sourpuss with long yellow hands which he kept folded over his kneecaps most of the time he talked to me. He was a detective-lieutenant attached to the 77th Street Division and we talked in a bare room with two small desks against opposite walls and room to move between them, if two people didn't try it at once. Dirty brown linoleum covered the floor and the smell of old cigar butts hung in the air. Nulty's shirt was frayed and his coat sleeves had been turned in at the cuffs. He looked poor enough to be honest, but he didn't look like a man who could deal with Moose Malloy.

He lit half of a cigar and threw the match on the floor, where a lot of company was waiting for it. His voice said bitterly:

'Shines. Another shine killing. That's what I rate after eighteen years in this man's police department. No pix, no space, not even four lines in the want-ad section.'

I didn't say anything. He picked my card up and read it again and threw it down.

'Philip Marlowe, Private Investigator. One of those guys, huh? Jesus, you look tough enough. What was you doing all that time?'

'All what time?'

'All the time this Malloy was twisting the neck of this smoke.'

'Oh, that happened in another room,' I said. 'Malloy hadn't promised me he was going to break anybody's neck.'

'Ride me,' Nulty said bitterly. 'Okey, go ahead and ride me. Everybody else does. What's another one matter? Poor old Nulty. Let's go on up and throw a couple of nifties at him. Always good for a laugh, Nulty is.'

'I'm not trying to ride anybody,' I said. 'That's the way it happened—in another room.'

'Oh, sure,' Nulty said through a fan of rank cigar smoke. 'I was down there and saw it, didn't I? Don't you pack no rod?'

'Not on that kind of a job.'

'What kind of a job?'

'I was looking for a barber who had run away from his wife. She thought he could be persuaded to come home.'

'You mean a dinge?'

'No, a Greek.'

'Okey,' Nulty said and spit into his waste-basket. 'Okey. You met the big guy how?'

'I told you already. I just happened to be there. He threw a negro out of the doors of Florian's and I unwisely poked my head in to see what was happening. So he took me upstairs.'

'You mean he stuck you up?'

'No, he didn't have the gun then. At least, he didn't show one. He took the gun away from Montgomery, probably. He just picked me up. I'm kind of cute sometimes.'

'I wouldn't know,' Nulty said. 'You seem to pick up awful easy.'

'All right,' I said. 'Why argue? I've seen the guy and you haven't. He could wear you or me for a watch charm. I didn't know he had killed anybody until after he left. I heard a shot, but I got the idea somebody had got scared and shot at Malloy and then Malloy took the gun away from whoever did it.'

'And why would you get an idea like that?' Nulty asked almost suavely. 'He used a gun to take that bank, didn't he?'

'Consider the kind of clothes he was wearing. He didn't go there to kill anybody; not dressed like that. He went there to look for this girl named Velma that had been his girl before he was pinched for the bank job. She worked there at Florian's or whatever place was there when it was still a white joint. He was pinched there. You'll get him all right.'

'Sure,' Nulty said. 'With that size and them clothes. Easy.'

'He might have another suit,' I said. 'And a car and a hideout and money and friends. But you'll get him.'

Nulty spit in the waste-basket again. 'I'll get him,' he said, 'about the time I get my third set of teeth. How many guys is put on it? One. Listen, you know why? No space. One time there was five smokes carved Harlem sunsets on each other down on East Eighty-four. One of them was cold already. There was blood on the furniture, blood on the walls, blood even on the ceiling. I go down and outside the house a guy that works on the *Chronicle*, a newshawk, is coming off the porch and getting into his car. He makes a face at us and says, "Aw, hell, shines," and gets in his heap and goes away. Don't even go in the house.'

'Maybe he's a parole breaker,' I said. 'You'd get some co-operation on that. But pick him up nice or he'll knock off a brace of prowlies for you. Then you'll get space.'

'And I wouldn't have the case no more neither,' Nulty sneered.

The phone rang on his desk. He listened to it and smiled sorrowfully. He hung up and scribbled on a pad and there was a faint gleam in his eyes, a light far back in a dusty corridor.

'Hell, they got him. That was Records. Got his prints, mug, and everything. Jesus, that's a little something anyway.' He read from his pad. 'Jesus, this is a man. Six five and one-half, two hundred sixty-four pounds, without his necktie. Jesus, that's a boy. Well, the hell with him. They got him on the air now. Probably at the end of the hot car list. Ain't nothing to do but just wait.' He threw his cigar into a spittoon.

'Try looking for the girl,' I said. 'Velma. Malloy will be looking for her. That's what started it all. Try Velma.'

'You try her,' Nulty said. 'I ain't been in a joy house in twenty years.'

I stood up. 'Okey,' I said, and started for the door.

'Hey, wait a minute,' Nulty said. 'I was only kidding. You ain't awful busy, are you?'

I rolled a cigarette around in my fingers and looked at him and waited by the door.

'I mean you got time to sort of take a gander around for this dame. That's a good idea you had there. You might pick something up. You can work under glass.'

'What's in it for me?'

He spread his yellow hands sadly. His smile was as cunning as a broken mousetrap. 'You been in jams with us boys before. Don't tell me no. I heard different. Next time it ain't doing you any harm to have a pal.'

'What good is it going to do me?'

'Listen,' Nulty urged. 'I'm just a quiet guy. But any guy in the department can do you a lot of good.'

'Is this for love—or are you paying anything in money?'

'No money,' Nulty said, and wrinkled his sad yellow nose. 'But I'm needing a little credit bad. Since the last shake-up, things is really tough. I wouldn't forget it, pal. Not ever.'

I looked at my watch. 'Okey, if I think of anything, it's yours. And when you get the mug, I'll identify it for you. After lunch.' We shook hands and I went down the mud-coloured hall and stairway to the front of the building and my car.

It was two hours since Moose Malloy had left Florian's with the Army Colt in his hand. I ate lunch at a drugstore, bought a pint of bourbon, and drove eastward to Central Avenue and north on Central again. The hunch I had was as vague as the heat waves that danced above the sidewalk.

Nothing made it my business except curiosity. But strictly speaking, I hadn't had any business in a month. Even a no-charge job was a change.

4

Florian's was closed up, of course. An obvious plainclothes-man sat in front of it in a car, reading a paper with one eye. I didn't know why they bothered. Nobody there knew anything about Moose Malloy. The bouncer and the barman had not been found. Nobody on the block knew anything about them, for talking purposes.

I drove past slowly and parked around the corner and sat looking at a negro hotel which was diagonally across the block from Florian's and beyond the nearest intersection. It was called the Hotel Sans Souci. I got out and walked back across the intersection and went into it. Two rows of hard empty chairs stared at each other across a strip of tan fibre carpet. A desk was back in the dimness and behind the desk a bald-headed man had his eyes shut and his soft brown hands clasped peacefully on the desk in front of him. He dozed, or appeared to. He wore an Ascot tie that looked as if it had been tied about the year 1880. The green stone in his stickpin was not quite as large as an apple. His large loose chin was folded down gently on the tie, and his folded hands were peaceful and clean, with manicured nails, and grey half-moons in the purple of the nails.

A metal embossed sign at his elbow said: 'This Hotel is Under the Protection of The International Consolidated Agencies Ltd. Inc.'

When the peaceful brown man opened one eye at me thoughtfully I pointed at the sign.

'H.P.D. man checking up. Any trouble here?'

H.P.D. means Hotel Protective Department, which is the department of a large agency that looks after cheque bouncers and people who move out by the back stairs leaving unpaid bills and second-hand suitcases full of bricks.

'Trouble, brother,' the clerk said in a high sonorous voice, 'is something we is fresh out of.' He lowered his voice four or five notches and added: 'What was the name again?'

'Marlowe. Philip Marlowe—'

'A nice name, brother. Clean and cheerful. You're looking right well to-day.' He lowered his voice again. 'But you ain't no H.P.D. man. Ain't seen one in years.' He unfolded his hands and pointed languidly at the sign. 'I acquired that second-hand, brother, just for the effect.'

'Okey,' I said. I leaned on the counter and started to spin a half dollar on the bare, scarred wood of the counter.

'Heard what happened over at Florian's this morning?'

'Brother, I forgit.' Both his eyes were open now and he was watching the blur of light made by the spinning coin.

'The boss got bumped off,' I said. 'Man named Montgomery. Somebody broke his neck.'

'May the Lawd receive his soul, brother.' Down went the voice again. 'Cop?'

'Private—on a confidential lay. And I know a man who can keep things confidential when I see one.'

He studied me, then closed his eyes and thought. He re-opened them cautiously and stared at the spinning coin. He couldn't resist looking at it.

'Who done it?' he asked softly. 'Who fixed Sam?'

'A tough guy out of the jailhouse got sore because it wasn't a white joint. It used to be, it seems. Maybe you remember?'

He said nothing. The coin fell over with a light ringing whirr and lay still.

'Call your play,' I said. 'I'll read you a chapter of the Bible or buy you a drink. Say which.'

'Brother, I kind of like to read my Bible in the seclusion of my family.' His eyes were bright, toadlike, steady.

'Maybe you've just had lunch,' I said.

'Lunch,' he said, 'is something a man of my shape and disposition aims to do without.' Down went the voice. 'Come 'round this here side of the desk.'

I went around and drew the flat pint of bonded bourbon out of my pocket and put it on the shelf. I went back to the front of the desk. He bent over and examined it. He looked satisfied.

'Brother, this don't buy you nothing at all,' he said. 'But I is pleased to take a light snifter in your company.'

He opened the bottle, put two small glasses on the desk and quietly poured each full to the brim. He lifted one, sniffed it carefully, and poured it down his throat with his little finger lifted.

He tasted it, thought about it, nodded and said: 'This come out of the correct bottle, brother. In what manner can I be of service to you? There ain't a crack in the sidewalk 'round here I don't know by its first name. Yessuh, this liquor has been keepin' the right company.' He refilled his glass.

I told him what had happened at Florian's and why. He stared at me solemnly and shook his bald head.

'A nice quiet place Sam run too,' he said. 'Ain't nobody been knifed there in a month.'

'When Florian's was a white joint some six or eight years ago or less, what was the name of it?'

'Electric signs come kind of high, brother.'

I nodded. 'I thought it might have had the same name. Malloy would probably have said something if the name had been changed. But who ran it?'

'I'm a mite surprised at you, brother. The name of that pore sinner was Florian. Mike Florian—'

'And what happened to Mike Florian?'

The negro spread his gentle brown hands. His voice was sonorous and sad. 'Daid, brother. Gathered to the Lawd. Nineteen hundred and thirty-four, maybe thirty-five. I ain't precise on that. A wasted life, brother, and a case of pickled kidneys, I heard say. The ungodly man drops like a polled steer, brother, but mercy waits for him up yonder.' His voice went down to the business level. 'Damn if I know why.'

'Who did he leave behind him? Pour another drink.'

He corked the bottle firmly and pushed it across the counter. 'Two is all, brother—before sundown. I thank you. Your method of approach is soothin' to a man's dignity. . . . Left a widow. Name of Jessie.'

'What happened to her?'

'The pursuit of knowledge, brother, is the askin' of many questions. I ain't heard. Try the phone book.'

There was a booth in the dark corner of the lobby. I went over and shut the door far enough to put the light on. I looked up the name in the chained and battered book. No Florian in it at all. I went back to the desk.

'No soap,' I said.

The negro bent regretfully and heaved a city directory up on top of the desk and pushed it towards me. He closed his eyes. He was getting bored. There was a Jessie Florian, Widow, in the book. She lived at 1644 West 54th Place. I wondered what I had been using for brains all my life.

I wrote the address down on a piece of paper and pushed the directory back across the desk. The negro put it back where he had found it, shook hands with me, then folded his hands on the desk exactly where they had been when I came in. His eyes drooped slowly and he appeared to fall asleep.

The incident for him was over. Half-way to the door I shot a glance back at him. His eyes were closed and he breathed softly and regularly, blowing a little with his lips at the end of each breath. His bald head shone.

I went out of the Hotel Sans Souci and crossed the street to my car. It looked too easy. It looked much too easy.

5

1644 West 54th Place was a dried-out brown house with a dried-out brown lawn in front of it. There was a large bare patch around a tough-looking palm tree. On the porch stood one lonely wooden rocker, and the afternoon breeze made the unpruned shoots of last year's poinsettias tap-tap against the cracked stucco wall. A line of stiff yellowish half-washed clothes jittered on a rusty wire in the side yard.

I drove on a quarter block, parked my car across the street and walked back.

The bell didn't work so I rapped on the wooden margin of the screen door. Slow steps shuffled and the door opened and I was looking into dimness at a blowsy woman who was blowing her nose as she opened the door. Her face was grey and puffy. She had weedy hair of that vague colour which is neither brown nor blonde, that hasn't enough life in it to be ginger, and isn't clean enough to be grey. Her body was thick in a shapeless outing flannel bathrobe many moons past colour and design. It was just something around her body. Her toes were large and obvious in a pair of man's slippers of scuffed brown leather.

I said: 'Mrs Florian? Mrs Jessie Florian?'

'Uh-huh,' the voice dragged itself out of her throat like a sick man getting out of bed.

'You are the Mrs Florian whose husband once ran a place of entertainment on Central Avenue? Mike Florian?'

She thumbed a wick of hair past her large ear. Her eyes glittered with surprise. Her heavy clogged voice said:

'Wha—what? My goodness sakes alive. Mike's been gone these five years. Who did you say you was?'

The screen door was still shut and hooked.

'I'm a detective,' I said. 'I'd like a little information.'

She stared at me a long dreary minute. Then with effort she unhooked the door and turned away from it.

'Come on in then. I ain't had time to get cleaned up yet,' she whined. 'Cops, huh?'

I stepped through the door and hooked the screen again. A large handsome cabinet radio droned to the left of the door in the corner of the room. It was the only decent piece of furniture the place had. It looked brand new. Everything else was junk—dirty overstuffed pieces, a wooden rocker that matched the one on the porch, a square arch into a dining-room with a stained table, finger marks all over the swing door to the kitchen beyond. A couple of frayed lamps with once gaudy shades that were now as gay as superannuated streetwalkers.

The woman sat down in the rocker and flopped her slippers and looked at me. I looked at the radio and sat down on the end of a davenport. She saw me looking at it. A bogus heartiness, as weak as a Chinaman's tea, moved into her face and voice. 'All the comp'ny I got,' she said. Then she tittered. 'Mike ain't done nothing new, has he? I don't get cops calling on me much.'

Her titter contained a loose alcoholic overtone. I leaned back against something hard, felt for it and brought up an empty quart gin bottle. The woman tittered again.

'A joke that was,' she said. 'But I hope to Christ they's enough cheap blondes where he is. He never got enough of them here.'

'I was thinking more about a redhead,' I said.

'I guess he could use a few of them too.' Her eyes, it seemed to me, were not so vague now. 'I don't call to mind. Any special redhead?'

'Yes. A girl named Velma. I don't know what last name she used except that it wouldn't be her real one. I'm trying to trace her for her folks. Your place on Central is a coloured place now, although they haven't changed the name, and of course the people there never heard of her. So I thought of you.'

'Her folks taken their time getting around to it—looking for her,' the woman said thoughtfully.

'There's a little money involved. Not much. I guess they have to get her in order to touch it. Money sharpens the memory.'

'So does liquor,' the woman said. 'Kind of hot to-day, ain't it? You said you was a copper though.' Cunning eyes, steady attentive face. The feet in the man's slippers didn't move.

I held up the dead soldier and shook it. Then I threw it to one side and reached back on my hip for the pint of bond bourbon the negro hotel clerk and I had barely tapped. I held it out on my knee. The woman's eyes became fixed in an incredulous stare. Then suspicion climbed all over her face, like a kitten, but not so playfully.

'You ain't no copper,' she said softly. 'No copper ever bought a drink of that stuff. What's the gag, mister?'

She blew her nose again, on one of the dirtiest handkerchiefs I ever saw.

Her eyes stayed on the bottle. Suspicion fought with thirst, and thirst was winning. It always does.

'This Velma was an entertainer, a singer. You wouldn't know her? I don't suppose you went there much.'

Seaweed-coloured eyes stayed on the bottle. A coated tongue coiled on her lips.

'Man, that's liquor,' she sighed. 'I don't give a damn who you are. Just hold it careful, mister. This ain't no time to drop anything.'

She got up and waddled out of the room and came back with two thick smeared glasses.

'No fixin's. Just what you brought is all,' she said.

I poured her a slug that would have made me float over a wall. She reached for it hungrily and put it down her throat like an aspirin tablet and looked at the bottle. I poured her another and a smaller one for me. She took it over to her rocker. Her eyes had turned two shades browner already.

'Man, this stuff dies painless with me,' she said and sat down. 'It never knows what hit it. What was we talkin' about?'

'A redhaired girl named Velma who used to work in your place on Central Avenue.'

'Yeah.' She used her second drink. I went over and stood the bottle on an end beside her. She reached for it. 'Yeah. Who you say you was?'

I took out a card and gave it to her. She read it with her tongue and lips, dropped it on a table beside her and set her empty glass on it.

'Oh, a private guy. You ain't said that, mister.' She waggled a finger at me with gay reproach. 'But your liquor says you're an all right guy at that. Here's to crime.' She poured a third drink for herself and drank it down.

I sat down and rolled a cigarette around in my fingers and waited. She either knew something or she didn't. If she knew something, she either would tell me or she wouldn't. It was that simple.

'Cute little redhead,' she said slowly and thickly. 'Yeah, I remember her. Song and dance. Nice legs and generous with 'em. She went off somewheres. How would I know what them tramps do?'

'Well, I didn't really think you would know,' I said. 'But it was natural to come and ask you, Mrs Florian. Help yourself to the whisky—I could run out for more when we need it.'

'You ain't drinkin',' she said suddenly.

I put my hand around my glass and swallowed what was in it slowly to make it seem more than it was.

'Where's her folks at?' she asked suddenly.

'What does that matter?'

'Okey,' she sneered. 'All cops is the same. Okey, handsome. A guy that buys me a drink is a pal.' She reached for the bottle and set up Number 4. 'I shouldn't ought to barter with you. But when I like a guy, the ceiling's the limit.' She simpered. She was as cute as a washtub. 'Hold on to your chair and don't step on no snakes,' she said. 'I got me an idea.'

She got up out of the rocker, sneezed, almost lost the bath-robe, slapped it back against her stomach and stared at me coldly.

'No peekin',' she said, and went out of the room again, hitting the door frame with her shoulder.

I heard her fumbling steps going into the back part of the house.

The poinsettia shoots tap-tapped dully against the front wall. The clothes line creaked vaguely at the side of the house. The ice cream peddler went by ringing his bell. The big new handsome radio in the corner whispered of dancing and love with a deep soft throbbing note like the catch in a torch singer's voice.

Then from the back of the house there were various types of crashing sounds. A chair seemed to fall over backwards, a bureau drawer was pulled out too far and crashed to the floor, there was fumbling and thudding and muttered thick language. Then the slow click of a lock and the squeak of a trunk top going up. More fumbling and banging. A tray landed on the floor. I got up from the davenport and sneaked into the dining-room and from that into a short hall. I looked around the edge of an open door.

She was in there swaying in front of the trunk, making grabs at what was in it, and then throwing her hair back over her forehead with anger. She was drunker than she thought. She leaned down and steadied herself on the trunk and coughed and sighed. Then she went down on her thick knees and plunged both hands into the trunk and groped.

They came up holding something unsteadily. A thick package tied with faded pink tape. Slowly, clumsily, she undid the tape. She slipped an envelope out of the package and leaned down again to thrust the envelope out of sight into the right-hand side of the trunk. She retied the tape with fumbling fingers.

I sneaked back the way I had come and sat down on the davenport. Breathing stertorous noises, the woman came back into the living-room and stood swaying in the doorway with the tape-tied package.

She grinned at me triumphantly, tossed the package and it fell somewhere near my feet. She waddled back to the rocker and sat down and reached for the whisky.

I picked the package off the floor and untied the faded pink tape.

'Look 'em over,' the woman grunted. 'Photos. Newspaper stills. Not that them tramps ever got in no newspapers except by way of the police blotter. People from the joint they are. They're all the bastard left me—them and his old clothes.'

I leafed through the bunch of shiny photographs of men and women in professional poses. The men had sharp foxy faces and racetrack clothes or eccentric clown-like make-up. Hoofers and comics from the filling station circuit. Not many of them would ever get west of Main Street. You would find them in tank town vaudeville acts, cleaned up, or down in the cheap burlesque houses, as dirty as the law allowed and once in a while just enough dirtier for a raid and a noisy police court trial, and then back in their shows again, grinning, sadistically filthy and as rank as the smell of stale sweat. The women had good legs and displayed their inside curves more than Will Hays would have liked. But their faces were as threadbare as a book-keeper's office cat. Blondes, brunettes, large cow-like eyes with a peasant dullness in them. Small sharp eyes with urchin greed in them. One or two of the faces obviously vicious. One or two of them might have had red hair. You couldn't tell from the photographs. I looked them over casually, without interest and tied the tape again.

'I wouldn't know any of these,' I said. 'Why am I looking at them?'

She leered over the bottle her right hand was grappling with unsteadily. 'Ain't you looking for Velma?'

'Is she one of these?'

Thick cunning played on her face, had no fun there and went somewhere else. 'Ain't you got a photo of her—from her folks?'

'No.'

That troubled her. Every girl has a photo somewhere, if it's only in short dresses with a bow in her hair. I should have had it.

'I ain't beginnin' to like you again,' the woman said almost quietly.

I stood up with my glass and went over and put it down beside hers on the end table.

'Pour me a drink before you kill the bottle.'

She reached for the glass and I turned and walked swiftly through the square arch into the dining-room, into the hall, into the cluttered bedroom with the open trunk and the spilled tray. A voice shouted behind me. I plunged ahead down into the right side of the trunk, felt an envelope and brought it up swiftly.

She was out of her chair when I got back to the living-room, but she had only taken two or three steps. Her eyes had a peculiar glassiness. A murderous glassiness.

'Sit down,' I snarled at her deliberately. 'You're not dealing with a simple-minded lug like Moose Malloy this time.'

It was a shot more or less in the dark, and it didn't hit anything. She blinked twice and tried to lift her nose with her upper lip. Some dirty teeth showed in a rabbit leer.

'Moose? The Moose? What about him?' she gulped.

'He's loose,' I said. 'Out of jail. He's wandering, with a forty-five gun in his hand. He killed a nigger over on Central this morning because he wouldn't tell him where Velma was. Now he's looking for the fink that turned him up eight years ago.'

A white look smeared the woman's face. She pushed the bottle against her lips and gurgled at it. Some of the whisky ran down her chin.

'And the cops are looking for *him*,' she said and laughed. 'Cops. Yah!'

A lovely old woman. I liked being with her. I liked getting her drunk for my own sordid purposes. I was a swell guy. I enjoyed being me. You find almost anything under your hand in my business, but I was beginning to be a little sick at my stomach.

I opened the envelope my hand was clutching and drew out a glazed still. It was like the others but it was different, much nicer. The girl wore a Pierrot costume from the waist up. Under the white conical hat with a black pompon on the top, her fluffed-out hair had a dark tinge that might have been red. The face was in profile but the visible eye seemed to have gaiety in it. I wouldn't say the face was lovely and unspoiled, I'm not that good at faces. But it was pretty. People had been nice to that face, or nice enough for their circle. Yet it was a very ordinary face and its prettiness was strictly assembly line. You would see a dozen faces like it on a city block in the noon hour.

Below the waist the photo was mostly legs and very nice legs at that. It was signed across the lower right-hand corner: 'Always yours—Velma Valento.'

I held it up in front of the Florian woman, out of her reach. She lunged but came short.

'Why hide it?' I asked.

She made no sound except thick breathing. I slipped the photo back into the envelope and the envelope into my pocket.

'Why hide it?' I asked again. 'What makes it different from the others? Where is she?'

'She's dead,' the woman said. 'She was a good kid, but she's dead, copper. Beat it.'

The tawny mangled brows worked up and down. Her hand opened and the whisky bottle slid to the carpet and began to gurgle. I bent to pick it up. She tried to kick me in the face. I stepped away from her.

'And that still doesn't say why you hid it,' I told her. 'When did she die? How?'

'I am a poor sick old woman,' she grunted. 'Get away from me, you son of a bitch.'

I stood there looking at her, not saying anything, not thinking of anything particular to say. I stepped over to her side after a moment and put the flat bottle, now almost empty, on the table at her side.

She was staring down at the carpet. The radio droned pleasantly in the corner. A car went by outside. A fly buzzed in a window. After a long time she moved one lip over the other and spoke to the floor, a meaningless jumble of words from which nothing emerged. Then she laughed and threw her head back and drooled. Then her right hand reached for the bottle and it rattled against her teeth as she drained it. When it was empty she held it up and shook it and threw it at me. It went off in the corner somewhere, skidding along the carpet and bringing up with a thud against the baseboard.

She leered at me once more, then her eyes closed and she began to snore.

It might have been an act, but I didn't care. Suddenly I had enough of the scene, too much of it, far too much of it.

I picked my hat off the davenport and went over to the door and opened it and went out past the screen. The radio still droned in the corner and the woman still snored gently in her chair. I threw a quick look back at her before I closed the door, then shut it, opened it again silently and looked again.

Her eyes were still shut but something gleamed below the lids. I went down the steps, along the cracked walk to the street.

In the next house a window curtain was drawn aside and a narrow intent face was close to the glass, peering, an old woman's face with white hair and a sharp nose.

Old Nosey checking up on the neighbours. There's always at least one like her to the block. I waved a hand at her. The curtain fell.

I went back to my car and got into it and drove back to the 77th Street Division, and climbed upstairs to Nulty's smelly little cubbyhole of an office on the second floor.

6

Nulty didn't seem to have moved. He sat in his chair in the same attitude of sour patience. But there were two more cigar stubs in his ash-tray and the floor was a little thicker in burnt matches.

I sat down at the vacant desk and Nulty turned over a photo that was lying face down on his desk and handed it to me. It was a police mug, front and profile, with a fingerprint classification underneath. It was Malloy all right, taken in a strong light, and looking as if he had no more eyebrows than a French roll.

'That's the boy.' I passed it back.

'We got a wire from Oregon State pen on him,' Nulty said. 'All time served except his copper. Things look better. We got him cornered. A prowl car was talking to a conductor the end of the Seventh Street line. The conductor mentioned a guy that size, looking like that. He got off Third and Alexandria. What he'll do is break into some big house where the folks are away. Lots of 'em there, old-fashioned places too far downtown now and hard to rent. He'll break in one and we got him bottled. What you been doing?'

'Was he wearing a fancy hat and white golf balls on his jacket?'

Nulty frowned and twisted his hands on his kneecaps. 'No, a blue suit. Maybe brown.'

'Sure it wasn't a sarong?'

'Huh? Oh yeah, funny. Remind me to laugh on my day off.'

I said: 'That wasn't the Moose. He wouldn't ride a street car. He had money. Look at the clothes he was wearing. He couldn't wear stock sizes. They must have been made to order.'

'Okey, ride me,' Nulty scowled. 'What you been doing?'

'What you ought to have done. This place called Florian's was under the same name when it was a white night trap. I talked to a negro hotel-man who knows the neighbourhood. The sign was expensive so the shines just went on using it when they took over. The man's name was Mike Florian. He's dead some years, but his widow is still around. She lives at 1644 West 54th Place. Her name is Jessie Florian. She's not in the phone book, but she is in the city directory.'

'Well, what do I do—date her up?' Nulty asked.

'I did it for you. I took in a pint of bourbon with me. She's a charming middle-aged lady with a face like a bucket of mud and if she has washed her hair since Coolidge's second term, I'll eat my spare tyre, rim and all.'

'Skip the wisecracks,' Nulty said.

'I asked Mrs Florian about Velma. You remember, Mr Nulty, the redhead named Velma that Moose Malloy was looking for? I'm not tiring you, am I, Mr Nulty?'

'What you sore about?'

'You wouldn't understand. Mrs Florian said she didn't remember Velma. Her home is very shabby except for a new radio, worth seventy or eighty dollars.'

'You ain't told me why that's something I should start screaming about.'

'Mrs Florian—Jessie to me—said her husband left her nothing but his old clothes and a bunch of stills of the gang who worked at his joint from time to time. I plied her with liquor and she is a girl who will take a drink if she had to knock you down to get the bottle. After the third or fourth she went into her modest bedroom and threw things around and dug the bunch of stills out of the bottom of an old trunk. But I was watching her without her knowing it and she slipped one out of the packet and hid it. So after a while I snuck in there and grabbed it.'

I reached into my pocket and laid the Pierrot girl on his desk. He lifted it and stared at it and his lips quirked at the corners.

'Cute,' he said. 'Cute enough. I could of used a piece of that once. Haw, haw. Velma Valento, huh? What happened to this doll?'

'Mrs Florian says she died—but that hardly explains why she hid the photo.'

'It don't do at that. Why did she hide it?'

'She wouldn't tell me. In the end, after I told her about the Moose being out, she seemed to take a dislike to me. That seems impossible, doesn't it?'

'Go on,' Nulty said.

'That's all. I've told you the facts and given you the exhibit. If you can't get somewhere on this set-up, nothing I could say would help.'

'Where would I get? It's still a shine killing. Wait'll we get the Moose. Hell, it's eight years since he saw the girl unless she visited him in the pen.'

'All right,' I said. 'But don't forget he's looking for her and he's a man who would bear down. By the way, he was in for a bank job. That means a reward. Who got it?'

'I don't know,' Nulty said. 'Maybe I could find out. Why?'

'Somebody turned him up. Maybe he knows who. That would be another job he would give time to.' I stood up. 'Well, good-bye and good luck.'

'You walking out on me?'

I went over to the door. 'I have to go home and take a bath and gargle my throat and get my nails manicured.'

'You ain't sick, are you?'

'Just dirty,' I said. 'Very, very dirty.'

'Well, what's your hurry? Sit down a minute.' He leaned back and hooked his thumbs in his vest, which made him look a little more like a cop, but didn't make him look any more magnetic.

'No hurry,' I said. 'No hurry at all. There's nothing more I can do. Apparently this Velma is dead, if Mrs Florian is telling the truth—and I don't at the moment know of any reason why she should lie about it. That was all I was interested in.'

'Yeah,' Nulty said suspiciously—from force of habit.

'And you have Moose Malloy all sewed up anyway, and that's that. So I'll just run on home now and go about the business of trying to earn a living.'

'We might miss out on the Moose,' Nulty said. 'Guys get away once in a while. Even big guys.' His eyes were suspicious also, in so far as they contained any expression at all. 'How much she slip you?'

'What?'

'How much this old lady slip you to lay off?'

'Lay off what?'

'Whatever it is you're layin' off from now on.' He moved his thumbs from his armholes and placed them together in front of his vest and pushed them against each other. He smiled.

'Oh, for Christ's sake,' I said, and went out of the office, leaving his mouth open.

When I was about a yard from the door, I went back and opened it again quietly and looked in. He was sitting in the same position, pushing his thumbs at each other. But he wasn't smiling any more. He looked worried.

His mouth was still open.

He didn't move or look up. I didn't know whether he heard me or not. I shut the door again and went away.

7

They had Rembrandt on the calendar that year, a rather smeary self-portrait due to imperfectly registered colour plates. It showed him holding a smeared palette with a dirty thumb and wearing a tam-o'-shanter which wasn't any too clean either. His other hand held a brush poised in the air, as if he might be going to do a little work after a while, if somebody made a down payment. His face was ageing, saggy, full of the disgust of life and the thickening effects of liquor. But it had a hard cheerfulness that I liked, and the eyes were as bright as drops of dew.

I was looking at him across my office desk at about four-thirty when the phone rang and I heard a cool, supercilious voice that sounded as if it thought it was pretty good. It said drawlingly, after I had answered:

'You are Philip Marlowe, a private detective?'

'Check.'

'Oh—you mean, yes. You have been recommended to me as a man who can be trusted to keep his mouth shut. I should like you to come to my house at seven o'clock this evening. We can discuss a matter. My name is Lindsay Marriott and I live at 4212 Cabrillo Street, Montemar Vista. Do you know where that is?'

'I know where Montemar Vista is, Mr Marriott.'

'Yes. Well, Cabrillo Street is rather hard to find. The streets down here are all laid out in a pattern of interesting but intricate curves. I should suggest that you walk up the steps from the sidewalk café. If you do that, Cabrillo is the third street you come to and my house is the only one on the block. At seven then?'

'What is the nature of the employment, Mr Marriott?'

'I should prefer not to discuss that over the phone.'

'Can't you give me some idea? Montemar Vista is quite a distance.'

'I shall be glad to pay your expenses, if we don't agree. Are you particular about the nature of the employment?'

'Not as long as it's legitimate.'

The voice grew icicles. 'I should not have called you, if it were not.'

A Harvard boy. Nice use of the subjunctive mood. The end of my foot itched, but my bank account was still trying to crawl under a duck. I put honey into my voice and said: 'Many thanks for calling me, Mr Marriott. I'll be there.'

He hung up and that was that. I thought Mr Rembrandt had a faint sneer on his face. I got the office bottle out of the deep drawer of the desk and took a short drink. That took the sneer out of Mr Rembrandt in a hurry.

A wedge of sunlight slipped over the edge of the desk and fell noiselessly to the carpet. Traffic lights bong-bonged outside on the boulevard, interurban cars pounded by, a typewriter clacked monotonously in the lawyer's office beyond the party wall. I had just filled and lit a pipe when the telephone rang again.

It was Nulty this time. His voice sounded full of baked potato. 'Well, I guess I ain't quite bright at that,' he said, when he knew who he was talking to. 'I miss one. Malloy went to see that Florian dame.'

I held the phone tight enough to crack it. My upper lip suddenly felt a little cold. 'Go on. I thought you had him cornered.'

'Was some other guy. Malloy ain't around there at all. We got a call from some old window-peeker on West Fifty-four. Two guys was to see the Florian dame. Number One parked the other side of the street and acted kind of cagey. Looked the dump over good before he went in. Was in about an hour. Six feet, dark hair, medium heavy built. Come out quiet.'

'He had liquor on his breath too,' I said.

'Oh, sure. That was you, wasn't it? Well, Number Two was the Moose. Guy in loud clothes as big as a house. He come in a car too but the old lady don't get the licence, can't read the number that far off. This was about a hour after you was there, she says. He goes in fast and is in about five minutes only. Just before he gets back in his car he takes a big gat out and spins the chamber. I guess that's what the old lady saw he done. That's why she calls up. She don't hear no shots though, inside the house.'

'That must have been a big disappointment,' I said.

'Yeah. A nifty. Remind me to laugh on my day off. The old lady misses one too. The prowl boys go down there and don't get no answer on the door, so they walk in, the front door not being locked. Nobody's dead on the floor. Nobody's home. The Florian dame has skipped out. So they stop by next door and tell the old lady and she's sore as a boil on account of she didn't see the Florian dame go out. So they report back and go on about the job. So about an hour, maybe hour and a half after that, the old lady phones in again and says Mrs Florian is home again. So they give the call to me and I ask her what makes that important and she hangs up in my face.'

Nulty paused to collect a little breath and wait for my comments. I didn't have any. After a moment he went on grumbling.

'What you make of it?'

'Nothing much. The Moose would be likely to go by there, of course. He must have known Mrs Florian pretty well. Naturally he wouldn't stick around very long. He would be afraid the law might be wise to Mrs Florian.'

'What I figure,' Nulty said calmly, 'Maybe I should go over and see her—kind of find out where she went to.'

'That's a good idea,' I said. 'If you can get somebody to lift you out of your chair.'

'Huh? Oh, another nifty. It don't make a lot of difference any more now though. I guess I won't bother.'

'All right,' I said. 'Let's have it whatever it is.'

He chuckled. 'We got Malloy all lined up. We really got him this time. We make him at Girard, headed north in a rented hack. He gassed up there and the service station kid recognized him from the description we broadcast a while back. He said everything jibed except Malloy had changed to a dark suit. We got county and state law on it. If he goes on north we get him at the Ventura line, and if he slides over to the Ridge Route, he has to stop at Castaic for his check ticket. If he don't stop, they phone ahead and block the road. We don't want no cop shot up, if we can help it. That sound good?'

'It sounds all right,' I said. 'If it really is Malloy, and if he does exactly what you expect him to do.'

Nulty cleared his throat carefully. 'Yeah. What you doing on it–just in case?'

'Nothing. Why should I be doing anything on it?'

'You got along pretty good with that Florian dame. Maybe she would have some more ideas.'

'All you need to find out is a full bottle,' I said.

'You handled her real nice. Maybe you ought to kind of spend a little more time on her.'

'I thought this was a police job.'

'Oh, sure. Was your idea about the girl though.'

'That seems to be out–unless the Florian is lying about it.'

'Dames lie about anything–just for practice,' Nulty said grimly. 'You ain't real busy, huh?'

'I've got a job to do. It came in since I saw you. A job where I get paid. I'm sorry.'

'Walking out, huh?'

'I wouldn't put it that way. I just have to work to earn a living.'

'Okey, pal. If that's the way you feel about it, okey.'

'I don't feel any way about it,' I almost yelled. 'I just don't have time to stooge for you or any other cop.'

'Okey, get sore,' Nulty said, and hung up.

I held the dead phone and snarled into it: 'Seventeen hundred and fifty cops in this town and they want me to do their leg work for them.'

I dropped the phone into its cradle and took another drink from the office bottle.

After a while I went down to the lobby of the building to buy an evening paper. Nulty was right in one thing at least. The Montgomery killing hadn't even made the want-ad section so far.

I left the office again in time for an early dinner.

8

I got down to Montemar Vista as the light began to fade, but there was still a fine sparkle on the water and the surf was breaking far out in long smooth curves. A group of pelicans was flying bomber formation just under the creaming lip of the waves. A lonely yacht was taking in toward the yacht harbour at Bay City. Beyond it the huge emptiness of the Pacific was purple-grey.

Montemar Vista was a few dozen houses of various sizes and shapes hanging by their teeth and eyebrows to a spur of mountain and looking as if a good sneeze would drop them down among the box lunches on the beach.

Above the beach the highway ran under a wide concrete arch which was in fact a pedestrian bridge. From the inner end of this a flight of concrete steps with a thick galvanized handrail on one side ran straight as a ruler up the side of the mountain. Beyond the arch the sidewalk café my client had spoken of was bright and cheerful inside, but the iron-legged tile-topped tables outside under the striped awning were empty save for a single dark woman in slacks who smoked and stared moodily out to sea, with a bottle of beer in front of her. A fox terrier was using one of the iron chairs for a lamp-post. She chided the dog absently as I drove past and gave the sidewalk café my business to the extent of using its parking space.

I walked back through the arch and started up the steps. It was a nice walk if you liked grunting. There were two hundred and eighty steps up to Cabrillo Street. They were drifted over with windblown sand and the handrail was as cold and wet as a toad's belly.

When I reached the top the sparkle had gone from the water and a seagull with a broken trailing leg was twisting against the offsea breeze. I sat down on the damp cold top step and shook the sand out of my shoes and waited for my pulse to come down into the low hundreds. When I was breathing more or less normally again I shook my shirt loose from my back and went along to the lighted house which was the only one within yelling distance of the steps.

It was a nice little house with a salt-tarnished spiral of staircase going up to the front door and an imitation coach-lamp for a porch light. The garage was underneath and to one side. Its door was lifted up and rolled back and the light of the porch-lamp shone obliquely on a huge black battleship of a car with chromium trimmings, a coyote tail tied to the Winged Victory on the radiator cap and engraved initials where the emblem should be. The car had a right-hand drive and looked as if it had cost more than the house.

I went up the spiral steps, looked for a bell, and used a knocker in the shape of a tiger's head. Its clatter was swallowed in the early evening fog. I heard no steps in the house. My damp shirt felt like an icepack on my back. The door opened silently, and I was looking at a tall blond man in a white flannel suit with a violet satin scarf around his neck.

There was a cornflower in the lapel of his white coat and his pale blue eyes looked faded out by comparison. The violet scarf was loose enough to show that he wore no tie and that he had a thick, soft brown neck, like the neck of a strong woman. His features were a little on the heavy side, but handsome; he had an inch more of height than I had, which made him six feet one. His blond hair was arranged, by art or nature, in three precise blond ledges which reminded me of steps, so that I didn't like them. I wouldn't have liked them anyway. Apart from all this he had the general appearance of a lad who would wear a white flannel suit with a violet scarf round his neck and a cornflower in his lapel.

He cleared his throat lightly and looked past my shoulder at the darkening sea. His cool supercilious voice said: 'Yes?'

'Seven o'clock,' I said. 'On the dot.'

'Oh yes. Let me see, your name is—' he paused and frowned in the effort of memory. The effect was as phony as the pedigree of a used car. I let him work at it for a minute, then I said:

'Philip Marlowe. The same as it was this afternoon.'

He gave me a quick darting frown, as if perhaps something ought to be done about that. Then he stepped back and said coldly:

'Ah yes. Quite so. Come in, Marlowe. My houseboy is away this evening.'

He opened the door wide with a fingertip, as though opening the door himself dirtied him a little.

I went in past him and smelled perfume. He closed the door. The entrance put us on a low balcony with a metal railing that ran around three sides of a big studio living-room. The fourth side contained a big fireplace and two doors. A fire was crackling in the fireplace. The balcony was lined with bookshelves and there were pieces of glazed metallic-looking bits of sculpture on pedestals.

We went down three steps to the main part of the living-room. The carpet almost tickled my ankles. There was a concert grand piano, closed down. On one corner of it stood a tall silver vase on a strip of peach-coloured velvet, and a single yellow rose in the vase. There was plenty of nice soft furniture, a great many floor cushions, some with golden tassels and some just naked. It was a nice room, if you didn't get rough. There was a wide damask-covered divan in a shadowy corner, like a casting couch. It was the kind of room where people sit with their feet in their laps and sip absinthe through lumps of sugar and talk with high affected voices and sometimes just squeak. It was a room where anything could happen except work.

Mr Lindsay Marriott arranged himself in the curve of the grand piano, leaned over to sniff at the yellow rose, then opened a French enamel cigarette case and lit a long brown cigarette with a gold tip. I sat down on a pink chair and hoped I wouldn't leave a mark on it. I lit a Camel, blew smoke through my nose and looked at a piece of black shiny metal on a stand. It showed a full, smooth curve with shallow fold in it and two protuberances on the curve. I stared at it. Marriott saw me staring at it.

'An interesting bit,' he said negligently, 'I picked it up just the other day. Asta Dial's *Spirit of Dawn.*'

'I thought it was Klopstein's *Two Warts on a Fanny,*' I said.

Mr Lindsay Marriott's face looked as if he had swallowed a bee. He smoothed it out with an effort.

'You have a somewhat peculiar sense of humour,' he said.

'Not peculiar,' I said. 'Just uninhibited.'

'Yes,' he said very coldly. 'Yes—of course. I've no doubt. . . . Well, what I wished to see you about is, as a matter of fact, a very slight matter indeed. Hardly worth bringing you down here for. I am meeting a couple of men to-night and paying them some money. I thought I might as well have someone with me. You carry a gun?'

'At times. Yes,' I said. I looked at the dimple in his broad, fleshy chin. You could have lost a marble in it.

'I shan't want you to carry that. Nothing of that sort at all. This is a purely business transaction.'

'I hardly ever shoot anybody,' I said. 'A matter of blackmail?'

He frowned. 'Certainly not. I'm not in the habit of giving people grounds for blackmail.'

'It happens to the nicest people. I might say particularly to the nicest people.'

He waved his cigarette. His aquamarine eyes had a faintly thoughtful expression, but his lips smiled. The kind of smile that goes with a silk noose.

He blew some more smoke and tilted his head back. This accentuated the soft firm lines of his throat. His eyes came down slowly and studied me.

'I'm meeting these men—most probably—in a rather lonely place. I don't know where yet. I expect a call giving me the particulars. I have to be ready to leave at once. It won't be very far away from here. That's the under-standing.'

'You've been making this deal some time?'

'Three or four days, as a matter of fact.'

'You left your bodyguard problem until pretty late.'

He thought that over. He snicked some dark ash from his cigarette. 'That's true. I had some difficulty making my mind up. It would be better for me to go alone, although nothing has been said definitely about my having someone with me. On the other hand I'm not much of a hero.'

'They know you by sight, of course?'

'I–I'm not sure. I shall be carrying a large amount of money and it is not my money. I'm acting for a friend. I shouldn't feel justified in letting it out of my possession, of course.'

I snubbed out my cigarette and leaned back in the pink chair and twiddled my thumbs. 'How much money–and what for?'

'Well, really—' it was a fairly nice smile now, but I still didn't like it. 'I can't go into that.'

'You just want me to go along and hold your hat?'

His hand jerked again and some ash fell off on his white cuff. He shook it off and stared down at the place where it had been.

'I'm afraid I don't like your manner,' he said, using the edge of his voice.

'I've had complaints about it,' I said. 'But nothing seems to do any good. Let's look at this job a little. You want a bodyguard, but he can't wear a gun. You want a helper, but he isn't supposed to know what he's supposed to do. You want me to risk my neck without knowing why or what for or what the risk is. What are you offering for all this?'

'I hadn't really got around to thinking about it.' His cheekbones were dusky red.

'Do you suppose you could get around to thinking about it?'

He leaned forward gracefully and smiled between his teeth. 'How would you like a swift punch on the nose?'

I grinned and stood up and put my hat on. I started across the carpet towards the front door, but not very fast.

His voice snapped at my back. 'I'm offering you a hundred dollars for a few hours of your time. If that isn't enough, say so. There's no risk. Some jewels were taken from a friend of mine in a hold-up–and I'm buying them back. Sit down and don't be so touchy.'

I went back to the pink chair and sat down again.

'All right,' I said. 'Let's hear about it.'

We stared at each other for all of ten seconds. 'Have you ever heard of Fei Tsui jade?' he asked slowly, and lit another of his dark cigarettes.

'No.'

'It's the only really valuable kind. Other kinds are valuable to some extent for the material, but chiefly for the workmanship on them. Fei Tsui is valuable in itself. All known deposits were exhausted hundreds of years ago. A friend of mine owns a necklace of sixty beads of about six carats each, intricately carved. Worth eighty or ninety thousand dollars. The Chinese Government has a very slightly larger one valued at a hundred and twenty-five thousand. My friend's necklace was taken in a hold-up a few nights ago. I was present, but quite helpless. I had driven my friend to an evening party and later to the Trocadero and we were on our way back to her home from there. A car brushed the left front fender and stopped, as I thought, to apologize. Instead of that it was a very quick and very neat hold-up. Either three or four men, I really saw only two, but I'm sure another stayed in the car behind the wheel, and I thought I saw a glimpse of still a fourth at the rear window. My friend was wearing the jade necklace. They took that and two rings and a bracelet. The one who seemed to be the leader looked the things over without any apparent hurry under a small flashlight. Then he handed one of the rings back and said that would give us an idea what kind of people we were dealing with and to wait for a phone call before reporting to the police or the insurance company. So we obeyed their instructions. There's plenty of that sort of thing going on, of course. You keep the affair to yourself and pay ransom, or you never see your jewels again. If they're fully insured, perhaps you don't mind, but if they happen to be rare pieces, you would rather pay ransom.'

I nodded. 'And this jade necklace is something that can't be picked up every day.'

He slid a finger along the polished surface of the piano with a dreamy expression, as if touching smooth things pleased him.

'Very much so. It's irreplaceable. She shouldn't have worn it out—ever. But she's a reckless sort of woman. The other things were good but ordinary.

'Uh-huh. How much are you paying?'

'Eight thousand dollars. It's dirt cheap. But if my friend couldn't get another like it, these thugs couldn't very easily dispose of it either. It's probably known to everyone in the trade, all over the country.'

'This friend of yours—does she have a name?'

'I'd prefer not to mention it at the moment.'

'What are the arrangements?'

He looked at me along his pale eyes. I thought he seemed a bit scared, but I didn't know him very well. Maybe it was a hangover. The hand that held the dark cigarette couldn't keep still.

'We have been negotiating by telephone for several days—through me. Everything is settled except the time and place of meeting. It is to be some time to-night. I shall presently be getting a call to tell me of that. It will not be very far away, they say, and I must be prepared to leave at once. I suppose this is so that no plant could be arranged. With the police, I mean.'

'Uh-huh. Is the money marked? I suppose it *is* money?'

'Currency, of course. Twenty-dollar bills. No, why should it be marked?'

'It can be done so that it takes black light to detect it. No reason—except that the cops like to break up these gangs—if they can get any co-operation. Some of the money might turn up on some lad with a record.'

He wrinkled his brow thoughtfully. 'I'm afraid I don't know what black light is.'

'Ultra-violet. It makes certain metallic inks glisten in the dark. I could get it done for you.'

'I'm afraid there isn't time for that now,' he said shortly.

'That's one of the things that worries me.'

'Why?'

'Why you only called me this afternoon. Why you picked on me. Who told you about me?'

He laughed. His laugh was rather boyish, but not a very young boy.

'Well, as a matter of fact I'll have to confess I merely picked your name at random out of the phone book. You see I hadn't intended to have anyone go with me. Then this afternoon I got to thinking why not.'

I lit another of my squashed cigarettes and watched his throat muscles. 'What's the plan?'

He spread his hands. 'Simply to go where I am told, hand over the package of money, and receive back the jade necklace.'

'Uh-huh.'

'You seem fond of that expression.'

'What expression?'

'Uh-huh.'

'Where will I be—in the back of the car?'

'I suppose so. It's a big car. You could easily hide in the back of it.'

'Listen,' I said slowly. 'You plan to go out with me hidden in your car to a destination you are to get over the phone some time to-night. You will have eight grand in currency on you and with that you are supposed to buy back a jade necklace worth ten or twelve times that much. What you will probably get will be a package you won't be allowed to open—providing you get anything at all. It's just as likely they will simply take your money, count it over in some other place, and mail you the necklace, if they feel big-hearted. There's nothing to prevent them double-crossing you. Certainly nothing I could do would stop them. These are heist guys. They're tough. They might even knock you on the head—not hard—just enough to delay you while they go on their way.'

'Well, as a matter of fact, I'm a little afraid of something like that,' he said quietly, and his eyes twitched. 'I suppose that's really why I wanted somebody with me.'

'Did they put a flash on you when they pulled the stick-up?'

He shook his head, no.

'No matter. They've had a dozen chances to look you over since. They probably knew all about you before that anyway. These jobs are cased. They're cased the way a dentist cases your tooth for a gold inlay. You go out with this dame much?'

'Well—not infrequently,' he said stiffly.

'Married?'

'Look here,' he snapped. 'Suppose we leave the lady out of this entirely.'

'Okey,' I said. 'But the more I know the fewer cups I break. I ought to walk away from this job, Marriott. I really ought. If the boys want to play ball, you don't need me. If they don't want to play ball, I can't do anything about it.'

'All I want is your company,' he said quickly.

I shrugged and spread my hands. 'Okey—but I drive the car and carry the money—and you do the hiding in the back. We're about the same height. If there's any question, we'll just tell them the truth. Nothing to lose by it.'

'No.' He bit his lip.

'I'm getting a hundred dollars for doing nothing. If anybody gets conked, it ought to be me.'

He frowned and shook his head, but after quite a long time his face cleared slowly and he smiled.

'Very well,' he said slowly. 'I don't suppose it matters much. We'll be together. Would you care for a spot of brandy?'

'Uh-huh. And you might bring me my hundred bucks. I like to feel money.'

He moved away like a dancer, his body almost motionless from the waist up.

The phone rang as he was on his way out. It was in a little alcove off the living-room proper, cut into the balcony. It wasn't the call we were thinking about though. He sounded too affectionate.

He danced back after a while with a bottle of Five-Star Martell and five nice crisp twenty-dollar bills. That made it a nice evening—so far.

9

The house was very still. Far off there was a sound which might have been beating surf or cars zooming along a highway, or wind in pine trees. It was the sea, of course, breaking far down below. I sat there and listened to it and thought long, careful thoughts.

The phone rang four times within the next hour and a half. The big one came at eight minutes past ten. Marriott talked briefly, in a very low voice, cradled the instrument without a sound and stood up with a sort of hushed movement. His face looked drawn. He had changed to dark clothes now. He walked silently back into the room and poured himself a stiff drink in a brandy glass. He held it against the light a moment with a queer unhappy smile, swirled it once quickly and tilted his head back to pour it down his throat.

'Well—we're all set, Marlowe. Ready?'

'That's all I've been all evening. Where do we go?'

'A place called Purissima Canyon.'

'I never heard of it.'

'I'll get a map.' He got one and spread it out quickly and the light blinked in his brassy hair as he bent over it. Then he pointed with his finger. The place was one of the many canyons off the foothill boulevard that turns into town from the coast highway north of Bay City. I had a vague idea where it was, but no more. It seemed to be at the end of a street called Camino de la Costa.

'It will be not more than twelve minutes from here,' Marriott said quickly. 'We'd better get moving. We only have twenty minutes to play with.'

He handed me a light-coloured overcoat which made me a fine target. It fitted pretty well. I wore my own hat. I had a gun under my arm, but I hadn't told him about that.

While I put the coat on, he went on talking in a light nervous voice and dancing on his hands the thick manila envelope with the eight grand in it.

'Purissima Canyon has a sort of level shelf at the inner end of it, they say. This is walled off from the road by a white fence of four-by-fours, but you can just squeeze by. A dirt road winds down into a little hollow and we are to wait there without lights. There are no houses around.'

'We?'

'Well, I mean "I"–theoretically.'

'Oh.'

He handed me the manila envelope and I opened it up and looked at what was inside. It was money all right, a huge wad of currency. I didn't count it. I snapped the rubber around again and stuffed the packet down inside my overcoat. It almost caved in a rib.

We went to the door and Marriott switched off all the lights. He opened the front door cautiously and peered out at the foggy air. We went out and down the salt-tarnished spiral stairway to the street level and the garage.

It was a little foggy, the way it always is down there at night. I had to start up the windshield wiper for a while.

The big foreign car drove itself, but I held the wheel for the sake of appearances.

For two minutes we figure-eighted back and forth across the face of the mountain and then popped out right beside the sidewalk café. I could understand now why Marriott had told me to walk up the steps. I could have driven about in those curving, twisting streets for hours without making any more yardage than an angle-worm in a bait can.

On the highway the lights of the streaming cars made an almost solid beam in both directions. The big corn-poppers were rolling north growling as they went and festooned all over with green and yellow overhang lights. Three minutes of that and we turned inland, by a big service station, and wound along the flank of the foothills. It got quiet. There was loneliness and the smell of kelp and the smell of wild sage from the hills. A yellow window hung here and there, all by itself, like the last orange. Cars passed, spraying the pavement with cold white light, then growled off into the darkness again. Wisps of fog chased the stars down the sky.

Marriott leaned forward from the dark rear seat and said:

'Those lights off to the right are the Belvedere Beach Club. The next canyon is Las Pulgas and the next after that Purissima. We turn right at the top of the second rise.' His voice was hushed and taut.

I grunted and kept on driving. 'Keep your head down,' I said over my shoulder. 'We may be watched all the way. This car sticks out like spats at an Iowa picnic. Could be the boys don't like your being twins.'

We went down into a hollow at the inward end of a canyon and then up on the high ground and after a little while down again and up again. Then Marriott's tight voice said in my ear:

'Next street on the right. The house with the square turret. Turn beside that.'

'You didn't help them pick this place out, did you?'

'Hardly,' he said, and laughed grimly. 'I just happen to know these canyons pretty well.'

I swung the car to the right past a big corner house with a square white turret topped with round tiles. The headlights sprayed for an instant on a street sign that read: Camino de la Costa. We slid down a broad avenue lined with unfinished electroliers and weed-grown sidewalks. Some realtor's dream had turned into a hangover there. Crickets chirped and bull-frogs whooped in the darkness behind the overgrown sidewalks. Marriott's car was that silent.

There was a house to a block, then a house to two blocks, then no houses at all. A vague window or two was still lighted, but the people around there seemed to go to bed with the chickens. Then the paved avenue ended abruptly in a dirt road packed as hard as concrete in dry weather. The dirt road narrowed and dropped slowly downhill between walls of brush. The lights of the Belvedere Beach Club hung in the air to the right and far ahead there was a gleam of moving water. The acrid smell of the sage filled the night. Then a white-painted barrier loomed across the dirt road and Marriott spoke at my shoulder again.

'I don't think you can get past it,' he said. 'The space doesn't look wide enough.'

I cut the noiseless motor, dimmed the lights and sat there, listening. Nothing. I switched the lights off altogether and got out of the car. The crickets stopped chirping. For a little while the silence was so complete that I could hear the sound of tyres on the highway at the bottom of the cliffs, a mile away. Then one by one the crickets started up again until the night was full of them.

'Sit tight. I'm going down there and have a look see,' I whispered into the back of the car.

I touched the gun butt inside my coat and walked forward. There was more room between the brush and the end of the white barrier than there had seemed to be from the car. Someone had hacked the brush away and there were car marks in the dirt. Probably kids going down there to neck on warm nights. I went on past the barrier. The road dropped and curved. Below was darkness and a vague far off sea-sound. And the lights of cars on the highway. I went on. The road ended in a shallow bowl entirely surrounded by brush. It was empty. There seemed to be no way into it but the way I had come. I stood there in the silence and listened.

Minute passed slowly after minute, but I kept on waiting for some new sound. None came. I seemed to have that hollow entirely to myself.

I looked across to the lighted beach club. From its upper windows a man with a good night glass could probably cover this spot fairly well. He could see a car come and go, see who got out of it, whether there was a group of men or just one. Sitting in a dark room with a good night glass you can see a lot more detail than you would think possible.

I turned to go back up the hill. From the base of a bush a cricket chirped loud enough to make me jump. I went on up around the curve and past the white barricade. Still nothing. The black car stood dimly shining against a greyness which was neither darkness nor light. I went over to it and put a foot on the running-board beside the driver's seat.

'Looks like a tryout,' I said under my breath, but loud enough for Marriott to hear me from the back of the car. 'Just to see if you obey orders.'

There was a vague movement behind but he didn't answer. I went on trying to see something besides bushes.

Whoever it was had a nice easy shot at the back of my head. Afterwards I thought I might have heard the swish of a sap. Maybe you always think that—afterwards.

10

'Four minutes,' the voice said. 'Five, possibly six. They must have moved quick and quiet. He didn't even let out a yell.'

I opened my eyes and looked fuzzily at a cold star. I was lying on my back. I felt sick.

The voice said: 'It could have been a little longer. Maybe even eight minutes altogether. They must have been in the brush, right where the car stopped. The guy scared easily. They must have thrown a small light in his face and he passed out—just from panic. The pansy.'

There was silence. I got up on one knee. Pains shot from the back of my head clear to my ankles.

'Then one of them got into the car,' the voice said, 'and waited for you to come back. The others hid again. They must have figured he would be afraid to come alone. Or something in his voice made them suspicious, when they talked to him on the phone.'

I balanced myself woozily on the flat of my hands, listening.

'Yeah, that was about how it was,' the voice said.

It was my voice. I was talking to myself, coming out of it. I was trying to figure the thing out subconsciously.

'Shut up, you damwit,' I said, and stopped talking to myself.

Far off the purl of motors, nearer the chirp of crickets, the peculiar long drawn ee-ee-ee of tree frogs. I didn't think I was going to like those sounds any more.

I lifted a hand off the ground and tried to shake the sticky sage ooze off it, then rubbed it on the side of my coat. Nice work, for a hundred dollars. The hand jumped at the inside pocket of the overcoat. No manila envelope, naturally. The hand jumped inside my own suit coat. My wallet was still there. I wondered if my hundred was still in it. Probably not. Something felt heavy against my left ribs. The gun in the shoulder holster.

That was a nice touch. They left me my gun. A nice touch of something or other—like closing a man's eyes after you knife him.

I felt the back of my head. My hat was still on. I took it off, not without discomfort, and felt the head underneath. Good old head, I'd had it a long time. It was a little soft now, a little pulpy, and more than a little tender. But a pretty light sapping at that. The hat had helped. I could still use the head. I could use it another year anyway.

I put my right hand back on the ground and took the left off and swivelled it around until I could see my watch. The illuminated dial showed 10.56, as nearly as I could focus on it.

The call had come at 10.08. Marriott had talked maybe two minutes. Another four had got us out of the house. Time passes very slowly when you are actually doing something. I mean, you can go through a lot of movements in very few minutes. Is that what I mean? What the hell do I care what I mean? Okey, better men than me have meant less. Okey, what I mean is, that would be 10.15, say. The place was about twelve minutes away. 10.27. I get out, walk down in the hollow, spend at the most eight minutes fooling around and come on back up to get my head treated. 10.35. Give me a minute to fall down and hit the ground with my face. The reason I hit it with my face, I got my chin scraped. It hurts. It feels scraped. That way I know it's scraped. No, I can't see it. I don't have to see it. It's my chin and I know whether it's scraped or not. Maybe you want to make something of it. Okey, shut up and let me think. What with? . . .

The watch showed 10.56 p.m. That meant I had been out for twenty minutes.

Twenty minutes' sleep. Just a nice doze. In that time I had muffed a mob and lost eight thousand dollars. Well, why not? In twenty minutes you can sink a battleship, down three or four planes, hold a double execution. You can die, get married, get fired and find a new job, have a tooth pulled, have your tonsils out. In twenty minutes you can even get up in the morning. You can get a glass of water at a night-club—maybe.

Twenty minutes' sleep. That's a long time. Especially on a cold night, out in the open. I began to shiver.

I was still on my knees. The smell of the sage was beginning to bother me. The sticky ooze from which wild bees get their honey. Honey was sweet, much too sweet. My stomach took a whirl. I clamped my teeth tight and just managed to keep it down my throat. Cold sweat stood out in lumps on my forehead, but I shivered just the same. I got up on one foot, then on both feet, straightened up, wobbling a little. I felt like an amputated leg.

I turned slowly. The car was gone. The dirt road stretched empty, back up the shallow hill towards the paved street, the end of Camino de la Costa. To the left the barrier of white-painted four-by-fours stood out against the darkness. Beyond the low wall of brush the pale glow in the sky would be the lights of Bay City. And over farther to the right and near by were the lights of Belvedere Club.

I went over where the car had stood and got a fountain pen flash unclipped from my pocket and poked the little light down at the ground. The soil was red loam, very hard in dry weather, but the weather was not bone dry. There was a little fog in the air, and enough of the moisture had settled on the surface of the ground to show where the car had stood. I could see, very faint, the tread marks of the heavy ten-ply Vogue tyres. I put the light on them and bent over and the pain made my head dizzy. I started to follow the tracks. They went straight ahead for a dozen feet, then swung over to the left. They didn't turn. They went towards the gap at the left-hand end of the white barricade. Then I lost them.

I went over to the barricade and shone the little light on the brush. Fresh-broken twigs. I went through the gap, on down the curving road. The ground was still softer here. More marks of the heavy tyres. I went on down, rounded the curve and was at the edge of the hollow closed in by brush.

It was there all right, the chromium and glossy paint shining a little even in the dark, and the red reflector glass of the tail-lights shining back at the pencil flash. It was there, silent, lightless, all the doors shut. I went towards it slowly, gritting my teeth at every step. I opened one of the rear doors and put the beam of the flash inside. Empty. The front was empty too. The ignition was off. The key hung in the lock on a thin chain. No torn upholstery, no scarred glass, no blood, no bodies. Everything neat and orderly. I shut the doors and circled the car slowly, looking for a sign and not finding any.

A sound froze me.

A motor throbbed above the rim of the brush. I didn't jump more than a foot. The flash in my hand went out. A gun slid into my hand all by itself. Then headlight beams tilted up towards the sky, then tilted down again. The motor sounded like a small car. It had that contented sound that comes with moisture in the air.

The lights tilted down still more and got brighter. A car was coming down the curve of the dirt road. It came two-thirds of the way and then stopped. A spotlight clicked on and swung out to the side, held there for a long moment, went out again. The car came on down the hill. I slipped the gun out of my pocket and crouched behind the motor of Marriott's car.

A small coupé of no particular shape or colour slid into the hollow and turned so that its headlights raked the sedan from one end to the other. I got my head down in a hurry. The lights swept above me like a sword. The coupé stopped. The motor died. The headlights died. Silence. Then a door opened and a light foot touched the ground. More silence. Even the crickets were silent. Then a beam of light cut the darkness low down, parallel to the ground and only a few inches above it. The beam swept, and there was no way I could get my ankles out of it quickly enough. The beam stopped on my feet. Silence. The beam came up and raked the top of the hood again.

Then a laugh. It was a girl's laugh. Strained, taut as a mandolin wire. A strange sound in that place. The white beam shot under the car again and settled on my feet.

The voice said, not quite shrilly: 'All right, you. Come out of there with your hands up and very damned empty. You're covered.'

I didn't move.

The light wavered a little, as though the hand that held it wavered. It swept slowly along the hood once more. The voice stabbed at me again.

'Listen, stranger. I'm holding a ten-shot automatic. I can shoot straight. Both your feet are vulnerable. What do you bid?'

'Put it up—or I'll blow it out of your hand!' I snarled. My voice sounded like somebody tearing slats off a chicken coop.

'Oh—a hard-boiled gentleman.' There was a quaver in the voice, a nice little quaver. Then it hardened again. 'Coming out? I'll count three. Look at the odds I'm giving you—twelve fat cylinders, maybe sixteen. But your feet will hurt. And ankle bones take years and years to get well and sometimes they never do really—'

I straightened up slowly and looked into the beam of the flashlight.

'I talk too much when I'm scared too,' I said.

'Don't—don't move another inch! Who are you?'

I moved around the front of the car towards her. When I was six feet from the slim dark figure behind the flash I stopped. The flash glared at me steadily.

'You stay right there,' the girl snapped angrily, after I had stopped. 'Who are you?'

'Let's see your gun.'

She held it forward into the light. It was pointed at my stomach. It was a little gun, it looked like a small Colt vest pocket automatic.

'Oh, that,' I said. 'That toy. It doesn't either hold ten shots. It holds six. It's just a little bitty gun, a butterfly gun. They shoot butterflies with them. Shame on you for telling a deliberate lie like that.'

'Are you crazy?'

'Me? I've been sapped by a hold-up man. I might be a little goofy.'

'Is that—is that your car?'

'No.'

'Who are you?'

'What were you looking at back there with your spotlight?'

'I get it. You ask the answers. He-man stuff. I was looking at a man.'

'Does he have blond hair in waves?'

'Not now,' she said quietly. 'He might have had—once.'

That jarred me. Somehow I hadn't expected it. 'I didn't see him,' I said lamely. 'I was following the tyre marks with a flashlight down the hill. Is he badly hurt?' I went another step towards her. The little gun jumped at me and the flash held steady.

'Take it easy,' she said quietly. 'Very easy. Your friend is dead.'

I didn't say anything for a moment. Then I said: 'All right, let's go look at him.'

'Let's stand right here and not move and you tell me who you are and what happened.' The voice was crisp. It was not afraid. It meant what it said.

'Marlowe. Philip Marlowe. An investigator. Private.'

'That's who you are—if it's true. Prove it.'

'I'm going to take my wallet out.'

'I don't think so. Just leave your hands where they happen to be. We'll skip the proof for the time being. What's your story?'

'This man may not be dead.'

'He's dead all right. With his brains on his face. The story, mister. Make it fast.'

'As I said—he may not be dead. We'll go look at him.' I moved one foot forward.

'Move and I'll drill you!' she snapped.

I moved the other foot forward. The flash jumped about a little. I think she took a step back.

'You take some awful chances, mister,' she said quietly. 'All right, go on ahead and I'll follow. You look like a sick man. If it hadn't been for that—'

'You'd have shot me. I've been sapped. It always makes me a little dark under the eyes.'

'A nice sense of humour—like a morgue attendant,' she almost wailed.

I turned away from the light and immediately it shone on the ground in front of me. I walked past the little coupé, an ordinary little car, clean and shiny under the misty starlight. I went on, up the dirt road, around the curve. The steps were close behind me and the flashlight guided me. There was no sound anywhere now except our steps and the girl's breathing. I didn't hear mine.

I I

Half-way up the slope I looked off to the right and saw his foot. She swung the light. Then I saw all of him. I ought to have seen him as I came down, but I had been bent over, peering at the ground with a fountain pen flash, trying to read tyre marks by a light the size of a quarter.

'Give me the flash,' I said and reached back.

She put it into my hand, without a word. I went down on a knee. The ground felt cold and damp through the cloth.

He lay smeared to the ground, on his back, at the base of a bush, in that bag-of-clothes position that always means the same thing. His face was a face I had never seen before. His hair was dark with blood, the beautiful blond ledges were tangled with blood, and some thick greyish ooze, like primeval slime.

The girl behind me breathed hard, but she didn't speak. I held the light on his face. He had been beaten to a pulp. One of his hands was flung out in a frozen gesture, the fingers curled. His overcoat was half twisted under him, as though he had rolled as he fell. His legs were crossed. There was a trickle as black as dirty oil at the corner of his mouth.

'Hold the flash on him,' I said, passing it back to her. 'If it doesn't make you sick.'

She took it and held it without a word, as steady as an old homicide veteran. I got my fountain pen flash out again and started to go through his pockets, trying not to move him.

'You shouldn't do that,' she said tensely. 'You shouldn't touch him until the police come.'

'That's right,' I said. 'And the prowl car boys are not supposed to touch him until the K-car men come and they're not supposed to touch him until the coroner's examiner sees him and the photographers have photographed him and the fingerprint man has taken his prints. And do you know how long all that is liable to take out here? A couple of hours.'

'All right,' she said. 'I suppose you're always right. I guess you must be that kind of person. Somebody must have hated him to smash his head in like that.'

'I don't suppose it was personal,' I growled. 'Some people just like to smash heads.'

'Seeing that I don't know what it's all about, I couldn't guess,' she said tartly.

I went through his clothes. He had loose silver and bills in one trouser pocket, a tooled leather keycase in the other, also a small knife. His left hip pocket yielded a small billfold with more currency, insurance cards, a driver's licence, a couple of receipts. In his coat loose match folders, a gold pencil clipped to a pocket, two thin cambric handkerchiefs as fine and white as dry powdered snow. Then the enamel cigarette case from which I had seen him take his brown gold-tipped cigarettes. They were South American, from Montevideo. And in the other inside pocket a second cigarette case I hadn't seen before. It was made of embroidered silk, a dragon on each side, a frame of imitation tortoiseshell so thin it was hardly there at all. I tickled the catch open and looked in at three oversize Russian cigarettes under the band of elastic. I pinched one. They felt old and dry and loose. They had hollow mouth-pieces.

'He smoked the others,' I said over my shoulder. 'These must have been for a lady friend. He would be a lad who would have a lot of lady friends.'

The girl was bent over, breathing on my neck now. 'Didn't you know him?'

'I only met him to-night. He hired me for a bodyguard.'

'Some bodyguard.'

I didn't say anything to that.

'I'm sorry,' she almost whispered. 'Of course I don't know the circumstances. Do you suppose those could be jujus? Can I look?'

I passed the embroidered case back to her.

'I knew a guy once who smoked jujus,' she said. 'Three highballs and three sticks of tea and it took a pipe wrench to get him off the chandelier.'

'Hold the light steady.'

There was a rustling pause. Then she spoke again.

'I'm sorry.' She handed the case down again and I slipped it back in his pocket. That seemed to be all. All it proved was that he hadn't been cleaned out.

I stood up and took my wallet out. The five twenties were still in it.

'High class boys,' I said. 'They only took the large money.'

The flash was drooping to the ground. I put my wallet away again, clipped my own small flash to my pocket and reached suddenly for the little gun she was still holding in the same hand with the flashlight. She dropped the flashlight, but I got the gun. She stepped back quickly and I reached down for the light. I put it on her face for a moment, then snapped it off.

'You didn't have to be rough,' she said, putting her hands down into the pockets of a long rough coat with flaring shoulders. 'I didn't think you killed him.'

I liked the cool quiet of her voice. I liked her nerve. We stood in the darkness, face to face, not saying anything for a moment. I could see the brush and light in the sky.

I put the light on her face and she blinked. It was a small neat vibrant face with large eyes. A face with bone under the skin, fine drawn like a Cremona violin. A very nice face.

'Your hair's red,' I said. 'You look Irish.'

'And my name's Riordan. So what? Put that light out. It's not red, it's auburn.'

I put it out. 'What's your first name?'

'Anne. And don't call me Annie.'

'What are you doing around here?'

'Sometimes at night I go riding. Just restless. I live alone. I'm an orphan. I know all this neighbourhood like a book. I just happened to be riding along and noticed a light flickering down in the hollow. It seemed a little cold for young love. And they don't use lights, do they?'

'I never did. You take some awful chances, Miss Riordan.'

'I think I said the same about you. I had a gun. I wasn't afraid. There's no law against going down there.'

'Uh-huh. Only the law of self-preservation. Here. It's not my night to be clever. I suppose you have a permit for the gun.' I held it out to her, butt first.'

She took it and tucked it down into her pocket. 'Strange how curious people can be, isn't it? I write a little. Feature articles.'

'Any money in it?'

'Very damned little. What were you looking for—in his pockets?'

'Nothing in particular. I'm a great guy to snoop around. We had eight thousand dollars to buy back some stolen jewellery for a lady. We got hijacked. Why they killed him I don't know. He didn't strike me as a fellow who would put up much of a fight. And I didn't hear a fight. I was down in the hollow when he was jumped. He was in the car, up above. We were supposed to drive down into the hollow but there didn't seem to be room for the car without scratching it up. So I went down there on foot and while I was down there they must have stuck him up. Then one of them got into the car and dry-gulched me. I thought he was still in the car, of course.'

'That doesn't make you so terribly dumb,' she said.

'There was something wrong with the job from the start. I could feel it. But I needed the money. Now I have to go to the cops and eat dirt. Will you drive me to Montemar Vista? I left my car there. He lived there.'

'Sure. But shouldn't somebody stay with him? You could take my car—or I could go call the cops.'

I looked at the dial of my watch. The faintly glowing hands said that it was getting towards midnight.

'No.'

'Why not?'

'I don't know why not. I just feel it that way. I'll play it alone.'

She said nothing. We went back down the hill and got into her little car and she started it and jockeyed it around without lights and drove it back up the hill and eased it past the barrier. A block away she sprang the lights on.

My head ached. We didn't speak until we came level with the first house on the paved part of the street. Then she said:

'You need a drink. Why not go back to my house and have one? You can phone the law from there. They have to come from West Los Angeles anyway. There's nothing up here but a fire station.'

'Just keep on going down to the coast. I'll play it solo.'

'But why? I'm not afraid of them. My story might help you.'

'I don't want any help. I've got to think. I want to be by myself for a while.'

'I—okey,' she said.

She made a vague sound in her throat and turned on to the boulevard. We came to the service station at the coast highway and turned north to Montemar Vista and the sidewalk café there. It was lit up like a luxury liner. The girl pulled over on to the shoulder and I got out and stood holding the door.

I fumbled a card out of my wallet and passed it in to her. 'Some day you may need a strong back,' I said. 'Let me know. But don't call me if it's brain work.'

She tapped the card on the wheel and said slowly: 'You'll find me in the Bay City phone book, 819 Twenty-fifth Street. Come around and pin a putty medal on me for minding my own business. I think you're still woozy from that crack on the head.'

She swung her car swiftly around on the highway and I watched its twin tail-lights fade into the dark.

I walked past the arch and the sidewalk café into the parking space and got into my car. A bar was right in front of me and I was shaking again. But it seemed smarter to walk into the West Los Angeles police station the way I did twenty minutes later, as cold as a frog and as green as the back of a new dollar bill.

12

It was an hour and a half later. The body had been taken away, the ground gone over, and I had told my story three or four times. We sat, four of us, in the day captain's room at the West Los Angeles station. The building was quiet except for a drunk in a cell who kept giving the Australian bush call while he waited to go downtown for sunrise court.

A hard white light inside a glass reflector shone down on the flat-topped table on which were spread the things that had come from Lindsay Marriott's pockets, things now that seemed as dead and homeless as their owner. The man across the table from me was named Randall and he was from Central Homicide in Los Angeles. He was a thin quiet man of fifty with smooth creamy-grey hair, cold eyes, a distant manner. He wore a dark red tie with black spots on it and the spots kept dancing in front of my eyes. Behind him, beyond the cone of light two beefy men lounged like bodyguards, each of them watching one of my ears.

I fumbled a cigarette around in my fingers and lit it and didn't like the taste of it. I sat watching it burn between my fingers. I felt about eighty years old and slipping fast.

Randall said coldly: 'The oftener you tell this story the sillier it sounds. This man Marriott had been negotiating for days, no doubt, about this pay-off and then just a few hours before the final meeting he calls up a perfect stranger and hires him to go with him as a bodyguard.'

'Not exactly as a bodyguard,' I said. 'I didn't even tell him I had a gun. Just for company.'

'Where did he hear of you?'

'First he said a mutual friend. Then that he just picked my name out of the book.'

Randall poked gently among the stuff on the table and detached a white card with an air of touching something not quite clean. He pushed it along the wood.

'He had your card. Your business card.'

I glanced at the card. It had come out of his billfold, together with a number of other cards I hadn't bothered to examine back there in the hollow of Purissima Canyon. It was one of my cards all right. It looked rather dirty at that, for a man like Marriott. There was a round smear across one corner.

'Sure,' I said. 'I hand those out whenever I get a chance. Naturally.'

'Marriott let you carry the money,' Randall said. 'Eight thousand dollars. He was rather a trusting soul.'

I drew on my cigarette and blew the smoke towards the ceiling. The light hurt my eyes. The back of my head ached.

'I don't have the eight thousand dollars,' I said. 'Sorry.'

'No. You wouldn't be here, if you had the money. Or would you?' There was a cold sneer on his face now, but it looked artificial.

'I'd do a lot for eight thousand dollars,' I said. 'But if I wanted to kill a man with a sap, I'd only hit him twice at the most–on the back of the head.'

He nodded slightly. One of the dicks behind him spat into the waste-basket.

'That's one of the puzzling features. It looks like an amateur job, but of course it might be meant to look like an amateur job. The money was not Marriott's was it?'

'I don't know. I got the impression not, but that was just an impression. He wouldn't tell me who the lady in the case was.'

'We don't know anything about Marriott–yet,' Randall said slowly. 'I suppose it's at least possible he meant to steal the eight thousand himself.'

'Huh?' I felt surprised. I probably looked surprised. Nothing changed in Randall's smooth face.

'Did you count the money?'

'Of course not. He just gave me a package. There was money in it and it looked like a lot. He said it was eight grand. Why would he want to steal it from me when he already had it before I came on the scene?'

Randall looked at a corner of the ceiling and drew his mouth down at the corners. He shrugged.

'Go back a bit,' he said. 'Somebody had stuck up Marriott and a lady and taken this jade necklace and stuff and had later offered to sell it back for what seems like a pretty small amount, in view of its supposed value. Marriott was to handle the pay-off. He thought of handling it alone and we don't know whether the other parties made a point of that or whether it was mentioned. Usually in cases like that they are rather fussy. But Marriott evidently decided it was all right to have you along. Both of you figured you were dealing with an organized gang and that they would play ball within the limits of their trade. Marriott was scared. That would be natural enough. He wanted company. You were the company. But you are a complete stranger to him, just a name on a card handed to him by some unknown party, said by him to be a mutual friend. Then at the last minute Marriott decides to have you carry the money and do the talking while he hides in the car. You say that was your idea, but he may have been hoping you would suggest it, and if you didn't suggest it, he would have had the idea himself.'

'He didn't like the idea at first,' I said.

Randall shrugged again. 'He pretended not to like the idea–but he gave in. So finally he gets a call and off you go to the place he describes. All this is coming from Marriott. None of it is known to you independently. When you get there, there seems to be nobody about. You are supposed to drive down into that hollow, but it doesn't look to be room enough for a big car. It wasn't, as a matter of fact, because the car was pretty badly scratched on the left side. So you get out and walk down into the hollow, see and hear nothing, wait a few minutes, come back to the car and then somebody in the car socks you on the back of the head. Now suppose Marriott wanted that money and wanted to make you the fall guy—wouldn't he have acted just the same way he did?'

'It's a swell theory,' I said. 'Marriott socked me, took the money, then he got sorry and beat his brains out, after first burying the money under a bush.'

Randall looked at me woodenly. 'He had an accomplice of course. Both of you were supposed to be knocked out, and the accomplice would beat it with the money. Only the accomplice double-crossed Marriott by killing him. He didn't have to kill you because you didn't know him.'

I looked at him with admiration and ground out my cigarette stub in a wooden tray that had once had a glass lining in it but hadn't any more.

'It fits the facts—so far as we know them,' Randall said calmly. 'It's no sillier than any other theory we could think up at the moment.'

'It doesn't fit one fact—that I was socked from the car, does it? That would make me suspect Marriott of having socked me—other things being equal. Although I didn't suspect him after he was killed.'

'The way you were socked fits best of all,' Randall said. 'You didn't tell Marriott you had a gun, but he may have seen the bulge under your arm or at least suspected you had a gun. In that case he would want to hit you when you suspected nothing. And you wouldn't suspect anything from the back of the car.'

'Okey,' I said. 'You win. It's a good theory, always supposing the money was not Marriott's and that he wanted to steal it and that he had an accomplice. So his plan is that we both wake up with bumps on our heads and the money is gone and we say so sorry and I go home and forget all about it. Is that how it ends? I mean is that how he expected it to end? It had to look good to him too, didn't it?'

Randall smiled wryly. 'I don't like it myself. I was just trying it out. It fits the facts—as far as I know them, which is not far.'

'We don't know enough to even start theorizing,' I said. 'Why not assume he was telling the truth and that he perhaps recognized one of the stick-up men?'

'You say you heard no struggle, no cry?'

'No. But he could have been grabbed quickly, by the throat. Or he could have been too scared to cry out when they jumped him. Say they were watching from the bushes and saw me go down the hill. I went some distance, you know. A good hundred feet. They go over to look into the car and see Marriott. Somebody sticks a gun in his face and makes him get out—quietly. Then he's sapped down. But something he says, or some way he looks, makes them think he has recognized somebody.'

'In the dark?'

'Yes,' I said. 'It must have been something like that. Some voices stay in your mind. Even in the dark people are recognized.'

Randall shook his head. 'If this was an organized gang of jewel thieves, they wouldn't kill without a lot of provocation.' He stopped suddenly and his eyes got a glazed look. He closed his mouth very slowly, very tight. He had an idea. 'Hijack,' he said.

I nodded. 'I think that's an idea.'

'There's another thing,' he said. 'How did you get here?'

'I drove my car.'

'Where was your car?'

'Down at Montemar Vista, in the parking lot by the sidewalk café.'

He looked at me very thoughtfully. The two dicks behind him looked at me suspiciously. The drunk in the cells tried to yodel, but his voice cracked and that discouraged him. He began to cry.

'I walked back to the highway,' I said. 'I flagged a car. A girl was driving it alone. She stopped and took me down.'

'Some girl,' Randall said. 'It was late at night, on a lonely road, and she stopped.'

'Yeah. Some of them will do that. I didn't get to know her, but she seemed nice.' I stared at them, knowing they didn't believe me and wondering why I was lying about it.

'It was a small car,' I said. 'A Chevvy coupé. I didn't get the licence number.'

'Haw, he didn't get the licence number,' one of the dicks said and spat into the waste-basket again.

Randall leaned forward and stared at me carefully. 'If you're holding anything back with the idea of working on this case yourself to make yourself a little publicity, I'd forget it, Marlowe. I don't like all the points in your story and I'm going to give you the night to think it over. To-morrow I'll probably ask you for a sworn statement. In the meantime let me give you a tip. This is a murder and a police job and we wouldn't want your help, even if it was good. All we want from you is facts. Get me?'

'Sure. Can I go home now? I don't feel any too well.'

'You can go home now.' His eyes were icy.

I got up and started towards the door in a dead silence. When I had gone four steps Randall cleared his throat and said carelessly:

Oh, one small point. Did you notice what kind of cigarettes Marriott smoked?'

I turned. 'Yes. Brown ones. South American, in a French enamel case.'

He leaned forward and pushed the embroidered silk case out of the pile of junk on the table and then pulled it towards him.

'Ever see this one before?'

'Sure. I was just looking at it.'

'I mean, earlier this evening.'

'I believe I did,' I said. 'Lying around somewhere. Why?'

'You didn't search the body?'

'Okey,' I said. 'Yes, I looked through his pockets. That was in one of them. I'm sorry. Just professional curiosity. I didn't disturb anything. After all he was my client.'

Randall took hold of the embroidered case with both hands and opened it. He sat looking into it. It was empty. The three cigarettes were gone.

I bit hard on my teeth and kept the tired look on my face. It was not easy.

'Did you see him smoke a cigarette out of this?'

'No.'

Randall nodded coolly. 'It's empty as you see. But it was in his pocket just the same. There's a little dust in it. I'm going to have it examined under a microscope. I'm not sure, but I have an idea it's marijuana.'

I said: 'If he had any of those, I should think he would have smoked a couple to-night. He needed something to cheer him up.'

Randall closed the case carefully and pushed it away.

'That's all,' he said. 'And keep your nose clean.'

I went out.

The fog had cleared off outside and the stars were as bright as artificial stars of chromium on a sky of black velvet. I drove fast. I needed a drink badly and the bars were closed.

13

I got up at nine, drank three cups of black coffee, bathed the back of my head with ice-water and read the two morning papers that had been thrown against the apartment door. There was a paragraph and a bit about Moose Malloy, in Part II, but Nulty didn't get his name mentioned. There was nothing about Lindsay Marriott, unless it was on the society page.

I dressed and ate two soft-boiled eggs and drank a fourth cup of coffee and looked myself over in the mirror. I still looked a little shadowy under the eyes. I had the door open to leave when the phone rang.

It was Nulty. He sounded mean.

'Marlowe?'

'Yeah. Did you get him?'

'Oh sure. We got him.' He stopped to snarl. 'On the Ventura line, like I said. Boy, did we have fun! Six foot six, built like a coffer dam, on his way to Frisco to see the Fair. He had five quarts of hooch in the front seat of the rent car, and he was drinking out of another one as he rode along, doing a quiet seventy. All we had to go up against him with was two county cops with guns and blackjacks.'

He paused and I turned over a few witty sayings in my mind, but none of them seemed amusing at the moment. Nulty went on:

'So he done exercises with the cops and when they were tired enough to go to sleep, he pulled one side off their car, threw the radio into the ditch, opened a fresh bottle of hooch, and went to sleep hisself. After a while the boys snapped out of it and bounced blackjacks off his head for about ten minutes before he noticed it. When he began to get sore they got handcuffs on him. It was easy. We got him in the icebox now, drunk driving, drunk in auto, assaulting police officer in performance of duty, two counts, malicious damage to official property, attempted escape from custody, assault less than mayhem, disturbing the peace, and parking on a stage highway. Fun, ain't it?'

'What's the gag?' I asked. 'You didn't tell me all that just to gloat.'

'It was the wrong guy,' Nulty said savagely. 'This bird is named Stoyanoffsky and he lives in Hemet and he just got through working as a sandhog on the San Jack tunnel. Got a wife and four kids. Boy, is she sore. What you doing on Malloy?'

'Nothing. I have a headache.'

'Any time you get a little free time—'

'I don't think so,' I said. 'Thanks just the same. When is the inquest on the nigger coming up?'

'Why bother?' Nulty sneered, and hung up.

I drove down to Hollywood Boulevard and put my car in the parking space beside the building and rode up to my floor. I opened the door of the little reception room which I always left unlocked, in case I had a client and the client wanted to wait.

Miss Anne Riordan looked up from a magazine and smiled at me.

She was wearing a tobacco brown suit with a high-necked white sweater inside it. Her hair by daylight was pure auburn and on it she wore a hat with a crown the size of a whisky glass and a brim you could have wrapped the week's laundry in. She wore it at an angle of approximately forty-five degrees, so that the edge of the brim just missed her shoulder. In spite of that it looked smart. Perhaps because of that.

She was about twenty-eight years old. She had a rather narrow forehead of more height than is considered elegant. Her nose was small and inquisitive, her upper lip a shade too long and her mouth more than a shade too wide. Her eyes were grey-blue with flecks of gold in them. She had a nice smile. She looked as if she had slept well. It was a nice face, a face you get to like. Pretty, but not so pretty that you would have to wear brass knuckles every time you took it out.

'I didn't know just what your office hours were,' she said. 'So I waited. I gather that your secretary is not here to-day.'

'I don't have a secretary.'

I went across and unlocked the inner door, then switched on the buzzer that rang on the outer door. 'Let's go into my private thinking parlour.'

She passed in front of me with a vague scent of very dry sandalwood and stood looking at the five green filing cases, the shabby rust-red rug, the half-dusted furniture, and the not too clean net curtains.

'I should think you would want somebody to answer the phone,' she said. 'And once in a while to send your curtains to the cleaners.'

'I'll send them out come St Swithin's Day. Have a chair. I might miss a few unimportant jobs. And a lot of leg art. I save money.'

'I see,' she said demurely, and placed a large suede bag carefully on the corner of the glass-topped desk. She leaned back and took one of my cigarettes. I burned my finger with a paper match lighting it for her.

She blew a fan of smoke and smiled through it. Nice teeth, rather large.

'You probably didn't expect to see me again so soon. How is your head?'

'Poorly. No, I didn't.'

'Were the police nice to you?'

'About the way they always are.'

'I'm not keeping you from anything important, am I?'

'No.'

'All the same I don't think you're very pleased to see me.'

I filled a pipe and reached for the packet of paper matches. I lit the pipe carefully. She watched that with approval. Pipe smokers were solid men. She was going to be disappointed in me.

'I tried to leave you out of it,' I said. 'I don't know why exactly. It's no business of mine any more anyhow. I ate my dirt last night and banged myself to sleep with a bottle and now it's a police case: I've been warned to leave it alone.'

'The reason you left me out of it,' she said calmly, 'was that you didn't think the police would believe just mere idle curiosity took me down into that hollow last night. They would suspect some guilty reason and hammer at me until I was a wreck.'

'How do you know I didn't think the same thing?'

'Cops are just people,' she said irrelevantly.

'They start out that way, I've heard.'

'Oh—cynical this morning.' She looked around the office with an idle but raking glance. 'Do you do pretty well in here? I mean financially? I mean, do you make a lot of money—with this kind of furniture?'

I grunted.

'Or should I try minding my own business and not asking impertinent questions?'

'Would it work, if you tried it?'

'Now we're both doing it. Tell me, why did you cover up for me last night? Was it on account of I have reddish hair and a beautiful figure?'

I didn't say anything.

'Let's try this one,' she said cheerfully. 'Would you like to know who that jade necklace belonged to?'

I could feel my face getting stiff. I thought hard but I couldn't remember for sure. And then suddenly I could. I hadn't said a word to her about a jade necklace.

I reached for the matches and relit my pipe. 'Not very much,' I said. 'Why?'

'Because I know.'

'Uh-huh.'

'What do you do when you get real talkative—wiggle your toes?'

'All right,' I growled. 'You came here to tell me. Go ahead and tell me.'

Her blue eyes widened and for a moment I thought they looked a little moist. She took her lower lip between her teeth and held it that way while she stared down at the desk. Then she shrugged and let go of her lip and smiled at me candidly.

'Oh I know I'm just a damned inquisitive wench. But there's a strain of bloodhound in me. My father was a cop. His name was Cliff Riordan and he was police chief of Bay City for seven years. I suppose that's what's the matter.'

'I seem to remember. What happened to him?'

'He was fired. It broke his heart. A mob of gamblers headed by a man named Laird Brunette elected themselves a mayor. So they put Dad in charge of the Bureau of Records and Identification, which in Bay City is about the size of a tea-bag. So Dad quit and pottered around for a couple of years and then died. And Mother died soon after him. So I've been alone for two years.'

'I'm sorry,' I said.

She ground out her cigarette. It had no lipstick on it. 'The only reason I'm boring you with this is that it makes it easy for me to get along with policemen. I suppose I ought to have told you last night. So this morning I found out who had charge of the case and went to see him. He was a little sore at you at first.'

'That's all right,' I said. 'If I had told him the truth on all points, he still wouldn't have believed me. All he will do is chew one of my ears off.'

She looked hurt. I got up and opened the other window. The noise of the traffic from the boulevard came in in waves, like nausea. I felt lousy. I opened the deep drawer of the desk and got the office bottle out and poured myself a drink.

Miss Riordan watched me with disapproval. I was no longer a solid man. She didn't say anything. I drank the drink and put the bottle away again and sat down.

'You didn't offer me one,' she said coolly.

'Sorry. It's only eleven o'clock or less. I didn't think you looked the type.'

Her eyes crinkled at the corners. 'Is that a compliment?'

'In my circle, yes.'

She thought that over. It didn't mean anything to her. It didn't mean anything to me either when I thought it over. But the drink made me feel a lot better.

She leaned forward and scraped her gloves slowly across the glass of the desk. 'You wouldn't want to hire an assistant, would you? Not if it only cost you a kind word now and then?'

'No.'

She nodded. 'I thought probably you wouldn't. I'd better just give you my information and go on home.'

I didn't say anything. I lit my pipe again. It makes you look thoughtful when you are not thinking.

'First of all, it occurred to me that a jade necklace like that would be a museum piece and would be well known,' she said.

I held the match in the air, still burning and watching the flame crawl close to my fingers. Then I blew it out softly and dropped it in the tray and said:

'I didn't say anything to you about a jade necklace.'

'No, but Lieutenant Randall did.'

'Somebody ought to sew buttons on his face.'

'He knew my father. I promised not to tell.'

'You're telling me.'

'You knew already, silly.'

Her hand suddenly flew up as if it was going to fly to her mouth, but it only rose half-way and then fell back slowly and her eyes widened. It was a good act, but I knew something else about her that spoiled it.

'You *did* know, didn't you?' She breathed the words hushedly.

'I thought it was diamonds. A bracelet, a pair of ear-rings, a pendant, three rings, one of the rings with emeralds too.'

'Not funny,' she said. 'Not even fast.'

'Fei Tsui jade. Very rare. Carved beads about six carats apiece, sixty of them. Worth eighty thousand dollars.'

'You have such nice brown eyes,' she said. 'And you think you're tough.'

'Well, who does it belong to and how did you find out?'

'I found out very simply. I thought the best jeweller in town would probably know, so I went and asked the manager of Block's. I told him I was a writer and wanted to do an article on rare jade—you know the line.'

'So he believed your red hair and your beautiful figure.'

She flushed clear to the temples. 'Well, he told me anyway. It belongs to a rich lady who lives in Bay City, in an estate on the canyon. Mrs Lewin Lockridge Grayle. Her husband is an investment banker or something, enormously rich, worth about twenty millions. He used to own a radio station in Beverly Hills, Station KFDK, and Mrs Grayle used to work there. He married her five years ago. She's a ravishing blonde. Mr Grayle is elderly, liverish, stays home and takes calomel while Mrs Grayle goes places and has a good time.'

'This manager of Block's,' I said. 'He's a fellow that gets around.'

'Oh, I didn't get all that from him, silly. Just about the necklace. The rest I got from Giddy Gertie Arbogast.'

I reached into the deep drawer and brought the office bottle up again.

'You're not going to turn out to be one of those drunken detectives, are you?' she asked anxiously.

'Why not? They always solve their cases and they never even sweat. Get on with the story.'

'Giddy Gertie is the society editor of the *Chronicle*. I've known him for years. He weighs two hundred and wears a Hitler moustache. He got out his morgue file on the Grayles. Look.'

She reached into her bag and slid a photograph across the desk, a five-by-three glazed still.

It was a blonde. A blonde to make a bishop kick a hole in a stained-glass window. She was wearing street clothes that looked black and white, and a hat to match and she was a little haughty, but not too much. Whatever you needed, wherever you happened to be—she had it. About thirty years old.

I poured a fast drink and burned my throat getting it down. 'Take it away,' I said. 'I'll start jumping.'

'Why, I got it for you. You'll want to see her, won't you?'

I looked at it again. Then I slid it under the blotter. 'How about to-night at eleven?'

'Listen, this isn't just a bunch of gag lines, Mr Marlowe. I called her up. She'll see you. On business.'

'It may start out that way.'

She made an impatient gesture, so I stopped fooling around and got my battle-scarred frown back on my face. 'What will she see me about?'

'Her necklace, of course. It was like this. I called her up and had a lot of trouble getting to talk to her, of course, but finally I did. Then I gave her the song and dance I had given the nice man at Block's and it didn't take. She sounded as if she had a hangover. She said something about talking to her secretary, but I managed to keep her on the phone and ask her if it was true she had a Fei Tsui jade necklace. After a while she said, yes. I asked if I might see it. She said, what for? I said my piece over again and it didn't take any better than the first time. I could hear her yawning and bawling somebody outside the mouthpiece for putting me on. Then I said I was working for Philip Marlowe. She said "So what?" Just like that.'

'Incredible. But all the society dames talk like tramps nowadays.'

'I wouldn't know,' Miss Riordan said sweetly. 'Probably some of them *are* tramps. So I asked her if she had a phone with no extension and she said what business was it of mine. But the funny thing was she hadn't hung up on me.'

'She had the jade on her mind and she didn't know what you were leading up to. And she may have heard from Randall already.'

Miss Riordan shook her head. 'No. I called him later and he didn't know who owned the necklace until I told him. He was quite surprised that I had found out.'

'He'll get used to you,' I said. 'He'll probably have to. What then?'

'So I said to Mrs Grayle: "You'd still like it back, wouldn't you?" Just like that. I didn't know any other way to say. I had to say something that would jar her a bit. It did. She gave me another number in a hurry. And I called that and I said I'd like to see her. She seemed surprised. So I had to tell her the story. She didn't like it. But she had been wondering why she hadn't heard from Marriott. I guess she thought he had gone south with the money or something. So I'm to see her at two o'clock. Then I'll tell her about you and how nice and discreet you are and how you would be a good man to help her get it back, if there's any chance and so on. She's already interested.'

I didn't say anything. I just stared at her. She looked hurt. 'What's the matter? Did I do right?'

'Can't you get it through your head that this is a police case now and that I've been warned to stay off it?'

'Mrs Grayle has a perfect right to employ you, if she wants to.'

'To do what?'

She snapped and unsnapped her bag impatiently. 'Oh, my goodness—a woman like that—with her looks—can't you see—' She stopped and bit her lip. 'What kind of man was Marriott?'

'I hardly knew him. I thought he was a bit of a pansy. I didn't like him very well.'

'Was he a man who would be attractive to women?'

'Some women. Others would want to spit.'

'Well, it looks as if he might have been attractive to Mrs Grayle. She went out with him.'

'She probably goes out with a hundred men. There's very little chance to get the necklace now.'

'Why?'

I got up and walked to the end of the office and slapped the wall with the flat of my hand, hard. The clacking typewriter on the other side stopped for a moment, and then went on. I looked down through the open window into the shaft between my building and the Mansion House Hotel. The coffee shop smell was strong enough to build a garage on. I went back to my desk, dropped the bottle of whisky back into the drawer, shut the drawer and sat down again. I lit my pipe for the eighth or ninth time and looked carefully across the half-dusted glass to Miss Riordan's grave and honest little face.

You could get to like that face a lot. Glamoured up blondes were a dime a dozen, but that was a face that would wear. I smiled at it.

'Listen, Anne. Killing Marriott was a dumb mistake. The gang behind this hold-up would never pull anything like that. What must have happened was that some gowed-up runt they took along for a gun-holder lost his head. Marriott made a false move and some punk beat him down and it was done so quickly nothing could be done to prevent it. Here is an organized mob with inside information on jewels and the movements of the women that wear them. They ask moderate returns and they would play ball. But here also is a back alley murder that doesn't fit at all. My idea is that whoever did it is a dead man hours ago, with weights on his ankles, deep in the Pacific Ocean. And either the jade went down with him or else they have some idea of its real value and they have cached it away in a place where it will stay for a long time—maybe for years before they dare bring it out again. Or, if the gang is big enough, it may show up on the other side of the world. The eight thousand they asked seems pretty low if they really knew the value of the jade. But it would be hard to sell. I'm sure of one thing. They never meant to murder anybody.'

Anne Riordan was listening to me with her lips slightly parted and a rapt expression on her face, as if she was looking at the Dalai Lama.

She closed her mouth slowly and nodded once. 'You're wonderful,' she said softly. 'But you're nuts.'

She stood up and gathered her bag to her. 'Will you go to see her or won't you?'

'Randall can't stop me—if it comes from her.'

'All right. I'm going to see another society editor and get some more dope on the Grayles if I can. About her love life. She would have one, wouldn't she?'

The face framed in auburn hair was wistful.

'Who hasn't?' I sneered.

'*I* never had. Not really.'

I reached up and shut my mouth with my hand. She gave me a sharp look and moved towards the door.

'You've forgotten something,' I said.

She stopped and turned. 'What?' She looked all over the top of the desk.

'You know damn well what.'

She came back to the desk and leaned across it earnestly. 'Why would they kill the man that killed Marriott, if they don't go in for murder?'

'Because he would be the type that would get picked up some time and would talk—when they took his dope away from him. I mean they wouldn't kill a customer.'

'What makes you so sure the killer took dope?'

'I'm not sure. I just said that. Most punks do.'

'Oh.' She straightened up and nodded and smiled. 'I guess you mean these,' she said and reached quickly into her bag and laid a small tissue bag package on the desk.

I reached for it, pulled a rubber band off it carefully and opened up the paper. On it lay three long thick Russian cigarettes with paper mouthpieces. I looked at her and didn't say anything.

'I know I shouldn't have taken them,' she said almost breathlessly. 'But I knew they were jujus. They usually come in plain papers but lately around Bay City they have been putting them out like this. I've seen several. I thought it was kind of mean for the poor man to be found dead with marijuana cigarettes in his pocket.'

'You ought to have taken the case too,' I said quietly. 'There was dust in it. And it being empty was suspicious.'

'I couldn't—with you there. I–I almost went back and did. But I didn't quite have the courage. Did it get you in wrong?'

'No,' I lied. 'Why should it?'

'I'm glad of that,' she said wistfully.

'Why didn't you throw them away?'

She thought about it, her bag clutched to her side, her wide-brimmed absurd hat tilted so that it hid one eye.

'I guess it must be because I'm a cop's daughter,' she said at last. 'You just don't throw away evidence.' Her smile was frail and guilty and her cheeks were flushed. I shrugged.

'Well—' the word hung in the air, like smoke in a closed room. Her lips stayed parted after saying it. I let it hang. The flush on her face deepened.

'I'm horribly sorry. I shouldn't have done it.'

I passed that too.

She went very quickly to the door and out.

14

I poked at one of the long Russian cigarettes with a finger, then laid them in a neat row, side by side and squeaked my chair. You just don't throw away evidence. So they were evidence. Evidence of what? That a man occasionally smoked a stick of tea, a man who looked as if any touch of the exotic would appeal to him. On the other hand lots of tough guys smoked marijuana, also lots of band musicians and high school kids, and nice girls who had given up trying. American hashish. A weed that would grow anywhere. Unlawful to cultivate now. That meant a lot in a country as big as the U.S.A.

I sat there and puffed my pipe and listened to the clacking typewriter behind the wall of my office and the bong-bong of the traffic lights changing on Hollywood Boulevard and spring rustling in the air, like a paper bag blowing along a concrete sidewalk.

They were pretty big cigarettes, but a lot of Russians are, and marijuana is a coarse leaf. Indian hemp. American hashish. Evidence. God, what hats the women wear. My head ached. Nuts.

I got my penknife out and opened the small sharp blade, the one I didn't clean my pipe with, and reached for one of them. That's what a police chemist would do. Slit one down the middle and examine the stuff under a microscope, to start with. There might just happen to be something unusual about it. Not very likely, but what the hell, he was paid by the month.

I slit one down the middle. The mouthpiece part was pretty tough to split. Okey, I was a tough guy, I slit it anyway. See can you stop me.

Out of the mouthpiece shiny segments of rolled thin cardboard partly straightened themselves and had printing on them. I sat up straight and pawed for them. I tried to spread them out on the desk in order, but they slid around on the desk. I grabbed another of the cigarettes and squinted inside the mouthpiece. Then I went to work with the blade of the pocket knife in a different way. I pinched the cigarette down to the place where the mouthpieces began. The paper was thin all the way, you could feel the grain of what was underneath. So I cut the mouthpiece off carefully and then still more carefully cut through the mouthpiece longways, but only just enough. It opened out and there was another card underneath, rolled up, not touched this time.

I spread it out fondly. It was a man's calling card. Thin pale ivory, just off-white. Engraved on that were delicately shaded words. In the lower left-hand corner a Stillwood Heights telephone number. In the lower right-hand corner the legend, 'By Appointment Only.' In the middle, a little larger, but still discreet: 'Jules Amthor.' Below, a little smaller: 'Psychic Consultant.'

I took hold of the third cigarette. This time, with a lot of difficulty, I teased the card out without cutting anything. It was the same. I put it back where it had been.

I looked at my watch, put my pipe in an ashtray, and then had to look at my watch again to see what time it was. I rolled the two cut cigarettes and the cut card in part of the tissue paper, the one that was complete with card inside in another part of the tissue paper and locked both little packages away in my desk.

I sat looking at the card. Jules Amthor, Psychic Consultant, By Appointment Only, Stillwood Heights phone number, no address. Three like that rolled inside three sticks of tea, in a Chinese or Japanese silk cigarette case with an imitation tortoise-shell frame, a trade article that might have cost thirty-five to seventy-five cents in any Oriental store, Hooey Phooey Sing–Long Sing Tung, that kind of place, where a nice-mannered Jap hisses at you, laughing heartily when you say that the Moon of Arabia incense smells like the girls in Frisco Sadie's back parlour.

And all this in the pocket of a man who was very dead, and who had another and genuinely expensive cigarette case containing cigarettes which he actually smoked.

He must have forgotten it. It didn't make sense. Perhaps it hadn't belonged to him at all. Perhaps he had picked it up in a hotel lobby. Forgotten he had it on him. Forgotten to turn it in. Jules Amthor, Psychic Consultant.

The phone rang and I answered it absently. The voice had the cool hardness of a cop who thinks he is good. It was Randall. He didn't bark. He was the icy type.

'So you didn't know who that girl was last night? And she picked you up on the boulevard and you walked over to there. Nice lying, Marlowe.'

'Maybe you have a daughter and you wouldn't like news camera-men jumping out of bushes and popping flashbulbs in her face.'

'You lied to me.'

'It was a pleasure.'

He was silent a moment, as if deciding something. 'We'll let that pass,' he said. 'I've seen her. She came in and told me her story. She's the daughter of a man I knew and respected, as it happens.'

'She told you,' I said, 'and you told her.'

'I told her a little,' he said coldly. 'For a reason. I'm calling you for the same reason. This investigation is going to be under cover. We have a chance to break this jewel gang and we're going to do it.'

'Oh, it's a gang murder this morning. Okey.'

'By the way, that was marijuana dust in that funny cigarette case–the one with the dragons on it. Sure you didn't see him smoke one out of it?'

'Quite sure. In my presence he smoked only the others. But he wasn't in my presence all the time.'

'I see. Well, that's all. Remember what I told you last night. Don't try getting ideas about this case. All we want from you is silence. Otherwise—'

He paused. I yawned into the mouthpiece.

'I heard that,' he snapped. 'Perhaps you think I'm not in a position to make that stick. I am. One false move out of you and you'll be locked up as a material witness.'

'You mean the papers are not to get the case?'

'They'll get the murder—but they won't know what's behind it.'

'Neither do you,' I said.

'I've warned you twice now,' he said. 'The third time is out.'

'You're doing a lot of talking,' I said, 'for a guy that holds cards.'

I got the phone hung in my face for that. Okey, the hell with him, let him work at it.

I walked around the office a little to cool off, made myself a short drink, looked at my watch again and didn't see what time it was, and sat down at the desk once more.

Jules Amthor, Psychic Consultant. Consultations By Appointment Only. Give him enough time and pay him enough money and he'll cure anything from a jaded husband to a grasshopper plague. He would be an expert in frustrated love affairs, women who slept alone and didn't like it, wandering boys and girls who didn't write home, sell the property now or hold it for another year, will this part hurt me with my public or make me seem more versatile? Men would sneak in on him too, big strong guys that roared like lions around their offices and were all cold mush under their vests. But mostly it would be women, fat women that panted and thin women that burned, old women that dreamed and young women that thought they might have Electra complexes, women of all sizes, shapes and ages, but with one thing in common—money. No Thursdays at the County Hospital for Mr Jules Amthor. Cash on the line for him. Rich bitches who had to be dunned for their milk bills would pay him right now.

A fakeloo artist, a hoopla spreader, and a lad who had his card rolled up inside sticks of tea, found on a dead man.

This was going to be good. I reached for the phone and asked the O-operator for the Stillwood Heights number.

15

A woman's voice answered, a dry, husky-sounding foreign voice: ''Allo.'

'May I talk to Mr Amthor?'

'Ah, no. I regret. I am ver-ry sor-ry. Amthor never speaks upon the telephone. I am hees secretary. Weel I take the message?'

'What's the address out there? I want to see him.'

'Ah, you weesh to consult Amthor professionally? He weel be ver-ry pleased. But he ees ver-ry beesy. When you weesh to see him?'

'Right away. Some time to-day.'

'Ah,' the voice regretted, 'that cannot be. The next week per'aps. I weel look at the book.'

'Look,' I said, 'never mind the book. You 'ave the pencil?'

'But certainly I 'ave the pencil. I—'

'Take this down. My name is Philip Marlowe. My address is 615 Cahuenga Building, Hollywood. That's on Hollywood Boulevard near Ivar. My phone number is Glenview 7537.' I spelled the hard ones and waited.

'Yes, Meester Marlowe. I 'ave that.'

'I want to see Mr Amthor about a man named Marriott.' I spelled that too. 'It is very urgent. It is a matter of life and death. I want to see him fast. F-a-s-t–fast. Sudden, in other words. Am I clear?'

'You talk ver-ry strange,' the foreign voice said.

'No.' I took hold of the phone standard and shook it. 'I feel fine. I always talk like that. This is a very queer business. Mr Amthor will positively want to see me. I'm a private detective. But I don't want to go to the police until I've seen him.'

'Ah,' the voice got as cool as a cafeteria dinner. 'You are of the police, no?'

'Listen,' I said. 'I am of the police, no. I am a private detective. Confidential. But it is very urgent just the same. You call me back, no? You 'ave the telephone number, yes?'

'Si. I 'ave the telephone number. Meester Marriott–he ees sick?'

'Well, he's not up and around,' I said. 'So you know him?'

'But no. You say a matter of life and death. Amthor he cure many people—'

'This is one time he flops,' I said. 'I'll be waiting for a call.'

I hung up and lunged for the office bottle. I felt as if I had been through a meat grinder. Ten minutes passed. The phone rang. The voice said:

'Amthor he weel see you at six o'clock.'

'That's fine. What's the address?'

'He weel send a car.'

'I have a car of my own. Just give me—'

'He weel send a car,' the voice said coldly, and the phone clicked in my ear.

I looked at my watch once more. It was more than time for lunch. My stomach burned from the last drink. I wasn't hungry. I lit a cigarette. It tasted like a plumber's handkerchief. I nodded across the office at Mr Rembrandt, then I reached for my hat and went out. I was half-way to the elevator before the thought hit me. It hit me without any reason or sense, like a dropped brick. I stopped and leaned against the marbled wall and pushed my hat around on my head and suddenly I laughed.

A girl passing me on the way from the elevators back to her work turned and gave me one of those looks which are supposed to make your spine feel like a run in a stocking. I waved my hand at her and went back to my office and grabbed the phone. I called up a man I knew who worked on the Lot Books of a title company.

'Can you find a property by the address alone?' I asked him.

'Sure. We have a cross-index. What is it?'

'1644 West 54th Place. I'd like to know a little something about the condition of the title.'

'I'd better call you back. What's that number?'

He called back in about three minutes.

'Get your pencil out,' he said. 'It's Lot 8 of Block 11 of Caraday's Addition to the Maplewood Tract Number 4. The owner of record, subject to certain things, is Jessie Pierce Florian, widow.'

'Yeah. What things?'

'Second half taxes, two ten-year street improvement bonds, one storm drain assessment bond also ten year, none of these delinquents, also a first trust deed of $2600.'

'You mean one of those things where they can sell you out on ten minutes' notice?'

'Not quite that quick, but a lot quicker than a mortgage. There's nothing unusual about it except the amount. It's high for that neighbourhood, unless it's a new house.'

'It's a very old house and in bad repair,' I said. 'I'd say fifteen hundred would buy the place.'

'Then it's distinctly unusual, because the refinancing was done only four years ago.'

'Okey, who holds it? Some investment company?'

'No. An individual. Man named Lindsay Marriott, a single man. Okey?'

I forgot what I said to him or what thanks I made. They probably sounded like words. I sat there, just staring at the wall.

My stomach suddenly felt fine. I was hungry. I went down to the Mansion House Coffee Shop and ate lunch and got my car out of the parking lot next to my building.

I drove south and east, towards West 54th Place. I didn't carry any liquor with me this time.

16

The block looked just as it had looked the day before. The street was empty except for an ice truck, two Fords in driveways and a swirl of dust going around a corner. I drove slowly past No. 1644 and parked farther along and studied the houses on either side of mine. I walked back and stopped in front of it, looking at the tough palm tree and the drab unwatered scrap of lawn. The house seemed empty, but probably wasn't. It just had that look. The lonely rocker on the front porch stood just where it had stood yesterday. There was a throw-away paper on the walk. I picked it up and slapped it against my leg and then I saw the curtain move next door, in the near front window.

Old Nosey again. I yawned and tilted my hat down. A sharp nose almost flattened itself against the inside of the glass. White hair above it, and eyes that were just eyes from where I stood. I strolled along the sidewalk and the eyes watched me. I turned in towards her house. I climbed the wooden steps and rang the bell.

The door snapped open as if it had been on a spring. She was a tall old bird with a chin like a rabbit. Seen from close her eyes were as sharp as lights on still water. I took my hat off.

'Are you the lady who called the police about Mrs Florian?'

She stared at me coolly and missed nothing about me, probably not even the mole on my right shoulder blade.

'I ain't sayin' I am, young man, and I ain't sayin' I ain't. Who are you?' It was a high twangy voice, made for talking over an eight party line.

'I'm a detective.'

'Land's sakes. Why didn't you say so? What's she done now? I ain't seen a thing and I ain't missed a minute. Henry done all the goin' to the store for me. Ain't been a sound out of there.'

She snapped the screen door unhooked and drew me in. The hall smelled of furniture oil. It had a lot of dark furniture that had once been in good style. Stuff with inlaid panels and scallops at the corners. We went into a front room that had cotton lace antimacassars pinned on everything you could stick a pin into.

'Say, didn't I see you before?' she asked suddenly, a note of suspicion crawling around in her voice. 'Sure enough I did. You was the man that—'

'That's right. And I'm still a detective. Who's Henry?'

'Oh, he's just a little coloured boy that goes errands for me. Well, what you want, young man?' She patted a clean red and white apron and gave me the beady eye. She clicked her store teeth a couple of times for practice.

'Did the officers come here yesterday after they went to Mrs Florian's house?'

'What officers?'

'The uniformed officers,' I said patiently.

'Yes, they was here a minute. They didn't know nothing.'

'Describe the big man to me—the one that had a gun and made you call up.'

She described him, with complete accuracy. It was Malloy all right.

'What kind of car did he drive?'

'A little car. He couldn't hardly get into it.'

'That's all you can say? This man's a murderer!'

Her mouth gaped, but her eyes were pleased. 'Land's sakes, I wish I could tell you, young man. But I never knew much about cars. Murder, eh? Folks ain't safe a minute in this town. When I come here twenty-two years ago we didn't lock our doors hardly. Now it's gangsters and crooked police and politicians fightin' each other with machine-guns, so I've heard. Scandalous is what it is, young man.'

'Yeah. What do you know about Mrs Florian?'

The small mouth puckered. 'She ain't neighbourly. Plays her radio loud late nights. Sings. She don't talk to anybody.' She leaned forward a little. 'I'm not positive, but my opinion is she drinks liquor.'

'She have many visitors?'

'She don't have no visitors at all.'

'You'd know, of course, Mrs—'

'Mrs Morrison. Land's sakes, yes. What else have I got to do but look out of the windows?'

'I bet it's fun. Mrs Florian has lived here a long time?'

'About ten years, I reckon. Had a husband once. Looked like a bad one to me. He died.' She paused and thought. 'I guess he died natural,' she added. 'I never heard different.'

'Left her money?'

Her eyes receded and her chin followed them. She sniffed hard. 'You been drinkin' liquor,' she said coldly.

'I just had a tooth out. The dentist gave it to me.'

'I don't hold with it.'

'It's bad stuff, except for medicine,' I said.

'I don't hold with it for medicine neither.'

'I think you're right,' I said. 'Did he leave her money? Her husband?'

'I wouldn't know.' Her mouth was the size of a prune and as smooth. I had lost out.

'Has anybody at all been there since the officers?'

'Ain't seen.'

'Thank you very much, Mrs Morrison. I won't trouble you any more now. You've been very kind and helpful.'

I walked out of the room and opened the door. She followed me and cleared her throat and clicked her teeth a couple more times.

'What number should I call?' she asked, relenting a little.

'University 4-5000. Ask for Lieutenant Nulty. What does she live on—relief?'

'This ain't a relief neighbourhood,' she said coldly.

'I bet that side piece was the admiration of Sioux Falls once,' I said, gazing at a carved sideboard that was in the hall because the dining-room was too small for it. It had curved ends, thin carved legs, was inlaid all over, and had a painted basket of fruit on the front.

'Mason City,' she said softly. 'Yessir, we had a nice home once, me and George. Best there was.'

I opened the screen door and stepped through it and thanked her again. She was smiling now. Her smile was as sharp as her eyes.

'Gets a registered letter first of every month,' she said suddenly.

I turned and waited. She leaned towards me. 'I see the mailman go up to the door and get her to sign. First day of every month. Dresses up then and goes out. Don't come home till all hours. Sings half the night. Times I could have called the police it was so loud.'

I patted the thin malicious arm.

'You're one in a thousand, Mrs Morrison,' I said. I put my hat on, tipped it to her and left. Half-way down the walk I thought of something and swung back. She was still standing inside the screen door, with the house door open behind her. I went back up on the steps.

'To-morrow's the first,' I said. 'First of April. April Fool's Day. Be sure to notice whether she gets her registered letter, will you, Mrs Morrison?'

The eyes gleamed at me. She began to laugh—a high-pitched old woman's laugh. 'April Fool's Day,' she tittered. 'Maybe she won't get it.'

I left her laughing. The sound was like a hen having hiccups.

17

Nobody answered my ring or knock next door. I tried again. The screen door wasn't hooked. I tried the house door. It was unlocked. I stepped inside.

Nothing was changed, not even the smell of gin. There were still no bodies on the floor. A dirty glass stood on the small table beside the chair where Mrs Florian had sat yesterday. The radio was turned off. I went over to the davenport and felt down behind the cushions. The same dead soldier and another one with him now.

I called out. No answer. Then I thought I heard a long slow unhappy breathing that was half groaning. I went through the arch and sneaked into the little hall-way. The bedroom door was partly open and the groaning sound came from behind it. I stuck my head in and looked.

Mrs Florian was in bed. She was lying flat on her back with a cotton comforter pulled up to her chin. One of the little fluffballs on the comforter was almost in her mouth. Her long yellow face was slack, half dead. Her dirty hair straggled on the pillow. Her eyes opened slowly and looked at me with no expression. The room had a sickening smell of sleep, liquor and dirty clothes. A sixty-nine cent alarm clock ticked on the peeling grey-white paint of the bureau. It ticked loud enough to shake the walls. Above it a mirror showed a distorted view of the woman's face. The trunk from which she had taken the photos was still open.

I said: 'Good afternoon, Mrs Florian. Are you sick?'

She worked her lips together slowly, rubbed one over the other, then slid a tongue out and moistened them and worked her jaws. Her voice came from her mouth sounding like a worn-out phonograph record. Her eyes showed recognition now, but not pleasure.

'You get him?'

'The Moose?'

'Sure.'

'Not yet. Soon, I hope.'

She screwed her eyes up and then snapped them open as if trying to get rid of a film over them.

'You ought to keep your house locked up,' I said. 'He might come back.'

'You think I'm scared of the Moose, huh?'

'You acted like it when I was talking to you yesterday.'

She thought about that. Thinking was weary work. 'Got any liquor?'

'No, I didn't bring any to-day, Mrs Florian. I was a little low on cash.'

'Gin's cheap. It hits.'

'I might go out for some in a little while. So you're not afraid of Malloy?'

'Why would I be?'

'Okey, you're not. What *are* you afraid of?'

Light snapped into her eyes, held for a moment, and faded out again. 'Aw beat it. You coppers give me an ache in the fanny.'

I said nothing. I leaned against the door frame and put a cigarette in my mouth and tried to jerk it up far enough to hit my nose with it. This is harder than it looks.

'Coppers,' she said slowly, as if talking to herself, 'will never catch that boy. He's good and he's got dough and he's got friends. You're wasting your time, copper.'

'Just the routine,' I said. 'It was practically a self-defence anyway. Where would he be?'

She snickered and wiped her mouth on the cotton comforter.

'Soap now,' she said. 'Soft stuff. Copper smart. You guys still think it gets you something.'

'I liked the Moose,' I said.

Interest flickered in her eyes. 'You known him?'

'I was with him yesterday—when he killed the nigger over on Central.'

She opened her mouth wide and laughed her head off without making any more sound than you would make cracking a breadstick. Tears ran out of her eyes and down her face.

'A big strong guy,' I said. 'Soft-hearted in spots too. Wanted his Velma pretty bad.'

The eyes veiled. 'Thought it was her folks was looking for her,' she said softly.

'They are. But she's dead, you said. Nothing there. Where did she die?'

'Dalhart, Texas. Got a cold and went to the chest and off she went.'

'You were there?'

'Hell, no. I just heard.'

'Oh. Who told you, Mrs Florian?'

'Some hoofer. I forget the name right now. Maybe a good stiff drink might help some. I feel like Death Valley.'

'And you look like a dead mule,' I thought, but didn't say it out loud. 'There's just one more thing,' I said, 'then I'll maybe run out for some gin. I looked up the title to your house, I don't know just why.'

She was rigid under the bedclothes, like a wooden woman. Even her eyelids were frozen half down over the clogged iris of her eyes. Her breath stilled.

'There's a rather large trust deed on it,' I said. 'Considering the low value of property round here. It's held by a man named Lindsay Marriott.'

Her eyes blinked rapidly, but nothing else moved. She stared.

'I used to work for him,' she said at last. 'I used to be a servant in his family. He kind of takes care of me a little.'

I took the unlighted cigarette out of my mouth and looked at it aimlessly and stuck it back in.

'Yesterday afternoon, a few hours after I saw you, Mr Marriott called me up at my office. He offered me a job.'

'What kind of job?' Her voice croaked now, badly.

I shrugged. 'I can't tell you that. Confidential. I went to see him last night.'

'You're a clever son of a bitch,' she said thickly and moved a hand under the bedclothes.

I stared at her and said nothing.

'Copper-smart,' she sneered.

I ran a hand up and down the door frame. It felt slimy. Just touching it made me want to take a bath.

'Well, that's all,' I said smoothly. 'I was just wondering how come. Might be nothing at all. Just a coincidence. It just looked as if it might mean something.'

'Copper-smart,' she said emptily. 'Not a real copper at that. Just a cheap shamus.'

'I suppose so,' I said. 'Well, good-bye, Mrs Florian. By the way, I don't think you'll get a registered letter to-morrow morning.'

She threw the bedclothes aside and jerked upright with her eyes blazing. Something glittered in her right hand. A small revolver, A Banker's Special. It was old and worn, but looked business-like.

'Tell it,' she snarled. 'Tell it fast.'

I looked at the gun and the gun looked at me. Not too steadily. The hand behind it began to shake, but the eyes still blazed. Saliva bubbled at the corners of her mouth.

'You and I could work together,' I said.

The gun and her jaw dropped at the same time. I was inches from the door. While the gun was still dropping, I slid through it and beyond the opening.

'Think it over,' I called back.

There was no sound, no sound of any kind.

I went fast back through the hall and dining-room and out of the house. My back felt queer as I went down the walk. The muscles crawled.

Nothing happened. I went along the street and got into my car and drove away from there.

The last day of March and hot enough for summer. I felt like taking my coat off as I drove. In front of the 77th Street Station, two prowl car men were scowling at a bent front fender. I went in through the swing doors and found a uniformed lieutenant behind the railing looking over the charge sheet. I asked him if Nulty was upstairs. He said he thought he was, was I a friend of his. I said yes. He said okey, go on up, so I went up the worn stairs and along the corridor and knocked at the door. The voice yelled and I went in.

He was picking his teeth, sitting in one chair with his feet on the other. He was looking at his left thumb, holding it up in front of his eyes and at arm's length. The thumb looked all right to me, but Nulty's stare was gloomy, as if he thought it wouldn't get well.

He lowered it to his thigh and swung his feet to the floor and looked at me instead of at his thumb. He wore a dark grey suit and a mangled cigar end was waiting on the desk for him to get through with the toothpick.

I turned the felt seat cover that lay on the other chair with its straps not fastened to anything, sat down, and put a cigarette in my face.

'You,' Nulty said, and looked at his toothpick, to see if it was chewed enough.'

'Any luck?'

'Malloy? I ain't on it any more.'

'Who is?'

'Nobody ain't. Why? The guy's lammed. We got him on the teletype and they got readers out. Hell, he'll be in Mexico long gone.'

'Well, all he did was kill a negro,' I said. 'I guess that's only a misdemeanour.'

'You still interested? I thought you was workin'?' His pale eyes moved damply over my face.

'I had a job last night, but it didn't last. Have you still got that Pierrot photo?'

He reached around and pawed under his blotter. He held it out. It still looked pretty. I stared at the face.

'This is really mine,' I said. 'If you don't need it for the file, I'd like to keep it.'

'Should be in the file, I guess,' Nulty said. 'I forgot about it. Okey, keep it under your hat. I passed the file in.'

I put the photo in my breast pocket and stood up. 'Well, I guess that's all,' I said, a little too airily.

'I smell something,' Nulty said coldly.

I looked at the piece of rope on the edge of his desk. His eyes followed my look. He threw the toothpick on the floor and stuck the chewed cigar in his mouth.

'Not this either,' he said.

'It's a vague hunch. If it grows more solid, I won't forget you.'

'Things is tough. I need a break, pal.'

'A man who works as hard as you deserves one,' I said.

He struck a match on his thumbnail, looked pleased because it caught the first time, and started inhaling smoke from the cigar.

'I'm laughing,' Nulty said sadly, as I went out.

The hall was quiet, the whole building was quiet. Down in front the prowl car men were still looking at their bent fender. I drove back to Hollywood.

The phone was ringing as I stepped into the office. I leaned down over the desk and said, 'Yes?'

'Am I addressing Mr Philip Marlowe?'

'Yes, this is Marlowe.'

'This is Mrs Grayle's residence. Mrs Lewin Lockridge Grayle. Mrs Grayle would like to see you here as soon as convenient.'

'Where?'

'The address is Number 862 Aster Drive, in Bay City. May I say you will arrive within the hour?'

'Are you Mr Grayle?'

'Certainly not, sir. I am the butler.'

'That's me you hear ringing the door bell,' I said.

18

It was close to the ocean and you could feel the ocean in the air but you couldn't see water from the front of the place. Aster Drive had a long smooth curve there and the houses on the inland side were just nice houses, but on the canyon side they were great silent estates, with twelve foot walls and wrought-iron gates and ornamental hedges; and inside, if you could get inside, a special brand of sunshine, very quiet, put up in noise-proof containers just for the upper classes.

A man in a dark blue Russian tunic and shiny black puttees and flaring breeches stood in the half-open gates. He was a dark, good-looking lad, with plenty of shoulders and shiny smooth hair and the peak on his rakish cap made a soft shadow over his eyes. He had a cigarette in the corner of his mouth and he held his head tilted a little, as if he liked to keep the smoke out of his nose. One hand had a smooth black gauntlet on it and the other was bare. There was a heavy ring on his third finger.

There was no number in sight, but this should be 862. I stopped my car and leaned out and asked him. It took him a long time to answer. He had to look me over very carefully. Also the car I was driving. He came over to me and as he came he carelessly dropped his ungloved hand towards his hip. It was the kind of carelessness that was meant to be noticed.

He stopped a couple of feet away from my car and looked me over again.

'I'm looking for the Grayle residence,' I said.

'This is it. Nobody in.'

'I'm expected.'

He nodded. His eyes gleamed like water. 'Name?'

'Philip Marlowe.'

'Wait there.' He strolled, without hurry, over to the gates and unlocked an iron door set into one of the massive pillars. There was a telephone inside. He spoke briefly into it, snapped the door shut, and came back to me.

'You have some identification?'

I let him look at the licence on the steering post. 'That doesn't prove anything,' he said. 'How do I know it's your car?'

I pulled the key out of the ignition and threw the door open and got out. That put me about a foot from him. He had a nice breath. Haig and Haig at least.

'You've been at the sideboy again,' I said.

He smiled. His eyes measured me. I said:

'Listen, I'll talk to the butler over that phone and he'll know my voice. Will that pass me in or do I have to ride on your back?'

'I just work here,' he said softly. 'If I didn't—' he let the rest hang in the air, and kept on smiling.

'You're a nice lad,' I said and patted his shoulder. 'Dartmouth or Dannemora?'

'Christ,' he said. 'Why didn't you say you were a cop?'

We both grinned. He waved his hand and I went in through the half-open gate. The drive curved and tall moulded hedges of dark green completely screened it from the street and from the house. Through a green gate I saw a Jap gardener at work weeding a huge lawn. He was pulling a piece of weed out of the vast velvet expanse and sneering at it the way Jap gardeners do. Then the tall hedge closed in again and I didn't see anything more for a hundred feet. Then the hedge ended in a wide circle in which half a dozen cars were parked.

One of them was a small coupé. There were a couple of very nice two-tone Buicks of the latest model, good enough to go for the mail in. There was a black limousine, with dull nickel louvres and hubcaps the size of bicycle wheels. There was a long sport phaeton with the top down. A short very wide all-weather concrete driveway led from these to the side entrance of the house.

Off to the left, beyond the parking space there was a sunken garden with a fountain at each of the four corners. The entrance was barred by a wrought-iron gate with a flying Cupid in the middle. There were busts on light pillars and a stone seat with crouching griffins at each end. There was an oblong pool with stone water-lilies in it and a big stone bullfrog sitting on one of the leaves. Still farther a rose colonnade led to a thing like an altar, hedged in at both sides, yet not so completely but that the sun lay in an arabesque along the steps of the altar. And far over to the left there was a wild garden, not very large, with a sundial in the corner near an angle of wall that was built to look like a ruin. And there were flowers. There were a million flowers.

The house itself was not so much. It was smaller than Buckingham Palace, rather grey for California, and probably had fewer windows than the Chrysler Building.

I sneaked over to the side entrance and pressed a bell and somewhere a set of chimes made a deep mellow sound like church bells.

A man in a striped vest and gilt buttons opened the door, bowed, took my hat and was through for the day. Behind him in dimness, a man in striped knife-edge pants and a black coat and wing collar with grey striped tie leaned his grey head forward about half an inch and said: 'Mr Marlowe? If you will come this way, please—'

We went down a hall. It was a very quiet hall. Not a fly buzzed in it. The floor was covered with Oriental rugs and there were paintings along the walls. We turned a corner and there was more hall. A French window showed a gleam of blue water far off and I remembered almost with a shock that we were near the Pacific Ocean and that this house was on the edge of one of the canyons.

The butler reached a door and opened it against voices and stood aside and I went in. It was a nice room with large chesterfields and lounging chairs done in pale yellow leather arranged around a fireplace in front of which, on the glossy but not slippery floor, lay a rug as thin as silk and as old as Æsop's aunt. A jet of flowers glistened in a corner, another on a low table, the walls were of dull painted parchment, there was comfort, space, cosiness, a dash of the very modern and a dash of the very old, and three people sitting in a sudden silence watching me cross the floor.

One of them was Anne Riordan, looking just as I had seen her last, except that she was holding a glass of amber fluid in her hand. One was a tall thin sad-faced man with a stony chin and deep eyes and no colour in his face but an unhealthy yellow. He was a good sixty, or rather a bad sixty. He wore a dark business suit, a red carnation, and looked subdued.

The third was the blonde. She was dressed to go out, in a pale greenish blue. I didn't pay much attention to her clothes. They were what the guy designed for her and she would go to the right man. The effect was to make her look very young and to make her lapis lazuli eyes look very blue. Her hair was of the gold of old paintings and had been fussed with just enough but not too much. She had a full set of curves which nobody had been able to improve on. The dress was rather plain except for a clasp of diamonds at the throat. Her hands were not small, but they had shape, and the nails were the usual jarring note–almost magenta. She was giving me one of her smiles. She looked as if she smiled easily, but her eyes had a still look, as if they thought slowly and carefully. And her mouth was sensual.

'So nice of you to come,' she said. 'This is my husband. Mix Mr Marlowe a drink, honey.'

Mr Grayle shook hands with me. His hand was cold and a little moist. His eyes were sad. He mixed a Scotch and soda and handed it to me.

Then he sat down in a corner and was silent. I drank half of the drink and grinned at Miss Riordan. She looked at me with a sort of absent expression, as if she had another clue.

'Do you think you can do anything for us?' the blonde asked slowly, looking down into her glass. 'If you think you can, I'd be delighted. But the loss is rather small, compared with having any more fuss with gangsters and awful people.'

'I don't know very much about it really,' I said.

'Oh, I hope you can.' She gave me a smile I could feel in my hip pocket.

I drank the other half of my drink. I began to feel rested. Mrs Grayle rang a bell set into the arm of the leather chesterfield and a footman came in. She half pointed to the tray. He looked around and mixed two drinks. Miss Riordan was still playing cute with the same one and apparently Mr Grayle didn't drink. The footman went out.

Mrs Grayle and I held our glasses. Mrs Grayle crossed her legs, a little carelessly.

'I don't know whether I can do anything,' I said. 'I doubt it. What is there to go on?'

'I'm sure you can.' She gave me another smile. 'How far did Lin Marriott take you into his confidence?'

She looked sideways at Miss Riordan. Miss Riordan just couldn't catch the look. She kept right on sitting. She looked sideways the other way. Mrs Grayle looked at her husband. 'Do you have to bother with this, honey?'

Mr Grayle stood up and said he was very glad to have met me and that he would go and lie down for a while. He didn't feel very well. He hoped I would excuse him. He was so polite I wanted to carry him out of the room just to show my appreciation.

He left. He closed the door softly, as if he was afraid to wake a sleeper. Mrs Grayle looked at the door for a moment and then put the smile back on her face and looked at me.

'Miss Riordan is in your complete confidence, of course.'

'Nobody's in my complete confidence, Mrs Grayle. She happens to know about this case—what there is to know.'

'Yes.' She drank a sip or two, then finished her glass at a swallow and set it aside.

'To hell with this polite drinking,' she said suddenly. 'Let's get together on this. You're a very good-looking man to be in your sort of racket.'

'It's a smelly business,' I said.

'I didn't quite mean that. Is there any money in it—or is that impertinent?'

'There's not much money in it. There's a lot of grief. But there's a lot of fun, too. And there's always a chance of a big case.'

'How does one get to be a private detective? You don't mind my sizing you up a little? And push that table over here, will you? So I can reach the drinks.'

I got up and pushed the huge silver tray on a stand across the glossy floor to her side. She made two more drinks. I still had half of my second.

'Most of us are ex-cops,' I said. 'I worked for the D.A. for a while. I got fired.'

She smiled nicely. 'Not for incompetence, I'm sure.'

'No, for talking back. Have you had any more phone calls?'

'Well—' She looked at Anne Riordan. She waited. Her look said things.

Anne Riordan stood up. She carried her glass, still full, over to the tray and set it down. 'You probably won't run short,' she said. 'But if you do—and thanks very much for talking to me, Mrs Grayle. I won't use anything. You have my word for it.'

'Heavens, you're not leaving,' Mrs Grayle said with her smile.

Anne Riordan took her lower lip between her teeth and held it there for a moment as if making up her mind whether to bite it off and spit it out or leave it on a while longer.

'Sorry, afraid I'll have to. I don't work for Mr Marlowe, you know. Just a friend. Good-bye, Mrs Grayle.'

The blonde gleamed at her. 'I hope you'll drop in again soon. Any time.' She pressed the bell twice. That got the butler. He held the door open.

Miss Riordan went out quickly and the door closed. For quite a while after it closed, Mrs Grayle stared at it with a faint smile. 'It's much better this way, don't you think?' she said after an interval of silence. I nodded. 'You're probably wondering how she knows so much if she's just a friend,' I said. 'She's a curious little girl. Some of it she dug out herself, like who you were and who owned the jade necklace. Some of it just happened. She came by last night to that dell where Marriott was killed. She was out riding. She happened to see a light and came down there.'

'Oh.' Mrs Grayle lifted a glass quickly and made a face. 'It's horrible to think of. Poor Lin. He was rather a heel. Most of one's friends are. But to die like that is awful.' She shuddered. Her eyes got large and dark.

'So it's all right about Miss Riordan. She won't talk. Her father was chief of police here for a long time,' I said.

'Yes. So she told me. You're not drinking.'

'I'm doing what *I* call drinking.'

'You and I should get along. Did Lin—Mr Marriott—tell you how the hold-up happened?'

'Between here and the Trocadero somewhere. He didn't say exactly. Three or four men.'

She nodded her golden gleaming head. 'Yes. You know there was something rather funny about that hold-up. They gave me back one of my rings, rather a nice one, too.'

'He told me that.'

'Then again I hardly ever wore the jade. After all, it's a museum piece, probably not many like it in the world, a very rare type of jade. Yet they snapped at it. I wouldn't expect them to think it had any value much, would you?'

'They'd know you wouldn't wear it otherwise. Who knew about its value?'

She thought. It was nice to watch her thinking. She still had her legs crossed, and still carelessly.

'All sorts of people, I suppose.'

'But they didn't know you would be wearing it that night? Who knew that?'

She shrugged her pale blue shoulders. I tried to keep my eyes where they belonged.

'My maid. But she's had a hundred chances. And I trust her—'

'Why?'

'I don't know. I just trust some people. I trust you.'

'Did you trust Marriott?'

Her face got a little hard. Her eyes a little watchful. 'Not in some things. In others, yes. There are degrees.' She had a nice way of talking, cool, half-cynical, and yet not hard-boiled. She rounded her words well.

'All right—besides the maid. The chauffeur?'

She shook her head, no. 'Lin drove me that night, in his own car. I don't think George was around at all. Wasn't it Thursday?'

'I wasn't there. Marriott said four or five days before in telling me about it. Thursday would have been an even week from last night.'

'Well, it was Thursday.' She reached for my glass and her fingers touched mine a little, and were soft to the touch. 'George gets Thursday evening off. That's the usual day, you know.' She poured a fat slug of mellow-looking Scotch into my glass and squirted in some fizz-water. It was the kind of liquor you think you can drink for ever and all you do is get reckless. She gave herself the same treatment.

'Lin told you my name?' she asked softly, the eyes still watchful.

'He was careful not to.'

'Then he probably misled you a little about the time. Let's see what we have. Maid and chauffeur out. Out of consideration as accomplices, I mean.'

'They're not out by me.'

'Well, at least I'm trying,' she laughed. 'Then there's Newton, the butler. He might have seen it on my neck that night. But it hangs down rather low and I was wearing a white fox evening wrap; no, I don't think he could have seen it.'

'I bet you looked a dream,' I said.

'You're not getting a little tight, are you?'

'I've been known to be soberer.'

She put her head back and went off into a peal of laughter. I have only known four women in my life who could do that and still look beautiful. She was one of them.

'Newton is okey,' I said. 'His type don't run with hoodlums. That's just guessing, though. How about the footman?'

She thought and remembered, then shook her head. 'He didn't see me.'

'Anybody ask you to wear the jade?'

Her eyes instantly got more guarded. 'You're not fooling me a damn bit,' she said.

She reached for my glass to refill it. I let her have it, even though it still had an inch to go. I studied the lovely lines of her neck.

When she had filled the glasses and we were playing with them again I said, 'Let's get the record straight and then I'll tell you something. Describe the evening.'

She looked at her wrist watch, drawing a full length sleeve back to do it. 'I ought to be—'

'Let him wait.'

Her eyes flashed at that. I liked them that way. 'There's such a thing as being just a little too frank,' she said.

'Not in my business. Describe the evening. Or have me thrown out on my ear. One or the other. Make your lovely mind up.'

'You'd better sit over here beside me.'

'I've been thinking that a long time,' I said. 'Ever since you crossed your legs, to be exact.'

She pulled her dress down. 'These damn things are always up around your neck.'

I sat beside her on the yellow leather chesterfield. 'Aren't you a pretty fast worker?' she asked quietly.

I didn't answer her.

'Do you do much of this sort of thing?' she asked with a sidelong look.

'Practically none. I'm a Tibetan monk, in my spare time.'

'Only you don't have any spare time.'

'Let's focus,' I said. 'Let's get what's left of our minds—or mine—on the problem. How much are you going to pay me?'

'Oh, that's the problem. I thought you were going to get my necklace back. Or try to.'

'I have to work in my own way. This way.' I took a long drink and it nearly stood me on my head. I swallowed a little air.

'And investigate a murder,' I said.

'That has nothing to do with it. I mean that's a police affair, isn't it?'

'Yeah—only the poor guy paid me a hundred bucks to take care of him—and I didn't. Makes me feel guilty. Makes me want to cry. Shall I cry?'

'Have a drink.' She poured us some more Scotch. It didn't seem to affect her any more than water affects Boulder Dam.

'Well, where have we got to?' I said, trying to hold my glass so that the whisky would stay inside it. 'No maid, no chauffeur, no butler, no footman. We'll be doing our own laundry next. How did the hold-up happen? Your version might have a few details Marriott didn't give me.'

She leaned forward and cupped her chin in her hand. She looked serious without looking silly-serious.

'We went to a party in Brentwood Heights. Then Lin suggested we run over to the Troc for a few drinks and a few dances. So we did. They were doing some work on Sunset and it was very dusty. So coming back Lin dropped down to Santa Monica. That took us past a shabby-looking hotel called the Hotel Indio, which I happened to notice for some silly meaningless reason. Across the street from it was a beer joint and a car was parked in front of that.'

'Only one car—in front of a beer joint?'

'Yes. Only one. It was a very dingy place. Well, this car started up and followed us and of course I thought nothing of that either. There was no reason to. Then before we got to where Santa Monica turns into Arguello Boulevard, Lin said, "Let's go over the other road" and turned up some curving residential street. Then all of a sudden a car rushed by us and grazed the fender and then pulled over to stop. A man in an overcoat and scarf and hat low on his face came back to apologize. It was a white scarf bunched out and it drew my eyes. It was about all I really saw of him except that he was tall and thin. As soon as he got close—and I remembered afterwards that he didn't walk in our headlights at all—'

'That's natural. Nobody likes to look into headlights. Have a drink. My treat this time.'

She was leaning forward, her fine eyebrows—not daubs of paint—drawn together in a frown of thought. I made two drinks. She went on:

'As soon as he got close to the side where Lin was sitting he jerked the scarf up over his nose and a gun was shining at us. "Stick-up," he said. "Be very quiet and everything will be jake." Then another man came over on the other side.'

'In Beverly Hills,' I said, 'the best policed four square miles in California.'

She shrugged. 'It happened just the same. They asked for my jewellery and bag. The man with the scarf did. The one on my side never spoke at all. I passed the things across Lin and the man gave me back my bag and one ring. He said to hold off calling the police and insurance people for a while. They would make us a nice smooth easy deal. He said they found it easier to work on a straight percentage. He seemed to have all the time in the world. He said they could work through the insurance people, if they had to, but that meant cutting in a shyster, and they preferred not to. He sounded like a man with some education.'

'It might have been Dressed-Up Eddie,' I said. 'Only he got bumped off in Chicago.'

She shrugged. We had a drink. She went on.

'Then they left and we went home and I told Lin to keep quiet about it. The next day I got a call. We have two phones, one with extensions and one in my bedroom with no extensions. The call was on this. It's not listed, of course.'

I nodded. 'They can buy the number for a few dollars. It's done all the time. Some movie people have to change their numbers every month.'

We had a drink.

'I told the man calling to take it up with Lin and he would represent me and if they were not too unreasonable, we might deal. He said okey, and from then on I guess they just stalled long enough to watch us a little. Finally, as you know, we agreed on eight thousand dollars and so forth.'

'Could you recognize any of them?'

'Of course not.'

'Randall know all this?'

'Of course. Do we have to talk about it any more? It bores me.' She gave me the lovely smile.

'Did he make any comment?'

She yawned. 'Probably. I forget.'

I sat with my empty glass in my hand and thought. She took it away from me and started to fill it again.

I took the refilled glass out of her hand and transferred it to my left and took hold of her left hand with my right. It felt smooth and soft and warm and comforting. It squeezed mine. The muscles in it were strong. She was a well built woman, and no paper flower.

'I think he had an idea,' she said. 'But he didn't say what it was.'

'Anybody would have an idea out of all that,' I said.

She turned her head slowly and looked at me. Then she nodded. 'You can't miss it, can you?'

'How long have you known him?'

'Oh, years. He used to be an announcer at the station my husband owned. K.F.D.K. That's where I met him. That's where I met my husband too.'

'I knew that. But Marriott lived as if he had money. Not riches, but comfortable money.'

'He came into some and quit radio business.'

'Do you know for a fact he came into money—or was that just something he said?'

She shrugged. She squeezed my hand.

'Or it may not have been very much money and he may have gone through it pretty fast,' I squeezed her hand back. 'Did he borrow from you?'

'You're a little old-fashioned, aren't you?' She looked down at the hand I was holding.

'I'm still working. And your Scotch is so good it keeps me half-sober. Not that I'd have to be drunk—'

'Yes.' She drew her hand out of mine and rubbed it. 'You must have quite a clutch—in your spare time. Lin Marriott was a high-class blackmailer, of course. That's obvious. He lived on women.'

'He had something on you?'

'Should I tell you?'

'It probably wouldn't be wise.'

She laughed. 'I will, anyhow. I got a little tight at his house once and passed out. I seldom do. He took some photos of me—with my clothes up to my neck.'

'The dirty dog,' I said. 'Have you got any of them handy?'

She slapped my wrist. She said softly:

'What's your name?'

'Phil. What's yours?'

'Helen. Kiss me.'

She fell softly across my lap and I bent down over her face and began to browse on it. She worked her eyelashes and made butterfly kisses on my cheeks. When I got to her mouth it was half open and burning and her tongue was a darting snake between her teeth.

The door opened and Mr Grayle stepped quietly into the room. I was holding her and didn't have a chance to let go. I lifted my face and looked at him. I felt as cold as Finnegan's feet, the day they buried him.

The blonde in my arms didn't move, didn't even close her lips. She had a half-dreamy, half-sarcastic expression on her face.

Mr Grayle cleared his throat slightly and said: 'I beg your pardon, I'm sure,' and went quietly out of the room. There was an infinite sadness in his eyes.

I pushed her away and stood up and got my handkerchief out and mopped my face.

She lay as I had left her, half sideways along the davenport, the skin showing in a generous sweep above one stocking.

'Who was that?' she asked thickly.

'Mr Grayle.'

'Forget him.'

I went away from her and sat down in the chair I had sat in when I first came into the room.

After a moment she straightened herself out and sat up and looked at me steadily.

'It's all right. He understands. What the hell can he expect?'

'I guess he knows.'

'Well, I tell you it's all right. Isn't that enough? He's a sick man. What the hell—'

'Don't go shrill on me. I don't like shrill women.'

She opened a bag lying beside her and took out a small handkerchief and wiped her lips, then looked at her face in a mirror.

'I guess you're right,' she said. 'Just too much Scotch. To-night at the Belvedere Club. Ten o'clock.' She wasn't looking at me. Her breath was fast.

'Is that a good place?'

'Laird Brunette owns it. I know him pretty well.'

'Right,' I said. I was still cold. I felt nasty, as if I had picked a poor man's pocket.

She got a lipstick out and touched her lips very lightly and then looked at me along her eyes. She tossed the mirror. I caught it and looked at my face. I worked at it with my handkerchief and stood up to give her back the mirror.

She was leaning back, showing all her throat, looking at me lazily down her eyes.

'What's the matter?'

'Nothing. Ten o'clock at the Belvedere Club. Don't be too magnificent. All I have is a dinner suit. In the bar?'

She nodded, her eyes still lazy.

I went across the room and out, without looking back. The footman met me in the hall and gave me my hat, looking like the Great Stone Face.

19

I walked down the curving driveway and lost myself in the shadow of the tall trimmed hedges and came to the gates. Another man was holding the fort now, a husky in plain clothes, an obvious bodyguard. He let me out with a nod.

A horn tooted. Miss Riordan's coupé was drawn up behind my car. I went over there and looked in at her. She looked cool and sarcastic. She sat there with her hands on the wheel, gloved and slim. She smiled.

'I waited. I suppose it was none of my business. What did you think of her?'

'I bet she snaps a mean garter.'

'Do you always have to say things like that?' She flushed bitterly. 'Sometimes I hate men. Old men, young men, football players, opera tenors, smart millionaires, beautiful men who are gigolos and almost-heels who are—private detectives.'

I grinned at her sadly. 'I know I talk too smart. It's in the air nowadays. Who told you he was a gigolo?'

'Who?'

'Don't be obtuse. Marriott.'

'Oh, it was a cinch guess. I'm sorry. I don't mean to be nasty. I guess you can snap her garter any time you want to, without much of a struggle. But there's one thing you can be sure of—you're a late comer to the show.'

The wide curving street dozed peacefully in the sun. A beautifully painted panel truck slid noiselessly to a stop before a house across the street, then backed a little and went up the driveway to a side entrance. On the side of the panel truck was painted the legend: 'Bay City Infant Service.'

Anne Riordan leaned towards me, her grey-blue eyes hurt and clouded. Her slightly too long upper lip pouted and then pressed back against her teeth. She made a sharp little sound with her breath.

'Probably you'd like me to mind my own business, is that it? And not have ideas you don't have first. I thought I was helping a little.'

'I don't need any help. The police don't want any from me. There's nothing I can do for Mrs Grayle. She has a yarn about a beer parlour where a car started from and followed them, but what does that amount to? It was a crummy dive on Santa Monica. This was a high-class mob. There was somebody in it that could even tell Fei Tsui jade when he saw it.'

'If he wasn't tipped off.'

'There's that too,' I said, and fumbled a cigarette out of a package. 'Either way there's nothing for me in it.'

'Not even about psychics?'

I stared rather blankly. 'Psychics?'

'My God,' she said softly. 'And I thought you were a detective.'

'There's a hush on part of this,' I said. 'I've got to watch my step. This

Grayle packs a lot of dough in his pants. And law is where you buy it in this town. Look at the funny way the cops are acting. No build-up, no newspaper handout, no chance for the innocent stranger to step in with the trifling clue that turns out to be all important. Nothing but silence and warnings to me to lay off. I don't like it at all.'

'You got most of the lipstick off,' Anne Riordan said. 'I mentioned psychics. Well, good-bye. It was nice to know you–in a way.'

She pressed her starter button and jammed her gears in and was gone in a swirl of dust.

I watched her go. When she was gone I looked across the street. The man from the panel truck that said Bay City Infant Service came out of the side door of the house dressed in a uniform so white and stiff and gleaming that it made me feel clean just to look at it. He was carrying a carton of some sort. He got into his panel truck and drove away.

I figured he had just changed a diaper.

I got into my own car and looked at my watch before starting up. It was almost five.

The Scotch, as good enough Scotch will, stayed with me all the way back to Hollywood. I took the red lights as they came.

'There's a nice little girl,' I told myself out loud, in the car, 'for a guy that's interested in a nice little girl.' Nobody said anything. 'But I'm not,' I said. Nobody said anything to that either. 'Ten o'clock at the Belvedere Club,' I said. Somebody said: 'Phooey.'

It sounded like my voice.

It was a quarter to six when I reached my office again. The building was very quiet. The typewriter beyond the party wall was stilled. I lit a pipe and sat down to wait.

20

The Indian smelled. He smelled clear across the little reception room when the buzzer sounded and I opened the door between to see who it was. He stood just inside the corridor door looking as if he had been cast in bronze. He was a big man from the waist up and he had a big chest. He looked like a bum.

He wore a brown suit of which the coat was too small for his shoulders and his trousers were probably a little tight under the armpits. His hat was at least two sizes too small and had been perspired in freely by somebody it fitted better than it fitted him. He wore it about where a house wears a wind vane. His collar had the snug fit of a horse-collar and was of about the same shade of dirty brown. A tie dangled outside his buttoned jacket, a black tie which had been tied with a pair of pliers in a knot the size of a pea. Around his bare and magnificent throat, above the dirty collar, he wore a wide piece of black ribbon, like an old woman trying to freshen up her neck.

He had a big flat face and a high-bridged fleshy nose that looked as hard as the prow of a cruiser. He had lidless eyes, drooping jowls, the shoulders of a blacksmith and the short and apparently awkward legs of a chimpanzee. I found out later that they were only short.

If he had been cleaned up a little and dressed in a white nightgown, he would have looked like a very wicked Roman senator.

His smell was the earthy smell of primitive man, and not the slimy dirt of cities.

'Huh,' he said. 'Come quick. Come now.'

I backed into my office and wiggled my finger at him and he followed me making as much noise as a fly makes walking on the wall. I sat down behind my desk and squeaked my swivel chair professionally and pointed to the customer's chair on the other side. He didn't sit down. His small black eyes were hostile.

'Come where?' I said.

'Huh. Me Second Planting. Me Hollywood Indian.'

'Have a chair, Mr Planting.'

He snorted and his nostrils got very wide. They had been wide enough for mouseholes to start with.

'Name Second Planting. Name no Mister Planting.'

'What can I do for you?'

He lifted his voice and began to intone in a deep-chested sonorous boom. 'He say come quick. Great white father say come quick. He say me bring you in fiery chariot. He say—'

'Yeah. Cut out the pig Latin,' I said. 'I'm no schoolmarm at the snake dances.'

'Nuts,' the Indian said.

We sneered at each other across the desk for a moment. He sneered better than I did. Then he removed his hat with massive disgust and turned it upside down. He rolled a finger around under the sweatband. That turned the sweatband up into view, and it had not been misnamed. He removed a paper clip from the edge and threw a fold of tissue paper on the desk. He pointed at it angrily, with a well-chewed fingernail. His lank hair had a shelf around it, high up, from the too-tight hat.

I unfolded the piece of tissue paper and found a card inside. The card was no news to me. There had been three exactly like it in the mouthpieces of three Russian-appearing cigarettes.

I played with my pipe, stared at the Indian and tried to ride him with my stare. He looked as nervous as a brick wall.

'Okey, what does he want?'

'He want you come quick. Come now. Come in fiery—'

'Nuts,' I said.

The Indian liked that. He closed his mouth slowly and winked an eye solemnly and then almost grinned.

'Also it will cost him a hundred bucks as a retainer,' I added, trying to look as if that was a nickel.

'Huh?' Suspicious again. Stick to basic English.

'Hundred dollars,' I said. 'Iron men. Fish. Bucks to the number of one hundred. Me no money, me no come. Savvy?' I began to count a hundred with both hands.

'Huh. Big shot,' the Indian sneered.

He worked under his greasy hatband and threw another fold of tissue paper on the desk. I took it and unwound it. It contained a brand-new hundred dollar bill.

The Indian put his hat back on his head without bothering to tuck the hatband back in place. It looked only slightly more comic that way. I sat staring at the hundred dollar bill, with my mouth open.

'Psychic is right,' I said at last. 'A guy that smart I'm afraid of.'

'Not got all day,' the Indian remarked, conversationally.

I opened my desk and took out a Colt .38 automatic of the type known as Super Match. I hadn't worn it to visit Mrs Lewin Lockridge Grayle. I stripped my coat off and strapped the leather harness on and tucked the automatic down inside it and strapped the lower strap and put my coat back on again.

This meant as much to the Indian as if I had scratched my neck.

'Gottum car,' he said. 'Big car.'

'I don't like big cars any more,' I said. 'I gottum own car.'

'You come my car,' the Indian said threateningly.

'I come your car,' I said.

I locked the desk and office up, switched the buzzer off and went out, leaving the reception room door unlocked as usual.

We went along the hall and down in the elevator. The Indian smelled. Even the elevator operator noticed it.

21

The car was a dark blue seven-passenger sedan, a Packard of the latest model, custom-built. It was the kind of car you wear your rope pearls in. It was parked by a fire-hydrant and a dark foreign-looking chauffeur with a face of carved wood was behind the wheel. The interior was upholstered in quilted grey chenille. The Indian put me in the back. Sitting there alone I felt like a high-class corpse, laid out by an undertaker with a lot of good taste.

The Indian got in beside the chauffeur and the car turned in the middle of the block and a cop across the street said: 'Hey,' weakly, as if he didn't mean it, and then bent down quickly to tie his shoe.

We went west, dropped over to Sunset and slid fast and noiseless along that. The Indian sat motionless beside the chauffeur. An occasional whiff of his personality drifted back to me. The driver looked as if he was half asleep but he passed the fast boys in the convertible sedans as though they were being towed. They turned on all the green lights for him. Some drivers are like that. He never missed one.

We curved through the bright mile or two of the Strip, past the antique shops with famous screen names on them, past the windows full of point lace and ancient pewter, past the gleaming new night-clubs with famous chefs and equally famous gambling rooms, run by polished graduates of the Purple Gang, past the Georgian-Colonial vogue, now old hat, past the handsome modernistic buildings in which the Hollywood flesh-peddlers never stop talking money, past a drive-in lunch which somehow didn't belong, even though the girls wore white silk blouses and drum majorettes' shakos and nothing below the hips but glazed kid Hessian boots. Past all this

and down a wide smooth curve to the bridle path of Beverly Hills and lights
to the south, all colours of the spectrum and crystal clear in an evening
without fog, past the shadowed mansions up on the hills to the north, past
Beverly Hills altogether and up into the twisting foothill boulevard and the
sudden cool dusk and the drift of wind from the sea.

It had been a warm afternoon, but the heat was gone. We whipped past a
distant cluster of lighted buildings and an endless series of lighted
mansions, not too close to the road. We dipped down to skirt a huge green
polo field with another equally huge practice field beside it, soared again to
the top of a hill and swung mountainward up a steep hill road of clean
concrete that passed orange groves, some rich man's pet because this is not
orange country, and then little by little the lighted windows of the
millionaires' homes were gone and the road narrowed and this was
Stillwood Heights.

The smell of sage drifted up from a canyon and made me think of a dead
man and a moonless sky. Straggly stucco houses were moulded flat to the
side of the hill, like bas-reliefs. Then there were no more houses, just the
still dark foothills with an early star or two above them, and the concrete
ribbon of road and a sheer drop on one side into a tangle of scrub oak and
manzanita where sometimes you can hear the call of the quails if you stop
and keep still and wait. On the other side of the road was a raw clay bank at
the edge of which a few unbeatable wild flowers hung on like naughty
children that won't go to bed.

Then the road twisted into a hairpin turn and the big tyres scratched over
loose stones, and the car tore less soundlessly up a long driveway lined with
wild geraniums. At the top of this, faintly lighted, lonely as a lighthouse,
stood an eyrie, an eagle's nest, an angular building of stucco and glass brick,
raw and modernistic and yet not ugly and altogether a swell place for a
psychic consultant to hang out his shingle. Nobody would be able to hear
any screams.

The car turned beside the house and a light flicked on over a black door
set into the heavy wall. The Indian climbed out grunting and opened the
rear door of the car. The chauffeur lit a cigarette with an electric lighter and
a harsh smell of tobacco came back to me softly in the evening. I got out.

We went over to the black door. It opened of itself, slowly almost with
menace. Beyond it a narrow hallway probed back into the house. Light
glowed from the glass brick walls.

The Indian growled, 'Huh. You go in, big shot.'

'After you, Mr Planting.'

He scowled and went in and the door closed after us as silently and
mysteriously as it had opened. At the end of the narrow hallway we
squeezed into a little elevator and the Indian closed the door and pressed a
button. We rose softly, without sound. Such smelling as the Indian had
done before was a mooncast shadow to what he was doing now.

The elevator stopped, the door opened. There was light and I stepped out
into a turret room where the day was still trying to be remembered. There
were windows all around it. Far off the sea flickered. Darkness prowled
slowly on the hills. There were panelled walls where there were no
windows, and rugs on the floor with the soft colours of old Persians, and
there was a reception desk that looked as if it had been made of carvings
stolen from an ancient church. And behind the desk a woman sat and smiled

at me, a dry tight withered smile that would turn to powder if you touched it.

She had sleek coiled hair and a dark, thin, wasted Asiatic face. There were heavy coloured stones in her ears and heavy rings on her fingers, including a moonstone and an emerald in a silver setting that may have been a real emerald but somehow managed to look as phony as a dime store slave bracelet. And her hands were dry and dark and not young and not fit for rings.

She spoke. The voice was familiar. 'Ah, Meester Marlowe, so ver-ry good of you to come. Amthor he weel be so ver-ry pleased.'

I laid the hundred dollar bill the Indian had given me down on the desk. I looked behind me. The Indian had gone down again in the elevator.

'Sorry. It was a nice thought, but I can't take this.'

'Amthor he–he weesh to employ you, is it not?' She smiled again. Her lips rustled like tissue paper.

'I'd have to find out what the job is first.'

She nodded and got up slowly from behind the desk. She swished before me in a tight dress that fitted her like a mermaid's skin and showed that she had a good figure if you like them four sizes bigger below the waist.

'I weel conduct you,' she said.

She pressed a button in the panelling and a door slid open noiselessly. There was a milky glow beyond it. I looked back at her smile before I went through. It was older than Egypt now. The door slid silently shut behind me.

There was nobody in the room.

It was octagonal, draped in black velvet from floor to ceiling, with a high remote black ceiling that may have been of velvet too. In the middle of a coal-black lustreless rug stood an octagonal white table, just large enough for two pairs of elbows and in the middle of it a milk-white globe on a black stand. The light came from this. How, I couldn't see. On either side of the table there was a white octagonal stool which was a smaller edition of the table. Over against one wall there was one more such stool. There were no windows. There was nothing else in the room, nothing at all. On the walls there was not even a light fixture. If there were other doors, I didn't see them. I looked back at the one by which I had come in. I couldn't see that either.

I stood there for perhaps fifteen seconds with the faint obscure feeling of being watched. There was probably a peephole somewhere, but I couldn't spot it. I gave up trying. I listened to my breath. The room was so still that I could hear it going through my nose, softly, like little curtains rustling.

Then an invisible door on the far side of the room slid open and a man stepped through and the door closed behind him. The man walked straight to the table with his head down and sat on one of the octagonal stools and made a sweeping motion with one of the most beautiful hands I have ever seen.

'Please be seated. Opposite me. Do not smoke and do not fidget. Try to relax, completely. Now how may I serve you?'

I sat down, got a cigarette into my mouth and rolled it along my lips without lighting it. I looked him over. He was thin, tall and straight as a steel rod. He had the palest finest white hair I ever saw. It could have been strained through silk gauze. His skin was as fresh as a rose petal. He might have been thirty-five or sixty-five. He was ageless. His hair was brushed straight back from as good a profile as Barrymore ever had. His eyebrows were coal black, like the walls and ceiling and floor. His eyes were deep, far too deep. They were the depthless drugged eyes of the somnambulist. They were like a well I read about once. It was nine hundred years old, in an old castle. You could drop a stone into it and wait. You could listen and wait and then you would give up waiting and laugh and then just as you were ready to turn away a faint, minute splash would come back up to you from the bottom of that well, so tiny, so remote that you could hardly believe a well like that possible.

His eyes were deep like that. And they were also eyes without expression, without soul, eyes that could watch lions tear a man to pieces and never change, that could watch a man impaled and screaming in the hot sun with his eyelids cut off.

He wore a double-breasted black business suit that had been cut by an artist. He stared vaguely at my fingers.

'Please do not fidget,' he said. 'It breaks the waves, disturbs my concentration.'

'It makes the ice melt, the butter run and the cat squawk,' I said.

He smiled the faintest smile in the world. 'You didn't come here to be impertinent, I'm sure.'

'You seem to forget why I did come. By the way, I gave that hundred dollar bill back to your secretary. I came, as you may recall, about some cigarettes. Russian cigarettes filled with marijuana. With your card rolled in the hollow mouthpieces.'

'You wish to find out why that happened?'

'Yeah. I ought to be paying you the hundred dollars.'

'That will not be necessary. The answer is simple. There are things I do not know. This is one of them.'

For a moment I almost believed him. His face was as smooth as an angel's wing.

'Then why send me a hundred dollars—and a tough Indian that stinks—and a car? By the way, does the Indian have to stink? If he's working for you, couldn't you sort of get him to take a bath?'

'He is a natural medium. They are rare—like diamonds, and like diamonds, are sometimes found in dirty places. I understand you are a private detective?'

'Yes.'

'I think you are a very stupid person. You look stupid. You are in a stupid business. And you came here on a stupid mission.'

'I get it,' I said. 'I'm stupid. It sank in after a while.'

'And I think I need not detain you any longer.'

'You're not detaining me,' I said. 'I'm detaining you. I want to know why those cards were in those cigarettes.'

He shrugged the smallest shrug that could be shrugged. 'My cards are available to anybody. I do not give my friends marijuana cigarettes. Your question remains stupid.'

'I wonder if this would brighten it up any. The cigarettes were in a cheap Chinese or Japanese case of imitation tortoise-shell. Ever see anything like that?'

'No. Not that I recall.'

'I can brighten it up a little more. The case was in the pocket of a man named Lindsay Marriott. Ever hear of him?'

He thought. 'Yes. I tried at one time to treat him for camera shyness. He was trying to get into pictures. It was a waste of time. Pictures did not want him.'

'I can guess that,' I said. 'He would photograph like Isadora Duncan. I've still got the big one left. Why did you send me the C-note?'

'My dear Mr Marlowe,' he said coldly, 'I am no fool. I am in a very sensitive profession. I am a quack. That is to say I do things which the doctors in their small frightened selfish guild cannot accomplish. I am in danger at all times–from people like you. I merely wish to estimate the danger before dealing with it.'

'Pretty trivial in my case, huh?'

'It hardly exists,' he said politely and made a peculiar motion with his left hand which made my eyes jump at it. Then he put it down very slowly on the white table and looked down at it. Then he raised his depthless eyes again and folded his arms.

'Your hearing—'

'I smell it now,' I said. 'I wasn't thinking of him.'

I turned my head to the left. The Indian was sitting on the third white stool against the black velvet.

He had some kind of a white smock on him over his other clothes. He was sitting without a movement, his eyes closed, his head bent forward a little, as if he had been asleep for an hour. His dark strong face was full of shadows.

I looked back at Amthor. He was smiling his minute smile.

'I bet that makes the dowagers shed their false teeth,' I said. 'What does he do for real money–sit on your knee and sing French songs?'

He made an impatient gesture. 'Get to the point, please.'

'Last night Marriott hired me to go with him on an expedition that involved paying some money to some crooks at a spot they picked. I got knocked on the head. When I came out of it Marriott had been murdered.'

Nothing changed much in Amthor's face. He didn't scream or run up the walls. But for him the reaction was sharp. He unfolded his arms and refolded them the other way. His mouth looked grim. Then he sat like a stone lion outside the Public Library.

'The cigarettes were found on him,' I said.

He looked at me coolly. 'But not by the police, I take it. Since the police have not been here.'

'Correct.'

'The hundred dollars,' he said very softly, 'was hardly enough.'

'That depends what you expect to buy with it.'

'You have these cigarettes with you?'

'One of them. But they don't prove anything. As you said, anybody could get your cards. I'm just wondering why they were where they were. Any ideas?'

'How well did you know Mr Marriott?' he asked softly.

'Not at all. But I had ideas about him. They were so obvious they stuck out.'

Amthor tapped lightly on the white table. The Indian still slept with his chin on his huge chest, his heavy-lidded eyes tight shut.

'By the way, did you ever meet a Mrs Grayle, a wealthy lady who lives in Bay City?'

He nodded absently. 'Yes, I treated her centres of speech. She had a very slight impediment.'

'You did a sweet job on her,' I said. 'She talks as good as I do now.'

That failed to amuse him. He still tapped on the table. I listened to the taps. Something about them I didn't like. They sounded like a code. He stopped, folded his arms again and leaned back against the air.

'What I like about this job everybody knows everybody,' I said. 'Mrs Grayle knew Marriott too.'

'How did you find that out?' he asked slowly.

I didn't say anything.

'You will have to tell the police—about those cigarettes,' he said.

I shrugged.

'You are wondering why I do not have you thrown out,' Amthor said pleasantly. 'Second Planting could break your neck like a celery stalk. I am wondering myself. You seem to have some sort of theory. Blackmail I do not pay. It buys nothing—and I have many friends. But naturally there are certain elements which would like to show me in a bad light. Psychiatrists, sex specialists, neurologists, nasty little men with rubber hammers and shelves loaded with the literature of aberrations. And of course they are all—doctors. While I am still a—quack. What is your theory?'

I tried to stare him down, but it couldn't be done. I felt myself licking my lips.

He shrugged lightly. 'I can't blame you for wanting to keep it to yourself. This is a matter that I must give thought to. Perhaps you are a much more intelligent man than I thought. I also make mistakes. In the meantime—' He leaned forward and put a hand on each side of the milky globe.

'I think Marriott was a blackmailer of women,' I said. 'And finger man for a jewel mob. But who told him what women to cultivate—so that he would know their comings and goings, get intimate with them, make love to them, make them load up with the ice and take them out, and then slip to a phone and tell the boys where to operate?'

'That,' Amthor said carefully, 'is your picture of Marriott—and of me. I am slightly disgusted.'

I leaned forward until my face was not more than a foot from his. 'You're in a racket. Dress it up all you please and it's still a racket. And it wasn't just the cards, Amthor. As you say, anybody could get those. It wasn't the marijuana. You wouldn't be in a cheap line like that—not with your chances. But on the back of each card there is a blank space. And on blank spaces, or even on written ones, there is sometimes invisible writing.'

He smiled bleakly, but I hardly saw it. His hands moved over the milky bowl.

The light went out. The room was as black as Carrie Nation's bonnet.

22

I kicked my stool back and stood up and jerked the gun out of the holster under my arm. But it was no good. My coat was buttoned and I was too slow. I'd have been too slow anyway, if it came to shooting anybody.

There was a soundless rush of air and an earthy smell. In the complete darkness the Indian hit me from behind and pinned my arms to my sides. He started to lift me. I could have got the gun out still and fanned the room with blind shots, but I was a long way from friends. It didn't seem as if there was any point in it.

I let go of the gun and took hold of his wrists. They were greasy and hard to hold. The Indian breathed gutturally and set me down with a jar that lifted the top of my head. He had my wrists now, instead of me having his. He twisted them behind me fast and a knee like a corner stone went into my back. He bent me. I can be bent. I'm not the City Hall. He bent me.

I tried to yell, for no reason at all. Breath panted in my throat and couldn't get out. The Indian threw me sideways and got a body scissors on me as I fell. He had me in a barrel. His hands went to my neck. Sometimes I wake up in the night. I feel them there and I smell the smell of him. I feel the breath fighting and losing and the greasy fingers digging in. Then I get up and take a drink and turn the radio on.

I was just about gone when the light flared on again, blood red, on account of the blood in my eyeballs and at the back of them. A face floated around and a hand pawed me delicately, but the other hands stayed on my throat.

A voice said softly, 'Let him breathe—a little.'

The fingers slackened. I wrenched loose from them. Something that glinted hit me on the side of the jaw.

The voice said softly: 'Get him on his feet.'

The Indian got me on my feet. He pulled me back against the wall, holding me by both twisted wrists.

'Amateur,' the voice said softly and the shiny thing that was as hard and bitter as death hit me again, across the face. Something warm trickled. I licked at it and tasted iron and salt.

A hand explored my wallet. A hand explored all my pockets. The cigarette in tissue paper came out and was unwrapped. It went somewhere in the haze that was in front of me.

'There were three cigarettes?' the voice said gently, and the shining thing hit my jaw again.

'Three,' I gulped.

'Just where did you say the others were?'

'In my desk—at the office.'

The shiny thing hit me again. 'You are probably lying—but I can find out.' Keys shone with funny little red lights in front of me. The voice said:

'Choke him a little more.'

The iron fingers went into my throat. I was strained back against him, against the smell of him and the hard muscles of his stomach. I reached up and took one of his fingers and tried to twist it.

The voice said softly: 'Amazing. He's learning.'

The glinting thing swayed through the air again. It smacked my jaw, the thing that had once been my jaw.

'Let him go. He's tame,' the voice said.

The heavy strong arms dropped away and I swayed forward and took a step and steadied myself. Amthor stood smiling very slightly, almost dreamily in front of me. He held my gun in his delicate, lovely hand. He held it pointed at my chest.

'I could teach you,' he said in his soft voice. 'But to what purpose? A dirty little man in a dirty little world. One spot of brightness on you and you would still be that. Is it not so?' He smiled, so beautifully.

I swung at his smile with everything I had left.

It wasn't so bad considering. He reeled and blood came out of both his nostrils. Then he caught himself and straightened up and lifted the gun again.

'Sit down, my child,' he said softly. 'I have visitors coming. I am so glad you hit me. It helps a great deal.'

I felt for the white stool and sat down and put my head down on the white table beside the milky globe which was now shining again softly. I stared at it sideways, my face on the table. The light fascinated me. Nice light, nice soft light.

Behind me and around me there was nothing but silence.

I think I went to sleep, just like that, with a bloody face on the table, and a thin beautiful devil with my gun in his hand watching me and smiling.

23

'All right,' the big one said. 'You can quit stalling now.'

I opened my eyes and sat up.

'Out in the other room, pally.'

I stood up, still dreamy. We went somewhere, through a door. Then I saw where it was—the reception room with the windows all around. It was black dark now outside.

The woman with the wrong rings sat at her desk. A man stood beside her.

'Sit here, pally.'

He pushed me down. It was a nice chair, straight but comfortable, but I wasn't in the mood for it. The woman behind the desk had a notebook open and was reading out loud from it. A short elderly man with a deadpan expression and a grey moustache was listening to her.

Amthor was standing by a window, with his back to the room, looking out at the placid line of the ocean, far off, beyond the pier lights, beyond the world. He looked at it as if he loved it. He half turned his head to look at me once, and I could see that the blood had been washed off his face, but his nose wasn't the nose I had first met, not by two sizes. That made me grin, cracked lips and all.

'You got fun, pally?'

I looked at what made the sound, what was in front of me and what had helped me get where I was. He was a wind-blown blossom of some two hundred pounds with freckled teeth and the mellow voice of a circus barker. He was tough, fast and he ate red meat. Nobody could push him around. He was the kind of cop who spits on his blackjack every night instead of saying his prayers. But he had humorous eyes.

He stood in front of me splay-legged, holding my open wallet in his hand, making scratches on the leather with his right thumbnail, as if he just liked to spoil things. Little things, if they were all he had. But probably faces would give him more fun.

'Peeper, huh, pally? From the big bad burg, huh? Little spot of blackmail, huh?'

His hat was on the back of his head. He had dusty brown hair darkened by sweat on his forehead. His humorous eyes were flecked with red veins.

My throat felt as though it had been through a mangle. I reached up and felt it. That Indian. He had fingers like pieces of tool steel.

The dark woman stopped reading out of her notebook and closed it. The elderly smallish man with the grey moustache nodded and came over to stand behind the one who was talking to me.

'Cops?' I asked, rubbing my chin.

'What do *you* think, pally?'

Policeman's humour. The small one had a cast in one eye, and it looked half blind.

'Not L.A.,' I said, looking at him. 'That eye would retire him in Los Angeles.'

The big man handed me my wallet. I looked through it. I had all the money still. All the cards. It had everything that belonged in it. I was surprised.

'Say something, pally,' the big one said. 'Something that would make us get fond of you.'

'Give me back my gun.'

He leaned forward a little and thought. I could see him thinking. It hurt his corns. 'Oh, you want your gun, pally?' He looked sideways at the one with the grey moustache. 'He wants his gun,' he told him. He looked at me again. 'And what would you want your gun for, pally?'

'I want to shoot an Indian.'

'Oh, you want to shoot an Indian, pally.'

'Yeah—just one Indian, pop.'

He looked at the one with the moustache again. 'This guy is very tough,' he told him. 'He wants to shoot an Indian.'

'Listen, Hemingway, don't repeat everything I say,' I said.

'I think the guy is nuts,' the big one said. 'He just called me Hemingway. Do you think he is nuts?'

The one with the moustache bit a cigar and said nothing. The tall beautiful man at the window turned slowly and said softly: 'I think possibly he is a little unbalanced.'

'I can't think of any reason why he should call me Hemingway,' the big one said. 'My name ain't Hemingway.'

The older man said: 'I didn't see a gun.'

They looked at Amthor. Amthor said: 'It's inside. I have it. I'll give it to you, Mr Blane.'

The big man leaned down from his hips and bent his knees a little and breathed in my face. 'What for did you call me Hemingway, pally?'

'There are ladies present.'

He straightened up again. 'You see.' He looked at the one with the moustache. The one with the moustache nodded and then turned and walked away, across the room. The sliding door opened. He went in and Amthor followed him.

There was silence. The dark woman looked down at the top of her desk and frowned. The big man looked at my right eyebrow and slowly shook his head from side to side, wonderingly.

The door opened again and the man with the moustache came back. He picked a hat up from somewhere and handed it to me. He took my gun out of his pocket and handed it to me. I knew by the weight it was empty. I tucked it under my arm and stood up.

The big man said: 'Let's go, pally. Away from here. I think maybe a little air will help you to get straightened out.'

'Okey, Hemingway.'

'He's doing that again,' the big man said sadly. 'Calling me Hemingway on account of there are ladies present. Would you think that would be some kind of dirty crack in his book?'

The man with the moustache said, 'Hurry up.'

The big man took me by the arm and we went over to the little elevator. It came up. We got into it.

24

At the bottom of the shaft we got out and walked along the narrow hallway and out of the black door. It was crisp clear air outside, high enough to be above the drift of foggy spray from the ocean. I breathed deeply.

The big man still had hold of my arm. There was a car standing there, a plain dark sedan, with private plates.

The big man opened the front door and complained: 'It ain't really up to your class, pally. But a little air will set you up fine. Would that be all right with you? We wouldn't want to do anything that you wouldn't like us to do, pally.'

'Where's the Indian?'

He shook his head a little and pushed me into the car. I got into the right side of the front seat. 'Oh, yeah, the Indian,' he said. 'You got to shoot him with a bow and arrow. That's the law. We got him in the back of the car.'

I looked in the back of the car. It was empty.

'Hell, he ain't there,' the big one said. 'Somebody must of glommed him off. You can't leave nothing in a unlocked car any more.'

'Hurry up,' the man with the moustache said, and got into the back seat. Hemingway went around and pushed his hard stomach behind the wheel.

He started the car. We turned and drifted off down the driveway lined with wild geraniums. A cold wind lifted off the sea. The stars were too far off. They said nothing.

We reached the bottom of the drive and turned out on to the concrete mountain road and drifted without haste along that.

'How come you don't have a car with you, pally?'

'Amthor sent for me.'

'Why would that be, pally?'

'It must have been he wanted to see me.'

'This guy is good,' Hemingway said. 'He figures things out.'

He spat out of the side of the car and made a turn nicely and let the car ride its motor down the hill. 'He says you called him up on the phone and tried to put the bite on him. So he figures he better have a look-see what kind of guy he is doing business with–if he is doing business. So he sends his own car.'

'On account of he knows he is going to call some cops he knows and I won't need mine to get home with,' I said. 'Okey, Hemingway.'

'Yeah, that again. Okey. Well, he has a dictaphone under his table and his secretary takes it all down and when we come she reads it back to Mister Blane here.'

I turned and looked at Mister Blane. He was smoking a cigar, peacefully, as though he had his slippers on. He didn't look at me.

'Like hell she did,' I said. 'More likely a stock bunch of notes they had all fixed up for a case like that.'

'Maybe you would like to tell us why you wanted to see this guy,' Hemingway suggested politely.

'You mean while I still have part of my face?'

'Aw, we ain't those kind of boys at all,' he said, with a large gesture.

'You know Amthor pretty well, don't you, Hemingway?

'Mr Blane kind of knows him. Me, I just do what the orders is.'

'Who the hell is Mister Blane?'

'That's the gentleman in the back seat.'

'And besides being in the back seat who the hell is he?'

'Why, Jesus, everybody knows Mr Blane.'

'All right,' I said, suddenly feeling very weary.

There was a little more silence, more curves, more winding ribbons of concrete, more darkness, and more pain.

The big man said: 'Now that we are all between pals and no ladies present we really don't give so much time to why you went back up there, but this Hemingway stuff is what really has me down.'

'A gag,' I said. 'An old, old gag.'

'Who is this Hemingway person at all?'

'A guy that keeps saying the same thing over and over until you begin to believe it must be good.'

'That must take a hell of a long time,' the big man said. 'For a private dick you certainly have a wandering kind of mind. Are you still wearing your own teeth?'

'Yeah, with a few plugs in them.'

'Well, you certainly have been lucky, pally.'

The man in the back seat said: 'This is all right. Turn right at the next.'

'Check.'

Hemingway swung the sedan into a narrow dirt road that edged along the flank of a mountain. We drove along that about a mile. The smell of the sage became overpowering.

'Here,' the man in the back seat said.

Hemingway stopped the car and set the brake. He leaned across me and opened the door.

'Well, it's nice to have met you, pally. But don't come back. Anyways not on business. Out.'

'I walk home from here?'

The man in the back seat said: 'Hurry up.'

'Yeah, you walk home from here, pally. Will that be all right with you?'

'Sure, it will give me time to think a few things out. For instance you boys are not L.A. cops. But one of you is a cop, maybe both of you. I'd say you are Bay City cops. I'm wondering why you were out of your territory.'

'Ain't that going to be kind of hard to prove, pally?'

'Good-night, Hemingway.'

He didn't answer. Neither of them spoke. I started to get out of the car and put my foot on the running board and leaned forward, still a little dizzy.

The man in the back seat made a sudden flashing movement that I sensed rather than saw. A pool of darkness opened at my feet and was far, far deeper than the blackest night.

I dived into it. It had no bottom.

25

The room was full of smoke.

The smoke hung straight up in the air, in thin lines, straight up and down like a curtain of small clear beads. Two windows seemed to be open in an end wall, but the smoke didn't move. I had never seen the room before. There were bars across the windows.

I was dull, without thought. I felt as if I had slept for a year. But the smoke bothered me. I lay on my back and thought about it. After a long time I took a deep breath that hurt my lungs.

I yelled: 'Fire!'

That made me laugh. I didn't know what was funny about it but I began to laugh. I lay there on the bed and laughed. I didn't like the sound of the laugh. It was the laugh of a nut.

The one yell was enough. Steps thumped rapidly outside the room and a key was jammed into a lock and the door swung open. A man jumped in sideways and shut the door after him. His right hand reached towards his hip.

He was a short thick man in a white coat. His eyes had a queer look, black and flat. There were bulbs of grey skin at the outer corners of them.

I turned my head on the hard pillow and yawned.

'Don't count that one, Jack. It slipped out,' I said.

He stood there scowling, his right hand hovering towards his right hip. Greenish malignant face and flat black eyes and grey-white skin and nose that seemed just a shell.

'Maybe you want some more straitjacket,' he sneered.

'I'm fine, Jack. Just fine. Had a long nap. Dreamed a little, I guess. Where am I?'

'Where you belong.'

'Seems like a nice place,' I said. 'Nice people, nice atmosphere. I guess I'll have me a short nap again.'

'Better be just that,' he snarled.

He went out. The door shut. The lock clicked. The steps growled into nothing.

He hadn't done the smoke any good. It still hung there in the middle of the room, all across the room. Like a curtain. It didn't dissolve, didn't float off, didn't move. There was air in the room, and I could feel it on my face. But the smoke couldn't feel it. It was a grey web woven by a thousand spiders. I wondered how they had got them to work together.

Cotton flannel pyjamas. The kind they have in the County Hospital. No front, not a stitch more than is essential. Coarse, rough material. The neck chafed my throat. My throat was still sore. I began to remember things. I reached up and felt the throat muscles. They were still sore. Just one Indian, pop. Okey, Hemingway. So you want to be a detective? Earn good money. Nine easy lessons. We provide badge. For fifty cents extra we send you a truss.

The throat felt sore but the fingers feeling it didn't feel anything. They might just as well have been a bunch of bananas. I looked at them. They looked like fingers. No good. Mail order fingers. They must have come with the badge and the truss. And the diploma.

It was night. The world outside the windows was a black world. A glass porcelain bowl hung from the middle of the ceiling on three brass chains. There was light in it. It had little coloured lumps around the edge, orange and blue alternately. I stared at them. I was tired of the smoke. As I stared they began to open up like little portholes and heads popped out. Tiny heads, but alive, heads like the heads of small dolls, but alive. There was a man in a yachting cap with a Johnnie Walker nose and a fluffy blonde in a picture hat and a thin man with a crooked bow tie. He looked like a waiter in a beach-town fly-trap. He opened his lips and sneered: 'Would you like your steak rare or medium, sir?'

I closed my eyes tight and winked them hard and when I opened them again it was just a sham porcelain bowl on three brass chains.

But the smoke still hung motionless in the moving air.

I took hold of the corner of a rough sheet and wiped the sweat off my face with the numb fingers the correspondence school had sent me after the nine easy lessons, one half in advance, Box Two Million Four Hundred and Sixty Eight Thousand Nine Hundred and Twenty Four, Cedar City, Iowa. Nuts. Completely nuts.

I sat up on the bed and after a while I could reach the floor with my feet. They were bare and they had pins and needles in them. Notions counter on the left, madam. Extra large safety-pins on the right. The feet began to feel the floor. I stood up. Too far up. I crouched over, breathing hard and held the side of the bed and a voice that seemed to come from under the bed said over and over again: 'You've got the dt's . . . you've got the dt's . . . you've got the dt's.'

I started to walk, wobbling like a drunk. There was a bottle of whisky on a small white enamel table between the two barred windows. It looked like a good shape. It looked about half full. I walked towards it. There are a lot of nice people in the world, in spite. You can crab over the morning paper and kick the shins of the guy in the next seat at the movies and feel mean and discouraged and sneer at the politicians, but there are a lot of nice people in the world just the same. Take the guy that left that half bottle of whisky there. He had a heart as big as one of Mae West's hips.

I reached it and put both my still half-numb hands down on it and hauled it up to my mouth, sweating as if I was lifting one end of the Golden Gate Bridge.

I took a long untidy drink. I put the bottle down again, with infinite care. I tried to lick underneath my chin.

The whisky had a funny taste. While I was realizing that it had a funny taste I saw a wash-bowl jammed into the corner of the wall. I made it. I just made it. I vomited. Dizzy Dean never threw anything harder.

Time passed—an agony of nausea and staggering and dazedness and clinging to the edge of the bowl and making animal sounds for help.

It passed. I staggered back to the bed and lay down on my back again and lay there panting, watching the smoke. The smoke wasn't quite so clear. Not quite so real. Maybe it was just something back of my eyes. And then quite suddenly it wasn't there at all and the light from the porcelain ceiling fixture etched the room sharply.

I sat up again. There was a heavy wooden chair against the wall near the door. There was another door besides the door the man in the white coat had come in at. A closet door, probably. It might even have my clothes in it. The floor was covered with green and grey linoleum in squares. The walls were painted white. A clean room. The bed on which I sat was a narrow iron hospital bed, lower than they usually are, and there were thick leather straps with buckles attached to the sides, about where a man's wrists and ankles would be.

It was a swell room—to get out of.

I had feeling all over my body now, soreness in my head and throat and in my arm. I couldn't remember about the arm. I rolled up the sleeve of the cotton pyjama thing and looked at it fuzzily. It was covered with pin pricks on the skin all the way from the elbow to the shoulder. Around each was a small discoloured patch, about the size of a quarter.

Dope. I had been shot full of dope to keep me quiet. Perhaps scopolamine too, to make me talk. Too much dope for the time. I was having the French fits coming out of it. Some do, some don't. It all depends how you are put together. Dope.

That accounted for the smoke and the little heads around the edge of the ceiling light and the voices and the screwy thoughts and the straps and bars and the numb fingers and feet. The whisky was probably part of somebody's forty-eight hour liquor cure. They had just left it around so that I wouldn't miss anything.

I stood up and almost hit the opposite wall with my stomach. That made me lie down and breathe very gently for quite a long time. I was tingling all over now and sweating. I could feel little drops of sweat form on my forehead and then slide slowly and carefully down the side of my nose to the corner of my mouth. My tongue licked at them foolishly.

I sat up once more and planted my feet on the floor and stood up.

'Okey, Marlowe,' I said between my teeth. 'You're a tough guy. Six feet of iron man. One hundred and ninety pounds stripped and with your face washed. Hard muscles and no glass jaw. You can take it. You've been sapped down twice, had your throat choked and been beaten half silly on the jaw with a gun barrel. You've been shot full of hop and kept under it until you're as crazy as two waltzing mice. And what does all that amount to? Routine. Now let's see you do something really tough, like putting your pants on.'

I lay down on the bed again.

Time passed again. I don't know how long. I had no watch. They don't make that kind of time in watches anyway.

I sat up. This was getting to be stale. I stood up and started to walk. No fun walking. Makes your heart jump like a nervous cat. Better lie down and go back to sleep. Better take it easy for a while. You're in bad shape, pally. Okey, Hemingway, I'm weak. I couldn't knock over a flower-vase. I couldn't break a fingernail.

Nothing doing. I'm walking. I'm tough. I'm getting out of here.

I lay down on the bed again.

The fourth time was a little better. I got across the room and back twice. I went over to the wash-bowl and rinsed it out and leaned on it and drank water out of the palm of my hand. I kept it down. I waited a little and drank more. Much better.

I walked. I walked. I walked.

Half an hour of walking and my knees were shaking but my head was clear. I drank more water, a lot of water. I almost cried into the bowl while I was drinking it.

I walked back to the bed. It was a lovely bed. It was made of rose-leaves. It was the most beautiful bed in the world. They had got it from Carole Lombard. It was too soft for her. It was worth the rest of my life to lie down in it for two minutes. Beautiful soft bed, beautiful sleep, beautiful eyes closing and lashes falling and the gentle sound of breathing and darkness and rest sunk in deep pillows. . . .

I walked.

They built the Pyramids and got tired of them and pulled them down and ground the stone up to make concrete for Boulder Dam and they built that and brought the water to the Sunny Southland and used it to have a flood with.

I walked all through it. I couldn't be bothered.

I stopped walking. I was ready to talk to somebody.

26

The closet door was locked. The heavy chair was too heavy for me. It was meant to be. I stripped the sheets and pad off the bed and dragged the mattress to one side. There was a mesh spring underneath fastened top and bottom by coil springs of black enamelled metal about nine inches long. I went to work on one of them. It was the hardest work I ever did. Ten minutes later I had two bleeding fingers and a loose spring. I swung it. It had a nice balance. It was heavy. It had a whip to it.

And when this was all done I looked across at the whisky bottle and it would have done just as well, and I had forgotten all about it.

I drank some more water. I rested a little, sitting on the side of the bare springs. Then I went over to the door and put my mouth against the hinge side and yelled:

'Fire! Fire! Fire!'

It was a short wait and a pleasant one. He came running hard along the hallway outside and his key jammed viciously into the lock and twisted hard.

The door jumped open. I was flat against the wall on the opening side. He had the sap out this time, a nice little tool about five inches long, covered with woven brown leather. His eyes popped at the stripped bed and then began to swing around.

I giggled and socked him. I laid the coil spring on the side of his head and he stumbled forward. I followed him down to his knees. I hit him twice more. He made a moaning sound. I took the sap out of his limp hand. He whined.

I used my knee on his face. It hurt my knee. He didn't tell me whether it hurt his face. While he was still groaning I knocked him cold with the sap.

I got the key from the outside of the door and locked it from the inside and went through him. He had more keys. One of them fitted my closet. In it my clothes hung. I went through my pockets. The money was gone from my wallet. I went back to the man with the white coat. He had too much money for his job. I took what I had started with and heaved him on to the bed and strapped him wrist and ankle and stuffed half a yard of sheet into his mouth. He had a smashed nose. I waited long enough to make sure he could breathe through it.

I was sorry for him. A simple hard-working little guy trying to hold his job down and get his weekly pay cheque. Maybe with a wife and kids. Too bad. And all he had to help him was a sap. It didn't seem fair. I put the doped whisky down where he could reach it, if his hands hadn't been strapped.

I patted his shoulder. I almost cried over him.

All my clothes, even my gun harness and gun, but no shells in the gun, hung in the closet. I dressed with fumbling fingers, yawning a great deal.

The man on the bed rested. I left him there and locked him in.

Outside was a wide silent hallway with three closed doors. No sounds came from behind any of them. A wine-coloured carpet crept down the middle and was as silent as the rest of the house. At the end there was a jog in the hall and then another hall at right angles and the head of a big old-fashioned staircase with white oak banisters. It curved graciously down into the dim hall below. Two stained-glass inner doors ended the lower hall. It was tessellated and thick rugs lay on it. A crack of light seeped past the edge of an almost closed door. But no sound at all.

An old house, built as once they built them and don't build them any more. Standing probably on a quiet street with a rose arbour at the side and plenty of flowers in front. Gracious and cool and quiet in the bright California sun. And inside it who cares, but don't let them scream too loud.

I had my foot out to go down the stairs when I heard a man cough. That jerked me around and I saw there was a half-open door along the other hallway at the end. I tiptoed along the runner. I waited, close to the partly open door, but not in it. A wedge of light lay at my feet on the carpet. The man coughed again. It was a deep cough, from a deep chest. It sounded peaceful and at ease. It was none of my business. My business was to get out of there. But any man whose door could be open in that house interested me. He would be a man of position, worth tipping your hat to. I sneaked a little into the wedge of light. A newspaper rustled.

I could see part of a room and it was furnished like a room, not like a cell. There was a dark bureau with a hat on it and some magazines. Windows with lace curtains, a good carpet.

Bed springs creaked heavily. A big guy, like his cough. I reached out fingertips and pushed the door an inch or two. Nothing happened. Nothing ever was slower than my head craning in. I saw the room now, the bed, and the man on it, the ash-tray heaped with stubs that overflowed on to a night table and from that to the carpet. A dozen mangled newspapers all over the bed. One of them in a pair of huge hands before a huge face. I saw the hair above the edge of the green paper. Dark, curly—black even—and plenty of it. A line of white skin under it. The paper moved a little more and I didn't breathe and the man on the bed didn't look up.

He needed a shave. He would always need a shave. I had seen him before, over on Central Avenue, in a negro dive called Florian's. I had seen him in a loud suit with white golf balls on the coat and a whisky sour in his hand. And I had seen him with an Army Colt looking like a toy in his fist, stepping softly through a broken door. I had seen some of his work and it was the kind of work that stays done.

He coughed again and rolled his buttocks on the bed and yawned bitterly and reached sideways for a frayed pack of cigarettes on the night table. One of them went into his mouth. Light flared at the end of his thumb. Smoke came out of his nose.

'Ah,' he said, and the paper went up in front of his face again.

I left him there and went back along the side hall. Mr Moose Malloy seemed to be in very good hands. I went back to the stairs and down.

A voice murmured behind the almost closed door. I waited for the answering voice. None. It was a telephone conversation. I went over close to the door and listened. It was a low voice, a mere murmur. Nothing carried that meant anything. There was finally a dry clicking sound. Silence continued inside the room after that.

This was the time to leave, to go far away. So I pushed the door open and stepped quietly in.

27

It was an office, not small, not large, with a neat professional look. A glass-doored bookcase with heavy books inside. A first aid cabinet on the wall. A white enamel and glass sterilizing cabinet with a lot of hypodermic needles and syringes inside it being cooked. A wide flat desk with a blotter on it, a bronze paper cutter, a pen set, an appointments book, very little else, except the elbows of a man who sat brooding, with his face in his hands.

Between the spread yellow fingers I saw hair the colour of wet brown sand, so smooth that it appeared to be painted on his skull. I took three more steps and his eyes must have looked beyond the desk and seen my shoes move. His head came up and he looked at me. Sunken colourless eyes in a parchment-like face. He unclasped his hands and leaned back slowly and looked at me with no expression at all.

Then he spread his hands with a sort of helpless but disapproving gesture and when they came to rest again, one of them was very close to the corner of the desk.

I took two steps more and showed him the blackjack. His index and second finger still moved towards the corner of the desk.

'The buzzer,' I said, 'won't buy you anything tonight. I put your tough boy to sleep.'

His eyes got sleepy. 'You have been a very sick man, sir. A very sick man. I can't recommend you being up and about yet.'

I said: 'The right hand.' I snapped the blackjack at it. It coiled into itself like a wounded snake.

I went around the desk grinning without there being anything to grin at. He had a gun in the drawer of course. They always have a gun in the drawer and they always get it too late, if they get it at all. I took it out. It was a .38 automatic, a standard model not as good as mine, but I could use its ammunition. There didn't seem to be any in the drawer. I started to break the magazine out of his.

He moved vaguely, his eyes still sunken and sad.

'Maybe you've got another buzzer under the carpet,' I said. 'Maybe it rings in the Chief's office down at headquarters. Don't use it. Just for an hour I'm a very tough guy. Anybody comes in that door is walking into a coffin.'

'There is no buzzer under the carpet,' he said. His voice had the slightest possible foreign accent.

I got his magazine out and my empty one and changed them. I ejected the shell that was in the chamber of his gun and let it lie. I jacked one up into the chamber of mine and went back to the other side of the desk again.

There was a spring lock on the door. I backed towards it and pushed it shut and heard the lock click. There was also a bolt. I turned that.

I went back to the desk and sat in a chair. It took my last ounce of strength.

'Whisky,' I said.

He began to move his hands around.

'Whisky,' I said.

He went to the medicine cabinet and got a flat bottle with a green revenue stamp on it and a glass.

'Two glasses,' I said. 'I tried your whisky once. I damn near hit Catalina Island with it.'

He brought two small glasses and broke the seal and filled the two glasses.

'You first,' I said.

He smiled faintly and raised one of the glasses.

'Your health, sir—what remains of it.' He drank. I drank. I reached for the bottle and stood it near me and waited for the heat to get to my heart. My heart began to pound, but it was back up in my chest again, not hanging on a shoelace.

'I had a nightmare,' I said. 'Silly idea. I dreamed I was tied to a cot and shot full of dope and locked in a barred room. I got very weak. I slept. I had no food. I was a sick man. I was knocked on the head and brought into a place where they did that to me. They took a lot of trouble. I'm not that important.'

He said nothing. He watched me. There was a remote speculation in his eyes, as if he wondered how long I would live.

'I woke up and the room was full of smoke,' I said. 'It was just a hallucination, irritation of the optic nerve or whatever a guy like you would call it. Instead of pink snakes I had smoke. So I yelled and a toughie in a white coat came in and showed me a blackjack. It took me a long time to get ready to take it away from him. I got his keys and my clothes and even took my money out of his pocket. So here I am. All cured. What were you saying?'

'I made no remark,' he said.

'Remarks want you to make them,' I said. 'They have their tongues hanging out waiting to be said. This thing here—' I waved the blackjack lightly, 'is a persuader. I had to borrow it from a guy.'

'Please give it to me at once,' he said with a smile you would get to love. It was like the executioner's smile when he comes to your cell to measure you for the drop. A little friendly, a little paternal, and a little cautious at the same time. You would get to love it if there was any way you could live long enough.

I dropped the blackjack into his palm, his left palm.

'Now the gun, please,' he said softly. 'You have been a very sick man, Mr Marlowe. I think I shall have to insist that you go back to bed.'

I stared at him.

'I am Dr Sonderborg,' he said, 'and I don't want any nonsense.'

He laid the blackjack down on the desk in front of him. His smile was as stiff as a frozen fish. His long fingers made movements like dying butterflies.

'The gun, please,' he said softly. 'I advise strongly—'

'What time is it, warden?'

He looked mildly surprised. I had my wristwatch on now but it had run down.

'It is almost midnight. Why?'

'What day is it?'

'Why, my dear sir—Sunday evening, of course.'

I steadied myself on the desk and tried to think and held the gun close enough to him so that he might try and grab it.

'That's over forty-eight hours. No wonder I had fits. Who brought me here?'

He stared at me and his left hand began to edge towards the gun. He belonged to the Wandering Hand Society. The girls would have had a time with him.

'Don't make me get tough,' I whined. 'Don't make me lose my beautiful manners and my flawless English. Just tell me how I got here.'

He had courage. He grabbed for the gun. It wasn't where he grabbed. I sat back and put it in my lap.

He reddened and grabbed for the whisky and poured himself another

drink and downed it fast. He drew a deep breath and shuddered. He didn't
like the taste of liquor. Dopers never do.

'You will be arrested at once, if you leave here,' he said sharply. 'You
were properly committed by an officer of the law—'

'Officers of the law can't do it.'

That jarred him, a little. His yellowish face began to work.

'Shake it up and pour it,' I said. 'Who put me in here, why and how? I'm
in a wild mood to-night. I want to go dance in the foam. I hear the banshees
calling. I haven't shot a man in a week. Speak out, Dr Fell. Pluck the
antique viol, let the soft music float.'

'You are suffering from narcotic poisoning,' he said coldly. 'You very
nearly died. I had to give you digitalis three times. You fought, you
screamed, you had to be restrained.' His words were coming so fast they
were leap-frogging themselves. 'If you leave my hospital in this condition,
you will get into serious trouble.'

'Did you say you were a doctor—a medical doctor?'

'Certainly. I am Dr Sonderborg, as I told you.'

'You don't scream and fight from narcotic poisoning, doc. You just lie in a
coma. Try again. And skim it. All I want is the cream. Who put me in your
private funny house?'

'But—'

'But me no buts. I'll make a sop of you. I'll drown you in a butt of
Malmsey wine. I wish I had a butt of Malmsey wine myself to drown in.
Shakespeare. He knew his liquor too. Let's have a little of our medicine.' I
reached for his glass and poured us a couple more. 'Get on with it, Karloff.'

'The police put you in here.'

'What police?'

'The Bay City police naturally.' His restless yellow fingers twisted his
glass. 'This is Bay City.'

'Oh. Did this police have a name?'

'A Sergeant Galbraith, I believe. Not a regular patrol car officer. He and
another officer found you wandering outside the house in a dazed condition
on Friday night. They brought you in because this place was close. I
thought you were an addict who had taken an overdose. But perhaps I was
wrong.'

'It's a good story. I couldn't prove it wrong. But why keep me here?'

He spread his restless hands. 'I have told you again and again that you
were a very sick man and still are. What would you expect me to do?'

'I must owe you some money then.'

He shrugged. 'Naturally. Two hundred dollars.'

I pushed my chair back a little. 'Dirt cheap. Try and get it.'

'If you leave here,' he said sharply, 'you will be arrested at once.'

I leaned back over the desk and breathed in his face. 'Not just for going
out of here, Karloff. Open that wall safe.'

He stood up in a smooth lunge. 'This has gone quite far enough.'

'You won't open it?'

'I most certainly will not open it.'

'This is a gun I'm holding.'

He smiled, narrowly and bitterly.

'It's an awful big safe.' I said. 'New too. This is a fine gun. You won't
open it?'

Nothing changed in his face.

'Damn it,' I said. 'When you have a gun in your hand, people are supposed to do anything you tell them to. It doesn't work, does it?'

He smiled. His smile held a sadistic pleasure. I was slipping back. I was going to collapse.

I staggered at the desk and he waited, his lips parted softly.

I stood leaning there for a long moment, staring into his eyes. Then I grinned. The smile fell off his face like a soiled rag. Sweat stood out on his forehead.

'So long,' I said. 'I leave you to dirtier hands than mine.'

I backed to the door and opened it and went out.

The front doors were unlocked. There was a roofed porch. The garden hummed with flowers. There was a white picket fence and a gate. The house was on a corner. It was a cool, moist night, no moon.

The sign on the corner said Descanso Street. Houses were lighted down the block. I listened for sirens. None came. The other sign said Twenty-third Street. I ploughed over to Twenty-fifth Street and started towards the eight-hundred block. No. 819 was Anne Riordan's number. Sanctuary.

I had walked a long time before I realized that I was still holding the gun in my hand. And I had heard no sirens.

I kept on walking. The air did me good, but the whisky was dying, and it writhed as it died. The block had fir trees along it, and brick houses, and looked like a house on Capitol Hill in Seattle more than Southern California.

There was a light still in No. 819. It had a white *porte-cochère*, very tiny, pressed against a tall cypress hedge. There were rose bushes in front of the house. I went up the walk. I listened before I pushed the bell. Still no sirens wailing. The bell chimed and after a little while a voice croaked through one of those electrical contraptions that let you talk with your front door locked.

'What is it, please?'

'Marlowe.'

Maybe her breath caught, maybe the electrical thing just made that sound being shut off.

The door opened wide and Miss Anne Riordan stood there in a pale green slack suit looking at me. Her eyes went wide and scared. Her face under the glare of the porchlight was suddenly pale.

'My God,' she wailed. 'You look like Hamlet's father!'

28

The living-room had a tan figured rug, white and rose chairs, black marble fireplace with very tall brass andirons, high bookcases built back into the walls, and tough cream drapes against the lowered venetian blinds.

There was nothing womanish in the room except a full-length mirror with a clear sweep of floor in front of it.

I was half-sitting and half-lying in a deep chair with my legs on a footstool. I had had two cups of black coffee, then I had had a drink, then I had had two soft-boiled eggs and a slice of toast broken into them, then some more black coffee with brandy laced in it. I had had all this in the breakfast room, but I couldn't remember what it looked like any more. It was too long ago.

I was in good shape again. I was almost sober and my stomach was bunting towards third base instead of trying for the centre-field flagpole.

Anne Riordan sat opposite me, leaning forward, her neat chin cupped in her neat hand, her eyes dark and shadowy under the fluffed out reddish-brown hair. There was a pencil stuck through her hair. She looked worried. I had told her some of it, but not all. Especially about Moose Malloy I had not told her.

'I thought you were drunk,' she said. 'I thought you had to be drunk before you came to see me. I thought you had been out with that blonde. I thought—I don't know what I thought.'

'I bet you didn't get all this writing,' I said, looking around. 'Not even if you got paid for what you thought you thought.'

'And my dad didn't get it grafting on the cops either,' she said. 'Like that fat slob they have for chief of police nowadays.'

'It's none of my business,' I said.

She said: 'We had some lots at Del Rey. Just sand lots they suckered him for. And they turned out to be oil lots.'

I nodded and drank out of the nice crystal glass I was holding. What was in it had a nice warm taste.

'A fellow could settle down here,' I said. 'Move right in. Everything set for him.'

'If he was that kind of fellow. And anybody wanted him to,' she said.

'No butler,' I said. 'That makes it tough.'

She flushed. 'But you—you'd rather get your head beaten to a pulp and your arm riddled with dope needles and your chin used for a backboard in a basketball game. God knows there's enough of it.'

I didn't say anything. I was too tired.

'At least,' she said, 'you had the brains to look in those mouthpieces. The way you talked over on Aster Drive I thought you had missed the whole thing.'

'Those cards don't mean anything.'

Her eyes snapped at me. 'You sit there and tell me that after the man had you beaten up by a couple of crooked policemen and thrown in a two-day liquor cure to teach you to mind your own business? Why the thing stands out so far you could break off a yard of it and still have enough left for a baseball bat.'

'I ought to have said that one,' I said. 'Just my style. Crude. What sticks out?'

'That this elegant psychic person is nothing but a high-class mobster. He picks the prospects and milks the minds and then tells the rough boys to go out and get the jewels.'

'You really think that?'

She stared at me. I finished my glass and got my weak look on my face again. She ignored it.

'Of course I think it,' she said. 'And so do you.'

'I think it's a little more complicated than that.'

Her smile was cosy and acid at the same time. 'I beg your pardon. I forgot for the moment you were a detective. It *would* have to be complicated, wouldn't it? I suppose there's a sort of indecency about a simple case.'

'It's more complicated than that,' I said.

'All right. I'm listening.'

'I don't know. I just think so. Can I have one more drink?'

She stood up. 'You know, you'll have to taste water sometime, just for the hell of it.' She came over and took my glass. 'This is going to be the last.' She went out of the room and somewhere ice cubes tinkled and I closed my eyes and listened to the small unimportant sounds. I had no business coming here. If they knew as much about me as I suspected, they might come here looking. That would be a mess.

She came back with the glass and her fingers cold from holding the cold glass touched mine and I held them for a moment and then let them go slowly as you let go of a dream when you wake with the sun in your face and you have been in an enchanted valley.

She flushed and went back to her chair and sat down and made a lot of business of arranging herself in it.

She lit a cigarette, watching me drink.

'Amthor's a pretty ruthless sort of lad,' I said. 'But I don't somehow see him as the brain guy of a jewel mob. Perhaps I'm wrong. If he was and he thought I had something on him, I don't think I'd have got out of that dope hospital alive. But he's a man who has things to fear. He didn't get really tough until I began to babble about invisible writing.'

She looked at me evenly. 'Was there some?'

I grinned. 'If there was, I didn't read it.'

'That's a funny way to hide nasty remarks about a person, don't you think? In the mouthpieces of cigarettes. Suppose they were never found.'

'I think the point is that Marriott feared something and that if anything happened to him, the cards *would* be found. The police would go over anything in his pockets with a fine-tooth comb. That's what bothers me. If Amthor's a crook, nothing would have been left to find.'

'You mean if Amthor murdered him—or had him murdered? But what Marriott knew about Amthor may not have had any direct connection with the murder.'

I leaned back and pressed my back into the chair and finished my drink and made believe I was thinking that over. I nodded.

'But the jewel robbery had a connection with the murder. And we're assuming Amthor had a connection with the jewel robbery.'

Her eyes were a little sly. 'I bet you feel awful,' she said. 'Wouldn't you like to go to bed?'

'Here?'

She flushed to the roots of her hair. Her chin stuck out. 'That was the idea. I'm not a child. Who the devil cares what I do or when or how?'

I put my glass aside and stood up. 'One of my rare moments of delicacy is coming over me,' I said. 'Will you drive me to a taxi stand, if you're not too tired?'

'You damned sap,' she said angrily. 'You've been beaten to a pulp and shot full of God knows how many kinds of narcotics and I suppose all you need is a night's sleep to get up bright and early and start out being a detective again.'

'I thought I'd sleep a little late.'

'You ought to be in a hospital, you damn fool!'

I shuddered. 'Listen,' I said. 'I'm not very clear-headed tonight and I don't think I ought to linger around here too long. I haven't a thing on any of these people that I could prove, but they seem to dislike me. Whatever I might say would be my word against the law, and the law in this town seems to be pretty rotten.'

'It's a nice town,' she said sharply, a little breathlessly. 'You can't judge—'

'Okey, it's a nice town. So is Chicago. You could live there a long time and not see a Tommy-gun. Sure, it's a nice town. It's probably no crookeder than Los Angeles. But you can only buy a piece of a big city. You can buy a town this size all complete, with the original box and tissue paper. That's the difference. And that makes me want out.'

She stood up and pushed her chin at me. 'You'll go to bed now and right here. I have a spare bedroom and you can turn right in and—'

'Promise to lock your door?'

She flushed and bit her lip. 'Sometimes I think you're a world-beater,' she said, 'and sometimes I think you're the worst heel I ever met.'

'On either count would you run me over to where I can get a taxi?'

'You'll stay here,' she snapped. 'You're not fit. You're a sick man.'

'I'm not too sick to have my brain picked,' I said nastily.

She ran out of the room so fast she almost tripped over the two steps from the living-room up to the hall. She came back in nothing flat with a long flannel coat on over her slack suit and no hat and her reddish hair looking as mad as her face. She opened a side door and threw it away from her, bounced through it and her steps clattered on the driveway. A garage door made a faint sound lifting. A car door opened and slammed shut again. The starter ground and the motor caught and the lights flared past the open French door of the living-room.

I picked my hat out of a chair and switched off a couple of lamps and saw that the French door had a Yale lock. I looked back a moment before I closed the door. It was a nice room. It would be a nice room to wear slippers in.

I shut the door and the little car slid up beside me and I went around behind it to get in.

She drove me all the way home, tight-lipped, angry. She drove like a fury. When I got out in front of my apartment house she said good-night in a frosty voice and swirled the little car in the middle of the street and was gone before I could get my keys out of my pocket.

They locked the lobby door at eleven. I unlocked it and passed into the always musty lobby and along to the stairs and the elevator. I rode up to my floor. Bleak light shone along it. Milk bottles stood in front of service doors. The red fire door loomed at the back. It had an open screen that let in a lazy trickle of air that never quite swept the cooking smell out. I was home in a sleeping world, a world as harmless as a sleeping cat.

I unlocked the door of my apartment and went in and sniffed the smell of it, just standing there, against the door for a little while before I put the light on. A homely smell, a smell of dust and tobacco smoke, the smell of a world where men live, and keep on living.

I undressed and went to bed. I had nightmares and woke out of them sweating. But in the morning I was a well man again.

29

I was sitting on the side of my bed in my pyjamas, thinking about getting up, but not yet committed. I didn't feel very well, but I didn't feel as sick as I ought to, not as sick as I would feel if I had a salaried job. My head hurt and felt large and hot and my tongue was dry and had gravel on it and my throat was stiff and my jaw was not untender. But I had had worse mornings.

It was a grey morning with high fog, not yet warm but likely to be. I heaved up off the bed and rubbed the pit of my stomach where it was sore from vomiting. My left foot felt fine. It didn't have an ache in it. So I had to kick the corner of the bed with it.

I was still swearing when there was a sharp tap at the door, the kind of bossy knock that makes you want to open the door two inches, emit the succulent raspberry and slam it again.

I opened it a little wider than two inches. Detective-Lieutenant Randall stood there, in a brown gabardine suit, with a pork-pie lightweight felt on his head, very neat and clean and solemn and with a nasty look in his eye.

He pushed the door lightly and I stepped away from it. He came in and closed it and looked around. 'I've been looking for you for two days,' he said. He didn't look at me. His eyes measured the room.

'I've been sick.'

He walked around with a light springy step, his creamy grey hair shining, his hat under his arm now, his hands in his pockets. He wasn't a very big man for a cop. He took one hand out of his pocket and placed the hat carefully on top of some magazines.

'Not here,' he said.

'In a hospital.'

'Which hospital?'

'A pet hospital.'

He jerked as if I had slapped his face. Dull colour showed behind his skin.

'A little early in the day, isn't it—for that sort of thing?'

I didn't say anything. I lit a cigarette. I took one draw on it and sat down on the bed again, quickly.

'No cure for lads like you, is there?' he said. 'Except to throw you in the sneezer.'

'I've been a sick man and I haven't had my morning coffee. You can't expect a very high grade of wit.'

'I told you not to work on this case.'

'You're not God. You're not even Jesus Christ.' I took another drag on the cigarette. Somewhere down inside me felt raw, but I liked it a little better.

'You'd be amazed how much trouble I could make you.'

'Probably.'

'Do you know why I haven't done it so far?'

'Yeah.'

'Why?' He was leaning over a little, sharp as a terrier, with that stony look in his eyes they all get sooner or later.

'You couldn't find me.'

He leaned back and rocked on his heels. His face shone a little. 'I thought you were going to say something else,' he said. 'And if you said it, I was going to smack you on the button.'

'Twenty million dollars wouldn't scare you. But you might get orders.'

He breathed hard, with his mouth a little open. Very slowly he got a packet of cigarettes out of his pocket and tore the wrapper. His fingers were trembling a little. He put a cigarette between his lips and went over to my magazine table for a match folder. He lit the cigarette carefully, put the match in the ash-tray and not on the floor, and inhaled.

'I gave you some advice over the telephone the other day,' he said. 'Thursday.'

'Friday.'

'Yes—Friday. It didn't take. I can understand why. But I didn't know at that time you had been holding out evidence. I was just recommending a line of action that seemed like a good idea in this case.'

'What evidence?'

He stared at me silently.

'Will you have some coffee?' I asked. 'It might make you human.'

'No.'

'*I* will.' I stood up and started for the kitchenette.

'Sit down,' Randall snapped. 'I'm far from through.'

I kept on going out to the kitchenette, ran some water into the kettle and put it on the stove. I took a drink of cold water from the tap, then another. I came back with a third glass in my hand to stand in the doorway and look at him. He hadn't moved. The veil of his smoke was almost a solid thing to one side of him. He was looking at the floor.

'Why was it wrong to go to Mrs Grayle when she sent for me?' I asked.

'I wasn't talking about that.'

'Yeah, but you were just before.'

'She didn't send for you.' His eyes lifted and had the stony look still. And the flush still dyed his sharp cheekbones. 'You forced yourself on her and talked about scandal and practically blackmailed yourself into a job.'

'Funny. As I remember it, we didn't even talk job. I didn't think there was anything in her story. I mean, anything to get my teeth into. Nowhere to start. And of course I supposed she had already told it to you.'

'She had. That beer joint on Santa Monica is a crook hideout. But that doesn't mean anything. I couldn't get a thing there. The hotel across the street smells too. Nobody we want. Cheap punks.'

'She tell you I forced myself on her?'

He dropped his eyes a little. 'No.'

I grinned. 'Have some coffee?'

'No.'

I went back into the kitchenette and made the coffee and waited for it to drip. Randall followed me out this time and stood in the doorway himself.

'This jewel gang has been working in Hollywood and around for a good ten years to my knowledge,' he said. 'They went too far this time. They killed a man. I think I know why.'

'Well, if it's a gang job and you break it, that will be the first gang murder solved since I lived in the town. And I could name and describe at least a dozen.'

'It's nice of you to say that, Marlowe.'

'Correct me if I'm wrong.'

'Damn it,' he said irritably. 'You're not wrong. There were a couple solved for the record, but they were just rappers. Some punk took it for the high pillow.'

'Yeah. Coffee?'

'If I drink some, will you talk to me decently, man to man, without wise-cracking?'

'I'll try. I don't promise to spill all my ideas.'

'I can do without those,' he said acidly.

'That's a nice suit you're wearing.'

The flush dyed his face again. 'This suit cost twenty-seven-fifty,' he snapped.

'Oh, Christ, a sensitive cop,' I said, and went back to the stove.

'That smells good. How do you make it?'

I poured. 'French drip. Coarse ground coffee. No filter papers.' I got the sugar from the closet and the cream from the refrigerator. We sat down on opposite sides of the nook.

'Was that a gag, about your being sick, in a hospital?'

'No gag. I ran into a little trouble–down in Bay City. They took me in. Not the cooler, a private dope and liquor cure.'

His eyes got distant. 'Bay City, eh? You like it the hard way, don't you, Marlowe?'

'It's not that I like it the hard way. It's that I get it that way. But nothing like this before. I've been sapped twice, the second time by a police officer or a man who looked like one and claimed to be one. I've been beaten with my own gun and choked by a tough Indian. I've been thrown unconscious into this dope hospital and kept there locked up and part of the time probably strapped down. And I couldn't prove any of it, except that I actually do have quite a nice collection of bruises and my left arm has been needled plenty.'

He stared hard at the corner of the table. 'In Bay City,' he said slowly.

'The name's like a song. A song in a dirty bathtub.'

'What were you doing down there?'

'I didn't go down there. These cops took me over the line. I went to see a guy in Stillwood Heights. That's in L.A.'

'A man named Jules Amthor,' he said quietly. 'Why did you swipe those cigarettes?'

I looked into my cup. The damned little fool, 'It looked funny, him–Marriott–having that extra case. With reefers in it. It seems they make them up like Russian cigarettes down in Bay City with hollow mouthpieces and the Romanoff arms and everything.'

He pushed his empty cup at me and I refilled it. His eyes were going over my face line by line, corpuscle by corpuscle, like Sherlock Holmes with his magnifying glass or Thorndyke with his pocket lens.

'You ought to have told me,' he said bitterly. He sipped and wiped his lips with one of those fringed things they give you in apartment houses for napkins. 'But you didn't swipe them. The girl told me.'

'Aw well, hell,' I said. 'A guy never gets to do anything in this country any more. Always women.'

'She likes you,' Randall said, like a polite F.B.I. man in a movie, a little sad, but very manly. 'Her old man was as straight a cop as ever lost a job. She had no business taking those things. She likes you.'

'She's a nice girl. Not my type.'

'You don't like them nice?' He had another cigarette going. The smoke was being fanned away from his face by his hand.

'I like smooth shiny girls, hard-boiled and loaded with sin.'

'They take you to the cleaners,' Randall said indifferently.

'Sure. Where else have I ever been? What do you call this session?'

He smiled his first smile of the day. He probably allowed himself four.

'I'm not getting much out of you,' he said.

'I'll give you a theory, but you are probably way ahead of me on it. This Marriott was a blackmailer of women, because Mrs Grayle just about told me so. But he was something else. He was the finger man for the jewel mob. The society finger, the boy who would cultivate the victims and set the stage. He would cultivate women he could take out, get to know them pretty well. Take this hold-up a week from Thursday. It smells. If Marriott hadn't been driving the car, or hadn't taken Mrs Grayle to the Troc or hadn't gone home the way he did, past that beer parlour, the hold-up couldn't have been brought off.'

'The chauffeur could have been driving,' Randall said reasonably. 'But that wouldn't have changed things much. Chauffeurs are not getting themselves pushed in the face with lead bullets by hold-up men–for ninety a month. But there couldn't be many stick-ups with Marriott alone with women or things would get talked about.'

'The whole point of this kind of racket is that things are not talked about,' I said. 'In consideration for that the stuff is sold back cheap.'

Randall leaned back and shook his head. 'You'll have to do better than that to interest me. Women talk about anything. It would get around that this Marriott was a kind of tricky guy to go out with.'

'It probably did. That's why they knocked him off.'

Randall stared at me woodenly. His spoon was stirring air in an empty cup. I reached over and he waved the pot aside. 'Go on with that one,' he said.

'They used him up. His usefulness was exhausted. It was about time for him to get talked about a little, as you suggest. But you don't quit in those rackets and you don't get your time. So this last hold-up was just that for him–the last. Look, they really asked very little for the jade considering its value. And Marriott handled the contact. But all the same Marriott was scared. At the last moment he thought he had better not go alone. And he figured a little trick that if anything did happen to him, something on him would point to a man, a man quite ruthless and clever enough to be the brains of that sort of mob, and a man in an unusual position to get information about rich women. It was a childish sort of trick but it did actually work.'

Randall shook his head. 'A gang would have stripped him, perhaps even have taken the body out to sea and dumped it.'

'No. They wanted the job to look amateurish. They wanted to stay in business. They probably have another finger lined up,' I said.

Randall still shook his head. 'The man these cigarettes pointed to is not the type. He has a good racket of his own. I've inquired. What did you think of him?'

His eyes were too blank, much too blank. I said: 'He looked pretty damn deadly to me. And there's no such thing as too much money, is there? And after all his psychic racket is a temporary racket for any one place. He has a vogue and everybody goes to him and after a while the vogue dies down and the business is licking its shoes. That is, if he's a psychic and nothing else. Just like movie stars. Give him five years. He could work it that long. But give him a couple of ways to use the information he must get out of these women and he's going to make a killing.'

'I'll look him up more thoroughly,' Randall said with the blank look. 'But right now I'm more interested in Marriott. Let's go back farther—much farther. To how you got to know him.'

'He just called me up. Picked my name out of the phone book. He said so, at any rate.'

'He had your card.'

I looked surprised. 'Sure. I'd forgotten that.'

'Did you ever wonder why he picked *your name*—ignoring that matter of your short memory?'

I stared at him across the top of my coffee cup. I was beginning to like him. He had a lot behind his vest besides his shirt.

'So that's what you really came up for?' I said.

He nodded. 'The rest, you know, is just talk.' He smiled politely at me and waited.

I poured some more coffee.

Randall leaned over sideways and looked along the cream-coloured surface of the table. 'A little dust,' he said absently, then straightened up and looked me in the eye. 'Perhaps I ought to go at this in a little different way,' he said. 'For instance, I think your hunch about Marriott is probably right. There's twenty-three grand in currency in his safe-deposit box—which we had a hell of a time to locate, by the way. There are also some pretty fair bonds and a trust deed to a property on West Fifty-fourth Place.'

He picked a spoon up and rapped it lightly on the edge of his saucer and smiled. 'That interest you?' he asked mildly. 'The number was 1644 West Fifty-fourth Place.'

'Yeah,' I said thickly.

'Oh, there was quite a bit of jewellery in Marriott's box too—pretty good stuff. But I don't think he stole it. I think it was very likely given to him. That's one up for you. He was afraid to sell it—on account of the association of thought in his own mind.'

I nodded. 'He'd feel as if it was stolen.'

'Yes. Now that trust deed didn't interest me at all at first, but here's how it works. It's what you fellows are up against in police work. We get all the homicide and doubtful death reports from outlying districts. We're supposed to read them the same day. That's a rule, like you shouldn't search without a warrant or frisk a guy for a gun without reasonable grounds. But we break rules. We have to. I didn't get around to some of the reports until this morning. Then I read one about a killing of a negro on Central, last Thursday. By a tough ex-con called Moose Malloy. And there was an identifying witness. And sink my putt, if you weren't the witness.'

He smiled, softly, his third smile. 'Like it?'

'I'm listening.'

'This was only this morning, understand. So I looked at the name of the man making the report and I knew him, Nulty. So I knew the case was a flop. Nulty is the kind of guy—well, were you ever up at Crestline?'

'Yeah.'

'Well, up near Crestline there's a place where a bunch of old box cars have been made into cabins. I have a cabin up there myself, but not a box car. These box cars were brought up on trucks, believe it or not, and there they stand without any wheels. Now Nulty is the kind of guy who would make a swell brakeman on one of those box cars.'

'That's not nice,' I said. 'A fellow officer.'

'So I called Nulty up and he hemmed and hawed around and spat a few times and then he said you had an idea about some girl called Velma something or other that Malloy was sweet on a long time ago and you went to see the widow of the guy that used to own the dive where the killing happened when it was a white joint, and where Malloy and the girl both worked at that time. And her address was 1644 West Fifty-fourth Place, the place Marriott had the trust deed on.'

'Yes?'

'So I just thought that was enough coincidence for one morning,' Randall said. 'And here I am. And so far I've been pretty nice about it.'

'The trouble is,' I said, 'it looks like more than it is. This Velma girl is dead, according to Mrs Florian. I have her photo.'

I went into the living-room and reached into my suit-coat and my hand was in mid-air when it began to feel funny and empty. But they hadn't even taken the photos. I got them out and took them to the kitchen and tossed the Pierrot girl down in front of Randall. He studied it carefully.

'Nobody I ever saw,' he said. 'That another one?'

'No, this is a newspaper still of Mrs Grayle. Anne Riordan got it.'

He looked at it and nodded. 'For twenty million, I'd marry her myself.'

'There's something I ought to tell you,' I said. 'Last night I was so damn mad I had crazy ideas about going down there and trying to bust it alone. This hospital is at Twenty-third and Descanso in Bay City. It's run by a man named Sonderborg who says he's a doctor. He's running a crook hide-out on the side. I saw Moose Malloy there last night. In a room.'

Randall sat very still, looking at me. 'Sure?'

'You couldn't mistake him. He's a big guy, enormous. He doesn't look like anybody you ever saw.'

He sat looking at me, without moving. Then very slowly he moved out from under the table and stood up.

'Let's go see this Florian woman.'

'How about Malloy?'

He sat down again. 'Tell me the whole thing, carefully.'

I told him. He listened without taking his eyes off my face. I don't think he even winked. He breathed with his mouth slightly open. His body didn't move. His fingers tapped gently on the edge of the table. When I had finished he said:

'This Dr Sonderborg—what did he look like?'

'Like a doper, and probably a dope peddler.' I described him to Randall as well as I could.

He went quietly into the other room and sat down at the telephone. He dialled his number and spoke quietly for a long time. Then he came back. I had just finished making more coffee and boiling a couple of eggs and making two slices of toast and buttering them. I sat down to eat.

Randall sat down opposite me and leaned his chin in his hand. 'I'm having a state narcotics man go down there with a fake complaint and ask to look around. He may get some ideas. He won't get Malloy. Malloy was out of there ten minutes after you left last night. That's one thing you can bet on.'

'Why not the Bay City cops?' I put salt on my eggs.

Randall said nothing. When I looked up at him his face was red and uncomfortable.

'For a cop,' I said, 'you're the most sensitive guy I ever met.'

'Hurry up with that eating. We have to go.'

'I have to shower and shave and dress after this.'

'Couldn't you just go in your pyjamas?' he asked acidly.

'So the town is as crooked as all that?' I said.

'It's Laird Brunette's town. They say he put up thirty grand to elect a mayor.'

'The fellow that owns the Belvedere Club?'

'And the two gambling boats.'

'But it's in our county,' I said.

He looked down at his clean, shiny fingernails.

'We'll stop by your office and get those other two reefers,' he said. 'If they're still there.' He snapped his fingers. 'If you'll lend me your keys, I'll do it while you get shaved and dressed.'

'We'll go together,' I said. 'I might have some mail.'

He nodded and after a moment sat down and lit another cigarette. I shaved and dressed and we left in Randall's car.

I had some mail, but it wasn't worth reading. The two cut up cigarettes in the desk drawer had not been touched. The office had no look of having been searched.

Randall took the two Russian cigarettes and sniffed at the tobacco and put them away in his pocket.

'He got one card from you,' he mused. 'There couldn't have been anything on the back of that, so he didn't bother about the others. I guess Amthor is not very much afraid—just thought you were trying to pull something. Let's go.'

30

Old Nosey poked her nose an inch outside the front door, sniffed carefully as if there might be an early violet blooming, looked up and down the street with a raking glance, and nodded her white head. Randall and I took our hats off. In that neighbourhood that probably ranked you with Valentino. She seemed to remember me.

'Good morning, Mrs Morrison,' I said. 'Can we step inside a minute? This is Lieutenant Randall from Headquarters.'

'Land's sakes, I'm all flustered. I got a big ironing to do,' she said.

'We won't keep you a minute.'

She stood back from the door and we slipped past her into her hallway with the side piece from Mason City or wherever it was and from that into the neat living-room with the lace curtains at the windows. A smell of ironing came from the back of the house. She shut the door in between as carefully as if it was made of short pie crust.

She had a blue and white apron on this morning. Her eyes were just as sharp and her chin hadn't grown any.

She parked herself about a foot from me and pushed her face forward and looked into my eyes.

'She didn't get it.'

I looked wise. I nodded my head and looked at Randall and Randall nodded his head. He went to a window and looked at the side of Mrs Florian's house. He came back softly, holding his pork-pie under his arm, debonair as a French count in a college play.

'She didn't get it,' I said.

'Nope, she didn't. Saturday was the first. April Fool's Day. He! He!' She stopped and was about to wipe her eyes with her apron when she remembered it was a rubber apron. That soured her a little. Her mouth got the pruny look.

'When the mailman come by and he didn't go up her walk she run out and called to him. He shook his head and went on. She went back in. She slammed the door so hard I figured a window'd break. Like she was mad.'

'I swan,' I said.

Old Nosey said to Randall sharply: 'Let me see your badge, young man. This young man had a whisky breath on him t'other day. I ain't never rightly trusted him.'

Randall took a gold and blue enamel badge out of his pocket and showed it to her.

'Looks like real police all right,' she admitted. 'Well, ain't nothing happened over Sunday. She went out for liquor. Come back with two square bottles.'

'Gin,' I said. 'That just gives you an idea. Nice folks don't drink gin.'

'Nice folks don't drink no liquor at all,' Old Nosey said pointedly.

'Yeah,' I said. 'Come Monday, that being to-day, and the mailman went by again. This time she was really sore.'

'Kind of smart guesser, ain't you, young man? Can't wait for folks to get their mouth open hardly.'

'I'm sorry, Mrs Morrison. This is an important matter to us—'

'This here young man don't seem to have no trouble keepin' his mouth in place.'

'He's married,' I said. 'He's had practice.'

Her face turned a shade of violet that reminded me, unpleasantly, of cyanosis. 'Get out of my house afore I call the police!' she shouted.

'There is a police officer standing before you, madam,' Randall said shortly. 'You are in no danger.'

'That's right there is,' she admitted. The violet tint began to fade from her face. 'I don't take to this man.'

'You have company, madam. Mrs Florian didn't get her registered letter to-day either—is that it?'

'No.' Her voice was sharp and short. Her eyes were furtive. She began to talk rapidly, too rapidly. 'People was there last night. I didn't even see them. Folks took me to the picture show. Just as we got back—no, just after they driven off—a car went away from next door. Fast without any lights. I didn't see the number.'

She gave a sharp sidelong look from her furtive eyes. I wondered why they were furtive. I wandered to the window and lifted the lace curtain. An official blue-grey uniform was nearing the house. The man wearing it wore a heavy leather bag over his shoulder and had a vizored cap.

I turned away from the window, grinning.

'You're slipping,' I told her rudely. 'You'll be playing shortstop in a Class C league next year.'

'That's not smart,' Randall said coldly.

'Take a look out of the window.'

He did and his face hardened. He stood quite still looking at Mrs Morrison. He was waiting for something, a sound like nothing else on earth. It came in a moment.

It was the sound of something being pushed into the front door mail slot. It might have been a handbill, but it wasn't. There were steps going back down the walk, then along the street, and Randall went to the window again. The mailman didn't stop at Mrs Florian's house. He went on, his blue-grey back even and calm under the heavy leather pouch.

Randall turned his head and asked with deadly politeness: 'How many mail deliveries a morning are there in this district, Mrs Morrison?'

She tried to face it out. 'Just the one,' she said sharply—'one mornings and one afternoons.'

Her eyes darted this way and that. The rabbit chin was trembling on the edge of something. Her hands clutched at the rubber frill that bordered the blue and white apron.

'The morning delivery just went by,' Randall said dreamily. 'Registered mail comes by the regular mailman?'

'She always got it Special Delivery,' the old voice cracked.

'Oh. But on Saturday she ran out and spoke to the mailman when he didn't stop at her house. And you said nothing about Special Delivery.'

It was nice to watch him working—on somebody else.

Her mouth opened wide and her teeth had the nice shiny look that comes from standing all night in a glass of solution. Then suddenly she made a squawking noise and threw the apron over her head and ran out of the room.

He watched the door through which she had gone. It was beyond the arch. He smiled. It was a rather tired smile.

'Neat, and not a bit gaudy,' I said. 'Next time you play the tough part. I don't like being rough with old ladies—even if they are lying gossips.'

He went on smiling. 'Same old story.' He shrugged. 'Police work. Phooey. She started with facts, as she knew facts. But they didn't come fast enough or seem exciting enough. So she tried a little lily-gilding.'

He turned and we went out into the hall. A faint noise of sobbing came from the back of the house. For some patient man, long dead, that had been the weapon of final defeat, probably. To me it was just an old woman sobbing, but nothing to be pleased about.

We went quietly out of the house, shut the front door quietly and made sure that the screen door didn't bang. Randall put his hat on and sighed.

Then he shrugged, spreading his cool well-kept hands out far from his body. There was a thin sound of sobbing still audible, back in the house.

The mailman's back was two houses down the street.

'Police work,' Randall said quietly, under his breath, and twisted his mouth.

We walked across the space to the next house. Mrs Florian hadn't even taken the wash in. It still jittered, stiff and yellowish on the wire line in the side yard. We went up on the steps and rang the bell. No answer. We knocked. No answer.

'It was unlocked last time,' I said.

He tried the door, carefully screening the movement with his body. It was locked this time. We went down off the porch and walked around the house on the side away from Old Nosey. The back porch had a hooked screen. Randall knocked on that. Nothing happened. He came back off the two almost paintless wooden steps and went along the disused and overgrown driveway and opened up a wooden garage. The doors creaked. The garage was full of nothing. There were a few battered old-fashioned trunks not worth breaking up for firewood. Rusted gardening tools, old cans, plenty of those, in cartons. On each side of the doors, in the angle of the wall a nice fat black widow spider sat in its casual untidy web. Randall picked up a piece of wood and killed them absently. He shut the garage up again, walked back along the weedy drive to the front and up the steps of the house on the other side from Old Nosey. Nobody answered his ring or knock.

He came back slowly, looking across the street over his shoulder.

'Back door's easiest,' he said. 'The old hen next door won't do anything about it now. She's done too much lying.'

He went up the two back steps and slid a knife blade neatly into the crack of the door and lifted the hook. That put us in the screen porch. It was full of cans and some of the cans were full of flies.

'Jesus, what a way to live!' he said.

The back door was easy. A five-cent skeleton key turned the lock. But there was a bolt.

'This jars me,' I said. 'I guess she's beat it. She wouldn't lock up like this. She's too sloppy.'

'Your hat's older than mine,' Randall said. He looked at the glass panel in the back door. 'Lend it to me to push the glass in. Or shall we do a neat job?'

'Kick it in. Who cares around here?'

'Here goes.'

He stepped back and lunged at the lock with his leg parallel to the floor. Something cracked idly and the door gave a few inches. We heaved it open and picked a piece of jagged cast metal off the linoleum and laid it politely on the wood-stone drainboard, beside about nine empty gin bottles.

Flies buzzed against the closed windows of the kitchen. The place reeked. Randall stood in the middle of the floor, giving it the careful eye.

Then he walked softly through the swing door without touching it except low down with his toe and using that to push it far enough back so that it stayed open. The living-room was much as I had remembered it. The radio was off.

'That's a nice radio,' Randall said. 'Cost money. If it's paid for. Here's something.'

He went down on one knee and looked along the carpet. Then he went to the side of the radio and moved a loose cord with his foot. The plug came into view. He bent and studied the knobs on the radio front.

'Yeah,' he said. 'Smooth and rather large. Pretty smart, that. You don't get prints on a light cord, do you?'

'Shove it in and see if it's turned on.'

He reached around and shoved it into the plug in the baseboard. The light went on at once. We waited. The thing hummed for a while and then suddenly a heavy volume of sound began to pour out of the speaker. Randall jumped at the cord and yanked it loose again. The sound was snapped off sharp.

When he straightened his eyes were full of light.

We went swiftly into the bedroom. Mrs Jessie Pierce Florian lay diagonally across her bed, in a rumpled cotton house dress, with her head close to one end of the footboard. The corner post of the bed was smeared darkly with something the flies liked.

She had been dead long enough.

Randall didn't touch her. He stared down at her for a long time and then looked at me with a wolfish baring of his teeth.

'Brains on her face,' he said. 'That seems to be the theme song of this case. Only this was done with just a pair of hands. But Jesus, what a pair of hands. Look at the neck bruises, the spacing of finger marks.'

'You look at them,' I said. I turned away. 'Poor old Nulty. It's not just a shine killing any more.'

31

A shiny black bug with a pink head and pink spots on it crawled slowly along the polished top of Randall's desk and waved a couple of feelers around, as if testing the breeze for a take-off. It wobbled a little as it crawled, like an old woman carrying too many parcels. A nameless dick sat at another desk and kept talking into an old-fashioned hushaphone telephone mouthpiece, so that his voice sounded like someone whispering in a tunnel. He talked with his eyes half closed, a big scarred hand on the desk in front of him holding a burning cigarette between the knuckles of the first and second fingers.

The bug reached the end of Randall's desk and marched straight off into the air. It fell on its back on the floor, waved a few thin worn legs in the air feebly and then played dead. Nobody cared, so it began waving the legs again and finally struggled over on its face. It trundled slowly off into a corner towards nothing, going nowhere.

The police loudspeaker box on the wall put out a bulletin about a hold-up on San Pedro south of Forty-fourth. The hold-up was a middle-aged man wearing a dark grey suit and grey felt hat. He was last seen running east on Forty-fourth and then dodging between two houses. 'Approach carefully,' the announcer said. 'This suspect is armed with a .32 calibre revolver and has just held up the proprietor of a Greek restaurant at Number

3966 South San Pedro.'

A flat click and the announcer went off the air and another one came on and started to read a hot car list, in a slow monotonous voice that repeated everything twice.

The door opened and Randall came in with a sheaf of letter size typewritten sheets. He walked briskly across the room and sat down across the desk from me and pushed some papers at me.

'Sign four copies,' he said.

I signed four copies.

The pink bug reached a corner of the room and put feelers out for a good spot to take off from. It seemed a little discouraged. It went along the baseboard towards another corner. I lit a cigarette and the dick at the hushaphone abruptly got up and went out of the office.

Randall leaned back in his chair, looking just the same as ever, just as cool, just as smooth, just as ready to be nasty or nice as the occasion required.

'I'm telling you a few things,' he said, 'just so you won't go having any more brainstorms. Just so you won't go masterminding all over the landscape any more. Just so maybe for Christ's sake you will let this one lay.'

I waited.

'No prints in the dump,' he said. 'You know which dump I mean. The cord was jerked to turn the radio off, but she turned it up herself probably. That's pretty obvious. Drunks like loud radios. If you have gloves on to do a killing and you turn up the radio to drown shots or something, you can turn it off the same way. But that wasn't the way it was done. And that woman's neck is broken. She was dead before the guy started to smack her head around. Now why did he start to smack her head around?'

'I'm just listening.'

Randall frowned. 'He probably didn't know he'd broken her neck. He was sore at her,' he said. 'Deduction.' He smiled sourly.

I blew some smoke and waved it away from my face.

'Well, why was he sore at her? There was a grand reward paid the time he was picked up at Florian's for the bank job in Oregon. It was paid to a shyster who is dead since, but the Florians likely got some of it. Malloy may have suspected that. Maybe he actually knew it. And maybe he was just trying to shake it out of her.'

I nodded. It sounded worth a nod. Randall went on:

'He took hold of her neck just once and his fingers didn't slip. If we get him, we might be able to prove by the spacing of the marks that his hands did it. Maybe not. The doc figures it happened last night, fairly early. Motion picture time, anyway. So far we don't tie Malloy to the house last night, not by any neighbours. But it certainly looks like Malloy.'

'Yeah,' I said. 'Malloy all right. He probably didn't mean to kill her, though. He's just too strong.'

'That won't help him any,' Randall said grimly.

'I suppose not. I just make the point that Malloy does not appear to me to be a killer type. Kill if cornered—but not for pleasure or money—and not women.'

'Is that an important point?' he asked dryly.

'Maybe you know enough to know what's important. And what isn't. I don't.'

He stared at me long enough for a police announcer to have time to put out another bulletin about the hold-up of the Greek restaurant on South San Pedro. The suspect was now in custody. It turned out later that he was a fourteen-year-old Mexican armed with a water-pistol. So much for eye-witnesses.

Randall waited until the announcer stopped and went on:

'We got friendly this morning. Let's stay that way. Go home and lie down and have a good rest. You look pretty peaked. Just let me and the police department handle the Marriott killing and find Moose Malloy and so on.'

'I got paid on the Marriott business,' I said. 'I fell down on the job. Mrs Grayle has hired me. What do you want me to do—retire and live on my fat?'

He stared at me again. 'I know. I'm human. They give you guys licences, which must mean they expect you to do something with them besides hang them on the wall in your office. On the other hand any acting-captain with a grouch can break you.'

'Not with the Grayles behind me.'

He studied it. He hated to admit I could be even half right. So he frowned and tapped his desk.

'Just so we understand each other,' he said after a pause. 'If you crab this case, you'll be in a jam. It may be a jam you can wriggle out of this time. I don't know. But little by little you will build up a body of hostility in this department that will make it damn hard for you to do any work.'

'Every private dick faces that every day of his life—unless he's just a divorce man.'

'You can't work on murders.'

'You've said your piece. I heard you say it. I don't expect to go out and accomplish things a big police department can't accomplish. If I have any small private notions, they are just that—small and private.'

He leaned slowly across the desk. His thin restless fingers tap-tapped, like the poinsettia shoots tapping against Mrs Jessie Florian's front wall. His creamy grey hair shone. His cool steady eyes were on mine.

'Let's go on,' he said. 'With what there is to tell. Amthor's away on a trip . His wife—and secretary—doesn't know or won't say where. The Indian has also disappeared. Will you sign a complaint against these people?'

'No. I couldn't make it stick.'

He looked relieved. 'The wife says she never heard of you. As to these two Bay City cops, if that's what they were—that's out of my hands. I'd rather not have the thing any more complicated than it is. One thing I feel pretty sure of—Amthor had nothing to do with Marriott's death. The cigarettes with his card in them were just a plant.'

'Doc Sonderborg?'

He spread his hands. 'The whole shebang skipped. Men from the D.A.'s office went down there on the quiet. No contact with Bay City at all. The house is locked up and empty. They got in, of course. Some hasty attempt had been made to clean up, but there are prints—plenty of them. It will take a week to work out what we have. There's a wall safe they're working on now. Probably had dope in it—and other things. My guess is that Sonderborg will have a record, not local, somewhere else, for abortion, or treating gunshot wounds or altering fingertips or for illegal use of dope. If it comes under Federal statutes, we'll get a lot of help.'

'He said he was a medical doctor,' I said.

Randall shrugged. 'May have been once. May never have been convicted. There's a guy practising medicine near Palm Springs right now who was indicted as a dope peddler in Hollywood five years ago. He was as guilty as hell—but the protection worked. He got off. Anything else worrying you?'

'What do you know about Brunette—for telling?'

'Brunette's a gambler. He's making plenty. He's making it an easy way.'

'All right,' I said, and started to get up. 'That sounds reasonable. But it doesn't bring us any nearer to this jewel heist gang that killed Marriott.'

'I can't tell you everything, Marlow.'

'I don't expect it,' I said. 'By the way, Jessie Florian told me—the second time I saw her—that she had been a servant in Marriott's family once. That was why he was sending her money. Anything to support that?'

'Yes. Letters in his safety-deposit box from her thanking him and saying the same thing.' He looked as if he was going to lose his temper. '*Now* will you for God's sake go home and mind your own business?'

'Nice of him to take such care of the letters, wasn't it?'

He lifted his eyes until their glance rested on the top of my head. Then he lowered the lids until half the iris was covered. He looked at me like that for a long ten seconds. Then he smiled. He was doing an awful lot of smiling that day. Using up a whole week's supply.

'I have a theory about that,' he said. 'It's crazy, but it's human nature. Marriott was by the circumstances of his life a threatened man. All crooks are gamblers, more or less, and all gamblers are superstitious—more or less. I think Jessie Florian was Marriott's lucky piece. As long as he took care of her, nothing would happen to him.'

I turned my head and looked for the pink-headed bug. He had tried two corners of the room now and was moving off disconsolately towards a third. I went over and picked him up in my handkerchief and carried him back to the desk.

'Look,' I said. 'This room is eighteen floors above ground. And this little bug climbs all the way up here just to make a friend. Me. *My* luck piece.' I folded the bug carefully into the soft part of the handkerchief and tucked the handkerchief into my pocket. Randall was pie-eyed. His mouth moved, but nothing came out of it.

'I wonder whose lucky piece Marriott was,' I said.

'Not yours, pal.' His voice was acid—cold acid.

'Perhaps not yours either.' My voice was just a voice. I went out of the room and shut the door.

I rode the express elevator down to the Spring Street entrance and walked out on the front porch of City Hall and down some steps and over to the flower beds. I put the pink bug down carefully behind a bush.

I wondered, in the taxi going home, how long it would take him to make the Homicide Bureau again.

I got my car out of the garage at the back of the apartment house and ate some lunch in Hollywood before I started down to Bay City. It was a beautiful cool sunny afternoon down at the beach. I left Arguello Boulevard at Third Street and drove over to the City Hall.

32

It was a cheap looking building for so prosperous a town. It looked more like something out of the Bible belt. Bums sat unmolested in a long row on the retaining wall that kept the front lawn—now mostly Bermuda grass—from falling into the street. The building was of three storeys and had an old belfry at the top, and the bell still hanging in the belfry. They had probably rung it for the volunteer fire brigade back in the good old chaw-and-spit days.

The cracked walk and the front steps led to open double doors in which a knot of obvious city hall fixers hung around waiting for something to happen so they could make something else out of it. They all had the well-fed stomachs, the careful eyes, the nice clothes and the reach-me-down manners. They gave me about four inches to get in.

Inside was a long dark hallway that had been mopped the day McKinley was inaugurated. A wooden sign pointed out the police department Information Desk. A uniformed man dozed behind a pint-sized PBX set into the end of a scarred wooden counter. A plainclothes man with his coat off and his hog's leg looking like a fire plug against his ribs took one eye off his evening paper, bonged a spittoon ten feet away from him, yawned, and said the Chief's office was upstairs at the back.

The second floor was lighter and cleaner, but that didn't mean that it was clean and light. A door on the ocean side, almost at the end of the hall, was lettered: John Wax, Chief of Police. Enter.

Inside there was a low wooden railing and a uniformed man behind it working a typewriter with two fingers and one thumb. He took my card, yawned, said he would see, and managed to drag himself through a mahogany door marked John Wax, Chief of Police. Private. He came back and held the door in the railing for me.

I went on in and shut the door of the inner office. It was cool and large and had windows on three sides. A stained wood desk was set far back like Mussolini's, so that you had to walk across an expanse of blue carpet to get to it, and while you were doing that you would be getting the beady eye.

I walked to the desk. A tilted embossed sign on it read: John Wax, Chief of Police. I figured I might be able to remember the name. I looked at the man behind the desk. No straw was sticking to his hair.

He was a hammered-down heavyweight, with short pink hair and a pink scalp glistening through it. He had small, hungry, heavy-lidded eyes, as restless as fleas. He wore a suit of fawn-coloured flannel, a coffee-coloured shirt and tie, a diamond ring, a diamond-studded lodge pin in his lapel, and the required three stiff points of handkerchief coming up a little more than the required three inches from his outside breast pocket.

One of his plump hands was holding my card. He read it, turned it over and read the back, which was blank, read the front again, put it down on his desk and laid on it a paperweight in the shape of a bronze monkey, as if he was making sure he wouldn't lose it.

He pushed a pink paw at me. When I gave it back to him, he motioned to a chair.

'Sit down, Mr Marlowe. I see you are in our business more or less. What can I do for you?'

'A little trouble, Chief. You can straighten it out for me in a minute, if you care to.'

'Trouble,' he said softly. 'A little trouble.'

He turned in his chair and crossed his thick legs and gazed thoughtfully towards one of his pairs of windows. That let me see handspun lisle socks and English brogues that looked as if they had been pickled in port wine. Counting what I couldn't see and not counting his wallet he had half a grand on him. I figured his wife had money.

'Trouble,' he said, still softly, 'is something our little city don't know much about, Mr Marlowe. Our city is small but very, very clean. I look out of my western windows and I see the Pacific Ocean. Nothing cleaner than that, is there?' He didn't mention the two gambling ships that were hull down on the brass waves just beyond the three-mile limit.

Neither did I. 'That's right, Chief,' I said.

He threw his chest a couple of inches farther. 'I look out of my northern windows and I see the busy bustle of Arguello Boulevard and the lovely California foothills, and in the near foreground one of the nicest little business sections a man could want to know. I look out of my southern windows, which I am looking out of right now, and I see the finest yacht harbour in the world, for a small yacht harbour. I don't have no eastern windows, but if I did have, I would see a residential section that would make your mouth water. No, sir, trouble is a thing we don't have a lot of on hand in our little town.'

'I guess I brought mine with me, Chief. Some of it at least. Do you have a man working for you named Galbraith, a plainclothes sergeant?'

'Why yes, I believe I do,' he said, bringing his eyes around. 'What about him?'

'Do you have a man working for you that goes like this?' I described the other man, the one who said very little, was short, had a moustache and hit me with a blackjack. 'He goes around with Galbraith, very likely. Somebody called him Mister Blane, but that sounded like a phony.'

'Quite on the contrary,' the fat Chief said as stiffly as a fat man can say anything. 'He is my Chief of Detectives. Captain Blane.'

'Could I see these two guys in your office?'

He picked my card up and read it again. He laid it down. He waved a soft glistening hand.

'Not without a better reason than you have given me so far,' he said suavely.

'I didn't think I could, Chief. Do you happen to know of a man named Jules Amthor? He calls himself a psychic adviser. He lives at the top of a hill in Stillwood Heights.'

'No. And Stillwood Heights is not in my territory,' the Chief said. His eyes now were the eyes of a man who has other thoughts.

'That's what makes it funny,' I said. 'You see, I went to call on Mr

Amthor in connection with a client of mine. Mr Amthor got the idea I was blackmailing him. Probably guys in his line of business get that idea rather easily. He had a tough Indian bodyguard I couldn't handle. So the Indian held me and Amthor beat me up with my own gun. Then he sent for a couple of cops. They happened to be Galbraith and Mister Blane. Could this interest you at all?'

Chief Wax flapped his hands on his desk top very gently. He folded his eyes almost shut, but not quite. The cool gleam of his eyes shone between the thick lids and it shone straight at me. He sat very still, as if listening. Then he opened his eyes and smiled.

'And what happened then?' he inquired, polite as a bouncer at the Stork Club.

'They went through me, took me away in their car, dumped me out on the side of a mountain and socked me with a sap as I got out.'

He nodded, as if what I had said was the most natural thing in the world. 'And this was in Stillwood Heights,' he said softly.

'Yeah.'

'You know what I think you are?' He leaned a little over the desk, but not far, on account of his stomach being in the way.

'A liar,' I said.

'The door is there,' he said, pointing to it with the little finger of his left hand.

I didn't move. I kept on looking at him. When he started to get mad enough to push his buzzer I said: 'Let's not both make the same mistake. You think I'm a small time private dick trying to push ten times his own weight, trying to make a charge against a police officer that, even if it was true, the officer would take damn good care couldn't be proved. Not at all. I'm not making any complaints. I think the mistake was natural. I want to square myself with Amthor and I want your man Galbraith to help me do it. Mister Blane needn't bother. Galbraith will be enough. And I'm not here without backing. I have important people behind me.'

'How far behind?' the Chief asked and chuckled wittily.

'How far is 862 Aster Drive, where Mr Merwin Lockridge Grayle lives?'

His face changed so completely that it was as if another man sat in his chair. 'Mrs Grayle happens to be my client,' I said.

'Lock the doors,' he said. 'You're a younger man than I am. Turn the bolt knobs. We'll make a friendly start on this thing. You have an honest face, Marlowe.'

I got up and locked the doors. When I got back to the desk along the blue carpet, the Chief had a nice looking bottle out and two glasses. He tossed a handful of cardamom seeds on his blotter and filled both glasses.

We drank. He cracked a few cardamom seeds and we chewed them silently, looking into each other's eyes.

'That tasted right,' he said. He refilled the glasses. It was my turn to crack the cardamom seeds. He swept the shells off his blotter to the floor and smiled and leaned back.

'Now let's have it,' he said. 'Has this job you are doing for Mrs Grayle anything to do with Amthor?'

'There's a connection. Better check that I'm telling you the truth, though.'

'There's that,' he said and reached for his phone. Then he took a small book out of his vest and looked up a number. 'Campaign contributors,' he said and winked. 'The Mayor is very insistent that all courtesies be extended. Yes, here it is.' He put the book away and dialled.

He had the same trouble with the butler that I had. It made his ears get red. Finally he got her. His ears stayed red. She must have been pretty sharp with him.

'She wants to talk to you,' he said and pushed the phone across his broad desk.

'This is Phil,' I said, winking naughtily at the Chief.

There was a cool provocative laugh. 'What are you doing with that fat slob?'

'There's a little drinking being done.'

'Do you have to do it with him?'

'At the moment, yes. Business. I said, is there anything new? I guess you know what I mean.'

'No. Are you aware, my good fellow, that you stood me up for an hour the other night? Did I strike you as the kind of girl that lets that sort of thing happen to her?'

'I ran into trouble. How about to-night?'

'Let me see—to-night is—what day of the week is it for heaven's sake?'

'I'd better call you,' I said. 'I may not be able to make it. This is Friday.'

'Liar.' The soft husky laugh came again. 'It's Monday. Same time, same place—and no fooling this time?'

'I'd better call you.'

'You'd better be there.'

'I can't be sure. Let me call you.'

'Hard to get? I see. Perhaps I'm a fool to bother.'

'As a matter of fact you are.'

'Why?'

'I'm a poor man, but I pay my own way. And it's not quite as soft a way as you would like.'

'Damn you, if you're not there—'

'I said I'd call you.'

She sighed. 'All men are the same.'

'So are all women—after the first nine.'

She damned me and hung up. The Chief's eyes popped so far out of his head they looked as if they were on stilts.

He filled both glasses with a shaking hand and pushed one at me.

'So it's like that,' he said very thoughtfully.

'Her husband doesn't care,' I said, 'so don't make a note of it.'

He looked hurt as he drank his drink. He cracked the cardamom seeds very slowly, very thoughtfully. We drank to each other's baby blue eyes. Regretfully the Chief put the bottle and glasses out of sight and snapped a switch on his call box.

'Have Galbraith come up, if he's in the building. If not, try and get in touch with him for me.'

I got up and unlocked the doors and sat down again. We didn't wait long. The side door was tapped on, the Chief called out, and Hemingway stepped into the room.

He walked solidly over to the desk and stopped at the end of it and looked at Chief Wax with the proper expression of tough humility.

'Meet Mr Philip Marlowe,' the Chief said genially. 'A private dick from L.A.'

Hemingway turned enough to look at me. If he had ever seen me before, nothing in his face showed it. He put a hand out and I put a hand out and he looked at the Chief again.

'Mr Marlowe has a rather curious story,' the Chief said, cunning, like Richelieu behind the arras. 'About a man named Amthor who has a place in Stillwood Heights. He's some sort of crystal-gazer. It seems Marlowe went to see him and you and Blane happened in about the same time and there was an argument of some kind. I forget the details.' He looked out of his windows with the expression of a man forgetting details.

'Some mistake,' Hemingway said. 'I never saw this man before.'

'There was a mistake, as a matter of fact,' the Chief said dreamily. 'Rather trifling, but still a mistake. Mr Marlowe thinks it of slight importance.'

Hemingway looked at me again. His face still looked like a stone face.

'In fact he's not even interested in the mistake,' the Chief dreamed on. 'But he is interested in going to call on this man Amthor who lives in Stillwood Heights. He would like someone with him. I thought of you. He would like someone who would see that he got a square deal. It seems that Mr Amthor has a very tough Indian bodyguard and Mr Marlowe is a little inclined to doubt his ability to handle the situation without help. Do you think you could find out where this Amthor lives?'

'Yeah,' Hemingway said. 'But Stillwood Heights is over the line, Chief. This just a personal favour to a friend of yours?'

'You might put it that way,' the Chief said, looking at his left thumb. 'We wouldn't want to do anything not strictly legal, of course.'

'Yeah,' Hemingway said. 'No.' He coughed. 'When do we go?'

The Chief looked at me benevolently. 'Now would be okey,' I said. 'If it suits Mr Galbraith.'

'I do what I'm told,' Hemingway said.

The Chief looked him over, feature by feature. He combed him and brushed him with his eyes. 'How is Captain Blane to-day?' he inquired, munching on a cardamom seed.

'Bad shape. Bust appendix,' Hemingway said. 'Pretty critical.'

The Chief shook his head sadly. Then he got hold of the arms of his chair and dragged himself to his feet. He pushed a pink paw across his desk.

'Galbraith will take good care of you, Marlowe. You can rely on that.'

'Well, you've certainly been obliging, Chief,' I said. 'I certainly don't know how to thank you.'

'Pshaw! No thanks necessary. Always glad to oblige a friend of a friend, so to speak.' He winked at me. Hemingway studied the wink but he didn't say what he added it up to.

We went out, with the Chief's polite murmurs almost carrying us down the office. The door closed. Hemingway looked up and down the office. The door closed. Hemingway looked up and down the hall and then he looked at me.

'You played that one smart, baby,' he said. 'You must got something we wasn't told about.'

33

The car drifted quietly along a quiet street of homes. Arching pepper trees almost met above it to form a green tunnel. The sun twinkled through their upper branches and their narrow light leaves. A sign at the corner said it was Eighteenth Street.

Hemingway was driving and I sat beside him. He drove very slowly, his face heavy with thought.

'How much you tell him?' he asked, making up his mind.

'I told him you and Blane went over there and took me away and tossed me out of the car and socked me on the back of the head. I didn't tell him the rest.'

'Not about Twenty-third and Descanso, huh?'

'No.'

'Why not?'

'I thought maybe I could get more co-operation from you if I didn't.'

'That's a thought. You really want to go over to Stillwood Heights, or was that just a stall?'

'Just a stall. What I really want is for you to tell me why you put me in that funny-house and why I was kept there?'

Hemingway thought. He thought so hard his cheek muscles made little knots under his greyish skin.

'That Blane,' he said. 'That sawed-off hunk of shin meat. I didn't mean for him to sap you. I didn't mean for you to walk home neither, not really. It was just an act, on account of we are friends with this swami guy and we kind of keep people from bothering him. You'd be surprised what a lot of people would try to bother him.'

'Amazed,' I said.

He turned his head. His grey eyes were lumps of ice. Then he looked ahead again through the dusty windshield and did some more thinking.

'Them old cops get sap-hungry once in a while,' he said. 'They just got to crack a head. Jesus, was I scared. You dropped like a sack of cement. I told Blane plenty. Then we run you over to Sonderborg's place on account of it was a little closer and he was a nice guy and would take care of you.'

'Does Amthor know you took me there?'

'Hell, no. It was our idea.'

'On account of Sonderborg is such a nice guy and he would take care of me. And no kickback. No chance for a doctor to back up a complaint if I made one. Not that a complaint would have much chance in this sweet little town, if I did make it.'

'You going to get tough?' Hemingway asked thoughtfully.

'Not me,' I said. 'And for once in your life neither are you. Because your job is hanging by a thread. You looked in the Chief's eyes and you saw that. I didn't go in there without credentials, not this trip.'

'Okey,' Hemingway said and spat out of the window. 'I didn't have any idea of getting tough in the first place except just the routine big mouth. What next?'

'Is Blane really sick?'

Hemingway nodded, but somehow failed to look sad. 'Sure is. Pain in the gut day before yesterday and it bust on him before they could get his appendix out. He's got a chance–but not too good.'

'We'd certainly hate to lose him,' I said. 'A fellow like that is an asset to any police force.'

Hemingway chewed that one over and spat it out of the car window.

'Okey, next question,' he sighed.

'You told me why you took me to Sonderborg's place. You didn't tell me why he kept me there over forty-eight hours, locked up and shot full of dope.'

Hemingway braked the car softly over beside the kerb. He put his large hands on the lower part of the wheel side by side and gently rubbed the thumbs together.

'I wouldn't have an idea,' he said in a far-off voice.

'I had papers on me showing I had a private licence,' I said. 'Keys, some money, a couple of photographs. If he didn't know you boys pretty well, he might think the crack on the head was just a gag to get into his place and look around. But I figure he knows you boys too well for that. So I'm puzzled.'

'Stay puzzled, pally. It's a lot safer.'

'So it is,' I said. 'But there's no satisfaction in it.'

'You got the L.A. law behind you on this?'

'On this what?'

'On this thinking about Sonderborg.'

'Not exactly.'

'That don't mean yes or no.'

'I'm not that important,' I said. 'The L.A. law can come in here any time they feel like it–two-thirds of them anyway. The Sheriff's boys and the D.A.'s boys. I have a friend in the D.A.'s office. I worked there once. His name is Bernie Ohls. He's Chief Investigator.'

'You give it to him?'

'No. I haven't spoken to him in a month.'

'Thinking about giving it to him?'

'Not if it interferes with a job I'm doing.'

'Private job?'

'Yes.'

'Okey, what is it you want?'

'What's Sonderborg's real racket?'

Hemingway took his hands off the wheel and spat out of the window. 'We're on a nice street here, ain't we? Nice homes, nice gardens, nice climate. You hear a lot about crooked cops, or do you?'

'Once in a while,' I said.

'Okey, how many cops do you find living on a street even as good as this, with nice lawns and flowers? I'd know four or five, all vice squad boys. They get all the gravy. Cops like me live in itty-bitty frame houses on the wrong side of town. Want to see where I live?'

'What would it prove?'

'Listen, pally,' the big man said seriously. 'You got me on a string, but it could break. Cops don't go crooked for money. Not always, not even often.

They got caught in the system. They get you where they have you do what is told them or else. And the guy that sits back there in the nice big corner office, with the nice suit and the nice liquor breath he thinks chewing on them seeds makes smell like violets, only it don't—he ain't giving the orders either. You get me?'

'What kind of man is the mayor?'

'What kind of guy is a mayor anywhere? A politician. You think he gives the orders? Nuts. You know what's the matter with this country, baby?'

'Too much frozen capital, I heard.'

'A guy can't stay honest if he wants to,' Hemingway said. 'That's what's the matter with this country. He gets chiselled out of his pants if he does. You gotta play the game dirty or you don't eat. A lot of bastards think all we need is ninety thousand F.B.I. men in clean collars and brief cases. Nuts. The percentage would get them just the way it does the rest of us. You know what I think? I think we gotta make this little world all over again. Now take Moral Rearmament. There you've got something. M.R.A. There you've got something, baby.'

'If Bay City is a sample of how it works, I'll take aspirin,' I said.

'You could get too smart,' Hemingway said softly. 'You might not think it, but it could be. You could get so smart you couldn't think about anything but bein' smart. Me, I'm just a dumb cop. I take orders. I got a wife and two kids and I do what the big shots say. Blane could tell you things. Me, I'm ignorant.'

'Sure Blane has appendicitis? Sure he didn't just shoot himself in the stomach for meanness?'

'Don't be that way,' Hemingway complained and slapped his hands up and down on the wheel. 'Try and think nice about people.'

'About Blane?'

'He's human—just like the rest of us,' Hemingway said. 'He's a sinner—but he's human.'

'What's Sonderborg's racket?'

'Okey, I was just telling you. Maybe I'm wrong. I had you figured for a guy that could be sold a nice idea.'

'You don't know what his racket is,' I said.

Hemingway took his handkerchief out and wiped his face with it. 'Buddy, I hate to admit it,' he said. 'But you ought to know damn well that if I knew or Blane knew Sonderborg had a racket, either we wouldn't of dumped you in there or you wouldn't ever have come out, not walking. I'm talking about a real bad racket, naturally. Not fluff stuff like telling old women's fortunes out of a crystal ball.'

'I don't think I was meant to come out walking,' I said. 'There's a drug called scopolamine, truth serum, that sometimes makes people talk without their knowing it. It's not sure fire, any more than hypnotism is. But it sometimes works. I think I was being milked in there to find out what I knew. But there are only three ways Sonderborg could have known that there was anything for me to know that might hurt him. Amthor might have told him, or Moose Malloy might have mentioned to him that I went to see Jessie Florian, or he might have thought putting me in there was a police gag.'

Hemingway stared at me sadly. 'I can't even see your dust,' he said. 'Who the hell is Moose Malloy?'

'A big hunk that killed a man over on Central Avenue a few days ago. He's on your teletype, if you ever read it. And you probably have a reader of him by now.'

'So what?'

'So Sonderborg was hiding him. I saw him there, on a bed reading news-papers, the night I snuck out.'

'How'd you get out? Wasn't you locked in?'

'I crocked the orderly with a bed spring. I was lucky.'

'This big guy see you?'

'No.'

Hemingway kicked the car away from the kerb and a solid grin settled on his face. 'Let's go collect,' he said. 'It figures. It figures swell. Sonderborg was hiding hot boys. If they had dough, that is. His set-up was perfect for it. Good money, too.'

He kicked the car into motion and whirled around a corner.

'Hell, I thought he sold reefers,' he said disgustedly. 'With the right protection behind him. But hell, that's a small time racket. A peanut grift.'

'Ever hear of the numbers racket? That's a small time racket too—if you're just looking at one piece of it.'

Hemingway turned another corner sharply and shook his heavy head. 'Right. And pin ball games and bingo houses and horse parlours. But add them all up and give one guy control and it makes sense.'

'What guy?'

He went wooden on me again. His mouth shut hard and I could see his teeth were biting at each other inside it. We were on Descanso Street and going east. It was a quiet street even in late afternoon. As we got towards Twenty-third, it became in some vague manner less quiet. Two men were studying a palm tree as if figuring out how to move it. A car was parked near Dr Sonderborg's place, but nothing showed in it. Halfway down the block a man was reading water meters.

The house was a cheeful spot by daylight. Tea rose begonias made a solid pale mass under the front windows and pansies a blur of colour around the base of a white acacia in bloom. A scarlet climbing rose was just opening its buds on a fan-shaped trellis. There was a bed of winter sweetpeas and a bronze-green humming bird prodding in them delicately. The house looked like the home of a well-to-do elderly couple who liked to garden. The late afternoon sun on it had a hushed and menacing stillness.

Hemingway slid slowly past the house and a tight little smile tugged at the corners of his mouth. His nose sniffed. He turned the next corner, and looked in his rear view mirror and stepped up the speed of the car.

After three blocks he braked at the side of the street again and turned to give me a hard level stare.

'L.A. law,' he said. 'One of the guys by the palm tree is called Donnelly. I know him. They got the house covered. So you didn't tell your pal uptown, huh?'

'I said I didn't.'

'The Chief'll love this,' Hemingway snarled. 'They come down here and raid a joint and don't even stop by to say hello.'

I said nothing.

'They catch this Moose Malloy?'

I shook my head. 'Not so far as I know.'

'How the hell far do you know, buddy?' he asked very softly.

'Not far enough. Is there any connection between Amthor and Sonderborg?'

'Not that I know of.'

'Who runs this town?'

Silence.

'I heard a gambler named Laird Brunette put up thirty grand to elect the mayor. I heard he owns the Belvedere Club and both the gambling ships out on the water.'

'Might be,' Hemingway said politely.

'Where can Brunette be found?'

'Why ask me, baby?'

'Where would you make for if you lost your hideout in this town?'

'Mexico.'

I laughed. 'Okey, will you do me a big favour?'

'Glad to.'

'Drive me back downtown.'

He started the car away from the kerb and tooled it neatly along a shadowed street towards the ocean. The car reached the City Hall and slid around into the police parking zone and I got out.

'Come round and see me some time,' Hemingway said. 'I'll likely be cleaning spittoons.'

He put his big hand out. 'No hard feelings?'

'M.R.A.' I said and shook the hand.

He grinned all over. He called me back when I started to walk away. He looked carefully in all directions and leaned his mouth close to my ear.

'Them gambling ships are supposed to be out beyond city and state jurisdiction,' he said. 'Panama registry. If it was me that was—' he stopped dead, and his bleak eyes began to worry.

'I get it,' I said. 'I had the same sort of idea. I don't know why I bothered so much to get you to have it with me. But it wouldn't work–not for just one man.'

He nodded, and then he smiled. 'M.R.A.' he said.

34

I lay on my back on a bed in a waterfront hotel and waited for it to get dark. It was a small front room with a hard bed and a mattress slightly thicker than the cotton blanket that covered it. A spring underneath me was broken and stuck into the left side of my back. I lay there and let it prod me.

The reflection of a red neon light glared on the ceiling. When it made the whole room red it would be dark enough to go out. Outside cars honked along the alley they called the Speedway. Feet slithered on the sidewalks below my window. There was a murmur and mutter of coming and going in the air. The air that seeped in through the rusted screens smelled of stale frying fat. Far off a voice of the kind that could be heard far off was shouting: 'Get hungry, folks. Get hungry. Nice hot doggies here. Get hungry.'

It got darker. I thought; and thought in my mind moved with a kind of sluggish stealthiness, as if it was being watched by bitter and sadistic eyes. I thought of dead eyes looking at a moonless sky, with black blood at the corners of the mouths beneath them. I thought of nasty old women beaten to death against the posts of their dirty beds. I thought of a man with bright blond hair who was afraid and didn't quite know what he was afraid of, who was sensitive enough to know that something was wrong, and too vain or too dull to guess what it was that was wrong. I thought of beautiful rich women who could be had. I thought of nice slim curious girls who lived alone and could be had too, in a different way. I thought of cops, tough cops that could be greased and yet were not by any means all bad, like Hemingway. Fat prosperous cops with Chamber of Commerce voices, like Chief Wax. Slim, smart and deadly cops like Randall, who for all their smartness and deadliness were not free to do a clean job in a clean way. I thought of sour old goats like Nulty who had given up trying. I thought of Indians and psychics and dope doctors.

I thought of lots of things. It got darker. The glare of the red neon sign spread farther and farther across the ceiling. I sat up on the bed and put my feet on the floor and rubbed the back of my neck.

I got up on my feet and went over to the bowl in the corner and threw cold water on my face. After a little while I felt a little better, but very little. I needed a drink, I needed a lot of life insurance, I needed a vacation, I needed a home in the country. What I had was a coat, a hat and a gun. I put them on and went out of the room.

There was no elevator. The hallways smelled and the stairs had grimed rails. I went down them, threw the key on the desk and said I was through. A clerk with a wart on his left eyelid nodded and a Mexican bellhop in a frayed uniform coat came forward from behind the dustiest rubber plant in California to take my bags. I didn't have any bags, so being a Mexican, he opened the door for me and smiled politely just the same.

Outside the narrow street fumed, the sidewalks swarmed with fat stomachs. Across the street a bingo parlour was going full blast and beside it a couple of sailors with girls were coming out of a photographer's shop where they had probably been having their photos taken riding on camels. The voice of the hot dog merchant split the dusk like an axe. A big blue bus blared down the street to the little circle where the street car used to turn on a turntable. I walked that way.

After a while there was a faint smell of ocean. Not very much, but as if they had kept this much just to remind people this had once been a clean open beach where the waves came in and creamed and the wind blew and you could smell something besides hot fat and cold sweat.

The little sidewalk car came trundling along the wide concrete walk. I got on it and rode to the end of the line and got off and sat on a bench where it was quiet and cold and there was a big brown heap of kelp almost at my feet. Out to sea they turned the lights on in the gambling boats. I got back on the sidewalk car the next time it came and rode back almost to where I had left the hotel. If anybody was tailing me, he was doing it without moving. I didn't think there was. In that clean little city there wouldn't be enough crime for the dicks to be very good shadows.

The black piers glittered their length and then disappeared into the dark background of night and water. You could still smell hot fat, but you could smell the ocean too. The hot dog man droned on:

'Get hungry, folks, get hungry. Nice hot doggies. Get hungry.'

I spotted him in a white barbecue stand tickling wienies with a long fork. He was doing a good business even that early in the year. I had to wait some time to get him alone.

'What's the name of the one farthest out?' I asked, pointing with my nose.

'*Montecito.*' He gave me the level steady look.

'Could a guy with reasonable dough have himself a time there?'

'What kind of a time?'

I laughed, sneeringly, very tough.

'Hot doggies,' he chanted. 'Nice hot doggies, folks.' He dropped his voice. 'Women?'

'Nix. I was figuring on a room with a nice sea breeze and good food and nobody to bother me. Kind of vacation.'

He moved away. 'I can't hear a word you say,' he said, and then went into his chant.

He did some more business. I didn't know why I bothered with him. He just had that kind of face. A young couple in shorts came up and bought hot dogs and strolled away with the boy's arm around the girl's brassiere and each eating the other's hot dog.

The man slid a yard towards me and eyed me over. 'Right now I should be whistling Roses of Picardy,' he said, and paused. 'That would cost you,' he said.

'How much?'

'Fifty. Not less. Unless they want you for something.'

'This used to be a good town,' I said. 'A cool-off town.'

'Thought it still was,' he drawled. 'But why ask me?'

'I haven't an idea,' I said. I threw a dollar bill on his counter. 'Put it in the baby's bank,' I said. 'Or whistle Roses of Picardy.'

He snapped the bill, folded it longways, folded it across and folded it again. He laid it on the counter and tucked his middle finger behind his thumb and snapped. The folded bill hit me lightly in the chest and fell noiselessly to the ground. I bent and picked it up and turned quickly. But nobody was behind me that looked like a dick.

I leaned against the counter and laid the dollar bill on it again. 'People don't throw money at me,' I said. 'They hand it to me. Do you mind?'

He took the bill, unfolded it, spread it out and wiped it off with his apron. He punched his cash-register and dropped the bill into the drawer.

'They say money don't stink,' he said. 'I sometimes wonder.'

I didn't say anything. Some more customers did business with him and went away. The night was cooling fast.

'I wouldn't try the *Royal Crown*,' the man said. 'That's for good little squirrels, that stick to their nuts. You look like dick to me, but that's your angle. I hope you swim good.'

I left him, wondering why I had gone to him in the first place. Play the hunch. Play the hunch and get stung. In a little while you wake up with your mouth full of hunches. You can't order a cup of coffee without shutting your eyes and stabbing the menu. Play the hunch.

I walked around and tried to see if anybody walked behind me in any particular way. Then I sought out a restaurant that didn't smell of frying grease and found one with a purple neon sign and a cocktail bar behind a reed curtain. A male cutie with henna'd hair drooped at a bungalow grand piano and tickled the keys lasciviously and sang Stairway to the Stars in a voice with half the steps missing.

I gobbled a dry martini and hurried back through the reed curtain to the dining-room.

The eighty-five cent dinner tasted like a discarded mailbag and was served to me by a waiter who looked as if he would slug me for a quarter, cut my throat for six bits, and bury me at sea in a barrel of concrete for a dollar and a half, plus sales tax.

35

It was a long ride for a quarter. The water taxi, an old launch painted up and glassed in for three-quarters of its length, slid through the anchored yachts and around the wide pile of stone which was the end of the breakwater. The swell hit us without warning and bounced the boat like a cork. But there was plenty of room to be sick that early in the evening. All the company I had was three couples and the man who drove the boat, a tough-looking citizen who sat a little on his left hip on account of having a black leather hip-holster inside his right hip pocket. The three couples began to chew each other's faces as soon as we left the shore.

I stared back at the lights of Bay City and tried not to bear down too hard on my dinner. Scattered points of light drew together and became a jewelled bracelet laid out in the show window of the night. Then the brightness faded and they were a soft orange glow appearing and disappearing over the edge of the swell. It was a long smooth even swell with no white caps, and just the right amount of heave to make me glad I hadn't pickled my dinner in bar whisky. The taxi slid up and down the swell now with a sinister smoothness, like a cobra dancing. There was cold in the air, the wet cold that sailors never get out of their joints. The red neon pencils that outlined the *Royal Crown* faded off to the left and dimmed in the gliding grey ghosts of the sea, then shone out again, as bright as new marbles.

We gave this one a wide berth. It looked nice from a long way off. A faint music came over the water and music over the water can never be anything but lovely. The *Royal Crown* seemed to ride as steady as a pier on its four hausers. Its landing stage was lit up like a theatre marquee. Then all this faded into remoteness and another, older, smaller boat began to sneak out of the night towards us. It was not much to look at. A converted seagoing freighter with scummed and rusted plates, the superstructure cut down to the boat deck level, and above that two stumpy masts just high enough for a radio antenna. There was light on the *Montecito* also and music floated across the wet dark sea. The spooning couples took their teeth out of each other's necks and stared at the ship and giggled.

The taxi swept around in a wide curve, careened just enough to give the passengers a thrill, and eased up to the hemp fenders along the stage. The taxi's motor idled and backfired in the fog. A lazy searchlight beam swept a circle about fifty yards out from the ship.

The taximan hooked to the stage and a sloe-eyed lad in a blue mess-jacket with bright buttons, a bright smile and a gangster mouth, handed the girls up from the taxi. I was last. The casual neat way he looked me over told me something about him. The casual neat way he bumped my shoulder clip told me more.

'Nix,' he said softly. 'Nix.'

He had a smoothly husky voice, a hard Harry straining himself through a silk handkerchief. He jerked his chin at the taximan. The taximan dropped a short loop over a bitt, turned his wheel a little, and climbed out on the stage. He stepped behind me.

'No gats on the boat, laddy. Sorry and all that rot,' Mess-jacket purred.

'I could check it. It's just part of my clothes. I'm a fellow who wants to see Brunette, on business.'

He seemed mildly amused. 'Never heard of him,' he smiled. 'On your way, bo.'

The taximan hooked a wrist through my right arm.

'I want to see Brunette,' I said. My voice sounded weak and frail, like an old lady's voice.

'Let's not argue,' the sloe-eyed lad said. 'We're not in Bay City now, not even in California, and by some good opinions not even in the U.S.A. Beat it.'

'Back in the boat,' the taximan growled behind me. 'I owe you a quarter. Let's go.'

I got back into the boat. Mess-jacket looked at me with his silent sleek smile. I watched it until it was no longer a smile, no longer a face, no longer anything but a dark figure against the landing lights. I watched it and hungered.

The way back seemed longer. I didn't speak to the taximan and he didn't speak to me. As I got off at the wharf he handed me a quarter.

'Some other night,' he said wearily, 'when we got more room to bounce you.'

Half a dozen customers waiting to get in stared at me, hearing him. I went past them, past the door of the little waiting-room on the float, towards the shallow steps at the landward end.

A big red-headed roughneck in dirty sneakers and tarry pants and what was left of a torn blue sailor's jersey and a streak of black down the side of his face straightened from the railing and bumped into me casually.

I stopped. He looked too big. He had three inches on me and thirty pounds. But it was getting to be time for me to put my fist into somebody's teeth even if all I got for it was a wooden arm.

The light was dim and mostly behind him. 'What's the matter, pardner?' he drawled. 'No soap on the hell ship?'

'Go darn your shirt,' I told him. 'Your belly is sticking out.'

'Could be worse,' he said. 'The gat's kind of bulgy under the light suit at that.'

'What pulls your nose into it?'

'Jesus, nothing at all. Just curiosity. No offence, pal.'

'Well, get the hell out of my way then.'

'Sure. I'm just resting here.'

He smiled a slow tired smile. His voice was soft, dreamy, so delicate for a big man that it was startling. It made me think of another soft-voiced big man I had strangely liked.

'You got the wrong approach,' he said sadly. 'Just call me Red.'

'Step aside, Red. The best people make mistakes. I feel one crawling up my back.'

He looked thoughtfully this way and that. He had me angled into a corner of the shelter on the float. We seemed to be more or less alone.

'You want on the *Monty*? Can be done. If you got a reason.'

People in gay clothes and gay faces went past us and got into the taxi. I waited for them to pass.

'How much is the reason?'

'Fifty bucks. Ten more if you bleed in my boat.'

I started around him.

'Twenty-five,' he said softly. 'Fifteen if you come back with friends.'

'I don't have any friends,' I said, and walked away. He didn't try to stop me.

I turned right along the cement walk down which the little electric cars come and go, trundling like baby carriages and blowing little horns that wouldn't startle an expectant mother. At the foot of the first pier there was a flaring bingo parlour, jammed full of people already. I went into it and stood against the wall behind the players, where a lot of other people stood and waited for a place to sit down.

I watched a few numbers go up on the electric indicator, listened to the table men call them off, tried to spot the house players and couldn't, and turned to leave.

A large blueness that smelled of tar took shape beside me. 'No got the dough—or just tight with it?' the gentle voice asked in my ear.

I looked at him again. He had the eyes you never see, that you only read about. Violet eyes. Almost purple. Eyes like a girl, a lovely girl. His skin was as soft as silk. Lightly reddened, but it would never tan. It was too delicate. He was bigger than Hemingway and younger, by many years. He was not as big as Moose Malloy, but he looked very fast on his feet. His hair was that shade of red that glints with gold. But except for the eyes he had a plain farmer face, with no stagy kind of handsomeness.

'What's your racket?' he asked. 'Private eye?'

'Why do I have to tell you?' I snarled.

'I kind of thought that was it,' he said. 'Twenty-five too high? No expense account?'

'No.'

He sighed. 'It was a bum idea I had anyway,' he said. 'They'll tear you to pieces out there.'

'I wouldn't be surprised. What's *your* racket?'

'A dollar here, a dollar there. I was on the cops once. They broke me.'

'Why tell me?'

He looked surprised. 'It's true.'

'You must have been levelling.'

He smiled faintly.

'Know a man named Brunette?'

The faint smile stayed on his face. Three bingoes were made in a row. They worked fast in there. A tall beak-faced man with sallow sunken cheeks and wrinkled suit stepped close to us and leaned against the wall and didn't look at us. Red leaned gently towards him and asked: 'Is there something we could tell you, pardner?'

The tall beak-faced man grinned and moved away. Red grinned and shook the building leaning against the wall again.

'I've met a man who could take you,' I said.

'I wish there was more,' he said gravely. 'A big guy costs money. Things ain't scaled for him. He costs to feed, to put clothes on, and he can't sleep with his feet in the bed. Here's how it works. You might not think this is a good place to talk, but it is. Any finks drift along I'll know them and the rest of the crowd is watching those numbers and nothing else. I got a boat with an under-water by-pass. That is, I can borrow one. There's a pier down the line without lights. I know a loading port on the *Monty* I can open. I take a load out there once in a while. There ain't many guys below decks.'

'They have a searchlight and lookouts,' I said.

'We can make it.'

I got my wallet out and slipped a twenty and a five against my stomach and folded them small. The purple eyes watched me without seeming to.

'One way?'

I nodded.

'Fifteen was the word.'

'The market took a spurt.'

A tarry hand swallowed the bills. He moved silently away. He faded into the hot darkness outside the doors. The beak-nosed man materialized at my left side and said quietly:

'I think I know that fellow in sailor clothes. Friend of yours? I think I seen him before.'

I straightened away from the wall and walked away from him without speaking, out of the doors, then left, watching a high head that moved along from electrolier to electrolier a hundred feet ahead of me. After a couple of minutes I turned into a space between two concession shacks. The beak-nosed man appeared, strolling with his eyes on the ground. I stepped out to his side.

'Good evening,' I said. 'May I guess your weight for a quarter?' I leaned against him. There was a gun under the wrinkled coat.

His eyes looked at me without emotion. 'Am I goin' to have to pinch you, son? I'm posted along this stretch to maintain law and order.'

'Who's dismaintaining it right now?'

'Your friend had a familiar look to me.'

'He ought to. He's a cop.'

'Aw hell,' the beak-nosed man said patiently. 'That's where I seen him. Good-night to you.'

He turned and strolled back the way he had come. The tall head was out of sight now. It didn't worry me. Nothing about that lad would ever worry me.

I walked on slowly.

36

Beyond the electroliers, beyond the beat and toot of the small sidewalk cars, beyond the smell of hot fat and popcorn and the shrill children and the barkers in the peep shows, beyond everything but the smell of the ocean and the suddenly clear line of the shore and the creaming fall of the waves into the pebbled spume. I walked almost alone now. The noises died behind me, the hot dishonest light became a fumbling glare. Then the lightless finger of a black pier jutted seaward into the dark. This would be the one. I turned to go out on it.

Red stood up from a box against the beginning of the piles and spoke upwards to me. 'Right,' he said. 'You go on out to the seasteps. I gotta go and get her and warm her up.'

'Waterfront cop followed me. That guy in the bingo parlour. I had to stop and speak to him.'

'Olson. Pickpocket detail. He's good too. Except once in a while he will lift a leather and plant it, to keep up his arrest record. That's being a shade too good, or isn't it?'

'For Bay City I'd say just about right. Let's get going. I'm getting the wind up. I don't want to blow this fog away. It doesn't look much but it would help a lot.'

'It'll last enough to fool a searchlight,' Red said. 'They got Tommy-guns on that boat deck. You go on out the pier. I'll be along.'

He melted into the dark and I went out the dark boards, slipping on fish-slimed planking. There was a low dirty railing at the far end. A couple leaned in a corner. They went away, the man swearing.

For ten minutes I listened to the water slapping the piles. A night bird whirred in the dark, the faint greyness of a wing cut across my vision and disappeared. A plane droned high in the ceiling. Then far off a motor barked and roared and kept on roaring like half a dozen truck engines. After a while the sound eased and dropped, then suddenly there was no sound at all.

More minutes passed. I went back to the seasteps and moved down them as cautiously as a cat on a wet floor. A dark shape slid out of the night and something thudded. A voice said: 'All set. Get in.'

I got into the boat and sat beside him under the screen. The boat slid out over the water. There was no sound from its exhaust now but an angry bubbling along both sides of the shell. Once more the lights of Bay City became something distantly luminous beyond the rise and fall of alien waves. Once more the garish lights of the *Royal Crown* slid off to one side, the ship seeming to preen itself like a fashion model on a revolving platform. And once again the ports of the good ship *Montecito* grew out of the black Pacific and the slow steady sweep of the searchlight turned around it like the beam of a lighthouse.

'I'm scared,' I said suddenly. 'I'm scared stiff.'

Red throttled down the boat and let it slide up and down the swell as though the water moved underneath and the boat stayed in the same place. He turned his face and stared at me.

'I'm afraid of death and despair,' I said. 'Of dark water and drowned men's faces and skulls with empty eyesockets. I'm afraid of dying, of being nothing, of not finding a man named Brunette.'

He chuckled. 'You had me going for a minute. You sure give yourself a pep talk. Brunette might be any place. On either of the boats, at the club he owns, back east, Reno, in his slippers at home. That all you want?'

'I want a man named Malloy, a huge brute who got out of the Oregon State pen a while back after an eight-year stretch for bank robbery. He was hiding out in Bay City.' I told him about it. I told him a great deal more than I intended to. It must have been his eyes.

At the end he thought and then spoke slowly and what he said had wisps of fog clinging to it, like the beads on a moustache. Maybe that made it seem wiser than it was, maybe not.

'Some of it makes sense,' he said. 'Some not. Some I wouldn't know about, some I would. If this Sonderborg was running a hideout and peddling reefers and sending boys out to heist jewels off rich ladies with a wild look in their eyes, it stands to reason that he had an in with the city government, but that don't mean they knew everything he did or that every cop on the force knew he had an in. Could be Blane did and Hemingway, as you call him, didn't. Blane's bad, the other guy is just tough cop, neither bad nor good, neither crooked nor honest, full of guts and just dumb enough, like me, to think being on the cops is a sensible way to make a living. This psychic fellow doesn't figure either way. He bought himself a line of protection in the best market, Bay City, and he used it when he had to. You never know what a guy like that is up to and so you never know what he has on his conscience or is afraid of. Could be he's human and fell for a customer once in a while. Them rich dames are easier to make than paper dolls. So my hunch about your stay in Sonderborg's place is simply that Blane knew Sonderborg would be scared when he found out who you were—and the story they told Sonderborg is probably what he told you, that they found you wandering with your head dizzy—and Sonderborg wouldn't know what to do with you and he would be afraid either to let you go or to knock you off, and after long enough Blane would drop around and raise the ante on him. That's all there was to that. It just happened they could use you and they did it. Blane might know about Malloy too. I wouldn't put it past him.'

I listened and watched the slow sweep of the searchlight and the coming and going of the water taxi far over to the right.

'I know how these boys figure,' Red said. 'The trouble with cops is not that they're dumb or crooked or tough, but that they think just being a cop gives them a little something they didn't have before. Maybe it did once, but not any more. They're topped by too many smart minds. That brings us to Brunette. He don't run the town. He couldn't be bothered. He put up big money to elect a mayor so his water taxis wouldn't be bothered. If there was anything in particular he wanted, they would give it to him. Like a while ago one of his friends, a lawyer, was pinched for drunk driving felony and Brunette got the charge reduced to reckless driving. They changed the blotter to do it, and that's a felony too. Which gives you an idea. His racket is gambling and all rackets tie together these days. So he might handle reefers, or touch a percentage from some of his workers he gave the business to. He might know Sonderborg and he might not. But the jewel heist is out. Figure the work these boys done for eight grand. It's a laugh to think Brunette would have anything to do with that.'

'Yeah,' I said. 'There was a man murdered too—remember?'

'He didn't do that either, nor have it done. If Brunette had that done, you wouldn't have found any body. You never know what might be stitched into a guy's clothes. Why chance it? Look what I'm doing for you for twenty-five bucks. What would Brunette get done with the money *he* has to spend?'

'Would he have a man killed?'

Red thought for a moment. 'He might. He probably has. But he's not a tough guy. These racketeers are a new type. We think about them the way we think about old time yeggs or needled-up punks. Big-mouthed police commissioners on the radio yell that they're all yellow rats, that they'll kill women and babies and howl for mercy if they see a police uniform. They ought to know better than to try to sell the public that stuff. There's yellow cops and there's yellow torpedoes—but damn few of either. And as for the top men, like Brunette—they didn't get there by murdering people. They got there by guts and brains—and they don't have the group courage the cops have either. But above all they're business men. What they do is for money. Just like other business men. Sometimes a guy gets badly in the way. Okey. Out. But they think plenty before they do it. What the hell am I giving a lecture for?'

'A man like Brunette wouldn't hide Malloy,' I said. 'After he had killed two people.'

'No. Not unless there was some other reason than money. Want to go back?'

'No.'

Red moved his hands on the wheel. The boat picked up speed. 'Don't think I *like* these bastards,' he said. 'I hate their guts.'

37

The revolving searchlight was a pale mist-ridden finger that barely skimmed the waves a hundred feet or so beyond the ship. It was probably more for show than anything else. Especially at this time in the evening. Anyone who had plans for hijacking the take on one of these gambling boats would need plenty of help and would pull the job about four in the morning, when the crowd was thinned down to a few bitter gamblers, and the crew were all dull with fatigue. Even then it would be a poor way to make money. It has been tried once.

A taxi curved to the landing stage, unloaded, went back shorewards. Red held his speedboat idling just beyond the sweep of the searchlight. If they lifted it a few feet, just for fun—but they didn't. It passed languidly and the dull water glowed with it and the speedboat slid across the line and closed in fast under the overhang, past the two huge scummy stern hausers. We sidled up to the greasy plates of the hull as coyly as a hotel dick getting set to ease a hustler out of his lobby.

Double iron doors loomed high above us, and they looked too high to reach and too heavy to open even if we could reach them. The speedboat scuffed the *Montecito*'s ancient sides and the swell slapped loosely at the shell under our feet. A big shadow rose in the gloom at my side and a coiled rope slipped upwards through the air, slapped, caught, and the end ran down and splashed in water. Red fished it out with a boat-hook, pulled it tight and fastened the end to something on the engine cowling. There was just enough fog to make everything seem unreal. The wet air was as cold as the ashes of love.

Red leaned close to me and his breath tickled my ear. 'She rides too high. Come a good blow and she'd wave her screws in the air. We got to climb those plates just the same.'

'I can hardly wait,' I said, shivering.

He put my hands on the wheel, turned it just as he wanted it, set the throttle, and told me to hold the boat just as she was. There was an iron ladder bolted close to the plates, curving with the hull, its rungs probably as slippery as a greased pole.

Going up it looked as tempting as climbing over the cornice of an office building. Red reached for it, after wiping his hands hard on his pants to get some tar on them. He hauled himself up noiselessly, without even a grunt, and his sneakers caught the metal rungs, and he braced his body out almost at right angles to get more traction.

The searchlight beam swept far outside us now. Light bounced off the water and seemed to make any face as obvious as a flare, but nothing happened. Then there was a dull creak of heavy hinges over my head. A faint ghost of yellowish light trickled out into the fog and died. The outline of one half of the loading port showed. It couldn't have been bolted from inside. I wondered why.

The whisper was a mere sound, without meaning. I left the wheel and started up. It was the hardest journey I ever made. It landed me panting and wheezing in a sour hold littered with packing boxes and barrels and coils of rope and clumps of rusted chain. Rats screamed in dark corners. The yellow light came from a narrow door on the far side.

Red put his lips against my ear. 'From here we take a straight walk to the boiler room catwalk. They'll have steam in one auxiliary, because they don't have no Diesels on this piece of cheese. There will be probably one guy below. The crew doubles in brass up on the play decks, table men and spotters and waiters and so on. They all got to sign on as something that sounds like ship. From the boiler room I'll show you a ventilator with no grating in it. It goes to the boat deck and the boat deck is out of bounds. But it's all yours—while you live.'

'You must have relatives on board,' I said.

'Funnier things have happened. Will you come back fast?'

'I ought to make a good splash from the boat deck,' I said, and got my wallet out. 'I think this rates a little more money. Here. Handle the body as if it was your own.'

'You don't owe me nothing more, pardner.'

'I'm buying the trip back—even if I don't use it. Take the money before I bust out crying and wet your shirt.'

'Need a little help up there?'

'All I need is a silver tongue and the one I have is like a lizard's back.'

'Put your dough away,' Red said. 'You paid me for the trip back. I think you're scared.' He took hold of my hand. His was strong, hard, warm and slightly sticky. 'I *know* you're scared,' he whispered.

'I'll get over it,' I said. 'One way or another.'

He turned away from me with a curious look I couldn't read in that light. I followed him among the cases and barrels, over the raised iron sill of the door, into a long dim passage with the ship smell. We came out of this on to a grilled steel platform, slick with oil, and went down a steel ladder that was hard to hold on to. The slow hiss of the oil burners filled the air now and blanketed all other sound. We turned towards the hiss through mountains of silent iron.

Around the corner we looked at a short dirty wop in a purple silk shirt who sat in a wired-together office chair, under a naked hanging light, and read the evening paper with the aid of a black forefinger and steel-rimmed spectacles that had probably belonged to his grandfather.

Red stepped behind him noiselessly. He said gently:

'Hi, Shorty. How's all the bambinos?'

The Italian opened his mouth with a click and threw a hand at the opening of his purple shirt. Red hit him on the angle of the jaw and caught him. He put him down on the floor gently and began to tear the purple shirt into strips.

'This is going to hurt him more than the poke on the button,' Red said softly. 'But the idea is a guy going up a ventilator ladder makes a lot of racket down below. Up above they won't hear a thing.'

He bound and gagged the Italian neatly and folded his glasses and put them in a safe place and we went along to the ventilator that had no grating in it. I looked up and saw nothing but blackness.

'Good-bye,' I said.

'Maybe you need a little help.'

I shook myself like a wet dog. 'I need a company of marines. But either I do it alone or I don't do it. So long.'

'How long will you be?' His voice still sounded worried.

'An hour or less.'

He stared at me and chewed his lip. Then he nodded. 'Sometimes a guy has to,' he said. 'Drop by that bingo parlour, if you get time.'

He walked away softly, took four steps, and came back. 'That open loading port,' he said. 'That might buy you something. Use it.' He went quickly.

38

Cold air rushed down the ventilator. It seemed a long way to the top. After three minutes that felt like an hour I poked my head out cautiously from the horn-like opening. Canvas-sheeted boats were grey blurs near by. Low voices muttered in the dark. The beam of the searchlight circled slowly. It came from a point still higher, probably a railed platform at the top of one of the stumpy masts. There would be a lad up there with a Tommy-gun too, perhaps even a light Browning. Cold job, cold comfort when somebody left the loading port unbolted so nicely.

Distant music throbbed like the phony bass of a cheap radio. Overhead a masthead light and through the higher layers of fog a few bitter stars stared down.

I climbed out of the ventilator, slipped my .38 from the shoulder clip and held it curled against my ribs, hiding it with my sleeve. I walked three silent steps and listened. Nothing happened. The muttering talk had stopped, but not on my account. I placed it now, between two lifeboats. And out of the night and the fog, as it mysteriously does, enough light gathered into one focus to shine on the dark hardness of a machine-gun mounted on a high tripod and swung down over the rail. Two men stood near it, motionless, not smoking, and their voices began to mutter again, a quiet whisper that never became words.

I listened to the muttering too long. Another voice spoke clearly behind me.

'Sorry, guests are not allowed on the boat deck.'

I turned, not too quickly, and looked at his hands. They were light blurs and empty.

I stepped sideways nodding and the end of a boat hid us. The man followed me gently, his shoes soundless on the damp deck.

'I guess I'm lost,' I said.

'I guess you are.' He had a youngish voice, not chewed out of marble. 'But there's a door at the bottom of the companion-way. It has a spring lock on it. It's a good lock. There used to be an open stairway with a chain and a brass sign. We found the livelier element would step over that.'

He was talking a long time, either to be nice, or to be waiting. I didn't know which. I said: 'Somebody must have left the door open.'

The shadowed head nodded. It was lower than mine.

'You can see the spot that puts us in, though. If somebody did leave it open, the boss won't like it a nickel. If somebody didn't, we'd like to know how you got up here. I'm sure you get the idea.'

'It seems a simple idea. Let's go down and talk to him about it.'

'You come with a party?'

'A very nice party.'

'You ought to have stayed with them.'

'You know how it is—you turn your head and some other guy is buying her a drink.'

He chuckled. Then he moved his chin slightly up and down.

I dropped and did a frogleap sideways and the swish of the blackjack was a long spent sigh in the quiet air. It was getting to be that every blackjack in the neighbourhood swung at me automatically. The tall one swore.

I said: 'Go ahead and be heroes.'

I clicked the safety catch loudly.

Sometimes even a bad scene will rock the house. The tall one stood rooted, and I could see the blackjack swinging at his wrist. The one I had been talking to thought it over without any hurry.

'This won't buy you a thing,' he said gravely. 'You'll never get off the boat.'

'I thought of that. Then I thought how little you'd care.'

It was still a bum scene.

'You want what?' he said quietly.

'I have a loud gun,' I said. 'But it doesn't have to go off. I want to talk to Brunette.'

'He went to San Diego on business.'

'I'll talk to his stand-in.'

'You're quite a lad,' the nice one said. 'We'll go down. You'll put the heater up before we go through the door.'

'I'll put the heater up when I'm sure I'm going through the door.'

He laughed lightly. 'Go back to your post, Slim. I'll look into this.'

He moved lazily in front of me and the tall one appeared to fade into the dark.

'Follow me, then.'

We moved Indian file across the deck. We went down brassbound slippery steps. At the bottom was a thick door. He opened it and looked at the lock. He smiled, nodded, held the door for me and I stepped through, pocketing the gun.

The door closed and clicked behind us. He said:

'Quiet evening, so far.'

There was a gilded arch in front of us and beyond it a gaming room, not very crowded. It looked much like any other room. At the far end there was a short glass bar and some stools. In the middle a stairway going down and up this the music swelled and faded. I heard roulette wheels. A man was dealing faro to a single customer. There were not more than sixty people in the room. On the faro table there was a pile of yellowbacks that would start a bank. The player was an elderly white-haired man who looked politely attentive to the dealer, but no more.

Two quiet men in dinner jackets came through the archway sauntering, looking at nothing. That had to be expected. They strolled towards us and the short slender man with me waited for them. They were well beyond the arch before they let their hands find their side pockets, looking for cigarettes of course.

'From now on we have to have a little organization here,' the short man said. 'I don't think you'll mind?'

'You're Brunette,' I said suddenly.

He shrugged. 'Of course.'

'You don't look so tough,' I said.

'I hope not.'

The two men in dinner jackets edged me gently.

'In here,' Brunette said, 'We can talk at ease.'

He opened the door and they took me into dock.

The room was like a cabin and not like a cabin. Two brass lamps swung in gimbals hung above a dark desk that was not wood, possibly plastic. At the end were two bunks in grained wood. The lower of them was made up and on the top one were half a dozen stacks of phonograph record books. A big combination radio-phonograph stood in the corner. There was a red leather chesterfield, a red carpet, smoking stands, a tabouret with cigarettes and a decanter and glasses, a small bar sitting cattycorners at the opposite end from the bunks.

'Sit down,' Brunette said and went around the desk. There were a lot of business-like papers on the desk, with columns of figures, done on a book-keeping machine. He sat in a tall-backed director's chair and tilted it a little and looked me over. Then he stood up again and stripped off his overcoat and scarf and tossed them to one side. He sat down again. He picked a pen up and tickled the lobe of one ear with it. He had a cat smile, but I like cats.

He was neither young nor old, neither fat nor thin. Spending a lot of time on or near the ocean had given him a good healthy complexion. His hair was nut-brown and waved naturally and waved still more at sea. His forehead was narrow and brainy and his eyes held a delicate menace. They were yellowish in colour. He had nice hands, not babied to the point of insipidity, but well kept. His dinner clothes were midnight blue, I judged, because they looked so black. I thought his pearl was a little too large, but that might have been jealousy.

He looked at me for quite a long time before he said: 'He has a gun.'

One of the velvety tough guys leaned against the middle of my spine with something that was probably not a fishing rod. Exploring hands removed the gun and looked for others.

'Anything else?' a voice asked.

Brunette shook his head. 'Not now.'

One of the gunners slid my automatic across the desk. Brunette put the pen down and picked up a letter opener and pushed the gun around gently on his blotter.

'Well,' he said quietly, looking past my shoulder. 'Do I have to explain what I want now?'

One of them went out quickly and shut the door. The other was so still he wasn't there. There was a long easy silence, broken by the distant hum of voices and the deep-toned music and somewhere down below a dull almost imperceptible throbbing.

'Drink?'

'Thanks.'

The gorilla mixed a couple at the little bar. He didn't try to hide the glasses while he did it. He placed one on each side of the desk, on black glass scooters.

'Cigarette?'

'Thanks.'

'Egyptian all right?'

'Sure.'

We lit up. We drank. It tasted like good Scotch. The gorilla didn't drink.

'What I want—' I began.

'Excuse me, but that's rather unimportant, isn't it?'

The soft catlike smile and the lazy half-closing of the yellow eyes.

The door opened and the other one came back and with him was Mess-jacket, gangster mouth and all. He took one look at me and his face went oyster-white.

'He didn't get past me,' he said swiftly, curling one end of his lips.

'He had a gun,' Brunette said, pushing it with the letter opener. 'This gun. He even pushed it into my back more or less, on the boat deck.'

'Not past me, boss,' Mess-jacket said just as swiftly.

Brunette raised his yellow eyes slightly and smiled at me. 'Well?'

'Sweep him out,' I said. 'Squash him somewhere else.'

'I can prove it by the taximan,' Mess-jacket snarled.

'You've been off the stage since five-thirty?'

'Not a minute, boss.'

'That's no answer. An empire can fall in a minute.'

'Not a second, boss.'

'But he can be had,' I said, and laughed.

Mess-jacket took the smooth gliding step of a boxer and his fist lashed like a whip. It almost reached my temple. There was a dull thud. His fist seemed to melt in mid-air. He slumped sideways and clawed at a corner of the desk, then rolled on his back. It was nice to see somebody else get sapped for a change.

Brunette went on smiling at me.

'I hope you're not doing him an injustice,' Brunette said. 'There's still the matter of the door to the companionway.'

'Accidentally open.'

'Could you think of any other idea?'

'Not in such a crowd.'

'I'll talk to you alone,' Brunette said, not looking at anyone but me.

The gorilla lifted Mess-jacket by the armpits and dragged him across the cabin and his partner opened an inner door. They went through. The door closed.

'All right,' Brunette said. 'Who are you and what do you want?'

'I'm a private detective and I want to talk to a man named Moose Malloy.'

'Show me you're a private dick.'

I showed him. He tossed the wallet back across the desk. His wind-tanned lips continued to smile and the smile was getting stagy.

'I'm investigating a murder,' I said. 'The murder of a man named Marriott on the bluff near your Belvedere Club last Thursday night. This murder happens to be connected with another murder, of a woman, done by Malloy, an ex-con and bank robber and all-round tough guy.'

He nodded. 'I'm not asking you yet what it has to do with me. I assume you'll come to that. Suppose you tell me how you got on my boat?'

'I told you.'

'It wasn't true,' he said gently. 'Marlowe is the name? It wasn't true, Marlowe. You know that. The kid down on the stage isn't lying. I pick my men carefully.'

'You own a piece of Bay City,' I said. 'I don't know how big a piece, but enough for what you want. A man named Sonderborg has been running a hideout there. He has been running reefers and stick-ups and hiding hot boys. Naturally, he couldn't do that without connections. I don't think he could do it without you. Malloy was staying with him. Malloy has left. Malloy is about seven feet tall and hard to hide. I think he could hide nicely on a gambling boat.'

'You're simple,' Brunette said softly. 'Supposing I wanted to hide him, why should I take the risk out here?' He sipped his drink. 'After all I'm in another business. It's hard enough to keep a good taxi service running without a lot of trouble. The world is full of places a crook can hide. If he has money. Could you think of a better idea?'

'I could, but to hell with it.'

'I can't do anything for you. So how did you get on the boat?'

'I don't care to say.'

'I'm afraid I'll have to have you made to say, Marlowe.' His teeth glinted in the light from the brass ship's lamps. 'After all, it can be done.'

'If I tell you, will you get word to Malloy?'

'What word?'

I reached for my wallet lying on the desk and drew a card from it and turned it over. I put the wallet away and got a pencil instead. I wrote five words on the back of the card and pushed it across the desk. Brunette took it and read what I had written on it. 'It means nothing to me,' he said.

'It will mean something to Malloy.'

He leaned back and stared at me. 'I don't make you out. You risk your hide to come out here and hand me a card to pass on to some thug I don't even know. There's no sense to it.'

'There isn't if you don't know him.'

'Why didn't you leave your gun ashore and come aboard the usual way?'

'I forgot the first time. Then I knew that toughie in the mess-jacket would never let me on. Then I bumped into a fellow who knew another way.'

His yellow eyes lighted as with a new flame. He smiled and said nothing.

'This other fellow is no crook but he's been on the beach with ears open. You have a loading port that has been unbarred on the inside and you have a ventilator shaft out of which the grating has been removed. There's one man to knock over to get to the boat deck. You'd better check your crew list, Brunette.'

He moved his lips softly, one over the other. He looked down at the card again. 'Nobody named Malloy is on board this boat,' he said. 'But if you're telling the truth about that loading port, I'll buy.'

'Go and look at it.'

He still looked down. 'If there's any way I can get word to Malloy, I will. I don't know why I bother.'

'Take a look at that loading port.'

He sat very still for a moment, then leaned forward and pushed the gun across the desk to me.

'The things I do,' he mused, as if he was alone. 'I run towns, I elect mayors, I corrupt police, I peddle dope, I hide out crooks, I heist old women strangled with pearls. What a lot of time I have.' He laughed shortly. 'What a lot of time.'

I reached for my gun and tucked it back under my arm.

Brunette stood up. 'I promise nothing,' he said, eyeing me steadily. 'But I believe you.'

'Of course not.'

'You took a long chance to hear so little.'

'Yes.'

'Well—' he made a meaningless gesture and then put his hand across the desk.

'Shake hands with a chump,' he said softly.

I shook hands with him. His hand was small and firm and a little hot.

'You wouldn't tell me how you found out about this loading port?'

'I can't. But the man who told me is no crook.'

'I could make you tell,' he said, and immediately shook his head. 'No. I believed you once. I'll believe you again. Sit still and have another drink.'

He pushed a buzzer. The door at the back opened and one of the nice-tough guys came in.

'Stay here. Give him a drink, if he wants it. No rough stuff.'

The torpedo sat down and smiled at me calmly. Brunette went quickly out of the office. I smoked. I finished my drink. The torpedo made me another. I finished that, and another cigarette.

Brunette came back and washed his hands over in the corner, then sat down at his desk again. He jerked his head at the torpedo. The torpedo went out silently.

The yellow eyes studied me. 'You win, Marlowe. And I have one hundred and sixty-four men on my crew list. Well—' he shrugged. 'You can go back by the taxi. Nobody will bother you. As to your message, I have a few contacts. I'll use them. Good-night. I probably should say thanks. For the demonstration.'

'Good-night,' I said, and stood up and went out.

There was a new man on the landing stage. I rode to shore on a different taxi. I went along to the bingo parlour and leaned against the wall in the crowd.

Red came along in a few minutes and leaned beside me against the wall.

'Easy, huh?' Red said softly, against the heavy clear voices of the table men calling the numbers.

'Thanks to you. He bought. He's worried.'

Red looked this way and that and turned his lips a little more close to my ear. 'Get your man?'

'No. But I'm hoping Brunette will find a way to get him a message.'

Red turned his head and looked at the tables again. He yawned and straightened away from the wall. The beak-nosed man was in again. Red stepped over to him and said: 'Hiya, Olson,' and almost knocked the man off his feet pushing past him.

Olson looked after him sourly and straightened his hat. Then he spat viciously on the floor.

As soon as he had gone, I left the place and went along to the parking lot back towards the tracks where I had left my car.

I drove back to Hollywood and put the car away and went up to the apartment.

I took my shoes off and walked around in my socks feeling the floor with my toes. They would still get numb again once in a while.

Then I sat down on the side of the pulled-down bed and tried to figure time. It couldn't be done. It might take hours or days to find Malloy. He might never be found until the police got him. If they ever did—alive.

39

It was about ten o'clock when I called the Grayle number in Bay City. I thought it would probably be too late to catch her, but it wasn't. I fought my way through a maid and the butler and finally heard her voice on the line. She sounded breezy and well primed for the evening.

'I promised to call you,' I said. 'It's a little late, but I've had a lot to do.'

'Another stand-up?' Her voice got cool.

'Perhaps not. Does your chauffeur work this late?'

'He works as late as I tell him to.'

'How about dropping by to pick me up? I'll be getting squeezed into my commencement suit.'

'Nice of you,' she drawled. 'Should I really bother?' Amthor had certainly done a wonderful job with her centres of speech—if anything had ever been wrong with them.

'I'd show you my etching.'

'Just one etching?'

'It's just a single apartment.'

'I heard they had such things,' she drawled again, then changed her tone. 'Don't act so hard to get. You have a lovely build, mister. And don't ever let anyone tell you different. Give me the address again.'

I gave it to her and the apartment number. 'The lobby door is locked,' I said. 'But I'll go down and slip the catch.'

'That's fine,' she said. 'I won't have to bring my jimmy.'

She hung up, leaving me with a curious feeling of having talked to somebody that didn't exist.

I went down to the lobby and slipped the catch and then took a shower and put my pyjamas on and lay down on the bed. I could have slept for a week. I dragged myself up off the bed again and set the catch on the door, which I had forgotten to do, and walked through a deep hard snowdrift out to the kitchenette and laid out glasses and a bottle of liqueur Scotch I had been saving for a really high-class seduction.

I lay down on the bed again. 'Pray,' I said out loud. 'There's nothing left but prayer.'

I closed my eyes. The four walls of the room seemed to hold the throb of a boat, the still air seemed to drip with fog and rustle with sea wind. I smelled the rank sour smell of a disused hold. I smelled engine oil and saw a wop in a purple shirt reading under a naked light bulb with his grandfather's spectacles. I climbed and climbed up a ventilator shaft. I climbed the Himalayas and stepped out on top and guys with machine-guns were all around me. I talked with a small and somehow very human yellow-eyed man who was a racketeer and probably worse. I thought of the giant with the red hair and the violet eyes, who was probably the nicest man I had ever met.

I stopped thinking. Lights moved behind my closed lids. I was lost in space. I was a gilt-edged sap come back from a vain adventure. I was a hundred dollar package of dynamite that went off with a noise like a pawnbroker looking at a dollar watch. I was a pink-headed bug crawling up the side of the City Hall.

I was asleep.

I woke slowly, unwillingly, and eyes stared at reflected light on the ceiling from the lamp. Something moved gently in the room.

The movement was furtive and quiet and heavy. I listened to it. Then I turned my head slowly and looked at Moose Malloy. There were shadows and he moved in the shadows, as noiselessly as I had seen him once before. A gun in his hand had a dark oily business-like sheen. His hat was pushed back on his black curly hair and his nose sniffed, like the nose of a hunting dog.

He saw me open my eyes. He came softly over to the side of the bed and stood looking down at me.

'I got your note,' he said. 'I make the joint clean. I don't make no cops outside. If this is a plant, two guys goes out in baskets.'

I rolled a little on the bed and he felt swiftly under the pillows. His face was still wide and pale and his deep-set eyes were still somehow gentle. He was wearing an overcoat to-night. It fitted him where it touched. It was burst out in one shoulder seam, probably just getting it on. It would be the largest size they had, but not large enough for Moose Malloy.

'I hoped you'd drop by,' I said. 'No copper knows anything about this. I just wanted to see you.'

'Go on,' he said.

He moved sideways to a table and put the gun down and dragged his overcoat off and sat down in my best easy chair. It creaked, but it held. He leaned back slowly and arranged the gun so that it was close to his right hand. He dug a pack of cigarettes out of his pocket and shook one loose and put it into his mouth without touching it with his fingers. A match flared on a thumbnail. The sharp smell of the smoke drifted across the room.

'You ain't sick or anything?' he said.

'Just resting. I had a hard day.'

'Door was open. Expecting someone?'

'A dame.'

He stared at me thoughtfully.

'Maybe she won't come,' I said. 'If she does, I'll stall her.'

'What dame?'

'Oh, just a dame. If she comes, I'll get rid of her. I'd rather talk to you.'

His very faint smile hardly moved his mouth. He puffed his cigarette awkwardly, as if it was too small for his fingers to hold with comfort.

'What made you think I was on the *Monty*?' he asked.

'A Bay City cop. It's a long story and too full of guessing.'

'Bay City cops after me?'

'Would that bother you?'

He smiled the faint smile again. He shook his head slightly.

'You killed a woman,' I said. 'Jessie Florian. That was a mistake.'

He thought. Then he nodded. 'I'd drop that one,' he said quietly.

'But that queered it,' I said. 'I'm not afraid of you. You're no killer. You didn't mean to kill her. The other one—over on Central—you could have squeezed out of. But not out of beating a woman's head on a bedpost until her brains were on her face.'

'You take some awful chances, brother,' he said softly.

'The way I've been handled,' I said, 'I don't know the difference any more. You didn't mean to kill her—did you?'

His eyes were restless. His head was cocked in a listening attitude.

'It's about time you learned your own strength,' I said.

'It's too late,' he said.

'You wanted her to tell you something,' I said. 'You took hold of her neck and shook her. She was already dead when you were banging her head against the bed-post.'

He stared at me.

'I know what you wanted her to tell you,' I said.

'Go ahead.'

'There was a cop with me when she was found. I had to break clean.'

'How clean?'

'Fairly clean,' I said. 'But not about to-night.'

He stared at me. 'Okey, how did you know I was on the *Monty*?' He had asked me that before. He seemed to have forgotten.

'I didn't. But the easiest way to get away would be by water. With the set-up they have in Bay City you could get out to one of the gambling boats. From there you could get clean away. With the right help.'

'Laird Brunette is a nice guy,' he said emptily. 'So I've heard. I never even spoke to him.'

'He got the message to you.'

'Hell, there's a dozen grapevines that might help him to do that, pal. When do we do what you said on the card? I had a hunch you were levelling. I wouldn't take the chance to come here otherwise. Where do we go?'

He killed his cigarette and watched me. His shadow loomed against the wall, the shadow of a giant. He was so big he seemed unreal.

'What made you think I bumped Jessie Florian?' he asked suddenly.

'The spacing of the finger marks on her neck. The fact that you had something to get out of her, and that you are strong enough to kill people without meaning to.'

'The johns tied me to it?'

'I don't know.'

'What did I want out of her?'

'You thought she might know where Velma was.'

He nodded silently and went on staring at me.

'But she didn't,' I said. 'Velma was too smart for her.'

There was a light knocking at the door.

Malloy leaned forward a little and smiled and picked up his gun. Somebody tried the doorknob. Malloy stood up slowly and leaned forward in a crouch and listened. Then he looked back at me from looking at the door.

I sat up on the bed and put my feet on the floor and stood up. Malloy watched me silently, without a motion. I went over to the door.

'Who is it?' I asked with my lips to the panel.

It was her voice all right. 'Open up, silly. It's the Duchess of Windsor.'

'Just a second.'

I looked back at Malloy. He was frowning. I went over close to him and said in a very low voice: 'There's no other way out. Go in the dressing-room behind the bed and wait. I'll get rid of her.'

He listened and thought. His expression was unreadable. He was a man who had now very little to lose. He was a man who would never know fear. It was not built into even that giant frame. He nodded at last and picked up his hat and coat and moved silently around the bed and into the dressing-room. The door closed, but did not shut tight.

I looked around for signs of him. Nothing but a cigarette butt that anybody might have smoked. I went to the room door and opened it. Malloy had set the catch again when he came in.

She stood there half smiling, in the high-necked white fox evening cloak she had told me about. Emerald pendants hung from her ears and almost buried themselves in the soft white fur. Her fingers were curled and soft on the small evening bag she carried.

The smile died off her face when she saw me. She looked me up and down. Her eyes were cold now.

'So it's like that,' she said grimly. 'Pyjamas and dressing gown. To show me his lovely little etching. What a fool I am.'

I stood aside and held the door. 'It's not like that at all. I was getting dressed and a cop dropped in on me. He just left.'

'Randall?'

I nodded. A lie with a nod is still a lie, but it's an easy lie. She hesitated a moment, then moved past me with a swirl of scented fur.

I shut the door. She walked slowly across the room, stared blankly at the wall, then turned quickly.

'Let's understand each other,' she said. 'I'm not this much of a pushover. I don't go for hall bedroom romance. There was a time in my life when I had too much of it. I like things done with an air.'

'Will you have a drink before you go?' I was still leaning against the door, across the room from her.

'Am I going?'

'You gave me the impression you didn't like it here.'

'I wanted to make a point. I have to be a little vulgar to make it. I'm not one of these promiscuous bitches. I can be had—but not just by reaching. Yes, I'll take a drink.'

I went out into the kitchenette and mixed a couple of drinks with hands that were not too steady. I carried them in and handed her one.

There was no sound from the dressing-room, not even a sound of breathing.

She took the glass and tasted it and looked across it at the far wall. 'I don't like men to receive me in their pyjamas,' she said. 'It's a funny thing. I liked you. I liked you a lot. But I could get over it. I have often got over such things.'

I nodded and drank.

'Most men are just lousy animals,' she said. 'In fact it's a pretty lousy world, if you ask me.'

'Money must help.'

'You think it's going to when you haven't always had money. As a matter of fact it just makes new problems.' She smiled curiously. 'And you forget how hard the old problems were.'

She got out a gold cigarette case from her bag and I went over and held a match for her. She blew a vague plume of smoke and watched it with half-shut eyes.

'Sit close to me,' she said suddenly.

'Let's talk a little first.'

'About what? Oh—my jade?'

'About murder.'

Nothing changed in her face. She blew another plume of smoke, this time more carefully, more slowly. 'It's a nasty subject. Do we have to?'

I shrugged.

'Lin Marriott was no saint,' she said. 'But I still don't want to talk about it.'

She stared at me coolly for a long moment and then dipped her hand into her open bag for a handkerchief.

'Personally, I don't think he was a finger man for a jewel mob, either,' I said. 'The police pretend that they think that, but they do a lot of pretending. I don't even think he was a blackmailer, in any real sense. Funny, isn't it?'

'Is it?' The voice was very, very cold now.

'Well, not really,' I agreed and drank the rest of my drink. 'It was awfully nice of you to come here, Mrs Grayle. But we seem to have hit the wrong mood. I don't even, for example, think Marriott was killed by a gang. I don't think he was going to that canyon to buy a jade necklace. I don't even think a jade necklace was ever stolen. I think he went to that canyon to be murdered, although he thought he went there to help commit a murder. But Marriott was a very bad murderer.'

She leaned forward a little and her smile became just a little glassy. Suddenly, without any real change in her, she ceased to be beautiful. She looked merely like a woman who would have been dangerous a hundred years ago, and twenty years ago daring, but who to-day was just Grade B Hollywood.

She said nothing, but her right hand was tapping the clasp of her bag.

'A very bad murderer,' I said. 'Like Shakespeare's Second Murderer in that scene in *King Richard III*. The fellow that had certain dregs of conscience, but still wanted the money, and in the end didn't do the job at all because he couldn't make up his mind. Such murderers are very dangerous. They have to be removed—sometimes with blackjacks.'

She smiled. 'And who was he about to murder, do you suppose?'

'Me.'

'That must be very difficult to believe—that anyone would hate you that much. And you said my jade necklace was never stolen at all. Have you any proof of all this?'

'I didn't say I had. I said I thought these things.'

'Then why be such a fool as to talk about them?'

'Proof,' I said, 'is always a relative thing. It's an overwhelming balance of probabilities. And that's a matter of how they strike you. There was a rather weak motive for murdering me—merely that I was trying to trace a former Central Avenue dive singer at the same time that a convict named Moose Malloy got out of jail and started to look for her too. Perhaps I was helping him find her. Obviously, it was possible to find her, or it wouldn't have been worth while to pretend to Marriott that I had to be killed and killed quickly. And obviously he wouldn't have believed it, if it wasn't so. But there was a much stronger motive for murdering Marriott, which he, out of vanity or love or greed or a mixture of all three, didn't evaluate. He was afraid, but not for himself. He was afraid of violence to which he was a part and for which he could be convicted. But on the other hand he was fighting for his meal ticket. So he took the chance.'

I stopped. She nodded and said: 'Very interesting. If one knows what you are talking about.'

'And one does,' I said.

We stared at each other. She had her right hand in her bag again now. I had a good idea what it held. But it hadn't started to come out yet. Every event takes time.

'Let's quit kidding,' I said. 'We're all alone here. Nothing either of us says has the slightest standing against what the other says. We cancel each other out. A girl who started in the gutter became the wife of a multi-millionaire. On the way up a shabby old woman recognized her—probably heard her singing at the radio station and recognized the voice and went to see—and this old woman had to be kept quiet. But she was cheap, therefore she only knew a little. But the man who dealt with her and made her monthly payments and owned a trust deed on her home and could throw her into the gutter any time she got funny—that man knew it all. He was expensive. But that didn't matter either, as long as nobody else knew. But some day a tough guy named Moose Malloy was going to get out of jail and start finding things out about his former sweetie. Because the big sap loved her—and still does. That's what makes it funny, tragic-funny. And about that time a private dick starts nosing in also. So the weak link in the chain, Marriott, is no longer a luxury. He has become a menace. They'll get to him and they'll take him apart. He's that kind of lad. He melts under heat. So he was murdered before he could melt. With a blackjack. By you.'

All she did was take her hand out of her bag, with a gun in it. All she did was point it at me and smile. All I did was nothing.

But that wasn't all that was done. Moose Malloy stepped out of the dressing-room with the Colt .45 still looking like a toy in his big hairy paw.

He didn't look at me at all. He looked at Mrs Lewin Lockridge Grayle. He leaned forward and his mouth smiled at her and he spoke to her softly.

'I thought I knew the voice,' he said. 'I listened to that voice for eight years—all I could remember of it. I kind of liked your hair red, though. Hiya, babe. Long time no see.'

She turned the gun.

'Get away from me, you son of a bitch,' she said.

He stopped dead and dropped the gun to his side. He was still a couple of feet from her. His breath laboured.

'I never thought,' he said quietly. 'It just came to me out of the blue. *You* turned me in to the cops. *You*. Little Velma.'

I threw a pillow, but it was too slow. She shot him five times in the stomach. The bullets made no more sound than fingers going into a glove.

Then she turned the gun and shot at me but it was empty. She dived for Malloy's gun on the floor. I didn't miss with the second pillow. I was around the bed and knocked her away before she got the pillow off her face. I picked the Colt up and went away around the bed again with it.

He was still standing, but he was swaying. His mouth was slack and his hands were fumbling at his body. He went slack at the knees and fell sideways on the bed, with his face down. His gasping breath filled the room.

I had the phone in my hand before she moved. Her eyes were a dead grey, like half-frozen water. She rushed for the door and I didn't try to stop her. She left the door wide, so when I had done phoning I went over and shut it. I turned his head a little on the bed, so he wouldn't smother. He was still alive, but after five in the stomach even a Moose Malloy doesn't live very long.

I went back to the phone and called Randall at his home. 'Malloy,' I said. 'In my apartment. Shot five times in the stomach by Mrs Grayle. I called the Receiving Hospital. She got away.'

'So you had to play clever,' was all he said and hung up quickly.

I went back to the bed. Malloy was on his knees beside the bed now, trying to get up, a great wad of bedclothes in one hand. His face poured sweat. His eyelids flickered slowly and the lobes of his ears were dark.

He was still on his knees and still trying to get up when the fast wagon got there. It took four men to get him on the stretcher.

'He has a slight chance—if they're .25s,' the fast wagon doctor said just before he went out. 'All depends what they hit inside. But he has a chance.'

'He wouldn't want it,' I said.

He didn't. He died in the night.

40

'You ought to have given a dinner party,' Anne Riordan said looking at me across her tan figured rug. 'Gleaming silver and crystal, bright crisp linen–if they're still using linen in the places where they give dinner parties–candlelight, the women in their best jewels and the men in white ties, the servants hovering discreetly with the wrapped bottles of wine, the cops looking a little uncomfortable in their hired evening clothes, as who the hell wouldn't, the suspects with their brittle smiles and restless hands, and you at the head of the long table telling all about it, little by little, with your charming light smile and a phony English accent like Philo Vance.'

'Yeah,' I said. 'How about a little something to be holding in my hand while you go on being clever?'

She went out to her kitchen and rattled ice and came back with a couple of tall ones and sat down again.

'The liquor bills of your lady friends must be something fierce,' she said and sipped.

'And suddenly the butler fainted,' I said. 'Only it wasn't the butler who did the murder. He just fainted to be cute.'

I inhaled some of my drink. 'It's not that kind of story,' I said. 'It's not lithe and clever. It's just dark and full of blood.'

'So she got away?'

I nodded. 'So far. She never went home. She must have had a little hideout where she could change her clothes and appearance. After all she lived in peril, like the sailors. She was alone when she came to see me. No chauffeur. She came in a small car and she left it a few dozen blocks away.'

'They'll catch her–if they really try.'

'Don't be like that. Wilde, the D.A. is on the level. I worked for him once. But if they catch her, what then? They're up against twenty million dollars and a lovely face and either Lee Farrell or Rennenkamp. It's going to be awfully hard to prove she killed Marriott. All they have is what looks like a heavy motive and her past life, if they can trace it. She probably has no record, or she wouldn't have played it this way.'

'What about Malloy? If you had told me about him before, I'd have known who she was right away. By the way, how did *you* know? Those two photos are not of the same woman.'

'No. I doubt if even old lady Florian knew they had been switched on her. She looked kind of surprised when I shoved the photo of Velma–the one that had Velma Valento written on it–in front of her nose. But she may have known. She may have just hid it with the idea of selling it to me later on. Knowing it was harmless, a photo of some other girl Marriott substituted.'

'It had to be that way. Just as when Marriott called me up and gave me a song and dance about a jewel ransom pay-off it had to be because I had been to see Mrs Florian asking about Velma. And when Marriott was killed, it had to be because he was the weak link in the chain. Mrs Florian didn't even know Velma had become Mrs Lewin Lockridge Grayle. She couldn't have. They bought her too cheap. Grayle says they went to Europe to be married and she was married under her real name. He won't tell where or when. He won't tell what her real name was. He won't tell where she is. I don't think he knows, but the cops don't believe that.'

'Why won't he tell?' Anne Riordan cupped her chin on the backs of her laced fingers and stared at me with shadowed eyes.

'He's so crazy about her he doesn't care whose lap she sat in.'

'I hope she enjoyed sitting in yours,' Anne Riordan said acidly.

'She was playing with me. She was a little afraid of me. She didn't want to kill me because it's bad business killing a man who is a sort of cop. But she probably would have tried in the end, just as she would have killed Jessie Florian, if Malloy hadn't saved her the trouble.'

'I bet it's fun to be played by handsome blondes,' Anne Riordan said. 'Even if there is a little risk. As, I suppose, there usually is.'

I didn't say anything.

'I suppose they can't do anything to her for killing Malloy, because he had a gun.'

'No. Not with her pull.'

The gold-flecked eyes studied me solemnly. 'Do you think she meant to kill Malloy?'

'She was afraid of him,' I said. 'She had turned him in eight years ago. He seemed to know that. But he wouldn't have hurt her. He was in love with her too. Yes, I think she meant to kill anybody she had to kill. She had a lot to fight for. But you can't keep that sort of thing up indefinitely. She took a shot at me in my apartment—but the gun was empty then. She ought to have killed me out on the bluff when she killed Marriott.'

'He was in love with her,' Anne said softly. 'I mean Malloy. It didn't matter to him she hadn't written to him in six years or ever gone to see him while he was in jail. It didn't matter to him that she had turned him in for a reward. He just bought some fine clothes and started to look for her the first thing when he got out. So she pumped five bullets into him, by way of saying hello. He had killed two people himself, but he was in love with her. What a world.'

I finished my drink and got the thirsty look on my face again. She ignored it. She said:

'And she had to tell Grayle where she came from and he didn't care. He went away to marry her under another name and sold his radio station to break contact with anybody who might know her and he gave her everything that money can buy and she gave him—what?'

'That's hard to say.' I shook the ice cubes at the bottom of my glass. That didn't get me anything either. 'I suppose she gave him a sort of pride that he, a rather old man, could have a young and beautiful and dashing wife. He loved her. What the hell are we talking about it for? These things happen all the time. It didn't make any difference what she did or who she played around with or what she had once been. He loved her.'

'Like Moose Malloy,' Anne said quietly.

'Let's go riding along the water.'

'You didn't tell me about Brunette or the cards that were in those reefers or Amthor or Dr Sonderborg or that little clue that set you on the path of the great solution.'

'I gave Mrs Florian one of my cards. She put a wet glass on it. Such a card was in Marriott's pocket, wet glass mark and all. Marriott was not a messy man. That was a clue, of sorts. Once you suspected anything it was easy to find out other connections, such as that Marriott owned a trust deed on Mrs Florian's house, just to keep her in line. As for Amthor, he's a bad hat. They picked him up in a New York hotel and they say he's an international con man. Scotland Yard has his prints, also Paris. How the hell they got all that since yesterday or the day before I don't know. These boys work fast when they feel like it. I think Randall has had this thing taped for days and was afraid I'd step on the tapes. But Amthor had nothing to do with killing anybody. Or with Sonderborg. They haven't found Sonderborg yet. They think he has a record too, but they're not sure until they get him. As for Brunette, you can't get anything on a guy like Brunette. They'll have him before the Grand Jury and he'll refuse to say anything, on his constitutional rights. He doesn't have to bother about his reputation. But there's a nice shake-up here in Bay City. The Chief has been canned and half the detectives have been reduced to acting patrolmen, and a very nice guy named Red Norgaard, who helped me get on the *Montecito*, has got his job back. The mayor is doing all this, changing his pants hourly while the crisis lasts.'

'Do you have to say things like that?'

'The Shakespearean touch. Let's go riding. After we've had another drink.'

'You can have mine,' Anne Riordan said, and got up and brought her untouched drink over to me. She stood in front of me holding it, her eyes wide and a little frightened.

'You're so marvellous,' she said. 'So brave, so determined, and you work for so little money. Everybody bats you over the head and chokes you and smacks your jaw and fills you with morphine, but you just keep right on hitting between tackle and end until they're all worn out. What makes you so wonderful?'

'Go on,' I growled. 'Spill it.'

Anne Riordan said thoughtfully: 'I'd like to be kissed, damn you!'

41

It took over three months to find Velma. They wouldn't believe Grayle didn't know where she was and hadn't helped her get away. So every cop and newshawk in the country looked in all the places where money might be hiding her. And money wasn't hiding her at all. Although the way she hid was pretty obvious once it was found out.

One night a Baltimore detective with a camera eye as rare as a pink zebra wandered into a night-club and listened to the band and looked at a handsome black-haired, black-browed torcher who could sing as if she meant it. Something in her face struck a chord and the chord went on vibrating.

He went back to Headquarters and got out the Wanted file and started through the pile of readers. When he came to the one he wanted he looked at it a long time. Then he straightened his straw hat on his head and went back to the night-club and got hold of the manager. They went back to the dressing-rooms behind the shell and the manager knocked on one of the doors. It wasn't locked. The dick pushed the manager aside and went in and locked it.

He must have smelled marijuana because she was smoking it, but he didn't pay any attention then. She was sitting in front of a triple mirror, studying the roots of her hair and eyebrows. They were her own eyebrows. The dick stepped across the room smiling and handed her the reader.

She must have looked at the face on the reader almost as long as the dick had down at Headquarters. There was a lot to think about while she was looking at it. The dick sat down and crossed his legs and lit a cigarette. He had a good eye, but he had over-specialized. He didn't know enough about women.

Finally she laughed a little and said: 'You're a smart lad, copper. I thought I had a voice that would be remembered. A friend recognized me by it once, just hearing it on the radio. But I've been singing with this band for a month—twice a week on a network—and nobody gave it a thought.'

'I never heard the voice,' the dick said and went on smiling.

She said: 'I suppose we can't make a deal on this. You know, there's a lot in it, if it's handled right.'

'Not with me,' the dick said. 'Sorry.'

'Let's go then,' she said and stood up and grabbed up her bag and got her coat from a hanger. She went over to him holding the coat out so he could help her into it. He stood up and held it for her like a gentleman.

She turned and slipped a gun out of her bag and shot him three times through the coat he was holding.

She had two bullets left in the gun when they crashed the door. They got half-way across the room before she used them. She used them both, but the second shot must have been pure reflex. They caught her before she hit the floor, but her head was already hanging by a rag.

'The dick lived until the next day,' Randall said, telling me about it. 'He talked when he could. That's how we have the dope. I can't understand him being so careless, unless he really was thinking of letting her talk him into a deal of some kind. That would clutter up his mind. But I don't like to think that, of course.'

I said I supposed that was so.

'Shot herself clean through the heart—twice,' Randall said. 'And I've heard experts on the stand say that's impossible, knowing all the time myself that it was. And you know something else?'

'What?'

'She was stupid to shoot that dick. We'd never have convicted her, not with her looks and money and the persecution story these high-priced guys would build up. Poor little girl from a dive climbs to be wife of rich man and the vultures that used to know her won't let her alone. That sort of thing. Hell, Rennenkamp would have half a dozen crummy old burlesque dames in court to sob that they'd blackmailed her for years, and in a way that you couldn't pin anything on them but the jury would go for it. She did a smart thing to run off on her own and leave Grayle out of it, but it would have been smarter to have come home when she was caught.'

'Oh you believe now that she left Grayle out of it?' I said.

He nodded. I said: 'Do you think she had any particular reason for that?'

He stared at me. 'I'll go for it, whatever it is.'

'She was a killer,' I said. 'But so was Malloy. And *he* was a long way from being all rat. Maybe that Baltimore dick wasn't so pure as the record shows. Maybe she saw a chance—not to get away—she was tired of dodging by that time—but to give a break to the only man who had ever really given her one.'

Randall stared at me with his mouth open and his eyes unconvinced.

'Hell, she didn't have to shoot a cop to do that' he said.

'I'm not saying she was a saint or even a half-way nice girl. Not ever. She wouldn't kill herself until she was cornered. But what she did and the way she did it, kept her from coming back here for trial. Think that over. And who would that trial hurt most? Who would be least able to bear it? And win, lose or draw, who would pay the biggest price for the show? An old man who had loved not wisely, but too well.'

Randall said sharply: 'That's just sentimental.'

'Sure. It sounded like that when I said it. Probably all a mistake anyway. So long. Did my pink bug ever get back up here?'

He didn't know what I was talking about.

I rode down to the street floor and went out on the steps of the City Hall. It was a cool day and very clear. You could see a long way—but not as far as Velma had gone.